PRAISE FOR SARAH J. MAAS'S
COURT OF THORNS AND ROSES SERIES

A COURT OF THORNS AND ROSES

"Simply dazzles." —*Booklist*, starred review

"Passionate, violent, sexy and daring. . . .
A true page-turner." —*USA Today*

"Suspense, romance, intrigue and action. This is
not a book to be missed!" —HuffPost

"Vicious and intoxicating. . . . A dazzling world, complex characters
and sizzling romance." —*RT Book Reviews*, Top Pick

"A sexy, action-packed fairytale." —Bustle

A COURT OF MIST AND FURY

"Fiercely romantic, irresistibly sexy and hypnotically magical.
A veritable feast for the senses." —*USA Today*

"Hits the spot for fans of dark, lush, sexy fantasy." —*Kirkus Reviews*

"An immersive, satisfying read." —*Publishers Weekly*

"Darkly sexy and thrilling." —Bustle

A COURT OF WINGS AND RUIN

"Fast-paced and explosively action-packed." —*Booklist*

"The plot manages to seduce you with its alluring
characters, irresistible world and never-ending action,
leaving you craving more." —*RT Book Reviews*

BOOKS BY SARAH J. MAAS

THE COURT OF THORNS AND ROSES SERIES

A Court of Thorns and Roses

A Court of Mist and Fury

A Court of Wings and Ruin

A Court of Frost and Starlight

A Court of Thorns and Roses Colouring Book

THE CRESCENT CITY SERIES

House of Earth and Blood

THE THRONE OF GLASS SERIES

The Assassin's Blade

Throne of Glass

Crown of Midnight

Heir of Fire

Queen of Shadows

Empire of Storms

Tower of Dawn

Kingdom of Ash

The Throne of Glass Colouring Book

A COURT OF FROST AND STARLIGHT

SARAH J. MAAS

BLOOMSBURY PUBLISHING
LONDON • OXFORD • NEW YORK • NEW DELHI • SYDNEY

BLOOMSBURY PUBLISHING
Bloomsbury Publishing Plc
50 Bedford Square, London, WC1B 3DP, UK
29 Earlsfort Terrace, Dublin 2, Ireland

First published in Great Britain 2018
This edition published 2020

A catalogue record for this book is available from the British Library

ISBN: PB: 978-1-5266-1718-7; eBook: 978-1-4088-9031-8

19 20 18

Typeset by Westchester Publishing Services
Printed and bound in Great Britain by CPI Group (UK) Ltd, Croydon CR0 4YY

MIX
Paper from
responsible sources
FSC® C020471

To the readers who look up at the stars and wish

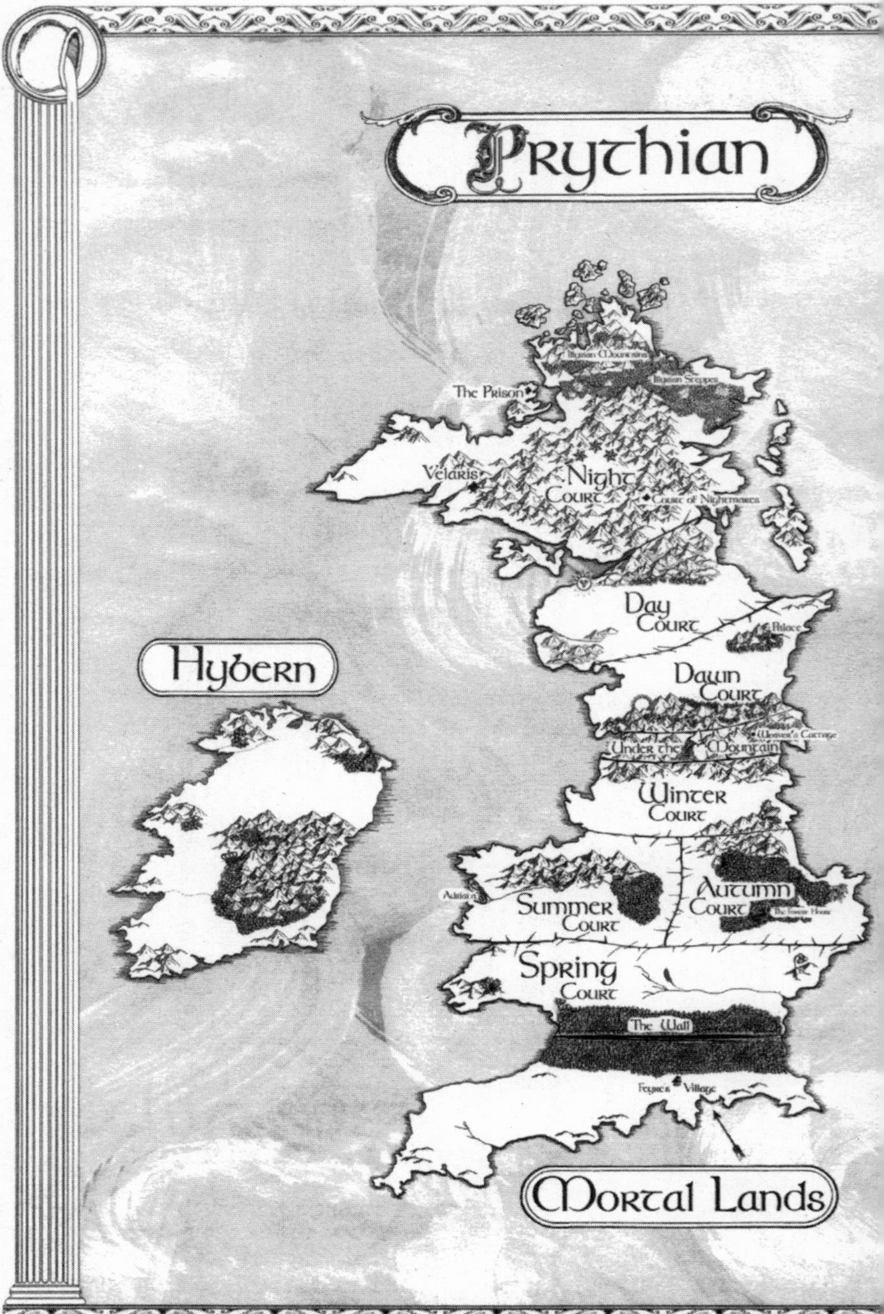
Prythian
The Prison
Velaris
Night Court
Court of Nightmares
Day Court
Palace
Hybern
Dawn Court
Under the Mountain
Winter Court
Summer Court
Autumn Court
Spring Court
The Wall
Feyre's Village
Mortal Lands

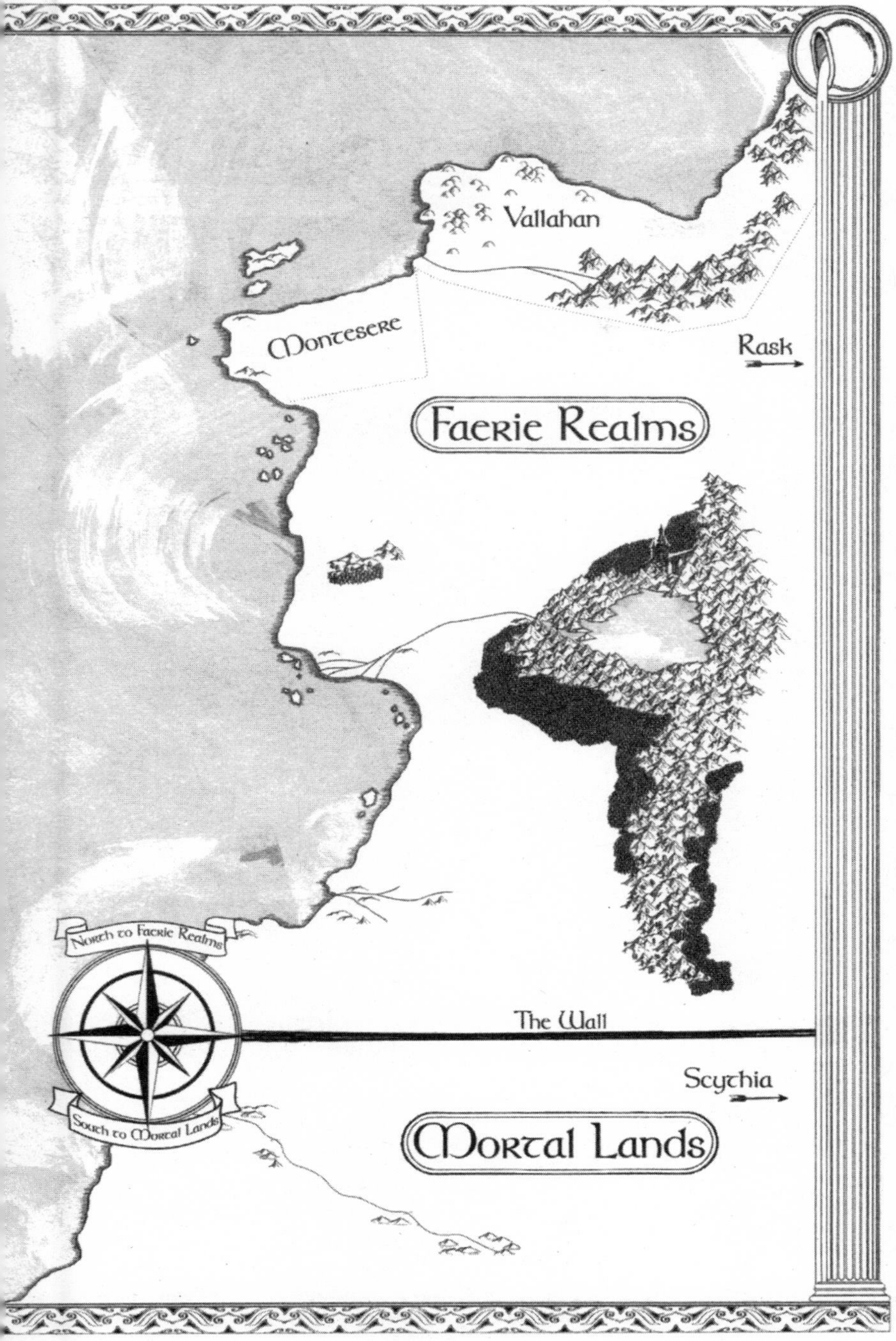
Vallahan
Montesere
Rask
Faerie Realms
The Wall
North to Faerie Realms
South to Mortal Lands
Scythia
Mortal Lands

CHAPTER 1

Feyre

The first snow of winter had begun whipping through Velaris an hour earlier.

The ground had finally frozen solid last week, and by the time I'd finished devouring my breakfast of toast and bacon, washed down with a heady cup of tea, the pale cobblestones were dusted with fine, white powder.

I had no idea where Rhys was. He hadn't been in bed when I'd awoken, the mattress on his side already cold. Nothing unusual, as we were both busy to the point of exhaustion these days.

Seated at the long cherrywood dining table at the town house, I frowned at the whirling snow beyond the leaded glass windows.

Once, I had dreaded that first snow, had lived in terror of long, brutal winters.

But it had been a long, brutal winter that had brought me so deep into the woods that day nearly two years ago. A long, brutal winter that had made me desperate enough to kill a wolf, that had eventually led me here—to this life, this . . . happiness.

The snow fell, thick clumps plopping onto the dried grass of the tiny front lawn, crusting the spikes and arches of the decorative fence beyond it.

Deep inside me, rising with every swirling flake, a sparkling, crisp power stirred. I was High Lady of the Night Court, yes, but also one blessed with the gifts of all the courts. It seemed Winter now wanted to play.

Finally awake enough to be coherent, I lowered the shield of black adamant guarding my mind and cast a thought down the soul-bridge between me and Rhys. *Where'd you fly off to so early?*

My question faded into blackness. A sure sign that Rhys was nowhere near Velaris. Likely not even within the borders of the Night Court. Also not unusual—he'd been visiting our war allies these months to solidify our relationships, build trade, and keep tabs on their post-wall intentions. When my own work allowed it, I often joined him.

I scooped up my plate, draining my tea to the dregs, and padded toward the kitchen. Playing with ice and snow could wait.

Nuala was already preparing for lunch at the worktable, no sign of her twin, Cerridwen, but I waved her off as she made to take my dishes. "I can wash them," I said by way of greeting.

Up to the elbows in making some sort of meat pie, the half-wraith gave me a grateful smile and let me do it. A female of few words, though neither twin could be considered shy. Certainly not when they worked—spied—for both Rhys and Azriel.

"It's still snowing," I observed rather pointlessly, peering out the kitchen window at the garden beyond as I rinsed off the plate, fork, and cup. Elain had already readied the garden for winter, veiling the more delicate bushes and beds with burlap. "I wonder if it'll let up at all."

Nuala laid the ornate lattice crust atop the pie and began pinching the edges together, her shadowy fingers making quick, deft work of it. "It'll be nice to have a white Solstice," she said, voice lilting and yet hushed. Full of whispers and shadows. "Some years, it can be fairly mild."

Right. The Winter Solstice. In a week. I was still new enough to being High Lady that I had no idea what my formal role was to be. If we'd have a High Priestess do some odious ceremony, as Ianthe had done the year before—

A year. Gods, nearly a year since Rhys had called in his bargain, desperate to get me away from the poison of the Spring Court, to save me from my despair. Had he been only a minute later, the Mother knew what would have happened. Where I'd now be.

Snow swirled and eddied in the garden, catching in the brown fibers of the burlap covering the shrubs.

My mate—who had worked so hard and so selflessly, all without hope that I would ever be with him.

We had both fought for that love, bled for it. Rhys had died for it.

I still saw that moment, in my sleeping and waking dreams. How his face had looked, how his chest had not risen, how the bond between us had shredded into ribbons. I still felt it, that hollowness in my chest where the bond had been, where *he* had been. Even now, with that bond again flowing between us like a river of star-flecked night, the echo of its vanishing lingered. Drew me from sleep; drew me from a conversation, a painting, a meal.

Rhys knew exactly why there were nights when I would cling tighter to him, why there were moments in the bright, clear sunshine that I would grip his hand. He knew, because *I* knew why his eyes sometimes turned distant, why he occasionally just blinked at all of us as if not quite believing it and rubbed his chest as if to ease an ache.

Working had helped. Both of us. Keeping busy, keeping focused—I sometimes dreaded the quiet, idle days when all those thoughts snared me at last. When there was nothing but me and my mind, and that memory of Rhys lying dead on the rocky ground, the King of Hybern snapping my father's neck, all those Illyrians blasted out of the sky and falling to earth as ashes.

Perhaps one day, even the work wouldn't be a battlement to keep the memories out.

Mercifully, plenty of work remained for the foreseeable future. Rebuilding Velaris after the attacks from Hybern being only one of many monumental tasks. For other tasks required doing as well—both in Velaris and beyond it: in the Illyrian Mountains, in the Hewn City, in the vastness of the entire Night Court. And then there were the other courts of Prythian. And the new, emerging world beyond.

But for now: Solstice. The longest night of the year. I turned from the window to Nuala, who was still fussing over the edges of her pie. "It's a special holiday here as well, right?" I asked casually. "Not just in Winter and Day." And Spring.

"Oh, yes," Nuala said, stooping over the worktable to examine her pie. Skilled spy—trained by Azriel himself—and master cook. "We love it dearly. It's intimate, warm, lovely. Presents and music and food, sometimes feasting under the starlight . . ." The opposite of the enormous, wild, days-long party I'd been subjected to last year. But—presents.

I had to buy presents for all of them. Not had to, but *wanted* to.

Because all my friends, now my family, had fought and bled and nearly died as well.

I shut out the image that tore through my mind: Nesta, leaning over a wounded Cassian, the two of them prepared to die together against the King of Hybern. My father's corpse behind them.

I rolled my neck. We could use something to celebrate. It had become so rare for all of us to be gathered for more than an hour or two.

Nuala went on, "It's a time of rest, too. And a time to reflect on the darkness—how it lets the light shine."

"Is there a ceremony?"

The half-wraith shrugged. "Yes, but none of us go. It's more for those who wish to honor the light's rebirth, usually by spending the entire night sitting in absolute darkness." A ghost of a smirk. "It's not quite such a novelty for my sister and me. Or for the High Lord."

I tried not to look too relieved that I wouldn't be dragged to a temple for hours as I nodded.

Setting my clean dishes to dry on the little wooden rack beside the sink, I wished Nuala luck on lunch, and headed upstairs to dress. Cerridwen had already laid out clothes, but there was still no sign of Nuala's twin as I donned the heavy charcoal sweater, the tight black leggings, and fleece-lined boots before loosely braiding back my hair.

A year ago, I'd been stuffed into fine gowns and jewels, made to parade in front of a preening court who'd gawked at me like a prized breeding mare.

Here . . . I smiled at the silver-and-sapphire band on my left hand. The ring I'd won for myself from the Weaver in the Wood.

My smile faded a bit.

I could see her, too. See Stryga standing before the King of

Hybern, covered in the blood of her prey, as he took her head in his hands and snapped her neck. Then threw her to his beasts.

I clenched my fingers into a fist, breathing in through my nose, out through my mouth, until the lightness in my limbs faded, until the walls of the room stopped pressing on me.

Until I could survey the blend of personal objects in Rhys's room—our room. It was by no means a small bedroom, but it had lately started to feel . . . tight. The rosewood desk against one wall was covered in papers and books from both of our own dealings; my jewelry and clothes now had to be divided between here and my old bedroom. And then there were the weapons.

Daggers and blades, quivers and bows. I scratched my head at the heavy, wicked-looking *mace* that Rhys had somehow dumped beside the desk without my noticing.

I didn't even want to know. Though I had no doubt Cassian was somehow behind it.

We could, of course, store everything in the pocket between realms, but . . . I frowned at my own set of Illyrian blades, leaning against the towering armoire.

If we got snowed in, perhaps I'd use the day to organize things. Find room for everything. Especially that mace.

It would be a challenge, since Elain still occupied a bedroom down the hall. Nesta had chosen her own home across the city, one that I opted to not think about for too long. Lucien, at least, had taken up residence in an elegant apartment down by the river the day after he'd returned from the battlefields. And the Spring Court.

I hadn't asked Lucien any questions about that visit—to Tamlin.

Lucien hadn't explained the black eye and cut lip, either. He'd only asked Rhys and me if we knew of a place to stay in Velaris, since he did not wish to inconvenience us further by staying at the town house, and did not wish to be isolated at the House of Wind.

He hadn't mentioned Elain, or his proximity to her. Elain had not asked him to stay, or to go. And whether she cared about the bruises on his face, she certainly hadn't let on.

But Lucien had remained, and found ways to keep busy, often gone for days or weeks at a time.

Yet even with Lucien and Nesta staying in their own apartments, the town house was a bit small these days. Even more so if Mor, Cassian, and Azriel stayed over. And the House of Wind was too big, too formal, too far from the city proper. Nice for a night or two, but . . . I loved this house.

It was my home. The first I'd really had in the ways that counted.

And it'd be nice to celebrate the Solstice here. With all of them, crowded as it might be.

I scowled at the pile of papers I had to sort through: letters from other courts, priestesses angling for positions, and kingdoms both human and faerie. I'd put them off for weeks now, and had finally set aside this morning to wade through them.

High Lady of the Night Court, Defender of the Rainbow and the . . . Desk.

I snorted, flicking my braid over a shoulder. Perhaps my Solstice gift to myself would be to hire a personal secretary. Someone to read and answer those things, to sort out what was vital and what could be put aside. Because a little extra time to myself, for *Rhys* . . .

I'd look through the court budget that Rhys never really cared to follow and see what could be moved around for the possibility of such a thing. For him and for me.

I knew our coffers ran deep, knew we could easily afford it and not make so much as a dent in our fortune, but I didn't mind the work. I loved the work, actually. This territory, its people—they were as much my heart as my mate. Until yesterday, nearly every waking hour had been packed with helping them. Until I'd been politely, graciously, told to *go home and enjoy the holiday.*

In the wake of the war, the people of Velaris had risen to the challenge of rebuilding and helping their own. Before I'd even come up with an idea of *how* to help them, multiple societies had been created to assist the city. So I'd volunteered with a handful of them for tasks ranging from finding homes for those displaced by the destruction to visiting families affected during the war to helping those without shelter or belongings ready for winter with new coats and supplies.

All of it was vital; all of it was good, satisfying work. And yet . . . there was more. There was *more* that I could do to help. Personally. I just hadn't figured it out yet.

It seemed I wasn't the only one eager to assist those who'd lost so much. With the holiday, a surge of fresh volunteers had arrived, cramming the public hall near the Palace of Thread and Jewels, where so many of the societies were headquartered. *Your help has been crucial, Lady*, one charity matron had said to me yesterday. *You have been here nearly every day—you have worked yourself to the bone. Take the week off. You've earned it. Celebrate with your mate.*

I'd tried to object, insisting that there were still more coats to hand out, more firewood to be distributed, but the faerie had just motioned to the crowded public hall around us, filled to the brim with volunteers. *We have more help than we know what to do with.*

When I'd tried objecting again, she'd shooed me out the front door. And shut it behind me.

Point taken. The story had been the same at every other organization I'd stopped by yesterday afternoon. *Go home and enjoy the holiday.*

So I had. At least, the first part. The *enjoying* bit, however . . .

Rhys's answer to my earlier inquiry about his whereabouts finally flickered down the bond, carried on a rumble of dark, glittering power. *I'm at Devlon's camp.*

It took you this long to respond? It was a long distance to the Illyrian Mountains, yes, but it shouldn't have taken minutes to hear back.

A sensual huff of laughter. *Cassian was ranting. He didn't take a breath.*

My poor Illyrian baby. We certainly do torment you, don't we?

Rhys's amusement rippled toward me, caressing my innermost self with night-veiled hands. But it halted, vanishing as quickly as it had come. *Cassian's getting into it with Devlon. I'll check in later.* With a loving brush against my senses, he was gone.

I'd get a full report about it soon, but for now . . .

I smiled at the snow waltzing outside the windows.

CHAPTER 2

Rhysand

It was barely nine in the morning, and Cassian was already pissed.

The watery winter sun tried and failed to bleed through the clouds looming over the Illyrian Mountains, the wind a boom across the gray peaks. Snow already lay inches deep over the bustling camp, a vision of what would soon befall Velaris.

It had been snowing when I departed at dawn—perhaps there would be a good coating already on the ground by the time I returned. I hadn't had a chance to ask Feyre about it during our brief conversation down the bond minutes ago, but perhaps she would go for a walk with me through it. Let me show her how the City of Starlight glistened under fresh snow.

Indeed, my mate and city seemed a world away from the hive of activity in the Windhaven camp, nestled in a wide, high mountain pass. Even the bracing wind that swept between the peaks, belying the camp's very name by whipping up dervishes of snow, didn't deter the Illyrians from going about their daily chores.

For the warriors: training in the various rings that opened onto a sheer drop to the small valley floor below, those not present out on patrol. For the males who hadn't made the cut: tending to various trades, whether merchants or blacksmiths or cobblers. And for the females: drudgery.

They didn't see it as such. None of them did. But their required tasks, whether old or young, remained the same: cooking, cleaning, child-rearing, clothes-making, laundry . . . There was honor in such tasks—pride and good work to be found in them. But not when every single one of the females here was *expected* to do it. And if they shirked those duties, either one of the half-dozen camp-mothers or whatever males controlled their lives would punish them.

So it had been, as long as I'd known this place, for my mother's people. The world had been reborn during the war months before, the wall blasted to nothingness, and yet some things did not alter. Especially here, where change was slower than the melting glaciers scattered amongst these mountains. Traditions going back thousands of years, left mostly unchallenged.

Until us. Until now.

Drawing my attention away from the bustling camp beyond the edge of the chalk-lined training rings where we stood, I schooled my face into neutrality as Cassian squared off against Devlon.

"The girls are busy with preparations for the Solstice," the camp-lord was saying, his arms crossed over his barrel chest. "The wives need all the help they can get, if all's to be ready in time. They can practice next week."

I'd lost count of how many variations of this conversation we'd had during the decades Cassian had been pushing Devlon on this.

The wind whipped Cassian's dark hair, but his face remained hard as granite as he said to the warrior who had begrudgingly trained us, "The girls can help their mothers *after* training is done for the day. We'll cut practice down to two hours. The rest of the day will be enough to assist in the preparations."

Devlon slid his hazel eyes to where I lingered a few feet away. "Is it an order?"

I held that gaze. And despite my crown, my power, I tried not to fall back into the trembling child I'd been five centuries ago, that first day Devlon had towered over me and then hurled me into the sparring ring. "If Cassian says it's an order, then it is."

It had occurred to me, during the years we'd been waging this same battle with Devlon and the Illyrians, that I could simply rip into his mind, all their minds, and make them agree. Yet there were some lines I could not, would not cross. And Cassian would never forgive me.

Devlon grunted, his breath a curl of steam. "An hour."

"Two hours," Cassian countered, wings flaring slightly as he held a hard line that I'd been called in this morning to help him maintain.

It had to be bad, then, if my brother had asked me to come. Really damn bad. Perhaps we needed a permanent presence out here, until the Illyrians remembered things like consequences.

But the war had impacted us all, and with the rebuilding, with the human territories crawling out to meet us, with other Fae kingdoms looking toward a wall-less world and wondering what shit they could get away with . . . We didn't have the resources to station someone out here. Not yet. Perhaps next summer, if the climate elsewhere was calm enough.

Devlon's cronies loitered in the nearest sparring ring, sizing up Cassian and me, the same way they had our entire lives. We'd slaughtered enough of them in the Blood Rite all those centuries ago that they still kept back, but . . . It had been the Illyrians who had bled and fought this summer. Who had suffered the most losses as they took on the brunt of Hybern and the Cauldron.

That any of the warriors survived was a testament to their skill and Cassian's leadership, but with the Illyrians isolated and idle up here, that loss was starting to shape itself into something ugly. Dangerous.

None of us had forgotten that during Amarantha's reign, a few of the war-bands had gleefully bowed to her. And I knew none of the Illyrians had forgotten that we'd spent those first few months after her downfall hunting down those rogue groups. And ending them.

Yes, a presence here was needed. But later.

Devlon pushed, crossing his muscled arms. "The boys need a nice Solstice after all they endured. Let the girls give one to them."

The bastard certainly knew what weapons to wield, both physical and verbal.

"Two hours in the ring each morning," Cassian said with that same hard tone that even I knew not to push unless I wanted a flat-out brawl. He didn't break Devlon's gaze. "The *boys* can help decorate, clean, and cook. They've got two hands."

"Some do," Devlon said. "Some came home without one."

I felt, more than saw, the wound strike deep in Cassian.

It was the cost of leading my armies: each injury, death, scar—he took them all as his own personal failings. And being around these warriors, seeing those missing limbs and brutal injuries still healing or that would never heal . . .

"They practice for ninety minutes," I said, soothing the dark power that began to roil in my veins, seeking a path into the world, and slid my chilled hands into my pockets. Cassian, wisely, pretended to look outraged, his wings spreading wide. Devlon opened his mouth, but I cut him off before he could shout something truly stupid. "An hour and a half every morning, then they do the housework, the males pitching in whenever they can." I glanced toward the permanent tents and small stone and wood houses scattered along the wide pass and up into the tree-crusted peaks behind us. "Do not forget that a great number of the females, Devlon, also suffered losses. Perhaps not a hand, but their husbands and sons and brothers were out on those battlefields. Everyone helps prepare for the holiday, and everyone gets to train."

I jerked my chin at Cassian, indicating for him to follow me to the house across the camp that we now kept as our semi-permanent base of operations. There wasn't a surface inside where I hadn't taken Feyre—the kitchen table being my particular favorite, thanks to those raw initial days after we'd first mated, when I could barely stand to be near her and not be buried inside her.

How long ago, how distant, those days seemed. Another lifetime ago.

I needed a holiday.

Snow and ice crunched under our boots as we aimed for the narrow, two-level stone house by the tree line.

Not a holiday to rest, not to visit anywhere, but just to spend more than a handful of hours in the same bed as my mate.

To get more than a few hours to sleep *and* bury myself in her. It seemed to be one or the other these days. Which was utterly unacceptable. And had turned me about twenty kinds of foolish.

Last week had been so stupidly busy and I'd been so desperate for the feel and taste of her that I'd taken her during the flight down from the House of Wind to the town house. High above Velaris—for all to see, if it weren't for the cloaking I had thrown into place. It'd required some careful maneuvering, and I'd planned for months now on actually making a moment of it, but with her against me like that, alone in the skies, all it had taken was one look into those blue-gray eyes and I was unfastening her pants.

A moment later, I'd been inside her, and had nearly sent us crashing into the rooftops like an Illyrian whelp. Feyre had just laughed.

I'd climaxed at the husky sound of it.

It had not been my finest moment, and I had no doubt I'd sink to lower levels before the Winter Solstice bought us a day's reprieve.

I choked my rising desire until it was nothing but a vague roaring in the back of my mind, and didn't speak until Cassian and I were nearly through the wooden front door.

"Anything else I should know about while I'm here?" I knocked the snow from my boots against the door frame and stepped into the house. That kitchen table lay smack in the middle of the front room. I banished the image of Feyre bent over it.

Cassian blew out a breath and shut the door behind him before tucking in his wings and leaning against it. "Dissension's brewing. With so many clans gathering for the Solstice, it'll be a chance for them to spread it even more."

A flicker of my power had a fire roaring in the hearth, the small downstairs warming swiftly. It was barely a whisper of magic, yet its release eased that near-constant strain of keeping all that I was, all that dark power, in check. I took up a spot against that damned table and crossed my arms. "We've dealt with this shit before. We'll deal with it again."

Cassian shook his head, the shoulder-length dark hair shining in the watery light leaking through the front windows. "It's not like it was before. Before, you, me, and Az—we were resented for what we are, who we are. But this time . . . *we* sent them to battle. *I* sent them, Rhys. And now it's not only the warrior-pricks who are grumbling, but also the females. They believe you and I marched them south as revenge for our own treatment as children; they think we specifically stationed some of the males on the front lines as payback."

Not good. Not good at all. "We have to handle this carefully, then. Find out where this poison comes from and put an end to it—peacefully," I clarified when he lifted his brows. "We can't kill our way out of this one."

Cassian scratched at his jaw. "No, we can't." It wouldn't be like hunting down those rogue war-bands who'd terrorized any in their path. Not at all.

He surveyed the dim house, the fire crackling in the hearth, where we'd seen my mother cook so many meals during our training. An old, familiar ache filled my chest. This entire house, every inch of it, was full of the past. "A lot of them are coming in for the Solstice," he went on. "I can stay here, keep an eye on things. Maybe hand out presents to the children, some of the wives. Things that they really need but are too proud to ask for."

It was a solid idea. But—"It can wait. I want you home for Solstice."

"I don't mind—"

"I want you home. In Velaris," I added when he opened his mouth to spew some Illyrian loyalist bullshit that he still believed, even after they had treated him like less than nothing his entire life. "We're spending Solstice together. All of us."

Even if I had to give them a direct order as High Lord to do it.

Cassian angled his head. "What's eating at you?"

"Nothing."

As far as things went, I had little to complain about. Taking my mate to bed on a regular basis wasn't exactly a pressing issue. Or anyone's concern but our own.

"Wound a little tight, Rhys?"

Of course he'd seen right through it.

I sighed, frowning at the ancient, soot-speckled ceiling. We'd celebrated the Solstice in this house, too. My mother always had gifts for Azriel and Cassian. For the latter, the initial Solstice we'd shared here had been the first time he'd received *any* sort of gift, Solstice or not. I could still see the tears Cassian had tried to hide as he'd opened his presents, and the tears in my mother's eyes as she watched him. "I want to jump ahead to next week."

"Sure that power of yours can't do it for you?"

I leveled a dry look at him. Cassian just gave me a cocky grin back.

I never stopped being grateful for them—my friends, my family, who looked at that power of mine and did not balk, did not become scented with fear. Yes, I could scare the shit out of them sometimes, but we *all* did that to each other. Cassian had terrified me more times than I wanted to admit, one of them being mere months ago.

Twice. Twice, in the span of a matter of weeks, it had happened.

I still saw him being hauled by Azriel off that battlefield, blood spilling down his legs, into the mud, his wound a gaping maw that sliced down the center of his body.

And I still saw him as Feyre had seen him—after she'd let me into her mind to reveal what, exactly, had occurred between her sisters and the King of Hybern. Still saw Cassian, broken and bleeding on the ground, begging Nesta to run.

Cassian had not yet spoken of it. About what had occurred in those moments. About Nesta.

Cassian and my mate's sister did not speak to each other at all.

Nesta had successfully cloistered herself in some slummy apartment across the Sidra, refusing to interact with any of us save for a few brief visits with Feyre every month.

I'd have to find a way to fix that, too.

I saw how it ate away at Feyre. I still soothed her after she awoke, frantic, from nightmares about that day in Hybern when her sisters had been Made against their will. Nightmares about the moment when Cassian was near death and Nesta was sprawled over him, shielding him from that killing blow, and Elain—*Elain*—had taken up Azriel's dagger and killed the King of Hybern instead.

I rubbed my brows between my thumb and forefinger. "It's rough now. We're all busy, all trying to hold everything together." Az, Cassian, and I had yet again postponed our annual five days of hunting up at the cabin this fall. Put off for next year—again. "Come home for Solstice, and we can sit down and figure out a plan for the spring."

"Sounds like a festive event."

With my Court of Dreams, it always was.

But I made myself ask, "Is Devlon one of the would-be rebels?"

I prayed it wasn't true. I resented the male and his backwardness, but he'd been fair with Cassian, Azriel, and me under his watch. Treated us to the same rights as full-blooded Illyrian warriors. Still did that for all the bastard-born under his command. It was his absurd ideas about females that made me want to throttle him. Mist him. But if he had to be replaced, the Mother knew who would take his position.

Cassian shook his head. "I don't think so. Devlon shuts down any talk like that. But it only makes them more secretive, which makes it harder to find out who's spreading this bullshit around."

I nodded, standing. I had a meeting in Cesere with the two priestesses who had survived Hybern's massacre a year ago regarding how to handle pilgrims who wanted to come from outside our territory. Being late wouldn't lend any favors to my arguments to delay such a thing until the spring. "Keep an eye on it for the next few days, then come home. I want you there two nights before Solstice. And for the day after."

A hint of a wicked grin. "I assume our Solstice-day tradition will still be on, then. Despite you now being such a grown-up, mated male."

I winked at him. "I'd hate for you Illyrian babies to miss me."

Cassian chuckled. There were indeed some Solstice traditions that never grew tiresome, even after the centuries. I was almost at the door when Cassian said, "Is . . ." He swallowed.

I spared him the discomfort of trying to mask his interest. "Both sisters will be at the house. Whether they want to or not."

"Nesta will make things unpleasant if she decides she doesn't want to be there."

"She'll be there," I said, grinding my teeth, "and she'll be pleasant. She owes Feyre that much."

Cassian's eyes flickered. "How is she?"

I didn't bother to put any sort of spin on it. "Nesta is Nesta. She does what she wants, even if it kills her sister. I've offered her job after job, and she refuses them all." I sucked on my teeth. "Perhaps you can talk some sense into her over Solstice."

Cassian's Siphons gleamed atop his hands. "It'd likely end in violence."

It indeed would. "Then don't say a word to her. I don't care—just keep Feyre out of it. It's her day, too."

Because this Solstice . . . it was her birthday. Twenty-one years old.

It hit me for a moment, how small that number was.

My beautiful, strong, fierce mate, shackled to me—

"I know what that look means, you bastard," Cassian said roughly, "and it's bullshit. She loves you—in a way I've never seen anybody love anyone."

"It's hard sometimes," I admitted, staring toward the snow-coated field outside the house, the training rings and dwellings beyond it, "to remember that she picked it. Picked me. That it's not like my parents, shoved together."

Cassian's face turned uncharacteristically solemn, and he remained quiet for a moment before he said, "I get jealous sometimes. I'd never begrudge you for your happiness, but what you two have, Rhys . . ." He dragged a hand through his hair, his crimson Siphon glinting in the light streaming through the window. "It's the legends, the lies, they spin us when we're children. About the glory and wonder of the mating bond. I thought it was all bullshit. Then you two came along."

"She's turning twenty-one. *Twenty-one*, Cassian."

"So? Your mother was eighteen to your father's nine hundred."

"And she was miserable."

"Feyre is not your mother. And you are not your father." He looked me over. "Where is this coming from, anyway? Are things . . . not good?"

The opposite, actually. "I get this feeling," I said, pacing a step, the ancient wood floorboards creaking beneath my boots, my power a writhing, living thing prowling through my veins, "that it's all some sort of joke. Some sort of cosmic trick, and that no one—*no one*—can be this happy and not pay for it."

"You've already paid for it, Rhys. Both of you. And then some."

I waved a hand. "I just . . ." I trailed off, unable to finish the words.

Cassian stared at me for a long moment.

Then he crossed the distance between us, gathering me in an embrace so tight I could barely breathe. "You made it. *We* made it. You both endured enough that no one would blame you if you danced off into the sunset like Miryam and Drakon and never bothered with anything else again. But you are bothering—you're both still working to make this peace last. *Peace*, Rhys. We have *peace*, and the true kind. Enjoy it—enjoy each other. You paid the debt before it was ever a debt."

My throat tightened, and I gripped him hard around his wings, the scales of his leathers digging into my fingers. "What about you?" I asked, pulling away after a moment. "Are you . . . happy?"

Shadows darkened his hazel eyes. "I'm getting there."

A halfhearted answer.

I'd have to work on that, too. Perhaps there were threads to be pulled, woven together.

Cassian jerked his chin toward the door. "Get going, you bastard. I'll see you in three days."

I nodded, opening the door at last. But paused on the threshold. "Thanks, brother."

Cassian's crooked grin was bright, even if those shadows still guttered in his eyes. "It's an honor, my lord."

CHAPTER 3

Cassian

Cassian wasn't entirely certain that he could deal with Devlon and his warriors without throttling them. At least, not for the next good hour or so.

And since that would do little to help quell the murmurings of discontent, Cassian waited until Rhys had winnowed out into the snow and wind before vanishing himself.

Not winnowing, though that would have been one hell of a weapon against enemies in battle. He'd seen Rhys do it with devastating results. Az, too—in the strange way that Az could move through the world *without* technically winnowing.

He'd never asked. Azriel certainly had never explained.

But Cassian didn't mind his own method of moving: flying. It certainly had served him well enough in battle.

Stepping out the front door of the ancient wooden house so that Devlon and the other pricks in the sparring rings would see him, Cassian made a good show of stretching. First his arms, honed and still aching to pummel in a few Illyrian faces. Then his wings, wider and broader than theirs. They'd always resented that, perhaps more than anything else. He flared them until the strain along the powerful muscles and sinews was a pleasurable burn, his wings casting long shadows across the snow.

And with a mighty flap, he shot into the gray skies.

The wind was a roar around him, the temperature cold enough that his eyes watered. Bracing—freeing. He flapped higher, then banked left, aiming for the peaks behind the camp pass. No need to do a warning sweep over Devlon and the sparring rings.

Ignoring them, projecting the message that they weren't important enough to even be considered threats were far better ways of pissing them off. Rhys had taught him that. Long ago.

Catching an updraft that sent him soaring over the nearest peaks and then into the endless, snow-coated labyrinth of mountains that made up their homeland, Cassian breathed in deep. His flying leathers and gloves kept him warm enough, but his wings, exposed to the chill wind . . . The cold was sharp as a knife.

He could shield himself with his Siphons, had done it in the past. But today, this morning, he wanted that biting cold.

Especially with what he was about to do. Where he was going.

He would have known the path blindfolded, simply by listening to the wind through the mountains, inhaling the smell of the pine-crusted peaks below, the barren rock fields.

It was rare for him to make the trek. He usually only did it when his temper was likely to get the better of him, and he had enough lingering control to know he needed to head out for a few hours. Today was no exception.

In the distance, small, dark shapes shot through the sky. Warriors on patrol. Or perhaps armed escorts leading families to their Solstice reunions.

Most High Fae believed the Illyrians were the greatest menace in these mountains.

They didn't realize that far worse things prowled between the peaks. Some of them hunting on the winds, some crawling out from deep caverns in the rock itself.

Feyre had braved facing some of those things in the pine forests of the Steppes. To save Rhys. Cassian wondered if his brother had ever told her what dwelled in these mountains. Most had been slain by the Illyrians, or sent fleeing to those Steppes. But the most cunning of them, the most ancient . . . they had found ways to hide. To emerge on moonless nights to feed.

Even five centuries of training couldn't stop the chill that skittered down his spine as Cassian surveyed the empty, quiet mountains below and wondered what slept beneath the snow.

He cut northward, casting the thought from his mind. On the horizon, a familiar shape took form, growing larger with each flap of his wings.

Ramiel. The sacred mountain.

The heart of not only Illyria, but the entirety of the Night Court.

None were permitted on its barren, rocky slopes—save for the Illyrians, and only once a year at that. During the Blood Rite.

Cassian soared toward it, unable to resist Ramiel's ancient summons. Different—the mountain was so different from the barren, terrible presence of the lone peak in the center of Prythian. Ramiel had always felt alive, somehow. Awake and watchful.

He'd only set foot on it once, on that final day of the Rite. When he and his brothers, bloodied and battered, had scaled its side to reach the onyx monolith at its summit. He could still feel the crumbling rock beneath his boots, hear the rasp of his breathing as he half hauled Rhys up the slopes, Azriel providing cover behind. As one, the three of them had touched the stone—the first to reach its peak at the end of that brutal week. The uncontested winners.

The Rite hadn't changed in the centuries since. Early each spring, it still went on, hundreds of warrior-novices deposited across the mountains and forests surrounding the peak, the territory off-limits during the rest of the year to prevent any of the novices from scouting ahead for the best routes and traps to lay. There were varying qualifiers throughout the year to prove a novice's readiness, each slightly different depending on the camp. But the rules remained the same.

All novices competed with wings bound, no Siphons—a spell restraining all magic—and no supplies beyond the clothes on your back. The goal: make it to the summit of that mountain by the end of that week and touch the stone. The obstacles: the distance, the natural traps, and each other. Old feuds played out; new ones were born. Scores were settled.

A week of pointless bloodshed, Az insisted.

Rhys often agreed, though he often *also* agreed with Cassian's point: the Blood Rite offered an escape valve for dangerous tensions within the Illyrian community. Better to settle it during the Rite than risk civil war.

Illyrians were strong, proud, fearless. But peacemakers, they were not.

Perhaps he'd get lucky. Perhaps the Rite this spring would ease some of the malcontent. Hell, he'd offer to participate *himself*, if it meant quieting the grumbling.

They'd barely survived this war. They didn't need another one. Not with so many unknowns gathering outside their borders.

Ramiel rose higher still, a shard of stone piercing the gray sky. Beautiful and lonely. Eternal and ageless.

No wonder that first ruler of the Night Court had made this his insignia. Along with the three stars that only appeared for a brief window each year, framing the uppermost peak of Ramiel like a crown. It was during that window when the Rite occurred. Which had come first: the insignia or the Rite, Cassian didn't know. Had never really cared to find out.

The conifer forests and ravines that dotted the landscape flowing to Ramiel's foot gleamed under fresh snow. Empty and clean. No sign of the bloodshed that would occur come the start of spring.

The mountain neared, mighty and endless, so wide that he might as well have been a mayfly in the wind. Cassian soared toward Ramiel's southern face, rising high enough to catch a glimpse of the shining black stone jutting from its top.

Who had put that stone atop the peak, he didn't know, either. Legend said it had existed before the Night Court formed, before the Illyrians migrated from the Myrmidons, before humans had even walked the earth. Even with the fresh snow crusting Ramiel, none had touched the pillar of stone.

A thrill, icy and yet not unwelcome, flooded his veins.

It was rare for anyone in the Blood Rite to make it to the monolith. Since he and his brothers had done it five centuries ago, Cassian could recall only a dozen or so who'd not only reached the mountain, but also survived the climb. After a week of fighting, of running, of having to find and make your own weapons and food, that climb was worse than every horror before it. It was the true test of will, of courage. To climb when you had nothing left; to climb when your body begged you to stop . . . It was when the breaking usually occurred.

But when he'd touched the onyx monolith, when he'd felt that ancient force sing into his blood in the heartbeat before it had whisked him back to the safety of Devlon's camp . . . It had been worth it. To feel that.

With a solemn bow of his head toward Ramiel and the living stone atop it, Cassian caught another swift wind and soared southward.

An hour's flight had him approaching yet another familiar peak.

One that no one but him and his brothers bothered to come to. What he'd so badly needed to see, to feel, today.

Once, it had been as busy a camp as Devlon's.

Once. Before a bastard had been born in a freezing, lone tent on the outskirts of the village. Before they'd thrown a young, unwed mother out into the snow only days after giving birth, her babe in her arms. And then taken that babe mere years later, tossing him into the mud at Devlon's camp.

Cassian landed on the flat stretch of mountain pass, the snowdrifts higher than at Windhaven. Hiding any trace of the village that had stood here.

Only cinders and debris remained anyway.

He'd made sure of it.

When those who had been responsible for her suffering and torment had been dealt with, no one had wanted to remain here a moment longer. Not with the shattered bone and blood coating every surface, staining every field and training ring. So they'd migrated, some blending into other camps, others making their own lives elsewhere. None had ever come back.

Centuries later, he didn't regret it.

Standing in the snow and wind, surveying the emptiness where he'd been born, Cassian didn't regret it for a heartbeat.

His mother had suffered every moment of her too-short life. It only grew worse after she'd given birth to him. Especially in the years after he'd been taken away.

And when he'd been strong and old enough to come back to look for her, she was gone.

They'd refused to tell him where she was buried. If they'd given her that honor, or if they'd thrown her body into an icy chasm to rot.

He still didn't know. Even with their final, rasping breaths, those who'd made sure she never knew happiness had refused to tell him. Had spat in his face and told him every awful thing they'd done to her.

He'd wanted to bury her in Velaris. Somewhere full of light and warmth, full of kind people. Far away from these mountains.

Cassian scanned the snow-covered pass. His memories here were murky: mud and cold and too-small fires. But he could recall a lilting, soft voice, and gentle, slender hands.

It was all he had of her.

Cassian dragged his hands through his hair, fingers catching on the wind-tangled snarls.

He knew why he'd come here, why he always came here. For all that Amren taunted him about being an Illyrian brute, he knew his own mind, his own heart.

Devlon was a fairer camp-lord than most. But for the females who were less fortunate, who were preyed upon or cast out, there was little mercy.

So training these women, giving them the resources and confidence to fight back, to look beyond their campfires . . . it was for her. For the mother buried here, perhaps buried nowhere. So it might never happen again. So his people, whom he still loved despite their faults, might one day become something *more*. Something better.

The unmarked, unknown grave in this pass was his reminder.

Cassian stood in silence for long minutes before turning his gaze westward. As if he might see all the way to Velaris.

Rhys wanted him home for the Solstice, and he'd obey.

Even if Nesta—

Nesta.

Even in his thoughts, her name clanged through him, hollow and cold.

Now wasn't the time to think of her. Not here.

He very rarely allowed himself to think of her, anyway. It usually didn't end well for whoever was in the sparring ring with him.

Spreading his wings wide, Cassian took a final glance around the camp he'd razed to the ground. Another reminder, too: of what he was capable of when pushed too far.

To be careful, even when Devlon and the others made him want to bellow. He and Az were the most powerful Illyrians in their long, bloody history. They wore an unprecedented seven Siphons each, just to handle the tidal wave of brute killing power they possessed. It was a gift and a burden that he'd never taken lightly.

Three days. He had three days until he was to go to Velaris.

He'd try to make them count.

CHAPTER 4

Feyre

The Rainbow was a hum of activity, even with the drifting veils of snow.

High Fae and faeries alike poured in and out of the various shops and studios, some perched on ladders to string up drooping garlands of pine and holly between the lampposts, some sweeping gathered clusters of snow from their doorsteps, some—no doubt artists—merely standing on the pale cobblestones and turning in place, faces uplifted to the gray sky, hair and skin and clothes dusted with fine powder.

Dodging one such person in the middle of the street—a faerie with skin like glittering onyx and eyes like swirling clusters of stars—I aimed for the front of a small, pretty gallery, its glass window revealing an assortment of paintings and pottery. The perfect place to do some Solstice shopping. A wreath of evergreen hung on the freshly painted blue door, brass bells dangling from its center.

The door: new. The display window: new.

Both had been shattered and stained with blood months ago. This entire street had.

It was an effort not to glance at the white-dusted stones of the street, sloping steeply down to the meandering Sidra at its base. To the walkway along the river, full of patrons and artists, where I had stood months ago and summoned wolves from those slumbering waters. Blood had been streaming down these cobblestones then, and there hadn't been singing and laughter in the streets, but screaming and pleading.

I took a sharp inhale through my nose, the chilled air tickling my nostrils. Slowly, I released it in a long breath, watching it cloud in front of me. Watching myself in the reflection of the store window: barely recognizable in my heavy gray coat, a red-and-gray scarf that I'd pilfered from Mor's closet, my eyes wide and distant.

I realized a heartbeat later that I was not the only one staring at myself.

Inside the gallery, no fewer than five people were doing their best not to gawk at me as they browsed the collection of paintings and pottery.

My cheeks warmed, heart a staccato beat, and I offered a tight smile before continuing on.

No matter that I'd spotted a piece that caught my eye. No matter that I *wanted* to go in.

I kept my gloved hands bundled in the pockets of my coat as I strode down the steep street, mindful of my steps on the slick cobblestones. While Velaris had plenty of spells upon it to keep the palaces and cafés and squares warm during the winter, it seemed that for this first snow, many of them had been lifted, as if everyone wanted to feel its chill kiss.

I'd indeed braved the walk from the town house, wanting to not only breathe in the crisp, snowy air, but to also just absorb the crackling excitement of those readying for Solstice, rather than merely winnowing or flying over them.

Though Rhys and Azriel still instructed me whenever they could, though I truly loved to fly, the thought of exposing sensitive wings to the cold made me shiver.

Few people recognized me while I strode by, my power firmly restrained within me, and most too concerned with decorating or enjoying the first snow to note those around them, anyway.

A small mercy, though I certainly didn't mind being approached. As High Lady, I hosted weekly open audiences with Rhys at the House of Wind. The requests ranged from the small—a faelight lamppost was broken—to the complicated—could we please stop importing goods from other courts because it impacted local artisans.

Some were issues Rhys had dealt with for centuries now, but he never acted like he had.

No, he listened to each petitioner, asked thorough questions, and then sent them on their way with a promise to send an answer to them soon. It had taken me a few sessions to get the hang of it—the questions he used, the *way* he listened. He hadn't pushed me to step in unless necessary, had granted me the space to figure out the rhythm and style of these audiences and begin asking questions of my own. And then begin writing replies to the petitioners, too. Rhys personally answered each and every one of them. And I now did, too.

Hence the ever-growing stacks of paperwork in so many rooms of the town house.

How he'd lasted so long without a team of secretaries assisting him, I had no idea.

But as I eased down the steep slope of the street, the bright-colored buildings of the Rainbow glowing around me like a shimmering memory of summer, I again mulled it over.

Velaris was by no means poor, its people mostly cared for, the buildings and streets well kept. My sister, it seemed, had managed to find the only thing relatively close to a slum. And insisted on living there, in a building that was older than Rhys and in dire need of repairs.

There were only a few blocks in the city like that. When I'd asked Rhys about them, about why they had not been improved, he merely said that he had tried. But displacing people while their homes were torn down and rebuilt . . . Tricky.

I hadn't been surprised two days ago when Rhys had handed me a piece of paper and asked if there was anything else I would like to add to it. On the paper had been a list of charities that he donated to around Solstice-time, everything from aiding the poor, sick, and elderly to grants for young mothers to start their own businesses. I'd added only two items, both to societies that I'd heard about through my own volunteering: donations to the humans displaced by the war with Hybern, as well as to Illyrian war widows and their families. The sums we allocated were sizable, more money than I'd ever dreamed of possessing.

Once, all I had wanted was enough food, money, and time to paint. Nothing more. I would have been content to let my sisters wed, to remain and care for my father.

But beyond my mate, my family, beyond being High Lady—the mere fact that I now lived *here*, that I could walk through an entire artists' quarter whenever I wished . . .

Another avenue bisected the street midway down its slope, and I turned onto it, the neat rows of houses and galleries and studios curving away into the snow. But even amongst the bright colors, there were patches of gray, of emptiness.

I approached one such hollow place, a half-crumbled building. Its mint-green paint had turned grayish, as if the very light had bled from the color as the building shattered. Indeed, the few buildings around it were also muted and cracked, a gallery across the street boarded up.

A few months ago, I'd begun donating a portion of my monthly salary—the idea of receiving such a thing was still utterly ludicrous—to rebuilding the Rainbow and helping its artists, but the scars remained, on both these buildings and their residents.

And the mound of snow-dusted rubble before me: who had dwelled there, worked there? Did they live, or had they been slaughtered in the attack?

There were many such places in Velaris. I'd seen them in my work, while handing out winter coats and meeting with families in their homes.

I blew out another breath. I knew I lingered too often, too long at such sites. I knew I should continue on, smiling as if nothing bothered me, as if all were well. And yet . . .

"They got out in time," a female voice said behind me.

I turned, boots slipping on the slick cobblestones. Throwing out a hand to steady me, I gripped the first thing I came into contact with: a fallen chunk of rock from the wrecked house.

But it was the sight of who, exactly, stood behind me, gazing at the rubble, that made me abandon any mortification.

I had not forgotten her in the months since the attack.

I had not forgotten the sight of her standing outside that shop door, a rusted pipe raised over one shoulder, squaring off against the gathered Hybern soldiers, ready to go down swinging for the terrified people huddled inside.

A faint rose blush glowed prettily on her pale green skin, her sable hair flowing past her chest. She was bundled against the cold in a brown coat, a pink scarf wrapped around her neck and lower half of her face, but her long, delicate fingers were gloveless as she crossed her arms.

Faerie—and not a kind I saw too frequently. Her face and body reminded me of the High Fae, though her ears were slenderer, longer than mine. Her form slimmer, sleeker, even with the heavy coat.

I met her eyes, a vibrant ochre that made me wonder what paints I'd have to blend and wield to capture their likeness, and offered a small smile. "I'm glad to hear it."

Silence fell, interrupted by the merry singing of a few people down the street and the wind gusting off the Sidra.

The faerie only inclined her head. "Lady."

I fumbled for words, for something High Lady–ish and yet accessible, and came up empty. Came up so empty that I blurted, "It's snowing."

As if the drifting veils of white could be anything else.

The faerie inclined her head again. "It is." She smiled at the sky, snow catching in her inky hair. "A fine first snow at that."

I surveyed the ruin behind me. "You—you know the people who lived here?"

"I did. They're living at a relative's farm in the lowlands now." She waved a hand toward the distant sea, to the flat expanse of land between Velaris and the shore.

"Ah," I managed to say, then jerked my chin at the boarded-up shop across the street. "What about that one?"

The faerie surveyed where I'd indicated. Her mouth—painted a berry pink—tightened. "Not so happy an ending, I'm afraid."

My palms turned sweaty within my wool gloves. "I see."

She faced me again, silken hair flowing around her. "Her name was Polina. That was her gallery. For centuries."

Now it was a dark, quiet husk.

"I'm sorry," I said, uncertain what else to offer.

The faerie's slim, dark brows narrowed. "Why should you be?" She added, "My lady."

I gnawed on my lip. Discussing such things with strangers . . . Perhaps not a good idea. So I ignored her question and asked, "Does she have any family?" I hoped they'd made it, at least.

"They live out in the lowlands, too. Her sister and nieces and nephews." The faerie again studied the boarded-up front. "It's for sale now."

I blinked, grasping the implied offer. "Oh—oh, I wasn't asking after it for *that* reason." It hadn't even entered my mind.

"Why not?"

A frank, easy question. Perhaps more direct than most people, certainly strangers, dared to be with me. "I—what use would I have for it?"

She gestured to me with a hand, the motion effortlessly graceful. "Rumor has it that you're a fine artist. I can think of many uses for the space."

I glanced away, hating myself a bit for it. "I'm not in the market, I'm afraid."

The faerie shrugged with one shoulder. "Well, whether you are or aren't, you needn't go skulking around here. Every door is open to you, you know."

"As High Lady?" I dared ask.

"As one of us," she said simply.

The words settled in, strange and yet like a piece I had not known was missing. An offered hand I had not realized how badly I wanted to grasp.

"I'm Feyre," I said, removing my glove and extending my arm.

The faerie clasped my fingers, her grip steel-strong despite her slender build. "Ressina." Not someone prone to excessive smiling, but still full of a practical sort of warmth.

Noon bells chimed in a tower at the edge of the Rainbow, the sound soon echoed across the city in the other sister-towers.

"I should be going," I said, releasing Ressina's hand and retreating a step. "It was nice to meet you." I tugged my glove back on, my fingers already stinging with cold. Perhaps I'd take some time this winter to master my fire gifts more precisely. Learning how to warm clothes and skin without burning myself would be mighty helpful.

Ressina pointed to a building down the street—across the intersection I had just passed through. The same building she'd defended, its walls painted raspberry pink, and doors and windows a bright turquoise, like the water around Adriata. "I'm one of the artists who uses that studio space over there. If you ever want a guide, or even some company, I'm there most days. I live above the studio." An elegant wave toward the tiny round windows on the second level.

I put a hand on my chest. "Thank you."

Again that silence, and I took in that shop, the doorway Ressina had stood before, guarding her home and others.

"We remember it, you know," Ressina said quietly, drawing my stare away. But her attention had landed on the rubble behind us, on the boarded-up studio, on the street, as if she, too, could see through the snow to the blood that had run between the cobblestones. "That you came for us that day."

I didn't know what to do with my body, my hands, so I opted for stillness.

Ressina met my stare at last, her ochre eyes bright. "We keep away to let you have your privacy, but don't think for one moment that there isn't a single one of us who doesn't know and remember, who isn't grateful that you came here and fought for us."

It hadn't been enough, even so. The ruined building behind me was proof of that. People had still died.

Ressina took a few unhurried steps toward her studio, then stopped. "There's a group of us who paint together at my studio. One night a week. We're meeting in two days' time. It would be an honor if you joined us."

"What sort of things do you paint?" My question was soft as the snow falling past us.

Ressina smiled slightly. "The things that need telling."

Even with the icy evening soon descending upon Velaris, people packed the streets, laden with bags and boxes, some lugging enormous fruit baskets from one of the many stands now occupying either Palace.

My fur-lined hood shielding me against the cold, I browsed through the vendor carts and storefronts in the Palace of Thread and Jewels, surveying the latter, mostly.

Some of the public areas remained heated, but enough of Velaris had now been temporarily left exposed to the bitter wind that I wished I'd opted for a heavier sweater that morning. Learning how to warm myself without summoning a flame would be handy indeed. If I ever had the time to do it.

I was circling back to a display in one of the shops built beneath the overhanging buildings when an arm looped through mine and Mor drawled, "Amren would love you forever if you bought her a sapphire that big."

I laughed, tugging back my hood enough to see her fully. Mor's cheeks were flushed against the cold, her braided golden hair spilling into the white fur lining her cloak. "Unfortunately, I don't think our coffers would return the feeling."

Mor smirked. "You *do* know that we're well-off, don't you? You could fill a bathtub with those things"—she jerked her chin toward the egg-sized sapphire in the window of the jewelry shop—"and barely make a dent in our accounts."

I knew. I'd seen the lists of assets. I still couldn't wrap my mind around the enormity of Rhys's wealth. *My* wealth. It didn't feel real, those numbers and figures. Like it was children's play money. I only bought what I needed.

But now . . . "I'm looking for something to get her for Solstice."

Mor surveyed the lineup of jewels, both uncut and set, in the window. Some gleamed like fallen stars. Others smoldered, as if they had been carved from the burning heart of the earth. "Amren does deserve a decent present this year, doesn't she?"

After what Amren had done during that final battle to destroy Hybern's armies, the choice she'd made to remain here . . . "We all do."

Mor nudged me with an elbow, though her brown eyes gleamed. "And will Varian be joining us, do you think?"

I snorted. "When I asked her yesterday, she hedged."

"I think that means yes. Or he'll at least be visiting *her*."

I smiled at the thought, and pulled Mor along to the next display window, pressing against her side for warmth. Amren and the Prince of Adriata hadn't officially declared anything, but I sometimes dreamed of it, too—that moment when she had shed her immortal skin and Varian had fallen to his knees.

A creature of flame and brimstone, built in another world to mete out a cruel god's judgment, to be his executioner upon the masses of helpless mortals. Fifteen thousand years, she had been stuck in this world.

And had not loved, not in the way that could alter history, alter fate, until that silver-haired Prince of Adriata. Or at least loved in the way that Amren was capable of loving anything.

So, yes: nothing was declared between them. But I knew he visited her, secretly, in this city. Mostly because some mornings, Amren would strut into the town house smirking like a cat.

But for what she'd been willing to walk away from, so that we could be saved . . .

Mor and I spied the piece in the window at the same moment. "That one," she declared.

I was already moving for the glass front door, a silver bell ringing merrily as we entered.

The shopkeeper was wide-eyed but beaming as we pointed to the piece, and swiftly laid it out on a black velvet pad. She made a sweet-tempered excuse to retrieve something from the back, granting us privacy to examine it as we stood before the polished wood counter.

"It's perfect," Mor breathed, the stones fracturing the light and burning with their own inner fire.

I ran a finger over the cool silver settings. "What do *you* want as a present?"

Mor shrugged, her heavy brown coat bringing out the rich soil of her eyes. "I've got everything I need."

"Try telling Rhys that. He says Solstice isn't about getting gifts you *need*, but rather ones you'd never buy for yourself." Mor rolled her eyes. Even though I was inclined to do the same, I pushed, "So what *do* you want?"

She ran a finger along a cut stone. "Nothing. I—there's nothing I want."

Beyond things she perhaps was not ready to ask for, search for.

I again examined the piece and casually asked, "You've been at Rita's a great deal lately. Is there anyone you might want to bring to Solstice dinner?"

Mor's eyes sliced to mine. "No."

It was her business, when and how to inform the others what she'd told me during the war. When and how to tell Azriel especially.

My only role in it was to stand by her—to have her back when she needed it.

So I went on, "What are *you* getting the others?"

She scowled. "After centuries of gifts, it's a pain in my ass to find something new for all of them. I'm fairly certain Azriel has a drawer full of all the daggers I've bought him throughout the centuries that he's too polite to throw away, but won't ever use."

"You honestly think he'd ever give up Truth-Teller?"

"He gave it to Elain," Mor said, admiring a moonstone necklace in the counter's glass case.

"She gave it back," I amended, failing to block out the image of the black blade piercing through the King of Hybern's throat. But

Elain *had* given it back—had pressed it into Azriel's hands after the battle, just as he had pressed it into hers before. And then walked away without looking back.

Mor hummed to herself. The jeweler returned a moment later, and I signed the purchase to my personal credit account, trying not to cringe at the enormous sum of money that just disappeared with a stroke of a golden pen.

"Speaking of Illyrian warriors," I said as we strode into the crammed Palace square and edged around a red-painted cart selling cups of piping hot molten chocolate, "what the hell *do* I get either of them?"

I didn't have the nerve to ask what I should get for Rhys, since, even though I adored Mor, it felt *wrong* to ask another person for advice on what to buy my mate.

"You *could* honestly get Cassian a new knife and he'd kiss you for it. But Az would probably prefer no presents at all, just to avoid the attention while opening it."

I laughed. "True."

Arm in arm, we continued on, the aromas of roasting hazelnuts, pine cones, and chocolate replacing the usual salt-and-lemon-verbena scent that filled the city. "Do you plan to visit Viviane during Solstice?"

In the months since the war had ended, Mor had remained in contact with the Lady of the Winter Court, perhaps soon to be *High* Lady, if Viviane had anything to do about it. They'd been friends for centuries, until Amarantha's reign had severed contact, and though the war with Hybern had been brutal, one of the good things to come of it had been the rekindling of their friendship. Rhys and Kallias had a still-lukewarm alliance, but it seemed

Mor's relationship with the High Lord of Winter's mate would be the bridge between our two courts.

My friend smiled warmly. "Perhaps a day or two after. Their celebrating lasts for a whole week."

"Have you been before?"

A shake of her head, golden hair catching in the faelight lamps. "No. They usually keep their borders closed, even to friends. But with Kallias now in power, and especially with Viviane at his side, they're starting to open up once more."

"I can only imagine their celebrations."

Her eyes glowed. "Viviane told me about them once. They make ours look positively dull. Dancing and drinking, feasting and gifting. Roaring fires made from entire tree trunks and cauldrons full of mulled wine, the singing of a thousand minstrels flowing throughout their palace, answered by the bells ringing on the large sleighs pulled by those beautiful white bears." She sighed. I echoed it, the image she'd crafted hovering in the frosty air between us.

Here in Velaris, we would celebrate the longest night of the year. In Kallias's territory, it seemed, they would celebrate the winter itself.

Mor's smile faded. "I did find you for a reason, you know."

"Not just to shop?"

She nudged me with an elbow. "We're to head to the Hewn City tonight."

I cringed. "*We* as in all of us?"

"You, me, and Rhys, at least."

I bit back a groan. "Why?"

Mor paused at a vendor, examining the neatly folded scarves

displayed. "Tradition. Around Solstice, we make a little visit to the Court of Nightmares to wish them well."

"Really?"

Mor grimaced, nodding to the vendor and continuing on. "As I said, tradition. To foster goodwill. Or as much of it as we have. And after the battles this summer, it wouldn't hurt."

Keir and his Darkbringer army had fought, after all.

We eased through the densely packed heart of the Palace, passing beneath a latticework of faelights just beginning to twinkle awake overhead. From a slumbering, quiet place inside me, the painting name flitted by. *Frost and Starlight*.

"So you and Rhys decided to tell me mere hours before we go?"

"Rhys has been away all day. *I* decided that we're to go tonight. Since we don't want to ruin the actual Solstice by visiting, now is best."

There were plenty of days between now and Solstice Eve to do it. But Mor's face remained carefully casual.

I still pushed, "You preside over the Hewn City, and deal with them all the time." She as good as ruled over it when Rhys wasn't there. And handled her awful father plenty.

Mor sensed the question within my statement. "Eris will be there tonight. I heard it from Az this morning."

I remained quiet, waiting.

Mor's brown eyes darkened. "I want to see for myself just how cozy he and my father have become."

It was good enough reason for me.

CHAPTER 5

Feyre

I was curled up on the bed, toasty and drowsy atop the layers of blankets and down quilts, when Rhys finally returned home as dusk fell.

I felt his power beckoning to me long before he got near the house, a dark melody through the world.

Mor had announced we wouldn't be going to the Hewn City for another hour or so, long enough that I'd forgone touching that paperwork on the rosewood writing desk across the room and had instead picked up a book. I'd barely managed ten pages before Rhys opened the bedroom door.

His Illyrian leathers gleamed with melted snow, and more of it shone on his dark hair and wings as he quietly shut the door. "Right where I left you."

I smiled, setting down the book beside me. It was nearly swallowed by the ivory down duvet. "Isn't this all I'm good for?"

A rogue smile tugging up one corner of his mouth, Rhys began removing his weapons, then the clothes. But despite the humor lighting his eyes, each movement was heavy and slow—as if he fought exhaustion with every breath.

"Maybe we should tell Mor to delay the meeting at the Court of Nightmares." I frowned.

He shucked off his jacket, the leathers thumping as they landed on the desk chair. "Why? If Eris will indeed be there, I'd like to surprise him with a little visit of my own."

"You look exhausted, that's why."

He put a dramatic hand over his heart. "Your concern warms me more than any winter fire, my love."

I rolled my eyes and sat up. "Did you at least eat?"

He shrugged, his dark shirt straining across his broad shoulders. "I'm fine." His gaze slid over my bare legs as I pushed back the covers.

Heat bloomed in me, but I shoved my feet into slippers. "I'll get you food."

"I don't want—"

"When did you last eat?"

A sullen silence.

"I thought so." I hauled a fleece-lined robe around my shoulders. "Wash up and change. We're leaving in forty minutes. I'll be back soon."

He tucked in his wings, the faelight gilding the talon atop each one. "You don't need to—"

"I want to, and I'm going to." With that, I was out the door and padding down the cerulean-blue hallway.

Five minutes later, Rhys held the door open for me wearing nothing but his undershorts as I strode in, tray in my hands.

"Considering that you brought the entire damn kitchen," he

mused as I headed for the desk, still not anywhere near dressed for our visit, "I should have just gone downstairs."

I stuck out my tongue, but scowled as I scanned the cluttered desk for any spare space. None. Even the small table by the window was covered with things. All important, vital things. I made do with the bed.

Rhys sat, folding his wings behind him before reaching to pull me into his lap, but I dodged his hands and kept a healthy distance away. "Eat the food first."

"Then I'll eat you after," he countered, grinning wickedly, but tore into the food.

The rate and intensity of that eating was enough to bank any rising heat in me at his words. "Did you eat *at all* today?"

A flash of violet eyes as he finished off his bread and began on the cold roast beef. "I had an apple this morning."

"Rhys."

"I was busy."

"*Rhys.*"

He set down his fork, his mouth twitching toward a smile. "Feyre."

I crossed my arms. "No one is too busy to eat."

"You're fussing."

"It's my job to fuss. And besides, *you* fuss plenty. Over far more trivial things."

"Your cycle *isn't* trivial."

"I was in a *little* bit of pain—"

"You were thrashing on the bed as if someone had gutted you."

"And *you* were acting like an overbearing mother hen."

"I didn't see you screaming at Cassian, Mor, or Az when *they* expressed concern for you."

"They didn't try to spoon-feed me like an invalid!"

Rhys chuckled, finishing off his food. "I'll eat regular meals if you allow me to turn into an overbearing mother hen twice a year."

Right—because my cycle was so different in this body. Gone were the monthly discomforts. I'd thought it a gift.

Until two months ago. When the first one had happened.

In place of those monthly, human discomforts was a biannual week of stomach-shredding *agony*. Even Madja, Rhys's favored healer, could do little for the pain short of rendering me unconscious. There had been a point during that week when I'd debated it, the pain slicing from my back and stomach down to my thighs, up to my arms, like living bands of lightning flashing through me. My cycle had never been pleasant as a human, and there had indeed been days when I couldn't get out of bed. It seemed that in being Made, the amplification of my attributes hadn't stopped at strength and Fae features. Not at all.

Mor had little to offer me beyond commiseration and ginger tea. At least it was only twice a year, she'd consoled me. That was two times too many, I'd managed to groan to her.

Rhys had stayed with me the entire time, stroking my hair, replacing the heated blankets that I soaked with sweat, even helping me clean myself off. Blood was blood, was all he said when I'd objected to him seeing me peel off the soiled undergarments. I'd been barely able to move at that point without whimpering, so the words hadn't entirely sunken in.

Along with the implication of that blood. At least the contraceptive brew he took was working. But conceiving amongst the Fae was rare and difficult enough that I sometimes wondered if waiting until I was ready for children might wind up biting me in the ass.

I hadn't forgotten the Bone Carver's vision, how he'd appeared to me. I knew Rhys hadn't, either.

But he hadn't pushed, or asked. I'd once told him that I wanted to live with him, experience *life* with him, before we had children. I still held to that. There was so much to do, our days too busy to even *think* about bringing a child into the world, my life full enough that even though it would be a blessing beyond measure, I would endure the twice-a-year agony for the time being. And help my sisters with them, too.

Fae fertility cycles had never been something I'd considered, and explaining them to Nesta and Elain had been uncomfortable, to say the least.

Nesta had only stared at me in that unblinking, cold way. Elain had blushed, muttering about the impropriety of such things. But they had been Made nearly six months ago. It was coming. Soon. If being Made somehow didn't interfere with it.

I'd have to find some way to convince Nesta to send word when hers started. Like hell would I allow her to endure that pain alone. I wasn't sure she *could* endure that pain alone.

Elain, at least, would be too polite to send Lucien away when he wanted to help. She was too polite to send him away on a normal day. She just ignored him or barely spoke to him until he got the hint and left. As far as I knew, he hadn't come within touching distance since the aftermath of that final battle. No, she tended to her gardens here, silently mourning her lost human life. Mourning Graysen.

How Lucien withstood it, I didn't know. Not that he'd shown any interest in bridging that gap between them.

"Where did you go?" Rhys asked, draining his wine and setting aside the tray.

If I wanted to talk, he'd listen. If I didn't want to, he would let it go. It had been our unspoken bargain from the start—to listen when the other needed, and give space when it was required. He was still slowly working his way through telling me all that had been done to him, all he'd witnessed Under the Mountain. There were still nights when I'd kiss away his tears, one by one.

This subject, however, was not so difficult to discuss. "I was thinking about Elain," I said, leaning against the edge of the desk. "And Lucien."

Rhys arched a brow, and I told him.

When I finished, his face was contemplative. "Will Lucien be joining us for the Solstice?"

"Is it bad if he does?"

Rhys let out a hum, his wings tucking in further. I had no idea how he withstood the cold while flying, even with a shield. Whenever I'd tried these past few weeks, I'd barely lasted more than a few minutes. The only time I'd managed had been last week, when our flight from the House of Wind had turned far warmer.

Rhys said at last, "I can stomach being around him."

"I'm sure he'd love to hear that thrilling endorsement."

A half smile that had me walking toward him, stopping between his legs. He braced his hands idly on my hips. "I can let go of the taunts," he said, scanning my face. "And the fact that he still harbors some hope of one day reuniting with Tamlin. But I cannot let go of how he treated you after Under the Mountain."

"I can. I've forgiven him for that."

"Well, you'll forgive *me* if I can't." Icy rage darkened the stars in those violet eyes.

"You still can barely talk to Nesta," I said. "Yet Elain you can talk to nicely."

"Elain is Elain."

"If you blame one, you have to blame the other."

"No, I don't. Elain is Elain," he repeated. "Nesta is . . . she's Illyrian. I mean that as a compliment, but she's an Illyrian at heart. So there is no excuse for her behavior."

"She more than made up for it this summer, Rhys."

"I cannot forgive anyone who made you suffer."

Cold, brutal words, spoken with such casual grace.

But he still didn't care about those who'd made *him* suffer. I ran a hand over the swirls and whorls of tattoos across his muscled chest, tracing the intricate lines. He shuddered under my fingers, wings twitching. "They're my family. You have to forgive Nesta at some point."

He rested his brow against my chest, right between my breasts, and wrapped his arms around my waist. For a long minute, he only breathed in the scent of me, as if taking it deep into his lungs. "Should that be my Solstice gift to you?" he murmured. "Forgiving Nesta for letting her fourteen-year-old sister go into those woods?"

I hooked a finger under his chin and tugged his head up. "You won't get any Solstice gift at all from *me* if you keep up this nonsense."

A wicked grin.

"Prick," I hissed, making to step back, but his arms tightened around me.

We fell silent, just staring at each other. Then Rhys said down the bond, *A thought for a thought, Feyre darling?*

I smiled at the request, the old game between us. But it faded as I answered, *I went into the Rainbow today.*

Oh? He nuzzled the plane of my stomach.

I dragged my hands through his dark hair, savoring the silken strands against my calluses. *There's an artist, Ressina. She invited me to come paint with her and some others in two nights.*

Rhys pulled back to scan my face, then arched a brow. "Why do you not sound excited about it?"

I gestured to our room, the town house, and blew out a breath. "I haven't painted anything in a while."

Not since we'd returned from battle. Rhys remained quiet, letting me sort through the jumble of words inside me.

"It feels selfish," I admitted. "To take the time, when there is so much to do and—"

"It is not selfish." His hands tightened on my hips. "If you want to paint, then paint, Feyre."

"People in this city still don't have homes."

"You taking a few hours every day to paint won't change that."

"It's not just that." I leaned down until my brow rested on his, the citrus-and-sea scent of him filling my lungs, my heart. "There are too many of them—things I want to paint. Need to. Picking one . . ." I took an unsteady breath and pulled back. "I'm not quite certain I'm ready to see what emerges when I paint some of them."

"Ah." He traced soothing, loving lines down my back. "Whether you join them this week, or two months from now, I think you should go. Try it out." He surveyed the room, the thick rug, as if he could see the entire town house beneath. "We can turn your old bedroom into a studio, if you want—"

"It's fine," I cut him off. "It—the light isn't ideal in there." At his raised brows, I admitted, "I checked. The only room that's good for it is the sitting room, and I'd rather not fill up the house with the reek of paint."

"I don't think anyone would mind."

"*I'd* mind. And I like privacy, anyway. The last thing I want is Amren standing behind me, critiquing my work as I go."

Rhys chuckled. "Amren can be dealt with."

"I'm not sure you and I are talking about the same Amren, then."

He grinned, tugging me close again, and murmured against my stomach, "It's your birthday on Solstice."

"So?" I'd been trying to forget that fact. And let the others forget it, too.

Rhys's smile became subdued—feline. "So, that means you get *two* presents."

I groaned. "I never should have told you."

"You were born on the longest night of the year." His fingers again stroked down my back. Lower. "You were meant to be at my side from the very beginning."

He traced the seam of my backside with a long, lazy stroke. With me standing before him like this, he could instantly smell the shift in my scent as my core heated.

I managed to say down the bond before words failed me, *Your turn. A thought for a thought.*

He pressed a kiss to my stomach, right over my navel. "Have I told you about that first time you winnowed and tackled me into the snow?"

I smacked his shoulder, the muscle beneath hard as stone. "*That's* your thought for a thought?"

He smiled against my stomach, his fingers still exploring, coaxing. "You tackled me like an Illyrian. Perfect form, a direct hit. But then you lay on top of me, panting. All I wanted to do was get us both naked."

"Why am I not surprised?" Yet I threaded my fingers through his hair.

The fabric of my dressing gown was barely more than cobwebs between us as he huffed a laugh onto my belly. I hadn't bothered putting on anything beneath. "You drove me out of my mind. All those months. I still don't quite believe I get to have this. Have you."

My throat tightened. That was the thought he wanted to trade, needed to share. "I wanted you, even Under the Mountain," I said softly. "I chalked it up to those horrible circumstances, but after we killed her, when I couldn't tell anyone how I felt—about how truly bad things were, I still told you. I've always been able to talk to you. I think my heart knew you were mine long before I ever realized it."

His eyes gleamed, and he buried his face between my breasts again, hands caressing my back. "I love you," he breathed. "More than life, more than my territory, more than my crown."

I knew. He'd given up that life to reforge the Cauldron, the fabric of the world itself, so I might survive. I hadn't had it in me to be furious with him about it afterward, or in the months since. He'd lived—it was a gift I would never stop being grateful for. And in the end, though, we'd saved each other. All of us had.

I kissed the top of his head. "I love you," I whispered onto his blue-black hair.

Rhys's hands clamped on the back of my thighs, the only warning before he smoothly twisted us, pinning me to the bed as he nuzzled my neck. "A week," he said onto my skin, gracefully folding his wings behind him. "A week to have you in this bed. That's all I want for Solstice."

I laughed breathlessly, but he flexed his hips, driving against me, the barriers between us little more than scraps of cloth. He brushed a kiss against my mouth, his wings a dark wall behind his shoulders. "You think I'm joking."

"We're strong for High Fae," I mused, fighting to concentrate as he tugged on my earlobe with his teeth, "but a week straight of sex? I don't think I'd be able to walk. Or you'd be able to function, at least with your favorite part."

He nipped the delicate arch of my ear, and my toes curled. "Then you'll just have to kiss my favorite part and make it better."

I slid a hand to that favorite part—*my* favorite part—and gripped him through his undershorts. He groaned, pressing himself into my touch, and the garment disappeared, leaving only my palm against the velvet hardness of him.

"We need to get dressed," I managed to say, even as my hand stroked over him.

"Later," he ground out, sucking on my lower lip.

Indeed. Rhys pulled back, tattooed arms braced on either side of my head. One was covered with his Illyrian markings, the other with the twin tattoo to the one on my arms: the last bargain we'd made. To remain together through all that waited ahead.

My core pounded, sister to my thunderous heartbeat, the need to have him buried inside me, to have him—

As if in mockery of those twin beats within me, a knocking rattled the bedroom door. "Just so you're aware," Mor chirped from the other side, "we *do* have to go soon."

Rhys let out a low growl that skittered over my skin, his hair slipping over his brow as he turned his head toward the door. Nothing but predatory intent in his glazed eyes. "We have thirty minutes," he said with remarkable smoothness.

"And it takes you two hours to get dressed," Mor quipped through the door. A sly pause. "And I'm not talking about Feyre."

Rhys grumbled a laugh and lowered his brow against mine. I closed my eyes, breathing him in, even while my fingers unfurled from around him. "This isn't finished," he promised me, his voice rough, before he kissed the hollow of my throat and pulled away. "Go terrorize someone else," he called to Mor, rolling his neck as his wings vanished and he stalked for the bathing room. "I need to primp."

Mor chuckled, her light footsteps soon fading away.

I slumped against the pillows and breathed deep, cooling the need that coursed through me. Water gurgled in the bathing room, followed by a soft yelp.

I wasn't the only one in need of cooling, it seemed.

Indeed, when I strode into the bathing room a few minutes later, Rhys was still cringing as he washed himself in the tub.

A dip of my fingers into the soapy water confirmed my suspicions: it was ice-cold.

CHAPTER 6

Morrigan

There was no light in this place.

There never had been.

Even the evergreen garlands, holly wreaths, and crackling birchwood fires in honor of the Solstice couldn't pierce the eternal darkness that dwelled in the Hewn City.

It was not the sort of darkness that Mor had come to love in Velaris, the sort of darkness that was as much a part of Rhys as his blood.

It was the darkness of rotting things, of decay. The smothering darkness that withered all life.

And the golden-haired male standing before her in the throne room, amongst the towering pillars carved with those scaled, slithering beasts—he had been created from it. Thrived in it.

"I apologize if we interrupted your festivities," Rhysand purred to him. To Keir. And to the male beside him.

Eris.

The throne room was empty now. A word from Feyre, and the

usual ilk who dined and danced and schemed here were gone, leaving only Keir and the High Lord of Autumn's eldest son.

The former spoke first, adjusting the lapels on his black jacket. "To what do we owe this pleasure?"

The sneering tone. She could still hear the hissed insults beneath it, whispered long ago in her family's private suite, whispered at every meeting and gathering when her cousin was not present. *Half-breed monstrosity. A disgrace to the bloodline.*

"High Lord."

The words came out of her without thought. And her voice, the voice she used here . . . Not her own. Never her own, never down here with them in the darkness. Mor kept her voice just as cold and unforgiving as she corrected, "To what do we owe this pleasure, *High Lord*."

She didn't bother to keep her teeth from flashing.

Keir ignored her.

His preferred method of insult: to act as if a person weren't worth the breath it'd take to speak with them.

Try something new, you miserable bastard.

Rhys cut in before Mor could contemplate saying just that, his dark power filling the room, the mountain, "We came, of course, to wish you and yours well for the Solstice. But it seems you already had a guest to entertain."

Az's information had been flawless, as it always was. When he'd found her reading up on Winter Court customs in the House of Wind's library this morning, she hadn't asked *how* he'd learned that Eris was to come tonight. She'd long since learned that Az was just as likely not to tell her.

But the Autumn Court male standing beside Keir . . . Mor made herself look at Eris. Into his amber eyes.

Colder than any hall of Kallias's court. They had been that way from the moment she'd met him, five centuries ago.

Eris laid a pale hand on the breast of his pewter-colored jacket, the portrait of Autumn Court gallantry. "I thought I'd extend some Solstice greetings of my own."

That voice. That silky, arrogant voice. It had not altered, not in tone or timbre, in the passing centuries, either. Had not changed since that day.

Warm, buttery sunlight through the leaves, setting them glowing like rubies and citrines. The damp, earthen scent of rotting things beneath the leaves and roots she lay upon. Had been thrown and left upon.

Everything hurt. Everything. She couldn't move. Couldn't do anything but watch the sun drift through the rich canopy far overhead, listen to the wind between the silvery trunks.

And the center of that pain, radiating outward like living fire with each uneven, rasping breath . . .

Light, steady steps crunched on the leaves. Six sets. A border guard, a patrol.

Help. Someone to help—

A male voice, foreign and deep, swore. Then went silent.

Went silent as a single pair of steps approached. She couldn't turn her head, couldn't bear the agony. Could do nothing but inhale each wet, shuddering breath.

"Don't touch her."

Those steps stopped.

It was not a warning to protect her. Defend her.

She knew the voice that spoke. Had dreaded hearing it.

She felt him approach now. Felt each reverberation in the leaves, the moss, the roots. As if the very land shuddered before him.

"No one touches her," he said. Eris. "The moment we do, she's our responsibility."

Cold, unfeeling words.

"But—but they nailed *a—"*

"No one touches her."

Nailed.

They had spiked nails into her.

Had pinned her down as she screamed, pinned her down as she roared at them, then begged them. And then they had taken out those long, brutal iron nails. And the hammer.

Three of them.

Three strikes of the hammer, drowned out by her screaming, by the pain.

She began shaking, hating it as much as she'd hated the begging. Her body bellowed in agony, those nails in her abdomen relentless.

A pale, beautiful face appeared above her, blocking out the jewel-like leaves above. Unmoved. Impassive. "I take it you do not wish to live here, Morrigan."

She would rather die here, bleed out here. She would rather die and return—return as something wicked and cruel, and shred them all apart.

He must have read it in her eyes. A small smile curved his lips. "I thought so."

Eris straightened, turning. Her fingers curled in the leaves and loamy soil.

She wished she could grow claws—grow claws as Rhys could—and rip out that pale throat. But that was not her gift. Her gift . . . her gift had left her here. Broken and bleeding.

Eris took a step away.

Someone behind him blurted, "We can't just leave her to—"

"We can, and we will," Eris said simply, his pace unfaltering as he strode away. "She chose to sully herself; her family chose to deal with her like garbage. I have already told them my decision in this matter." A long pause, crueler than the rest. "And I am not in the habit of fucking Illyrian leftovers."

She couldn't stop it, then. The tears that slid out, hot and burning.

Alone. They would leave her alone here. Her friends did not know where she had gone. She barely knew where she was.

"But—" That dissenting voice cut in again.

"Move out."

There was no dissension after that.

And when their steps faded away, then vanished, the silence returned.

The sun and the wind and the leaves.

The blood and the iron and the soil beneath her nails.

The pain.

A subtle nudge of Feyre's hand against her own drew her out, away from that bloody clearing just over the border of the Autumn Court.

Mor threw her High Lady a grateful glance, which Feyre smartly ignored, already returning her attention to the conversation. Never having taken her focus off it in the first place.

Feyre had fallen into the role of mistress of this horrible city with far more ease than she had. Clad in a sparkling onyx gown, the crescent-moon diadem atop her head, her friend looked every part the imperious ruler. As much a part of this place as the twining, serpentine beasts carved and etched everywhere. What Keir, perhaps, had one day pictured for Mor herself.

Not the red gown Mor wore, bright and bold, or the gold

jewelry at her wrists, her ears, shimmering like sunlight down here in the gloom.

"If you wanted this little liaison to remain private," Rhys was saying with lethal calm, "perhaps a public gathering was not the wisest place to meet."

Indeed.

The Steward of the Hewn City waved a hand. "Why should we have anything to hide? After the war, we're all such good friends."

She often dreamed of gutting him. Sometimes with a knife; sometimes with her own bare hands.

"And how does your father's court fare, Eris?" A mild, bored question from Feyre.

His amber eyes held nothing but distaste.

A roaring filled Mor's head at that look. She could barely hear his drawled answer. Or Rhys's reply.

It had once been her delight to taunt Keir and this court, to keep them on their toes. Hell, she'd even snapped a few of the Steward's bones this spring—after Rhys had shattered his arms into uselessness. Had been glad to do it, after what Keir had said to Feyre, and then delighted when her mother had banished her from their private quarters. An order that still held. But from the moment Eris had walked into that council chamber all those months ago . . .

You are over five hundred years old, she often reminded herself. She could face it, handle it better than this.

I am not in the habit of fucking Illyrian leftovers.

Even now, even after Azriel had found her in those woods, after Madja had healed her until no trace of those nails marred her stomach . . . She should not have come here tonight.

Her skin became tight, her stomach roiling. *Coward*.

She had faced down enemies, fought in many wars, and yet this, these two males together—

Mor felt more than saw Feyre stiffen beside her at something Eris had said.

Her High Lady answered Eris, "Your father is forbidden to cross into the human lands." No room for compromise with that tone, with the steel in Feyre's eyes.

Eris only shrugged. "I don't think it's your call."

Rhys slid his hands into his pockets, the portrait of casual grace. Yet the shadows and star-flecked darkness that wafted from him, that set the mountain shuddering beneath his every step—that was the true face of the High Lord of the Night Court. The most powerful High Lord in history. "I would suggest reminding Beron that territory expansion is not on the table. For any court."

Eris wasn't fazed. Nothing had ever disturbed him, ruffled him. Mor had hated it from the moment she'd met him—that distance, that coldness. That lack of interest or feeling for the world. "Then I would suggest to you, High Lord, that you speak to your dear friend Tamlin about it."

"Why." Feyre's question was sharp as a blade.

Eris's mouth curved in an adder's smile. "Because Tamlin's territory is the only one that borders the human lands. I'd think that anyone looking to expand would have to go through the Spring Court first. Or at least obtain his permission."

Another person she'd one day kill. If Feyre and Rhys didn't do it first.

It didn't matter what Tamlin had done in the war, if he'd brought Beron and the human forces with him. If he'd played Hybern.

It was another day, another female lying on the ground, that Mor would not forget, could not forgive.

Rhys's cold face turned contemplative, though. She could easily read the reluctance in his eyes, the annoyance at having Eris tip him off, but information was information.

Mor glanced toward Keir and found him watching her.

Save for her initial order to the Steward, she had not spoken a word. Contributed to this meeting. Stepped up.

She could see that in Keir's eyes. The satisfaction.

Say something. Think of something to say. To strip him down to nothing.

But Rhys deemed they were done, linking his arm through Feyre's and guiding them away, the mountain indeed trembling beneath their steps. What he'd said to Eris, Mor had no idea.

Pathetic. Cowardly and pathetic.

Truth is your gift. Truth is your curse.

Say something.

But the words to strike down her father did not come.

Her red gown flowing behind her, Mor turned her back on him, on the smirking heir to Autumn, and followed her High Lord and Lady through the darkness and back into the light.

CHAPTER 7

Rhysand

"You really do know how to give Solstice presents, Az."

I turned from the wall of windows in my private study at the House of Wind, Velaris awash in the hues of early morning.

My spymaster and brother remained on the other side of the sprawling oak desk, the maps and documents he'd presented littering the surface. His expression might as well have been stone. Had been that way from the moment he'd knocked on the double doors to the study just after dawn. As if he'd known that sleep had been futile for me last night after Eris's not-so-subtle warning about Tamlin and his borders.

Feyre hadn't mentioned it when we'd returned home. Hadn't seemed ready to discuss it: how to deal with the High Lord of Spring. She'd quickly fallen asleep, leaving me to brood before the fire in the sitting room.

It was little wonder I'd flown up here before sunrise, eager for the biting cold to chase the weight of the sleepless night away from me. My wings were still numb in spots from the flight.

"You wanted information," Az said mildly. At his side, Truth-Teller's obsidian hilt seemed to absorb the first rays of the sun.

I rolled my eyes, leaning against the desk and gesturing to what he'd compiled. "You couldn't have waited until after Solstice for this particular gem?"

One glance at Azriel's unreadable face and I added, "Don't bother to answer that."

A corner of Azriel's mouth curled up, the shadows about him sliding over his neck like living tattoos, twins to the Illyrian ones marked beneath his leathers.

Shadows different from anything my powers summoned, spoke to. Born in a lightless, airless prison meant to break him.

Instead, he had learned its language.

Though the cobalt Siphons were proof that his Illyrian heritage ran true, even the rich lore of that warrior-people, *my* warrior-people, did not have an explanation for where the shadowsinger gifts came from. They certainly weren't connected to the Siphons, to the raw killing power most Illyrians possessed and channeled through the stones to keep from destroying everything in its path. The bearer included.

Drawing my eyes from the stones atop his hands, I frowned at the stack of papers Az had presented moments ago. "Have you told Cassian?"

"I came right here," Azriel said. "He'll arrive soon enough, anyway."

I chewed on my lip as I studied the territory map of Illyria. "It's more clans than I expected," I admitted and sent a flock of shadows skittering across the room to soothe the power now stirring, restless, in my veins. "Even in my worst-case calculations."

"It's not every member of these clans," Az said, his grim face undermining his attempt to soften the blow. "This overall number just reflects the places where discontent is spreading, not where the majorities lie." He pointed with a scarred finger to one of the camps. "There are only two females here who seem to be spewing poison about the war. One a widow, and one a mother to a soldier."

"Where there's smoke, there's fire," I countered.

Azriel studied the map for a long minute. I gave him the silence, knowing that he'd speak only when he was damn well ready. As boys, Cassian and I had devoted hours to pummeling Az, trying to get him to speak. He'd never once yielded.

"The Illyrians are pieces of shit," he said too quietly.

I opened my mouth and shut it.

Shadows gathered around his wings, trailing off him and onto the thick red rug. "They train and train as warriors, and yet when they don't come home, their families make *us* into villains for sending them to war?"

"Their families have lost something irreplaceable," I said carefully.

Azriel waved a scarred hand, his cobalt Siphon glinting with the movement as his fingers cut through the air. "They're hypocrites."

"And what would you have me do, then? Disband the largest army in Prythian?"

Az didn't answer.

I held his gaze, though. Held that ice-cold stare that still sometimes scared the shit out of me. I'd seen what he'd done to his half brothers centuries ago. Still dreamed of it. The act itself wasn't what lingered. Every bit of it had been deserved. Every damn bit.

But it was the frozen precipice that Az had plummeted into that sometimes rose from the pit of my memory.

The beginnings of that frost cracked over his eyes now. So I said calmly, yet with little room for argument, "I am not going to disband the Illyrians. There is nowhere for them to go, anyway. And if we try to drag them out of those mountains, they might launch the very assault we're trying to defuse."

Az said nothing.

"But perhaps more pressing," I went on, jabbing a finger on the sprawling continent, "is the fact that the human queens have not returned to their own territories. They linger in that joint palace of theirs. Beyond that, Hybern's general populace is not too thrilled to have lost this war. And with the wall gone, who knows what other Fae territories might make a grab for human lands?" My jaw tightened at that last one. "This peace is tenuous."

"I know that," Az said at last.

"So we might need the Illyrians again before it is over. Need them willing to shed blood."

Feyre knew. I'd been filling her in on every report and meeting. But this latest one . . . "We will keep an eye on the dissenters," I finished, letting Az sense a rumble of the power that prowled inside me, let him *feel* that I meant every word. "Cassian knows it's growing amongst the camps and is willing to do whatever it takes to fix it."

"He doesn't know just how many there are."

"And perhaps we should wait to tell him. Until after the holiday." Az blinked. I explained quietly, "He's going to have enough to deal with. Let him enjoy the holiday while he can."

Az and I made a point not to mention Nesta. Not amongst each other, and certainly not in front of Cassian. I didn't let myself contemplate it, either. Neither did Mor, given her unusual silence on the matter since the war had ended.

"He'll be pissed at us for keeping it from him."

"He already suspects much of it, so it's only confirmation at this point."

Az ran a thumb down Truth-Teller's black hilt, the silver runes on the dark scabbard shimmering in the light. "What about the human queens?"

"We continue to watch. *You* continue to watch."

"Vassa and Jurian are still with Graysen. Do we loop them in?"

A strange gathering, down in the human lands. With no queen ever having been appointed to the slice of territory at the base of Prythian, only a council of wealthy lords and merchants, Jurian had somehow stepped in to lead. Using Graysen's family estate as his seat of command.

And Vassa . . . She had stayed. Her *keeper* had granted her a reprieve from her curse—the enchantment that turned her into a firebird by day, woman again by night. And bound her to his lake deep in the continent.

I'd never seen such spell work. I'd sent my power over her, Helion too, hunting for any possible threads to unbind it. I found none. It was as if the curse was woven into her very blood.

But Vassa's freedom would end. Lucien had said as much months ago, and still visited her often enough that I knew nothing in that regard had improved. She would have to return to the lake, to the sorcerer-lord who kept her prisoner, sold to him by the very queens who had again gathered in their joint castle. Formerly Vassa's castle, too.

"Vassa knows that the Queens of the Realm will be a threat until they are dealt with," I said at last. Another tidbit that Lucien had told us. Well, Az and me at least. "But unless the queens step out of line, it's not for us to face. If we sweep in, even to stop them from triggering another war, we'll be seen as conquerors, not heroes. We need the humans in other territories to trust us, if we can ever hope to achieve lasting peace."

"Then perhaps Jurian and Vassa should deal with them. While Vassa is free to do so."

I'd contemplated it. Feyre and I had discussed it long into the night. Several times. "The humans must be given a chance to rule themselves. Decide for themselves. Even our allies."

"Send Lucien, then. As our human emissary."

I studied the tenseness in Azriel's shoulders, the shadows veiling half of him from the sunlight. "Lucien is away right now."

Az's brows rose. "Where?"

I winked at him. "You're my spymaster. Shouldn't you know?"

Az crossed his arms, face as elegant and cold as the legendary dagger at his side. "I don't make a point of looking after his movements."

"Why?"

Not a flicker of emotion. "He is Elain's mate."

I waited.

"It would be an invasion of her privacy to track him."

To know when and if Lucien sought her out. What they did together.

"You sure about that?" I asked quietly.

Azriel's Siphons guttered, the stones turning as dark and foreboding as the deepest sea. "Where did Lucien go."

I straightened at the pure order in the words. But I said, voice slipping into a drawl, "He went to the Spring Court. He'll be there for Solstice."

"Tamlin kicked him out the last time."

"He did. But he invited him for the holiday." Likely because Tamlin realized he'd be spending it alone in that manor. Or whatever was left of it.

I had no pity where that was concerned.

Not when I could still feel Feyre's undiluted terror as Tamlin tore through the study. As he locked her in that house.

Lucien had let him do it, too. But I'd made my peace with him. Or tried to.

With Tamlin, it was more complicated than that. More complicated than I let myself usually dwell on.

He was still in love with Feyre. I couldn't blame him for it. Even if it made me want to rip out his throat.

I shoved the thought away. "I'll discuss Vassa and Jurian with Lucien when he returns. See if he's up for another visit." I angled my head. "Do you think he can handle being around Graysen?"

Az's expressionless face was precisely the reason he'd never lost to us at cards. "Why should I be the judge of that?"

"You mean to tell me that you *weren't* bluffing when you said you didn't track Lucien's every movement?"

Nothing. Absolutely nothing on that face, on his scent. The shadows, whatever the hell they were, hid too well. Too much. Azriel only said coldly, "If Lucien kills Graysen, then good riddance."

I was inclined to agree. So was Feyre—and Nesta.

"I'm half tempted to give Nesta hunting rights for Solstice."

"You're getting her a gift?"

No. Sort of. "I'd think bankrolling her apartment and drinking was gift enough."

Az ran a hand through his dark hair. "Are we . . ." Unusual for him to stumble with words. "Are we supposed to get the sisters presents?"

"No," I said, and meant it. Az seemed to loose a sigh of relief. Seemed to, since all but a breath of air passed from his lips. "I don't think Nesta gives a shit, and I don't think Elain expects to receive anything from us. I'd leave the sisters to exchange presents amongst themselves."

Az nodded distantly.

I drummed my fingers on the map, right over the Spring Court. "I can tell Lucien myself in a day or two. About going to Graysen's manor."

Azriel arched a brow. "You mean to visit the Spring Court?"

I wished I could say otherwise. But I instead told him what Eris had implied: that Tamlin either might not care to enforce his borders with the human realm or might be open to letting anyone through them. I doubted I'd get a decent night's rest until I found out for myself.

When I finished, Az picked at an invisible speck of dust on the leather scales of his gauntlet. The only sign of his annoyance. "I can go with you."

I shook my head. "It's better to do this on my own."

"Are you talking about seeing Lucien or Tamlin?"

"Both."

Lucien, I could stomach. Tamlin . . . Perhaps I didn't want any witnesses for what might be said. Or done.

"Will you ask Feyre to join you?" One look in Azriel's hazel eyes and I knew he was well aware of my reasons for going alone.

"I'll ask her in a few hours," I said, "but I doubt she will want to come. And I doubt I will try my best to convince her to change her mind."

Peace. We had peace within our grasp. And yet there were debts left unpaid that I was not above righting.

Az nodded knowingly. He'd always understood me best—more than the others. Save my mate. Whether it was his gifts that allowed him to do so, or merely the fact that he and I were more similar than most realized, I'd never learned.

But Azriel knew a thing or two about old scores to settle. Imbalances to be righted.

So did most of my inner circle, I supposed.

"No word on Bryaxis, I take it." I peered toward the marble beneath my boots, as if I could see all the way to the library beneath this mountain and the now-empty lower levels that had once been occupied.

Az studied the floor as well. "Not a whisper. Or a scream, for that matter."

I chuckled. My brother had a sly, wicked sense of humor. I'd planned to hunt Bryaxis down for months now—to take Feyre and let her track down the entity that, for lack of a better explanation, seemed to be fear itself. But, as with so many of my plans for my mate, running this court and figuring out the world beyond it had gotten in the way.

"Do you want me to hunt it down?" An easy, unruffled question.

I waved a hand, my mating band catching in the morning light. That I hadn't heard from Feyre yet told me enough: still asleep. And as tempting as it was to wake her just to hear the sound of her voice, I had little desire to have my balls nailed to the wall for disrupting her sleep. "Let Bryaxis enjoy the Solstice as well," I said.

A rare smile curled Az's mouth. "Generous of you."

I inclined my head dramatically, the portrait of regal magnanimity, and dropped into my chair before propping my feet on the desk. "When do you head out for Rosehall?"

"The morning after Solstice," he supplied, turning toward the glittering sprawl of Velaris. He winced—slightly. "I still need to do some shopping before I go."

I offered my brother a crooked smile. "Buy her something from me, will you? And put it on my account this time."

I knew Az wouldn't, but he nodded all the same.

CHAPTER 8

Cassian

A storm was coming.

Right in time for Solstice. It wouldn't hit for another day or two, but Cassian could smell it on the wind. The others in the Windhaven camp could as well, the usual flurry of activity now a swift, efficient thrum. Houses and tents checked, stews and roasts being prepared, people departing or arriving earlier than expected to outrace it.

Cassian had given the girls the day off because of it. Had ordered all training and exercises, males included, to be postponed until after the storm. Limited patrols would still go out, only by those skilled and eager to test themselves against the sure-to-be-brutal winds and frigid temperatures. Even in a storm, enemies could strike.

If the storm was as great as he sensed it would be, this camp would be buried under snow for a good few days.

Which is why he wound up standing in the small craftsman center of the camp, beyond the tents and handful of permanent houses. Only a few shops occupied either side of the unpaved road, usually just a dirt track in warmer months. A general goods store, which had already posted a sold-out sign, two blacksmiths, a cobbler, a wood-carver, and a clothier.

The wooden building of the clothier was relatively new. At least by Illyrian standards—perhaps ten years old. Above the first-floor store seemed to be living quarters, lamps burning brightly within. And in the glass display window of the store: exactly what he'd come seeking.

A bell above the leaded-glass door tinkled as Cassian entered, tucking his wings in tight even with the broader-than-usual doorway. Warmth hit him, welcome and delicious, and he quickly shut the door behind him.

The slender young female behind the pine counter was already standing still. Watching him.

Cassian noticed the scars on her wings first. The careful, brutal scars down the center tendons.

Nausea roiled in his gut, even as he offered a smile and strode toward the polished counter. Clipped. She'd been clipped.

"I'm looking for Proteus," he said, meeting the female's brown eyes. Sharp and shrewd. Taken aback by his presence, but unafraid. Her dark hair was braided simply, offering a clear view of her tan skin and narrow, angular face. Not a face of beauty, but striking. Interesting.

Her eyes did not lower, not in the way Illyrian females had been ordered and trained to do. No, even with the clipping scars that proved traditional ways ran brutally deep in her family, she held his stare.

It reminded him of Nesta, that stare. Frank and unsettling.

"Proteus was my father," she said, untying her white apron to reveal a simple brown dress before she emerged from behind the counter. *Was*.

"I'm sorry," he said.

"He didn't come home from the war."

Cassian kept his chin from lowering. "I am even sorrier, then."

"Why should you be?" An unmoved, uninterested question. She extended a slender hand. "I'm Emerie. This is my shop now."

A line in the sand. And an unusual one. Cassian shook her hand, unsurprised to find her grip strong and unfaltering.

He'd known Proteus. Had been surprised when the male had joined the ranks during the war. Cassian knew he'd had one daughter and no sons. No close male relatives, either. With his death, the store would have gone to one of them. But for his daughter to step up, to insist this store was *hers*, and to keep running it . . . He surveyed the small, tidy space.

Glanced through the front window to the shop across the street, the sold-out sign there.

Stock filled Emerie's store. As if she'd just gotten a fresh shipment. Or no one had bothered to come in. Ever.

For Proteus to have owned and built this place, in a camp where the idea of shops was one that had only started in the past fifty or so years, meant he'd had a good deal of money. Enough perhaps for Emerie to coast on. But not forever.

"It certainly seems like it's your shop," he said at last, turning his attention back to her. Emerie had drifted a few feet away, her back straight, chin upraised.

He'd seen Nesta in that particular pose, too. He called it her *I Will Slay My Enemies* pose.

Cassian had named about two dozen poses for Nesta at this point.

Ranging from *I Will Eat Your Eyes for Breakfast* to *I Don't Want Cassian to Know I'm Reading Smut*. The latter was his particular favorite.

Suppressing his smile, Cassian gestured to the pretty piles of shearling-lined gloves and thick scarves that bedecked the window display. "I'll take every bit of winter gear you have."

Her dark brows rose toward her hairline. "Really?"

He fished a hand into the pocket of his leathers to pull out his money pouch and extended it to her. "That should cover it."

Emerie weighed the small leather pouch in her palm. "I don't need charity."

"Then take whatever the cost is for your gloves and boots and scarves and coats out of it and give the rest back to me."

She made no answer before chucking the pouch on the counter and bustling to the window display. Everything he asked for she gathered onto the counter in neat piles and stacks, even going into the back room behind the counter and emerging with more. Until there wasn't an empty bit of space on the polished counter, and only the sound of clinking coins filled the shop.

She wordlessly handed him back his pouch. He refrained from mentioning that she was one of the few Illyrians who'd ever accepted his money. Most had spat on it, or thrown it on the ground. Even after Rhys had become High Lord.

Emerie surveyed the piles of winter goods on the counter. "Do you want me to find some bags and boxes?"

He shook his head. "That won't be necessary."

Again, her dark brows rose.

Cassian reached into his money pouch and set three heavy coins onto the only sliver of empty space he could find on the counter. "For the delivery charges."

"To whom?" Emerie blurted.

"You live above the shop, don't you?" A terse nod. "Then I assume you know enough about this camp and who has plenty, and who has nothing. A storm is going to hit in a few days. I'd like you to distribute this amongst those who might feel its impact the hardest."

She blinked, and he saw her reassessment. Emerie studied the piled goods. "They—a lot of them don't like me," she said, more softly than he'd heard.

"They don't like me, either. You're in good company."

A reluctant curl of her lips at that. Not quite a smile. Certainly not with a male she didn't know.

"Consider it good advertising for this shop," he went on. "Tell them it was a gift from their High Lord."

"Why not you?"

He didn't want to answer that. Not today. "Better to leave me out of it."

Emerie took his measure for a moment, then nodded. "I'll make sure this has been delivered to those who need it most by sundown."

Cassian bowed his head in thanks and headed for the glass door. The door and windows on this building alone had likely cost more than most Illyrians could afford in years.

Proteus had been a wealthy man—a good businessman. And a decent warrior. To have risked this by going to war, he had to have possessed some shred of pride.

But the scars on Emerie's wings, proof that she'd never taste the wind again . . .

Half of him wished that Proteus were still alive. If only so he could kill the male himself.

Cassian reached for the brass handle, the metal cold against his palm.

"Lord Cassian."

He peered over a shoulder to where Emerie still stood behind the counter. He didn't bother to correct her, to say that he did not and would never accept using *lord* before his name. "Happy Solstice," she said tersely.

Cassian flashed her a smile. "You, too. Send word if you have any trouble with the deliveries."

Her narrow chin rose. "I'm sure I won't need to."

Fire in those words. Emerie would make the families take them, whether they wanted to or not.

He'd seen that fire before—and the steel. He half wondered what might happen if the two of them ever met. What might come of it.

Cassian shouldered his way out of the shop and into the freezing day, the bell tinkling in his wake. A herald of the storm to come.

Not just the storm that was barreling toward these mountains.

But perhaps one that had been brewing here for a long, long time.

CHAPTER 9

Feyre

I shouldn't have eaten dinner.

It was the thought tumbling through my head as I neared the studio Ressina occupied, darkness full overhead. As I saw the lights spilling into the frosted street, mixing with the glow from the lamps.

At this hour, three days before Solstice, it was packed with shoppers—not just residents of the quarter, but those from across the city and its countryside. So many High Fae and faeries, many of the latter kinds that I had never seen before. But all smiling, all seeming to shimmer with merriment and goodwill. It was impossible not to feel the thrum of that energy under my skin, even as nerves threatened to send me flying home, frigid wind or no.

I'd hauled a pack full of supplies down here, a canvas tucked under my arm, unsure whether they would be provided or if it would look rude to show up at Ressina's studio and appear to have *expected* to be given them. I'd walked from the town house, not wanting to winnow with so many things, and not wanting to risk losing the canvas to the tug of the bitter wind if I flew.

Staying warm aside, shielding against the wind while still *flying* on the wind was something I'd yet to master, despite my now-occasional lessons with Rhys or Azriel, and with additional weight in my arms, plus the cold . . . I didn't know how the Illyrians did it, up in their mountains, where it was cold all year.

Perhaps I'd find out soon, if the grumblings and malcontent spread across the war-camps.

Not the time to think about it. My stomach was already uneasy enough.

I paused a house away from Ressina's studio, my palms sweating within my gloves.

I'd never painted with a group before. I rarely liked to share my paintings with anyone.

And this first time back in front of a canvas, unsure of what might come spilling out of me . . .

A tug on the bond.

Everything all right?

A casual, soft question, the cadence of Rhys's voice soothing the tremors along my nerves.

He'd told me where he planned to go tomorrow. What he planned to inquire about.

He'd asked me if I'd like to go with him.

I'd said no.

I might owe Tamlin my mate's life, I might have told Tamlin that I wished him peace and happiness, but I did not wish to see him. Speak with him. Deal with him. Not for a good long while. Perhaps forever.

Maybe it was because of that, because I'd felt worse after declining Rhys's invitation than I had when he'd asked, that I'd ventured out into the Rainbow tonight.

But now, faced with Ressina's communal studio, already hearing the laughter flitting out from where she and others had gathered for their weekly paint-in, my resolve sputtered out.

I don't know if I can do this.

Rhys was quiet for a moment. *Do you want me to come with you? To paint?*

I'd be an excellent nude model.

I smiled, not caring that I was by myself in the street with countless people streaming past me. My hood concealed most of my face, anyway. *You'll forgive me if I don't feel like sharing the glory that is you with anyone else.*

Perhaps I'll model for you later, then. A sensuous brush down the bond that had my blood heating. *It's been a while since we had paint involved.*

That cabin and kitchen table flashed into my mind, and my mouth went a bit dry. *Rogue.*

A chuckle. *If you want to go in, then go in. If you don't, then don't. It's your call.*

I frowned down at the canvas tucked under one arm, the box of paints cradled in the other. Frowned toward the studio thirty feet away, the shadows thick between me and that golden spill of light.

I know what I want to do.

No one noticed me winnow inside the boarded-up gallery and studio space down the street.

And with the boards over the windows, no one noticed the balls of faelight that I kindled and set to floating in the air on a gentle wind.

Of course, with the boards over empty windows, and no occupant for months, the main room was freezing. Cold enough that I set down my supplies and bounced on my toes as I surveyed the space.

It had probably been lovely before the attack: a massive window faced southward, letting in endless sunshine, and skylights—also boarded up—dotted the vaulted ceiling. The gallery in the front was perhaps thirty feet wide, fifty feet deep, with a counter against one wall halfway back, and a door to what had to be the studio space or storage in the rear. A quick examination told me I was half right: storage was in the back, but no natural light for painting. Only narrow windows above a row of cracked sinks, a few metal counters still stained with paint, and old cleaning supplies.

And paint. Not paint itself, but the *smell* of it.

I breathed in deep, feeling it settle into my bones, letting the quiet of the space settle, too.

The gallery up front had been her studio as well. Polina must have painted while she chatted with customers surveying the hung art whose outlines I could barely make out against the white walls.

The floors beneath them were gray stone, kernels of shattered glass still shining between the cracks.

I didn't want to do this first painting in front of others.

I could barely do it in front of myself. It was enough to drive away any guilt in regard to ignoring Ressina's offer to join her. I'd made her no promises.

So I summoned my flame to begin warming the space, setting little balls of it burning midair throughout the gallery. Lighting it further. Warming it back to life.

Then I went in search of a stool.

CHAPTER 10

Feyre

I painted and painted and painted.

My heart thundered the entire time, steady as a war-drum.

I painted until my back cramped and my stomach gurgled with demands for hot cocoa and dessert.

I'd known what needed to come out of me the moment I perched on the rickety stool I'd dusted off from the back.

I'd barely been able to hold the paintbrush steady enough to make the first few strokes. From fear, yes. I was honest enough with myself to admit that.

But also from the sheer unleashing of it, as if I were a racehorse freed from my pen, the image in my mind a dashing vision that I sprinted to keep up with.

But it began to emerge. Began to take form.

And in its wake, a sort of quiet followed, as if it were a layer of snow blanketing the earth. Clearing away what was beneath.

More cleansing, more soothing than any of the hours I'd spent rebuilding this city. Equally as fulfilling, yes, but the painting, the unleashing and facing it, was a release. A first stitch to close a wound.

The tower bells of Velaris sang twelve before I stopped.

Before I lowered my brush and stared at what I'd created.

Stared at what gazed back.

Me.

Or how I'd been in the Ouroboros, that beast of scale and claw and darkness; rage and joy and cold. All of me. What lurked beneath my skin.

I had not run from it. And I did not run from it now.

Yes—the first stitch to close a wound. That's how it felt.

With my brush dangling between my knees, with that beast forever on canvas, my body went a bit limp. Boneless.

I scanned the gallery, the street behind the boarded-up windows. No one had come to inquire about the lights in the hours I'd been here.

I stood at last, groaning as I stretched. I couldn't take it with me. Not when the painting had to dry, and the damp night air off the river and distant sea would be terrible for it.

I certainly wasn't going to bring it back to the town house for someone to find. Even Rhys.

But here . . . No one would know, should someone come in, who had painted it. I hadn't signed my name. Didn't want to.

If I left it here to dry overnight, if I came back tomorrow, there would certainly be some closet in the House of Wind where I might hide it afterward.

Tomorrow, then. I'd come back tomorrow to claim it.

CHAPTER 11

Rhysand

It was Spring, and yet it wasn't.

It was not the land I had once roamed in centuries past, or even visited almost a year ago.

The sun was mild, the day clear, distant dogwoods and lilacs still in eternal bloom.

Distant—because on the estate, nothing bloomed at all.

The pink roses that had once climbed the pale stone walls of the sweeping manor house were nothing but tangled webs of thorns. The fountains had gone dry, the hedges untrimmed and shapeless.

The house itself had looked better the day after Amarantha's cronies had trashed it.

Not for any visible signs of destruction, but for the general quiet. The lack of life.

Though the great oak doors were undeniably worse for wear. Deep, long claw marks had been slashed down them.

Standing on the top step of the marble staircase that led to those front doors, I surveyed the brutal gashes. My money was on Tamlin having inflicted them after Feyre had duped him and his court.

But Tamlin's temper had always been his downfall. Any bad day could have produced the gouge marks.

Perhaps today would produce more of them.

The smirk was easy to summon. So was the casual stance, a hand in the pocket of my black jacket, no wings or Illyrian leathers in sight, as I knocked on the ruined doors.

Silence.

Then—

Tamlin answered the door himself.

I wasn't sure what to remark on: the haggard male before me, or the dark house behind him.

An easy mark. Too easy of a mark, to mock the once-fine clothes desperate for a wash, the shaggy hair that needed a trim. The empty manor, not a servant in sight, no Solstice decorations to be found.

The green eyes that met mine weren't the ones I was accustomed to, either. Haunted and bleak. Not a spark.

It would be a matter of minutes to fillet him, body and soul. To finish what had undoubtedly started that day Feyre had called out silently at their wedding, and I had come.

But—peace. We had peace within our sights.

I could rip him apart after we attained it.

"Lucien claimed you would come," Tamlin said by way of greeting, voice as flat and lifeless as his eyes, a hand still braced on the door.

"Funny, I thought his mate was the seer."

Tamlin only stared at me, either ignoring or missing the humor. "What do you want."

No whisper of sound behind him. On any acre of this estate. Not even a note of birdsong. "I came to have a little chat." I offered him a half grin that I knew made him see red. "Can I trouble you for a cup of tea?"

The halls were dim, the embroidered curtains drawn.

A tomb.

This place was a tomb.

With each step toward what had once been the library, the dust and silence pressed in.

Tamlin didn't speak, didn't offer any explanations for the vacant house. For the rooms we passed, some of the carved doors cracked open enough for me to behold the destruction inside.

Shattered furniture, shredded paintings, cracked walls.

Lucien had not come here to make amends during Solstice, I realized as Tamlin opened the door to the dark library.

Lucien had come here out of pity. Mercy.

My sight adjusted to the darkness before Tamlin waved a hand, igniting the faelights in their glass bowls.

He hadn't destroyed this room yet. Had likely taken me to the one chamber in this house that had usable furniture.

I kept my mouth shut as we strode for a large desk in the center of the space, Tamlin claiming an ornate cushioned chair on one side of it. The only thing he had that was close to a throne these days.

I slid into the matching seat across from him, the pale wood groaning in protest. The set had likely been meant to accommodate tittering courtiers, not two full-grown warriors.

Quiet fell, as thick as the emptiness in this house.

"If you've come to gloat, you can spare yourself the effort."

I put a hand on my chest. "Why should I bother?"

No humor. "What did you want to talk about?"

I made a good show of surveying the books, the vaulted, painted ceiling. "Where's my dear friend Lucien?"

"Hunting for our dinner."

"No taste for such things these days?"

Tamlin's eyes remained dull. "He left before I was awake."

Hunting for dinner—because there were no servants here to make food. Or buy it.

I couldn't say I felt bad for him.

Only for Lucien, once again stuck with being his crony.

I crossed an ankle over a knee and leaned back in my chair. "What's this I hear about you not enforcing your borders?"

A beat of quiet. Then Tamlin gestured toward the door. "Do you see any sentries around to do it?"

Even they had abandoned him. Interesting. "Feyre did her work thoroughly, didn't she."

A flash of white teeth, a glimmer of light in his eyes. "With your coaching, I have no doubt."

I smiled. "Oh, no. That was all her. Clever, isn't she."

Tamlin gripped the curved arm of his chair. "I thought the High Lord of the Night Court couldn't be bothered to brag."

I didn't smile as I countered with, "I suppose you think I should be thanking you, for stepping up to assist in reviving me."

"I have no illusions that the day you thank me for anything, Rhysand, is the day the burning fires of hell go cold."

"Poetic."

A low snarl.

Too easy. It was far too easy to bait him, rile him. And though

I reminded myself of the wall, of the peace we needed, I said, "You saved my mate's life on several occasions. I will always be thankful for that."

I knew the words found their mark. *My mate*.

Low. It was a low blow. I had everything—*everything* I'd wished for, dreamed of, begged the stars to grant me.

He had nothing. Had been given everything and squandered it. He didn't deserve my pity, my sympathy.

No, Tamlin deserved what he'd brought upon himself, this husk of a life.

He deserved every empty room, every snarl of thorns, every meal he had to hunt for himself.

"Does she know you're here?"

"Oh, she certainly does." One look at Feyre's face yesterday when I'd invited her along had given me her answer before she'd voiced it: she had no interest in ever seeing the male across from me again.

"And," I went on, "she was as disturbed as I was to learn that your borders are not as enforced as we'd hoped."

"With the wall gone, I'd need an army to watch them."

"That can be arranged."

A soft snarl rumbled from Tamlin, and a hint of claws gleamed at his knuckles. "I'm not letting your ilk onto my lands."

"My *ilk*, as you call them, fought most of the war that *you* helped bring about. If you need patrols, I will supply the warriors."

"To protect humans from us?" A sneer.

My hands ached to wrap around his throat. Indeed, shadows curled at my fingertips, heralds of the talons lurking just beneath.

This house—I hated this house. Had hated it from the moment

I'd set foot in it that night, when Spring Court blood had flowed, payment for a debt that could never be repaid. Payment for two sets of wings, pinned in the study.

Tamlin had burned them long ago, Feyre had told me. It made no difference. He'd been there that day.

Had given his father and brothers the information on where my sister and mother would be waiting for me to meet them. And done nothing to help them as they were butchered.

I still saw their heads in those baskets, their faces still etched with fear and pain. And saw them again as I beheld the High Lord of Spring, both of us crowned in the same blood-soaked night.

"To protect humans from us, yes," I said, my voice going dangerously quiet. "To maintain the peace."

"What peace?" The claws slid back under his skin as he crossed his arms, less muscled than I'd last seen them on the battlefields. "Nothing is different. The wall is gone, that's all."

"We can make it different. Better. But only if we start off the right way."

"I'm not allowing one Night Court brute onto my lands."

His people despised him enough, it seemed.

And at that word—*brute*—I had enough. Dangerous territory. For me, at least. To let my own temper get the better of me. At least around him.

I rose from the chair, Tamlin not bothering to stand. "You brought every bit of this upon yourself," I said, my voice still soft. I didn't need to yell to convey my rage. I never had.

"You won," he spat, sitting forward. "You got your *mate*. Is that not enough?"

"No."

The word echoed through the library.

"You nearly destroyed her. In every way possible."

Tamlin bared his teeth. I bared mine back, temper be damned. Let some of my power rumble through the room, the house, the grounds.

"She survived it, though. Survived *you*. And you still felt the need to humiliate her, belittle her. If you meant to win her back, old friend, that wasn't the wisest route."

"Get out."

I wasn't finished. Not even close. "You deserve everything that has befallen you. You deserve this pathetic, empty house, your ravaged lands. I don't care if you offered that kernel of life to save me, I don't care if you still love my mate. I don't care that you saved her from Hybern, or a thousand enemies before that." The words poured out, cold and steady. "I hope you live the rest of your miserable life alone here. It's a far more satisfying end than slaughtering you." Feyre had once arrived at the same decision. I'd agreed with her then, still did, but now I truly understood.

Tamlin's green eyes went feral.

I braced for it, readied for it—*wanted* it. For him to explode out of that chair and launch himself at me, for his claws to start slashing.

My blood hammered in my veins, my power coiling inside me.

We could wreck this house in our fight. Bring it down to rubble. And then I'd turn the stones and wood into nothing but black dust.

But Tamlin only stared. And after a heartbeat, his eyes lowered to the desk. "Get out."

I blinked, the only sign of my surprise. "Not in the mood for a brawl, Tamlin?"

He didn't bother to look at me again. "Get out" was all he said.

A broken male.

Broken, from his own actions, his own choices.

It was not my concern. He did not deserve my pity.

But as I winnowed away, the dark wind ripping around me, a strange sort of hollowness took root in my stomach.

Tamlin didn't have shields around the house. None to prevent anyone from winnowing in, to guard against enemies appearing in his bedroom and slitting his throat.

It was almost as if he was waiting for someone to do it.

I found Feyre walking home from presumably doing some shopping, a few bags dangling from her gloved hands.

Her smile when I landed beside her, snow whipping around us, was like a fist to my heart.

It faded immediately, however, when she read my face.

Even in the middle of the busy city street, she put a hand to my cheek. "That bad?"

I nodded, leaning into her touch. The most I could manage.

She pressed a kiss to my mouth, her lips warm enough that I realized I'd gone cold.

"Walk home with me," she said, looping her arm through mine and pressing close.

I obeyed, taking the bags from her other hand. As the blocks passed and we crossed over the icy Sidra, then up the steep hills, I told her. Everything I'd said to Tamlin.

"Having heard you rip into Cassian, I'd say you were fairly mild," she observed when I'd finished.

I snorted. "Profanity wasn't necessary here."

She contemplated my words. "Did you go because you were concerned about the wall, or just because you wanted to say those things to him?"

"Both." I couldn't bring myself to lie to her about it. "And perhaps slaughter him."

Alarm flared in her eyes. "Where is this coming from?"

I didn't know. "I just . . ." Words failed me.

Her arm tightened around mine, and I turned to study her face. Open, understanding. "The things you said . . . they weren't wrong," she offered. No judgment, no anger.

Something still a bit hollow inside me filled slightly. "I should have been the bigger male."

"You're the bigger male most days. You're entitled to a slipup." She smiled broadly. Bright as the full moon, lovelier than any star.

I still had not gotten her a Solstice gift. And birthday present.

She angled her head at my frown, her braid slipping over a shoulder. I ran my hand along it, savoring the silken strands against my frozen fingers. "I'll meet you at home," I said, handing her the bags once more.

It was her turn to frown. "Where are you going?"

I kissed her cheek, breathing in her lilac-and-pear scent. "I have some errands that need tending to." And looking at her, walking beside her, did little to cool the rage that still roiled in me. Not when that beautiful smile made me want to winnow back to the Spring Court and punch my Illyrian blade through Tamlin's gut.

Bigger male indeed.

"Go paint my nude portrait," I told her, winking, and shot into the bitterly cold sky.

The sound of her laughter danced with me all the way to the Palace of Thread and Jewels.

✝

I surveyed the spread my preferred jeweler had laid out on black velvet atop the glass counter. In the lights of her cozy shop bordering the Palace, they flickered with an inner fire, beckoning.

Sapphires, emeralds, rubies . . . Feyre had them all. Well, in moderate amounts. Save for those cuffs of solid diamond I'd given her for Starfall.

She'd worn them only twice:

That night I had danced with her until dawn, barely daring to hope that she might be starting to return a fraction of what I felt for her.

And the night we'd returned to Velaris, after that final battle with Hybern. When she had worn *only* those cuffs.

I shook my head, and said to the slim, ethereal faerie behind the counter, "Beautiful as they are, Neve, I don't think milady wants jewels for Solstice."

A shrug that wasn't at all disappointed. I was a frequent enough customer that Neve knew she'd make a sale at some point.

She slid the tray beneath the counter and pulled out another, her night-veiled hands moving smoothly.

Not a wraith, but something similar, her tall, lean frame wrapped in permanent shadows, only her eyes—like glowing coals—visible. The rest tended to come in and out of view, as if the shadows parted to reveal a dark hand, a shoulder, a foot. Her people all master jewel smiths, dwelling in the deepest mountain mines in our court. Most of the heirlooms of our house had been Tartera-made, Feyre's cuffs and crowns included.

Neve waved a shadowed hand over the tray she'd laid out. "I had selected these earlier, if it's not too presumptuous, to consider for Lady Amren."

Indeed, these all *sang* Amren's name. Large stones, delicate settings. Mighty jewelry, for my mighty friend. Who had done so much for me, my mate—our people. The world.

I surveyed the three pieces. Sighed. "I'll take all of them."

Neve's eyes glowed like a living forge.

CHAPTER 12

Feyre

"What the hell is that?"

Cassian was grinning the next evening as he waved a hand toward the pile of pine boughs dumped on the ornate red rug in the center of the foyer. "Solstice decorations. Straight from the market."

Snow clung to his broad shoulders and dark hair, and his tan cheeks were flushed with cold. "You call that a decoration?"

He smirked. "A heap of pine in the middle of the floor is Night Court tradition."

I crossed my arms. "Funny."

"I'm serious." I glared, and he laughed. "It's for the mantels, the banister, and whatever else, smartass. Want to help?" He shrugged off his heavy coat, revealing a black jacket and shirt beneath, and hung it in the hall closet. I remained where I was and tapped my foot.

"What?" he said, brows rising. It was rare to see Cassian in anything but his Illyrian leathers, but the clothes, while not as fine as anything Rhys or Mor usually favored, suited him.

"Dumping a bunch of trees at my feet is really how you say hello these days? A little time in that Illyrian camp and you forget all your manners."

Cassian was on me in a second, hoisting me off the ground to twirl me until I was going to be sick. I beat at his chest, cursing at him.

Cassian set me down at last. "What'd you get me for Solstice?"

I smacked his arm. "A heaping pile of shut the hell up." He laughed again, and I winked at him. "Hot cocoa or wine?"

Cassian curved a wing around me, turning us toward the cellar door. "How many good bottles does little Rhysie have left?"

We drank two of them before Azriel arrived, took one look at our drunken attempts at decorating, and set about fixing it before anyone else could see the mess we'd made.

Lounging on a couch before the birch fire in the living room, we grinned like devils as the shadowsinger straightened the wreaths and garlands we'd chucked over things, swept up pine needles we'd scattered over the carpets, and generally shook his head at everything.

"Az, relax for a minute," Cassian drawled, waving a hand. "Have some wine. Cookies."

"Take off your coat," I added, pointing the bottle toward the shadowsinger, who hadn't even bothered to do so before fixing our mess.

Azriel straightened a sagging section of garland over the windowsill. "It's almost like you two *tried* to make it as ugly as possible."

Cassian clutched at his heart. "We take offense to that."

Azriel sighed at the ceiling.

"Poor Az," I said, pouring myself another glass. "Wine will make you feel better."

He glared at me, then the bottle, then Cassian . . . and finally stormed across the room, took the bottle from my hand, and chugged the rest. Cassian grinned with delight.

Mostly because Rhys drawled from the doorway, "Well, at least now I know who's drinking all my good wine. Want another one, Az?"

Azriel nearly spewed the wine into the fire, but made himself swallow and turn, red-faced, to Rhys. "I would like to explain—"

Rhys laughed, the rich sound bouncing off the carved oak moldings of the room. "Five centuries, and you think I don't know that if my wine's gone, Cassian's usually behind it?"

Cassian raised his glass in a salute.

Rhys surveyed the room and chuckled. "I can tell exactly which ones you two did, and which ones Azriel tried to fix before I got here." Azriel was indeed now rubbing his temple. Rhys lifted a brow at me. "I expected better from an artist."

I stuck out my tongue at him.

A heartbeat later, he said in my mind, *Save that tongue for later. I have ideas for it.*

My toes curled in their thick, high socks.

"It's cold as hell!" Mor called from the front hall, startling me from the warmth pooling in my core. "And who the hell let Cassian and Feyre decorate?"

Azriel choked on what I could have sworn was a laugh, his normally shadowed face lighting up as Mor bustled in, pink with cold and puffing air into her hands. She, however, scowled. "You two couldn't wait until I got here to break into the good wine?"

I grinned as Cassian said, "We were just getting started on Rhys's collection."

Rhys scratched his head. "It *is* there for anyone to drink, you know. Help yourself to whatever you want."

"Dangerous words, Rhysand," Amren warned, strutting through the door, nearly swallowed up by the enormous white fur coat she wore. Only her chin-length dark hair and solid silver eyes were visible above the collar. She looked—

"You look like an angry snowball," Cassian said.

I clamped my lips together to keep the laugh in. Laughing at Amren wasn't a wise move. Even now, with her powers mostly gone and permanently in a High Fae body.

The angry snowball narrowed her eyes at him. "Careful, boy. Wouldn't want to start a war you can't win." She unbuttoned the collar so we all heard her clearly as she purred, "Especially with Nesta Archeron coming for Solstice in two days."

I felt the ripple that went through them—between Cassian, and Mor, and Azriel. Felt the pure temper that rumbled from Cassian, all half-drunk merriness suddenly gone. He said in a low voice, "Shut it, Amren."

Mor was watching closely enough that it was hard not to stare. I glanced at Rhys instead, but a contemplative look had overtaken his face.

Amren merely grinned, those red lips spreading wide enough to show most of her white teeth as she stalked toward the front hall closet and said over a shoulder, "I'm going to enjoy seeing her shred into you. That's if she shows up sober."

And that was enough. Rhys seemed to arrive at the same idea, but before he could say something, I cut in, "Leave Nesta out of it, Amren."

Amren gave me what might have been considered an apologetic

glance. But she merely declared, shoving her enormous coat into the closet, "Varian's coming, so deal with it."

✣

Elain was in the kitchen, helping Nuala and Cerridwen prepare the evening meal. Even with Solstice two nights away, everyone had descended upon the town house.

Except one.

"Any word from Nesta?" I said to my sister by way of greeting.

Elain straightened from the piping-hot loaves of bread she'd hauled from the oven, her hair half up, the apron over her rose-pink gown dusted with flour. She blinked, her large brown eyes clear. "No. I told her to join us tonight, and to let me know when she'd decided. I didn't hear back."

She waved a dishcloth over the bread to cool it slightly, then lifted a loaf to tap the bottom. A hollow sound thumped back, answer enough for her.

"Do you think it's worth fetching her?"

Elain slung the dishcloth over her slim shoulder, rolling her sleeves up to the elbow. Her skin had gained color these months—at least, before the cold weather had set in. Her face had filled in, too. "Are you asking me that as her sister, or as a seer?"

I kept my face calm, pleasant, and leaned against the worktable.

Elain had not mentioned any further visions. And we had not asked her to use her gifts. Whether they still existed, with the Cauldron's destruction and then re-forming, I didn't know. Didn't want to ask.

"You know Nesta best," I answered carefully. "I thought you'd like to weigh in."

"If Nesta doesn't want to be here tonight, then it's more trouble than it's worth to bring her in."

Elain's voice was colder than usual. I glanced at Nuala and Cerridwen, the latter giving me a shake of her head as if to say, *Not a good day for her.*

Like the rest of us, Elain's recovery was ongoing. She'd wept for hours the day I'd taken her to a wildflower-covered hill on the outskirts of the city—to the marble headstone I'd had erected there in honor of our father.

I'd turned his body to ashes after the King of Hybern had killed him, but he still deserved a resting place. For all he'd done in the end, he deserved the beautiful stone I'd had carved with his name. And Elain had deserved a place to visit with him, talk with him.

She went at least once a month.

Nesta had never been at all. Had ignored my invitation to come with us that first day. And every time afterward.

I took up a spot beside Elain, grabbing a knife from the other side of the table to begin cutting the bread. Down the hall, the sounds of my family echoed toward us, Mor's bright laughter ringing out above Cassian's rumble.

I waited until I had a stack of steaming slices before I said, "Nesta is still a part of this family."

"Is she?" Elain sawed deep into the next loaf. "She certainly doesn't act like it."

I hid my frown. "Did something happen when you saw her today?"

Elain didn't answer. She just kept slicing the bread.

So I continued as well. I didn't appreciate when other people pushed me to speak. I'd grant her that same courtesy, too.

In silence, we worked, then set about filling the platters with the food Nuala and Cerridwen signaled was ready, their shadows veiling them more than usual. To grant us some sense of privacy. I threw them a look of gratitude, but they both shook their heads. No thanks necessary. They'd spent more time with Elain than even I had. They understood her moods, what she sometimes needed.

It was only when Elain and I were hauling the first of the serving dishes down the hall toward the dining room that she spoke. "Nesta said she didn't want to come to Solstice."

"That's fine." Even though something in my chest twisted a bit.

"She said she didn't want to come to *anything*. Ever."

I paused, scanning the pain and fear now shining in Elain's eyes. "Did she say why?"

"No." Anger—there was anger in Elain's face, too. "She just said . . . She said that we have our lives, and she has hers."

To say that to me, fine. But to *Elain*?

I blew out a breath, my stomach gurgling at the platter of slow-roasted chicken I held between my hands, the scent of sage and lemon filling my nose. "I'll talk to her."

"Don't," Elain said flatly, starting once more into a walk, veils of steam drifting past her shoulders from the roasted rosemary potatoes in her hands, as if they were Azriel's shadows. "She won't listen."

Like hell she wouldn't.

"And you?" I made myself say. "Are you—all right?"

Elain looked over a shoulder at me as we entered the foyer, then turned left—to the dining room. In the sitting room across the way, all conversation halted at the smell of food. "Why wouldn't I be all right?" she asked, a smile lighting up her face.

I'd seen those smiles before. On my own damn face.

But the others came barreling in from the sitting room, Cassian kissing Elain's cheek in greeting before he nearly lifted her out of the way to get to the dining table. Amren came next, giving my sister a nod, her ruby necklace sparkling in the faelights speckled throughout the garlands in the hall. Then Mor, with a smacking kiss for either cheek. Then Rhys, shaking his head at Cassian, who began helping himself to the platters Nuala and Cerridwen winnowed in. As Elain lived here, my mate gave her only a smile of greeting before taking up his seat at Cassian's right.

Azriel emerged from the sitting room, a glass of wine in hand and wings tucked back to reveal his fine, yet simple black jacket and pants.

I felt, more than saw, my sister go still as he approached. Her throat bobbed.

"Are you just going to hold that chicken all night?" Cassian asked me from the table.

Scowling, I stomped toward him, plunking the platter onto the wooden surface. "I spat in it," I said sweetly.

"Makes it all the more delicious," Cassian crooned, smiling right back. Rhys snickered, drinking deeply from his wine.

But I strode to my seat—nestled between Amren and Mor—in time to see Elain say to Azriel, "Hello."

Az said nothing.

No, he just moved toward her.

Mor tensed beside me.

But Azriel only took Elain's heavy dish of potatoes from her hands, his voice soft as night as he said, "Sit. I'll take care of it."

Elain's hands remained in midair, as if the ghost of the dish remained between them. With a blink, she lowered them, and noticed her apron. "I—I'll be right back," she murmured, and hurried down the hall before I could explain that no one cared if she showed up to dinner covered in flour and that she should just *sit*.

Azriel set the potatoes in the center of the table, Cassian diving right in. Or he tried to.

One moment, his hand was spearing toward the serving spoon. The next, it was stopped, Azriel's scarred fingers wrapped around his wrist. "Wait," Azriel said, nothing but command in his voice.

Mor gaped wide enough that I was certain the half-chewed green beans in her mouth were going to tumble onto her plate. Amren just smirked over the rim of her wineglass.

Cassian gawked at him. "Wait for *what*? Gravy?"

Azriel didn't let go. "Wait until everyone is seated before eating."

"Pig," Mor supplied.

Cassian gave a pointed look to the plate of green beans, chicken, bread, *and* ham already half eaten on Mor's plate. But he relaxed his hand, leaning back in his chair. "I never knew you were a stickler for manners, Az."

Azriel only released Cassian's hand, and stared at his wineglass.

Elain swept in, apron gone and hair rebraided. "Please don't wait on my account," she said, taking the seat at the head of the table.

Cassian glared at Azriel. Az pointedly ignored him.

But Cassian waited until Elain had filled her plate before he took another scoop of anything. As did the others.

I met Rhys's stare across the table. *What was that about?*

Rhys sliced into his glazed ham in smooth, skilled strokes. *It had nothing to do with Cassian.*

Oh?

Rhys took a bite, gesturing with his knife for me to eat. *Let's just say it hit a little close to home.* At my beat of confusion, he added, *There are some scars when it comes to how his mother was treated. Many scars.*

His mother, who had been a servant—near-slave—when he was born. And afterward. *None of us bother to wait for everyone to sit, least of all Cassian.*

It can strike at odd times.

I did my best not to look toward the shadowsinger. *I see.*

Turning to Amren, I studied her plate. Small portions of everything. "Still getting used to it?"

Amren grunted, rolling around her roasted, honeyed carrots. "Blood tastes better."

Mor and Cassian choked.

"And it didn't take so much *time* to consume," Amren groused, lifting the teensiest scrap of roast chicken to her red-painted lips.

Small, slow meals for Amren. The first normal meal she'd eaten after returning—a bowl of lentil soup—had made her vomit for an hour. So it had been a gradual adjustment. She still couldn't dive into a meal the way the rest of us were prone to. Whether it was wholly physical or perhaps some sort of personal adjustment period, none of us knew.

"And then there are the other unpleasant results of eating," Amren went on, slicing her carrots into tiny slivers.

Azriel and Cassian swapped a glance, then both seemed to find their plates *very* interesting. Even as smiles tugged on their faces.

Elain asked, "What sort of results?"

"Don't answer that," Rhys said smoothly, pointing to Amren with his fork.

Amren hissed at him, her dark hair swaying like a curtain of liquid night, "Do you know what an inconvenience it is to need to find a place to relieve myself *everywhere I go*?"

A fizzing noise came from Cassian's side of the table, but I clamped my lips together. Mor gripped my knee beneath the table, her body shaking with the effort of keeping her laugh reined in.

Rhys drawled to Amren, "Shall we start building public toilets for you throughout Velaris, Amren?"

"I mean it, Rhysand," Amren snapped. I didn't dare meet Mor's stare. Or Cassian's. One look and I'd completely dissolve. Amren waved a hand down at herself. "I should have selected a male form. At least *you* can whip it out and go wherever you like without having to worry about spilling on—"

Cassian lost it. Then Mor. Then me. And even Az, chuckling faintly.

"You really don't know how to pee?" Mor roared. "After all this time?"

Amren seethed. "I've seen animals—"

"Tell me you know how a toilet works," Cassian burst out, slapping a broad hand on the table. "Tell me you know that much."

I clapped a hand over my mouth, as if it would push the laugh back in. Across the table, Rhys's eyes were brighter than stars, his mouth a quivering line as he tried and failed to remain serious.

"I know how to sit on a toilet," Amren growled.

Mor opened her mouth, laughter dancing on her face, but Elain asked, "Could you have done it? Decided to take a male form?"

The question cut through the laughter, an arrow fired between us.

Amren studied my sister, Elain's cheeks red from our unfiltered talk at the table. "Yes," she said simply. "Before, in my other form, I was neither. I simply *was*."

"Then why did you pick this body?" Elain asked, the faelight of the chandelier catching in the ripples of her golden-brown braid.

"I was more drawn to the female form," Amren answered simply. "I thought it was more symmetrical. It pleased me."

Mor frowned down at her own form, ogling her considerable assets. "True."

Cassian snickered.

Elain asked, "And once you were in this body, you couldn't change?"

Amren's eyes narrowed slightly. I straightened, glancing between them. Unusual, yes, for Elain to be so vocal, but she'd been improving. Most days, she was lucid—perhaps quiet and prone to melancholy, but aware.

Elain, to my surprise, held Amren's gaze.

Amren said after a moment, "Are you asking out of curiosity for my past, or your own future?"

The question left me too stunned to even reprimand Amren. The others, too.

Elain's brow furrowed before I could leap in. "What do you mean?"

"There's no going back to being human, girl," Amren said, perhaps a tad gently.

"Amren," I warned.

Elain's face reddened further, her back straightening. But she didn't bolt. "I don't know what you're talking about." I'd never heard Elain's voice so cold.

I glanced at the others. Rhys was frowning, Cassian and Mor were both grimacing, and Azriel . . . It was pity on his beautiful face. Pity and sorrow as he watched my sister.

Elain hadn't mentioned being Made, or the Cauldron, or

Graysen in months. I'd assumed that perhaps she was becoming accustomed to being High Fae, that she'd perhaps begun to let go of that mortal life.

"Amren, you have a spectacular gift for ruining dinner conversation," Rhys said, swirling his wine. "I wonder if you could make a career out of it."

His Second glared at him. But Rhys held her stare, silent warning in his face.

Thank you, I said down the bond. A warm caress echoed in answer.

"Pick on someone your own size," Cassian said to Amren, shoveling roast chicken into his mouth.

"I'd feel bad for the mice," Azriel muttered.

Mor and Cassian howled, earning a blush from Azriel and a grateful smile from Elain—and no shortage of scowling from Amren.

But something in me eased at that laughter, at the light that returned to Elain's eyes.

A light I wouldn't see dimmed further.

I need to go out after dinner, I said to Rhys as I dug into my meal again. *Care for a flight across the city?*

Nesta didn't open her door.

I knocked for perhaps a good two minutes, scowling at the dim wooden hallway of the ramshackle building that she'd chosen to live in, then sent a tether of magic through the apartment beyond.

Rhys had erected wards around the entire thing, and with our magic, our souls' bond, there was no resistance to the thread of power I unspooled through the door and into the apartment itself.

Nothing. No sign of life or—or worse beyond.

She wasn't at home.

I had a good idea of where she'd be.

Winnowing into the freezing street, I pinwheeled my arms to keep upright as my boots slid on the ice coating the stones.

Leaning against a lamppost, faelight gilding the talons atop his wings, Rhys chuckled. And didn't move an inch.

"Asshole," I muttered. "Most males would *help* their mates if they're about to break their heads on the ice."

He pushed off the lamppost and prowled toward me, every movement smooth and unhurried. Even now, I'd gladly spend hours just watching him.

"I have a feeling that if I *had* stepped in, you would have bitten my head off for being an overbearing mother hen, as you called me."

I grumbled an answer he chose not to hear.

"Not at home, then?"

I grumbled again.

"Well, that leaves precisely ten other places where she could be."

I grimaced.

Rhys asked, "Do you want me to look?"

Not physically, but use his power to find Nesta. I hadn't wanted him to do it earlier, since it felt like some sort of violation of privacy, but given how damned *cold* it was . . . "Fine."

Rhys wrapped his arms, then his wings around me, tucking me into his heat as he murmured onto my hair, "Hold on."

Darkness and wind tumbled around us, and I buried my face in his chest, breathing in the scent of him.

Then laughter and singing, music blaring, the tangy smell of stale ale, the bite of cold—

I groaned as I beheld where he'd winnowed us, where he'd detected my sister.

"There are wine rooms in this city," Rhys said, cringing. "There are concert halls. Fine restaurants. Pleasure clubs. And yet your sister . . ."

And yet my sister managed to find the seediest, most miserable taverns in Velaris. There weren't many. But she patronized all of them. And this one—the Wolf's Den—was by far the worst.

"Wait here," I said over the fiddles and drums spilling from the tavern as I pulled out of his embrace. Down the street, a few drunk revelers spotted us and fell silent. Felt Rhys's power, perhaps my own as well, and found somewhere else to be for a while.

I had no doubt the same would happen in the tavern, and had no doubt Nesta would resent us for ruining her night. At least I could slip inside mostly unnoticed. If both of us went in there, I knew my sister would see it as an attack.

So it would be me. Alone.

Rhys kissed my brow. "If someone propositions you, tell them we'll both be free in an hour."

"Och." I waved him off, banking my powers to a near-whisper within me.

He blew me a kiss.

I waved that away, too, and slipped through the tavern door.

CHAPTER
13
Feyre

My sister didn't have drinking companions. As far as I knew, she went out alone, and made them as the night progressed. And every now and then, one of them went home with her.

I hadn't asked. Wasn't even sure when the first time had been.

I also didn't dare ask Cassian if he knew. They had barely exchanged more than a few words since the war.

And as I entered the light and rolling music of the Wolf's Den and immediately spotted my sister seated with three males at a round table in the shadowed back, I could almost see the specter of that day against Hybern looming behind her.

Every ounce of weight that Elain had gained it seemed Nesta had lost. Her already proud, angular face had turned more so, her cheekbones sharp enough to slice. Her hair remained up in her usual braided coronet, she wore her preferred gray gown, and she was, as ever, immaculately clean despite the hovel she chose to occupy. Despite the reeking, hot tavern that had seen better years. Centuries.

A queen without a throne. That was what I'd call the painting that swept into my mind.

Nesta's eyes, the same blue-gray as my own, lifted the moment I shut the wooden door behind me. Nothing flickered across her face beyond vague disdain. The three High Fae males at her table were all fairly well dressed considering the place they patronized.

Likely wealthy young bucks out for the night.

I reined in my scowl as Rhys's voice filled my head. *Mind your own business.*

Your sister is handily beating them at cards, by the way.

Snoop.

You love it.

I pressed my lips together, sending a vulgar gesture down the bond as I approached my sister's table. Rhys's laughter rumbled against my shields in answer, like star-flecked thunder.

Nesta simply went back to staring at the fan of cards she held, her posture the epitome of glorious boredom. But her companions peered up at me when I stopped at the edge of their stained and scarred wooden table. Half-consumed glasses of amber liquid sweated with moisture, kept chilled through some magic of the tavern's.

The male across the table—a handsome, rakish-looking High Fae, with hair like spun gold—met my eyes.

His hand of cards slumped to the table as he bowed his head. The others followed suit.

Only my sister, still studying her cards, remained uninterested.

"My lady," said a thin, dark-haired male, throwing a wary glance toward my sister. "How may we be of assistance?"

Nesta didn't so much as look up as she adjusted one of her cards.

Fine.

I smiled sweetly at her companions. "I hate to interrupt your night out, gentlemen." Gentle*males*, I supposed. A holdover from my human life—one that the third male noted with a hint of a raised, thick brow. "But I would like a word with my sister."

The dismissal was clear enough.

As one, they rose, cards abandoned, and swiped up their drinks. "We'll get a refill," the golden-haired one declared.

I waited until they were at the bar, pointedly not gazing over their shoulders, before I slid into the rickety seat the dark-haired one had vacated.

Slowly, Nesta's eyes lifted toward mine.

I leaned back in the chair, wood groaning. "So which one was going home with you tonight?"

Nesta snapped her cards together, setting the stack facedown on the table. "I hadn't decided."

Icy, flat words. The perfect accompaniment to the expression on her face.

I simply waited.

Nesta waited, too.

Still as an animal. Still as death.

I'd once wondered if that was her power. Her curse, granted by the Cauldron.

Nothing I'd seen of it, glimpsed in those moments against Hybern, had seemed *like* death. Just brute power. But the Bone Carver had whispered of it. And I'd seen it, shining cold and bright in her eyes.

But not for months now.

Not that I'd seen much of her.

A minute passed. Then another.

Utter silence, save for the merry music from the four-piece band on the other side of the room.

I could wait. I'd wait here all damn night.

Nesta settled back in her chair, inclined to do the same.

My money's on your sister.

Quiet.

I'm getting cold out here.

Illyrian baby.

A dark chuckle, then the bond went silent again.

"Is that mate of yours going to stand in the cold all night?"

I blinked, wondering if she'd somehow sensed the thoughts between us. "Who says he's here?"

Nesta snorted. "Where one goes, the other follows."

I refrained from voicing all of the potential retorts that leaped onto my tongue.

Instead, I asked, "Elain invited you to dinner tonight. Why didn't you come?"

Nesta's smile was slow, sharp as a blade. "I wanted to hear the musicians play."

I cast a pointed look to the band. More skilled than the usual tavern set, but not a real excuse. "She wanted you there." *I wanted you there.*

Nesta shrugged. "She could have eaten with me here."

"You know Elain wouldn't feel comfortable in a place like this."

She arched a well-groomed brow. "A place like this? What sort of place is that?"

Indeed, some people were turning our way. High Lady—I was

High Lady. Insulting this place and the people in it wouldn't win me any supporters. "Elain is overwhelmed by crowds."

"She didn't used to be that way." Nesta swirled her glass of amber liquid. "She loved balls and parties."

The words hung unspoken. *But you and your court dragged us into this world. Took that joy away from her.*

"If you bothered to come by the house, you'd see that she's readjusting. But balls and parties are one thing. Elain never patronized taverns before this."

Nesta opened her mouth, no doubt to lead me down a path away from the reason I'd come here. So I cut in before she could. "That's beside the point."

Steel-cold eyes held mine. "Can you get to it, then? I'd like to return to my game."

I debated scattering the cards to the ale-slick ground. "Solstice is the day after tomorrow."

Nothing. Not a blink.

I interlaced my fingers and set them on the table between us. "What will it take to get you to come?"

"For Elain's sake or yours?"

"Both."

Another snort. Nesta surveyed the room, everyone carefully *not* watching us now. I knew without asking that Rhys had slid a sound barrier around us.

Finally, my sister looked back at me. "So you're bribing me, then?"

I didn't flinch. "I'm seeing if you're willing to be reasoned with. If there's a way to make it worth your while."

Nesta planted the tip of her pointer finger atop her stack of cards and fanned them out across the table. "It's not even our holiday. We don't *have* holidays."

"Perhaps you should try it. You might enjoy yourself."

"As I told Elain: you have your lives, and I have mine."

Again, I cast a pointed glance to the tavern. "Why? Why this insistence on distancing yourself?"

She settled back in her seat, crossing her arms. "Why do I have to be a part of your merry little band?"

"You're my sister."

Again, that empty, cold look.

I waited.

"I'm not going to your party," she said.

If Elain hadn't been able to convince her, I certainly wouldn't succeed. I didn't know why I hadn't realized it before. Before wasting my time. But I tried—one last time. For Elain's sake. "Father would want you to—"

"Don't you finish that sentence."

Despite the sound shield around us, there was nothing to block the view of my sister baring her teeth. The view of her fingers curling into invisible claws.

Nesta's nose crinkled with undiluted rage as she snarled, "*Leave.*"

A scene. This was about to become a scene in the worst way.

So I rose, hiding my trembling hands by balling them into tight fists at my sides. "Please come," was all I said before turning back toward the door, the walk between her table and the exit feeling so much longer. All the staring faces I'd have to pass looming.

"My rent," Nesta said when I'd walked two steps.

I paused. "What about your rent?"

She swigged from her glass. "It's due next week. In case you forgot."

She was completely serious.

I said flatly, "Come to Solstice and I'll make sure it's delivered."

Nesta opened her mouth, but I turned again, staring down every gaping face that peered up at me as I passed.

I felt my sister's gaze piercing the space between my shoulder blades the entire walk to that front door. And the entire flight home.

CHAPTER 14

Rhysand

Even with workers seldom halting their repairs, the rebuilding was still years from being finished. Especially along the Sidra, where Hybern had hit hardest.

Little more than rubble remained of the once-great estates and homes along the southeastern bend of the river, their gardens overgrown and private boathouses half sunken in the gentle flow of the turquoise waters.

I'd grown up in these houses, attending the parties and feasts that lasted long into the night, spending bright summer days lazing on the sloping lawns, cheering the summer boat races on the Sidra. Their facades had been as familiar as any friend's face. They'd been built long before I was born. I'd expected them to last long after I was gone.

"You haven't heard from the families about when they'll be returning, have you?"

Mor's question floated to me above the crunch of pale stone beneath our feet as we ambled along the snow-dusted grounds of one such estate.

She'd found me after lunch—a rare, solitary meal these days. With Feyre and Elain out shopping in the city, when my cousin had appeared in the foyer of the town house, I hadn't hesitated to invite her for a walk.

It had been a long while since Mor and I had walked together.

I wasn't stupid enough to believe that though the war had ended, all wounds had been healed. Especially between Mor and me.

And I wasn't stupid enough to delude myself into thinking that I hadn't put off this walk for a while now—and so had she.

I'd seen her eyes go distant the other night at the Hewn City. Her silence after her initial snarled warning at her father had told me enough about where her mind had drifted.

Another casualty of this war: working with Keir and Eris had dimmed something in my cousin.

Oh, she hid it well. Save for when she was face-to-face with the two males who had—

I didn't let myself finish the thought, summon the memory. Even five centuries later, the rage threatened to swallow me until I'd left the Hewn City and Autumn Court in ruins.

But those were her deaths to claim. They always had been. I had never asked why she'd waited so long.

We'd quietly meandered through the city for half an hour now, going mostly unnoticed. A small blessing of Solstice: everyone was too busy with their own preparations to mark who strolled through the packed streets.

How we'd wound up here, I had no idea. But here we were, nothing but the fallen and cracked blocks of stone, winter-dry weeds, and gray sky for company.

"The families," I said at last, "are at their other estates." I knew them all, wealthy merchants and nobles who had defected from the

Hewn City long before the two halves of my realm had been officially severed. "With no plans to return anytime soon." Perhaps forever. I'd heard from one of them, a matriarch of a merchant empire, that they were likely going to sell rather than face the ordeal of building from scratch.

Mor nodded absently, the chill wind whipping strands of her hair over her face as she paused in the middle of what had once been a formal garden sloping from the house to the icy river itself. "Keir is coming here soon, isn't he."

So rarely would she ever refer to him as her father. I didn't blame her. That male hadn't been her father for centuries. Long before that unforgivable day.

"He is."

I'd managed to keep Keir at bay since the war had ended—had prepared for him to inevitably decide that no matter the work I dumped in his lap, no matter how I might interrupt his little visits with Eris, he would visit this city.

Perhaps I had brought this upon myself, by enforcing the Hewn City's borders for so long. Perhaps their horrible traditions and narrow minds had only grown worse while being contained. It was their territory, yes, but I'd given them nothing else. No wonder they were so curious about Velaris. Though Keir's desire to visit only stemmed from one need: to torment his daughter.

"When."

"Likely in the spring, if I'm guessing correctly."

Mor's throat bobbed, her face going cold in a way I so rarely witnessed. In a way I hated, if only because I was to blame for it.

I'd told myself it had been worth it. Keir's Darkbringers had been crucial in our victory. And he'd suffered losses because of it.

The male was a prick in every sense of the word, but he'd come through on his end.

I had little choice but to hold up my own.

Mor scanned me from head to toe. I'd opted for a black jacket crafted from heavier wool, and forgone wings entirely. Just because Cassian and Azriel had to suffer through having them be freezing all the time didn't mean I had to. I remained still, letting Mor arrive at her own conclusions. "I trust you," she said at last.

I bowed my head. "Thank you."

She waved a hand, launching into a walk again down the pale gravel paths of the garden. "But I still wish there had been another way."

"I do, too."

She twisted the ends of her thick red scarf before tucking them into her brown overcoat.

"If your father comes here," I offered, "I can make sure you're away." No matter that she had been the one to push for the minor confrontation with the Steward and Eris the other night.

She scowled. "He'll see it for what it is: hiding. I won't give him that satisfaction."

I knew better than to ask if she thought her mother would come along. We didn't discuss Mor's mother. Ever.

"Whatever you decide, I'll support you."

"I know that." She paused between two low-lying boxwoods and watched the icy river beyond.

"And you know that Az and Cassian are going to be monitoring them like hawks for the entire visit. They've been planning the security protocols for months now."

"They have?"

I nodded gravely.

Mor blew out a breath. "I wish we were still able to threaten to unleash Amren on the entire Hewn City."

I snorted, gazing across the river to the quarter of the city just barely visible over the rise of a hill. "Half of me wonders if Amren wishes the same."

"I assume you're getting her a *very* good present."

"Neve was practically skipping with glee when I left the shop."

A small laugh. "What did you get Feyre?"

I slid my hands into my pockets. "This and that."

"So, nothing."

I dragged a hand through my hair. "Nothing. Any ideas?"

"She's your mate. Shouldn't this sort of thing be instinctual?"

"She's impossible to shop for."

Mor gave me a wry look. "Pathetic."

I nudged her with an elbow. "What did *you* get her?"

"You'll have to wait until Solstice evening to see."

I rolled my eyes. In the centuries I'd known her, Mor's present-buying abilities had never improved. I had a drawer full of downright hideous cuff links that I'd never worn, each gaudier than the next. I was lucky, though: Cassian had a trunk crammed with silk shirts of varying colors of the rainbow. Some even had ruffles on them.

I could only imagine the horrors in store for my mate.

Thin sheets of ice lazily drifted down the Sidra. I didn't dare ask Mor about Azriel—what she'd gotten him, what she planned to *do* with him. I had little interest in being chucked right into that icy river.

"I'm going to need you, Mor," I said quietly.

The amusement in Mor's eyes sharpened to alertness. A predator. There was a reason she'd held her own in battle, and could hold her own against any Illyrian. My brothers and I had overseen much of the training ourselves, but she'd spent years traveling to other lands, other territories, to learn what they knew.

Which was precisely why I said, "Not with Keir and the Hewn City, not with holding the peace long enough for things to stabilize."

She crossed her arms, waiting.

"Az can infiltrate most courts, most lands. But I might need you to win those lands over." Because the pieces that were now strewn on the table . . . "Treaty negotiations are dragging on too long."

"They're not happening at all."

Truth. With the rebuilding, too many tentative allies had claimed they were busy and would reconvene in the spring to discuss the new terms.

"You wouldn't need to be gone for months. Just visits here and there. Casual."

"Casual, but make the kingdoms and territories realize that if they push too far or enter into human lands, we'll obliterate them?"

I huffed a laugh. "Something like that. Az has lists of the kingdoms most likely to cross the line."

"If I'm flitting about the continent, who will deal with the Court of Nightmares?"

"I will."

Her brown eyes narrowed. "You're not doing this because you think I can't handle Keir, are you?"

Careful, careful territory. "No," I said, and wasn't lying. "I think you can. I know you can. But your talents are better wielded elsewhere for now. Keir wants to build ties to the Autumn Court—let him. Whatever he and Eris are scheming up, they know we're watching, and know how stupid it would be for either of them to push us. One word to Beron, and Eris's head will roll."

Tempting. So damn tempting to tell the High Lord of Autumn that his eldest son coveted his throne—and was willing to take it by force. But I'd made a bargain with Eris, too. Perhaps a fool's bargain, but only time would tell in that regard.

Mor fiddled with her scarf. "I'm not afraid of them."

"I know you're not."

"I just—being near them, *together* . . ." She shoved her hands into her pockets. "It's probably what it feels like for you to be around Tamlin."

"If it's any consolation, cousin, I behaved rather poorly the other day."

"Is he dead?"

"No."

"Then I'd say you controlled yourself admirably."

I laughed. "Bloodthirsty of you, Mor."

She shrugged, again watching the river. "He deserves it."

He did indeed.

She glanced sidelong at me. "When would I need to leave?"

"Not for another few weeks, maybe a month."

She nodded, and fell quiet. I debated asking her if she wished to know *where* Azriel and I thought she might go first, but her silence said enough. She'd go anywhere.

Too long. She'd been cooped up within the borders of this court for too long. The war barely counted. And it wouldn't happen in a month, or perhaps a few years, but I could see it: the invisible noose tightening around her neck with every day spent here.

"Take a few days to think about it," I offered.

She whipped her head toward me, golden hair catching in the light. "You said you needed me. It didn't seem like there was much room for choice."

"You always have a choice. If you don't want to go, then it's fine."

"And who would do it instead? Amren?" A knowing look.

I laughed again. "Certainly not Amren. Not if we want peace." I added, "Just—do me a favor and take some time to think about it before you say yes. Consider it an offer, not an order."

She fell silent once more. Together, we watched the ice floes drift down the Sidra, toward the distant, wild sea. "Does he win if I go?" A quiet, tentative question.

"You have to decide that for yourself."

Mor turned toward the ruined house and grounds behind us. Staring not at them, I realized, but eastward.

Toward the continent and the lands within. As if wondering what might be waiting there.

CHAPTER 15

Feyre

I had yet to find or even come up with a vague idea for what to give Rhysand for Solstice.

Mercifully, Elain quietly approached me at breakfast, Cassian still passed out on the couch in the sitting room across the foyer and no sign of Azriel where he'd fallen asleep on the couch across from him, both too lazy—and perhaps a little drunk, after all the wine we'd had last night—to make the trek up to the tiny spare bedroom they'd be sharing during Solstice. Mor had taken my old bedroom, not minding the clutter I'd added, and Amren had gone back to her own apartment when we'd finally drifted to sleep in the early hours of the morning. Both my mate and Mor were still sleeping, and I'd been content to let them continue doing so. They'd earned that rest. We all had.

But Elain, it seemed, was as sleepless as me, especially after my stinging talk with Nesta that even the wine I'd returned home to drink couldn't dull, and she wanted to see if I was game for a walk about the city, providing me with the perfect excuse to head out for more shopping.

Decadent—it felt decadent, and selfish, to shop, even if it was for people I loved. There were so many in this city and beyond it who had next to nothing, and every additional, unnecessary moment I spent peering into window displays and running my fingers over various goods grated against my nerves.

"I know it's not easy for you," Elain observed as we drifted through a weaver's shop, admiring the fine tapestries, rugs, and blankets she'd crafted into images of various Night Court scenes: Velaris under the glow of Starfall; the rocky, untamed shores of the northern isles; the stelae of the temples of Cesere; the insignia of this court, the three stars crowning a mountain peak.

I turned from a wall covering depicting that very image. "What's not easy?"

We kept our voices to a near-murmur in the quiet, warm space, more out of respect to the other browsers admiring the work.

Elain's brown eyes roved over the Night Court insignia. "Buying things without a dire need to do so."

In the back of the vaulted, wood-paneled shop, a loom thrummed and clicked as the dark-haired artist who made the pieces continued her work, pausing only to answer questions from customers.

So different. This space was so different from the cottage of horrors that had belonged to the Weaver in the Wood. To Stryga.

"We have everything we need," I admitted to Elain. "Buying presents feels excessive."

"It's their tradition, though," Elain countered, her face still flushed with the cold. "One that they fought and died to protect in the war. Perhaps that's the better way to think of it, rather than feeling guilty. To remember that this day means something to them. All of them, regardless of who has more, who has less, and in celebrating the traditions, even through the presents, we honor those who fought for its very existence, for the peace this city now has."

For a moment, I just stared at my sister, the wisdom she'd spoken. Not a whisper of those oracular abilities. Just clear eyes and an open expression. "You're right," I said, taking in the insignia rising before me.

The tapestry had been woven from fabric so black it seemed to devour the light, so black it almost strained the eye. The insignia, however, had been rendered in silver thread—no, not silver. A sort of iridescent thread that shifted with sparks of color. Like woven starlight.

"You're thinking of getting it?" Elain asked. She hadn't bought anything in the hour we'd already been out, but she'd stopped often enough to contemplate. A gift for Nesta, she'd said. She was looking for a gift for our sister, regardless of whether Nesta deigned to join us tomorrow.

But Elain had seemed more than content to simply watch the humming city, to take in the sparkling strands of faelights strung between buildings and over the squares, to sample any tidbit of food offered by an eager vendor, to listen to minstrels busking by the now-silent fountains.

As if my sister, too, had merely been looking for an excuse to get out of the house today.

"I don't know *who* I'd get it for," I admitted, extending a finger toward the black fabric of the tapestry. The moment my nail touched the velvet-soft surface, it seemed to vanish. As if the material truly did gobble up all color, all light. "But . . ." I looked toward the weaver at the other end of the space, another piece half-formed on her loom. Leaving my thought unfinished, I strode for her.

The weaver was High Fae, full-figured and pale-skinned. A sheet of black hair had been braided back from her face, the length of the plait dropping over the shoulder of her thick, red sweater. Practical brown pants and shearling-lined boots completed her attire. Simple, comfortable clothes. What I might wear while painting. Or doing anything.

What I was wearing beneath my heavy blue overcoat, to be honest.

The weaver halted her work, deft fingers stilling, and lifted her head. "How can I help you?"

Despite her pretty smile, her gray eyes were . . . quiet. There was no way of explaining it. Quiet, and a little distant. The smile tried to offset it, but failed to mask the heaviness lingering within.

"I wanted to know about the tapestry with the insignia," I said. "The black fabric—what is it?"

"I get asked that at least once an hour," the weaver said, her smile remaining yet no humor lighting her eyes.

I cringed a bit. "Sorry to add to that." Elain drifted to my side, a fuzzy pink blanket in one hand, a purple blanket in the other.

The weaver waved off my apology. "It's an unusual fabric. Questions are expected." She smoothed a hand over the wooden frame of her loom. "I call it Void. It absorbs the light. Creates a complete lack of color."

"You made it?" Elain asked, now staring over her shoulder toward the tapestry.

A solemn nod. "A newer experiment of mine. To see how darkness might be made, woven. To see if I could take it farther, deeper than any weaver has before."

Having been in a void myself, the fabric she'd woven came unnervingly close. "Why?"

Her gray eyes shifted toward me again. "My husband didn't return from the war."

The frank, open words clanged through me.

It was an effort to hold her gaze as she continued, "I began trying to create Void the day after I learned he'd fallen."

Rhys hadn't asked anyone in this city to join his armies, though. Had deliberately made it a choice. At the confusion on my face, the weaver added softly, "He thought it was right. To help fight. He left with several others who felt the same, and joined up with a Summer Court legion they found on their way south. He died in the battle for Adriata."

"I'm sorry," I said softly. Elain echoed the words, her voice gentle.

The weaver only stared toward the tapestry. "I thought we'd have a thousand more years together." She began to coax the loom back into movement. "In the three hundred years we were wed, we never had the chance to have children." Her fingers moved beautifully, unfaltering despite her words. "I don't even have a piece of him in that way. He's gone, and I am not. Void was born of that feeling."

I didn't know what to say as her words settled in. As she continued working.

It could have been me.

It could have been Rhys.

That extraordinary fabric, created and woven in grief that I had briefly touched and never wished to know again, contained a loss I could not imagine recovering from.

"I keep hoping that every time I tell someone who asks about Void, it will get easier," the weaver said. If people asked about it as frequently as she'd claimed . . . I couldn't have endured it.

"Why not take it down?" Elain asked, sympathy written all over her face.

"Because I do not want to keep it." The shuttle swept across the loom, flying with a life of its own.

Despite her poise, her calm, I could almost feel her agony radiating into the room. A few touches of my daemati gifts and I might ease that grief, make the pain less. I'd never done so for anyone, but . . .

But I could not. Would not. It would be a violation, even if I made it with good intentions.

And her loss, her unending sorrow—she had created something from it. Something extraordinary. I couldn't take that away from her. Even if she asked me to.

"The silver thread," Elain asked. "What is that called?"

The weaver paused the loom again, the colorful strings vibrating. She held my sister's gaze. No attempt at a smile this time. "I call it Hope."

My throat became unbearably tight, my eyes stinging enough that I had to turn away, to walk back toward that extraordinary tapestry.

The weaver explained to my sister, "I made it after I mastered Void."

I stared and stared at the black fabric that was like peering into a pit of hell. And then stared at the iridescent, living silver thread that cut through it, bright despite the darkness that devoured all other light and color.

It could have been me. And Rhys. Had very nearly gone that way.

Yet he had lived, and the weaver's husband had not. *We* had lived, and their story had ended. She did not have a piece of him left. At least, not in the way she wished.

I was lucky—so tremendously *lucky* to even be complaining about shopping for my mate. That moment when he had died had been the worst of my life, would likely remain so, but we had survived it. These months, the *what-if* had haunted me. All of the *what-ifs* that we'd so narrowly escaped.

And this holiday tomorrow, this chance to celebrate being together, living . . .

The impossible depth of blackness before me, the unlikely defiance of Hope shining through it, whispered the truth before I knew it. Before I knew what I wanted to give Rhys.

The weaver's husband had not come home. But mine had.

"Feyre?"

Elain was again at my side. I hadn't heard her steps. Hadn't heard any sound for moments.

The gallery had emptied out, I realized. But I didn't care, not as I again approached the weaver, who had stopped once more. At the mention of my name.

The weaver's eyes were slightly wide as she bowed her head. "My lady."

I ignored the words. "How." I gestured to the loom, the half-finished piece taking form on its frame, the art on the walls. "How do you keep creating, despite what you lost?"

Whether she noted the crack in my voice, she didn't let on. The weaver only said, her sad, sorrowful gaze meeting mine, "I have to."

The simple words hit me like a blow.

The weaver went on, "I *have* to create, or it was all for nothing. I *have* to create, or I will crumple up with despair and never leave my bed. I *have* to create because I have no other way of voicing *this*."

Her hand rested on her heart, and my eyes burned. "It is hard," the weaver said, her stare never leaving mine, "and it hurts, but if I were to stop, if I were to let this loom or the spindle go silent . . ." She broke my gaze at last to look to her tapestry. "Then there would be no Hope shining in the Void."

My mouth trembled, and the weaver reached over to squeeze my hand, her callused fingers warm against mine.

I had no words to offer her, nothing to convey what surged in my chest. Nothing other than, "I would like to buy that tapestry."

✠

The tapestry was a gift for no one but myself, and would be delivered to the town house later that afternoon.

Elain and I browsed various stores for another hour before I left my sister to do her own shopping at the Palace of Thread and Jewels.

I winnowed right into the abandoned studio in the Rainbow.

I needed to paint. Needed to get out what I'd seen, felt in the weaver's gallery.

I wound up staying for three hours.

Some paintings were quick, swift renderings. Some I began plotting out with pencil and paper, mulling over the canvas needed, the paint I'd like to use.

I painted through the grief that lingered at the weaver's story, painted *for* her loss. I painted all that rose within me, letting the past bleed onto the canvas, a blessed relief with each stroke of my brush.

It was little surprise I was caught.

I barely had time to leap off my stool before the front door opened and Ressina entered, a mop and bucket in her green hands. I certainly didn't have enough time to hide all the paintings and supplies.

Ressina, to her credit, only smiled as she stopped short. "I suspected you'd be in here. I saw the lights the other night and thought it might be you."

My heart pounded through my body, my face as warm as a forge, but I managed to offer a close-lipped smile. "Sorry."

The faerie gracefully crossed the room, even with the cleaning supplies in hand. "No need to apologize. I was just headed in to do some cleaning up."

She dumped the mop and bucket against one of the empty white walls with a faint thud.

"Why?" I laid my paintbrush atop the palette I'd placed on a stool beside mine.

Ressina set her hands on her narrow hips and surveyed the place.

By some mercy or lack of interest, she didn't look too long at my paintings. "Polina's family hasn't discussed whether they're selling, but I figured she, at least, wouldn't want the place to be a mess."

I bit my lip, nodding awkwardly as I lingered by the mess I'd added. "Sorry I . . . I didn't come by your studio the other night."

Ressina shrugged. "Again, no need to apologize."

So rarely did anyone outside the Inner Circle speak to me with such casualness. Even the weaver had become more formal after I'd offered to buy her tapestry.

"I'm just glad someone's using this place. That *you* are using it," Ressina added. "I think Polina would have liked you."

Silence fell when I didn't answer. When I began scooping up supplies. "I'll get out of your way." I moved to set down a still-drying painting against the wall. A portrait I'd been thinking about for some time now. I sent it to that pocket between realms, along with all the others I'd been working on.

I bent to pick up my pack of supplies.

"You could leave those."

I paused, a hand looped around the leather strap. "It's not my space."

Ressina leaned against the wall beside her mop and bucket. "Perhaps you could talk to Polina's family about that. They're motivated sellers."

I straightened, taking the supply pack with me. "Perhaps," I hedged, sending the rest of the supplies and paintings tumbling into that pocket realm, not caring if they crashed into each other as I headed for the door.

"They live out on a farm in Dunmere, by the sea. In case you're ever interested."

Not likely. "Thanks."

I could practically hear her smile as I reached the front door. "Happy Solstice."

"You, too," I threw over my shoulder before I vanished onto the street.

And slammed right into the hard, warm chest of my mate.

I rebounded off Rhys with a curse, scowling at his laugh as he gripped my arms to steady me against the icy street. "Going somewhere?"

I frowned at him, but linked my arm through his and launched into a brisk walk. "What are you doing here?"

"Why are you running out of an abandoned gallery as if you've stolen something?"

"I was not *running*." I pinched his arm, earning another deep, husky laugh.

"Walking suspiciously quickly, then."

I didn't answer until we'd reached the avenue that sloped down to the river. Thin crusts of ice drifted along the turquoise waters. Beneath them, I could feel the current still flowing past—not as strongly as I did in warmer months, though. As if the Sidra had fallen into a twilight slumber for the winter.

"That's where I've been painting," I said at last as we halted at the railed walkway beside the river. A damp, cold wind brushed past, ruffling my hair. Rhys tucked a strand of it behind my ear. "I went back today—and was interrupted by an artist, Ressina. But the studio belonged to a faerie who didn't survive the attack this spring. Ressina was cleaning up the space on her behalf. Polina's behalf, in case Polina's family wants to sell it."

"We can buy you a studio space if you need somewhere to paint by yourself," he offered, the thin sunlight gilding his hair. No sign of his wings.

"No—no, it's not being alone so much as . . . the right space to do it. The right *feel* to it." I shook my head. "I don't know. The painting helps. Helps me, I mean." I blew out a breath and surveyed him, the face dearer to me than anything in the world, the weaver's words echoing through me.

She had lost her husband. I had not. And yet she still wove, still created. I cupped Rhys's cheek, and he leaned into the touch as I quietly asked, "Do you think it's stupid to wonder if painting might help others, too? Not *my* painting, I mean. But teaching others to paint. Letting them paint. People who might struggle the same way I do."

His eyes softened. "I don't think that's stupid at all."

I traced my thumb over his cheekbone, savoring every inch of contact. "It makes me feel better—perhaps it would do the same for others."

He remained quiet, offering me that companionship that demanded nothing, asked nothing as I kept stroking his face. We had been mated for less than a year. If things had not gone well during that final battle, how many regrets would have consumed me? I knew—knew which ones would have hit the hardest, struck the deepest. Knew which ones were in my power to change.

I lowered my hand from his face at last. "Do you think anyone would come? If such a space, such a thing, were available?"

Rhys considered, scanning my eyes before kissing my temple, his mouth warm against my chilled face. "You'll have to see, I suppose."

I found Amren in her loft an hour later. Rhys had another meeting to attend with Cassian and their Illyrian commanders out at Devlon's war-camp, and had walked me to the door of her building before winnowing.

My nose crinkled as I entered Amren's toasty apartment. "It smells . . . interesting in here."

Amren, seated at the long worktable in the center of the space, gave me a slashing grin before gesturing to the four-poster bed.

Rumpled sheets and askew pillows said enough about what scents I was detecting.

"You could open a window," I said, waving to the wall of them at the other end of the apartment.

"It's cold out," was all she said, going back to—

"A jigsaw puzzle?"

Amren fitted a tiny piece into the section she'd been working on. "Am I supposed to be doing something else during my Solstice holiday?"

I didn't dare answer that as I shrugged off my overcoat and scarf. Amren kept the fire in the hearth near-sweltering. Either for herself, or her Summer Court companion, no sign of whom could I detect. "Where's Varian?"

"Out buying more presents for me."

"More?"

A smaller smile this time, her red mouth quirking to the side as she fitted another piece into her puzzle. "He decided the ones he brought from the Summer Court were not enough."

I didn't want to get into that comment, either.

I took a seat across from her at the long, dark wood table, examining the half-finished puzzle of what seemed to be some sort of autumnal pastoral. "A new hobby of yours?"

"Without that odious Book to decipher, I've found I miss such things." Another piece snapped into place. "This is my fifth this week."

"We're only three days into the week."

"They don't make them hard enough for me."

"How many pieces is this one?"

"Five thousand."

"Show-off."

Amren tutted to herself, then straightened in her chair, rubbing her back and wincing. "Good for the mind, but bad for the posture."

"Good thing you have Varian to exercise with."

Amren laughed, the sound like a crow's caw. "Good thing indeed." Those silver eyes, still uncanny, still limned with some trace of power, scanned me. "You didn't come here to keep me company, I suppose."

I leaned back in the rickety old chair. None at the table matched. Indeed, each seemed from a different decade. Century. "No, I didn't."

The High Lord's Second waved a hand tipped in long red nails and stooped over her puzzle again. "Proceed."

I took a steadying breath. "It's about Nesta."

"I suspected as much."

"Have you spoken to her?"

"She comes here every few days."

"Really?"

Amren tried and failed to fit a piece into her puzzle, her eyes darting over the color-sorted pieces around her. "Is it so hard to believe?"

"She doesn't come to the town house. Or the House of Wind."

"No one likes going to the House of Wind."

I reached for a piece and Amren clicked her tongue in warning. I set my hand back on my lap.

"I was hoping you might have some insight into what she's going through."

Amren didn't reply for a while, scanning the pieces laid out instead. I was about to repeat myself when she said, "I like your sister."

One of the few.

Amren lifted her eyes to me, as if I'd said the words aloud. "I like her because so few do. I like her because she is not easy to be around, or to understand."

"But?"

"But nothing," Amren said, returning to the puzzle. "Because I like her, I am not inclined to gossip about her current state."

"It's not gossip. I'm concerned." We all were. "She is starting down a path that—"

"I will not betray her confidence."

"She's talked to you?" Too many emotions cascaded through me at that. Relief that Nesta had talked to anyone, confusion that it had been *Amren*, and perhaps even some jealousy that my sister had not turned to me—or Elain.

"No," Amren said. "But I know she would not like me to be musing over her *path* with anyone. With you."

"But—"

"Give her time. Give her space. Give her the opportunity to sort through this on her own."

"It's been months."

"She's an immortal. Months are inconsequential."

I clenched my jaw. "She refuses to come home for Solstice. Elain will be heartbroken if she doesn't—"

"Elain, or you?"

Those silver eyes pinned me to the spot.

"Both," I said through my teeth.

Again, Amren sifted through her pieces. "Elain has her own problems to focus on."

"Such as?"

Amren just gave me a Look. I ignored it.

"If Nesta deigns to visit you," I said, the ancient chair groaning as I pushed it back and rose, grabbing my coat and scarf from the bench by the door, "tell her that it would mean a great deal if she came on Solstice."

Amren didn't bother to look up from her puzzle. "I will make no promises, girl."

It was the best I could hope for.

CHAPTER 16

Rhysand

That afternoon, Cassian dumped his leather bag on the narrow bed against the wall of the fourth bedroom in the town house, the contents rattling.

"You brought weapons to Solstice?" I asked, leaning against the door frame.

Azriel, setting his own bag on the bed opposite Cassian's, threw our brother a vague look of alarm. After passing out on the sitting room couches last night, and a likely uncomfortable sleep, they'd finally bothered to settle into the bedroom designated for them.

Cassian shrugged, plopping onto the bed, which was better suited for a child than an Illyrian warrior. "Some might be gifts."

"And the rest?"

Cassian toed off his boots and leaned against the headboard, folding his arms behind his head as his wings draped to the floor. "The females bring their jewelry. I bring my weapons."

"I know a few females in this house who might take offense to that."

Cassian offered me a wicked grin in response. The same grin

he'd given Devlon and the commanders at our meeting an hour ago. All was ready for the storm; all patrols accounted for. A standard meeting, and one I didn't need to attend, but it was always good to remind them of my presence. Especially before they all gathered for Solstice.

Azriel strode to the lone window at the end of the room and peered into the garden below. "I've never stayed in this room." His midnight voice filled the space.

"That's because you and I have been shoved to the bottom of the ladder, brother," Cassian answered, his wings draping over the bed and to the wooden floor. "Mor gets the good bedroom, Elain is living in the other, and so we get this one." He didn't mention that the final, empty bedroom—Nesta's old room—would remain open. Azriel, to his credit, didn't, either.

"Better than the attic," I offered.

"Poor Lucien," Cassian said, smiling.

"If Lucien shows up," I corrected. No word about whether he would be joining us. Or remaining in that mausoleum Tamlin called a home.

"My money's on yes," Cassian said. "Want to make a wager?"

"No," Azriel said, not turning from the window.

Cassian sat up, the portrait of outrage. "No?"

Azriel tucked in his wings. "Would *you* want people betting on you?"

"You assholes bet on me all the time. I remember the last one you did—you and Mor, making wagers about whether my wings would heal."

I snorted. True.

Azriel remained at the window. "Will Nesta stay here if she comes?"

Cassian suddenly found the Siphon atop his left hand to be in need of polishing.

I decided to spare him and said to Azriel, "Our meeting with the commanders went as well as could be expected. Devlon actually had a schedule drawn up for the girls' training, whenever this oncoming storm blows out. I don't think it was for show."

"I'd still be surprised if they remember once the storm clears," Azriel said, turning from the garden window at last.

Cassian grunted in agreement. "Anything new about the grumbling in the camps?"

I kept my face neutral. Az and I had agreed to wait until after the holiday to divulge to Cassian the full extent of what we knew, *who* we suspected or knew was behind it. We'd told him the basics, though. Enough to assuage any sort of guilt.

But I knew Cassian—as well as myself. Perhaps more so. He wouldn't be able to leave it alone if he knew now. And after all he'd been putting up with these months, and long before it, my brother deserved a break. At least for a few days.

Of course that *break* had already included the meeting with Devlon and a grueling training session atop the House of Wind this morning. Out of all of us, the concept of relaxing was the most foreign to Cassian.

Azriel leaned against the carved wood footboard at the end of his bed. "Little to add to what you already know." Smooth, easy liar. Far better than me. "But they sensed that it's growing. The best time to assess is after Solstice, when they've all returned home. See who spreads the discord then. If it's grown while they were all celebrating together or snowed in with this storm."

The perfect way to then reveal the full extent of what we knew.

If the Illyrians revolted . . . I didn't want to think that far down the road. What it would cost me. What it would cost Cassian, to fight the people he still so desperately wanted to be a part of. To kill them. It'd be far different from what we'd done to the Illyrians who'd gladly served Amarantha, and done such terrible things in her name. Far different.

I shut out the thought. Later. After Solstice. We'd deal with it then.

Cassian, mercifully, seemed inclined to do the same. Not that I blamed him, given the hour of bullshit posturing he'd endured before we'd winnowed here. Even now, centuries later, the camp-lords and commanders still challenged him. Spat on him.

Cassian toed his own footboard, his legs not even fully stretched out. "Who used this bed anyway? It's Amren-sized."

I snorted. "Careful how you whine. Feyre calls us Illyrian babies often enough."

Azriel chuckled. "Her flying has improved enough that I think she's entitled to do so."

Pride rippled through me. Perhaps she wasn't a natural, but she made up for it with sheer grit and focus. I'd lost count of the hours we spent in the air—the precious time we'd managed to steal for ourselves.

I said to Cassian, "I can see about finding you two longer beds." With Solstice Eve here, it would take a minor miracle. I'd have to turn Velaris upside down.

He waved a hand. "No need. Better than the couch."

"You being too drunk to climb the stairs last night aside," I said wryly, earning a vulgar gesture in response, "space in this house does indeed seem to be an issue. You could stay up at the House if you'd prefer. I can winnow you in."

"The House is boring." Cassian yawned for emphasis. "Az sneaks off into shadows and I'm left all alone."

Azriel gave me a look that said, *Illyrian baby indeed*.

I hid my smile and said to Cassian, "Perhaps you should get a place of your own, then."

"I have one in Illyria."

"I meant here."

Cassian lifted a brow. "I don't need a house here. I need a *room*." He again toed the footboard, rocking the wood panel. "This one would be fine, if it didn't have a doll's bed."

I chuckled again, but held in my retort. My suggestion that he might *want* a place of his own. Soon.

Not that anything was happening on that front. Not anytime soon. Nesta had made it clear enough she had no interest in Cassian—not even in being in the same room as him. I knew why. I'd seen it happen, had felt that way plenty.

"Perhaps that will be your Solstice present, Cassian," I replied instead. "A new bed here."

"Better than Mor's presents," Az muttered.

Cassian laughed, the sound booming off the walls.

But I peered in the direction of the Sidra and lifted a brow.

She looked radiant.

Solstice Eve had fully settled upon Velaris, quieting the thrum that had pulsed through the city for the past few weeks, as if everyone paused to listen to the falling snow.

A gentle fall, no doubt, compared with the wild storm unleashing itself upon the Illyrian Mountains.

We'd gathered in the sitting room, the fire crackling, wine opened and flowing. Though neither Lucien nor Nesta had shown their faces, the mood was far from somber.

Indeed, as Feyre emerged from the kitchen hallway, I took a moment to simply drink her in from where I sat in an armchair near the fire.

She went right to Mor—perhaps because Mor was holding the wine, the bottle already outreached.

I admired the view from behind as Feyre's glass was filled.

It was an effort to leash every raging instinct at that particular view. At the curves and hollows of my mate, the color of her—so vibrant, even in this room of so many personalities. Her midnight-blue velvet gown hugged her perfectly, leaving little to the imagination before it pooled to the floor. She'd left her hair down, curling slightly at the ends—hair I knew I later wanted to plunge my hands into, scattering the silver combs pinning up the sides. And then I'd peel off that dress. Slowly.

"You'll make me vomit," Amren hissed, kicking me with her silver silk shoe from where she sat in the armchair adjacent to mine. "Rein in that scent of yours, boy."

I cut her an incredulous look. "Apologies." I threw a glance to Varian, standing to the side of her armchair, and silently offered him my condolences.

Varian, clad in Summer Court blue and gold, only grinned and inclined his head toward me.

Strange—so strange to see the Prince of Adriata here. In my town house. Smiling. Drinking my liquor.

Until—

"Do you even celebrate Solstice in the Summer Court?"

Until Cassian decided to open his mouth.

Varian turned his head toward where Cassian and Azriel lounged on the sofa, his silver hair sparkling in the firelight. "In the summer, obviously. As there are two Solstices."

Azriel hid his smile by taking a sip from his wine.

Cassian slung an arm across the back of the sofa. "Are there really?"

Mother above. It was going to be this sort of night, then.

"Don't bother answering him," Amren said to Varian, sipping from her own wine. "Cassian is precisely as stupid as he looks. And sounds," she added with a slashing glance.

Cassian lifted his glass in salute before drinking.

"I suppose your Summer Solstice is the same in theory as ours," I said to Varian, though I knew the answer. I'd seen many of them—long ago. "Families gather, food is eaten, presents shared."

Varian gave me what I could have sworn was a grateful nod. "Indeed."

Feyre appeared beside my seat, her scent settling into me. I tugged her down to perch on the rolled arm of my chair.

She did so with a familiarity that warmed something deep in me, not even bothering to look my way before her arm slid around my shoulders. Just resting there—just because she could.

Mate. My mate.

"So Tarquin doesn't celebrate Winter Solstice at all?" she asked Varian.

A shake of the head.

"Perhaps we should have invited him," Feyre mused.

"There's still time," I offered. The Cauldron knew we needed alliances more than ever. "The call is yours, Prince."

Varian peered down at Amren, who seemed to be entirely focused on her goblet of wine. "I'll think about it."

I nodded. Tarquin was his High Lord. Should he come here, Varian's focus would be elsewhere. Away from where he wished that focus to be—for the few days he had with Amren.

Mor plopped onto the sofa between Cassian and Azriel, her golden curls bouncing. "I like it to be just us anyway," she declared. "And you, Varian," she amended.

Varian offered her a smile that said he appreciated the effort.

The clock on the mantel chimed eight. As if it had summoned her, Elain slid into the room.

Mor was instantly on her feet, offering—*insisting* on wine. Typical.

Elain politely refused, taking up a spot in one of the wooden chairs set in the bay of windows. Also typical.

But Feyre was staring at the clock, her brow furrowed. *Nesta isn't coming.*

You invited her for tomorrow. I sent a soothing caress down the bond, as if it could wipe away the disappointment rippling from her.

Feyre's hand tightened on my shoulder.

I lifted my glass, the room quieting. "To family old and new. Let the Solstice festivities begin."

We all drank to that.

CHAPTER 17

Feyre

The glare of sunlight on snow filtering through our heavy velvet curtains awoke me on Solstice morning.

I scowled at the sliver of brightness and turned my head away from the window. But my cheek collided with something crinkly and firm. Definitely not my pillow.

Peeling my tongue from the roof of my mouth, rubbing at the headache that had formed by my left brow thanks to the hours of drinking, laughing, and more drinking that we'd done until the early hours of the morning, I lifted myself enough to see what had been set beside my face.

A present. Wrapped in black crepe paper and tied with silver thread. And beside it, smiling down at me, was Rhys.

He'd propped his head on a fist, his wings draped across the bed behind him. "Happy birthday, Feyre darling."

I groaned. "How are you smiling after all that wine?"

"I didn't have a whole bottle to myself, that's how." He traced a finger down the groove of my spine.

I rose onto my elbows, surveying the present he'd laid out. It was rectangular and almost flat—only an inch or two thick. "I was hoping you'd forget."

Rhys smirked. "Of course you were."

Yawning, I dragged myself into a kneeling position, stretching my arms high above my head before I pulled the gift to me. "I thought we were opening presents tonight with the others."

"It's your birthday," he drawled. "The rules don't apply to you."

I rolled my eyes at that, even as I smiled a bit. Easing away the wrapping, I pulled out a stunning notebook bound in black, supple leather, so soft it was almost like velvet. On the front, stamped in simple silver letters, were my initials.

Opening the floppy front cover, it revealed page after page of beautiful, thick paper. All blank.

"A sketchbook," he said. "Just for you."

"It's beautiful." It was. Simple, yet exquisitely made. I would have picked it for myself, had such a luxury not seemed excessive.

I leaned down to kiss him, a brush of our mouths. From the corner of my eye, I saw another item appear on my pillow.

I pulled back to see a second present waiting, the large box wrapped in amethyst paper. "More?"

Rhys waved a lazy hand, pure Illyrian arrogance. "Did you think a sketchbook would suffice for my High Lady?"

My face heating, I opened the second present. A sky-blue scarf of softest wool lay folded inside.

"So you can stop stealing Mor's," he said, winking.

I grinned, wrapping the scarf around myself. Every inch of skin it touched felt like a decadence.

"Thank you," I said, stroking the fine material. "The color is beautiful."

"Mmmm." Another wave of his hand, and a third present appeared.

"This is getting excessive."

Rhys only arched a brow, and I chuckled as I opened the third gift. "A new satchel for my painting supplies," I breathed, running my hands over the fine leather as I admired all the various pockets and straps. A set of pencils and charcoals already lay within. The front had also been monogrammed with my initials—along with a tiny Night Court insignia. "Thank you," I said again.

Rhysand's smile deepened. "I had a feeling jewels wouldn't be high on your list of desired gifts."

It was true. Beautiful as they were, I had little interest in them. And had plenty already. "This is exactly what I would have asked for."

"Had you not been hoping that your own mate would forget your birthday."

I snorted. "Had I not been hoping for that." I kissed him again, and when I made to pull away, he slid a hand behind my head and kept me there.

He kissed me deeply, lazily—as if he'd be content to do nothing but that all day. I might have considered it.

But I managed to extract myself, and crossed my legs as I settled back on the bed and reached for my new sketchbook and satchel of supplies. "I want to draw you," I said. "As my birthday present to *me*."

His smile was positively feline.

I added, flipping open my sketchbook and turning to the first page, "You said once that nude would be best."

Rhys's eyes glowed, and a whisper of his power through the room had the curtains parting, flooding the space with midmorning sunshine. Showing every glorious naked inch of him sprawled across the bed, illuminating the faint reds and golds of his wings. "Do your worst, Cursebreaker."

My very blood sparking, I pulled out a piece of charcoal and began.

It was nearly eleven by the time we emerged from our room. I'd filled pages and pages of my sketchbook with him—drawings of his wings, his eyes, his Illyrian tattoos. And enough of his naked, beautiful body that I knew I'd never share this sketchbook with anyone but him. Rhys had indeed hummed his approval when he'd leafed through my work, smirking at the accuracy of my drawings regarding certain areas of his body.

The town house was still silent as we descended the stairs, my mate opting for Illyrian leathers—for whatever strange reason. If Solstice morning included one of Cassian's grueling training sessions, I'd gladly stay behind and start eating the feast I could already smell cooking in the kitchen down the hall.

Entering the dining room to find breakfast waiting, but none of our companions present, Rhys helped me into my usual seat midway down the table, then slid into the chair beside me.

"I'm assuming Mor's still asleep upstairs." I plopped a chocolate pastry onto my plate, then another onto his.

Rhys sliced into the leek-and-ham quiche and set a chunk on my plate. "She drank even more than you, so I'm guessing we won't see her until sundown."

I snorted, and held out my cup to receive the tea he now offered, steam curling from the pot's spout.

But two massive figures filled the archway of the dining room, and Rhys paused.

Azriel and Cassian, having crept up on cat-soft feet, were also wearing their Illyrian leathers.

And from their shit-eating grins, I knew this would not end well.

They moved before Rhys could, and only a flare of his power kept the teapot from falling onto the table before they hauled him out of his seat. And aimed right for the front door.

I only bit into my pastry. "Please bring him back in one piece."

"We'll take good care of him," Cassian promised, wicked humor in his eyes.

Even Azriel was still grinning as he said, "If he can keep up."

I lifted a brow, and just as they vanished out the front door, still dragging Rhys along, my mate said to me, "Tradition."

As if that was an explanation.

And then they were gone, off to the Mother knew where.

But at least neither of the Illyrians had remembered my birthday—thank the Cauldron.

So with Mor asleep and Elain likely in the kitchen helping to prepare that delicious food whose aroma now filled the house, I indulged in a rare, quiet meal. Helped myself to the pastry I'd put on Rhys's plate, along with his portion of the quiche. And another after that.

Tradition indeed.

With little to do beyond resting until the festivities began the hour before sundown, I settled in at the desk in our bedroom to do some paperwork.

Very festive, Rhys purred down the bond.

I could practically see his smirk.

And where, exactly, are you?

Don't worry about it.

I scowled at the eye on my palm, though I knew Rhys no longer used it. *That makes it sound like I* should *be worried.*

A dark laugh. *Cassian says you can pummel him when we get home.*

Which will be when?

A too-long pause. *Before dinner?*

I chuckled. *I really don't want to know, do I?*

You really don't.

Still smiling, I let the thread between us drop, and sighed at the papers staring up at me. Bills and letters and budgets . . .

I lifted a brow at the last, hauling a leather-bound tome toward me. A list of household expenses—just for Rhys and me. A drop of water compared with the wealth contained across his various assets. Our assets. Pulling out a piece of paper, I began counting the expenses so far, working through a tangle of mathematics.

The money *was* there—if I wanted to use it. To buy that studio. There was money in the "miscellaneous purchases" funds to do it.

Yes, I could buy that studio in a heartbeat with the fortune now in my name. But using that money so lavishly, even for a studio that wouldn't be just for me . . .

I shut the ledger, sliding my calculations into the pages, and rose. Paperwork could wait. Decisions like that could wait. Solstice, Rhys had told me, was for family. And since he was currently spending it with his brothers, I supposed I should find at least one of my sisters.

Elain met me halfway to the kitchen, bearing a tray of jam tarts toward the table in the dining room. Where an assortment of baked goods had already begun to take form, tiered cakes and iced cookies. Sugar-frosted buns and caramel-drizzled fruit pies. "Those look pretty," I told her by way of greeting, nodding toward the heart-shaped cookies on her tray. *All* of it looked pretty.

Elain smiled, her braid swishing with each step toward the growing mound of food. "They taste as good as they look." She set down the tray and wiped her flour-coated hands on the apron she wore over her dusty-pink gown. Even in the middle of winter, she was a bloom of color and sunshine.

She handed me one of the tarts, sugar sparkling. I bit in without hesitation and let out a hum of pleasure. Elain beamed.

I surveyed the food she was assembling and asked between bites, "How long have you been working on this?"

A one-shouldered shrug. "Since dawn." She added, "Nuala and Cerridwen were up hours earlier."

I'd seen the Solstice bonus Rhys had given each of them. It was more than most families made in a year. They deserved every damned copper mark.

Especially for what they'd done for my sister. The companionship, the purpose, the small sense of normalcy in that kitchen. She'd bought them those cozy, fuzzy blankets from the weaver, one raspberry pink and the other lilac.

Elain surveyed me in turn as I finished off the tart and reached for another. "Have you had any word from her?"

I knew who she meant. Just as I opened my mouth to tell her no, a knock thudded on the front door.

Elain moved fast enough that I could barely keep up, flinging open the fogged glass antechamber door in the foyer, then unlatching the heavy oak front door.

But it wasn't Nesta who stood on the front step, cheeks flushed with cold.

No, as Elain took a step back, hand falling away from the doorknob, she revealed Lucien smiling tightly at us both.

"Happy Solstice," was all he said.

CHAPTER 18

Feyre

"You look well," I said to Lucien when we'd settled in the armchairs before the fire, Elain perched silently on the couch nearby.

Lucien warmed his hands in the glow of the birch fire, the light casting his face in reds and golds—golds that matched his mechanical eye. "You as well." A sidelong glance toward Elain, swift and fleeting. "Both of you."

Elain said nothing, but at least she bowed her head in thanks. In the dining room, Nuala and Cerridwen continued to add food to the table, their presence now little more than twin shadows as they walked through the walls.

"You brought presents," I said uselessly, nodding toward the small stack he'd set by the window.

"It's Solstice tradition here, isn't it?"

I stifled my wince. The last Solstice I'd experienced had been at the Spring Court. With Ianthe. And Tamlin.

"You're welcome to stay for the night," I said, since Elain certainly wasn't going to.

Lucien lowered his hands into his lap and leaned back in the armchair. "Thank you, but I have other plans."

I prayed he didn't catch the slightly relieved glimmer on Elain's face.

"Where are you going?" I asked instead, hoping to keep his focus on me. Knowing it was an impossible task.

"I . . ." Lucien fumbled for the words. Not out of some lie or excuse, I realized a moment later. Realized when he said, "I've been at the Spring Court every now and then. But if I'm not here in Velaris, I've mostly been staying with Jurian. And Vassa."

I straightened. "Really? Where?"

"There's an old manor house in the southeast, in the humans' territory. Jurian and Vassa were . . . gifted it."

From the lines that bracketed his mouth, I knew who had likely arranged for the manor to fall into their hands. Graysen—or his father. I didn't dare glance at Elain.

"Rhys mentioned that they were still in Prythian. I didn't realize it was such a permanent base."

A short nod. "For now. While things are sorted out."

Like the world without a wall. Like the four human queens who still squatted across the continent. But now wasn't the time to talk of it. "How are they—Jurian and Vassa?" I'd learned enough from Rhys about how Tamlin was faring. I didn't care to hear any more of it.

"Jurian . . ." Lucien blew out a breath, scanning the carved wood ceiling above. "Thank the Cauldron for him. I never thought I'd say that, but it's true." He ran a hand through his silken red hair. "He's keeping everything running. I think he'd have been crowned king by now if it wasn't for Vassa." A twitch of the lips, a spark in that russet eye. "She's doing well enough. Savoring every second of her temporary freedom."

I had not forgotten her plea to me that night after the last battle with Hybern. To break the curse that kept her human by night, firebird by day. A once-proud queen—still proud, yes, but desperate to reclaim her freedom. Her human body. Her kingdom.

"She and Jurian are getting along?"

I hadn't seen them interact, could only imagine what the two of them would be like in the same room together. Both trying to lead the humans who occupied the sliver of land at the southernmost end of Prythian. Left ungoverned for so long. Too long.

No king or queen remained in these lands. No memory of their name, their lineage.

At least amongst humans. The Fae might know. Rhys might know.

But all that lingered of whoever had once ruled the southern tip of Prythian was a motley assortment of lords and ladies. Nothing else. No dukes or earls or any of the titles I'd once heard my sisters mention while discussing the humans on the continent. There were no such titles in the Fae lands. Not in Prythian.

No, there were just High Lords and lords. And now a High Lady.

I wondered if the humans had taken to using only *lord* as a title thanks to the High Fae who lurked above the wall.

Lurked—but no longer.

Lucien considered my question. "Vassa and Jurian are two sides of the same coin. Mercifully, their vision for the future of the human territories is mostly aligned. But the methods on how to attain that . . ." A frown to Elain, then a wince at me. "This isn't very Solstice-like talk."

Definitely not, but I didn't mind. And as for Elain . . .

My sister rose to her feet. "I should get refreshments."

Lucien rose as well. "No need to trouble yourself. I'm—"

But she was already out of the room.

When her footsteps had faded from earshot, Lucien slumped into his armchair and blew out a long breath. "How is she?"

"Better. She makes no mention of her abilities. If they remain."

"Good. But is she still . . ." A muscle flickered in his jaw. "Does she still mourn him?"

The words were little more than a growl.

I chewed on my lip, weighing how much of the truth to reveal. In the end, I opted for all of it. "She was deeply in love with him, Lucien."

His russet eye flashed with simmering rage. An uncontrollable instinct—for a mate to eliminate any threat. But he remained sitting. Even as his fingers dug into the arms of his chair.

I continued, "It has only been a few months. Graysen made it clear that the engagement is ended, but it might take her a while longer to move past it."

Again that rage. Not from jealousy, or any threat, but—"He's as fine a prick as any I've ever encountered."

Lucien *had* encountered him, I realized. Somehow, in living with Jurian and Vassa at that manor, he'd run into Elain's former betrothed. And managed to leave the human lord breathing.

"I would agree with you on that," I admitted. "But remember that they were engaged. Give her time to accept it."

"To accept a life shackled to me?"

My nostrils flared. "That's not what I meant."

"She wants nothing to do with me."

"Would *you*, if your positions were reversed?"

He didn't answer.

I tried, "After Solstice wraps up, why don't you come stay for a week or two? Not in your apartment, I mean. Here, at the town house."

"And do what?"

"Spend time with her."

"I don't think she'll tolerate two minutes alone with me, so forget about two weeks." His jaw worked as he studied the fire.

Fire. His mother's gift.

Not his father's.

Yes, it was Beron's gift. The gift of the father who the world believed had sired him. But not the gift of Helion. His true father.

I still hadn't mentioned it. To anyone other than Rhys.

Now wasn't the time for that, either.

"I'd hoped," I ventured to say, "that when you rented the apartment, it meant you would come work here. With us. Be our human emissary."

"Am I not doing that now?" He arched a brow. "Am I not sending twice-weekly reports to your spymaster?"

"You could come *live* here, is all I'm saying," I pushed. "Truly live here, stay in Velaris for longer than a few days at a time. We could get you nicer quarters—"

Lucien got to his feet. "I don't need your charity."

I rose as well. "But Jurian and Vassa's is fine?"

"You'd be surprised to see how the three of us get along."

Friends, I realized. They had somehow become his *friends*. "So you'd rather stay with them?"

"I'm not staying *with* them. The manor is *ours*."

"Interesting."

His golden eye whirred. "What is."

Not feeling very festive at all, I said sharply, "That you now feel more comfortable with humans than with the High Fae. If you ask me—"

"I'm not."

"It seems like you've decided to fall in with two people without homes of their own as well."

Lucien stared at me, long and hard. When he spoke, his voice was rough. "Happy Solstice to you, Feyre."

He turned toward the foyer, but I grabbed his arm to halt him. The corded muscle of his forearm shifted beneath the fine silk of his sapphire jacket, but he made no move to shake me off. "I didn't mean that," I said. "You have a home here. If you want it."

Lucien studied the sitting room, the foyer beyond and dining room on its other side. "The Band of Exiles."

"The what?"

"That's what we call ourselves. The Band of Exiles."

"You have a name for yourselves." I fought my incredulous tone.

He nodded.

"Jurian isn't an exile," I said. Vassa, yes. Lucien, two times over now.

"Jurian's kingdom is nothing but dust and half-forgotten memory, his people long scattered and absorbed into other territories. He can call himself whatever he likes."

Yes, after the battle with Hybern, after Jurian's aid, I supposed he could.

But I asked, "And what, exactly, does this Band of Exiles plan to do? Host events? Organize party-planning committees?"

Lucien's metal eye clicked faintly and narrowed. "You can be as much of an asshole as that mate of yours, you know that?"

True. I sighed again. "I'm sorry. I just—"

"I don't have anywhere else to go." Before I could object, he said, "You ruined any chance I have of going back to Spring. Not to Tamlin, but to the court beyond his house. Everyone either still believes the lies you spun or they believe me complicit in your deceit. And as for here . . ." He shook off my grip and headed for the door. "*I* can't stand to be in the same room as her for more than two minutes. *I* can't stand to be in this court and have your mate pay for the very clothes on my back."

I studied the jacket he wore. I'd seen it before. Back in—

"Tamlin sent it to our manor yesterday," Lucien hissed. "My clothes. My belongings. All of it. He had it sent from the Spring Court and dumped on the doorstep."

Bastard. Still a bastard, despite what he'd done for Rhys and me during that last battle. But the blame for that behavior was not on Tamlin's shoulders alone. I'd created that rift. Ripped it apart with my own two hands.

I didn't quite feel guilty enough to warrant apologizing for it. Not yet. Possibly not ever.

"Why?" It was the only question I could think to ask.

"Perhaps it had something to do with your mate's visit the other day."

My spine stiffened. "Rhys didn't involve you in that."

"He might as well have. Whatever he said or did, Tamlin decided he wishes to remain in solitude." His russet eye darkened. "Your mate should have known better than to kick a downed male."

"I can't say I'm particularly sorry that he did."

"You will need Tamlin as an ally before the dust has settled. Tread carefully."

I didn't want to think about it, consider it, today. Any day. "My business with him is done."

"Yours might be, but Rhys's isn't. And you'd do well to remind your mate of that fact."

A pulse down the bond, as if in answer. *Everything all right?*

I let Rhys see and hear all that had been said, the conversation conveyed in the blink of an eye. *I'm sorry to have caused him trouble*, Rhys said. *Do you need me to come home?*

I'll handle it.

Let me know if you need anything, Rhys said, and the bond went silent.

"Checking in?" Lucien asked quietly.

"I don't know what you're talking about," I said, my face the portrait of boredom.

He gave me a knowing look, continuing to the door and grabbing his heavy overcoat and scarf from the hooks mounted on the wood paneling beside it. "The bigger box is for you. The smaller one is for her."

It took me a heartbeat to realize he meant the presents. I glanced over my shoulder to the careful silver wrapping, the blue bows atop both boxes.

When I looked back, Lucien was gone.

I found my sister in the kitchen, watching the kettle scream.

"He's not staying for tea," I said.

No sign of Nuala or Cerridwen.

Elain simply removed the kettle from the heat.

I knew I wasn't truly angry with her, not angry with anyone but myself, but I said, "You couldn't say a single word to him? A pleasant greeting?"

Elain only stared at the steaming kettle as she set it on the stone counter.

"He brought you a present."

Those doe-brown eyes turned toward me. Sharper than I'd ever seen them. "And that entitles him to my time, my affections?"

"No." I blinked. "But he is a *good* male." Despite our harsh words. Despite this Band of Exiles bullshit. "He cares for you."

"He doesn't know me."

"You don't give him the chance to even try to do so."

Her mouth tightened, the only sign of anger in her graceful countenance. "I don't want a mate. I don't want a *male*."

She wanted a human man.

Solstice. Today was Solstice, and everyone was supposed to be cheerful and happy. Certainly *not* fighting left and right. "I know you don't." I loosed a long breath. "But . . ."

But I had no idea how to finish that sentence. Just because Lucien was her mate didn't mean he had a claim on her time. Her affection. She was her own person, capable of making her own choices. Assessing her own needs.

"He is a good male," I repeated. "And it . . . it just . . ." I fought for the words. "I don't like to see either of you unhappy."

Elain stared at the worktable, baked goods both finished and incomplete arrayed on the surface, the kettle now cooling on the counter. "I know you don't."

There was nothing else to be said. So I touched her shoulder and strode out.

Elain didn't say a word.

I found Mor sitting on the bottom steps of the stairs, wearing a pair of peach-colored loose pants and a heavy white sweater. A combination of Amren's usual style and my own.

Gold earrings flashing, Mor offered a grim smile. "Drink?" A decanter and pair of glasses appeared in her hands.

"Mother above, yes."

She waited until I'd sat beside her on the oak steps and downed a mouthful of amber liquid, the stuff burning its way along my throat and warming my belly, before she asked, "Do you want my advice?"

No. Yes.

I nodded.

Mor drank deeply from her glass. "Stay out of it. She's not ready, and neither is he, no matter how many presents he brings."

I lifted a brow. "Snoop."

Mor leaned back against the steps, utterly unrepentant. "Let him live with his Band of Exiles. Let him deal with Tamlin in his own way. Let him figure out where he wants to be. *Who* he wants to be. The same goes with her."

She was right.

"I know you still blame yourself for your sisters being Made." Mor nudged my knee with her own. "And because of that, you want to fix everything for them now that they're here."

"I always wanted to do that," I said glumly.

Mor smiled crookedly. "That's why we love you. Why they love you."

Nesta, I wasn't so sure about.

Mor continued, "Just be patient. It'll sort itself out. It always does."

Another kernel of truth.

I refilled my glass, set the crystal decanter on the step behind us, and drank again. "I want them to be happy. All of them."

"They will be."

She said the simple words with such unflagging conviction that I believed her.

I arched a brow. "And you—are you happy?"

Mor knew what I meant. But she just smiled, swirling the liquor in her glass. "It's Solstice. I'm with my family. I'm drinking. I'm *very* happy."

A skilled evasion. But one I was content to partake in. I clinked my heavy glass against hers. "Speaking of our family . . . Where the *hell* are they?"

Mor's brown eyes lit up. "Oh—oh, he didn't tell you, did he?"

My smile faltered. "Tell me what."

"What the three of them do every Solstice morning."

"I'm beginning to be nervous."

Mor set down her glass, and gripped my arm. "Come with me."

Before I could object, she'd winnowed us out.

Blinding light hit me. And cold.

Brisk, brutal cold. Far too cold for the sweaters and pants we wore.

Snow. And sun. And wind.

And mountains.

And—a cabin.

The cabin.

Mor pointed to the endless field atop the mountain. Covered in snow, just as I'd last seen it. But rather than a flat, uninterrupted expanse . . .

"Are those *snow forts?*"

A nod.

Something white shot across the field, white and hard and glistening, and then—

Cassian's yowl echoed off the mountains around us. Followed by, "You *bastard!*"

Rhys's answering laugh was bright as the sun on snow.

I surveyed the three walls of snow—the *barricades*—that bordered the field as Mor erected an invisible shield against the bitter wind. It did little to drive away the cold, though. "They're having a snowball fight."

Another nod.

"Three Illyrian warriors," I said. "The *greatest* Illyrian warriors. Are having a snowball fight."

Mor's eyes practically glowed with wicked delight. "Since they were children."

"They're over five hundred years old."

"Do you want me to tell you the running tally of victories?"

I gaped at her. Then at the field beyond. At the snowballs that were indeed flying with brutal, swift precision as dark heads popped over the walls they'd built.

"No magic," Mor recited, "no wings, no breaks."

"They've been out here since noon." It was nearly three. My teeth began chattering.

"I've always stayed in to drink," Mor supplied, as if that were an answer.

"How do they even decide who *wins?*"

"Whoever doesn't get frostbite?"

I gaped at her again over my clacking teeth. "This is ridiculous."

"There's more alcohol in the cabin."

Indeed, none of the males seemed to even notice us. Not as Azriel popped up, launched two snowballs sky-high, and vanished behind his wall of snow again.

A moment later, Rhys's vicious curse barked toward us. *"Asshole."*

Laughter laced every syllable.

Mor looped her arm through mine again. "I don't think your mate is going to be the victor this year, my friend."

I leaned into her warmth, and we waded through the shin-high snow toward the cabin, the chimney already puffing against the clear blue sky.

Illyrian babies indeed.

CHAPTER 19

Feyre

Azriel won.

His one-hundred-ninety-ninth victory, apparently.

The three of them had entered the cabin an hour later, dripping snow, skin splotched with red, grinning from ear to ear.

Mor and I, snuggled together beneath a blanket on the couch, only rolled our eyes at them.

Rhys just dropped a kiss atop my head, declared the three of them were going to take a steam in the cedar-lined shed attached to the house, and then they were gone.

I blinked at Mor as they vanished, letting the image settle.

"Another tradition," she told me, the bottle of amber-colored alcohol mostly empty. And my head now spinning with it. "An Illyrian custom, actually—the heated sheds. The birchin. A bunch of naked warriors, sitting together in the steam, sweating."

I blinked again.

Mor's lips twitched. "About the only good custom the Illyrians ever came up with, to be honest."

I snorted. "So the three of them are just in there. Naked. Sweating."

Mother above.

Interested in taking a look? The dark purr echoed into my mind.

Lech. Go back to your sweating.

There's room for one more in here.

I thought mates were territorial.

I could feel him smile as if he were grinning against my neck. *I'm always eager to learn what sparks your interest, Feyre darling.*

I surveyed the cabin around me, the surfaces I'd painted nearly a year ago. *I was promised a wall, Rhys.*

A pause. A long pause. *I've taken you against a wall before.*

These walls.

Another long, long pause. *It's bad form to be at attention while in the birchin.*

My lips curved as I sent him an image. A memory.

Of me on the kitchen table just a few feet away. Of him kneeling before me. My legs wrapped around his head.

Cruel, wicked thing.

I heard a door slamming somewhere in the house, followed by a distinctly male yelp. Then banging—as if someone was trying to get back inside.

Mor's eyes sparkled. "You got him kicked out, didn't you?"

My answering smile set her roaring.

The sun was sinking toward the distant sea beyond Velaris when Rhys stood at the black marble mantel of the town house sitting room and lifted his glass of wine.

All of us—in our finery for once—lifted ours in suit.

I'd opted to wear my Starfall gown, forgoing my crown but wearing the diamond cuffs at my wrists. It sparkled and gleamed in my line of vision as I stood at Rhys's side, taking in every plane of his beautiful face as he said, "To the blessed darkness from which we are born, and to which we return."

Our glasses rose, and we drank.

I glanced to him—my mate, in his finest black jacket, the silver embroidery gleaming in the faelight. *That's it?*

He arched a brow. *Did you want me to keep droning on, or did you want to start celebrating?*

My lips twitched. *You really do keep things casual.*

Even after all this time, you still don't believe me. His hand slid behind me and pinched. I bit my lip to keep from laughing. *I hope you got me a good Solstice present.*

It was my turn to pinch him, and Rhys laughed, kissing my temple once before sauntering out of the room to no doubt grab more wine.

Beyond the windows, darkness had indeed fallen. The longest night of the year.

I found Elain studying it, beautiful in her amethyst-colored gown. I made to move toward her, but someone beat me to it.

The shadowsinger was clad in a black jacket and pants similar to Rhysand's—the fabric immaculately tailored and built to fit his wings. He still wore his Siphons atop either hand, and shadows trailed his footsteps, curling like swirled embers, but there was little sign of the warrior otherwise. Especially as he gently said to my sister, "Happy Solstice."

Elain turned from the snow falling in the darkness beyond and smiled slightly. "I've never participated in one of these."

Amren supplied from across the room, Varian at her side, resplendent in his princely regalia, "They're highly overrated."

Mor smirked. "Says the female who makes out like a bandit every year. I don't know how you don't get robbed going home with so much jewelry stuffed into your pockets."

Amren flashed her too-white teeth. "Careful, Morrigan, or I'll return the pretty little thing I got you."

Mor, to my surprise, shut right up.

And so did the others, as Rhys returned with—

"You didn't." I blurted out the words.

He grinned at me over the giant tiered cake in his arms—over the twenty-one sparkling candles lighting up his face.

Cassian clapped me on the shoulder. "You thought you could sneak it past us, didn't you?"

I groaned. "You're all insufferable."

Elain floated to my side. "Happy birthday, Feyre."

My friends—my family—echoed the words as Rhys set the cake on the low-lying table before the fire. I glanced toward my sister. "Did you . . . ?"

A nod from Elain. "Nuala did the decorating, though."

It was then that I realized what the three different tiers had been painted to look like.

On the top: flowers. In the middle: flames.

And on the bottom, widest layer . . . stars.

The same design of the chest of drawers I'd once painted in that dilapidated cottage. One for each of us—each sister. Those stars and moons sent to me, my mind, by my mate, long before we'd ever met.

"I asked Nuala to do it in that order," Elain said as the others gathered round. "Because you're the foundation, the one who lifts us. You always have been."

My throat tightened unbearably, and I squeezed her hand in answer.

Mor, Cauldron bless her, shouted, "Make a wish and let us get to the presents!"

At least one tradition did not change on either side of the wall.

I met Rhys's stare over the sparkling candles. His smile was enough to make the tightness in my throat turn into burning in my eyes.

What are you going to wish for?

A simple, honest question.

And looking at him, at that beautiful face and easy smile, so many of those shadows vanished, our family gathered around us, eternity a road ahead . . . I knew.

I truly knew what I wanted to wish for, as if it were a piece of Amren's puzzle clicking into place, as if the threads of the weaver's tapestry finally revealed the design they'd formed to make.

I didn't tell him, though. Not as I gathered my breath and blew.

Cake before dinner was utterly acceptable on Solstice, Rhys informed me as we set aside our plates on whatever surface was nearest in the sitting room. Especially before presents.

"What presents?" I asked, surveying the room empty of them, save for Lucien's two boxes.

The others grinned at me as Rhys snapped his fingers, and—

"Oh."

Boxes and bags, all brightly wrapped and adorned, filled the bay windows.

Piles and mountains and *towers* of them. Mor let out a squeal of delight.

I twisted toward the foyer. I'd left mine in a broom closet on the third level—

No. There they were. Wrapped and by the back of the bay.

Rhys winked at me. "I took it upon myself to add your presents to the communal trove."

I lifted my brows. "Everyone gave you their gifts?"

"He's the only one who can be trusted not to snoop," Mor explained.

I looked toward Azriel.

"Even him," Amren said.

Azriel gave me a guilty cringe. "Spymaster, remember?"

"We started doing it two centuries ago," Mor went on. "After Rhys caught Amren literally *shaking* a box to figure out what was inside."

Amren clicked her tongue as I laughed. "What they didn't see was Cassian down here ten minutes earlier, *sniffing* each box."

Cassian threw her a lazy smile. "I wasn't the one who got caught."

I turned to Rhys. "And somehow *you're* the most trustworthy one?"

Rhys looked outright offended. "I am a High Lord, Feyre darling. Unwavering honor is built into my bones."

Mor and I snorted.

Amren strode for the nearest pile of presents. "I'll go first."

"Of course she will," Varian muttered, earning a grin from me and Mor.

Amren smiled sweetly at him before bending to pick up a gift. Varian had the good sense to shudder only when she'd turned her back on him.

But she plucked up a pink-wrapped present, read the label, and ripped into it.

Everyone tried and failed to hide their wince.

I'd seen some animals tear into carcasses with less ferocity.

But she beamed as she turned to Azriel, a set of exquisite pearl-and-diamond earrings dangling from her small hands. "Thank you, Shadowsinger," she said, inclining her head.

Azriel only inclined his head in return. "I'm glad they pass inspection."

Cassian elbowed his way past Amren, earning a hiss of warning, and began chucking presents. Mor caught hers easily, shredding the paper with as much enthusiasm as Amren. She grinned at the general. "Thank you, darling."

Cassian smirked. "I know what you like."

Mor held up—

I choked. Azriel did, too, whirling on Cassian as he did.

Cassian only winked at him as the barely there red negligee swayed between Mor's hands.

Before Azriel could undoubtedly ask what we were all thinking, Mor hummed to herself and said, "Don't let him fool you: he couldn't think of a damn thing to get me, so he gave up and asked me outright. I gave him precise orders. For once in his life, he obeyed them."

"The perfect warrior, through and through," Rhys drawled.

Cassian leaned back on the couch, stretching his long legs before him. "Don't worry, Rhysie. I got one for you, too."

"Shall I model it for you?"

I laughed, surprised to hear the sound echo across the room. From Elain.

Her present . . . I hurried to the pile of gifts before Cassian could lob one across the room again, hunting for the parcel I'd carefully wrapped yesterday. I just spied it behind a larger box when I heard it. The knock.

Just once. Quick and hard.

I knew. I knew, before Rhys even looked toward me, who was standing at that door.

Everyone did.

Silence fell, interrupted only by the crackling fire.

A beat, and then I was moving, dress swishing around me as I crossed into the foyer, heaved open the leaded glass door and the oak one beyond it, then braced myself against the onslaught of cold.

Against the onslaught of Nesta.

CHAPTER 20

Feyre

Snow clung to Nesta's hair as we stared at each other across the threshold.

Pink tinged her cheeks from the frigid night, but her face remained solemn. Cold as the snow-dusted cobblestones.

I opened the door a bit wider. "We're in the sitting room."

"I saw."

Conversation, tentative and halting, carried to the foyer. No doubt a noble attempt by everyone to give us some privacy and sense of normalcy.

When Nesta remained on the doorstep, I extended a hand toward her. "Here—I'll take your coat."

I tried not to hold my breath as she glanced past me, into the house. As if weighing whether to take that step over the threshold.

From the edge of my vision, purple and gold flashed—Elain. "You'll fall ill if you just stand there in the cold," she tutted to Nesta, smiling broadly. "Come sit with me by the fire."

Nesta's blue-gray eyes slid to mine. Wary. Assessing.

I held my ground. Held that door open.

Without a word, my sister crossed the threshold.

It was the matter of a moment to remove her coat, scarf, and gloves to reveal one of those simple yet elegant gowns she favored. She'd opted for a slate gray. No jewelry. Certainly no presents, but at least she'd come.

Elain linked elbows to lead Nesta into the room, and I followed, watching the group beyond as they paused.

Watching Cassian especially, now standing with Az at the fire.

He was the portrait of relaxed, an arm braced against the carved mantel, his wings tucked in loosely, a faint grin on his face and a glass of wine in his hand. He slid his hazel eyes toward my sister without him moving an inch.

Elain had plastered a smile onto her face as she led Nesta not toward the fire as she'd promised, but the liquor cabinet.

"Don't take her to the wine—take her to the food," Amren called to Elain from her perch on the armchair as she slid the pearl earrings Az had given her into her lobes. "I can see her bony ass even through that dress."

Nesta halted halfway across the room, spine stiff. Cassian went still as death.

Elain paused beside our sister, that plastered-on smile faltering.

Amren just smirked at Nesta. "Happy Solstice, girl."

Nesta stared at Amren—until a ghost of a smile curved her lips. "Pretty earrings."

I felt, more than saw, the room relax slightly.

Elain said brightly, "We were just getting to presents."

It occurred to me only when she said the words that none of the gifts in this room had Nesta's name on them.

"We haven't eaten yet," I supplied, lingering in the threshold between the sitting room and foyer. "But if you're hungry, we can get you a plate—"

Nesta accepted the glass of wine Elain pressed into her hand. I didn't fail to note that when Elain turned again to the liquor cabinet, she poured a finger of amber-colored liquor into a glass and knocked back the contents with a grimace before facing Nesta again.

A soft snort from Amren at that, missing nothing.

But Nesta's attention had gone to the birthday cake still sitting on the table, its various tiers delved into many times over.

Her eyes lifted to mine in the silence. "Happy birthday."

I offered a nod of thanks. "Elain made the cake," I offered somewhat uselessly.

Nesta only nodded before heading for a chair near the back of the room, by one of the bookcases. "You can return to your presents," she said softly, but not weakly, as she sat.

Elain rushed toward a box near the front of the pile. "This one's for you," she declared to our sister.

I threw Rhys a pleading glance. *Please start talking again. Please.*

Some of the light had vanished from his violet eyes as he studied Nesta while she drank from her glass. He didn't respond down the bond, but instead said to Varian, "Does Tarquin host a formal party for the Summer Solstice, or does he have a more casual gathering?"

The Prince of Adriata didn't miss a beat, and launched into a perhaps unnecessarily detailed description of the Summer Court's celebrations. I'd thank him for it later.

Elain had reached Nesta by then, offering her what seemed to be a heavy, paper-wrapped box.

By the windows, Mor sprang into motion, handing Azriel his gift.

Torn between watching the two, I remained in the doorway.

Azriel's composure didn't so much as falter as he opened her present: a set of embroidered blue towels—with his initials on them. Bright blue.

I had to look away to keep from laughing. Az, to his credit, gave Mor a smile of thanks, a blush creeping over his cheeks, his hazel eyes fixed on her. I looked away at the heat, the yearning that filled them.

But Mor waved him off and moved to pass Cassian his gift; but the warrior didn't take it. Or take his eyes off Nesta as she undid the brown paper wrapping on the box and revealed a set of five novels in a leather box. She read the titles, then lifted her head to Elain.

Elain smiled down at her. "I went into that bookshop. You know the one by the theater? I asked them for recommendations, and the woman—female, I mean . . . She said this author's books were her favorite."

I inched close enough to read one of the titles. Romance, from the sound of it.

Nesta pulled out one of the books and fanned through the pages. "Thank you."

The words were stiff—gravelly.

Cassian at last turned to Mor, tearing open her present with a disregard for the fine wrapping. He laughed at whatever was inside the box. "Just what I always wanted." He held up a pair of what seemed to be red silk undershorts. The perfect match to her negligee.

With Nesta pointedly preoccupied with flipping through her new books, I moved to the presents I'd wrapped yesterday.

For Amren: a specially designed folding carrier for her puzzles. So she didn't need to leave them at home if she were to visit sunnier, warmer lands. This earned me both an eye roll and a smile of appreciation. The ruby-and-silver brooch, shaped like a pair of feathered wings, earned me a rare peck on the cheek.

For Elain: a pale blue cloak with armholes, perfect for gardening in the chillier months.

And for Cassian, Azriel, and Mor . . .

I grunted as I hauled over the three wrapped paintings. Then waited in foot-shifting silence while they opened them.

While they beheld what was inside and smiled.

I hadn't any idea what to get them, other than this. The pieces I'd worked on recently—glimpses of their stories.

None of them explained what the paintings meant, what they beheld. But each of them kissed me on the cheek in thanks.

Before I could hand Rhys his present, I found a heap of them in my lap.

From Amren: an illuminated manuscript, ancient and beautiful. From Azriel: rare, vibrant paint from the continent. From Cassian: a proper leather sheath for a blade, to be set down the groove of my spine like a true Illyrian warrior. From Elain: fine brushes monogrammed with my initials and the Night Court insignia on the handles. And from Mor: a pair of fleece-lined slippers. Bright pink, fleece-lined slippers.

Nothing from Nesta, but I didn't care. Not one bit.

The others passed around their gifts, and I finally found a moment to haul the last painting over to Rhys. He'd lingered by the bay window, quiet and smiling. Last year had been his first Solstice since Amarantha—this year, his second. I didn't want to know what it had been like, what she'd done to him, during those forty-nine Solstices he'd missed.

Rhys opened my present carefully, lifting the painting so the others wouldn't see it.

I watched his eyes rove over what was on it. Watched his throat bob.

"Tell me that's not your new pet," Cassian said, having snuck behind me to peer at it.

I shoved him away. "Snoop."

Rhys's face remained solemn, his eyes star-bright as they met mine. "Thank you."

The others continued on a tad more loudly—to give us privacy in that crowded room.

"I have no idea where you might hang it," I said, "but I wanted you to have it."

To see.

For on that painting, I'd shown him what I had not revealed to anyone. What the Ouroboros had revealed to me: the creature inside myself, the creature full of hate and regret and love and sacrifice, the creature that could be cruel and brave, sorrowful and joyous.

I gave him *me*—as no one but him would ever see me. No one but him would ever understand.

"It's beautiful," he said, voice still hoarse.

I blinked away the tears that threatened at those words and leaned into the kiss he pressed to my mouth. *You are beautiful*, he whispered down the bond.

So are you.

I know.

I laughed, pulling away. *Prick.*

There were only a few presents left—Lucien's. I opened mine to find a gift for me and my mate: three bottles of fine liquor. *You'll need it*, was all the note said.

I handed Elain the small box with her name on it. Her smile faded as she opened it.

"Enchanted gloves," she read from the card. "That won't tear or become too sweaty while gardening." She set aside the box without looking at it for longer than a moment. And I wondered if she *preferred* to have torn and sweaty hands, if the dirt and cuts were proof of her labor. Her joy.

Amren squealed—actually *squealed*—with delight when she beheld Rhys's present. The jewels glittering inside the multiple boxes. But her delight turned quieter, more tender when she opened Varian's gift. She didn't show any of us what was inside the small box before offering him a small, private smile.

There was a tiny box left on the table by the window—a box that Mor lifted, squinted at the name tag, and said, "Az, this one's for you."

The shadowsinger's brows lifted, but his scarred hand extended to take the present.

Elain turned from where she'd been speaking to Nesta. "Oh, that's from me."

Azriel's face didn't so much as shift at the words. Not even a smile as he opened the present and revealed—

"I had Madja make it for me," Elain explained. Azriel's brows narrowed at the mention of the family's preferred healer. "It's a powder to mix in with any drink."

Silence.

Elain bit her lip and then smiled sheepishly. "It's for the headaches everyone always gives you. Since you rub your temples so often."

Silence again.

Then Azriel tipped his head back and *laughed*.

I'd never heard such a sound, deep and joyous. Cassian and Rhys joined him, the former grabbing the glass bottle from Azriel's hand and examining it. "Brilliant," Cassian said.

Elain smiled again, ducking her head.

Azriel mastered himself enough to say, "Thank you." I'd never seen his hazel eyes so bright, the hues of green amid the brown and gray like veins of emerald. "This will be invaluable."

"Prick," Cassian said, but laughed again.

Nesta watched warily from her chair, Elain's present—her only present—in her lap. Her spine stiffened slightly. Not at the words, but at Elain, laughing with them. With us.

As if Nesta were looking at us through some sort of window. As if she were still standing out in the front yard, watching us in the house.

I forced myself to smile, though. To laugh with them.

I had a feeling Cassian was doing the same.

✣

The night was a blur of laughter and drinking, even with Nesta sitting in near-silence at the packed dinner table.

It was only when the clock chimed two that the yawns began to appear. Amren and Varian were the first to leave, the latter bearing all of her presents in his arms, the former nestled in the fine ermine coat that he'd given her—a second gift to whatever one he'd put in that small box.

Settled again in the sitting room, Nesta got to her feet half an hour later. She quietly bid Elain good night, dropping a kiss to the top of her hair, and drifted for the front door.

Cassian, nestled with Mor, Rhys, and Azriel on the couch, didn't so much as move.

But I did, rising from my own chair to follow Nesta to where she was donning her layers at the front door. I waited until she'd entered the antechamber before extending my hand.

"Here."

Nesta half turned toward me, focus darting to what was in my hand. The small slip of paper.

The banker's note for her rent. And then some.

"As promised," I said.

For a moment, I prayed she wouldn't take it. That she would tell me to tear it up.

But Nesta's lips only tightened, her fingers unwavering as she took the money.

As she turned her back on me and walked out the front door, into the freezing darkness beyond.

I remained in the chilly antechamber, hand still outstretched, the phantom dryness of that check lingering on my fingers.

The floorboards thudded behind me, and then I was being gently but forcibly moved to the side. It happened so fast I barely had time to realize that Cassian had gone storming past—right out the front door.

To my sister.

CHAPTER 21

Cassian

He'd had enough.

Enough of the coldness, the sharpness. Enough of the sword-straight spine and razor-sharp stare that had only honed itself these months.

Cassian could barely hear over the roaring in his head as he charged into the snowy night. Could barely register moving aside his High Lady to get to the front door. To get to Nesta.

She'd already made it to the gate, walking with that unfaltering grace despite the icy ground. Her collection of books tucked under an arm.

It was only when Cassian reached her that he realized he had nothing to say. Nothing to say that wouldn't make her laugh in his face.

"I'll walk you home," was all that came out instead.

Nesta paused just past the low iron gate, her face cold and pale as moonlight.

Beautiful. Even with the weight loss, she was as beautiful

standing in the snow as she'd been the first time he'd laid eyes on her in her father's house.

And infinitely more deadly. In so many ways.

She looked him over. "I'm fine."

"It's a long walk, and it's late."

And you didn't say one gods-damned word to me the entire night.

Not that he'd said a word to her.

She'd made it clear enough in those initial days after that last battle that she wanted nothing to do with him. With any of them.

He understood. He really did. It had taken him months—*years*—after his first battles to readjust. To cope. Hell, he was still reeling from what had happened in that final battle with Hybern, too.

Nesta held her ground, proud as any Illyrian. More vicious, too. "Go back into the house."

Cassian gave her a crooked grin, one he knew sent that temper of hers boiling. "I think I need some fresh air, anyway."

She rolled her eyes and launched into a walk. He wasn't stupid enough to offer to carry her books.

Instead, he easily kept pace, an eye out for any treacherous patches of ice on the cobblestones. They'd barely survived Hybern. He didn't need her snapping her neck on the street.

Nesta lasted all of a block, the green-roofed houses merry and still full of song and laughter, before she halted. Whirled on him.

"Go back to the house."

"I will," he said, flashing a grin again. "After I drop you off at your front door."

At that piece-of-shit apartment she insisted on living in. Across the city.

Nesta's eyes—the same as Feyre's and yet wholly different, sharp and cold as steel—went to his hands. What was in them. "What is that."

Another grin as he lifted the small, wrapped parcel. "Your Solstice present."

"I don't want one."

Cassian continued past her, tossing the present in his hands. "You'll want this one."

He prayed she would. It had taken him months to find it.

He hadn't wanted to give it to her in front of the others. Hadn't even known she'd be there tonight. He'd been well aware of Elain's and Feyre's cajoling. Just as he'd been well aware of the money he'd seen Feyre give to Nesta moments before she left.

As promised, his High Lady had said.

He wished she hadn't. Wished for a lot of things.

Nesta fell into step beside him, huffing as she kept up with his long strides. "I don't want *anything* from you."

He made himself arch an eyebrow. "You sure about that, sweetheart?"

I have no regrets in my life, but this. That we did not have time.

Cassian shut out the words. Shut out the image that chased him from his dreams, night after night: not Nesta holding up the King of Hybern's head like a trophy; not the way her father's neck had twisted in Hybern's hands. But the image of her leaning over him, *covering* Cassian's body with her own, ready to take the full brunt of the king's power for him. To die for him—with him. That slender, beautiful body, arching over him, shaking in terror, willing to face that end.

He hadn't seen a glimpse of that person in months. Had not seen her smile or laugh.

He knew about the drinking, about the males. He told himself he didn't care.

He told himself he didn't want to know who the bastard was who had taken her maidenhead. Told himself he didn't want to know if the males meant anything—if *he* meant anything.

He didn't know why the hell he cared. Why he'd bothered. Even from the start. Even after she'd kneed him in the balls that one afternoon at her father's house.

Even as she said, "I've made my thoughts clear enough on what I want from *you*."

He'd never met someone able to imply so much in so few words, in placing so much emphasis on *you* as to make it an outright insult.

Cassian clenched his jaw. And didn't bother to restrain himself when he said, "I'm tired of playing these bullshit games."

She kept her chin high, the portrait of queenly arrogance. "I'm not."

"Well, everyone else is. Perhaps you can find it in yourself to try a little harder this year."

Those striking eyes slid toward him, and it was an effort to stand his ground. "Try?"

"I know that's a foreign word to you."

Nesta stopped at the bottom of the street, right along the icy Sidra. "Why should I have to *try* to do anything?" Her teeth flashed. "I was dragged into this world of yours, this court."

"Then go somewhere else."

Her mouth formed a tight line at the challenge. "Perhaps I will."

But he knew there was no other place to go. Not when she had no money, no family beyond this territory. "Be sure to write."

She launched into a walk again, keeping along the river's edge.

Cassian followed, hating himself for it. "You could at least come live at the House," he began, and she whirled on him.

"*Stop*," she snarled.

He halted in his tracks, wings spreading slightly to balance him.

"*Stop* following me. *Stop* trying to haul me into your happy little circle. *Stop doing all of it*."

He knew a wounded animal when he saw one. Knew the teeth they could bare, the viciousness they displayed. But it couldn't keep him from saying, "Your sisters love you. I can't for the life of me understand why, but they do. If you can't be bothered to try for my happy little circle's sake, then at least try for them."

A void seemed to enter those eyes. An endless, depthless void.

She only said, "Go home, Cassian."

He could count on one hand the number of times she'd used his name. Called him anything other than *you* or *that one*.

She turned away—toward her apartment, her grimy part of the city.

It was instinct to lunge for her free hand.

Her gloved fingers scraped against his calluses, but he held firm. "Talk to me. Nesta. Tell me—"

She ripped her hand out of his grip. Stared him down. A mighty, vengeful queen.

He waited, panting, for the verbal lashing to begin. For her to shred him into ribbons.

But Nesta only stared at him, her nose crinkling. Stared, then snorted—and walked away.

As if he were nothing. As if he weren't worth her time. The effort.

A low-born Illyrian bastard.

This time, when she continued onward, Cassian didn't follow.

He watched her until she was a shadow against the darkness—and then she vanished completely.

He remained staring after her, that present in his hands.

Cassian's fingertips dug into the soft wood of the small box.

He was grateful the streets were empty when he hurled that box into the Sidra. Hurled it hard enough that the splash echoed off the buildings flanking the river, ice cracking from the impact.

Ice instantly re-formed over the hole he'd blown open. As if it, and the present, had never been.

Nesta

Nesta sealed the fourth and final lock on her apartment door and slumped against the creaking, rotting wood.

Silence settled in around her, welcome and smothering.

Silence, to soothe the trembling that had chased her across this city.

He'd followed.

She'd known it in her bones, her blood. He'd kept high in the skies, but he'd followed until she'd entered the building.

She knew he was now waiting on a nearby rooftop to see her light kindle.

Twin instincts warred within her: to leave the faelight untouched and make him wait in the freezing dark, or to ignite that bowl and just get rid of his presence. Get rid of everything he was.

She opted for the latter.

In the dim, thick silence, Nesta lingered by the table against the wall near her front door. Slid her hand into her pocket and pulled out the folded banknote.

Enough for three months' rent.

She tried and failed to muster the shame. But nothing came.

Nothing at all.

There was anger, occasionally. Sharp, hot anger that sliced her.

But most of the time it was silence.

Ringing, droning silence.

She hadn't felt anything in months. Had days when she didn't really know where she was or what she'd done. They passed swiftly and yet dripped by.

So did the months. She'd blinked, and winter had fallen. Blinked, and her body had turned too thin. As hollow as she felt.

The night's frosty chill crept through the worn shutters, drawing another tremble from her. But she didn't light the fire in the hearth across the room.

She could barely stand to hear the crack and pop of the wood. Had barely been able to endure it in Feyre's town house. *Snap; crunch*.

How no one ever remarked that it sounded like breaking bones, like a snapping neck, she had no idea.

She hadn't lit one fire in this apartment. Had kept warm with blankets and layers.

Wings rustled, then boomed outside the apartment.

Nesta loosed a shuddering sigh and slid down the wall until she was sitting against it.

Until she drew her knees to her chest and stared into the dimness.

Still the silence raged and echoed around her.

Still she felt nothing.

CHAPTER 22

Feyre

It was three by the time the others went to bed. By the time Cassian returned, quiet and brooding, and knocked back a glass of liquor before stalking upstairs. Mor followed him, worry dancing in her eyes.

Azriel and Elain remained in the sitting room, my sister showing him the plans she'd sketched to expand the garden in the back of the town house, using the seeds and tools my family had given her tonight. Whether he cared about such things, I had no idea, but I sent him a silent prayer of thanks for his kindness before Rhys and I slipped upstairs.

I reached to remove my diamond cuffs when Rhys stopped me, his hands wrapping around my wrists. "Not yet," he said softly.

My brows bunched.

He only smiled. "Hold on."

Darkness and wind swept in, and I clung to him as he winnowed—

Candlelight and crackling fire and colors . . .

"The cabin?" He must have altered the wards to allow us to winnow directly inside.

Rhys grinned, letting go of me to swagger to the couch before the fireplace and plop down, his wings draping to the floor. "For some peace and quiet, mate."

Dark, sensual promise lay in his star-flecked eyes.

I bit my lip as I approached the rolled arm of the couch and perched on it, my dress glittering like a river in the firelight.

"You look beautiful tonight." His words were low, rough.

I stroked a hand down the lap of my gown, the fabric shimmering beneath my fingers. "You say that every night."

"And mean it."

I blushed. "Cad."

He inclined his head.

"I know High Ladies are probably supposed to wear a new dress every day," I mused, smiling at the gown, "but I'm rather attached to this one."

He ran his hand down my thigh. "I'm glad."

"You never told me where you got it—where you got all my favorite dresses."

Rhys arched a dark brow. "You never figured it out?"

I shook my head.

For a moment, he said nothing, his head dipping to study the dress. "My mother made them."

I went still.

Rhys smiled sadly at the shimmering gown. "She was a seamstress, back at the camp where she'd been raised. She didn't just do the work because she was ordered to. She did it because she loved it. And when she mated my father, she continued."

I grazed a reverent hand down my sleeve. "I—I had no idea."

His eyes were star-bright. "Long ago, when I was still a boy, she made them—all your gowns. A trousseau for my future bride." His throat bobbed. "Every piece . . . Every piece I have ever given you to wear, she made them. For you."

My eyes stung as I breathed, "Why didn't you tell me?"

He shrugged with one shoulder. "I thought you might be . . . disturbed to wear gowns made by a female who died centuries ago."

I put a hand over my heart. "I am honored, Rhys. Beyond words."

His mouth trembled a bit. "She would have loved you."

It was as great a gift as any I'd been given. I leaned down until our brows touched. *I would have loved her.*

I felt his gratitude without him saying a word as we remained there, breathing each other in for long minutes.

When I could finally speak again, I pulled away. "I've been thinking."

"Should I be worried?"

I slapped his boots, and he laughed, deep and rasping, the sound curling around my core.

I showed him my palms, the eye in both of them. "I want these changed."

"Oh?"

"Since you're no longer using them to snoop on me, I figured they could be something else."

He set a hand on his broad chest. "I never snoop."

"You're the greatest busybody I've ever met."

Another laugh. "And what, exactly, do you want on your palms?"

I smiled at the paintings I'd done on the walls, the mantel, the tables. Thought of the tapestry I'd bought. "I want a mountain—with three stars." The Night Court insignia. "The same that you have on your knees."

Rhys was quiet for a long time, his face unreadable. When he spoke, his voice was low. "Those are markings that can never be altered."

"It's a good thing I plan to be here for a while, then."

Rhys slowly sat up, unbuttoning the top of his tight black jacket. "You're sure?"

I nodded slowly.

He moved to stand before me, gently taking my hands in his, turning them palm-up. To the cat's eye that stared at us. "I never snooped, you know."

"You certainly did."

"Fine, I did. Can you forgive me?"

He meant it—the worry that I'd deemed his glimpses a violation. I rose onto my toes and kissed him softly. "I suppose I could find it in me."

"Hmmm." He brushed a thumb over the eye inked into both of my palms. "Any last words before I mark you forever?"

My heart thundered, but I said, "I have one last Solstice gift for you."

Rhys went still at my soft voice, the tremble in it. "Oh?"

Our hands linked, I caressed the adamant walls of his mind. The barriers immediately fell, allowing me in. Allowing me to show him that last gift.

What I hoped he'd deem as a gift, too.

His hands began shaking around mine, but he said nothing until I'd retreated from his mind. Until we were staring at each other again in silence.

His breathing turned ragged, his eyes silver-lined. "You're sure?" he repeated.

Yes. More than anything. I'd realized it, felt it, in the weaver's gallery. "Would it be . . . Would it indeed be a gift for you?" I dared ask.

His fingers tightened around mine. "Beyond measure."

As if in answer, light flared and sizzled along my palms, and I peered down to find my hands altered. The mountain and three stars gracing the heart of each palm.

Rhys was still staring at me, his breathing uneven.

"We can wait," he said quietly, as if fearful of the snow falling outside hearing our whispered words.

"I don't want to," I said, and meant it. The weaver had made me realize that, too. Or perhaps just see clearly what I'd quietly wanted for some time now.

"It could take years," he murmured.

"I can be patient." He lifted a brow at that, and I smiled, amending, "I can *try* to be patient."

His own answering smile set me grinning.

Rhys leaned in, brushing a kiss to my neck, right beneath my ear. "Shall we begin tonight, mate?"

My toes curled. "That was the plan."

"Mmm. Do you know what my plan was?" Another kiss, this one to the hollow of my throat as his hands slipped around my back and began to undo the hidden buttons of my dress. That precious, beautiful dress. I arched my neck to give him better access, and he obliged, his tongue flicking over the spot he'd just kissed.

"My plan," he went on, the dress sliding from me to pool on the rug, "involved this cabin, and a wall."

My eyes opened just as his hands began to trace long lines along my bare back. Lower.

I found Rhys smiling down at me, his eyes heavy-lidded while he surveyed my naked body. Naked, save for the diamond cuffs at my wrists. I went to remove them, but he murmured, "Leave them."

My stomach tightened in anticipation, my breasts turning achingly heavy.

I unbuttoned the rest of his jacket, fingers shaking, and peeled it from him, along with his shirt. And his pants.

Then he was standing naked before me, wings slightly flared, muscled chest heaving, showing me the full evidence of just how ready he was.

"Do you want to begin at the wall, or finish there?" His words were guttural, barely recognizable, and the gleam in his eyes turned into something predatory. He slid a hand down the front of my torso in brazen possessiveness. "Or shall it be the wall the entire time?"

My knees buckled, and I found myself beyond words. Beyond anything but him.

Rhys didn't wait for my answer before kneeling before me, his wings draping over the rug. Before he pressed a kiss to my abdomen, as if in reverence and benediction. Then pressed a kiss lower.

Lower.

My hand slid into his hair, just as he gripped one of my thighs and hoisted my leg over his shoulder. Just as I found myself somehow leaning against the wall near the doorway, as if he'd winnowed us. My head hit the wood with a soft thud as Rhys lowered his mouth to me.

He took his time.

Licked and stroked me until I'd shattered, then laughed against me, dark and rich, before he rose to his full height.

Before he hoisted me up, my legs wrapping around his waist, and pinned me against that wall.

One arm braced on the wall, the other holding me aloft, Rhys met my eyes. "How shall it be, mate?"

In his stare, I could have sworn galaxies swirled. In the shadows between his wings, the glorious depths of the night dwelled.

"Hard enough to make the pictures fall off," I reminded him, breathless.

He laughed again, low and wicked. "Hold on tight, then."

Mother above and Cauldron save me.

My hands slid onto his shoulders, digging into the hard muscle.

But he slowly, *so slowly*, pushed into me.

So I felt every inch of him, every place where we were joined. I tipped my head back again, a moan slipping out of me.

"Every time," he gritted out. "Every time, you feel *exquisite*."

I clenched my teeth, panting through my nose. He worked his way in, thrusting in small movements, letting me adjust to each thick inch of him.

And when he was seated inside me, when his hand tightened on my hip, he just . . . stopped.

I moved my hips, desperate for any friction. He shifted with me, denying it.

Rhys licked his way up my throat. "I think about you, about this, every damn hour," he purred against my skin. "About the way you taste."

Another slight withdrawal—then a plunge in. I panted and panted, leaning my head into the hard wall behind me.

Rhys let out an approving sound, and withdrew slightly. Then pushed back in. Hard.

A low rattle sounded down the wall to my left.

I stopped caring. Stopped caring if we did indeed make the pictures fall off the wall as Rhys halted once more.

"But mostly I think about this. How you feel around me, Feyre." He drove into me, exquisite and relentless. "How you taste on my tongue." My nails cut into his broad shoulders. "How even if we have a thousand years together, I will never tire of *this*."

Release began to gather along my spine, shutting out all sound and sense beyond where he met me, touched me.

Another thrust, longer and harder. The wood groaned beneath his hand.

He lowered his mouth to my breast and nipped—nipped, and then licked away the hurt that sent pleasure zinging through my blood. "How you let me do such naughty, terrible things to you."

His voice was a caress that had my hips moving, begging him to go *faster*.

Rhys only chuckled softly, cruelly, as he withheld that all-out, unhinged joining I craved.

I opened my eyes long enough to peer down, to where I could see him joined with me, moving so achingly slowly in and out of me. "Do you like watching?" he breathed. "Watching me move in you?"

In answer, beyond words, I shot my mind down the bridge between us, brushing against his adamant shields.

He let me in instantly, mind-to-mind and soul-to-soul, and then I was looking through his eyes—looking down at *me* as he gripped my hip and thrust.

He purred, *Look at how I fuck you, Feyre.*

Gods, was my only answer.

Mental hands ran along my mind, my soul. *Look at how perfectly we fit.*

My flushed body was arched against the wall—perfect indeed for receiving him, for taking every inch of him.

Do you see why I can't stop thinking of this—of you?

Again, he withdrew and drove in, and released the damper on his power.

Stars flickered around us, sweet darkness sweeping in. As if we were the only souls in a galaxy. And still Rhys remained before me, my legs wrapped around his waist.

I brushed my own mental hands down him and breathed, *Can you fuck me in here, too?*

That wicked delight faltered. Went silent.

The stars and darkness paused, too.

Then undiluted, utter predator answered, *It would be my pleasure.*

And then I didn't have the words for what happened.

He gave me everything I wanted: the unleashed pounding of him inside my body—the unrelenting thrust and filling and slap of skin on skin, the slam of our bodies against wood. Night singing all around us, stars sweeping by like snow.

And then there was us. Mind-to-mind, lain out on that bridge between our souls.

We had no bodies here, but I felt him as he seduced me, his dark power wrapping around mine, licking at my flames, sucking on my ice, scraping claws against my own.

I felt him as his power blended with mine, ebbing and flowing, in and out, until my magic lashed out, latching onto him, both of us raging and burning together.

All while he moved in me, relentless and driving as the sea. Over and over, power and flesh and soul, until I think I was screaming, until I think he was roaring, and my mortal body clenched around him, shattering.

Then *I* shattered, everything I was rupturing into stars and galaxies and comets, nothing but pure, shining joy. Rhys held me, enveloped me, his darkness absorbing the light that sparkled and blasted, keeping me whole, keeping me together.

And when my mind could form words, when I could again feel his essence around me, his body still moving in my own, I sent him that image one last time, into the dark and stars—my gift.

Perhaps our gift, one day.

Rhys spilled into me with a roar, his wings splaying wide.

And in our minds, down that bond, his magic erupted, his soul washing over mine, filling every crack and pit so that there was not one part of me that was not full of him, brimming with his dark, glorious essence and undimming love.

He remained buried in me, leaning heavily against the wall as he panted against my neck, "*FeyreFeyreFeyre*."

He was shaking. We both were.

I worked up the presence of mind to crack open my eyes.

His face was wrecked. Stunned. His mouth remained partially open as he gaped at me, the glow still radiating from my skin, bright against the star-kissed shadows along his.

For long moments, we only stared. Breathed.

And then Rhys glanced sidelong toward the rest of the room.

Toward what we'd done.

A sly smile formed on his lips as we took in the pictures that had indeed come off the wall, their frames cracked on the floor. A vase atop a nearby side table had even been knocked to the ground, shattered into little blue pieces.

Rhys kissed beneath my ear. "That'll come out of your salary, you know."

I whipped my head to him and released my grip on his shoulders to flick his nose. He laughed, brushing his lips against my temple.

But I stared at the marks I'd left on his skin, already fading. Stared at the tattoos across his chest, his arms. Even an immortal's lifetime of painting wouldn't be enough to capture every facet of him. Of us.

I lifted my eyes to his again and found stars and darkness waiting. Found *home* waiting.

Never enough. Not to paint him, know him. Eons would never be enough for all I wanted to do, see with him. For all I wanted to love him.

The painting shone before me: *Night Triumphant—and the Stars Eternal.*

"Do it again," I breathed, my voice hoarse.

Rhys knew what I meant.

And I'd never been so glad for a Fae mate when he hardened again a heartbeat later, lowered me to the floor and flipped me onto my stomach, then plunged deep into me with a growling purr.

And even when we eventually collapsed on the rug, barely avoiding the broken pictures and vase shards, unable to move for a good long while, that image of my gift remained between us, shimmering as bright as any star.

That beautiful, blue-eyed, dark-haired boy that the Bone Carver had once shown me.

That promise of the future.

Velaris was still sleeping when Rhys and I returned the next morning.

He didn't bring us to the town house, however. But to an estate along the river, the building in ruins, the gardens a tangle.

Mist hung over much of the city in the hour before dawn.

The words we'd exchanged last night, what we'd done, flowed between us, as invisible and solid as our mating bond. He hadn't taken his contraceptive tonic with breakfast. Wouldn't be taking it again anytime soon.

"You never asked about your Solstice present," Rhys said after a while, our steps crunching in the frosted gravel of the gardens along the Sidra.

I lifted my head from where I'd been leaning it against his shoulder while we'd ambled along. "I suppose you were waiting to make a dramatic reveal."

"I suppose I was." He halted, and I paused beside him as he turned to the house behind us. "This."

I blinked at him. At the rubble of the estate. "This?"

"Consider it a Solstice and birthday present in one." He gestured to the house, the gardens, the grounds that flowed to the river's edge. With a perfect view of the Rainbow at night, thanks to the land's curve. "It's yours. Ours. I purchased it on Solstice Eve. Workers are coming in two days to begin clearing the rubble and knock down the rest of the house."

I blinked again, long and slow. "You bought me an *estate*."

"Technically, it will be *our* estate, but the house is yours. Build it to your heart's content. Everything you want, everything you need—build it."

The cost alone, the sheer size of this gift had to be beyond astronomical. "Rhys."

He paced a few steps, running his hands through his blue-black hair, his wings tucked in tight. "We have no space at the town house. You and I can barely fit everything in the bedroom. And no one wants to be at the House of Wind." He again gestured to the magnificent estate around us. "So build a house for us, Feyre. Dream as wildly as you want. It's yours."

I didn't have words for it. What cascaded through me. "It—the *cost—*"

"Don't worry about the cost."

"But . . ." I gaped at the sleeping, tangled land, the ruined house. Pictured what I might want there. My knees wobbled. "Rhys—it's too much."

His face became deadly serious. "Not for you. Never for you." He slid his arms around my waist, kissing my temple. "Build a house with a painting studio." He kissed my other temple. "Build a house with an office for you, and one for me. Build a house with a bathtub big enough for two—and for wings." Another kiss, this time to my cheek. "Build a house with rooms for all our family." He kissed my other cheek. "Build a house with a garden for Elain, a training ring for the Illyrian babies, a library for Amren, and an enormous dressing room for Mor." I choked on a laugh at that. But Rhys silenced it with a kiss to my mouth, lingering and sweet. "Build a house with a nursery, Feyre."

My heart tightened to the point of pain, and I kissed him back. Kissed him again, and again, the property wide and clear around us. "I will," I promised.

CHAPTER 23

Rhysand

The sex had destroyed me.

Utterly ruined me.

Any lingering scrap of my soul that hadn't already belonged to her had unconditionally surrendered last night.

And seeing Feyre's expression when I showed her the riverfront estate . . . I held the memory of her shining, beautiful face close to me as I knocked on the cracked front doors of Tamlin's manor.

No answer.

I waited a minute. Two.

I unspooled a thread of power through the house, sensing. Half dreading what I might find.

But there—in the kitchens. A level below. Alive.

I saw myself in, my steps echoing on the splintered marble floors. I didn't bother to veil them. He likely sensed my arrival the moment I'd winnowed onto his front step.

It was a matter of a few minutes to reach the kitchen.

I wasn't entirely prepared for what I saw.

A great elk lay dead on the long worktable in the center of the dark space, the arrow through its throat illumined by the watery light leaking through the small windows. Blood pooled on the gray stone floor, its drip the only sound.

The only sound as Tamlin sat in a chair before it. Staring at the felled beast.

"Your dinner is leaking," I told him by way of greeting, nodding toward the mess gathering on the floor.

No reply. The High Lord of Spring didn't so much as look up at me.

Your mate should have known better than to kick a downed male.

Lucien's words to Feyre yesterday had lingered. Perhaps it was why I'd left Feyre to explore the new paints Azriel had given her and winnowed here.

I surveyed the mighty elk, its dark eyes open and glazed. A hunting knife lay embedded in the wood beside its shaggy head.

Still no words, not even a whisper of movement. Very well, then.

"I spoke to Varian, Prince of Adriata," I said, lingering on the other side of the table, the rack of antlers like a briar of thorns between us. "I requested that he ask Tarquin to dispatch soldiers to your border." I'd done it last night, pulling Varian aside during dinner. He'd readily agreed, swearing it would be done. "They will arrive within a few days."

No reply.

"Is that acceptable to you?" As part of the Seasonal Courts, Summer and Spring had long been allies—until this war.

Slowly, Tamlin's head lifted, his unbound golden hair dull and matted.

"Do you think she will forgive me?" The question was a rasp. As if he'd been screaming.

I knew whom he meant. And I didn't know. I didn't know if her wishing him happiness was the same as forgiveness. If Feyre would ever want to offer that to him. Forgiveness could be a gift to both, but what he'd done . . . "Do you want her to?"

His green eyes were empty. "Do I deserve it?"

No. Never.

He must have read it on my face, because he asked, "Do you forgive me—for your mother and sister?"

"I don't recall ever hearing an apology."

As if an apology would ever right it. As if an apology would ever cover the loss that still ate at me, the hole that remained where their bright, lovely lives had once glowed.

"I don't think one will make a difference, anyway," Tamlin said, staring at the felled elk once more. "For either of you."

Broken. Utterly broken.

You will need Tamlin as an ally before the dust has settled, Lucien had warned my mate. Perhaps that was why I'd come, too.

I waved a hand, my magic slicing and sundering, and the elk's coat slid to the floor in a rasp of fur and slap of wet flesh. Another flicker of power, and slabs of meat had been carved from its sides, piled next to the dark stove—which soon kindled.

"Eat, Tamlin," I said. He didn't so much as blink.

It was not forgiveness—it was not kindness. I could not, would not, ever forget what he'd done to those I loved most.

But it was Solstice, or had been. And perhaps because Feyre had given me a gift greater than any I could dream of, I said, "You can waste away and die after we've sorted out this new world of ours."

A pulse of my power, and an iron skillet slid onto the now-hot stove, a steak of meat thumping into it with a sizzle.

"Eat, Tamlin," I repeated, and vanished on a dark wind.

CHAPTER 24

Morrigan

She'd lied to Feyre.

Sort of.

She *was* going to the Winter Court. Just not as soon as she'd said. Viviane, at least, knew when to truly expect her. Although they'd been exchanging letters for months now, Mor still hadn't told even the Lady of the Winter Court where she'd be between Solstice in Velaris and her visit to Viviane and Kallias's mountain home.

She didn't like telling people about this place. Had never mentioned it to the others.

And as Mor galloped over the snowy hills, her mare, Ellia, a solid, warm weight beneath her, she remembered why.

Early-morning mist hung between the bumps and hollows of the sprawling estate. Her estate. Athelwood.

She'd bought it three hundred years ago for the quiet. Had kept it for the horses.

Ellia took the hills with unfaltering grace, flowing fast as the west wind.

Mor hadn't been raised to ride. Not when winnowing was infinitely faster.

But with winnowing, it never felt as if she were actually *traveling* anywhere. As if she were going, running, racing to the next place. She wished it, and there she was.

The horses, though . . . Mor felt every inch of land they galloped across. Felt the wind and smelled the hills and snow and could see the passing wall of dense forest to her left.

Alive. It was all alive, and her ever more so, when she rode.

Athelwood had come with six horses, the previous owner having grown bored with them. All of them rare and coveted breeds. They'd been worth as much as the sprawling estate and three hundred pristine acres northwest of Velaris. A land of rolling hills and burbling streams, of ancient forests and crashing seas.

She did not like being alone for long periods of time—couldn't stand it. But a few days here and there were necessary, vital for her soul. And getting out on Ellia was as rejuvenating as any day spent basking in the sun.

She pulled Ellia to a halt atop one of the larger hills, letting the mare rest, even as Ellia yanked on the reins. She'd run until her heart gave out—had never been quite as docile as her handlers desired. Mor loved her all the greater for it.

She had always been drawn to the untamed, wild things of the world.

Horse and rider breathing hard, Mor surveyed her rolling grounds, the gray sky. Nestled in her Illyrian leathers and heated from the ride, she was comfortably warm. An afternoon reading by the crackling fire in Athelwood's extensive library followed by a hearty dinner and early bed would be bliss.

How far away the continent seemed, Rhys's request with it. To go, to play spy and courtier and ambassador, to see those kingdoms long closed, where friends had once dwelled . . . *Yes*, her blood called to her. *Go as far and wide as you can. Go on the wind.*

But to leave, to let Keir believe he had *made* her go with his bargain with Eris . . .

Coward. Pathetic coward.

She shut out the hissing in her head, running a hand down Ellia's snowy mane.

She had not mentioned it these past few days in Velaris. Had wanted to make this choice on her own, and had understood how the news might cast a shadow over the merriment.

She knew Azriel would say no, would want her safe. As he had always done. Cassian would have said yes, Amren with him, and Feyre would have worried but agreed. Az would have been pissed, and withdrawn even further into himself.

She hadn't wanted to take his joy away from him. Any more than she already did.

But she'd have to tell them, regardless of what she decided, at some point.

Ellia's ears went flat against her head.

Mor stiffened, following the mare's line of sight.

To the tangle of wood to their left, little more than a thatch of trees from this distance.

She rubbed Ellia's neck. "Easy," she breathed. "Easy."

Even in these woods, ancient terrors had been known to emerge.

But Mor scented nothing, saw nothing. The tendril of power she speared toward the woods revealed only the usual birds and small beasts. A hart drinking from a hole in an iced-over stream.

Nothing, except—

There, between a snarl of thorns. A patch of darkness.

It did not move, did not seem to do anything but linger. And watch.

Familiar and yet foreign.

Something in her power whispered not to touch it, not to go near it. Even from this distance.

Mor obeyed.

But she still watched that darkness in the thorns, as if a shadow had fallen asleep amongst them.

Not like Azriel's shadows, twining and whispering.

Something different.

Something that stared back, watching her in turn.

Best left undisturbed. Especially with the promise of a crackling fire and glass of wine at home.

"Let's take the short route back," she murmured to Ellia, patting her neck.

The horse needed no further encouragement before launching into a gallop, turning them from the woods and its shadowy watcher.

Over and between the hills they rode, until the woods were hidden in the mists behind them.

What else might she see, witness, in lands where none in the Night Court had ventured for millennia?

The question lingered with every thunderous step from Ellia over snow and brook and hill.

Its answer echoed off the rocks and trees and gray clouds overhead.

Go. Go.

CHAPTER 25

Feyre

Two days later, I stood in the doorway of Polina's abandoned studio.

Gone were the boarded-up windows, the drooping cobwebs. Only open space remained, clean and wide.

I was still gaping when Ressina found me, halting on her path down the street, no doubt coming from her own studio. "Happy Solstice, my lady," she said, smiling brightly.

I didn't return the smile as I stared and stared at the open door. The space beyond.

Ressina laid a hand on my arm. "Is something wrong?"

My fingers curled at my sides, wrapping around the brass key in my palm. "It's mine," I said quietly.

Ressina's smile began to grow again. "Is it, now?"

"They—her family gave it to me."

It had happened this morning. I'd winnowed to Polina's family farm, somehow surprising no one when I'd appeared. As if they'd been waiting.

Ressina angled her head. "So why the face?"

"They *gave* it to me." I splayed my arms. "I tried to buy it. I offered her family money." I shook my head, still reeling. I hadn't even been back to the town house. Hadn't even told Rhys. I'd woken at dawn, Rhys already off to meet with Az and Cassian at Devlon's camp, and decided to hell with waiting. Putting *life* off didn't make a lick of sense. I knew what I wanted. There was no reason to delay. "They handed me the deed, told me to sign my name to it, and gave me the key." I rubbed my face. "They refused my money."

Ressina let out a long whistle. "I'm not surprised."

"Polina's sister, though," I said, my voice shaking as I pocketed the key in my overcoat, "suggested I use the money for something else. That if I wanted to give it away, I should donate it to the Brush and Chisel. Do you know what that is?"

I'd been too stunned to ask, to do anything other than nod and say I would.

Ressina's ochre eyes softened. "It's a charity for artists in need of financial help—to provide them and their families with money for food or rent or clothes. So they needn't go hungry or want for anything while they create."

I couldn't stop the tears that blurred my vision. Couldn't stop myself from remembering those years in that cottage, the hollow ache of hunger. The image of those three little containers of paint that I'd savored.

"I didn't know it existed," I managed to whisper. Even with all the committees that I volunteered to help, they had not mentioned it.

I didn't know that there was a place, a world, where artists might be valued. Taken care of. I'd never dreamed of such a thing.

A warm, slender hand landed on my shoulder, gently squeezing.

Ressina asked, "So what are you going to do with it? The studio."

I surveyed the empty space before me. Not empty—*waiting.*

And from far away, as if it was carried on the cold wind, I heard the Suriel's voice.

Feyre Archeron, a request. Leave this world a better place than how you found it.

I swallowed down my tears, and brushed a stray strand of my hair back into my braid before I turned to the faerie. "You wouldn't be looking for a wholly inexperienced business partner, would you?"

CHAPTER 26

Rhysand

The girls were in the training ring.

Only six of them, and none looking too pleased, but they were there, cringing their way through Devlon's halfhearted orders on how to handle a dagger. At least Devlon had given them something relatively simple to learn. Unlike the Illyrian bows, a stack of them lingering by the girls' chalk-lined ring. As if in a taunt.

A good number of males couldn't muster the strength to wield those mighty bows. I could still feel the whip of the string against my cheek, my wrist, my fingers during the years it had taken to master it.

If one of the girls decided to take up the Illyrian bow, I'd oversee her lessons myself.

I lingered with Cassian and Azriel at the far end of the sparring rings, the Windhaven camp glaringly bright with the fresh snow that had been dumped by the storm.

As expected, the storm had finished yesterday—two days after Solstice. And as promised, Devlon had the girls in the ring. The youngest was around twelve, the eldest sixteen.

"I thought there were more," Azriel muttered.

"Some left with their families for Solstice," Cassian said, eyes on the training, hissing every now and then when one of the girls did a painfully wrong maneuver that went uncorrected. "They won't be back for a few more days."

We'd shown him the lists Az had compiled of the possible troublemakers in these camps. Cassian had been distant ever since. More malcontents than we'd expected. A good number of them from the Ironcrest camp, notorious rival of this clan, where Kallon, son of its lord, was taking pains to stir up as much dissent as possible. All directed toward Cassian and myself.

A ballsy move, considering Kallon was still a warrior-novice. Not even due to take the Rite until this spring or the next. But he was as bad as his brute of a father. Worse, Az claimed.

Accidents happen in the Rite, I'd only suggested when Cass's face had tightened with the news.

We won't dishonor the Rite by tampering with it, was his only reply.

Accidents happen in the skies all the time, then, Azriel had coolly countered.

If the whelp wants to bust my balls, he can grow a pair himself and do it to my face, Cassian had growled, and that was that.

I knew him well enough to leave him to it—to decide how and when to deal with Kallon.

"Despite the grumblings in the camps," I said to Cassian, gesturing toward the training rings. The males kept a healthy distance from where the few females trained, as if frightened of catching some deadly disease. Pathetic. "This *is* a good sign, Cass."

Azriel nodded his agreement, his shadows twining around him. Most of the camp women had ducked into their homes when he'd appeared.

A rare visit from the shadowsinger. Both myth and terror. Az looked just as displeased to be here, but he'd come when I asked.

It was healthy, perhaps, for Az to sometimes remember where he'd come from. He still wore the Illyrian leathers. Had not tried to get the tattoos removed. Some part of him was Illyrian still. Always would be. Even if he wished to forget it.

Cassian said nothing for a minute, his face a mask of stone. He'd been distant even before we'd gathered around the table in my mother's old house to deliver the report this morning. Distant since Solstice. I'd bet decent money on why.

"It will be a good sign," Cassian said at last, "when there are twenty girls out there and they've shown up for a month straight."

Az snorted softly. "I'll bet you—"

"No bets," Cassian said. "Not on this."

Az held Cassian's stare for a moment, cobalt Siphons flickering, and then nodded. Understood. This mission of Cassian's, hatched years ago and perhaps close to fruition . . . It went beyond bets for him. Went down to a wound that had never really healed.

I slung my arm around Cassian's shoulders. "Small steps, brother." I threw him a grin, knowing it didn't meet my eyes. "Small steps."

For all of us.

Our world might very well depend on it.

CHAPTER 27

Feyre

The city bells chimed eleven in the morning.

A month later, Ressina and I stood near the front door, both of us in nearly identical clothes: thick, long sweaters, warm leggings, and sturdy, shearling-lined work boots.

Boots that were already splattered with paint.

In the weeks since Polina's family had gifted me the studio, Ressina and I had been here nearly every day. Readying the place. Figuring out our strategy. The lessons.

"Any minute now," Ressina murmured, glancing to the small clock mounted on the bright white walls of the studio. *That* had been an endless debate: what color to paint the space? We'd wanted yellow, then decided that it might not display the art well enough. Black and gray were too dreary for the atmosphere we wanted, beige could also clash with the art . . . So we'd gone with white. The back room, at least, we'd painted brightly—a different color on each wall. Green and pink and red and blue.

But this front space . . . Empty. Save for the tapestry I'd hung on one wall, the black of the Void mesmerizing. And a reminder. As much of a reminder as the impossible iridescence of Hope, glittering throughout. To work through loss, no matter how overwhelming. To create.

And then there were the ten easels and stools set in a circle in the middle of the gallery floor.

Waiting.

"Will they come?" I murmured to Ressina.

The faerie shifted on her feet, the only sign of her worry. "They said they would."

In the month that we'd been working together, she'd become a good friend. A dear friend. Ressina's eye for design was impeccable, good enough that I'd asked her to help me plan the river-house. That's what I was calling it. Since *river-manor* . . . No. *House* it would be, even if it was the largest home in this city. Not from any preening, but simply from practicality. From the size of our court, our family. A family that would perhaps keep growing.

But that was later. For now . . .

A minute passed by. Then two.

"Come on," Ressina muttered.

"Perhaps they had the wrong time?"

But as I said it, they emerged. Ressina and I held our breath as the pack of them rounded the corner, aiming for the studio.

Ten children, High Fae and faerie, and some of their parents.

Some of them—since others were no longer alive.

I kept a warm smile on my face, even as my heart thundered with each child that passed through our door, wary and unsure, clustering near the easels. My palms sweated as the parents gathered with them, their faces less guarded, but still hesitant. Hesitant, yet hopeful.

Not just for themselves, but the children they'd brought with them.

We hadn't advertised broadly. Ressina had reached out to some friends and acquaintances, and requested they ask around. If there were children in this city who might need a place to express the horrors that had happened during the war. If there were children who might not be able to talk about what they'd endured, but could perhaps paint or draw or sculpt it. Perhaps they wouldn't do any of those things, but the act of creating *something* . . . it could be a balm to them.

As it was for me.

As it was for the weaver, and Ressina, and so many of the artists in this city.

Once word had gotten out, inquiries had poured in. Not just from parents or guardians, but from potential instructors. Artists in the Rainbow who were eager to help—to teach classes.

I'd instruct one a day, depending on what was required of me as High Lady. Ressina would do another. And a rotating schedule of other teachers to teach the third and fourth classes of the day. Including the weaver, Aranea, herself.

Because the response from parents and family had been overwhelming.

How soon do classes start? was the most frequent question. The close second being *How much does it cost?*

Nothing. Nothing, we told them. It was free. No child or family would ever pay for classes here—or the supplies.

The room filled, and Ressina and I swapped a quick, relieved look. A nervous look, too.

And when I faced the families gathered, the room open and sunny around us, I smiled once more and began.

CHAPTER 28

Feyre

He was waiting for me an hour and a half later.

As the last of the children flitted out, some laughing, some still solemn and hollow-eyed, he held the door open for them and their families. They all gawked, bowing their heads, and Rhys offered them a wide, easy smile in return.

I loved that smile. Loved that casual grace as he strode into the gallery, no sign of his wings today, and surveyed the still-drying paintings. Surveyed the paint splattered on my face and sweater and boots. "Rough day at the office?"

I pushed back a strand of my hair. Knowing it was likely streaked with blue paint. Since my fingers were covered in it. "You should see Ressina."

Indeed, she'd gone into the back moments ago to wash off a face full of red paint. Courtesy of one of the children, who'd deemed it a good idea to form a bubble of *all* the paint to see what color it would turn, and then float it across the room. Where it collided with her face.

Rhys laughed when I showed him down the bond. "Excellent use of their budding powers, at least."

I grinned, surveying one of the paintings beside him. "That's what I said. Ressina didn't find it so funny."

Though she had. Smiling had been a little difficult, though, when so many of the children had both visible and unseen scars.

Rhys and I studied a painting by a young faerie whose parents had been killed in the attack. "We didn't give them any detailed prompts," I said as Rhys's eyes roved around the painting. "We only told them to paint a memory. This is what she came up with."

It was hard to look at. The two figures in it. The red paint. The figures in the sky, their vicious teeth and reaching claws.

"They don't take their paintings home?"

"These will dry first, but I asked her if she wanted me to keep this somewhere special. She said to throw it out."

Rhys's eyes danced with worry.

I said quietly, "I want to keep it. To put in my future office. So we don't forget."

What had happened, what we were working for. Exactly why Aranea's tapestry of the Night Court insignia hung on the wall here.

He kissed my cheek in answer and moved to the next painting. He laughed. "Explain this one."

"This boy was *immensely* disappointed in his Solstice presents. Especially since it didn't include a puppy. So his 'memory' is one he hopes to make in the future—of him and his 'dog.' With his parents in a doghouse instead, while he and the dog live in the proper house."

"Mother help his parents."

"He was the one who made the bubble."

He laughed again. "Mother help *you*."

I nudged him, laughing now. "Walk me home for lunch?"

He sketched a bow. "It would be my honor, lady."

I rolled my eyes, shouting to Ressina that I'd be back in an hour. She called that I should take my time. The next class didn't come until two. We'd decided to both be at these initial classes, so the parents and guardians got to know us. And the children as well. It would be two full weeks of this before we got through the entire roster of classes.

Rhys helped me with my coat, stealing a kiss before we walked out into the sunny, frigid day. The Rainbow bustled around us, artists and shoppers nodding and waving our way as we strode for the town house.

I linked my arm through his, nestling into his warmth. "It's strange," I murmured.

Rhys angled his head. "What is?"

I smiled. At him, at the Rainbow, at the city. "This feeling, this excitement to wake up every day. To see you, and to work, and to just *be* here."

Nearly a year ago, I'd told him the opposite. Wished for the opposite. His face softened, as if he, too, remembered it. And understood.

I went on, "I know there's much to do. I know there are things we'll have to face. A few sooner than later." Some of the stars in his eyes banked at that. "I know there's the Illyrians, and the human queens, and the humans themselves, and all of it. But despite them . . ." I couldn't finish. Couldn't find the right words. Or speak them without falling apart in public.

So I leaned into him, into that unfailing strength, and said down the bond, *You make me so very happy. My* life *is happy, and I will never stop being grateful that you are in it.*

I looked up to find him not at all ashamed to have tears slipping down his cheeks in public. I brushed a few away before the chill wind could freeze them, and Rhys whispered in my ear, "I will never stop being grateful to have you in my life, either, Feyre darling. And no matter what lies ahead"—a small, joyous smile at that—"we will face it together. Enjoy every moment of it together."

I leaned into him again, his arm tightening around my shoulders. Around the top of the arm inked with the tattoo we both bore, the promise between us. To never part, not until the end.

And even after that.

I love you, I said down the bond.

What's not to love?

Before I could elbow him, Rhys kissed me again, breathless and swift. *To the stars who listen, Feyre.*

I brushed a hand over his cheek to wipe away the last of his tears, his skin warm and soft, and we turned down the street that would lead us home. Toward our future—and all that waited within it.

To the dreams that are answered, Rhys.

ACKNOWLEDGMENTS

In the course of writing this tale, I wound up going through two of the biggest events of my life. This past summer, I was about a third of the way into drafting *A Court of Frost and Starlight* when I got the worst sort of phone call from my mom: my father had suffered a massive heart attack, and it was unlikely that he would survive. What happened next was nothing short of a miracle, and the fact that my dad is alive today to see this book come out fills me with more joy than I can express.

The incredible ICU team at the University of Vermont in Burlington will forever have my deepest gratitude. Not only for saving my father's life, but also for the unparalleled care and compassion that he (and my entire family) received during the two weeks we spent camped out in the hospital. The ICU nurses will always be my heroes—your tireless hard work, unfailing positivity, and remarkable intelligence are the stuff of legends. You offered my family a ray of hope during the darkest days of our lives, and never once made us feel the tremendous weight of the odds stacked against us. Thank you, thank you, thank you for all that you do and have done, both for my family and for countless others.

I managed to finish writing *A Court of Frost and Starlight* after that (thanks to a few healing weeks spent up in beautiful Maine), but it wasn't until early autumn that the second life-changing thing happened: I found out that I was pregnant. To go from a summer that ranks among the worst days of my life to that sort of joy was such an enormous blessing, and though this tale will release a few weeks before I'm due to give birth, *A Court of Frost and Starlight* will always hold a special place in my heart because of it.

But I couldn't have gotten through these long months of working on this project without my husband, Josh. (I couldn't get through *life* without Josh.) So, thank you to the greatest husband in any world, for taking such good care of me, both before and during this pregnancy, and making sure that I had everything I needed to stay focused and make this book a reality (some prime examples: endless plates of snacks, tea on demand, finding me the comfiest of pillows to prop my swollen feet on). I love you to the stars and back, and I can't wait for this next epic chapter in our journey together.

And Annie. My sweet, sassy baby pup, Annie. Thank you for the warm cuddles and whiskery kisses, for being such a joy and a comfort on both the brightest and darkest of days. There is no greater or more faithful canine companion than you. I love you forever.

As always, I owe a huge debt to my agent, Tamar Rydzinski. Thank you, thank you, thank you for being in my corner, for keeping me sane, and for your wisdom and guidance. None of this would be possible without you.

To the badass team at the Laura Dail Literary Agency: you guys rock. Thank you for *everything*. And Cassie Homer: you are the absolute best, and I am so grateful for all that you do.

Bethany Buck: thank you for all your help with this book, and for being such a lovely person. And thank you x infinity to the entire team at Bloomsbury: Cindy Loh, Cristina Gilbert, Kathleen Farrar, Nigel Newton, Rebecca McNally, Sonia Palmisano, Emma Hopkin, Ian Lamb, Emma Bradshaw, Lizzy Mason, Courtney Griffin, Erica Barmash, Emily Ritter, Alona Fryman, Alexis Castellanos, Grace Whooley, Alice Grigg, Elise Burns, Jenny Collins, Beth Eller, Kelly de Groot, Lucy Mackay-Sim, Hali Baumstein, Melissa Kavonic, Diane Aronson, Donna Mark, John Candell, Nicholas Church, Anna Bernard, Kate Sederstrom, and the entire foreign rights team: I'm so thrilled to be published by you.

Charlie Bowater: Your art is such an inspiration to me on so many levels. Thank you for all of your tremendous work, and for the truly stunning border on the cover. It's such a dream come true to collaborate with you, and I can't wait to work with you more in the future.

To my family: Thank you for the love and support you gave my dad and me this summer. You flew and drove in from all across the country to be there for us in Vermont, and almost a year later, I still don't have the words to convey my gratitude or how much I love you all. I am so very blessed to have you in my life.

To my parents: it's been one hell of a year, but we made it. I'll never stop being amazed and grateful that I can even say those words. I love you both.

To my marvelous friends (you know who you are): Thank you for being there when I needed you most, for checking on me and my family, and for never failing to bring a smile to my face.

And lastly, to everyone out there who has picked up my books: thank you. You are the greatest group of people that I've ever met, and I'm honored to have you as readers. To the stars who listen—and the dreams that are answered.

The Court of Thorns and Roses series continues in

Read on for a sneak peek!

The black water nipping at her thrashing heels was freezing.

Not the bite of winter chill, or even the burn of solid ice, but something colder. Deeper.

The cold of the gaps between stars, the cold of a world before light.

The cold of hell—true hell, she realized as she bucked against the strong hands trying to shove her into that Cauldron.

True hell, because that was Elain lying on the stone floor with the red-haired, one-eyed Fae male hovering over her. Because those were pointed ears poking through her sister's sodden gold-brown hair, and an immortal glow radiating from Elain's fair skin.

True hell—worse than the inky depths mere inches from her toes.

Put her under, the hard-faced Fae king ordered.

And the sound of that voice, the voice of the male who had done this to Elain . . .

She knew she was going into the Cauldron. Knew she would lose this fight.

Knew no one was coming to save her: not sobbing Feyre, not Feyre's gagged former lover, not her devastated new mate.

Not Cassian, broken and bleeding on the floor. The warrior was still trying to rise on trembling arms. To reach her.

The King of Hybern—he had done this. To Elain. To Cassian.

And to her.

The icy water bit into the soles of her feet.

It was a kiss of venom, a death so permanent that every inch of her roared in defiance.

She was going in—but she would not go gently.

The water gripped her ankles with phantom talons, tugging her down. She twisted, wrenching her arm free from the guard who held it.

And Nesta Archeron pointed. One finger—at the King of Hybern.

A death-promise. A target marked.

Hands shoved her into the water's waiting claws.

Nesta laughed at the fear that crept into the king's eyes just before the water devoured her whole.

In the beginning

And in the end

There was Darkness

And nothing more

She did not feel the cold as she sank into a sea that had no bottom, no horizon, no surface. But she felt the burning.

Immortality was not a serene youth.

It was fire.

It was molten ore poured into her veins, boiling her human blood until it was nothing but steam, forging her brittle bones until they were fresh steel.

And when she opened her mouth to scream, when the pain ripped her very self in two, there was no sound. There was nothing in this place but darkness and agony and power—

They would pay. All of them.

Starting with this Cauldron.

Starting *now*.

She tore into the darkness with talons and teeth. Rent and cleaved and shredded.

And the dark eternity around her shuddered. Bucked. Thrashed.

She laughed as it recoiled. Laughed around the mouthful of raw power she ripped out and swallowed whole; laughed at the fistfuls of eternity she shoved into her heart, her veins.

The Cauldron struggled like a bird under a cat's paw. She refused to relent.

Everything it had stolen from her, from Elain, she would take from it.

Wrapped in black eternity, Nesta and the Cauldron twined, burning through the darkness like a newborn star.

NOVICE

Cassian raised his fist to the green door in the dim hallway—and hesitated.

He'd cut down more enemies than he cared to tally, had stood knee-deep in gore on countless battlefields and kept swinging, had made choices that cost him the lives of skilled warriors, had been a general and a grunt and an assassin, and yet . . . here he was, lowering his fist.

Balking.

The building on the north side of the Sidra River was in need of new paint. And new floors, if the creaking boards beneath his boots as he'd climbed the two flights had been any indication. But at least it was clean. Definitely grim by Velaris's standards, but when the city itself had no slums, that wasn't saying much. He'd seen and stayed in far worse.

He'd never understood, though, why Nesta insisted on dwelling here. He got why she wouldn't take up rooms in the House of Wind—it was too far from the city, and she couldn't fly or winnow in. Which meant dealing with the ten thousand steps up and down. But why live in this dump, when the town house was sitting empty? Since construction had finished on Feyre and Rhys's sprawling home on the river, the town house had been left open to any of their friends who needed or wanted it. He knew for a fact that Feyre had offered Nesta a room there—and had been rejected.

He frowned at the door's peeling paint. No sounds trickled through the sizable gap between the door and the floor, wide enough for even the fattest of rats to meander through; no fresh scents lingered in the cramped hallway.

Maybe he'd get lucky and she'd be out—perhaps sleeping under the bar of whatever seedy tavern she'd frequented last night. Though that might be worse, since he'd need to track her down there instead.

Cassian lifted his fist again, the red of his Siphon flickering in the ancient faelights tucked into the ceiling.

Coward. Grow some damned balls.

Cassian knocked once. Twice.

Silence.

Cassian almost sighed his relief aloud. Thank the fucking Mother—

Clipped, precise footsteps sounded from the other side of the door. Each more pissed off than the last.

He tucked his wings in tight, squaring his shoulders as he braced his feet apart. A traditional fighting stance, beaten into him during his training years, now mere muscle memory. He didn't dare consider why the sound of those footsteps sent his body falling into it.

The snap as she unlatched each of her four locks might as well have been the beating of a war-drum.

Cassian ran through the list of things he was to say, how Feyre had suggested he say them.

The door was yanked open, the knob twisting so hard Cassian wondered if she was imagining it as his neck.

Nesta Archeron already wore a scowl. But there she was.

She looked like hell.

"What do you want?" She didn't open the door wider than a hand's breadth.

When had he last seen her? The end-of-summer party on that barge in the Sidra last month? She hadn't looked this bad. Though he supposed a night trying to drown oneself in wine and liquor never left anyone looking particularly good the next morning. Especially at—

"It's seven in the morning," she went on, raking him over with that gray-blue stare that always kindled his temper.

She wore a male's shirt. Worse, she wore *only* a male's shirt.

Cassian propped a hand on the doorjamb and gave her a half grin he knew brought out her claws. "Rough night?"

Rough year, really. Her beautiful face was pale, far thinner than it had been before the war with Hybern, her lips bloodless, and those eyes . . . Cold and sharp, like a winter morning in the mountains.

No joy, no laughter, in any plane of it. Of her.

She made to shut the door on his hand.

He shoved a booted foot into the gap before she could break his fingers. Her nostrils flared slightly.

"Feyre wants you at the house."

"Which one?" Nesta said, frowning at the foot he'd wedged in the door. "She has five."

He bit back his retort. This wasn't the battlefield—and he wasn't her opponent. His job was to transport her to the assigned spot. And then pray that the lovely home Feyre and Rhys had just moved into wouldn't be reduced to rubble.

"The new one."

"Why didn't my sister fetch me herself?" He knew that suspicious gleam in her eye, the slight stiffening of her back. His own instincts surged to meet her defiance, to push and push and discover what might happen.

Since Winter Solstice, they'd exchanged only a handful of words. Most had been at the barge party last month. They'd consisted of:

Move.

Hello, Nes.

Move.

Gladly.

After months and months of nothing, of barely seeing her at all, that had been it.

He hadn't even understood why she'd shown up to the party, especially when she knew she'd be stuck on the water with them for hours. Amren likely deserved the credit for the rare appearance, due to whatever bit of sway the female held over Nesta. But by the end of that night, Nesta had been at the front of the line to get off the boat, arms tight around herself, and Amren had been brooding at the other end of it, nearly shaking with rage and disgust.

No one had asked what had happened between them, not even Feyre. The boat had docked, and Nesta had practically run off, and no one had spoken to her since. Until today. Until this conversation, which felt like the longest they'd had since the battles against Hybern.

Cassian said at last, "Feyre is High Lady. She's busy running the Night Court."

Nesta cocked her head, gold-brown hair sliding over a bony shoulder. On anyone else, the movement would have been contemplative. On her, it was the warning of a predator, sizing up prey.

"And my sister," she said in that flat voice that refused to yield any sign of emotion, "deemed my *immediate presence* necessary?"

"She knew you'd likely need to clean yourself up, and wanted to give you a head start. You're expected at nine."

He waited for the explosion as she did the math.

Her eyes flared. "Do I look like I need *two hours* to become presentable?"

He took the invitation to survey her: long bare legs, an elegant sweep of hips, tapered waist—too damn thin—and full, inviting breasts that were at odds with the new, sharp angles of her body.

On any other female, those magnificent breasts might have been enough cause for him to begin courting her the moment he met her. But from the instant he'd met Nesta, the cold fire in her eyes had been a temptation of a different sort.

And now that she was High Fae, all inherent dominance and aggression—and piss-poor attitude—he avoided her as much as possible. Especially with what had happened during and after the war against Hybern. She'd made her feelings about him more than clear.

Cassian said at last, "You look like you could use a few big meals, a bath, and some real clothes."

Nesta rolled her eyes, but fingered the hem of her shirt.

Cassian added, "Kick out the sorry bastard, get washed, and I'll bring you some tea."

Her brows rose a fraction of an inch.

He gave her a crooked smile. "You think I can't hear that male in your bedroom, trying to quietly put on his clothes and sneak out the window?"

As if in answer, a muffled thud came from the bedroom. Nesta hissed.

"I'll be back in an hour to see how things are proceeding." Cassian put enough bite behind the words that his soldiers would know not to push him—they'd remember that he required seven Siphons to keep his magic under control for good reason. But Nesta did not fly in his legions, did not fight under his command, and certainly did not seem to recall that he was over five hundred years old and—

"Don't bother. I'll be there on time."

He pushed off the doorjamb, wings flaring slightly as he backed away a few steps. "That's not what I was asked to do. I'm to see you from door to door."

Her face tightened. "Go perch on a chimney."

He sketched a bow, not daring to take his eyes off her. She'd emerged from the Cauldron with . . . gifts. Considerable gifts—dark ones. But no one had seen nor felt any sign of them since that last battle with Hybern, since Amren had shattered the Cauldron and Feyre and Rhys had managed to heal it. Elain, too, had revealed no indication of her seer's abilities since then.

But if Nesta's power remained, still capable of leveling battlefields . . . Cassian knew better than to make himself vulnerable to another predator. "Do you want your tea with milk or lemon?"

She slammed the door in his face.

Then locked each of those four locks.

Whistling to himself and wondering if that poor bastard inside the apartment would indeed flee out the window—mostly to escape *her*—Cassian strode down the dim hallway and went to find some food.

He'd need the sustenance today. Especially once Nesta learned precisely why her sister had summoned her.

Nesta Archeron didn't know the name of the male in her apartment.

She ransacked her wine-soaked memory as she returned to the bedroom, dodging piles of books and lumps of clothing, recalling heated glances at the tavern, the wet, hot meeting of their mouths, the sweat coating her as she rode him until pleasure and drink sent her into blessed oblivion, but not his name.

The male had already leaned out the window, with Cassian no doubt lurking on the street below to witness his spectacularly pathetic exit, when Nesta reached the dim, cramped bedroom. The brass-poster bed was rumpled, the sheets half-spilled on the creaky, uneven wood floor, and the cracked window banged against the wall on its loose hinges. The male twisted toward her.

He was handsome, in the way most High Fae males were handsome. A bit thinner than she liked them—practically a boy compared to the towering mass of muscle that had just filled her doorway. He winced as she padded in, his expression turning pained as he noted what she wore. "I . . . That's . . ."

Nesta tugged off his shirt, leaving nothing but bare skin in its wake.

His eyes widened, but the scent of his fear remained—not fear of her, but of the male he'd heard at the front door. As he remembered who her sister was. Who her sister's mate was. Who her sister's friends were. As if any of that meant something.

What would his fear smell like if he learned she'd used him, slept with him, to keep herself at bay? To settle that writhing darkness that had simmered inside her from the moment she'd emerged from the Cauldron? Sex, music, and drink, she'd learned this past year—all of it helped. Not entirely, but it kept the power from boiling over. Even if she could still feel it streaming through her blood, coiled tight around her bones.

She chucked the white shirt at him. "You can use the front door now."

He slung the shirt over his head. "I— Is he still—" His gaze kept snagging on her breasts, peaked against the chill morning; her bare skin. The apex of her thighs.

"Good-bye." Nesta entered the rusty, leaky bathroom attached to her bedroom. At least the place had hot running water.

Sometimes.

Feyre and Elain had tried to convince her to move. She'd always ignored their advice. Just as she'd ignore whatever was said today. She knew Feyre planned a scolding. Perhaps something to do with the fact that Nesta had signed last night's outrageous tab at the tavern to her sister's bank account.

Nesta snorted, twisting the handle in the bath. It groaned, the metal icy to the touch, and water sputtered, then sprayed into the cracked, stained tub.

This was her residence. No servants, no eyes monitoring and judging every move, no company unless she invited them. Or unless prying, swaggering warriors made it their business to stop by.

It took five minutes for the water to actually heat enough to start filling the tub. There had been some days in the past year when she hadn't even bothered to take the time. Some days when she'd climbed into the icy water, not feeling its bite but that of the Cauldron's dark depths as it devoured her whole. As it ripped away her humanity, her mortality, and made her into *this*.

It had taken her months of battling it—the body-tensing panic that made her very bones tremble to be submerged. But she'd forced herself to face it down. Had learned to sit in the icy water, nauseated and shaking, teeth gritted; had refused to move until her body recognized that she was in a tub and not the Cauldron, that she was in her apartment and not the stone castle across the sea, that she was alive, immortal. Even though her father was not.

No, her father was ashes in the wind, his existence marked only by a headstone on a hill outside this city. Or so her sisters had told her.

I loved you from the first moment I held you in my arms, her father had said to her in those last moments together.

Don't you lay your filthy hands on my daughter. Those had been his final words, spat at the King of Hybern. Her father had squandered those final words on that worm of a king.

Her father. The man who had never fought for his children, not until the end. When he had come to save them—to save the humans and the Fae, yes, but most of all, his daughters. Her.

A grand, stupid waste.

Unholy dark power flowed through her, and it had not been enough to stop the King of Hybern from snapping his neck.

She had hated her father, hated him deeply, and yet he had loved her, for some inexplicable reason. Not enough to try to spare them from poverty or keep them from starving. But somehow it had been enough for him to raise an army on the continent. To sail a ship named for her into battle.

She had still hated her father in those last moments. And then his neck had cracked, his eyes not full of fear as he died, but of that foolish love for her.

That was what had lingered—the look in his eyes. The resentment in her heart as he died for her. It had festered, gnawing at her like the power she buried deep, running rampant through her head until no icy baths could numb it away.

She could have saved him.

It was the King of Hybern's fault. She knew that. But it was hers, too. Just as it was her fault that Elain had been captured by the Cauldron after Nesta spied on it with that scrying, her fault that Hybern had done such terrible things to hunt her and her sister down like a deer.

Some days, the sheer dread and panic locked Nesta's body up so thoroughly that nothing could get her to breathe. Nothing could stop the awful power from beginning to rise, rise, rise in her. Nothing beyond the music at those taverns, the card games with strangers, the endless bottles of wine, and the sex that made her feel nothing—but offered a moment of release amid the roaring inside her.

Nesta finished washing away the sweat and other remnants of last night. The sex hadn't been bad—she'd had better, but also much worse. Even immortality wasn't enough time for some males to master the art of the bedroom.

So she'd taught herself what she liked. She'd obtained a monthly contraceptive tea from her local apothecary, and then she'd brought that first male here. He had no idea that her maidenhead had been intact until he'd spied the smeared blood on the sheets. His face had tightened with distaste—then a glimmer of fear that she might report an unsatisfactory first bedding to her sister. To her sister's insufferable mate. Nesta hadn't bothered to tell him that she avoided both of them at all costs. Especially the latter. These days, Rhysand seemed content to do the same.

After the war with Hybern, Rhysand had offered her jobs. Positions in his court.

She didn't want them. They were pity offerings, thin attempts to get her to be a part of Feyre's life, to be gainfully employed. But the High Lord had never liked her. Their conversations were coldly civil at best.

She'd never told him that the reasons he hated her were the same reasons she lived here. Took cold baths some days. Forgot to eat on others. Couldn't stand the crack and snap of a fireplace. And drowned herself in wine and music and pleasure each night. Every damning thing Rhysand thought about her was true—and she'd known it long before he had ever shadowed her doorstep.

Any offering Rhysand threw her way was made solely out of love for Feyre. Better to spend her time the way she wished. They kept paying for it, after all.

The knock on the door rattled the entire apartment.

She glared toward the front room, debating whether to pretend she'd left, but Cassian could hear her, smell her. And if he broke down the door, which he was likely to do, she'd just have the headache of explaining it to her stingy landlord.

So Nesta donned the dress she'd left on the floor last night, and then again freed all four locks. She'd installed them the first day she'd arrived. Locking them each night was practically a ritual. Even when the nameless male had been here, even out of her mind on wine, she'd remembered to lock them all.

As if that would keep the monsters of this world at bay.

Nesta tugged open the door enough to see Cassian's cocky grin, and left it ajar as she stormed away to search for her shoes.

He strode in after her, a mug of tea in his hand—the cup probably borrowed from the shop at the corner. Or outright given to him, considering how people tended to worship the ground his muddy boots walked on. He'd already been adored in this city before the Hybern conflict. His heroism and sacrifice—the feats he'd performed on the battlefields—had won him even more awe after its end.

She didn't blame his admirers. She'd experienced the pleasure and sheer terror of watching him on those battlefields. Still woke with sweat coating her at the memories: how she couldn't breathe while she'd witnessed him fight, enemies swarming him; how it had felt when the Cauldron's power had surged and she'd known it was going to strike where their army was strongest—him.

She hadn't been able to save the one thousand Illyrians who had fallen in the moment after she'd summoned him to safety. She turned away from that memory, too.

Cassian surveyed her apartment and let out a low whistle. "Ever thought of hiring a cleaner?"

Nesta scanned the small living area—a sagging crimson couch, a soot-stained brick hearth, a moth-eaten floral armchair, then the ancient kitchenette, piled with leaning columns of dirty dishes. Where had she thrown her shoes last night? She shifted her search to her bedroom.

"Some fresh air would be a good start," Cassian added from the other room. The window groaned as he cracked it open.

She found her brown shoes in opposite corners of the bedroom. One reeked of spilled wine.

Nesta perched on the edge of the mattress to slide them on, tugging at the laces. She didn't bother to look up as Cassian's steady steps approached, then halted at the threshold.

He sniffed once. Loudly.

"I'd hoped you at least changed the sheets between visitors, but apparently that doesn't bother you."

Nesta tied the laces on the first shoe. "What business is it of yours?"

He shrugged, though the tightness on his face didn't reflect such nonchalance. "If I can smell a few different males in here, then surely your companions can, too."

"Hasn't stopped them yet." She tied the other shoe, Cassian's hazel eyes tracking the movement.

"Your tea is getting cold." His teeth flashed.

Nesta ignored him and searched the bedroom again. Her coat . . .

"Your coat is on the ground by the front door," he said. "And it's going to be brisk out, so bring a scarf."

She ignored that, too, but breezed by him, careful to avoid touching him, and found her dark blue overcoat exactly where he'd claimed it was. She opened the front door, pointing for him to leave first.

Cassian held her gaze as he stalked for her, then reached out an arm—

And plucked the cerulean-and-cream scarf Elain had given her for her birthday this spring off the hook on the wall. He gripped it in his fist, dangling it like a strangled snake as he brushed past her.

Something was eating at him. Usually, Cassian held out a bit longer before yielding to his temper. Perhaps it had to do with whatever Feyre wanted to say up at the house.

Nesta's gut twisted as she set each lock.

She wasn't stupid. She knew there had been unrest since the war had ended, both in these lands and on the continent. Knew that without the barrier of the wall, some Fae territories were pushing the limits on what they could get away with in terms of border claims and how they treated humans. And she knew that those four human queens still squatted in their shared palace, their armies unused and intact.

They were monsters, all of them. They'd killed the golden-haired queen who'd betrayed them and sold another—Vassa—to a sorcerer-lord. It seemed only fitting that the youngest of the four remaining queens had been transformed into a crone by the Cauldron. Made into a long-lived Fae, yes, but aged into a withered shell as punishment for the power Nesta had taken from the Cauldron. How she'd ripped it apart while it had torn her mortal body into something new.

That wizened queen blamed her. Had wanted to kill her, if Hybern's Ravens had been correct before Bryaxis and Rhysand had destroyed them for infiltrating the House of Wind's library.

There had been no whisper of that queen in the fourteen months since the war.

But if some new threat had arisen . . .

The four locks seemed to laugh at her before Nesta followed Cassian out of the building and into the bustling city beyond.

The riverfront "house" was actually an estate, and so new and clean and beautiful that Nesta remembered her shoes were covered in stale wine precisely as she strode through the towering marble archway and into the shining front hall, tastefully decorated in shades of ivory and sand.

A mighty staircase bisected the enormous space, a chandelier of handblown glass—made by Velaris artisans—drooping from the carved ceiling above it. The faelights in each nest-shaped orb cast shimmering reflections on the polished pale wood floors, interrupted only by potted ferns, wood furniture also made in Velaris, and an outrageous array of art. She didn't bother to remark on any of it. Plush blue rugs broke up the pristine floors, a long runner flowing along the cavernous halls on either side, and one ran beneath the arch of the stairs, straight to a wall of windows on its other side, which looked out onto the sloping lawn and gleaming river at its feet.

Cassian headed to the left—toward the formal rooms for business, Feyre had informed Nesta during that first and only tour two months ago. Nesta had been half-drunk at the time, and had hated every second of it, each perfect room.

Most males bought their wives and mates jewelry for an outrageous Winter Solstice present.

Rhys had bought Feyre a palace.

No—he'd purchased the war-decimated land, and then given his mate free rein to design the residence of their dreams.

And somehow, Nesta thought as she silently followed an unnaturally quiet Cassian down the hall toward one of the studies whose doors were cracked open, Feyre and Rhys *had* managed to make this place seem cozy, welcoming. A behemoth of a building, but still a home. Even the formal furniture seemed designed for comfort and lounging, for long conversations over hearty food. Every piece of art had been picked by Feyre herself, or painted by her, many of them portraits and depictions of *them*—her friends, her . . . new family.

There were none of Nesta, naturally.

Even their gods-damned father had a portrait on the wall along one side of the grand staircase: him and Elain, smiling and happy, as they'd been before the world went to shit. Sitting on a stone bench amid bushes bursting with pink and blue hydrangea. The formal gardens of their first home, that lovely manor near the sea. Nesta and their mother were nowhere in sight.

That was how it had been, after all: Elain and Feyre doted on by their father. Nesta prized and trained by their mother.

During that first tour, Nesta had noted the lack of herself here. The lack of their mother. She said nothing, of course, but it was a pointed absence.

It was enough to now set her teeth on edge, to make her grab the invisible, internal leash that kept the horrible power within her at bay and pull tight, as Cassian slipped into the study and said to whoever awaited them, "She's here."

Nesta braced herself, but Feyre merely chuckled. "You're five minutes early. I'm impressed."

"Seems like a good omen for gambling. We should head to Rita's," Cassian drawled just as Nesta stepped into the wood-paneled room.

The study opened into a lush garden courtyard. The space was warm and rich, and she might have admitted she liked the floor-to-ceiling bookshelves, the sapphire velvet furniture before the black marble hearth, had she not seen who was sitting inside.

Feyre perched on the rolled arm of the couch, clad in a heavy white sweater and dark leggings.

Rhys, in his usual black, leaned against the mantel, arms crossed. No wings today.

And Amren, in her preferred gray, sat cross-legged in the leather armchair by the roaring hearth, those muted silver eyes sweeping over Nesta with distaste.

So much had changed between her and the female.

Nesta had seen to that—the destruction. She didn't let herself think about that argument at the end-of-summer party on the river barge. Or the silence between herself and Amren since then.

No more visits to Amren's apartment. No more chats over jigsaw puzzles. Certainly no more lessons in magic. She'd made sure of that last part, too.

Feyre, at least, smiled at her. "I heard you had quite the night."

Nesta glanced between where Cassian had claimed the armchair across from Amren, the empty spot on the couch beside Feyre, and where Rhys stood by the hearth.

She kept her spine straight, her chin high, hating that they all eyed her as she opted to sit on the couch beside her sister. Hating that Rhys and Amren noted her filthy shoes, and probably still smelled that male on her despite the bath.

"You look atrocious," Amren said.

Nesta wasn't stupid enough to glare at the . . . whatever Amren was. She was High Fae now, yes, but she'd once been something different. Not of this world. Her tongue was still sharp enough to wound.

Like Nesta, Amren did not possess court-specific magic related to the High Fae. It didn't make her influence in this court any less mighty. Nesta's own High Fae powers had never materialized—she had only what she'd taken from the Cauldron, rather than letting it deign to gift her with power, as it had with Elain. She had no idea what she'd ripped from the Cauldron while it had stolen her humanity from her—but she knew they were things she did not and would never wish to understand, to master. The very thought had her stomach churning.

"Though I bet it's hard to look good," Amren went on, "when you're out until the darkest hours of the night, drinking yourself stupid and fucking anything that comes your way."

Feyre whipped her head to the High Lord's Second. Rhys seemed inclined to agree with Amren. Cassian kept his mouth shut. Nesta said smoothly, "I wasn't aware that my activities were under your jurisdiction."

Cassian loosed a murmur that sounded like a warning. To which one of them, she didn't know. Or care.

Amren's eyes glowed, a remnant of the power that had once burned inside her. All that was left now. Nesta knew her own power could shine like that, too—but while Amren's had revealed itself to be light and heat, Nesta knew that her silver flame came from a colder, darker place. A place that was old—and yet wholly new.

Amren challenged, "They are when you spend that much of our gold on wine."

Perhaps she had pushed them too far with last night's tab.

Nesta looked to Feyre, who winced. "So you really did make me come all the way here for a scolding?"

Feyre's eyes—mirror images of her own—softened slightly. "No, it's not a scolding." She cut a sharp glance at Rhys, still icily silent against the mantel, and then to Amren, seething in her chair. "Think of this as a discussion."

Nesta shot to her feet. "My life is not your concern, or up for any sort of *discussion*."

"*Sit down*," Rhys snarled.

The raw command in that voice, the utter dominance and power . . .

Nesta froze, fighting it, hating that Fae part of her that bowed to such things. Cassian leaned forward in his chair, as if he'd leap between them. She could have sworn something like pain had etched itself across his face.

But Nesta held Rhysand's gaze. Threw every ounce of defiance she could into it, even as his order made her knees *want* to bend, to sit.

Rhys said, "You are going to stay. You are going to listen."

She let out a low laugh. "You're not my High Lord. You don't give me orders." But she knew how powerful he was. Had seen it, felt it. Still trembled to be near him.

Rhys scented that fear. One side of his mouth curled up in a cruel smile. "You want to go head-to-head, Nesta Archeron?" he purred. The High Lord of the Night Court gestured to the sloping lawn beyond the windows. "We've got plenty of space out there for a brawl."

Nesta bared her teeth, silently roaring at her body to obey *her* orders. She'd sooner die than bow to him. To any of them.

Rhys's smile grew, well aware of that fact.

"That's enough," Feyre snapped at Rhys. "I told you to keep out of it."

He dragged his star-flecked eyes to his mate, and it was all Nesta could do to keep from collapsing onto the couch as her knees gave out at last. Feyre angled her head, nostrils flaring, and said to Rhysand, "You can either *leave*, or you can stay and keep your mouth shut."

Rhys again crossed his arms, but said nothing.

"You too," Feyre spat to Amren. The female harrumphed and nestled into her chair.

Nesta didn't bother to look pleasant as Feyre twisted to face her, taking a proper seat on the couch, the velvet cushions sighing beneath her. Her sister swallowed. "We need to make some changes, Nesta," Feyre said hoarsely. "You do—and *we* do."

Where the hell was Elain?

"I'll take the blame," Feyre went on, "for allowing things to get this far, and this bad. After the war with Hybern, with everything else that was going on, it . . . You . . . I should have been there to help you, but I wasn't, and I am ready to admit that this is partially my fault."

"That *what* is your fault?" Nesta hissed.

"You," Cassian said. "This bullshit behavior."

He'd said that at the Winter Solstice. And just as it had then, her spine locked at the insult, the *arrogance*—

"Look," Cassian went on, holding up his hands, "it's not some moral failing, but—"

"I understand how you're feeling," Feyre cut in.

"You know *nothing* about how I'm feeling."

Feyre plowed ahead. "It's time for some changes. Starting now."

"Keep your self-righteous do-gooder nonsense out of my life."

"You don't have a life," Feyre retorted. "And I'm not going to sit by for another moment and watch you destroy yourself." She put a tattooed hand on her heart, like it meant something. "I decided after the war to give you time, but it seems that was wrong. *I* was wrong."

"Oh?" The word was a dagger thrown between them.

Rhys tensed at the sneer, but still said nothing.

"You're done," Feyre breathed, voice shaking. "This behavior, that apartment, all of it—you are *done*, Nesta."

"And where," Nesta said, her tone mercifully icy, "am I supposed to go?"

Feyre looked to Cassian.

For once, Cassian wasn't grinning. "You're coming with me," he said. "To train."

Don't miss
Sarah J. Maas's bestselling
Court of Thorns and Roses series:

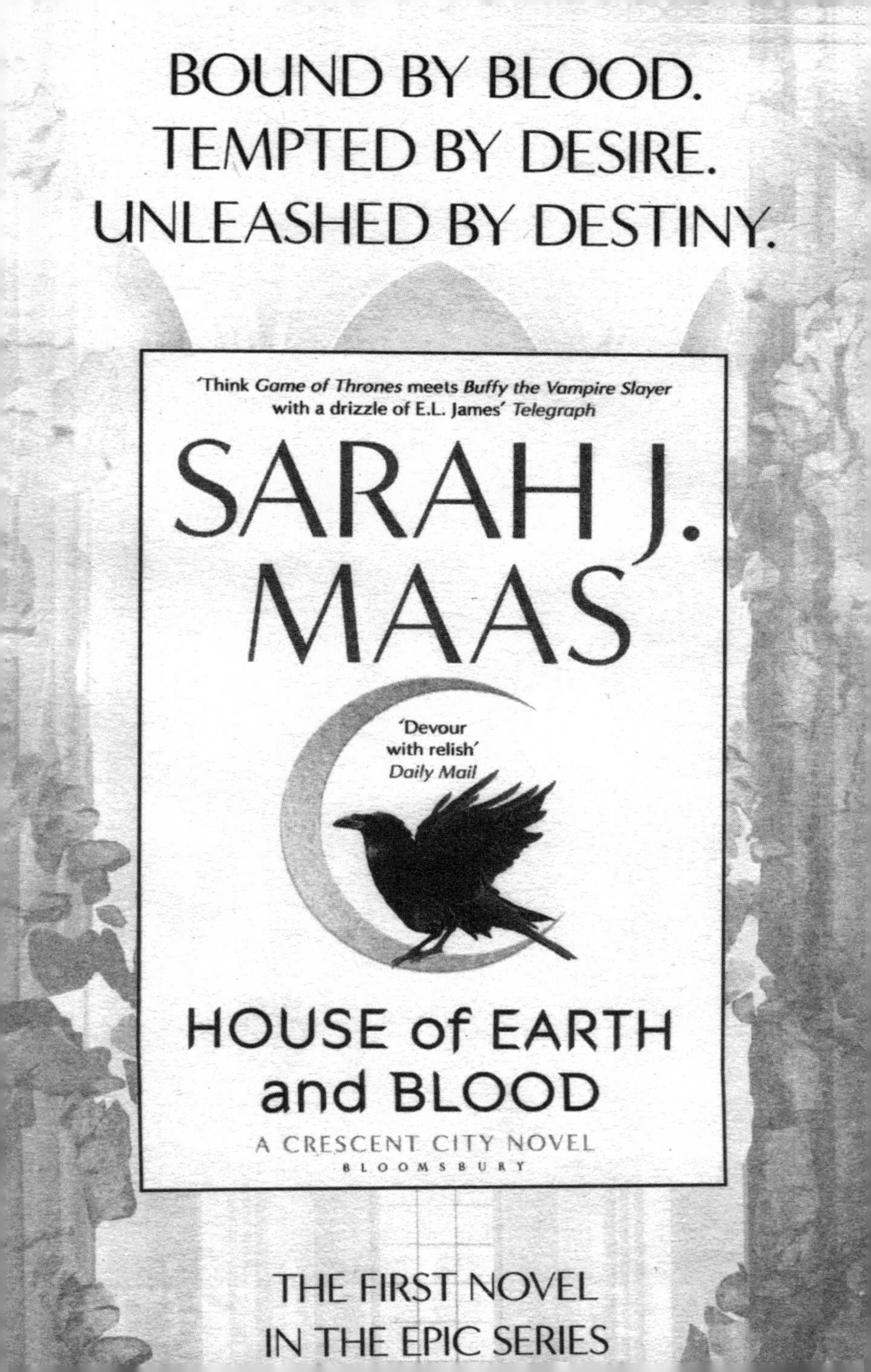
BOUND BY BLOOD.
TEMPTED BY DESIRE.
UNLEASHED BY DESTINY.
'Think Game of Thrones meets Buffy the Vampire Slayer with a drizzle of E.L. James' Telegraph
SARAH J. MAAS
'Devour with relish' Daily Mail
HOUSE of EARTH and BLOOD
A CRESCENT CITY NOVEL
BLOOMSBURY
THE FIRST NOVEL
IN THE EPIC SERIES

PRAISE FOR SARAH J. MAAS'S
COURT OF THORNS AND ROSES SERIES

A COURT OF THORNS AND ROSES

"Simply dazzles." —*Booklist*, starred review

"Passionate, violent, sexy and daring. . . .
A true page-turner." —*USA Today*

"Suspense, romance, intrigue and action. This is
not a book to be missed!" —HuffPost

"Vicious and intoxicating. . . . A dazzling world, complex characters
and sizzling romance." —*RT Book Reviews*, Top Pick

"A sexy, action-packed fairytale." —Bustle

A COURT OF MIST AND FURY

"Fiercely romantic, irresistibly sexy and hypnotically magical.
A veritable feast for the senses." —*USA Today*

"Hits the spot for fans of dark, lush, sexy fantasy." —*Kirkus Reviews*

"An immersive, satisfying read." —*Publishers Weekly*

"Darkly sexy and thrilling." —Bustle

A COURT OF WINGS AND RUIN

"Fast-paced and explosively action-packed." —*Booklist*

"The plot manages to seduce you with its alluring
characters, irresistible world and never-ending action,
leaving you craving more." —*RT Book Reviews*

BOOKS BY SARAH J. MAAS

THE COURT OF THORNS AND ROSES SERIES

A Court of Thorns and Roses

A Court of Mist and Fury

A Court of Wings and Ruin

A Court of Frost and Starlight

A Court of Thorns and Roses Colouring Book

THE CRESCENT CITY SERIES

House of Earth and Blood

THE THRONE OF GLASS SERIES

The Assassin's Blade

Throne of Glass

Crown of Midnight

Heir of Fire

Queen of Shadows

Empire of Storms

Tower of Dawn

Kingdom of Ash

The Throne of Glass Colouring Book

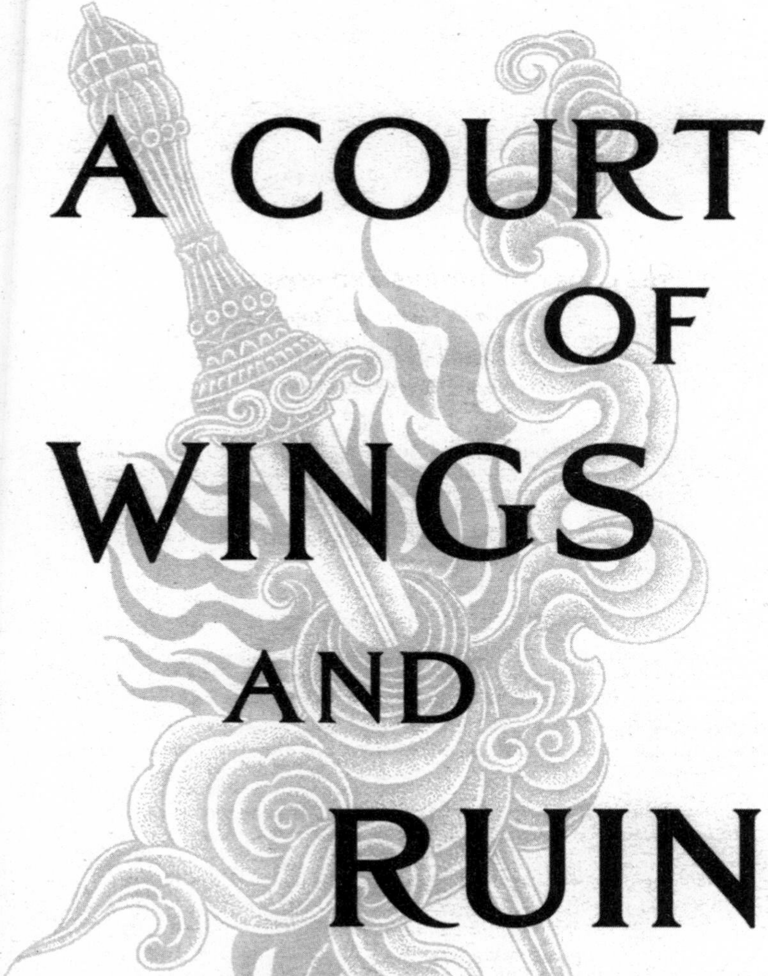

A COURT OF WINGS AND RUIN

SARAH J. MAAS

BLOOMSBURY PUBLISHING
LONDON • OXFORD • NEW YORK • NEW DELHI • SYDNEY

BLOOMSBURY PUBLISHING
Bloomsbury Publishing Plc
50 Bedford Square, London, WC1B 3DP, UK
29 Earlsfort Terrace, Dublin 2, Ireland

BLOOMSBURY, BLOOMSBURY PUBLISHING and the Diana logo are trademarks of Bloomsbury Publishing Plc

First published in Great Britain 2017
This edition published 2020

A catalogue record for this book is available from the British Library

ISBN: PB: 978-1-5266-1717-0; eBook: 978-1-4088-5791-5

19 20 18

Typeset by Westchester Publishing Services
Printed and bound in Great Britain by CPI Group (UK) Ltd, Croydon CR0 4YY

FSC www.fsc.org MIX Paper from responsible sources FSC® C020471

For Josh and Annie—
A gift. All of it.

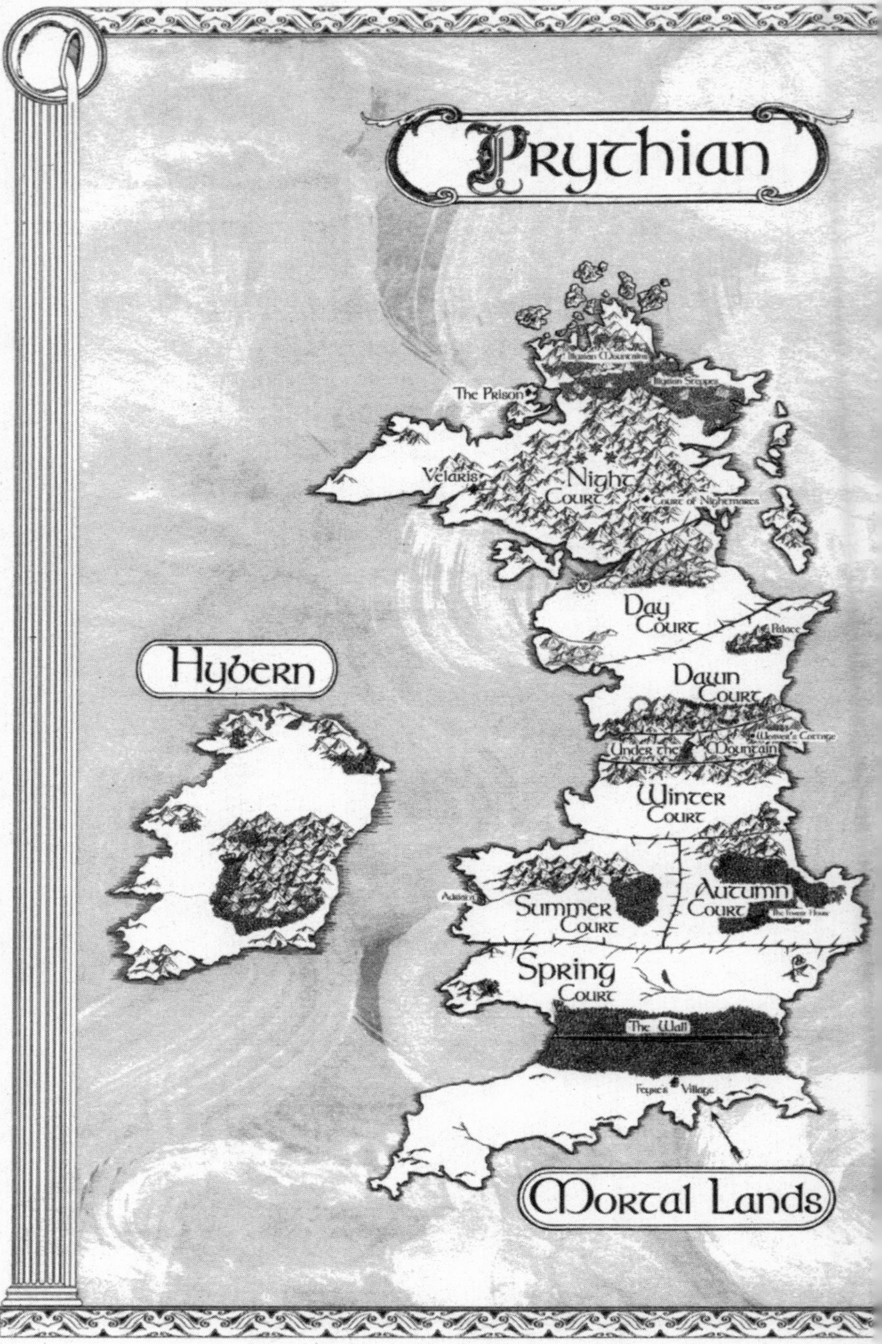
Prythian
The Prison
Velaris
Night Court
Court of Nightmares
Day Court
Palace
Dawn Court
Under the Mountain
Winter Court
Summer Court
Autumn Court
Spring Court
The Wall
Hybern
Mortal Lands

Vallahan
Montesere
Rask
Faerie Realms
North to Faerie Realms
South to Mortal Lands
The Wall
Scythia
Mortal Lands

A COURT
OF
WINGS
AND
RUIN

Rhysand
Two Years Before the Wall

The buzzing flies and screaming survivors had long since replaced the beating war-drums.

The killing field was now a tangled sprawl of corpses, human and faerie alike, interrupted only by broken wings jutting toward the gray sky or the occasional bulk of a felled horse.

With the heat, despite the heavy cloud cover, the smell would soon be unbearable. Flies already crawled along eyes gazing unblinkingly upward. They didn't differentiate between mortal and immortal flesh.

I picked my way across the once-grassy plain, marking the banners half-buried in mud and gore. It took most of my lingering strength to keep my wings from dragging over corpse and armor. My own power had been depleted well before the carnage had stopped.

I'd spent the final hours fighting as the mortals beside me had: with sword and fist and brute, unrelenting focus. We'd held the lines against Ravennia's legions—hour after hour, we'd held the lines, as I had been ordered to do by my father, as I knew I must do. To falter here would have been the killing blow to our already-sundering resistance.

The keep looming at my back was too valuable to be yielded to the

Loyalists. Not just for its location in the heart of the continent, but for the supplies it guarded. For the forges that smoldered day and night on its western side, toiling to stock our forces.

The smoke of those forges now blended with the pyres already being kindled behind me as I kept walking, scanning the faces of the dead. I made a note to dispatch any soldiers who could stomach it to claim weapons from either army. We needed them too desperately to bother with honor. Especially since the other side did not bother with it at all.

So still—the battlefield was so still, compared with the slaughter and chaos that had finally halted hours ago. The Loyalist army had retreated rather than surrender, leaving their dead for the crows.

I edged around a fallen bay gelding, the beautiful beast's eyes still wide with terror, flies crusting his bloodied flank. The rider was twisted beneath it, the man's head partially severed. Not from a sword blow. No, those brutal gashes were claws.

They wouldn't yield easily. The kingdoms and territories that wanted their human slaves would not lose this war unless they had no other choice. And even then . . . We'd learned the hard way, very early on, that they had no regard for the ancient rules and rites of battle. And for the Fae territories that fought beside mortal warriors . . . We were to be stomped out like vermin.

I waved away a fly that buzzed in my ear, my hand caked with blood both my own and foreign.

I'd always thought death would be some sort of peaceful homecoming—a sweet, sad lullaby to usher me into whatever waited afterward.

I crunched down with an armored boot on the flagpole of a Loyalist standard-bearer, smearing red mud across the tusked boar embroidered on its emerald flag.

I now wondered if the lullaby of death was not a lovely song, but the droning of flies. If flies and maggots were all Death's handmaidens.

The battlefield stretched toward the horizon in every direction save the keep at my back.

Three days, we had held them off; three days, we had fought and died here.

But we'd held the lines. Again and again, I'd rallied human and faerie, had refused to let the Loyalists break through, even when they'd hammered our vulnerable right flank with fresh troops on the second day.

I'd used my power until it was nothing but smoke in my veins, and then I'd used my Illyrian training until swinging my shield and sword was all I knew, all I could manage against the hordes.

A half-shredded Illyrian wing jutted from a cluster of High Fae corpses, as if it had taken all six of them to bring the warrior down. As if he'd taken them all out with him.

My heartbeat pounded through my battered body as I hauled away the piled corpses.

Reinforcements had arrived at dawn on the third and final day, sent by my father after my plea for aid. I had been too lost in battle-rage to note who they were beyond an Illyrian unit, especially when so many had been wielding Siphons.

But in the hours since they'd saved our asses and turned the tide of the battle, I had not spotted either of my brothers amongst the living. Did not know if Cassian or Azriel had even fought on the plain.

The latter was unlikely, as my father kept him close for spying, but Cassian . . . Cassian could have been reassigned. I wouldn't have put it past my father to shift Cassian to a unit most likely to be slaughtered. As this one had been, barely half limping off the battlefield earlier.

My aching, bloodied fingers dug into dented armor and clammy, stiff flesh as I heaved away the last of the High Fae corpses piled atop the fallen Illyrian soldier.

The dark hair, the golden-brown skin . . . The same as Cassian's.

But it was not Cassian's death-gray face that gaped at the sky.

My breath whooshed from me, my lungs still raw from roaring, my lips dry and chapped.

I needed water—badly. But nearby, another set of Illyrian wings poked up from the piled dead.

I stumbled and lurched toward it, letting my mind drift someplace dark and quiet while I righted the twisted neck to peer at the face beneath the simple helm.

Not him.

I picked my way through the corpses to another Illyrian.

Then another. And another.

Some I knew. Some I didn't. Still the killing field stretched onward under the sky.

Mile after mile. A kingdom of the rotting dead.

And still I looked.

PART ONE

PRINCESS OF CARRION

CHAPTER 1

Feyre

The painting was a lie.

A bright, pretty lie, bursting with pale pink blooms and fat beams of sunshine.

I'd begun it yesterday, an idle study of the rose garden lurking beyond the open windows of the studio. Through the tangle of thorns and satiny leaves, the brighter green of the hills rolled away into the distance.

Incessant, unrelenting spring.

If I'd painted this glimpse into the court the way my gut had urged me, it would have been flesh-shredding thorns, flowers that choked off the sunlight for any plants smaller than them, and rolling hills stained red.

But each brushstroke on the wide canvas was calculated; each dab and swirl of blending colors meant to portray not just idyllic spring, but a sunny disposition as well. Not too happy, but gladly, finally healing from horrors I carefully divulged.

I supposed that in the past weeks, I had crafted my demeanor as intricately as one of these paintings. I supposed that if I had also chosen to show myself as I truly wished, I would have been adorned with flesh-shredding talons, and hands that choked the life out of those now in my company. I would have left the gilded halls stained red.

But not yet.

Not yet, I told myself with every brushstroke, with every move I'd made these weeks. Swift revenge helped no one and nothing but my own, roiling rage.

Even if every time I spoke to them, I heard Elain's sobbing as she was forced into the Cauldron. Even if every time I looked at them, I saw Nesta fling that finger at the King of Hybern in a death-promise. Even if every time I scented them, my nostrils were again full of the tang of Cassian's blood as it pooled on the dark stones of that bone-castle.

The paintbrush snapped between my fingers.

I'd cleaved it in two, the pale handle damaged beyond repair.

Cursing under my breath, I glanced to the windows, the doors. This place was too full of watching eyes to risk throwing it in the rubbish bin.

I cast my mind around me like a net, trawling for any others near enough to witness, to be spying. I found none.

I held my hands before me, one half of the brush in each palm.

For a moment, I let myself see past the glamour that concealed the tattoo on my right hand and forearm. The markings of my true heart. My true title.

High Lady of the Night Court.

Half a thought had the broken paintbrush going up in flames.

The fire did not burn me, even as it devoured wood and brush and paint.

When it was nothing but smoke and ash, I invited in a wind that swept them from my palms and out the open windows.

For good measure, I summoned a breeze from the garden to snake through the room, wiping away any lingering tendril of smoke, filling it with the musty, suffocating smell of roses.

Perhaps when my task here was done, I'd burn this manor to the ground, too. Starting with those roses.

Two approaching presences tapped against the back of my mind, and I snatched up another brush, dipping it in the closest swirl of paint, and lowered the invisible, dark snares I'd erected around this room to alert me of any visitors.

I was working on the way the sunlight illuminated the delicate veins in a rose petal, trying not to think of how I'd once seen it do the same to Illyrian wings, when the doors opened.

I made a good show of appearing lost in my work, hunching my shoulders a bit, angling my head. And made an even better show of slowly looking over my shoulder, as if the struggle to part myself from the painting was a true effort.

But the battle was the smile I forced to my mouth. To my eyes—the real tell of a smile's genuine nature. I'd practiced in the mirror. Over and over.

So my eyes easily crinkled as I gave a subdued yet happy smile to Tamlin.

To Lucien.

"Sorry to interrupt," Tamlin said, scanning my face for any sign of the shadows I remembered to occasionally fall prey to, the ones I wielded to keep him at bay when the sun sank beyond those foothills. "But I thought you might want to get ready for the meeting."

I made myself swallow. Lower the paintbrush. No more than the nervous, unsure girl I'd been long ago. "Is—you talked it over with Ianthe? She's truly coming?"

I hadn't seen her yet. The High Priestess who had betrayed my sisters to Hybern, betrayed *us* to Hybern.

And even if Rhysand's murky, swift reports through the mating bond had soothed some of my dread and terror . . . She was responsible for it. What had happened weeks ago.

It was Lucien who answered, studying my painting as if it held the proof I knew he was searching for. "Yes. She . . . had her reasons. She is willing to explain them to you."

Perhaps along with her reasons for laying her hands on whatever males she pleased, whether they wished her to or not. For doing it to Rhys, and Lucien.

I wondered what Lucien truly made of it. And the fact that the collateral in her friendship with Hybern had wound up being *his* mate. Elain.

We had not spoken of Elain save for once, the day after I'd returned. *Despite what Jurian implied regarding how my sisters will be treated by Rhysand*, I had told him, *despite what the Night Court is like*, *they won't hurt Elain or Nesta like that—not yet. Rhysand has more creative ways to harm them.*

Lucien still seemed to doubt it.

But then again, I had also implied, in my own "gaps" of memory, that perhaps I had not received the same creativity or courtesy.

That they believed it so easily, that they thought Rhysand would ever force someone . . . I added the insult to the long, long list of things to repay them for.

I set down the brush and pulled off the paint-flecked smock, carefully laying it on the stool I'd been perched on for two hours now.

"I'll go change," I murmured, flicking my loose braid over a shoulder.

Tamlin nodded, monitoring my every movement as I neared them. "The painting looks beautiful."

"It's nowhere near done," I said, dredging up that girl who had shunned praise and compliments, who had wanted to go unnoticed. "It's still a mess."

Frankly, it was some of my best work, even if its soullessness was only apparent to me.

"I think we all are," Tamlin offered with a tentative smile.

I reined in the urge to roll my eyes, and returned his smile, brushing my hand over his shoulder as I passed.

Lucien was waiting outside my new bedroom when I emerged ten minutes later.

It had taken me two days to stop going to the old one—to turn right at the top of the stairs and not left. But there was nothing in that old bedroom.

I'd looked into it once, the day after I returned.

Shattered furniture; shredded bedding; clothes strewn about as if he'd gone looking for me inside the armoire. No one, it seemed, had been allowed in to clean.

But it was the vines—the thorns—that had made it unlivable. My old bedroom had been overrun with them. They'd curved and slithered over the walls, entwined themselves amongst the debris. As if they'd crawled off the trellises beneath my windows, as if a hundred years had passed and not months.

That bedroom was now a tomb.

I gathered the soft pink skirts of my gauzy dress in a hand and shut the bedroom door behind me. Lucien remained leaning against the door across from mine.

His room.

I didn't doubt he'd ensured I now stayed across from him. Didn't doubt that the metal eye he possessed was always turned toward my own chambers, even while he slept.

"I'm surprised you're so calm, given your promises in Hybern," Lucien said by way of greeting.

The promise I'd made to kill the human queens, the King of Hybern, Jurian, and Ianthe for what they'd done to my sisters. To my friends.

"You yourself said Ianthe had her reasons. Furious as I might be, I can hear her out."

I had not told Lucien of what I knew regarding her true nature. It would mean explaining that Rhys had thrown her out of his own home, that Rhys had done it to defend himself and the members of his court, and it would raise too many questions, undermine too many carefully crafted lies that had kept him and his court—*my* court—safe.

Though I wondered if, after Velaris, it was even necessary. Our enemies knew of the city, knew it was a place of good and peace. And had tried to destroy it at the first opportunity.

The guilt for the attack on Velaris after Rhys had revealed it to those human queens would haunt my mate for the rest of our immortal lives.

"She's going to spin a story that you'll want to hear," Lucien warned.

I shrugged, heading down the carpeted, empty hall. "I can decide for myself. Though it sounds like you've already chosen not to believe her."

He fell into step beside me. "She dragged two innocent women into this."

"She was working to ensure Hybern's alliance held strong."

Lucien halted me with a hand around my elbow.

I allowed it because *not* allowing it, winnowing the way I'd done in the woods those months ago, or using an Illyrian defensive maneuver to knock him on his ass, would ruin my ruse. "You're smarter than that."

I studied the broad, tan hand wrapped around my elbow. Then I met one eye of russet and one of whirring gold.

Lucien breathed, "Where is he keeping her?"

I knew who he meant.

I shook my head. "I don't know. Rhysand has a hundred places where they could be, but I doubt he'd use any of them to hide Elain, knowing that I'm aware of them."

"Tell me anyway. List all of them."

"You'll die the moment you set foot in his territory."

"I survived well enough when I found you."

"You couldn't see that he had me in thrall. You let him take me back." Lie, lie, lie.

But the hurt and guilt I expected weren't there. Lucien slowly released his grip. "I need to find her."

"You don't even know Elain. The mating bond is just a physical reaction overriding your good sense."

"Is that what it did to you and Rhys?"

A quiet, dangerous question. But I made fear enter my eyes, let myself drag up memories of the Weaver, the Carver, the Middengard Wyrm so that old terror drenched my scent. "I don't want to talk about that," I said, my voice a rasping wobble.

A clock chimed on the main level. I sent a silent prayer of thanks to the Mother and launched into a quick walk. "We'll be late."

Lucien only nodded. But I felt his gaze on my back, fixed right on my spine, as I headed downstairs. To see Ianthe.

And at last decide how I was going to shred her into pieces.

The High Priestess looked exactly as I remembered, both in those memories Rhys had shown me and in my own daydreamings of using the talons hidden beneath my nails to carve out her eyes, then her tongue, then open up her throat.

My rage had become a living thing inside my chest, an echoing heartbeat that soothed me to sleep and stirred me to waking. I quieted it as I stared at Ianthe across the formal dining table, Tamlin and Lucien flanking me.

She still wore the pale hood and silver circlet set with its limpid blue stone.

Like a Siphon—the jewel in its center reminded me of Azriel's and Cassian's Siphons. And I wondered if, like the Illyrian warriors', the jewel somehow helped shape an unwieldy gift of magic into something more refined, deadlier. She had never removed it—but then again, I had never seen Ianthe summon any greater power than igniting a ball of faelight in a room.

The High Priestess lowered her teal eyes to the dark wood table, the hood casting shadows on her perfect face. "I wish to begin by saying how truly sorry I am. I acted out of a desire to . . . to grant what I believed you perhaps yearned for but did not dare voice, while also keeping our allies in Hybern satisfied with our allegiance."

Pretty, poisoned lies. But finding her true motive . . . I'd been waiting these weeks for this meeting. Had spent these weeks pretending to convalesce, pretending to *heal* from the horrors I'd survived at Rhysand's hands.

"Why would I ever wish for my sisters to endure that?" My voice came out trembling, cold.

Ianthe lifted her head, scanning my unsure, if not a bit aloof, face. "So you could be with them forever. And if Lucien had discovered that Elain was his mate beforehand, it would have been . . . devastating to realize he'd only have a few decades."

The sound of Elain's name on her lips sent a snarl rumbling up my throat. But I leashed it, falling into that mask of pained quiet, the newest in my arsenal.

Lucien answered, "If you expect our gratitude, you'll be waiting a while, Ianthe."

Tamlin shot him a warning look—both at the words and the tone. Perhaps Lucien would kill Ianthe before I had the chance, just for the horror she'd put his mate through that day.

"No," Ianthe breathed, eyes wide, the perfect picture of remorse and guilt. "No, I don't expect gratitude in the least. Or forgiveness. But understanding . . . This is my home, too." She lifted a slender hand clad in silver rings and bracelets to encompass the room, the manor. "We have all had to make alliances we didn't believe we'd ever forge—perhaps unsavory ones, yes, but . . . Hybern's force is too great to stop. It now can only be weathered like any other storm." A glance toward Tamlin. "We have worked so hard to prepare ourselves for Hybern's inevitable arrival—all these months. I made a grave mistake, and I will always regret any pain I caused, but let us continue this good work together. Let us find a way to ensure our lands and people survive."

"At the cost of how many others?" Lucien demanded.

Again, that warning look from Tamlin. But Lucien ignored him.

"What I saw in Hybern," Lucien said, gripping the arms of his chair hard enough that the carved wood groaned. "Any promises he made of peace and immunity . . ." He halted, as if remembering that Ianthe might very well feed this back to the king. He loosened his grip on the chair, his long fingers flexing before settling on the arms again. "We have to be careful."

"We will be," Tamlin promised. "But we've already agreed to certain conditions. Sacrifices. If we break apart now . . . even with Hybern as our ally, we have to present a solid front. Together."

He still trusted her. Still thought that Ianthe had merely made a bad call. Had no idea what lurked beneath the beauty, the clothes, and the pious incantations.

But then again, that same blindness kept him from realizing what prowled beneath my skin as well. Ianthe bowed her head again. "I will endeavor to be worthy of my friends."

Lucien seemed to be trying very, very hard not to roll his eyes.

But Tamlin said, "We'll all try."

That was his new favorite word: *try*.

I only swallowed, making sure he heard it, and nodded slowly, keeping my eyes on Ianthe. "Don't ever do anything like that again."

A fool's command—one she'd expected me to make, from the quickness with which she nodded. Lucien leaned back in his seat, refusing to say anything else.

"Lucien is right, though," I blurted, the portrait of concern. "What of the people in this court during this conflict?" I frowned at Tamlin. "They were brutalized by Amarantha—I'm not sure how well they will endure living beside Hybern. They have suffered enough."

Tamlin's jaw tightened. "Hybern has promised that our people shall remain untouched and undisturbed." *Our* people. I nearly scowled—even as I nodded again in understanding. "It was a part of our . . . bargain." When he'd sold out all of Prythian, sold out everything decent and good in himself, to *retrieve* me. "Our people will be safe when Hybern arrives. Though I've sent out word that families should . . . relocate to the eastern part of the territory. For the time being."

Good. At least he'd considered those potential casualties—at least he cared that much about his people, understood what sorts of sick games Hybern liked to play and that he might swear one thing but mean another. If he was already moving those most at risk during this conflict out of the way . . . It made my work here all the easier. And east—a bit of information I tucked away. If east was safe, then the west . . . Hybern would indeed be coming from that direction. Arriving there.

Tamlin blew out a breath. "That brings me to the other reason behind this meeting."

I braced myself, schooling my face into bland curiosity, as he declared, "The first delegation from Hybern arrives tomorrow." Lucien's golden skin paled. Tamlin added, "Jurian will be here by noon."

CHAPTER 2

I'd barely heard a whisper of Jurian these past weeks—hadn't seen the resurrected human commander since that night in Hybern.

Jurian had been reborn through the Cauldron using the hideous remnants of him that Amarantha had hoarded as trophies for five hundred years, his soul trapped and aware within his own magically preserved eye. He was mad—had gone mad long before the King of Hybern had resurrected him to lead the human queens down a path of ignorant submission.

Tamlin and Lucien had to know. Had to have seen that gleam in Jurian's eyes.

But . . . they also did not seem to entirely mind that the King of Hybern possessed the Cauldron—that it was capable of cleaving this world apart. Starting with the wall. The only thing standing between the gathering, lethal Fae armies and the vulnerable human lands below.

No, that threat certainly didn't seem to keep Lucien or Tamlin awake at night. Or from inviting these monsters into their home.

Tamlin had promised upon my return that I was to be included in the planning, in every meeting. And he was true to his word when he explained that Jurian would arrive with two other commanders from Hybern, and I would be present for it. They indeed wished to survey the wall, to test for the perfect spot to rend it once the Cauldron had recovered its strength.

Turning my sisters into Fae, apparently, had drained it.

My smugness at the fact was short-lived.

My first task: learn where they planned to strike, and how long the Cauldron required to return to its full capacity. And then smuggle that information to Rhysand and the others.

I took extra care dressing the next day, after sleeping fitfully thanks to a dinner with a guilt-ridden Ianthe, who went to excessive lengths to kiss my ass and Lucien's. The priestess apparently wished to wait until the Hybern commanders were settled before making her appearance. She'd cooed about wanting to ensure they had the chance to get to know us before she intruded, but one look at Lucien told me that he and I, for once, agreed: she had likely planned some sort of grand entrance.

It made little difference to me—to my plans.

Plans that I sent down the mating bond the next morning, words and images tumbling along a night-filled corridor.

I did not dare risk using the bond too often. I had communicated with Rhysand only once since I'd arrived. Just once, in the hours after I'd walked into my old bedroom and spied the thorns that had conquered it.

It had been like shouting across a great distance, like speaking underwater. *I am safe and well*, I'd fired down the bond. *I'll tell you what I know soon.* I'd waited, letting the words travel into the dark. Then I'd asked, *Are they alive? Hurt?*

I didn't remember the bond between us being so hard to hear, even when I'd dwelled on this estate and he'd used it to see if I was still breathing, to make sure my despair hadn't swallowed me whole.

But Rhysand's response had come a minute later. *I love you. They are alive. They are healing.*

That was it. As if it was all that he could manage.

I had drifted back to my new chambers, locked the door, and enveloped the entire place in a wall of hard air to keep any scent from my silent tears escaping as I curled up in a corner of the bathing room.

I had once sat in such a position, watching the stars during the long, bleak hours of the night. Now I took in the cloudless blue sky beyond the open window, listened to the birds singing to one another, and wanted to roar.

I had not dared to ask for more details about Cassian and Azriel—or my sisters. In terror of knowing just how bad it had been—and what I'd do if their healing turned grim. What I'd bring down upon these people.

Healing. Alive and healing. I reminded myself of that every day.

Even when I still heard their screams, smelled their blood.

But I did not ask for more. Did not risk touching the bond beyond that first time.

I didn't know if someone could monitor such things—the silent messages between mates. Not when the mating bond could be scented, and I was playing such a dangerous game with it.

Everyone believed it had been severed, that Rhys's lingering scent was because he'd forced me, had planted that scent in me.

They believed that with time, with distance, his scent would fade. Weeks or months, likely.

And when it didn't fade, when it remained . . . That's when I'd have to strike, with or without the information I needed.

But out of the possibility that communicating down the bond kept its scent strong . . . I had to minimize how much I used it. Even if not talking to Rhys, not hearing that amusement and cunning . . . I would hear those things again, I promised myself over and over. See that wry smile.

And I was again thinking of how pained that face had been the last time I'd seen it, thinking of Rhys, covered in Azriel's and Cassian's blood, as Jurian and the two Hybern commanders winnowed into the gravel of the front drive the next day.

Jurian was in the same light leather armor, his brown hair whipping across his face in the blustery spring breeze. He spied us standing on the white marble steps into the house and his mouth curled in that crooked, smug smile.

I willed ice into my veins, the coldness from a court I had never set foot in. But I wielded its master's gift on myself, turning burning rage into frozen calm as Jurian swaggered toward us, a hand on the hilt of his sword.

But it was the two commanders—one male, one female—that had a sliver of true fear sliding into my heart.

High Fae in appearance, their skin the same ruddy hue and hair the identical inky black as their king. But it was their vacant, unfeeling faces that snagged the eye. A lack of emotion honed from millennia of cruelty.

Tamlin and Lucien had gone rigid by the time Jurian halted at the foot of the sweeping front stairs. The human commander smirked. "You're looking better than the last time I saw you."

I dragged my eyes to his. And said nothing.

Jurian snorted and gestured the two commanders forward. "May I present Their Highnesses, Prince Dagdan and Princess Brannagh, nephew and niece to the King of Hybern."

Twins—perhaps linked in power and mental bonds as well.

Tamlin seemed to remember that these were now his allies and marched down the stairs. Lucien followed.

He'd sold us out. Sold out Prythian—for me. To get me back.

Smoke curled in my mouth. I willed frost to fill it again.

Tamlin inclined his head to the prince and princess. "Welcome to my home. We have rooms prepared for all of you."

"My brother and I shall reside in one together," the princess said. Her voice was deceptively light—almost girlish. The utter lack of feeling, the utter authority was anything but.

I could practically feel the snide remark simmering in Lucien. But I stepped down the stairs and said, ever the lady of the house that these people, that Tamlin, had once expected me to gladly embrace, "We can easily make adjustments."

Lucien's metal eye whirred and narrowed on me, but I kept my face impassive as I curtsied to them. To my enemy. Which of my friends would face them on the battlefield?

Would Cassian and Azriel have even healed enough to fight, let alone lift a sword? I did not allow myself to dwell on it—on how Cassian had screamed as his wings had been shredded.

Princess Brannagh surveyed me: the rose-colored dress, the hair that Alis had curled and braided over the top of my head in a coronet, the pale pink pearls at my ears.

A harmless, lovely package, perfect for a High Lord to mount whenever he wished.

Brannagh's lip curled as she glanced at her brother. The prince deemed the same thing, judging by his answering sneer.

Tamlin snarled softly in warning. "If you're done staring at her, perhaps we can move on to the business between us."

Jurian let out a low chuckle and strode up the stairs without being given leave to do so. "They're curious." Lucien stiffened at the impudence of the gesture, the words. "It's not every century that the contested possession of a female launches a war. Especially a female with such . . . talents."

I only turned on a heel and stalked up the steps after him. "Perhaps if you'd bothered going to war over Miryam, she wouldn't have left you for Prince Drakon."

A ripple seemed to go through Jurian. Tamlin and Lucien tensed at my back, torn between monitoring our exchange and escorting the two Hybern royals into the house. Upon my own explanation that Azriel and his network of spies were well trained, we'd cleared any unnecessary servants, wary of spying ears and eyes. Only the most trusted among them remained.

Of course, I'd forgotten to mention that I knew Azriel had pulled his spies weeks ago, the information not worth the cost of their lives. Or that it served *my* own purposes to have fewer people watching me.

Jurian halted at the top of the stairs, his face a mask of cruel death as I took the last steps to him. "Careful what you say, girl."

I smiled, breezing past. "Or what? You'll throw me in the Cauldron?"

I strode between the front doors, edging around the table in the heart of the entry hall, its towering vase of flowers arching to meet the crystal chandelier.

Right there—just a few feet away, I had crumpled into a ball of terror and despair all those months ago. Right there in the center of the foyer, Mor had picked me up and carried me out of this house and into freedom.

"Here's the first rule of this visit," I said to Jurian over my shoulder as I headed for the dining room, where lunch awaited. "Don't threaten me in my own home."

The posturing, I knew a moment later, had worked.

Not on Jurian, who glowered as he claimed a seat at the table.

But on Tamlin, who brushed a knuckle over my cheek as he passed by, unaware of how carefully I had chosen the words, how I had baited Jurian to serve up the opportunity on a platter.

That was my first step: make Tamlin believe, truly believe, that I loved him and this place, and everyone in it.

So that he would not suspect when I turned them on each other.

Prince Dagdan yielded to his twin's every wish and order. As if he were the blade she wielded to slice through the world.

He poured her drinks, sniffing them first. He selected the finest cuts of meat from the platters and neatly arranged them on her plate. He always let her answer, and never so much as looked at her with doubt in his eyes.

One soul in two bodies. And from the way they glanced to each other in wordless exchanges, I wondered if they were perhaps . . . perhaps like me. *Daemati*.

My mental shields had been a wall of black adamant since arriving. But as we dined, beats of silence going on longer than conversation, I found myself checking them over and over.

"We will set out for the wall tomorrow," Brannagh was saying to Tamlin. More of an order than a request. "Jurian will accompany us. We require the use of sentries who know where the holes in it are located."

The thought of them so close to the human lands . . . But my sisters were not there. No, my sisters were somewhere in the vast territory of my own court, protected by my friends. Even if my father would return home from his business dealings on the continent in a matter of a month or two. I still had not figured out how I'd tell him.

"Lucien and I can escort you," I offered.

Tamlin whipped his head to me. I waited for the refusal, the shutdown.

But it seemed the High Lord had indeed learned his lesson, was indeed willing to *try*, as he merely gestured to Lucien. "My emissary knows the wall as well as any sentry."

You are letting them do this; you are rationally allowing them to bring down that wall and prey upon the humans on the other side. The words tangled and hissed in my mouth.

But I made myself give Tamlin a slow, if not slightly displeased, nod. He knew I'd never be happy about it—the girl he believed had been returned to him would always seek to protect her mortal homeland. Yet he thought I'd stomach it for him, for us. That Hybern wouldn't feast on the humans once that wall came down. That we'd merely absorb them into our territory.

"We'll leave after breakfast," I told the princess. And I added to Tamlin, "With a few sentries as well."

His shoulders loosened at that. I wondered if he'd heard how I'd defended Velaris. That I had protected the Rainbow against a legion of beasts like the Attor. That I had slaughtered the Attor, brutally, cruelly, for what it had done to me and mine.

Jurian surveyed Lucien with a warrior's frankness. "I always wondered who made that eye after she carved it out."

We did not speak of Amarantha here. We had never allowed her presence into this house. And it had stifled me for those months I'd lived here after Under the Mountain, killed me day by day to shove those fears and pain down deep.

For a heartbeat, I weighed who I had been with who I was now supposed to be. Slowly healing—emerging back into the girl Tamlin had fed and sheltered and loved before Amarantha had snapped my neck after three months of torture.

So I shifted in my seat. Studied the table.

Lucien merely leveled a hard look at Jurian as the two Hybern royals watched with impassive faces. "I have an old friend at the Dawn Court. She's skilled at tinkering—blending magic and machinery. Tamlin got her to craft it for me at great risk."

A hateful smile from Jurian. "Does your little mate have a rival?"

"My mate is none of your concern."

Jurian shrugged. "She shouldn't be any of yours, either, considering she's probably been fucked by half the Illyrian army by now."

I was fairly certain that only centuries of training kept Lucien from leaping over the table to rip out Jurian's throat.

But it was Tamlin's snarl that rattled the glasses. "You will behave as a proper guest, Jurian, or you will sleep in the stables like the other beasts."

Jurian merely sipped from his wine. "Why should I be punished for stating the truth? Neither of you were in the War, when my forces allied with the Illyrian brutes." A sidelong glance at the two Hybern royals. "I suppose you two had the delight of fighting against them."

"We kept the wings of their generals and lords as trophies," Dagdan said with a small smile.

It took every bit of concentration not to glance at Tamlin. Not to demand the whereabouts of the two sets of wings his father had kept as trophies after he'd butchered Rhysand's mother and sister.

Pinned in the study, Rhys had said.

But I hadn't spotted any trace when I'd gone hunting for them upon returning here, feigning exploration out of sheer boredom on a rainy day. The cellars had yielded nothing, either. No trunks or crates or locked rooms containing those wings.

The two bites of roasted lamb I'd forced down now rebelled against me. But at least any hint of disgust was a fair reaction to what the Hybern prince had claimed.

Jurian indeed smiled at me as he sliced his lamb into little pieces. "You know that we fought together, don't you? Me and your High Lord. Held the lines against the Loyalists, battled side by side until gore was up to our shins."

"He is not her High Lord," Tamlin said with unnerving softness.

Jurian only purred at me, "He must have told you where he hid Miryam and Drakon."

"They're dead," I said flatly.

"The Cauldron says otherwise."

Cold fear settled into my gut. He'd tried it already—to resurrect Miryam for himself. And had found that she was not amongst the deceased.

"I was told they were dead," I said again, trying to sound bored, impatient. I took a bite of my lamb, so bland compared to the wealth of spices in Velaris. "I'd think you'd have better things to do, Jurian, than obsess over the lover who jilted you."

His eyes gleamed, bright with five centuries of madness, as he skewered a morsel of meat with his fork. "They say you were fucking Rhysand before you ever jilted your own lover."

"That is *enough*," Tamlin growled.

But I felt it then. The tap against my mind. Saw their plan, clear and simple: rile us, distract us, while the two quiet royals slid into our minds.

Mine was shielded. But Lucien's—Tamlin's—

I reached out with my night-kissed power, casting it like a net. And found two oily tendrils spearing for Lucien's and Tamlin's minds, as if they were indeed javelins thrown across the table.

I struck. Dagdan and Brannagh jolted back in their seats as if I'd landed a physical blow, while their powers slammed into a barrier of black adamant around Lucien's and Tamlin's minds.

They shot their dark eyes toward me. I held each of their gazes.

"What's wrong?" Tamlin asked, and I realized how quiet it had become.

I made a good show of furrowing my brow in confusion. "Nothing." I offered a sweet smile to the two royals. "Their Highnesses must be tired after such a long journey."

And for good measure, I lunged for their own minds, finding a wall of white bone.

They flinched as I dragged black talons down their mental shields, gouging deep.

The warning blow cost me, a low, pulsing headache forming around my temples. But I merely dug back into my food, ignoring Jurian's wink.

No one spoke for the rest of the meal.

CHAPTER 3

The spring woods fell silent as we rode between the budding trees, birds and small furred beasts having darted for cover long before we passed.

Not from me, or Lucien, or the three sentries trailing a respectful distance behind. But from Jurian and the two Hybern commanders who rode in the center of our party. As if they were as awful as the Bogge, as the naga.

We reached the wall without incident or Jurian trying to bait us into distraction. I'd been awake most of the night, casting my awareness through the manor, hunting for any sign that Dagdan and Brannagh were working their daemati influence on anyone else. Mercifully, the curse-breaking ability I'd inherited from Helion Spell-Cleaver, High Lord of the Day Court, had detected no tangles, no spells, save for the wards around the house itself, preventing anyone from winnowing in or out.

Tamlin had been tense at breakfast, but had not asked me to remain behind. I'd even gone so far as to test him by asking what was wrong—to which he'd only replied that he had a headache. Lucien had just patted him on the shoulder and promised to look after me. I'd nearly laughed at the words.

But laughter was now far from my lips as the wall pulsed and throbbed, a heavy, hideous presence that loomed from half a mile away. Up close, though . . . Even our horses were skittish, tossing their heads and stomping their hooves on the mossy earth as we tied them to the low-hanging branches of blooming dogwoods.

"The gap in the wall is right up here," Lucien was saying, sounding about as thrilled as me to be in such company. Stomping over the fallen pink blossoms, Dagdan and Brannagh slid into step beside him, Jurian slithering off to survey the terrain, the sentries remaining with our mounts.

I followed Lucien and the royals, keeping a casual distance behind. I knew my elegant, fine clothes weren't fooling the prince and princess into forgetting that a fellow daemati now walked at their backs. But I'd still carefully selected the embroidered sapphire jacket and brown pants—adorned only with the jeweled knife and belt that Lucien had once gifted me. A lifetime ago.

"Who cleaved the wall here?" Brannagh asked, surveying the hole that we could not see—no, the wall itself was utterly invisible—but rather felt, as if the air had been sucked from one spot.

"We don't know," Lucien replied, the dappled sunlight glinting along the gold thread adorning his fawn-brown jacket as he crossed his arms. "Some of the holes just appeared over the centuries. This one is barely wide enough for one person to get through."

An exchanged glance between the twins. I came up behind them, studying the gap, the wall around it that made every instinct recoil at its . . . *wrongness*. "This is where I came through—that first time."

Lucien nodded, and the other two lifted their brows. But I took a step closer to Lucien, my arm nearly brushing his, letting him be a barrier between us. They'd been more careful at breakfast this morning about pushing against my mental shields. Yet now, letting them think I was physically cowed by them . . . Brannagh studied how closely I stood to Lucien; how he shifted slightly to shield me, too.

A little, cold smile curled her lips. "How many holes are in the wall?"

"We've counted three along our entire border," Lucien said tightly. "Plus one off the coast—about a mile away."

I didn't let my cool mask falter as he offered up the information.

But Brannagh shook her head, dark hair devouring the sunlight. "The sea entrances are of no use. We need to break it on the land."

"The continent surely has spots, too."

"Their queens have an even weaker grasp on their people than you do," Dagdan said. I plucked up that gem of information, studied it.

"We'll leave you to explore it, then," I said, waving toward the hole. "When you're done, we'll ride to the next."

"It's two days from here," Lucien countered.

"Then we'll plan a trip for that excursion," I said simply. Before Lucien could object, I asked, "And the third hole?"

Lucien tapped a foot against the mossy ground, but said, "Two days past that."

I turned to the royals, arching a brow. "Can both of you winnow?"

Brannagh flushed, straightening. But it was Dagdan who admitted, "I can." He must have carried both Brannagh and Jurian when they arrived. He added, "Only a few miles if I bear others."

I merely nodded and headed toward a tangle of stooping dogwoods, Lucien following close behind. When there was nothing but ruffling pink blossoms and trickling sunlight through the thatch of branches, when the royals had busied themselves with the wall, out of sight and sound, I took up a perch on a smooth, bald rock.

Lucien sat against a nearby tree, folding one booted ankle over another. "Whatever you're planning, it'll land us knee-deep in shit."

"I'm not planning anything." I plucked up a fallen pink blossom and twirled it between my thumb and forefinger.

That golden eye narrowed, clicking softly.

"What do you even see with that thing?"

He didn't answer.

I chucked the blossom onto the soft moss between us. "Don't trust me? After all we've been through?"

He frowned at the discarded blossom, but still said nothing.

I busied myself by sorting through my pack until I found the canteen of water. "If you'd been alive for the War," I asked him, taking a swig, "would you have fought on their side? Or fought for the humans?"

"I would have been a part of the human-Fae alliance."

"Even if your father wasn't?"

"Especially if my father wasn't."

But Beron had been part of that alliance, if I correctly recalled my lessons with Rhys all those months ago.

"And yet here you are, ready to march with Hybern."

"I did it for you, too, you know." Cold, hard words. "I went with him to get you back."

"I never realized what a powerful motivator guilt can be."

"That day you—went away," he said, struggling to avoid that other word—*left*. "I beat Tamlin back to the manor—received the message when we were out on the border and raced here. But the only trace of you was that ring, melted between the stones of the parlor. I got rid of it a moment before Tam arrived home to see it."

A probing, careful statement. Of the facts that pointed not toward abduction.

"They melted it off my finger," I lied.

His throat bobbed, but he just shook his head, the sunlight leaking through the forest canopy setting the ember-red of his hair flickering.

We sat in silence for minutes. From the rustling and murmuring, the royals were finishing up, and I braced myself, calculating the words I'd need to wield without seeming suspicious.

I said quietly, "Thank you. For coming to Hybern to get me."

He pulled at the moss beside him, jaw tight. "It was a trap. What I thought we were to do there . . . it did not turn out that way."

It was an effort not to bare my teeth. But I walked to him, taking up a place at his side against the wide trunk of the tree. "This situation is terrible," I said, and it was the truth.

A low snort.

I knocked my knee against his. "Don't let Jurian bait you. He's doing it to feel out any weaknesses between us."

"I know."

I turned my face to him, resting my knee against his in silent demand. "Why?" I asked. "*Why* does Hybern want to do this beyond some horrible desire for conquest? What drives him—his people? Hatred? Arrogance?"

Lucien finally looked at me, the intricate pieces and carvings on the metal eye much more dazzling up close. "Do you—"

Brannagh and Dagdan shoved through the bushes, frowning to find us sitting there.

But it was Jurian—right on their heels, as if he'd been divulging the details of his surveying—who smiled at the sight of us, knee to knee and nearly nose to nose.

"Careful, Lucien," the warrior sneered. "You see what happens to males who touch the High Lord's belongings."

Lucien snarled, but I shot him a warning glare.

Point proven, I said silently.

And despite Jurian, despite the sneering royals, a corner of Lucien's mouth tugged upward.

Ianthe was waiting at the stables when we returned.

She'd made her grand arrival at the end of breakfast hours before, breezing into the dining room when the sun was shining in shafts of pure gold through the windows.

I had no doubt she'd planned the timing, just as she had planned the stop in the middle of one of those sunbeams, angled so her hair glowed and the jewel atop her head burned with blue fire. I would have titled the painting *Model Piety*.

After she'd been briefly introduced by Tamlin, she'd mostly cooed over Jurian—who had only scowled at her like some insect buzzing in his ear.

Dagdan and Brannagh had listened to her fawning with enough boredom that I was starting to wonder if the two of them perhaps preferred no one's company but each other's. In whatever unholy capacity. Not a blink of interest toward the beauty who often made males and females stop to gape. Perhaps any sort of physical passion had long ago been drained away, alongside their souls.

So the Hybern royals and Jurian had tolerated Ianthe for about a minute before they'd found their food more interesting. A slight that no doubt explained why she had decided to meet us here, awaiting our return as we rode in.

It was my first time on a horse in months, and I was stiff enough that I could barely move as the party dismounted. I gave Lucien a subtle, pleading look, and he barely hid his smirk as he sauntered over to me.

Our dispersing party watched as he braced my waist in his broad hands and easily hefted me off the horse, none more closely than Ianthe.

I only patted Lucien on the shoulder in thanks. Ever the courtier, he bowed back.

It was hard, sometimes, to remember to hate him. To remember the game I was already playing.

Ianthe trilled, "A successful journey, I hope?"

I jerked my chin toward the royals. "They seemed pleased."

Indeed, whatever they'd been looking for, they'd found agreeable. I hadn't dared ask too many prying questions. Not yet.

Ianthe bowed her head. "Thank the Cauldron for that."

"What do you want," Lucien said a shade too flatly.

She frowned but lifted her chin, folding her hands before her as she said, "We're to have a party in honor of our guests—and to coincide with the Summer Solstice in a few days. I wished to speak to Feyre about it." A two-faced smile. "Unless you have an objection to that."

"He doesn't," I answered before Lucien could say something he'd regret. "Give me an hour to eat and change, and I'll meet you in the study."

Perhaps a tinge more assertive than I'd once been, but she nodded all the same. I linked my elbow with Lucien's and steered him away. "See you soon," I told her, and felt her gaze on us as we walked from the dim stables and into the bright midday light.

His body was taut, near-trembling.

"What happened between you?" I hissed when we were lost among the hedges and gravel paths of the garden.

"It's not worth repeating."

"When I—was taken," I ventured, almost stumbling on the word, almost saying *left*. "Did she and Tamlin . . ."

I was not faking the twisting low in my gut.

"No," he said hoarsely. "No. When Calanmai came along, he refused. He flat-out refused to participate. I replaced him in the Rite, but . . ."

I'd forgotten. Forgotten about Calanmai and the Rite. I did a mental tally of the days.

No wonder I'd forgotten. I'd been in that cabin in the mountains. With Rhys buried in me. Perhaps we'd generated our own magic that night.

But Lucien . . . "You took Ianthe into that cave on Calanmai?"

He wouldn't meet my gaze. "She insisted. Tamlin was . . . Things were bad, Feyre. I went in his stead, and I did my duty to the court. I went of my own free will. And we completed the Rite."

No wonder she'd backed off him. She'd gotten what she wanted.

"Please don't tell Elain," he said. "When we—when we find her again," he amended.

He might have completed the Great Rite with Ianthe of his own free will, but he certainly hadn't enjoyed it. Some line had been blurred—badly.

And my heart shifted a bit in my chest as I said to him with no guile whatsoever, "I won't tell anyone unless you say so." The weight of that jeweled knife and belt seemed to grow. "I wish I had been there to stop it. I should have been there to stop it." I meant every word.

Lucien squeezed our linked arms as we rounded a hedge, the house rising up before us. "You are a better friend to me, Feyre," he said quietly, "than I ever was to you."

Alis frowned at the two dresses hanging from the armoire door, her long brown fingers smoothing over the chiffon and silk.

"I don't know if the waist can be taken out," she said without peering back at where I sat on the edge of the bed. "We took so much of it in that there's not much fabric left to play with . . . You might very well need to order new ones."

She faced me then, running an eye over my robed body.

I knew what she saw—what lies and poisoned smiles couldn't hide: I had become wraith-thin while living here after Amarantha. Yet for all Rhys had done to harm me, I'd gained back the weight I'd lost, put on muscle, and discarded the sickly pallor in favor of sun-kissed skin.

For a woman who had been tortured and tormented for months, I looked remarkably well.

Our eyes held across the room, the silence hewn only by the humming of the few remaining servants in the hallway, busy with preparations for the solstice tomorrow morning.

I'd spent the past two days playing the pretty pet, allowed into meetings with the Hybern royals mostly because I remained quiet. They were as cautious as we were, hedging Tamlin and Lucien's questions about the movements of their armies, their foreign allies—and other allies within

Prythian. The meetings went nowhere, as all *they* wanted to know was information about our own forces.

And about the Night Court.

I fed Dagdan and Brannagh details both true and false, mixing them together seamlessly. I laid out the Illyrian host amongst the mountains and steppes, but selected the strongest clan as their weakest; I mentioned the efficiency of those blue stones from Hybern against Cassian's and Azriel's power but failed to mention how easily they'd worked around them. Any questions I couldn't evade, I feigned memory loss or trauma too great to bear recalling.

But for all my lying and maneuvering, the royals were too guarded to reveal much of their own information. And for all my careful expressions, Alis seemed the only one who noted the tiny tells that even I couldn't control.

"Do you think there are any gowns that will fit for solstice?" I said casually as her silence continued. "The pink and green ones fit, but I've worn them thrice already."

"You never cared for such things," Alis said, clicking her tongue.

"Am I not allowed to change my mind?"

Those dark eyes narrowed slightly. But Alis yanked open the armoire doors, the dresses swaying with it, and riffled through its dark interior. "You could wear this." She held up an outfit.

A set of turquoise Night Court clothes, cut so similarly to Amren's preferred fashion, dangled from her spindly fingers. My heart lurched.

"That—why—" Words stumbled out of me, bulky and slippery, and I silenced myself with a sharp yank on my inner leash. I straightened. "I have never known you to be cruel, Alis."

A snort. She chucked the clothes back into the armoire. "Tamlin shredded the two other sets—missed this one because it was in the wrong drawer."

I wove a mental thread into the hallway to ensure no one was listening. "He was upset. I wish he'd destroyed that pair, too."

"I was there that day, you know," Alis said, folding her spindly arms across her chest. "I saw the Morrigan arrive. Saw her reach into that cocoon of power and pick you up like a child. I begged her to take you out."

My swallow wasn't feigned.

"I never told him that. Never told any of them. I let them think you'd been abducted. But you clung to her, and she was willing to slaughter all of us for what had happened."

"I don't know why you'd assume that." I tugged the edges of my silk robe tighter around me.

"Servants talk. And Under the Mountain, I never heard of or saw Rhysand laying a hand on a servant. Guards, Amarantha's cronies, the people he was ordered to kill, yes. But never the meek. Never those unable to defend themselves."

"He's a monster."

"They say you came back different. Came back wrong." A crow's laugh. "I never bother to tell them I think you came back right. Came back right at last."

A precipice yawned open before me. Lines—there were lines here, and my survival and that of Prythian depended upon navigating them. I rose from the bed, hands shaking slightly.

But then Alis said, "My cousin works in the palace at Adriata."

Summer Court. Alis had originally been from the Summer Court, and had fled here with her two nephews after her sister had been brutally murdered during Amarantha's reign.

"Servants in that palace are not meant to be seen or heard, but they see and hear plenty when no one believes they're present."

She was my friend. She had helped me at great risk Under the Mountain. Had stood by me in the months after. But if she jeopardized everything—

"She said you visited. And that you were healthy, and laughing, and happy."

"It was a lie. He made me act that way." The wobble in my voice didn't take much to summon.

A knowing, crooked smile. "If you say so."

"I *do* say so."

Alis pulled out a dress of creamy white. "You never got to wear this one. I had it ordered for after your wedding day."

It wasn't exactly bride-like, but rather pure. Clean. The kind of gown I'd have resented when I returned from Under the Mountain, desperate to avoid any comparison to my ruined soul. But now . . . I held Alis's stare, and wondered which of my plans she'd deciphered.

Alis whispered, "I will only say this once. Whatever you plan to do, I beg you leave my boys out of it. Take whatever retribution you desire, but please spare them."

I would never—I almost began. But I only shook my head, knotting my brows, utterly confused and distressed. "All I want is to settle back into life here. To heal."

Heal the land of the corruption and darkness spreading across it.

Alis seemed to understand it, too. She set the dress on the armoire door, airing out the loose, shining skirts.

"Wear this on solstice," she said quietly.

So I did.

CHAPTER 4

Summer Solstice was exactly as I had remembered: streamers and ribbons and garlands of flowers everywhere, casks of ale and wine hauled out to the foothills surrounding the estate, High Fae and lesser faeries alike flocking to the celebrations.

But what had not existed here a year ago was Ianthe.

The celebrating would be sacrilege, she intoned, if we did not give thanks first.

So we all were up two hours before the dawn, bleary-eyed and none of us too keen to endure her ceremony as the sun crested the horizon on the longest day of the year. I wondered if Tarquin had to weather such tedious rituals in his shining palace by the sea. Wondered what sort of celebrations would occur in Adriata today, with the High Lord of Summer who had come so very close to being a friend.

As far as I knew, despite the murmurings between servants, Tarquin still had never sent word to Tamlin about the visit Rhys, Amren, and I had made. What did the Summer lord now think of my changed circumstances? I had little doubt Tarquin had heard. And I prayed he stayed out of it until my work here was finished.

Alis had found me a luxurious white velvet cloak for the brisk ride into the hills, and Tamlin had lifted me onto a moon-pale mare with wildflowers woven into her silver mane. If I had wanted to paint a picture of serene purity, it would have been the image I cast that morning, my hair braided above my head, a crown of white hawthorn blossoms upon it. I'd dabbed rouge onto my cheeks and lips—a slight hint of color. Like the first blush of spring across a winter landscape.

As our procession arrived at the hill, a gathered crowd of hundreds already atop it, all eyes turned to me. But I kept my gaze ahead, to where Ianthe stood before a rudimentary stone altar bedecked in flowers and the first fruits and grains of summer. The hood was off her pale blue robe for once, the silver circlet now resting directly atop her golden head.

I smiled at her, my mare obediently pausing at the northern arc of the half circle that the crowd had formed around the hill's edge and Ianthe's altar, and wondered if Ianthe could spy the wolf grinning beneath.

Tamlin helped me off the horse, the gray light of predawn shimmering along the golden threads in his green jacket. I forced myself to meet his eyes as he set me on the soft grass, aware of every other stare upon us.

The memory gleamed in his gaze—in the way his gaze dipped to my mouth.

A year ago, he had kissed me on this day. A year ago, I'd danced amongst these people, carefree and joyous for the first time in my life, and had believed it was the happiest I'd ever been and ever would be.

I gave him a little, shy smile and took the arm he extended. Together, we crossed the grass toward Ianthe's stone altar, the Hybern royals, Jurian, and Lucien trailing behind.

I wondered if Tamlin was also remembering another day all those months ago, when I'd worn a different white gown, when there had also been flowers strewn about.

When my mate had rescued me after I'd decided not to go through with the wedding, some fundamental part of me knowing it wasn't right. I had believed I didn't deserve it, hadn't wanted to burden Tamlin for an eternity with someone as broken as I'd been at the time. And Rhys . . . Rhys would have let me marry him, believing me to be happy, wanting me to be happy even if it killed him. But the moment I had said no . . . He had saved me. Helped me save myself.

I glanced sidelong at Tamlin.

But he was studying my hand, braced on his arm. The empty finger where that ring had once perched.

What did he make of it—where did he think that ring had gone, if Lucien had hidden the evidence? For a heartbeat, I pitied him.

Pitied that not only Lucien had lied to him, but Alis as well. How many others had seen the truth of my suffering—and tried to spare *him* from it?

Seen my suffering and done nothing to help *me*.

Tamlin and I paused before the altar, Ianthe offering us a serene, regal nod.

The Hybern royals shifted on their feet, not bothering to hide their impatience. Brannagh had made barely veiled complaints about the solstice at dinner last night, declaring that in Hybern they did not bother with such odious things and got on with the revelry. And implying, in her way, that soon, neither would we.

I ignored the royals as Ianthe lifted her hands and called to the crowd behind us, "A blessed solstice to us all."

Then began an endless string of prayers and rituals, her prettiest young acolytes assisting with the pouring of sacred wine, with the blessing of the harvest goods on the altar, with beseeching the sun to rise.

A lovely, rehearsed little number. Lucien was half-asleep behind me.

But I'd gone over the ceremony with Ianthe, and knew what was coming when she lifted the sacred wine and intoned, "As the light is strongest today, let it drive out unwanted darkness. Let it banish the black stain of evil."

Jab after jab at my mate, my home. But I nodded along with her.

"Would Princess Brannagh and Prince Dagdan do us the honor of imbibing this blessed wine?"

The crowd shifted. The Hybern royals blinked, frowning to each other.

But I stepped aside, smiling prettily at them and gesturing to the altar.

They opened their mouths, no doubt to refuse, but Ianthe would not be denied. "Drink, and let our new allies become new friends," she declared. "Drink, and wash away the endless night of the year."

The two daemati were likely testing that cup for poison through whatever magic and training they possessed, but I kept the bland smile on my face as they finally approached the altar and Brannagh accepted the outstretched silver cup.

They each barely had a sip before they made to step back. But Ianthe cooed at them, insisting they come behind the altar to witness our ceremony at her side.

I had made sure she knew precisely how disgusted they were with her rituals. How they would do their best to stomp out her usefulness as a leader of her people once they arrived. She now seemed inclined to convert them.

More prayers and rituals, until Tamlin was summoned to the other side of the altar to light a candle for the souls extinguished in the past year—to now bring them back into the light's embrace when the sun rose.

Pink began to stain the clouds behind them.

Jurian was also called forward to recite one final prayer I'd requested Ianthe add, in honor of the warriors who fought for our safety each day.

And then Lucien and I were standing alone in the circle of grass, the altar and horizon before us, the crowd at our backs and sides.

From the rigidity of his posture, the dart of his gaze over the site, I knew he was now running through the prayers and how I had worked with Ianthe on the ceremony. How he and I remained on this side of the line right as the sun was about to break over the world, and the others had been maneuvered away.

Ianthe stepped toward the hill's edge, her golden hair tumbling freely down her back as she lifted her arms to the sky. The location was intentional, as was the positioning of her arms.

She'd made the same gesture on Winter Solstice, standing in the precise spot where the sun would rise between her upraised arms, filling them with light. Her acolytes had discreetly marked the place in the grass with a carved stone.

Slowly, the golden disc of the sun broke over the hazy greens and blues of the horizon.

Light filled the world, clear and strong, spearing right for us.

Ianthe's back arched, her body a mere vessel for the solstice's light to fill, and what I could see of her face was already limned in pious ecstasy.

The sun rose, a held, gilded note echoing through the land.

The crowd began to murmur.

Then cry out.

Not at Ianthe.

But at me.

At me, resplendent and pure in white, beginning to glow with the light of day as the sun's path flowed directly over me instead.

No one had bothered to confirm or even notice that Ianthe's marker stone had moved five feet to the right, too busy with my parading arrival to spy a phantom wind slide it through the grass.

It took Ianthe longer than anyone else to look.

To turn to see that the sun's power was not filling her, blessing her.

I released the damper on the power that I had unleashed in Hybern, my body turning incandescent as light shone through. Pure as day, pure as starlight.

"Cursebreaker," some murmured. "Blessed," others whispered.

I made a show of looking surprised—surprised and yet accepting of the Cauldron's choice. Tamlin's face was taut with shock, the Hybern royals' nothing short of baffled.

But I turned to Lucien, my light radiating so brightly that it bounced off his metal eye. A friend beseeching another for help. I reached a hand toward him.

Beyond us, I could feel Ianthe scrambling to regain control, to find some way to spin it.

Perhaps Lucien could, too. For he took my hand, and then knelt upon one knee in the grass, pressing my fingers to his brow.

Like stalks of wheat in a wind, the others fell to their knees as well.

For in all of her preening ceremonies and rituals, never had Ianthe revealed any sign of power or blessing. But Feyre Cursebreaker, who had led Prythian from tyranny and darkness . . .

Blessed. Holy. Undimming before evil.

I let my glow spread, until it, too, rippled from Lucien's bowed form.

A knight before his queen.

When I looked to Ianthe and smiled again, I let a little bit of the wolf show.

The festivities, at least, remained the same.

Once the uproar and awe had ebbed, once my own glow had vanished when the sun crested higher than my head, we made our way to the nearby hills and fields, where those who had not attended the ceremony had already heard about my small miracle.

I kept close to Lucien, who was inclined to indulge me, as everyone seemed to be torn between joy and awe, question and concern.

Ianthe spent the next six hours trying to explain what had happened. The Cauldron had blessed her chosen friend, she told whoever would listen. The sun had altered its very path to show how glad it was for my return.

Only her acolytes really paid attention, and half of them appeared only mildly interested.

Tamlin, however, seemed the wariest—as if the blessing had somehow upset me, as if he remembered that same light in Hybern and could not figure out why it disturbed him so.

But duty had him fielding thanks and good wishes from his subjects, warriors, and the lesser lords, leaving me free to wander. I was stopped every now and then by fervent, adoring faeries who wished to touch my hand, to weep a bit over me.

Once, I would have cringed and winced. Now I received their thanks and prayers beatifically, thanking them, smiling at them.

Some of it was genuine. I had no quarrel with the people of these lands, who had suffered alongside the rest. None. But the courtiers and sentries who sought me out . . . I put on a better show for them. Cauldron-blessed, they called me. *An honor*, I merely replied.

On and on I repeated those words, through breakfast and lunch, until I returned to the house to freshen up and take a moment for myself.

In the privacy of my room, I set my crown of flowers on the dressing table and smiled slightly at the eye tattooed into my right palm.

The longest day of the year, I said into the bond, sending along flickers of all that had occurred atop that hill. *I wish I could spend it with you.*

He would have enjoyed my performance—would have laughed himself hoarse afterward at the expression on Ianthe's face.

I finished washing up and was about to head out into the hills again when Rhysand's voice filled my mind.

It'd be an honor, he said, laughter in every word, *to spend even a moment in the company of Feyre Cauldron-blessed.*

I chuckled. The words were distant, strained. Keep it quick—I had to keep it quick, or risk exposure. And more than anything, I needed to ask, to know—

Is everyone all right?

I waited, counting the minutes. *Yes. As well as we can be. When do you come home to me?*

Each word was quieter than the last.

Soon, I promised him. *Hybern is here. I'll be done soon.*

He didn't reply—and I waited another few minutes before I again donned my flower crown and strode down the stairs.

As I emerged into the bedecked garden, though, Rhysand's faint voice filled my head once more. *I wish I could spend today with you, too.*

The words wrapped a fist around my heart, and I forced them from my mind as I returned to the party in the hills, my steps heavier than they'd been when I floated into the house.

But lunch had been cleared away, and dancing had begun.

I saw him waiting on the outskirts of one of the circles, observing every move I took.

I glanced between the grass and the crowd and the cluster of musicians coaxing such lively music from drums and fiddles and pipes as I approached, no more than a shy, hesitant doe.

Once, those same sounds had shaken me awake, had made me dance and dance. I supposed they were now little more than weapons in my arsenal as I stopped before Tamlin, lowered my lashes, and asked softly, "Will you dance with me?"

Relief, happiness, and a slight edge of concern. "Yes," he breathed. "Yes, of course."

So I let him lead me into the swift dance, spinning and tilting me, people gathering to cheer and clap. Dance after dance after dance, until sweat was running down my back as I worked to keep up, keep that smile on my face, to remember to laugh when my hands were within strangling distance of his throat.

The music eventually shifted into something slower, and Tamlin eased us into the melody. When others had found their own partners more interesting to watch, he murmured, "This morning . . . Are you all right?"

My head snapped up. "Yes. I—I don't know what that was, but yes. Is Ianthe . . . mad?"

"I don't know. She didn't see it coming—I don't think she handles surprises very well."

"I should apologize."

His eyes flashed. "What for? Perhaps it was a blessing. Magic still surprises *me*. If she's angry, it's her problem."

I made a show of considering, then nodded. Pressed closer, loathing every place where our bodies touched. I didn't know how Rhys had endured it—endured Amarantha. For five decades.

"You look beautiful today," Tamlin said.

"Thank you." I made myself peer up into his face. "Lucien—Lucien told me that you didn't complete the Rite at Calanmai. That you refused."

And you let Ianthe take him into that cave instead.

His throat bobbed. "I couldn't stomach it."

And yet you could stomach making a deal with Hybern, as if I were a stolen item to be returned. "Maybe this morning was not just a blessing for me," I offered.

A stroke of his hand down my back was his only reply.

That was all we said for the next three dances, until hunger dragged me toward the tables where dinner had now been laid out. I let him fill a plate for me, let him serve me himself as we found a spot under a twisted old oak and watched the dancing and the music.

I nearly asked if it was worth it—if giving up this sort of peace was worth it, in order to have me back. For Hybern would come here, use these lands. And there would be no more singing and dancing. Not once they arrived.

But I kept quiet as the sunlight faded and night finally fell.

The stars winked into existence, dim and small above the blazing fires.

I watched them through the long hours of celebrating, and could have sworn that they kept me company, my silent and stalwart friends.

CHAPTER 5

I crawled back to the manor two hours after midnight, too exhausted to last until dawn.

Especially when I noted the way Tamlin looked at me, remembering that dawn last year when he'd led me away and kissed me as the sun rose.

I asked Lucien to escort me, and he'd been more than happy to do so, given that his own status as a mated male made him uninterested in any sort of female company these days. And given that Ianthe had been trying to corner him all day to ask about what had happened at the ceremony.

I changed into my nightgown, a small, lacy thing I'd once worn for Tamlin's enjoyment and now was glad to don thanks to the day's sweat still clinging to my skin, and flopped into bed.

For nearly half an hour, I kicked at the sheets, tossing and turning, thrashing.

The Attor. The Weaver. My sisters being thrown into the Cauldron. All of them twined and eddied around me. I let them.

Most of the others were still celebrating when I yelped, a sharp, short cry that had me bouncing from the bed.

My heart thundered along my veins, my bones, as I cracked open the door, sweating and haggard, and padded across the hall.

Lucien answered on the second knock.

"I heard you—what's wrong." He scanned me, russet eye wide as he noted my disheveled hair, my sweaty nightgown.

I swallowed, a silent question on my face, and he nodded, retreating into the room to let me inside. Bare from the waist up, he'd managed to haul on a pair of pants before opening the door, and hastily buttoned them as I strode past.

His room had been bedecked in Autumn Court colors—the only tribute to his home he'd ever let show—and I surveyed the night-dark space, the rumpled bedsheets. He perched on the rolled arm of a large chair before the blackened fire, watching me wring my hands in the center of the crimson carpet.

"I dream about it," I rasped. "Under the Mountain. And when I wake up, I can't remember where I am." I lifted my now-unmarred left arm before me. "I can't remember *when* I am."

Truth—and half a lie. I still dreamed of those horrible days, but no longer did they consume me. No longer did I run to the bathroom in the middle of the night to hurl my guts up.

"What did you dream of tonight?" he asked quietly.

I dragged my eyes to his, haunted and bleak. "She had me spiked to the wall. Like Clare Beddor. And the Attor was—"

I shuddered, running my hands over my face.

Lucien rose, stalking to me. The ripple of fear and pain at my own words masked my scent enough, masked my own power as my dark snares picked up a slight vibration in the house.

Lucien paused half a foot from me. He didn't so much as object as I threw my arms around his neck, burying my face against his warm, bare chest. It was seawater from Tarquin's own gift that slipped from my eyes, down my face, and onto his golden skin.

Lucien loosed a heavy sigh and slid an arm around my waist, the other threading through my hair to cradle my head. "I'm sorry," he murmured. "I'm sorry."

He held me, stroking soothing lines down my back, and I calmed my weeping, those seawater tears drying up like wet sand in the sun.

I lifted my head from his sculpted chest at last, my fingers digging into the hard muscles of his shoulders as I peered into his concerned face. I took deep, heaving breaths, my brows knotting and mouth parting as I—

"What's going on."

Lucien whipped his head toward the door.

Tamlin stood there, face a mask of cold calm. The beginnings of claws glinted at his knuckles.

We pushed away, too swiftly to be casual. "I had a nightmare," I explained, straightening my nightgown. "I—I didn't want to wake the house."

Tamlin was just staring at Lucien, whose mouth had tightened into a thin line as he marked those claws, still half-drawn.

"I had a nightmare," I repeated a bit sharply, gripping Tamlin's arm and leading him from the room before Lucien could so much as open his mouth.

I closed the door, but could still feel Tamlin's attention fixed on the male behind it. He didn't sheath his claws. Didn't summon them any further, either.

I strode the few feet to my room, watching Tamlin assess the hall. The distance between my door and Lucien's. "Good night," I said, and shut the door in Tamlin's face.

I waited the five minutes it took Tamlin to decide not to kill Lucien, and then smiled.

I wondered if Lucien had pieced it together. That I had known Tamlin would come to my room tonight, after I had given him so many shy touches and glances today. That I had changed into my most indecent nightgown not for the heat, but so that when my invisible snares in the house informed me that Tamlin had finally worked up the nerve to come to my bedroom, I'd look the part.

A feigned nightmare, the evidence set into place with my thrashed sheets. I'd left Lucien's door open, with him too distracted and unsuspecting of why I'd really be there to bother to shut it, or notice the shield of hard air I'd placed around the room so that he wouldn't hear or scent Tamlin as he arrived.

Until Tamlin saw us there, limbs entwined, my nightgown askew, staring at each other so intently, so full of *emotion* that we'd either just been starting or finishing up. That we didn't even notice until Tamlin was right there—and that invisible shield vanished before he could sense it.

A nightmare, I'd told Tamlin.

I was the nightmare.

Preying on what Tamlin had feared from my very first days here.

I had not forgotten that long-ago fight he'd picked with Lucien. The warning he'd given him to stop flirting with me. To stay away. The fear that I'd preferred the red-haired lord over him and that it would threaten every plan he had. *Back off*, he'd told Lucien.

I had no doubt Tamlin was now running through every look and conversation since then. Every time Lucien had intervened on my behalf, both Under the Mountain and afterward. Weighing how much that new mating bond with Elain held sway over his friend.

Considering how this very morning, Lucien had knelt before me, swearing fealty to a newborn god, as if we had both been Cauldron-blessed.

I let myself smile for a moment longer, then dressed.

There was more work to do.

CHAPTER 6

A set of keys to the estate gates had gone missing.

But after last night's incident, Tamlin didn't appear to care.

Breakfast was silent, the Hybern royals sullen at being kept waiting so long to see the second cleft in the wall, and Jurian, for once, too tired to do anything but shovel meat and eggs into his hateful mouth.

Tamlin and Lucien, it seemed, had spoken before the meal, but the latter made a point to keep a healthy distance from me. To not look at or speak to me, as if still needing to convince Tamlin of our innocence.

I debated asking Jurian outright if he'd stolen the keys from whatever guard had lost them, but the silence was a welcome reprieve.

Until Ianthe breezed in, carefully avoiding acknowledging me, as if I was indeed the blinding sun that had been stolen from her.

"I am sorry to interrupt your meal, but there is a matter to discuss, High Lord," Ianthe said, pale robes swirling at her feet as she halted halfway to the table.

All of us perked up at that.

Tamlin, brooding and snarly, demanded, "What is it."

She made a show of realizing the Hybern royals were present.

Listening. I tried not to snort at the oh-so-nervous glance she threw their way, then to Tamlin. The next words were no surprise whatsoever. "Perhaps we should wait until after the meal. When you are alone."

No doubt a power play, to remind them that she did, in fact, have sway here—with Tamlin. That Hybern, too, might want to remain on her good side, considering the *information* she bore. But I was cruel enough to say sweetly, "If we can trust our allies in Hybern to go to war with us, then we can trust them to use discretion. Go ahead, Ianthe."

She didn't so much as look in my direction. But now caught between outright insult and politeness . . . Tamlin weighed our company against Ianthe's posture and said, "Let's hear it."

Her white throat bobbed. "There is . . . My acolytes discovered that the land around my temple is . . . dying."

Jurian rolled his eyes and went back to his bacon.

"Then tell the gardeners," Brannagh said, returning to her own food. Dagdan snickered into his cup of tea.

"It is not a matter of gardening." Ianthe straightened. "It is a blight upon the land. Grass, root, bud—all of it, shriveled up and sickly. It reeks of the naga."

It was an effort not to glance to Lucien—to see if he also noticed the too-eager gleam in her eye. Even Tamlin loosed a sigh, as if he saw it for what it was: an attempt to regain some ground, perhaps a scheme to poison the earth and then miraculously heal it.

"There are other spots in the woods where things have died and are not coming back," Ianthe went on, pressing a silver-adorned hand to her chest. "I fear it's a warning that the naga are gathering—and plan to attack."

Oh, I'd gotten under her skin. I'd been wondering what she'd do after yesterday's solstice, after I'd robbed her of her moment and power. But this . . . Clever.

I hid my smirk down deep and said gently, "Ianthe, perhaps it *is* a case for the groundskeepers."

She stiffened, at last facing me. *You think you're playing the game*, I itched to tell her, *but you have no idea that every choice you made last night and this morning were only steps I nudged you toward.*

I jerked my chin toward the royals, then Lucien. "We're heading out this afternoon to survey the wall, but if the problem remains when we return in a few days, I'll help you look into it."

Those silver-ringed fingers curled into loose fists at her sides. But like the true viper she was, Ianthe said to Tamlin, "Will you be joining them, High Lord?"

She looked to me and Lucien—the assessment too lingering to be casual.

A faint, low headache was already forming, made worse with every word out of her mouth. I'd been up too late, and had gotten too little sleep—and I needed my strength for the days ahead. "He will not," I said, cutting off Tamlin before he could reply.

He set down his utensils. "I think I will."

"I don't need an escort." Let him unravel the layers of defensiveness in that statement.

Jurian snorted. "Starting to doubt our good intentions, High Lord?"

Tamlin snarled at him. "Careful."

I placed a hand flat on the table. "I'll be fine with Lucien and the sentries."

Lucien seemed inclined to sink into his seat and disappear forever.

I surveyed Dagdan and Brannagh and smiled a bit. "I can defend myself, if it comes to that," I said to Tamlin.

The daemati smiled back at me. I hadn't felt another touch on my mental barriers, or the ones I'd been working to keep around as many people here as possible. The constant use of my power was wearing on me, however—being away from this place for four or five days would be a welcome relief.

Especially as Ianthe murmured to Tamlin, "Perhaps you *should* go, my friend." I waited—waited for whatever nonsense was about to come out of that pouty mouth— "You never know when the Night Court will attempt to snatch her away."

I had a blink to debate my reaction. To opt for leaning back in my chair, shoulders curling inward, hauling up those images of Clare, of Rhys with those ash arrows through his wings—any sort of way to dredge my scent in fear. "Have you news?" I whispered.

Brannagh and Dagdan looked *very* interested at that.

The priestess opened her mouth, but Jurian cut her off, drawling, "There is no news. Their borders are secure. Rhysand would be a fool to push his luck by coming here."

I stared at my plate, the portrait of bowed terror.

"A fool, yes," Ianthe countered, "but one with a vendetta." She faced Tamlin, the morning sun catching in the jewel atop her head. "Perhaps if you returned to him his family's wings, he might . . . settle."

For a heartbeat, silence rippled through me.

Followed by a wave of roaring that drowned out nearly every thought, every self-preserving instinct. I could barely hear over that bellowing in my blood, my bones.

But the words, the offer . . . A cheap attempt at snaring me. I pretended not to hear, not to care. Even as I waited and waited for Tamlin's reply.

When Tamlin answered, his voice was low. "I burned them a long time ago."

I could have sworn there was something like remorse—remorse and shame—in his words.

Ianthe only tsked. "Too bad. He might have paid handsomely for them."

My limbs ached with the effort of not leaping over the table to smash her head into the marble floor.

But I said to Tamlin, soothing and gentle, "I'll be fine out there." I touched his hand, brushing my thumb over the back of his palm. Held his stare. "Let's not start down this road again."

As I pulled away, Tamlin merely fixed Lucien with a look, any trace of that guilt gone. His claws slid free, embedding in the scar-flecked wood of his chair's arm. "Be careful."

None of us pretended it was anything but a threat.

It was a two-day ride, but took us only a day to get there with winnowing-walking-winnowing. We could manage a few miles at a time, but Dagdan was slower than I'd anticipated, given that he had to carry his sister and Jurian.

I didn't fault him for it. With each of us bearing another, the drain was considerable. Lucien and I both bore a sentry, minor lords' sons who had been trained to be polite and watchful. Supplies, as a result, were limited. Including tents.

By the time we made it to the cleft in the wall, darkness was falling.

The few supplies we'd hauled also had encumbered our winnowing through the world, and I let the sentries erect the tents for us, ever the lady keen to be waited on. Our dinner around the small fire was near-silent, none of us bothering to speak, save for Jurian, who questioned the sentries endlessly about their training. The twins retreated to their own tent after they'd picked at the meat sandwiches we'd packed, frowning at them as if they were full of maggots instead, and Jurian wandered off into the woods soon after, claiming he wanted a walk before he retired.

I hauled myself into the canvas tent when the fire was dying out, the space barely big enough for Lucien and me to sleep shoulder to shoulder.

His red hair gleamed in the faint firelight a moment later as he shoved through the flaps and swore. "Maybe I should sleep out there."

I rolled my eyes. "Please."

A wary, considering glance as he knelt and removed his boots. "You know Tamlin can be . . . sensitive about things."

"He can also be a pain in my ass," I snapped, and slithered under the blankets. "If you yield to him on every bit of paranoia and territorialism, you'll just make it worse."

Lucien unbuttoned his jacket but remained mostly dressed as he slid onto his sleeping roll. "I think it's made worse because you two haven't . . . I mean, you haven't, right?"

I stiffened, tugging the blanket higher onto my shoulders. "No. I don't want to be touched like that—not for a while."

His silence was heavy—sad. I hated the lie, hated it for how filthy it felt to wield it. "I'm sorry," he said. And I wondered what else he was apologizing for as I faced him in the darkness of our tent.

"Isn't there some way to get out of this deal with Hybern?" My words were barely louder than the murmuring embers outside. "I'm back, I'm safe. We could find some way around it—"

"No. The King of Hybern crafted his bargain with Tamlin too cleverly, too clearly. Magic bound them—magic will strike him if he does not allow Hybern into these lands."

"In what way? Kill him?"

Lucien's sigh ruffled my hair. "It will claim his own powers, maybe kill him. Magic is all about balance. It's why he couldn't interfere with your bargain with Rhysand. Even the person who tries to sever the bargain faces consequences. If he'd kept you here, the magic that bound you to Rhys might have come to claim *his* life as payment for yours. Or the life of someone else he cared about. It's old magic—old and strange. It's why we avoid bargains unless it's necessary: even the scholars at the Day Court don't know how it works. Believe me, I've asked."

"For me—you asked them for me."

"Yes. I went last winter to inquire about breaking your bargain with Rhys."

"Why didn't you tell me?"

"I—we didn't want to give you false hope. And we didn't dare let Rhysand get wind of what we were doing, in case he found a way to interfere. To stop it."

"So Ianthe pushed Tamlin to Hybern instead."

"He was frantic. The scholars at the Day Court worked too slowly. I begged him for more time, but you'd already been gone for months. He wanted to act, not wait—despite that letter you sent. *Because* of that letter you sent. I finally told him to go ahead with it after—after that day in the forest."

I turned onto my back, staring at the sloped ceiling of the tent.

"How bad was it?" I asked quietly.

"You saw your room. He trashed it, the study, his bedroom. He—he killed the sentries who'd been on guard. After he got the last bit of information from them. He executed them in front of everyone in the manor."

My blood chilled. "You didn't stop him."

"I tried. I begged him for mercy. He didn't listen. He *couldn't* listen."

"The sentries didn't try to stop him, either?"

"They didn't dare. Feyre, he's a High Lord. He's a different *breed*."

I wondered if he'd say the same thing if he knew what I was.

"We were backed into a corner with no options. None. It was either go to war with the Night Court *and* Hybern, or ally with Hybern, let them try to stir up trouble, and then use that alliance to our own advantage further down the road."

"What do you mean," I breathed.

But Lucien realized what he'd said, and hedged, "We have enemies in every court. Having Hybern's alliance will make them think twice."

Liar. Trained, clever liar.

I loosed a heaving, sleepy breath. "Even if they're now our allies," I mumbled, "I still hate them."

A snort. "Me too."

✢

"Get up."

Blinding sunlight cut into the tent, and I hissed.

The order was drowned out by Lucien's snarl as he sat up. "*Out*," he ordered Jurian, who looked us over once, sneered, and stalked away.

I'd rolled onto Lucien's bedroll at some point, any schemes indeed second to my most pressing demand—warmth. But I had no doubt Jurian would tuck away the information to throw in Tamlin's face when we returned: we'd shared a tent, and had been *very* cozy upon awakening.

I washed in the nearby stream, my body stiff and aching from a night on the ground, with or without the help of a bedroll.

Brannagh was prowling for the stream by the time I'd finished. The princess gave me a cold, thin smile. "I'd pick Beron's son, too."

I stared at the princess beneath lowered brows.

She shrugged, her smile growing. "Autumn Court males have fire in their blood—and they fuck like it, too."

"I suppose you know from experience?"

A chuckle. "Why do you think I had so much fun in the War?"

I didn't bother to hide my disgust.

Lucien caught me cringing at him when her words replayed for the tenth time an hour later, while we hiked the half mile toward the crack in the wall. "What?" he demanded.

I shook my head, trying not to imagine Elain subject to that . . . fire. "Nothing," I said, just as Jurian swore ahead.

We were both moving at his barked curse—and then broke into a run at the sound of a sword whining free of its sheath. Leaves and branches whipped at me, but then we were at the wall, that invisible, horrible marker humming and throbbing in my head.

And staring right at us through the hole were three Children of the Blessed.

CHAPTER 7

Brannagh and Dagdan looked like they'd just found second breakfast waiting for them.

Jurian had his sword out, the two young women and one young man gaping between him and the others. Then at us, their eyes widening further as they noted Lucien's cruel beauty.

They dropped to their knees. "Masters and Mistresses," they beseeched us, their silver jewelry glinting in the dappled sunlight through the leaves. "You have found us on our journey."

The two royals smiled so broadly I could see all of their too-white teeth.

Jurian, for once, seemed torn before he snapped, "What are you doing here?"

The dark-haired girl at the front was lovely, her honey-gold skin flushed as she lifted her head. "We have come to dwell in the immortal lands; we have come as tribute."

Jurian cut cold, hard eyes to Lucien. "Is this true?"

Lucien stared him down. "We accept no tribute from the human lands. Least of all children."

Never mind that the three of them appeared only a few years younger than myself.

"Why don't you come through," Brannagh cooed, "and we can . . . enjoy ourselves." She was indeed sizing up the brown-haired young man and the other girl, her hair a ruddy brown, face sharp but interesting. From the way Dagdan was leering at the beautiful girl in front, I knew he'd silently made his claim already.

I shoved in front of them and said to the three mortals, "Get out. Go back to your villages, back to your families. You cross this wall, and you will die."

They balked, rising to their feet, faces taut with fear—and awe. "We have come to live in peace."

"There is no such thing here. There is only death for your kind."

Their eyes slid to the immortals behind me. The dark-haired girl blushed at Dagdan's intent stare, seeing the High Fae beauty and none of the predator.

So I struck.

The wall was a screeching, terrible vise, crushing my magic, battering my head.

But I speared my power through that gap, and slammed into their minds.

Too hard. The young man flinched a bit.

So soft—defenseless. Their minds yielded like butter melting on my tongue.

I beheld pieces of their lives like shards in a broken mirror, flashing every which way: the dark-haired girl was rich, educated, headstrong—had wanted to escape an arranged marriage and believed Prythian was a better option. The ruddy-haired girl had known nothing but poverty and her father's fists, which had turned more violent after they'd ended her mother's life. The young man had sold himself on the streets of a large village until the Children had come one day and offered him something better.

I worked quickly. Neatly.

I was finished before three heartbeats had passed, before Brannagh had even drawn breath to say, "There is no death here. Only pleasure, if you are willing."

Even if they weren't willing, I wanted to add.

But the three of them now blinked—balking.

Beholding us for what we were: deadly, merciless. The truth behind the spun stories.

"We—perhaps have . . . made a mistake," their leader said, retreating a step.

"Or perhaps this was fate," Brannagh countered with a snake's smile.

They kept backing away. Kept seeing the histories I'd planted into their minds—that we were here to hurt and kill them, that we had done so with all their friends, that we'd use and discard them. I showed them the naga, the Bogge, the Middengard Wyrm; I showed them Clare and the golden-haired queen, skewered on that lamppost. The memories I gave them became stories they had ignored—but now understood with us before them.

"Come here," Dagdan ordered.

The words were kindling to their fear. The three of them turned, heavy pale robes twisting with them, and bolted for the trees.

Brannagh tensed, as if she'd charge through the wall after them, but I gripped her arm and hissed, "If you pursue them, then you and I will have a problem."

In emphasis, I dragged mental talons down her own shield.

The princess snarled at me.

But the humans were already gone.

I prayed they'd listen to the other command I'd woven into their minds: to get on a boat, get as many friends as they could, and flee for the continent. To return here only when the war was over, and to warn as many humans as possible to get out before it was too late.

The Hybern royals growled their displeasure, but I ignored it as I took up a spot against a tree and settled in to wait, not trusting them to stay on this side of the border.

The royals resumed their work, stalking up and down the wall.

A moment later, a male body came up beside mine.

Not Lucien, I realized with a jolt, but did not so much as flinch.

Jurian's eyes were on the place where the humans had been.

"Thank you," he said, his voice rough.

"I don't know what you're talking about," I replied, well aware that Lucien carefully watched from the shade of a nearby oak.

Jurian gave me a knowing smirk and sauntered after Dagdan.

They took all day.

Whatever it was they were inspecting, whatever they were hunting for, the royals didn't inform us.

And after the confrontation that morning, I knew pushing them into revealing it wouldn't happen. I'd used up my allotted tolerance for the day.

So we spent another night in the woods, which was precisely how I wound up sitting across the fire from Jurian after the twins had crawled into their tent and the sentries had taken up their watch positions. Lucien had gone to the stream to get more water, and I watched the flame dance amongst the logs, feeling it echo inside myself.

Spearing my power through the wall had left me with a lingering, pounding headache all day, more than a bit dizzy. I had no doubt sleep would claim me fast and hard, but the fire was too warm and the spring night too brisk to willingly breach that long gap of darkness between the flame and my tent.

"What happens to the ones who do make it through the wall?" Jurian asked, the hard panes of his face cast in flickering relief by the fire.

I ground the heel of my boot into the grass. "I don't know. They never came back once they went over. But while Amarantha ruled, creatures prowled these woods, so . . . I don't think it ended well. I've never encountered a mention of them being at any court."

"Five hundred years ago, they'd have been flogged for that nonsense," Jurian said. "We were their slaves and whores and laborers for millennia—men and women fought and died so we'd never have to serve them again. Yet there they are, in those costumes, unaware of the danger, the history."

"Careful, or you might not sound like Hybern's faithful pet."

A low, hateful laugh. "That's what you think I am, isn't it. His dog."

"What's the end goal, then?"

"I have unfinished business."

"Miryam is dead."

That madness danced again, replacing the rare lucidity. "Everything I did during the War, it was for Miryam and me. For our people to survive and one day be free. And she *left me* for that pretty-faced prince the moment I put my people before her."

"I heard she left you because you became so focused on wringing information from Clythia that you lost sight of the real conflict."

"Miryam told me to go ahead and fuck her for information. Told me to seduce Clythia until she'd sold out all of Hybern and the Loyalists. She had no qualms with that. None."

"So all of this is to get Miryam back?"

He stretched his long legs before him, crossing one ankle over the other. "It's to draw her out of her little nest with that winged prick and make her regret it."

"You get a second shot at life and that's what you wish to do? Revenge?"

Jurian smiled slowly. "Isn't that what you're doing?"

Months of working with Rhys had me remembering to furrow my brow in confusion. "Against Rhys, I would one day like it."

"That's what they all say, when they pretend he's a sadistic murderer. You forget I knew him in the War. You forget he risked his legion to save Miryam from our enemy's fort. That's how Amarantha captured him, you know. Rhys knew it was a trap—for Prince Drakon. So Rhys went against orders, and marched in his whole legion to get Miryam out. For his friend, for *my* lover—and for that bastard Drakon's sake. Rhys sacrificed his legion in the process, got all of them captured and tortured afterward. Yet everyone insists Rhysand is soulless, wicked. But the male I knew was the most decent of them all. Better than that prick-prince. You don't lose that quality, no matter the centuries, and Rhys was too smart to do anything but have the vilification of his character be a calculated move. And yet here you are—his mate. The most powerful High Lord in the world lost his mate, and has not yet come to claim her, even when she is defenseless in the woods." Jurian chuckled. "Perhaps that's because Rhysand has not lost you at all. But rather unleashed you upon us."

I had never heard that story, but it seemed so like my mate that I knew the flames between us now smoldered in my eyes as I said, "You love to hear yourself talk, don't you."

"Hybern will kill all of you," was all Jurian replied.

Jurian wasn't wrong.

Lucien woke me the next morning with a hand over my mouth, warning gleaming in his russet eye. I smelled it a moment later: the coppery tang of blood.

We shoved into our clothes and boots, and I did a quick inventory of the weapons we'd squeezed into the tent with us. I had three daggers. Lucien had two, as well as an elegant short sword. Better than nothing, but not much.

A glance from him communicated our plan well enough: play casual until we assessed the situation.

I had a heartbeat to realize that this was perhaps the first time he and I had worked in tandem. Hunting had never been a joint effort, and Under the Mountain had been one of us looking out for the other—never a team. A unit.

Lucien slid from the tent, limbs loose and ready to shift into a defensive position. He'd been trained, he once told me—at the Autumn Court and at this one. Like Rhys, he usually opted for words to win his battles, but I'd seen him and Tamlin in the practice ring. He knew how to handle a weapon. How to kill, if need be.

I pushed past him, devouring the details of my surroundings as if I were a starving man at a feast.

The forest was the same. Jurian was crouched before the fire, stirring the embers back to alertness, his face a hard, brooding mask. But the sentries—they were pale as Lucien stalked to them. I followed their shifting attention to the trees behind Jurian.

No sign of the royals.

The blood—

A coppery tang, yes. But laced with earth and marrow and—rot. Mortality.

I stormed for the trees and dense brush.

"You're too late," Jurian said as I passed him, still poking the embers. "They finished two hours ago."

Lucien was on my heels as I shoved into the brambles, thorns tearing at my hands.

The Hybern royals hadn't bothered to clean up their mess.

From what was left of the three bodies, their shredded pale robes like fallen ashes through the small clearing, Dagdan and Brannagh must have shut out their screams with some sort of shield.

Lucien swore. "They went through the wall last night. To hunt them down."

Even with hours separating them, the royals were Fae—swift, immortal. The three Children of the Blessed would have tired after running, would have camped somewhere.

Blood was already drying on the grass, on the trunks of the surrounding trees.

Hybern's brand of torture wasn't very creative: Clare, the golden queen, and these three . . . A similar mutilating and torment.

I unfastened my cloak and carefully laid it over the biggest remains of them I could find: the torso of the young man, clawed up and bloodless. His face was still etched in pain.

Flame heated at my fingertips, begging me to burn them, to give them at least that sort of burial. But— "Do you think it was for sport, or to send us a message?"

Lucien laid his own cloak across the remains of the two young women. His face was as serious as I'd ever seen it. "I think they aren't accustomed to being denied. I'd call this an immortal temper tantrum."

I closed my eyes, trying to calm my roiling stomach.

"You aren't to blame," he added. "They could have killed them out in the mortal lands, but they brought them here. To make a statement about their power."

He was right. The Children of the Blessed would have been dead even if I hadn't interfered. "They're threatened," I mused. "And proud to a fault." I toed the blood-soaked grass. "Do we bury them?"

Lucien considered. "It sends a message—that we're willing to clean up their messes."

I surveyed the clearing again. Considered everything at stake. "Then we send another sort of message."

CHAPTER 8

Tamlin paced in front of the hearth in his study, every turn as sharp as a blade.

"They are our *allies*," he growled at me, at Lucien, both of us seated in armchairs flanking the mantel.

"They're monsters," I countered. "They butchered three innocents."

"And you should have left it alone for me to deal with." Tamlin heaved a jagged breath. "Not *retaliated* like children." He threw a glare in Lucien's direction. "I expected better from you."

"But not from me?" I asked quietly.

Tamlin's green eyes were like frozen jade. "You have a personal connection to those people. *He* does not."

"That's the sort of thinking," I snapped, clutching the armrests, "that has allowed for a *wall* to be the only solution between our two peoples; for the Fae to look at these sorts of *murders* and not care." I knew the guards outside could hear. Knew anyone walking by could hear. "The loss of *any* life on either side is a *personal connection*. Or is it only High Fae lives that matter to you?"

Tamlin stopped short. And snarled at Lucien, "Get out. I'll deal with you later."

"Don't you talk to him like that," I hissed, shooting to my feet.

"You have jeopardized this alliance with that stunt you two pulled—"

"Good. They can burn in *hell* for all I care!" I shouted. Lucien flinched.

"*You sent the Bogge after them!*" Tamlin roared.

I didn't so much as blink. And I knew the sentries had heard indeed by the cough of one outside—a sound of muffled shock.

And I made sure those sentries could still hear as I said, "They terrorized those humans—made them suffer. I figured the Bogge was one of the few creatures that could return the favor."

Lucien had tracked it down—and we'd lured it, carefully, over hours, back to that camp. Right to where Dagdan and Brannagh had been gloating over their kill. They'd managed to get away—but only after what had sounded like a good bit of screaming and fighting. Their faces remained bloodless even hours later, their eyes still brimming with hate whenever they deigned to look at us.

Lucien cleared his throat. Stood as well. "Tam—those humans were barely more than children. Feyre gave the royals an order to stand down. They ignored it. If we let Hybern walk all over us, we stand to lose more than their alliance. The Bogge reminded them that we aren't without our claws, too."

Tamlin didn't take his eyes off me as he said to Lucien, "*Get. Out.*"

There was enough violence in the words that neither Lucien nor I objected this time as he slipped from the room and shut the double doors behind him. I speared my power into the hall, sensing him sitting on the foot of the stairs. Listening. As the six sentries in the hall were listening.

I said to Tamlin, my back ramrod straight, "You don't get to speak to me like that. You *promised* you wouldn't act this way."

"You have no idea what's at risk—"

"Don't you talk down to me. Not after what *I* went through to get back here, to you. To our *people*. You think any of us are happy to be working with Hybern? You think I don't see it in their faces? The question of whether *I* am worth the dishonor of it?"

His breathing turned ragged again. Good, I wanted to urge him. *Good.*

"You sold us out to get me back," I said, low and cold. "You whored us out to Hybern. Forgive me if *I* am now trying to regain some of what we lost."

Claws slid free. A feral growl rippled out of him.

"They hunted down and butchered those humans for sport," I went on. "You might be willing to get on your knees for Hybern, but I certainly am not."

He exploded.

Furniture splintered and went flying, windows cracked and shattered.

And this time, I did not shield myself.

The worktable slammed into me, throwing me against the bookshelf, and every place where flesh and bone met wood barked and ached.

My knees slammed into the carpeted floor, and Tamlin was instantly in front of me, hands shaking—

The doors burst open.

"What have you done," Lucien breathed, and Tamlin's face was the picture of devastation as Lucien shoved him aside. He *let* Lucien shove him aside and help me stand.

Something wet and warm slid down my cheek—blood, from the scent of it.

"Let's get you cleaned up," Lucien said, an arm around my shoulders as he eased me from the room. I barely heard him over the ringing in my ears, the slight spinning to the world.

The sentries—Bron and Hart, two of Tamlin's favorite lord-warriors among them—were gaping, attention torn between the wrecked study and my face.

With good reason. As Lucien led me past a gilded hall mirror, I beheld what had drawn such horror. My eyes were glassy, my face pallid—save for the scratch just beneath my cheekbone, perhaps two inches long and leaking blood.

Little scratches peppered my neck, my hands. But I willed that cleansing, healing power—that of the High Lord of Dawn—to keep from seeking them out. From smoothing them away.

"Feyre," Tamlin breathed from behind us.

I halted, aware of every eye that watched. "I'm fine," I whispered. "I'm sorry." I wiped at the blood dribbling down my cheek. "I'm fine," I told him again.

No one, not even Tamlin, looked convinced.

And if I could have painted that moment, I would have named it *A Portrait in Snares and Baiting.*

Rhysand sent word down the bond the second I was soaking in the bathtub.

Are you hurt?

The question was faint, the bond quieter and tenser than it had been days ago.

Sore, but fine. Nothing I can't handle. Though my injuries still lingered. And showed no signs of a speedy healing. Perhaps I'd been too good at keeping those healing powers at bay.

The reply was a long time coming. Then it came all at once, as if he wanted to cram every word in before the difficulty of the distance silenced us.

I know better than to tell you to be careful, or to come home. But I want you home. Soon. And I want him dead for putting a hand on you.

Even with the entirety of the land between us, his rage rippled down the bond.

I answered, my tone soothing, dry, *Technically,* his magic *touched me, not his hand.*

The bathwater was cold by the time his reply came through. *I'm glad you have a sense of humor about this. I certainly don't.*

I sent back an image of me sticking out my tongue at him.

My clothes were back on when his answer arrived.

Like mine, it was wordless, a mere image. Like mine, Rhysand's tongue was out.

But it was occupied with doing something else.

I made a point to take a ride the next day. Made sure it was when Bron and Hart were on duty, and asked them to escort me.

They didn't say much, but I felt their assessing glances at my every wince as we rode the worn paths through the spring wood. Felt them study the cut on my face, the bruises beneath my clothes that had me hissing every now and then. Still not fully healed to my surprise—though I supposed it worked to my advantage.

Tamlin had begged my forgiveness at dinner yesterday—and I'd given it to him. But Lucien hadn't spoken to him all evening.

Jurian and the Hybern royals had sulked at the delay after I'd quietly admitted my bruises made it too difficult to accompany them to the wall. Tamlin hadn't possessed the nerve to suggest they go without me, to rob me of that duty. Not when he saw the purplish markings and knew that if they were on a human, I might have been dead.

And the royals, after Lucien and I had sent the Bogge's invisible malice after them, had backed off. For now. I kept my shields up—around myself and the others, the strain now a constant headache that had any extra sort of magic feeling feeble and thin. The reprieve on the border hadn't done much—no, it'd made the strain worse after I'd sent my power through the wall.

I'd invited Ianthe to the house, subtly requesting her comforting presence. She arrived knowing the full details of what had transpired in that study—letting it conveniently slip that Tamlin had confessed it to her, pleading for absolution from the Mother and Cauldron and whoever else. I prattled about my own forgiveness to her that evening, and made a show of taking her good counsel, telling the courtiers and others at our crowded table that night how lucky we were to have Tamlin *and* Ianthe guarding our lands.

Honestly, I don't know how none of them connected it.

How none of them saw my words as not a strange coincidence but a dare. A threat.

That last little nudge.

Especially when seven naga broke into the estate grounds just past midnight.

They were dispatched before they reached the house—an attack halted by a Cauldron-sent warning vision from none other than Ianthe herself.

The chaos and screaming woke the estate. I remained in my room, guards beneath my windows and outside my door. Tamlin himself, blood-drenched and panting, came to inform me that the grounds were again secure. That the naga had been found with the keys to the gate, and the sentry who had lost them would be dealt with in the morning. A freak accident, a final show of power from a tribe that had not gone gently after Amarantha's reign.

All of us saved from further harm by Ianthe.

We all gathered outside the barracks the next morning, Lucien's face pallid and drawn, purple smudges beneath his glazed eyes. He hadn't returned to his room last night.

Beside me, the Hybern royals and Jurian were silent and grim as Tamlin paced before the sentry strung up between two posts.

"You were entrusted with guarding this estate and its people," Tamlin said to the shuddering male, already stripped down to his pants. "You were found not only asleep at the gate last night, but it was *your* set of keys that originally went missing." Tamlin snarled softly. "Do you deny this?"

"I—I never fall asleep. It's never happened until now. I must have just nodded off for a minute or two," the sentry stammered, the ropes restraining him groaning as he strained against them.

"You jeopardized the lives of everyone in this manor."

And it could not go unpunished. Not with the Hybern royals here, seeking any sign of weakness.

Tamlin held out a hand. Bron, stone-faced, approached to give him a whip.

All the sentries, his most trusted warriors, shifted about. Some outright glaring at Tamlin, some trying not to watch what was about to unfold.

I grabbed Lucien's hand. It wasn't entirely for show.

Ianthe stepped forward, hands folded over her stomach. "Twenty lashes. And one more, for the Cauldron's forgiveness."

The guards turned baleful eyes toward her now.

Tamlin unfurled the whip onto the dirt.

I made my move. Slid my power into the bound sentry's mind and freed the memory I'd coiled up tightly in his head—freed his tongue, too.

"It was her," he panted, jerking his chin to Ianthe. "*She* took the keys."

Tamlin blinked—and everyone in that courtyard looked right to Ianthe.

Her face didn't so much as flinch at the accusation—the truth he'd flung her way.

I'd been waiting to see how she'd counter my showing of power at the solstice, tracking her movements that entire day and night. Within moments of my leaving the party she'd gone to the barracks, used some glimmer of power to lull him to sleep, and taken his keys. Then planted her warnings about the naga's impending attacks . . . after she gave the creatures the keys to the gates.

So she could sound the alarm last night. So *she* could save us from a real threat.

Clever idea—had it not played right into everything I'd laid out.

Ianthe said smoothly, "Why should I take the keys? I warned you of the attack."

"You were at the barracks—I *saw* you that night," the sentry insisted, then turned pleading eyes to Tamlin. It wasn't fear of pain that propelled him, I realized. No, the lashings would have been deserved and earned and borne well. It was the fear of honor lost.

"I would have thought one of your sentries, Tamlin, would have more dignity than to spread lies to spare himself from some fleeting pain." Ianthe's face remained serene as always.

Tamlin, to his credit, studied the sentry for a long moment.

I stepped forward. "I will hear his story."

Some of the guards loosed sighs. Some looked at me with pity and affection.

Ianthe lifted her chin. "With all due respect, milady, it is not your judgment to make."

And there it was. The attempt to knock me down a few pegs.

Just because it would make her see red, I ignored her completely and said to the sentry, "I will hear your story."

I kept my focus on him, even as I counted my breaths, even as I prayed that Ianthe would take the bait—

"You'll take the word of a sentry over that of a High Priestess?"

My disgust at her blurted words wasn't entirely feigned—even though hiding my faint smile was an effort. The guards shifted on their feet at the insult, the tone. Even if they had not already trusted their fellow sentry, from her words alone, they realized her guilt.

I looked to Tamlin then—saw his eyes sharpen as well. With understanding. Too many protests from Ianthe.

Oh, he was well aware that Ianthe had perhaps planned that naga attack to reclaim some shred of power and influence—as a savior of these people.

Tamlin's mouth tightened in disapproval.

I'd given them both a length of rope. I supposed now would be the moment to see whether they'd hang themselves with it.

I dared one more step forward, upturning my palms to Tamlin. "Perhaps it was a mistake. Don't take it from his hide—or his honor. Let's hear him out."

Tamlin's eyes softened a fraction. He remained silent—considering.

But behind me, Brannagh snorted.

"Pathetic," she murmured, though everyone could hear it.

Weak. Vulnerable. Ripe for conquest. I saw the words slam through Tamlin's face, as if they were shutting doors in their wake.

There was no other interpretation—not for Tamlin.

But Ianthe assessed me, standing before the crowd, the influence I'd made so very clear I was capable of stealing. If she admitted guilt . . . whatever she had left would come crumbling down.

Tamlin opened his mouth, but Ianthe cut him off. "There are laws to be obeyed," she told me, gently enough that I wanted to drag my nails down her face. "Traditions. He has broken our trust, has let our blood be spilled for his carelessness. Now he seeks to accuse a High Priestess of *his* failings. It cannot go unpunished." She nodded to Tamlin. "Twenty-one lashes, High Lord."

I glanced between them, my mouth going dry. "Please. Just listen to him."

The guard hanging between the posts had such hope and gratitude in his eyes.

In this . . . in this, my revenge edged toward something oily, something foreign and queasy. He would heal from the pain, but the blow to his honor . . . It'd take a little piece out of mine as well.

Tamlin stared at me, then Ianthe. Then glanced to the smirking Hybern royals—to Jurian, who crossed his arms, his face unreadable.

And like I'd gambled, Tamlin's need for control, for strength, won out.

Ianthe was too important an ally to risk isolating. The word of a low sentry . . . no, it did not matter as much as hers.

Tamlin turned to the sentry tied to the posts. "Put the bit in," he quietly ordered Bron.

There was a heartbeat of hesitation from Bron—as if the shock of Tamlin's order had rippled through him. Through all the guards. Siding with Ianthe—over them. His sentries.

Who had gone over the wall, again and again, to try to break that curse for him. Who had gladly done it, gladly *died*, hunted down as those wolves, for him. And the wolf I'd felled, Andras . . . He'd gone willingly, too. Tamlin had sent them all over, and not all of them had come back. They had gone willingly, yet this . . . this was his thanks. His gratitude. His trust.

But Bron did as commanded, sliding the small piece of wood into the now-trembling sentry's mouth.

Judging by the barely concealed disdain in the guards' faces, at least they were aware of what had occurred—or what they believed had occurred: the High Priestess had orchestrated this entire attack to cast herself as a savior, offering up the reputation of one of their own as the asking price. They had no idea—none—that I'd goaded her into it, pushed and pushed her to reveal just what a snake she was. How little anyone without a title meant to her.

How Tamlin listened to her without question—to a fault.

It wasn't much of an act when I put a hand to my throat, backing up a step, then another, until Lucien's warmth was against me, and I leaned fully into him.

The sentries were sizing up Ianthe, the royals. Tamlin had always been one of them—fought for them.

Until now. Until Hybern. Until he put these foreign monsters before them.

Until he put a scheming High Priestess before them.

Tamlin's eyes were on us, on the hand Lucien put on my arm to steady me, as he drew back the whip.

The thunderous crack as it cleaved the air snapped through the barracks, the estate.

Through the very foundations of the court.

CHAPTER 9

Ianthe wasn't done.

I knew it—braced myself for it. She didn't flit back to her temple a few miles away.

Rather, she remained at the house, seizing her chance to worm her way closer to Tamlin. She believed she'd gained a foothold, that her declaration of justice served at the bloody end of the whipping hadn't been anything but a final slap in the face to the guards who watched.

And when that sentry had sagged from his bindings, when the others came to gently untie him, Ianthe merely ushered the Hybern party and Tamlin into the manor for lunch. But I'd remained at the barracks, tending to the groaning sentry, drawing away bloodied bowls of water while the healer quietly patched him up.

Bron and Hart personally escorted me back to the estate hours later. I thanked them each by name. Then apologized that I hadn't been able to prevent it—Ianthe's scheming or the unjust punishment of their friend. I meant every word, the crack of the whip still echoing in my ears.

Then they spoke the words I'd been waiting for. They were sorry they hadn't stopped *any* of it, either.

Not just today. But the bruises now fading—at last. The other incidents.

If I had asked them, they would have handed me their own knives to slit their throats.

The next evening, I was hurrying back to my room to change for dinner when Ianthe made her next move.

She was to come with us to the wall tomorrow morning.

Her, and Tamlin, too.

If we were all to be a united front, she'd declared over dinner, then she wished to see the wall herself.

The Hybern royals didn't care. But Jurian winked at me, as if he, too, saw the game in motion.

I packed my own bags that night.

Alis entered right before bed, a third pack in her hands. "Since it's a longer trip, I brought you supplies."

Even with Tamlin joining us, it was too many people for him to winnow us directly.

So we'd go, as we'd done before, in segments. A few miles at a time.

Alis laid the pack she'd prepared beside my own. Picked up the brush on the vanity and beckoned me to sit on the cushioned bench before it.

I obeyed. For a few minutes, she brushed my hair in silence.

Then she said, "When you leave tomorrow, I leave, too."

I lifted my eyes to hers in the mirror.

"My nephews are packed, the ponies ready to take us back to Summer Court territory at last. It has been too long since I saw my home," she said, though her eyes shone.

"I know the feeling," was all I said.

"I wish you well, lady," Alis said, setting down the brush and beginning to braid back my hair. "For the rest of your days, however long they may be, I wish you well."

I let her finish the plait, then pivoted on the bench to grip her thin fingers in mine. "Don't ever tell Tarquin you know me well."

Her brows rose.

"There is a blood ruby with my name on it," I clarified.

Even her tree-bark skin seemed to blanch. She understood it well enough: I was a hunted enemy of the Summer Court. Only my death would be accepted as payment for my crimes.

Alis squeezed my hand. "Blood rubies or no, you will always have one friend in the Summer Court."

My throat bobbed. "And you will always have one in mine," I promised her.

She knew which court I meant. And did not look afraid.

The sentries did not glance at Tamlin, or so much as speak to him unless absolutely necessary. Bron, Hart, and three others were to join us. They had spotted me checking on their friend before dawn—a courtesy I knew none of the others had extended.

Winnowing felt like wading through mud. In fact, my powers had become more of a burden than a help. I had a throbbing headache by noon, and spent the last leg of the journey dizzy and disoriented as we winnowed again and again.

We arrived and set up camp in near-silence. I quietly, shyly asked to share a tent with Ianthe instead of Tamlin, appearing eager to mend the rift the whipping had torn between us. But I did it more to spare Lucien from her attention than to keep Tamlin at bay. Dinner was made and eaten, bedrolls laid out, and Tamlin ordered Bron and Hart on the first watch.

Lying beside Ianthe without slitting her throat was an exercise in patience and control.

But whenever the knife beneath my pillow seemed to whisper her name, I'd remind myself of my friends. The family that was alive—healing in the North.

I repeated their names silently, over and over into the darkness. Rhysand. Mor. Cassian. Amren. Azriel. Elain. Nesta.

I thought of how I had last seen them, so bloodied and hurting. Thought of Cassian's scream as his wings were shredded; of Azriel's threat to the king as he advanced on Mor. Nesta, fighting every step toward the Cauldron.

My goal was bigger than revenge. My purpose greater than personal retribution.

Dawn broke, and I found my palm curled around the hilt of my knife anyway. I drew it out as I sat up, staring down at the sleeping priestess.

The smooth column of her neck seemed to glow in the early-morning sun leaking through the tent flaps.

I weighed the knife in my hand.

I wasn't sure I'd been born with the ability to forgive. Not for terrors inflicted on those I loved. For myself, I didn't care—not nearly as much. But there was some fundamental pillar of steel in me that could not bend or break in this. Could not stomach the idea of letting these people get away with what they'd done.

Ianthe's eyes opened, the teal as limpid as her discarded circlet. They went right to the knife in my hand. Then to my face.

"You can't be too careful while sharing a camp with enemies," I said.

I could have sworn something like fear shone in her eyes. "Hybern is not our enemy," she said a tad breathlessly.

From her paleness as I left the tent, I knew my answering smile had done its job well.

Lucien and Tamlin showed the twins where the crack in the wall lay.

And as they had done with the first two, they spent hours surveying it, the surrounding land.

I kept close this time, watching them, my presence now deemed relatively unthreatening if not a nuisance. We'd played our little power games, established I could bite if I wished, but we'd tolerate each other.

"Here," Brannagh murmured to Dagdan, jerking her chin to the invisible divider. The only markings were the different trees: on our side, they were the bright, fresh green of spring. On the other, they were dark, broad, curling slightly with heat—the height of summer.

"The first one was better," Dagdan countered.

I sat atop a small boulder, peeling an apple with a paring knife.

"Closer to the western coast, too," he added to his twin.

"This is closer to the continent—to the strait."

I sliced deep into the flesh of the apple, carving out a hunk of white meat.

"Yes, but we'd have more access to the High Lord's supplies."

Said High Lord was currently off with Jurian, hunting for food more filling than the sandwiches we'd packed. Ianthe had gone to a nearby spring to pray, and I had no idea whatsoever where Lucien or the sentries were.

Good. Easier for me as I shoved the apple slice into my mouth and said around it, "I say go for this one."

They twisted toward me, Brannagh sneering and Dagdan's brows high. "What do you know of any of it?" Brannagh demanded.

I shrugged, cutting another piece of apple. "You two talk louder than you realize."

Shared accusatory glares between them. Proud, arrogant, cruel. I'd been taking their measure this fortnight. "Unless you want to risk the other courts having time to rally and intercepting you before you can cross to the strait, I'd pick this one."

Brannagh rolled her eyes.

I went on, rambling and bored, "But what do I know? You two have squatted on a little island for five hundred years. Clearly you know more about Prythian and moving armies than me."

Brannagh hissed, "This is not about armies, so I will trust you to keep that mouth *shut* until we have use for you."

I snorted. "You mean to tell me all of this nonsense hasn't been to find a place to break through the wall and use the Cauldron to *also* transport the mass of your armies here?"

She laughed, swinging her dark curtain of hair over a shoulder. "The Cauldron is not for transporting grunt armies. It is for remaking worlds. It is for bringing down this hideous wall and reclaiming what we were."

I merely crossed my legs. "I'd think that with an army of ten thousand you wouldn't need any magical objects to do your dirty work."

"Our army is ten times that, girl," Brannagh sneered. "And twice *that* number if you count our allies in Vallahan, Montesere, and Rask."

Two hundred thousand. Mother save us.

"You've certainly been busy all these years." I surveyed them, utterly nonplussed. "Why not strike when Amarantha had the island?"

"The king had not yet found the Cauldron, despite years of searching. It served his purposes to let her be an experiment for how we might break these people. And served as good motivation for our allies on the continent to join us, knowing what would await them."

I finished off my apple and chucked the core into the woods. They watched it fly like two hounds tracking a pheasant.

"So they're all going to converge here? I'm supposed to play hostess to so many soldiers?"

"Our own force will take care of Prythian before uniting with the others. Our commanders are preparing for it as we speak."

"You must think you stand a shot at losing if you're bothering to use the Cauldron to help you win."

"The Cauldron *is* victory. It will wipe this world clean again."

I lifted my brows in irreverent cynicism. "And you need this exact spot to unleash it?"

"This exact spot," Dagdan said, a hand on the hilt of his sword, "exists because a person or object of mighty power passed through it. The Cauldron will study the work they've already done—and magnify it until the wall collapses entirely. It is a careful, complex process, and one I doubt your mortal mind can grasp."

"Probably. Though this mortal mind did manage to solve Amarantha's riddle—and destroy her."

Brannagh merely turned back to the wall. "Why do you think Hybern let her live for so long in these lands? Better to have someone else do his dirty work."

I had what I needed.

Tamlin and Jurian were still off hunting, the royals were preoccupied, and I'd sent the sentries to fetch me more water, claiming that some of my bruises still ached and I wanted to make a poultice for them.

They'd looked positively murderous at that. Not at me—but at who had given me those bruises. Who had picked Ianthe over them—and Hybern over their honor and people.

I'd brought three packs, but I'd only need one. The one I'd carefully repacked with Alis's new supplies, now tucked beside everything I'd anticipated needing to get clear of them and go. The one I'd brought with me on every trip out to the wall, just in case. And now . . .

I had numbers, I had a purpose, I had a specific location, and the names of foreign territories.

But more than that, I had a people who had lost faith in their High Priestess. I had sentries who were beginning to rebel against their High Lord. And as a result of those things, I had Hybern royals doubting the strength of their allies here. I'd primed this court to fall. Not from outside forces—but its own internal warring.

And I had to be clear of it before it happened. Before the last sliver of my plan fell into place.

The party would return without me. And to maintain that illusion of strength, Tamlin and Ianthe would lie about it—where I'd gone.

And perhaps a day or two after that, one of these sentries would reveal the news, a carefully sprung trap that I'd coiled into his mind like one of my snares.

I'd fled for my life—after being nearly killed by the Hybern prince and princess. I'd planted images in his head of my brutalized body, the markings consistent with what Dagdan and Brannagh had already revealed to be their style. He'd describe them in detail—describe how he helped me get away before it was too late. How I ran for my life when Tamlin and Ianthe refused to intervene, to risk their alliance with Hybern.

And when the sentry revealed the truth, no longer able to stomach keeping quiet when he saw how my sorry fate was concealed by Tamlin and Ianthe, just as Tamlin had sided with Ianthe the day he'd flogged that sentry . . .

When he described what Hybern had done to me, their Cursebreaker, their newly anointed Cauldron-blessed, before I'd fled for my life . . .

There would be no further alliance. For there would be no sentry or denizen of this court who would stand with Tamlin or Ianthe after this. After *me*.

I ducked into my tent to grab my pack, my steps light and swift. Listening, barely breathing, I scanned the camp, the woods.

A few seconds extra had me snatching Tamlin's bandolier of knives from where he'd left them inside his tent. They'd get in the way while using a bow and arrow, he'd explained that morning.

Their weight was considerable as I slung it across my chest. Illyrian fighting knives.

Home. I was going *home*.

I didn't bother to look back at that camp as I slipped into the northern tree line. If I winnowed without stopping between leaps, I'd be at the foothills in an hour—and would vanish through one of the caves not long after that.

I made it about a hundred yards into the cover of the trees before I halted.

I heard Lucien first.

"Back off."

A low female laugh.

Everything in me went still and cold at that sound. I'd heard it once before—in Rhysand's memory.

Keep going. They were distracted, horrible as it was.

Keep going, keep going, keep going.

"I thought you'd seek me out after the Rite," Ianthe purred. They couldn't be more than thirty feet through the trees. Far enough away not to hear my presence, if I was quiet enough.

"I was obligated to perform the Rite," Lucien snapped. "That night wasn't the product of desire, believe me."

"We had fun, you and I."

"I'm a mated male now."

Every second was the ringing of my death knell. I'd primed everything to fall; I'd long since stopped feeling any sort of guilt or doubt about my plan. Not with Alis now safely away.

And yet—and yet—

"You don't act that way with Feyre." A silk-wrapped threat.

"You're mistaken."

"Am I?" Twigs and leaves crunched, as if she was circling him. "You put your hands all over her."

I had done my job too well, provoked her jealousy too much with every instance I'd found ways to get Lucien to touch me in her presence, in Tamlin's presence.

"Do *not* touch me," he growled.

And then I was moving.

I masked the sound of my footfalls, silent as a panther as I stalked to the little clearing where they stood.

Where Lucien stood, back against a tree—twin bands of blue stone shackled around his wrists.

I'd seen them before. On Rhys, to immobilize his power. Stone hewn from Hybern's rotted land, capable of nullifying magic. And in this case . . . holding Lucien against that tree as Ianthe surveyed him like a snake before a meal.

She slid a hand over the broad panes of his chest, his stomach.

And Lucien's eyes shot to me as I stepped between the trees, fear and humiliation reddening his golden skin.

"That's enough," I said.

Ianthe whipped her head to me. Her smile was innocent, simpering. But I saw her note the pack, Tamlin's bandolier. Dismiss them. "We were in the middle of a game. Weren't we, Lucien?"

He didn't answer.

And the sight of those shackles on him, however she'd trapped him, the sight of her *hand* still on his stomach—

"We'll return to the camp when we're done," she said, turning to him again. Her hand slid lower, not for his own pleasure, but simply to throw it in my face that she *could*—

I struck.

Not with my knives or magic, but my mind.

I ripped down the shield I'd kept up around her to avoid the twins' control—and slammed myself into her consciousness.

A mask over a face of decay. That's what it was like to go inside that beautiful head and find such hideous thoughts inside it. A trail of males she'd used her power on or outright forced to bed, convinced of her entitlement to them. I pulled back against the tug of those memories, mastering myself. "Take your hands off him."

She did.

"Unshackle him."

Lucien's skin drained of color as Ianthe obeyed me, her face queerly vacant, pliant. The blue stone shackles thumped to the mossy ground.

Lucien's shirt was askew, the top button on his pants already undone.

The roaring that filled my mind was so loud I could barely hear myself as I said, "Pick up that rock."

Lucien remained pressed against that tree. And he watched in silence as Ianthe stooped to pick up a gray, rough rock about the size of an apple.

"Put your right hand on that boulder."

She obeyed, though a tremor went down her spine.

Her mind thrashed and struggled against me, like a fish snared on a line. I dug my mental talons in deeper, and some inner voice of hers began screaming.

"Smash your hand with the rock as hard as you can until I tell you to stop."

The hand she'd put on him, on so many others.

Ianthe brought the stone up. The first impact was a muffled, wet thud.

The second was an actual crack.

The third drew blood.

Her arm rose and fell, her body shuddering with the agony.

And I said to her very clearly, "You will never touch another person against their will. You will never convince yourself that they truly want your advances; that they're playing games. You will never know another's touch unless they initiate, unless it's desired by *both* sides."

Thwack; crack; thud.

"You will not remember what happened here. You will tell the others that you fell."

Her ring finger had shifted in the wrong direction.

"You are allowed to see a healer to set the bones. But not to erase the scarring. And every time you look at that hand, you are going to remember that touching people against their will has consequences, and if you do it again, everything you are will cease to exist. You will live with that terror every day, and never know where it originates. Only the fear of something chasing you, hunting you, waiting for you the instant you let your guard down."

Silent tears of pain flowed down her face.

"You can stop now."

The bloodied rock tumbled onto the grass. Her hand was little more than cracked bones wrapped in shredded skin.

"Kneel here until someone finds you."

Ianthe fell to her knees, her ruined hand leaking blood onto her pale robes.

"I debated slitting your throat this morning," I told her. "I debated it all last night while you slept beside me. I've debated it every single day since I learned you sold out my sisters to Hybern." I smiled a bit.

"But I think this is a better punishment. And I hope you live a long, long life, Ianthe, and never know a moment's peace."

I stared down at her for a moment longer, tying off the tapestry of words and commands I'd woven into her mind, and turned to Lucien. He'd fixed his pants, his shirt.

His wide eyes slid from her to me, then to the bloodied stone.

"The word you're looking for, Lucien," crooned a deceptively light female voice, "is *daemati*."

We whirled toward Brannagh and Dagdan as they stepped into the clearing, grinning like wolves.

CHAPTER 10

Brannagh ran her fingers through Ianthe's golden hair, clicking her tongue at the bloodied pulp cradled in her lap. "Going somewhere, Feyre?"

I let my mask drop.

"I have places to be," I told the Hybern royals, noting the flanking positions they were too casually establishing around me.

"What could be more important than assisting us? You are, after all, sworn to assist our king."

Time—biding their time until Tamlin returned from hunting with Jurian.

Lucien shoved off the tree, but didn't come to my side. Something like agony flickered across his face as he finally noted the stolen bandolier, the pack on my shoulders.

"I have no allegiance to you," I told Brannagh, even as Dagdan began to edge past my line of sight. "I am a free person, allowed to go where and when I will it."

"Are you?" Brannagh mused, sliding a hand to her sword at her hip. I pivoted slightly to keep Dagdan from slipping into my blind spot. "Such careful plotting these weeks, such skilled maneuvering. You didn't seem to worry that we'd be doing the same."

They weren't letting Lucien leave this clearing alive. Or at least with his mind intact.

He seemed to realize it at the same moment I did, understanding that there was no way they'd reveal this without knowing they'd get away with it.

"Take the Spring Court," I said, and meant it. "It's going to fall one way or another."

Lucien snarled. I ignored him.

"Oh, we intend to," Brannagh said, sword inching free of its dark sheath. "But then there's the matter of you."

I thumbed free two of the Illyrian fighting knives.

"Haven't you wondered at the headaches? How things seem a little muffled on certain mental bonds?"

My powers had tired so swiftly, had become weaker and weaker these weeks—

Dagdan snorted and finally observed to his sister, "I'd give her about ten minutes before the apple sets in."

Brannagh chuckled, toeing the blue stone shackle. "We gave the priestess the powder at first. Crushed faebane stone, ground so fine you couldn't see or scent or taste it in your food. She'd add a little at a time, nothing suspicious—not too much, lest it stifle all your powers at once."

Unease began to clench my gut.

"We've been daemati for a thousand years, girl," Dagdan sneered. "But we didn't even need to slip into her mind to get her to do our bidding. But you . . . what a valiant effort you put up, trying to shield them all from us."

Dagdan's mind speared for Lucien's, a dark arrow shot between them. I slammed up a shield between them. And my head—my very bones *ached*—

"What *apple*," I bit out.

"The one you shoved down your throat an hour ago," Brannagh said. "Grown and tended in the king's personal garden, fed a steady diet of water laced with faebane. Enough to knock out your powers for a few days straight, no shackles required. And here you are, thinking no one had noticed you planned to vanish today." She clicked her tongue again. "Our uncle would be most displeased if we allowed that to happen."

I was running out of borrowed time. I could winnow, but then I'd abandon Lucien to them if he somehow couldn't manage to himself with the faebane in his system from the food at the camp—

Leave him. I should and *could* leave him.

But to a fate perhaps worse than death—

His russet eye gleamed. "Go."

I made my choice.

I exploded into night and smoke and shadow.

And even a thousand years wasn't enough for Dagdan to adequately prepare as I winnowed in front of him and struck.

I sliced through the front of his leather armor, not deep enough to kill, and as steel snagged on its plates, he twisted expertly, forcing me to either expose my right side or lose the knife—

I winnowed again. This time, Dagdan went with me.

I was not fighting Hybern cronies unaware in the woods. I was not fighting the Attor and its ilk in the streets of Velaris. Dagdan was a Hybern prince—a commander.

He fought like one.

Winnow. Strike. Winnow. Strike.

We were a black whirlwind of steel and shadow through the clearing, and months of Cassian's brutal training clicked into place as I kept my feet under me.

I had the vague sense of Lucien gaping, even Brannagh taken aback by my show of skill against her brother.

But Dagdan's blows weren't hard—no, they were precise and swift, but he didn't throw himself into it wholly.

Buying time. Wearing me down until my body fully absorbed that apple and its power rendered me nearly mortal.

So I hit him where he was weakest.

Brannagh screamed as a wall of flame slammed into her.

Dagdan lost his focus for all of a heartbeat. His roar as I sliced deep into his abdomen shook the birds from the trees.

"You little bitch," he spat, dancing back from my next blow as the fire cleared and Brannagh was revealed on her knees. Her physical shield had been sloppy—she'd expected me to attack her mind.

She was shuddering, gasping with agony. The reek of charred skin now drifted to us, directly from her right arm, her ribs, her thigh.

Dagdan lunged for me again, and I brought up both of my knives to meet his blade.

He didn't pull the blow this time.

I felt its reverberation in every inch of my body.

Felt the rising, stifling silence, too. I'd felt it once before—that day in Hybern.

Brannagh surged to her feet with a sharp cry.

But Lucien was there.

Her focus wholly on me, on taking from me the beauty I'd burned from her, Brannagh did not see him winnow until it was too late.

Until Lucien's sword refracted the light of the sun leaking through the canopy. And then met flesh and bone.

A tremor shuddered through the clearing—like some thread between the twins had been snipped as Brannagh's dark head thudded onto the grass.

Dagdan screamed, launching himself at Lucien, winnowing across the fifteen feet between us.

Lucien had barely heaved his blade out of Brannagh's severed neck when Dagdan was before him, sword shoving forward to ram through his throat.

Lucien only had enough time to stumble back from Dagdan's killing blow.

I had enough time to stop it.

I parried Dagdan's blade aside with one knife, the male's eyes going wide as I winnowed between them—and punched the other into his eye. Right into the skull behind it.

Bone and blood and soft tissue scraped and slid along the blade, Dagdan's mouth still open with surprise as I yanked out the knife.

I let him fall atop his sister, the thud of flesh on flesh the only sound.

I merely looked at Ianthe, my power guttering, a hideous ache building in my gut, and made my last command, amending my earlier ones. "You tell them I killed them. In self-defense. After they hurt me so badly while you and Tamlin did *nothing*. Even when they torture you for the truth, you say that I fled after I killed them—to save this court from their horrors."

Blank, vacant eyes were my only answer.

"Feyre."

Lucien's voice was a hoarse rasp.

I merely wiped my two knives on Dagdan's back before going to reclaim my fallen pack.

"You're going back. To the Night Court."

I shouldered my heavy pack and finally looked at him. "Yes."

His tan face had paled. But he surveyed Ianthe, the two dead royals. "I'm going with you."

"No," was all I said, heading for the trees.

A cramp formed deep in my belly. I had to get away—had to use the last of my power to winnow to the hills.

"You won't make it without magic," he warned me.

I just gritted my teeth against the sharp pain in my abdomen as I rallied my strength to winnow to those distant foothills. But Lucien gripped my arm, halting me.

"I'm going with you," he said again, face splattered with blood as bright as his hair. "I'm getting my mate back."

There was no time for this argument. For the truth and debate and the answers I saw he desperately wanted.

Tamlin and the others would have heard the shouting by now.

"Don't make me regret this," I told him.

Blood coated the inside of my mouth by the time we reached the foothills hours later.

I was panting, my head throbbing, my stomach a twisting knot of aching.

Lucien was barely better off, his winnowing as shaky as my own before we halted amongst the rolling green and he doubled over, hands braced on his knees. "It's—gone," he said, gasping for breath. "My magic—not an ember. They must have dosed all of us today."

And given me a poisoned apple just to make sure it kept me down.

My power pulled away from me like a wave reeling back from the shore. Only there was no return. It just went farther and farther out into a sea of nothing.

I peered at the sun, now a hand's width above the horizon, shadows already thick and heavy between the hills. I took my bearings, sorting through the knowledge I'd compiled these weeks.

I stepped northward, swaying. Lucien gripped my arm. "You're taking a door?"

I slid aching eyes toward him. "Yes." The caves—doors, they called them—in those hollows led to other pockets of Prythian. I'd taken one straight Under the Mountain. I would now take one to get me home. Or as close to it as I could get. No door to the Night Court existed, here or anywhere.

And I would not risk my friends by bringing them here to retrieve me. No matter that the bond between Rhys and me . . . I couldn't so much as feel it.

A numbness had spread through me. I needed to get out—now.

"The Autumn Court portal is that way." Warning and reproach.

"I can't go into Summer. They'll kill me on sight."

Silence. He released my arm. I swallowed, my throat so dry I could barely do so. "The only other door here leads Under the Mountain. We sealed off all the other entrances. If we go there, we could wind up trapped—or have to return."

"Then we go to Autumn. And from there . . ." I trailed off before I finished. *Home*. But Lucien gleaned it anyway. And seemed to realize then—that's what the Night Court was. *Home*.

I could almost see the word in his russet eye as he shook his head. *Later*.

I gave him a silent nod. Yes—later, we'd have it all out. "The Autumn Court will be as dangerous as Summer," he warned.

"I just need somewhere to hide—to lie low until . . . until we can winnow again."

A faint buzzing and ringing filled my ears. And I felt my magic vanish entirely.

"I know a place," Lucien said, walking toward the cave that would take us to his home.

To the lands of the family who'd betrayed him as badly as this court had betrayed mine.

We hurried through the hills, swift and silent as shadows.

The cave to the Autumn Court had been left unguarded. Lucien looked at me over his shoulder as if to ask if I, too, had been responsible for the lack of guards who were always stationed here.

I gave him another nod. I'd slid into their minds before we'd left, making sure this door would be left open. Cassian had taught me to always have a second escape route. Always.

Lucien paused before the swirling gloom of the cave mouth, the blackness like a wyrm poised to devour us both. A muscle feathered in his jaw.

I said, "Stay, if you want. What's done is done."

For Hybern was coming—already here. I had debated it for weeks: whether it was better to claim the Spring Court for ourselves, or to let it fall to our enemies.

But it could not remain neutral—a barrier between our forces in the North and the humans in the South. It would have been easy to call in Rhys and Cassian, to have the latter bring in an Illyrian legion to claim the territory when it was weakest after my own maneuverings. Depending on how much mobility Cassian had retained—if he was still healing.

Yet then we'd hold one territory—with five other courts between us. Sympathy might have swayed for the Spring Court; others might have joined Hybern against us, considering our conquest here proof of our wickedness. But if Spring fell to Hybern . . . We could rally the other courts to us. Charge as one from the North, drawing Hybern in close.

"You were right," Lucien declared at last. "That girl I knew did die Under the Mountain."

I wasn't sure if it was an insult. But I nodded all the same. "At least we can agree on that." I stepped into the awaiting cold and dark.

Lucien fell into step beside me as we strode beneath the archway of carved, crude stone, our blades out as we left behind the warmth and green of eternal spring.

And in the distance, so faint I thought I might have imagined it, a beast's roar cleaved the land.

PART TWO

CURSEBREAKER

CHAPTER 11

The cold was what hit me first.

Brisk, crisp cold, laced with loam and rotting things.

In the twilight, the world beyond the narrow cave mouth was a latticework of red and gold and brown and green, the trees thick and old, the mossy ground strewn with rocks and boulders that cast long shadows.

We emerged, blades out, barely breathing beyond a trickle of air.

But there were no Autumn Court sentries guarding the entrance to Beron's realm—none that we could see or scent.

Without my magic, I was blind again, unable to sweep a net of awareness through the ancient, vibrant trees to catch any traces of nearby Fae minds.

Utterly helpless. That's how I'd been before. How I'd survived so long without it . . . I didn't want to consider.

We crept on cat-soft feet into the moss and stone and wood, our breath curling in front of us.

Keep moving, keep striding north. Rhys would have realized by now that our bond had gone dark—was likely trying to glean whether I had planned for that. Whether it was worth the risk of revealing our scheming to find me.

But until he did . . . until he could hear me, find me . . . I had to keep moving.

So I let Lucien lead the way, wishing I'd at least been able to shift my eyes to something that could pierce the darkening wood. But my magic was still and frozen. A crutch I'd become too reliant upon.

We picked our way through the forest, the chill deepening with each vanishing shaft of sunlight.

We hadn't spoken since we'd entered that cave between courts. From the stiffness of his shoulders, the hard angle of his jaw as he moved on silent, steady feet, I knew only our need for stealth kept his simmering questions at bay.

Night was fully overhead, the moon not yet risen, when he led us into another cave.

I balked at the entrance.

Lucien merely said, voice flat and as icy as the air, "It doesn't lead anywhere. It curves away in the back—it'll keep us out of sight."

I let him go inside first nonetheless.

Every limb and movement turned sluggish, aching. But I trailed him into the cave, and around the bend he'd indicated.

Flint struck, and I found myself gazing at a makeshift camp of sorts.

The candle Lucien had ignited sat on a natural stone ledge, and on the floor nearby lay three bedrolls and old blankets, crusted with leaves and cobwebs. A little fire pit lay in the sloped center of the space, the ceiling above it charred.

No one had been here in months. Years.

"I used to stay here while hunting. Before—I left," he said, examining a dusty, leather-bound book left on the stone ledge beside the candle. He set the tome down with a thump. "It's just for the night. We'll find something to eat in the morning."

I only lifted the closest bedroll and smacked it a few times, leaves and clouds of dust flying off before I laid it upon the ground.

"You truly planned this," he said at last.

I sat on the bedroll and began sorting through my pack, hauling out the warmer clothes, food, and supplies Alis herself had placed within. "Yes."

"That's all you have to say?"

I sniffed at the food, wondering what was laced with faebane. It could be in everything. "It's too risky to eat," I admitted, evading his question.

Lucien was having none of it. "I knew. I knew you were lying the moment you unleashed that light in Hybern. My friend at the Dawn Court has the same power—her light is identical. And it does not do whatever horseshit you lied about it doing."

I shoved my pack off my bedroll. "Then why not tell him? You were his faithful dog in every other sense."

His eye seemed to simmer. As if being in his own lands set that molten ore inside him rising to the surface, even with the damper on his power. "Glad to see the mask is off, at least."

Indeed, I let him see it all—didn't alter or shape my face into anything but coldness.

Lucien snorted. "I didn't tell him for two reasons. One, it felt like kicking a male already down. I couldn't take that hope away from him." I rolled my eyes. "Two," he snapped, "I knew if I was correct and called you on it, you'd find a way to make sure I never saw her."

My nails dug into my palms hard enough to hurt, but I remained seated on the bedroll as I bared my teeth at him. "And that's why you're here. Not because it's right and he's always been wrong, but just so you can get what *you* think you're owed."

"She is my *mate* and in my enemy's hands—"

"I've made no secret from the start that Elain is safe and cared for."

"And I'm supposed to believe you."

"Yes," I hissed. "You are. Because if I believed for one moment that my sisters were in danger, no High Lord or king would have kept me from going to save them."

He just shook his head, the candlelight dancing over his hair. "You have the gall to question my priorities regarding Elain—yet what was *your* motive where I was concerned? Did you plan to spare me from your path of destruction because of any genuine friendship, or simply for fear of what it might do to her?"

I didn't answer.

"Well? What *was* your grand plan for me before Ianthe interfered?"

I pulled at a stray thread in the bedroll. "You would have been fine," was all I said.

"And what about Tamlin? Did you plan to disembowel him before you left and simply not get the chance?"

I ripped the loose thread right out of the bedroll. "I debated it."

"But?"

"But I think letting his court collapse around him is a better punishment. Certainly longer than an easy death." I slung off Tamlin's bandolier of knives, leather scraping against the rough stone floor. "You're his emissary—surely you realize that slitting his throat, however satisfying, wouldn't win us many allies in this war." No, it'd give Hybern too many openings to undermine us.

He crossed his arms. Digging in for a good, long fight. Before he could do just that, I cut in, "I'm tired. And our voices echo. Let's have it out when it's not likely to get us caught and killed."

His gaze was a brand.

But I ignored it as I nestled down on the bedroll, the material reeking of dust and rot. I pulled my cloak over me, but didn't close my eyes.

I didn't dare sleep—not when he might very well change his mind. Yet just lying down, not moving, not thinking . . . Some of the tightness in my body eased.

Lucien blew out the candle and I listened to the sounds of him settling down as well.

"My father will hunt you for taking his power if he finds out," he said into the frigid dark. "And kill you for learning how to wield it."

"He can get in line," was all I said.

My exhaustion was a blanket over my senses as gray light stained the cave walls.

I'd spent most of the night shivering, jolting at every snap and sound in the forest outside, keenly aware of Lucien's movements on his bedroll.

From his own haggard face as he sat up, I knew he hadn't slept, either, perhaps wondering if I'd abandon him. Or if his family would find us first. Or mine.

We took each other's measure.

"What now," he rasped, scrubbing a broad hand over his face.

Rhys had not come—I had not heard a whisper of him down the bond.

I felt for my magic, but only ashes greeted me. "We head north," I said. "Until the faebane is out of our systems and we can winnow." Or I could contact Rhys and the others.

"My father's court lies due northward. We'll have to go to the east or west to avoid it."

"No. East takes us too close to the Summer Court border. And I won't lose time by going too far west. We go straight north."

"My father's sentries will easily spot us."

"Then we'll have to remain unseen," I said, rising.

I dumped the last of the contaminated food from my pack. Let the scavengers have it.

Walking through the woods of the Autumn Court felt like striding inside a jewel box.

Even with all that potentially hunted us now, the colors were so vivid it was an effort not to gawk and gape.

By midmorning, the rime had melted away under the buttery sun to reveal what was suitable for eating. My stomach growled with every step, and Lucien's red hair gleamed like the leaves above us as he scanned the woods for anything to fill our bellies.

His woods, by blood and law. He was a son of this forest, and here . . . He looked crafted from it. For it. Even that gold eye.

Lucien eventually stopped at a jade stream wending through a granite-flanked gully, a spot he claimed had once been rich with trout.

I was in the process of constructing a rudimentary fishing pole when he waded into the stream, boots off and pants rolled to his knees, and caught one with his bare hands. He'd tied his hair up, a few strands of it falling into his face as he swooped down again and threw a second trout onto the sandy bank where I'd been trying to find a substitute for fishing twine.

We remained silent as the fish eventually stopped flapping, their sides catching and gleaming with all the colors so bright above us.

Lucien picked them up by their tails, as if he'd done it a thousand times. He might very well have, right here in this stream. "I'll clean them while you start the fire." In the daylight, the glow of the flames wouldn't be noticed. Though the smoke . . . a necessary risk.

We worked and ate in silence, the crackling fire offering the only conversation.

We hiked north for five days, hardly exchanging a word.

Beron's seat was so vast it took us three days to enter, pass through, and clear it. Lucien led us through the outskirts, tense at every call and rustle.

The Forest House was a sprawling complex, Lucien informed me during the few times we risked or bothered to speak to each other. It had been built in and around the trees and rocks, and only its uppermost levels were visible above the ground. Below, it tunneled a few levels into the stone. But its sprawl generated its size. You might walk from one end of the House to the other and it would take you half the morning. There were layers and circles of sentries ringing it: in the trees, on the ground, atop the moss-coated shingles and stones of the House itself.

No enemies approached Beron's home without his knowledge. None left without his permission.

I knew we'd passed beyond Lucien's known map of their patrol routes and stations when his shoulders sagged.

Mine were slumped already.

I had barely slept, only letting myself do so when Lucien's breathing slid into a different, deeper rhythm. I knew I couldn't keep it up for long, but without the ability to shield, to sense any danger . . .

I wondered if Rhys was looking for me. If he'd felt the silence.

I should have gotten a message out. Told him I was going and how to find me.

The faebane—that was why the bond had sounded so muffled. Perhaps I should have killed Ianthe outright.

But what was done was done.

I was rubbing at my aching eyes, taking a moment's rest beneath our new bounty: an apple tree, laden with fat, succulent fruit.

I'd filled my bag with what I could fit inside. Two cores already lay discarded beside me, the sweet rotting scent as lulling as the droning of the bees gorging themselves on fallen apples. A third apple was already primed and poised for eating atop my outstretched legs.

After what the Hybern royals had done, I should have sworn off apples forever, but hunger had always blurred lines for me.

Lucien, sitting a few feet away, chucked his fourth apple into the bushes as I bit into mine. "The farmlands and fields are near," he announced. "We'll have to stay out of sight. My father doesn't pay well for his crops, and the land-workers will earn any extra coin they can."

"Even selling out the location of one of the High Lord's sons?"

"*Especially* that way."

"They didn't like you?"

His jaw tightened. "As the youngest of seven sons, I wasn't particularly needed or wanted. Perhaps it was a good thing. I was able to study for longer than my father allowed my brothers before shoving them out the door to rule over some territory within our lands, and I could train for as long as I liked, since no one believed I'd be dumb enough to kill my way up the long list of heirs. And when I grew bored with studying and fighting . . . I learned what I could of the land from its people. Learned about the people, too."

He eased to his feet with a groan, his unbound hair glimmering as the midday sun overhead set the blood and wine hues aglow.

"I'd say that sounds more High-Lord-like than the life of an idle, unwanted son."

A long, steely look. "Did you think it was mere hatred that prompted my brothers to do their best to break and kill me?"

Despite myself, a shudder rippled down my spine. I finished off the apple and uncoiled to my feet, plucking another off a low-hanging branch. "Would you want it—your father's crown?"

"No one's ever asked me that," Lucien mused as we moved on, dodging fallen, rotting apples. The air was sticky-sweet. "The bloodshed that would be required to earn that crown wouldn't be worth it. Neither would its festering court. I'd gain a crown—only to rule over a crafty, two-faced people."

"Lord of Foxes," I said, snorting as I remembered that mask he'd once worn. "But you never answered my question—about why the people here would sell you out."

The air ahead lightened, and a golden field of barley undulated toward a distant tree line.

"After Jesminda, they would."

Jesminda. He'd never spoken her name.

Lucien slid between the swaying, bobbing stalks. "She was one of them." The words were barely audible over the sighing barley. "And when I didn't protect her . . . It was a betrayal of their trust, too. I ran to some of their houses while fleeing my brothers. They turned me out for what I let happen to her."

Waves of gold and ivory rolled around us, the sky a crisp, unmarred blue.

"I can't blame them for it," he said.

We cleared the fertile valley by the late afternoon. When Lucien offered to stop for the night, I insisted we keep going—right into the steep foothills that leaped into gray, snowcapped mountains that marked the start of the shared range with the Winter Court. If we could get over the border in a day or two, perhaps my powers would have returned enough to contact Rhys—or winnow the rest of the way home.

The hike wasn't an easy one.

Great, craggy boulders made up the ascent, flecked with moss and long, white grasses that hissed like adders. The wind ripped at our hair, the temperature dropping the higher we climbed.

Tonight . . . We might have to risk a fire tonight. Just to stay alive.

Lucien was panting as we scaled a hulking boulder, the valley sprawling away behind, the wood a tangled river of color beyond it. There had to be a pass *into* the range at some point—out of sight.

"How are you not winded," he panted, hauling himself onto the flat top.

I shoved back the hair that had torn free of my braid to whip my face. "I trained."

"I gathered that much after you took on Dagdan and walked away from it."

"I had the element of surprise on my side."

"No," Lucien said quietly as I reached for a foothold in the next boulder. "That was all you." My nails barked as I dug my fingers into the rock and heaved myself up. Lucien added, "You had my back—with them, with Ianthe. Thank you."

The words hit something low in my gut, and I was glad for the wind that kept roaring around us, if only to hide the burning in my eyes.

I slept—finally.

With the crackling fire in our latest cave, the heat and the relative remoteness were enough to finally drag me under.

And in my dreams, I think I swam through Lucien's mind, as if some small ember of my power was at last returning.

I dreamed of our cozy fire, and the craggy walls, the entire space barely big enough to fit us and the fire. I dreamed of the howling, dark night beyond, of all the sounds that Lucien so carefully sorted through while he kept watch.

His attention slid to me at one point and lingered.

I had never known how young, how human I looked when I slept. My braid was a rope over my shoulder, my mouth slightly parted, my face haggard with days of little rest and food.

I dreamed that he removed his cloak and added it over my blanket.

Then I ebbed away, flowing out of his head as my dreams shifted and sailed elsewhere. I let a sea of stars rock me into sleep.

A hand gripped my face so hard the groaning of my bones jolted me awake.

"Look who we found," a cold male voice drawled.

I knew that face—the red hair, the pale skin, the smirk. Knew the faces of the other two males in the cave, a snarling Lucien pinned beneath them.

His brothers.

CHAPTER 12

"Father," the one now holding a knife to my throat said to Lucien, "is rather put out that you didn't stop by to say hello."

"We're on an errand and can't be delayed," Lucien answered smoothly, mastering himself.

That knife pressed a fraction harder into my skin as he let out a humorless laugh. "Right. Rumor has it you two have run off together, cuckolding Tamlin." His grin widened. "I didn't think you had it in you, little brother."

"He had it *in* her, it seems," one of the others sniggered.

I slid my gaze to the male above me. "You will release us."

"Our esteemed father wishes to see you," he said with a snake's smile. The knife didn't waver. "So you will come with us to his home."

"Eris," Lucien warned.

The name clanged through me. Above me, mere inches away . . . Mor's former betrothed. The male who had abandoned her when he found her brutalized body on the border. The High Lord's heir.

I could have sworn phantom talons bit into my palms.

A day or two more, and I might have been able to slash them across his throat.

But I didn't have that time. I only had now. I had to make it count.

Eris merely said to me, cold and bored, "Get up."

I felt it then—stirring awake as if some stick had poked it. As if being here, in this territory, amongst its blooded royals, had somehow sparked it to life, boiling past that poison. Turning that poison to steam.

With his knife still angled against my neck, I let Eris haul me to my feet, the other two dragging Lucien before he could stand on his own.

Make it count. Use my surroundings.

I caught Lucien's eye.

And he saw the sweat beading on my temple, my upper lip, as my blood heated.

A slight bob of his chin was his only sign of understanding.

Eris would bring us to Beron, and the High Lord would either kill us for sport, sell us to the highest bidder, or hold us indefinitely. And after what they had done to Lucien's lover, what they'd done to Mor . . .

"After you," Eris said smoothly, lowering that knife at last. He shoved me a step.

I'd been waiting. Balance, Cassian had taught me, was crucial to winning a fight.

And as Eris's shove caused him to get on uneven footing, I turned my propelled step on him.

Twisting, so fast he didn't see me get into his open guard, I drove my elbow into his nose.

Eris stumbled back.

Flame slammed into the other two, and Lucien hurtled out of the way as they shouted and fell deeper into the cave.

I unleashed every drop of the flame in me, a wall of it between us and them. Sealing his brothers inside the cave.

"*Run*," I gasped out, but Lucien was already at my side, a steadying hand under my arm as I burned that flame hotter and hotter. It wouldn't keep them contained for long, and I could indeed feel someone's power rising to challenge mine.

But there was another force to wield.

Lucien understood the same moment I did.

Sweat simmered on Lucien's brow as a pulse of flame-licked power slammed into the stones just above us. Dust and debris rained down.

I threw any trickle of magic into Lucien's next blow.

His next.

As Eris's livid face emerged from my net of flame, glowing like a new-forged god of wrath, Lucien and I brought down the cave ceiling.

Fire burst through the small cracks like a thousand flaming serpents' tongues—but the cave-in did not so much as tremble.

"Hurry," Lucien panted, and I didn't waste breath agreeing as we staggered into the night.

Our packs, our weapons, our food . . . all inside that cave.

I had two daggers on me, Lucien one. I'd been wearing my cloak, but . . . he'd indeed given me his. He shivered against the cold as we dragged and clawed our way up the mountain slope, and did not dare stop.

Had I still remained human, I would have been dead.

The cold was bone-deep, the screaming wind lashing us like burning whips. My teeth clacked against each other, my fingers so stiff I could scarcely grapple onto the icy granite with each mile we staggered through the mountains. Perhaps both of us were spared from an icy death by the kernel of flame that had just barely kindled inside our veins.

We didn't pause once, an unspoken fear that if we did, the cold would leech any lingering warmth and we'd never again move. Or Lucien's brothers would gain ground.

I tried, over and over, to shout down the bond to Rhys. To winnow. To grow wings and attempt to fly us out of the mountain pass we trudged through, the snow waist-deep and so densely packed in places we had to crawl over it, our skin scraped raw from the ice.

But the faebane's stifling grip still held the majority of my power in check.

We had to be close to the Winter Court border, I told myself as we squinted against a blast of icy wind through the other end of the narrow mountain pass. Close—and once we were over it, Eris and the others wouldn't dare set foot into another court's territory.

My muscles screamed with every step, my boots soaked through with snow, my feet perilously numb. I'd spent enough human winters in the forest to know the dangers of exposure—the threat of cold and wet.

Lucien, a step behind me, panted hard as the walls of rock and snow parted to reveal a bitter, star-flecked night—and more mountains beyond. I almost whimpered.

"We've got to keep going," he said, snow crusting the stray strands of his hair, and I wondered if the sound had indeed left me.

Ice tickled my frozen nostrils. "We can't last long—we need to get warm and rest."

"My brothers—"

"We will die if we continue." Or lose fingers and toes at the best. I pointed to the mountain slope ahead, a hazardous plunge down. "We can't risk that at night. We need to find a cave and try to make a fire."

"With *what*?" he snapped. "Do you see any wood?"

I only continued on. Arguing just wasted energy—and time.

And I didn't have an answer, anyway.

I wondered if we'd make it through the night.

✣

We found a cave. Deep and shielded from wind or sight. Lucien and I carefully covered our tracks, making sure the wind blew in our favor, veiling our scents.

That was where our luck ran out. No wood to be found; no fire in either of our veins.

So we used our only option: body heat. Huddled in the farthest reaches of the cave, we sat thigh to thigh and arm to arm beneath my cloak, shuddering with cold and dripping wet.

I could scarcely hear the hollow scream of the wind over my chattering teeth. And his.

Find me, find me, find me, I tried shouting down that bond. But my mate's wry voice didn't answer.

There was only the roaring void.

"Tell me about her—about Elain," Lucien said quietly. As if the death that squatted in the dark beside us had drawn his thoughts to his own mate as well.

I debated not saying anything, shaking too hard to dredge up speech, but . . . "She loves her garden. Always loved growing things. Even when we were destitute, she managed to tend a little garden in the warmer months. And when—when our fortune returned, she took to tending and planting the most beautiful gardens you've ever seen. Even in Prythian. It drove the servants mad, because they were supposed to do the work and ladies were only meant to clip a rose here and there, but Elain would put on a hat and gloves and kneel in the dirt, weeding. She acted like a pure-bred lady in every regard but that."

Lucien was silent for a long moment. "Acted," he murmured. "You talk about her as if she's dead."

"I don't know what changes the Cauldron wrought on her. I don't think going home is an option. No matter how she might yearn to."

"Surely Prythian is a better alternative, war or no."

I steeled myself before saying, "She is engaged, Lucien."

I felt every inch of him go stiff beside me. "To whom."

Flat, cold words. With the threat of violence simmering beneath.

"To a human lord's son. The lord hates faeries—has dedicated his life and wealth to hunting them. Us. I was told that though it's a love match, her betrothed's father was keen to have access to her considerable dowry to continue his crusade against faerie-kind."

"Elain loves this lord's son." Not quite a question.

"She says she does. Nesta—Nesta thought the father and his obsession with killing faeries was bad enough to raise some alarms. She never voiced the concern to Elain. Neither did I."

"My mate is engaged to a human male." He spoke more to himself than to me.

"I'm sorry if—"

"I want to see her. Just once. Just—to know."

"To know what?"

He hitched my damp cloak higher around us. "If she is worth fighting for."

I couldn't bring myself to say she was, to give him that sort of hope when Elain might very well do everything in her power to hold to her engagement. Even if immortality had already rendered it impossible.

Lucien leaned his head back against the rock wall behind us. "And then I'll ask your mate how he survived it—knowing you were engaged to someone else. Sharing another male's bed."

I tucked my freezing hands under my arms, gazing toward the gloom ahead.

"Tell me when you knew," he demanded, his knee pressing into mine. "That Rhysand was your mate. Tell me when you stopped loving Tamlin and started loving *him* instead."

I chose not to answer.

"Was it going on before you even left?"

I whipped my head to him, even if I could barely make out his features in the dark. "I never touched Rhysand like that until months later."

"You kissed Under the Mountain."

"I had as little choice in that as I did in the dancing."

"And yet this is the male you now love."

He didn't know—he had no inkling of the personal history, the secrets, that had opened my heart to the High Lord of the Night Court. They were not my stories to tell.

"One would think, Lucien, that you'd be glad I fell in love with my mate, given that you're in the same situation Rhys was in six months ago."

"You *left* us."

Us. Not Tamlin. *Us*. The words echoed into the dark, toward the howling wind and lashing snow beyond the bend.

"I told you that day in the woods: you abandoned me long before I ever physically left." I shivered again, hating every point of contact, that I so desperately needed his warmth. "You fit into the Spring Court as little as I did, Lucien. You enjoyed its pleasures and diversions. But don't pretend you weren't made for something *more* than that."

His metal eye whirred. "And where, exactly, do you believe I will fit in? The Night Court?"

I didn't answer. I didn't have one, honestly. As High Lady, I could likely offer him a position, if we survived long enough to make it home. I'd do it mostly to keep Elain from ever going to the Spring Court, but I had little doubt Lucien would be able to hold his own against my friends. And some small, horrible part of me enjoyed the thought of taking one more thing away from Tamlin, something vital, something essential.

"We should leave at dawn," was my only reply.

We lasted the night.

Every part of me was stiff and aching when we began our careful trek down the mountain. Not a whisper or trace of Lucien's brothers—or any sort of life.

I didn't care, not when we at last passed over the border and into Winter Court lands.

Beyond the mountain, a great ice-plain sparkled into the distance. It would take days to cross, but it didn't matter: I'd awoken with enough power in my veins to warm us with a small fire. Slowly—so slowly, the effects of the faebane ebbed.

I was willing to wager that we'd be halfway across the ice by the time we could winnow out of here. If our luck held and no one else found us.

I ran through every lesson Rhys had taught me about the Winter Court and its High Lord, Kallias.

Towering, exquisite palaces, full of roaring hearths and bedecked in evergreens. Carved sleighs were the court's preferred method of transportation, hauled by velvet-antlered reindeer whose splayed hooves were ideal for the ice and snow. Their forces were well trained, but they often relied on the great, white bears that stalked the realm for any unwanted visitors.

I prayed none of them waited on the ice, their coats perfectly blended into the terrain.

The Night Court's relationship with Winter was fine enough, still tenuous, as all our bonds were, after Amarantha. After she'd butchered so many of them—including, I remembered with no small surge of nausea, dozens of Winter Court children.

I couldn't imagine it—the loss, the rage and grief. I'd never had the nerve to ask Rhys, in those months of training, who the children had belonged to. What the consequences had been. If it was considered the worst of Amarantha's crimes, or just one of countless others.

But despite any tentative bonds, Winter was one of the Seasonal Courts. It might side with Tamlin, with Tarquin. Our best allies remained the Solar Courts: Dawn and Day. But they lay far to the north—above the demarcation line between the Solar and Seasonal Courts. That slice of sacred, unclaimed land that held Under the Mountain. And the Weaver's cottage.

We'd be gone before we ever had to set foot in that lethal, ancient forest.

It was another day and night before we cleared the mountains entirely and set foot on the thick ice. Nothing grew, and I could only tell when we were on solid land by the dense snow packed beneath. Otherwise, too frequently, the ice was clear as glass—revealing dark, depthless lakes beneath.

At least we didn't encounter any of the white bears. But the real threat, we both quickly realized, was the utter lack of shelter: out on the ice, there was none to be found against the wind and cold. And if we lit a fire with our feeble magic, anyone nearby would spot it. No matter the practicality of lighting a fire atop a frozen lake.

The sun was just slipping above the horizon, staining the plain with gold, the shadows still a bruised blue, when Lucien said, "Tonight, we'll melt some of the ice pack enough to soften it—and build a shelter."

I considered. We were barely a hundred feet onto what seemed to be an endless lake. It was impossible to tell where it ended. "You think we'll be out on the ice for that long?"

Lucien frowned toward the dawn-stained horizon. "Likely, but who knows how far it extends?" Indeed, the snowdrifts hid much of the ice beneath.

"Perhaps there's some other way around . . . ," I mused, glancing back toward our abandoned little camp.

We looked at the same time. And both beheld the three figures now standing at the lake edge. Smiling.

Eris lifted a hand wreathed in flame.

Flame—to melt the ice on which we stood.

CHAPTER 13

"Run," Lucien breathed.

I didn't dare take my eyes off his brothers. Not as Eris lowered that hand to the frozen edge of the lake. "Run where, exactly?"

Flesh met ice and steam rippled. The ice went opaque, thawing in a line that shot for us—

We ran. The slick ice made for a treacherous sprint, my ankles roaring with the effort of keeping me upright.

Ahead, the lake stretched on forever. And with the sun barely awake, the dangers would be even harder to spot—

"Faster," Lucien ordered. "Don't look!" he barked as I began to turn my head to see if they'd followed. He lashed out a hand to grip my elbow, steadying me before I could even register that I'd stumbled.

Where would we go where would we go where would we go

Water splashed beneath my boots—thawed ice. Eris had to either be expending all his power to get through millennia of ice, or was just doing it slowly to torture us—

"Zag," Lucien panted. "We need to—"

He shoved me aside, and I staggered, arms wheeling.

Just as an arrow ricocheted off the ice where I'd been standing.

"*Faster*," Lucien snapped, and I didn't hesitate.

I hurtled into a flat-out sprint, Lucien and I weaving in and out of each other's paths as those arrows continued firing. Ice sprayed where they landed, and no matter how fast we ran, the ground beneath us melted and melted—

Ice. I had ice in my veins, and now that we were over the border of the Winter Court—

I didn't care if they saw it—my power. Kallias's power. Not when the alternatives were far worse.

I threw out a hand before us as a melting splotch began to spread, ice groaning.

A spray of ice shot from my palm, freezing the lake once more.

With each pump of my arms as I ran, I fired that ice from my palms, solidifying what Eris sought to melt ahead of us. Maybe—just maybe we could clear the lake, and if they were stupid enough to be atop it when we did . . . If I could form ice, I could certainly un-form it.

I crossed paths with Lucien again, meeting his wide eyes as we did, and opened my mouth to tell him my plan, when Eris appeared.

Not behind. Ahead.

But it was the other brother at his side, arrow aimed and already flying for me, who drew the shout from my throat.

I lunged to the side, rolling.

Not fast enough.

The arrow's edge sliced the shell of my ear, my cheek, leaving a stinging wake. Lucien shouted, but another arrow was flying.

It went clean through my right forearm this time.

Ice sliced into my face, my hands, as I went down, knees barking, arm shrieking in agony at the impact—

Behind, steps thudded on ice as the third brother closed in.

I bit my lip hard enough to draw blood as I ripped away the cloth of my jacket and shirt from my forearm, snapped the arrow in two, and tore the pieces from my flesh. My roar shattered and bounced across the ice.

Eris had taken one step toward me, smiling like a wolf, when I was up again, my last two Illyrian knives in my palms, my right arm screaming at the movement—

Around me, the ice began to melt.

"This can end with you going under, begging me to get you out once that ice instantly refreezes," Eris drawled. Behind him, cut off by his brothers, Lucien had drawn his own knife and now sized up the other two. "Or this can end with you agreeing to take my hand. But either way, you will be coming with me."

Already, the flesh in my arm was knitting together. Healing—from Dawn's powers reawakening in my veins—

And if that was working—

I didn't give Eris time to read my move.

I sucked in a sharp breath.

White, blinding light erupted from me. Eris swore, and I ran.

Not toward him, not when I was still too injured to wield my knives. But away—toward that distant shore. Half-blinded myself, I stumbled and staggered until I was clear of the treacherous, melting splotches, then sprinted.

I made it all of twenty feet before Eris winnowed in front of me and struck.

A backhanded blow to the face, so hard my teeth went through my lip.

He struck again before I could even fall, a punch to my gut that ripped the air from my lungs. Beyond me, Lucien had unleashed himself upon his two brothers. Metal and fire blasted and collided, ice spraying.

I'd no sooner hit the ice than Eris grabbed me by the hair, right at the roots, the grip so brutal tears stung my eyes. But he dragged me back toward that shore, back across the ice—

I fought against the blow to my gut, fought to get a wisp of air down my throat, into my lungs. My boots scraped against the ice as I feebly kicked, yet Eris held firm—

I think Lucien shouted my name.

I opened my mouth, but a gag of fire shoved its way between my lips. It didn't burn, but was hot enough to tell me it would if Eris willed it. Equal bands of flame wrapped around my wrists, my ankles. My throat.

I couldn't remember—couldn't remember what to do, how to move, how to *stop* this—

Closer and closer to the shore, to the awaiting party of sentries that winnowed in out of nowhere. *No, no, no*—

A shadow slammed into the earth before us, cracking the ice toward every horizon.

Not a shadow.

An Illyrian warrior.

Seven red Siphons glinted over his scaled black armor as Cassian tucked in his wings and snarled at Eris with five centuries' worth of rage.

Not dead. Not hurt. Whole.

His wings repaired and strong.

I loosed a shuddering sob over the burning gag. Cassian's Siphons flickered in response, as if the sight of me, at Eris's hand—

Another impact struck the ice behind us. Shadows skittered in its wake.

Azriel.

I began crying in earnest, some leash I'd kept on myself snapping free as my friends landed. As I saw that Azriel, too, was alive, was healed. As Cassian drew twin Illyrian blades, the sight of them like home, and said to Eris with lethal calm, "I suggest you drop my lady."

Eris's grip on my hair only tightened, wringing a whimper from me.

The wrath that twisted Cassian's face was world-ending.

But his hazel eyes slid to mine. A silent command.

He had spent months training me. Not just to attack, but to defend. Had taught me, over and over, how to get free of a captor's grasp. How to manage not only my body, but my mind.

As if he'd known that it was a very real possibility that this scenario would one day happen.

Eris had bound my limbs, but—I could still move them. Still use parts of my magic.

And getting him off balance long enough to let go, to let Cassian jump between us and take on the High Lord's son . . .

Towering over me, Eris didn't so much as glance down as I twisted, spinning on the ice, and slammed my bound legs up between his.

He lurched, bending over with a grunt.

Right into the fisted, bound hands I drove into his nose. Bone crunched, and his hand sprang free of my hair.

I rolled, scrambling away. Cassian was already there.

Eris hardly had time to draw his sword as Cassian brought his own down upon him.

Steel against steel rang out across the ice. Sentries on the shore unleashed arrows of wood and magic—only to bounce against a shield of blue.

Azriel. Across the ice, he and Lucien were engaging the other two brothers. That any of Lucien's siblings held out against the Illyrians was a testament to their own training, but—

I focused the ice in my veins on the gag in my mouth, the binds around my wrists and ankles. Ice to smother fire, to sing it to sleep . . .

Cassian and Eris clashed, danced back, clashed again.

Ropes of fire snapped free, dissolving with a hiss of steam.

I was on my feet again, reaching for a weapon I did not have. My daggers had been lost forty feet away.

Cassian got past Eris's guard with brutal efficiency. And Eris screamed as the Illyrian blade punched through his gut.

Blood, red as rubies, stained the ice and snow.

For a heartbeat, I saw how it would play out: three of Beron's sons dead at our hands. A temporary satisfaction for me, five centuries of satisfaction for Cassian, Azriel, and Mor, but if Beron still debated what side to support in this war . . .

I had other weapons to use.

"Stop," I said.

The word was a soft, cold command.

And Azriel and Cassian obeyed.

Lucien's other two brothers were back-to-back, bloody and gaping. Lucien himself was panting, sword still raised, as Azriel flicked the blood off his own blade and stalked toward me.

I met the hazel eyes of the shadowsinger. The cool face that hid such pain—and kindness. He had come. Cassian had come.

The Illyrians fell into place beside me. Eris, a hand pressed to his gut, was breathing wetly, glaring at us.

Glaring—then considering. Watching the three of us as I said to Eris, to his other two brothers, to the sentries on the shore, "You all deserve to die for this. And for much, much more. But I am going to spare your miserable lives."

Even with a wound through his gut, Eris's lip curled.

Cassian snarled his warning.

I only removed the glamour I'd kept on myself these weeks. With the sleeve of my jacket and shirt gone, there was nothing but smooth skin where that wound had been. Smooth skin that now became adorned with swirls and whorls of ink. The markings of my new title—and my mating bond.

Lucien's face drained of color as he strode for us, stopping a healthy distance from Azriel's side.

"I am High Lady of the Night Court," I said quietly to them all.

Even Eris stopped sneering. His amber eyes widened, something like fear now creeping into them.

"There's no such thing as a High Lady," one of Lucien's brothers spat.

A faint smile played on my mouth. "There is now."

And it was time for the world to know it.

I caught Cassian's gaze, finding pride glimmering there—and relief.

"Take me home," I ordered him, my chin high and unwavering.

Then to Azriel, "Take us both home." I said to the Autumn Court's scions, "We'll see you on the battlefield."

Let them decide whether it was better to be fighting beside us or against us.

I turned to Cassian, who opened his arms and tucked me in tight before launching us skyward in a blast of wings and power. Beside us, Azriel and Lucien did the same.

When Eris and the others were nothing but specks of black on white below, when we were sailing high and fast, Cassian observed, "I don't know who looks more uncomfortable: Az or Lucien Vanserra."

I chuckled, glancing over my shoulder to where the shadowsinger carried my friend, both of them making a point not to speak, look, or talk. "Vanserra?"

"You never knew his family name?"

I met those laughing, fierce hazel eyes.

Cassian's smile softened. "Hello, Feyre."

My throat tightened to the point of pain, and I threw my arms around his neck, embracing him tightly.

"I missed you, too," Cassian murmured, squeezing me.

We flew until we reached the border of the sacred, eighth territory. And when Cassian set us down in a snowy field before the ancient wood, I took one look at the blond female in Illyrian leathers pacing between the gnarled trees and launched into a sprint.

Mor held me as tightly as I gripped her.

"Where is he?" I asked, refusing to let go, to lift my head from her shoulder.

"He—it's a long story. Far away, but racing home. Right now." Mor pulled back enough to scan my face. Her mouth tightened at the lingering injuries, and she gently scraped away flecks of dried blood caked on my ear. "He picked up on you—the bond—minutes ago. The three of us were closest. I winnowed in Cassian, but with Eris and the others there . . ." Guilt dimmed her eyes. "Relations with the Winter Court are strained—we thought if I was out here on the border, it might keep Kallias's forces from looking south. At least long enough to get you." And to avoid an interaction with Eris that Mor was perhaps not ready for.

I shook my head at the shame still shadowing her usually bright features. "I understand." I embraced her again. "I understand."

Mor's answering squeeze was rib-crushing.

Azriel and Lucien landed, plumes of snow spraying in the former's wake. Mor and I released each other at last, my friend's face going grave as she sized up Lucien. Snow and blood and dirt coated him—coated us both.

Cassian explained to Mor, "He fought against Eris and the other two."

Mor's throat bobbed, noting the blood staining Cassian's hands—realizing it wasn't his own. Scenting it, no doubt, as she blurted, "Eris. Did you—"

"He remains alive," Azriel answered, shadows curling around the clawed tips of his wings, so stark against the snow beneath our boots. "So do the others."

Lucien was glancing between all of them, wary and quiet. What he knew of Mor's history with his eldest brother . . . I'd never asked. Never wanted to.

Mor tossed her mass of golden waves over a shoulder. "Then let's go home."

"Which one?" I asked carefully.

Mor swept her attention over Lucien once more. I almost pitied Lucien for the weight in her gaze, the utter judgment. The stare of the Morrigan—whose gift was pure truth.

Whatever she beheld in Lucien was enough for her to say, "The town house. You have someone waiting there for you."

CHAPTER 14

I had not let myself imagine it: the moment I'd again stand in the wood-paneled foyer of the town house. When I'd hear the song of the gulls soaring high above Velaris, smell the brine of the Sidra River that wended through the heart of the city, feel the warmth of the sunshine streaming through the windows upon my back.

Mor had winnowed us all, and now stood behind me, panting softly, as we watched Lucien survey our surroundings.

His metal eye whirred, while the other warily scanned the rooms flanking the foyer: the dining room and sitting room overlooking the little front yard and street; then the stairs to the second level; then the hallway beside it that led to the kitchen and courtyard garden.

Then finally to the shut front door. To the city waiting beyond.

Cassian took up a place against the banister, crossing his arms with an arrogance I knew meant trouble. Azriel remained beside me, shadows wreathing his knuckles. As if battling High Lords' sons was how they usually spent their days.

I wondered if Lucien knew that his first words here would either damn or save him. I wondered what my role in it would be.

No—it was my call.

High Lady. I—outranked them, my friends. It was my call to make whether Lucien was allowed to keep his freedom.

But their watchful silence was indication enough: let him decide his own fate.

At last, Lucien looked at me. At us.

He said, "There are children laughing in the streets."

I blinked. He said it with such . . . quiet surprise. As if he hadn't heard the sound in a long, long time.

I opened my mouth to reply, but someone else spoke for me.

"That they do so at all after Hybern's attack is testament to how hard the people of Velaris have worked to rebuild."

I whirled, finding Amren emerging from wherever she'd been sitting in the other room, the plush furniture hiding her small body.

She appeared exactly as she had the last time I'd seen her: standing in this very foyer, warning us to be careful in Hybern. Her chin-length, jet-black hair gleamed in the sunlight, her silver, unearthly eyes unusually bright as they met mine.

The delicate female bowed her head. As much of a gesture of obedience as a fifteen-thousand-year-old creature would make to a newly minted High Lady. And friend. "I see you brought home a new pet," she said, nose crinkling with distaste.

Something like fear had entered Lucien's eye, as if he, too, beheld the monster that lurked beneath that beautiful face.

Indeed, it seemed he had heard of her already. Before I could introduce him, Lucien bowed at the waist. Deeply. Cassian let out an amused grunt, and I shot him a warning glare.

Amren smiled slightly. "Already trained, I see."

Lucien slowly straightened, as if he were standing before the open maw of some great plains-cat he did not wish to startle with sudden movements.

"Amren, this is Lucien . . . Vanserra."

Lucien stiffened. "I don't use my family's name." He clarified to Amren with another incline of his head, "Lucien will do."

I suspected he'd ceased using that name the moment his lover's heart had stopped beating.

Amren was studying that metal eye. "Clever work," she said, then surveyed me. "Looks like someone clawed you up, girl."

The wound in my arm, at least, had healed, though a nasty red mark remained. I assumed my face wasn't much better. Before I could answer her, Lucien asked, "What is this place?"

We all looked at him. "Home," I said. "This is—my home."

I could see the details now sinking in. The lack of darkness. The lack of screaming. The scent of the sea and citrus, not blood and decay. The laughter of children that indeed continued.

The greatest secret in Prythian's history.

"This is Velaris," I explained. "The City of Starlight."

His throat bobbed. "And you are High Lady of the Night Court."

"Indeed she is."

My blood stopped at the voice that drawled from behind me.

At the scent that hit me, awoke me. My friends began smiling.

I turned.

Rhysand leaned against the archway into the sitting room, arms crossed, wings nowhere to be seen, dressed in his usual immaculate black jacket and pants.

And as those violet eyes met mine, as that familiar half smile faded . . .

My face crumpled. A small, broken noise cracked from me.

Rhys was instantly moving, but my legs had already given out. The foyer carpet cushioned the impact as I sank to my knees.

I covered my face with my hands while the past month crashed into me.

Rhys knelt before me, knee to knee.

Gently, he pulled my hands away from my face. Gently, he took my cheeks in his hands and brushed away my tears.

I didn't care that we had an audience as I lifted my head and beheld the joy and concern and love shining in those remarkable eyes.

Neither did Rhys as he murmured, "My love," and kissed me.

I'd no sooner slid my hands into his hair than he scooped me into his arms and stood in one smooth movement. I pulled my mouth from his, glancing toward a pallid Lucien, but Rhysand said to our companions without so much as looking at them, "Go find somewhere else to be for a while."

He didn't wait to see if they obeyed.

Rhys winnowed us up the stairs and launched into a steady, swift walk down the hallway. I peered down at the foyer in time to spy Mor grabbing Lucien's arm and nodding to the others before they all vanished.

"Do you want to go over what happened at the Spring Court?" I asked, voice raw, as I studied my mate's face.

No amusement, nothing but that predatory intensity, focused on my every breath. "There are other things I'd rather do first."

He carried me into our bedroom—once *his* room, now full of our belongings. It was exactly as I'd last seen it: the enormous bed that he now strode for, the two armoires, the desk by the window that overlooked the courtyard garden now bursting with purple and pink and blue amid the lush greens.

I braced myself to be sprawled on the bed, but Rhys paused halfway across the room, the door snicking shut on a star-kissed wind.

Slowly, he set me on the plush carpet, blatantly sliding me down his body as he did so. As if he was as powerless to resist touching me, as reluctant to let go as I was with him.

And every place where our bodies met, all of him so warm and solid and *real* . . . I savored it, my throat tight as I placed a hand on his sculpted chest, the thunderous heartbeat beneath his black jacket echoing into my palm. The only sign of whatever torrent coursed through him as he skimmed his hands up my arms in a lingering caress and gripped my shoulders.

His thumbs stroked a gentle rhythm over my filthy clothes as he scanned my face.

Beautiful. He was even more beautiful than I had remembered, dreamed of during those weeks at the Spring Court.

For a long moment, we only breathed in each other's air. For a long moment, all I could do was take the scent of him deep into my lungs, letting it settle inside me. My fingers tightened on his jacket.

Mate. My mate.

As if he'd heard it down the bond, Rhys finally murmured, "When the bond went dark, I thought . . ." Fear—genuine terror shadowed his eyes, even as his thumbs continued stroking my shoulders, gentle and steady. "By the time I got to the Spring Court, you'd vanished. Tamlin was raging through that forest, hunting for you. But you hid your scent. And even I couldn't—couldn't find you—"

The snag in his words was a knife to my gut. "We went to the Autumn Court through one of the doors," I said, setting my other hand on his arm. The corded muscles beneath shifted at my touch. "You couldn't find me because two Hybern commanders drugged my food and drink with faebane—enough to extinguish my powers. I—I still don't have full use."

Cold rage now flickered across that beautiful face as his thumbs halted on my shoulders. "You killed them."

Not entirely a question, but I nodded.

"Good."

I swallowed. "Has Hybern sacked the Spring Court?"

"Not yet. Whatever you did . . . it worked. Tamlin's sentries abandoned him. Over half his people refused to appear for the Tithe two days ago. Some are leaving for other courts. Some are murmuring of rebellion. It seems you made yourself quite beloved. Holy, even." Amusement at last warmed his features. "They were rather upset when they believed he'd allowed Hybern to terrorize you into fleeing."

I traced the faint silver whorl of embroidery on the breast of his jacket, and I could have sworn he shuddered beneath the touch. "I suppose they'll learn soon enough I'm well cared for." Rhys's hands tightened on my shoulders in agreement, as if he were about to show me just how well cared for I was, but I angled my head. "What about Ianthe—and Jurian?"

Rhysand's powerful chest heaved beneath my hand as he blew out a breath. "Reports are murky on both. Jurian, it seems, has returned to the hand that feeds him. Ianthe . . ." Rhys lifted his brows. "I assume *her* hand is courtesy of you, and not the commanders."

"She fell," I said sweetly.

"Must have been some fall," he mused, a dark smile dancing on those lips as he drifted even closer, the heat of his body seeping into me while his hands migrated from my shoulders to brush lazy lines down my back. I bit my lip, focusing on his words and not the urge to arch into the touch, to bury my face in his chest and do some exploring of my own. "She's currently convalescing after her ordeal, apparently. Won't leave her temple."

It was my turn to murmur, "Good." Perhaps one of those pretty acolytes of hers would get sick of her sanctimonious bullshit and smother Ianthe in her sleep.

I braced my hands on his hips, fully ready to slide beneath his jacket, *needing* to touch bare skin, but Rhys straightened, pulling back. Still close enough that one of his hands remained on my waist, but the other—

He reached for my arm, gently examining the angry welt where my skin had been torn by an arrow. Darkness rumbled in the corner of the room. "Cassian let me into his mind just now—to show me what happened on the ice." He stroked a thumb over the hurt, the touch featherlight. "Eris was always a male of limited days. Now Lucien might find himself closer to inheriting his father's throne than he ever expected to be."

My spine locked. "Eris is precisely as horrible as you painted him to be."

Rhys's thumb glided over my forearm again, leaving gooseflesh in its wake. A promise—not of the retribution he was contemplating, but of what awaited us in this room. The bed a few feet away. Until he murmured, "You declared yourself High Lady."

"Was I not supposed to?"

He released my arm to brush his knuckles across my cheek. "I've wanted to roar it from the rooftops of Velaris from the moment the priestess anointed you. How typical of you to upend my grand plans."

A smile tugged on my lips. "It happened less than an hour ago. I'm sure you could go crow from the chimney right now and everyone would give you credit for breaking the news."

His fingers threaded through my hair, tilting my face up. That wicked smile grew, and my toes curled in their boots. "There's my darling Feyre."

His head dipped, his gaze fixated on my mouth, hunger lighting those violet eyes—

"Where are my sisters?" The thought clanged through me, jarring as a pealing bell.

Rhys paused, hand slipping from my hair as his smile faded. "At the House of Wind." He straightened, swallowing—as if it somehow checked him. "I can—take you to them." Every word seemed to be an effort.

But he would, I realized. He'd shove down his need for me and take me to them, if that was what I wanted. My choice. It had always been my choice with him.

I shook my head. I wouldn't see them—not yet. Not until *I* was steady enough to face them. "They're well, though?"

His hesitation told me enough. "They're safe."

Not really an answer, but I wasn't going to fool myself into thinking my sisters would be thriving. I leaned my brow against his chest. "Cassian and Azriel are healed," I murmured against his jacket, breathing in the scent of him over and over as a tremor shuddered through me. "You told me that—and yet I didn't . . . it didn't sink in. Until now."

Rhys ran a hand down my back, the other sliding to grip my hip.

"Azriel healed within a few days. Cassian's wings . . . it was complex. But he's been training every day to regain his strength. The healer had to rebuild most of his wings—but he'll be fine."

I swallowed down the tightness in my throat and wrapped my arms around his waist, pressing my face wholly against his chest. His hand tightened on my hip in answer, the other resting at my nape, holding me to him as I breathed, "Mor said you were far away—that was why you weren't there."

"I'm sorry I wasn't."

"No," I said, lifting my head to scan his eyes, the guilt dampening them. "I didn't mean it like that. I just . . ." I savored the feel of him beneath my palms. "Where were you?"

Rhys stilled, and I braced myself as he said casually, "I couldn't very well let you do *all* the work to undermine our enemies, could I?"

I didn't smile. "Where. Were. You."

"With Az only recently back on his feet, I took it upon myself to do some of his work."

I clenched my jaw. "Such as?"

He leaned down, nuzzling my throat. "Don't you want to comfort your mate, who has missed you terribly these weeks?"

I planted a hand on his face and pushed him back, scowling. "I want my mate to tell me where the hell he was. *Then* he can get his *comfort*."

Rhys nipped at my fingers, teeth snapping playfully. "Cruel, beautiful female."

I watched him beneath lowered brows.

Rhys rolled his eyes, sighing. "I was on the continent. At the human queens' palace."

I choked. "You were *where*?"

"Technically, I was flying above it, but—"

"You went *alone*?"

He gaped at me. "Despite what our mistakes in Hybern might have suggested, I *am* capable of—"

"You went to the human world, to our enemies' compound, *alone*?"

"I'd rather it be me than any of the others."

That had been his problem from the start. Always him, always sacrificing—

"Why," I demanded. "Why risk it? Is something happening?"

Rhys peered toward the window, as if he could see all the way to the mortal lands. His mouth tightened. "It's the quiet on their side of the sea that bothers me. No whisper of armies gathered, no other human allies summoned. Since Hybern, we've heard nothing. So I thought to see for myself why that is." He flicked my nose, tugging me closer again. "I'd just neared the edge of their territory when I felt the bond awaken again. I knew the others were closer, so I sent them."

"You don't need to explain."

Rhys rested his chin atop my head. "I wanted to be there—to get you. Find you. Bring you home."

"You do certainly enjoy a dramatic entrance."

He chuckled, his breath warming my hair as I listened to the sound rumble through his body.

Of course he would have been working against Hybern while I was away. Had I expected them all to be sitting on their asses for over a month? And Rhys, constantly plotting, always a step ahead . . . He would have used this time to his advantage. I debated asking about it, but right now, breathing him in, feeling his warmth . . . Let it wait.

Rhys pressed a kiss to my hair. "You're home."

A shuddering, small sound came out of me as I nodded, squeezing him tighter. Home. Not just Velaris, but wherever he was, our family was.

Ebony claws stroked along the barrier in my mind—in affection and request.

I lowered my shields for him, just as his own dropped. His mind curled around mine, as surely as his body now held me.

"I missed you every moment," Rhys said, leaning down to kiss the corner of my mouth. "Your smile." His lips grazed over the shell of my ear and my back arched slightly. "Your laugh." He pressed a kiss to my neck, right beneath my ear, and I tilted my head to give him access, biting down the urge to beg him to take more, to take faster as he murmured, "Your scent."

My eyes fluttered closed, and his hands coasted around my hips to cup my rear, squeezing as he bent to kiss the center of my throat. "The sounds you make when I'm inside you."

His tongue flicked over the spot where he'd kissed, and one of those sounds indeed escaped me. Rhys kissed the hollow of my collarbone, and my core went utterly molten. "My brave, bold, brilliant mate."

He lifted his head, and it was an effort to open my eyes. To meet his stare as his hands roved in lazy lines down my back, over my rear, then up again. "I love you," he said. And if I hadn't already believed him, felt it in my very bones, the light in his face as he said the words . . .

Tears burned my eyes again, slipping free before I could control myself.

Rhys leaned in to lick them away. One after another. As he'd once done Under the Mountain.

"You have a choice," he murmured against my cheekbone. "Either I lick every inch of you clean . . ." His hand grazed the tip of my breast, circling lazily. As if we had days and days to do this. "Or you can get into the bath that should be ready by now."

I pulled away, lifting a brow. "Are you suggesting that I smell?"

Rhys smirked, and I could have sworn my core pounded in answer. "Never. But . . ." His eyes darkened, the desire and amusement fading as he took in my clothes. "There is blood on you. Yours, and others'. I thought I'd be a good mate and offer you a bath before I ravish you wholly."

I huffed a laugh and brushed back his hair, savoring the silken, sable strands between my fingers. "So considerate. Though I can't believe you kicked everyone out of the house so you could take me to bed."

"One of the many benefits to being High Lord."

"What a terrible abuse of power."

That half smile danced on his mouth. "Well?"

"As much as I'd like to see you attempt to lick off a week's worth of dirt, sweat, and blood . . ." His eyes gleamed with the challenge, and I laughed again. "Normal bath, please."

He had the nerve to look vaguely disappointed. I poked him in the chest as I pushed away, aiming for the large bathing room attached to the bedroom. The massive porcelain tub was already filled with steaming water, and—

"Bubbles?"

"Do you have a moral objection to them?"

I grinned, unbuttoning my jacket. My fingers were near-black with dirt and caked blood. I cringed. "I might need more than one bath to get clean."

He snapped his fingers, and my skin was instantly pristine again. I blinked. "If you can do that, then what's the point of the bath?" He'd done it Under the Mountain for me a few times—that magical cleaning. I'd somehow never asked.

He leaned against the doorway, watching me peel off my torn and stained jacket. As if it were the most important task he'd ever been given. "The essence of the dirt remains." His voice roughened as he tracked each movement of my fingers while I unlaced my boots. "Like a layer of oil."

Indeed, my skin, while it looked clean, felt . . . unwashed. I kicked off the boots, letting them land on my filthy jacket. "So it's more for aesthetic purposes."

"You're taking too long," he said, jerking his chin toward the bath.

My breasts tightened at the slight growl lacing his words. He watched that, too.

And I smiled to myself, arching my back a bit more than necessary as I removed my shirt and tossed it to the marble floor. Sunlight streamed in through the steam rising from the tub, casting the space between us in gold and white. Rhys made a low noise that sounded vaguely like a whimper as he took in my bare torso. As he took in my breasts, now heavy and aching, badly enough that I had to swallow my plea to forget this bath entirely.

But I pretended not to notice as I unbuttoned my pants and let them fall to the floor. Along with my undergarments.

Rhys's eyes simmered.

I smirked, daring a look at his own pants. At the evidence of what, exactly, this was doing to him, pressing against the black material with impressive demand. I simply crooned, "Too bad there isn't room in the tub for two."

"A design flaw, and one I shall remedy tomorrow." His voice was rough, quiet—and it slid invisible hands down my breasts, between my legs.

Mother save me. I somehow managed to walk, to climb into the tub. Somehow managed to remember how to bathe myself.

Rhys remained leaning against the doorway the entire time, silently watching with that unrelenting focus.

I might have taken longer washing certain areas. And might have made sure he saw it.

He only gripped the threshold hard enough that the wood groaned beneath his hand.

But Rhys made no move to pounce, even when I toweled off and brushed out my tangled hair. As if the restraint . . . it was part of the game, too.

My bare toes curled on the marble floor as I set down my brush on the sink vanity, every inch of my body aware of where he stood in the doorway, aware of his eyes upon me in the mirror's reflection.

"All clean," I declared, my voice hoarse as I met his stare in the mirror. I could have sworn only darkness and stars swirled beyond his shoulders. A blink, and they were gone. But the predatory hunger on his face . . .

I turned, my fingers trembling slightly as I clutched my towel around me.

Rhys only extended a hand, his own fingers shaking. Even the towel was abrasive against my too-sensitive skin as I laid my hand on his, his calluses scraping as they closed over my fingers. I wanted them scraping all over me.

But he simply led me into the bedroom, step after step, the muscles of his broad back shifting beneath his jacket. And lower, the sleek, powerful cut of thighs, his ass—

I was going to devour him. From head to toe. I was going to *devour* him—

But Rhys paused before the bed, releasing my hand and facing me from the safety of a step away. And it was the expression on his face as he traced a still-tender spot on my cheekbone that checked the heat threatening to raze my senses.

I swallowed, my hair dripping on the carpet. “Is the bruise bad?”

“It’s nearly gone.” Darkness flickered in the room once more.

I scanned that perfect face. Every line and angle. The fear and rage and love—the wisdom and cunning and strength.

I let my towel drop to the carpet.

Let him look me over as I put a hand on his chest, his heart raging beneath my palm.

“Ready for ravishing.” My words didn’t come out with the swagger I’d intended.

Not when Rhys’s answering smile was a dark, cruel thing. “I hardly know where to begin. So many possibilities.”

He lifted a finger, and my breath came hard and fast as he idly circled one of my breasts, then the other. In ever-tightening rings. “I could start here,” he murmured.

I clenched my thighs together. He noted the movement, that dark smile growing. And just before his finger reached the tip of my breast, just before he gave me what I was about to beg for, his finger slid upward—to my chest, my neck, my chin. Right to my mouth.

He traced the shape of my lips, a whisper of touch. "Or I could start here," he breathed, slipping the tip of his finger into my mouth.

I couldn't help myself from closing my lips around him, from flicking my tongue against the pad of his finger.

But Rhys withdrew his finger with a soft groan, making a downward path. Along my neck. Chest. Straight over a nipple. He paused there, flicking it once, then smoothed his thumb over the small hurt.

I was shaking now, barely able to keep standing as his finger continued past my breast.

He drew patterns on my stomach, scanning my face as he purred, "Or . . ."

I couldn't think beyond that single finger, that one point of contact as it drifted lower and lower, to where I wanted him. "Or?" I managed to breathe.

His head dipped, hair sliding over his brow as he watched—we both watched—his broad finger venture down. "Or I could start here," he said, the words guttural and raw.

I didn't care—not as he dragged that finger down the center of me. Not as he circled that spot, light and taunting. "Here would be nice," he observed, his breathing uneven. "Or maybe even here," he finished, and plunged that finger inside me.

I groaned, gripping his arm, nails digging into the muscles beneath—muscles that shifted as he pumped his finger once, twice. Then slid it out and drawled, brows rising. "Well? Where shall I begin, Feyre darling?"

I could barely form words, thoughts. But—I'd had enough of playing.

So I took that infernal hand of his, guiding it to my heart, and placed it there, half over the curve of my breast. I met his hooded gaze as I spoke the words that I knew would be his undoing in this little game, the words that were rising up in me with every breath. "You're mine."

It snapped the tether he'd kept on himself.

His clothes vanished—all of them—and his mouth angled over my own.

It wasn't a gentle kiss. Wasn't soft or searching.

It was a claiming, wild and unchecked—it was an unleashing. And the taste of him . . . the heat of him, the demanding stroke of his tongue against my own . . . Home. I was *home*.

My hands shot into his hair, pulling him closer as I answered each of his searing kisses with my own, unable to get enough, unable to touch and feel enough of him.

Skin to skin, Rhys nudged me toward the bed, his hands kneading my rear as I ran my own over the velvet softness of him, over every hard plane and ripple. His beautiful, mighty wings tore from his back, splaying wide before neatly tucking in.

My thighs hit the bed behind us, and Rhys paused, trembling. Giving me time to reconsider, even now. My heart strained, but I pulled my mouth from his. Held his gaze as I lowered myself onto the white sheets and inched back.

Further and further onto the bed, until I was bare before him. Until I took in the considerable, proud length of him and my core tightened in answer. "Rhys," I breathed, his name a plea on my tongue.

His wings flared, chest heaving as stars sparked in his eyes. And it was the longing there—beneath the desire, beneath the need—it was the longing in those beautiful eyes that made me glance to the mountains tattooed on his knees.

The insignia of this court—our court. The promise that he would kneel for no one and nothing but his crown.

And me.

Mine—he was *mine*. I sent the thought down the bond.

No playing, no delaying—I wanted him on me, in me. I *needed* to feel him, hold him, share breath with him. He heard the edge of desperation, felt it through the mating bond flowing between us.

His eyes did not leave mine as he prowled over me, every movement graceful as a stalking plains-cat. Interlacing our fingers, his breathing uneven, Rhys used a knee to nudge my legs apart and settle between them.

Carefully, lovingly, he laid our joined hands beside my head as he guided himself into me and whispered in my ear, "You're mine, too."

At the first nudge of him, I surged forward to claim his mouth.

I dragged my tongue over his teeth, swallowing his groan of pleasure as his hips rolled in gentle thrusts and he pushed in, and in, and in.

Home. This was *home*.

And when Rhys was seated to the hilt, when he paused to let me adjust to the fullness of him, I thought I might explode into moonlight and flame, thought I might die from the sheer force of what swept through me.

My pants were edged with sobs as I dug my fingers into his back, and Rhys withdrew slightly to study my face. To read what was there. "Never again," he promised as he pulled out, then thrust back in with excruciating slowness. He kissed my brow, my temple. "My darling Feyre."

Beyond words, I moved my hips, urging him deeper, harder. Rhys obliged me.

With every movement, every shared breath, every whispered endearment and moan, that mating bond I'd hidden so far inside myself grew brighter. Clearer.

And when it again shone as brilliantly as adamant, my release cascaded through me, leaving my skin glowing like a newborn star in its wake.

At the sight of it, right as I dragged a finger down the sensitive inside of his wing, Rhys shouted my name and found his pleasure.

I held him through every heaving breath, held him as he at last stilled, lingering inside me, and relished the feel of his skin on mine.

For long minutes, we remained there, tangled together, listening to our breathing even out, the sound of it finer than any music.

After a while, Rhys lifted his chest enough to take my right hand. To examine the tattoos inked there. He kissed one of the whorls of near-black blue ink.

His throat bobbed. "I missed you. Every second, every breath. Not just this," he said, shifting his hips for emphasis and dragging a groan from deep in my throat, "but . . . talking to you. Laughing with you. I missed having you in my bed, but missed having you as my friend even more."

My eyes burned. "I know," I managed to say, stroking a hand down his wings, his back. "I know." I kissed his bare shoulder, right over a whorl of Illyrian tattoo. "Never again," I promised him, and whispered it over and over as the sunlight drifted across the floor.

CHAPTER 15

My sisters had been living in the House of Wind since they'd arrived in Velaris.

They did not leave the palace built into the upper parts of a flat-topped mountain overlooking the city. They did not ask for anything, or anyone.

So I would go to them.

Lucien was waiting in the sitting room when Rhys and I came downstairs at last, my mate having given the silent order for them to return.

Unsurprisingly, Cassian and Azriel were *casually* seated in the dining room across the hall, eating lunch and marking every single breath Lucien emitted. Cassian smirked at me, brows flicking up.

I shot him a warning glare that dared him to comment. Azriel, thankfully, just kicked Cassian under the table.

Cassian gawked at Azriel as if to declare *I wasn't going to* say *anything* while I approached the open archway into the sitting room, Lucien rising to his feet.

I fought my cringe as I halted in the threshold. Lucien was still in his travel-worn, filthy clothes. His face and hands, at least, were clean, but . . . I should have gotten him something else. Remembered to offer him—

The thought rippled away into nothing as Rhys appeared at my side.

Lucien did not bother to hide the slight curling of his lip.

As if he could see the mating bond glowing between Rhys and me.

His eyes—both russet and golden—slid down my body. To my hand.

To the ring now on my finger, at the star sapphire sky-bright against the silver. A simple silver band sat on Rhysand's matching finger.

We'd slid them onto each other's hands before coming downstairs—more intimate and searing than any publicly made vows.

I'd told Rhys before we did so that I had half a mind to deposit his ring at the Weaver's cottage and make him retrieve it.

He'd laughed and said that if I truly felt it was necessary to settle the score between us, perhaps I could find some other creature for him to battle—one that wouldn't delight in removing *my* favorite part from his body. I'd only kissed him, murmuring about someone thinking rather highly of themselves, and had placed the ring he'd selected for himself, bought here in Velaris while I'd been away, onto his finger.

Any joy, any lingering laughter from that moment, those silent vows . . . It curled up like leaves in a fire as Lucien sneered at our rings. How close we stood. I swallowed.

Rhys noted it, too. It was impossible to miss.

My mate leaned against the carved archway and drawled to Lucien, "I assume Cassian or Azriel has explained that if you threaten anyone in this house, this territory, we'll show you ways to die you've never even imagined."

Indeed, the Illyrians smirked from where they lingered in the dining room threshold. Azriel was by far the more terrifying of the pair.

Something twisted in my gut at the threat—the smooth, sleek aggression.

Lucien was—had been—my friend. He wasn't my enemy, not entirely—

"But," Rhys continued, sliding his hands into his pockets, "I can understand how difficult this past month has been for you. I know Feyre explained we aren't exactly as rumor suggests . . ." I'd let him into my mind before we'd come down—shown him all that had occurred at the Spring Court. "But hearing it and seeing it are two different things." He shrugged with one shoulder. "Elain has been cared for. Her participation in life here has been entirely her choice. No one but us and a few trusted servants have entered the House of Wind."

Lucien remained silent.

"I was in love with Feyre," Rhys said quietly, "long before she ever returned the feeling."

Lucien crossed his arms. "How fortunate that you got what you wanted in the end."

I closed my eyes for a heartbeat.

Cassian and Azriel stilled, waiting for the order.

"I will only say this once," warned the High Lord of the Night Court. Even Lucien flinched. "I suspected Feyre was my mate before I ever knew she was involved with Tamlin. And when I learned of it . . . If it made her happy, I was willing to step back."

"You came to our house and stole her away on her wedding day."

"I was going to call the wedding off," I cut in, taking a step toward Lucien. "You knew it."

Rhysand went on before Lucien could snap a reply, "I was willing to lose my mate to another male. I was willing to let them marry, if it brought her joy. But what I was not willing to do was let her suffer. To let her fade away into a shadow. And the moment that piece of shit blew apart his study, the moment he *locked her in that house* . . ." His wings ripped from him, and Lucien started.

Rhys bared his teeth. My limbs turned light, trembling at the dark power curling in the corners of the room. Not fear—never fear of him. But at the shattered control as Rhys snarled at Lucien, "My mate may one day find it in herself to forgive him. Forgive you. But I will never forget how it felt to sense her *terror* in those moments." My cheeks heated, especially as Cassian and Azriel stalked closer, those hazel eyes now filled with a mix of sympathy and wrath.

I had never talked about it to them—what had gone on that day Tamlin had destroyed his study, or the day he'd sealed me inside the manor. I'd never asked Rhys if he'd informed them. From the fury rippling from Cassian, the cold rage seeping from Azriel . . . I didn't think so.

Lucien, to his credit, didn't back away a step. From Rhys, or me, or the Illyrians.

The Clever Fox Stares Down Winged Death. The painting flashed into my mind.

"So, again, I will say this only once," Rhys went on, his expression smoothing into lethal calm, dragging me from the colors and light and shadows gathering in my mind. "Feyre did not dishonor or betray Tamlin. I revealed the mating bond months later—and she gave me hell for it, don't worry. But now that you've found your mate in a similar situation, perhaps you will try to understand how it felt. And if you can't be bothered, then I hope you're wise enough to keep your mouth shut, because the next time you look at my mate with that disdain and disgust, I won't bother to explain it again, and I will rip out your fucking throat."

Rhys said it so mildly that the threat took a second to register. To settle in me like a stone plunked into a pool.

Lucien only shifted on his feet. Wary. Considering. I counted the heartbeats, debating how much I'd interfere if he said something truly stupid, when he at last murmured, "There is a longer story to be told, it seems."

Smart answer. The rage ebbed from Rhys's face—and Cassian's and Azriel's shoulders relaxed ever so slightly.

Just once, Lucien had said to me, during those days on the run. That was all he wanted—to see Elain only once.

And then . . . I'd have to figure out what to do with him. Unless my mate already had some plan in motion.

One look at Rhys, who lifted his brows as if to say *He's all yours*, told me it was my call. But until then . . . I cleared my throat.

"I'm going to see my sisters up at the House," I said to Lucien, whose eyes snapped to mine, the metal one tightening and whirring. I forced a grim smile to my face. "Would you like to come?"

Lucien weighed my offer—and the three males monitoring his every blink and breath.

He only nodded. Another wise decision.

We were gone within minutes, the quick walk up to the roof of the town house serving as Lucien's tour of my home. I didn't bother to point out the bedrooms. Lucien certainly didn't ask.

Azriel left us as we took to the skies, murmuring that he had some pressing business to attend to. From the glare Cassian gave him, I wondered if the shadowsinger had invented it to avoid carrying Lucien to the House of Wind, but Rhys's subtle nod to Azriel told me enough.

There were indeed matters afoot. Plans in motion, as they always were. And once I finished visiting my sisters . . . I'd get answers of my own.

So Cassian bore a stone-faced Lucien into the skies, and Rhys swept me into his arms, shooting us gracefully into the cloudless blue.

With every wing beat, with every deep inhale of the citrus-and-salt breeze . . . some tightness in my body uncoiled.

Even if every wing beat brought us closer to the House looming above Velaris. To my sisters.

✢

The House of Wind had been carved into the red, sun-warmed stone of the flat-topped mountains that lurked over one edge of the city, with countless balconies and patios jutting to overhang the thousand-foot drop to the valley floor. Velaris's winding streets flowed right to the sheer wall of the mountain itself, and snaking through it wove the Sidra, a glittering, bright band in the midday sun.

As we landed on the veranda that edged our usual dining room, Cassian and Lucien alighting behind us, I let it sink in: the city and the river and the distant sea, the jagged mountains on the other side of Velaris and the blazing blue of the sky above. And the House of Wind, my other home. The grand, formal sister to the town house—our *public* home, I supposed. Where we would hold meetings and receive guests who weren't family.

A far more pleasant alternative to my other residence. The Court of Nightmares. At least there, I could stay in the moonstone palace high atop the mountain under which the Hewn City had been built. Though the people I'd rule over . . . I shut them from my thoughts as I adjusted my braid, tucking in strands that had been whipped free by the gentle wind Rhys had allowed through his shield while flying.

Lucien just walked to the balcony rail and stared out. I didn't quite blame him.

I glanced over a shoulder to where Rhys and Cassian now stood. Rhys lifted a brow.

Wait inside.

Rhys's smile was sharp. *So you won't have any witnesses when you push him over the railing?*

I gave him an incredulous look and strode for Lucien, Rhys's murmur to Cassian about getting a drink in the dining room the only indication of their departure. That, and the near-silent opening and closing of the glass doors that led into the dining room beyond. The same room where I'd first met most of them—my new family.

I came up beside Lucien, the wind ripping strands of his red hair free from where he'd tied it at his nape.

"This isn't what I expected," he said, taking in the sprawl of Velaris.

"The city is still rebuilding after the Hybern attack."

His eyes dropped to the carved balcony rail. "Even though we had no part in that . . . I'm sorry. But—that's not what I meant." He glanced behind us, to where Rhys and Cassian waited inside the dining room, drinks now in hand, leaning all too casually against the giant oak table in its center.

They became immensely interested in some spot or stain on the surface between them.

I scowled at them, but swallowed. And even though my sisters waited inside, even though the urge to see them was so tangible I wouldn't have been surprised to find a rope tugging me into the House, I said to Lucien, "Rhys saved my life on Calanmai."

So I told him. All of it—the story that perhaps would help him understand. And realize how truly safe Elain was—*he* now was. I eventually summoned Rhys to explain his own history—and he gave Lucien the barest details. None of the vulnerable, sorrowful bits that had reduced me to tears in that mountain cabin. But it painted a clear enough picture.

Lucien said nothing while Rhys spoke. Or when I continued with my tale, Cassian often chiming in with his own account of how it'd been to live with two mated-yet-un-mated people, to pretend Rhys wasn't courting me, to welcome me into their little circle.

I didn't know how long had passed when we finished, though Rhys and Cassian used the time to unabashedly sun their wings by the open balcony ledge. I left off our story at Hybern—at the day I'd gone back to the Spring Court.

Silence fell, and Rhys and Cassian again walked away, understanding the emotion swimming in Lucien's eye—the meaning of the long breath he blew out.

When we were alone, Lucien rubbed his eyes. "I've seen Rhysand do such . . . horrible things, seen him play the dark prince over and over. And yet you tell me it was all a lie. A mask. All to protect this place, these people. And I would have laughed at you for believing it, and yet . . . this city exists. Untouched—or until recently, I suppose. Even the Dawn Court's cities are nothing so lovely as this."

"Lucien—"

"And you love him. And he—he truly does love you." Lucien dragged a hand through his red hair. "And all these people I have spent my centuries hating, even fearing . . . They are your family."

"I think Amren would probably deny that she feels any affection for us—"

"Amren is a bedtime story they told us as younglings to make us behave. Amren was who would drink my blood and carry me to hell if I acted out of line. And yet there she was, acting more like a cranky old aunt than anything."

"We don't—we don't enforce protocol and rank here."

"Obviously. Rhys lives in a *town house*, by the Cauldron." He waved an arm to encompass the city.

I didn't know what to say, so I kept silent.

"I hadn't realized I was a villain in your narrative," Lucien breathed.

"You weren't." Not entirely.

The sun danced on the distant sea, turning the horizon into a glittering sprawl of light.

"She doesn't know anything about you. Only the basics that Rhys gave her: you are a High Lord's son, serving in the Spring Court. And you helped me Under the Mountain. Nothing else."

I didn't add that Rhys had told me my sister hadn't asked about him at all.

I straightened. "I would like to see them first. I know you're anxious—"

"Just do it," Lucien said, bracing his forearms on the stone rail of the veranda. "Come get me when she's ready."

I almost patted his shoulder—almost said something reassuring.

But words failed me again as I headed for the dim interior of the House.

⸸

Rhys had given Nesta and Elain a suite of connecting rooms, all with views overlooking the city and river and distant mountains beyond.

But it was in the family library that Rhys tracked down Nesta.

There was a coiled, razor-sharp tension in Cassian as the three of us strode down the stairways of the House, the red stone halls dim and echoing with the rustle of Cassian's wings and the faint howl of wind rattling at every window. A tension that grew more taut with every step toward the double doors of the library. I hadn't asked if they had seen each other, or spoken, since that day in Hybern.

Cassian volunteered no information.

And I might have asked Rhys down the bond had he not opened one of the doors.

Had I not immediately spied Nesta curled in an armchair, a book on her knees, looking—for once—very *un*-Nesta-like. Casual. Perhaps relaxed.

Perfectly content to be alone.

The moment my shoes scuffed against the stone floor, she shot straight up, back going stiff, closing her book with a muffled thud. Yet her gray-blue eyes didn't so much as widen as they beheld me.

As I took her in.

Nesta had been beautiful as a human woman.

As High Fae, she was devastating.

From the utter stillness with which Cassian stood beside me, I wondered if he thought the same thing.

She was in a pewter-colored gown, its make simple, yet the material fine. Her hair was braided over the crown of her head, accentuating her long, pale neck—a neck Cassian's eyes darted to, then quickly away from, as she sized us up and said to me, "You're back."

With her hair styled like that, it hid the pointed ears. But there was nothing to hide the ethereal grace as she took one step. As her focus again returned to Cassian and she added, "What do you want?"

I felt the blow like a punch to my gut. "At least immortality hasn't changed some things about you."

Nesta's look was nothing short of icy. "Is there a purpose to this visit, or may I return to my book?"

Rhys's hand brushed mine in silent comfort. But his face . . . hard as stone. And even less amused.

But Cassian sauntered over to Nesta, a half smile spreading across his face. She stood stiffly while he picked up the book, read the title, and chuckled. "I wouldn't have pegged you for a romance reader."

She gave him a withering glare.

Cassian leafed through the pages and drawled to me, "You haven't missed much while you were off destroying our enemies, Feyre. It's mostly been this."

Nesta whirled to me. "You—accomplished it?"

I clenched my jaw. "We'll see how it plays out. I made sure Ianthe suffered." At the hint of rage and fear that crept into Nesta's eyes, I amended, "Not enough, though."

I glanced at her hand—the one she'd pointed with at the King of Hybern. Rhys had mentioned no signs of special powers from either of my sisters. Yet that day in Hybern, when Nesta had opened her eyes . . . I had seen it. Seen something great and terrible within them.

"And, again, why are you here?" She snatched her book from Cassian, who allowed her to do so, but remained standing beside her. Watching every breath, every blink.

"I wanted to see you," I said quietly. "See how you were doing."

"See if I've accepted my lot and found myself grateful for becoming one of *them*?"

I steeled my spine. "You're my sister. I watched them hurt you. I wanted to see if you were all right."

A low, bitter laugh. But she turned to Cassian, looked him over as if she were a queen on a throne, and then declared to all of us, "What do I care? I get to be young and beautiful forever, and I never have to go back to those sycophantic fools over the wall. I get to do as I wish, since apparently no one here has any regard for rules or manners or our traditions. Perhaps I *should* thank you for dragging me into this."

Rhys put a hand on the small of my back before the words even struck their target.

Nesta snorted. "But it's not me you should be checking on. I had as little at stake on the other side of the wall as I do here." Hate rippled over her features—enough hate that I felt sick. Nesta hissed. "She will not leave her room. She will not stop crying. She will not eat, or sleep, or drink."

Rhys's jaw clenched. "I have asked you over and over if you needed—"

"Why should I allow any of *you*"—the last word was shot at Cassian with as much venom as a pit viper—"to get near her? It is no one's business but our own."

"Elain's mate is here," I said.

And it was the wrong thing to utter in Nesta's presence.

She went white with rage.

"He is no such thing to her," she snarled, advancing on me enough that Rhys slid a shield into place between us.

As if he, too, had glimpsed that mighty power in her eyes that day in Hybern. And did not know how it would manifest.

"If you bring that *male* anywhere near her, I'll—"

"You'll what?" Cassian crooned, trailing her at a casual pace as she stopped perhaps five feet from me. He lifted a brow as she whirled on him. "You won't join me for practice, so you sure as hell aren't going to hold your own in a fight. You won't talk about your powers, so you certainly aren't going to be able to wield them. And you—"

"Shut your mouth," she snapped, every inch the conquering empress. "I told you to stay the hell away from me, and if you—"

"You come between a male and his mate, Nesta Archeron, and you're going to learn about the consequences the hard way."

Nesta's nostrils flared. Cassian only gave her a crooked grin.

I cut in, "If Elain is not up for it, then she won't see him. I won't force the meeting on her. But he does wish to see her, Nesta. I'll ask on his behalf, but the decision will be hers."

"The male who sold us out to Hybern."

"It's more complicated than that."

"Well, it will certainly be more complicated when Father returns and finds us gone. What do you plan to tell *him* about all this?"

"Seeing as he hasn't sent word from the continent in months, I'll worry about that later," I sniped back. And thank the Cauldron for it—that he was off trading in some lucrative territory.

Nesta only shook her head, turning toward the chair and her book. "I don't care. Do what you want."

A stinging dismissal, if not admission that she still trusted me enough to consider Elain's needs first. Rhys jerked his chin at Cassian in a silent order to leave, and as I followed them, I said softly, "I'm sorry, Nesta."

She didn't answer as she sat stiffly in her chair, picked up her book, and dutifully ignored us. A blow to the face would have been better.

When I looked ahead, I found Cassian staring back at Nesta as well.

I wondered why no one had yet mentioned what now shone in Cassian's eyes as he gazed at my sister.

The sorrow. And the longing.

The suite was filled with sunlight.

Every curtain shoved back as far as it could go, to let in as much sun as possible.

As if any bit of darkness was abhorrent. As if to chase it away.

And seated in a small chair before the sunniest of the windows, her back to us, was Elain.

Where Nesta had been in contented silence before we found her, Elain's silence was . . . hollow.

Empty.

Her hair was down—not even braided. I couldn't remember the last time I'd seen it unbound. She wore a moon-white silk dressing robe.

She did not look, or speak, or even flinch as we entered.

Her too-thin arms rested on her chair. That iron engagement ring still encircled her finger.

Her skin was so pale it looked like fresh snow in the harsh light.

I realized then that the color of death, of sorrow, was white.

The lack of color. Of vibrancy.

I left Cassian and Rhys by the door.

Nesta's rage was better than this . . . shell.

This void.

My breath caught as I edged around her chair. Beheld the city view she stared so blankly at.

Then beheld the hollowed-out cheeks, the bloodless lips, the brown eyes that had once been rich and warm, and now seemed utterly dull. Like grave dirt.

She didn't so much as look at me as I said softly, "Elain?"

I didn't dare reach for her hand.

I didn't dare get too close.

I had done this. I had brought this upon them—

"I'm back," I added a bit limply. Uselessly.

All she said was, "I want to go home."

I closed my eyes, my chest unbearably tight. "I know."

"He'll be looking for me," she whispered.

"I know," I said again. Not Lucien—she wasn't talking about him at all.

"We were supposed to be married next week."

I put a hand on my chest, as if it'd stop the cracking in there. "I'm sorry."

Nothing. Not even a flicker of emotion. "Everyone keeps saying that." Her thumb brushed the ring on her finger. "But it doesn't fix anything, does it?"

I couldn't get enough air in. I couldn't—I couldn't *breathe*, looking at this broken, carved-out thing my sister had become. What I'd robbed her of, what I'd taken from her—

Rhys was there, an arm sliding around my waist. "Can we get you anything, Elain?" He spoke with such gentleness I could barely stand it.

"I want to go home," she repeated.

I couldn't ask her—about Lucien. Not now. Not yet.

I turned away, fully prepared to bolt and completely fall apart in another room, another section of the House. But Lucien was standing in the doorway.

And from the devastation on his face, I knew he'd heard every word. Seen and heard and felt the hollowness and despair radiating from her.

Elain had always been gentle and sweet—and I had considered it a different sort of strength. A better strength. To look at the hardness of the world and choose, over and over, to love, to be kind. She had been always so full of light.

Perhaps that was why she now kept all the curtains open. To fill the void that existed where all of that light had once been.

And now nothing remained.

CHAPTER 16

Rhysand silently led Lucien to the suite he'd be occupying at the opposite end of the House of Wind. Cassian and I trailed behind, none of us speaking until my mate opened a set of onyx doors to reveal a sunny sitting room carved from more red stone. Beyond the wall of windows, the city flowed far below, the view stretching to the distant jagged mountains and glittering sea.

Rhys paused in the center of a midnight-blue handwoven rug and gestured to the sealed doors on his left. "Bedroom." He waved a lazy hand toward the single door on the opposite wall. "Bathing room."

Lucien surveyed it all with cool indifference. What he felt about Elain, what he planned to do . . . I didn't want to ask.

"I assume you'll need clothes," Rhys went on, nodding toward Lucien's filthy jacket and pants—which he'd worn for the past week while we scrambled through territories. Indeed, that was . . . blood splattered in several spots. "Any preferences for attire?"

That drew Lucien's attention, the male shifting enough to take in Rhys—to note Cassian and me lurking in the doorway. "Is there a cost?"

"If you're trying to say that you have no money, don't worry—the clothes are complimentary." Rhys gave him a half smile. "If you're trying to ask if this is some sort of bribe . . ." A shrug. "You are a High Lord's son. It would be bad manners not to house and clothe you in your time of need."

Lucien bristled.

Stop baiting him, I shot down the bond.

But it's so fun, came the purred reply.

Something had rattled him. Rattled Rhys enough that taunting Lucien was an easy way to take the edge off. I stepped closer, Cassian remaining behind me as I told Lucien, "We'll be back for dinner in a few hours. Rest a while—bathe. If you need anything, pull that rope by the door."

Lucien stiffened—not at what I'd said, I realized, but at the tone. A hostess. But he asked, "What of—Elain?"

Your call, Rhys offered.

"I need to think about it," I answered plainly. "Until I figure out what to do with her, with Nesta, stay out of their way." I added perhaps too tightly, "This house is warded against winnowing, both from outside and within. There's one way out—the stairs to the city. It, too, is warded—and guarded. Please don't do anything stupid."

"So am I a prisoner?"

I could feel the response simmering in Rhys, but I shook my head. "No. But understand while you may be her mate, Elain is *my* sister. I'll do what I must to protect her from further harm."

"I would never hurt her."

A bleak sort of honesty in his words.

I simply nodded, loosening a breath, and met Rhysand's stare in silent urging.

My mate gave no indication of my wordless plea as he said, "You are free to wander where you wish, into the city itself if you feel like braving the stairs, but there are two conditions: you are not to take either sister, and you are not to enter their floor. If you require a book from the library, you will ask the servants. If you wish to speak to Elain or Nesta, you will also ask the servants, who will ask us. If you disregard those rules, I'll lock you in a room with Amren."

Then Rhys turned away, hands sliding into his pockets as he offered his hooked elbow to me. I looped my arm through his, but said to Lucien, "We'll see you in a few hours."

We were almost to the door, Cassian already in the hall, when Lucien said to me, "Thank you."

I didn't dare ask him for what.

✠

We flew right to Amren's loft, more than a few people waving as we soared over the rooftops of Velaris. My smile wasn't faked when I waved back to them—my people. Rhys only held me a bit tighter while I did so, his own smile as bright as the sun on the Sidra.

Mor and Azriel were already waiting inside Amren's apartment, seated like scolded children on the threadbare divan against the wall while the dark-haired female flipped through the pages of books sprawled around her on the floor.

Mor gave me a grateful, relieved look as we entered, Azriel's own face revealing nothing while he stood, keeping a careful, too-casual distance from her side. But it was Amren who said from the floor, "You should kill Beron and his sons and set up the handsome one as High Lord of Autumn, self-imposed exile or no. It will make life easier."

"I'll take that into consideration," Rhys said, striding toward her while I remained with the others. If they were hanging back . . . Amren had to be in some mood.

I blew out a breath. "Who else thinks it's a terrible idea to leave the three of them up at the House of Wind?"

Cassian raised his hand as Rhys and Mor chuckled. The High Lord's general said, "I give him an hour before he tries to see her."

"Thirty minutes," Mor countered, sitting back down on the divan and crossing her legs.

I cringed. "I guarantee Nesta is now guarding Elain. I think she might honestly kill him if he so much as tries to touch her."

"Not without training she won't," Cassian grumbled, tucking in his wings as he claimed the seat beside Mor that Azriel had vacated. The shadowsinger didn't so much as look at it. No, Azriel just walked to the wall beside Cassian and leaned against the wood paneling.

But Rhys and the others remained quiet enough that I knew to proceed carefully as I asked Cassian, "Nesta spoke as if you've been up at the House . . . often. You've offered to train her?"

Cassian's hazel eyes shuttered as he crossed a booted ankle over another, stretching his muscled legs before him. "I go up there every other day. It's good exercise for my wings." Those wings shifted in emphasis. Not a scratch marred them.

"And?"

"And what you saw in the library is a pleasanter version of the conversation we always have."

Mor's lips pressed into a thin line, as if she was trying her best *not* to say anything. Azriel was trying *his* best to shoot a warning stare at Mor to remind her to indeed keep her mouth shut. As if they'd already discussed this. Many times.

"I don't blame her," Cassian said, shrugging despite his words. "She was—violated. Her body stopped belonging wholly to her." His jaw clenched. Even Amren didn't dare say anything. "And I am going to peel the King of Hybern's skin off his bones the next time I see him."

His Siphons flickered in answer.

Rhys said casually, "I'm sure the king will thoroughly enjoy the experience."

Cassian glowered. "I mean it."

"Oh, I have no doubt that you do." Rhys's violet eyes were dazzling in the dimness of the loft. "But before you lose yourself in plans for revenge, do remember that we have a war to plan first."

"Asshole."

A corner of my mate's mouth tugged upward. And—Rhys was goading him, working Cassian into a temper to keep that brittle edge of guilt from consuming him. The others letting him take on the task, likely having done it several times themselves these weeks. "I am most definitely that," Rhys said, "but the fact still remains that revenge is secondary to winning this war."

Cassian opened his mouth as if he'd keep arguing, but Rhys peered at the books scattered on the lush carpet. "Nothing?" he asked Amren.

"I don't know why you sent those two buffoons"—a narrowed glance toward Mor and Azriel—"to monitor me." So this was where Azriel had gone—right to the loft. To no doubt spare Mor from enduring Amren Duty alone. But Amren's tone . . . cranky, yes, but perhaps a bit of a front, too. To banish that too-fragile gleam in Cassian's eyes.

"We're not monitoring you," Mor said, tapping her foot on the carpet. "We're monitoring the Book."

And as she said it . . . I felt it. Heard it.

Amren had placed the Book of Breathings on her nightstand.

A glass of old blood atop it.

I didn't know whether to laugh or cringe. The latter won out as the Book murmured, *Hello, sweet-faced liar. Hello, princess with—*

"Oh, be quiet," Amren hissed toward the Book, who—shut up. "Odious thing," she muttered, and went back to the tome before her.

Rhys gave me a wry smile. "Since the two halves of the Book were joined back together, it has been . . . known to speak every now and then."

"What does it say?"

"Utter nonsense," Amren spat, scowling at the Book. "It just likes to hear itself talk. Like most of the people cramping up my apartment."

Cassian smirked. "Did someone forget to feed Amren again?"

She pointed a warning finger at him without so much as looking up. "Is there a reason, Rhysand, why you dragged your yapping pack into my home?"

Her home was little more than a giant, converted attic, but none of us dared argue as Mor, Cassian, and Azriel finally came closer, forming a small circle around Amren's sprawl in the center of the room.

Rhys said to me, "The information you got from Dagdan and Brannagh confirms what we've been gathering ourselves while you were gone. Especially Hybern's potential allies in other territories—on the continent."

"Vultures," Mor muttered, and Cassian looked inclined to agree.

But Rhys—Rhys had indeed been spying, while Azriel had been—

Rhys snorted. "I *can* stay hidden, mate."

I glared at him, but Azriel cut in. "Having Hybern's movements confirmed by you, Feyre, is what we needed."

"Why?"

Cassian crossed his arms. "We barely stand a chance of surviving Hybern's armies on our own. If armies from Vallahan, Montesere, and Rask join them . . ." He drew a line across his tan throat.

Mor elbowed him in the ribs. Cassian nudged her right back as Azriel shook his head at both of them, shadows coiling around the tips of his wings.

"Are those three territories . . . that powerful?" Perhaps it was a foolish question, showing how little I knew of the faerie lands on the continent—

"Yes," Azriel said, no judgment in his hazel eyes. "Vallahan has the numbers, Montesere has the money, and Rask . . . it is large enough to have both."

"And we have no potential allies amongst the other overseas territories?"

Rhys pulled at a stray thread on the cuff of his black jacket. "Not ones that would sail here to help."

My stomach turned. "What of Miryam and Drakon?" He'd once refused to consider, but— "You fought for Miryam and Drakon centuries ago," I said to Rhys. He'd done a great deal more than that, if Jurian was to be believed. "Perhaps it's time to call in that debt."

But Rhys shook his head. "We tried. Azriel went to Cretea." The island where Miryam, Drakon, and their unified human and Fae peoples had secretly lived for the past five centuries.

"It was abandoned," Azriel said. "In ruin. With no trace of what happened or where they went."

"You think Hybern—"

"There was no sign of Hybern, or of any harm," Mor cut in, her face taut. They had been her friends, too—during the War. Miryam, and Drakon, and the human queens who had gotten the Treaty signed. And it was worry—true, deep worry—that guttered in her brown eyes. In all their eyes.

"Then do you think they heard about Hybern and ran?" I asked. Drakon had a winged legion, Rhys had once told me. If there was any chance of finding them—

"The Drakon and Miryam I knew wouldn't have run—not from this," Rhys said.

Mor leaned forward, her golden hair spilling over her shoulders. "But with Jurian now a player in this conflict . . . Miryam and Drakon, whether they like it or not, have always been tied to him. I don't blame them for running, if he truly hunts them."

Rhys's face slackened for a heartbeat. "That is what the King of Hybern has on Jurian," he murmured. "Why Jurian works for him."

My brow furrowed.

"Miryam died—a spear through her chest during that last battle at the sea," Rhys explained. "She bled out while she was carried to safety. But Drakon knew of a sacred, hidden island where an object of great and terrible power had been concealed. An object made by the Cauldron itself, legend claimed. He brought her there, to Cretea—used the item to resurrect her, make her immortal. As you were Made, Feyre."

Amren had said it—months ago. That Miryam had been *Made* as I was.

Amren seemed to remember it, too, as she said, "The King of

Hybern must have promised Jurian to use the Cauldron to track the item. To where Miryam and Drakon now live. Perhaps they figured that out—and left as fast as they could."

And for revenge, for that insane rage that hounded Jurian . . . he'd do whatever the King of Hybern asked. So he could kill Miryam himself.

"But where did they go?" I looked to Azriel, the shadowsinger still standing with preternatural stillness against the wall. "You found no trace at all of where they might have vanished to?"

"None," Rhys answered for him. "We've sent messengers back since—to no avail."

I rubbed at my face, sealing off that path of hope. "Then if they are not a possible ally . . . How do we keep those other territories on the continent from joining with Hybern—from sending their armies here?" I winced. "That's our plan—isn't it?"

Rhys smiled grimly. "It is. One we've been working on while you were away." I waited, trying not to pace as Amren's silver eyes seemed to glow with amusement. "I looked at Hybern first. At its people. As best I could."

He'd *gone* to Hybern—

Rhys smirked at the concern flaring across my face. "I'd hoped that Hybern might have some internal conflict to exploit—to get them to collapse from within. That its people might not want this war, might see it as costly and dangerous and unnecessary. But five hundred years on that island, with little trade, little opportunity . . . Hybern's people are hungry for change. Or rather . . . a change back to the old days, when they had human slaves to do their work, when there were no barriers keeping them from what they now perceive as their right."

Amren slammed shut the book she'd been perusing. "Fools." She shook her head, inky hair swaying, as she scowled up at me. "Hybern's wealth has been dwindling for centuries. Most of their trade routes before the War dealt with the South—with the Black Land. But once it went to the humans . . . We don't know if Hybern's king deliberately failed to establish new trade routes and opportunities for his people in order to one day fuel this war, or if he was just that shortsighted and let everything fall apart. But for centuries now, Hybern's people have been festering. Hybern *let* their resentment of their growing stagnation and poverty fester."

"There are many High Fae," Mor said carefully, "who believed before the War, and still believe now, that humans . . . that they are property. There were many High Fae who knew nothing but privilege thanks to those slaves. And when that privilege was ripped away from them, when they were forced to leave their homelands or forced to make room for other High Fae and re-form territories—create new ones—above that wall . . . They have not forgotten that anger, even centuries later. Especially not in places like Hybern, where their territory and population remained mostly untouched by change. They were one of the few who did not have to yield any land to the wall—and did not yield any land to the Fae territories now looking for a new home. Isolated, growing poorer, with no slaves to do their labor . . . Hybern has long viewed the days before the War as a golden era. And these centuries since as a dark age."

I rubbed at my chest. "They're all insane, to think that."

Rhys nodded. "Yes—they certainly are. But don't forget that their king has encouraged these limited world views. He did not expand their trade routes, did not allow other territories to take any of his land and bring their cultures. He considered where things went wrong for the Loyalists in the War. How they ultimately yielded not from being overwhelmed but because they began arguing amongst themselves. Hybern has had a long, long while to think on those mistakes. And how to avoid them at any cost. So he made sure his people are completely for this war, completely for the idea of the wall coming down, because they think it will somehow restore this . . . gilded vision of the past. Hybern's people see their king and their armies not as conquerors, but as liberators of High Fae and those who stand with them."

Nausea churned in my gut. "How can anyone *believe* that?"

Azriel ran a scarred hand through his hair. "That's what we've been learning. Listening in Hybern. And in territories like Rask and Montesere and Vallahan."

"We're to be made an example of, girl," Amren explained. "Prythian. We were among the fiercest defenders and negotiators of the Treaty. Hybern wants to claim Prythian not only to clear the path to the continent, but to make an example of what happens to High Fae territories that defend the Treaty."

"But surely other territories would protect it," I said, scanning their faces.

"Not as many as we'd hoped," Rhys admitted, wincing. "There are many—too many—who have also felt squashed and suffocated during these centuries. They want their old lands back beneath the wall, and the power and prosperity that came with it. Their vision of the past has been colored by five hundred years of struggling to adjust and thrive."

"Perhaps we did them a disservice," Mor mused, "in not sharing enough of our wealth, our territory. Perhaps we are to blame for allowing some of this to rot and fester."

"That remains to be discussed," Amren said, waving a delicate hand. "The point is that we are not facing an army hell-bent on destruction. They are hell-bent on what they believe is *liberation*. Of High Fae stifled by the wall, and what they believe still belongs to them."

I swallowed. "So how do the other territories play into it—the three Hybern claims will ally with them?" I looked between Rhys and Azriel. "You said you were . . . over there?"

Rhys shrugged. "Over there, in Hybern, in the other territories . . ." He winked at my gaping mouth. "I had to keep myself busy to avoid missing you."

Mor rolled her eyes. But it was Cassian who said, "We can't afford to let those three territories join with Hybern. If they send armies to Prythian, we're done."

"So what do we do?"

Rhys leaned against the carved post of Amren's bed. "We've been keeping them busy." He jerked his chin to Azriel. "We planted information—truth and lies and a blend of both—for them to find. And also scattered some of it among our old allies, who are now balking at supporting us." Azriel's smile was a slash of white. Lies and truth—the shadowsinger and his spies had sowed them in foreign courts.

My brow narrowed. "You've been playing the territories on the continent off each other?"

"We've been making sure that they're kept busy with each other," Cassian said, a hint of wicked humor glinting in his hazel eyes. "Making sure that longtime enemies and rival-nations of Rask, Vallahan, and Montesere have suddenly received information that has them worried about being attacked. And raising their own defenses. Which in turn has made Rask, Vallahan, and Montesere start looking toward their own borders and not our own."

"If our allies from the War are too scared to come here to fight," Mor said, folding her arms over her chest, "then as long as they're keeping the others occupied—keeping them from sailing *here*—we don't care."

I blinked at them. At Rhys.

Brilliant. Utterly brilliant, to keep them so focused and fearful of each other that they stayed away. "So . . . they won't be coming?"

"We can only pray," Amren said. "And pray we deal with this fast enough that they don't figure out we've played them all."

"What of the human queens, though?" I chewed on the tip of my thumb. "They have to be aware that no bargain with Hybern would ultimately work to their advantage."

Mor braced her forearms on her thighs. "Who knows what Hybern promised them—lied about? He already granted them immortality through the Cauldron in exchange for their cooperation. If they were foolish enough to agree to it, then I don't doubt they've already thrown open the gates to him."

"But we don't know that for certain," Amren countered. "And none of it explains why they've been so quiet—locked up in that palace."

Rhys and Azriel shook their heads in silent confirmation.

I surveyed them, their fading amusement. "It drives you mad, doesn't it, that no one has been able to get inside that palace."

A low growl from both of them before Azriel muttered, "You have no idea."

Amren just clicked her tongue, her upswept eyes settling on me. "Those Hybern commanders were fools to reveal their plans in regard to breaking the wall. Or perhaps they knew the information would return to us, and their master wants us to stew."

I angled my head. "You mean shattering the wall through the holes already in it?"

A bob of her sharp chin as she gestured to the books around her. "It's complex spell work—a loophole through the magic that binds the wall."

"And it implies," Mor said, frowning deeply, "that something might be amiss with the Cauldron."

I raised my brows, considering. "Because the Cauldron should be able to bring that wall down on its own, right?"

"Right," Rhysand said, striding to the Book on the nightstand. He didn't dare touch it. "Why bother seeking out those holes to help the Cauldron when he could unleash its power and be done with it?"

"Maybe he used too much of its power transforming my sisters and those queens."

"It's likely," Rhys said, stalking back to my side. "But if he's going to exploit those tears in the wall, we need to find a way to *fix* them before he can act."

I asked Amren, "Are there spells to patch it up?"

"I'm looking," she said through her teeth. "It'd help if *someone* dragged their ass to a library to do more research."

"We are at your disposal," Cassian offered with a mock bow.

"I wasn't aware you could read," Amren said sweetly.

"It could be a fool's errand," Azriel cut in before Cassian could voice the retort dancing in his eyes. "To get us to focus on the wall as a decoy—while he strikes from another direction."

I grimaced at the Book. "Why not just try to nullify the Cauldron again?"

"Because it nearly killed you the last time," Rhys said in a sort of calm, steady voice that told me enough: there was no way in hell he'd risk me attempting it again.

I straightened. "I wasn't prepared in Hybern. None of us were. If I tried again—"

Mor cut in. "If you tried again, it might very well kill you. Not to mention, we'd have to actually *get* to the Cauldron, which isn't an option."

"The king," Azriel clarified at my furrowed brow, "won't allow the Cauldron out of his sight. And he's rigged it with more spells and traps than the last time." I opened my mouth to object, but the shadowsinger added, "We looked into it. It's not a viable path."

I believed him—the stark honesty in those hazel eyes was confirmation enough that they'd weighed it thoroughly. "Well, if it's too risky to nullify the Cauldron," I mused, "then can *I* somehow fix the wall? If the wall was made *by* faeries coming together, and my very magic is a blend of so many . . ."

Amren considered in the silence that fell. "Perhaps. The relationship would be tenuous, but . . . yes, perhaps you could patch it up. Though your sisters, directly forged by the Cauldron itself, might bear the sort of magic we—"

"My sisters play no part in this."

Another beat of silence, interrupted only by the rustle of Azriel's wings.

"I asked them to help once—and look what happened. I won't risk them again."

Amren snorted. "You sound exactly like Tamlin."

I felt the words like a blow.

Rhys slid a hand against my back, having appeared so fast I didn't see him move. But before he could reply, Mor said quietly, "Don't you ever say that sort of bullshit again, Amren."

There was nothing on Mor's face beyond cold calm—fury.

I'd never seen her look so . . . terrifying. She had been furious with the mortal queens, but this . . . This was the face of the High Lord's third in command.

"If you're cranky because you're hungry, then tell us," Mor went on with that frozen quiet. "But if you say anything like that again, I will throw you in the gods-damned Sidra."

"I'd like to see you try."

A little smile was Mor's only answer.

Amren slid her attention to me. "We need your sisters—if not for this, then to convince others to join us, of the risk. Since any would-be ally might have some . . . difficulty believing us after so many years of lies."

"Apologize," said Mor.

"Mor," I murmured.

"*Apologize*," she hissed at Amren.

Amren said nothing.

Mor took a step toward her, and I said, "She's right."

They both looked to me, brows raised.

I swallowed. "Amren is right." I walked out of Rhys's touch—realizing he'd kept silent to let me sort it out. Let me figure out how to deal with both of them, as family, but mostly as their High Lady.

Mor's face tightened, but I shook my head. "I can—ask my sisters. See if they have any sort of power. See if they'd be willing to . . . talk to others about what they endured. But I won't force them to help, if they do not wish to participate. The choice will be theirs." I glanced at my mate—the male who had always presented me with a choice not as a gift, but as my own gods-given *right*. Rhys's violet eyes flickered in acknowledgment. "But I'll make our . . . desperation clear."

Amren huffed, hardly more than a bird of prey puffing its feathers.

"Compromise, Amren," Rhys purred. "It's called compromise."

She ignored him. "If you want to start convincing your sisters, get them out of the House. Being cooped up never helped anyone."

Rhys said smoothly, "I'm not entirely sure Velaris is prepared for Nesta Archeron."

"My sister's not some feral animal," I snapped.

Rhys recoiled a bit, the others suddenly finding the carpet, the divan, the books incredibly fascinating. "I didn't mean that."

I didn't answer.

Mor frowned in disapproval at Rhys, who I felt watching me carefully, but asked me, "What of Elain?"

I shifted slightly, pushing past the words still hanging between me and Rhys. "I can ask, but . . . she might not be ready to be around so many people." I clarified, "She was supposed to be married next week."

"So she keeps saying, over and over," Amren grumbled.

I shot her a glare. "Careful." Amren blinked up at me in surprise. But I went on, "So, we need to find a way to patch up the wall before Hybern uses the Cauldron to break it. And fight this war before any other territories join Hybern's assault. And eventually get the Cauldron itself. Anything else?"

Rhys said behind me, his own voice carefully casual, "That covers it. As soon as a force can be assembled, we take on Hybern."

"The Illyrian legions are nearly ready," Cassian said.

"No," Rhys said. "I mean a bigger force. A force not just from the Night Court, but from all of Prythian. Our only decent shot at finding allies in this war."

None of us spoke, none of us moved as Rhys said simply, "Tomorrow, invitations go out to every High Lord in Prythian. For a meeting in two weeks. It's time we see who stands with us. And make sure they understand the consequences if they don't."

CHAPTER 17

I let Cassian carry me to the House two hours later, just because he admitted he was still working to strengthen his wings and needed to push himself.

Heat rippled off the tiled roofs and red stone as we soared high over them, the sea breeze a cool kiss against my face.

We'd barely finished debating thirty minutes ago, only stopping when Mor's stomach had grumbled as loudly as a breaking thunderhead. We'd spent our time weighing the merits of where to meet, who to bring along to the meeting with the High Lords.

Invitations would go out tomorrow—but not specify the meeting place. There was no point in selecting one, Rhys said, when the High Lords would no doubt refuse our initial selection and counter with their own choice of where to gather. All we had chosen was the day and the time—the two weeks a cushion against the bickering that was sure to ensue. The rest . . . We'd just have to prepare for every possibility.

We'd quickly returned to the town house to change before heading back up to the House—and I'd found Nuala and Cerridwen waiting in my room, smiles on their shadowy faces.

I'd embraced them both, even if Rhys's hello had been less . . . enthusiastic. Not for dislike of the half-wraiths, but . . .

I'd snapped at him. In Amren's apartment. He hadn't seemed angry, and yet . . . I'd felt him carefully watching me these past few hours. It'd made it . . . strange to look at him. Strange enough that the appetite I'd been steadily building had gone a bit queasy. I'd challenged him before, but . . . not as High Lady. Not with the . . . tone.

So I didn't get to ask him about it as Nuala and Cerridwen helped me dress and he headed into the bathing room to wash up.

Not that there was much finery to bother with. I'd opted for my Illyrian leather pants and a loose, white shirt—and a pair of embroidered slippers that Cassian kept snorting at as we flew.

When he did so for the third time in two minutes, I pinched his arm and said, "It's hot. Those boots are stuffy."

His brows rose, the portrait of innocence. "I didn't say anything."

"You grunted. *Again.*"

"I've been living with Mor for five hundred years. I've learned the hard way not to question shoe choices." He smirked. "However stupid they may be."

"It's dinner. Unless there's some battle planned afterward?"

"Your sister will be there—I'd say that's battle aplenty."

I casually studied his face, noting how hard he worked to keep his features neutral, to keep his gaze fixed anywhere but on my own. Rhys flew nearby, far enough to remain out of earshot as I said, "Would you use her to see if she can somehow fix the wall?"

Hazel eyes shot to me, fierce and clear. "Yes. Not only for our sakes, but . . . she needs to get out of the House. She needs to . . ." Cassian's wings kept up a steady booming beat, the new sections only detectable by their lack of scarring. "She'll destroy herself if she stays cooped up in there."

My chest tightened. "Do . . ." I thought through my words. "The day she was changed, she . . . I felt something different with her." I fought against the tensing in my muscles as I recalled those moments. The screaming and the blood and the nausea as I watched my sisters taken against their will, as I could do nothing, as we—

I swallowed down the fear, the guilt. "It was like . . . everything she was, that steel and fire . . . It became magnified. Cataclysmic. Like . . . looking at a house cat and suddenly finding a panther standing there instead." I shook my head, as if it would clear away the memory of the predator, the rage simmering in those blue-gray eyes.

"I will never forget those moments," Cassian said quietly, scenting or sensing the memories wreaking havoc on me. "As long as I live."

"Have you seen any glimpse of it since?"

"Nothing." The House loomed, golden lights at the walls of windows and doorways beckoning us closer. "But I can feel it—sometimes." He added a bit ruefully, "Usually when she's pissed at me. Which is . . . most of the time."

"Why?" They'd always been at each other's throats, but this . . . yes, the dynamic between them had been different earlier. Sharper.

Cassian shook his dark hair out of his eyes, slightly longer than the last time I'd seen it. "I don't think Nesta will ever forgive me for what happened in Hybern. To her—but mostly to Elain."

"Your wings were shredded. You were barely alive." For that was guilt—ravaging and poisonous—in each of Cassian's words. What the others had been fighting against in the loft. "You were in no position to save anyone."

"I made her a promise." The wind ruffled Cassian's hair as he squinted at the sky. "And when it mattered, I didn't keep it."

I still dreamed of him trying to crawl toward her, reaching for her even in the semi-unconscious state the pain and blood loss had thrown him into. As Rhysand had once done for me during those last moments with Amarantha.

Perhaps only a few wing beats separated us from the broad landing veranda, but I asked, "Why do you bother, Cassian?"

His hazel eyes shuttered as we smoothly landed. And I thought he wouldn't answer, especially not as we heard the others already in the dining room beyond the veranda, especially not when Rhys gracefully landed beside us and strode in ahead with a wink.

But Cassian said quietly as we headed for the dining room, "Because I can't stay away."

Elain, not surprisingly, didn't leave her room.

Nesta, surprisingly, did.

It wasn't a formal dinner by any means—though Lucien, standing near the windows and watching the sun set over Velaris, was wearing a fine green jacket embroidered with gold, his cream-colored pants showing off muscled thighs, and his knee-high black boots polished enough that the chandeliers of faelight reflected off them.

He'd always had a casual grace about him, but here, tonight, with his hair tied back and jacket buttoned to his neck, he truly looked the part of a High Lord's son. Handsome, powerful, a bit rakish—but well-mannered and elegant.

I aimed for him as the others helped themselves to the wine breathing in decanters on the ancient wood table, keenly aware that while my friends chatted, they kept one eye on us. Lucien ran *his* one eye over me—my casual attire, then the Illyrians in their leathers, and Amren in her usual gray, and Mor in her flowing red gown, and said, "What *is* the dress code?"

I shrugged, passing him the glass of wine I'd brought over. "It's . . . whatever we feel like."

That gold eye clicked and narrowed, then returned to the city ahead. "What did you do with yourself this afternoon?"

"Slept," he said. "Washed. Sat on my ass."

"I could give you a tour of the city tomorrow morning," I offered. "If you like."

Never mind that we had a meeting to plan for. A wall to heal. A war to fight. I could set aside half a day. Show him *why* this place had become my home, why I had fallen in love with its ruler.

As if sensing my thoughts, Lucien said, "You don't need to waste your time convincing me. I get it. I get . . . I get that we were not what you wanted. Or needed. How small and isolated our home must have been for you, once you saw this." He jerked his chin toward the city, where lights were now sparking into view amid the falling twilight. "Who could compare?"

I almost said *Don't you mean* what *could compare?* but held my tongue.

His focus shifted behind me before he replied—and Lucien shut his mouth. His metal eye whirred softly.

I followed his glance, and tried not to tense as Nesta stepped into the room.

Yes, *devastating* was a good word for how lovely she'd become as High Fae. And in a long-sleeved, dark blue gown that clung to her curves before falling gracefully to the ground in a spill of fabric . . .

Cassian looked like someone had punched him in the gut.

But Nesta stared right at me, the faelight shimmering along the silver combs in her upswept hair. The others, she dutifully ignored, chin lifting as she strode for us. I prayed that Mor and Amren, their brows high, wouldn't say any—

"*Where* did that dress come from?" Mor said, red gown flowing behind her as she breezed toward Nesta. My sister drew up short, shoulders tensing, readying to—

But Mor was already there, fingering the heavy blue fabric, surveying every stitch. "I want one," she pouted. Her attempt, no doubt, to segue into an invitation to shop for a larger wardrobe with me. As High Lady, I'd need clothes—fancier ones. Especially for this meeting. My sisters, too.

Mor's brown eyes flicked to mine, and I had to fight the crushing gratitude that threatened to make my own burn as I approached them.

"I assume my mate dug it up somewhere," I said, throwing a glance over my shoulder at Rhys, who was perched on the edge of the dining table, flanked by Az and Cassian, all three Illyrians pretending that they weren't listening to every word as they poured the wine amongst themselves.

Busybodies. I sent the thought down the bond, and Rhys's dark laughter echoed in return.

"He gets all the credit for clothes," Mor said, examining the fabric of Nesta's skirt while my sister monitored like a hawk, "and he never tells me where he finds them. He still won't tell me where he found Feyre's dress for Starfall." She threw a glare over her shoulder. "Bastard."

Rhys chuckled. Cassian, however, didn't smile, every pore of him seemingly fixed on Nesta and Mor.

On what my sister would do.

Mor only examined the silver combs in Nesta's hair. "It's a good thing we're not the same size—or else I might be tempted to steal that dress."

"Likely right off her," Cassian muttered.

Mor's answering smirk wasn't reassuring.

But Nesta's face remained blank. Cold. She looked Mor up and down—noting the dress that exposed much of her midriff, back, and chest, then the flowing skirts with sheer panels that revealed glimpses of her legs. Scandalous, by human fashions. "Fortunately for you," Nesta said flatly, "I don't return the sentiment."

Azriel coughed into his wine.

But Nesta only walked to the table and claimed a seat.

Mor blinked, but confided to me with a wince, "I think we're going to need a lot more wine."

Nesta's spine stiffened. But she said nothing.

"I'll raid the collection," Cassian offered, disappearing through the inner hall doors too quickly to be casual.

Nesta stiffened a bit more.

Teasing my sister, poking fun at her . . . I snatched a seat at Nesta's side and murmured, "They mean well."

Nesta just ran a finger over her ivory-and-obsidian place setting, examining the silverware with vines of night-blooming jasmine engraved around the hilts. "I don't care."

Amren slid into the seat across from me, right as Cassian returned, a bottle in each hand, and cringed. Amren said to my sister, "You're a real piece of work."

Nesta's eyes flicked up. Amren idly swirled a goblet of blood, watching her like a cat with a new, interesting toy.

Nesta only said, "Why do your eyes glow?"

Little curiosity—just a blunt need for explanation.

And no fear. None.

Amren angled her head. "You know, none of these busybodies have ever asked me that."

Those busybodies were trying not to look too concerned. As was I.

Nesta only waited.

Amren sighed, her dark bob swaying. "They glow because it was the one part of me the containment spell could not quite get right. The one glimpse into what lurks beneath."

"And what is beneath?"

None of the others spoke. Or even moved. Lucien, still by the window, had turned the color of fresh paper.

Amren traced a finger along the rim of her goblet, her red-tinted nail gleaming as bright as the blood inside. "They never dared ask me that, either."

"Why."

"Because it is not polite to ask—and they are afraid."

Amren held Nesta's stare, and my sister did not balk. Did not flinch.

"We are the same, you and I," Amren said.

I wasn't sure I was breathing. Through the bond, I wasn't sure Rhys was, either.

"Not in flesh, not in the thing that prowls beneath our skin and bones . . ." Amren's remarkable eyes narrowed. "But . . . I see the kernel, girl." Amren nodded, more to herself than anyone. "You did not fit—the mold that they shoved you into. The path you were born upon and forced to walk. You tried, and yet you did not, *could* not, fit. And then the path changed." A little nod. "I know—what it is to be that way. I remember it, long ago as it was."

Nesta had mastered the Fae's preternatural stillness far more quickly than I had. And she sat there for a few heartbeats, simply staring at the strange, delicate female across from her, weighing the words, the power that radiated from Amren . . . And then Nesta merely said, "I don't know what you're talking about."

Amren's red lips parted in a wide, serpentine smile. "When you erupt, girl, make sure it is felt across worlds."

A shiver slithered down my skin.

But Rhys drawled, "Amren, it seems, has been taking drama lessons at the theater down the street from her house."

She shot him a glare. "I mean it, Rhysand—"

"I'm sure you do," he said, claiming the seat to my right. "But I'd prefer to eat *something* before you make us lose our appetites."

His broad hand warmed my knee as he clasped it beneath the table, giving me a reassuring squeeze.

Cassian took the seat on Amren's left, Azriel beside him, Mor grabbing the seat opposite him, leaving Lucien . . .

Lucien frowned at the remaining place setting at the head of the table, then at the blank, barren spot across from Nesta. "I—shouldn't you sit at the head?"

Rhys raised an eyebrow. "I don't care where you sit. I only care about eating something right"—he snapped his fingers—"now."

The food, prepared by cooks I made a point to go meet in the belly of the House, appeared across the table in platters and spreads and bowls. Roast meats, various sauces and gravies, rice and bread, steamed vegetables fresh from the surrounding farms . . . I nearly sighed at the smells curling around me.

Lucien slid into his seat, looking for all the world like he was perching atop a pincushion.

I leaned past Nesta to explain to Lucien, "You get used to it—the informality."

"You say that, Feyre darling, like it's a bad thing," Rhys said, helping himself to a platter of pan-fried trout before passing it to me.

I rolled my eyes, sliding a few crispy pieces onto my plate. "It took me by surprise that first dinner we all had, just so you know."

"Oh, I know." Rhys grinned.

Cassian sniggered.

"Honestly," I said to Lucien, who wordlessly stacked a pile of buttery green beans onto his plate but didn't touch it, perhaps marveling at the simple fare, so at odds with the overwrought dishes of Spring, "Azriel is the only polite one." A few cries of outrage from Mor and Cassian, but a ghost of a smile danced on the shadowsinger's mouth as he dipped his head and hauled a platter of roast beets sprinkled with goat cheese toward himself. "Don't even try to pretend that it's not true."

"Of course it's true," Mor said with a loud sigh, "but you needn't make us sound like *heathens*."

"I would have thought you'd find that term to be a compliment, Mor," Rhys said mildly.

Nesta was watching the volley of words as if it were a sporting match, eyes darting between us. She didn't reach for any food, so I took the liberty of dumping spoonfuls of various things onto her plate.

She watched that, too.

And when I paused, moving on to further fill my own plate, Nesta said, "I understand—what you meant about the food."

It took me a moment to recall—to remember that particular conversation back at our father's estate, when she and I had been at each other's throats over the differences between human and Fae food. It was the same in terms of *what* was served, but it just . . . *tasted* better above the wall.

"Is that a compliment?"

Nesta didn't return my smile as she speared some asparagus with her fork and dug in.

And I figured it was as good a time as any as I said to Cassian, "What time are we back in the training ring tomorrow?"

To his credit, Cassian didn't so much as glance at Nesta as he replied with a lazy smile, "I'd say dawn, but since I'm feeling rather grateful that you're back in one piece, I'll let you sleep in. Let's meet at seven."

"I'd hardly call that sleeping in," I said.

"For an Illyrian, it is," Mor muttered.

Cassian's wings rustled. "Daylight is a precious resource."

"We live in the *Night Court*," Mor countered.

Cassian only grimaced at Rhys and Azriel. "I told you that the moment we started letting females into our group, they'd be nothing but trouble."

"As far as I can recall, Cassian," Rhys countered drily, "you actually said you needed a reprieve from staring at our ugly faces, and that some *ladies* would add some much-needed prettiness for you to look at all day."

"Pig," Amren said.

Cassian gave her a vulgar gesture that made Lucien choke on his green beans. "I was a young Illyrian and didn't know better," he said, then pointed his fork at Azriel. "Don't try to blend into the shadows. You said the same thing."

"He did not," Mor said, and the shadows that Azriel had indeed been subtly weaving around himself vanished. "Azriel has never once said anything that awful. Only you, Cassian. Only you."

The general of the High Lord's armies stuck out his tongue. Mor returned the gesture.

Amren scowled at Rhys. "You'd be wise to leave *both* of them at home for the meeting with the others, Rhysand. They'll cause nothing but trouble."

I dared a peek at Lucien—just to gauge his reaction.

His face was indeed controlled, but—a hint of surprise twinkled there. Wariness, too, but . . . surprise. I risked another glance at Nesta, but she was watching her plate, dutifully ignoring the others.

Rhys said, "It remains to be seen if they'll be joining us." Lucien looked at him then, the curiosity in that one eye unmistakable. Rhys noted it and shrugged. "You'll find out soon enough, I suppose. Invitations are going out tomorrow, calling all the High Lords to gather to discuss this war."

Lucien's hand tightened on his fork. "All?"

I wasn't sure if he meant Tamlin or his father, but Rhys nodded nonetheless.

Lucien considered. "Can I offer my unsolicited advice?"

Rhys smirked. "I think that's the first time anyone at this table has ever asked such a thing."

Mor and Cassian now stuck out their tongues at him.

But Rhys waved a lazy hand at Lucien. "By all means, advise away."

Lucien studied my mate, then me. "I assume Feyre is going."

"I am."

Amren sipped from her glass of blood—the only sound in the room as Lucien considered again. "Are you planning to hide her powers?"

Silence.

Rhys at last said, "That was something I'd planned to discuss with my mate. Are you leaning one way or another, Lucien?"

There was still something sharp in his tone, something just a little vicious.

Lucien studied me again, and it was an effort not to squirm. "My father would likely join with Hybern if he thought he stood a chance of getting his power back that way—by killing you."

A snarl from Rhys.

"Your brothers saw me, though," I said, setting down my fork. "Perhaps they could mistake the flame as yours, but the ice . . ."

Lucien jerked his chin to Azriel. "That's the information you need to gather. What my father knows—if my brothers realized what she was doing. You need to start from there, and build your plan for this meeting accordingly."

Mor said, "Eris might keep that information to himself and convince the others to as well, if he thinks it'll be more useful that way." I wondered if Mor looked at that red hair, the golden-brown skin that was a few shades darker than his brothers', and still saw Eris.

Lucien said evenly, "Perhaps. But we need to find that out. If Beron or Eris has that information, they'll use it to their advantage in that meeting—to control it. Or control you. Or they might not show up at all, and instead go right to Hybern."

Cassian swore softly, and I was inclined to echo the sentiment.

Rhys swirled his wine once, set it down, and said to Lucien, "You and Azriel should talk. Tomorrow."

Lucien glanced toward the shadowsinger—who only nodded at him. "I'm at your disposal."

None of us were dumb enough to ask if he'd be willing to reveal details on the Spring Court. If he thought that Tamlin would arrive. That was perhaps a conversation best left for another time. With just him and me.

Rhys leaned back in his seat. Contemplating—something. His jaw tightened, then he let out a near-silent huff of air. Steeling himself.

For whatever he was about to reveal, whatever plans he had decided not to reveal until now. And even as my stomach tightened, some sort of thrill went through me at it—at that clever mind at work.

Until Rhys said, "There is another meeting that needs to be had—and soon."

CHAPTER 18

"Please don't say we need to go to the Court of Nightmares," Cassian grumbled around a mouthful of food.

Rhys lifted a brow. "Not in the mood to terrorize our friends there?"

Mor's golden face paled. "You mean to ask my father to fight in this war," she said to Rhys.

I reined in my sharp intake of breath.

"What is the Court of Nightmares?" Nesta demanded.

Lucien answered for us. "The place where the rest of the world believes the majority of the Night Court to be." He jerked his chin at Rhys. "The seat of his power. Or it was."

"Oh, it still is," Rhys said. "To everyone outside Velaris." He leveled a steady look at Mor. "And yes. Keir's Darkbringer legion is considerable enough that a meeting is warranted."

The last meeting had resulted in Keir's arm being shattered in so many places it had gone saggy. I doubted the male would be inclined to help us anytime soon—perhaps why Rhys wanted this meeting.

Nesta's brows narrowed. "Why not just order them? Don't they answer to you?"

Cassian set down his fork, food forgotten. "Unfortunately, there are protocols in place between our two subcourts regarding this sort of thing. They mostly govern themselves—with Mor's father their steward."

Mor's throat bobbed. Azriel watched her carefully, his mouth a tight line.

"The steward of the Hewn City is legally entitled to refuse to aid my armies," Rhys explained to Nesta, to me. "It was part of the agreement my ancestor made with the Court of Nightmares all those thousands of years ago. They would remain within that mountain, would not challenge or disturb us beyond its borders . . . and would retain the right to decide *not* to assist in war."

"And have they—refused?" I asked.

Mor nodded gravely. "Twice. Not my father." She nearly choked on the word. "But . . . there were two wars. Long, long ago. They chose not to fight. We won, but . . . barely. At great cost."

And with this war upon us . . . we would need every ally we could muster. Every army.

"We leave in two days," Rhys said.

"He'll say no," Mor countered. "Don't waste your time."

"Then I shall have to find a way to convince him otherwise."

Mor's eyes flashed. "What?"

Azriel and Cassian shifted in their seats, and Amren clicked her tongue at Rhys. Disapproval.

"He fought in the War," Rhys said calmly. "Perhaps we'll be lucky this time, too."

"I'll remind you that the Darkbringer legion was nearly as bad as the enemy when it came to their behavior," Mor said, pushing her plate away.

"There will be new rules."

"You will not be in a position to make rules, and you know it," Mor snapped.

Rhys only swirled his wine again. "We'll see."

I glanced to Cassian. The general shook his head subtly. *Stay out of this one. For now.*

I swallowed, nodding back with equal faintness.

Mor whipped her head toward Azriel. "What do *you* think?"

The shadowsinger held her stare, his face unreadable. Considering. I tried not to hold my breath. Defending the female he loved or siding with his High Lord . . . "It's not my call to make."

"That's a bullshit answer," Mor challenged.

I could have sworn hurt flickered in Azriel's eyes, but he only shrugged, his face again a mask of cold indifference. Mor's lips pursed.

"You don't need to come, Mor," Rhys said with that calm, even voice.

"Of course I'm coming. It'll make it worse if I'm not there." She drained her wine in one swift tilt of her head. "I suppose I have two days now to find a dress suitable to horrify my father."

Amren, at least, chuckled at that, Cassian rumbling a laugh as well.

But Rhys watched Mor for a long minute, some of the stars in his eyes winking out. I debated asking if there was some other way, some path to avoid *this* awfulness between us, but . . . Earlier, I had snapped at him. And with Lucien and my sister here . . . I kept my mouth shut.

Well, about that matter. In the silence that fell, I scrambled for any scrap of normalcy and turned again to Cassian. "Let's train at *eight* tomorrow. I'll meet you in the ring."

"Seven thirty," he said with a disarming grin—one that most of his enemies would likely run from. Lucien went back to picking at his food. Mor refilled her wineglass, Azriel monitoring every move she made, his fork clenched in his scarred hand.

"Eight," I countered with a flat look. I turned to Nesta, silent and watchful through all of this. "Care to join?"

"No."

The beat of silence was too pointed to be dismissed. But I gave my sister a casual shrug, reaching for the wine jug. Then I said to none of them in particular, "I want to learn how to fly."

Mor spewed her wine across the table, splattering it right across Azriel's chest and neck. The shadowsinger was too busy gawking at me to even notice.

Cassian looked torn between howling at Azriel and gaping.

My magic was still too weak to grow those Illyrian wings, but I gestured to the Illyrians and said, "I want you to teach me."

Mor blurted, "Really?" while Lucien—*Lucien*—said, "Well, that explains the wings."

Nesta leaned forward to appraise me. "What wings?"

"I can—shape-shift," I admitted. "And with the oncoming conflict," I declared to all of them, "knowing how to fly might be . . . useful." I jerked my chin toward Cassian, who now studied me with unnerving intensity—sizing me up. "I assume the battles against Hybern will include Illyrians." A shallow nod from the general. "Then I plan to fight with you. In the skies."

I waited for the objections, for Rhys to shut it down.

There was only the howling wind outside the dining room windows.

Cassian whooshed out a breath. "I don't know if it's technically even possible—time-wise. You'd have to learn not only how to fly, but how to bear the weight of your shield and weapons—and how to work within an Illyrian unit. It takes us decades to master that last part alone. We have months at best—weeks at worst."

My chest sank a bit.

"Then we'll teach her what we know until then," Rhys said. But the stars in his eyes turned stone-cold as he added, "I'll give her any shot at an advantage—at getting away if things go to shit. Even a day of training might make a difference."

Azriel tucked in his wings, his beautiful features uncharacteristically soft. Contemplative. "I'll teach you."

"Are you . . . certain?" I asked.

The unreadable mask slipped back over Azriel's face. "Rhys and Cass were taught how to fly so young that they barely remember it."

But Azriel, locked in his hateful father's dungeons like some criminal until he was eleven, denied the ability to fly, to fight, to do anything his Illyrian instincts screamed at him to do . . .

Darkness rumbled down the bond. Not anger at me, but . . . as Rhys, too, remembered what had been done to his friend. He'd never forgotten. None of them had. It was an effort not to look at the brutal scars coating Azriel's hands. I prayed Nesta wouldn't inquire about it.

"We've taught plenty of younglings the basics," Cassian countered.

Azriel shook his head, shadows twining around his wrists. "It's not the same. When you're older, the fears, the mental blocks . . . it's different."

None of them, not even Amren, said anything.

Azriel only said to me, "I'll teach you. Train with Cass for a few hours, and I'll meet you when you're through." He added to Lucien, who did not balk from those writhing shadows, "After lunch, we'll meet."

I swallowed, but nodded. "Thank you." And perhaps Azriel's kindness snapped some sort of tether in me, but I turned to Nesta. "The King of Hybern is trying to bring down the wall by using the Cauldron to expand the holes already in it." Her blue-gray eyes revealed nothing—only simmering rage at the king's name. "I might be able to patch up those holes, but you . . . being made of the Cauldron itself . . . if the Cauldron can widen those holes, perhaps you can close them, too. With training—in whatever time we have."

"I can show you," Amren clarified to my sister. "Or, in theory I can. If we start soon—tomorrow morning." She considered, then declared to Rhys, "When you go to the Court of Nightmares, we will go with you."

I whipped my head to Amren. "What?" The thought of Nesta in that place—

"The Hewn City is a trove of objects of power," Amren explained. "There may be opportunities to practice. Let the girl get a feel for what something like the wall or the Cauldron might be like." She added when Azriel seem poised to object, "*Covertly*."

Nesta said nothing.

I waited for her outright refusal, the cold shutdown of all hope.

But Nesta only asked, "Why not just kill the King of Hybern before he can act?"

Utter silence.

Amren said a bit softly, "If you want his killing blow, girl, it's yours."

Nesta's gaze drifted toward the open interior doors of the dining room. As if she could see all the way to Elain. "What happened to the human queens?"

I blinked. "What do you mean?"

"Were they made immortal?" This question went to Azriel.

Azriel's Siphons smoldered. "Reports have been murky and inconsistent. Some say yes, others say no."

Nesta examined her wineglass.

Cassian braced his forearms on the table. "Why?"

Nesta's eyes shot right to his face. She spoke quietly to me, to all of us, even as she held Cassian's gaze as if he were the only one in the room. "By the end of this war, I want them dead. The king, the queens—all of them. Promise me you'll kill them all, and I'll help you patch up the wall. I'll train with her"—a jerk of her chin to Amren—"I'll go to the Hewn City or whatever it is . . . I'll do it. But only if you promise me that."

"Fine," I said. "And we might need your assistance during the meeting with the High Lords—to provide testimony to other courts and allies of what Hybern is capable of. What was done to you."

"No."

"You don't mind fixing the wall or going to the Court of Nightmares, but speaking to people is where you draw your line?"

Nesta's mouth tightened. "No."

High Lady or sister; sister or High Lady . . . "People's lives might depend on your account of it. The success of this meeting with the High Lords might depend upon it."

She gripped the arms of her chair, as if restraining herself. "Don't talk down to me. My answer is no."

I angled my head. "I understand that what happened to you was horrible—"

"You have *no idea* what it was or was not. None. And I am not going to grovel like one of those Children of the Blessed, begging High Fae who would have gladly killed me as a mortal to help us. I'm not going to tell them *that* story—*my* story."

"The High Lords might not believe our account, which makes you a valuable witness—"

Nesta shoved her chair back, chucking her napkin on her plate, gravy soaking through the fine linen. "Then it is not my problem if you're unreliable. I'll help you with the wall, but I am not going to whore my story around to everyone on your behalf." She shot to her feet, color rising to her ordinarily pale face, and hissed, "And if you even *dare* suggest to Elain that she do such a thing, I will rip out your *throat*."

Her eyes lifted from mine to sweep over everyone—extending the threat.

None of us spoke as she left the dining room and slammed the door shut behind her.

I slumped in my chair, resting my head against the back.

Something thumped in front of me. A bottle of wine. "It's fine if you drink directly from it," was all Mor said.

"I'd say Nesta rivals Amren for sheer bloodthirstiness," Rhys mused hours later as he and I walked alone through the streets of Velaris. "The only difference is that Amren actually drinks it."

I snorted, shaking my head as we turned onto the broad street beside the Sidra and meandered along the star-flecked river.

So many scars still marred the lovely buildings of Velaris, streets gouged from fallen debris and claws. Most of it had been repaired, but some storefronts had been left boarded up, some homes along the river no more than mounds of rubble. We'd flown down from the House as soon as we'd finished dinner—well, the wine, I supposed. Mor had taken another bottle with her when she'd disappeared into the House, Azriel frowning after her.

Rhys and I hadn't invited anyone else with us. He'd only asked me through the bond, *Walk with me?* And I'd merely given him a subtle nod.

And here we were. We'd walked for over an hour now, mostly quiet, mostly . . . thinking. Of the words and information and threats shared today. Neither of us slowed our steps until we reached that little restaurant where we had all dined under the stars one night.

Something tight in my chest eased as I beheld the untouched building, the potted citrus plants sighing in the river breeze. And on that breeze . . . those delectable, rich spices, garlicky meat, simmering tomatoes . . . I leaned my back against the rail along the river walkway, watching the restaurant workers serve the packed tables.

"Who knows," I murmured, answering him at last. "Perhaps Nesta will take up the blood-drinking habit, too. I certainly believe her threat to rip out my throat. Maybe she'll enjoy the taste."

Rhys chuckled, the sound rumbling into my bones as he took up a spot beside me, his elbows braced on the rail, wings tucked in tight. I breathed in deeply, taking the citrus-and-sea scent of him into my lungs, my blood. His mouth grazed my neck. "Will you hate me if I say that Nesta is . . . difficult?"

I laughed softly. "I'd say this went fairly well, all things considered. She agreed to one thing, at least." I chewed on my lower lip. "I shouldn't have asked her in public. I made a mistake."

He remained silent, listening.

"With the others," I asked, "how do you find that balance—between High Lord and family?"

Rhys considered. "It isn't easy. I've made plenty of bad calls over the centuries. So I hate to tell you that tonight might only be the start of it."

I loosed a long sigh. "I should have considered that telling strangers what happened to her in Hybern might . . . might not be something she was comfortable with. My sister has been a private person her entire life, even amongst us."

Rhys leaned in to kiss my neck again. "Earlier today—at the loft," he said, pulling back to meet my eyes. Unflinching. Open. "I didn't mean to insult her."

"I'm sorry I snapped at you."

He lifted a dark brow. "Why in hell would you be? I insulted your sister; you defended her. You had every right to kick my ass for it."

"I didn't mean to . . . undermine you."

Shadows flickered in his eyes. "Ah." He twisted toward the Sidra, and I followed suit. The water meandered past, its dark surface rippling with golden faelights from the streetlamps and the bright jewels of the Rainbow. "That was why it was . . . strange between us this afternoon." He cringed and faced me fully. "Mother above, Feyre."

My cheeks heated and I interrupted before he could continue. "I get why, though. A solid, unified front is important." I scratched at the smooth wood of the rail with a finger. "Especially for us."

"Not amongst our family."

Warmth spread through me at the words—*our* family.

He took my hand, interlacing our fingers. "We can make whatever rules we want. You have every right to question me, push me—both in private and in public." A snort. "Of course, if you decide to truly kick my ass, I might request that it's done behind closed doors so I don't have to suffer centuries of teasing, but—"

"I won't undermine you in public. And you won't undermine me."

He remained quiet, letting me think, speak.

"We can question each other through the bond if we're around people other than our friends," I said. "But for now, for these initial years, I'd like to show the world a unified front . . . That is, if we survive."

"We'll survive." Uncompromising will in those words, that face. "But I want you to feel comfortable pushing me, calling me out—"

"When have I ever *not* done that?" He smiled. But I added, "I want you to do the same—for me."

"Deal. But amongst our family . . . call me on my bullshit all you want. I insist, actually."

"Why?"

"Because it's fun."

I nudged him with an elbow.

"Because you're my equal," he said. "And as much as that means having each other's backs in public, it also means that we grant each other the gift of honesty. Of truth."

I surveyed the bustling city around us. "Can I give you a bit of truth, then?"

He stilled, but said, "Always."

I blew out a breath. "I think you should be careful—working with Keir. Not for how despicable he is, but because . . . I think you could truly wound Mor if you don't play it right."

Rhys dragged a hand through his hair. "I know. I know."

"Is it worth it—whatever troops he can offer? If it means hurting her?"

"We've been working with Keir for centuries. She should be used to it by now. And yes—his troops are worth it. The Darkbringers are well trained, powerful, and have been idle too long."

I considered. "The last time we went to the Court of Nightmares, I played your whore."

He winced at the word.

"But I am now your High Lady," I went on, stroking a finger over the back of his hand. He tracked the movement. My voice dropped lower. "To get Keir to agree to aid us . . . Any tips on what mask I should wear to the Hewn City?"

"It's for you to decide," he said, still watching my finger trace idle circles on his skin. "You've seen how I am there—how we are. It is for you to decide how to play into that."

"I suppose I'd better decide soon—not just for this, but the meeting with the other High Lords in two weeks."

Rhys slid a sidelong glance to me. "Every court is invited."

"I doubt he'll come, given that he is Hybern's ally and knows we'd kill him."

The river breeze stirred his blue-black hair. "The meeting will occur with a binding spell that forces us all into cease-fire. If someone breaks it while the meeting occurs, the magic will demand a steep cost. Probably their life. Tamlin wouldn't be stupid enough to attack—nor us him."

"Why invite him at all?"

"Excluding him will only give him more ammunition against us. Believe me, I have little desire to see him. Or Beron. Who perhaps is higher on my kill list than Tamlin right now."

"Tarquin will be there. And *we* are pretty high on his kill list."

"Even with the blood rubies, he wouldn't be stupid enough to attack during the meeting." Rhys sighed through his nose.

"How many allies can we count on? Beyond Keir and the Hewn City, I mean." I glanced down the river walkway. The diners and revelers were too busy enjoying themselves to even note our presence, even with Rhys's recognizable wings. Still—perhaps not the best place for this conversation.

"I'm not sure," Rhys admitted. "Helion and his Day Court, probably. Kallias . . . maybe. Things have been strained with the Winter Court since Under the Mountain."

"I assume Azriel is going to be finding out more."

"He's already on the hunt."

I nodded. "Amren claimed she and Nesta needed help researching ways to repair the wall." I gestured to the city. "Point me toward the best library to find that sort of thing."

Rhys's brows lifted. "Right now? Your work ethic puts mine to shame."

I hissed, "*Tomorrow*, smartass."

He chuckled, wings flaring and tucking in tight. Wings . . . wings he'd allowed Lucien to see.

"You trust Lucien."

Rhys angled his head at the not-quite question. "I trust in the fact that we currently have possession of the one thing he wants above all else. And as long as that remains, he'll try to stay on our good side. But if that changes . . . His talent was wasted in the Spring Court. There was a reason he had that fox mask, you know." His mouth tugged to the side. "If he got Elain away, back to Spring or wherever . . . do you believe, deep down, that he wouldn't sell what he knows? Either for gain, or to ensure she stays safe?"

"You let him hear everything tonight, though."

"None of it is information that would let Hybern wreck us. The king likely already knows that we'll go for Keir's alliance—that we'll try to find a way to stop him from bringing down the wall. He wasn't subtle with Dagdan and Brannagh's searching. And he'll expect us to try to band the High Lords together. Which is why the meeting location will not be decided until later. Will I tell Lucien then? Bring him along?"

I considered his question: Did *I* trust Lucien? "I don't know, either," I admitted, and sighed. "I don't like that Elain is a pawn in this."

"I know. It's never easy."

He'd dealt with such things for centuries. "I want to wait—see what Lucien does over the next two weeks. How he acts, with us and Elain. What Azriel thinks of him." I frowned. "He's not a bad person—he's not evil."

"He certainly isn't."

"I just . . ." I met his calm, steady stare. "There is risk in trusting him without question."

"Did he discuss what he feels regarding Tamlin?"

"No. I didn't want to push on that. He was . . . remorseful about what happened with me, and Hybern, and Elain. Would he have felt that way without Elain in the mix? I don't know—maybe. I don't think he would have left, though."

Rhys brushed the hair from my face. "It's all part of the game, Feyre darling. Who to trust, when to trust them—what information to barter."

"Do you enjoy it?"

"Sometimes. Right now, I don't. Not when the risks are this high." His fingers grazed my brow. "When I have so much to lose."

I laid my palm on his chest, right over those Illyrian tattoos beneath his clothes, right over his heart. Felt the sturdy beat echoing into my skin and bones.

I forgot the city around us as he met my eyes, lips hovering over my skin, and murmured, "We will keep planning for the future, war or no war. *I* will keep planning for our future."

My throat burned, and I nodded.

"We deserve to be happy," he said, his eyes sparkling enough to tell me that he recalled the words I'd given him on the town house roof after the attack. "And I will fight with everything I have to ensure it."

"*We* will fight," I said hoarsely. "Not just you—not anymore."

Too much. He had given too much already, and still seemed to think it was not enough.

But Rhys only peered over his broad shoulder, to the cheerful restaurant behind us. "That first night we all came here," he said, and I followed his gaze, watching the workers set the tables with loving precision. "When you told Sevenda that you felt awake while eating her food . . ." He shook his head. "It was the first time you had looked . . . peaceful. Like you were indeed awake, *alive* again. I was so relieved I thought I'd puke right onto the table."

I recalled the long, strange look he'd given me when I'd finally spoken. Then the long walk we'd taken home, when we'd heard that music he'd sent to my cell Under the Mountain.

I pushed off the rail and tugged him toward the bridge that spanned the Sidra—the bridge to take us home. Let the debate over who'd give the most in this war rest for now. "Walk with me—through the Rainbow." The glittering, colorful jewel of the city, the beating heart that housed the artists' quarter. Vibrant and thrumming at this hour of the night.

I linked arms with him before saying, "You and this city helped wake me up—helped bring me back to life." His eyes flickered as I smiled up at him. "I will fight with everything I have, too, Rhys. Everything."

He only kissed the top of my head, tugging me closer as we crossed the Sidra under the starry sky.

CHAPTER 19

It was a good thing I'd insisted on meeting Cassian at eight, because even though I awoke at dawn, one look at Rhysand's sleeping face had me deciding to spend the morning slowly, sweetly waking him up.

I was still flushed by the time Rhys dropped me at the sparring ring atop the House of Wind, the space surrounded by a wall of red rock, the top open to the elements. He promised to meet me after lunch to show me the library for my researching, then gave me a roguish wink and kiss on the cheek before he shot back into the sky with a powerful flap of his wings.

Leaning against the wall beside the weapons rack, Cassian only said, "I hope you didn't exert yourself too much already, because this is *really* going to hurt."

I rolled my eyes, even as I tried to shut out the image of Rhysand laying me on my stomach, then kissing his way down my spine. Lower. Tried to shut out the feeling of his strong hands gripping my hips and lifting them up, up, until he lay beneath them and feasted on me, until I was quietly begging him and he rose behind me and I had to bite my pillow to keep from waking the whole house with my moaning.

Rhysand in the morning was . . . I didn't have words for what it was when he was unhurried and lazy and wicked, when his hair was still mussed with sleep and his eyes got that glazed, purely male gleam in them. They'd still had that lazy, satisfied glint a moment ago, and his mockingly chaste kiss on my cheek had sent a red-hot line through me.

Later. I'd torture him later.

For now . . . I strode to where Cassian stood, rotating my shoulders. "Two Illyrian males making me sweat in one morning. What's a female to do?"

Cassian barked a laugh. "At least you showed up with some spirit."

I grinned, bracing my hands on my hips as I surveyed the weapons rack. "Which one?"

"None." He jerked his chin toward the ring etched in white chalk behind us. "It's been a while since we trained. We're spending today going over the basics."

The words were laced with enough tightness that I said, "It hasn't been that long."

"It's been a month and a half."

I studied him, the wings tucked in tight, the shoulder-length dark hair. "What's wrong?"

"Nothing." He stalked past me to the ring.

"Is it Nesta?"

"Not everything in my life is about your sister, you know."

I kept my mouth shut on that front. "Is it something with the Court of Nightmares visit tomorrow?"

Cassian shucked off his shirt, revealing rippling muscles covered in beautiful, intricate tattoos. Illyrian markings for luck and glory. "It's nothing. Get into position."

I obeyed, even as I eyed him carefully. "You're . . . angry."

He refused to speak until I started my circuit of warm-ups: various lunges, kicks, and stretches designed to loosen my muscles. And only when we'd begun sparring, his hands wrapped against my onslaught of punching, did he say, "You and Rhys hid the truth from us. And we went into Hybern blind about it."

"About what?"

"That you're High Lady."

I jabbed at his raised hands in a one-two combination, breathing hard. "What difference would it have made?"

"It would have changed *everything*. None of it would have gone down like that."

"Perhaps that's why Rhys decided to keep it a secret."

"Hybern was a *disaster*."

I halted my punching. "You knew I was his mate when we went. I don't see how being High Lady alters anything."

"It does."

I put my hands on my hips, ignoring his motion to continue. "Why?"

Cassian dragged a hand through his hair. "Because . . . because as his mate, you were still . . . his to protect. Oh, don't get that look. He's yours to protect, too. I would have laid my life down for you as his mate—and as your friend. But you were still . . . his."

"And as High Lady?"

Cassian loosed a rough breath. "As High Lady, you are *mine*. And Azriel's, and Mor's and Amren's. You belong to all of us, and we belong to *you*. We would not have . . . put you in so much danger."

"Maybe that's why Rhys wanted to keep it a secret. It would have changed your focus."

"This is between you and me. And trust me, Rhys and I had . . . *words* about this."

I lifted a brow. "You're mad at me?"

He shook his head, eyes shuttering.

"Cassian."

He just held up his hands in a silent order to continue.

I sighed and began again. It was only after I'd gotten through fifteen repetitions and was panting heavily that Cassian said, "You didn't think you were essential. You saved our asses, yes, but . . . you didn't think you were essential here."

One-two, one-two, one-two. "I'm not." He opened his mouth, but I charged ahead, speaking around my gasps for breath. "You all have a . . . duty—you're all vital. Yes, I have my own abilities, but . . . You and Azriel were hurt, my sisters were . . . you know what happened to them. I did what I could to get us out. I'd rather it was me than any of you. I couldn't have lived with the alternative."

His upraised hands were unfaltering as I pummeled them. "Anything could have happened to you at the Spring Court."

I stopped again. "If Rhys isn't grilling me with the overprotective bullshit, then I don't see why *you*—"

"Don't for one moment think that Rhys wasn't beside himself with worry. Oh, he seems collected enough, Feyre, but I know him. And every moment you were gone, he was in a *panic*. Yes, he knew—we knew—you could handle yourself. But it doesn't stop us from worrying."

I shook out my sore hands, then rubbed my already-aching arms. "You were mad at him, too."

"If I hadn't been healing, I would have kicked his ass from one end of Velaris to the other."

I didn't reply.

"We were all terrified for you."

"I managed just fine."

"Of course you did. We knew you would. But . . ." Cassian crossed his arms. "Rhys pulled the same shit fifty years ago. When he went to that damned party Amarantha threw."

Oh. *Oh*.

"I'll never forget it, you know," he said, blowing out a breath. "The moment when he spoke to us all, mind to mind. When I realized what was happening, and that . . . he'd saved us. Trapped us here and tied our hands, but . . ." He scratched at his temple. "It went quiet—in my head. In a way it hadn't been before. Not since . . ." Cassian squinted at the cloudless sky. "Even with utter hell unleashing here, across our territory, I just went . . . quiet." He tapped the side of his head with a finger, and frowned. "After Hybern, the healer kept me asleep while she worked on my wings. So when I woke up two weeks later . . . that's when I heard. And when Mor told me what happened to you . . . It went quiet again."

I swallowed against the constriction of my throat. "You found me when I needed you most, Cassian."

"Pleased to be of service." He gave me a grim smile. "You can rely on us, you know. Both of you. He's inclined to do everything himself—to *give* everything of himself. He can't stand to let anyone else offer up anything." That smile faded. "Neither can you."

"And you can?"

"It's not easy, but yes. I'm general of his armies. Part of that includes knowing how to delegate. I've been with Rhys for over five hundred years and he still tries to do everything himself. Still thinks it's not enough."

I knew that—too well. And the thought of Rhys, in this war, trying to take on all that faced us . . . Nausea churned in my gut. "He gives orders all the time."

"Yes. And he's good at knowing what we excel at. But when it comes down to it . . ." Cassian adjusted the wrappings on his hands. "If the High Lords and Keir don't step up, he'll still face Hybern. And will take the brunt of it so we don't have to."

An unshakable, queasy sort of tightness pushed in on me. Rhys would survive—he wouldn't dare sacrifice everything to make sure we—

Rhys would. He had with Amarantha, and he'd do it again without hesitation.

I shut it out. Shoved it down. Focused on my breathing.

Something drew Cassian's attention behind me. And even as his body remained casual, a predatory gleam flickered in his eyes.

I didn't need to turn to know who was standing there.

"Care to join?" Cassian purred.

Nesta said, "It doesn't look like you're exercising anything other than your mouths."

I looked over my shoulder. My sister was in a dress of pale blue that turned her skin golden, her hair swept up, her back a stiff column. I scrambled to say something, to apologize, but . . . not in front of him. She wouldn't want this conversation in front of Cassian.

Cassian extended a wrapped hand, his fingers curling in a come-hither motion. "Scared?"

I wisely kept my mouth shut as Nesta stepped from the open doorway into the blinding light of the courtyard. "Why should I be scared of an oversized bat who likes to throw temper tantrums?"

I choked, and Cassian shot me a warning glare, daring me to laugh. But I felt for that bond in my mind, lowering my mental shields enough to say to Rhysand, wherever he was in the city, *Please come spare me from Cassian and Nesta's bickering.*

A heartbeat later, Rhys crooned, *Regretting becoming High Lady?*

I savored that voice—that humor. But I shoved that simmering panic down again as I countered, *Is this part of my duties?*

A sensual, dark laugh. *Why do you think I was so desperate for a partner? I've had almost five centuries to deal with this alone. It's only fair you have to endure it now.*

Cassian was saying to Nesta, "Seems like you're a little on edge, Nesta. And you left so abruptly last night . . . Any way I can help ease that tension?"

Please, I begged Rhys.

What will you give me?

I wasn't sure if I could *hiss* down the bond between us, but from the chuckle that echoed into my mind a heartbeat later, I knew the feeling had been conveyed. *I'm in a meeting with the governors of the Palaces. They might be a little pissy if I vanish.* I tried not to sigh.

Nesta picked at her nails. "Amren is coming to instruct me in a few—"

Shadow rippled across the courtyard, cutting her off. And it wasn't Rhysand who landed between us, but—

I sent another pretty face for you to admire, Rhys said. *Not as beautiful as mine, of course, but a close second.*

As the shadows wreathing him cleared, Azriel sized up Nesta and Cassian, then threw a vaguely sympathetic look in my direction. "I need to start our lesson early."

A piss-poor lie, but I said, "Right. No problem at all."

Cassian glowered at me, then Azriel. We both ignored him as I strode to the shadowsinger, unwrapping my hands as I went.

Thank you, I said down the bond.

You can make it up to me tonight.

I tried not to blush at the image Rhys sent into my head detailing precisely how I'd repay him, and slammed down my mental shields. On the other side of them, I could have sworn talon-tipped fingers trailed down the black adamant in a sensual, silent promise. I swallowed hard.

Azriel's wings spread, dark reds and golds shining through in the bright sun, and he opened his arms to me. "The pine forest will be good—the one by the lake."

"Why?"

"Because water is better to fall into than hard rock," Cassian replied, crossing his arms.

My stomach clenched. But I let Azriel scoop me up, his scent of night-chilled mist and cedar wrapping around me as he flapped his wings once, stirring the dirt of the courtyard.

I caught Cassian's narrowed gaze and grinned widely. "Good luck," I said, and Azriel, Cauldron bless him, shot into the cloudless sky.

Neither of us missed Cassian's barked, filthy curse, though we didn't deign to comment.

Cassian was a general—*the* general of the Night Court.

Surely Nesta wasn't anything he couldn't handle.

"I dropped Amren off at the House on my way in," Azriel told me as we landed at the shore of a turquoise mountain lake flanked by pines and granite. "I told her to get to the training ring immediately." A half smile. "After a few minutes, that is."

I snorted and stretched my arms. "Poor Cassian."

Azriel gave a huff of amusement. "Indeed."

I shifted on my feet, small gray rocks along the shore skittering beneath my boots. "So . . ."

Azriel's black hair seemed to gobble up the blinding sunlight. "In order to fly," he said drily, "you'll need wings."

Right.

My face heated. I rolled and cracked my wrists. "It's been a while since I summoned them."

His piercing stare didn't stray from my face, my posture. As immovable and steady as the granite this lake had been carved into. I might as well have been a flitting butterfly by comparison. "Do you need me to turn around?" He lifted a dark brow in emphasis.

I cringed. "No. But . . . it might take me a few tries."

"We started our lesson early—we've got plenty of time."

"I appreciate you making the effort to pretend that it wasn't because I was desperate to avoid Cassian and Nesta's early-morning bickering."

"I'd never let my High Lady suffer through that." He said it completely stone-faced.

I chuckled, rubbing at a sore spot on my shoulder. "Are you . . . ready to meet with Lucien this afternoon?"

Azriel angled his head. "*Should* I be preparing for it?"

"No. I just . . ." I shrugged. "When do you leave to gather information on the High Lords?"

"After I talk to him." His eyes were shining—lit with amusement. As if he knew I was buying time.

I blew out a breath. "Right. Here we go."

Touching that part of me, the part Tamlin had given me . . . Some vital piece of my heart recoiled. Even as something sharp and vicious in my gut preened at what I'd taken. All that I'd taken.

I shoved out the thoughts, focusing on those Illyrian wings. I'd summoned them that day in the Steppes from pure memory and fear. Creating them now . . . I let my mind slip into my recollections of Rhys's wings, how they felt and moved and weighed . . .

"The frame needs to be a bit thicker," Azriel offered as a weight began to drag at my back. "Strengthen the muscles leading to it."

I obeyed, my magic listening in turn. He provided more feedback, where to add and where to ease up, where to smooth and where to toughen.

I was rasping for breath, sweat sliding down my spine, by the time he said, "Good." He cleared his throat. "I know you're not Illyrian, but . . . amongst their kind, it is considered . . . inappropriate to touch someone's wings without permission. Especially females."

Their kind. Not his.

It took me a moment to realize what he was asking. "Oh—oh. Go ahead."

"I need to ascertain if they *feel* right."

"Right." I put my back to him, my muscles groaning as they worked to spread the wings. Everything—from my neck to my shoulders to my ribs to my spine to my ass—seemed to now control them, and was barking in protest at the weight and movement.

I'd only had them for a few seconds with Lucien in the Steppes—I hadn't realized how heavy they were, how complex the muscles.

Azriel's hands, for all their scarring, were featherlight as he grasped and touched certain areas, patting and tapping others. I gritted my teeth, the sensation like . . . like having the arch of my foot tickled and poked. But he made quick work of it, and I rolled my shoulders again as he stepped around me to murmur, "It's—amazing. They're the same as mine."

"I think the magic did most of the work."

A shake of the head. "You're an artist—it was your attention to detail."

I blushed a bit at the compliment, and braced my hands on my hips. "Well? Do we jump into the skies?"

"First lesson: don't let them drag on the ground."

I blinked. My wings were indeed resting on the rocks. "Why?"

"Illyrians think it's lazy—a sign of weakness. And from a practical standpoint, the ground is full of things that could hurt your wings. Splinters, shards of rock . . . They can not only get stuck and lead to infection, but also impact the way the wing catches the wind. So keep them off the ground."

Knife-sharp pain rippled down my back as I tried to lift them. I managed getting the left upright. The right just drooped like a loose sail.

"You need to strengthen your back muscles—and your thighs. And your arms. And core."

"So everything, then."

Again, that dry, quiet smile. "Why do you think Illyrians are so fit?"

"Why did no one warn me about this cocky side of yours?"

Azriel's mouth twitched upward. "Both wings up."

A quiet but unyielding demand.

I winced, contorting my body this way and that as I fought to get the right one to rise. No luck.

"Try spreading them, then tucking in, if you can't lift it up like that."

I obeyed, and hissed at the sharp pain along every muscle in my back as I flared the wings. Even the slightest breeze off the lake tickled and tugged, and I braced my feet apart on the rocky shore, seeking some semblance of balance—

"Now fold inward."

I did, snapping them shut—the movement so fast that I toppled forward.

Azriel caught me before I could eat stone, gripping me tightly under the shoulder and hauling me up. "Building your core muscles will also help with the balance."

"So, back to Cassian, then."

A nod. "Tomorrow. Today, focus on lifting and folding, spreading and lifting." Azriel's wings gleamed with red and gold as the sun gilded them. "Like this." He demonstrated, flaring his wings wide, tucking them in, flaring, angling, tucking them in. Over and over.

Sighing, I followed his movements, my back throbbing and aching. Perhaps flying lessons were a waste of time.

CHAPTER 20

"I've never been to a library before," I admitted to Rhys after lunch, as we strode down level after level beneath the House of Wind, my words echoing off the carved red stone. I winced with every step, rubbing at my back.

Azriel had given me a tonic that would help with the soreness, but I knew that by tonight, I'd be whimpering. If hours of researching any way to patch up those holes in the wall didn't make me start first.

"I mean," I clarified, "not counting the private libraries here and at the Spring Court, and my family had one as well, but not . . . Not a real one."

Rhys glanced sidelong at me. "I've heard that the humans have free libraries on the continent—open to anyone."

I wasn't sure if it was a question or not, but I nodded. "In one of the territories, they allow anyone in, regardless of their station or bloodline." I considered his words. "Did . . . were there libraries before the War?"

Of course there had been, but what I meant—

"Yes. Great libraries, full of cranky scholars who could find you tomes dating back thousands of years. But humans were not allowed inside—unless you were someone's slave on an errand, and even then you were closely watched."

"Why?"

"Because the books were full of magic, and things they wanted to keep humans from knowing." Rhys slid his hands into his pockets, leading me down a corridor lit only by bowls of faelight upraised in the hands of beautiful female statues, their forms High Fae and faerie alike. "The scholars and librarians refused to keep slaves of their own—some for personal reasons, but mainly because they didn't want them accessing the books and archives."

Rhys gestured down another curving stairwell. We must have been far beneath the mountain, the air dry and cool—and heavy. As if it had been trapped inside for ages. "What happened to the libraries once the wall was built?"

Rhys tucked in his wings as the stairs became tighter, the ceiling dropping. "Most scholars had enough time to evacuate—and were able to winnow the books out. But if they didn't have the time or the brute power . . ." A muscle ticked in his jaw. "They burned the libraries. Rather than let the humans access their precious information."

A chill snaked down my spine. "They'd rather have lost that information forever?"

He nodded, the dim light gilding his blue-black hair. "Prejudices aside, the fear was that the humans would find dangerous spells—and use them on us."

"But we—I mean, *they* don't have magic. Humans don't have magic."

"Some do. Usually the ones who can claim distant Fae ancestry. But some of those spells don't require magic from the wielder—only the right words, or use of ingredients."

His words snagged on something in my mind. "Could—I mean, obviously they did, but . . . Humans and Fae once interbred. What happened to the offspring? If you were half Fae, half human, where did you go once the wall went up?"

Rhys stepped into a hall at the foot of the stairs, revealing a wide passageway of carved red stone and a sealed set of obsidian doors, veins of silver running throughout. Beautiful—terrifying. Like some great beast was kept behind them.

"It did not go well for the half-breeds," he said after a moment. "Many were offspring of unwanted unions. Most usually chose to stay with their human mothers—their human families. But once the wall went up, amongst humans, they were a . . . reminder of what had been done, of the enemies lurking above the wall. At best, they were outcasts and pariahs, their children—if they bore the physical traits—as well. At worst . . . Humans were angry in those initial years, and that first generation afterward. They wanted someone to pay for the slavery, for the crimes against them. Even if the half-breed had done nothing wrong . . . It did not end well."

He approached the doors, which opened on a phantom wind, as if the mountain itself lived to serve him.

"And the ones above the wall?"

"They were deemed even lower than lesser faeries. Either they were unwanted everywhere they went, or . . . many found work on the streets. Selling themselves."

"Here in Velaris?" My words were a bare brush of air.

"My father was still High Lord then," Rhys said, his back stiffening. "We had not allowed any humans, slave or free, into our territory in centuries. He did not allow them in—either to whore or to find sanctuary."

"And once you were High Lord?"

Rhys halted before the gloom that spread beyond us. "By then, it was too late for most of them. It is hard to . . . offer refuge to someone without being able to explain *where* we were offering them a safe place. To get the word out about it while maintaining our illusion of ruthless cruelty." The starlight guttered in his eyes. "Over the years, we encountered a few. Some were able to make it here. Some were . . . beyond our help."

Something moved in the darkness beyond the doors, but I kept my focus on his face, on his tensed shoulders. "If the wall comes down, will . . . ?" I couldn't finish the words.

Rhys slid his fingers through mine, interlacing our hands. "Yes. If there are those, human or faerie, who need a safe place . . . this city will be open to them. Velaris has been closed off for so long—too long, perhaps. Adding new people, from different places, different histories and cultures . . . I do not see how that could be a bad thing. The transition might be more complex than we anticipate, but . . . yes. The gates to this city will be open for those who need its protection. To any who can make it here."

I squeezed his hand, savoring the hard-earned calluses on it. No, I would not let him bear the burden of this war, its cost, alone.

Rhys glanced to the open doors—to the hooded and cloaked figure patiently waiting in the shadows beyond them. Every aching sinew and bone locked up as I took in the pale robes, the hood crowned with a limpid blue stone, the panel that could be lowered over the eyes—

Priestess.

"This is Clotho," Rhys said calmly, releasing my hand to guide me toward the awaiting female. The weight of his hand on my lower back told me enough about how much he realized the sight of her would jar me. "She's one of the dozens of priestesses who work here."

Clotho lowered her head in a bow, but said nothing.

"I—I didn't know that the priestesses left their temples."

"A library is a temple of sorts," Rhys said with a wry smile. "But the priestesses here . . ." As we entered the library proper, golden lights flickered to life. As if Clotho had been in utter darkness until we'd entered. "They are special. Unique."

She angled her head in what might have been amusement. Her face remained in shadow, her slim body concealed in those pale, heavy robes. Silence—and yet life danced around her.

Rhys smiled warmly at the priestess. "Did you find the texts?"

And it was only when she bobbed her head in a sort of "so-so" motion that I realized either she could not or would not speak. Clotho gestured to her left—into the library itself.

And I dragged my eyes away from the mute priestess long enough to take in the library.

Not a cavernous room in a manor. Not even close.

This was . . .

It was as if the base of the mountain had been hollowed out by some massive digging beast, leaving a pit descending into the dark heart of the world. Around that gaping hole, carved into the mountain itself, spiraled level after level of shelves and books and reading areas, leading into the inky black. From what I could see of the various levels as I drifted toward the carved stone railing overlooking the drop, the stacks shot far into the mountain itself, like the spokes of a mighty wheel.

And through it all, fluttering like moth's wings, the rustle of paper and parchment.

Silent, and yet alive. Awake and humming and restless, some many-limbed beast at constant work. I peered upward, finding more levels rising toward the House above. And lurking far below . . . Darkness.

"What's at the bottom of the pit?" I asked as Rhys came up beside me, his shoulder brushing mine.

"I once dared Cassian to fly down and see." Rhys braced his hands on the railing, gazing down into the gloom.

"And?"

"And he came back up, faster than I've ever seen him fly, white as death. He never told me what he saw. The first few weeks, I thought it was a joke—just to pique my curiosity. But when I finally decided to see for myself a month later, he threatened to tie me to a chair. He said some things were better left unseen and undisturbed. It's been two hundred years, and he still won't tell me what he saw. If you even mention it, he goes pale and shaky and won't talk for a few hours."

My blood chilled. "Is it . . . some sort of monster?"

"I have no idea." Rhys jerked his chin toward Clotho, the priestess patiently waiting a few steps behind us, her face still in shadow. "They don't speak or write of it, so if they know . . . They certainly won't tell me. So if it doesn't bother us, then I won't bother it. That is, if it's even an *it*. Cassian never said if he saw anything living down there. Perhaps it's something else entirely."

Considering the things I'd already witnessed . . . I didn't want to think about what lay at the bottom of the library. Or what could make Cassian, who had seen more dreadful and deadly parts of the world than I could ever imagine, so terrified.

Robes rustling, Clotho aimed for the sloping walkway into the library, and we fell into step behind her. The floors were red stone, like the rest of the place, but smooth and polished. I wondered if any of the priestesses had ever gone sledding down the spiraling path.

Not that I know of, Rhys said into my mind. *But Mor and I once tried when we were children. My mother caught us on our third level down, and we were sent to bed without supper.*

I clamped down on my smile. *Was it such a crime?*

It was when we'd oiled up the floor, and the scholars were falling on their faces.

I coughed to cover my laugh, lowering my head, even with Clotho a few steps ahead.

We passed stacks of books and parchment, the shelves either built into the stone itself or made of dark, solid wood. Hallways lined with both vanished into the mountain itself, and every few minutes, a little reading area popped up, full of tidy tables, low-burning glass lamps, and deep-cushioned chairs and couches. Ancient woven rugs adorned the floors beneath them, usually set before fireplaces that had been carved into the rock and kept well away from any shelves, their grates fine-meshed enough to retain any wandering embers.

Cozy, despite the size of the space; warm, despite the unknown terror lurking below.

If the others piss me off too much, I like to come down here for some peace and quiet.

I smiled slightly at Rhys, who kept looking ahead as we spoke mind to mind.

Don't they know by now that they can find you down here?

Of course. But I never go to the same spot twice in a row, so it usually takes them so long to find me that they don't bother. Plus, they know that if I'm here, it's because I want to be alone.

Poor baby High Lord, I crooned. *Having to run away to find solitude perfect for brooding.*

Rhys pinched my behind, and I clamped down on my lip to keep from yelping.

I could have sworn Clotho's shoulders shook with laughter.

But before I could bite off Rhys's head for the rippling pain my aching back muscles felt in the wake of the sudden movement, Clotho led us into a reading area about three levels down, the massive worktable laden with fat, ancient books bound in various dark leathers.

A neat stack of paper was set to one side, along with an assortment of pens, and the reading lamps were at full glow, merry and sparkling in the gloom. A silver tea service gleamed on a low-lying table between the two leather couches before the grumbling fireplace, steam curling from the arched spout of the kettle. Biscuits and little sandwiches filled the platter beside it, along with a fat pile of napkins that subtly hinted we use them before touching the books.

"Thank you," Rhys told the priestess, who only pulled a book off the pile she'd undoubtedly gathered and opened it to a marked page. The ancient velvet ribbon was the color of old blood—but it was her hand that struck me as it met the golden light of the lamps.

Her fingers were crooked. Bent and twisted at such angles I would have thought her born with them were it not for the scarring.

For a heartbeat, I was in a spring wood. For a heartbeat, I heard the crunch of stone on flesh and bone as I made another priestess smash her hand. Over and over.

Rhys put a hand on my lower back. The effort it must have taken Clotho to move everything into place with those gnarled hands . . .

But she looked toward another book—or at least her head turned that way—and it slid over to her.

Magic. Right.

She gestured with a finger that was bent in two different directions to the page she'd selected, then to the book.

"I'll look," Rhys said, then inclined his head. "We'll give a shout if we need anything."

Clotho bowed her head again and began striding away, careful and silent.

"Thank you," I said to her.

The priestess paused, looking back, and bowed her head, hood swaying.

Within seconds, she was gone.

I stared after her, even as Rhys slid into one of the two chairs before the piles of books.

"A long time ago, Clotho was hurt very badly by a group of males," Rhys said quietly.

I didn't need details to know what that had entailed. The edge in Rhys's voice implied enough.

"They cut out her tongue so she couldn't tell anyone who had hurt her. And smashed her hands so she couldn't write it." Every word was more clipped than the last, and darkness snarled through the small space.

My stomach turned. "Why not kill her?"

"Because it was more entertaining for them that way. That is, until Mor found her. And brought her to me."

When he'd undoubtedly looked into her mind and seen their faces.

"I let Mor hunt them." His wings tucked in tightly. "And when she finished, she stayed down here for a month. Helping Clotho heal as best as could be expected, but also . . . wiping away the stain of them."

Mor's trauma had been different, but . . . I understood why she'd done it, wanted to be here. I wondered if it had granted her any measure of closure.

"Cassian and Azriel were healed completely after Hybern. Nothing could be done for Clotho?"

"The males were . . . healing her as they hurt her. Making the injuries permanent. When Mor found her, the damage had been set. They hadn't finished her hands, so we were able to salvage them, give her some use, but . . . To heal her, the wounds would have needed to be ripped open again. I offered to take the pain away while it was done, but . . . She could not endure it—what having the wounds open again would trigger in her mind. Her heart. She has lived down here since then—with others like her. Her magic helps with her mobility."

I knew we should begin working, but I asked, "Are . . . all the priestesses in this library like her?"

"Yes."

The word held centuries of rage and pain.

"I made this library into a refuge for them. Some come to heal, work as acolytes, and then leave; some take the oaths to the Cauldron and Mother to become priestesses and remain here forever. But it belongs to them whether they stay a week or a lifetime. Outsiders are allowed to use the library for research, but only if the priestesses approve. And only if they take binding oaths to do no harm while they visit. This library belongs to them."

"Who was here before them?"

"A few cranky old scholars, who cursed me soundly when I relocated them to other libraries in the city. They still get access, but when and where is always approved by the priestesses."

Choice. It had always been about my choice with him. And for others as well. Long before he'd ever learned the hard way about it. The question must have been in my eyes because Rhys added, "I came here a great deal in those weeks after Under the Mountain."

My throat tightened as I leaned in to brush a kiss to his cheek. "Thank you for sharing this place with me."

"It belongs to you, too, now." And I knew he meant not just in terms of us being mates, but . . . in the ways it belonged to the other females here. Who had endured and survived.

I gave him a half smile. "I suppose it's a miracle that I can even stand to be underground."

But his features remained solemn, contemplative. "It is." He added softly, "I'm very proud of you."

My eyes burned, and I blinked as I faced the books. "And I suppose," I said with an effort at lightness, "that it's a miracle I can actually *read* these things."

Rhys's answering smile was lovely—and just a bit wicked. "I believe my little lessons helped."

"Yes, '*Rhys is the greatest lover a female can hope for*' is undoubtedly how I learned to read."

"I was only trying to tell you what you now know."

My blood heated a bit. "Hmmm," was all I said, pulling a book toward me.

"I'll take that *hmmm* as a challenge." His hand slid down my thigh, then cupped my knee, his thumb brushing along its side. Even through my leathers, the heat of him seeped to my very bones. "Maybe I'll haul you between the stacks and see how quiet you can be."

"Hmmm." I flipped through the pages, not seeing any of the text.

His hand began a lethal, taunting exploration up my thigh, his fingers grazing along the sensitive inside. Higher, higher. He leaned in to drag a book toward himself, but whispered in my ear, "Or maybe I'll spread you out on this desk and lick you until you scream loud enough to wake whatever is at the bottom of the library."

I whipped my head toward him. His eyes were glazed—almost sleepy.

"I was fully committed to that plan," I said, even as his hand stopped very, *very* close to the apex of my thighs, "until you brought in that *thing* down below."

A feline smile. He held my stare as his tongue brushed his bottom lip.

My breasts tightened beneath my shirt, and his gaze dropped—watching. "I would have thought," he mused, "that our bout this morning would be enough to tide you over until tonight." His hand slid between my legs, brazenly cupping me, his thumb pushing down on an aching spot. A low groan slipped from me, and my cheeks heated in its wake. "Apparently, I didn't do a good enough job sating you, if you're so easily riled after a few hours."

"Prick," I breathed, but the word was ragged. His thumb pressed down harder, circling roughly.

Rhys leaned in again, kissing my neck—that place right under my ear—and said against my skin, "Let's see what names you call me when my head is between your legs, Feyre darling."

And then he was gone.

He'd winnowed away, half the books with him. I started, my body foreign and cold, dizzy and disoriented.

Where the hell are you? I scanned around me, and found nothing but shadow and merry flame and books.

Two levels below.

And why *are you two levels below?* I shoved out of my chair, back aching in protest as I stormed for the walkway and rail beyond, then peered down into the gloom.

Sure enough, in a reading area two levels below, I could spy his dark hair and wings—could spy him leaning back in his chair before an identical desk, an ankle crossed over a knee. Smirking up at me. *Because I can't work with you distracting me.*

I scowled at him. I'm *distracting* you*?*

If you're sitting next to me, the last thing on my mind is reading dusty old books. Especially when you're in all that tight leather.

Pig.

His chuckle echoed up through the library amid the fluttering papers and scratching pens of the priestesses working throughout.

How can you winnow inside the House? I thought there were wards against it.

The library makes its own rules, apparently.

I snorted.

Two hours of work, he promised me, turning back to the table and flaring his wings—a veritable screen to block my view of him. And his view of me. *Then we can play.*

I gave him a vulgar gesture.

I saw that.

I did it again, and his laugh floated to me as I faced the books stacked before me and began to read.

✣

We found a myriad of information about the wall and its forming. When we compared our notes two hours later, many of the texts were conflicting, all of them claiming absolute authority on the subject. But there were a few similar details that Rhys had not known.

He had been healing at the cabin in the mountains when they'd formed the wall, when they'd signed that Treaty. The details that emerged had been murky at best, but the various texts Clotho had dug up on the wall's formation and rules agreed on one thing: it had never been made to last.

No, initially, the wall had been a temporary solution—to cleave human and faerie until peace settled long enough for them to later reconvene. And decide how they were to live together—as one people.

But the wall had remained. Humans had grown old and died, and their children had forgotten the promises of their parents, their grandparents, their ancestors. And the High Fae who survived . . . it was a new world, without slaves. Lesser faeries stepped in to replace the missing free labor; territory boundaries had been redrawn to accommodate those displaced. Such a great shift in the world in those initial centuries, so many working to move past war, to heal, that the wall . . . the wall became permanent. The wall became legend.

"Even if all seven courts ally," I said as we plucked grapes from a silver bowl in a quiet sitting room in the House of Wind, having left the dim library for some much-needed sunshine, "even if Keir and the Court of Nightmares join, too . . . Will we stand a chance in this war?"

Rhys leaned back in the embroidered chair before the floor-to-ceiling window. Velaris was a glittering sprawl below and beyond—serene and lovely, even with the scars of battle now peppering it. "Army against army, the possibility of victory is slim." Blunt, honest words.

I shifted in my own identical chair on the other side of the low-lying table between us. "Could you . . . If you and the King of Hybern went head to head . . ."

"Would I win?" Rhys lifted a brow, and studied the city. "I don't know. He's been smart about keeping the extent of his power hidden. But he had to resort to trickery and threats to beat us that day in Hybern. He has thousands of years of knowledge and training. If he and I fought . . . I doubt he will let it come to that. He stands a better chance at sure victory by overwhelming us with numbers, in stretching us thin. If we fought one-on-one, if he'd even accept an open challenge from me . . . the damage would be catastrophic. And that's without him wielding the Cauldron."

My heart stumbled. Rhys went on, "I'm willing to take the brunt of it, if it means the others will at least *stand* with us against him."

I clenched the tufted arms of the chair.

"You shouldn't have to."

"It might be the only choice."

"I don't accept that as an option."

He blinked at me. "Prythian might need me as an option." Because with that power of his . . . He'd take on the king and his entire army. Burn himself out until he was—

"*I* need you. As an option. In *my* future."

Silence. And even with the sun warming my feet, a terrible cold spread through me.

His throat bobbed. "If it means giving you a future, then I'm willing to do—"

"You will do no such *thing*." I panted through my bared teeth, leaning forward in my chair.

Rhys only watched me, eyes shadowed. "How can you ask me not to give everything I have to ensure that you, that my family and people, survive?"

"You've given *enough*."

"Not enough. Not yet."

It was hard to breathe, to see past the burning in my eyes. "Why? Where does this *come* from, Rhys?"

For once, he didn't answer.

And there was something brittle enough in his expression, some long unhealed wound that glimmered there, that I sighed, rubbed my face, and then said, "Just—work with me. With all of us. *Together*. This isn't your burden alone."

He plucked another grape from its stem, chewed. His lips tilted in a faint smile. "So what do you propose, then?"

I could still see that vulnerability in his eyes, still feel it in that bond between us, but I angled my head. I sorted through all I knew, all that had happened. Considered the books I'd read in the library below. A library that housed—

"Amren warned us to never put the two halves of the Book together," I mused. "But we—*I* did. She said that older things might be . . . awoken by it. Might come sniffing."

Rhys crossed an ankle over a knee.

"Hybern might have the numbers," I said, "but what if we had the monsters? You said Hybern will see an alliance with all the courts coming—but perhaps not one with things wholly unconnected." I leaned forward. "And I'm not talking about the monsters roaming across the world. I am talking about one in particular—who has nothing to lose and everything to gain."

One that I would do everything in my power to use, rather than let Rhys face the brunt of this alone.

His brows rose. "Oh?"

"The Bone Carver," I clarified. "He and Amren have both been looking for a way back to their own worlds." The Carver had been insistent, relentless, in asking me that day in the Prison about where I had gone during death. I could have sworn Rhys's golden-brown skin paled, but I added, "I wonder if it's time to ask him what he'd give to go back home."

CHAPTER 21

The aching muscles along my back, core, and thighs had gone into complete revolt by the time Rhys and I parted ways, my mate heading off to track down Cassian—who would be my escort tomorrow morning to the Prison. If both of us had gone, it would perhaps look too . . . desperate, too vital. But if the High Lady and her general went to visit the Carver to pose some hypothetical questions . . .

It would still show our hand, but perhaps not quite how badly we needed any extra bit of assistance. And Cassian, unsurprisingly, knew more about the Carver than anyone thanks to some morbid fascination with all of the Prison's inmates. Especially since he was responsible for jailing some of them.

But while Rhys sought out Cassian, I had a task of my own.

I was wincing and hissing as I strode through the murky red halls of the House to find my sister and Amren. To see which of them was still standing after their first lesson. Among other things.

I found them in a quiet, forgotten workroom, coldly watching the other.

Books lay scattered on the table between them. A ticking clock by the dusty cabinets was the only sound.

"Sorry to interrupt your staring contest," I said, lingering in the doorway. I rubbed at a spot low in my back. "I wanted to see how the first lesson was going."

"Fine." Amren didn't take her eyes off my sister, a faint smile playing about her red mouth.

I studied Nesta, who gazed at Amren, utterly stone-faced.

"What are you doing?"

"Waiting," Amren said.

"For what?"

"For busybodies to leave us alone."

I straightened, clearing my throat. "Is this part of her training?"

Amren turned her head to me with exaggerated slowness, her chin-length, razor-straight hair shifting with the movement. "Rhys has his own method of training you. I have mine." Her white teeth flashed with every word. "We visit the Court of Nightmares tomorrow night—she needs *some* basic training before we do."

"Like what?"

Amren sighed at the ceiling. "Shielding herself. From prying minds and powers."

I blinked. I should have thought of that. That if Nesta were to join us, be at the Hewn City . . . she would need some defenses beyond what we could offer her.

Nesta at last looked to me, her face as cold as ever.

"Are you all right?" I asked her.

Amren clicked her tongue. "She's fine. Stubborn as an ass, but as you're related, I'm not surprised."

I scowled. "How am I supposed to know what your methods are? For all I know, you picked up some terrible techniques in that Prison."

Careful. So, so careful.

Amren hissed, "That place taught me plenty of things, but certainly not this."

I angled my head, the portrait of curiosity. "Did you ever interact with the others?"

The fewer people who knew about my trip tomorrow to see the Carver, the safer it was—the less chance of Hybern catching wind of it. Not for any fear of betrayal, but . . . there was always risk.

Azriel, now off hunting for information on the Autumn Court, would be told when he returned tonight. Mor . . . I'd tell her eventually. But Amren . . . Rhys and I had decided to wait to tell Amren. The last time we'd gone to the Prison, she'd been . . . testy. Telling her we planned to unleash one of her fellow inmates? Perhaps not the best thing to mention while we waited for her to find a way to heal that wall—and train my sister.

Impatience rippled across Amren's face, those silver eyes flaring. "I only spoke to them in whispers and echoes through rock, girl. And I was glad of it."

"What's the Prison?" Nesta asked at last.

"A hell entombed in stone," Amren said. "Full of creatures you should thank the Mother no longer walk the earth freely."

Nesta frowned deeply, but shut her mouth.

"Like who?" I asked. Any extra information she might have—

Amren bared her teeth. "I am giving a magic lesson, not a history one." She waved a dismissive hand. "If you want someone to gossip with, go find one of the dogs. I'm sure Cassian's still sniffing around upstairs."

Nesta's lips twitched upward.

Amren pointed at her with a slender finger ending in a sharp, manicured nail. "*Concentrate*. Vital organs *must* be shielded at all times."

I tapped a hand against the open doorway. "I'll keep looking for more information for you in the library, Amren." No response. "Good luck," I added.

"She doesn't need luck," Amren said. Nesta huffed a laugh.

I took that as the only farewell I'd get. Perhaps letting Amren and Nesta train together was . . . a bad choice. Even if the prospect of unleashing them upon the Court of Nightmares . . . I smiled a bit at the thought.

By the time Mor, Rhys, Cassian, and I gathered for dinner at the town house—Azriel still off spying—my muscles were so sore I could barely walk up the front stairs. Sore enough that any plans I had to visit Lucien up at the House after the meal vanished. Mor was testy and quiet throughout, no doubt in anticipation of the visit tomorrow night.

She'd had to work with Keir plenty throughout the centuries, and yet tomorrow . . . She'd only warned Rhys once while we ate that he should thoroughly consider any offer Keir might give him in exchange for his army. Rhys had shrugged, saying he'd think about it when the time came. A non-answer—and one that made Mor grit her teeth.

I didn't blame her. Long before the War, her family had brutalized her in ways I didn't let myself consider. Not a day before I was to meet with them again—ask *them* for help. Work with them.

Rhys, Mother bless him, had a bath waiting for me after the meal.

I'd need all my strength for tomorrow. For the monsters I was to face beneath two very different mountains.

I had not visited this place for months. But the carved stone walls were just as I'd last seen them, the darkness still interrupted by bracketed torches.

Not the Prison. Under the Mountain.

But instead of Clare's mutilated body spiked high to the wall above me . . .

Her blue-gray eyes were still wide with terror. Gone was the haughty iciness, the queenly jut to her chin.

Nesta. They'd done precisely to her, wound for wound, what they'd done to Clare.

And behind me, screaming and pleading—

I turned, finding Elain, naked and weeping, tied to that enormous spit. What I had once been threatened to endure. Gnarled, masked faeries rotated the iron handles, turning her over—

I tried to move. Tried to lunge.

But I was frozen—utterly bound by invisible chains to the floor.

Feminine laughter flitted from the other end of that throne room. From the dais. Now empty.

Empty, because that was Amarantha, strutting into the gloom, down some hall that hadn't been there before but now stretched away into nothing.

Rhysand followed a step behind her. Going with her. To that bedroom.

He looked over his shoulder at me, only once.

Over his wings. His wings, which were out, which she'd see and destroy, right after she—

I was screaming for him to stop. Thrashing at those bonds. Elain's pleading rose, higher and higher. Rhys kept walking with Amarantha. Let her take his hand and tug him along.

I couldn't move, couldn't stop it, any of it—

I was hauled out of the dream like a thrashing fish from a net cast deep into the sea.

And when I surfaced . . . I remained half there. Half in my body, half Under the Mountain, watching as—

"Breathe."

The word was an order. Laced with that primal command he so rarely wielded.

But my eyes focused. My chest expanded. I slipped a bit further back into my body.

"Again."

I did so. His face came into view, faelights murmuring to life inside their lamps and bowls in our bedroom. His wings were tucked in tight, framing his disheveled hair, his drawn face.

Rhys.

"Again," he only said. I obeyed.

My bones had turned brittle, my stomach a roiling mess. I closed my eyes, fighting the nausea. Rippling terror kept its talons buried deep. I could still see it: the way she'd led him down that hall. To—

I surged, rolling to the edge of the mattress and clamping down hard as my body tried to heave up its contents onto the carpet. His hand was instantly on my back, rubbing soothing circles. Utterly willing to let me vomit right over the side of the bed. But I focused on my breathing.

On closing down those memories, one by one. Memories repainted.

I lay half sprawled over the edge for uncounted minutes. He rubbed my back throughout.

When I could finally move, when the nausea had subsided . . . I twisted back over. And the sight of that face . . . I slid my arms around his waist, gripping tightly as he pressed a silent kiss to my hair, reminding myself over and over that we were out. We had survived. Never again—never again would I let someone hurt him like that. Hurt my sisters like that.

Never again.

CHAPTER 22

I felt Rhys's attention on me while we dressed the next morning, and throughout our hearty breakfast. Yet he didn't push, didn't demand to know what had dragged me into that screaming hell.

It had been a long while since those nightmares had hauled either of us from sleep. Blurred the lines.

It was only when we stood in the foyer, waiting for Cassian before we winnowed to the Prison, that Rhys asked from where he leaned against the stair banister, "Do you need to talk about it?"

My Illyrian leathers groaned as I turned toward him.

Rhys clarified, "With me—or anyone."

I answered him truthfully, tugging at the end of my braid. "With everything bearing down on us, everything at stake . . ." I let my braid drop. "I don't know. I think it's torn open some . . . part of me that was slowly repairing." Repairing thanks to both of us.

He nodded, no fear or reproach in his eyes.

So I told him. All of it. Stumbling over the parts that still made me ill. He only listened.

And when I was done, that shakiness remained, but . . . Speaking it, voicing it aloud to him . . .

The savage grip of those terrors lightened. Cleared away like dew in the sun. I freed a long breath, as if blowing those fears from me, letting my body loosen in its wake.

Rhys silently pushed off the banister and kissed me. Once. Twice.

Cassian stalked through the front door a heartbeat later and groaned that it was too early to stomach the sight of us kissing. My mate only snarled at him before he took us both by the hand and winnowed us to the Prison.

Rhys gripped my fingers tighter than usual as the wind ripped around us, Cassian now wisely keeping silent. And as we emerged from that black, tumbling wind, Rhys leaned over to kiss me a third time, sweet and soft, before the gray light and roaring wind greeted us.

Apparently, the Prison was cold and misty no matter the time of year.

Standing at the base of the mossy, rocky mountain under which the Prison was built, Cassian and I frowned up the slope.

Despite the Illyrian leathers, the chill seeped into my bones. I rubbed at my arms, lifting my brows at Rhys, who had remained in his usual attire, so out of place in this damp, windy speck of green in the middle of a gray sea.

The wind ruffled his black hair as he surveyed us, Cassian already sizing up the mountain like some opponent. Twin Illyrian blades were crossed over the general's muscled back. "When you're in there," Rhys said, the words barely audible over the wind and silver streams running down the mountainside, "you won't be able to reach me."

"Why?" I rubbed my already-freezing hands together before puffing a hot breath into the cradle of my palms.

"Wards and spells far older than Prythian," was all Rhys said. He jerked his chin to Cassian. "Don't let each other out of your sight."

It was the dead seriousness with which Rhys spoke that kept me from retorting.

Indeed, my mate's eyes were hard—unflinching. While we were

here, he and Azriel were to discuss what he'd found out about Autumn's leanings in this war. And then adjust their strategy for the meeting with the High Lords. But I could sense it, the urge to request he join us. Watch over us.

"Shout down the bond when you're out again," Rhys said with a mildness that didn't reach his gaze.

Cassian looked back over a shoulder. "Get back to Velaris, you mother hen. We'll be fine."

Rhys leveled another uncharacteristically hard stare at him. "Remember who you put in here, Cassian."

Cassian just tucked in his wings, as if every muscle shifted toward battle. Steady and solid as the mountain we were about to climb.

With a wink at me, Rhys vanished.

Cassian checked the buckles on his swords and motioned me to start the long trek up the hill. My gut tightened at the climb ahead. The shrieking hollowness of this place.

"Who did you put in here?" The mossy earth cushioned my steps.

Cassian put a scar-flecked finger to his lips. "Best left for another time."

Right. I fell into step beside him, my thighs burning with the steep hike. Mist chilled my face. Conserving his strength—Cassian wasn't wasting a drop of energy on shielding us from the elements.

"You really think unleashing the Carver will do the trick against Hybern?"

"You're the general," I panted, "you tell me."

He considered, the wind tossing his dark hair over his tan face. "Even if you promise to find a way to send him back to his own world with the Book, or give him whatever unholy thing he wants," Cassian mused, "I think you'd better find a way to control him in *this* world, or else we'll be fighting enemies on all fronts. And I know which one will hand our asses to us."

"The Carver's that bad."

"You're asking this right before we're to meet with him?"

I hissed, "I assumed Rhys would have put his foot down if it was *that* risky."

"Rhys has been known to hatch plans that make my heart stop dead," Cassian grumbled. "So, I wouldn't count on him to be the voice of reason."

I scowled at Cassian, earning a wolfish grin in return.

But Cassian scanned the heavy gray sky, as if hunting for spying eyes. Then the moss and grass and rocks beneath our boots for listening ears below. "There was life here," he said, answering my question at last, "before the High Lords took Prythian. Old gods, we call them. They ruled the forests and the rivers and the mountains—some *were* those things. Then the magic shifted to the High Fae, who brought the Cauldron and Mother along with them, and though the old gods were still worshipped by a select few, most people forgot them."

I grappled onto a large gray rock as I climbed over it. "The Bone Carver was an old god?"

He dragged a hand through his hair, the Siphon gleaming in the watery light. "That's what legend says. Along with whispers of being able to fell hundreds of soldiers with one breath."

A chill rippled down my skin that had nothing to do with the brisk wind. "Useful on a battlefield."

Cassian's golden-brown skin paled while his eyes churned with the thought. "Not without the proper precautions. Not without him being bound to obey us within an inch of his life." Which I'd have to figure out as well, I supposed.

"How did he wind up here—in the Prison?"

"I don't know. No one does." Cassian helped me over a boulder, his hand gripping mine tightly. "But *how* do you plan on freeing him from the Prison?"

I winced. "I suppose our friend would know, since she got out." Careful—we had to be careful when mentioning Amren's name here.

Cassian's face grew solemn. "She doesn't talk about how she did it, Feyre. I'd be careful how you push her." Since we still had not told Amren where we were today. What we were doing.

I thought about saying more, but ahead, far up the slope, the massive bone gates opened.

I'd forgotten it—the weight of the air inside the Prison. Like wading through the unstirred air of a tomb. Like stealing a breath from the open mouth of a skull.

We both bore an Illyrian blade in one hand, the faelight bobbing ahead to show the way, occasionally dancing and sliding along the shining metal. Our other hands . . . Cassian clenched my fingers as tightly as I clutched his while we descended into the eternal blackness of the Prison, our steps crunching on the dry ground. There were no doors—none that we could see.

But behind that solid, black rock, I could still feel them. Could have sworn a faint scratching sound filled the passage. From the other side of that rock.

As if someone were running their nails down it. Something huge—and old. And quiet as the wind through a field of wheat.

Cassian kept utterly silent, tracking something—counting something.

"This could be . . . a very bad idea," I admitted, my grip tightening on his hand.

"Oh, it most certainly is," Cassian said with a faint smile as we continued down and down into the heavy black and thrumming silence. "But this is war. We don't have the luxury of good ideas—only picking between the bad ones."

The Bone Carver's cell door swung open the moment I laid my palm to it.

"Worth the misery of being Rhys's mate," Cassian quipped as the white bone swung away into darkness.

A light chuckle within.

The amusement faded from Cassian's face at the sound—as we walked into the cell, still hand in hand.

The orb of faelight bobbed ahead, illuminating the stone-hewn cell.

Cassian growled at what it revealed. Who it revealed.

Wholly different, no doubt, from the same young boy who now smiled at me.

Dark-haired, with eyes of crushing blue.

I started at the child's face—what I had not noticed that first time. What I had not understood.

It was Rhysand's face. The coloring, the eyes . . . it was my mate's face.

But the Carver's full, wide mouth, curled into that hideous smile . . . That was my mouth. My father's mouth.

The hair on my arms rose. The Carver inclined his head in greeting—in greeting and in confirmation, as if he knew precisely what I realized. Who I had seen and was still seeing.

The High Lord's son. My son. *Our* son. Should we survive long enough to bear him.

Should I not fail in my task to recruit the Carver. Should we not fail to unify the High Lords and the Court of Nightmares. And keep that wall intact.

It was an effort to keep my knees from buckling. Cassian's face was pale enough that I knew whatever he was seeing . . . it wasn't a beautiful young boy.

"I was wondering when you'd return," the Carver said, that boy's voice sweet and yet dreadful—from the ancient creature that lurked beneath it. "High Lady," he added to me. "Please accept my congratulations on your union." A glance at Cassian. "I can smell the wind on you." Another little smile. "Have you brought me a gift?"

I reached into the pocket of my jacket and chucked a small shard of bone, no bigger than my hand, at the Carver's feet.

"This is all that's left of the Attor after I splattered him on the streets of Velaris."

Those blue eyes flared with unholy delight. I hadn't even known we'd kept this fragment. It had been stored until now—precisely for this sort of thing.

"So bloodthirsty, my new High Lady," the Carver purred, picking up the cracked bone and turning it over in those small, delicate hands. And then the Carver said, "I smell my sister on you, Cursebreaker."

My mouth went dry. His sister—

"Did you steal from her? Did she weave a thread of your life into her loom?"

The Weaver of the Wood. My heart thundered. No breathing could steady it. Cassian's hand tightened around mine.

The Carver purred to Cassian, "If I tell you a secret, warrior-heart, what will you give me?"

Neither of us spoke. Carefully—we'd have to phrase and do this so carefully.

The Carver stroked the shard of bone in his palm, attention fixed upon a stone-faced Cassian. "What if I tell you what the rock and darkness and sea beyond whispered to me, Lord of Bloodshed? How they shuddered in fear, on that island across the sea. How they trembled when *she* emerged. She took something—something precious. She ripped it out with her teeth."

Cassian's golden-brown face had drained of color, his wings tucking in tight.

"What did you wake that day in Hybern, Prince of Bastards?"

My blood went cold.

"What came out was not what went in." A rasping laugh as the Carver laid the shard of bone on the ground beside him. "How lovely she is—new as a fawn and yet ancient as the sea. How she calls to you.

A queen, as my sister once was. Terrible and proud; beautiful as a winter sunrise."

Rhys had warned me of the inmates' capacity to lie, to sell anything, to get free.

"Nesta," the Bone Carver murmured. "*Nes-ta.*"

I squeezed Cassian's hand. Enough. It was *enough* of this teasing and taunting. But he didn't look at me.

"How the wind moans her name. Can you hear it, too? Nesta. *Nesta. Nesta.*"

I wasn't sure Cassian was breathing.

"What did she do, drowning in the ageless dark? What did she *take*?"

It was the bite in the last word that snapped my tether of restraint. "If you wish to find out, perhaps you should stop talking long enough for us to explain."

My voice seemed to shake Cassian free of whatever trance he'd been in. His breathing surged, tight and fast, and he scanned my face—apology in his eyes.

The Carver chuckled. "I so rarely get company. Forgive me for wanting to make idle talk." He crossed an ankle over a foot. "And why have you sought my services?"

"We attained the Book of Breathings," I said casually. "There are . . . interesting spells inside. Codes within codes within codes. Someone we know cracked most of them. She is still looking for others. Spells that could . . . send someone like her home. Others like her, too."

The Carver's violet eyes flared bright as flame. "I'm listening."

CHAPTER 23

"War is upon us," I said to the Carver. "Rumor suggests you have . . . gifts that may be useful upon the battlefield."

A smile at Cassian, as if understanding why he'd joined me. "In exchange for a price," the Carver mused.

"Within reason," Cassian countered.

The Carver surveyed his cell. "And you think that I wish to go . . . back."

"Don't you?"

The Carver folded his legs beneath his small frame. "Where we came from . . . I do not believe it is now anything more than dust drifting across a plain. There is no home to return to. Not one that I desire."

For if he'd been here before even Amren had arrived . . . Tens of thousands of years—longer, perhaps. I shoved against the sinking sensation in my gut. "Then perhaps improving your . . . living conditions might entice you, if this world is where you wish to be."

"This cell, Cursebreaker, is where I wish to be." The Carver patted the dirt beside him. "Do you think I let them trap me without good reason?"

Cassian's entire body seemed to shift—seemed to go aware and focused. Ready to haul us out of there.

The Carver traced three overlapping, interlocked circles in the dirt. "You have met my sister—my twin. The Weaver, as you now call her. I knew her as Stryga. She, and our older brother, Koschei. How they delighted in this world when we fell into it. How those ancient Fae feared and worshipped them. Had I been braver, I might have bided my time—waited for their power to fade, for that long-ago Fae warrior to trick Stryga into diminishing her power and becoming confined to the Middle. Koschei, too—confined and bound by his little lake on the continent. All before Prythian, before the land was carved up and any High Lord was crowned."

Cassian and I waited, not daring to interrupt.

"Clever, that Fae warrior. Her bloodline is long gone now—though a trace still runs through some human line." He smiled, perhaps a bit sadly. "No one remembers her name. But I do. She would have been my salvation, had I not made my choice long before she walked this earth."

I waited and waited and waited, picking apart the story he laid out like crumbs of bread.

"She could not kill them in the end—they were too strong. They could only be contained." The Carver wiped a hand through the circles he'd drawn, erasing them wholly. "I knew that long before she ever trapped them—took it upon myself to find my way here."

"To spare the world from yourself?" Cassian asked, brows narrowing.

The Carver's eyes burned like the hottest flame. "To *hide* from my siblings."

I blinked. "Why?"

"They are death-gods, girl," the Carver hissed. "You are immortal—or long-lived enough to seem that way. But my siblings and I . . . We are different. And the two of them . . . Stronger. So much stronger than I ever was. My sister . . . she found a way to *eat* life itself. To stay young and beautiful forever thanks to the lives she steals."

The weaving—the threads inside that house, the roof made of hair . . . I made a note to throw Rhys in the Sidra for sending me into that cottage.

But the Carver himself . . . "If they are death-gods," I said, "then what are you?"

Death. He had asked me, over and over, about death. About what waited beyond it, what it felt like. Where I had gone. I'd thought it mere curiosity, but . . .

That boy's face crinkled with amusement. My son's face. The vision of the future that had once been shown to me all those months ago, as some sort of taunt or embodiment of what I hadn't dared yet admit to myself. What I was most uncertain of. And now . . . now that young boy . . . A different sort of taunt, for the future I now stood to lose.

"I am forgotten, that's what I am. And that's how I prefer to be." The Carver rested his head against the wall of rock behind him. "So you will find that I do not wish to leave. That I have no desire to remind my sister and brother that I am alive and in the world. Contained and diminished as they are, their influence remains . . . considerable."

"If Hybern wins this war," Cassian said roughly, "you might find the gates of this place blown wide open. And your sister and brother unleashed from their own territories—and interested in paying a visit."

"Even Hybern is not that foolish." A satisfied huff of air. "I'm sure there are other inmates here who will find your offer . . . tempting."

My blood roared. "You will not even consider assisting us." I waved a hand to the cell. "This is what you would prefer—for eternity?"

"If you knew my brother and sister, Cursebreaker, you would find this a much wiser and more comfortable alternative."

I opened my mouth, but Cassian squeezed my hand in warning. Enough. We'd said enough, revealed enough. Looking so desperate . . . It would help nothing.

"We should go," Cassian said to me, the very picture of unruffled calm. "The delights of the Hewn City await."

We'd indeed be late if we didn't leave now. I threw a glare at the

Carver by way of farewell, letting Cassian lead me toward the open cell door.

"You are going to the Hewn City," the Carver said—not entirely a question.

"I don't see how that is any business of yours," I said over my shoulder.

The Carver's beat of silence echoed around us. Made us pause on the threshold.

"One last attempt," the Carver mused, eyes skating over us, "to rally the entirety of the Night Court, I suppose."

"Again, it is none of your concern," I said coolly.

The Carver smiled. "You will be bargaining with him." A glance at the tattoo on my right hand. "I wonder what Keir's asking price will be." A low laugh. "Interesting."

Cassian let out a long-suffering sigh. "Out with it."

The Bone Carver again fell silent, toying with the shard of the Attor's bone in the dirt beside him. "The eddies of the Cauldron swirl in strange ways," he murmured, more to himself than us.

"We're going," I said, making to turn again, hauling Cassian with me.

"My sister had a collection of mirrors in her black castle," the Carver said.

We halted once more.

"She admired herself day and night in those mirrors, gloating over her youth and beauty. There was one mirror—the Ouroboros, she called it. It was old even when we were young. A window to the world. All could be seen, all could be told through its dark surface. Keir possesses it—an heirloom of his household. Bring it to me. That is my price. The Ouroboros, and I am yours to wield. If you can find a way to free me." A hateful smile.

I exchanged a glance with Cassian, and we both shrugged at the Carver. "We'll see," was all I said before we walked out.

Cassian and I sat on a boulder overlooking a silver stream, breathing in the chill mists. The Prison loomed at our backs, a dreadful weight blocking out the horizon.

"You said that you knew the Carver was an old god," I mused softly. "Did you know he was a death-god?"

Cassian's face was taut. "I guessed." When I lifted a brow, he clarified, "He carves deaths into bones. Sees them. Enjoys them. It wasn't hard to figure out."

I considered. "Was it you or Rhys who suggested you come here with me?"

"I wanted to come. But Rhys . . . he guessed it, too."

Because what we'd seen in Nesta's eyes that day . . .

"Like calls to like," I murmured.

Cassian nodded tightly. "I don't think even the Carver knows what Nesta is. But I wanted to see—just in case."

"Why?"

"I want to help."

It was answer enough.

We fell into silence, the stream gurgling as it rushed by.

"Would you be frightened of her, if Nesta *was*—Death? Or if her power came from it?"

Cassian was quiet for a long moment.

He said at last, "I'm a warrior. I've walked beside Death my entire life. I would be more afraid *for* her, to have that power. But not afraid *of* her." He considered, and added after a heartbeat, "Nothing about Nesta could frighten me."

I swallowed, and squeezed his hand. "Thank you."

I wasn't sure why I even said it, but he nodded all the same.

I felt him before he appeared, a spark of star-kissed joy flaring through me right as Rhys stepped out of the air itself. "Well?"

Cassian hopped off the boulder, extending a hand to help me down. "You're not going to like his asking price."

Rhys held out both hands to winnow us back to Velaris. "If he wants the fancy dinner plates, he can have them."

Neither Cassian nor I could muster a laugh as we both reached for Rhys's outstretched hands. "You better bring your bargaining skills tonight," was all Cassian muttered to my mate before we vanished into shadow.

CHAPTER 24

When we returned to the town house in the height of summer afternoon heat, Cassian and Azriel drew sticks for who would remain in Velaris that night.

Both wanted to join us at the Hewn City, but someone had to guard the city—part of their long-held protocol. And someone had to guard Elain, though I certainly wasn't about to tell Lucien that. Cassian, swearing and pissy, got the short stick, and Azriel only clapped him on the shoulder before heading up to the House to prepare.

I followed after him a few minutes later, leaving Cassian to tell Rhys the rest of what the Carver had said. What he wanted.

There were two people I needed to see up at the House before we left. I should have checked in on Elain earlier, should have remembered that her would-have-been wedding was in a few days, but . . . I cursed myself for forgetting it. And as for Lucien . . . It wouldn't hurt, I told myself, to keep tabs on where he was. How that conversation with Azriel had gone yesterday. Make sure he remembered the rules we'd set.

But fifteen minutes later, I was trying not to wince as I walked down the halls of the House of Wind, grateful Azriel had gone ahead. I'd winnowed into the sky above the highest balcony—and since I figured now was as good a time as any to practice flying, I'd summoned wings.

And fallen twenty feet onto hard stone.

A rallied wind kept the fall from cracking any bones, but both my knees and my pride were significantly bruised by my graceless tumble through the air.

At least no one had witnessed it.

My stiff, limping steps, at least, had eased into a smoother gait by the time I found Elain in the family library.

Still staring at the window, but she was out of her room.

Nesta was reading in her usual chair, one eye on Elain, the other on the book spread in her lap. Only Nesta glanced my way as I slipped through the carved wooden doors.

I murmured, "Hello," and shut the doors behind me.

Elain didn't turn. She was wearing a pale pink gown that did little to complement her sallow skin, her brown-gold hair hanging in loose, heavy ringlets down her thin back.

"It's a fine day," I said to them.

Nesta arched an elegant eyebrow. "Where's your menagerie of friends?"

I leveled a steely look back at her. "Those friends have offered you shelter and comfort." And training—or whatever Amren was doing. "Are you ready for tonight?"

"Yes." Nesta merely resumed reading the book in her lap. Pure dismissal.

I let out a little snort that I knew would make her see red, and strode for Elain. Nesta monitored my every step, a panther readying to strike at the merest hint of danger.

"What are you looking at?" I asked Elain, keeping my voice soft. Casual.

Her face was wan, her lips bloodless. But they moved—barely—as she said, "I can see so very far now. All the way to the sea."

Indeed, the sea beyond the Sidra was a distant sparkle. "It takes some getting used to."

"I can hear your heartbeat—if I listen carefully. I can hear her heartbeat, too."

"You can learn to drown out the sounds that bother you." I had—entirely on my own. I wondered if Nesta had as well, or if they both suffered, hearing each other's heartbeats day and night. I didn't look to my other sister to confirm it.

Elain's eyes at last slid to mine. The first time she'd done so.

Even wasted away by grief and despair, Elain's beauty was remarkable. Hers was a face that could bring kings to their knees. And yet there was no joy in it. No light. No life.

She said, "I can hear the sea. Even at night. Even in my dreams. The crashing sea—and the screams of a bird made of fire."

It was an effort not to glance to Nesta. Even the town house was too far to hear anything from the nearby coast. And as for some fire-bird . . .

"There is a garden—at my other house," I said. "I'd like for you to come tend it, if you're willing."

Elain only turned toward the sunny windows again, the light dancing in her hair. "Will I hear the earthworms writhing through the soil? Or the stretching of roots? Will the bird of fire come to sit in the trees and watch me?"

I wasn't sure if I should answer. It was an effort to keep from shaking.

But I caught Nesta's eye, noting the glimmer of pain on my eldest sister's face before it was hidden beneath that cool mask. "There's a book I need you to help me find, Nesta," I said, giving a pointed stare to the stacks to my left.

Far enough away for privacy, but close enough to remain nearby should Elain need anything. Do anything.

Something in my chest cracked as Nesta's eyes also went to the windows before Elain.

To check, as I did, for whether they could be easily opened.

Mercifully, they were permanently sealed, likely to protect against some careless fool forgetting to close them and ruining the books. Likely Cassian.

Nesta wordlessly set down her book and followed me into the small labyrinth of stacks, both of us keeping an ear on the main sitting area.

When we were far enough away, I threw up a shield of hard wind around us. Keeping any sound inside. "How did you get her to leave her room?"

"I didn't," Nesta said, leaning against a shelf and crossing her slim arms. "I found her in here. She wasn't in bed when I awoke."

Nesta must have panicked upon finding her room empty—"Did she eat anything?"

"No. I managed to get her to drink some broth last night. She refused anything else. She's been talking in those half riddles all day."

I dragged a hand through my hair, freeing strands from my braid. "Did anything happen to trigger—"

"I don't know. I check on her every few hours." Nesta clenched her jaw. "I was gone for longer yesterday, though." While she trained with Amren. Rhys had informed me that by the end of it, Nesta's rudimentary shields were solid enough that Amren deemed my sister ready for tonight.

But there, beneath that cool demeanor—guilt. Panic.

"I doubt anything happened," I said quickly. "Maybe it's just . . . part of the recovery process. Her adjustment to being Fae."

Nesta didn't look convinced. "Does she have powers? Like mine."

And what, exactly, are those powers, Nesta? "I—don't know. I don't think so. Unless this is the first sign of something manifesting." It was an effort not to add, *If you'd talk about what went on in the Cauldron, perhaps we'd have a better understanding of it.* "Let's give her a day or two—see what happens. If she improves."

"Why not see now?"

"Because we're going to the Hewn City in a few hours. And you don't seem inclined to want us shoving into your business," I told her as evenly as I could. "I doubt Elain does, too."

Nesta stared me down, not a flicker of emotion on her face, and gave a curt nod. "Well, at least she left the room."

"And the chair."

We exchanged a rare, calm glance.

But then I said, "Why won't you train with Cassian?"

Nesta's spine locked up. "Why is it only Cassian that I may train with? Why not the other one?"

"Azriel?"

"Him, or the blond one who won't shut up."

"If you're referring to Mor—"

"And why must I train at all? I am no warrior, nor do I desire to be."

"It could make you strong—"

"There are many types of strength beyond the ability to wield a blade and end lives. Amren told me that yesterday."

"You said you wanted our enemies dead. Why not kill them yourself?"

She inspected her nails. "Why bother when someone else can do it for me?"

I avoided the urge to rub my temples. "We're—"

But the doors to the library opened, and I snapped my barrier of hard air down entirely at the thud of stalking footsteps, then their sudden halting.

I gripped Nesta's arm to keep her still just as Lucien's voice blurted, "You—you left your room."

Nesta bristled, teeth flashing. I gripped her harder, and threw a new wall of air around us—holding her there.

Weeks of cloistering Elain had done nothing to improve her state. Perhaps the half riddles were proof of that. And even if Lucien was currently breaking the rules we had set—

More steps—no doubt closer to where Elain stood at the window.

"Is . . . is there anything I can get for you?"

I'd never heard my friend's voice so soft. So tentative and concerned.

Perhaps it made me the lowest sort of wretch, but I cast my mind toward them. Toward him.

And then I was in his body, his head.

Too thin.

She must not be eating at all.

How can she even stand?

The thoughts flowed through his head, one after another. His heart was a raging, thunderous beat, and he didn't dare move from his position a mere five feet away. She hadn't yet turned toward him, but the ravages of her fasting were evident enough.

Touch her, smell her, taste her—

The instincts were a running river. He fisted his hands at his sides.

He hadn't expected her to be here. The other sister—the viper—was a possibility, but one he was willing to risk. Aside from talking to the shadowsinger yesterday—which had been just about as unnerving as he'd expected, though Azriel seemed like a decent enough male—he'd been cooped up in this wind-blasted House for two days. The thought of another one had been enough to make him risk Rhysand's wrath.

He just wanted a walk—and a few books. It had been an age since he'd even had free time to read, let alone do so for pleasure.

But there she was.

His mate.

She was nothing like Jesminda.

Jesminda had been all laughter and mischief, too wild and free to be contained by the country life that she'd been born into. She had teased him, taunted him—seduced him so thoroughly that he hadn't wanted anything but her. She'd seen him not as a High Lord's seventh son, but as a male. Had loved him without question, without hesitation. She had chosen him.

Elain had been . . . thrown at him.

He glanced toward the tea service spread on a low-lying table nearby. "I'm going to assume that one of those cups belongs to your sister." *Indeed, there was a discarded book in the viper's usual chair. Cauldron help the male who wound up shackled to her.*

"Do you mind if I help myself to the other?"

He tried to sound casual—comfortable. Even as his heart raced and raced, so swift he thought he might vomit on the very expensive, very old carpet. From Sangravah, if the patterns and rich dyes were any indication.

Rhysand was many things, but he certainly had good taste.

This entire place had been decorated with thought and elegance, with a penchant for comfort over stuffiness.

He didn't want to admit he liked it. Didn't want to admit that he found the city beautiful.

That the circle of people who now claimed to be Feyre's new family . . . It was what, long ago, he'd once thought life at Tamlin's court would be.

An ache like a blow to the chest went through him, but he crossed the rug. Forced his hands to be steady while he poured himself a cup of tea and sat in the chair opposite Nesta's vacated one.

"There's a plate of biscuits. Would you like one?"

He didn't expect her to answer, and he gave himself all of one more minute before he'd rise from this chair and leave, hopefully avoiding Nesta's return.

But sunlight on gold caught his eye—and Elain slowly turned from her vigil at the window.

He had not seen her entire face since that day in Hybern.

Then, it had been drawn and terrified, then utterly blank and numb, her hair plastered to her head, her lips blue with cold and shock.

Looking at her now . . .

She was pale, yes. The vacancy still glazing her features.

But he couldn't breathe *as she faced him fully.*

She was the most beautiful female he'd ever seen.

Betrayal, queasy and oily, slid through his veins. He'd said the same to Jesminda once.

But even as shame washed through him, the words, the sense chanted, Mine. You are mine, and I am yours. Mate.

Her eyes were the brown of a fawn's coat. And he could have sworn something sparked in them as she met his gaze.

"Who are you?"

He knew without demanding clarification that she was aware of what *he was to her.*

"I am Lucien. Seventh son of the High Lord of the Autumn Court."

And a whole lot of nothing. He'd told the shadowsinger all he knew—of his surviving brothers, of his father. His mother . . . he'd kept some details, irrelevant and utterly personal, to himself. Everything else—his father's closest allies, the most conniving courtiers and lords . . . He'd handed it over. Granted, it was dated by a few centuries, but in his time as emissary, from the information he'd gathered, not much had changed. They'd all acted the same Under the Mountain, anyway. And after what had happened with his brothers a few days ago . . . There was no tinge of guilt when he told Azriel what he knew. None of what he felt when he looked toward the south—toward both of the courts he'd called home.

For a long moment, Elain's face did not shift, but those eyes seemed to focus a bit more. "Lucien," she said at last, and he clenched his teacup to keep from shuddering at the sound of his name on her mouth. "From my sister's stories. Her friend."

"Yes."

But Elain blinked slowly. "You were in Hybern."

"Yes." It was all he could say.

"You betrayed us."

He wished she'd shoved him out the window behind her. "It—it was a mistake."

Her eyes went frank and cold. "I was to be married in a few days."

He fought against the bristling rage, the irrational urge to find the male who'd claimed her and shred him apart. The words were a rasp as he instead said, "I know. I'm sorry."

She did not love him, want him, need him. Another male's bride.

A mortal man's wife. Or she would have been.

She looked away—toward the windows. "I can hear your heart," she said quietly.

He wasn't sure how to respond, so he said nothing, and drained his tea, even as it burned his mouth.

"When I sleep," she murmured, "I can hear your heart beating through the stone." She angled her head, as if the city view held some answer. "Can you hear mine?"

He wasn't sure if she truly meant to address him, but he said, "No, lady. I cannot."

Her too-thin shoulders seemed to curve inward. "No one ever does. No one ever looked—not really." A bramble of words. Her voice strained to a whisper. "He did. He saw me. He will not now."

Her thumb brushed the iron ring on her finger.

Another male's ring, another marker that she was claimed—

It was enough. I had listened enough, learned enough. I pulled out of Lucien's mind.

Nesta was gaping at me, even as her face had leeched of color at every word uttered between them. "Have you ever gone into *my*—"

"No," I rasped.

How she knew what I had done, I didn't want to ask. Not as I dropped the shield around us and headed for the sitting area.

Lucien, no doubt having heard our steps, was flushed as he glanced between me and Nesta. No inkling whatsoever that I'd slid into his mind. Rifled through it like a bandit in the night. I shoved down the mild nausea.

My eldest sister merely said to him, "Get out."

I flashed Nesta a glare, but Lucien rose. "I came for a book."

"Well, find one and leave."

Elain only stared out the window, unaware—or uncaring.

Lucien didn't head for the stacks. He just went to the open doors. He paused right between them and said to me, to Nesta, "She needs fresh air."

"We'll judge what she needs."

I could have sworn his ruby hair gleamed like molten metal as his temper rose. But it faded, his russet eye fixing on me. "Take her to the sea. Take her to some garden. But get her out of this house for an hour or two."

Then he walked away.

I looked at my two sisters. Cloistered up here, high above the world.

"You're moving into the town house right now," I said to them. To Lucien, who paused in the dim hallway outside.

Nesta, to my shock, did not object.

Neither did Rhys when I sent my order down the bond, asking him, Cassian, and Azriel to help move them. No, my mate just promised to assign two bedrooms to my sisters down the hall, on the other side of the stairs. And a third for Lucien—on our side of the hall. Well away from Elain's.

Thirty minutes later, Azriel carried Elain down, my sister silent and unresponsive in his arms.

Nesta had looked ready to walk off the balcony rather than let Cassian, already dressed and armed for guarding the town house tonight, hold her, so I nudged her toward Rhys, pushed Lucien toward Cassian, and flew myself back.

Or tried to—again. I soared for about half a minute, savoring the cleansing scream of the wind, before my wings wobbled, my back strained, and the fall became unbearably deadly. I winnowed the rest of the way to the town house, and adjusted vases and figurines in the sitting room while waiting for them.

Azriel arrived first, no shadows to be seen, my sister a pale, golden mass in his arms. He, too, wore his Illyrian armor, Elain's golden-brown hair snagging in some of the black scales across his chest and shoulders.

He set her down gently on the foyer carpet, having carried her in through the front door.

Elain peered up at his patient, solemn face.

Azriel smiled faintly. "Would you like me to show you the garden?"

She seemed so small before him, so fragile compared to the scales of his fighting leathers, the breadth of his shoulders. The wings peeking over them.

But Elain did not balk from him, did not shy away as she nodded—just once.

Azriel, graceful as any courtier, offered her an arm. I couldn't tell if she was looking at his blue Siphon or at his scarred skin beneath as she breathed, "Beautiful."

Color bloomed high on Azriel's golden-brown cheeks, but he inclined his head in thanks and led my sister toward the back doors into the garden, sunlight bathing them.

A moment later, Nesta was stomping through the front door, her face a remarkable shade of green. "I need—a toilet."

I met Rhys's stare as he prowled in behind her, hands in his pockets. *What did you do?*

His brows shot up. But I wordlessly pointed Nesta toward the powder room beneath the stairs, and she vanished, slamming the door behind her.

Me? Rhys leaned against the bottom post of the banister. *She complained that I was flying deliberately slow. So I went fast.*

Cassian and Lucien appeared, neither looking at the other. But Lucien's attention went right to the hallway toward the back, his nostrils flaring as he scented Elain's direction. And who she'd gone with.

A low snarl slipped out of him—

"Relax," Rhys said. "Azriel isn't the ravishing type."

Lucien cut him a glare.

Mercifully, or perhaps not, Nesta's retching filled the silence. Cassian gaped at Rhys. "What did you *do*?"

"I asked him the same thing," I said, crossing my arms. "He said he '*went fast*.' "

Nesta vomited again—then silence.

Cassian sighed at the ceiling. "She'll never fly again."

The doorknob twisted, and we tried—or at least Cassian and I did—not to seem like we'd been listening to her. Nesta's face was still greenish-pale, but . . . Her eyes burned.

There was no way of describing that burning—and even painting it might have failed.

Her eyes remained the same blue-gray as my own. And yet . . . Molten ore was all I could think of. Quicksilver set aflame.

She advanced a step toward us. All her attention fixed on Rhys.

Cassian casually stepped in her path, wings folded in tight. Feet braced apart on the carpet. A fighting stance—casual, but . . . his Siphons glimmered.

"Do you know," Cassian drawled to her, "that the last time I got into a brawl in this house, I was kicked out for a month?"

Nesta's burning gaze slid to him, still outraged—but hinted with incredulity.

He just went on, "It was Amren's fault, of course, but no one believed me. And no one dared banish *her*."

She blinked slowly.

But the burning, molten gaze became mortal. Or as mortal as one of us could be.

Until Lucien breathed, "What *are* you?"

Cassian didn't seem to dare take his focus off Nesta. But my sister slowly looked at Lucien.

"I made it give something back," she said with terrifying quiet. The Cauldron. The hairs along my arms rose. Nesta's gaze flicked to the carpet, then to a spot on the wall. "I wish to go to my room."

It took a moment to realize she'd spoken to me. I cleared my throat. "Up the stairs, on your right. Second door. Or the third—whichever suits you. The other is for Elain. We need to leave in . . ." I squinted at the clock in the sitting room. "Two hours."

A shallow nod was her only acknowledgment and thanks.

We watched as she headed up the steps, her lavender gown trailing after her, one slender hand braced on the rail.

"I'm sorry," Rhys called up after her.

Her hand tightened on the rail, the whites of her knuckles poking through her pale skin, but she didn't say anything as she continued on.

"Is that sort of thing even possible?" Cassian murmured when the door to her room had shut. "For someone to *take* from the Cauldron's essence?"

"It would seem so," Rhys mused, then said to Lucien, "The flame in her eyes was not of your usual sort, I take it."

Lucien shook his head. "No. It spoke to nothing in my own arsenal. That was . . . Ice so cold it burned. Ice and yet . . . fluid like flame. Or flame made of ice."

"I think it's death," I said quietly.

I held Rhys's gaze, as if it were again the tether that had kept me in this world. "I think the power is death—death made flesh. Or whatever power the Cauldron holds over such things. That's why the Carver heard it—heard about her."

"Mother above," Lucien said, dragging a hand through his hair.

Cassian gave him a solemn nod.

But Rhys rubbed his jaw, weighing, thinking. Then he said simply, "Only Nesta would not just conquer Death—but pillage it."

No wonder she didn't wish to speak to anyone about it—didn't wish to bear witness on our behalf. It had been mere seconds for us while she'd gone under.

I had never asked either of my sisters how long it had been for *them* inside that Cauldron.

"Azriel knows you're watching," Rhys drawled from where he stood before the mirror in our bedroom, adjusting the lapels of his black jacket.

The town house was a quiet flurry of activity as we prepared to leave. Mor and Amren had arrived half an hour ago, the former heading for the sitting room, the latter bearing a dress for my sister. I didn't dare ask Amren to see what she'd selected for Nesta.

Training, Amren had said days ago. There were magical objects in the Court of Nightmares that my sister could study tonight, while we were occupied with Keir. I wondered if the Ouroboros was one of them—and made a note to ask Amren what she knew of the mirror the Carver so badly desired. Which I'd somehow have to convince Keir to part with tonight.

Lucien had offered to make himself useful while we were gone by reading through some of the texts now piled on the tables throughout the sitting room. Amren had only grunted at the offer, which I told Lucien amounted to a yes.

Cassian was already on the roof, casually sharpening his blades. I'd asked him if *nine* swords were really necessary, and he merely told me that it didn't hurt to be prepared, and that if I had enough time to question him, then I should have enough time to do another workout. I'd quickly left, throwing a vulgar gesture his way.

My hair still damp from the bath I'd just taken, I slid my heavy earrings through my lobes and peered out our bedroom window, monitoring the garden below.

Elain sat silently at one of the wrought-iron tables, a cup of tea before her. Azriel was sprawled on the chaise longue across the gray stones, sunning his wings and reading what looked to be a stack of reports—likely information on the Autumn Court that he planned to present to Rhys once he'd sorted through it all. Already dressed for the Hewn City—the brutal, beautiful armor so at odds with the lovely garden. And my sister sitting within it.

"Why not make *them* mates?" I mused. "Why Lucien?"

"I'd keep that question from Lucien."

"I'm serious." I turned toward him and crossed my arms. "What decides it? *Who* decides it?"

Rhys straightened his lapels before plucking an invisible piece of lint from them. "Fate, the Mother, the Cauldron's swirling eddies . . ."

"*Rhys.*"

He watched me in the reflection of the mirror as I strode for my armoire, flinging open the doors to yank out the dress I'd selected. Scraps of shimmering black—a slightly more modest version of what I'd worn to the Court of Nightmares months ago. "You said your mother and father were wrong for each other; *Tamlin* said his own parents were wrong for each other." I peeled off my dressing robe. "So it can't be a perfect system of matching. What if"—I jerked my chin toward the window, to my sister and the shadowsinger in the garden—"*that* is what she needs? Is there no free will? What if Lucien wishes the union but she doesn't?"

"A mating bond can be rejected," Rhys said mildly, eyes flickering in the mirror as he drank in every inch of bare skin I had on display. "There is choice. And sometimes, yes—the bond picks poorly. Sometimes, the bond is nothing more than some . . . preordained guesswork at who will provide the strongest offspring. At its basest level, it's perhaps only that. Some natural function, not an indication of true, paired souls." A smile at me—at the rareness, perhaps, of what we had. "Even so," Rhys went on, "there will always be a . . . tug. For the females, it is usually easier to ignore, but the males . . . It can drive them mad. It is their burden to fight through, but some believe they are entitled to the female. Even after the bond is rejected, they see her as belonging to them. Sometimes they return to challenge the male she chooses for herself. Sometimes it ends in death. It is savage, and it is ugly, and it mercifully does not happen often, but . . . Many mated pairs will try to make it work, believing the Cauldron selected them for a reason. Only years later will they realize that perhaps the pairing was not ideal in spirit."

I scrounged up the jeweled, dark belt from an armoire drawer and slung it low over my hips. "So you're saying she could walk away—and Lucien would have free rein to kill whoever she wishes to be with."

Rhys turned from the mirror at last, his dark clothes pristine—cut perfectly to his body. No wings tonight. "Not free rein—not in my lands. It has been illegal in our territory for a long, long time for males to do that. Even before I was born. Other courts, no. On the continent, there are territories that believe the females literally *belong* to their mate. But not here. Elain would have our full protection if she rejects the bond. But it will still be a bond, however weakened, that will trail her for the rest of her existence."

"Do you think she and Lucien match well?" I pulled out a pair of sandals that laced up my bare thighs and jammed my feet into them before beginning work on the bindings.

"You know them better than I do. But I will say that Lucien is loyal—fiercely so."

"So is Azriel."

"Azriel," Rhys said, "has been preoccupied with the same female for the past five hundred years."

"Wouldn't the mating bond have snapped into place for them if it exists?"

Rhys's eyes shuttered. "I think that is a question Azriel has been asking himself every day since he met Mor." He sighed as I finished one foot and started on the other. "Am I allowed to request that you *not* play matchmaker? Let them sort it out."

I rose, bracing my hands on my hips. "I would never meddle in someone else's affairs!"

He only raised a brow in silent challenge. And I knew precisely what he referred to.

My gut tightened as I took a seat at the vanity and began braiding my hair into a coronet atop my head. Perhaps I was a coward, for not being able to ask it aloud, but I said down the bond, *Was it a violation—going into Lucien's mind like that?*

I can't answer that for you. Rhys came over and handed me a hairpin.

I slid it into a section of braid. *I needed to be sure—that he wasn't about to try to grab her, to sell us out.*

He handed me another. *And did you get an answer to that?*

We worked in unison, pinning my hair into place. *I think so. It wasn't just about what he thought—it was the . . . feeling. I sensed no ill will, no conniving. Only concern for her. And . . . sorrow. Longing.* I shook my head. *Do I tell him? What I did?*

Rhys pinned a hard-to-reach section of my hair. *You have to deem whether the cost is worth assuaging your guilt.*

The cost being Lucien's tentative trust in me, this place. *I crossed a line.*

But you did it to ensure the safety of people you love.

I didn't realize . . . I trailed off, shaking my head again.

He squeezed my shoulder. *Didn't realize what?*

I shrugged, slouching on the cushioned stool. *That it'd be so complicated.* My face warmed. *I know that sounds terribly naïve—*

It's always complicated, and it never gets easier, no matter how many centuries I've been doing it.

I pushed around the extra hairpins on the vanity. *It's the second time I've gone into his mind.*

Then say it's the last, and be done with it.

I blinked, lifting my head. I'd painted my lips in a shade of red so dark it was nearly black, and they now pressed into a thin line.

He clarified, *What's done is done. Agonizing over it won't change anything. You realized it was a line you didn't like crossing, and so you won't make that mistake again.*

I shifted in my seat. *Would you have done it?*

Rhys considered. *Yes. And I would have felt just as guilty afterward.*

Hearing that settled something, deep down. I nodded once—twice.

If you want to make yourself feel a little better, he added, *Lucien did technically violate the rules we set. So you were entitled to look into his mind, if only to ensure the safety of your sister. He crossed the line first.*

That thing deep in me eased a bit more. *You're right.*

And it was done.

I watched Rhys in the mirror as a dark crown appeared in his hands. The one of ravens' feathers that I'd seen him wear—or its feminine twin. A tiara—which he gently, reverently, set before the braid we'd pinned into place atop my head. The original crown . . . it appeared atop Rhys's head a moment later.

Together, we stared at our reflection. Lord and Lady Night.

"Ready to be wicked?" he purred in my ear.

My toes curled at the caress in that voice—at the memory of the last time we'd gone to the Court of Nightmares. How I'd sat in his lap—where his fingers had drifted.

I rose from the bench, facing him fully. His hands skimmed the bare skin along my ribs. Between my breasts. Down the outside of my thighs. Oh, he remembered, too.

"This time," I breathed, kissing the tendril of tattoo that peeked just above the collar of Rhys's black jacket, "I get to make Keir beg."

CHAPTER 25

Amren hadn't dressed Nesta in cobwebs and stardust, as Mor and I were clothed. And she hadn't dressed Nesta in her own style of loose pants and a cropped blouse.

She had kept it simple. Brutal.

A dress of impenetrable black flowed to the dark marble floors of the throne room of the Hewn City, tight through the bodice and sleeves, its neckline skimming the base of her pale throat. Nesta's hair had been swept into a simple style to reveal the panes of her face, the savage clarity of her eyes as she took in the assembled crowd, the towering carved pillars and the scaled beasts twined around them, the mighty dais and the throne atop it . . . and did not balk.

Indeed, Nesta's chin only lifted with each step we took toward that dais.

One throne, I realized—that mighty throne of those twined, scaly beasts.

Rhys realized it, too. Planned for it.

My sister and the others peeled away at the foot of the dais, taking flanking positions at its base. No fear, no joy, no light in their faces.

Azriel, at Mor's side, looked murderously calm as he surveyed those gathered. As he beheld Keir, waiting beside a golden-haired woman who had to be Mor's mother, sneering at us. *Promise them nothing*, Mor had warned me.

Rhys held out a hand for me to ascend the dais steps. I kept my head high, back straight, as I gripped his fingers and strode up the few stairs. Toward that solitary throne.

Rhys only winked as he gracefully escorted me right into that throne, the movement as easy and smooth as a dance.

The crowd murmured as I sat, the black stone bitingly cold against my bare thighs.

They outright gasped as Rhys simply perched on the arm of the throne, smirked at me, and said to the Court of Nightmares, "Bow."

For they had not. And with me seated on that throne . . .

Their faces were still a mixture of shock and disdain as they all dropped to their knees.

I avoided looking at Nesta while she had no choice but to follow suit.

But I made myself look at Keir, at the female beside him, at anyone who dared meet my gaze. Made myself remember what they had done to Mor, now bowing with a grin on her face, when she was barely more than a child. Some of the court averted their eyes.

"I will interpret the lack of two thrones to be due to the fact that this visit came upon you quickly," Rhys said with lethal calm. "And I will let you all escape without having your skin flayed from your bones as *my* mating gift to *you*. Our loyal subjects," he added, smiling faintly.

I traced a finger over the scaly coil of one of the beasts that made up the arms of the throne. Our court. Part of it.

And we needed them to fight with us. To agree to it—tonight.

The mouth I'd painted that dark, dark red parted into a lazy smile. Tendrils of power snaked toward the dais, but didn't dare venture past the first step. Testing me—what power I might have. But not getting close enough to offend Rhysand.

I let them creep closer, sniffing around, as I said to Rhys, to the throne room, "Surely, my love, they would like to stand now."

Rhys smiled down at me, then at the crowd. "Rise."

They did. And some of those tendrils of power dared climb up the first step.

I pounced.

Three gasps choked through the murmuring room as I slammed talon-sharp magic down upon those too-curious powers. Dug in deep and hard. A cat with a bird under its paw. Several of them.

"Do you wish to have this back?" I asked quietly to no one in particular.

Near the foot of the dais, Keir was scowling over a shoulder, his silver circlet glinting atop his golden hair. Someone whimpered in the back of the room.

"Don't you know," Rhys purred to the crowd, "that it's not polite to touch a lady without her permission?"

In answer, I sank those dark talons in further, the magic of whoever had dared try to test me thrashing and buckling. "Play nice," I crooned to the crowd.

And let go.

Three separate flurries of motion warred for my attention. Someone had winnowed outright, fleeing. Another had fainted. And a third was clinging to whoever stood beside them, trembling. I marked all their faces.

Amren and Nesta approached the foot of the dais. My sister was staring as if she'd never seen me before. I didn't dare break my mask of bemused coolness. Didn't dare ask if Nesta's shields were holding up—if someone had just tried to test her as well. Nesta's own imperious face yielded nothing.

Amren bowed her head to Rhys, to me. "By your leave, High Lord."

Rhys waved an idle hand. "Go. Enjoy yourselves." He jerked his chin to the watching crowd. "Food and music. Now."

He was obeyed. Instantly.

My sister and Amren vanished before the crowd could begin milling about, striding right through those towering doors and into the gloom. To go play with some of the magical trove kept here—to give Nesta some practice for whenever Amren figured out how to fix the wall.

A few heads turned in their direction—then quickly looked away as Amren noticed them.

Let some of the monster inside show.

We still had not told her of the Bone Carver—of the Prison visit. Something a bit like guilt coiled in my stomach. Though I supposed I had to get used to it as Rhys curled a finger toward Keir and said, "The council room. Ten minutes."

Keir's eyes narrowed at the order, the female beside him keeping her head down—the portrait of subservience. What Mor was supposed to have been.

My friend was indeed watching her parents, cold indifference on her face. Azriel kept a step away, monitoring everything.

I didn't let myself look too interested—too worried—as Rhys offered me a hand and we rose from the throne. And went to talk of war.

The council chamber of the Hewn City was nearly as large as the throne room. It was carved from the same dark rock, its pillars fashioned after those entangled beasts.

Far below the high, domed ceiling, a mammoth table of black glass split the room in two like a lightning strike, its corners left long and jagged. Sharp as a razor.

Rhys claimed a seat at the head of the table. I took the one at the opposite end. Azriel and Mor found seats on one side, and Keir settled into the seat on the other.

A chair beside him sat empty.

Rhys leaned back in his dark chair, swirling the wine that had been poured by a stone-faced servant a moment before. It had been an effort not to thank the male who'd filled my goblet.

But here, I did not thank anyone.

Here, I took what was mine, and offered no gratitude or apologies for it.

"I know why you're here," Keir said without any sort of preamble.

"Oh?" Rhys's eyebrow arched beautifully.

Keir surveyed us, distaste lingering on his handsome face. "Hybern is swarming. Your legions"—a sneer at Azriel, at the Illyrians he represented—"are gathering." Keir interlaced his long fingers and set them upon the dark glass. "You mean to ask for my Darkbringers to join your army."

Rhys sipped from his wine. "Well, at least you've spared me the effort of dancing around the subject."

Keir held his gaze without blinking. "I will confess that I find myself . . . sympathetic to Hybern's cause."

Mor shifted slightly in her seat. Azriel just pinned that icy, all-seeing stare on Keir.

"You would not be the only one," Rhys countered coolly.

Keir frowned up at the obsidian chandelier, fashioned after a wreath of night-blooming flowers—the center of each a twinkling silver faelight. "There are many similarities between Hybern's people and my own. Both of us trapped—stagnant."

"Last I checked," Mor cut in, "you have been free to do as you wish for centuries. Longer."

Keir didn't so much as look at her, earning a flicker of rage from Azriel at the dismissal. "Ah, but *are* we free here? Not even the entirety of this mountain belongs to us—not with your palace atop it."

"*All* of this belongs to me, I'll remind you," Rhys said wryly.

"It's that mentality that allows me to find Hybern's stifled people to be . . . kindred spirits."

"You want the palace upstairs, Keir, then it's yours." Rhys crossed his legs. "I didn't know you were lusting after it for so long."

Keir's answering smile was near-serpentine. "You must need my army rather desperately, Rhysand." Again, that hateful glance at Azriel. "Are the overgrown bats not up to snuff anymore?"

"Come train with them," Azriel said softly, "and you'll learn for yourself."

In his centuries of miserable existence, Keir had certainly mastered the art of sneering.

And the way he sneered at Azriel . . . Mor's teeth flashed in the dim light. It was an effort to keep myself from doing the same.

"I have no doubt," Rhys said, the portrait of glorious boredom, "that you've already decided upon your asking price."

Keir peered down the table—to me. Looked his fill as I held his stare. "I did."

My stomach turned at that gaze, the words.

Dark power rumbled through the chamber, setting the onyx chandelier tinkling. "Tread carefully, Keir."

Keir only smiled at me, then at Rhys. Mor had gone utterly still.

"What would you give me for a shot at this war, Rhysand? You whored yourself to Amarantha—but what about your mate?"

He had not forgotten how we'd treated him. How we'd humiliated him months ago.

And Rhys . . . there was only eternal, unforgiving death in his face, in the darkness gathering behind his chair. "The bargain our ancestors struck grants you the right to choose how and when your army assists my own. But it does not grant you the right to keep your life, Keir, when I grow tired of your existence."

As if in answer, invisible claws gouged deep marks in the table, the glass shrieking. I flinched. Keir blanched at the lines now inches from him.

"But I thought you might be . . . hesitant to assist me," Rhys went on. I'd never seen him so calm. Not calm—but filled with icy rage.

The sort I sometimes glimpsed in Azriel's eyes.

Rhys snapped his fingers and said to no one in particular, "Bring him in."

The doors opened on a phantom wind.

I didn't know where to look as a servant escorted in the tall male figure.

At Mor, whose face went white with dread. At Azriel, who reached for his dagger—Truth-Teller—his every breath alert, focused, but unsurprised. Not a hint of shock.

Or at Eris, heir to the Autumn Court, as he strolled into the room.

CHAPTER 26

That's who the final, empty seat was for.

And Rhys . . .

He remained sprawled in his chair, sipping from his wine. "Welcome back, Eris," he drawled. "It's been what—five centuries since you last set foot in here?"

Mor slid her eyes toward Rhys. Betrayal and—hurt. That was hurt flashing there.

For not warning us. For this . . . surprise.

I wondered if I schooled my features with any more success than my friend as Eris claimed the vacant seat at the table, not bothering to so much as nod to a wary-eyed Keir. "It has indeed been a while."

He'd healed since that day on the ice—not a sign of the gut-wound Cassian had given him. His red hair was unbound, a silken drape over his well-tailored cobalt jacket.

What is he doing here, I speared down the bond, not bothering to hide any of what coursed through me.

Making sure Keir agrees to help, was all Rhys said, the words tight and clipped. Restrained.

As if he were still holding the full might of his rage in check.

Shadows curled around Azriel's shoulders, whispering in his ear as he stared down Eris.

"You once wanted to build ties to Autumn, Keir," said Rhys, setting down his goblet of wine. "Well, here's your chance. Eris is willing to offer you a formal alliance—in exchange for your services in this war."

How the hell did you get him to agree to that?

Rhys didn't answer.

Rhysand.

Keir leaned back in his chair. "It is not enough."

Eris snorted, pouring himself a goblet of wine from the decanter in the center of the table. "I'd forgotten why I was so relieved when our bargain fell apart the last time."

Rhys shot him a warning look. Eris just drank deeply.

"What is it that you want, then, Keir?" Rhys purred.

I had the feeling if Keir suggested me again, he'd wind up splattered on the wall.

But Keir must have known, too. And said simply to Rhysand, "I want out. I want space. I want my people to be free of this mountain."

"You have every comfort," I finally said. "And yet it is not enough?"

Keir ignored me as well. As I'm sure he ignored most women in his life.

"You have been keeping secrets, High Lord," Keir said with a hateful smile, interlacing his hands and resting them on the mauled table. Right atop the nearest deep gouge. "I always wondered—where all of you *went* when you weren't here. Hybern answered the question at last—thanks to that attack on . . . what is its name? Velaris. Yes. On Velaris. The City of Starlight."

Mor went utterly still.

"I want access to the city," Keir said. "For me, and my court."

"No," Mor said. The word echoed off the pillars, the glass, the rock.

I was inclined to agree. The thought of these people, of Keir, in

Velaris . . . Tainting it with their presence, their hatred and small-mindedness, their disdain and cruelty . . .

Rhys did not refuse. Did not shoot down the suggestion.

You can't be serious.

Rhys only watched Keir as he answered down the bond, *I anticipated this—and I took precautions.*

I contemplated it. *The meeting with the Palace governors . . . That was tied to this?*

Yes.

Rhysand said to Keir, "There would be conditions."

Mor opened her mouth, but Azriel laid a scarred hand atop hers.

She snatched her hand back as if she'd been burned—burned as he had been.

Azriel's mask of cold didn't so much as waver at the rejection. Though Eris chuckled softly. Enough to make Azriel's hazel eyes glaze with rage as he settled them upon the High Lord's son. Eris only inclined his head to the shadowsinger.

"I want unrestricted access," Keir said to Rhys.

"You will not get it," Rhys said. "There will be limited stays, limited numbers allowed in. To be decided later."

Mor turned pleading eyes to Rhys. Her city—the place that she loved so much—

I could almost hear it. The crack I knew was about to sound amongst our own circle.

Keir looked to Mor at last—noted the despair and anger. And smiled.

He had no real desire to get out of here.

Only a desire to take something he'd undoubtedly gleaned that his daughter cherished.

I could have gladly shredded through his throat as Keir said, "Done."

Rhys didn't so much as smile. Mor was only staring and staring at him, that beseeching expression crumpling her face.

"There is one more thing," I added, squaring my shoulders. "One more request."

Keir deigned to acknowledge me. "Oh?"

"I have need of the Ouroboros mirror," I said, willing ice into my veins. "Immediately."

Interest and surprise flared in Keir's brown eyes. Mor's eyes.

"Who told you that I have it?" he asked quietly.

"Does it matter? I want it."

"Do you even know what the Ouroboros *is*?"

"Consider your tone, Keir," Rhys warned.

Keir leaned forward, bracing his forearms on the table. "The mirror . . ." He laughed under his breath. "Consider it my mating present." He added with sweet venom, "If you can take it."

Not a threat to face him, but— "What do you mean?"

Keir rose to his feet, smirking like a cat with a canary in its mouth. "To take the Ouroboros, to claim it, you must first look into it." He headed for the doors, not waiting to be dismissed. "And everyone who has attempted to do so has either gone mad or been broken beyond repair. Even a High Lord or two, if legend is true." A shrug. "So it is yours, if you dare to face it." Keir paused at the threshold as the doors opened on a phantom wind. He said to Rhys, perhaps the closest he'd come to asking for permission to leave, "Lord Thanatos is having . . . difficulties with his daughter again. He requires my assistance." Rhys only waved a hand, as if he hadn't just yielded our city to the male. Keir jerked his chin at Eris. "I will wish to speak with you—soon."

Once he was done gloating over his victory tonight. What we'd given.

And lost.

If the Ouroboros could not be retrieved, at least without such terrible risk . . . I shut out the thought, sealing it away for later, as Keir left. Leaving us alone with Eris.

The heir of Autumn just sipped his wine.

And I had the terrible sense that Mor had gone somewhere far, far away as Eris set down his goblet and said, "You look well, Mor."

"You don't speak to her," Azriel said softly.

Eris gave a bitter smile. "I see you're still holding a grudge."

"This arrangement, Eris," Rhys said, "relies solely upon you keeping your mouth shut."

Eris huffed a laugh. "And haven't I done an excellent job? Not even my father suspected when I left tonight."

I glanced between my mate and Eris. "How did this come about?"

Eris looked me over. The crown and dress. "You didn't think that I knew your shadowsinger would come sniffing around to see if I'd told my father about your . . . powers? Especially after my brothers so mysteriously *forgot* about them, too. I knew it was a matter of time before one of you arrived to take care of my memory as well." Eris tapped the side of his head with a long finger. "Too bad for you, I learned a thing or two about daemati. Too bad for my brothers that I never bothered to teach them."

My chest tightened. *Rhys.*

To keep me safe from Beron's wrath, to keep this potential alliance with the High Lords from falling apart before it began . . . *Rhys.*

It was an effort to keep my eyes from burning.

A gentle caress down the bond was his only answer.

"Of course I didn't tell my father," Eris went on, drinking from his wine again. "Why waste that sort of information on the bastard? His answer would be to hunt you down and kill you—not realizing how much shit we're in with Hybern and that you might be the key to stopping it."

"So he plans to join us, then," Rhys said.

"Not if he learns about your little secret." Eris smirked.

Mor blinked—as if realizing that Rhys's contact with Eris, his invitation here . . . The glance she gave me, clear and settled, told me enough. Hurt and anger still swirled, but understanding, too.

"So what's the asking price, Eris?" Mor demanded, leaning her bare arms on the dark glass. "Another little bride for you to torture?"

Something flickered in Eris's eyes. "I don't know who fed you those lies to begin with, Morrigan," he said with vicious calm. "Likely the bastards you surround yourself with." A sneer at Azriel.

Mor snarled, rattling the glasses. "You never gave any evidence to the contrary. Certainly not when you left me in those woods."

"There were forces at work that you have never considered," Eris said coldly. "And I am not going to waste my breath explaining them to you. Believe what you want about me."

"You hunted me down like an animal," I cut in. "I think we'll choose to believe the worst."

Eris's pale face flushed. "I was given an order. And sent to do it with two of my . . . brothers."

"And what of the brother you hunted down alongside me? The one whose lover you helped to execute before his eyes?"

Eris laid a hand flat on the table. "You know *nothing* about what happened that day. *Nothing*."

Silence.

"Indulge me," was all I said.

Eris stared me down. I stared right back.

"How do you think he made it to the Spring border," he said quietly. "I wasn't there—when they did it. Ask him. I refused. It was the first and only time I have denied my father anything. He punished me. And by the time I got free . . . They were going to kill him, too. I made sure they didn't. Made sure Tamlin got word—anonymously—to get the hell over to his own border."

Where two of Eris's brothers had been killed. By Lucien and Tamlin.

Eris picked at a stray thread on his jacket. "Not all of us were so lucky in our friends and family as you, Rhysand."

Rhys's face was a mask of boredom. "It would seem so."

And none of this entirely erased what he'd done, but . . . "What is the asking price," I repeated.

"The same thing I told Azriel when I found him snooping through my father's woods yesterday."

Hurt flared in Mor's eyes as she whipped her head toward the shadowsinger. But Azriel didn't so much as acknowledge her as he announced, "When the time comes . . . we are to support Eris's bid to take the throne."

Even as Azriel spoke, that frozen rage dulled his face. And Eris was wise enough to finally pale at the sight. Perhaps that was why Eris had kept knowledge of my powers to himself. Not just for this sort of bargaining, but to avoid the wrath of the shadowsinger. The blade at his side.

"The request still stands, Rhysand," Eris said, mastering himself, "to just kill my father and be done with it. I can pledge troops right now."

Mother above. He didn't even try to hide it—to look at all remorseful. It was an effort to keep my jaw from dropping to the table at his intent, the casualness with which he spoke it.

"Tempting, but too messy," Rhys replied. "Beron sided with us in the War. Hopefully he'll sway that way again." A pointed stare at Eris.

"He will," Eris promised, running a finger over one of the claw marks gouged into the table. "And will remain blissfully unaware of Feyre's . . . gifts."

A throne—in exchange for his silence. And sway.

"Promise Keir nothing you care about," Rhys said, waving a hand in dismissal.

Eris just rose to his feet. "We'll see." A frown at Mor as he drained his wine and set down the goblet. "I'm surprised you still can't control yourself around him. You had every emotion written right on that pretty face of yours."

"Watch it," Azriel warned.

Eris looked between them, smiling faintly. Secretly. As if he knew something that Azriel didn't. "I wouldn't have touched you," he said to Mor, who blanched again. "But when you fucked that other bastard—" A snarl ripped from Rhys's throat at that. And my own. "I knew why you did it." Again that secret smile that had Mor shrinking. *Shrinking*. "So I gave you your freedom, ending the betrothal in no uncertain terms."

"*And what happened next*," Azriel growled.

A shadow crossed Eris's face. "There are few things I regret. That is one of them. But . . . perhaps one day, now that we are allies, I shall tell you why. What it cost me."

"I don't give a shit," Mor said quietly. She pointed to the door. "Get out."

Eris gave a mocking bow to her. To all of us. "See you at the meeting in twelve days."

CHAPTER 27

We found Nesta and Amren waiting outside the throne room, both of them looking pissy and tired.

Well, that made six of us.

I didn't doubt Keir's claim about the mirror—and risking gazing into it . . . None of us could afford it. To be broken. Driven mad. None of us—not right now. Perhaps the Bone Carver had known that. Had sent me on a fool's errand to amuse himself.

We did not bother with good-byes to the whispering court as we winnowed to the town house. To Velaris—the peace and beauty that now felt infinitely more fragile.

Cassian had come off the roof at some point to join Lucien in the sitting room, the books from the wall spread on the low-lying table between them. Both got to their feet at the expressions on our faces.

Cassian was halfway to Mor when she whirled on Rhys and said, "*Why?*"

Her voice broke.

And something in my chest cracked, too, at the tears that began running down her face.

Rhys just stood there, staring down at her. His face unreadable.

Watching as she slammed her hands into his chest and shouted, "*Why?*"

He yielded a step. "Eris found Azriel—our hands were tied. I made the best of it." His throat bobbed. "I'm sorry."

Cassian was sizing them up, frozen halfway across the room. And I assumed Rhys was telling him mind to mind, assumed he was telling Amren and perhaps even Lucien and Nesta, from their surprised blinks.

Mor whirled on Azriel. "*Why didn't you say anything?*"

Azriel held her gaze unflinchingly. Didn't so much as rustle his wings. "Because you would have tried to stop it. And we can't afford to lose Keir's alliance—and face the threat of Eris."

"You're working with that prick," Cassian cut in, whatever catching-up now over, apparently. He moved to Mor's side, a hand on her back. He shook his head at Azriel and Rhys, disgust curling his lip. "You should have spiked Eris's fucking head to the front gates."

Azriel only watched them with that icy indifference. But Lucien crossed his arms, leaning against the back of the couch. "I have to agree with Cassian. Eris is a snake."

Perhaps Rhys had not filled him in on everything, then. On what Eris had claimed about saving his youngest brother in whatever way he could. Of his defiance.

"Your whole family is despicable," Amren said to Lucien from where she and Nesta lingered in the archway. "But Eris may prove a better alternative. If he can find a way to kill Beron off and make sure the power shifts to himself."

"I'm sure he will," Lucien said.

But Mor was still staring at Rhys, those silent tears streaming down her flushed cheeks. "It's not about Eris," she said, voice wobbling. "It's about *here*." She waved a hand to the town house, the city. "This is my *home*, and you are going to let Keir *destroy it*."

"I took precautions," Rhys said—an edge to his voice I had not heard in some time. "Many of them. Starting with meeting with the governors of the Palaces and getting them to agree never to serve, shelter, or entertain Keir or anyone from the Court of Nightmares."

Mor blinked. Cassian's hand moved to her shoulder and squeezed.

"They have been sending out the word to every business owner in the city," Rhys went on, "every restaurant and shop and venue. So Keir and his ilk may come here . . . But they will not find it a welcoming place. Or one where they can even procure lodgings."

Mor shook her head as she whispered, "He'll still destroy it."

Cassian slid his arm around her shoulders, his face harder than I'd ever seen it as he studied Rhys. Then Azriel. "You should have warned us."

"I should have," Rhys said—though he didn't sound sorry for it. Azriel just remained a foot away, wings tucked in tight and Siphons glimmering.

I stepped in at last. "We'll set limitations—on when and how often they come."

Mor shook her head, still not looking anywhere but at Rhys. "If Amarantha were alive . . ." The word slithered through the room, darkening the corners. "If she were alive and I offered to *work* with her—even if it was to save us all—how would you feel?"

Never—they had never come this close to discussing what had happened to him.

I approached Rhys's side, brushing my fingers against his. His own curled around mine.

"If Amarantha offered us a slim shot at survival," Rhys said, his gaze unflinching, "then I would not give a *shit* that she made me fuck her for all those years."

Cassian flinched. The entire *room* flinched.

"If Amarantha showed up at that door right now," Rhys snarled, pointing toward the foyer entry, "and said she could buy us a chance at defeating Hybern, at keeping all of *you* alive, *I would thank the fucking Cauldron.*"

Mor shook her head, tears slipping free again. "You don't mean that."

"I do."

Rhys.

But the bond, the bridge between us . . . it was a howling void. A raging, dark tempest.

Too far—this was pushing them both too far. I tried to catch Cassian's gaze, but he was monitoring them closely, his golden-brown skin unnaturally pale. Azriel's shadows gathered close, half veiling him from view. And Amren—

Amren stepped between Rhys and Mor. They both towered over her.

"I kept this unit from breaking for forty-nine years," Amren said, eyes flaring bright as lightning. "I am not going to let you rip it to shreds now." She faced Mor. "Working with Keir and Eris is not forgiving them. And when this war is over, I will hunt them down and butcher them with you, if that is what you wish." Mor said nothing—though she at last looked away from Rhys.

"My father will poison this city."

"I will not allow him to," Amren said.

I believed her.

And I think Mor did, too, for the tears that continued sliding free . . . they seemed to shift, somehow.

Amren turned to Rhys, whose face had now edged toward—devastation.

I slid my hand through his. *I see you,* I said, giving him the words I'd once whispered all those months ago. *And it does not frighten me.*

Amren said to him, "You're a sneaky bastard. You always have been, and likely always will be. But it doesn't excuse you, boy, from not warning us. Warning her, not where those two monsters are involved. Yes, you made the right call—played it well. But you also played it badly."

Something like shame dimmed his eyes. "I'm sorry."

The words—to Mor, to Amren.

Amren's dark hair swayed as she assessed them. Mor just shook her head at last—more acceptance than denial.

I swallowed, my voice rough as I said, "This is war. Our allies are few and already don't trust us." I met each of them in the eye—my sister, Lucien, Mor, and Azriel and Cassian. Then Amren. Then my mate. I squeezed his hand at the guilt now sinking its claws deep into him. "You all have been to war and back—when I've never even set foot on a battlefield. But . . . I have to imagine that we will not last long if . . . we cleave apart. From within."

Stumbling, near-incoherent words, but Azriel said at last, "She's right."

Mor didn't so much as look in his direction. I could have sworn guilt clouded Azriel's eyes, there and gone in a blink.

Amren stepped back to Nesta's side as Cassian asked me, "What happened with the mirror?"

I shook my head. "Keir says it's mine, if I dare to take it. Apparently, what you see inside will break you—or drive you insane. No one's ever walked away from it."

Cassian swore.

"Exactly," I said. It was a risk perhaps none of us were entirely prepared to face. Not when we were all needed—each one of us.

Mor added a bit hoarsely, straightening the ebony pleats and panels of her gossamer gown, "My father spoke true about that. I was raised with legends of the mirror. None were pleasant. Or successful."

Cassian frowned at me, at Rhys. "So what—"

"You are talking about the Ouroboros," Amren said.

I blinked. Shit. *Shit*—

"Why do you want that mirror?" Her voice had slipped to a low timbre.

Rhys slid his free hand into his pocket. "If honesty is the theme of the night . . . Because the Bone Carver requested it."

Amren's nostrils flared. "You went to the Prison."

"Your old friends say hello," Cassian drawled, leaning a shoulder against the sitting room archway.

Amren's face tightened, Nesta glancing between them—carefully. Reading us. Especially as Amren's quicksilver eyes swirled. "Why did you go."

I opened my mouth, but the gold of Lucien's eye caught my attention. Snared it.

My hesitation must have been indication enough of my wariness.

Jaw tight with a hint of frustration, Lucien excused himself to his room. Frustration—and perhaps disappointment. I blocked it out—what it did to my stomach.

"We had some questions for the Carver." Cassian gave Amren a slash of a smile when Lucien was gone. "And we have some for you."

Amren's smoke-filled eyes flared. "You are going to unleash the Carver."

I said simply, "Yes." A one-monster army.

"That is impossible."

"I'll remind you that *you*, sweet Amren, escaped," Rhys countered smoothly. "And have stayed free. So it can be done. Perhaps you could tell us how you did it."

Cassian had stationed himself by the doorway, I realized, to be closer to Nesta. To grab her if Amren decided she didn't particularly care for where this conversation was headed. Or for any of the furniture in this room.

Precisely why Rhys now placed himself on Amren's other side—to draw her attention away from me, and Mor behind us, every muscle in her lithe body on alert.

Cassian was staring at Nesta—hard enough that my sister at last twisted toward him. Met his gaze. His head tilted—slightly. A silent order.

Nesta, to my shock, obeyed. Drifted over to Cassian's side as Amren replied to Rhys, "No."

"It wasn't a request," Rhys said.

He'd once admitted that merely questioning Amren had been something she'd allowed him to do only in recent years. But giving her an order, pushing her like this . . .

"Feyre and Cassian spoke to the Bone Carver. He wants the Ouroboros in exchange for serving us—fighting Hybern for us. But we need you to explain how to get him out." The bargain Rhys or I would strike with him would suffice to hold him to our will.

"Anything else?" Her voice was too calm, too sweet.

"When we're done with all of this," Rhys said, "then my promise from months ago still holds: use the Book to send yourself home, if you want."

Amren stared up at him. It was so quiet that the clock on the sitting room mantel could be heard. And beyond that—the fountain in the garden—

"Call off your dog," Amren said with that lethal tone.

Because the shadow in the corner behind Amren . . . that was Azriel. The obsidian hilt of Truth-Teller in his scarred hand. He'd moved without my realizing it—though I had no doubt the others had likely been aware.

Amren bared her teeth at him. Azriel's beautiful face didn't so much as shift.

Rhys remained where he was as he asked Amren, "Why won't you tell us?"

Cassian casually slid Nesta behind him, his fingers snagging in the skirts of her black gown. As if to reassure himself that she wasn't in Amren's direct path. Nesta only rose onto her toes to peer over his shoulder.

"Because the stone beneath this house has ears, the wind has ears—all of it listening," Amren said. "And if it reports back . . . They will remember, Rhysand, that they have not caught me. And I will not let them put me in that black pit again."

My ears hollowed out as a shield clicked into place. "No one will hear beyond this room."

Amren surveyed the books lying forgotten on the low table in the sitting room.

Her brows narrowed. "I had to give something up. I had to give *me* up. To walk out, I had to become something else entirely, something the Prison would not recognize. So I—I bound myself into this body."

I'd never heard her stumble over a word before.

"You said someone else bound you," Rhys questioned carefully.

"I lied—to cover what I'd done. So none could know. To escape the Prison, I made myself mortal. Immortal as you are, but . . . mortal compared to—to what I was. And what I was . . . I did not feel, the way you do. The way I do now. Some things—loyalty and wrath and curiosity—but not the full spectrum." Again, that faraway look. "I was perfect, according to some. I did not regret, did not mourn—and pain . . . I did not experience it. And yet . . . yet I wound up *here*, because I was not quite like the others. Even as—as what I was, I was different. Too curious. Too questioning. The day the rip appeared in the sky . . . it was curiosity that drove me. My brothers and sisters fled. Upon the orders of our ruler, we had just laid waste to twin cities, smote them wholly into rubble on the plain, and yet they *fled* from that rip in the world. But I wanted to look. I *wanted*. I was not built or bred to feel such selfish things as *want*. I'd seen what happened to those of my kind who strayed, who learned to place their needs first. Who developed . . . feeling. But I went through the tear in the sky. And here I am."

"And you gave all that up to get out of the Prison?" Mor asked softly.

"I yielded my grace—my perfect immortality. I knew that once I did . . . I would feel pain. And regret. I would want, and I would burn with it. I would . . . fall. But I was—the time locked away down there . . . I didn't care. I had not felt the wind on my face, had not smelled the rain . . . I did not even remember what they felt like. I did not remember sunlight."

It was to Azriel that her attention drifted—the shadowsinger's darkness pulling away to reveal eyes full of understanding. *Locked away.*

"So I bound myself into this body. I shoved my burning grace deep into me. I gave up everything I was. The cell door just . . . unlocked. And so I walked out."

A burning grace . . . That still smoldered far within her, visible only through the smoke in her gray eyes.

"That will be the cost of freeing the Carver," Amren said. "You will have to bind him into a body. Make him . . . Fae. And I doubt he will agree to it. Especially without the Ouroboros."

We were silent.

"You should have asked me before you went," she said, that sharpness returning to her tone. "I would have spared you the visit."

Rhysand swallowed. "Can you be—unbound?"

"Not by me."

"What would happen if you were?"

Amren stared at him for a long while. Then me. Cassian. Azriel. Mor. Nesta. Finally back to my mate. "I would not remember you. I would not care for any of you. I would either smite you or abandon you. What I feel now . . . it would be foreign to me—it would hold no sway. Everything I am, this body . . . it would cease to be."

"What *were* you," Nesta breathed, coming around Cassian to stand at his side.

Amren toyed with one of her black pearl earrings. "A messenger—and soldier-assassin. For a wrathful god who ruled a young world."

I could feel the questions of the others brewing. Rhys's eyes were near-glowing with them.

"Was Amren your name?" Nesta asked.

"No." The smoke swirled in her eyes. "I do not remember the name I was given. I used Amren because—it's a long story."

I almost begged her to tell it, but soft footsteps thudded, and then—

"Oh."

Elain started—enough so that I realized she couldn't hear us. Had no idea we were here, thanks to the shield that kept sound from escaping.

It instantly dropped. But my sister remained near the stairs. She'd covered her nightgown with a silk shawl of palest blue, her fingers grappling into the fabric as she held herself.

I went to her immediately. "Do you need anything?"

"No. I . . . I was sleeping, but I heard . . ." She shook her head. Blinked at our formal attire, the dark crown atop my head—and Rhysand's. "I didn't hear you."

Azriel stepped forward. "But you heard something else."

Elain seemed about to nod, but only backed away. "I think I was dreaming," she murmured. "I think I'm always dreaming these days."

"Let me get you some hot milk," I said, putting a hand on her elbow to guide her into the sitting room.

But Elain shook me off, heading back to the stairs. She said as she climbed the first steps, "I can hear her—crying."

I gripped the bottom post of the banister. "Who?"

"Everyone thinks she's dead." Elain kept walking. "But she's not. Only—different. Changed. As I was."

"Who," I pushed.

But Elain continued up the stairs, that shawl drooping down her back. Nesta stalked from Cassian's side to approach my own. We both sucked in a breath, to say what, I didn't know but—

"What did you see," Azriel said, and I tried not to flinch as I found him at my other side, not having seen him move. Again.

Elain paused halfway up the stairs. Slowly, she turned to look back at him. "I saw young hands wither with age. I saw a box of black stone. I saw a feather of fire land on snow and melt it."

My stomach dropped to the floor. One glance at Nesta confirmed that she felt it, too. Saw it.

Mad. Elain might very well have gone mad—

"It was angry," Elain said quietly. "It was so, so angry that something was taken. So it took something from them as punishment."

We said nothing. I didn't know *what* to say—what to even ask or demand. If the Cauldron had done something to *her* as well . . .

I faced Azriel, exposing my palms to him. "What does that *mean*?"

Azriel's hazel eyes churned as he studied my sister, her too-thin body. And without a word, he winnowed away. Mor watched the space where he'd been standing long after he was gone.

I waited until the others had left—Cassian and Rhys slipping away to ponder the possibilities or lack thereof of our would-be allies, Amren storming off to be rid of us entirely, and Mor striding out to enjoy what she deemed as her last few days of peace in this city, a brittleness still in her voice—before I cornered Nesta in the sitting room.

"What happened at the Hewn City—with you and Amren? You didn't mention it."

"It was fine."

I clenched my jaw. "What happened?"

"She brought me to a room full of treasure. Strange objects. And it . . ." She tugged at the tight sleeve of her gown. "Some of it wanted to *hurt* us. As if it were alive—aware. Like . . . like in all those stories and lies we were fed over the wall."

"Are you all right?" I couldn't find any signs of harm on either of them, and neither had said anything to suggest—

"It was a training exercise. With a form of magic designed to repel intruders." The words were recited. "As the wall will likely be. She wanted me to breach the defenses—find weaknesses."

"And repair them?"

"Just find the weaknesses. Repairing is another thing," Nesta said, her eyes going distant as she frowned at the still-open books on the low table before the fireplace.

I sighed. "So . . . that went right, at least."

Those eyes went razor-sharp again. "I failed. Every time. So, no. It did not go right."

I didn't know what to say. Sympathy would likely earn me a

tongue-lashing. So I opted for another route. "We need to do something about Elain."

Nesta stiffened. "And what solution do you propose, exactly? Letting your mate into her mind to scramble things around?"

"I'd never do that. I don't think Rhys can even . . . fix things like that."

Nesta paced in front of the darkened fireplace. "Everything has a cost. Maybe the cost of her youth and immortality was losing part of her sanity."

My knees wobbled enough that I took a seat on the deep-cushioned couch. "What was your cost?"

Nesta stopped moving. "Perhaps it was to see Elain suffer—while I got away unscathed."

I shot to my feet. "Nesta—"

"Don't bother." But I trailed her as she strode for the stairs. To where Lucien was now descending the steps—and winced at the sight of her approach.

He gave her a wide berth as she stormed past him. One look at his taut face had me bracing myself—and returning to the sitting room.

I slumped into the nearest armchair, surprised to find myself still in my black dress as the fabric scraped against my bare skin. How long had I been back from the Hewn City? Thirty minutes? Less? And had the Prison only been that morning?

It felt like days ago. I rested my head against the embroidered back of the chair and watched Lucien take a seat on the rolled arm of the nearest couch. "Long day?"

I grunted my response.

That metal eye tightened. "I thought the Prison was another myth."

"Well, it's not."

He weighed my tone, and crossed his arms. "Let me do something. About Elain. I heard—from my room. Everything that happened just now. It wouldn't hurt to have a healer look her over. Externally and internally."

I was tired enough that I could barely summon the breath to ask, "Do you think the Cauldron made her insane?"

"I think she went through something terrible," Lucien countered carefully. "And it wouldn't hurt to have your best healer do a thorough examination."

I rubbed my hand over my face. "All right." My breath snagged on the words. "Tomorrow morning." I managed a shallow nod, rallying my strength to rise from the chair. Heavy—there was an old heaviness in me. Like I could sleep for a hundred years and it wouldn't be enough.

"Please tell me," Lucien said when I crossed the threshold into the foyer. "What the healer says. And if—if you need me for anything."

I gave him one final nod, speech suddenly beyond me.

I knew Nesta still wasn't asleep as I walked past her room. Knew she'd heard every word of our conversation thanks to that Fae hearing. And I knew she heard as I listened at Elain's door, knocked once, and poked my head in to find her asleep—breathing.

I sent a request to Madja, Rhysand's preferred healer, to come the next day at eleven. I did not explain why or who or what. Then went into my bedroom, crawled onto the mattress, and cried.

I didn't really know why.

Strong, broad hands rubbed down my spine, and I opened my eyes to find the room wholly black, Rhysand perched on the mattress beside me. "Do you want anything to eat?" His voice was soft—tentative.

I didn't raise my head from the pillow. "I feel . . . heavy again," I breathed, voice breaking.

Rhys said nothing as he gathered me up into his arms. He was still in his jacket, as if he'd just come in from wherever he'd been talking with Cassian.

In the dark, I breathed in his scent, savored his warmth. "Are you all right?"

Rhys was quiet for a long minute. "No."

I slid my arms around him, holding him tightly.

"I should have found another way," he said.

I stroked my fingers through his silken hair.

Rhys murmured, "If she . . ." His swallow was audible. "If she showed up at this house . . ." I knew who he meant. "I would kill her. Without even letting her speak. I would kill her."

"I know." I would, too.

"You asked me at the library," he whispered. "Why I . . . Why I'd rather take all of this upon myself. Tonight is why. Seeing Mor *cry* is why. I made a bad call. Tried to find some other way around this shit-hole we're in." And had lost something—*Mor* had lost something—in the process.

We held each other in silence for minutes. Hours. Two souls, twining in the dark. I lowered my shields, let him in fully. His mind curled around mine.

"Would you risk looking into it—the Ouroboros?" I asked.

"Not yet," was all Rhys said, holding me tighter. "Not yet."

CHAPTER 28

I dragged myself out of bed by sheer will the next morning.

Amren had said the Carver wouldn't bind himself into a Fae body—had *claimed* that.

But it wouldn't hurt to try. If it gave us the slightest chance of holding out, of keeping Rhys from giving everything . . .

He was already gone by the time I awoke. I gritted my teeth as I dressed in my leathers and winnowed to the House of Wind.

I had my wings ready as I hit the wards protecting it, and managed a decent-enough glide into the open-air training ring on its flat top.

Cassian was already waiting, hands on his hips. Watching as I eased down, down . . .

Too fast. My feet skipped over the dirt, bouncing me up, up—

"*Backflap*—"

His warning was too late.

I slammed into a wall of crimson before I could get a face full of the ruddy rock, but—I swore, pride skinned as much as my palms as I staggered back, my wings unwieldy behind me. Cassian's shoulders shook as he reined in a laugh, and I gave him a vulgar gesture in return.

"If you go in for a landing that way, make sure you have room."

I scowled. "Lesson learned."

"Or space to bank and circle until you slow—"

"I get it."

Cassian held up his hands, but the amusement faded as he watched me dismiss the wings and stalk toward him. "You want to go hard today, or take it easy?"

I didn't think the others gave him enough credit—for noticing the shift in someone's emotional current. To command legions, I supposed, he needed to be able to read that sort of thing, judge when his soldiers or enemies were strong or breaking or broken.

I peered inside, to that place where I now felt like quicksand, and said, "Hard. I want to limp out of here." I peeled off the leather jacket and rolled up the sleeves of my white shirt.

Cassian swept an assessing stare over me. He murmured, "It helps me, too—the physical activity, the training." He rolled his shoulders as I began to stretch. "It's always helped me focus and center myself. And after last night . . ." He tied back his dark hair. "I definitely need it—this."

I held my leg folded behind me, my muscles protesting at the stretch. "I suppose there are worse methods of coping."

A lopsided grin. "Indeed there are."

Azriel's lesson afterward consisted of standing in a breeze and trying to memorize his instructions on currents and downdrafts, on how heat and cold could shape wind and speed. Throughout it, he was quiet—removed. Even by his standards.

I made the mistake of asking if he'd spoken to Mor since he'd left last night.

No, he had not. And that was that.

Even if he kept flexing his scarred hand at his side. As if recalling the sensation of the hand she'd whipped free of his touch during that meeting. Over and over. I didn't dare tell him that he'd made the right call—that perhaps he should talk to Mor, rather than let the guilt eat at him. The two of them had enough between them without me shoving myself into it.

I was indeed limping by the time I returned to the town house hours later, finding Mor at the dining table, munching on a giant pastry she'd grabbed from a bakery on her way in.

"You look like a team of horses trampled you," she said around her food.

"Good," I said, taking the pastry out of her hand and finishing it off. She squawked in outrage, but snapped her fingers, and a plate of carved melon from the kitchen down the hall appeared on the polished table before her.

Right atop the pile of what looked to be letters on various pieces of stationery. "What's that?" I said, wiping the crumbs from my mouth.

"The first of the High Lords' responses," she said sweetly, plucking up a slice of the green fruit and biting off a chunk. No hint of last night's rage and fear.

"That pleasant, hmm?"

"Helion's came first this morning. Between all the innuendo, I think he said he'd be willing to . . . join us."

I lifted my brows. "That's good—isn't it?"

A shrug. "Helion, we weren't worried about. The other two . . ." She finished off the melon, chewing wetly. "Thesan says he'll come, but won't do it unless it's in a truly neutral and safe location. Kallias . . . he doesn't trust any of us after . . . Under the Mountain. He wants to bring armed guards."

Day, Dawn, and Winter. Our closest allies. "No word from anyone else?" My gut tightened.

"No. Spring, Autumn, and Summer haven't sent a reply."

"We don't have much time until the meeting. What if they refuse to reply at all?" I didn't have the nerve to wonder aloud if Eris would be good to his word and make sure his father attended—and joined our cause. Not with the light back in her face.

Mor picked up another slice of melon. "Then we'll have to decide if Rhys and I will go drag them by their necks to this meeting, or if we'll have it without them."

"I'd suggest the second option." Mor furrowed her brows. "The first," I clarified, "doesn't sound conducive to actually forming an alliance."

Though I was surprised that Tarquin hadn't responded. Even with his blood feud with us . . . The male I'd met, whom I still admired so much . . . Surely he'd want to ally against Hybern. Unless he now wanted to ally *with* them to ensure Rhys and I were wiped off the map forever.

"We'll see," was all Mor said.

I blew out a breath through my nose. "About last night—"

"It's fine. It's nothing." The swiftness with which she spoke suggested anything but.

"It's not nothing. You're *allowed* to feel that way."

Mor fluffed her hair. "Well, it won't help us win this war."

"No. But . . . I'm not sure what to say."

Mor stared toward the window for a long moment. "I understand why Rhys did it. The position we were in. Eris is . . . You know what he is like. And if he was indeed threatening to sell information about your gifts to his father . . . Mother above, *I* would have made the same bargain with Eris to keep Beron from hunting you." Something in my chest eased at that. "It's just . . . My father knew—the second he heard of this place, he probably knew what it meant to me. There would have been no other asking price for my father's help in this war. None. Rhys knew that as well. Tried to bring Eris into it to sweeten the deal for my father—to possibly avoid this outcome with Velaris altogether."

I raised my brows in silent question.

"We talked—Rhys and I. This morning. While Cassian was kicking your ass."

I snorted. "What about Azriel?" So much for my decision to stay out of it.

Mor resumed picking at the melon. "Az . . . He had a tough call to make, when Eris found him. He . . ." She chewed on her lip. "I don't know why I expected him to side with me, why it caught me so off guard." I refrained from suggesting she tell him that. Mor shrugged. "It just . . . it all took me by surprise. And I will never be happy about any of these terms, but . . . My father wins, Eris wins, all the males like them *win* if I let it get to me. If I let it impact my joy, my life. My relationships with all of you." She sighed at the ceiling. "I hate war."

"Likewise."

"Not just for the death and awfulness," Mor went on. "But because of what it does to us. These decisions."

I nodded, even if I was only starting to understand. The choices and the costs.

I opened my mouth, but a knock on the front door sounded. I glanced to the clock in the sitting room across the foyer. Right. The healer.

I'd mentioned to Elain this morning that Madja was coming to see her at eleven, and I'd gotten a noncommittal response. Better than outright refusal, I supposed.

"Are you going to answer the door, or should I?"

I made a vulgar gesture at the sheer sass in Mor's question, but my friend gripped my hand as I rose from my chair.

"If you need anything . . . I'll be right here."

I gave Mor a small, grateful smile. "As will I."

She was still smiling at me as I took a deep breath before heading for the entry.

The healer found nothing.

I believed her—if only because Madja was one of the few High Fae I'd seen whose dark skin was etched with wrinkles, her hair spin-drift fine with age. Her brown eyes were still clear and kindled with an inner warmth, and her knobby hands remained steady as she passed them over Elain's body while my sister lay patiently, silently, on the bed.

Magic, sweet and cooling, had thrummed from the female, filling Elain's bedroom. And when she had gently laid her hands on either side of Elain's head and I'd started, Madja had only smiled wryly over her thin shoulder and told me to relax.

Nesta, sharp-eyed in the corner, had kept quiet.

After a long minute, Madja asked us to join her in fetching Elain a cup of tea—with a pointed glance to the door. We both took the invitation and left our sister in her sunlit room.

"What do you mean, *nothing* is wrong with her?" Nesta hissed under her breath as the ancient female braced a hand on the stair railing to help herself down. I kept beside the healer, a hand in easy reach of her elbow, should she need it.

Madja, I reminded myself, had healed Cassian and Azriel—and countless injuries beyond that. She'd healed Rhys's wings during the War. She looked ancient, but I had no doubt of her stamina—or sheer will to help her patients.

Madja didn't deign to answer Nesta until we were at the bottom of the steps. Lucien was already waiting in the sitting room, Mor still lingering in the dining room. Both of them rose to their feet, but remained in their respective rooms, flanking the foyer.

"What I mean," Madja said at last, sizing up Nesta, then me, "is that I can find nothing wrong with her. Her body is fine—too thin and in need of more food and fresh air, but nothing amiss. And as for her mind . . . I cannot enter it."

I blinked. "She has a shield?"

"She is Cauldron-Made," the healer said, again looking over Nesta. "You are not like the rest of us. I cannot pierce the places it left its mark most deeply." The mind. The soul. She shot me a warning glance. "And I would not try if I were you, Lady."

"But do you think there's something wrong, even if there are no signs?" Nesta pushed.

"I have seen the victims of trauma before. Her symptoms match well with many of those invisible wounds. But . . . she was also Made by something I do not understand. Is there something wrong with her?" Madja chewed over the words. "I do not like that word—*wrong*. Different, perhaps. Changed."

"Does she need further help?" Nesta said through her teeth.

The ancient healer jerked her chin toward Lucien. "See what he can do. If anyone can sense if something is amiss, it's a mate."

"How." The word was barely more than a barked command.

I braced myself to warn Nesta to be polite, but Madja said to my sister, as if she were a small child, "The mating bond. It is a bridge between souls."

The healer's tone made my sister stiffen, but Madja was already hobbling for the front door. She pointed at Lucien as she saw herself out. "Try sitting down with her. Just talking—sensing. See what you pick up. But don't push." Then she was gone.

I whirled on Nesta. "A little *respect*, Nesta—"

"Call another healer."

"Not if you're going to bark them out of the house."

"Call another healer."

Mor strode for us with deceptive calm, and Nesta gave her a withering glare.

I caught Lucien's eye. "Would you try it?"

Nesta snarled, "Don't you even *attempt*—"

"Be quiet," I snapped.

Nesta blinked.

I bared my teeth at her. "He will *try*. And if he doesn't find anything amiss, we'll consider bringing another healer."

"You're just going to drag her down here?"

"I'm going to invite her."

Nesta faced Mor, still watching from the archway. "And what will *you* be doing?"

Mor gave my sister a half smile. "I'll be sitting with Feyre. Keeping an eye on things."

Lucien muttered something about not needing to be monitored, and we all looked at him with raised brows.

He just lifted his hands, claimed he wanted to freshen up, and headed down the hall.

CHAPTER 29

It was the most uncomfortable thirty minutes I could recall.

Mor and I sipped chilled mint tea by the bay window, the replies of the three High Lords piled on the little table between our twin chairs, pretending to be watching the summer-kissed street beyond us, the children, High Fae and faerie, darting about with kites and streamers and all manner of toys.

Pretending, while Lucien and Elain sat in stilted silence by the dim fireplace, an untouched tea service between them. I didn't dare ask if he was trying to get into her head, or if he was feeling a bond similar to that black adamant bridge between Rhys's mind and my own. If a normal mating bond felt wholly different.

A teacup rattled and rasped against a saucer, and Mor and I glanced over.

Elain had picked up the teacup, and now sipped from it without so much as looking toward him.

In the dining room across the hall, I knew Nesta was craning her neck to look.

Knew, because Amren snapped at my sister to pay attention.

They were building walls—in their minds, Amren had told me as she ordered Nesta to sit at the dining room table, directly across from her.

Walls that Amren was teaching her to sense—to find the holes she'd laid throughout. And repair them. If the fell objects at the Court of Nightmares had not allowed my sister to grasp what must be done, then this was their next attempt—a different, invisible route. Not all magic was flash and glittering, Amren had declared, and then shooed me out.

But any sign of that power within my sister . . . I did not hear it or see it or feel it. And neither offered any explanation for what it was, exactly, that they were trying to coax from within her.

Outside the house, movement again caught our eye, and we found Rhys and Cassian strolling in through the low front gate, returning from their first meeting with Keir's Darkbringer army commanders—already rallying and preparing. At least that much had gone right yesterday.

Both of them spotted us in the window within a heartbeat. Stopped cold.

Don't come in, I warned him through the bond. *Lucien is trying to sense what's wrong with Elain. Through the bond.*

Rhys murmured what I'd said to Cassian, who now angled his head, much in the way I had no doubt Nesta had done, to peer beyond us.

Rhys said wryly, *Does Elain know this?*

She was invited down for tea. So we're having it.

Rhys muttered again to Cassian, who choked on a laugh and turned right around, heading into the street. Rhys lingered, sliding his hands into his pockets. *He's getting a drink. I'm inclined to join him. When can I return without fearing for my life?*

I gave him a vulgar gesture through the window. *Such a big, strong Illyrian warrior.*

Illyrian warriors know when to pick their battles. And with Nesta watching everything like a hawk and you two circling like vultures . . . I know who will walk away from that fight.

I made the gesture again, and Mor figured out enough of what was being said that she echoed the movement. Rhys laughed quietly and sketched a bow.

The High Lords sent replies, I said as he strolled away. *Day, Dawn, and Winter will come.*

I know, he said. *And I just received word from Cresseida that Tarquin is contemplating it.*

Better than nothing. I said as much.

Rhys smiled at me over his shoulder. *Enjoy your tea, you overbearing chaperone.*

I could have used a chaperone around you, you realize.

You had four *of them in this house.*

I smiled as he finally reached the low front gate where Cassian waited, apparently using the momentary delay to stretch out his wings, to the delight of the half-dozen children now gawking at them.

Amren hissed from the other room, "*Focus.*" The dining table rattled.

The sound seemed to startle Elain, who swiftly set down her teacup. She rose to her feet, and Lucien shot to his.

"I'm sorry," he blurted.

"What—what was that?"

Mor put a hand on my knee to keep me from rising, too.

"It—it was a tug. On the bond."

Amren snapped, "*Don't you*—wicked girl."

Then Nesta was standing in the threshold. "What did you do." The words were as sharp as a blade.

Lucien looked to her, then over to me. A muscle feathered in his jaw. "Nothing," he said, and again faced his mate. "I'm sorry—if that unsettled you."

Elain sidled toward Nesta, who seemed to be at a near-simmer. "It felt . . . strange," Elain breathed. "Like you pulled on a thread tied to a rib."

Lucien exposed his palms to her. "I'm sorry."

Elain only stared at him for a long moment. And any lucidity faded away as she shook her head, blinking twice, and said to Nesta, "Twin ravens are coming, one white and one black."

Nesta hid the devastation well. The frustration. "What can I get you, Elain?"

Only with Elain did she use that voice.

But Elain shook her head once more. "Sunshine."

Nesta cut me a furious stare before guiding our sister down the hall—to the sunny garden in the back.

Lucien waited until the glass door had opened and closed before he loosed a long breath.

"There's a bond—it's a real thread," he said, more to himself than us.

"And?" Mor asked.

Lucien ran both hands through his long red hair. His skin was darker—a deep golden-brown, compared to the paleness of Eris's coloring. "And I got to Elain's end of it when she ran off."

"Did you sense anything?"

"No—I didn't have time. I *felt* her, but . . ." A blush stained his cheek. Whatever he'd felt, it wasn't what we were looking for. Even if we had no idea what, precisely, that was.

"We can try again—another day," I offered.

Lucien nodded, but looked unconvinced.

Amren snapped from the dining room, "Someone go retrieve your sister. Her lesson isn't over."

I sighed. "Yes, Amren."

Lucien's attention slid behind me, to the various letters on different styles and makes of paper. That golden eye narrowed. As Tamlin's emissary, he no doubt recognized them. "Let me guess: they said yes, but picking the location is now going to be the headache."

Mor frowned. "Any suggestions?"

Lucien tied back his hair with a strap of brown leather. "Do you have a map?"

I supposed that left me to retrieve Nesta.

"That pine tree wasn't there a moment ago."

Azriel let out a quiet laugh from where he sat atop a boulder two days later, watching me pluck pine needles out of my hair and jacket. "Judging by its size, I'd say it's been there for . . . two hundred years at least."

I scowled, brushing off the shards of bark and my bruised pride.

That coldness, that aloofness that had been there in the wake of Mor's anger and rejection . . . It'd warmed. Either from Mor choosing to sit next to him at dinner last night—a silent offer of forgiveness—or simply needing time to recover from it. Even if I could have sworn some kernel of guilt had flickered every time Azriel had looked at Mor. What Cassian had thought of it, of his own anger toward Azriel . . . he'd been all smiles and lewd comments. Glad all was back to normal—for now at least.

My cheeks burned as I scaled the boulder he perched on, the drop at least fifteen feet to the forest floor below, the lake a sparkling sprawl peeking through the pine trees. Including the tree I'd collided with face-first on my latest attempt to leap off the boulder and simply *sail* to the lake.

I braced my hands on my hips, examining the drop, the trees, the lake beyond. "What did I do wrong?"

Azriel, who had been sharpening Truth-Teller in his lap, flicked his hazel eyes up to me. "Aside from the tree?"

The shadowsinger had a sense of humor. Dry and quiet, but . . . alone together, it came out far more often than it did amongst our group.

I'd spent these past two days either poring over ancient volumes for any hint on repairing the wall to hand over to Amren and Nesta, who continued to silently, invisibly build and mend walls within their minds, or debating with Rhys and the others about how to reply to the volley of letters now being exchanged with the other High Lords regarding where the meeting would take place. Lucien had indeed given us an initial location, and several more when those were struck down. But that was to be expected, Lucien had said, as if he'd arranged such things countless times. Rhys had only nodded in agreement—and approval.

And when I wasn't doing that . . . I was combing through *more* books, any and all Clotho could find me, all regarding the Ouroboros. How to master it.

The mirror was notorious. Every known philosopher had ruminated on it. Some had dared face it—and gone mad. Some had approached—and run away in terror.

I could not find an account of anyone who had mastered it. Faced what lurked within and walked away with the mirror in their possession.

Save for the Weaver in the Wood—who certainly seemed insane enough, perhaps thanks to the mirror she'd so dearly loved. Or perhaps whatever evil lurked in her had tainted the mirror, too. Some of the philosophers had suggested as much, though they hadn't known her name—only that a dark queen had once possessed it, cherished it. Spied on the world with it—and used it to hunt down beautiful young maidens to keep her eternally young.

I supposed Keir's family owning the Ouroboros for millennia suggested the success rate of walking away was low. It was not heartening. Not when all the texts agreed on one thing: there was no way around it. No loophole. Facing the terror within . . . that was the only route to claim it.

Which meant I perhaps had to consider alternatives—other ways to entice the Bone Carver to join us. When I found a moment.

Azriel sheathed his legendary fighting knife and examined the wings I'd spread wide. "You're trying to steer with your arms. The muscles are in the wings themselves—and in your back. Your arms are unnecessary—they're more for balancing than anything. And even that's mostly a mental comfort."

It was more words than I'd ever heard from him.

He lifted a brow at my gaping, and I shut my mouth. I frowned at the drop ahead. "Again?" I grumbled.

A soft laugh. "We can find a lower ledge to jump from, if you want."

I cringed. "You said *this* was low."

Azriel leaned back on his hands and waited. Patient, cool.

But I felt the bark tear into my palms, the thud of my knees into its rough side—

"You are immortal," he said quietly. "You are very hard to break." A pause. "That's what I told myself."

"Hard to break," I said glumly, "but it still *hurts*."

"Tell that to the tree."

I huffed a laugh. "I know the drop isn't far, and I know it won't kill me. Can't you just . . . *push* me?"

For it was that initial leap of utter faith, that initial lurch into motion that had my limbs locking up.

"No." A simple answer.

I still hesitated.

Useless—this fear. I had faced down the Attor, falling through the sky for a thousand feet.

And the rage at its memory, at what it had done with its miserable life, what more like it might do again, had me gritting my teeth and sprinting off the boulder.

I snapped my wings out wide, my back protesting as they caught the wind, but my lower half began to drop, my legs a dead weight as my core yielded—

The infernal tree rose up before me, and I swerved hard to the right.

Right into another tree.

Wings first.

The sound of bone and sinew on wood, then earth, hit me before the pain did. So did Azriel's soft curse.

A small noise came out of me. The stinging of my palms registered first—then in my knees.

Then my back—

"Shit," was all I could say as Azriel knelt before me.

"You're all right. Just stunned."

The world was still reordering itself.

"You banked well," he offered.

"Into another tree."

"Being aware of your surroundings is half of flying."

"You said that already," I snapped. He had. A dozen times just this morning.

Azriel only sat on his heels and offered me a hand up. My flesh burned as I gripped his fingers, a mortifying number of pine needles and splinters tumbling off me. My back throbbed enough that I lowered my wings, not caring if they dragged in the dirt as Azriel led me toward the lake edge.

In the blinding sun off the turquoise water, his shadows were gone, his face stark and clear. More . . . human than I had ever seen him.

"There's no chance that I'll be able to fly in the legions, is there?" I asked, kneeling beside him as he tended to my skinned palms with expert care and gentleness. The sun was brutal against his scars, hiding not one twisted, rippling splotch.

"Likely not," he said. My chest hollowed out at that. "But it doesn't hurt to practice until the last possible moment. You never know when any measure of training may be useful."

I winced as he fished out a large splinter from my palm, then washed it clean.

"It was very hard for me to learn how to fly," he said. I didn't dare respond. "Most Illyrians learn as toddlers. But . . . I assume Rhysand told you the particulars of my early childhood."

I nodded. He finished the one hand and started on the other. "Because I was so old, I had a fear of flying—and did not trust my instincts. It was an . . . embarrassment to be taught so late. Not just to me, but to all in the war-camp once I arrived. But I learned, often going off by myself. Cassian, of course, found me first. Mocked me, beat me to hell, then offered to train me. Rhys was there the next day. They taught me to fly."

He finished my other hand, and sat on the shore, the stones murmuring as they shifted beneath him. I sat beside him, bracing my sore palms faceup on my knees, letting my wings sag behind me.

"Because it was such an effort . . . A few years after the War, Rhys brought me back a story. It was a gift—the story. For me. He—he went to see Miryam and Drakon in their new home, the visit so secret even we hadn't known it was happening until he returned. We knew their people hadn't drowned in the sea, as everyone believed, as they wanted people to believe. You see, when Miryam freed her people from the queen of the Black Land, she led all of them—nearly fifty thousand of them—across the desert, all the way to the shores of the Erythrian Sea, Drakon's aerial legion providing cover. But they got to the sea and found the ships they'd arranged to transport them over the narrow channel to the next kingdom had been destroyed. Destroyed by the queen herself, who sent her lingering armies to drag her former slaves back.

"Drakon's people—the Seraphim—are winged. Like us, but their wings are feathered. And unlike us, their army and society allow women to lead, to fight, to rule. All of them are gifted with mighty magic of wind and air. And when they beheld that army charging after them, they knew their own force was too small to face them. So they cleaved the sea itself—made a path through the water, all the way through the channel, and ordered the humans to run.

"They did, but Miryam insisted on remaining behind until every last one of her people had crossed. Not one human would she leave behind. Not one. They were about halfway through the crossing when the army reached them. The Seraphim were spent—their magic could barely hold the sea passage. And Drakon knew that if they held it any longer . . . that army would make it across and butcher the humans on the other side. The Seraphim fought off the vanguard on the floor of the sea, and it was bloody and brutal and chaotic . . . And during the melee, they didn't see Miryam skewered by the queen herself. Drakon didn't see. He thought she made it out, carried by one of his soldiers. He ordered the parted sea to come down to drown the enemy force.

"But a young Seraphim cartographer named Nephelle saw Miryam go down. Nephelle's lover was one of Drakon's generals, and it was she who realized Miryam and Nephelle were missing. Drakon was frantic, but their magic was spent and no force in the world could hold back the sea as it barreled down, and no one could reach his mate in time. But Nephelle did.

"Nephelle, you see, was a cartographer because she'd been rejected from the legion's fighting ranks. Her wings were too small, the right one somewhat malformed. And she was slight—short enough that she'd be a dangerous gap in the front lines when they fought shield to shield. Drakon had let her try out for the legion as a courtesy to her lover, but Nephelle failed. She could barely carry the Seraphim shield, and her smaller wings hadn't been strong enough to keep up with the others. So she had made herself invaluable as a cartographer during the War, helping Drakon and her lover find the geographical advantages in their battles. And she became Miryam's dearest friend during those long months as well.

"And that day on the seafloor, Nephelle remembered that her friend had been in the back of the line. She returned for her, even as all others fled for the distant shore. She found Miryam skewered on the queen's spear, bleeding out. The sea wall started to come down—on the opposite shore. Killing the approaching army first—racing toward them.

"Miryam told Nephelle to save herself. But Nephelle would not abandon her friend. She picked her up and flew."

Azriel's voice was soft with awe.

"When Rhys spoke to Drakon about it years later, he still didn't have words to describe what happened. It defied all logic, all training. Nephelle, who had never been strong enough to hold a Seraphim shield, carried Miryam—triple the weight. And more than that . . . She *flew*. The sea was crashing down upon them, but Nephelle flew like the best of Seraphim warriors. The seafloor was a labyrinth of jagged rocks, too narrow for the Seraphim to fly through. They'd tried during their escape and crashed into them. But Nephelle, with her smaller wings . . . Had they been *one inch* wider, she would not have fit. And more than that . . . Nephelle soared through them, Miryam dying in her arms, as fast and skilled as the greatest of Seraphim. Nephelle, who had been passed over, who had been forgotten . . . She outraced death itself. There was not a foot of room between her and the water on either side of her when she shot up from the seafloor; not half of that rising up at her feet. And yet her too-small wingspan, that deformed wing . . . they did not fail her. Not once. Not for one wing beat."

My eyes burned.

"She made it. Suffice to say her lover made Nephelle her wife that night, and Miryam . . . well, she is alive today because of Nephelle." Azriel picked up a flat, white stone and turned it over in his hands. "Rhys told me the story when he returned. And since then we have privately adapted the Nephelle Philosophy with our own armies."

I raised a brow. Azriel shrugged. "We—Rhys, Cass, and I—will occasionally remind each other that what we think to be our greatest weakness can sometimes be our biggest strength. And that the most unlikely person can alter the course of history."

"The Nephelle Philosophy."

He nodded. "Apparently, every year in their kingdom, they have the Nephelle Run to honor her flight. On dry land, but . . . She and her wife crown a new victor every year in commemoration of what happened that day." He chucked the stone back amongst its brethren on the shore, the sound clattering over the water. "So we'll train, Feyre, until the last possible day. Because we never know if just one extra hour will make the difference."

I weighed his words, Nephelle's story. I rose to my feet and spread my wings. "Then let's try again."

I groaned as I limped into our bedroom that night to find Rhys sitting at the desk, poring over more books.

"I warned you that Azriel's a hard bastard," he said without looking at me. He lifted a hand, and water gurgled in the adjacent bathing room.

I grumbled a thank-you and trudged toward it, gritting my teeth against the agony in my back, my thighs, my bones. Every part *hurt*, and since the muscles needed to re-form around the wings, I had to carry *them*, too. Their scraping along the wood and carpet, then wood again, was the only sound beyond my weary feet. I beheld the steaming bath that would require some balancing to get into and whimpered.

Even removing my clothes would entail using muscles that had nearly given out.

A chair scraped in the bedroom, followed by cat-soft feet, then—

"I'm sure you already know this, but you need to actually climb into a bath to get clean—not stare at it."

I didn't have the strength to even glare at him, and I managed all of one stumbling, stiff step toward the water when he caught me.

My clothes vanished, presumably to the laundry downstairs, and Rhys swept me into his arms, lowering my naked body into the water. With the wings, the fit was tight, and—

I groaned from deep in my throat at the glorious heat and didn't bother to do anything other than lean my head against the back of the tub.

"I'll be right back," he said, and left the bathroom, then the bedroom itself.

By the time he returned, I only knew I'd fallen asleep thanks to the hand he put on my shoulder. "Out," he said, but lifted me himself, toweled me off, and led me to the bed.

He lay me down belly-first, and I noted the oils and balms he'd set there, the faint odor of rosemary and—something I was too tired to notice but smelled lovely floating to me. His hands gleamed as he applied generous amounts to his palms, and then his hands were on me.

My groan was about as undignified as they came as he kneaded the aching muscles of my back. The sorer areas drew out rather pathetic-sounding whimpers, but he rubbed them gently, until the tension was a dull ache rather than sharp, blinding pain.

And then he started on my wings.

Relief and ecstasy, as muscles eased and those sensitive areas were lovingly, tauntingly grazed over.

My toes curled, and just as he reached the sensitive spot that had my stomach clenching, his hands slid to my calves. He began a slow progression, higher and higher, up my thighs, teasing strokes between them that left me panting through my nose. Rising up until he got to my backside, where his massaging was equally professional and sinful. And then up—up my lower back, to my wings.

His touch turned different. Exploring. Broad strokes and feather-light ones, arches and swirls and direct, searing lines.

My core heated, turning molten, and I bit down on my lip as he lightly scraped a fingernail so, so close to that inner, sensitive spot. "Too bad you're so sore from training," Rhys mused, making idle, lazy circles.

I could only manage a garbled strand of words that were both plea and insult.

He leaned in, his breath warming the space of skin between my wings. "Did I ever tell you that you have the dirtiest mouth I've ever heard?"

I muttered words that only offered more proof of that claim.

He chuckled and skimmed the edge of that sensitive spot, right as his other hand slid between my legs.

Brazenly, I lifted my hips in silent demand. But he just circled with a finger, as lazy as the strokes along my wing. He kissed my spine. "How shall I make love to you tonight, Feyre darling?"

I writhed, rubbing against the folds of the blankets beneath me, desperate for any sort of friction as he dangled me over that edge.

"So impatient," he purred, and that finger glided into me. I moaned, the sensation too much, too consuming, with his hand between my legs and the other stroking closer and closer to that spot on my wing, a predator circling prey.

"Will it ever stop?" he mused, more to himself than me as another finger joined the one sliding in and out of me with taunting, indolent strokes. "Wanting you—every hour, every breath. I don't think I can stand a thousand years of this." My hips moved with him, driving him deeper. "Think of how my productivity will plummet."

I growled something at him that was likely *not* very romantic, and he chuckled, slipping out both fingers. I made a little whining noise of protest.

Until his mouth replaced where his fingers had been, his hands gripping my hips to raise me up, to lend him better access as he feasted on me. I groaned, the sound muffled by the pillow, and he only delved deeper, taunting and teasing with every stroke.

A low moan broke from me, my hips rolling. Rhys's grip on them tightened, holding me still for his ministrations. "I never got to take you in the library," he said, dragging his tongue right up my center. "We'll have to remedy that."

"Rhys." His name was a plea on my lips.

"Hmmm," was all he said, a rumble of the sound against me . . . I panted, hands fisting in the sheets.

His hands drifted from my hips at last, and I again breathed his name, in thanks and relief and anticipation of him at last giving me what I wanted—

But his mouth closed around the bundle of nerves at the apex of my thighs while his hand . . . He went right to that damned spot at the inner edge of my left wing and stroked lightly.

My climax tore through me with a hoarse cry, sending me soaring out of my body. And when the shuddering ripples and starlight faded . . .

A bone-weary exhaustion settled over me, permanent and unending as the mating bond between us. Rhys curled into bed behind me, tucking my wings in so he could fold me against him. "That was a fun experiment," he murmured into my ear.

I could feel him against my backside, hard and ready, but when I made to reach for him, Rhys's arms only tightened around me. "Sleep, Feyre," he told me.

So I laid a hand on his forearm, savoring the corded strength beneath, and nestled my head back against his chest. "I wish I had days to spend with you—like this," I managed to say as my eyelids drooped. "Just me and you."

"We will." He kissed my hair. "We will."

CHAPTER 30

I was still sore enough the next day that I had to send word to Cassian I wasn't training with him. Or Azriel.

A mistake, perhaps, given that both of them showed up at the door to the town house within minutes, the former demanding what the hell was wrong with me, the latter bearing a tin of salve to help with the aches in my back.

I thanked Azriel for the salve and told Cassian to mind his own business.

And then asked him to fly Nesta up to the House of Wind for me, since I certainly couldn't fly her in—even for a few feet after winnowing.

My sister, it seemed, had found nothing in her books about repairing the wall—and since no one had yet shown her the library . . . I'd volunteered. Especially since Lucien had left before breakfast for a library across the city to look up anything in regard to fixing the wall, a task I'd been more than willing to hand over. I might have felt guilty for never giving him a proper tour of Velaris, but . . . he seemed eager. More than eager—he seemed to be itching to head into the city on his own.

The two Illyrians paused their inspection of me long enough to note my sisters finishing up breakfast, Nesta in a pale gray gown that brought out the steel in her eyes, Elain in dusty pink.

Both males went a bit still. But Azriel sketched a bow—while Cassian stalked for the dining table, reached right over Nesta's shoulder, and grabbed a muffin from its little basket. "Morning, Nesta," he said around a mouth of blueberry-lemon. "Elain."

Nesta's nostrils flared, but Elain peered up at Cassian, blinking twice. "He snapped your wings, broke your bones."

I tried to shut out the sound of Cassian's scream—the memory of the spraying blood.

Nesta stared at her plate. Elain, at least, was out of her room, but . . .

"It'll take more than that to kill me," Cassian said with a smirk that didn't meet his eyes.

Elain only said to Cassian, "No, it will not."

Cassian's dark brows narrowed. I dragged a hand over my face before going to Elain and touching her too-bony shoulder. "Can I set you up in the garden? The herbs you planted are coming in nicely."

"I can help her," said Azriel, stepping to the table as Elain silently rose. No shadows at his ear, no darkness ringing his fingers as he extended a hand.

Nesta monitored him like a hawk, but kept silent as Elain took his hand, and out they went.

Cassian finished the muffin, licking his fingers. I could have sworn Nesta watched the entire thing with a sidelong glance. He grinned at her as if he knew it, too. "Ready for some flying, Nes?"

"Don't call me that."

The wrong thing to say, from the way Cassian's eyes lit up.

I chose that moment to winnow to the skies above the House, chuckling as wind carried me through the world. Some sisterly payback, I supposed. For Nesta's general attitude.

Mercifully, no one saw my slightly better crash landing on the veranda, and by the time Cassian's dark figure appeared in the sky, Nesta's hair bright as bronze in the morning sun, I'd brushed off the dirt and dust from my leathers.

My sister's face was wind-flushed as Cassian gently set her down. Then she strode for the glass doors without a single look back.

"You're welcome," Cassian called after her, more than a bite to his voice. His hands clenched and slackened at his sides—as if he were trying to loosen the feel of her from his palms.

"Thank you," I said to him, but Cassian didn't bother saying farewell as he launched skyward and vanished into the clouds.

The library beneath the House was shadowed, quiet. The doors opened for us, the same way they'd opened when Rhys and I had first visited.

Nesta said nothing, only surveying every stack and alcove and dangling chandelier as I led her down to the level where Clotho had found those books. I showed her the small reading area where I'd been stationed, and gestured to the desk. "I know Cassian gets under your skin, *but* I'm curious, too. How *do* you know what to look for in regard to the wall?"

Nesta ran a finger over the ancient wood desk. "Because I just do."

"How."

"I don't know how. Amren told me to just . . . see if the information clicks." And perhaps that frightened her. Intrigued her, but frightened her. And she hadn't told Cassian not out of spite, but because she didn't wish to reveal that vulnerability. That lack of control.

I didn't push. Even as I stared at her for a long moment. I didn't know how—how to broach that subject, how to ask if she was all right, if I could help her. I had never been affectionate with her—I'd never held her. Kissed her cheek. I didn't know where to begin.

So I just said, "Rhys gave me a layout of the stacks. I think there might be more on the Cauldron and wall a few levels down. You can wait here, or—"

"I'll help you look."

We followed the sloping path in silence, the rustle of paper and occasional whisper of a priestess's robes along the stone floors the only sounds. I quietly explained to her who the priestesses were—why they were here. I explained that Rhys and I planned to offer sanctuary to any humans who could make it to Velaris.

She said nothing, quieter and quieter as we descended, that black pit on my right seeming to grow thicker the deeper we went.

But we reached a path of stacks that veered into the mountain in a long hall, faelights flickering into life within glass globes along the wall as we passed. Nesta scanned the shelves while we walked, and I read the titles—a bit more slowly, still needing a little time to process what was instinct for my sister.

"I didn't know you couldn't really read," Nesta said as she paused before a nondescript section, noticing the way I silently sounded out the words of a title. "I didn't know where you were in your lessons—when it all happened. I assumed you could read as easily as us."

"Well, I couldn't."

"Why didn't you ask us to teach you?"

I trailed a finger over the neat row of spines. "Because I doubted you would agree to help."

Nesta stiffened like I'd hit her, coldness blooming in those eyes. She tugged a book from a shelf. "Amren said Rhysand taught you to read."

My cheeks heated. "He did." And there, deep beneath the world, with only darkness for company, I asked, "Why do you push everyone away but Elain?" *Why have you always pushed* me *away?*

Some emotion guttered in her eyes. Her throat bobbed. Nesta shut her eyes for a moment, breathing in sharply. "Because—"

The words stopped.

I felt it at the same moment she did.

The ripple and tremor. Like . . . like some piece of the world shifted, like some off-kilter chord had been plucked.

We turned toward the illuminated path that we'd just taken through the stacks, then to the dark far, far beyond.

The faelights along the ceiling began to sputter and die. One by one. Closer and closer to us.

I only had an Illyrian knife at my side.

"What is that," Nesta breathed.

"Run," was all I said.

I didn't give her the chance to object as I grabbed her by the elbow and sprinted into the stacks ahead. Faelights flickered to life as we passed—only to be devoured by the dark surging for us.

Slow—my sister was so damned slow with her dress, her general lack of exercising—

Rhys.

Nothing.

If the wards around the Prison were thick enough to keep out communication . . . Perhaps the same applied here.

A wall approached—with a hall before it. A second slope: left rising, right plunging down—

Darkness slithered down from above. But the inky gloom leading deeper . . . fresh and open.

I went right. "Faster," I said to her. If we could lead whoever it was deep, perhaps we could cut back, right to the pit. I could winnow—

Winnow. I could winnow *now*—

I grabbed for Nesta's arm.

Right as the darkness behind us paused, and two High Fae stepped out of it. Both male.

One dark-haired, one light. Both in gray jackets embroidered with bone-white thread.

I knew their coat of arms on the upper right shoulder. Knew their dead eyes.

Hybern. Hybern was *here*—

I didn't move fast enough as one of them blew out a breath toward us.

As that blue faebane dust sprayed into my eyes, my mouth, and my magic died out.

Nesta's gasp told me she felt something similar.

But it was on my sister that the two focused as I staggered back, tears streaming the dust from my eyes, spitting out the faebane. I gripped her arm, trying to winnow. Nothing.

Behind them, a hooded priestess slumped to the ground.

"So easy to get into their minds once our master let us through the wards," said one of them—the dark-haired male. "To make them think we were scholars. We'd planned to come for you . . . But it seems you found us first."

All spoken to my sister. Nesta's face was near-white, though her eyes showed no fear. "Who are you."

The white-haired one smiled broadly as they approached. "We're the king's Ravens. His far-flying eyes and talons. And we've come to take you back."

The king—their master. He'd . . . Mother above.

Was the king here—in Velaris?

Rhys. I slammed a mental hand into the bond. Over and over. *Rhys*.

Nothing.

Nesta's breath began to come quickly. Swords hung at their sides—two apiece. Their shoulders were broad, arms wide enough to indicate muscle filled those fine clothes.

"You're not taking her anywhere," I said, palming my knife. How had the king done it—arrived here unnoted, and fractured our wards? And if he was in Velaris . . . I shoved down my terror at the thought. At what he might be doing beyond this library, unseen and hidden—

"You're an unexpected prize, too," the black-haired one said to me. "But your sister . . ." A smile that showed all of his too-white teeth. "You took something from that Cauldron, girl. The king wants it back."

That was why the Cauldron couldn't shatter the wall. Not because its power was spent.

But because Nesta had stolen too much of it.

CHAPTER 31

I laid my options before me.

I doubted the king's Ravens were stupid enough to be kept talking long enough for my powers to return. And if the king was indeed here . . . I had to warn everyone. *Immediately*.

It left me with three choices.

Take them on in hand-to-hand combat with only a knife, when they were each armed with twin blades and were muscled enough to know how to use them.

Make a run for it, and try to get out of the library—and risk the lives and further trauma of the priestesses in the levels above.

Or . . .

Nesta was saying to them, "If he wants what I took, he can come get it himself."

"He's too busy to bother," the white-haired male purred, advancing another step.

"Apparently you're not."

I gripped Nesta's fingers in my free hand. She glanced at me.

I need you to trust me, I tried to convey to her.

Nesta read the emotion in my eyes—and gave the barest dip of her chin.

I said to them, "You made a grave mistake coming here. To *my* house."

They sniggered.

I gave them a returning smirk as I said, "And I hope it rips you into bloody ribbons."

Then I ran, hauling Nesta with me. Not toward the upper levels.

But down.

Down into the eternal blackness of the pit at the heart of the library.

And into the arms of whatever lurked inside it.

Around and down, around and down—

Shelves and paper and furniture and darkness, the smell turning musty and damp, the air thickening, the darkness like dew on my skin—

Nesta's breath was ragged, her skirts rustling with each sprinting step we took.

Time—only a matter of time before one of those priestesses contacted Rhys.

But even a minute might be too late.

There was no choice. None.

Faelights stopped appearing ahead.

Low, hideous laughter trickled behind us. "Not so easy, is it—to find your way in the dark."

"Don't stop," I panted to Nesta, flinging us farther into the dark.

A high-pitched scratching sounded. Like talons on stone. One of the Ravens crooned, "Do you know what happened to them—the queens?"

"Keep going," I breathed, gripping a hand against the wall to remain rooted.

Soon—we'd reach the bottom soon, and then . . . And then face some horror awful enough that Cassian wouldn't speak of it.

The lesser of two evils—or the worse of them.

"The youngest one—that pinched-faced bitch—went into the Cauldron first. Practically trampled the others to get in after it saw what it did to you and your sister."

"Don't stop," I repeated as Nesta stumbled. "If I go down, you *run*."

That was a choice that I did not need to debate. That did not frighten me. Not for a heartbeat.

Stone screamed beneath twin sets of talons. "But the Cauldron . . . Oh, it *knew* that something had been taken from it. Not sentient, but . . . it knew. It was furious. And when that young queen went in . . ."

The Ravens laughed. Laughed as the slope leveled out and we found ourselves at the bottom of the library.

"Oh, it gave her immortality. It made her Fae. But since something had been taken from it . . . the Cauldron took what she valued most. Her youth." They sniggered again. "A young woman went in . . . but a withered crone came out."

And from the catacombs of my memory, Elain's voice sounded: *I saw young hands wither with age*.

"The other queens won't go into the Cauldron for terror of the same happening now. And the youngest one . . . Oh, you should hear how she talks, Nesta Archeron. The things *she* wants to do to you when Hybern is done . . ."

Twin ravens are coming.

Elain had known. *Sensed* it. Had tried to warn us.

There were ancient stacks down here. Or, at least I felt them as we bumped into countless hard edges in our blind sprint. Where was it, where *was* it—

Deeper into the dark, we ran.

"We're growing bored of this pursuit," one of them said. "Our master is waiting for us to retrieve you."

I snorted loudly enough for them to hear. "I'm shocked he could even muster the strength to break the wards—he seems to need a trove of magical objects to do his work for him."

The other one hissed, talons scratching louder, "Whose spell book do you think Amarantha stole many decades ago? Who suggested the amusement of sticking the masks to Spring's faces as punishment? Another little spell, the one he burned through today—to crack through your wards here. Only once could it be wielded—such a pity."

I studied the faint trickle of light I could make out—far away and high up. "Run toward the light," I breathed to Nesta. "I'll hold them off."

"No."

"Don't try to be noble, if that's what you're whispering about," one of the Ravens cawed from behind. "We'll catch you both anyway."

We didn't have time—for whatever was down here to find us. We didn't have time—

"*Run*," I breathed. "Please."

She hesitated.

"*Please*," I begged her, my voice breaking.

Nesta squeezed my hand once.

And between one breath and the next, she bolted to the side—toward the center of the pit. The light high above.

"What—" one of them snapped, but I struck.

Every bone in my body barked in pain as I slammed into one of the stacks. Then again. Again.

Until it teetered and fell, collapsing onto the one beside it. And the next. And the next.

Blocking the way Nesta had gone.

And any chance of my exit, too. Wood groaned and snapped, books thudded on stone.

But ahead . . .

I clawed and patted the wall as I plunged farther into the pit floor. My magic was a husk in my veins.

"We'll still catch her, don't worry," one of them crooned. "Wouldn't want dear sisters to be separated."

Where are you where are you where are you

I didn't see the wall in front of me.

My teeth sang as I collided face-first. I patted blindly, feeling for a break, a corner—

The wall continued on. Dead end. If it was a dead end—

"Nowhere to go down here, Lady," one of them said.

I kept moving, gritting my teeth, gauging the power still frozen inside me. Not even an ember to summon to light the way, to show where I was—

To show any holes ahead—

The terror of it had my bones locking up. No. No, keep moving, keep going—

I reached out, desperate for a bookshelf to grab. Surely they wouldn't put a shelf near a gaping hole in the earth—

Empty blackness met my fingers, slipped between them. Again and again.

I stumbled a step.

Leather met my fingers—solid leather. I fumbled, the hard spines of books meeting my palms, and bit down my sob of relief. A lifeline in a violent sea; I felt my way down the stack, running now. It ended too soon. I took another blind step forward, touched my way around a corner of another stack. Just as the Ravens hissed with displeasure.

The sound said enough.

They'd lost me—for a moment.

I inched along, keeping my back to a shelf, calming my heaving lungs until my breaths became near-silent.

"Please," I breathed into the dark, barely more than a whisper. "Please, help me."

In the distance, a *boom* shuddered through the ancient floor.

"High Lady of the Night Court," one of the Ravens sang. "What sort of cage shall our king build for you?"

Fear would get me killed, fear would—

A soft voice whispered in my ear, *You are the High Lady?*

The voice was both young and old, hideous and beautiful. "Y-yes," I whispered.

I could sense no body heat, detect no physical presence, but . . . I felt it behind me. Even with my back to the shelf, I felt the mass of it lurking behind me. Around me. Like a shroud.

"We can smell you," the other Raven said. "How your mate shall rage when he's found we've taken you."

"Please," I breathed to the thing crouched behind me, over me.

What shall you give me?

Such a dangerous question. Never make a bargain, Alis had once warned me before Under the Mountain. Even if the bargains I'd made . . . they'd saved us. And brought me to Rhys.

"What do you want?"

One of the Ravens snapped, "Who is she talking to?"

The stone and wind hear all, speak all. They whispered to me of your desire to wield the Carver. To trade.

My breath came hard and fast. "What of it?"

I knew him once—long ago. Before so many things crawled the earth.

The Ravens were close—far too close when one of them hissed, "What is she mumbling?"

"Does she know a spell, as the master did?"

I whispered to the lurking dark behind me, "What is your price?"

The Ravens' footsteps sounded so nearby they couldn't have been more than twenty feet away. "Who are you talking to?" one of them demanded.

Company. Send me company.

I opened my mouth, but then said, "To—eat?"

A laugh that made my skin crawl. *To tell me of* life.

The air ahead shifted—as the Hybern Ravens closed in. "There you are," one seethed.

"It's a bargain," I breathed. The skin along my left forearm tingled. The thing behind me . . . I could have sworn I felt it smile.

Shall I kill them?

"P-please do."

Light sputtered before me, and I blinked at the blinding ball of faelight.

I saw the twin Ravens first, that faelight at their shoulder—to illuminate me for their taking.

Their attention went to me. Then rose over my shoulder. My head.

Absolute, unfiltered terror filled their faces. At what stood behind me.

Close your eyes, the thing purred in my ear.

I obeyed, trembling.

Then all I heard was screaming.

High-pitched shrieking and pleading. Bones snapping, blood splattering like rain, cloth ripping, and screaming, screaming, *screaming*—

I squeezed my eyes shut so hard it hurt. Squeezed them shut so hard I was shaking.

Then there were warm, rough hands on me, dragging me away, and Cassian's voice at my ear, saying, "Don't look. *Don't look.*"

I didn't. I let him lead me away. Just as I felt Rhys arrive. Felt him land on the floor of the pit so hard the entire mountain shuddered.

I opened my eyes then. Found him storming toward us, night rippling off him, such fury on his face—

"Get them out."

The order was given to Cassian.

The screaming was still erupting behind us.

I lurched toward Rhys, but he was already gone, a plume of darkness spreading from him.

To shield the view of what he walked into.

Knowing I would look.

The screaming stopped.

In the terrible silence, Cassian hauled me out—toward the dim center of the pit. Nesta was standing there, arms around herself, eyes wide.

Cassian only stretched out an arm for her. As if in a trance, she walked right to his side. His arms tightened around both of us, Siphons flaring, gilding the darkness with bloodred light.

Then we launched skyward.

Just as the screaming began anew.

CHAPTER 32

Cassian gave us both a glass of brandy. A tall glass.

Seated in an armchair in the family library high above, Nesta drank hers in one gulp.

I claimed the chair across from her, took a sip, shuddered at the taste, and made to set it down on the low-lying table between us.

"Keep drinking," Cassian ordered. The wrath wasn't toward me.

No—it was toward whatever was below. What had happened.

"Are you hurt?" Cassian asked me. Each word was clipped—brutal.

I shook my head.

That he didn't ask Nesta . . . he must have found her first. Ascertained for himself.

I started, "Is the king—the city—"

"No sign of him." A muscle twitched in his jaw.

We sat in silence. Until Rhys appeared between the open doors, shadows trailing in his wake.

Blood coated his hands—but nothing else.

So much blood, ruby-bright in the midmorning sun.

Like he'd clawed through them with his bare hands.

His eyes were wholly frozen with rage.

But they dipped to my left arm, the sleeve filthy but still rolled up—

Like a slim band of black iron around my forearm, a tattoo now lay there.

It's custom in my court for bargains to be permanently marked upon flesh, Rhys had told me Under the Mountain.

"What did you give it." I hadn't heard that voice since that visit to the Court of Nightmares.

"It—it said it wanted company. Someone to tell it about life. I said yes."

"Did you volunteer *yourself*."

"No." I drained the rest of the brandy at the tone, his frozen face. "It just said *someone*. And it didn't specify *when*." I grimaced at the solid black band, no thicker than the width of my finger, interrupted only by two slender gaps near the side of my forearm. I tried to stand, to go to him, to take those bloody hands. But my knees still wobbled enough that I couldn't move. "Are the king's Ravens dead?"

"They nearly were when I arrived. It left enough of their minds functioning for me to have a look. And finish them when I was done."

Cassian was stone-faced, glancing between Rhys's bloody hands and his ice-cold eyes.

But it was to my sister that my mate turned. "Hybern hunts you because of what you took from the Cauldron. The queens want you dead for vengeance—for robbing them of immortality."

"I know." Nesta's voice was hoarse.

"What did you take."

"I don't know." The words were barely more than a whisper. "Even Amren can't figure it out."

Rhys stared her down. But Nesta looked to me—and I could have sworn fear shone there, and guilt and . . . some other feeling. "You told me to run."

"You're my sister," was all I said. She'd once tried to cross the wall to save me.

But she started. "Elain—"

"Elain is fine," Rhys said. "Azriel was at the town house. Lucien is headed back, and Mor is nearly there. They know of the threat."

Nesta leaned her head back against the armchair's cushion, going a bit boneless.

I said to Rhys, "Hybern infiltrated our city. Again."

"The prick held on to that fleeting spell until he really needed it."

"Fleeting spell?"

"A spell of mighty power, able to be wielded only once—to great effect. One capable of cleaving wards . . . He must have been biding his time."

"Are the wards here—"

"Amren is currently adapting them against such things. And will then begin combing through this city to find if the king also deposited any other cronies before he vanished."

Beneath the cold rage, there was a sharpness—honed enough that I said, *What's wrong?*

"What's wrong?" he replied—verbally, as if he could no longer distinguish between the two. "What's wrong is that those pieces of *shit* got into my house and attacked my *mate*. What's wrong is that my own damn wards worked against me, and you had to make a bargain with that *thing* to keep yourself from being taken. What's wrong—"

"Calm down," I said quietly, but not weakly.

His eyes glowed, like lightning had struck an ocean. But he inhaled deeply, blowing out the breath through his nose, and his shoulders loosened—barely.

"Did you see what it was—that thing down there?"

"I guessed enough about it to close my eyes," he said. "I only opened them when it had stepped away from their bodies."

Cassian's skin had turned ashen. He'd seen it. He'd seen it again. But he said nothing.

"Yes, the king got past our defenses," I said to Rhys. "Yes, things went badly. But we weren't hurt. And the Ravens revealed some key pieces of information."

Sloppy, I realized. Rhys had been sloppy in killing them. Normally, he would have kept them alive for Azriel to question. But he'd taken what he needed, quickly and brutally, and ended it. He'd shown more restraint about the Attor—

"We know why the Cauldron doesn't work at its full strength now," I went on. "We know that Nesta is more of a priority for the king than I am."

Rhys mulled it over. "Hybern showed part of his hand, in bringing them here. He has to have a sliver of doubt of his conquest if he'd risk it."

Nesta looked like she was going to be sick. Cassian wordlessly refilled her glass. But I asked, "How—how did you know that we were in trouble?"

"Clotho," Rhys said. "There's a spelled bell inside the library. She rang it, and it went out to all of us. Cassian got there first."

I wondered what had happened in those initial moments, when he'd found my sister.

As if he'd read my thoughts, Rhys sent the image to me, no doubt courtesy of Cassian.

Panic—and rage. That was all he knew as he shot down into the heart of the pit, spearing for that ancient darkness that had once shaken him to his very marrow.

Nesta was there—and Feyre.

It was the former he saw first, stumbling out of the dark, wide-eyed, her fear a tang that whetted his rage into something so sharp he could barely think, barely breathe—

She let out a small, animal sound—like some wounded stag—as she saw him. As he landed so hard his knees popped.

He said nothing as Nesta launched herself toward him, her dress filthy and disheveled, her arms stretching for him. He opened his own for her, unable to stop his approach, his reaching—

She gripped his leathers instead. "Feyre," *she rasped, pointing behind her with a free hand, shaking him solidly with the other. Strength—such untapped strength in that slim, beautiful body. "Hybern."*

That was all he needed to hear. He drew his sword—then Rhys was arrowing for them, his power like a gods-damned volcanic eruption. Cassian charged ahead into the gloom, following the screaming—

I pulled away, not wanting to see any further. See what Cassian had witnessed down there.

Rhys strode to me, and lifted a hand to brush my hair—but stopped upon seeing the blood crusting his fingers. He instead studied the tattoo now marring my left arm. "As long as we don't have to invite it to solstice dinner, I can live with it."

"*You* can live with it?" I lifted my brows.

A ghost of a smile, even with all that had happened, that now lay before us. "At least now if one of you misbehaves, I know the perfect punishment. Going down there to *talk* to that thing for an hour."

Nesta scowled with distaste, but Cassian let out a dark laugh. "I'll take scrubbing toilets, thank you."

"Your second encounter seemed less harrowing than the first."

"It wasn't trying to *eat* me this time." But shadows still darkened his eyes.

Rhys saw them, too. Saw them and said quietly, again with that High Lord's voice, "Warn whoever needs to know to stay indoors tonight. Children off the streets at sundown, none of the Palaces will remain open past moonrise. Anyone on the streets faces the consequences."

"Of what?" I asked, the liquor in my stomach now burning.

Rhys's jaw tightened, and he surveyed the sparkling city beyond the windows. "Of Amren on the hunt."

+

Elain was nestled beside a too-casual Mor on the sitting room couch when we arrived at the town house. Nesta strode past me, right to Elain, and took up a seat on her other side, before turning her attention to where we remained in the foyer. Waiting—somehow sensing the meeting that was about to unfold.

Lucien, stationed by the front window, turned from watching the street. Monitoring it. A sword and dagger hung from his belt. No humor, no warmth graced his face—only fierce, grim determination.

"Azriel's coming down from the roof," Rhys said to none of us in particular, leaning against the archway into the sitting room and crossing his arms.

And as if he'd summoned him, Azriel stepped out of a pocket of shadow by the stairs and scanned us from head to toe. His eyes lingered on the blood crusting Rhys's hands.

I took up a spot at the opposite doorway post while Cassian and Azriel remained between us.

Rhys was quiet for a moment before he said, "The priestesses will keep silent about what happened today. And the people of this city won't learn *why* Amren is now preparing to hunt. We can't afford to let the other High Lords know. It would unnerve them—and destabilize the image we have worked so hard to create."

"The attack on Velaris," Mor countered from her place on the couch, "already showed we're vulnerable."

"That was a surprise attack, which we handled quickly," Cassian said, Siphons flickering. "Az made sure the information came out portraying *us* as victors—able to defeat any challenge Hybern throws our way."

"We did that today," I said.

"It's different," Rhys said. "The first time, we had the element of their surprise to excuse us. This second time . . . it makes us look unprepared. Vulnerable. We can't risk that getting out before the meeting in ten days. So for all appearances, we will remain unruffled as we prepare for war."

Mor sagged against the couch cushions. "A war where we have no allies beyond Keir, either in Prythian or beyond it."

Rhys gave her a sharp look. But Elain said quietly, "The queen might come."

Silence.

Elain was staring at the unlit fireplace, eyes lost to that vague murkiness.

"What queen," Nesta said, more tightly than she usually spoke to our sister.

"The one who was cursed."

"Cursed by the Cauldron," I clarified to Nesta, pushing off the archway. "When it threw its tantrum after you . . . left."

"No." Elain studied me, then her. "Not that one. The other."

Nesta took a steadying breath, opening her mouth to either whisk Elain upstairs or move on.

But Azriel asked softly, taking a single step over the threshold and into the sitting room, "What other?"

Elain's brows twitched toward each other. "The queen—with the feathers of flame."

The shadowsinger angled his head.

Lucien murmured to me, eye still fixed on Elain, "Should we—does she need . . . ?"

"She doesn't need anything," Azriel answered without so much as looking at Lucien.

Elain was staring at the spymaster now—unblinkingly.

"We're the ones who need . . ." Azriel trailed off. "A seer," he said, more to himself than us. "The Cauldron made you a seer."

CHAPTER 33

Seer.

The word clanged through me.

She'd known. She'd *warned* Nesta about the Ravens. And in the chaos of the attack, that little realization had slipped from me. Slipped from me as reality and dream slipped and entwined for Elain. *Seer.*

Elain turned to Mor, who was now gaping at my sister from her spot beside her on the couch. "Is that what this is?"

And the words, the tone . . . they were so *normal*-sounding that my chest tightened.

Mor's gaze darted across my sister's face, as if weighing the words, the question, the truth or lie within.

Mor at last blinked, mouth parting. Like that magic of hers had at last solved some puzzle. Slowly, clearly, she nodded. Lucien silently slid into one of the chairs, before the window, that metal eye whirring as it roved over my sister.

It made sense, I supposed, that Azriel alone had listened to her. The male who heard things others could not . . . Perhaps he, too, had suffered as Elain had before he understood what gift he possessed. He asked Elain, "There is another queen?"

Elain squinted, as if the question required some inner clarification, some . . . path into looking the right way at whatever had addled and plagued her. "Yes."

"The sixth queen," Mor breathed. "The queen who the golden one said wasn't ill . . ."

"She said not to trust the other queens because of it," I added.

And as soon as the words left my mouth . . . It was like stepping back from a painting to see the entire picture. Up close, the words had been muddled and messy. But from a distance . . .

"You stole from the Cauldron," I said to Nesta, who seemed ready to jump between all of us and Elain. "But what if the Cauldron *gave* something to Elain?"

Nesta's face drained of color. "What?"

Equally ashen, Lucien seemed inclined to echo Nesta's hoarse question.

But Azriel nodded. "You knew," he said to Elain. "About the young queen turning into a crone."

Elain blinked and blinked, eyes clearing again. As if the understanding, *our* understanding . . . it freed her from whatever murky realm she'd been in.

"The sixth queen is alive?" Azriel asked, calm and steady, the voice of the High Lord's spymaster, who had broken enemies and charmed allies.

Elain cocked her head, as if listening to some inner voice. "Yes."

Lucien just stared and stared at my sister, as if he'd never seen her before.

I whipped my face to Rhys. *A potential ally?*

I don't know, he answered. *If the others cursed her* . . .

"What sort of curse?" my mate asked before he'd even finished speaking to me.

Elain shifted her face toward him. Another blink. "They sold her—to . . . to some darkness, to some . . . sorcerer-lord . . ." She shook her head. "I can never see him. What he is. There is an onyx box that he possesses, more vital than anything . . . save for them. The girls. He keeps other girls—others so like her—but she . . . By day, she is one form, by night, human again."

"A bird of burning feathers," I said.

"Firebird by day," Rhys mused, "woman by night . . . So she's held captive by this sorcerer-lord?"

Elain shook her head. "I don't know. I hear her—her screaming. With rage. Utter rage . . ." She shuddered.

Mor leaned forward. "Do you know why the other queens cursed her—sold her to him?"

Elain studied the table. "No. No—that is all mist and shadow."

Rhys blew out a breath. "Can you sense where she is?"

"There is . . . a lake. Deep in—in the continent, I think. Hidden amongst mountains and ancient forests." Elain's throat bobbed. "He keeps them all at the lake."

"Other women like her?"

"Yes—and no. Their feathers are white as snow. They glide across the water—while she rages through the skies above it."

Mor said to Rhys, "What information do we have on this sixth queen?"

"Little," Azriel answered for him. "We know little. Young—somewhere in her mid-twenties. Scythia lies along the wall, to the east. It's smallest amongst the human queens' realms, but rich in trade and arms. She goes by Vassa, but I never got a report with her full name."

Rhys considered. "She must have posed a considerable threat to the queens if they turned on her. And considering their agenda . . ."

"If we can find Vassa," I cut in, "she could be vital in convincing the human forces to fight. And giving us an ally on the continent."

"*If* we can find her," Cassian countered, stepping up to Azriel's side, his wings flaring slightly. "It could take months. Not to mention, facing the male who holds her captive could be harder than expected. We can't afford all those potential risks. Or the time it'd take. We should focus on this meeting with the other High Lords first."

"But we could stand to gain much," Mor said. "Perhaps she has an army—"

"Perhaps she does," Cassian cut her off. "But if she's cursed, who will lead it? And if her kingdom is so far away . . . they have to travel the mortal way, too. You remember how slowly they moved, how quickly they died—"

"It's worth a try," Mor sniped.

"You're needed here," Cassian said. Azriel looked inclined to agree, even as he kept quiet. "I need you on a battlefield—not traipsing through the continent. The *human* half of it. If those queens have rallied armies to offer Hybern, they're no doubt standing between you and Queen Vassa."

"You don't give me orders—"

"No, but I do," Rhys said. "Don't give me that look. He's right—we need you here, Mor."

"Scythia," Mor said, shaking her head. "I remember them. They're horse people. A mounted cavalry could travel far faster—"

"No." Sheer will blazed in Rhys's eyes. The order was final.

But Mor tried again. "There is a reason why Elain is seeing these things. She was right about the other queen turning old, about the Ravens' attack—*why* is she being sent this image? *Why* is she hearing this queen? It must be vital. If we ignore it, perhaps we'll deserve to fail."

Silence. I surveyed them all. Vital. Each of them was vital *here*. But me . . .

I sucked in a breath.

"I'll go."

Lucien was staring at Elain as he spoke.

We all looked at him.

Lucien shifted his focus to Rhys, to me. "I'll go," he repeated, rising to his feet. "To find this sixth queen."

Mor opened and shut her mouth.

"What makes you think you could find her?" Rhys asked. Not rudely, but—from a commander's perspective. Sizing up the skills Lucien offered against the risks, the potential benefits.

"This eye . . ." Lucien gestured to the metal contraption. "It can see things that others . . . can't. Spells, glamours . . . Perhaps it can help me find her. And break her curse." He glanced at Elain, who was again studying her lap. "I'm not needed here. I'll fight if you need me to, but . . ." He offered me a grim smile. "I do not belong in the Autumn Court. And I'm willing to bet I'm no longer welcome at h—the Spring Court." *Home*, he had almost said. "But I cannot sit here and do *nothing*. Those queens with their armies—there is a threat in that regard, too. So use me. Send me. I will find Vassa, see if she can . . . bring help."

"You will be going into the human territory," Rhys warned. "I can't spare a force to guard you—"

"I don't need one. I travel faster on my own." His chin lifted. "I will find her. And if there's an army to bring back, or at least some way for her own story to sway the human forces . . . I'll find a way to do that, too."

My friends glanced to each other. Mor said, "It will be—very dangerous."

A half smile curved Lucien's mouth. "Good. It'd be boring otherwise."

Only Cassian returned the grin. "I'll load you up with some Illyrian steel."

Elain now watched Lucien warily. Blinking every now and then. She revealed no hint of whatever she might be seeing—sensing. None.

Rhys pushed off the archway. "I'll winnow you as close as we can get—to wherever you need to be to begin your hunt." Lucien had indeed been studying all those maps lately. Perhaps at the quiet behest of whatever force had guided us all. My mate added, "Thank you."

Lucien shrugged. And it was that gesture alone that made me say at last, "Are you sure?"

He only glanced at Elain, whose face was again a calm void while she traced a finger over the embroidery on the couch cushions. "Yes. Let me help in whatever way I can."

Even Nesta seemed relatively concerned. Not for him, no doubt, but the fact that if he were hurt, or killed . . . What would it do to Elain? The severing of the mating bond . . . I shut out the thought of what it'd do to me.

I asked Lucien, "When do you want to leave?"

"Tomorrow." I hadn't heard him sound so assertive in . . . a long time. "I'll prepare for the rest of today, and leave after breakfast tomorrow morning." He added to Rhys, "If that works for you."

My mate waved an idle hand. "For what you're about to do, Lucien, we'll make it work."

Silence fell once more. If he could find that missing queen and perhaps bring back some sort of human army, or at least sway the mortal forces from Hybern's thrall . . . If I could find a way to get the Carver to fight for us that did not involve using that terrible mirror . . . Would it be enough?

The meeting with the High Lords, it seemed, would decide that.

Rhys jerked his chin at Azriel, who took it as an order to vanish—to no doubt check in on Amren.

"Find out if Keir and his Darkbringers had any attacks," my mate ordered Mor and Cassian, who nodded and left as well. Alone with my sisters and Lucien, Rhys and I caught Nesta's eye.

And for once, my sister rose to her feet and came toward us, the three of us not so subtly heading upstairs. Leaving Lucien and Elain alone.

It was an effort not to linger atop the landing, to listen to what was said.

If anything was said at all.

But I made myself take Rhys's hand, flinching at the blood still caked on his skin, and led him to our bathing room. Nesta's bedroom door clicked shut down the hall.

Rhys wordlessly watched me as I turned on the bathtub faucet and grabbed a washcloth from the chest against the wall. I took up a seat at the edge of the tub, testing the water temperature against my wrist, and patted the porcelain rim beside me. "Sit."

He obeyed, his head drooping as he sat.

I took one of his hands, guided it to the gurgling stream of water, and held it beneath.

Red flowed off his skin, eddying in the water beneath. I plucked up the cloth and scrubbed gently, more blood flaking off, water splashing onto the still-immaculate sleeves of his jacket. "Why not shield your hands?"

"I wanted to feel it—their lives ending beneath my fingers."

Cold, flat words.

I scrubbed at his nails, the blood wedged into the cracks where it met his skin. The arcs beneath. "Why is it different this time?" Different from the Attor's ambush, Hybern's attack in the woods, the attack on Velaris . . . all of it. I'd seen him in a rage before, but never . . . never so detached. As if morality and kindness were things that lurked on a surface far, far above the frozen depths he'd plunged into.

I turned his palm into the spray, getting at the space between his fingers.

"What is the point of it," he said, "of all this power . . . if I can't protect those who are most vulnerable in my city? If it can't detect an incoming attack?"

"Even Azriel didn't learn of it—"

"The king used an archaic spell and walked in the *front door*. If I can't . . ." Rhys shook his head, and I lowered his now-clean hand and reached for the other. More blood stained the water. "If I can't protect them here . . . How can . . ." His throat bobbed. I lifted his chin with a hand. Icy rage had slipped into something a bit shattered and aching. "Those priestesses have endured enough. I failed them today. That library . . . it will no longer feel safe for them. The one place they've had to themselves, where they knew they were protected . . . Hybern took that away today."

And from him. He had gone to that library for his own need for healing—for safety.

He said, "Perhaps it's punishment for taking away Velaris from Mor—in granting Keir access here."

"You can't think like that—it won't end well." I finished washing his other hand, rinsed the cloth, then began swiping it along his neck, his temples . . . Soothing, warm presses, not to clean but to relax.

"I'm not angry about the bargain," he said, closing his eyes as I swiped the cloth over his brow. "In case you were . . . worried."

"I wasn't."

Rhys opened his eyes, as if he could hear the smile in my voice, and studied me while I chucked the cloth into the tub with a wet slap and turned off the faucet.

He was still studying me when I took his face in my damp hands. "What happened today was not your fault," I said, the words filling the sun-drenched bathing room. "None of it. It all lies on Hybern—and when we face the king again, we will remember these attacks, these injuries to our people. We forgot Amarantha's spell book—to our own loss. But we have a Book of our own—hopefully with the spell we need. And for now . . . for now, we will prepare, and we will face the consequences. For now, we move ahead."

He turned his head to kiss my palm. "Remind me to give you a salary raise."

I choked on a cough. "For what?"

"For the sage counsel—and the other vital services you provide me." He winked.

I laughed in earnest, and squeezed his face as I pressed a swift kiss to his mouth. "Shameless flirt."

The warmth returned to his eyes at last.

So I reached for an ivory towel and bundled his hands, now clean and warm, into the folds of soft fabric.

CHAPTER 34

Amren found no other Hybern assassins or spies during her long night of hunting through Velaris. How she sought them, how she distinguished friend from foe . . . Some people, Mor told me the next morning—after we *all* had a sleepless night—painted their thresholds in lamb's blood. A sort of offering to her. And payment to stay away. Some left cups of it on their doorsteps.

As if everyone in the city knew that the High Lord's Second, that small-boned female . . . she was the monster that defended them from the other horrors of the world.

Rhys had spent much of the previous day and night reassuring the priestesses of their safety, walking them through the new wards. The priestess who had let them in . . . for whatever reason, Hybern had left her alive. She allowed Rhys into her mind to see what had happened: once the king had sundered the wards with that fleeting spell, his Ravens had appeared as two old scholars to get the priestess to open the door, then forced their way into her mind so that she'd welcome them in without being vetted. The violation of that alone . . . Rhys had spent hours with those priestesses yesterday. Mor, too.

Talking, listening to the ones who *could* speak, holding the hands of the ones who couldn't.

And when they at last left . . . There was a peace between my mate and his cousin. Some lingering jagged edge that had somehow been soothed.

We didn't have long. I knew that. Felt it with every breath. Hybern wasn't coming; Hybern was *here*.

Our meeting with the High Lords was now over a week away—and still Nesta refused to join us.

But it was fine. We'd manage. I'd manage.

We didn't have another choice.

Which was why I found myself standing in the foyer the next morning, watching Lucien shoulder his heavy pack. He wore Illyrian leathers under a heavier jacket, along with layers of clothes beneath to help him survive in varying climates. He'd braided back his red hair, the length of it snaking across his back—right in front of the Illyrian sword strapped down his spine.

Cassian had given him free rein yesterday afternoon to loot his personal cache of weapons, though my friend had been economical about which ones he'd selected. The blade, plus a short sword, plus an assortment of daggers. A quiver of arrows and an unstrung bow were tied to his pack.

"You know precisely where you want Rhys to take you?" I asked at last.

Lucien nodded, glancing to where my mate now waited by the front door. He'd bring Lucien to the edge of the human continent—to wherever Lucien had decided would be the best landing spot. No farther, Azriel had insisted. His reports indicated it was too watched, too dangerous. Even for one of our own. Even for the most powerful High Lord in history.

I stepped forward, and didn't give Lucien time to step back as I hugged him tightly. "Thank you," I said, trying not to think about all the steel on him—if he'd need to use it.

"It was time," Lucien said quietly, giving me a squeeze. "For me to do something."

I pulled away, surveying his scarred face. "Thank you," I said again. It was all I could think of to say.

Rhys extended a hand to Lucien.

Lucien studied it—then my mate's face. I could nearly see all the hateful words they'd spoken. Dangling between them, between that outstretched hand and Lucien's own.

But Lucien took Rhys's hand. That silent offer of not only transportation.

Before that dark wind swept in, Lucien looked back.

Not to me, I realized—to someone behind me.

Pale and thin, Elain stood atop the stairs.

Their gazes locked and held.

But Elain said nothing. Did not so much as take one step downward.

Lucien inclined his head in a bow, the movement hiding the gleam in his eye—the longing and sadness.

And when Lucien turned to signal to Rhys to go . . . He did not glance back at Elain.

Did not see the half step she took toward the stairs—as if she'd speak to him. Stop him.

Then Rhys was gone, and Lucien with him.

When I turned to offer Elain breakfast, she'd already walked away.

I waited in the foyer for Rhys to return.

In the dining room to my left, Nesta silently practiced building those invisible walls in her mind—no sign of Amren since her hunt last night. When I asked if she was making any progress, my sister had only said, "Amren thinks I'm getting close enough to begin trying on something tangible."

And that was that. I left her to it, not bothering to ask if Amren had *also* come close to figuring out some sort of spell in the Book to repair that wall.

In silence, I counted the minutes, one by one.

Then a familiar dark wind swirled through the foyer, and I loosed a too-tight breath as Rhys appeared in the middle of the hall carpet. No indication of any sort of trouble, no sign of hurt or harm, but I slid my arms around his waist, needing to feel him, smell him. "Did everything go well?"

Rhys brushed a kiss to the top of my head. "As well as can be expected. He's now on the continent, heading eastward."

He marked Nesta studying at the dining table. "How's our new seer holding up?"

I pulled back to explain that I'd left Elain to her own thoughts, but Nesta said, "Don't call her that."

Rhys gave me an incredulous look, but Nesta just went back to flipping through a book, her face going vacant—while she practiced with whatever wall-building exercises Amren had ordered. I poked him in the ribs. *Don't provoke her.*

A corner of his mouth lifted—the expression full of wicked delight. *Can I provoke you instead?*

I clamped my lips to keep from smiling—

The front door blew open and Amren stormed in.

Rhys was instantly facing her. "What."

Gone was the slick amusement, the relaxed posture.

Amren's pale face remained calm, but her eyes . . . They swirled with rage.

"Hybern has attacked the Summer Court. They lay siege to Adriata as we speak."

CHAPTER 35

Hybern had made its grand move at last. And we had not anticipated it.

I knew Azriel would take the blame upon himself. One look at the shadowsinger as he prowled through the front door of the town house minutes later, Cassian on his heels, told me that he already did.

We stood in the foyer, Nesta lingering at the dining table behind me.

"Has Tarquin called for aid?" Cassian asked Amren.

None of us dared question how she knew.

Amren's jaw tightened. "I don't know. I got the message, and—nothing else."

Cassian nodded once and turned to Rhys. "Did the Summer Court have a mobile fighting force readied when you were there?"

"No," Rhys said. "His armada was scattered along the coast." A glance at Azriel.

"Half is in Adriata—the other dispersed," the shadowsinger supplied. "His terrestrial army was moved to the Spring Court border . . . after Feyre. The closest legion is perhaps three days' march away. Very few can winnow."

"How many ships?" Rhys asked.

"Twenty in Adriata, fully armed."

A calculating look at Amren. "Numbers on Hybern?"

"I don't know. Many. It—I think they are overwhelmed."

"What was the exact message?" Pure, unrelenting command laced every word.

Amren's eyes glittered like fresh silver. "It was a warning. From Varian. To prepare our own defenses."

Utter silence.

"Prince Varian sent you a warning?" Cassian asked a bit quietly.

Amren glared at him. "It is a thing that friends do."

More silence.

I met Rhys's stare, sensed the weight and dread and anger simmering behind the cool features. "We cannot leave Tarquin to face them alone," I said. Perhaps Hybern had sent the Ravens yesterday to distract us from looking beyond our own borders. To have our focus on Hybern, not our own shores.

Rhys's attention cut to Cassian. "Keir and his Darkbringer army are nowhere near ready to march. How soon can the Illyrian legions fly?"

Rhys immediately winnowed Cassian into the war-camps to give the orders himself. Azriel had vanished with them, going ahead to scout Adriata, taking his most trusted spies with him.

Nausea had churned in my gut as Cassian and Azriel tapped the Siphons atop their hands and that scaled armor unfurled across their body. As seven Siphons appeared on each. As the shadowsinger's scarred hands checked the buckles on his knife belts and his quiver, while Rhys summoned extra Illyrian blades for Cassian—two at his back, one at each side.

Then they were gone—stone-faced and steady. Ready for bloodshed.

Mor arrived moments later, heavily armed, her hair braided back and every inch of her thrumming with impatience.

But Mor and I waited—for the order to go. To join them. Cassian had positioned the Illyrian legions closer to the southern border the weeks I'd been away, but even so, they wouldn't be able to fly without a few hours of preparation. And it would require Rhys to winnow them in. *All* of them. To Adriata.

"Will you fight?"

Nesta was now standing a few steps up the staircase of the town house, watching as Mor and I readied. Soon—Azriel or Rhys would contact us soon with the all-clear to winnow to Adriata.

"We'll fight if it's required," I said, checking once more that the belt of knives was secure at my hips.

Mor wore Illyrian leathers as well, but the blades on her were different. Slimmer, lighter, some of their tips slightly curved. Like lightning given flesh. Seraphim blades, she told me. Gifted to her by Prince Drakon himself during the War.

"What do you know of battle?"

I couldn't tell if my sister's tone was insulting or merely inquisitive.

"We know plenty," Mor said tightly, arranging her long braid between the blades crossed over her back. Elain and Nesta would remain here, with Amren watching over them. And watching over Velaris, along with a small legion of Illyrians Cassian had ordered to camp in the mountains above the city. Mor had passed Amren on her way in, the small female apparently heading to the butcher to fill up on provisions before she'd return to stay here—for however long we'd be in Adriata. If we returned at all.

I met Nesta's gaze again. Only wary distance greeted me. "We'll send word when we can."

A rumble of midnight thunder brushed against the walls of my mind. A silent signal, speared over land and mountains. As if Rhys's concentration was now wholly focused elsewhere—and he did not dare break it.

My heart stumbled a beat. I gripped Mor's arm, the leather scales cutting into my palm. "They've arrived. Let's go."

Mor turned to my sister, and I had never seen her seem so . . . warriorlike. I'd known it lurked beneath the surface, but here was the Morrigan. The female who had *fought* in the War. Who knew how to end lives with blade and magic.

"It's nothing we can't handle," Mor said to Nesta with a cocky smile, and then we were gone.

Black wind roared and tore at me, and I clung to Mor as she winnowed us through the courts, her breath a ragged beat in my ear—

Then blinding light and suffocating heat and screams and thunderous booming and metal on metal—

I swayed, bracing my feet apart as I blinked. As I took in my surroundings.

Rhys and the Illyrians had already joined the fray.

Mor had winnowed us to the barren top of one of the hills flanking the half-moon bay of Adriata, offering perfect views of the island-city in its center and the city on the mainland below.

The waters of the bay were red.

Smoke rose in gnarled black columns from buildings and foundering ships.

People screamed, soldiers shouted—

So many.

I had not anticipated the scope of how many soldiers there would be. On either side.

I'd thought it would be neat lines. Not chaos everywhere. Not Illyrians in the skies above the city and the harbor, blasting their power and arrows into the Hybern army that rained hell upon the city. Ship after ship squatted toward the horizon, hemming either entrance to the bay. And in the bay . . .

"Those are Tarquin's ships," Mor said, her face taut as she pointed to the white sails colliding with terrible force against the gray sails of Hybern's fleet. Utterly outnumbered, and yet plumes of magic—water and wind and whips of vines—kept attacking any boat that neared. And those that broke through the magic faced soldiers armed with spears and bows and swords.

And ahead of them, pushing against the fleet . . . the Illyrian lines.

So many. Rhys had winnowed them in—all of them. The drain on his power . . .

Mor's throat bobbed. "No one else has come," she murmured. "No other courts."

No sign of Tamlin and the Spring Court on Hybern's side, either.

A thunderous boom of dark power blasted into Hybern's fleet, scattering ships—but not many. As if . . . "Rhys's power is either already nearly spent or . . . they've got something working against it," I said. "More of that faebane?"

"Hybern would be stupid not to use it." Her fingers curled and uncurled at her sides. Sweat beaded on her temple.

"Mor?"

"I knew it was coming," she murmured. "Another war, at some point. I knew battles would come for *this* war. But . . . I forgot how terrible it is. The sounds. The smells."

Indeed, even from the rocky outcropping so high above, it was . . . overwhelming. The tang of blood, the pleading and screaming . . . Getting into the midst of it . . .

Alis. Alis had left the Spring Court, fearing the hell I'd unleash there—only to come here. To *this*. I prayed she was not in the city proper, prayed she and her nephews were keeping safe.

"We're to go to the palace," Mor said, squaring her shoulders. I hadn't dared break Rhysand's concentration by opening up a channel in the bond, but it seemed he was still capable of giving orders. "Soldiers have reached its northern side, and their defenses are surrounded."

I nodded once, and Mor drew her slender, curving blade. It gleamed as brightly as Amren's eyes, that Seraphim steel.

I unsheathed my Illyrian blade from across my back, the metal dark and ancient by comparison to the living silver flame in her hand.

"We stick close—you don't get out of sight," Mor said, smoothly and precisely. "We don't go down a hall or stairwell without assessing first."

I nodded again, at a loss for words. My heart beat at a gallop, my palms turning sweaty. Water—I wished I'd had some water. My mouth had gone bone-dry.

"If you can't bring yourself to make the kill," she added without a hint of judgment, "then shield me from behind."

"I can do it—the . . . killing," I rasped. I'd done plenty of it that day in Velaris.

Mor assessed the grip I maintained on my blade, the set of my shoulders. "Don't stop, and don't linger. We press forward until I say we retreat. Leave the wounded to the healers."

None of them enjoyed this, I realized. My friends—they had gone to war and back and had not found it worthy of glorification, had not let its memory become rose-tinted in the centuries following. But they were willing to dive into its hell once again for the sake of Prythian.

"Let's go," I said. Every moment we wasted here could spell someone's doom in that gleaming palace in the bay.

Mor swallowed once and winnowed us into the palace.

She must have visited a few times throughout the centuries, because she knew where to arrive.

The middle levels of Tarquin's palace had been communal space between the lower floors that the servants and lesser faeries were shoved into and the shining residential quarters for the High Fae above. When I had last seen the vast greeting hall, the light had been clear and white, flitting off the seashell-encrusted walls, dancing along the running rivers built into the floor. The sea beyond the towering windows had been turquoise mottled with vibrant sapphire.

Now that sea was choked with mighty ships and blood, the clear skies full of Illyrian warriors swooping down upon them in determined, unflinching lines. Thick metal shields glinted as the Illyrians dove and rose, emerging each time covered in blood. If they returned to the skies at all.

But my task was here. This building.

We scanned the floor, listening.

Frantic murmurs echoed from the stairwells leading upward, along with heavy thudding.

"They're barricading themselves into the upper levels," Mor observed as my brows narrowed.

Leaving the lesser fae trapped below. With no aid.

"Bastards," I breathed.

The lesser fae did not have as much magic between them—not in the way the High Fae did.

"This way," Mor said, jerking her chin toward the descending stairs. "They're three levels down, and climbing. Fifty of them."

A ship's worth.

CHAPTER 36

The first and second kills were the hardest. I didn't waste physical strength on the cluster of five Hybern soldiers—High Fae, not Attor-like underlings—forcing their way into a barricaded room full of terrified servants.

No, even as my body hesitated at the kills, my magic did not.

The two soldiers nearest me had feeble shields. I tore through them with a sizzling wall of fire. Fire that then found its way down their throats and burned every inch of the way.

And then sizzled through skin and tendon and bone and severed the heads from their bodies.

Mor just killed the soldier nearest her with good old-fashioned beheading.

She whirled, the soldier's head still falling, and sliced off the head of the one just nearing us.

The fifth and final soldier stopped his assault on the battered door.

Looked between us with flat, hate-bright eyes.

"Do it, then," he said, his accent so like that of the Ravens.

His thick sword rose, blood sliding down the groove of the fuller.

Someone was sobbing in terror on the other side of that door.

The soldier lunged for us, and Mor's blade flashed.

But I struck first, an asp of pure water striking his face—stunning him. Then shoving down his open mouth, his throat, up his nose. Sealing off any air.

He slumped to the ground, clawing at his neck as if he'd free a passage for the water now drowning him.

We left him without looking back, the grunting of his choking soon turning to silence.

Mor slid me a sidelong glance. "Remind me not to get on your bad side."

I appreciated the attempt at humor, but . . . laughter was foreign. There was only the breath in my heaving lungs and the roiling of magic through my veins and the clear, unyielding crispness of my vision, assessing all.

We found eight more in the midst of killing and hurting, a dormitory turned into Hybern's own sick pleasure hall. I did not care to linger on what they did, and only marked it so that I knew how fast and easily to kill.

The ones merely slaughtering died fast.

The others . . . Mor and I lingered. Not much, but those deaths were slower.

We left two of them alive—hurt and disarmed but alive—for the surviving faeries to kill.

I gave them two Illyrian knives to do it.

The Hybern soldiers began screaming before we cleared the level.

The hallway on the floor below was splattered in blood. The din was deafening. A dozen soldiers in the silver-and-blue armor of Tarquin's court battled against the bulk of the Hybern force, holding the corridor.

They were nearly pushed back to the stairs we'd just exited, steadily overwhelmed by the solid numbers against them, the Hybern soldiers stepping over—stepping *on*—the bodies of the fallen Summer Court warriors.

Tarquin's soldiers were flagging, even as they kept swinging, kept fighting. The closest one beheld us—opened his mouth to order us to run. But then he noted the armor, the blood on us and our blades.

"Don't be afraid," Mor said—as I stretched out a hand and darkness fell.

Soldiers on both sides shouted, scrambling back, armor clanging.

But I shifted my eyes, made them night-seeing. As I had done in that Illyrian forest, when I had first drawn Hybern blood.

Mor, I think, was born able to see in the darkness.

We winnowed through the ebon-veiled corridor in short bursts.

I could see their terror as I killed them. But they could not see me.

Every time we appeared in front of Hybern soldiers, frantic in the impenetrable dark, their heads fell. One after another. Winnow; slash. Winnow; thump.

Until there were none left, only the mounds of their bodies, the puddles of their blood.

I banished the darkness from the corridor, finding the Summer Court soldiers panting and gaping. At us. At what we had done in a matter of a minute.

I didn't look too long at the carnage. Mor didn't, either.

"Where else?" was all I asked.

We cleared the palace to its lowest levels. Then we took to the city streets, the steep hill leading down to the water rampant with Hybern soldiers.

The morning sun rose higher, beating down on us, making our skin slick and swollen with sweat beneath our leathers. I stopped discerning the sweat on my palms from the blood coating it.

I stopped being able to feel a great many things as we killed and killed, sometimes engaging in outright combat, sometimes with magic, sometimes earning our own bruises and small wounds.

But the sun continued its arc across the sky, and the battle continued in the bay, the Illyrian lines battering the Hybern fleet from above while Tarquin's armada pushed from behind.

Slowly, we purged the streets of Hybern soldiers. All I knew was the sun baking the blood coating my skin, the coppery tang of it clinging to my nostrils.

We had just cleared a narrow street, Mor striding through the felled Hybern soldiers to make sure any survivors . . . stopped surviving. I leaned against a blood-bathed stone wall just outside the shattered front window of a clothier, watching Mor's quicksilver blade rise and fall in lightning-bright flashes.

Beyond us, all around us, the screams of the dying were like the never-ending pealing of the city's warning bells.

Water—I needed water. If only to wash the blood from my mouth.

Not my own blood, but that of the soldiers we'd cut down. Blood that had sprayed into my mouth, up my nose, into my eyes, when we'd ended them.

Mor reached the last of the dead, and terrified High Fae and faeries finally poked their heads out of the doorways and windows flanking the cobblestoned street. No sign of Alis, her nephews, or cousin—or anyone who looked like them, amongst the living or the fallen. A small blessing.

We had to keep moving. There were more—so many more.

As Mor began striding back to me, boots sloshing through puddles of blood, I reached a mental hand toward the bond. Toward Rhys—toward anything that was solid and familiar.

Wind and darkness answered me.

I became only half-aware of the narrow street and the blood and the sun as I peered down the bridge between us. *Rhys*.

Nothing.

I speared myself along it, stumbling blindly through that raging tempest of night and shadow. If the bond sometimes felt like a living band of light, it now had turned into a bridge of ice-kissed obsidian.

And rising up on its other end . . . his mind. The walls—his shields . . . They had turned into a fortress.

I laid a mental hand to the black adamant, my heart thundering. What was he facing—what was he *seeing* to have made his shields so impenetrable?

I couldn't feel him on the other side.

There was only the stone and the dark and the wind.

Rhys.

Mor had nearly reached me when his answer came.

A crack in the shield—so swift that I did not have time to do anything more than lunge for it before it had closed behind me. Sealing me inside with him.

The streets, the sun, the city vanished.

There was only here—only him. And the battle.

Looking through Rhysand's eyes as I once had that day Under the Mountain . . . I felt the heat of the sun, the sweat and blood sliding down his face, slipping beneath the neck of his black Illyrian armor—smelled the brine of the sea and the tang of blood all around me. Felt the exhaustion ripping at him, in his muscles and in his magic.

Felt the Hybern warship shudder beneath him as he landed on its main deck, an Illyrian blade in each hand.

Six soldiers died instantly, their armor and bodies turning into red-and-silver mist.

The others halted, realizing who'd landed amongst them, in the heart of their fleet.

Slowly, Rhys surveyed the helmeted heads before him, counted the weapons. Not that it mattered. All of them would soon be crimson mist or food for the beasts circling the waters around the clashing armada. And then this ship would be splinters on the waves.

Once he was done. It was not the common foot soldiers he'd sought out.

Because where power should have been thrumming from him, obliterating them . . . It was a muffled rumble. Stifled.

He'd tracked it here—that strange damper on his power, on the Siphons' power. As if some sort of spell had turned his power oily in his grip. Harder to wield.

It was why the battle had gone on so long. The clean, precise blow he'd intended to land upon arriving—the single shot that would have saved so many lives . . . It had slipped from his grasp.

So he'd hunted it down, that damper. Battled his way across Adriata to get to this ship. And now, exhaustion starting to rip at him . . . The armed soldiers around Rhysand parted—and he appeared.

Trapped within Rhysand's mind, his powers stifled and body weary, there was nothing I could do but watch as the King of Hybern stepped from belowdecks and smiled at my mate.

CHAPTER 37

Blood slid from the tips of Rhys's twin blades onto the deck. One drop—two. Three.

Mother above. The king—

The King of Hybern wore his own colors: slate gray, embroidered with bone-colored thread. Not a weapon on him. Not a speckle of blood.

Within Rhys's mind, there was no jagged breath for me to take, no heartbeat to thunder in my chest. There was nothing I could do but watch—watch and keep quiet, so I didn't distract him, didn't risk taking his focus away for one blink . . .

Rhys met the king's dark eyes, bright beneath heavy brows, and smiled. "Glad to see you're still not fighting your own battles."

The king's answering smile was a brutal slash of white. "I was waiting for more interesting quarry to find me." His voice was colder than the highest peak of the Illyrian mountains.

Rhys didn't dare look away from him. Not as his magic unfurled, sniffing out every angle to kill the king. A trap—it had been a trap to discover which High Lord hunted down the source of that damper first.

Rhys had known one of them—the king, his cronies—would be waiting here.

He'd known, and come. Known and not asked us to *help* him—

If I was smart, Rhys said to me, his voice calm and steady, *I'd find some way to take him alive, make Azriel break him—get him to yield the Cauldron. And make an example of him to the other bastards thinking of bringing down that wall.*

Don't, I begged him. *Just kill him—kill him and be done with it, Rhys. End this war before it can truly begin.*

A pause of consideration. *But a death here, quick and brutal . . . His followers would turn it against me, no doubt.*

If he could manage it. The king had not been fighting. Had not depleted his reserves of power. But Rhys . . .

I felt Rhys size up the odds alongside me. *Let one of us come to you. Don't face him alone—*

Because trying to take the king alive without full access to his power . . .

Information rippled into me, brimming with all Rhys had seen and learned. Taking the king alive depended on whether Azriel was in good enough shape to help. He and Cassian had taken a few blows themselves, but—nothing they couldn't handle. Nothing to spook the Illyrians still fighting under their command. Yet.

"Seems like the tide is turning," Rhys observed as the armada around them indeed pushed Hybern's forces out to sea. He had not seen Tarquin. Or Varian and Cresseida. But the Summer Court still fought. Still pushed Hybern back, back, back from the harbor.

Time. Rhys needed *time*—

Rhys lunged toward the king's mind—and met *nothing*. Not a trace, not a whisper. As if he were nothing but wicked thought and ancient malice—

The king clicked his tongue. "I'd heard that you were a charmer, Rhysand. Yet here you are, groping and pawing at me like a green youth."

A corner of Rhys's mouth twitched up. "Always a delight to disappoint Hybern."

"Oh, on the contrary," the king said, crossing his arms—muscle shifting beneath. "You've always been such a source of entertainment. Especially for my darling Amarantha."

I felt it—the thought that escaped Rhys.

He wanted to wipe that name from living memory. Perhaps one day he would. One day he'd erase it from every mind in this world, one by one, until she was no one and nothing.

But the king knew that. From that smile, he knew.

And everything he had done . . . All of it . . .

Kill him, Rhys. Kill him and be done with it.

It's not that easy, was his even reply. *Not without searching this ship, searching him for that source of the spell on our power, and breaking it.*

But if he lingered much longer . . . I had no doubt the king had some nasty surprise waiting. Designed to spring shut at any moment. I knew Rhys was aware of it, too.

Knew, because he rallied his magic, assessing and weighing, an asp readying to strike.

"The last report I received from Amarantha," the king went on, sliding his hands into his pockets, "she was still enjoying you." The soldiers laughed.

My mate was used to it—that laughter. Even if it made me want to roar at them, rend them to pieces. But Rhys didn't so much as grit his teeth, though the king gave him a smile that told me he was well aware of what sort of scars lingered. What my mate had done to keep Amarantha distracted. Why he'd done it.

Rhys smirked. "Too bad it didn't end so pleasantly for her." His magic slithered through the ship, hunting down that tether for the power holding back our forces . . .

Kill him—kill him now. The word was a chant in my blood, my mind.

In his, too. I could hear it, clear as my own thoughts.

"Such a remarkable girl—your mate," the king mused. No emotion, not so much as a bit of anger beyond that cold amusement. "First Amarantha, then my pet, the Attor . . . And then she broke past all the wards around my palace to aid your escape. Not to mention . . ." A low laugh. "My niece and nephew." Rage—that was rage starting to blacken in his eyes. "She savaged Dagdan and Brannagh—and for what reason?"

"Perhaps you should ask Tamlin." Rhys raised a brow. "Where is he, by the way?"

"Tamlin." Hybern savored the name, the sound of it. "He has plans for you, after what you and your mate did to him. His court. What a mess for him to clean up—though she certainly made it easier for me to plant more of my troops in his lands."

Mother above—Mother above, I'd *done* that—

"She'll be happy to hear that."

Too long. Rhys had lingered too long, and facing him now . . . Fight or run. Run or fight.

"Where did her gifts come from, I wonder? Or who?"

The king knew. What I was. What I possessed.

"I'm a lucky male to have her as my mate."

The king smiled again. "For the little time you have remaining."

I could have sworn Rhys blocked out the words.

The king went on casually, "It will take everything, you know. To try to stop me. Everything you have. And it still won't be enough. And when you have given everything and you are dead, Rhysand, when your mate is mourning over your corpse, I am going to take her."

Rhys didn't let a flicker of emotion show, sliding on that cool, amused mask over the roaring rage that surrounded me at the thought, the threat. That settled before me like a beast ready to lunge, to defend. "She defeated Amarantha and the Attor," Rhys countered. "I doubt you'll be much of an effort, either."

"We'll see. Perhaps I'll give her to Tamlin when I'm done."

Fury heated Rhys's blood. And my own.

Strike or flee, Rhys, I begged again. *But do it* now.

Rhys rallied his power, and I felt it rise within him, felt him grappling to sustain his grip on it.

"The spell will wear off," the king said, waving a hand. "Another little trick I picked up while rotting away in Hybern."

"I don't know what you're talking about," Rhys said mildly.

They only smiled at each other.

And then Rhys asked, "Why?"

The king knew what he meant.

"There was room at the table for everyone, you and your ilk claimed." The king snorted. "For humans, lesser faeries, for half-breeds. In this new world of yours, there was room at the table for everyone—so long as they thought like you. But the Loyalists . . . How you delighted in shutting us out. Looking down your noses at us." He gestured to the soldiers monitoring them, the battle in the bay. "You want to know why? Because we suffered—when you stifled us, when you shut us out." Some of his soldiers grunted their agreement. "I have no interest in spending another five centuries seeing my people bow before human pigs—seeing them claw out a living while you shield and coddle those mortals, granting them our resources and wealth in exchange for *nothing*." He inclined his head. "So we shall reclaim what is ours. What was always ours, and will always be ours."

Rhys offered him a sly grin. "You can certainly try."

My mate didn't bother saying more as he hurled a slender javelin of power at him, the shot as precise as an arrow.

And when it reached the king—

It went right through him.

He rippled—then steadied.

An illusion. A shade.

The king rumbled a laugh. "Did you think I'd appear at this battle myself?" He waved a hand toward the soldiers still watching. "A taste—this battle is only a taste for you. To whet your appetite."

Then he was gone.

The magic leaking from the boat, the oily sheen it'd laid over Rhys's power . . . it vanished, too.

Rhys allowed the Hybern soldiers aboard the ship, aboard the ones around him, the honor of at least lifting their blades.

Then he turned them all into nothing but red mist and splinters floating on the waves.

CHAPTER 38

Mor was shaking me. I only knew it because Rhys threw me out of his mind the moment he unleashed himself upon those soldiers.

You were here too long, was all he said, caressing a dark talon down my face. Then I was out, stumbling down the bond, his shield slamming shut behind me.

"Feyre," Mor was saying, fingers digging into my shoulders through my leathers. "*Feyre*."

I blinked, the sun and blood and narrow street coming into focus.

Blinked—and then vomited all over the cobblestones between us.

People, shaken and petrified, only stared.

"This way," Mor said, and looped her arm around my waist as she led me into a dusty, empty alley. Far from watching eyes. I barely took in the city and bay and sea beyond—barely noticed that a mighty maelstrom of darkness and water and wind was now shoving Hybern's fleet back over the horizon. As if Tarquin's and Rhys's powers had been unleashed by the king's vanishing.

I made it to a pile of fallen stones from the half-wrecked building beside us when I vomited again. And again.

Mor put a hand on my back, rubbing soothing circles as I retched. "I did the same after my first battle. We all did."

It wasn't even a battle—not in the way I'd pictured: army against army on some unremarkable battlefield, chaotic and muddy. Even the real battle today had been out on the sea—where the Illyrians were now sailing inland.

I couldn't bear to start counting how many made the return trip.

I didn't know how Mor or Rhys or Cassian or Azriel could bear it.

And what I'd just seen . . . "The king was here," I breathed.

Mor's hand stilled on my back. "What?"

I leaned my brow against the sun-warmed brick of the building before me and told her—what I'd seen in Rhys's mind.

The king—he had been here and yet not here. Another trick—another spell. No wonder Rhys hadn't been able to attack his mind: the king hadn't been present to do so.

I closed my eyes as I finished, pressing my brow harder into the brick.

Blood and sweat still coated me. I tried to remember the usual fit of my soul in my body, the priority of things, my way of looking at the world. What to do with my limbs in the stillness. How did I usually position my hands without a blade between them? How did I *stop* moving?

Mor squeezed my shoulder, as if she understood the racing thoughts, the foreignness of my body. The War had raged for seven years. *Years*. How long would this one last?

"We should find the others," she said, and helped me straighten before winnowing us back to the palace towering high above.

I couldn't bring myself to send another thought down the bond. See where Rhys was. I didn't want him to see me—*feel* me—in such a state. Even if I knew he wouldn't judge.

He, too, had spilled blood on the battlefield today. And many others before it. All of my friends had.

And I could understand—just for a heartbeat, as the wind tore around us—why some rulers, human and Fae, had bowed before Hybern. Bowed, rather than face this.

It wasn't only the cost of life that ripped and devastated and sundered. It was the altering of a soul with it—the realization that I could perhaps go back home to Velaris, perhaps see peace achieved and cities rebuilt . . . but this battle, this war . . . *I* would be the thing forever changed.

War would linger with me long after it had ended, some invisible scar that would perhaps fade, but never wholly vanish.

But for my home, for Prythian and the human territory and so many others . . .

I would clean my blades, and wash the blood from my skin.

And I would do it again and again and again.

✣

The middle level of the palace was a flurry of motion: blood-drenched Summer Court soldiers limped around healers and servants rushing to the injured being laid on the floor.

The stream through the center of the hall ran red.

More and more winnowed in, borne by wide-eyed High Fae.

A few Illyrians—just as bloody but eyes clear—hauled in their own wounded through the open windows and balcony doors.

Mor and I scanned the space, the throngs of people, the reek of death and screams of the injured.

I tried to swallow, but my mouth was too dry. "Where are—"

I recognized the warrior the same moment he spied me.

Varian, kneeling over an injured soldier with his thigh in ribbons, went utterly still as our eyes met. His brown skin was splattered in blood as bright as the rubies they'd sent to us, his white hair plastered to his head, as if he'd just chucked off his helmet.

He whistled through his teeth, and a soldier appeared at his side, taking up his position of tying a tourniquet around the hurt male's thigh. The Prince of Adriata rose to his feet.

I did not have any magic left in me to shield. After seeing Rhys with the king, there was only an empty pit where my fear had been a wild sea within me. But I felt Mor's power slide into place between us.

There was a death-promise on my head. From them.

Varian approached—slowly. Stiffly. As if his entire body ached. Though his handsome face revealed nothing. Only bone-weary exhaustion.

His mouth opened—then shut. I didn't have words, either.

So Varian rasped, his voice hoarse enough that I knew he'd been screaming for a long, long time, "He's in the oak dining room."

The one where I had first dined with them.

I just nodded at the prince and began easing my way through the crowd, Mor keeping close to my side.

I'd thought Varian meant Rhysand.

But it was Tarquin who stood in gore-flecked silver armor at the dining table, maps and charts before him, Summer Court Fae either blood-soaked or pristine filling the sunny chamber.

The High Lord of the Summer Court looked up from the table as we paused on the threshold. Took in me, then Mor.

The kindness, the consideration that I had last seen on the High Lord's face was gone. Replaced by a grim, cold thing that made my stomach turn.

Blood had clotted from a thick slice down his neck, the caked bits crumbling away as Tarquin glanced to the people in the room and said, "Leave us."

No one even dared glance twice at him as they filed out.

I had done a horrible thing the last time we were here. I had lied, and stolen. I had torn into his mind and tricked him into believing me innocent. Harmless. I did not blame him for the blood ruby he had sent. But if he sought to exact his vengeance now . . .

"I heard you two cleared the palace. And helped clear the island."

His words were low—lifeless.

Mor inclined her head. "Your soldiers fought bravely beside us."

Tarquin ignored her, his crushing turquoise eyes upon me. Taking in the blood, the wounds, the leathers. Then the mating band on my finger, the star sapphire dull, blood crusted between the delicate folds and arcs of metal.

"I thought you came to finish the job," Tarquin said to me.

I didn't dare move.

"I heard Tamlin took you. Then I heard the Spring Court fell. Collapsed from within. Its people in revolt. And you had vanished. And when I saw the Illyrian legion sweeping in . . . I thought you had come for me, too. To help Hybern finish us off."

Varian had not told him—of the message he'd snuck to Amren. Not a call for aid, but a frantic warning for Amren to save herself. Tarquin hadn't known that we'd be coming.

"We would never ally with Hybern," Mor said.

"I am talking to Feyre Archeron."

I'd never heard Tarquin use that tone. Mor bristled, but said nothing.

"Why?" Tarquin demanded, sunlight glinting on his armor—whose delicate, overlapping scales were fashioned after a fish's.

I didn't know what he meant. Why had we deceived and stolen from him? Why had we come to help? Why to both?

"Our dreams are the same," was all I could think to say.

A united realm, in which lesser faeries were no longer shoved down. A better world.

The opposite of what Hybern fought for. What his allies fought for.

"Is that how you justified stealing from me?"

My heart stumbled a beat.

Rhysand said from behind me, no doubt having winnowed in, "My mate and I had our reasons, Tarquin."

My knees nearly buckled at the evenness in his voice, at the blood-speckled face that still revealed no sign of great injury, at the dark armor—the twin to Azriel's and Cassian's—that had held intact despite a few deep scratches I could barely stand to note. *Cassian and Azriel?*

Fine. Overseeing the Illyrian injured and setting up camp in the hills.

Tarquin glanced between us. "Mate."

"Wasn't it obvious?" Rhysand asked with a wink. But there was an edge in his eyes—sharp and haunted.

My chest tightened. *Did the king leave some sort of trap to—*

He slid a hand against my back. *No. No—I'm all right. Pissed I didn't see that he was an illusion, but . . . Fine.*

Tarquin's face didn't so much as shift from that cold wrath. "When you went into the Spring Court and deceived Tamlin as well about your true nature, when you destroyed his territory . . . You left the door open for Hybern. They docked in his harbors." No doubt to wait for the wall to collapse and then sail south. Tarquin snarled, "It was an easy trip to my doorstep. You did this."

I could have sworn I felt Rhys flinch through the bond. But my mate said calmly, "We did nothing. Hybern chooses its actions, not us." He jerked his chin toward Tarquin. "My force shall remain camped in the hills until you've deemed the city secure. Then we will go."

"And do you plan to steal anything else before you do?"

Rhys went utterly still. Debating, I realized, whether to apologize. Explain.

I spared him from the choice. "Tend to your wounded, Tarquin."

"Don't give me orders."

The face of the former Summer Court admiral—the prince who had commanded the fleet in the harbor until the title was thrust upon him. I took in the weariness fogging his eyes, the anger and grief.

People had died. Many people. The city he had fought so hard to rebuild, the people who had tried to fight past the scars of Amarantha . . .

"We are at your disposal," I said to him, and walked out.

Mor kept close, and we emerged into the hall to find a cluster of his advisers and soldiers watching us carefully. Behind us, Rhys said to Tarquin, "I didn't have a choice. I did it to try to *avoid* this, Tarquin. To stop Hybern before he got this far." His voice was strained.

Tarquin only said, "Get out. And take your army with you. We can hold the bay now that they don't have surprise on their side."

Silence. Mor and I lingered just outside the open doors, not turning back, but both of us listening. Listening as Rhysand said, "I saw enough of Hybern in the War to tell you this attack is just a fraction of what the king plans to unleash." A pause. "Come to the meeting, Tarquin. We need you—Prythian needs you."

Another beat of quiet. Then Tarquin said, "Get out."

"Feyre's offer holds: we are at your disposal."

"Take your mate and leave. And I'd suggest warning her not to give High Lords orders."

I stiffened, about to whirl around, when Rhys said, "She is High Lady of the Night Court. She may do as she wishes."

The wall of Fae standing before us withdrew slightly. Now studying me, some gaping. A murmur rippled through them. Tarquin let out a low, bitter laugh. "You do love to spit on tradition."

Rhys didn't say anything more, his strolling footsteps sounding over the tiled floor until his hand warmed my shoulder. I looked up at him, aware of all who gawked at us. At me.

Rhys pressed a kiss to my sweaty, blood-crusted temple and we vanished.

CHAPTER 39

The Illyrian camp remained in the hills above Adriata.

Mostly because there were so many injured that we couldn't move them until they'd healed enough to survive it.

Wings shredded, guts dangling out, faces mauled . . .

I don't know how my friends were still standing as they tended to the wounded as much as they could. I barely saw Azriel, who had set up a tent to organize the information pouring in from his scouts: the Hybern fleet had retreated. Not to the Spring Court, but across the sea. No sign of any other forces waiting to strike. No whisper of Tamlin or Jurian.

Cassian, though . . . He limped through the injured laid out on the rocky, dry ground, offering kernels of praise or comfort to the soldiers who had not yet been tended. With the Siphons, he could do quick battlefield patching, but . . . nothing extensive. Nothing intricate.

His face, whenever we crossed paths as I fetched supplies for the healers working without rest, was grave. Gaunt. He still wore his armor, and though he'd rinsed the blood from his skin, it clung near the neck of his breastplate. The dullness in his hazel eyes was the same as that glazing my own. And Mor's.

But Rhys . . . His eyes were clear. Alert. His expression grim, but . . . It was to him the soldiers looked. And he was everything he should be: a High Lord confident in his victory, whose forces had smashed through the Hybern fleet and saved a city of innocents. The toll it had taken on his own soldiers was difficult, but a worthy cost for victory. He strolled through the camp—overseeing the wounded, the information Azriel handed him, checking in with his commanders—still in his Illyrian armor. But wings gone. They'd vanished before he'd appeared in Tarquin's chamber.

The sun set, leaving a blanket of darkness over the city lying below. So much darker than I'd last beheld it, alive and glittering with light. But this new darkness . . . We had seen it in Velaris after the attack—we now knew it too well.

Faelights bobbed over our camp, gilding the talons of all those Illyrian wings as they worked or lay injured. I knew many looked to me—their High Lady.

But I could not muster Rhys's ease. His quiet triumph.

So I kept fetching bowls of fresh water, kept hauling away the bloodied ones. Helped pin down screaming soldiers until my teeth clacked against each other with the force of their thrashing.

I sat down only when my legs could no longer keep me upright, upon an overturned bucket outside the healers' tent. Just a few minutes—I'd sit for just a few minutes.

I awoke inside another tent, laid upon a pile of furs, the faelight dim and soft.

Rhys sat beside me, legs crossed, his hair in unusual disarray. Streaked with blood—as if it had coated his hands when he dragged them through it.

"How long was I out?" My words were a rasp.

He lifted his head from where he'd been studying some array of papers spread on the fur before him. "Three hours. Dawn is still far off—you should sleep."

But I propped myself on my elbows. "You're not."

He shrugged, sipping from the water goblet set beside him. "I'm not the one who fell face-first off a bucket into the mud." His wry smile faded. "How are you feeling?"

I almost said *Fine*, but . . . "I'm still figuring out what to feel."

A careful nod. "Open war is like that . . . It takes a while to decide how to deal with everything that it brings. The costs."

I sat up fully, scanning the papers he'd laid out. Casualty lists. Only a hundred or so names on them, but . . . "Did you know them—the ones who died?"

His violet eyes shuttered. "A few. Tarquin lost many more than we did."

"Who tells their families?"

"Cassian. He'll send out lists once dawn arrives—when we see who survives the night. He'll visit their families if he knew them."

I remembered that Rhys had once told me he'd scanned casualty lists for his friends in the War—the dread they'd all felt, waiting to see if a familiar name was on them.

So many shadows clouded those violet eyes. I laid a hand on his own. He studied my fingers on his, the arcs of dirt beneath my fingernails.

"The king only came today," he said at last, "to taunt me. The library attack, this battle . . . It was a way to toy with me. Us."

I touched his jaw. Cold—his skin was cold, despite the warm summer night pressing on us. "You are not going to die in this war, Rhysand."

His attention snapped to me.

I cupped his face in both hands now. "Don't you listen to a word he says. He knows—"

"He knows about us. Our histories."

And that scared Rhys to death.

"He knew the library . . . He picked it for what it meant to *me*, not just to take Nesta."

"So we learn where to hit him, and strike hard. Better yet, we kill him before he can do any further harm."

Rhys shook his head slightly, removing his face from my hands. "If it was only the king to contend with . . . But with the Cauldron in his arsenal . . ."

And it was the way his shoulders began to curve in, the way his chin dipped ever so slightly . . . I grabbed his hand again. "We need allies," I said, my eyes burning. "We can't face the brunt of this war alone."

"I know." The words were heavy—weary.

"Move the meeting with the High Lords sooner. Three days from now."

"I will." I'd never heard that tone—that quiet.

And it was precisely because of it that I said, "I love you."

His head lifted, eyes churning. "There was a time when I dreamed of hearing that," he murmured. "When I never thought I'd hear it from you." He gestured to the tent—to Adriata beyond it. "Our trip here was the first time I let myself . . . hope."

To the stars who listen—and the dreams that are answered.

And yet today, with Tarquin . . .

"The world should know," I said. "The world should know how good you are, Rhysand—how wonderful all of you are."

"I can't tell if I should be worried that you're saying such nice things about me. Maybe the king's taunting *did* get to you."

I pinched his arm, and he let out a low laugh before raising my face to study my eyes. He angled his head. "*Should* I be worried?"

I put a hand to his cheek once more, the silken skin now warm. "You are selfless, and brave, and kind. You are more than I ever dreamed for myself, more than I . . ." The words choked off, and I swallowed, taking a deep breath. I wasn't sure if he needed to hear it after what the king had said, but *I* needed to say it. Starlight now danced in his eyes. But I went on, "At this meeting with the other High Lords, what role will you play?"

"The usual one."

I nodded, having anticipated his answer. "And the others will play their usual roles, too."

"And?"

I slid my hand from his face and put it over his heart. "I think the time has come for us to remove the masks. To stop playing the part."

He waited, hearing me out.

"Velaris is secret no longer. The king knows too much about us—who we are. What we are. And if we're to ally with the other High Lords . . . I think they need the truth. They will need the truth in order to trust us. The truth about who you really are—who Mor and Cassian and Azriel really are. Look at how poorly things went with Tarquin today. We can't—we can't let it continue like this. So no more masks, no more roles to play. We go as ourselves. As a family."

If anything, the king's taunting had told me that. Games were over. There would be no more disguises, no more lies. Perhaps he thought it'd drive us toward continuing to do such things. But to stand a chance . . . perhaps victory lay in the other direction. In honesty. With us standing together—as precisely who we were.

I waited for Rhys to tell me that I was young and inexperienced, that I knew nothing of politics and war.

Yet Rhys only brushed his thumb over my cheek. "They may be angry at the lies we've fed them over the centuries."

"Then we will make it clear that we understand their feelings—and make it clear that we had no alternative way to protect our people."

"We'll show them the Court of Dreams," he said quietly.

I nodded. We'd show them—and also show Keir, and Eris, and Beron. Show who we were to our allies—and our enemies.

Stars glimmered and burned out in those beautiful eyes. "And what of your powers?" The king had known of them, too—or guessed at it.

I knew from his cautious tone that he'd already formed an opinion. But the choice was mine—he'd face it at my side no matter what I decided.

And as I thought it through . . . "I think they'll see the revealing of our good sides as manipulative if it also comes out that your mate has stolen power from them all. If the king plans to use that information against us—we'll deal with that later."

"Technically, that power was *gifted*, but . . . you're right. We'll have to walk a fine enough line regarding how we show ourselves—spin it the right way so they don't think it's a trap or scheme. But when it comes to you . . ." Darkness blotted out the stars in his eyes. The darkness of assassins and thieves, the darkness of uncompromising death. "You could tip the scale in Hybern's favor if any of them are considering an alliance. Beron alone might try to kill you, with or without this war. I doubt even Eris could keep him from it."

I could have sworn the war-camp shuddered at the power that rumbled awake—the wrath. Voices outside the tent dropped to whispers. Or outright silence.

But I leaned over and kissed him lightly. "We'll deal with it," I said onto his mouth.

He pulled his mouth from mine, his face grave. "We keep all your powers but the ones I gave you hidden. As my High Lady, you will have been expected to have received some."

I swallowed hard, nodding, and took a long drink from his goblet of water. No more lies, no more deceptions—beyond my magic. Let Tarquin be the first and last casualty of our deceit.

I chewed on my lip. "What about Miryam and Drakon? Have you learned anything about where they might have gone?" *Along with that legion of aerial warriors?*

The question seemed to drag him up from wherever he'd gone while contemplating what now lay before us.

Rhys sighed, scanning those casualty lists again. The dark ink seemed to absorb the dim faelight. "No. Az's spies have found no trace of them in any of the surrounding territories." He rubbed his temple. "How do you vanish an entire people?"

I frowned. "I suppose Jurian's tactic to draw them out worked against him." Jurian—there hadn't been a whisper of him at the battle today.

"It would seem so." He shook his head, the light dancing in the raven-black locks of his hair. "I should have established protocols with them—centuries ago. Ways to contact them, for them to contact us, if we ever needed help."

"Why didn't you?"

"They wanted to be forgotten by the world. And when I saw how peaceful Cretea became . . . I did not want the world to intrude on them, either." A muscle flickered in his jaw.

"If we did somehow find them . . . would that be enough, though? If we can stop the wall from sundering first, I mean. Our forces and Drakon's, perhaps even Queen Vassa if Lucien can find her, against all of Hybern?" Against whatever gambits or spells the king still planned to unleash.

Rhys was quiet for a moment. "It might have to be."

It was the way his voice went hoarse, the way his eyes guttered, that made me press a kiss to his mouth as I laid a hand upon his chest and pushed him down upon the furs.

His brows rose, but a half smile appeared on his lips. "There's little privacy in a war-camp," he warned, some of the light coming back to his eyes.

I only straddled him, unfastening the button at the top of his dark jacket. The one below it. "Then I suppose you'll have to be quiet," I said, working my way down the front of the jacket until it gaped open to reveal the shirt beneath. I traced a finger of the whorl of tattoo peeking out near his neck. "When I saw you facing the king today . . ."

He brushed his fingers against my thighs. "I know. I felt you."

I tugged on the hem of his shirt, and he rose onto his elbows, helping me remove his jacket, then the shirt beneath. A bruise marred his ribs, an angry splotch—

"It's fine," he said before I could speak. "A lucky shot."

"With *what?*"

Again, that half smile. "A spear?"

My heart stopped. "A . . ." I delicately brushed the bruise, swallowing hard.

"Tipped in faebane. My shield blocked most of it—but not enough to avoid the impact."

Dread curled in my stomach. But I leaned down and brushed a kiss over the bruise.

Rhys loosed a long breath, his body seeming to settle. Calm.

So I kissed the bruise again. Moved lower. He drew idle circles on my shoulder, my back.

I felt his shield settle around our tent as I unbuttoned his pants. As I kissed my way across the muscled pane of his stomach.

Lower. Rhys's hands slid into my hair as the rest of his clothes vanished.

I stroked my hand over him once, twice—luxuriating in the feel of him, in knowing he was here, we were *both* here. Safe.

Then I echoed the movement with my mouth.

His growls of pleasure filled the tent, drowning out the distant cries of the injured and dying. Life and death—hovering so close, whispering in our ears.

But I tasted Rhys, worshipped him with my hands and mouth and then my body—and hoped that this shard of life we offered up, this undimming light between us, would drive death a bit further away. At least for another day.

Only a few more Illyrians died during the night. But high up in the hills, the screams and wails of Tarquin's people rose to us on plumes of smoke from the still-burning fires Hybern had set. They continued burning when we left in the early hours after dawn, winnowing back to Velaris.

Cassian and Azriel remained to lead the Illyrian legions to their new camp on our southern borders—and the former left from there to fly into the Steppes. To offer his condolences to a few of those families.

Nesta was waiting for us in the foyer of the town house, Amren seething in a chair before the unlit fireplace of the sitting room.

No sign of Elain, but before I could ask, Nesta demanded, "What happened?"

Rhys glanced to me, then to Amren, who had shot to her feet and was now watching us with the same expression as Nesta's. My mate said to my sister, "There was a battle. We won."

"We know that," Amren said, her small feet near-silent on the rugs as she strode for us. "What happened with Tarquin?"

Mor took a breath to say something about Varian that would likely not end well for any of us, so I cut in, "Well, he didn't try to slaughter us on sight, so . . . things went decently?"

Rhys gave me a bemused look. "The royal family remains alive and well. Tarquin's armada suffered losses, but Cresseida and Varian were unscathed."

Something tight in Amren's face seemed to relax at the words—his careful, diplomatic words.

But Nesta was glancing between us all, her back still stiff, mouth a thin line. "Where is he?"

"Who?" Rhys crooned.

"Cassian."

I didn't think I'd ever heard his name from her lips. Cassian had always been *him* or *that one*. And Nesta had been . . . pacing in the foyer.

As if she was worried.

I opened my mouth, but Mor beat me to it. "He's busy."

I'd never heard her voice so . . . sharp. Icy.

Nesta held Mor's stare. Her jaw tightened, then relaxed, then tightened—as if fighting some battle to keep questions in. Mor didn't drop her gaze.

Mor had never seemed ruffled by mention of Cassian's past lovers. Perhaps because they'd never meant much—not in the ways that counted. But if the Illyrian warrior no longer stood as a physical and emotional buffer between her and Azriel . . . And worse, if the person who caused that vacancy was Nesta . . .

Mor said flatly, "When he gets back, keep your forked tongue behind your teeth."

My heart leaped into a furious beat, my arms slack at my sides at the insult, the threat.

But Rhys said, "Mor."

She slowly—so slowly—looked at him.

There was nothing but uncompromising will in Rhys's face. "We now leave for the meeting in three days. Send out dispatches to the other High Lords to inform them. And I'm done debating where to meet. Pick a place and be done with it."

She stared him down for a heartbeat, then dragged her gaze back to my sister.

Nesta's face had not altered, the coldness limning it unbending. She was so still she seemed to barely be breathing. But she did not balk. She did not avert her eyes from the Morrigan.

Mor vanished with hardly a blink.

Nesta only turned and headed for the sitting room, where I noticed books had been laid on the low-lying table before the hearth.

Amren flowed in behind her, tossing a backward look over a shoulder at Rhys. The motion shifted her gray blouse enough that I caught the sparkle of red peeking beneath the fabric.

The necklace of rubies that she wore, hidden, beneath her shirt. Gifted from Varian.

But Rhys nodded to Amren, and the female asked my sister, "Where were we?"

Nesta sat in the armchair, holding herself tightly enough that the whites of her knuckles arced through her skin. "You were explaining how the territory lines were formed between courts."

The words were distant—brittle. And—*They've also taken up history lessons?*

I'm as shocked as you are that the house is still standing.

I swallowed my laugh, linking my arm through his and tugging him down the hall. It had been a while since I'd seen him so . . . dirty. We both needed a bath, but there was something I had to do first. Needed to do.

Behind us, Amren murmured to Nesta, "Cassian has gone to war many times, girl. He isn't general of Rhys's forces for nothing. This battle was a skirmish compared to what lies ahead. He's likely visiting the families of the fallen as we speak. He'll be back before the meeting."

Nesta said, "I don't care."

At least she was talking again.

I halted Rhys halfway down the hall.

With so many listening ears in the house, I said down the bond, *Take me to the Prison. Right now.*

Rhys asked no questions.

CHAPTER 40

I had no bone to bring with me. And though every step up that hillside and then down into the dark ripped and weighed on me, I kept moving. Kept planting one foot in front of the other.

I had the feeling Rhys did the same.

Standing before the Bone Carver two hours later, the ancient death-god still wearing my would-be son's skin, I said, "Find another object that you desire."

The Carver's violet eyes flared. "Why does the High Lord linger in the hall?"

"He has little interest in seeing you."

Partially true. Rhys had wondered if the blow to his pride would work in our favor.

"You reek of blood—and death." The Carver breathed in a great lungful of air. Of my scent.

"Pick another object than the Ouroboros," was all I said.

Hybern knew about our histories, our would-be allies. There remained a shred of hope that he would not see the Carver coming.

"I desire nothing else than my window to the world."

I avoided the urge to clench my hands into fists.

"I could offer you so many other things." My voice turned low, honeyed.

"You are afraid to claim the mirror." The Bone Carver angled his head. "Why?"

"You are not afraid of it?"

"No." A little smile. He leaned to the side. "Are you frightened of it, too, Rhysand?"

My mate didn't bother to answer from the hall, though he did come to lean against the threshold, crossing his arms. The Carver sighed at the sight of him—the dirt and blood and wrinkled clothes, and said, "Oh, I much prefer you bloodied up."

"Pick something else," I replied. *And not a fool's errand this time.*

"What would you give me? Riches do me no good down here. Power holds no sway over the stone." He chuckled. "What about your firstborn?" A secret smile as he gestured with that small boy's hand to himself.

Rhys's attention slid to me, surprise—surprise and something deeper, more tender—flickering on his face. *Not just any boy, then.*

My cheeks heated. *No. Not just any boy.*

"It is rude, Majesties, to speak when no one can hear you."

I sliced a glare toward the Carver. "There is nothing else, then." *Nothing else that won't break me if I so much as look upon it?*

"Bring me the Ouroboros and I am yours. You have my word."

I weighed the beatific expression on the Carver's face before I strode out.

"Where is my bone?" The demand cracked through the gloom.

I kept walking. But Rhys chucked something at him. "From lunch."

The Carver's hiss of outrage as a chicken bone skittered over the floor followed us out.

In silence, we began the trek up through the Prison. The mirror—I'd have to find some way to get it. After the meeting. Just in case it did indeed . . . destroy me.

What does he look like?

The question was soft—tentative. I knew who he meant.

I interlaced my fingers through Rhysand's and squeezed tightly. *Let me show you.*

And as we walked through the darkness, toward that distant, still-hidden light, I did.

We were starving by the time we returned to the town house. And since neither of us felt like waiting for food to be prepared, Rhys and I headed right for the kitchen, passing by Amren and Nesta with little more than a wave.

My mouth was already watering as Rhys shouldered open the swinging door into the kitchen.

But we beheld what was within and halted.

Elain stood between Nuala and Cerridwen at the long worktable. All three of them covered in flour. Some sort of doughy mess on the surface before them.

The two handmaiden-spies instantly bowed to Rhys, and Elain—

There was a slight sparkle in her brown eyes.

As if she'd been enjoying herself with them.

Nuala swallowed hard. "The lady said she was hungry, so we went to make her something. But—she said she wanted to learn how, so . . ." Hands wreathed in shadows lifted in a helpless gesture, flour drifting off them like veils of snow. "We're making bread."

Elain was glancing between all of us, and as her eyes began to shutter, I gave her a broad smile and said, "I hope it'll be done soon—I'm starved."

Elain offered a faint smile in return and nodded.

She was hungry. She was . . . doing something. *Learning* something.

"We're going to bathe," I announced, even as my stomach grumbled. "We'll leave you to your baking."

I tugged Rhys into the hall before they'd finished saying good-bye, the kitchen door swinging shut behind us.

I put a hand on my chest, leaning against the wood panels of the stair wall. Rhys's hand covered my own a heartbeat later.

"That was what I felt," he said, "when I saw you smile that night we dined along the Sidra."

I leaned forward, resting my brow against his chest, right over his heart. "She still has a long way to go."

"We all do."

He stroked a hand over my back. I leaned into the touch, savoring his warmth and strength.

For long minutes, we stood there. Until I said, "Let's go find somewhere to eat—outside."

"Hmmm." He showed no sign of letting go.

I looked up at last. Found his eyes shining with that familiar, wicked light. "I think I'm hungry for something else," he purred.

My toes curled in my boots, but I lifted my brows and said coolly, "Oh?"

Rhys nipped at my earlobe, then whispered in my ear as he winnowed us up to our bedroom, where two plates of food now waited on the desk. "I owe you for last night, mate."

He gave me the courtesy, at least, of letting me pick what he consumed first: me or the food.

I picked wisely.

Nesta was waiting at the breakfast table the next morning.

Not for me, I realized as her gaze slipped over me as if I were no more than a servant. But for someone else.

I kept my mouth shut, not bothering to tell her Cassian was still up at the war-camps. If she wouldn't ask . . . I wasn't getting in the middle of it.

Not when Amren claimed that my sister was close—so close—to grasping whatever skill was involved in potentially patching up the wall. If she would only *unleash* herself, Amren said. I didn't dare suggest that perhaps the world wasn't quite ready for that.

I ate my breakfast in silence, my fork scraping across the plate. Amren said she was close to finding what we needed in the Book, too—whatever spell my sister would wield. How Amren knew, I had no idea. It didn't seem wise to ask.

Nesta only spoke when I rose to my feet. "You're going to that meeting in two days."

"Yes."

I braced myself for whatever she intended to say.

Nesta glanced toward the front windows, as if still waiting, still watching.

"You went off into battle. Without a second thought. Why?"

"Because I had to. Because people needed help."

Her blue-gray eyes were near-silver in the trickle of morning light. But Nesta said nothing else, and after waiting for another moment, I left, winnowing up to the House for my flying lesson with Azriel.

CHAPTER 41

The next two days were so busy that the lesson with Azriel was the only time I trained with him. The spymaster had returned from dispatching the messages Mor had written about the meeting moving up. They had agreed on the date, at least. But Mor's declaration of the spot, despite her unyielding language, had been universally rejected. Thus continued the endless back-and-forth between courts.

Under the Mountain had once been their neutral meeting place.

Even if it hadn't been sealed, no one was inclined to meet there now.

So the debate raged about who would host the gathering of all the High Lords.

Well, six of them. Beron, at last, had deigned to join. But no word had come from the Spring Court, though we knew the messages had been received.

All of us would go—save Amren and Nesta, who the former insisted needed to practice more. Especially when Amren had found a passage in the Book last night that *might* be what we needed to fix the wall.

With only hours to spare the evening before, it was finally agreed that the meeting would take place in the Dawn Court. It was close enough to the middle of the land, and since Kallias, High Lord of Winter, would not allow anyone into his territory after the horrors Amarantha had wrought upon its people, it was the only other area flanking that neutral middle land.

Rhys and Thesan, High Lord of the Dawn Court, were on decent terms. Dawn was mostly neutral in any conflict, but as one of the three Solar Courts, their allegiance always leaned toward each other. Not as strong an ally as Helion Spell-Cleaver in the Day Court, but strong enough.

It didn't stop Rhys, Mor, and Azriel from gathering around the dining table at the town house the night before to go over every kernel of information they'd ever learned about Thesan's palace—about possible pitfalls and traps. And escape routes.

It was an effort not to pace, not to ask if perhaps the risks outweighed the benefits. So much had gone wrong in Hybern. So much was going wrong throughout the world. Every time Azriel spoke, I heard his roar of pain as that bolt went through his chest. Every time Mor countered an argument, I saw her pale-faced and backing away from the king. Every time Rhys asked for my opinion, I saw him kneeling in his friends' blood, begging the king not to sever our bond.

Nesta and Amren paused their practicing in the sitting room every so often so that the latter could chime in with some bit of advice or warning regarding the meeting. Or so that Amren could snap at Nesta to concentrate, to push harder. While she herself combed through the Book.

A few more days, Amren declared when Nesta at last went upstairs, complaining of a headache. A few more days, and my sister, through whatever mysterious power, might be able to *do* something. That is, Amren added, if *she* could crack that promising section of the Book in time. And with that, the dark-haired female bid us good night—to go read until her eyes were bleeding, she claimed.

Considering how awful the Book was, I wasn't entirely sure if she was joking.

The others weren't, either.

I barely touched my dinner. And I barely slept that night, twisting in the sheets until Rhys woke and patiently listened to me murmur my fears until they were nothing but shadows.

Dawn broke, and as I dressed, the morning unfurled into a sunny, dry day.

Though we would be going to the meeting as we truly were, our usual attire remained the same: Rhys in his preferred black jacket and pants, Azriel and Cassian in their Illyrian armor, all seven Siphons polished and gleaming. Mor had forgone her usual red gown for one of midnight blue. It was cut with the same revealing panels and flowing, gauzy skirts, but there was something . . . restrained in it. Regal. A princess of the realm.

The usual attire—except my own.

I had not found a new gown. For there was no other gown that could top the one I now wore as I stood in the foyer while the clock on the sitting room mantel struck eleven.

Rhys hadn't yet come downstairs, and there was no sign of Amren or Nesta to see us off. We'd gathered a few minutes earlier, but . . . I looked down at myself again. Even in the warm faelight of the foyer, the gown glittered and gleamed like a fresh-cut jewel.

We had taken my gown from Starfall and refashioned it, adding sheer silk panels to the back shoulders, the glittering material like woven starlight as it flowed behind me in lieu of a veil or cape. If Rhysand was Night Triumphant, I was the star that only glowed thanks to his darkness, the light only visible because of him.

I scowled up the stairs. That is, if he bothered to show up on time.

My hair, Nuala had swept into an ornate, elegant arc across my head, and in front of it . . .

I caught Cassian glancing at me for the third time in less than a minute and demanded, "What?"

His lips twitched at the corners. "You just look so . . ."

"Here we go," Mor muttered from where she picked at her red-tinted nails against the stair banister. Rings glinted at every knuckle, on every finger; stacks of bracelets tinkled against each other on either wrist.

"Official," Cassian said with an incredulous look in her direction. He waved a Siphon-topped hand to me. "*Fancy.*"

"Over five hundred years old," Mor said, shaking her head sadly, "a skilled warrior and general, famous throughout territories, and complimenting ladies is still something he finds next to impossible. Remind me why we bring you on diplomatic meetings?"

Azriel, wreathed in shadows by the front door, chuckled quietly. Cassian shot him a glare. "I don't see *you* spouting poetry, brother."

Azriel crossed his arms, still smiling faintly. "I don't need to resort to it."

Mor let out a crow of laughter, and I snorted, earning a jab in the ribs from Cassian. I batted his hand away, but refrained from the shove I wanted to give him, only because it was the first I'd seen of him since Adriata and shadows still dimmed his eyes—and because of the precarious-feeling thing atop my head.

The crown.

Rhys had crowned me at each and every meeting and function we'd had, long before I was his mate, long before I was his High Lady. Even Under the Mountain.

I'd never questioned the tiaras and diadems and crowns that Nuala or Cerridwen wove into my hair. Never objected to them—even before things between us had been this way. But this one . . . I peered up the stairs as Rhys's strolling, unhurried footsteps thudded on the carpet.

This crown was heavier. Not unwelcome, but . . . strange. And as Rhys appeared at the top of the stairs, resplendent in that black jacket, his wings out and gleaming as if he'd polished them, I was again in that room he'd brought me to late last night, after I'd awoken him with my thrashing and twisting in bed.

It was contained a level above the library in the House of Wind, and warded with so many spells that it had taken him a few moments to work through them. Only he and I—and any future offspring, he added with a soft smile—were able to enter. Unless we brought guests.

The chamber was a cool, chill black—as if we'd stepped inside the mind of some sleeping beast. And within its round space gleamed glittering islands of light. Of jewels.

Ten thousand years' worth of treasure.

It was neatly organized, in podiums and open drawers and busts and racks.

"The family jewels," Rhys said with a devious grin. "Some of the pieces we don't like are kept at the Court of Nightmares, just so they don't get pissy and because we sometimes loan them to Mor's family, but these . . . these are for the family."

He led me past displays that sparkled like small constellations, the worth of each . . . Even as a merchant's daughter, I could not calculate the worth of any of it.

And toward the back of the chamber, shrouded in a heavier darkness . . .

I'd heard of catacombs on the continent, where skulls of beloved or infamous people were kept in little alcoves—dozens or hundreds of them to a wall.

The concept here was the same: carved into the rock was an entire wall of crowns. They each had their own resting place, lined with black velvet, each illuminated by—

"Glowworms," Rhys told me as the tiny, bluish globs crusted in the arches of each nook seemed to glitter like the entire night sky. In fact . . . What I'd taken for small faelights in the ceiling high above . . . It was all glowworms. Pale blue and turquoise, their light as silken as moonlight, illumining the jewels with their ancient, silent fire.

"Pick one," Rhys whispered in my ear.

"A glowworm?"

He nipped at my earlobe. "Smartass." He steered me back toward the wall of crowns, each wholly different—as individual as skulls. "Pick whichever crown you like."

"I can't just—take one."

"You most certainly can. They belong to you."

I lifted a brow. "They don't—not really."

"By law and tradition, this is all yours. Sell it, melt it, wear them—do whatever you want."

"You don't care about it?" I gestured to the trove worth more than most kingdoms.

"Oh, I have favorite pieces that I might convince you to spare, but . . . This is yours. Every last piece of it."

Our eyes met, and I knew he, too, recalled the words that I'd whispered to him months ago. That every piece of my still-healing heart belonged to him. I smiled, and brushed a hand down his arm before approaching the wall of crowns.

I had been terrified once, in Tamlin's court, of being given a crown. Had dreaded it. And I supposed that I indeed had never fretted over it when it came to Rhys. As if some small part of me had always known that this was where I was meant to be: at his side, as his equal. His queen.

Rhys inclined his head as if to say yes—he saw and understood and had always known.

Now striding down the town house stairs, Rhys's attention went right to that crown atop my head. And the emotion that rippled across his face was enough to make even Mor and Cassian look away.

I'd let the crown call to me. I hadn't picked it for style or comfort, but for the draw I felt to it, as if it were that ring in the Weaver's cottage.

My crown was crafted of silver and diamond, all fashioned into swirls of stars and various phases of the moon. Its arching apex held aloft a crescent moon of solid diamond, flanked by two exploding stars. And with the glittering dress from Starfall . . .

Rhys stepped off the stairs and took my hand.

Night Triumphant—and the Stars Eternal.

If he was the sweet, terrifying darkness, I was the glittering light that only his shadows could make clear.

"I thought you were leaving," Nesta's voice cut in from atop the stairs.

I braced myself, dragging my attention away from Rhys.

Nesta was in a gown of darkest blue, no jewelry to be seen, her hair swept up and unadorned as well. I supposed that with her stunning beauty, she needed no ornamentation. It would have been like putting jewelry on a lion. But for her to be dressed like that . . .

She strode down the stairs, and when the others were silent, I realized . . .

I tried not to look too obvious as I glanced at Cassian.

They had not seen each other since Adriata.

But the warrior only gave her a cursory once-over and turned toward Azriel to say something. Mor was watching both carefully—the warning she'd given my sister ringing silently between them. And Nesta, Mother damn it all, seemed to remember. Seemed to rein in whatever words she'd been about to spit and just approached me.

And nearly made my heart stop dead with shock as she said, "You look beautiful."

I blinked at her.

Mor said, "That, Cassian, was what you were attempting to say."

He grumbled something we chose not to hear. I said to Nesta, "Thank you. You do as well."

Nesta only shrugged.

I pushed, "Why *are* you dressed so nicely? Shouldn't you be practicing with Amren?"

I felt Cassian's attention slide to us, felt them all look as Nesta said, "I'm going with you."

CHAPTER 42

No one said anything.

Nesta only lifted her chin. "I . . ." I'd never seen her stumble for words. "I do not want to be remembered as a coward."

"No one would say that," I offered quietly.

"I would." Nesta surveyed us all, her gaze jumping past Cassian. Not to slight him, but . . . avoid answering the look he was giving her. Approval—more. "It was some distant thing," she said. "War. Battle. It . . . it's not anymore. I will help, if I can. If it means . . . telling them what happened."

"You've given enough," I said, my dress rustling as I braved a solitary step toward her. "Amren claimed you were close to mastering whatever skill you need. You should stay—focus on that."

"No." The word was steady, clear. "A day or two delay with my training won't make any difference. Perhaps by the time we return, Amren will have decoded that spell in the Book." She shrugged with a shoulder. "You went off to battle for a court you barely know—who barely see you as friends. Amren showed me the blood ruby. And when I asked you why . . . you said because it was the right thing. People needed help." Her throat bobbed. "No one is going to fight to save the humans beneath the wall. No one cares. But I do." She toyed with a fold in her dress. "I do."

Rhys stepped up to my side. "As High Lady, Feyre is no longer my emissary to the human world." He gave Nesta a tentative smile. "Want the job?"

Nesta's face yielded nothing, but I could have sworn some spark flared. "Consider this meeting a trial basis. And I'll make you pay through the teeth for my services."

Rhys sketched a bow. "I would expect nothing less of an Archeron sister." I poked him in the ribs, and he huffed a laugh. "Welcome to the court," he said to her. "You're about to have one hell of a first day."

And to my eternal shock, a smile tugged at Nesta's mouth.

"No going back now," Cassian said to Rhys, gesturing to his wings.

Rhys slid his hands into his pockets. "I figure it's time for the world to know who really has the largest wingspan."

Cassian laughed, and even Azriel smiled. Mor gave me a look that had me biting my lip to keep from howling.

"Twenty gold marks says there's a fight in the first hour," Cassian said, still not really looking at Nesta.

"Thirty, and I say within forty-five minutes," Mor said, crossing her arms.

"You do remember there are vows and wards of neutrality," Rhys said mildly.

"You lot don't need fists or magic to fight," Mor chirped.

Azriel said from the door, "Fifty, and I say within thirty minutes. Started by Autumn."

Rhys rolled his eyes. "Try *not* to look like you're all gambling on them. And no cheating by provoking fights." Their answering grins were anything but reassuring. Rhys sighed. "A hundred marks on a fight within fifteen minutes."

Nesta let out a soft snort. But they all looked to me, waiting.

I shrugged. "Rhys and I are a team. He can gamble away our money on this bullshit."

They all looked deeply offended.

Rhys looped his elbow through mine. "A queen in appearance—"

"Don't even finish that," I said.

He laughed. "Shall we?"

He'd winnow me in, Mor would now take Cassian *and* Nesta, and Azriel would carry himself. Rhys glanced toward the sitting room clock and gave the shadowsinger a nod.

Azriel instantly vanished. First to arrive—first to see if any trap awaited.

In silence, we waited. One minute. Two.

Then Rhys blew out a breath and said, "Clear." He threaded his fingers through mine, gripping tightly.

Mor sagged a bit, jewelry glinting with the movement, and went to take Cassian's arm.

But he'd at last approached Nesta. And as the world began to turn to shadows and wind, I saw Cassian tower over my sister, saw her chin lift defiantly, and heard him growl, "Hello, Nesta."

Rhys seemed to halt his winnowing as my sister said, "So you're alive."

Cassian bared his teeth in a feral grin, wings flaring slightly. "Were you hoping otherwise?"

Mor was watching—watching so closely, every muscle tense. She again reached for his arm, but Cassian angled out of reach, not tearing his eyes from Nesta's blazing gaze.

Nesta blurted, "You didn't come to—" She stopped herself.

The world seemed to go utterly still at that interrupted sentence, nothing and no one more so than Cassian. He scanned her face as if furiously reading some battle report.

Mor just watched as Cassian took Nesta's slim hand in his own, interlacing their fingers. As he folded in his wings and blindly reached his other hand back toward Mor in a silent order to transport them.

Cassian's eyes did not leave Nesta's; nor did hers leave his. There was no warmth, no tenderness on either of their faces. Only that raging intensity, that blend of contempt and understanding and fire.

Rhys began to winnow us again, and just as the dark wind swept in, I heard Cassian say to Nesta, his voice low and rough, "The next time, Emissary, I'll come say hello."

I'd learned enough from Rhys about what to expect of the Dawn Court, but even the vistas he'd painted for me didn't do the sight justice.

It was the clouds I saw first.

Enormous clouds drifting in the cobalt sky, soft and magnanimous, still tinged by the rose remnants of sunrise, their round edges gilded with the golden light. The dewy freshness of morning lingered in the balmy air as we peered up at the mountain-palace spiraling into the heavens above.

If the palace above the Court of Nightmares had been crafted of moonstone, this was made from . . . sunstone. I didn't have a word for the near-opalescent golden stone that seemed to hold the gleaming of a thousand sunrises within it.

Steps and balconies and archways and verandas and bridges linked the towers and gilded domes of the palace, periwinkle morning glories climbing the pillars and neatly cut blocks of stone to drink in the gilded mists wafting by.

Wafting by, because the mountain on which the palace stood . . . There was a reason I beheld the clouds first.

The veranda that we'd appeared on was empty, save for Azriel and a slim-hipped attendant in the gold-and-ruby livery of Dawn. Light, loose robes—layered and yet flattering.

The male bowed, his brown skin smooth with youth and beauty. "This way, High Lord."

Even his voice was as lovely as the first glimmer of gold on the horizon. Rhys returned his bow with a shallow nod, and offered his arm to me.

Mor muttered behind us, falling into rank with Nesta at her side, "If you ever feel like building a new house, Rhys, let's use this one for inspiration."

Rhys threw her an incredulous look over a shoulder. Cassian and Azriel snorted softly.

I glanced to Nesta as the attendant led us not to the archway beyond the veranda, but the spiral stairs climbing upward—along the bare face of a tower.

Nesta seemed as out of place as all of us—save Mor—but . . .

That was awe on my sister's face.

Utter awe at the castle in the clouds, at the verdant countryside rippling away far below, speckled with red-roofed little villages and broad, sparkling rivers. A lush, eternal countryside, rich with the weight of summer upon it.

And I wondered if my face had appeared like that—the day I'd first seen Velaris. The mix of awe and anger and the realization that the world was large, and beautiful, and sometimes so overwhelming in its wonder that it was impossible to drink it down all at once.

There were other palaces within Dawn's territory—set in small cities that specialized in tinkering and clockwork and clever things. Here . . . beyond those little villages nestled in the country hills, there was no industry. Nothing beyond the palace and the sky and the clouds.

We ascended the spiral stairs, the drop off the too-near edge falling away into warm-colored rock peppered with clusters of pale roses and fluffy, magenta peonies. A beautiful, colorful death.

Every step had me bracing myself as we wound up and up the tower, Rhys's grip on my hand unwavering.

The wings remained out. He did not falter a single step.

His eyes slid to mine, amused and questioning. He said down the bond, *And do* you *think I need to redecorate our home?*

We passed open-air chambers full of fat, silk pillows and plush carpets, passed windows whose panes were arranged in colorful medleys, passed urns overflowing with lavender and fountains gurgling clearest water under the mild rays of the sun.

It's not a competition, I trilled to him.

His hand tightened on mine. *Well, even if Thesan has a prettier palace, I'm the only one blessed with a High Lady at my side.*

I couldn't help my blush.

Especially as Rhys added, *Tonight, I want you to wear that crown to bed. Only the crown.*

Scoundrel.

Always.

I smiled, and he leaned in smoothly to brush a kiss to my cheek.

Mor muttered a plea for mercy from mates.

Muted voices reached us from the open-air chamber atop the sunstone tower—some deep, some sharp, some lilting—before we finished the last rotation around it, the arched, glassless windows offering no barrier to the conversation within.

Three others are here already, Rhys warned me, and I had the feeling that was what Azriel was now murmuring to Mor and Cassian. *Helion, Kallias, and Thesan.*

The High Lords of Day, Winter, and our host, Dawn.

Meaning Autumn and Summer—Beron and Tarquin—had not arrived yet. Or Spring.

I still doubted Tamlin would come at all, but Beron and Tarquin . . . Perhaps the battle had changed Tarquin's mind. And Beron was awful enough to perhaps have sided with Hybern already, regardless of Eris's manipulating.

I caught the bob of Rhys's throat as we cleared the final steps to the open doorway. A long bridge connected the other half of the tower to the palace interior, its rails drooping with dawn-pale wisteria. I wondered if the others had been led up these stairs, or if it was somehow meant to be an insult.

Shields up? Rhys asked, but I knew he was aware mine had been raised since Velaris.

Just as I was aware that he'd put a shield, mental and physical, around all of us, terms of peace or no.

And though his face was calm, his shoulders thrown back, I said, *I see all of you, Rhys. And there is not one part that I do not love with everything that I am.*

His hand squeezed mine in answer before he laid my fingers on his arm, raising it enough that we must have painted a rather courtly portrait as we entered the chamber.

You bow to no one, was all he replied.

CHAPTER 43

The chamber was and was not what I expected. Deep-cushioned oak chairs had been arranged in a massive circle in the heart of the room—enough for all the High Lords and their delegates. Some, I realized, had been shaped to accommodate wings.

It seemed it was not unusual. For clustered around a beautiful, slender male who I immediately remembered from Under the Mountain were winged Fae. If the Illyrians had batlike wings, these . . . they were like birds.

The Peregryns are distantly related to Drakon's Seraphim people and provide Thesan with a small aerial legion, Rhys said to me of the muscular, golden-armored males and females gathered. *The male on his left is his captain and lover.* Indeed, the handsome male stood just a tad closer to his High Lord, one hand on the fine sword at his side. *No mating bond yet*, Rhys went on, *but I think Thesan didn't dare acknowledge it while Amarantha reigned. She delighted in ripping out their feathers—one by one. She made a dress out of them once.*

I tried not to wince as we stepped onto the polished marble floor, the stone warmed with the sun streaming through the open archways. The others had looked toward us, some murmuring at the sight of

Rhys's wings, but my attention went to the true gem of the chamber: the reflection pool.

Rather than a table occupying the space between that circle of chairs, a shallow, circular reflection pool was carved into the floor itself. Its dark water was laden with pink and gold water lilies, the pads broad and flat as a male's hand, and beneath them pumpkin-and-ivory fish lazily swam about.

This, I admitted to Rhys, *I might need to have.*

A wry pulse of humor down the bond. *I'll make a note of it for your birthday.*

More wisteria twined about the pillars flanking the space, and along the tables set against the few walls, bunches of wine-colored peonies unfurled their silken layers. Between the vases, platters and baskets of food had been laid—small pastries, cured meats, and garlands of fruit beckoned before sweating pewter ewers of some refreshment.

Then there were the three High Lords themselves.

We were not the only ones to have dressed well.

Rhys and I halted halfway through the space.

I knew them all—remembered them from those months Under the Mountain. Rhys had taught me their histories while we'd trained. I wondered if they sensed their power within me as their attention slid between us.

Thesan glided forward, his embroidered, exquisite shoes silent on the floor. His tunic was tight-fitting through his slender chest, but flowing pants—much like those Amren favored—whispered with movement as he approached. His brown skin and hair were kissed with gold, as if the sunrise had permanently gilded them, but his upswept eyes, the rich brown of freshly tilled fields, were his loveliest feature. He paused a few feet away, taking in Rhys and me, our entourage. The wings that Rhys kept folded behind him.

"Welcome," Thesan said, his voice as deep and rich as those eyes. His lover monitored our every breath from a few feet behind, no doubt realizing our own companions were doing the same behind us. "Or," Thesan mused, "since you've called this meeting, perhaps you should be doing the welcoming?"

A faint smile ghosted Rhys's perfect face, shadows twining between the strands of his hair. He'd loosened the damper on his power—just a bit. They all had. "I may have requested the meeting, Thesan, but you were the one gracious enough to offer up your beautiful residence."

Thesan gave a nod of thanks, perhaps deeming it impolite to inquire about Rhysand's newly revealed wings, then turned to me.

We stared at each other while my companions bowed behind me. As a High Lord's wife should have done with them.

Yet I simply stood. And stared.

Rhys did not interfere—not at this first test.

Dawn—the gift of healing. It was his gift that had allowed me to save Rhysand's life. That had sent me to the Suriel, that day I had learned the truth that would alter my eternity.

I offered Thesan a restrained smile. "Your home is lovely."

But Thesan's attention had gone to the tattoo. I knew he realized it the moment he noticed the ink covered the wrong hand. Then the crown atop my head. His brows flicked up.

Rhys only shrugged.

The other two High Lords had approached now.

"Kallias," Rhys said to the white-haired one, whose skin was so pale it looked frozen. Even his crushing blue eyes seemed like chips hewn from a glacier as he studied Rhys's wings and seemed to instantly dismiss them. He wore a jacket of royal blue embroidered with silver thread, its collar and sleeves dusted with white rabbit fur. I would have thought it too warm for the mild day, especially the fur-lined, knee-high brown boots, but given the utter iciness of his expression, perhaps his blood ran frozen. A trio of similarly colored High Fae remained in their seats, one of them a stunning young female who looked right at Mor—and grinned.

Mor returned the beam, hopping from one foot to another as Kallias opened his mouth—

And then my friend squealed.

Squealed.

Both females hurtled for each other, and Mor's squeal had turned to a quiet sob as she flung her arms around the slender stranger and hugged her tight. The female's own arms were shaking as she gripped Mor.

Then they were laughing and crying and dancing around each other, pausing to study each other's faces, to wipe away tears, and then embracing again.

"You look the same," the stranger was saying, beaming from ear to ear. "I think that's the same dress I saw you in—"

"*You* look the same! Wearing fur in the middle of summer—how utterly typical—"

"You brought the usual suspects, it seems—"

"Thankfully, the company has been improved by some new arrivals—" Mor waved me over. It had been ages since I'd seen her shining so brightly. "Viviane, meet Feyre. Feyre, meet Viviane—Kallias's wife."

I glanced at Thesan and Kallias, the latter of whom watched his wife and Mor with raised brows. "I tried to suggest she stay at home," Kallias said drily, "but she threatened to freeze my balls off."

Rhys let out a dark chuckle. "Sounds familiar."

I threw him a glare over a sparkling shoulder—just in time to see the smirk fade from Kallias's face as he truly took in Rhys. Not just the wings this time. My mate's own amusement dimmed, some thread of tension going taut between him and Kallias—

But I'd reached Mor and Viviane, and wiped the curiosity from my face as I shook the female's hand, surprised to find it warm.

Her silver hair glittered in the sun like fresh snow. "Wife," Viviane said, clicking her tongue. "You know, it still sounds strange to me. Every time someone says it, I keep looking over my shoulder as if it'll be someone else."

Kallias said to none of us in particular, from where he remained facing Rhys, stiff-backed, "I have yet to decide if I find it insulting. Since she says it every day."

Viviane stuck out her tongue at him.

But Mor gripped her shoulder and squeezed. "It's about time."

A blush stained Viviane's pale face. "Yes, well—everything was different after Under the Mountain." Her sapphire eyes slid to mine and she bowed her head. "Thank you—for returning my mate to me."

"Mates?" Mor fizzed, glancing between them. "Married *and* mates?"

"You two do realize that this is a serious meeting," Rhys said.

"And that the fish in the pool are very sensitive to high-pitched sounds," Kallias added.

Viviane gave them both a vulgar gesture that made me instantly like her.

Rhys looked to Kallias with what I assumed was some sort of long-suffering male expression. But the High Lord did not return it.

He only stared at Rhys, amusement again gone—that coldness settling in across his face.

There had been . . . tension with the Winter Court, Mor had explained when they'd rescued Lucien and me on the ice. A lingering anger over something that had occurred Under the Mountain—

But the third High Lord had at last approached from across the pool.

My father had once bought and traded a gold and lapis lazuli pendant that hailed from the ruins of an arid southeastern kingdom, where the Fae had ruled as gods amid swaying date palms and sand-swept palaces. I'd been mesmerized by the colors, the artistry, but more interested in the shipment of myrrh and figs that had come with it—a few of the latter my father had snuck to me while I loitered in his office. Even now, I could still taste their sweetness on my tongue, still smell that earthy scent, and I couldn't quite explain why, but . . . I remembered that ancient necklace and those exquisite delicacies as he prowled toward us.

His clothes had been formed from a single bolt of white fabric—not a robe, not a dress, but rather something in between, pleated and draped over his muscular body. A golden cuff of an upright serpent encircled one powerful bicep, offsetting his near-glowing dark skin, and a radiant crown of golden spikes—the rays of the sun, I realized—glistened atop his onyx hair.

The sun personified. Powerful, lazy with grace, capable of kindness and wrath. Nearly as beautiful as Rhysand. And somehow—somehow colder than Kallias.

His High Fae entourage was almost as large as ours, clad in similar robes of varying rich dyes—cobalt and crimson and amethyst—some with expertly kohl-lined eyes, all of them fit and gleaming with health.

But perhaps the physical power of them—of *him* was the sleight of hand.

For Helion's other title was Spell-Cleaver, and his one thousand libraries were rumored to contain the knowledge of the world. Perhaps all that knowledge had made him too aware, too cold behind those bright eyes.

Or perhaps that had come after Amarantha had looted some of those libraries for herself. I wondered if he'd reclaimed what she'd taken—or if he mourned what she'd burned.

Even Mor and Viviane halted their reunion as Helion stopped a wise distance away.

It was his power that had gotten my friends out of Hybern. His power that made me glow whenever Rhys and I were tangled in each other and every heartbeat ached with mirth.

Helion jerked his square chin to Rhys, the only one of them, it seemed, not surprised by my mate's wings. But his eyes—a striking amber—fell on me.

"Does Tamlin know what she is?"

His voice was indeed colder than Kallias's. And the question—so carefully worded.

Rhys drawled, "If you mean beautiful and clever, then yes—I think he does."

Helion leveled a flat look at him. "Does he know she is your mate—and High Lady?"

"*High Lady?*" Viviane squeaked, but Mor shushed her, drawing her away to whisper.

Thesan and Kallias took me in. Slowly.

Cassian and Azriel casually slid closer, no more than a night breeze.

"If he arrives," Rhys said smoothly, "I suppose we'll find out."

Helion let out a dark laugh. Dangerous—he was utterly lethal, this High Lord kissed by the sun. "I always liked you, Rhysand."

Thesan stepped forward, ever the good host. For that laugh indeed promised violence. His lover and the other Peregryns seemed to shift into defensive positions—either to guard their High Lord or simply to remind us that we were guests in their home.

But Helion's attention snagged on Nesta.

Lingered.

She only stared right back at him. Unruffled, unimpressed.

"Who is your guest?" the High Lord of Day asked a bit too quietly for my liking.

Cassian revealed nothing—not even a glimmer that he *knew* Nesta. But he didn't move an inch from his casual defensive position. Neither did Azriel.

"She is my sister, and our emissary to the human lands," I said at last to him, stepping to her side. "And she will tell her story when the others are here."

"She is Fae."

"No shit," Viviane muttered under her breath, and Mor's snort was cut off as Kallias raised his brows at them. Helion ignored them.

"Who Made her?" Thesan asked politely, angling his head.

Nesta surveyed Thesan. Then Helion. Then Kallias.

"Hybern did," she said simply. Not a flicker of fear in her eyes, in her upraised chin.

Stunned silence.

But I'd had enough of my sister being ogled. I linked elbows with her, heading toward the low-backed chairs that I assumed were for us. "They threw her in the Cauldron," I said. "Along with my other sister, Elain." I sat, placing Nesta beside me, and gazed at the three assembled High Lords without an inch of manners or niceness or flattery. "After the High Priestess Ianthe and Tamlin sold out Prythian and my family to them."

Nesta nodded her silent confirmation.

Helion's eyes blazed like a forge. "That is a heavy accusation to make—especially of your former lover."

"It is no accusation," I said, folding my hands in my lap. "We were all there. And now we're going to do something about it."

Pride flickered down the bond.

And then Viviane muttered to Kallias, jabbing him in the ribs, "Why can't *I* be High Lady as well?"

The others arrived late.

We took our seats around the reflection pool, Thesan's impeccably mannered attendants bringing us plates of food and goblets of exotic juices from the tables against the wall. Conversation halted and flowed, Mor and Viviane sitting next to each other to catch up on what seemed like fifty years' worth of gossip.

Viviane had not been Under the Mountain. As her childhood friend, Kallias had been protective of her to a fault over the years—had placed the sharp-minded female on border duty for decades to avoid the scheming of his court. He didn't let her near Amarantha, either. Didn't let anyone get a whiff of what he felt for his white-haired friend, who had no clue—not one—that he had loved her his entire life. And in those last moments, when his power had been ripped from him by that spell . . . Kallias had flung out the remnants to warn her. To tell Viviane he loved her. And then he begged her to protect their people.

So she had.

As Mor and my friends had protected Velaris, Viviane had veiled and guarded the small city under her watch, offering safe harbor to those who made it.

Never forgetting the High Lord and friend trapped Under the Mountain, never ceasing her hunt for finding a way to free him. Especially while Amarantha unleashed her horrors upon his court to break them, punish them. Yet Viviane held them together. And through that reign of terror—during all those years—she realized what Kallias was to her, what she felt for him in return.

The day he'd returned home, he'd winnowed right to her.

She'd kissed him before he could speak a word. He'd then knelt down and asked her to be his wife.

They went an hour later to a temple and swore their vows. And that night—*during the you-know*, Viviane grinned at Mor—the mating bond at last snapped into place.

The story occupied our time while we waited, since Mor wanted details. Lots of them. Ones that pushed the boundaries of propriety and left Thesan choking on his elderberry wine. But Kallias smiled at his wife and mate, warm and bright enough that despite his icy coloring, *he* should have been the High Lord of Day.

Not the sharp-tongued, brutal Helion, who watched my sister and me like an eagle. A great, golden eagle—with very sharp talons.

I wondered what his beast form was; if he grew wings like Rhysand. And claws.

If Thesan did, too—white wings like the watchful Peregryns who kept silent, his own fierce-eyed lover not uttering a word to anyone. Perhaps the High Lords of the Solar Courts all possessed wings beneath their skin, a gift from the skies that their courts claimed ownership of.

It was an hour before Thesan announced, "Tarquin is here."

My mouth went dry. An uncomfortable silence spread.

"Heard about the blood rubies." Helion smirked at Rhys, toying with the golden cuff on his bicep. "*That* is a story I want you to tell."

Rhys waved an idle hand. "All in good time." *Prick*, he said to me with a wink.

But then Tarquin cleared the top step into the chamber, Varian and Cresseida flanking him.

Varian glanced among us for someone who was not there—and glowered when he beheld Cassian, seated to Nesta's left. Cassian just gave him a cocky grin.

I wrecked one building, Cassian had said once of his last visit to the Summer Court. Where he was now *banned*. Apparently, even assisting them in battle hadn't lifted it.

Tarquin ignored Rhysand and me—ignored all of us, Rhys's wings included—as he made vague apologies for the tardiness, blaming it on the attack. Possibly true. Or he'd been deciding until the last minute whether to come, despite his acceptance of the invitation.

He and Helion were nearly as tense, and only Thesan seemed to be on decent terms with him. Neutral indeed. Kallias had become even colder—distant.

But the introductions were done, and then . . .

An attendant whispered to Thesan that Beron and *all* of his sons had arrived. The smile instantly vanished from Mor's mouth, her eyes.

From my own as well.

The violence simmering off my friends was enough to boil the pool at our toes as the High Lord of Autumn filed through the archway, his sons in rank behind him, his wife—Lucien's mother—at his side. Her russet eyes scanned the room, as if looking for that missing son. They settled instead on Helion, who gave her a mocking incline of his dark head. She quickly averted her gaze.

She had saved my life once—Under the Mountain. In exchange for my sparing Lucien's.

Did she wonder where her lost son was now? Had she heard the rumors I'd crafted, the lies I'd spun? I couldn't tell her that Lucien currently hunted the continent, dodging armies, for an enchanted queen. To find a scrap of salvation.

Beron—slender-faced and brown-haired—didn't bother to look anywhere but at the High Lords assembled. But his remaining sons sneered at us. Sneered enough that the Peregryns ruffled their feathers. Even Varian flashed his teeth in warning at the leer Cresseida earned from one of them. Their father didn't bother to check them.

But Eris did.

A step behind his father, Eris murmured, "Enough," and his younger brothers fell into line. All three of them.

Whether Beron noticed or cared, he did not let on. No, he merely stopped halfway across the room, hands folded before him, and scowled—as if we were a pack of mongrels.

Beron, the oldest among us. The most awful.

Rhys smoothly greeted him, though his power was a dark mountain shuddering beneath us, "It's no surprise that you're tardy, given that your own sons were too slow to catch my mate. I suppose it runs in the family."

Beron's lips curled slightly as he looked to me, my crown. "Mate—and High Lady."

I leveled a flat, bored stare at him. Turned it on his hateful sons. On—Eris.

Eris only smiled at me, amused and aloof. Would he wear that mask when he ended his father's life and stole his throne?

Cassian was watching the would-be High Lord like a hawk studying his next meal. Eris deigned a glance at the Illyrian general and inclined his head in invitation, subtly patting his stomach. Ready for round two.

Then Eris's attention shifted to Mor, sweeping over her with a disdain that made me see red. Mor only stared blankly at him. Bored.

Even Viviane was biting her lip. So she knew of what had been done to Mor—what Eris's presence would trigger.

Unaware of the meeting that had already occurred, the unholy alliance struck. Azriel was so still I wasn't sure he was breathing. Whether Mor noticed, whether she knew that though she'd tried to move past the bargain we'd made, the guilt of it still haunted Azriel, she didn't let on.

They sat—filling in the final seats.

Not one empty chair left.

It said enough about Tamlin's plans.

I tried not to sag in my chair as the attendants took care of the Autumn Court, as we all settled.

Thesan, as host, began. "Rhysand, you have called this meeting. Pushed us to gather sooner than we intended. Now would be the time to explain what is so urgent."

Rhys blinked—slowly. "Surely the invading armies landing on our shores explain enough."

"So you have called us to do what, exactly?" Helion challenged, bracing his forearms on his muscled, gleaming thighs. "Raise a unified army?"

"Among other things," Rhys said mildly. "We—"

It was almost the same—the entrance.

Almost the same as that night in my family's old cottage, when the door had shattered and a beast had charged in with the freezing cold and roared at us.

He did not bother with the landing balcony, or the escorts. He did not have an entourage.

Like a crack of lightning, vicious as a spring storm, he winnowed into the chamber itself.

And my blood went colder than Kallias's ice as Tamlin appeared, and smiled like a wolf.

CHAPTER 44

Absolute silence. Absolute stillness.

I felt the tremor of magic slide through the room as shield after shield locked into place around each High Lord and his retinue. The one Rhysand had already snapped around us, now reinforcing . . . Rage laced its essence. Wrath and rage. Even if my mate's face was bored—lazy.

I tried to school mine into the cold caution with which Nesta regarded him, or the vague distaste on Mor's. I tried—and failed utterly.

I knew his moods, his temper.

Here was the High Lord who had shredded those naga into bloody ribbons; here was the High Lord who had impaled Amarantha on Lucien's sword and ripped out her throat with his teeth.

All of it, gleaming in those green eyes as they fixed on me, on Rhys. Tamlin's teeth were white as crow-picked bones as he smiled broadly.

Thesan rose, his captain remaining seated beside him—albeit with a hand on his sword. "We were not expecting you, Tamlin." Thesan gestured with a slender hand toward his cringing attendants. "Fetch the High Lord a chair."

Tamlin did not tear his gaze from me. From us.

His smile turned subdued—yet somehow more unnerving. More vicious.

He wore his usual green tunic—no crown, no adornments. No sign of another bandolier to replace the one I'd stolen.

Beron drawled, "I will admit, Tamlin, that I am surprised to see you here." Tamlin didn't alter his focus from me. From every breath I took. "Rumor claims your allegiance now lies elsewhere."

Tamlin's gaze shifted—but down. To the ring on my finger. To the tattoo adorning my right hand, flowing beneath the glittering, pale blue sleeve of my gown. Then it rose—right to that crown I'd picked for myself.

I didn't know what to say. What to do with my body, my breathing.

No more masks, no more lies and deceptions. The truth, now sprawled bare and open before him. What I'd done in my rage, the lies I'd fed him. The people and land I'd laid vulnerable to Hybern. And now that I'd returned to my family, my mate . . .

My molten wrath had cooled into something sharp-edged and brittle.

The attendants hauled over a chair—setting it between one of Beron's sons and Helion's entourage. Neither looked thrilled about it, though they weren't stupid enough to physically recoil as Tamlin sat.

He said nothing. Not a word.

Helion waved a scar-flecked hand. "Let's get on with it, then."

Thesan cleared his throat. No one looked toward him.

Not as Tamlin surveyed the hand Rhys had resting on my sparkling knee.

The loathing in Tamlin's eyes practically simmered.

No one, not even Amarantha, had ever looked at me with such hatred.

No, Amarantha hadn't really known me—her loathing had been superficial, driven from a personal history that poisoned everything. Tamlin . . . Tamlin knew me. And now hated every inch of what I was.

He opened his mouth, and I braced myself.

"It would seem congratulations are in order."

The words were flat—flat and yet sharp as his claws, currently hidden beneath his golden skin.

I said nothing.

Rhys only held Tamlin's stare. Held it with a face like ice, and yet utter rage roiled beneath it. Cataclysmic rage, surging and writhing down the bond between us.

But my mate addressed Thesan, who had reclaimed his seat, yet seemed far from any sort of ease, "We can discuss the matter at hand later."

Tamlin said calmly, "Don't stop on my account."

The light in Rhysand's eyes guttered, as if a hand of darkness wiped away those stars. But he reclined in his chair, withdrawing his hand from my knee to trace idle circles on his seat's wooden arm. "I'm not in the business of discussing our plans with enemies."

Helion, across the reflection pool, grinned like a lion.

"No," Tamlin said with equal ease, "you're just in the business of fucking them."

Every thought and sound eddied out of my head.

Cassian, Azriel, and Mor were still as death—their fury rippling off them in silent waves. But whether Tamlin noticed or cared that three of the deadliest people in this room were currently contemplating his demise, he didn't let on.

Rhys shrugged, smiling faintly. "Seems a far less destructive alternative to war."

"And yet here you are, having started it in the first place."

Rhysand's blink was the only sign of his confusion.

A claw slid out of Tamlin's knuckle.

Kallias tensed, a hand drifting to the arm of Viviane's chair—as if he'd throw himself in front of it. But Tamlin only dragged that claw lightly down the carved arm of his own chair—as he'd once dragged them down my skin. He smiled as if he knew precisely what memory it triggered, but said to my mate, "If you hadn't stolen my bride away in the night, Rhysand, I would not have been forced to take such drastic measures to get her back."

I said quietly, "The sun was shining when I left you."

Those green eyes slid to me, glazed and foreign. He let out a low snort, then looked away again.

Dismissal.

Kallias asked, "Why are you here, Tamlin?"

Tamlin's claw dug into the wood, puncturing deep even as his voice remained mild. I had no doubt that gesture was meant for me, too. "I bartered access to my lands to get back the woman I love from a sadist who plays with minds as if they are toys. I meant to fight Hybern—to find a way around the bargain I made with the king once she was back. Only Rhysand and his cabal had turned her into one of them. And she delighted in ripping open my territory for Hybern to invade. All for a petty grudge—either her own or her . . . master's."

"You don't get to rewrite the narrative," I breathed. "You don't get to spin this to your advantage."

Tamlin only angled his head at Rhys. "When you fuck her, have you ever noticed that little noise she makes right before she climaxes?"

Heat stained my cheeks. This wasn't outright battle, but a steady, careful shredding of my dignity, my credibility. Beron beamed, delighted—while Eris carefully monitored.

Rhys turned his head, looking me over from head to toe. Then back to Tamlin. A storm about to be unleashed.

But it was Azriel who said, his voice like cold death, "Be careful how you speak about my High Lady."

Surprise flashed in Tamlin's eyes—then vanished. Vanished, swallowed by pure fury as he realized what that tattoo coating my hand was for. "It was not enough to sit at my side, was it?" A hateful smile curled his lips. "You once asked me if you'd be my High Lady, and when I said no . . ." A low laugh. "Perhaps I underestimated you. Why serve in my court, when you could rule in his?"

Tamlin at last faced the other gathered High Lords and their retinues. "They peddle tales of defending our land and peace. And yet *she* came to my lands and laid them bare for Hybern. *She* took my High Priestess and warped her mind—after she shattered her bones for spite. And if you are asking yourself what happened to that human girl who went Under the Mountain to save us . . . Look to the male sitting beside her. Ask what he stands to gain—what *they* stand to gain from this war, or lack of it. Would we fight Hybern, only to find ourselves with a Queen and King of Prythian? She's proved her ambition—and you saw how he was more than happy to serve Amarantha to remain unscathed."

It was an effort not to snarl, not to grip the arms of my chair and roar at him.

Rhys let out a dark laugh. "Well played, Tamlin. You're learning."

Ire contorted Tamlin's face at the condescension. But he faced Kallias. "You asked why I'm here? I might ask the same of you." He jerked his chin at the High Lord of Winter, at Viviane—the few other members of their retinue who had remained silent. "You mean to tell me that after Under the Mountain, you can stomach working with him?" A finger flung in Rhysand's direction.

I wanted to rip that finger right off Tamlin's hand. And feed it to the Middengard Wyrm.

The silvery glow about Kallias dulled.

Even Viviane seemed to dim. "We came here to decide that for ourselves."

Mor was staring at her friend in quiet question. Viviane, for the first time since we'd arrived, did not look toward her. Only at her mate.

Rhys said softly to them, to everyone, "I had no involvement in that. None."

Kallias's eyes flared like blue flame. "You stood beside her throne while the order was given."

I watched, stomach twisting, as Rhys's golden skin paled. "I tried to stop it."

"Tell that to the parents of the two dozen younglings she butchered," Kallias said. "That you *tried*."

I had forgotten. Forgotten that bit of Amarantha's despicable history. It had happened while I was still at the Spring Court—a report one of Lucien's contacts at the Winter Court managed to smuggle out. Of two dozen children killed by the "blight." By Amarantha.

Rhys's mouth tightened. "There is not one day that passes when I don't remember it," he said to Kallias, to Viviane. To their companions. "Not one day."

I hadn't known.

He had told me once, all those months ago, that there were memories he could not bring himself to share—even with me. I had assumed it was only in regard to what Amarantha had done to him. Not . . . what he might have been forced to witness, too. Forced to endure, bound and trapped.

And standing by, leashed to Amarantha, while she ordered the murder of those children—

"Remembering," Kallias said, "doesn't bring them back, does it?"

"No," Rhys said plainly. "No, it doesn't. And I am now fighting to make sure it never happens again."

Viviane glanced between her husband and Rhys. "I was not present Under the Mountain. But I would hear, High Lord, how you tried to—stop her." Pain tightened her face. She, too, had been unable to prevent it while she guarded her small slice of the territory.

Rhys said nothing.

Beron snorted. "Finally speechless, Rhysand?"

I put a hand on Rhys's arm. I had no doubt Tamlin marked it. And I didn't care. I said to my mate, not bothering to keep my voice down, "I believe you."

"Says the woman," Beron countered, "who gave an innocent girl's name in her stead—for Amarantha to butcher as well."

I blocked out the words, the memory of Clare.

Rhys swallowed. I tightened my grip on his arm.

His voice was rough as he said to Kallias, "When your people rebelled . . ." They had, I recalled. Winter had rebelled against Amarantha. And the children . . . that had been Amarantha's answer. Her punishment for the disobedience. "She was furious. She wanted you dead, Kallias."

Viviane's face drained of color.

Rhys went on, "I . . . convinced her that it would serve little purpose."

"Who knew," Beron mused, "that a cock could be so persuasive?"

"Father." Eris's voice was low with warning.

For Cassian, Azriel, Mor, and I had fixed our gazes upon Beron. And none of us were smiling.

Perhaps Eris would be High Lord sooner than he planned.

But Rhys went on to Kallias, "She backed off the idea of killing you. Your rebels were dead—I convinced her it was enough. I thought it was the end of it." His breathing hitched slightly. "I only found out when you did. I think she viewed my defense of you as a warning sign—she didn't tell me any of it. And she kept me . . . confined. I tried to break into the minds of the soldiers she sent, but her damper on my power was too strong to hold them—and it was already done. She . . . she sent a daemati with them. To . . ." He faltered. The children's minds—they'd been shattered. Rhys swallowed. "I think she wanted you to suspect me. To keep us from ever allying against her."

What he must have witnessed within those soldiers' minds . . .

"Where did she confine you?" The question came from Viviane, her arms wrapped around her middle.

I wasn't entirely ready for it when Rhys said, "Her bedroom."

My friends did not hide their rage, their grief at the details he'd kept even from them.

"Stories and words," Tamlin said, lounging in his chair. "Is there any proof?"

"*Proof*—" Cassian snarled, half rising in his seat, wings starting to flare.

"No," Rhys cut in as Mor blocked Cassian with an arm, forcing him to sit. Rhys added to Kallias, "But I swear it—upon my mate's life." His hand at last rested atop mine.

For the first time since I'd known him, Rhys's skin was clammy.

I reached down the bond, even as Rhys held Kallias's stare. I did not have any words. Only myself—only my soul, as I curled up against his towering shields of black adamant.

He'd known what coming here, presented just as we were, would cost him. What he might have to reveal beyond the wings he loved so dearly.

Tamlin rolled his eyes. It took every scrap of restraint to keep me from lunging for him—from ripping out those eyes.

But whatever Kallias read in Rhys's face, his words . . . He pinned Tamlin with a hard stare as he asked again, "Why are you *here*, Tamlin?"

A muscle flickered in Tamlin's jaw. "I am here to help you fight against Hybern."

"Bullshit," Cassian muttered.

Tamlin glowered at him. Cassian, folding his wings in neatly as he leaned back in his chair once more, just offered a crooked grin in return.

"You will forgive us," Thesan interrupted gracefully, "if we are doubtful. And hesitant to share any plans."

"Even when I have information on Hybern's movements?"

Silence. Tarquin, across the pool, watched and listened—either because he was the youngest of them, or perhaps he knew some advantage lay in letting us battle it out ourselves.

Tamlin smiled at me. "Why do you think I invited them to the house? Into my lands?" He let out a low snarl, and I felt Rhys tensing as Tamlin said to me, "I once told you I would fight against tyranny, against that sort of evil. Did you think *you* were enough to turn me from that?" His teeth shone white as bone. "It was so *easy* for you to call me a monster, despite all I did for you, for your family." A sneer toward Nesta, who was frowning with distaste. "Yet you witnessed all that *he* did Under the Mountain, and still spread your legs for him. Fitting, I suppose. He whored for Amarantha for decades. Why shouldn't you be his whore in return?"

"Watch your mouth," Mor snapped. I was having difficulty swallowing—breathing.

Tamlin ignored her wholly and waved a hand toward Rhysand's wings. "I sometimes forget—what you are. Have the masks come off now, or is this another ploy?"

"You're beginning to become tedious, Tamlin," Helion said, propping his head on a hand. "Take your lovers' spat elsewhere and let the rest of us discuss this war."

"You'd be all too happy for war, considering how well you made out in the last one."

"No one says war can't be lucrative," Helion countered. Tamlin's lip curled in a silent snarl that made me wonder if he'd gone to Helion to break my bargain with Rhys—if Helion had refused.

"Enough," Kallias said. "We have our opinions on how the conflict with Hybern should be dealt with." Those glacial eyes hardened as he again took in Tamlin. "Are you here as an ally of Hybern or Prythian?"

The mocking, hateful gleam faded into granite resolve. "I stand against Hybern."

"Prove it," Helion goaded.

Tamlin lifted his hand, and a stack of papers appeared on the little table beside his chair. "Charts of armies, ammunition, caches of faebane . . . Everything carefully gleaned these months."

All of this directed at me, as I refused to so much as lower my chin. My back ached from keeping it so straight, a twinge of pain flanking either side of my spine.

"Noble as it sounds," Helion went on, "who is to say that information is correct—or that you aren't Hybern's agent, trying to mislead us?"

"Who is to say that Rhysand and his cronies are not agents of Hybern, all of this a ruse to get you to yield without realizing it?"

Nesta murmured, "You can't be serious." Mor gave my sister a look as if to say that he certainly was.

"If we need to ally against Hybern," Thesan said, "you are doing a good job of convincing us not to band together, Tamlin."

"I am simply warning you that they might present the guise of honesty and friendship, but the fact remains that *he* warmed Amarantha's bed for fifty years, and only worked against her when it seemed the tide was turning. I'm warning you that while he claims his own city was attacked by Hybern, they made off remarkably well—as if they'd been anticipating it. Don't think he wouldn't sacrifice a few buildings and lesser faeries to lure you into an alliance, into thinking you had a common enemy. Why is it that only the Night Court got word about the attack on Adriata—and were the only ones to arrive in time to play savior?"

"They received word," Varian cut in coolly, "because *I* warned them of it."

Tarquin whipped his head to his cousin, brows high with surprise.

"Perhaps you're working with them, too," Tamlin said to the Prince of Adriata. "You're next in line, after all."

"You're insane," I breathed to Tamlin as Varian bared his teeth. "Do you hear what you're *saying*?" I pointed toward Nesta. "Hybern turned my sisters into Fae—after *your* bitch of a priestess sold them out!"

"Perhaps Ianthe's mind was already in Rhysand's thrall. And what a tragedy to remain young and beautiful. You're a good actress—I'm sure the trait runs in the family."

Nesta let out a low laugh. "If you want someone to blame for all of this," she said to Tamlin, "perhaps you should first look in the mirror."

Tamlin snarled at her.

Cassian snarled right back, "*Watch it.*"

Tamlin looked between my sister and Cassian—his gaze lingering on Cassian's wings, tucked in behind him. Snorted. "Seems like other preferences run in the Archeron family, too."

My power began to rumble—a behemoth rising up, yawning awake.

"What do you want?" I hissed. "An apology? For me to crawl back into your bed and play nice, little wife?"

"Why should I want spoiled goods returned to me?"

My cheeks heated.

Tamlin growled, "The moment you let him fuck you like an—"

One heartbeat, the poisoned words were spewing from his mouth—where fangs lengthened.

Then they stopped.

Tamlin's mouth simply stopped emitting *sounds*. He shut his mouth, opened it—tried again.

No sound, not even a snarl, came out.

There was no smile on Rhysand's face, not a glint of that irreverent amusement as he rested his head against the back of his chair. "The gasping-fish look is a good one for you, Tamlin."

The others, who had been watching with disdain and amusement and boredom, now turned to my mate. Now possessed a shadow of fear in their eyes as they realized who and what, exactly, sat amongst them.

Brethren, and yet not. Tamlin was a High Lord, as powerful as any of them.

Except for the one at my side. Rhys was as different from them as humans were to Fae.

They forgot it, sometimes—how deep that well of power went. What manner of power Rhys bore.

But as Rhysand ripped away Tamlin's ability to speak, they remembered.

CHAPTER 45

Only my friends didn't seem surprised.

Tamlin's eyes were green flame, golden light flickering around him as his magic sought to wrest free from Rhysand's control. As he tried and tried to speak.

"If you want proof that we are not scheming with Hybern," Rhysand said blandly to them all, "consider the fact that it would be far less time-consuming to slice into your minds and make you do my bidding."

Only Beron was stupid enough to scoff. Eris was just angling his body in his chair—blocking the path to his mother.

"Yet here I am," Rhysand went on, not deigning to give Beron a glance of acknowledgment. "Here we all are."

Absolute silence.

Then Tarquin, silent and watchful, cleared his throat.

I waited for it—for the blow that would surely doom us. We were thieves who had deceived him, we had come to his house in peace and stolen from him, had ripped into their minds to ensure our success.

But Tarquin said to me, to Rhysand, "Despite Varian's unsanctioned warning . . ." A glare at his cousin, who didn't so much as look sorry about it, "You were the only ones who came to help. The only ones. And yet you asked for nothing in return. Why?"

Rhys's voice was a bit hoarse as he asked, "Isn't that what friends do?"

A subtle, quiet offer.

Tarquin took him in. Then me. And the others. "I rescind the blood rubies. Let there be no debts between us."

"Don't expect Amren to return hers," Cassian muttered. "She's grown attached to it."

I could have sworn a smile tugged on Varian's mouth.

But Rhys faced Tamlin, whose own mouth remained shut. His eyes still livid. And my mate said to him, "I believe you. That you will fight for Prythian."

Kallias didn't appear so convinced. Neither did Helion.

Rhys loosened his grasp on Tamlin's voice. I only knew because a low snarl slipped from him. But Tamlin made no move to attack, to even speak.

"War is upon us," Rhysand declared. "I have no interest in wasting energy arguing amongst ourselves."

The better man—male. His restraint, his choice of words . . . All of it a careful portrayal of reason and power. But Rhysand . . . I knew he meant what he said. Even if Tamlin had been a part of killing his own family, even if he had played his part in Hybern . . . For our home, for Prythian, he'd set it aside. A sacrifice that would harm no one but his own soul.

But Beron said, "You may be inclined to believe him, Rhysand, but as someone who shares a border with his court, I am not so easily swayed." A wry look. "Perhaps my errant son can clarify. Pray, where is he?"

Even Tamlin looked toward us—toward me.

"Helping to guard our city," was all I said. Not a lie, not entirely.

Eris snorted and surveyed Nesta, who stared back at him with steel in her face. "Pity you didn't bring the other sister. I hear our little brother's mate is quite the beauty."

If they knew Elain was Lucien's mate . . . It was now another avenue, I realized with no small amount of horror. Another way to strike at the youngest brother they hated so fiercely, so unreasonably. Eris's bargain with us had not included protection of Lucien. My mouth went dry.

But Mor replied smoothly, "You still certainly like to hear yourself talk, Eris. Good to know some things don't change over the centuries."

Eris's mouth curled into a smile at the words, the careful game of pretending that they had not seen each other in years. "Good to know that after five hundred years, you still dress like a slut."

One moment, Azriel was seated.

The next, he'd blasted through Eris's shield with a flare of blue light and tackled him backward, wood shattering beneath them.

"Shit," Cassian spat, and was instantly there—

And met a wall of blue.

Azriel had sealed them in, and as his scarred hands wrapped around Eris's throat, Rhys said, "Enough."

Azriel squeezed, Eris thrashing beneath him. No physical brawling—there had been a rule against that, but Azriel, with whatever power those shadows gave him . . .

"*Enough*, Azriel," Rhys ordered. Perhaps those shadows that now slid and eddied around the shadowsinger *hid* him from the wrath of the binding magic. The others made no move to interfere, as if wondering the same.

Azriel dug his knee—and all his weight—into Eris's gut. He was silent, utterly silent as he ripped the air from Eris's body. Beron's flames struck the blue shield, over and over, but the fire skittered off and fizzled out on the water. Any that escaped were torn to shreds by shadows.

"Call off your overgrown bat," Beron ordered Rhys.

Rhys was enjoying it, bargain with Eris or no—could have ended it seconds ago. He gave me a glance as if to say so. And an invitation.

I rose on surprisingly steady knees.

Felt all of them tense, Tamlin's gaze like a brand as I walked toward the shadowsinger, my sparkling gown hissing along the floor behind me. As I put a tattooed hand on the hard, near-invisible curve of the shield and said, "Come, Azriel."

Azriel stopped.

Eris gasped for air as those scarred hands loosened. As Azriel turned his face toward me—

The frozen rage there rooted me to the spot.

But beneath it, I could almost see the images that haunted him: the hand Mor had yanked away, her weeping, distraught face as she had screamed at Rhys.

And now, behind us, Mor was shaking in her chair. Pale and shaking.

I only offered my hand to Azriel. "Come sit beside me."

Nesta had already moved her seat, and an extra chair appeared beside mine.

I didn't let my hand tremble as I kept it extended. And waited.

Azriel's eyes slid to Eris, the High Lord's son panting beneath him. And the shadowsinger leaned down to whisper something in his ear that made Eris blanch further.

But the shield dropped. The shadows lightened into sunshine.

Beron struck—only for his fire to bounce off a hard barrier of my own. I lifted my gaze to the High Lord of Autumn. "That's twice now we've handed you your asses. I'd think you'd be sick of the humiliation."

Helion laughed. But my attention returned to Azriel, who took my still-offered hand and rose. The scars were rough against my fingers, but his skin was like ice. Pure ice.

Mor opened her mouth to say something to Azriel, but Cassian put a hand on her bare knee and shook his head. I led the shadowsinger to the empty chair beside mine—then walked to the table myself to pour him a glass of wine.

No one spoke until I offered it to him and sat down.

"They are my family," I said at the raised brows I received for my waiting on him. Tamlin just shook his head in disgust and finally slid that claw back into his hand. But I met Eris's fuming gaze, my voice as cold as Azriel's face as I said, "I don't care if we are allies in this war. If you insult my friend again, I won't stop him the next time."

Only Eris knew how far that alliance went—information that could damn this meeting if either side revealed it. Information that could get him wiped off the earth by his father.

Mor was staring and staring at Azriel, who refused to look at her, who refused to do anything but give Eris that death-gaze.

Eris, wisely, averted his eyes. And said, "Apologies, Morrigan."

His father actually gawked at the words. But something like approval shone on the Lady of Autumn's face as her eldest son settled himself once more.

Thesan rubbed his temples. "This does not bode well."

But Helion smirked at his retinue, crossing an ankle over a knee and flashing those powerful, sleek thighs. "Looks like you owe me ten gold marks."

It seemed like we weren't the only ones who'd placed bets. Even if not one of Helion's entourage answered his mocking smile with one of their own.

Helion waved a hand, and the stacks of papers Tamlin had compiled drifted over to him on a phantom wind. With a snap of his fingers—scar-flecked from swordplay—other stacks appeared before every chair in the room. Including my own. "Replicas," he said without looking up as he leafed through the documents.

A handy trick—for a male whose trove was not in gold, but in knowledge.

No one made any move to touch the papers before us.

Helion clicked his tongue. "If all of this is true," he announced, Tamlin snarling at the haughty tone, "then I'd suggest two things: first, destroying Hybern's caches of faebane. We won't last long if they've made them into so many versatile weapons. It's worth the risk to destroy them."

Kallias arched a brow. "How would you suggest we do that?"

"We'll handle it," Tarquin offered. Varian nodded. "We owe them for Adriata."

Thesan said, "There is no need."

We all blinked at him. Even Tamlin. The High Lord of Dawn just folded his hands in his lap. "A master tinkerer of mine has been waiting for the past several hours. I would like for her to now join us."

Before anyone could reply, a High Fae female appeared at the edge of the circle. She bowed so quickly that I barely glimpsed more than her light brown skin and long, silken black hair. She wore clothes similar to Thesan's, and yet—her sleeves had been rolled up to the forearms, the tunic unbuttoned to her chest. And her hand—

I guessed who she was before she rose. Her right hand was solid gold—mechanical. The way Lucien's was. It clicked and whirred quietly, drawing the eye of every immortal in the room as she faced her High Lord. Thesan smiled in warm welcome.

But her face . . . I wondered if Amren had modeled her own features after a similar bloodline when she'd bound herself into her Fae body: the sharp chin, round cheeks, and stunning uptilted eyes. But where Amren's were that unholy silver, this female's were dark as onyx. And aware—utterly aware of us gawking at her hand, her arrival—as she said to Thesan, "My Lord."

Thesan gestured to the female standing tall before the assembled group. "Nuan is one of my most skilled craftspeople."

Rhys leaned back in his seat, brows rising with recognition at the name, and jerked his chin to Beron, to Eris. "You might know her as the person responsible for granting your . . . errant son, as you called him, the ability to use his left eye after Amarantha removed it."

Nuan nodded once in confirmation, her lips pressing into a thin line as she took in Lucien's family. She didn't so much as turn in Tamlin's direction—and he certainly didn't bother to acknowledge her, regardless of the past binding them, their mutual friend.

"And what has this to do with the faebane?" Helion demanded.

Thesan's lover seethed at the High Lord of Day's tone, but one glance from Thesan had the male relaxing.

Nuan turned, her dark hair slipping over a shoulder as she studied Helion. And did not seem impressed. "Because I found a solution for it."

Thesan waved a hand. "We heard rumors of faebane being used in this war—used in the attack on your city, Rhysand. We thought to look into the issue before it became a deadly weakness for all of us." He nodded to Nuan. "Beyond her unparalleled tinkering, she is a skilled alchemist."

Nuan crossed her arms, the sun glinting off her metal hand. "Thanks to samples attained after the attack in Velaris, I was able to create an . . . antidote, of sorts."

"How did you get those samples?" Cassian demanded.

A flush crept over Nuan's cheeks. "I—heard the rumors and assumed Lucien Vanserra would be residing there after . . . what happened." She still didn't look at Tamlin, who remained silent and brooding. "I managed to contact him a few days ago—asked him to send samples. He did—and did not tell you," she added quickly to Rhysand, "because he did not want to raise your hopes. Not until I'd found a solution."

No wonder he'd been so eager to head alone into Velaris that day he'd gone to help us research. I shot a look at Rhys. *Seems like Lucien can still play the fox.*

Rhys didn't look at me, though his lips twitched as he replied, *Indeed.*

Nuan went on, "The Mother has provided us with everything we need on this earth. So it has been a matter of finding what, exactly, she gave us in Prythian to combat a material from Hybern capable of wiping out our powers."

Helion shifted with impatience, that glistening, white fabric slipping over his muscled chest.

Thesan read that impatience, too, and said, "Nuan has been able to quickly create a powder for us to ingest in drink, food, however you please. It grants immunity from the faebane. I already have workers in three of my cities manufacturing as much of it as possible to hand out to our unified armies."

Even Rhys seemed impressed at the stealth, the unveiling. *I'm surprised you didn't have a grand reveal of your own today*, I quipped down the bond.

Cruel, beautiful High Lady, he purred, eyes twinkling.

Tarquin asked, "But what of physical objects made from faebane? They possessed gauntlets at the battle to smash through shields." He jerked his chin to Rhys. "And when they attacked your own city."

"Against that," Nuan said, "you only have your wits to protect you." She did not break Tarquin's stare, and he straightened, as if surprised she did so. "The compound I've made will only protect you—your powers—from being rendered void by the faebane. Perhaps if you are pierced with a weapon tipped in faebane, having the compound in your system will negate its impact."

Quiet fell.

Beron said, "And we are supposed to trust you"—a look at Thesan, then at Nuan—"with this . . . substance we're to blindly ingest."

"Would you rather face Hybern without any power?" Thesan demanded. "My master alchemists and tinkerers are no fools."

"No," Beron said, frowning, "but where did she come from? *Who* are you?" The last bit directed at Nuan.

"I am the daughter of two High Fae from Xian, who moved here to give their children a better life, if that is what you are demanding to know," Nuan answered tightly.

Helion demanded of Beron, "What does this have to do with anything?"

Beron shrugged. "If her family is from Xian—which I'll have you remember fought for the Loyalists—then whose interests does she serve?"

Helion's amber eyes flashed.

Thesan cut in sharply, "I will have *you* remember, Beron, that my own mother hailed from Xian. And a large majority of my court did as well. Be careful what you say."

Before Beron could hiss a retort, Nuan said to the Lord of Autumn, her chin high, "I am a child of Prythian. I was born here, on this land, as your sons were."

Beron's face darkened. "Watch your tone, girl."

"She doesn't have to watch anything," I cut in. "Not when you fling that sort of horseshit at her." I looked to the alchemist. "I will take your antidote."

Beron rolled his eyes.

But Eris said, "Father."

Beron lifted a brow. "You have something to add?"

Eris didn't flinch, but he seemed to choose his words very, very carefully. "I have seen the effects of faebane." He nodded toward me. "It truly renders us unable to tap our power. If it's wielded against us in war or beyond it—"

"If it is, we shall face it. I will not risk my people or family in testing out a *theory*."

"It is no theory," Nuan said, that mechanical hand clicking and whirring as it curled into a fist. "I would not stand here unless it had been proved without a doubt."

A female of pride and hard work.

Eris said, "I will take it."

It was the most . . . decent I'd ever heard him sound. Even Mor blinked at it.

Beron studied his son with a scrutiny that made some small, small part of me wonder if Eris might have grown to be a good male if he'd had a different father. If one still lurked there, beneath centuries of poison.

Because Eris . . . What had it been like for him, Under the Mountain? What games had he played—what had he endured? Trapped for forty-nine years. I doubted he would risk such a thing happening again. Even if it set him in opposition to his father—or perhaps because of that.

Beron only said, "No, you will not. Though I'm sure your brothers will be sorry to hear it."

Indeed, the others seemed rather put-out that their first barrier to the throne wasn't about to risk his life in testing Nuan's solution.

Rhys said simply, "Then don't take it. I will. My entire court will, as will my armies." He gave a thankful nod to Nuan.

Thesan did the same—in thanks and dismissal—and the master tinkerer bowed once more and left.

"At least you have armies to give it to," Tamlin said mildly, breaking his roiling silence. A smile at me. "Though perhaps that was part of the plan. Disable my force while your own swept in. Or was it just to see my people suffer?"

A headache was beginning to pound at my right temple.

Those claws poked through his knuckles again. "Surely you knew that when you turned my forces on me, it would leave my people defenseless against Hybern."

I said nothing. Even as I blocked the images from my mind.

"You primed my court to fall," Tamlin said with venomous quiet. "And it did. Those villages you wanted so badly to help rebuild? They're nothing more than cinders now."

I shut out that, too. He'd said they'd remain untouched, that Hybern had *promised*—

"And while you've been making antidotes and casting yourselves as saviors, I've been piecing together my forces—regaining their trust, their numbers. Trying to gather my people in the East—where Hybern has not yet marched."

Nesta said drily, "So you won't be taking the antidote, then."

Tamlin ignored her, even as his claws sank into the arm of his chair. But I believed him—that he'd moved as many of his people as he could to the eastern edge of the territory. He'd said as much long before I'd returned home.

Thesan cleared his throat and said to Helion, "You said you had two suggestions based on the information you analyzed."

Helion shrugged, the sun catching in the embroidered gold thread of his tunic. "Indeed, though it seems Tamlin is already ahead of me.

The Spring Court must be evacuated." His amber eyes darted between Tarquin and Beron. "Surely your northern neighbors will welcome them."

Beron's lip curled. "We do not have the resources for such a thing."

"Right," Viviane said, "because everyone's too busy polishing every jewel in that trove of yours."

Beron threw her a glare that had Kallias tensing. "Wives were invited as a courtesy, not as consultants."

Viviane's sapphire eyes flared as if struck by lightning. "If this war goes poorly, we'll be bleeding out right alongside you, so I think we damn well get a say in things."

"Hybern will do far worse things than kill you," Beron countered coolly. "A young, pretty thing like you especially."

Kallias's snarl rippled the water in the reflection pool, echoed by Mor's own growl.

Beron smiled a bit. "Only three of us were present for the last war." A nod to Rhys and Helion, whose face darkened. "One does not easily forget what Hybern and the Loyalists did to captured females in their war-camps. What they reserved for High Fae females who either fought for the humans or had families who did." He put a heavy hand on his wife's too-thin arm. "Her two sisters bought her time to run when Hybern's forces ambushed their lands. The two ladies did not walk out of that war-camp again."

Helion was watching Beron closely, his stare simmering with reproach.

The Lady of the Autumn Court kept her focus on the reflection pool. Any trace of color drained from her face. Dagdan and Brannagh flashed through my mind—along with the corpses of those humans. What they'd done to them before and after they'd died.

"We will take your people," Tarquin cut in quietly to Tamlin. "Regardless of your involvement with Hybern . . . your people are innocent. There is plenty of room in my territory. We will take all of them, if need be."

A curt nod was Tamlin's only acknowledgment and gratitude.

Beron said, "So the Seasonal Courts are to become the charnel houses and hostels, while the Solar Courts remain pristine here in the North?"

"Hybern has focused its efforts on the southern half," Rhys said. "To be close to the wall—and human lands."

At this, Nesta and I exchanged looks.

Rhys went on, "Why bother to go through the northern climes—through faerie territories on the continent, when you could claim the South and use it to go directly to the human lands of the continent?"

Thesan asked, "And you believe the human armies there will bow to Hybern?"

"Its queens sold us out," Nesta said. She lifted her chin, poised as any emissary. "For the gift of immortality, the human queens will allow Hybern in to sweep away any resistance. They might very well hand over control of their armies to him." Nesta looked to me, to Rhys. "Where do the humans on our island go? We cannot evacuate them to the continent, and with the wall intact . . . Many might rather risk waiting than cross over the wall anyway."

"The fate of the humans below the wall," Beron cut in, "is none of our concern. Especially in a spit of land with no queen, no army."

"It is my concern," I said, and the voice that came out of me was not Feyre the huntress or Feyre the Cursebreaker, but Feyre the High Lady. "Humans are nearly defenseless against our kind."

"So go waste your own soldiers defending them," Beron said. "I will not send my own forces to protect chattel."

My blood heated, and I took a breath to cool it, to cool the magic crackling at the insult. It did nothing. If it was this impossible to get all of them to ally against Hybern . . .

"You're a coward," I breathed to the High Lord of Autumn. Even Rhys tensed.

Beron just said, "The same could be claimed of you."

My stomach churned. "I don't need to explain myself to you."

"No, but perhaps to that girl's family—but they're dead, too, aren't they? Butchered and burned to death in their own beds. Funny, that you should now seek to defend humans when you were all too happy to offer them up to save yourself."

My palms heated, as if twin suns built and swirled beneath them. *Easy*, Rhys purred. *He's a cranky old bastard.*

But I could barely hear the words behind the tangle of images: Clare's mutilated body nailed to the wall; the cinders of the Beddors' house staining the snow like wisps of shadow; the smile of the Attor as it hauled me through those stone halls Under the Mountain—

"As my lady said," Rhys drawled, "she does not need to explain herself to you."

Beron leaned back in his chair. "Then I suppose I don't need to explain my motivations, either."

Rhys lifted a brow. "Your staggering generosity aside, *will* you be joining our forces?"

"I have not yet decided."

Eris went so far as to give his father a look bordering on reproach. From genuine alarm or for what that refusal might mean for our *own* covert alliance, I couldn't tell.

"Armies take time to raise," Cassian said. "You don't have the luxury of sitting on your ass. You need to rally your soldiers now."

Beron only sneered. "I don't take orders from the bastards of lesser fae whores."

My heartbeat was so wild I could hear it in every corner of my body, feel it pounding in my arms, my gut. But it was nothing compared to the wrath on Cassian's face—or the icy rage on Azriel's and Rhys's. And the disgust on Mor's.

"That bastard," Nesta said with utter coolness, though her eyes began to burn, "may wind up being the only person standing in the way of Hybern's forces and your people."

She didn't so much as look at Cassian as she said it. But he stared at her—as if he'd never seen her before.

This argument was pointless. And I didn't care who they were or who I was as I said to Beron, "Get out if you're not going to be helpful."

At his side, Eris had the wits to actually look worried. But Beron continued to ignore his son's pointed stare and hissed at me, "Did you know that while your *mate* was warming Amarantha's bed, most of our people were locked beneath that mountain?"

I didn't deign responding.

"Did you know that while he had his head between her legs, most of us were fighting to keep our families from becoming the nightly entertainment?"

I tried to shut out the images. The blinding fury at what had been done, what he'd done to keep Amarantha distracted—the secrets he still kept from shame or disinterest in sharing, I didn't know. Cassian was now trembling two seats down—with restraint. And Rhys said nothing.

Tarquin murmured, "That's enough, Beron."

Tarquin, who had guessed at Rhysand's sacrifice, his motives.

Beron ignored him. "And now Rhysand wants to play hero. Amarantha's Whore becomes Hybern's Destroyer. But if it goes badly . . ." A cruel, cold smile. "Will he get on his knees for Hybern? Or just spread his—"

I stopped hearing the words. Stopped hearing anything other than my heart, my breathing.

Fire exploded out of me.

Raging, white-hot flame that blasted into Beron like a lance.

CHAPTER 46

Beron shielded barely fast enough to block me, but the wake singed Eris's arm—right through the cloth. And the pale, lovely arm of Lucien's mother.

The others shouted, shooting to their feet, but I couldn't think, couldn't hear *anything* but Eris's words, see those moments Under the Mountain, see that nightmare of Amarantha leading Rhys down the hall, what Rhys had endured—

Feyre.

I ignored it as I stood. And sent a wave of water from the reflection pond to encircle Beron and his chair. A bubble without air.

Flame pounded against it, turning water to steam, but I pushed harder.

I'd kill him. Kill him and gladly be done with it.

Feyre.

I couldn't tell if Rhysand was yelling it, if he was murmuring it down the bond. Maybe both.

Beron's flame barrier slammed into my water, hard enough that ripples began to form, steam hissing amongst them.

So I bared my teeth and sent a fist of white light punching into that fiery shield—the white light of Day. Spell-breaker. Ward-cleaver.

Beron's eyes widened as his shields began to fray. As that water pushed in.

Then hands were on my face. And violet eyes were before mine, calm and yet insistent. "You've proved your point, my love," Rhys said. "Kill him, and horrible Eris will take his place."

Then I'll kill all of them.

"As interesting an experiment as that might be," Rhys crooned, "it would only complicate the matters at hand."

Into my mind he whispered, *I love you. The words of that hateful bastard don't mean anything. He has nothing of joy in his life. Nothing good. We do.*

I began to hear things—the trickling water of the pool, the crackle of flames, the quick breathing of those around us, the cursing of Beron trapped in that tightening cocoon of light and water.

I love you, Rhys said again.

And I let go of my magic.

Beron's flames exploded like an unfurling flower—and bounced harmlessly off the shield Rhys had thrown around us.

Not to shield against Beron.

But the other High Lords were now on their feet.

"That was how you got through my wards," Tarquin murmured.

Beron was panting so hard he looked like he might spew fire.

But Helion rubbed his jaw as he sat down once more. "I wondered where it went—that little bit. So small—like a fish missing a single scale. But I still felt whenever something brushed against that empty spot." A smirk at Rhys. "No wonder you made her High Lady."

"I made her High Lady," Rhys said simply, lowering his hands from my face but not leaving my side, "because I love her. Her power was the last thing I considered."

I was beyond words, beyond basic feelings. Helion asked Tamlin, "You knew of her powers?"

Tamlin was only watching me and Rhys, my mate's declaration hanging between us. "It was none of your business," was all Tamlin said to Helion. To all of them.

"The power belongs to *us*. I think it is," Beron seethed.

Mor leveled a look at Beron that would have sent lesser males running.

The Lady of Autumn was clutching her arm, angry red splattered along the moon-white skin. No glimmer of pain on that face, though. I said to her as I reclaimed my seat, "I'm sorry."

Her eyes lifted toward mine, round as saucers.

Beron spat, "Don't talk to her, you human filth."

Rhys shattered through Beron's shield, his fire, his defenses.

Shattered through them like a stone hurled into a window, and slammed his dark power into Beron so hard he rocked back in his seat. Then that seat disintegrated into black, sparkling dust beneath him.

Leaving Beron to fall on his ass.

Glittering ebony dust drifted away on a phantom wind, staining Beron's crimson jacket, clinging like clumps of ash to his brown hair.

"Don't ever," Rhys said, hands sliding into his pockets, "speak to my mate like that again."

Beron shot to his feet, not bothering to brush off the dust, and declared to no one in particular, "This meeting is over. I hope Hybern butchers you all."

But Nesta rose from her chair. "This meeting is *not* over."

Even Beron paused at her tone. Eris sized up the space between my sister and his father.

She stood tall, a pillar of steel. "You are all there is," she said to Beron, to all of us. "You are all that there is between Hybern and the end of everything that is good and decent." She settled her stare on Beron, unflinching and fierce. "You fought against Hybern in the last war. Why do you refuse to do so now?"

Beron did not deign to answer. But he did not leave. Eris subtly motioned his brothers to sit.

Nesta marked the gesture—hesitated. As if realizing she indeed held their complete attention. That every word mattered. "You may hate us. I don't care if you do. But I do care if you let innocents suffer and die. At least stand for them. Your people. For Hybern will make an example of them. Of all of us."

"And you know this how?" Beron sneered.

"I went into the Cauldron," Nesta said flatly. "It showed me his heart. He will bring down the wall, and butcher those on either side of it."

Truth or lie, I could not tell. Nesta's face revealed nothing. And no one dared contradict her.

She looked to Kallias and Viviane. "I am sorry for the loss of those children. The loss of one is abhorrent." She shook her head. "But beneath the wall, I witnessed children—entire families—starve to death." She jerked her chin at me. "Were it not for my sister . . . I would be among them."

My eyes burned, but I blinked it away.

"Too long," Nesta said. "For too long have humans beneath the wall suffered and died while you in Prythian thrived. Not during that—queen's reign." She recoiled, as if hating to even speak Amarantha's name. "But long before. If you fight for anything—fight now, to protect those you forgot. Let them know they're not forgotten. Just this once."

Thesan cleared his throat. "While a noble sentiment, the details of the Treaty did not demand we provide for our human neighbors. They were to be left alone. So we obeyed."

Nesta remained standing. "The past is the past. What I care about is the road ahead. What I care about is making sure no children—Fae or human—are harmed. You have been entrusted with protecting this land." She scanned the faces around her. "How can you not fight for it?"

She looked to Beron and his family as she finished. Only the Lady and Eris seemed to be considering—impressed, even, by the strange, simmering woman before them.

I didn't have the words in me—to convey what was in my heart. Cassian seemed the same.

Beron only said, "I shall consider it." A look at his family, and they vanished.

Eris was the last to winnow, something conflicted dancing over his face, as if this was not the outcome he'd planned for. Expected.

But then he, too, was gone, the space where they'd been empty save for that black, glittering dust.

Slowly, Nesta sat, her face again cold—as if it were a mask to conceal whatever raged in her at Beron's disappearance.

Kallias asked me quietly, "Did you master the ice?"

I gave a shallow nod. "All of it."

Kallias scrubbed at his face as Viviane set a hand on his arm. "Does it make a difference, Kal?"

"I don't know," he admitted.

That fast, this alliance unraveled. That fast—because of my lack of control, my—

It either would have been this or something else, Rhys said from where he stood beside my chair, one hand toying with the glittering panels on the back of my gown. *Better now than later. Kallias won't break—he just needs to sort it through on his own.*

But Tarquin said, "You saved us Under the Mountain. Losing a kernel of power seems a worthy payment."

"It seems she took far more than that," Helion argued, "if she could be within seconds of drowning Beron despite the wards." Perhaps I'd gotten around them simply by being Made—outside anything the wards knew to recognize.

Helion's power, warm and clear, brushed against the shield, trawling through the air between us. As if testing for a tether. As if I were some parasite, leeching power from him. And he'd gladly sever it.

Thesan declared, "What's done is done. Short of killing her"—Rhys's power roiled through the room at the words—"there is nothing we can do."

It wasn't entirely placating, his tone. Words of peace, yet the tone was terse. As if, were it not for Rhys and his power, he'd consider tying me down on an altar and cutting me open to see where his power was—and how to take it back.

I stood, looking Thesan in the eye. Then Helion. Tarquin. Kallias. Exactly as Nesta had done. "I did not take your power. You gave it to me, along with the gift of my immortal life. I am grateful for both. But they are mine now. And I will do with them what I will."

My friends had risen to their feet, now in rank behind me, Nesta at my left. Rhys stepped up to my right, but did not touch me. Let me stand on my own, stare them all down.

I said quietly, but not weakly, "I will use these powers—*my* powers—to smash Hybern to bits. I will burn them, and drown them, and freeze them. I will use these powers to heal the injured. To shatter through Hybern's wards. I have done so already, and I will do so again. And if you think that my possession of a kernel of your magic is your biggest problem, then your priorities are *severely* out of order."

Pride flickered down the bond. The High Lords and their retinues said nothing.

But Viviane nodded, chin high, and rose. "I will fight with you."

Cresseida stood a heartbeat later. "As will I."

Both of them looked to the males in their court.

Tarquin and Kallias rose.

Then Helion, smirking at me and Rhys.

And finally Thesan—Thesan and Tamlin, who did not so much as breathe in my direction, had barely moved or spoken these past few minutes. It was the least of my concerns, so long as they all were standing.

Six out of seven. Rhys chuckled down the bond. *Not bad, Cursebreaker. Not bad at all.*

CHAPTER 47

Our alliance did not begin well.

Even though we talked for a good two hours afterward . . . the bickering, the back-and-forth, continued. With Tamlin there, none would declare what numbers they had, what weapons, what weaknesses.

As the afternoon slipped into evening, Thesan pushed back his chair. "You are all welcome to stay the night and resume this discussion in the morning—unless you wish to return to your own homes for the evening."

We're staying, Rhysand said. *I need to talk to some of the others alone.*

Indeed, the others seemed to have similar thoughts, for all decided to stay.

Even Tamlin.

We were shown toward the suites appointed for us—the sunstone turning a deep gold in the late-afternoon sun. Tamlin was escorted away first, by Thesan himself and a trembling attendant. He had wisely chosen not to attack Rhys or me during the debating, though his refusal to even acknowledge us did not go unnoticed. And as he left, back stiff and steps clipped, he did not say a word. Good.

Then Tarquin was led out, then Helion. Until only Kallias's party and our own waited.

Rhys rose from his seat and dragged a hand through his hair. "That went well. It would seem *none* of us won our bet about who'd fight first."

Azriel stared at the floor, stone-faced. "Sorry." The word was emotionless—distant.

He had not spoken, had barely moved, since his savage attack. It had taken Mor thirty minutes after it to stop shaking.

"He had it coming," Viviane said. "Eris is a piece of shit."

Kallias turned to his mate with high brows.

"What?" She put a hand on her chest. "He is."

"Be that as it may," Kallias said with cool humor, "the question remains about whether Beron will fight with us."

"If all the others are allying," Mor said hoarsely, her first words in hours, "Beron will join. He's too smart to risk siding with Hybern and losing. And I'm sure if things go badly, he'll easily switch over."

Rhys nodded, but faced Kallias. "How many troops do you have?"

"Not enough. Amarantha did her job well." Again, that ripple of guilt that pulsed down the bond. "We've got the army that Viv commanded and hid, but not much else. You?"

Rhys didn't reveal a whisper of the tension that tightened in me, as if it were my own. "We have sizable forces. Mostly Illyrian legions. And a few thousand Darkbringers. But we'll need every soldier who can march."

Viviane walked to where Mor remained seated, still pale, and braced her hands on my friend's shoulders. "I always knew we'd fight alongside each other one day."

Mor dragged her brown eyes up. But she glanced toward Kallias, who seemed to be trying his best not to appear worried. Mor gave the High Lord a look as if to say *I'll take care of her* before she smiled at Viviane. "It's almost enough to make me feel bad for Hybern."

"Almost." Viviane grinned wickedly. "But not quite."

We were led to a suite built around a lavish sitting area and private dining room. All of it carved from that sunstone, bedecked in jewel-toned fabrics, broad cushions clumped along the thick carpets, and overlooked by ornate golden cages filled with birds of all shapes and sizes. I'd spied peacocks parading about the countless courtyards and gardens as we'd walked through Thesan's home, some preening in the shade beneath potted fig trees.

"How did Thesan keep Amarantha from trashing this place?" I asked Rhys as we surveyed the sitting room that opened to the hazy sprawl of countryside far, far below.

"It's his private residence." Rhys dismissed his wings and slumped onto a pile of emerald cushions near the darkened fireplace. "He likely shielded it the same way Kallias and I did."

A decision that would weigh heavily on them for many centuries, I had no doubt.

But I looked to Azriel, currently leaning against the wall beside the floor-to-ceiling window, shadows fluttering around him. Even the birds in their cages nearby remained silent.

I said down the bond, *Is he all right?*

Rhys tucked his hands behind his head, though his mouth tightened. *Likely not, but if we try to talk to him about it, it'll only make it worse.*

Mor was indeed sprawled on a couch—one wary eye on Azriel. Cassian sat beside her, holding her feet in his lap. He'd taken the spot closer to Azriel—right between them. As if he'd leap into their path if need be.

You handled it beautifully, Rhys added. *All of it.*

Despite my explosion?

Because *of your explosion.*

I met his stare, sensing the emotions swirling beneath as I claimed a seat in an overstuffed chair near my mate's pillow-mound. *I knew that you were powerful. But I didn't realize that you had such an advantage on the others.*

Rhys's eyes shuttered, even as he gave me a half smile. *I'm not sure even Beron knew until today. Suspected, maybe, but . . . He'll now be wishing he'd found a way to kill me in the cradle.*

A shiver skittered down my spine. *He knows about Elain being Lucien's mate. He makes a move to harm or take her, and he's dead.*

Uncompromising will swept over the stars in his eyes. *I'll kill him myself if he does. Or hold him long enough for you to do the job. I think I'd enjoy watching you.*

I'll keep it in mind for your next birthday. I drummed my fingers on the polished arm of the chair, the wood as smooth as glass. *Do you really believe Tamlin's claim that he's been working for our side?*

Yes. A beat of silence down the bond. *And perhaps we did him a disservice by not even considering the possibility. Perhaps even I started to think him some warrior brute.*

I felt tired—in my bones, my breath. *Does it change anything, though?*

In some ways, yes. In others . . . Rhys surveyed me. *No. No, it does not.*

I blinked, realizing I'd been lost in the bond, but found Azriel still by the window, Cassian now rubbing Mor's feet. Nesta had retired to her own room without a word—and remained there. I wondered if Beron's leaving despite her words . . . Perhaps it had thrown her.

I got to my feet, straightening the folds of my shimmering gown. *I should check on Nesta. Talk to her.*

Rhys nestled deeper into his spread of pillows, tucking his hands behind his head. *She did well today.*

Pride fluttered at the praise as I crossed the room. But I got as far as the foyer archway when a knock thudded on the door that opened into the sunny hallway. I halted, the sheer panels of my dress swaying, sparkling like pale blue fire in the golden light.

"Don't open it," Mor warned from her spot on the couch. "Even with the shield, don't open it."

Rhys uncoiled to his feet. "Wise," he said, prowling past me to the front door, "but unnecessary." He opened the door, revealing Helion—alone.

Helion braced a hand on the door frame and grinned. "How'd you convince Thesan to give you the better view?"

"He finds my males to be prettier than yours, I think."

"I think it's a wing fetish."

Rhys laughed and opened the door wider, beckoning him in. "You've really mastered the swaggering prick performance, by the way. Expertly done."

Helion's robe swayed with his graceful steps, brushing his powerful thighs. He spied me standing by the round table in the center of the foyer and bowed. Deeply.

"Apologies for the bastard act," he said to me. "Old habits and all."

Here it was—the amusement and joy in his amber eyes. The lightness that led to my own glow when lost to pure bliss. Helion frowned at Rhys. "*You* were on unnaturally nice behavior today. I was betting Beron would be dead by the end of it—you can't imagine my shock that he walked out alive."

"My mate suggested it would be in our favor to appear as we truly are."

"Well, now I look as bad as Beron." He strode straight past me with a wink, stalking into the sitting room. He grinned at Azriel. "You handing Eris's ass to him will be my new fantasy at night, by the way."

Azriel didn't so much as bother to look over his shoulder at the High Lord. But Cassian snorted. "I was wondering when the come-ons would begin."

Helion threw himself onto the couch across from Cassian and Mor. He'd ditched that radiant crown somewhere, but kept that gold armband of the upright serpent. "It's been what—four centuries now, and you three still haven't accepted my offer."

Mor lolled her head to the side. "I don't like to share, unfortunately."

"You never know until you try," Helion purred.

The three of them in bed . . . with him? I must have been blinking like a fool because Rhys said to me, *Helion favors both males and females.*

Usually together in his bed. And has been hounding after that trio for centuries.

I considered—Helion's beauty and the others . . . *Why the hell haven't they said yes?*

Rhys barked a laugh that had all of them looking at him with raised brows.

My mate just came up behind me and slid his arms around my waist, pressing a kiss to my neck. *Would you like someone to join us in bed, Feyre darling?*

My skin stretched tight over my bones at the tone, the suggestion. *You're incorrigible.*

I think you'd like two males worshipping you.

My toes curled.

Mor cleared her throat. "Whatever you're saying mind to mind, either share it or go to another room so we don't have to sit here, stewing in your scents."

I stuck out my tongue. Rhys laughed again, kissing my neck once more before saying, "Apologies for offending your delicate sensibilities, cousin."

I pushed out of his embrace, out of the touch that still made me dizzy enough that basic thought became difficult, and claimed a chair adjacent to Mor and Cassian's couch.

Cassian said to Helion, "Are your forces ready?"

Helion's amusement faded—reshaping into that hard, calculating exterior. "Yes. They'll rendezvous with yours in the Myrmidons."

The mountain range we shared at our border. He'd refused to divulge such information earlier.

"Good," Cassian said, rubbing at the arch of Mor's foot. "We'll push south from there."

"With the final encampment being where?" Mor asked, withdrawing her foot from Cassian's hands and tucking both feet beneath her. Helion traced the curve of her bare leg, his amber eyes a bit glazed as he met hers.

Mor didn't balk from the heated look. And a keen sort of awareness seemed to overtake her—like every nerve in her body shook awake. I didn't dare look toward Azriel.

There must have been multiple shields around the room, around every crack and opening where spying eyes and ears might be waiting, because Cassian said, "We join Thesan's forces, then eventually make camp along Kallias's southwestern border—near the Summer Court."

Helion drew his gaze from Mor long enough to ask Rhys, "You and pretty Tarquin had a moment today. Do you truly think he'll join us?"

"If you mean in bed, definitely not," Rhys said with a wry smile as he again sprawled on his spread of cushions. "But if you mean in this war . . . Yes. I believe he means to fight. Beron, on the other hand . . ."

"Hybern is focusing on the South," Helion said. "And regardless of what *you* think Tamlin's up to, the Spring Court is now mostly occupied. Beron has to realize his court will be a battleground if he doesn't join us to push southward—especially if Summer has joined us."

Meaning the Spring Court and human lands would see the brunt of the battles.

"Will Beron choose to listen to reason, though?" Mor mused.

Helion tapped a finger against the carved arm of his couch. "He played games in the War and it cost him—dearly. His people still remember those choices—those losses. His own damn wife remembers."

Helion had looked at the Lady of Autumn repeatedly during the meeting. I asked, carefully and casually, "What do you mean?"

Mor shook her head—not at what I'd said, but at whatever had occurred.

Helion fixed his full attention upon me. It was an effort not to flinch at the weight of that focus, the simmering intensity. The muscled body was only a mask—to hide that cunning mind beneath. I wondered if Rhys had picked that up from him.

Helion folded an ankle over a knee. "The Lady of the Autumn

Court's two older sisters were indeed . . ." He searched for a word. "Butchered. Tormented, and then butchered, during the War."

I shut out Nesta's screaming, shut out Elain's sobbing as she was hauled toward that Cauldron.

Lucien's aunts. Dead before he'd ever existed. Had his mother ever told him this story?

Rhys explained to me, "Hybern's forces had swarmed our lands by that point."

Helion's jaw clenched. "The Lady of the Autumn Court was sent to stay with her sisters, her younger children packed off to other relatives. To spread out the bloodline." He dragged a hand through his sable hair. "Hybern attacked their estate. Her sisters bought her time to run. Not because she was married to Beron, but because they loved each other. Fiercely. She tried to stay, but they convinced her to go. So she did—she ran and ran, but Hybern's beasts were still faster. Stronger. They cornered her at a ravine, where she became trapped atop a ledge, the beasts snapping at her feet."

He didn't speak for a long moment.

Too many details. He knew so many details.

I said quietly, "You saved her. You found her, didn't you?"

A coronet of light seemed to flicker over that thick black hair. "I did."

There was enough weight, anger, and something else in those two words that I studied the High Lord of Day.

"What happened?"

Helion didn't break my stare. "I tore the beasts apart with my bare hands."

A chill slid down my spine. "Why?"

He could have ended it a thousand other ways. Easier ways. Cleaner ways.

Rhys's bloody hands after the Ravens' attack flashed through my mind.

Helion didn't so much as shift in his chair. "She was still young—though she'd been married to that delightful male for nearly two decades. Married too young, the marriage arranged when she was twenty."

The words were clipped. And twenty—so young. Nearly as young as Mor had been when her own family tried to marry her to Eris.

"So?" A dangerous, taunting question.

And how his eyes burned at that, flaring bright as suns.

But it was Mor who said coolly, "I heard a rumor once, Helion, that she waited before agreeing to that marriage. For a certain someone who had met her by chance at an equinox ball the year before."

I tried not to blink, not to let any of my rising interest surface.

The fire banked to embers and Helion threw a half smile in Mor's direction. "Interesting. I heard her family wanted internal ties to power, and that they didn't give her a choice before they sold her to Beron."

Sold her. Mor's nostrils flared. Cassian ran a hand down the back of her hair. Azriel didn't so much as turn from his vigil at the window, though I could have sworn his wings tucked in a bit tighter.

"Too bad they're just rumors," Rhys cut in smoothly, "and can't be confirmed by anyone."

Helion merely toyed with the gold cuff on his sculpted arm, twisting the serpent to the center of his bicep. But I furrowed my brows. "Does Beron know you saved his wife in the War?" He hadn't mentioned anything during the meeting.

Helion let out a dark laugh. "Cauldron, no." There was enough wry, knowing humor that I straightened.

"You had—an affair after you rescued her?"

The amusement only grew, and Helion pushed a finger against his lips in mock warning. "Careful, High Lady. Even the birds report to Thesan here."

I frowned at the birds in cages throughout the room, still silent in Azriel's shadowy presence.

I threw shields around them, Rhys said down the bond.

"How long did the affair last?" I asked. That withdrawn female . . . I couldn't imagine it.

Helion snorted. "Is that a polite question for a High Lady to be asking?"

But the way he spoke, that smile . . .

I only waited, using silence to push him instead.

Helion shrugged. "On and off for decades. Until Beron found out. They say the lady was all brightness and smiles before that. And after Beron was through with her . . . You saw what she is."

"What did he do to her?"

"The same things he does now." Helion waved a hand. "Belittle her, leave bruises where no one but him will see them."

I clenched my teeth. "If you were her lover, why didn't you stop it?"

The wrong thing to say. Utterly wrong, by the dark fury that rippled across Helion's face. "Beron is a High Lord, and she is his wife, mother of his brood. She chose to stay. *Chose*. And with the protocols and rules, *Lady*, you will find that most situations like the one you were in do *not* end well for those who interfere."

I didn't back down, didn't apologize. "You barely even looked at her today."

"We have more important matters at hand."

"Beron never called you out for it?"

"To publicly do so would be to admit that his *possession* made a fool of him. So we continue our little dance, these centuries later." I somehow doubted that beneath that roguish charm and irreverence, Helion felt it was a dance at all.

But if it had ended centuries ago, and she'd never seen him again, had let Beron treat her so abominably . . .

Whatever you've just figured out, Rhys said, *you'd better stop looking so shocked by it.*

I forced a smile to my face. "You High Lords really do love your melodrama, don't you?"

Helion's own smile didn't reach his eyes. But Rhys asked, "In your libraries, have you ever encountered a mention of how the wall might be repaired?"

Helion began asking why we wanted to know, what Hybern was doing with the Cauldron . . . and Rhys fed him answers, easily and smoothly.

While we spoke, I said down the bond, *Helion is Lucien's father.*

Rhys was silent. Then—

Holy burning hell.

His shock was a shooting star between us.

I let my gaze dart through the room, half paying attention to Helion's musing on the wall and how to repair it, then dared study the High Lord for a heartbeat. *Look at him. The nose is the same, the smile. The voice. Even Lucien's skin is darker than his brothers'.* A golden brown compared to their pale coloring.

It would explain why his father and brothers detest him so much—why they have tormented him his entire life.

My heart squeezed at that. *And why Eris didn't want him dead. He wasn't a threat to Eris's power—his throne.* I swallowed. *Helion has no idea, does he?*

It would seem not.

The Lady of Autumn's favorite son—not only from Lucien's goodness. But because he was the child she'd dreamed of having . . . with the male she undoubtedly loved.

Beron must have discovered the affair when she was pregnant with Lucien.

He likely suspected, but there was no way to prove it—not if she was sharing his bed, too. Rhys's disgust was a tang in my mouth. *I have no doubt Beron debated killing her for the betrayal, and even afterward. When Lucien could be passable as his own offspring—just enough to make him doubt who had sired his last son.*

I wrapped my head around it. Lucien not Beron's son, but Helion's. *His power is flame, though. They've mused Beron's title could go to him.*

His mother's family is strong—that was why Beron wanted a bride from their line. The gift could be hers.

You never suspected?

Not once. I'm mortified I didn't even consider it.

What does this mean, though?

Nothing—ultimately nothing. Other than the fact that Lucien might be Helion's sole heir.

And that . . . it changed nothing in this war. Especially not with Lucien on the continent, hunting that enchanted queen. A bird of flame . . . and a lord of fire. I wondered if they'd found each other yet.

A door opened and shut in the foyer beyond, and I braced myself as Nesta appeared. Helion paused his debating the wall to survey her carefully, as he had done earlier.

Spell-Cleaver. That was his title.

She surveyed *him* with her usual disdain.

But Helion gave her the same bow he'd offered me—though his smile was edged with enough sensuality that even my heart raced a bit. No wonder the Lady of Autumn hadn't stood a chance. "I don't think we were introduced properly earlier," he crooned to Nesta. "I'm—"

"I don't care," Nesta said with a snap of her wrist, striding right past him and up to my side. "I'd like a word," she said. "Now."

Cassian was biting his knuckle to keep from laughing—at the utter surprise and shock on Helion's face. It wasn't every day, I supposed, that anyone of either sex dismissed him so thoroughly. I threw the High Lord a semi-apologetic glance and led my sister out of the room.

"What is it?" I asked when Nesta and I had entered her bedroom, the space bedecked in pink silk and gold, accents of ivory scattered throughout. The lavishness of it indeed put our various homes to shame.

"We need to leave," Nesta said. "Right now."

Every sense went on alert. "Why?"

"It feels wrong. Something feels wrong."

I studied her, the clear sky beyond the towering, drape-framed windows. "Rhys and the others would sense it. You're likely just picking up on all the power gathered here."

"Something is *wrong*," Nesta insisted.

"I'm not doubting you feel that way but . . . If none of the others are picking it up—"

"I am not *like* the others." Her throat bobbed. "We need to leave."

"I can send you back to Velaris, but we have things to discuss here—"

"I don't care about me, I—"

The door opened, and Cassian stalked in, face grave. The sight of the wings, the Illyrian armor in this opulent, pink-filled room planted itself in my mind, the painting already taking form, as he said, "What's wrong."

He studied every inch of her. As if there were nothing and no one else here, anywhere.

But I said, "She senses something is off—says we need to leave right away."

I waited for the dismissal, but Cassian angled his head. "What, precisely, feels wrong?"

Nesta stiffened, mouth pursing as she weighed his tone. "It feels like there's this . . . dread. This sense that . . . that I forgot something but can't remember what."

Cassian stared at her for a moment longer. "I'll tell Rhys."

And he did.

Within moments, Rhys, Cassian, and Azriel had vanished, leaving Mor and Helion in alert silence. I waited with Nesta. Five minutes. Ten. Fifteen.

Thirty minutes later, they returned, shaking their heads. Nothing.

Not in the palace, not in the lands around it, not in the skies above or the earth below. Not for miles and miles. Nothing. Rhys even checked with Amren, and found nothing amiss in Velaris—Elain, mercifully, safe and sound.

None of them, however, were stupid enough to suggest that Nesta had made it up. Not with that otherworldly power in her veins. Or that perhaps the dread was a lingering effect of her time in Hybern. Like the crushing panic that I'd struggled to face down, that still stalked me some nights.

So we stayed. We ate in our private dining room, Helion joining us, no sign of Tarquin or Thesan—certainly not Tamlin.

Kallias and Viviane appeared midway through the meal, and Mor kicked Cassian out of his seat to make space for her friend. They chatted and gossiped—even though Mor kept glancing at Helion.

And the High Lord of Day kept glancing at her.

Azriel barely spoke, those shadows still perched on his shoulders. Mor barely looked at him.

But we dined and drank for hours, until night was overhead. And though Rhys and Kallias were tense, careful around each other . . . By the end of the meal, they were at least talking.

Nesta was the first to leave the table, still wary and on edge. The others made one final check of the grounds before we tumbled into the silk sheets of our cloud-soft beds.

Rhys and I left Mor and Helion talking knee to knee on the sitting room cushions, Viviane and Kallias long returned to their suite. I had no idea where Azriel went off to—or Cassian, for that matter.

And when I emerged from washing up in the ivory-and-gold bathing room and Helion's deep murmur and Mor's sultry laugh flitted in from the hall—when it moved past our door and then *her* door creaked open and closed . . .

Rhysand's wings were folded in tightly as he surveyed the stars beyond the bedroom windows. Quieter and smaller here, somehow.

"Why?"

He knew what I meant.

"Mor gets spooked. And what Az did today scared the shit out of her."

"The violence?"

"The violence as a result of what he feels, lingering guilt over the deal with Eris—and what neither of them will face."

"Don't you think it's been long enough? And that taking Helion to bed is likely the *worst* possible thing to do?"

But I had no doubt Helion needed a distraction as much as Mor did. From thinking too long about the people they loved—who they could not have.

"Mor and Azriel have both taken lovers throughout the centuries," he said, wings shifting slightly. "The only difference here is the close proximity."

"You sound remarkably fine with this."

Rhys glanced over a shoulder to where I lingered by the foot of the massive ivory bed, its carved headboard fashioned after overlapping waterlilies. "It's their life—their relationship. They have both had plenty of opportunities to confess what they feel. Yet they have not. Mor especially. For private reasons of her own, I'm sure. My meddling isn't going to make it any better."

"But—but he *loves* her. How can he sit idly by?"

"He thinks she's happier without him." His eyes shone with the memory—of his own choice to sit back. "He thinks he's unworthy of her."

"It seems like an Illyrian trait."

Rhys snorted, returning to the stars. I came up to his side and slid my arm around his waist. He opened his arm to me, cupping my shoulder as I rested my head against that soft spot where his own shoulder met his chest. A heartbeat later, his wing curved around me, too, enveloping me in his shadowed warmth. "There will come a day when Azriel has to decide if he is going to fight for her or let her go. And it won't be because some other male insults her or beds her."

"And what about Cassian? He's entangled—and enabling this nonsense."

A wry smile. "Cassian is going to have to decide some things, too. In the near future, I think."

"Are he and Nesta . . . ?"

"I don't know. Until the bond snaps into place, it can be hard to detect." Rhys swallowed once, gaze fixed on the stars. I simply waited. "Tamlin still loves you, you know."

"I know."

"That was an ugly encounter."

"All of it was ugly," I said. What Beron and Tamlin had brought up with Amarantha, what Rhys had been forced to reveal . . . "Are you all right?" I could still feel the clamminess of his hand upon mine as he spoke of what Amarantha had done.

He brushed a thumb down my shoulder. "It wasn't . . . easy." He amended, "I thought I'd vomit all over the floor."

I squeezed him a little tighter. "I'm sorry you had to share those things—sorry you . . . sorry for all of it, Rhys." I breathed in his scent, taking it deep into my lungs. Out—we had made it out. "And I know it likely means nothing, but . . . I'm proud of you. That you were brave enough to tell them."

"It doesn't mean nothing," he said softly. "That you feel that way about me—about today." He kissed my temple, and warmth flickered along the bond. "It means . . ." His wing curved closer around me. "I don't have the words to tell you what it means." But as that love, that joy and light shimmered through the bond . . . I understood.

He peered down at me. "And are you . . . all right?"

I nestled my head further into his chest. "I just feel . . . tired. Sad. Sad that it turned so awful—and yet . . . yet *furious* about everything that happened to me, to my sisters. I . . ." I blew out a long breath. "When I was back at the Spring Court . . ." I swallowed. "I looked—for their wings."

Rhys went utterly still, and I took his hand, squeezing hard as he only said, "Did you find them?" The words were barely a brush of air.

I shook my head, but said before the grief on his face could grow, "I learned that he burned them—long ago."

Rhys said nothing for a lingering moment, his attention returning to the stars. "Thank you for even thinking—for risking to look for them."

The only trace—the horrific remnants—of his mother and sister. "I didn't . . . I'm glad he burned them," Rhys admitted. "I could happily kill him, for so many things, and yet . . ." He rubbed his chest. "I'm glad he offered them that peace, at least."

I nodded. "I know." I ran my thumb over the back of his hand. And perhaps because of the raw, stark quiet, I confessed, "It feels strange, to share a room, a bed, with you under the same roof as him."

"I can imagine."

For somewhere in this palace, Tamlin *was* lying in bed—well aware that I was about to enter this one with Rhysand. The past tangled and snarled, and I whispered, "I don't think—I don't think I can have sex here. With him so close." Rhys remained quiet. "I'm sorry if—"

"You don't need to apologize. Ever."

I looked up, finding his gaze on me—not angry or frustrated, but . . . sad. Knowing. "I want to share this bed with you, though," I breathed. "I want you to hold me."

Stars flickered to life in his eyes. "Always," he promised, kissing my brow, his wings now enveloping me completely. "Always."

CHAPTER 48

Helion slipped from Mor's room before we were awake—though I certainly heard them throughout the night. Enough so that Rhys put a shield around our room. Azriel and Cassian didn't return at all.

Mor didn't look like a female who had been tumbling with a gorgeous High Lord, however, as she picked at her breakfast. There was something vacant in her brown eyes, a paleness to her ordinarily golden skin.

Cassian strutted in at last, greeting Mor with a chipper, "You look terrible—Helion keep you up all night?"

She threw her spoon at him. Then her porridge.

Cassian caught the first and shielded against the other, his Siphon blazing like an awakening ember. Porridge slid to the floor.

"Helion wanted you to join," she mildly replied, refilling her tea. "Quite badly."

"Maybe next time," Cassian said, dropping into the seat beside me. "How's your sister?"

"She seemed fine—still worried." I didn't ask where he and Azriel had been all night. If only because I wasn't sure Mor wanted to hear the answer.

Cassian served himself from the platters of fruits and pastries, frowning at the lack of meat. "Ready for another day full of arguing and plotting?"

Mor and I grumbled. Rhys strode in, hair still damp from his bath, and grinned. "That's the spirit."

Despite the fraught day ahead, I smiled at my mate.

He'd held me all night, tucked against his chest, his wing draped over me. A different sort of intimacy than the sex—deeper. Our souls entwined, holding tight.

I'd awoken to his wing still over me, his breath tickling my ear. My throat had closed up as I'd studied his sleeping face, my chest tightening to the point of pain. I was well aware how wildly I loved him, but looking at him then . . . I felt it in every pore of my body, felt it as if it might crush me, consume me. And the next time someone insulted him . . .

The thought was still prowling through my mind as we finished breakfast, dressed, and returned to that chamber atop the palace. To begin forming the backbone of this alliance.

I kept the crown from yesterday, but swapped my Starfall gown for one of glittering black, the dress made up of solid ebony silk overlaid with shimmering obsidian gossamer. Its skirts flowed behind me, the tight sleeves tapered to points that brushed the center of my hand, looped into place around my middle finger with an attached onyx ring. If I was a fallen star yesterday, today Rhys's mysterious clothier had made me into the Queen of the Night.

The rest of my companions had dressed accordingly.

Yesterday, we had been ourselves—open and friendly and caring. Today we showed the other courts what we'd unleash upon our enemies. What we were capable of if provoked.

Helion was back to his edged, swaggering aloofness, lounging in his chair as we entered that lovely chamber atop one of the palace's many gilded towers. He gave Mor an extra glance, lips curving in sensual amusement. He was resplendent today in robes of cobalt edged in gold that offset his gleaming brown skin, golden sandals upon his feet. Azriel, shadows wafting from his shoulders and trailing at his feet, ignored him as he passed. The shadowsinger hadn't shown a flicker of emotion, however, to Mor when he'd met us in the foyer.

She hadn't asked where he'd been all night and morning, and Azriel had volunteered nothing. But he didn't seem inclined to ignore her, at least. No, he'd just settled back into his usual watchful quiet, and Mor had been content to let him, slumping a bit in relief as soon as he'd turned to lead us to the meeting, likely having already scouted the walk minutes ago.

Thesan was the only person who bothered to greet us when we passed through that wisteria-draped archway, but he took one look at our attire, our faces, and muttered a prayer to the Cauldron. His lover, clad in his captain's armor once more, sized us up, his wings flaring slightly, but kept seated with the other Peregryns.

Tamlin arrived last, raking his gaze over all of us as he sat. I didn't bother to acknowledge him.

And Helion didn't wait for Thesan to beckon to begin. He merely crossed an ankle over a knee and said, "I thoroughly reviewed the charts and figures you've compiled, Tamlin."

"And?" Tamlin bit out. Today would go *incredibly* well, then.

"And," Helion said simply, no trace of the laughing, easy male of the night before, "if you can rally your forces quickly, you and Tarquin might be able to hold the front line long enough for those of us above the Middle to bring the larger hosts."

"It's not that easy," Tamlin said through his teeth. "I have a third of them left." A seething look toward me. "After Feyre destroyed their faith in me."

I had done that—in my rage, my need for vengeance . . . I had not thought long-term. Had not considered that perhaps we would *need* that army. But—

Nesta let out a breathy, sharp noise and surged from her chair.

I lunged for her, nearly tripping over the skirts of my dress as she staggered back, a hand clutching at her chest.

Another step would have taken her stumbling into the reflection pool, but Mor sprang forward, gripping her. "What's wrong?" Mor demanded, holding my sister upright as her face contorted in what looked to be—pain. Confusion and pain.

Sweat beaded on Nesta's brow, though her face went deathly pale. "Something . . ." The word was cut off by a low groan. She sagged, and Mor caught her fully, scanning Nesta's face. Cassian was instantly there, his hand at her back, teeth bared at the invisible threat.

"Nesta," I said, reaching for her.

Nesta seized—then twisted past Cassian to empty her stomach into the reflection pool.

"Poison?" Kallias asked, pushing Viviane behind him. She merely stepped around his arm. Tamlin remained seated, his jaw a hard line, monitoring us all.

But Helion and Thesan strode forward, grim and focused. Helion's power flickered around him like blindingly bright fireflies, darting to my sister, landing on her gently.

Thesan, glowing gold and rosy, laid a hand on Nesta's arm. Healing.

"Nothing," they said together.

Nesta rested her head against Mor's shoulder, her breathing ragged. "Something is wrong," she managed to say. "Not with me. Not me."

But with the Cauldron.

Rhys was having some sort of silent conversation with Azriel and Cassian, the latter monitoring every breath my sister took. But the two Illyrians nodded to Rhys, and began stalking for the open windows—to fly out.

Nesta moaned, body tensing as if she'd vomit again. But then we felt it.

A shuddering through the earth. Through air and stone and green, growing things.

As if some great god blew a breath across the land.

Then the impact came.

Rhys threw himself over me so fast I didn't register wholly that the mountain itself *shook*, that the building *swayed*. We hit the stones as debris rained, and I felt him readying to winnow—

Then it stopped.

Screaming rose up from the valley below. But silence reigned in the palace. Amongst us.

Nesta vomited again, and Mor let her sag to the floor this time.

"What in *hell*—" Helion began.

But Rhys hauled his body off mine, his tan face draining of color. His lips going bloodless as he stared southward. Far, far southward.

I felt his magic spear from him, a shooting star across the land.

And when he looked back at us, his eyes went right to me. It was the fear in them—the sorrow and fear—that made my mouth go wholly dry. That made my blood run cold.

Rhys swallowed. Once. Twice. Then he declared hoarsely, "The King of Hybern just used the Cauldron to attack the wall."

Murmuring—some gasps.

Rhys swallowed a third time, and the ground slid out from under me as he clarified, "The wall is gone. Shattered. Across Prythian, and on the continent." He said again, as if convincing himself, "We were too late—too slow. Hybern just destroyed the wall."

CHAPTER 49

Nesta's connection to the Cauldron, Rhys mused as we gathered around the dining table in the town house, had allowed her to sense that the King of Hybern was rallying its power.

The same way I was able to wield the connection to the High Lords to track their traces of power, and to find the Book and Cauldron, Nesta's own power—own immortality—was so closely bound to the Cauldron that its dreadful presence, when awoken, brushed through her, too.

That was why he hunted her. Not just for the power she'd taken . . . but for the fact that Nesta was a warning bell.

We'd all departed the Dawn Court within minutes, Thesan promising large shipments of faebane antidote to every High Lord and army within two days, and that his Peregryns would begin readying themselves under his captain's command—to join the Illyrians in the skies.

Kallias and Helion swore their own terrestrial armies would march as soon as possible. Only Tamlin, whose southern border covered the entire wall, was unaccounted for—his armies in shambles. Helion just said to Tamlin before the latter left, "Get your people out. Bring whatever host you can muster." Whatever remained after me.

Tarquin echoed the sentiment, along with his promise to offer safe harbor for the Spring Court. Tamlin didn't reply to either of them. Didn't confirm that he would be bringing forces before he winnowed—without a glance at me. A small relief, since I hadn't decided whether to demand his sworn help or spit on him.

Good-byes were brief. Viviane had embraced Mor tightly—then me, to my surprise. Kallias only clasped Rhys's hand, a taut, tentative gesture, and vanished with his mate. Then Helion, with a wink at all of us. Tarquin was the last to go, Varian and Cresseida flanking him. His armada, they'd decided, would be left to guard his own cities while the bulk of his soldiers would march on land.

Tarquin's crushing blue eyes flared as his power rallied to winnow them. But Varian said—to me, to Rhys—"Tell her thank you." He put a hand on his chest, the fine gold-and-silver thread of his teal jacket glinting in the morning sun. "Tell her . . ." The Prince of Adriata shook his head. "I'll tell her myself the next time I see her." It seemed like more of a promise—that Varian *would* see Amren again, war or no. Then they were gone.

No word arrived from Beron before we uttered our farewells and gratitude to Thesan. Not a whisper that Beron might have changed his mind. Or that Eris might have persuaded him.

But that was not my concern. Or Nesta's.

If the wall had come down . . . Too late. We'd been too late. All of that research . . . I should have insisted that if Amren deemed Nesta nearly ready, then we should have gone directly to the wall. Seen what she could do, spell from the Book or no.

Perhaps it was my fault, for wanting to shelter her, build her strength, for letting her remain withdrawn. But if I had pushed and pushed . . .

Even now, seated around the town house dining table in Velaris, I hadn't decided whether the potential of breaking my sister permanently was worth the cost of saving lives. I didn't know how Rhys and the others had made such decisions—for years. Especially during Amarantha's reign.

"We should have evacuated months ago," Nesta said, her plate of roast chicken and vegetables untouched. It was the first words any of us had spoken in minutes while we'd all picked at our food.

Elain had been told—by Amren. She now sat at the table, more straight-backed and clear-eyed than I'd seen her. Had she beheld this, in whatever wanderings that new, inner sight granted her? Had the Cauldron whispered of it while we'd been away? I hadn't the heart to ask her.

Rhys was saying to Nesta, "We can go to your estate tonight—evacuate your household and bring them back here."

"They will not come."

"Then they will likely die."

Nesta straightened her fork and knife beside her plate. "Can't you spirit them away somewhere south—far from here?"

"That many people? Not without first finding a safe place, which would take time we don't have." Rhys considered. "If we get a ship, they can sail—"

"They will demand their families and friends come."

A beat of silence. Not an option. Then Elain said quietly, "We could move them to Graysen's estate."

We all faced her at the evenness of her voice.

She swallowed, her slender throat so pale, and explained, "His father has high walls—made of thick stone. With space for plenty of people and supplies." All of us made a point *not* to look at that ring she still wore. Elain went on, "His father has been planning for something like this for . . . a long time. They have defenses, stores . . ." A shallow breath. "And a grove of ash trees, with a cache of weapons made from them."

A snarl from Cassian. Despite their power, their might . . . However those trees had been created, something in the ash wood cut right through Fae defenses. I'd seen it firsthand—killed one of Tamlin's sentinels with an arrow through the throat.

"If the faeries who attack possess magic," Cassian said, and Elain recoiled at the harsh tone, "then thick stone won't do much."

"There are escape tunnels," Elain whispered. "Perhaps it is better than nothing."

A glance between the Illyrians. "We can set up a guard—" Cassian began.

"No," Elain interrupted, her voice louder than I'd heard in months. "They . . . Graysen and his father . . ."

Cassian's jaw tightened. "Then we cloak—"

"They have hounds. Bred and trained to hunt you. Detect you."

A stiff silence as my friends contemplated how, exactly, those hounds had been trained.

"You can't mean to leave their castle undefended," Cassian tried a shade more gently. "Even with the ash, it won't be enough. We'd need to set wards at the very minimum."

Elain considered. "I can speak to him."

"No," I said—at the same moment Nesta did.

But Elain cut us off. "If—if you and . . . they"—a glance at Rhys, my friends—"come with me, your Fae scents might distract the dogs."

"You're Fae, too," Nesta reminded her.

"Glamour me," Elain said—to Rhys. "Make me look human. Just long enough to convince him to open his gates to those seeking sanctuary. Perhaps even let you set those wards around the estate."

And with our scents to confuse the hounds . . . "This could end very badly, Elain."

She brushed her thumb over the iron-and-diamond engagement ring. "It's already ended badly. Now it's just a matter of deciding how we meet the consequences."

"Wisely said," Mor offered, smiling softly at Elain. She looked to Cassian. "You need to move the Illyrian legions today."

Cassian nodded, but said to Rhys, "With the wall down, we need you to make a few things clear to the Illyrians. I need you at the camp with me—to give one of your pretty speeches before we go."

Rhys's mouth twitched toward a smile. "We can all go—then head to the human lands." He surveyed us, the town house. "We have an hour to prepare. Meet back here—then we leave."

Mor and Azriel instantly winnowed out, Cassian striding for Rhys to ask him about the Court of Nightmares soldiers and their preparation.

Nesta and I aimed for Elain, both of us speaking at once. "Are you sure?" I demanded at the same time Nesta said, "I can go—let me talk to him."

Elain only rose to her feet. "He doesn't know you," she said to me. Then she faced Nesta with a frank, bemused look. "And he hates you."

Some rotten part of me wondered if their broken engagement was for the best, then. Or if Elain had somehow suggested this visit, right after Lucien had left Prythian, for some chance to . . . I didn't let myself finish the thought.

I said, watching the space where my friends had vanished from the town house, "I need you to understand, Elain, that if this goes badly . . . if he tries to harm you, or any of us . . ."

"I know. You will defend your own."

"I will defend *you*."

The vacancy fogged over her eyes. But Elain lifted her chin. "No matter what, don't kill him. Please."

"We'll try—"

"*Swear it.*" I'd never heard that tone from her. Ever.

"I can't make that promise." I wouldn't back down, not on this. "But I will do everything in my power to avoid it."

Elain seemed to realize it, too. She peered down at herself, at the simple blue gown she wore. "I need to dress."

"I'll help you," Nesta offered.

But Elain shook her head. "Nuala and Cerridwen will help me."

Then she was gone—shoulders a little squarer.

Nesta's throat bobbed. I murmured, "It wasn't your fault—that the wall came down before we could stop it."

Steel-filled eyes cut to me. "If I had stayed to practice—"

"Then you just would have been here while you waited for us to return from the meeting."

Nesta smoothed a hand down her dark dress. "What do I do now?"

A purpose, I realized. Assigning her the task of finding a way to repair the holes in the wall . . . it had given my sister what perhaps our human lives had never granted her: a bearing.

"You come with us—to Graysen's estate, and then travel with the army. If you're connected with the Cauldron, then we'll need you close. Need you to tell us if it's being wielded again."

Not quite a mission, but Nesta nodded all the same.

Right as Cassian clapped Rhys on the shoulder and prowled toward us. He paused a foot away, and frowned. "Dresses aren't good for flying, ladies."

Nesta didn't reply.

He lifted a brow. "No barking and biting today?"

But Nesta didn't rise to meet him, her face still drained and sallow. "I've never worn pants," was all she said.

I could have sworn concern flashed across Cassian's features. But he brushed it aside and drawled, "I have no doubt you'd start a riot if you did."

No reaction. Had the Cauldron—

Cassian stepped in Nesta's path when she tried to walk past him. Put a tan, callused hand on her forehead. She shook off the touch, but he gripped her wrist, forcing her to meet his stare. "Any one of those human pricks makes a move to hurt you," he breathed, "and you kill them."

He wouldn't be coming—no, he'd be mustering the full might of the Illyrian legions. Azriel would be joining us, though.

Cassian pressed one of his knives into Nesta's hand. "Ash can kill you now," he said with lethal quiet as she stared down at the blade. "A scratch can make you queasy enough to be vulnerable. Remember where the exits are in every room, every fence and courtyard—mark them when you go in, and mark how many men are around you. Mark where Rhys and the others are. Don't forget that you're stronger and faster. Aim for the soft parts," he added, folding her fingers around the hilt. "And if someone gets you into a hold . . ." My sister said nothing as Cassian showed her the sensitive areas on a man. Not just the groin, but the inside of the foot, pinching the thigh, using her elbow like a weapon. When he finished, he stepped back, his hazel eyes churning with some emotion I couldn't place.

Nesta surveyed the fine dagger in her hand. Then lifted her head to look at him.

"I told you to come to training," Cassian said with a cocky grin, and strode off.

I studied Nesta, the dagger, her quiet, still face.

"Don't even start," she warned me, and headed for the stairs.

✠

I found Amren in her apartment, cursing at the Book.

"We're leaving within the hour," I said. "Do you have everything you need here?"

"Yes." Amren lifted her head, those uptilted silver eyes swirling with ire. Not at me, I realized with no small relief. At the fact that Hybern had beaten us to the wall. Beaten *her*.

That wasn't my problem.

Not as the words of that meeting with the High Lords eddied. Not as I again saw Beron walk out, no soldiers or help promised. Not as I heard Rhys and Cassian discussing how few soldiers the others possessed compared to Hybern's forces.

The king's taunt to Rhys had been roiling through my mind for days now.

Hybern expected him to give everything—*everything*—to stop them. Had claimed only that would give us a fighting shot. And I knew my mate. Perhaps better than I knew myself. I knew Rhys would spend all of himself, destroy himself, if it meant a chance at winning. At survival.

The other High Lords . . . I couldn't afford to risk counting on them. Helion, strong as he was, wouldn't even step in to save his own lover. Tarquin, perhaps. But the others . . . I didn't know them. Didn't have time to. And I would not gamble their tentative allegiance. I would not gamble Rhys.

"What do you want?" Amren snapped when I remained staring at her.

"There is a creature beneath the library. Do you know it?"

Amren shut the Book. "Its name is Bryaxis."

"What is it."

"You do not want to know, girl."

I shoved back the arm of my ebony dress, the finery so at odds with the loft, its messiness. "I made a bargain with it." I showed her the band of tattoo around my forearm. "So I suppose I do."

Amren stood, brushing dust off her gray pants. "I heard about that. Foolish girl."

"I had no choice. And now we are bound to each other."

"And what of it?"

"I want to ask it for another bargain. I need you to examine the wards holding it down there—and to explain things." I didn't bother to look pleasant. Or desperate. Or grateful. I didn't bother to wipe the cold, hard mask from my face as I added, "You're coming with me. Right now."

CHAPTER 50

There was no priestess waiting to lead us into the black pit at the heart of the library. And Amren, for once, kept quiet.

We reached that bottom level, that impenetrable dark, our steps the only sound.

"I want to talk to you," I said into the blackness beckoning beyond the end of the light leaking down from high above.

One does not summon me.

"I summon you. I'm here to offer you company. As part of our bargain."

Silence.

Then I felt it, snaking and curling around us, gobbling up the light. Amren swore softly.

You brought—what is it you brought?

"Someone like you. Or you could be like them."

You speak in riddles.

A cool, insubstantial hand brushed against my nape and I tried not to inch back toward the light. "Bryaxis. Your name is Bryaxis. And someone locked you down here a long time ago."

The darkness paused.

"I'm here to offer you another bargain."

Amren remained still and silent, as I'd told her to, offering me a single nod of confirmation. She could indeed sever the wards holding Bryaxis down here—when the time was right.

"There is a war," I said, fighting to keep my voice steady. "A terrible war about to break across the land. If I can free you, will you fight for me? For me and my High Lord?"

The thing—Bryaxis—did not reply.

I nudged Amren with my elbow.

She said, her voice as young and old as the creature's, "We will offer you freedom from this place in exchange for it."

A bargain. A simple, powerful magic. As great as any the Book could muster.

This is my home.

I considered. "Then what is it you want in exchange?"

Silence.

Sunlight. And moonlight. The stars.

I opened my mouth to say I wasn't entirely sure that even as High Lady of the Night Court I could promise such things, but Amren stepped on my foot and murmured, "A window. High above."

Not a mirror, as the Carver wanted. But a window in the mountain. We'd have to carve far, far up, but—

"That's it?"

Amren stomped on my foot this time.

Bryaxis whispered in my ear, *Will I be able to hunt without restraint on the battlefields? Drink in their fear and dread until I am sated?*

I felt slightly bad for Hybern as I said, "Yes—only Hybern. And only until the war is over." One way or another.

A beat of silence. *What would you have me do, then?*

I gestured to Amren. "She will explain. She will disable the wards—when we need you."

Then I will wait.

"Then it's a bargain. You will obey our orders in this war, fight for us until we no longer need you, and in exchange . . . we shall bring the sun and moon and stars to you. In your home." Another prisoner who had come to love its cell. Perhaps Bryaxis and the Carver should meet. An ancient death-god and the face of nightmares. The painting, dreadful yet alluring, began to creep roots deep within my mind.

I kept my shoulders loose, posture as casual as I could summon while the darkness slid around me, winding between me and Amren, and whispered into my ear, *It is a bargain.*

✠

I made the hour count. When we all gathered in the town house foyer once more to winnow to the Illyrian camp, I'd changed into my fighting leathers, my new tattoo concealed beneath.

No one asked where I'd gone. Though Mor looked me over and said, "Where's Amren?"

"Still poring over the Book," I answered just as Rhys winnowed into the town house. Not a lie. Amren would stay here—until we needed her at the battlefields.

Rhys angled his head. "Looking for what? The wall is gone."

"For anything," I said. "For another way to nullify the Cauldron that doesn't involve the insides of my head leaking out through my nose."

Rhys cringed and opened his mouth to object, but I cut him off. "There must be another way—Amren thinks there *must* be another way. It doesn't hurt to look. And have her hunt for any other spell that might stop the king."

And when Amren was not doing that . . . she'd bring down those complex wards containing Bryaxis beneath the library—to be severed only when I called for Bryaxis. Only when the might of Hybern's army was fully upon us. If I could not get the Ouroboros for the Carver . . . then Bryaxis was better than nothing.

I wasn't entirely certain why I didn't mention it to the others.

Rhys's eyes flickered, no doubt warring with the idea of what role any other route would require of me in regard to the Cauldron, but he nodded.

I interlaced my fingers with his, and he squeezed once.

Behind me, Mor took Nesta and Cassian by the hand, readying to winnow them to the camp, while shadows gathered around Azriel, Elain at his side, wide-eyed at the spymaster's display.

But we hesitated—all of us. And I allowed myself one last time to drink it in, the furniture and the wood and the sunlight. To listen to the sounds of Velaris, the laughing of children in the streets, the song of the gulls.

In the silence, I knew my friends were, too.

Rhys cleared his throat, and nodded to Mor. Then she was gone, Cassian and Nesta with her. Then Azriel, gently taking Elain's hand in his own, as if afraid his scars would hurt her.

Alone with Rhys, I savored the buttery sunshine leaking in from the windows of the front door. Breathed in the smell of the bread Nuala and Cerridwen had baked that morning with Elain.

"The creature in the library," I murmured. "Its name is Bryaxis."

Rhys lifted a brow. "Oh?"

"I offered it a bargain. To fight for us."

Stars danced in those violet eyes. "And what did Bryaxis say?"

"Only that it wants a window—to see the stars and moon and sun."

"You did explain that we need it to slaughter our enemies, didn't you?"

I nudged him with a hip. "The library is its home. It only wanted some adjustments made to it."

A crooked smile tugged on Rhys's mouth. "Well, I suppose if I now have to redecorate my own lodgings to match Thesan's splendor, I might as well add a window for the poor thing."

I elbowed him in the ribs that time. He still wore his finery from the meeting. Rhys chuckled. "So our army grows by one. Poor Cassian will never recover when he sees his newest recruit."

"With any luck, Hybern won't, either."

"And the Carver?"

"He can rot down there. I don't have time for his games. Bryaxis will have to be enough."

Rhys glanced at my arm, as if he could see the new, second band beside the first one. He lifted our joined hands and pressed a kiss to the back of my palm.

Again, we silently looked around the town house, taking in every last detail, the quiet that now lay like a layer of dust upon it.

Rhys said softly, "I wonder if we'll see it again."

I knew he wasn't just talking about the house. But I rose up on my toes and kissed his cheek. "We will," I promised as a dark wind gathered to sweep us to the Illyrian war-camp. I held tightly to him as I added, "We'll see it all again."

And when that night-kissed wind winnowed us away, away into war, away into untold danger . . . I prayed that my promise held true.

PART THREE

HIGH LADY

CHAPTER 51

Even at the height of summer, the Illyrian mountain-camp was damp. Brisk. There were some truly lovely days, Rhys assured me when I scowled as we winnowed in, but cooler weather was better anyway, when an army was involved. Heat made tempers rise. Especially when it was too hot to sleep comfortably. And considering the Illyrians were a testy lot to begin with . . . It was a blessing that the sky was cloudy and the wind mist-kissed.

But even the weather wasn't enough to make the greeting party look pleasant.

I only recognized one of the muscle-bound Illyrians in full armor waiting for us. Lord Devlon. The sneer was still on his face—though milder compared to the outright contempt contorting the features of a few. Like Azriel and Cassian, they possessed dark hair and eyes of assorted hazel and brown. And like my friends, their skin was rich shades of golden brown, some flecked with bone-white scars of varying severity.

But unlike my friends, one or two Siphons adorned their hands. The seven Azriel and Cassian wore seemed almost vulgar by comparison.

But the gathered males only looked at Rhys, as if the two Illyrians flanking him were little more than trees. Mor and I remained on either side of Nesta, who had changed into a dark blue, practical dress and now surveyed the camp, the winged warriors, the sheer *size* of the host assembled in the camp around us . . .

We kept Elain half-hidden behind the wall of our bodies. Considering the backward view of the Illyrians toward females, I'd suggested we remain a step away on this meeting—literally. There were only a few female fighters in the legion . . . Now was not the time to test the tolerance of the Illyrians. Later—later, if we won this war. If we survived.

Devlon was speaking, "It's true, then. The wall came down."

"A temporary failure," Rhys crooned. He was still wearing his fine jacket and pants from the meeting with the High Lords. For whatever reason, he hadn't chosen to wear the Illyrian leathers. Or the wings.

It's because they already know I trained with them, am one of them. They need to remember that I'm also their High Lord. And I have no intention of loosening the leash.

The words were a silk-covered scrape of nails down my mind.

Rhys began giving unwavering, cold instructions about the impending push southward. The voice of the High Lord—the voice of a warrior who had fought in the War and had no intention of losing this one. Cassian frequently added his own orders and clarifications.

Azriel—Azriel just stared them all down. He had not wanted to come to the camp months ago. Disliked being back here. Hated these people, his heritage.

The other lords kept glancing to the shadowsinger in dread and rage and disgust. He only leveled that lethal gaze back at them.

On and on they went, until Devlon looked over Rhys's shoulder—to where we stood.

A scowl at Mor. A frown at me—wisely subdued. Then he noticed Nesta.

"What is *that*," Devlon asked.

Nesta merely stared at him, one hand clamping the edges of her gray cloak together at her chest. One of the other camp-lords made some sign against evil.

"*That*," Cassian said too quietly, "is none of your concern."

"Is she a witch."

I opened my mouth, but Nesta said flatly, "Yes."

And I watched as nine full-grown, weathered Illyrian warlords flinched.

"She may act like one sometimes," Cassian clarified, "but no—she is High Fae."

"She is no more High Fae than we are," Devlon countered.

A pause that went on for too long. Even Rhys seemed at a loss for words. Devlon had complained when we'd first met that Amren and I were *Other*. As if he possessed some sense for such things. Devlon muttered, "Keep her away from the females and children."

I clutched Nesta's free hand in silent warning to remain quiet.

Mor let out a snort that made the Illyrians stiffen. But she shifted, revealing Elain behind her. Elain was just blinking, wide-eyed, at the camp. The army.

Devlon let out a grunt at the sight of her. But Elain wrapped her own blue cloak around herself, averting her eyes from all of those towering, muscled warriors, the army camp bustling toward the horizon . . . She was a rose bloom in a mud field. Filled with galloping horses.

"Don't be afraid of them," Nesta said beneath lowered brows.

If Elain was a blooming flower in this army camp, then Nesta . . . she was a freshly forged sword, waiting to draw blood.

Take them into our war tent, Rhys said silently to me. *Devlon honestly might throw a hissy fit if he has to face Nesta for another minute.*

I'd pay good money to see that.

So would I.

I hid my smile. "Let's find something warm to drink," I said to my sisters, beckoning Mor to join. We aimed for the largest of the tents in the camp, a black banner sewn with a mountain and three silver stars flapping from its apex. Warriors and females laboring around the fires silently monitored us. Nesta stared them all down. Elain kept her focus on the dry, rocky ground.

The tent's interior was simple yet luxurious: thick carpets covered the low wooden platform on which the tent had been erected to keep out the damp; braziers of faelights flickered throughout, chairs and a few chaise longues were scattered around, covered in thick furs. A massive desk with several chairs occupied one half of the main space. And behind a curtain in the back . . . I assumed our bed waited.

Mor flung herself onto the nearest chaise. "Welcome to an Illyrian war-camp, ladies. Try to keep your awe contained."

Nesta drifted toward the desk, the maps atop it. "What is the difference," she asked none of us in particular, "between a faerie and a witch?"

"Witches amass power beyond their natural reserve," Mor answered with sudden seriousness. "They use spells and archaic tools to harness more power to them than the Cauldron allotted—and use it for whatever they desire, good or ill."

Elain silently surveyed the tent, head tipping back. Her mass of heavy brown-gold hair shifted with the movement, the faelight dancing among the silken strands. She'd left it half-up, the style arranged to hide her ears should the glamours fail at Graysen's estate. Tamlin's hadn't worked on Nesta—perhaps Graysen and his father would have a similar immunity to such things.

Elain at last slid into the chair near Mor's, her dawn-pink dress—finer than the ones she usually wore—crinkling beneath her. "Will—will many of these soldiers die?"

I cringed, but Nesta said, "Yes." I could almost see the unspoken words Nesta reined in. *Your mate might die sooner than them, though.*

Mor said, "Whenever you're ready, Elain, I'll glamour you."

"Will it hurt?" Elain asked.

"It didn't when Tamlin glamoured your memories," Nesta said, leaning against the desk.

Mor still said, "No. It might . . . tingle. Just act as you would as a human."

"It's the same as how I act now." Elain began wringing her slender fingers.

"Yes," I said, "but . . . try to keep the vision-talk . . . to yourself. While we're there." I added quickly, "Unless it's something that you can't—"

"I can," Elain said, squaring her slim shoulders. "I will."

Mor smiled tightly. "Deep breath."

Elain obeyed. I blinked, and it was done.

Gone was the faint glow of immortal health; the face that had become a bit sharper. Gone were the pointed ears, the grace. Muted. Drab—or in the way that someone as beautiful as Elain could be drab. Even her hair seemed to have lost its luster, the gold now brassy, the brown mousy.

Elain studied her hands, turning them over. "I hadn't realized . . . how ordinary it looked."

"You're still lovely," Mor said a bit gently.

Elain offered a half smile. "I suppose that war makes wanting things like that unimportant."

Mor was quiet for a heartbeat. "Perhaps. But you should not let war steal it from you regardless."

Elain's palm was clammy in mine as Rhys winnowed us into the human lands, Mor taking Azriel and Nesta. And though her face was calm when we found ourselves blinking at the heat and sunshine of a full mortal summer, her grip on my hand was as strong as the iron ring around her finger.

The heat lay heavy over the estate we now faced—the stone guardhouse the only opening I could see in either direction.

The only opening in the towering stone wall rising up before us, solid as some mammoth beast, so high I had to crane my neck back to spy the spikes jutting from its top.

The guards at the thick iron gates . . .

Rhys slid his hands into his pockets, a shield already around us. Mor and Azriel took up defensive positions at our sides.

Twelve guards at this gate. All armed, faces hidden beneath thick helmets, despite the heat. Their bodies were equally covered in plated armor, right down to their boots.

Any of us could end their lives without lifting a hand. And the wall they guarded, the gates they held . . . I did not think they would last long, either.

But . . . if we could place wards here, perhaps set up a bastion of Fae warriors . . . Through those open gates, I glimpsed sprawling lands—fields and pastures and groves and a lake . . . And beyond it . . . a solid, bulky fortress of dark brown stone.

Nesta had been right. It was like a prison, this place. Its lord had prepared to weather the storm from inside, a king over these resources. But there was room. Plenty of room for people.

And the would-be mistress of this prison . . . Head high, Elain said to the guards, to the dozen arrows now pointed at her slender throat, "Tell Graysen that his betrothed has come for him. Tell him . . . tell him that Elain Archeron begs for sanctuary."

CHAPTER 52

We waited outside the gates while a guard mounted a horse and galloped down the long, dusty road to the fortress itself. A second curtain wall lay around the bulky building. With our Fae sight, we could see as *those* gates opened, then another pair.

"How did you even *meet* him," I murmured to Elain as we lingered beneath the shade of the looming oaks outside the gate, "if he's locked up in here?"

Elain stared and stared at the distant fortress. "At a ball—his father's ball."

"I've been to funerals that were merrier," Nesta muttered.

Elain cut her a look. "This house has needed a woman's touch for years."

Neither of us said that it didn't seem likely she would be the one.

Azriel kept a few steps away, little more than the shade of one of the oaks behind us. But Mor and Rhys . . . they monitored everything. The guards whose fear . . . the salty, sweaty tang of it grated on every nerve.

But they held firm. Held those ash-tipped arrows at us.

Long minutes passed. Then finally a yellow flag was raised at the distant fortress gates. We braced ourselves.

But one of the guards before us grunted, "He'll come out to see you."

✣

We were not to be allowed within the keep. To see their defenses, their resources.

The guardhouse was as far as they'd allow us.

They led us inside, and though we tried to keep our otherness to a minimum . . . The hounds leashed to the walls within snarled. Viciously enough that the guards led them out.

The main room of the guardhouse was stuffy and cramped, more so with all of us in there, and though I offered Elain a seat by the sealed window, she remained standing—at the front of our company. Staring at the shut iron door.

I knew Rhys was listening to every word the guards uttered outside, his tendrils of power waiting to sense any turn in their intentions. I doubted the stone and iron of the building could hold any of us, certainly not together, but . . . Letting them shut us in here to wait . . . It rubbed against some nerve. Made my body restless, a cold sweat breaking out. Too small, not enough air—

It's all right, Rhys soothed. *This place cannot hold you.*

I nodded, though he hadn't spoken, trying to swallow the feeling of the walls and ceiling pushing on me.

Nesta was watching me carefully. I admitted to her, "Sometimes . . . I have problems with small spaces."

Nesta studied me for a long moment. And then she said with equal quiet, though we could all hear, "I can't get into a bathtub anymore. I have to use buckets."

I hadn't known—hadn't even thought that bathing, submerging in water . . .

I knew better than to touch her hand. But I said, "When we get home, we'll install something else for you."

I could have sworn there was gratitude in her eyes—that she might have said something else when horses approached.

"Two dozen guards," Azriel murmured to Rhys. A glance at Elain. "And Lord Graysen and his father, Lord Nolan."

Elain went still as a doe as footsteps crunched outside. I caught Nesta's eye, read the understanding there, and nodded.

Any attempt to hurt Elain . . . I did not care what I had promised my sister. I'd leave Nesta to shred him. Indeed, my eldest sister's fingers had curled—as if invisible talons crowned them.

But the door banged open, and—

The panting young man was so . . . human-looking.

Handsome, brown-haired, blue-eyed, but . . . human. Solidly built beneath his light armor, tall—perhaps a mortal ideal of a knight who would swoop a beautiful maiden onto his horse and ride off into the sunset.

So at odds from the savage strength of the Illyrians, the cultivated lethalness of Mor and Amren. From my own clawing and shredding—and Nesta's.

But a small sound came out of Elain as she beheld Graysen. As he gasped for breath, scanning her from head to toe. He staggered toward her a step—

A broad, scar-flecked hand gripped the back of Graysen's armor, hauling him to a stop.

The man who held the young lord fully entered the cramped room.

Tall and thin, hawk-nosed and gray-eyed . . . "What is the meaning of this."

We all stared at him beneath lowered brows.

Elain was shaking. "Sir—Lord Nolan . . ." Words failed her as she again looked at her betrothed, who had not taken his earnest blue eyes from her, not for a heartbeat.

"The wall has come down," Nesta said, stepping to Elain's side.

Graysen looked to Nesta at that. Shock flared at what he beheld: the ears, the beauty, the . . . otherworldly power that thrummed around her. "How," he said, his voice low and raspy.

"I was kidnapped," Nesta answered coolly, not one flicker of fear in her eyes. "I was taken by the army invading these lands and turned against my will."

"How," Nolan echoed.

"There is a Cauldron—a weapon. It grants its owner power to . . . do such things. I was a test." Nesta then launched into a sharp, short explanation of the queens, of Hybern, of why the wall had fallen.

When she finished Lord Nolan only demanded, "And who are your companions?"

It was a gamble—we knew it was. To say who we were, when we knew full well the terror of *any* Fae, let alone High Lords . . .

But I stepped forward. "My name is Feyre Archeron. I am High Lady of the Night Court. This is Rhysand, my—husband." I doubted *mate* would go over well as a term.

Rhys came to my side. Some of the guards shifted and murmured with terror. Some flinched at the hand Rhys lifted—to gesture behind him. "Our third in command, Morrigan. And our spymaster, Azriel."

Lord Nolan, to his credit, did not blanch. Graysen did, but remained steady. "Elain," Graysen breathed. "Elain—why are you *with* them?"

"Because she is our sister," Nesta answered, her fingers still curled with those invisible talons. "And there is no safer place for her during this war than with us."

Elain whispered, "Graysen—we've come to beg you . . ." A pleading glance at his father. "Both of you . . . Open your gates to any humans who can get here. To families. With the wall down . . . We—they believe . . . There is not enough time for an evacuation. The queens will not send aid from the continent. But here—they might stand a chance."

Neither man responded, though Graysen now looked at Elain's engagement ring. His blue eyes rippled with pain. "I would be inclined to believe you," he said quietly, "if you were not lying to me with your every breath."

Elain blinked. "I—I am not, I—"

"Did you think," Lord Nolan said, and Nesta and I closed ranks around Elain as he took a step toward us, "that you could come to *my* house and deceive me with your faerie magic?"

Rhys said, "We don't care what you believe. We only come to ask you to help those who cannot defend themselves."

"At what gain? What risk of your own?"

"You have an arsenal of ash weapons," I said. "I'd think the risk to us is apparent."

"And to your sister as well," Nolan spat toward Elain. "Don't forget to include her."

"Any weapon can hurt a mortal," Mor said blandly.

"But she isn't a mortal, is she?" Nolan sneered. "No, I have it on good authority that it was Elain Archeron who was turned Fae first. And who now has a High Lord's son as a *mate*."

"And who, exactly, told you this?" Rhys said with a lift of the brow, not showing one ounce of ire, of surprise.

Steps sounded.

But we all went for our weapons as Jurian strolled into the guardhouse and said, "I did."

CHAPTER 53

Jurian held up his tanned hands, new calluses dotting his palms and fingers. New—for the remade body he'd had to train to handle weapons these months.

"I came alone," Jurian said. "You can stop snarling."

Elain began shaking—either at the truth revealed, or the memories that pelted her, pelted Nesta, at the sight of him. Jurian inclined his head to my sisters. "Ladies."

"They are no ladies," Lord Nolan sneered.

"Father," Graysen warned.

Nolan ignored him. "Upon his arrival, Jurian explained what had been done to you—*both* of you. What the queens on the continent desire."

"And what is that?" Rhys asked, his voice a deceptive croon.

"Power. Youth," Jurian said with a shrug. "The usual things."

"Why are you *here*," I demanded. Kill him—we should kill him *now* before he could hurt us any further, kill him for that bolt he'd put through Azriel's chest and the threat he'd made to Miryam and Drakon, perhaps causing them to vanish and leave us to fight this war on our own—

"The queens are snakes," Jurian said, leaning against the edge of a table shoved by the wall. "They deserve to be butchered for their treachery. It took no effort on my part when Hybern sent me to woo them to our cause. Only one of them was noble enough to play the game—to know we'd been dealt a shitty hand and to play it the best she could. But when she helped you, the others found out. And they gave her to the Attor." Jurian's eyes gleamed bright—not with madness, I realized.

But clarity.

And I had the sense of the world sliding out from beneath my feet as Jurian said, "He resurrected me to turn them to his cause, believing I had gone mad during the five hundred years Amarantha trapped me. So I was reborn, and found myself surrounded by my old enemies—faces I had once marked to kill. I found myself on the wrong side of a wall, with the human realm poised to shatter beneath it."

Jurian looked right to Mor, whose mouth was a tight line. "You were my friend," he said, voice straining. "We fought back-to-back during some battles. And yet you believed me at first sight—believed that I'd ever let them *turn* me."

"You went mad with—with Clythia. It was *madness*. It destroyed you."

"And I was glad to do it," Jurian snarled. "I was *glad* to do it, if it bought us an edge in that war. I didn't *care* what it did to me, what it broke in me. If it meant we could be *free*. And I have had five hundred years to think about it. While being held prisoner by my enemy. Five hundred years, Mor." The way he said her name, so familiar and knowing—

"You played the villain convincingly enough, Jurian," Rhys purred.

Jurian snapped his face toward Rhys. "You should have looked. I expected you to *look* into my mind, to see the truth. Why didn't you?"

Rhys was quiet for a long moment. Then he said softly, "Because I didn't want to see her."

See any trace of Amarantha.

"You mean to imply," Mor pushed, "that you've been working to help *us* during this?"

"Where better to plot your enemy's demise, to learn their weaknesses, than at their side?"

We were silent, Lord Graysen and his father watching—or the latter did. Graysen and Elain were just staring at each other.

"Why this obsession to find Miryam and Drakon?" Mor asked.

"It's what the world expects of me. What Hybern expects. And if he grants my asking price to find them . . . Drakon has a legion capable of turning the tide in battle. It was why I allied with him during the War. I don't doubt Drakon still has it trained and ready. Word will have reached him by now. Especially that I am looking for them."

A warning. The only way Jurian could send one—by making himself the hunter.

I said to Jurian, "You don't want to kill Miryam and Drakon."

There was stark honesty in Jurian's eyes as he shook his head once. "No," he said roughly. "I want to beg their forgiveness."

I looked to Mor. But tears lined her eyes, and she blinked them furiously away.

"Miryam and Drakon have vanished," Rhys said. "Their people with them."

"Then find them," Jurian said. He jerked his chin to Azriel. "Send the shadowsinger, send whomever you trust, but *find* them."

Silence.

"Look into my head," Jurian said to Rhys. "Look, and see for yourself."

"Why now," Rhys said. "Why here."

Jurian held his stare. "Because the wall came down, and now I can move freely—to warn the humans here. Because . . ." He loosed a long breath. "Because Tamlin ran right back to Hybern after your meeting ended this morning. Right to their camp in the Spring Court, where Hybern now plans to launch a land assault on Summer tomorrow."

CHAPTER 54

Jurian was not my enemy.

I couldn't wrap my mind around it. Even as Rhys and I *both* looked.

I didn't linger for long.

The pain and guilt and rage, what he had seen and endured . . .

But Jurian spoke true. Laid himself bare to us.

He knew the spot they planned to attack. Where and when and how many.

Azriel vanished without a glance at any of us—to warn Cassian and move the legion.

Jurian was saying to Mor, "They didn't kill the sixth queen. Vassa. She saw through me—or thought she did—from the start. Warned them against this. Told them that if I was reborn, it was a bad sign, and to rally their armies to face the threat before it grew too large. But Vassa is too brash, too young. She didn't play the game the way the golden one, Demetra, did. Didn't see the lust in their eyes when I told them of the Cauldron's powers. Didn't know that from the moment I began to spin Hybern's lies . . . they became her enemies. They couldn't kill Vassa—the next in line to her throne is far more willful. So they found an old death-lord above the wall, with a penchant for enslaving young women. He cursed her, and stole her away . . . The entire world believes she's been sick these past months."

"We know," Mor said, and none of us dared glance at Elain. "We learned about it."

And even with the truth laid bare . . . none of us told him that Lucien had gone after her.

Elain seemed to remember, though. Who was hunting for that missing queen. And she said to Graysen, stone-faced and sorrowful through all of this, "I did not mean to deceive you."

His father answered, "I find I have trouble believing that."

Graysen swallowed. "Did you think you could come back here—live with me as this . . . lie?"

"No. Yes. I—I don't know what I wanted—"

"And you are bound to some . . . Fae male. A High Lord's son."

A different High Lord's heir, likely, I wanted to say.

"His name is Lucien." I wasn't certain if I'd ever heard his name from her lips.

"I don't care what his name is." The first sharp words from Graysen. "You are his *mate*. Do you even know what that means?"

"It means *nothing*," Elain said, her voice breaking. "It means *nothing*. I don't *care* who decided it or why they did—"

"You belong to *him*."

"I belong to *no one*. But my heart belongs to *you*."

Graysen's face hardened. "I don't want it."

He would have been better off hitting her, that's how deep the hurt in her eyes went. And seeing her face crumple . . .

I stepped close, pushing her behind me. "Here is what is going to happen. You are going to take in any people who can make it here. We will supply these walls with wards."

"We don't need them," sneered Nolan.

"Shall I demonstrate for you," I said, "how wrong you are? Or shall you take my word for it that I could reduce this wall to rubble with half a thought? And that is to say nothing of my friends. You will find, Lord Nolan, that you *want* our wards, and our help. All in exchange for taking in whatever humans need the safety."

"I don't want riffraff wandering through here."

"So only the rich and chosen will walk through the gates?" Rhys asked, arching a brow. "I can't imagine the aristocracy being content to work your land and fish in your lake or butcher your meat."

"We have plenty of workers here to do that."

It was happening again. Another fight with narrow-minded, hateful people . . .

But Jurian said to the lords, "I fought beside your ancestor. And he would be ashamed if you locked out those who needed it. You would spit on his grave to do so. I hold a position of trust with Hybern. One word from me, and I will make sure his legion takes a visit here. To you."

"You'll threaten to bring the very enemy you seek to protect us from?"

Jurian shrugged. "I can also convince Hybern to steer clear. He trusts me that much. You let in those people . . . I will do my best to keep his armies far away."

He gave Rhys a look, daring him to doubt it.

We were still too stunned to even try to look neutral.

But then Nolan said, "I do not pretend to have a large army. Only a considerable unit of soldiers. If what you say is true . . ." A glance at Graysen. "We will take them. Whoever can make it."

I wondered if the elder lord might be the one who could actually be reasoned with. Especially as Graysen said to Elain, "Take that ring off."

Elain's fingers curved into a fist. "No."

Ugly. This was about to get ugly in the worst way—

"Take. It. Off."

It was Nolan's turn to murmur a warning to his son. Graysen ignored him. Elain did not move.

"*Take it off!*" The roared words barked over the stones.

"That's enough," Rhys said, his voice lethally calm. "The lady keeps the ring, if she wants it. Though none of us will be particularly sad to see it go. Females tend to prefer gold or silver to iron."

Graysen leveled a seething look at Rhysand. "Is this the start of it? You Fae *males* will come to take our women? Are your own not fuckable enough?"

"Watch your tongue, boy," his father said. Elain turned white at the coarse language.

Graysen only said to her, "I am not marrying you. Our engagement is over. I will take whatever people occupy your lands. But not you. Never *you*."

Tears began sliding down Elain's face, their scent filling the room with salt.

Nesta stepped forward. Then another step. And another.

Until she was in front of Graysen, faster than anyone could see.

Until Nesta smacked him hard enough that his head snapped to the side.

"You never deserved her," Nesta snarled into the stunned silence as Graysen cupped his face and swore, bending over. Nesta only looked back at me. Rage, unfiltered and burning, roiled in her eyes. But her voice was stone-cold as she said to me, "I assume we're done here."

I gave her a wordless nod. And proud as any queen, Nesta took Elain's arm and led her from the guardhouse. Mor trailed behind, guarding their backs as they entered the veritable field of weapons and snarling hounds waiting outside.

The two lords saw themselves out without so much as a good-bye.

Alone, Jurian said, "Tell the shadowsinger I'm sorry about the arrow to the chest."

Rhys shook his head. "What's the next move, then? I assume you're doing more than warning humans to flee or hide."

Jurian pushed off the table. "The next move, Rhysand, is me going back to that Hybern war-camp and throwing a fit that my search for

Miryam and Drakon's whereabouts wasn't fruitful. My step after that is to take another trip to the continent and sow the seeds of discord amongst the queens' courts. To let some *vital* things slip about their agenda. Who they really support. What they really want. It will keep them busy—too worried about their own internal conflict to consider sailing here. And once that's done . . . who knows? Perhaps I'll join you on the battlefield."

Rhys rubbed his brows with a thumb and forefinger, the locks of his hair sliding forward as he dipped his head. "I wouldn't believe a word, except I looked into that head of yours."

Jurian tapped a hand on the door frame. "Tell Cassian to hammer the left flank hard tomorrow. Hybern is putting his untrained nobles there for some seasoning—they're spoiled and untested. Buckle the ranks there, and it'll spook the grunts. Hit them with everything you've got, and fast—don't give them time to rally or find their courage." Jurian gave me a grim smile. "I never congratulated you for slaughtering Dagdan and Brannagh. Good riddance."

"I did it for those Children of the Blessed," I said. "Not for glory."

"I know," Jurian said, flicking up his brows. "Why do you think I decided to trust you?"

CHAPTER 55

"I'm too old for these sorts of surprises," Mor groused as the war-tent groaned in the howling mountain wind at the northern border of the Winter Court, the Illyrian army settling down for the night. To wait for the attack tomorrow. They'd flown all day, the location remote enough to keep even an army of our size hidden. Until tomorrow, at least.

We'd warned Tarquin—and dispatched messages to Helion and Kallias to join if they could make it in time. But come the hour before dawn, the Illyrian legion would take to the skies and fly hard for that southern battlefield. They would land, hopefully, before it began. Right as Keir and his commanders winnowed in the Darkbringer legion from the Night Court.

And then the slaughter would begin. On either side.

If what Jurian claimed was true. Cassian had choked when we'd told him Jurian's battle advice. A milder reaction, Azriel said, than his initial response.

I asked Mor from where I sat at the foot of the fur-covered chaise we currently shared, "You never suspected Jurian might be . . . good?"

She swigged from her wine and leaned back against the cushions piled before the rolled headrest. My sisters were in another tent, not quite as big but equally luxurious, their lodgings flanked by Cassian's and Azriel's tents, and Mor's before it. No one would get to them without my friends knowing. Even if Mor was currently here with me.

"I don't know," she said, hauling a heavy wool throw blanket over her legs. "I was never as close to Jurian as I was to some of the others, but . . . we did fight together. Saved each other. I just assumed Amarantha broke him."

"Parts of him are broken," I said, shuddering to recall those memories I'd seen, the feelings. I pulled some of her blanket over my lap.

"We're all broken," Mor said. "In our own ways—in places no one might see."

I angled my head to inquire, but she asked, "Is Elain . . . all right?"

"No," was all I said. Elain was not all right.

She had quietly cried while we winnowed here. And in the hours afterward, while the army arrived and the camp was rebuilt. She did not take off her ring. She only lay on the cot in her tent, nestled among the furs and blankets, and stared at nothing.

Any bit of good, any advancement . . . gone. I debated returning to smash every bone in Graysen's body, but resisted—if only because it would give Nesta license to unleash herself upon him. And death at Nesta's hands . . . I wondered if they'd have to invent a new word for *killing* when she was done with Graysen.

So Elain silently cried, the tears so unending that I wondered if it was some sign of her heart bleeding out. Some sliver of hope that had shattered today. That Graysen would still love her, still marry her—and that love would trump even a mating bond.

A final tether had been snapped—to her life in the human lands.

Only our father, wherever he was, remained as any sort of connection.

Mor read whatever was on my face and set down the wine on the small wood table beside the chaise. "We should sleep. I don't even know why I'm drinking."

"Today was . . . unexpected."

"It's so much harder," she said, groaning as she chucked the rest of the blanket into my lap and rose to her feet. "When enemies turn into friends. And the opposite, I suppose. What didn't I see? What did I overlook or dismiss? It always makes me reassess *myself* more than them."

"Another joy of war?"

She snorted, heading for the tent flaps. "No—of life."

I barely slept that night.

Rhys didn't come to the tent—not once.

I slipped from our bed when the darkness was just starting to yield to gray, following the tug of the mating bond as I had done that day Under the Mountain.

He stood atop a rocky outcropping crusted with patches of ice, watching the stars fade away one by one over the still-slumbering camp.

I wordlessly slid my arm around his waist, and he shifted his wings to fold me into his side.

"A lot of soldiers are going to die today," he said quietly.

"I know."

"It never gets easier," he whispered.

The strong panes of his face were taut, and silver lined his eyes as he studied the stars. Only here, only now, would he show that grief—that worry and pain. Never before his armies; never before his enemies.

He loosed a long breath. "Are you ready?" I would stay near the back of the lines with Mor to get a feel for battle. The flow and terror and structure. My sisters would remain here until it was safe to winnow them afterward. If things didn't go to hell first.

"No," I admitted. "But I have no other choice than to be ready."

Rhys kissed the top of my head, and we stared at the dying stars in silence.

"I'm grateful," he said after a while, as the camp beneath us stirred in the building light. "To have you at my side. I don't know if I ever told you that—how grateful I am to have you stand with me."

I blinked back the burning in my eyes and took his hand. I laid it over my heart, letting him feel its beating while I kissed him one final time, the last of the stars vanishing as the army below us awoke to do battle.

CHAPTER 56

Jurian was right.

We'd seen inside his head, yet we'd still doubted. Still wondered if we'd arrive to find Hybern had changed their position, or attacked elsewhere.

But Hybern's horde was precisely where Jurian claimed they'd be.

And as the Illyrian army swept for them while they marched over the Spring border and into Summer . . . Hybern's forces certainly seemed shocked.

Rhys had cloaked our forces—all of them. Sweat had slid down his temple at the strain, at keeping the mass of us hidden from sight and sound and scent as we flew mile after mile. My wings weren't strong enough—so Mor winnowed us through the sky, keeping pace with them.

But we arrived together. And as Rhys ripped the sight shield away, revealing battle-hungry Illyrians spearing from the skies in neat, precise lines . . . As he revealed the legion of Keir's Darkbringers charging on foot, swathed in wisps of night and armed with star-bright steel . . . It was hard not to be smug at the panic that rippled over the marching mass of Hybern.

But Hybern's army . . . It stretched far—deep and long. Meant to sweep away everything in its path.

"*SHIELDS,*" Cassian bellowed at the front line.

One by one by one, shields of red and blue and green flickered into life around the Illyrians and their weapons, overlapping like the scales of a fish. Overlapping like the solid metal shields they each bore on their left arms, locking into place from ankle to shoulder.

Below, Keir's troops rippled with shadowy shields flaring into place before them.

Mor winnowed us to the tree-covered hill that overlooked the field Cassian had deemed would be the best place to hit them based on Azriel's scouting. There was a slope to the grass—in our advantage. We held the high ground; a narrow, shallow river lay not too far back from Hybern's army. Success in battle, Cassian had told me that morning over a swift breakfast, was often decided not by numbers, but by picking where to fight.

The Hybern army seemed to realize their disadvantage within moments.

But the Illyrians had landed beside Keir's soldiers. Cassian, Azriel, and Rhys spread out amongst the front line, all clad in that black Illyrian armor, all armed as the other winged soldiers were: shield gripped in the left hand, Illyrian blade in the right, an assortment of daggers on them, and helmets.

The helmets were the only markers of who they were. Unlike the smooth domes of the others, Rhys, Azriel, and Cassian wore black helmets whose cheek-guards had been fashioned and swept upward like ravens' wings. Albeit razor-sharp ravens' wings that jutted up on either side of the helmet, right above the ear, but . . . The effect, I admitted, was terrifying. Especially with the two other swords strapped across their backs, the gauntlets that covered every inch of their hands, and the Siphons gleaming amongst Cassian's and Azriel's ebony armor.

Rhys's own power roiled around him, readying to hammer the right flank while Cassian aimed for the left. Rhys was to conserve his power—in case the king arrived. Or worse—the Cauldron.

This army, however huge . . . It did not seem that the king was even there to lead it. Or Tamlin. Or Jurian. Merely an invading harbinger of the force to come, but sizable enough that the damage . . . We could easily spy the damage behind the army, the plumes of smoke staining the cloudless summer sky.

Mor and I said little in the hours that followed.

I did not have it in me for words, for any sort of coherent speech as we watched. Either through our surprise or pure luck, there was no sign of that faebane. I was inclined to thank the Mother for that.

Even if every soldier in our camp this morning had mixed Nuan's antidote into their gruel, it would do nothing against *blocking* weapons tipped in faebane from shattering shields. Only stop against the stifling of magic, should it come into contact either through that damned powder . . . or by being impaled by a weapon tipped in it. Lucky—so lucky it was not in use today.

Because seeing the carnage, the fine line of control . . . There was no place for me on those front lines, where the Illyrians fought by the strength of their sword, their power, and their trust in the male on either side of them. Even Keir's soldiers fought as one—obedient and unfaltering, lashing out with shadows and steel. I would have been a fissure in that impenetrable armor—and what Cassian and the Illyrians unleashed upon Hybern . . .

Cassian slammed into that left flank. Siphons unleashed bursts of power that sometimes bounced off shields, sometimes found their mark and shredded flesh and bone.

But where Hybern's magic shields held out . . . Rhys, Azriel, and Cassian sent out blasts of their own power to shatter them. Leaving them vulnerable to those Siphons—or pure Illyrian steel. And if that did not fell them . . . Keir and his Darkbringers cleaned up the rest. Precisely. Coolly.

The field became a blood-drenched mud pit. Bodies gleamed in the morning sun, light bouncing off their armor. Hybern panicked at the unbreakable Illyrian lines that pushed and pushed them back. That battered them.

And as that left flank broke apart, as its nobles fell or turned and fled . . . The other Hybern soldiers began descending into panic, too.

There was one mounted commander who did not go easily. Who didn't turn his horse toward that river behind them to flee.

Cassian selected him as his opponent.

Mor gripped my hand tight enough to hurt as Cassian stepped out of that impenetrable front line of shields and swords, the soldiers around him immediately closing the gap. Mud and blood splattered Cassian's dark helmet, his armor.

He ditched his tall shield for a round one strapped across his back, crafted from the same ebony metal.

And then he launched into a run.

I could have sworn even Rhys paused on the other end of the battlefield to watch as Cassian cut his way through those enemy soldiers, aiming for the mounted Hybern commander. Who realized what and who was coming for him and started to search for a better weapon.

Cassian had been born for this—these fields, this chaos and brutality and calculation.

He didn't stop moving, seemed to know where every opponent fought both ahead and behind, seemed to breathe in the flow of the battle around him. He even let his Siphons' shield drop—to get close, to *feel* the impact of the arrows that he took in that ebony shield. If he slammed that shield into a soldier, his other arm was already swinging his sword at the next opponent.

I'd never seen anything like it—the skill and precision. It was like a dance.

I must have said it aloud because Mor replied, "For him, that's what battle is. A symphony."

Her eyes did not stray from Cassian's death-dance.

Three soldiers were brave or stupid enough to try to charge him. Cassian had them down and dying with four maneuvers.

"Holy Mother," I breathed.

That was who had been training me. Why Fae trembled at his name.

Why the high-born Illyrian warriors had been jealous enough to want him dead.

But there Cassian was, no one between him and the commander.

The commander had found a discarded spear. He threw it.

Fast and sure, I skipped a heartbeat as it spiraled for Cassian.

His knees bent, wings tucked in tight, shield twisting—

He took the spear in the shield with an impact I could have sworn I heard, then sliced off the shaft and kept running.

Within a heartbeat, Cassian had sheathed both shield and sword across his back.

And I would have asked why but he'd already picked up another fallen spear.

Already hurled it, his entire body going into the throw, the movement so perfect that I knew I'd one day paint it.

Both armies seemed to stop at the throw.

Even with the distance, Cassian's spear hit home.

It went right through the commander's chest, so hard it knocked the male clean off his horse.

By the time he was done falling, Cassian was there.

His sword caught the sunlight as it lifted and plunged down.

Cassian had picked his mark well. Hybern fled now. Outright turned and fled for the river.

But Hybern found Tarquin's army waiting on its opposite bank, exactly where Cassian had ordered it to appear.

Trapped with the Illyrians and Keir's Darkbringers at their backs and Tarquin's two thousand soldiers on the other side of the narrow river . . .

It was harder to watch—that slaughter.

Mor said to me, "It's over."

The sun was high in the sky, heat rising with every minute.

"You don't need to see this," she added.

Because some of the Hybern soldiers were surrendering. On their knees.

As it was Tarquin's territory, Rhys yielded the decision about what to do with prisoners.

From the distance, I picked out Tarquin from his armor—more ornate than Rhysand's, but still brutal. Fish fins and scales seemed to be the motif, and his azure cloak flowed through the mud behind him as he stepped over fallen bodies to get to the few hundred surviving enemy.

Tarquin stared at where the enemy had knelt, his helmet masking his features.

Nearby, Rhys, Cassian, and Azriel monitored, speaking to Keir and the Illyrian captains. I did not see many wings amongst the fallen on the field. A mercy.

The only mercy, it seemed, as Tarquin made a motion with his hand.

Some of the Hybern soldiers began screaming for clemency, their offers to sell information ringing out, even to us.

Tarquin pointed at a few of them, and they were hauled away by his soldiers. To be questioned. And I doubted it would be pleasant.

But the others . . .

Tarquin stretched out his hand toward them.

It took me a heartbeat to realize why the Hybern soldiers were thrashing and clawing at themselves, some trying to crawl away. But then one of them collapsed, and sunlight caught on his face. And even with the distance, I could tell—could tell it was water now bubbling out of his lips.

Out the lips of all the Hybern soldiers as Tarquin drowned them on dry land.

I didn't see Rhys or the others for hours—not when he gave the order that the Illyrian war-camp was to be moved from the border of the Winter Court and rebuilt at the edge of the battlefield. So Mor and I winnowed to and from the camps as the exodus began. We brought my sisters last, waiting until many of the bodies had been turned to black dust by Rhysand. The blood and mud remained, but the camp maintained too good a position to yield—or waste time finding another one.

Elain didn't seem to care. Didn't seem to even notice that we winnowed her. She just went from her tent to Mor's arms, then into the same tent rebuilt in the new camp.

Nesta, however . . . I told her upon arriving that everyone was fine. But when we winnowed to the battlefield . . . She stared at that bloody, muddy plain. At the weapons soldiers of both courts were plundering from the fallen enemy.

Nesta listened to the low-level Illyrian soldiers whispering about how Cassian had thrown that spear, how he'd cut down soldiers like stalks of wheat, how he'd fought like Enalius—their most ancient warrior-god and the first of the Illyrians.

It had been a while, it seemed, since they had seen Cassian in open battle. Since they'd realized that he'd been young in the War, and now . . . the looks they gave Cassian as he passed . . . they were the same as those the High Lords had given Rhys upon seeing his power. Like them, and yet Other.

Nesta watched, and listened to it all, while the camp was built around us.

She did not ask where the bodies had gone before her arrival. She wholly ignored the camp Keir and his Darkbringers built beside ours—the ebony-armored soldiers who sneered at her, at me, at the Illyrians. No, Nesta only made sure that Elain was dozing in her tent, and then offered to help cut up linen for bandages.

We were doing just that around the early-evening fire when Rhys and Cassian approached, still in their armor, Azriel nowhere to be found.

Rhys took a seat on the log I was perched atop of, armor thudding, and silently pressed a kiss to my temple. He reeked of metal and blood and sweat.

His helmet clunked on the ground at our feet. I silently handed him a pitcher of water, and made to grab a glass when Rhys just lifted the pewter container and drank right from it. It sloshed over the sides, water pinging against the black metal coating his thighs, and when he at last set it down, he looked . . . tired. In his eyes, Rhys seemed weary.

But Nesta had jolted to her feet, staring at Cassian, at the helmet he had tucked into the crook of his arm, the weapons still poking above his shoulder, in need of cleaning. His dark hair hung limp with sweat, his face was mud-splattered where even the helmet had not kept it out.

But she surveyed his seven Siphons, the dim red stones. And then she said, "You're hurt."

Rhys snapped to attention at that.

Cassian's face was grim—his eyes glassy. "It's fine." Even the words were laced with exhaustion.

But she reached for his arm—his shield arm.

Cassian seemed to hesitate, but offered it to her, tapping the Siphon atop his palm. The armor slid back a fraction over his forearm, revealing—

"You know better than to walk around with an injury," Rhys said a bit tensely.

"I was busy," Cassian said, not taking his focus off Nesta as she studied the swollen wrist. How she'd detected it through the armor . . . She must have read it in his eyes, his stance.

I hadn't realized she'd been observing the Illyrian general enough to notice his tells.

"And it'll be fixed by morning," Cassian added, daring Rhys to say otherwise.

But Nesta's pale fingers gently probed his golden-brown skin, and he hissed through his teeth.

"How do I fix it?" she asked. Her hair had been tied in a loose knot atop her head earlier in the day, and in the hours that we'd worked to ready and distribute supplies to the healers, through the heat and humidity, stray tendrils had come free to curl about her temple, her nape. Faint color had stained her cheeks from the sun, and her forearms, bare beneath the sleeves she'd rolled up, were flecked with mud.

Cassian slowly sat on the log where she'd been perched a moment before, groaning softly—as if even that movement taxed him. "Icing it usually helps, but wrapping it will just lock it in place long enough for the sprain to repair itself—"

She reached for the basket of bandages she'd been preparing, then for the pitcher at her feet.

I was too tired to do anything other than watch as she washed his wrist, his hand, her own fingers gentle. Too tired to ask if she possessed the magic to heal it herself. Cassian seemed too weary to speak as well while she wrapped bandages around his wrist, only grunting to confirm if it was too tight or too loose, if it helped at all. But he watched her—didn't take his eyes off her face, the brows bunched and lips pursed in concentration.

And when she'd tied it neatly, his wrist wrapped in white, when Nesta made to pull back, Cassian gripped her fingers in his good hand. She lifted her gaze to his. "Thank you," he said hoarsely.

Nesta did not yank her hand away.

Did not open her mouth for some barbed retort.

She only stared and stared at him, at the breadth of his shoulders, even more powerful in that beautiful black armor, at the strong column of his tan neck above it, his wings. And then at his hazel eyes, still riveted to her face.

Cassian brushed a thumb down the back of her hand.

Nesta opened her mouth at last, and I braced myself—

"You're hurt?"

At the sound of Mor's voice, Cassian snatched his hand back and pivoted toward Mor with a lazy smile. "Nothing for you to cry over, don't worry."

Nesta dragged her stare from his face—down to her now-empty hand, her fingers still curled as if his palm lay there. Cassian didn't look at Nesta as she rose, snatching up the pitcher, and muttered something about getting more water from inside the tent.

Cassian and Mor fell into their banter, laughing and taunting each other about the battle and the ones ahead.

Nesta didn't come back out again for some time.

I helped with the wounded long into the night, Mor and Nesta working alongside me.

A long day for all of us, yes, but the others . . . They had fought for hours. From the tight angle of Mor's jaw as she tended to injured Darkbringers and Illyrians alike, I knew the various recountings of the battle wore on her—not for the tales of glory and gore, but for the sole fact that she had not been there to fight beside them.

But between the Darkbringer forces and the Illyrians . . . I wondered where she'd fight. Whom she'd command or answer to. Definitely not Keir, but . . . I was still chewing it over when I at last slipped between the warm sheets of my bed and curled my body into Rhys's.

His arm instantly slid over my waist, tugging me in closer. "You smell like blood," he murmured into the dimness.

"Sorry," I said. I'd washed my hands and forearms before sliding into bed, but a full bath . . . I had barely managed the walk through the camp moments ago.

He stroked a hand over my waist, down to my hip. "You must be exhausted."

"And *you* should be sleeping," I chided, shifting closer, letting his warmth and scent wrap around me.

"Can't," he admitted, his lips brushing over my temple.

"Why?"

His hand drifted to my back, and I arched into the long, trailing strokes along my spine. "It takes a while—to settle myself after battle." It had been hours and hours since the fighting had ceased. Rhys's lips began a journey from my temple down my jaw.

And even with the weight of exhaustion pressing on me, as his mouth grazed over my chin, as he nipped at my bottom lip . . . I knew what he was asking.

Rhys sucked in a breath as I traced the contours of his muscled stomach, as I marveled at the softness of his skin, the strength of the body beneath it.

He pressed a featherlight kiss to my lips. "If you're too tired," he began, even as he went wholly still while my fingers continued their journey, past the sculpted muscles of his abdomen.

I answered him with a kiss of my own. Another. Until his tongue slid over the seam of my lips and I opened for him.

Our joining was fast, and hard, and I was clawing at his back before the end shattered through both of us, dragging my hands over his wings.

For long minutes afterward, we remained there, my legs thrown over his shoulders, the rise and fall of his chest pushing into mine in a lingering echo of our bodies' movements.

Then he withdrew, gently lowering my legs from his shoulders. He kissed the inside of each of my knees as he did so, setting them on either side of him as he rose up to kneel before me.

The tattoos on his knees were nearly obscured by the rumpled sheets, the design stretched with the position. But I traced my fingers over the tops of those mountains, the three stars inked atop them, as he remained kneeling between my legs, gazing down at me.

"I thought about you every moment I was on that battlefield," he said softly. "It focused me, centered me—let me get through it."

I stroked those tattoos on his knees again. "I'm glad. I think . . . I think some part of me was down there on that battlefield with you, too." I glanced to his suit of armor, cleaned and displayed on a dummy near the small dressing area. His winged helmet shone like a dark star in the dimness. "Seeing that battle today . . . It felt different from the one in Adriata." Rhys only listened, those star-flecked eyes patient. "In Adriata, I didn't . . ." I struggled for the words. "The chaos of the battle in Adriata was easier, somehow. Not *easy*, I mean—"

"I know what you meant."

I sighed, sitting up so that we were knee-to-knee and face-to-face. "What I'm trying and failing miserably to explain is that attacks like the one in Adriata, in Velaris . . . I can fight in those. There are people to defend, and the disorder of it . . . I can—I'll gladly fight in those battles. But what I saw today, that sort of warfare . . ." I swallowed. "Will you be ashamed of me if I admit that I'm not sure if I'm ready for that sort of battling?" Line against line, swinging and stabbing until I didn't know up from down, until mud and gore blurred the line between enemy and foe, relying as much upon the warriors beside me as my own skill set. And the closeness of it, the sounds and sheer scale of the bloodbath . . .

He took my face in his hands, kissing me once. "Never. I can never be ashamed of you. Certainly not over this." He kept his mouth close to mine, sharing breath. "Today's battle *was* different from Adriata, and Velaris. If we had more time to train you with a unit, you could easily fight amongst the lines and hold your own. But only if you wanted to. And for now, these initial battles . . . Being down in that slaughterhouse is not something I'd wish upon you." He kissed me again. "We are a pair," he said against my lips. "If you ever wish to fight by my side, it will be my honor."

I pulled my head back, frowning at him. "I feel like a coward now."

He stroked a thumb over my cheek. "No one would ever think that of you—not with all you have done, Feyre." A pause. "War is ugly, and messy, and unforgiving. The soldiers doing the fighting are only a fraction of it. Don't underestimate how far it goes for them to see you here—to see you tending to the wounded and participating in these meetings and councils."

I considered, letting my fingers drift across the Illyrian tattoos over his chest and shoulders.

And perhaps it was the afterglow of our joining, perhaps it was the battle today, but . . . I believed him.

Tarquin's army didn't blend into ours as Keir's did, but rather camped beside it. Azriel led team after team of scouts to find the rest of Hybern's host, discover their next movement . . . But nothing.

I wondered if Tamlin was with them—if he'd whispered to Hybern everything that had been discussed in that meeting. The weaknesses between courts. I didn't dare ask anyone.

But I did dare to question Nesta about whether she felt the Cauldron's power stirring. Mercifully, she reported feeling nothing amiss. Even so . . . I knew Rhys was frequently checking with Amren in Velaris—asking if she had made any discoveries with the Book.

And even if she found some alternative way to stop that Cauldron . . . We needed to know where the king was hiding the rest of his army first. And not so we could face it—not alone. No, so we could bring others to finish the job.

But only once we knew where the rest of Hybern's army was—where I was to unleash Bryaxis. It would do no good to have Hybern learn of Bryaxis's existence and adjust its plans. No, only when that full army was upon us . . . Only then would I set it upon them.

The first three days after the battle, the armies healed their wounded and rested. By the fourth, Cassian ordered them to do menial tasks to stave off any restlessness and chances for dangerous grumbling. His first order: dig a trench around the entire camp.

But the fifth day, the trench halfway finished . . . Azriel appeared, panting, in the middle of our war-tent.

Hybern had somehow skirted us entirely, and sent a force marching up the seam between the Autumn and Summer Courts. Heading for the Winter Court border.

We couldn't glean a reason why. Azriel hadn't discovered one, either. They were half a day's flight from us. He'd already sent warnings to Kallias and Viviane.

Rhys, Tarquin, and the others debated for hours, weighing the possibilities. Abandon this spot by the border, and we could be playing into Hybern's plans. But leave that northward army unattended and it could keep going north as far as it pleased. We could not afford to split our own army in two—there weren't enough soldiers to spare.

Until Varian came up with an idea.

He dismissed all the captains and generals, Keir and Devlon looking none too pleased at the order as they stormed out, dismissed everyone but his sister, Tarquin, and my own family.

"We march north—*and* we stay."

Rhys lifted a brow. Cassian frowned.

But Varian jabbed a finger on the map spread on the table we'd gathered around. "Spin a glamour—a good one. So that if anyone walks by here, they see and hear and smell an army. Put whatever spells in place to repel them from actually coming up to it. But let Hybern's eyes report that we are still here. That we choose to stay here."

"While we march north under a sight shield," Cassian murmured, rubbing his jaw. "It could work." He added with a grin to Varian, "You ever get sick of all that sunshine, you can come play with us in Velaris."

Though Varian frowned, something glinted in his eye.

But Tarquin said to Rhys, "You could make such a deception?"

Rhys nodded and winked at me. "With assistance from my mate."

I prayed that I'd rested enough as they all looked to me.

I was nearly drained by the time Rhys and I were finished that night. I followed his instructions, marking faces and details, willing that shape-shifting magic to craft them out of thin air, to give them life of their own.

It was like . . . applying a thin film over all those living in the camp, that would then separate when we moved out—separate and grow into its own entity that walked and talked and did all manner of things here. While we marched to intercept Hybern's army, hidden from sight by Rhys.

But it worked. Cresseida, skilled with glamours herself, worked personally on the Summer Court soldiers. She and I were both panting and sweaty hours later, and I nodded my thanks as she handed me a skein of water. She was not a trained warrior like her brother, but she was a solid, needed presence amongst the army—the soldiers looked to her for guidance and stability.

We moved out again, a far larger beast than the one that had flown down here. The Summer Court soldiers and Keir's legion could not fly, but Tarquin dug deep into his reservoirs and winnowed them along with us. He'd be wholly empty by the time we reached the enemy, but he insisted he was better at fighting with steel anyway.

We found the Hybern army at the northern edge of the mighty forest that stretched along the Summer Court's eastern border.

Azriel had scouted the land ahead for Cassian, laid it out in precise detail. It was late enough in the afternoon that Hybern was readying to settle down for the night.

Cassian had let our army rest all day, anticipating that. Knowing that at the end of a long day of marching, Hybern's forces would be exhausted, muddled. Another rule of war, he told me. Knowing *when* to pick your battles could be equally as important as where you fought them.

With rain-heavy clouds sweeping in from the east and the sun sinking toward the trees behind us—sycamores and oaks that towered high—we landed. Rhys ripped off the glamour surrounding us.

He wanted word to get out—wanted word to spread amongst Hybern's forces *who* was meeting them at every turn. Slaughtering them.

But they already knew.

Again, I watched from the camp itself, atop a broad rim leading into the grassy little valley where Hybern had planned to rest. Elain ducked into her tent the moment the Illyrian warriors built it for her. Only Nesta strode toward the edge of the tents to watch the battle on the valley floor below. Mor joined her, then me.

Nesta did not flinch at the clash and din of battle. She only stared toward one black-armored figure, leading the lines, his occasional order to *push* or to *hold that flank* barking across the battle.

Because this battle . . . Hybern had been ready. And the appearance they'd given, of a tired army ready to rest for the night . . . It had been a ruse, as our own had been.

Keir's soldiers started going down first, shadows sputtering out. Their front lines buckling.

Mor watched it, stone-faced. I had no doubt she was half hoping her father joined the dead now piling up. Even as Keir managed to rally the Darkbringers, reassembled that front line—only after Cassian had roared at him to fix it. And on the other side of the field . . .

Rhys and Tarquin were drained enough that they were actually battling sword to sword against soldiers. And again, no sign of the king or Jurian or Tamlin.

Mor was hopping from one foot to another, glancing at me every now and then. The bloodshed, the brutality—it sang to some part of her. Being up here with me . . . It was not where she wished to be.

But this . . . this running after armies, scrambling to stay ahead . . .

It would not provide a solution. Not for long.

The skies opened up, and the battle turned into outright muddy slaughter. Siphons flared, soldiers died. Hybern wielded its own magic upon our forces, arrows tipped in faebane finally making an appearance, along with clouds of it, that mercifully didn't last long in the rain. And did not impact us—not one bit—with Nuan's antidote in our systems. Only those arrows, which were skillfully avoided with shields or outright destruction to their shafts, leaving the stone to fall harmlessly from the sky.

Still Cassian, Azriel, and Rhys kept fighting, kept killing. Tarquin and Varian held their own—spreading out their soldiers to aid Keir's once-again foundering line.

Too late.

From the distance, through the rain, we could see perfectly as the dark line of Keir's soldiers caved to an onslaught of Hybern cavalry.

"Shit," Mor breathed, gripping my arm tight enough to bruise, warm summer rain soaking our clothes, our hair. "*Shit.*"

Like a burst dam, Hybern's soldiers poured through, cleaving Keir's force in half. Cassian's bellowing was audible even from the hilltop—then he was soaring, dodging arrows and spears, his Siphons so dim they barely guarded him against it. I could have sworn Rhys roared some order to him—that Cassian disregarded as he landed in the middle, the *middle* of those enemy forces sundering our lines, and unleashed himself.

Nesta inhaled in a sharp, high gasp.

More and more—Hybern spread us farther and farther apart. Rhys's power slammed into the flank of them, trying to shove them back. But his power was drained, exhausted from last night. Dozens fell to those snapping shadows, rather than hundreds.

"Re-form the lines," Mor was muttering, releasing me to pace, rain sluicing down her face. "Re-form the damned lines!"

Cassian was trying. Azriel had lunged into the fray, nothing more than shadows edged in blue light, battling his way toward where Cassian fought, utterly surrounded.

"Mother above," Nesta said softly. Not in awe. No—no, that was dread in her voice.

And within my own as I said, "They can fix this." Or I prayed they could.

Even if this battle . . . this was not all that Hybern had to offer against us.

This was not all they had to offer, and yet we were being pushed back, back, back—

Red flared in the heart of that battle like an exploding ember. A circle of soldiers died.

But more of Hybern's soldiers pushed in around Cassian. Even Azriel could not get to his side. My stomach turned, over and over.

Hybern had hidden the majority of its force somewhere. Our scouts could not find it. *Azriel* could not find it. And Elain . . . She could not see that mighty army, she'd said. In her dreams awake and asleep.

I knew little of war, of battle. But this . . . it felt like patching up holes in a boat while it sank.

As the rain drenched us, as Mor paced and swore at the slaughter, the bodies starting to pile up on our side, the foundering lines . . . I realized what I had to do, if I could not be down there, fighting.

Who I had to hunt down—and ask about the location of Hybern's true army.

The Suriel.

CHAPTER 57

"Absolutely not," Mor said when I pulled her a few feet away from Nesta, the din of battle and rain drowning out our voices. "*Absolutely not.*"

I jerked my head toward the valley below. "Go join them. You're wasted here. They need you." It was true. "Cassian and Az *need* you to push back the front lines." For Cassian's Siphons were beginning to sputter.

"Rhys will *kill* me if I leave you here."

"Rhys will do no such thing, and you know it. He's got wards around this camp, and I'm not entirely defenseless, you know."

I wasn't *lying*, exactly, but . . . The Suriel might very well not appear if Mor was there. And if I told her where I was going . . . I had no doubt she *would* insist on coming with me.

We didn't have the luxury of waiting for Jurian to give us information. About many things. I needed to leave—now.

"Go fight. Make those Hybern pricks scream a bit."

Nesta drew her attention away from the slaughter enough to add, "Help them."

For that was Cassian, making another charge toward a Hybern commander. Hoping to spook the soldiers again.

Mor frowned deeply, bounced once on her toes. "Just—be on your guard. Both of you."

I gave her a wry look—right before she rushed for her tent. I waited until she'd emerged again, buckling on weapons, and saluted me before she winnowed away. To the battlefield.

Right to Azriel's side—just as a soldier nearly landed a blow to his back.

Mor punched her sword through the soldier's throat before he could land that strike.

And then Mor began cutting a path toward Cassian, toward the broken front line beyond him, her damp golden hair a ray of sunshine amid the mud and dark armor.

Soldiers began screaming. Screamed some more when Azriel, blue Siphons flaring, fell into place beside her. Together, they plowed a path to Cassian—or tried to.

They made it perhaps ten feet before they were swarmed again. Before the press of bodies made even Mor's hair vanish in mud and rain.

Nesta laid a hand against her bare, rain-slick throat. Cassian began another assault on a Hybern captain—slower this time than he'd been.

Now. I had to go now—quickly. I took a step away from the outlook.

My sister narrowed her brows at me. "You're leaving?"

"I'll be back soon," was all I said. I didn't dare wonder how much of our army would be left when I did.

By the time I strode away, Nesta had already faced the battle once more, rain plastering her hair to her head. Resuming her unending vigil of the general battling on the valley floor below.

I had to track the Suriel.

And even though Elain could not see the Hybern host . . . It was worth a try.

Her tent was dim, and quiet—the sounds of slaughter far away, dreamlike.

She was awake, staring blankly at the canvas ceiling.

"I need you to find something for me," I said, dripping water everywhere as I laid a map across her thighs. Perhaps not as gentle as I should have been, but she at least sat up at my tone. Blinked at the map of Prythian.

"It's called the Suriel—it's one of many who bear that name. But . . . but it looks like this," I said, and reached for her hand to show her. I hesitated. "*May* I show it to you?"

My sister's brown eyes were glazed.

"Plant the image in your mind," I clarified. "So you know where to look."

"I don't know how to look," Elain mumbled.

"You can try." I should have asked Amren to train her, too.

But Elain studied me, the map, then nodded.

She had no mental shields, no barriers. The gates to her mind . . . Solid iron, covered in vines of flowers—or it would have been. The blossoms were all sealed, sleeping buds tucked into tangles of leaves and thorns.

I took a step beyond them, just into the antechamber of her mind, and planted the image of the Suriel there, trying to infuse it with safety—the truth that it looked terrifying, but had not harmed me.

Still, Elain shuddered when I pulled out. "Why?"

"It has answers I need. Immediately." Or else we might not have much of an army *left* to fight that entire Hybern host once I located it.

Elain again glanced at the map. At me. Then closed her eyes.

Her eyes shifted beneath her lids, the skin so delicate and colorless that the blue veins beneath were like small streams. "It moves . . . ," she whispered. "It moves through the world like . . . like the breath of the western wind."

"Where is it headed?"

Her finger lifted, hovering over the map, the courts.

Slowly, she set it down.

"There," she breathed. "It is going there. Now."

I looked at where she had laid her finger and felt the blood rush from my face.

The Middle.

The Suriel was headed to that ancient forest in the Middle. Just south—miles, perhaps . . .

From the Weaver of the Wood.

I winnowed in five leaps. I was breathless, my power nearly drained thanks to the glamouring I'd done yesterday, the summoned flame I'd used to dry myself off, and the winnowing that had taken me from the battle and right into the heart of that ancient wood.

The heavy, ripe air was as awful as I remembered, the forest thick with moss that choked the gnarled beeches and the gray stones scattered throughout. Then there was the silence.

I wondered if I should have indeed brought Mor with me as I listened. As I felt with my lingering magic for any sign of it.

The moss cushioned my steps as I eased into a walk. Scanning, listening. How far away, how small, that battle to the south felt.

My swallow was loud in my ears.

Things other than the Weaver prowled these woods. And the Weaver herself . . . Stryga, the Bone Carver had called her. His sister. Both siblings to an awful, male creature lurking in another part of the world.

I drew my Illyrian blade, the metal singing in the thick air.

But an ancient, rasping voice asked behind me, "Have you come to kill me, or to beg for my help once again, Feyre Archeron?"

CHAPTER 58

I turned, but did not sheath my blade across my back.

The Suriel was standing a few feet away, clad not in the cloak I had given it months ago, but a different one—heavier and darker, the fabric already torn and shredded. As if the wind it traveled on had ripped through it with invisible talons.

Only a few months since I had last seen it—when it had told me that Rhys was my mate. It might as well have been a lifetime ago.

Its over-large teeth clacked faintly. "Thrice now, we have met. Thrice now, you have hunted for me. This time, you sent the trembling fawn to find me. I did not expect to see those doe-eyes peering at me from across the world."

"I'm sorry if it was a violation," I said as steadily as I could. "But it's an urgent matter."

"You wish to know where Hybern is hiding its army."

"Yes. And other things. But let's start with that."

A hideous, horrific smile. "Even I cannot see it."

My stomach tightened. "You can see everything but that?"

The Suriel angled its head in a way that reminded me it was indeed a predator. And there was no snare this time to hold it back.

"He uses magic to cloak it—magic far older than I."

"The Cauldron."

Another awful smile. "Yes. That mighty, wicked thing. That bowl of death and life." It shivered with what I could have sworn was delight. "You have one already who can find Hybern."

"Elain says she cannot see it—see past his magic."

"Then use the other to track it."

"Nesta. Use *Nesta* to track the Cauldron?"

"Like calls to like. The King of Hybern does not travel without the Cauldron. So where it is, he and his army shall be. Tell the beautiful thief to find it."

The hair on my arms rose. "How?"

It angled its head, as if listening. "If she is unskilled . . . bones will do the talking for her."

"Scrying—you mean scrying with bones?"

"Yes." Those tattered robes flitted in a phantom wind. "Bones and stones."

I swallowed again. "Why did the Cauldron not react when I joined the Book and spoke the spell to nullify its power?"

"Because you did not hold on for long enough."

"It was killing me."

"Did you think you could leash its power without a cost?"

My heart stuttered. "I need to—to die for it to be stopped?"

"So dramatic, human-heart. But yes—yes, that spell would have drained the life from you."

"Is there—is there another spell to use instead? To nullify its powers."

"If there were such a thing, you would still have to get close enough to the Cauldron to do it. Hybern will not make that mistake twice."

I swallowed. "Even if we nullify the Cauldron . . . will it be enough to stop Hybern?"

"It depends on your allies. If they survive long enough to battle afterward."

"Would the Bone Carver make a difference?" *And Bryaxis.*

The Suriel had no eyelids. But its milky eyes flared with surprise. "I cannot see—not him. He is not . . . born of this earth. His thread has not been woven in." Its twisted mouth tightened. "You wish to save Prythian so much that you would risk unleashing him."

"Yes." The moment I located that army, I'd unleash Bryaxis upon it. But as for the Carver . . . "He wanted a—gift. In exchange. The Ouroboros."

The Suriel let out a sound that might have been a gasp—delight or horror, I did not know. "The Mirror of Beginnings and Endings."

"Yes—but . . . I cannot retrieve it."

"You are afraid to look. To see what is within."

"Will it drive me—mad? Break me?"

It was an effort not to flinch at that monstrous face, at the milky eyes and lipless mouth. All focused upon me. "Only you can decide what breaks you, Cursebreaker. Only you." Not an answer—not really. Certainly not enough to risk retrieving the mirror. The Suriel again listened to that phantom wind. "Tell the silver-eyed messenger that the answer lies on the second and penultimate pages of the Book. Together they hold the key."

"The key to *what*?"

The Suriel clicked its bony fingers together, like the many-jointed limbs of a crustacean, tip-tapping against each other. "The answer to what you need to stop Hy—"

It took me a heartbeat to register what happened.

To identify the wooden thing that burst through the Suriel's throat as an ash arrow. To realize that what sprayed in my face, landing on my tongue and tasting like soil, was black blood.

To realize that the thudding before the Suriel could even scream . . . more arrows.

The Suriel stumbled to its knees, a choking sound coming out of that mouth.

It had been afraid of the naga that day in the woods. Had known it could be killed.

I surged toward it, palming a knife with my left hand, sword angling up.

Another arrow fired, and I ducked behind a gnarled tree.

The Suriel let out a scream at the impact. Birds scattered into flight, and my ears rang—

And then its labored, wet breathing filled the wood. Until a lilting female voice crooned, "Why does it talk to you, Feyre, when it would not even deign to speak with me?"

I knew that voice. That laughter beneath the words.

Ianthe.

Ianthe was here. With two Hybern soldiers behind her.

CHAPTER 59

Concealed behind the tree, I took in my surroundings. I was exhausted, but . . . I could winnow. I could winnow and be gone. The ash arrows they'd put into the Suriel, however . . .

I met its eyes as it lay there, bleeding out on the moss.

The same ash arrows that had brought down Rhys. But my mate's had been carefully placed to disable him.

These had been aimed to kill.

That mouth of too-big teeth formed a silent word. *Run*.

"It took the King of Hybern *days* to unravel what you did to me," Ianthe purred, her voice drawing closer. "I still can't use most of my hand."

I didn't reply. Winnow—I should winnow.

Black blood dribbled out of the Suriel's neck, that arrow tip vulgar as it jutted up from its thick skin. I couldn't heal it—not with those ash arrows still in its flesh. Not until they were out.

"I'd heard from Tamlin how you captured this one," Ianthe went on, coming closer and closer. "So I adapted your methods. And it would not tell me *anything*. But since you have made contact so many times, the robe *I* gave it . . ." I could hear the smile in her voice. "A simple tracking spell, a gift from the king. To be triggered in your presence. If you should come calling again."

Run, the Suriel mouthed once more, blood dribbling past its withered lips.

That was pain in its eyes. Real pain, as mortal as any creature. And if Ianthe took it alive to Hybern . . . The Suriel knew it was a possibility. It had begged me for freedom once . . . yet it was willing to be taken. For me to run.

Its milky eyes narrowed—in pain and understanding. *Yes*, it seemed to say. *Go*.

"The king built shields in my mind," Ianthe prattled on, "to keep you from harming me again when I found you."

I peered around the tree to spy her standing at the edge of the clearing, frowning at the Suriel. She wore her pale robes, that blue stone crowning her hood. Only two guards with her. Even after all this time . . . She still underestimated me.

I ducked back around before she could spot me. Met the Suriel's stare one more time.

And I let it read every one of the emotions that solidified in me with absolute clarity.

The Suriel began to shake its head. Or tried to.

But I gave it a smile of farewell. And stepped into the clearing.

"I should have slit your throat that night in the tent," I said to the priestess.

One of the guards shot an arrow at me.

I blocked it with a wall of hard air that instantly buckled. Drained—mostly drained. And if it took another hit from an ash arrow . . .

Ianthe's face tightened. "You'll find you want to reconsider how you speak to me. I'll be your best advocate in Hybern."

"I suppose you'll have to catch me first," I said coolly—and ran.

I could have sworn that ancient forest moved to make room for me.

Could have sworn it, too, read my final thoughts to the Suriel, and cleared the way.

But not for them.

I hurled every scrap of strength into my legs, into keeping upright, as I sprinted through the trees, leaping over rocks and streams, dodging moss-coated boulders.

Yet those guards, yet *Ianthe*, managed to keep close behind, even as they swore at the snapping trunks that seemed to shift into their way, the rocks that went loose beneath their feet. I only had to outrun them for so long.

Only for a few miles. Draw them away from the Suriel, buy it time to flee.

And make sure they *paid* for what they had done. All of it.

I opened my senses, letting them lead the way. The forest did the rest.

Perhaps she was waiting for me. Perhaps she had ordered the woods to open a path.

The Hybern guards gained on me. My feet flew beneath me, swift as a deer.

I began to recognize the trees, the rocks. There, I had stood with Rhys—there, I had flirted with him. There, he had lounged atop a branch while waiting for me.

The air behind me parted—an arrow.

I veered left, nearly slamming into a tree. The arrow went wide.

The light shifted ahead—brighter. The clearing.

I let out a whimper of relief that I made sure they heard.

I broke from the tree line in a leap, knees popping as I flew over the stones leading to that hair-thatched cottage.

"*Help me*," I breathed, making sure they heard that, too.

The wooden door was already half-open. The world slowed and cleared with each step, each heartbeat, as I hurtled over the threshold.

And into the Weaver's cottage.

CHAPTER 60

I gripped the door handle as I passed the threshold, digging in my heels and throwing every scrap of strength into my arms to keep that door from shutting. From locking me in.

Invisible hands shoved against it, but I gritted my teeth and braced a foot against the wall, iron biting into my hands.

The room behind me was dark. "Thief," intoned a lovely voice in the blackness.

"You do know," Ianthe tittered from outside the cottage, her steps slowing into a walk, "that we'll have to kill whoever is inside there with you. Selfish of you, Feyre."

I panted, holding the door open, making sure they couldn't see me on the other side.

"You have seen my twin," the Weaver hissed softly—with a hint of wonder. "I smell him on you."

Outside, Ianthe and the guard grew closer. Closer and closer.

Somewhere deep in the room, I *felt* her move. Felt her stand. And take a step toward me.

"What are you," the Weaver breathed.

"Feyre, you can be quite tedious," Ianthe said. Right outside. I could barely make out her pale robes through the crack between the door and threshold. "Do you think you can ambush us in there? I saw your shield. You're drained. And I do not think your *glowing* trick will help."

The Weaver's dress rustled as she crept closer in the gloom. "Who did you bring, little wolf? Who did you bring to me?"

Ianthe and her two guards stepped over the threshold. Then another step. Past the open door. They didn't see me in the shadows behind it.

"Dinner," I said to the Weaver, whirling around the door—to its outside face. And let go of the handle.

Just as the door slammed shut hard enough to rattle the cottage, I saw the ball of faelight that Ianthe lifted to illuminate the room.

Saw the horrible face of the Weaver, that mouth of stumped teeth opening wide with delight and unholy hunger. A death-god of old—starved for life. With a beautiful priestess before her.

I was already hurtling for the trees when the guards and Ianthe began screaming.

Their unending screams followed me for half a mile. By the time I reached the spot where I'd seen the Suriel fall, they'd faded.

Sprawled out, the Suriel's bony chest heaved unevenly, its breaths few and far between.

Dying.

I slid to my knees before it, sinking into the bloody moss. "Let me help you. I can heal you."

I'd do it the same way I'd helped Rhysand. Remove those arrows—and offer it my blood.

I reached for the first one, but a dry, bony hand settled on my wrist. "Your magic . . . ," it rasped, "is spent. Do not . . . waste it."

"I can save you."

It only gripped my wrist. "I am already gone."

"What—what can I do?" The words turned thin—brittle.

"Stay . . . ," it breathed. "Stay . . . until the end."

I took its hand in mine. "I'm sorry." It was all I could think to say. I had done this—I had brought it here.

"I knew," it gasped, sensing my shift in thoughts. "The tracking . . . I knew of it."

"Then why come at all?"

"You . . . were kind. You . . . fought your fear. You were . . . kind," it said again.

I began crying.

"And you were kind to me," I said, not brushing away the tears that fell onto its bloodied, tattered robe. "Thank you—for helping me. When no one else would."

A small smile on that lipless mouth. "Feyre Archeron." A labored breath. "I told you—to stay with the High Lord. And you did."

Its warning to me that first time we'd met. "You—you meant Rhys." All this time. All this time—

"Stay with him . . . and live to see everything righted."

"Yes. I did—and it was."

"No—not yet. *Stay with him.*"

"I will." I always would.

Its chest rose—then fell.

"I don't even know your name," I whispered. The Suriel—it was a title, a name for its kind.

That small smile again. "Does it matter, Cursebreaker?"

"Yes."

Its eyes dimmed, but it did not tell me. It only said, "You should go now. Worse things—worse things are coming. The blood . . . draws them."

I squeezed its bony hand, the leathery skin growing colder. "I can stay a while longer."

I had killed enough animals to know when a body neared death. Soon, now—it would be a matter of breaths.

"Feyre Archeron," the Suriel said again, gazing at the leafy canopy, the sky peeking through it. A painful inhale. "A request."

I leaned close. "Anything."

Another rattling breath. "Leave this world . . . a better place than how you found it."

And as its chest rose and stopped altogether, as its breath escaped in one last sigh, I understood why the Suriel had come to help me, again and again. Not just for kindness . . . but because it was a dreamer.

And it was the heart of a dreamer that had ceased beating inside that monstrous chest.

Its sudden silence echoed into my own.

I laid my head on its chest, on that now-silent vault of bone, and wept.

I wept and wept, until there was a strong hand at my shoulder.

I didn't know the scent, the feel of that hand. But I knew the voice as Helion said softly to me, "Come, Feyre. It is not safe here. Come."

I lifted my head. Helion was there, features grim, his brown skin ashen.

"I can't leave it here like this," I said, refusing to let go of its hand. I didn't care how Helion had found me. Why he'd found me.

He looked to the fallen creature, mouth tightening. "I'll take care of it."

Burn it—with the power of the sun.

I let him help me to my feet. Let him extend a hand toward that body—

"Wait."

Helion obeyed.

"Give me your cloak. Please."

Brows narrowing, Helion unfastened the rich crimson cloak pinned at each shoulder.

I didn't bother to explain as I covered the Suriel's body with the fine fabric. Far finer than the hateful rags Ianthe had given it. I tucked the High Lord's cloak gently around its broad shoulders, its bony arms.

"Thank you," I said one last time to the Suriel, and stepped away.

Helion's flame was a pure, blinding white.

It burned the Suriel into ashes within a heartbeat.

"Come," Helion said again, extending a hand. "Let's get you to the camp."

It was the kindness in his voice that cracked my chest. But I took Helion's hand.

As warm light whisked us away, I could have sworn that the pile of ashes was stirred by a phantom wind.

CHAPTER 61

Helion winnowed me into the camp. Right into Rhys's war-tent.

My mate was pale. Blood-splattered and filthy, from his skin to his armor to his hair.

I opened my mouth—to ask how the battle had gone, to say what had happened, I don't know.

But Rhys just reached for me, folding me into his chest.

And at the smell and warmth and solidity of him . . . I began weeping again.

I didn't know who was in the tent. Who had survived the battle. But they all left.

Left, while my mate held me, rocking me gently, as I cried and cried.

He only told me what had happened when my tears had quieted. When he'd washed the Suriel's black blood from my hands, my face.

I was out of the tent a heartbeat later, charging through the mud, dodging exhausted and weary soldiers. Rhys was a step behind me, but said nothing as I shoved through flaps of another tent and took stock of what and who was before me.

Mor and Azriel were standing before the cot, monitoring every move the healer sitting beside it made.

As she held her glowing hands over Cassian.

I understood then—the quiet Cassian had once mentioned to me.

It was now in my head as I looked at his muddy, pained face—pained, even in unconsciousness. As I heard his labored, wet breathing.

As I beheld the slice curving up from his navel to the bottom of his sternum. The split flesh. The blood—mostly just a trickle.

I swayed—only for Rhys to grip me beneath the elbows.

The healer didn't turn to look at me as her brow bunched in concentration, hands flaring with white light. Beneath them—slowly, the lips of the wound reached toward each other.

If it was this bad now—

"How," I rasped. Rhys had told me three things a moment ago:

We'd won—barely. Tarquin had again decided what to do with any survivors. And Cassian had been gravely injured.

"Where were you," was all Mor said to me. She was soaked, bloody, and coated in mud. Azriel was, too. No sign of injuries beyond minor cuts, mercifully.

I shook my head. I'd let Rhys into my mind while he held me. Showed him everything—explained Ianthe and the Suriel and the Weaver. What it had told me. Rhys's eyes had gone distant for a moment, and I knew Amren was on her way, the Book in tow. To help Nesta track that Cauldron—or try to. He could explain to Mor.

He'd only known I was gone after the battle stopped—when he realized Mor had been fighting. And that I was not at the camp anymore. He'd just reached Elain's tent when Helion sent word he'd found me. Using whatever gift he possessed that allowed him to sense such things. And was bringing me back. Vague, brief details.

"Is he—is he going to—" I couldn't finish the rest. Words had become as foreign and hard to reach as the stars.

"No," the healer said without looking at me. "He'll be sore for a few days, though."

Indeed, she'd gotten either side of the wound to touch—to now start weaving together.

Bile surged up my throat at the sight of that raw flesh—

"How," I asked again.

"He wouldn't wait for us," Mor said flatly. "He kept charging—trying to re-form the line. One of their commanders engaged him. He wouldn't turn away. By the time Az got there, he was down."

Azriel's face was stone-cold, even as his hazel eyes fixed unrelentingly upon that knitting wound.

Mor said again, "Where did you *go*?"

"If you're about to fight," the healer said sharply, "take it outside. My patient doesn't need to hear this."

None of us moved.

Rhys brushed a hand down my arm. "You are, as always, free to go wherever and whenever you wish. But what I think Mor is saying is . . . try to leave a note the next time."

The words were casual, but that was panic in his eyes. Not—not the controlling fear Tamlin had once succumbed to, but . . . genuine terror of not knowing where I was, if I needed help. Just as I would want to know where he was, if he needed help, if he vanished when our enemies surrounded us. "I'm sorry," I said. To him, to the others.

Mor didn't so much as look at me.

"You have nothing to be sorry for," Rhys replied, hand sliding to cup my cheek. "You decided to take things into your own hands, and got us valuable information in the process. But . . ." His thumb stroked over my cheekbone. "We have been lucky," he breathed. "Keeping a step ahead—keeping out of Hybern's claws. Even if today . . . today wasn't so fortunate on the battlefield. But the cynic in me wonders if our luck is about to expire. And I would rather it not end with you."

They all had to think me young and reckless.

No, Rhys said through the bond, and I realized I'd left my shields open. *Believe me, if you knew half of the shit Cassian and Mor have pulled, you'd get why we don't. I just . . . Leave a note. Or tell me the next time.*

Would you have let me go if I had?

I do not let *you do anything.* He tilted my face up, Mor and Azriel looking away. *You are your own person, you make your own choices. But we are mates—I am yours, and you are mine. We do not let each other do things, as if we dictate the movements of each other. But . . . I might have insisted I go with you. More for my own mental well-being, just to know you were safe.*

You were occupied.

A slash of a smile. *If you were hell-bent on going into the Middle, I would have unoccupied myself from battle.*

I waited for him to chide me about not waiting until they were done, about all of it, but . . . he angled his head. "I wonder if the Weaver forgives you now," he mused aloud.

Even the healer seemed to start at the name—the words.

A shiver ran down my spine. "I don't want to know."

Rhys let out a low laugh. "Then let's never find out."

But the amusement faded as he again surveyed Cassian. The wound that was now sealed over.

The Suriel wasn't your fault.

I loosed a breath as Cassian's eyelids began to shift and flutter. *I know.*

I'd already added its death to my ever-growing list of things I'd soon make Hybern pay for.

Long minutes passed, and we stood in silence. I did not ask where Nesta was. Mor barely acknowledged me. And Rhys . . .

He perched on the foot of the cot as Cassian's eyes at last opened, and the general let out a groan of pain.

"That's what you get," the healer chided, gathering her supplies, "for stepping in front of a sword." She frowned at him. "Rest tonight and tomorrow. I know better than to insist on a third day after that, but try *not* to leap in front of blades anytime soon."

Cassian just blinked rather dazedly at her before she bowed to Rhys and me and left.

"How bad," he asked, his voice hoarse.

"How bad was your injury," Rhys said mildly, "or how badly did we have our asses kicked?"

Cassian blinked again. Slowly. As if whatever sedative he'd been given still held sway.

"To answer the second question," Rhys went on, Mor and Azriel backing away a step or two as something sharpened in my mate's voice, "we managed. Keir took heavy hits, but . . . we won. Barely. To answer the first . . ." Rhys bared his teeth. "Don't you *ever* pull that kind of shit again."

The glaze wore off Cassian's eyes as he heard the challenge, the anger, and tried to sit up. He hissed, scowling down at the red, angry slice down his chest.

"Your guts were hanging out, you stupid prick," Rhys snapped. "Az held them in for you."

Indeed, the shadowsinger's hands were caked in blood—Cassian's blood. And his face . . . cold with—anger.

"I'm a soldier," Cassian said flatly. "It's part of the job."

"I gave you an order to *wait*," Rhys growled. "You ignored it."

I glanced to Mor, to Azriel—a silent question of whether we should remain. They were too busy watching Rhys and Cassian to notice.

"The line was breaking," Cassian retorted. "Your order was bullshit."

Rhys braced his hands on either side of Cassian's legs and snarled in his face, "I am your *High Lord*. You don't get to disregard orders you don't like."

Cassian sat up this time, swearing at the pain lingering in his body. "Don't you pull rank because you're pissed off—"

"You and your damned theatrics on the battlefield nearly got you *killed*." And even as Rhys spat the words—that was panic, again, in his eyes. His voice. "I'm not pissed. I'm *furious*."

"So you're allowed to be mad about our choices to protect *you*—and we're not allowed to be furious with you for *your* self-sacrificing bullshit?"

Rhys just stared at him. Cassian stared right back.

"You could have died," was all Rhys said, his voice raw.

"So could you."

Another beat of silence—and in its wake, the anger shifted.

Rhys said quietly, "Even after Hybern . . . I can't stomach it."

Seeing him hurt. Any of us hurt.

And the way Rhys spoke, the way Cassian leaned forward, wincing again, and gripped Rhys's shoulder . . .

I strode out of the tent. Left them to talk. Azriel and Mor followed behind me.

I squinted at the watery light—the very last before true dark. When my vision adjusted . . . Nesta stood by the nearest tent, an empty water bucket between her feet. Her hair a damp mess atop her mud-flecked head. Watching us emerge, grim-faced—

"He's fine. Healed and awake," I said quickly.

Nesta's shoulders sagged a bit.

She'd saved me the trouble of hunting her down to ask her about tracking the Cauldron. Better to do it now, with some privacy. Especially before Amren arrived.

But Mor said coldly, "Shouldn't you be refilling that bucket?"

Nesta went stiff. Sized up Mor. But Mor didn't flinch from that look.

After a moment, Nesta picked up her bucket, mud caked up to her shins, and continued on, steps squelching.

I turned, finding Azriel striding for the commanders' tent, but Mor—

Livid. She was absolutely *livid* as she faced me. "She didn't bother to tell anyone that you left."

Hence the anger. "Nesta is many things, but she's certainly loyal."

Mor didn't smile. Not as she said, "You lied."

She stormed for her own tent, and with *that* comment . . . I had no choice but to follow her in.

The space was mostly occupied with her bed and a small desk littered with weapons and maps. "I didn't *lie*," I said, wincing. "I just . . . didn't tell you what I planned to do."

She gaped at me. "You nudged me to *leave you*, insisting you would be safe *at the camp*."

"I'm sorry," I said.

"Sorry? *Sorry?*" She splayed her arms. Bits of mud flew off.

I didn't know what to do with my own—how to even look her in the eye. I'd seen her mad before, but never . . . never at me. I'd never had a friend to quarrel with—who cared enough.

"I know everything you're about to say, every excuse for why I couldn't go with you," Mor snapped. "But none of it excuses you for *lying* to me. If you'd explained, I would have let you go—if you'd *trusted* me, I would have let you go. Or maybe talked you out of an idiotic idea that nearly got you *killed*. They are *hunting* for you. They want to get their hands on you and *use you*. *Hurt you*. You've only seen a *taste* of what Hybern can do, what they delight in. And to break you to his will, the king will do *anything*."

I didn't know what to say other than, "We needed this information."

"Of course we did. But do you know what it felt like to look Rhys in the eye and tell him I had *no idea* where you were? To realize—for myself—that you had *vanished*, and likely duped me into enabling it?" She scrubbed at her filthy face, smearing the mud and gore further. "I thought you were smarter than that. *Better* than that sort of thing."

The words sent a line of fire searing across my vision, burning down my spine. "I'm not going to listen to this."

I turned to leave, but Mor was already there, gripping my arm. "Oh, yes, you are. Rhys might be all smiles and forgiveness, but you still have *us* to answer to. You are my *High Lady*. Do you understand what it means when you imply you don't trust us to help you? To respect your wishes if you want to do something alone? When you *lie* to us?"

"You want to talk about lying?" I didn't even know what came out of my mouth. I wished I'd killed Ianthe myself, if only to get rid of the rage that writhed along my bones. "How about the fact that you lie to yourself and all of us *every single day*?"

She went still, but didn't loosen her hold on my arm. "You don't know what you're talking about."

"Why haven't you ever made a move for Azriel, Mor? Why did you invite Helion to your bed? You clearly found no pleasure in it—I saw the way you looked the next day. So before you accuse me of being a liar, I'd suggest you look long and hard at *yourself*—"

"That's enough."

"Is it? Don't like someone pushing you about it? About *your* choices? Well, neither do I."

Mor dropped my arm. "Get out."

"Fine."

I didn't glance back as I left. I wondered if she could hear my thunderous heartbeat with every storming step I took through the muddy camp.

Amren found me within twenty steps, a wrapped bundle in her arms. "Every time you lot leave me at home, *someone* manages to get gutted."

CHAPTER 62

I couldn't bring myself to smile at Amren. I could barely keep my chin high.

She peered behind me, as if she could see the path I'd taken from Mor's tent, smell the fight on me. "Be careful," Amren warned as I fell into step beside her, heading for our tent again, "of how you push her. There are some truths that even Morrigan has not herself faced."

The hot anger was swiftly slipping into something cold and queasy and heavy.

"We all fight from time to time, girl," Amren said. "Both of you should cool your heels. Talk tomorrow."

"Fine."

Amren shot me a sharp look, her hair swinging with the motion, but we'd reached my tent.

Rhys and Azriel were holding Cassian between them as they gently set him into a chair at the paper-strewn desk. The general's face was still grayish, but someone had found a shirt for him—and washed off the blood. From the way Cassian sagged in that seat . . . He must have insisted he come. And from the way Rhys lightly mussed his hair as he strode to the other side of the desk . . . That wound, too, had been patched up.

Rhys lifted a brow as I entered, still stomping a bit. I shook my head. *I'll tell you later.*

A caress of claws down my innermost barrier—a comforting touch.

Amren laid the Book onto the desk with a thud that echoed in the earth beneath our feet.

"The second and penultimate pages," I said, trying not to flinch at the power of the Book slithering through the tent. "The Suriel claimed the key you were looking for is there. To nullify the Cauldron's power."

I assumed Rhys had told Amren what had occurred—and assumed that he'd told someone to fetch Nesta, since she pushed through the heavy flaps a moment later.

"Did you bring them?" Rhys asked Amren as Nesta silently approached the table.

Still coated in mud up to her shins, my sister paused on the other side—away from where Cassian now sat. Looked him over. Her face revealed nothing, yet her hands . . . I could have sworn a faint tremor rippled through her fingers before she balled them into fists and faced Amren. Cassian watched her for a moment longer before turning his head toward Amren as well. How long had Nesta stood atop that hill, watching the battle? Had she seen him fall?

Amren reached into the pocket of her pewter cloak and chucked a black velvet bag onto the desk. It clacked and thunked as it hit the wood. "Bones and stones."

Nesta only angled her head at the sight of the bag.

Your sister came immediately when I explained what we needed, Rhys said. *I think seeing Cassian hurt convinced her not to pick a fight today.*

Or convinced my sister to pick a fight with someone else entirely.

Nesta lifted the bag. "So, I scatter these like some backstreet charlatan and it'll find the Cauldron?"

Amren let out a low laugh. "Something like that."

Arcs of mud lay beneath Nesta's nails. She didn't seem to notice as she untied the small pouch and dumped out its contents. Three stones, four bones. The latter were brown and gleamed with age; the former were white as the moon and smooth as glass, each marked with a thin, reedy letter I did not recognize.

"Three stones for the faces of the Mother," Amren said upon seeing Nesta's raised brows. "Four bones . . . for whatever reason the *charlatans* came up with that I can't be bothered to remember."

Nesta snorted. Rhys echoed the sentiment. My sister said, "So what—I just shake them around in my hands and chuck them? How am I to make sense of any of it?"

"We can figure it out," Cassian said, his voice rough and weary. "But start with holding them in your hands and thinking—about the Cauldron."

"Don't just *think* about it," Amren corrected. "You must cast your mind *toward* it. Find the bond that links you."

Even I paused at that. And Nesta, stones and bones now in hand . . . She made no move to close her eyes. "I—am I to . . . touch it?"

"No," Amren warned. "Just come close. Find it, but do not interact."

Nesta still didn't move. She could not use the bathtub, she'd told me. Because the memories it dragged up—

Cassian said to her, "Nothing can harm you here." He sucked in a breath, groaning softly, and rose to his feet. Azriel tried to stop him, but Cassian brushed him off and strode for my sister's side. He braced a hand on the desk when he at last stopped. "Nothing can harm you," he repeated.

Nesta was still looking at him when she finally shut her eyes. I shifted, and the angle allowed me to see what I hadn't detected before.

Nesta stood before the map, a fist of bones and stones clenched over it. Cassian remained at her side—his other hand on her lower back.

And I marveled at the touch she allowed—marveled at it as much as I did the mud-splattered hand she held out. The concentration that settled over her face.

Her eyes shifted beneath their lids, as if scanning the world. "I don't see anything."

"Go deeper," Amren urged. "Find that tether between you."

She stiffened, but Cassian stepped closer, and she settled again.

A minute went by. Then another.

A muscle twitched on Nesta's brow. Her hand bobbed.

Her breath then came fast and hard, her lips curling back as she panted through her teeth.

"Nesta," Cassian warned.

"Quiet," Amren snapped.

A small noise came out of her—one of terror.

"Where is it, girl," Amren coaxed. "Open your hand. Let us see."

Nesta's fingers only clutched tighter, the whites of her knuckles as stark as the stones held within them.

Too deep—whatever she had done—

I lunged for her. Not physically, but with my mind.

If Elain's mental gates were those of a sleeping garden, Nesta's . . . They belonged to an ancient fortress, sharp and brutal. The sort I imagined they once impaled people upon.

But they were open wide. And inside . . .

Dark.

Dark like I had never known, even with Rhysand.

Nesta.

I took a step into her mind.

The images slammed into me.

One after one after one, I saw them.

The army that stretched into the horizon. The weapons, the hate, the sheer size.

I saw the king standing over a map in a war-tent, flanked by Jurian and several commanders, the Cauldron squatting in the center of the room behind them.

And there was Nesta.

Standing in that tent, watching the king, the Cauldron.

Frozen in place.

With undiluted fear.

"Nesta."

She did not seem to hear me as she stared at them.

I reached for her hand. "You found it. I see—I see where it is."

Nesta's face was bloodless. But she at last dragged her attention to me. "Feyre."

Surprise lit her terror-wide eyes.

"Let's go back," I said.

She nodded, and we turned. But we felt it—we both did.

Not the king or the commanders plotting with him. Not Jurian as he played his deadly game of deception. But the Cauldron. As if some great sleeping beast opened an eye.

The Cauldron seemed to sense us watching. Sense us *there*.

I felt it stir—like it would lunge for Nesta. I grabbed my sister and ran.

"Open your fist," I ordered her as we sprinted for the iron gates to her mind. "Open it *now*."

She only panted, and that monstrous force swelled behind us, a black wave rising up.

"Open it *now*, or it will get in here. Open it *now*, Nesta!"

I heard the words as I threw myself out of her mind—heard them because I'd been shouting in that tent.

With a gasp, Nesta's fingers splayed wide, scattering stones and bones over the map.

Cassian caught her with an arm around the waist as she swayed. He hissed in pain at the movement. "What the *hell*—"

"Look," Amren breathed.

There was no throw that could have done it—save for one blessed by magic.

The stones and bones formed a perfect, tight circle around a spot on the map.

Nesta and I went pale. I had seen the size of that army—we both had. While Hybern had been driving us northward, letting us chase them in these two battles . . .

The king had amassed his host along the western edge of the human territory.

Perhaps no more than a hundred miles from our family's estate.

⁜

Rhys called in Tarquin and Helion to show them what we'd discovered.

Too few. We had too few soldiers, even with three armies here, to take on that host. I'd shown Rhysand what I'd seen—and he'd shown it to the others.

"Kallias will arrive soon," Helion said, dragging his hands through his onyx hair.

"He'd have to bring forty thousand soldiers," Cassian said. "I doubt he has half that."

Rhys was staring and staring at that cluster of stones and bones on the map. I could feel the wrath rippling off him—not just at Hybern, but himself for not thinking Hybern might be deliberately toying with us. Positioning us here.

We'd won the high ground these two battles—Hybern had won the high ground in this war.

He knew what waited in the Middle.

And Hybern had now forced us to gather here—in this spot—so that he and his behemoth army could drive us northward. A clean sweep from the south, eventually pushing us into the Middle or forcing us to break apart to avoid the lethal tangle of trees and denizens.

And if we took the battle to them . . . We might court death.

None of us were foolish enough to risk building any plans around Jurian, regardless of where his true allegiance lay. Our best chance was in buying time for other allies to arrive. Kallias. Thesan.

Tamlin had chosen who to back in this war. And even if he'd picked Prythian, he would have been left with the problem of mustering a Spring Court force after I'd destroyed their faith in him.

And Miryam and Drakon . . . *Not enough time*, Rhys said to me. *To hunt for them—find them, and bring back their army. We could return to find Hybern has wiped our own off the map.*

But there was the Carver—if I dared risk retrieving his prize. I didn't mention it, didn't offer it. Not until I could know for certain—once I wasn't about to faint from exhaustion.

"We'll rest on it," Tarquin said, blowing out a breath. "Meet at dawn tomorrow. Making a decision after a long day never helped anyone."

Helion agreed, and saw himself out. It was hard not to stare, not to compare his features to Lucien's. Their nose was the same—eerily identical. How had no one ever called him out for it?

I supposed it was the least of my worries. Tarquin frowned at the map one last time and declared, "We'll find a way to face this."

Rhys nodded, while Cassian's mouth quirked to the side. He'd slid back into his chair for the discussion, and now nursed a cup of some healing brew Azriel had fetched for him.

Tarquin turned from the table, just as the tent flaps parted for a pair of broad shoulders—

Varian. He didn't so much as look at his High Lord, his focus going right to where Amren sat at the head of the table. As if he'd sensed she was here—or someone had reported. And he'd come running.

Amren's eyes flicked up from the Book as Varian halted. A coy smile curved her red lips.

There was still blood and dirt splattered on Varian's brown skin, coating his silver armor and close-cropped white hair. He didn't seem to notice or care as he strode for Amren.

And none of us dared to speak as Varian dropped to his knees before Amren's chair, took her shocked face in his broad hands, and kissed her soundly.

CHAPTER 63

None of us lasted long after dinner.

Amren and Varian didn't even bother to join us.

No, she'd just wrapped her legs around his waist, right there in front of us, and he'd stood, lifting her in one swift movement. I wasn't entirely sure how Varian managed to walk them out of the tent while still kissing her, Amren's hands dragging through his hair, letting out noises that were unnervingly like purring as they vanished into the camp.

Rhys had let out a low laugh as we all gawked in their wake. "I suppose that's how Varian decided he'd tell Amren he was feeling rather grateful she ordered us to go to Adriata."

Tarquin cringed. "We'll alternate who has to deal with them on holidays."

Cassian chuckled hoarsely, and looked to Nesta, who remained pale and quiet. What she'd seen, what *I'd* seen in her mind . . .

The size of that army . . .

"Eat or bed?" Cassian had asked Nesta, and I honestly couldn't tell if he'd meant it as some invitation. I debated telling him he was in no shape.

Nesta only said, "Bed." And there was certainly *no* invitation in the exhausted reply.

Rhys and I managed to eat, quietly discussing what we'd seen. Exhaustion weighted my every breath, and I'd barely finished my plate of roast mutton before I crawled into bed and passed out atop the blankets. Rhys woke me only to tug off my boots and jacket.

Tomorrow morning. We'd figure out how to deal with everything tomorrow morning. I'd talk to Amren about finally mustering Bryaxis to help us wipe out that army.

Maybe there was something else we weren't seeing. Some additional shot at salvation beyond that nullifying spell.

My dreams were a tangled garden, thorns snagging on me as I stumbled through them.

I dreamed of the Suriel, bleeding out and smiling. I dreamed of the Weaver's open mouth ripping into Ianthe while she still screamed. I dreamed of Lord Graysen—so mortal and young—standing at the edge of the camp, beckoning to Elain. Telling her he'd come for her. To come home with him. That he'd found a way to undo what had been done to her—to make her human again.

I dreamed of that Cauldron in the King of Hybern's war-tent, so dark and slumbering . . . Awakening as Nesta and I stood there, invisible and unseen.

How it had watched back. *Known* us.

I could feel it watching me, even then. In my dreams. Feel it extend an ancient, black tendril toward me—

I jolted awake.

Rhys's naked body was wrapped around mine, his face softened with sleep. In the blackness of the tent, I listened.

Crackling fires outside. The drowsy murmurs of the soldiers on watch. The wind sighing along the canvas tents, snapping at the banners crowning them.

I scanned the dark, listening.

The skin on my arms pebbled.

"Rhys."

He was instantly awake—sitting upright. "What is it?"

"Something . . ." I listened so hard my ears strained. "Something is here. Something is wrong."

He moved, hauling on his pants and knife-belt. I followed suit, still trying to listen, fingers stumbling over the buckles. "I dreamed," I whispered. "I dreamed about the Cauldron . . . that it was *watching* again."

"*Shit.*" The word was a hiss of breath.

"I think we opened a door," I breathed, shoving my feet into my boots. "I think . . . I think . . ." I couldn't finish the sentence as I hurried for the tent flaps, Rhys at my heels. Nesta. I had to find Nesta—

Gold-brown hair flashed in the firelight, and she was already there, hurrying for me, still in her nightgown. "You hear it, too," she panted.

Hear—I couldn't hear, but just *feel*—

Amren's small figure darted around a tent, wearing what looked to be Varian's shirt. It came down to her knees, and its owner was indeed behind her, bare-chested as Rhys was, and wide-eyed.

Amren's bare feet were splattered in mud and grass. "It came here—its power. I can feel it—slithering around. *Looking.*"

"The Cauldron," Varian said, brows narrowing. "But—it's *aware*?"

"We pried too deep," Amren said. "Battle aside, it knows where we are as much as we now know its location."

Nesta raised a hand. "*Listen.*"

And I heard it then.

It was a song and invitation, a cluster of notes sung by a voice that was male and female, young and old, haunting and alluring and—

"I can't hear anything," Rhys said.

"You were not Made," Amren snapped. But we were. The three of us . . .

Again, the Cauldron sang its siren song.

My very bones recoiled. "What does it *want*?"

I felt it pulling away—felt it sliding off into the night.

Azriel stepped out of a shadow. "What *is* that," he hissed.

My brows rose. "You hear it?"

A shake of the head. "No—but the shadows, the wind . . . They recoil."

The Cauldron sang again.

Distant—withdrawing.

"I think it's leaving," I whispered.

Cassian stumbled and staggered for us a moment later, a hand braced on his chest, Mor on his heels. She did not so much as look at me, nor I her, as Rhys told them. Standing together in the dead of night—

The Cauldron sang one final note—then went silent.

The presence, the weight . . . vanished.

Amren loosed a sigh. "Hybern knows where we are by now. The Cauldron likely wanted to have a look for itself. After we taunted it."

I rubbed at my face. "Let's pray that's the last we see of it."

Varian angled his head. "So you three . . . because you were *Made*, you can hear it? Sense it?"

"It would appear so," Amren said, looking inclined to tug him back to wherever they'd been, to finish what they'd no doubt still been in the middle of doing.

But Azriel asked softly, "What about Elain?"

Something cold went through me. Nesta was just staring at Azriel. Staring and staring—

Then she broke into a run.

Her bare feet slid through the mud, splattering me as we charged for our sister's tent.

"Elain—" Nesta shoved open the tent.

She stopped short so fast I slammed into her. The tent—the tent was empty.

Nesta flung herself inside, tossing away blankets, as if Elain had somehow sunk into the ground. *"Elain!"*

I whirled into the camp, scanning the tents nearby. One look at Rhys conveyed what we'd found inside. An Illyrian blade appeared in his hand just before he winnowed.

Azriel stalked to my side, right into the tent where Nesta had now come to her feet. He tucked his wings in tightly as he squeezed through the narrow space, ignoring Nesta's snarl of warning, and knelt at the cot.

He ran a scarred hand over the rumpled blankets. "They're still warm."

Outside, Cassian was barking orders, the camp rousing.

"The Cauldron," I breathed. "The Cauldron was fading away—going somewhere—"

Nesta was already moving, sprinting for where we'd heard that voice. *Luring* Elain out.

I knew how it had done it.

I'd dreamed of it.

Graysen standing on the edge of camp, calling to her, promising her love and healing.

We reached the copse of trees at the edge of the camp, just as Rhys appeared out of the night, his blade now sheathed across his back. There was something in his hands. No emotion on his carefully neutral face.

Nesta let out a sound that might have been a sob as I realized what he'd found at the edge of the forest. What the Cauldron had left behind in its haste to return to Hybern's war-camp. Or as a mocking gift.

Elain's dark blue cloak, still warm from her body.

CHAPTER 64

Nesta sat with her head in her hands inside my tent. She did not speak, did not move. Coiled in on herself, clinging to stay whole—that's how she looked. How I felt.

Elain—taken to Hybern's army.

Nesta had stolen something vital from the Cauldron. And in those moments Nesta had hunted it down for us . . . The Cauldron had learned what was vital to *her*.

So the Cauldron had stolen something in return.

"We'll get her back," Cassian rasped from where he perched on the rolled arm of the chaise longue across the small sitting area, watching her carefully. Rhys, Amren, and Mor were meeting with the other High Lords, informing them what had been done. Seeing if they knew anything. Had any way of helping.

Nesta lowered her hands, lifting her head. Her eyes were red-rimmed, lips thin. "No, you will not." She pointed to the map on the table. "I saw that army. Its size, who is in it. I *saw* it, and there is no chance of *any* of you getting into its heart. Even you," she added when Cassian opened his mouth again. "*Especially* not when you're injured."

And what Hybern would do to Elain, might already be doing—

From the shadows near the entrance to the tent, Azriel said, as if in answer to some unspoken debate, "I'm getting her back."

Nesta slid her gaze to the shadowsinger. Azriel's hazel eyes glowed golden in the shadows.

Nesta said, "Then you will die."

Azriel only repeated, rage glazing that stare, "I'm getting her back."

With the shadows, he might stand a chance of slipping in. But there were wards to consider, and ancient magic, and the king with those spells and the Cauldron . . .

For a moment, I saw that set of paints Elain had once bought me with the extra money she'd saved. The red, yellow, and blue I'd savored, used to paint that dresser in our cottage. I had not painted in years at that point, had not dared spend the money on myself . . . But Elain had.

I stood. Met Azriel's wrathful stare.

"I'm going with you," I said.

Azriel only nodded.

"You'll never get far enough into the camp," Cassian warned.

"I'm going to walk right in."

And as they narrowed their brows, I shifted myself. Not a glamour, but a true changing of features.

"Shit," Cassian breathed when I was done.

Nesta rose to her feet. "They might already know she's dead."

For it was Ianthe's face, her hair, that I now possessed. It nearly drained what was left of my depleted magic. Anything more . . . I might not have enough left to keep her features in place. But there were other ways. Routes. For the rest of what I needed.

"I need one of your Siphons," I said to Azriel. The blue was slightly deeper, but at night . . . they might not notice the difference.

He held out his palm, a round, flat blue stone appearing in it, and chucked it to me. I wrapped my fingers around the warm stone, its power throbbing in my veins like an unearthly heartbeat as I looked to Cassian. "Where is the blacksmith."

✣

The camp blacksmith did not ask any questions when I handed over the silver candlesticks from my tent and Azriel's Siphon. When I asked him to craft that circlet. Immediately.

A mortal blacksmith might have taken a while—days. But a Fae one . . .

By the time he finished, Azriel had gone to the camp priestess and retrieved a spare set of her robes. Perhaps not identical to Ianthe's, but close enough. As High Priestess, none would dare look too closely at her. Ask questions.

I had just set the circlet atop my hood when Rhys prowled into our tent. Azriel was honing Truth-Teller with relentless focus, Cassian sharpening the weapons I was to fasten beneath the robe—atop the Illyrian leathers.

"He'll sense your power," I said to Rhys before he could speak.

"I know," Rhys said hoarsely. And I realized—realized the other High Lords had come up empty.

My hands began shaking. I knew the odds. Knew what I'd face in there. I'd seen it in Nesta's mind hours ago.

Rhys closed the distance between us, clutching my hands. Gazing at *me*, and not Ianthe's face, as if he could see the soul beneath. "There are wards around the camp. You can't winnow. You have to walk in—and out. Then you can make the jump back here."

I nodded.

He brushed a kiss to my brow. "Ianthe sold out your sisters," he said, his voice turning sharp and hard. "It's only fitting that you use her to get Elain back."

He gripped the sides of my face, bringing us nose to nose.

"Do not get distracted. Do not linger. You are a warrior, and warriors know when to pick their fights."

I nodded, our breath mingling.

Rhys growled. "They took what is ours. And we do not allow those crimes to go unpunished."

His power rippled and swirled around me.

"You do not fear," Rhys breathed. "You do not falter. You do not yield. You go in, you get her, and you come out again."

I nodded again, holding his stare.

"Remember that you are a wolf. And you cannot be caged."

He kissed my brow one more time, my blood thrumming and boiling in me, howling to draw blood.

I began to buckle on the weapons Cassian had lined up in neat rows on the table, Rhys helping me with the straps and loops, positioning them so that they wouldn't be visible beneath my robe. The only one I couldn't fit was the Illyrian blade—no way to hide it and be able to easily draw it. Cassian gave me an extra dagger to make up for its absence.

"You get them in and out again, shadowsinger," Rhys said to Azriel as I walked to the spymaster's side, getting a feel for the weight of the weapons and the flow of the heavy robe. "I don't care how many of them you have to kill to do it. They both come out."

Azriel gave a grave, steady nod. "I swear it, High Lord."

Formal words, formal titles.

I gripped Azriel's scarred hand, the weight of his Siphon pressing on my brow through the hood. We looked to Rhys, to Cassian and Nesta, to Mor—right as she appeared, breathless, between the tent flaps. Her eyes went to me, then the shadowsinger, and flared with shock and fear—

But we were gone.

Azriel's dark breeze was different from Rhys's. Colder. Sharper. It cut through the world like a blade, spearing us toward that army camp.

Night was still overhead, dawn perhaps two hours away, when he landed us in a thick forest on a hilltop that overlooked the outskirts of the mighty camp.

The king had used the same spells that Rhys had put around Velaris and our own forces. Spells to hide it from sight, and dispel people who got too close.

We'd landed inside of them, thanks to Nesta's specifics. With a perfect view of the city of soldiers that sprawled away into the night.

Campfires burned, as numerous as the stars. Beasts snapped and snarled, yanking on leashes and chains. On and on and on that army went, a squatting terror drinking the life from the earth.

Azriel silently faded into blackness—until he was my own shadow and nothing more.

I fluffed out the priestess's pale robe, adjusted the circlet atop my head, and began to pick my way down the hill.

Into the heart of Hybern's army.

CHAPTER 65

The first test would be the most dangerous—and informative.

Passing through the guards stationed at the edge of the camp—and learning if they'd heard of Ianthe's demise. Learning what sort of power Ianthe truly wielded here.

I kept my features in that beatific, pretty mask she'd always plastered on her face, head held just so, my mating ring turned facedown and put onto my other hand, a few silver bracelets Azriel had borrowed from the camp priestess dangling at my wrists. I let them jangle loudly, as she had, like a cat with a bell on its collar.

A pet—I supposed Ianthe was no more than a pet of the king.

I couldn't see Azriel, but I could feel him, as if the Siphon parading itself as Ianthe's jewel was a tether. He dwelled in every pocket of shadow, darting ahead and behind.

The six guards flanking the camp entrance monitored Ianthe, strutting out of the dark, with unmasked distaste. I steadied my heart, *became* her, preening and coy, vain and predatory, holy and sensual.

They did not stop me as I walked past them and onto the long avenue that cut through the endless camp. Did not look confused or expectant.

I didn't dare let my shoulders slump, or even heave a sigh of utter relief. Not as I headed down the broad artery lined by tents and forges, fires and—and things I did not look at, did not even turn toward as the sounds coming out of them charged at me.

This place made the Court of Nightmares seem like a human sitting room filled with chaste maidens embroidering pillows.

And somewhere in this hell-pit . . . Elain. Had the Cauldron presented her to the king? Or was she in some in-between, trapped in whatever dark world the Cauldron occupied?

I'd seen the king's tent in Nesta's scrying. It had not seemed as far away as it did now, rising like a gargantuan, spiny beast from the center of the camp. Entrance to it would present another set of obstacles.

If we made it that far without being noticed.

The time of night worked to our advantage. The soldiers who were awake were either engaged in activities of varying awfulness, or were on guard and wishing they could be. The rest were asleep.

It was strange, I realized with each bouncing step and jangle of jewelry toward the heart of camp, to consider that Hybern actually needed rest.

I'd somehow assumed they were beyond it—mythic, unending in their strength and rage.

But they, too, tired. And ate. And slept.

Perhaps not as easily or as much as humans, but, with two hours until dawn, we were lucky. Once the sun chased away the shadows, though . . . Once it made some gaps in my costume all too clear . . .

It was hard to scan the tents we passed, hard to focus on the sounds of the camp while pretending to be someone wholly used to it. I didn't even know if Ianthe *had* a tent here—if she was allowed near the king whenever she wished.

I doubted it—doubted we'd be able to stroll right into his personal tent and find wherever the hell Elain was.

A massive bonfire smoldered and crackled near the center of camp, the sounds of revelry reaching us long before we got a good visual.

I knew within a few heartbeats that most of the soldiers were *not* sleeping.

They were here.

Celebrating.

Some danced in wicked circles around the fire, their contorted shapes little more than twisted shadows flinging through the night. Some drank from enormous oak barrels of beer I recognized—right from Tamlin's stores. Some writhed with each other—some merely watched.

But through the laughter and singing and music, over the roar of the fire . . . Screaming.

A shadow gripped my shoulder, reminding me not to run.

Ianthe would not run—would not show alarm.

My mouth went dry as that scream sounded again.

I couldn't bear it—to let it go on, to see what was being done—

Azriel's shadow-hand grasped my own, tugging me closer. His rage rippled off his invisible form.

We made a lazy circuit of the revelry, other parts of it becoming clear. The screaming—

It was not Elain.

It was not Elain who hung from a rack near a makeshift dais of granite.

It was one of the Children of the Blessed, young and slender—

My stomach twisted, threatening to surge up my throat. Two others were chained up beside her. From the way they sagged, the injuries on their naked bodies—

Clare. It was like Clare, what had been done to them. And like Clare, they had been left there to rot, left for the crows surely to arrive at dawn.

This one had held out for longer.

I couldn't. I couldn't—couldn't *leave* her there—

But if I lingered too long, they'd see. And drawing attention to myself . . .

Could I live with it? I'd once killed two innocents to save Tamlin and his people. I'd be as good as killing her if I left her there in favor of saving my sister . . .

Stranger. She was a *stranger*—

"He's been looking for you," drawled a hard male voice.

I pivoted to find Jurian striding from between two tents, buckling his sword-belt. I glanced at the dais. And as if an invisible hand wiped away the smoke . . .

There sat the King of Hybern. He lounged in his chair, head propped on a fist, face a mask of vague amusement as he surveyed the revelry, the torture and torment. The adulation of the crowd that occasionally turned to toast or bow to him.

I willed my voice to soften, adapted that lilt. "I have been busy with my sisters."

Jurian stared at me for a long moment, eyes sliding to the Siphon atop my head.

I knew the moment he realized who I was. Those brown eyes flared—barely.

"Where is she," was all I breathed.

Jurian gave a cocky grin. Not directed at me, but anyone watching us. "You've been lusting after me for weeks now," he purred. "Act like it."

My throat constricted. But I laid a hand on his forearm, batting my eyelashes at him as I stepped closer.

A bemused snort. "I have trouble believing that's how you won his heart."

I tried not to scowl. "*Where* is she."

"Safe. Untouched."

My chest caved in at the word.

"Not for long," Jurian said. "It gave him a shock when she appeared before the Cauldron. He had her contained. Came here to brood over what to do with her. And how to make you pay for it."

I ran a hand up his arm, then rested it over his heart. "Where. Is. She."

Jurian leaned in as if he'd kiss me, and brought his mouth to my ear. "Were you smart enough to kill her before you took her skin?"

My hands tightened on his jacket. "She got what she deserved."

I could feel Jurian's smile against my ear. "She's in his tent. Chained with steel and a little spell from his favorite book."

Shit. *Shit.* Perhaps I should have gotten Helion, who could break almost any—

Jurian caught my chin between his thumb and forefinger. "Come to my tent with me, Ianthe. Let me see what that pretty mouth can do."

It was an effort not to recoil, but I let Jurian put a hand on my lower back. He chuckled. "Seems like you've already got some steel in you. No need for mine."

I gave him a pretty, sunshine smile. "What of the girl on the rack?"

Darkness flickered in those eyes. "There have been many before her, and many will come after."

"I can't leave her here," I said through my teeth.

Jurian led me into the labyrinth of tents, heading for that inner circle. "Your sister or her—you won't be able to take two out."

"Get her to me, and I'll make it happen."

Jurian muttered, "Say you would like to pray before the Cauldron before we retire."

I blinked, and realized there were guards—guards and that giant, bone-colored tent ahead of us. I clasped my hands before me and said to Jurian, "Before we . . . retire, I should like to pray before the great Cauldron. To give thanks for today's bounty."

Jurian glowered—a man ready for rutting who had been delayed. "Make it quick," he said, jerking his chin to the guards on either side of the tent flaps. I caught the look he gave them—male to male. They didn't bother to hide their leering as I passed.

And since I was *Ianthe* . . . I gave them each a sultry smile, sizing them up for conquest of a different kind than the one they'd come to Prythian to do.

The one on the right's answering grin told me he was mine for the taking.

Later, I willed my eyes to say. *When I'm done with the human.*

He adjusted his belt a bit as I slipped into the tent.

Dim—cold. Like the sky before dawn, that's how the tent felt.

No crackling braziers, no faelights. And in the center of the massive tent . . . a darkness that devoured the light. The Cauldron.

The hair on my arms rose.

Jurian whispered in my ear, "You have five minutes to get her out. Take her to the western edge—there's a cliff overlooking the river. I'll meet you there."

I blinked at him.

Jurian's grin was a slash of white in the gloom. "If you hear screaming, don't panic." His diversion. He smirked toward the shadows. "I hope you can carry three, shadowsinger."

Azriel did not confirm that he was there, that he'd heard.

Jurian studied me for a heartbeat longer. "Save a dagger for your own heart. If they catch you alive, the king will—" He shook his head. "Don't let them catch you alive."

Then he was gone.

Azriel emerged from the deep shadows in the corner of the tent a heartbeat later. He jerked his chin toward the curtains in the back. I began intoning one of Ianthe's many prayers, a pretty speech I'd heard her say a thousand times at the Spring Court.

We rushed across the rugs, dodging tables and furniture. I chanted her prayers all the while.

Azriel slid back the curtain—

Elain was in her nightgown. Gagged, wrists wrapped in steel that glowed violet. Her eyes went wide as she saw us—Azriel and *me*—

I shifted my face back into my own, raising a hand to my lips as Azriel knelt before her. I kept up my litany of praying, beseeching the Cauldron to make my womb fruitful, on and on—

Azriel gently removed the gag from her mouth. "Are you hurt?"

She shook her head, devouring the sight of him as if not quite believing it. "You came for me." The shadowsinger only inclined his head.

"Hurry," I whispered, then resumed my prayer. We had until it ran out.

Azriel's Siphons flared, the one atop my head warming.

The magic did nothing when it came into contact with those bonds. Nothing.

Only a few more verses of my prayer left to chant.

Her wrists and ankles were bound. She couldn't run out of here with them on.

I reached a hand toward her, scrambling for a thread of Helion's power to unravel the king's spell on the chains. But my magic was still depleted, in shambles—

"We don't have time," Azriel murmured. "He's coming."

The screaming and shouting began.

Azriel scooped up Elain, looping her bound arms around his neck. "Hold tight," he ordered her, "and don't make a sound."

Barking and baying rent the night. I drew off the robe, and pocketed Azriel's Siphon before palming two knives. "Out the back?"

A nod. "Get ready to run."

My heart thundered. Elain glanced between us, but did not tremble. Did not cringe.

"Run, and don't stop," he told me. "We sprint for the western edge—the cliff."

"If Jurian's not there with the girl in time—"

"Then you will go. I'll get her."

I blew out a breath, steadying myself.

The barking and growling grew louder—closer.

"Now," Azriel hissed, and we ran.

His Siphons blazed, and the canvas of the back of the tent melted into nothing. We bolted through it before the guards nearby noticed.

They didn't react to us. Only peered at the hole.

Azriel had made us invisible—shadow-bound.

We sprinted between tents, feet flying over the grass and dirt. "Hurry," he whispered. "The shadows won't last long."

For in the east, behind us . . . the sun was beginning to rise.

A piercing howl split the dying night. And I knew they'd realized what we'd done. That we were *here*. And even if they couldn't see us . . . the King of Hybern's hounds could scent us.

"*Faster*," Azriel snarled.

The earth shuddered behind us. I didn't dare look behind.

We neared a rack of weapons. I sheathed my knives, freeing my hands as we hurtled past and I snatched a bow and quiver of arrows from their stand. *Ash* arrows.

The arrows clacked as I slung the quiver over a shoulder. As I nocked an arrow into place.

Azriel cut right, swerving around a tent.

And with the angle . . . I turned and fired.

The nearest hound—it was not a hound, I realized as the arrow spiraled for its head.

But some cousin of the naga—some monstrous, scaled thing that thundered on all fours, serpentine face snarling and full of bone-shredding white teeth—

My arrow went right through its throat.

It went down, and we rounded the tent, hurtling for that still-dim western horizon.

I nocked another arrow.

Three others. Three more behind us, gaining with every clawed step—

I could feel them around us—Hybern commanders, racing along

with the hounds, tracking the beasts because they still could not see us. That arrow I'd fired had told them enough about the distance. But the moment the hounds caught up . . . those commanders would appear. Kill us or drag us away.

Row after row of tents, slowly awakening at the ruckus in the center of the camp.

The air rippled, and I looked up to see the rain of ash arrows unleashed from behind, so many they were a blind attempt to hit *any* target—

Azriel's blue shield shuddered at the impact, but held. Yet our shadows shivered and faded.

The hounds closed in, two breaking away—to cut to the side. To herd us.

For that was a *cliff* at the other edge of the camp. A cliff with a very, *very* long drop, and unforgiving river below.

And standing at its end, huddled in a dark cloak . . .

That was the girl.

Jurian had left her there—for us. Where he'd gone . . . I saw no sign of him.

But behind us, filling the air as if he'd used magic to do so . . . The king spoke.

"What intrepid thieves," he drawled, the words everywhere and nowhere. "How shall I punish you?"

I had no doubt the wards ended just beyond the cliff's edge. It was confirmed by the snarls of the hounds, who seemed to know that their prey would escape in less than a hundred yards. If we could jump far enough to be clear of them.

"*Get her out, Azriel,*" I begged him, panting. "I'll get the other."

"We're *all*—"

"*That's an order.*"

A clean shot, an unimpeded path right to that cliff's edge, and to freedom beyond—

"You need to—" My words were cut off.

I felt the impact before the pain. The searing, *burning* pain that erupted through my shoulder. An ash arrow—

My feet snagged beneath me, blood spraying, and I hit the rocky ground so hard my bones groaned. Azriel swore, but with Elain in his arms, fighting—

The hounds were there in a second.

I fired an arrow at one, my shoulder screaming with the movement. The hound fell, clearing the view behind.

Revealing the king striding down the line of tents, unhurried and assured of our capture, a bow dangling from his hand. The bow that had delivered the arrow now piercing through my body.

"Torturing you would be so dull," the king mused, voice still magnified. "At least, the traditional sort of torture." Every step was slow, intentional. "How Rhysand shall rage. How he shall panic. His mate, at last come to see me."

Before I could warn Azriel to hurry, the other two hounds were on me.

One leaped right for me. I lifted my bow to intercept its jaws.

The hound snapped it in two, hurling the wood away. I grabbed for a knife, just as the second one leaped—

A roar deafened me, made my head ring. Just as one of the hounds was thrown off me.

I knew that roar, knew—

A golden-furred beast with curling horns tore into the hounds.

"Tamlin," I got out, but his green eyes narrowed. *Run*, he seemed to say.

That was who had been running alongside us. Trying to find us.

He ripped and shredded, the hounds launching themselves wholly on him. The king paused, and though he remained far off, I could clearly make out the surprise slackening his face.

Now. I had to go *now*—

I scrambled to my feet, whipping the arrow out with a swallowed scream. Azriel was already there, no more than a few heartbeats having passed—

Azriel gripped me by the collar, and a web of blue light fastened itself at my shoulder. Holding the blood in, a bandage until a healer—

"You need to fly," he panted.

Six more hounds closed in. Tamlin still fought the others, gaining ground—holding the line.

"We need to get airborne," Azriel said, one eye now on the king as he resumed his mockingly slow approach. "Can you make it?"

The young woman was still standing at the edge of the cliff. Watching us with wide eyes, black hair whipping over her face.

I'd never made a running takeoff before. I'd barely been able to keep in the skies.

Even if Azriel took the girl in his free arm . . .

I didn't let myself consider the alternative. I *would* get airborne. Only long enough to sail over that cliff, and winnow out when we'd passed the wards' edge.

Tamlin let out a yelp of what sounded like pain, followed by another earth-shuddering roar. The rest of the hounds had reached him. He did not falter, did not yield an inch to them—

I summoned the wings. The drag and weight of them . . . Even with the Siphon-bandage, pain razed my senses at the tug on my muscles.

I panted through my gritted teeth as Azriel plunged ahead, wings beginning to flap. Not enough space on the jutting ledge for us to do this side by side. I gobbled down details of his takeoff, the beating of his wings, the shifting angle of his body.

"Grab onto him!" Elain ordered the wide-eyed human girl as Azriel thundered toward her. The girl looked like a doe about to be run down by a wolf.

The girl did not open her arms as they neared.

Elain screamed at her, *"If you want to live, do it now!"*

The girl dropped her cloak, opened her arms wide.

Her black hair streamed behind Azriel, catching amongst his wings as he practically tackled her into the sky. But I saw, even as I ran, Elain's pale hands lurch—gripping the girl by her neck, holding her as tightly as she could.

And just in time.

One of the hounds broke free from Tamlin in a mighty leap. I ducked, bracing for impact.

But it was not aiming for me. Two bounding strides down the stone ledge and another leap—

Azriel's roar echoed off the rocks as the hound slammed into him, dragging those shredding talons down his spine, his wings—

The girl screamed, but Elain moved. As Azriel battled to keep them airborne, keep his grip on them, my sister sent a fierce kick into the beast's face. Its eye. Another. Another.

It bellowed, and Elain slammed her bare, muddy foot into its face again. The blow struck home.

With a yelp of pain, it released its claws—and plunged into the ravine.

So fast. It happened so fast. And blood—blood sprayed from his back, his wings—

But Azriel remained in the air. Blue light splayed over the wounds. Staunching the blood, stabilizing his wings. I was still running for the cliff as he whirled, revealing a pain-bleached face, while he gripped the two women tightly.

But he beheld what charged after me. The sprint ahead. And for the first time since I had known him, there was terror in Azriel's eyes as he watched me make that run.

I flapped my wings, an updraft hauling my feet up, then crashing them down onto the rock. I stumbled, but kept running, kept flapping, back screaming—

Another one of the hounds broke past Tamlin's guard. Came barreling down that narrow stretch of rock, claws gouging the stone beneath. I could have sworn the king laughed from behind.

"Faster!" Azriel roared, blood oozing with each wing beat. I could see the dawn through the shreds in the membrane. *"Push up!"*

The stone echoed with the thunderous steps of the hound at my heels.

The end of the rock loomed. Freefall lay beyond. And I knew the hound would leap with me. The king would have it retrieve me by any means necessary, even if my body was broken on the river far, far below. This high, I would splatter like an egg dropped from a tower.

And he'd keep whatever was left of me, as Jurian had been kept, alive and aware.

"Hold them high!"

I stretched my wings as far as they would go. Thirty steps between me and the edge.

"Legs up!"

Twenty steps. The sun broke over the eastern horizon, gilding Azriel's bloody armor with gold.

The king fired another arrow—two. One for me, one soaring for Elain's exposed back. Azriel slammed both away with a blue shield. I didn't look to see if that shield extended to Tamlin.

Ten steps. I beat my wings, muscles screaming, blood sliding past even that Siphon's bandage. Beat them as I sent a wave of wind rising up beneath me, air filling the flexible membrane, even as the bone and sinews strained to snapping.

My feet lifted from the ground. Then hit again. I pushed with the wind, flapping like hell. The hound gained on me.

Five steps. I knew—I knew that whatever force had compelled me to learn to fly . . . Somehow, it had known. That this moment was coming. All of it—all of it, for this moment.

And with barely three steps to the edge of that cliff . . . A warm wind, kissed with lilac and new grass, blasted up from beneath me. A wind of—spring. Lifting me, filling my wings.

My feet rose. And rose. And rose.

The hound leaped after me.

"Bank!"

I threw my body sideways, wings swinging me wide. The rising dawn and drop and sky tilted and spun before I evened out.

I looked behind to see that naga-hound snap at where my heels had been. And then plunge down, down, down into the ravine and river below.

The king fired again, the arrow tipped with glimmering amethyst power. Azriel's shield held—barely. Whatever magic the king had wrapped around it—Azriel grunted in pain.

But he snarled, "*Fly*," and I veered toward the way I'd come, back trembling with the effort to keep my body upright. Azriel turned, the girl moaning in terror as he lost a few feet to the sky—before he leveled out and soared beside me.

The king barked a command, and a barrage of arrows arced up from the camp—rained down upon us.

Azriel's shield buckled, but held solid. I flapped my wings, back shrieking.

I pressed a hand to my wound, just as the wards pushed against me. Pushed as if they tried and tried to contain me, to hold Azriel where he now flapped like hell against them, blood spraying from those wounded wings, sliding down his shredded back—

I unleashed a flare of Helion's white light. Burning, singeing, melting.

A hole ripped through the wards. Barely wide enough.

We didn't hesitate as we sailed through, as I gasped for breath. But I looked back. Just once.

Tamlin was surrounded by the hounds. Bleeding, panting, still in that beast form.

The king was perhaps thirty feet away, livid—utterly livid as he beheld the hole I'd again ripped through his wards. Tamlin made the most of his distraction.

He did not glance toward us as he made a break for the cliff edge.

He leaped far—far and wide. Farther than any beast or Fae should be able to. That wind he'd sent my way now bolstering him, guiding him toward that hole we'd swept through.

Tamlin cleared it and winnowed away, still not looking at me as I gripped Azriel's hand and we vanished as well.

⁜

Azriel's power gave out on the outskirts of our camp.

The girl, despite the burns and lashings on her moon-white skin, was able to walk.

The gray light of morning had broken over the world, mist clinging to our ankles as we headed into that camp, Azriel still cradling Elain to his chest. He dripped blood behind him the entire time—a trickle compared to the torrent that should be leaking out. Contained only by the patches of power he'd slapped on it. Help—he needed a healer immediately.

We both did. I pressed a hand against the wound in my shoulder to keep the bleeding minimal. The girl went so far as to even offer to use her lingering scraps of clothing to bind it.

I didn't have the breath to explain that I was Fae, and there had been ash in my skin. I needed to see a healer before it set and sealed in any splinters. So I just asked for her name.

Briar, she said, her voice raw from screaming. Her name was Briar.

She did not seem to mind the mud that squelched under her feet and splattered her bare shins. She only gazed at the tents, the soldiers who stumbled out. One saw Azriel and shouted for a healer to hurry for the spymaster's tent.

Rhys winnowed into our path before we'd made it past the first line of tents. His eyes went right to Azriel's wings, then the wound in my shoulder, the paleness of my face. To Elain, then Briar.

"I couldn't leave her," I said, surprised to find my own voice raw.

Running steps approached, and then Nesta rounded a tent, skidding to a halt in the mud.

She let out a sob at the sight of Elain, still in Azriel's arms. I'd never heard a sound like that from her. Not once.

She isn't hurt, I said to her, into that chamber in her mind. Because words . . . I couldn't form them.

Nesta broke into another sprint. I reached for Rhysand, his face taut as he stalked for us—

But Nesta got there first.

I swallowed my shout of pain as Nesta's arms went around my neck and she embraced me so hard it snatched my breath away.

Her body shook—shook as she sobbed and said over and over and over, "Thank you."

Rhys lunged for Azriel, taking Elain from him and gently setting my sister down. Azriel rasped, swaying on his feet, "We need Helion to get these chains off her."

Yet Elain didn't seem to notice them as she rose up on her toes and kissed the shadowsinger's cheek. And then walked to me and Nesta, who pulled back long enough to survey Elain's clean face, her clear eyes.

"We need to get you to Thesan," Rhys said to Azriel. "Right now."

Before I could turn back, Elain threw her arms around me. I did not remember when I began to cry as I felt those slender arms hold me, tight as steel.

I did not remember the healer who patched me up, or how Rhys bathed me. How I told him what happened with Jurian, and Tamlin, Nesta hovering around Elain as Helion came to remove her chains, cursing the king's handiwork, even as he admired its quality.

But I did remember lying down on the bearskin rug once it was done. How I felt Elain's slim body settle next to mine and curl into my side, careful not to touch the bandaged wound in my shoulder. I had not realized how cold I was until her warmth seeped into me.

A moment later, another warm body nestled on my left. Nesta's scent drifted over me, fire and steel and unbending will.

Distantly, I heard Rhys usher everyone out—to join him in checking on Azriel, now under Thesan's care.

I didn't know how long my sisters and I lay there together, just like we had once shared that carved bed in that dilapidated cottage. Then—back then, we had kicked and twisted and fought for any bit of space, any breathing room.

But that morning, as the sun rose over the world, we held tight. And did not let go.

CHAPTER 66

Kallias and his army arrived by noon.

It was only the sound of it that woke me from where my sisters and I dozed on the floor. That, and a thought that clanged through me.

Tamlin.

His actions would cover Jurian's betrayal. I had no doubt Tamlin hadn't gone back to Hybern's army after the meeting to betray us—but to play spy.

Though after last night . . . it was unlikely he'd get close to Hybern again. Not when the king himself had witnessed everything.

I didn't know what to make of it.

That he'd saved me—that he'd given up his deception to do so. Where had he gone to when he'd winnowed? We hadn't heard anything about the Spring Court forces.

And that wind he'd sent . . . I'd never seen him use such a power.

The Nephelle Philosophy indeed. The weakness that had transformed into a strength hadn't been my wings, my flying. But Tamlin. If he hadn't interfered . . . I didn't let myself consider.

Elain and Nesta were still dozing on the bearskin rug when I eased out from their tangle of limbs. Washed my face in the copper basin set near my bed. A glimpse in the mirror above it revealed I'd seen better days. Weeks. Months.

I peeled back the neck of my white shirt to frown at the wound bandaged at my shoulder. I winced, rotating the joint—marveling at how much it had already healed. My back, however . . .

Aching pain jolted and rippled all along it. In my abdomen, too. Muscles I'd pushed to the breaking point to get airborne. Frowning at the mirror, I braided my hair and shrugged on my jacket, hissing at the movement in my shoulder. Another day or two, and the pain might be minimal enough to wield a sword. Maybe.

I prayed Azriel would be in better shape. If Thesan himself had been healing him, perhaps he was. If we were lucky.

I didn't know how Azriel had managed to stay aloft—stay conscious during those minutes in the sky. I didn't let myself think about how and when and why he'd learned to manage pain like that.

I quietly asked the nearest camp-mother to dig up some platters of food for my sisters. Elain was likely starving, and I doubted Nesta had eaten anything during the hours we'd been gone.

The winged matron only asked if *I* needed anything, and when I told her I was fine, she just clicked her tongue and said she'd make sure food found its way to me, too.

I didn't have the nerve to request she find some of Amren's preferred food as well. Even if I had no doubt Amren would need it—after her . . . activities with Varian last night. Unless he'd—

I didn't let myself think about that as I aimed for her tent. We'd found Hybern's army. And having seen it last night . . . I'd offer Amren any help I could in decoding that spell the Suriel had pointed her toward. Anything, if it meant stopping the Cauldron. And when we'd picked our final battlefield . . . then, only then, would I unleash Bryaxis upon Hybern.

I was nearly to her tent, offering grim smiles in exchange for the nods and wary glances the Illyrian warriors gave me, when I spied the commotion just near the edge of camp. A few extra steps had me staring out across a thin demarcation line of grass and mud—to the Winter Court camp now nearly constructed in its full splendor.

Kallias's army was still winnowing in supplies and units of warriors, his court made up of High Fae with either his snow-white hair or hair of blackest night, skin ranging from moon pale to rich brown. The lesser fae . . . he'd brought more lesser faeries than any of us, if you excluded the Illyrians. It was an effort not to gawk as I lingered at the edge of where their camp began.

Long-limbed creatures like shards of ice given form stalked past, tall enough to plant the cobalt-and-silver banners atop various tents; wagons were hauled by sure-footed reindeer and lumbering white bears in ornate armor, some so keenly aware when they ambled by that I wouldn't have been surprised if they could talk. White foxes scuttled about underfoot, bearing what looked to be messages strapped to their little embroidered vests.

Our Illyrian army was brutal, basic—few frills and sheer rank reigned. Kallias's army—or, I suppose, the army that Viviane had held together during Amarantha's reign—was a complex, beautiful, teeming thing. Orderly, and yet thrumming with life. Everyone had a purpose, everyone seemed keen on doing it efficiently and proudly.

I spotted Mor walking with Viviane and a stunningly beautiful young woman who looked like either Viviane's twin or sister. Viviane was beaming, Mor perhaps more subdued for once, and as she twisted—

My brows rose. The human girl—Briar—was with them. Now tucked beneath Viviane's arm, face still bruised and swollen in spots, but . . . smiling timidly at the Winter Court ladies.

Viviane began to lead Briar away, chattering merrily, and Mor and Viviane's possible-sister lingered to watch them. Mor said something to the stranger that made her smile—well, slightly.

It was a restrained smile, and it faded quickly. Especially as a High

Fae soldier strode past, grinned at her with some teasing remark, and then continued on. Mor watched the female's face carefully—and swiftly looked away as she turned back to her, clapped Mor on the shoulder, and strode off after her possible-sister and Briar.

I remembered our argument the moment Mor turned toward me. Remembered the words we'd left unsaid, the ones I probably shouldn't have spoken. Mor flipped her hair over a shoulder and headed right for me.

I spoke before she could get the first word out, "You gave Briar over to them?"

We fell into step back toward our own camp. "Az explained the state you found her in. I didn't think being exposed to battle-ready Illyrians would do much to soothe her."

"And the Winter Court army is much better?"

"They've got fuzzy animals."

I snorted, shaking my head. Those enormous bears were indeed fuzzy—if you ignored the claws and teeth.

Mor glanced sidelong at me. "You did a very brave thing in saving Briar."

"Anyone would have done it."

"No," she said, adjusting her tight Illyrian jacket. "I'm not sure . . . I'm not sure even *I* would have tried to get her. If I would have deemed the risk worth it. I've made enough calls like that where it went badly that I . . ." She shook her head.

I swallowed. "How's Azriel?"

"Alive. His back is fine. But Thesan hasn't healed many Illyrian wings, so the healing is . . . slow. Different from repairing Peregryn wings, apparently. Rhys sent for Madja." The healer in Velaris. "She'll be here either later today or tomorrow to work on him."

"Will he—fly again?"

"Considering Cassian's wings were in worse shape, I'd say yes. But . . . perhaps not in battle. Not anytime soon."

My stomach tightened. "He won't be happy about that."

"None of us are."

To lose Azriel on the field . . .

Mor seemed to read what I was thinking and said, "Better than being dead." She dragged a hand through her golden hair. "It would have been so easy—for things to have gone wrong last night. And when I saw you two vanish . . . I had this thought, this terror, that I might not get to see you again. To make things right."

"I said things I didn't really mean to—"

"We both did." She led me up to the tree line at the border of both our camps, and I knew from that alone . . . I knew she was about to tell me something she didn't wish anyone overhearing. Something worth delaying my meeting with Amren for a little while.

She leaned against a towering oak, foot tap-tapping on the ground. "No more lies between us."

Guilt tugged on my gut. "Yes," I said. "I—I'm sorry about deceiving you. I just . . . I made a mistake. And I'm sorry."

Mor rubbed her face. "You were right about me, though. You were . . ." Her hand shook as she lowered it. She gnawed on her lip, throat bobbing. Her eyes at last met mine—bright and fearful and anguished. Her voice broke as she said, "I don't love Azriel."

I remained perfectly still. Listening.

"No, that's not true, either. I—I do love him. As my family. And sometimes I wonder if it can be . . . more, but . . . I do not love him. Not the way he—he feels for me." The last words were a trembling whisper.

"Have you ever loved him? That way?"

"No." She wrapped her arms around herself. "No. I don't . . . You see . . ." I'd never seen her at such a loss for words. She closed her eyes, fingers digging into her skin. "I *can't* love him like that."

"Why?"

"Because I prefer females."

For a heartbeat, only silence rippled through me. "But—you sleep with males. You slept with Helion . . ." And had looked terrible the next day. Tortured and not at all sated.

Not just because of Azriel, but . . . because it wasn't what she wanted.

"I do find pleasure in them. In both." Her hands were shaking so fiercely that she gripped herself even tighter. "But I've known, since I was little more than a child, that I prefer females. That I'm . . . attracted to them more over males. That I connect with them, care for them more on that soul-deep level. But at the Hewn City . . . All they care about is breeding their bloodlines, making alliances through marriage. Someone like me . . . If I were to marry where my heart desired, there would be no offspring. My father's bloodline would have *ended* with me. I knew it—knew that I could never tell them. Ever. People like me . . . we're reviled by them. Considered selfish, for not being able to pass on the bloodline. So I never breathed a word of it. And then . . . then my father betrothed me to Eris, and . . . And it wasn't just the prospect of marriage to *him* that scared me. No, I knew I could survive his brutality, his cruelty and coldness. I was—I *am* stronger than him. It was . . . It was the idea of being bred like a prize mare, of being forced to give up that one part of me . . ." Her mouth wobbled, and I reached for her hand, prying it off her arm. I squeezed gently as tears began sliding down her flushed face.

"I slept with Cassian because I knew it would mean little to him, too. Because I knew doing it would buy me a shot at freedom. If I had told my parents that I preferred females . . . You've met my father. He and Beron would have tied me to that marriage bed for Eris. Literally. But sullied . . . I knew my shot at freedom lay there. And I saw how Azriel looked at me . . . knew how he felt. And if I'd chosen him . . ." She shook her head. "It wouldn't have been fair to him. So I slept with Cassian, and Azriel thought I deemed him unsuitable, and then everything happened and . . ." Her fingers tightened on mine. "After Azriel found me with that note nailed to my womb . . . I tried to explain. But he started to confess what he felt, and I panicked, and . . . and to get him to *stop*, to keep him from saying he loved me, I just turned and left, and . . . and I couldn't face explaining it after that. To Az, to the others."

She loosed a shuddering breath. "I sleep with males in part because I enjoy it, but . . . also to keep people from looking too closely."

"Rhys wouldn't care—I don't think anyone in Velaris would."

A nod. "Velaris is . . . a haven for people like me. Rita's . . . the owner is like me. A lot of us go there—without anyone really ever picking up on it."

No wonder she practically lived at the pleasure hall.

"But this part of me . . ." Mor wiped at her tears with her free hand. "It didn't matter as much, when my family disowned me. When they called me a whore and a piece of trash. When they hurt me. Because those things . . . they weren't part of me. Weren't true, and weren't . . . intrinsic. They couldn't break me because . . . because they never touched that innermost part of me. They never even guessed. But I hid it . . . I've hidden it because . . ." She tilted back her head, looking skyward. "Because I live in terror of my family finding out—and shaming me, *hurting* me about this one thing that has remained wholly mine. This one part of me. I won't let them . . . won't let them destroy it. Or try to. So I've rarely . . . During the War, I finally took my first—female lover."

She was quiet for a long moment, blinking away tears. "It was Nephelle and her lover—now her wife, I suppose—who made me dare to try. They made me so jealous. Not of them personally, but just . . . of what they had. Their openness. That they lived in a place, with a people who thought nothing of it. But with the War, with the traveling across the world . . . No one from home was with me for months at a time. It was safe, for once. And one of the human queens . . ."

The friends she had so passionately mentioned, had known so intimately.

"Her name was Andromache. And she was . . . so beautiful. And kind. And I loved her . . . so much."

Human. Andromache had been human. My eyes burned.

"But she was human. And a queen—who needed to continue her royal line, especially during such a tumultuous time. So I left—went home after the last battle. And when I realized what a mistake it was, that I didn't care if I only had sixty more years with her . . . The wall went up that day." A small sob came out of her.

"And I could not . . . I was not allowed or able to cross it. I tried. For three years, I tried over and over. And by the time I managed to find a hole to cross . . . She had married. A man. And had an infant daughter—with another on the way. I didn't set foot inside her castle. Didn't even try to see her. I just turned around and went home."

"I'm so sorry," I breathed, my voice breaking.

"She bore five children. And died an old woman, safe in her bed. And I saw her spirit again—in that golden queen. Her descendant."

Mor closed her eyes, breath rippling past her shaking lips. "For a while, I mourned her. Both while she lived and after she died. For a few decades, there were no lovers—of any kind. But then . . . one day I woke up, and I wanted . . . I don't know what I wanted. The opposite of her. I found them—female, male. A few lovers over these past centuries, the females always secret—and I think that's why it wore on them, why they always ended it. I could never be . . . open about it. Never be seen with them. And as for the males . . . it never went as deep. The bond, I mean. Even if I did still crave—you know, every now and then." A huff of a laugh that I echoed. "But all of them . . . It wasn't the same as Andromache. It doesn't feel the same—in here," she breathed, putting a hand over her heart.

"And the male lovers I took . . . it became a way to keep Azriel from wondering why—why I wouldn't notice him. Make that move. You see—you see how marvelous he is. How special. But if I slept with him, even once, just to *try* it, to make sure . . . I think after all this time, he'd think it was a culmination—a happy ending. And . . . I think it might shatter him if I revealed afterward that . . . I'm not sure I can give my entire heart to him that way. And . . . and I love him enough to want him to find someone who can truly love him like he deserves. And I love myself . . . I love myself enough to not want to settle until I find that person, too." A shrug. "If I can even work up the courage to tell the world first. My gift is truth—and yet I have been living a lie my entire existence."

I squeezed her hand once more. "You'll tell them when you're ready. And I'll stand by you no matter what. Until then . . . Your secret is safe. I won't tell anyone—even Rhys."

"Thank you," she breathed.

I shook my head. "No—thank you for telling me. I'm honored."

"I wanted to tell you; I realized I wanted to tell you the moment you and Azriel winnowed to Hybern's camp. And the thought of not being able to tell you . . ." Her fingers tightened around mine. "I promised the Mother that if you made it back safely, I would tell you."

"It seemed she was happy to take the bargain," I said with a smile.

Mor wiped at her face and grinned. It faded almost instantly. "You must think I'm horrible for stringing along Azriel—and Cassian."

I considered. "No. No, I don't." So many things—so many things now made sense. How Mor had looked away from the heat in Azriel's eyes. How she'd avoided that sort of romantic intimacy, but had been fine to defend him if she felt his physical or emotional well-being was at stake.

Azriel loved her, of that I had no doubt. But Mor . . . I'd been blind not to see. Not to realize that there was a damn good reason why five hundred years had passed and Mor had not accepted what Azriel so clearly offered to her.

"Do you think Azriel suspects?" I asked.

Mor drew her hand from mine and paced a few steps. "Maybe. I don't know. He's too observant not to, but . . . I think it confuses him whenever I take a male home."

"So the thing with Helion . . . Why?"

"He wanted a distraction from his own problems, and I . . ." She sighed. "Whenever Azriel makes his feelings clear, like he did with Eris . . . It's stupid, I know. It's so *stupid* and cruel that I do this, but . . . I slept with Helion just to remind Azriel . . . Gods, I can't even say it. It sounds even worse saying it."

"To remind him that you're not interested."

"I should tell him. I *need* to tell him. Mother above, after last night, I should. But . . ." She twisted her mass of golden hair over a shoulder. "It's gone on for so long. So long. I'm petrified to face him—to tell him he's spent five hundred years pining for someone and something that won't ever exist. The potential fallout . . . I like things the way they are. Even if I can't . . . can't really be *me*, I . . . things are good enough."

"I don't think you should settle for 'good enough,'" I said quietly. "But I understand. And, again . . . when you decide the time is right, whether it's tomorrow or in another five hundred years . . . I'll have your back."

She blinked away tears again. I turned toward the camp, and a faint smile bloomed on my mouth.

"What?" she asked, coming to my side.

"I was just thinking," I said, smile growing, "that whenever you're ready . . . I was thinking about how much fun I'm going to have playing matchmaker for you."

Mor's answering grin was brighter than the entirety of the Day Court.

Amren had secluded herself in a tent, and would not let anyone in. Not me, or Varian, or Rhysand.

I certainly tried, hissing as I pushed against her wards, but even Helion's magic could not break them. And no matter how I demanded and coaxed and pleaded, she did not answer. Whatever the Suriel had told me to suggest to her about the Book . . . she'd deemed it more vital, it seemed, than even why I'd come to speak to her: to join me in retrieving Bryaxis. I could likely do it without her since she'd already disabled the wards to contain Bryaxis, but . . . Amren's presence would be . . . welcome. On my end, at least.

Perhaps it made me a coward, but facing Bryaxis on my own, to bind it into a slightly more tangible body and summon it here at last to smash through Hybern's army . . . Amren would be better—at the talking, the ordering.

But since I wasn't about to start shouting about my plans in the middle of that camp . . . I cursed Amren soundly and stormed back to my war-tent.

Only to find that my plans were to be upended anyway. For even if I brought Bryaxis to Hybern's army . . . That army was no longer where it was supposed to be.

Standing beside the enormous worktable in the war-tent, every side flanked with High Lords and their commanders, I crossed my arms as Helion slid an unnerving number of figures across the lower half of Prythian's map. "My scouts say Hybern is on the move as of this afternoon."

Azriel, perched on a stool, his wings and back heavily bandaged and face still grayish with blood loss, nodded once. "My spies say the same." His voice was still hoarse from screaming.

Helion's blazing amber eyes narrowed. "He shifted directions, though. He'd planned to move that army north—drive us back that way. Now he marches due east."

Rhys braced his hands on the table, his sable hair sliding forward as he studied the map. "So he's now heading straight across the island—to what end? He would have been better off sailing around. And I doubt he's changed his mind about meeting us in battle. Even with Tamlin now revealed as an enemy." They'd all been quietly shocked, some relieved, to hear it. Though we'd had no whisper of whether Tamlin would be now marching his small force to us. And nothing from Beron, either.

Tarquin frowned. "Losing Tamlin won't cost him many troops, but Hybern could be going to meet another ally on the eastern coast—to rendezvous with the army of those human queens from the continent."

Azriel shook his head, wincing at the movement and what it surely did to his back. "He sent the queens back to their homes—and there they remain, their armies not even raised. He'll wait to wield that host until he arrives on the continent."

Once he was done annihilating us. And if we failed tomorrow . . . would there be anyone at all to challenge Hybern on the continent? Especially once those queens rallied their human armies to his banner—

"Perhaps he's leading us on another chase," Kallias mused with a frown, Viviane peering at the map beside him.

"Not Hybern's style," Mor said. "He doesn't establish patterns—he knows we're onto his first method of stretching us thin. Now he'll try another way."

As she spoke, Keir—standing with two silent Darkbringer captains—studied her closely. I braced myself for any sort of sneer, but the male merely resumed examining the map. These meetings had been the only place where she'd bothered to acknowledge her father's role in this war—and even then, even now, she barely glanced his way.

But it was better than outright hostility, though I had no doubt Mor was wise enough not to lay into Keir when we still needed his Darkbringers. Especially after Keir's legion had suffered so many losses at that second battle. Whether Keir was furious about those casualties, he had not let on—neither had any of his soldiers, who did not speak with anyone outside their own ranks beyond what was necessary. Silence, I supposed, was far preferable. And Keir's sense of self-preservation no doubt kept his mouth shut in these meetings—and bade him take whatever orders were sent his way.

"Hybern is delaying the conflict," Helion murmured. "Why?"

I glanced over at Nesta, sitting with Elain by the faelight braziers. "He still doesn't have the missing piece. Of the Cauldron's power."

Rhys angled his head, studying the map, then my sisters. "Cassian." He pointed to the massive river snaking inland through the Spring Court. "If we were to cut south from where we are now—to head right down to the human lands . . . would you cross that river, or go west far enough to avoid it?"

Cassian lifted a brow. Gone was yesterday's pallid face and pain. A small mercy.

On the opposite side of the table, Lord Devlon seemed inclined to open his mouth to give his opinion. Unlike Keir, the Illyrian commander had no such qualms about making his disdain for us known. Especially in regard to Cassian's command.

But before Devlon could shove his way in, Cassian said, "A river crossing like that would be time-consuming and dangerous. The river's too wide. Even with winnowing, we'd have to construct boats or bridges to get across. And an army this size . . . We'd have to go west, then cut south—"

As the words faded, Cassian's face paled. And I looked at where Hybern's army was now marching eastward, below that mighty river. From where we were now—

"He wanted us exhausting ourselves on winnowing armies around," Helion said, picking up the thread of Cassian's thought. "On fighting those battles. So that when it counted, we would not have the strength to winnow past that river. We'd have to go on foot—and take the long way around to avoid the crossing."

Tarquin swore now. "So he could march south, knowing we're days behind. And enter the human lands with no resistance."

"He could have done that from the start," Kallias countered. My knees began to shake. "Why now?"

It was Nesta who said from her seat across the room beside the faelight brazier, "Because we insulted him. Me—and my sisters."

All eyes went to us.

Elain put a hand on her throat. She breathed, "He's going to march on the human lands—butcher them. To spite us?"

"I killed his priestess," I murmured. "You took from his Cauldron," I said to Nesta. "And you . . ." I examined Elain. "Stealing you back was the final insult."

Kallias said, "Only a madman would wield the might of his army just to get revenge on three women."

Helion snorted. "You forget that some of us fought in the War. We know firsthand how unhinged he can be. And that something like this would be exactly his style."

I caught Rhys's eye. *What do we do?*

Rhys's thumb brushed down the back of my hand. "He knows we'll come."

"I'd say he's assuming quite a lot about how much we care for humans," Helion said. Keir looked inclined to agree, but wisely remained silent.

Rhys shrugged. "He'll have seen our prioritizing of Elain's safety as proof that the Archeron sisters hold sway here. He thinks they'll convince us to haul our asses down there, likely to a battlefield with few advantages, and be annihilated."

"So we're not going to?" Tarquin frowned.

"Of course we're going to," Rhys said, straightening to his full height and lifting his chin. "We will be outnumbered, and exhausted, and it will not end well. But this has nothing to do with my mate, or her sisters. The wall is down. It is gone. It is a new world, and we must decide how we are to end this old one and begin it anew. We must decide if we will begin it by allowing those who cannot defend themselves to be slaughtered. If that is the sort of people we are. Not individual courts. We, as a Fae *people*. Do we let the humans stand alone?"

"We'll all die together, then," Helion said.

"Good," Cassian said, glancing at Nesta. "If I end my life defending those who need it most, then I will consider it a death well spent." Lord Devlon, for once, nodded his approval. I wondered if Cassian noticed it—if he cared. His face revealed nothing, not as his focus remained wholly on my sister.

"So will I," Tarquin said.

Kallias looked to Viviane, who was smiling sadly up at him. I could see the regret there—for the time they had lost. But Kallias said, "We'll need to leave by tomorrow if we are to stand a chance at staunching the slaughter."

"Sooner than that," Helion said, flashing a dazzling smile. "A few hours." He jerked his chin at Rhys. "You realize humans will be slaughtered before we can get there."

"Not if we can act faster," I said, rotating my shoulder. Still stiff and sore, but healing fast.

They all raised their brows.

"Tonight," I said. "We winnow—those of us who can. To human homes—towns. And we winnow out as many of them as we can before dawn."

"And where will we put them?" Helion demanded.

"Velaris."

"Too far," Rhys murmured, scanning the map before us. "To do all that winnowing."

Tarquin tapped a finger on the map—on his territory. "Then bring them to Adriata. I will send Cresseida back—let her oversee them."

"We'll need all the strength we have to fight Hybern," Kallias said carefully. "Wasting it on winnowing humans—"

"It is no waste," I said. "One life may change the world. Where would you all be if someone had deemed saving my life to be a waste of time?" I pointed to Rhys. "If *he* had deemed saving my life Under the Mountain a waste of time? Even if it's only twenty families, or ten . . . They are not a waste. Not to me—or to you."

Viviane was giving her mate a sharp, reproachful glare, and Kallias had the good sense to mumble an apology.

Then Amren said from behind us, striding through the tent flaps, "I hope you all voted to face Hybern in battle."

Rhys arched a brow. "We did. Why?"

Amren set the Book upon the table with a thump. "Because we will need it as a distraction." She smiled grimly at me. "We need to get to the Cauldron, girl. *All* of us."

And I knew she didn't mean the High Lords.

But rather the four of us—who had been Made. Me, Amren . . . and my sisters.

"You found another way to stop it?" Tarquin asked.

Amren's sharp chin bobbed in a nod. "Even better. I found a way to stop his entire army."

CHAPTER 67

We'd need access to the Cauldron—be able to touch it. Together.

Alone, it had nearly killed me. But split amongst others who were Made . . . We could withstand its lethal power.

If we got it under our control, in one fell swoop we could harness its might to bind the king and his army. And wipe them off the earth.

Amren had found the spell to do it. Right where the Suriel had claimed it'd be encoded in the Book. Rather than nullify the Cauldron's powers . . . we would nullify the person controlling it. *And* his entire host.

But we had to attain the Cauldron first. And with the two armies poised to fight . . .

We would move only when the carnage was at its peak. When Hybern might be distracted in the chaos. Unless he planned to wield that Cauldron on the killing field.

Which was a high possibility.

There was no chance we'd infiltrate that army camp again—not after we'd stolen Elain. So we would have to wait until we walked into the trap he'd set for us. Wait until we took up disadvantageous positions on that battlefield he'd selected, and arrive exhausted from the battles before it, the trek there. Exhausted from winnowing those human families out of his path.

Which we did. That night, any of us who could winnow . . .

I went to my old village with Rhysand.

I went to the houses where I had once left gold as a mortal woman.

At first, they did not recognize me.

Then they realized what I was.

Rhys held their minds gently, soothing them, as I explained. What had happened to me, what was coming. What we needed to do.

They did not have time to pack more than a few things. And they were all trembling as we swept them across the world, to the warmth of a lush forest just outside Adriata, Cresseida already waiting with food and a small army of servants to help and organize.

The second family did not believe us. Thought it was some faerie trick. Rhys tried to hold their minds, but their panic was too deep, their hatred too tangible.

They wanted to stay.

Rhys didn't give them a choice after that. He winnowed their entire family, all of them screaming. They were still shrieking when we left them in that forest, more humans around them, our companions winnowing in new arrivals for Cresseida to document and soothe.

So we continued. House to house. Family to family. Anyone in Hybern's path.

All night. Every High Lord in our army, any commander or noble with the gift and strength.

Until we were panting. Until there was a small city of humans huddled together in that summer-ripe forest. Until even Rhys's strength flagged and he could barely winnow back to our tent.

He passed out before his head had hit the pillow, his wings splayed across the bed.

Too much strain, too much relying on his power.

I watched him sleep, counting his breaths.

We knew—all of us did. We knew that we wouldn't walk away from that battlefield.

Maybe it would inspire others to fight, but . . . We knew. My mate, my family . . . they would fight, buy us time with their lives while Amren and my sisters and I tried to stop that Cauldron. Some would go down before we could reach it.

And they were willing to do it. If they were afraid, none of them let on.

I brushed Rhys's sweat-damp hair back from his brow.

I knew he'd give everything before any of us could offer it. Knew he'd try.

It was as much a part of him as his limbs, this need to sacrifice, to protect. But I wouldn't let him do it—not without trying myself.

Amren had not mentioned Bryaxis in our talks earlier. Had seemed to have forgotten it. But we still had a battle to wage tomorrow. And if Bryaxis could buy my friends, could buy Rhys, any extra time while I hunted down that Cauldron . . . If it could buy them the slimmest shot of survival . . . Then the Bone Carver could as well.

I didn't care about the cost. Or the risk. Not as I looked at my sleeping mate, exhaustion lining his face.

He had given enough. And if this broke me, drove me mad, ripped me apart . . . All Amren would need was my presence, my body, tomorrow with the Cauldron. Anything else . . . if it was what I had to give, my own cost to buy them any sliver of survival . . . I would gladly pay it. Face it.

So I rallied the dregs of my power and winnowed away—winnowed north.

To the Court of Nightmares.

There was a winding stair, deep within the mountain. It led to only one place: a chamber near the uppermost peak. I had learned as much from my research.

I stood at the base of that stairwell, peering up into the impenetrable gloom, my breath clouding in front of me.

A thousand stairs. That was how many steps stood between me and the Ouroboros. The Mirror of Beginnings and Endings.

Only you can decide what breaks you, Cursebreaker. Only you.

I kindled a ball of faelight over my head and began my ascent.

CHAPTER 68

I did not expect the snow.

Or the moonlight.

The chamber must have lain beneath the palace of moonstone—shafts in the rough rock leading outside, welcoming in snowdrifts and moonlight.

I gritted my teeth against the bitter cold, the wind howling through the cracks like wolves raging along the mountainside beyond.

The snow glittered over the walls and floor, slithering over my boots with the wind gusts. Moonlight peered in, bright enough that I vanished my ball of faelight, bathing the entire chamber in blues and silvers.

And there, against the far wall of the chamber, snow crusting its surface, its bronze casing . . .

The Ouroboros.

It was a massive, round disc—as tall as I was. Taller. And the metal around it had been fashioned after a massive serpent, the mirror held within its coils as it devoured its own tail.

Ending and beginning.

From across the room, with the snow . . . I could not see it. What lay within.

I forced myself to take a step forward. Another.

The mirror itself was black as night—yet . . . wholly clear.

I watched myself approach. Watched the arm I had upraised against the wind and snow, the pinched expression on my face. The exhaustion.

I stopped three feet away. I did not dare touch it.

It only showed me myself.

Nothing.

I scanned the mirror for any signs of . . . *something* to push or touch with my magic. But there was only the devouring head of the serpent, its maw open wide, frost sparkling on its fangs.

I shuddered against the cold, rubbing my arms. My reflection did the same.

"Hello?" I whispered.

There was nothing.

My hands burned with cold.

Up close, the surface of the Ouroboros was like a gray, calm sea. Undisturbed. Sleeping.

But in its upper corner—movement.

No—not movement in the mirror.

Behind me.

I was not alone.

Crawling down the snow-kissed wall, a massive beast of claws and scales and fur and shredding teeth inched toward the floor. Toward me.

I kept my breathing steady. Did not let it scent a tendril of my fear—whatever it was. Some guardian of this place, some creature that had crawled in through the cracks—

Its enormous paws were near-silent on the floor, the fur on them a blend of black and gold. Not a beast designed to hunt in these mountains. Certainly not with the ridge of dark scales down its back. And the large, shining eyes—

I didn't have time to remark on those blue-gray eyes as the beast pounced.

I whirled, Illyrian dagger in my freezing hand, ducking low and aiming up—for the heart.

But no impact came. Only snow, and cold, and wind.

There was nothing before me. Behind me.

No paw prints in the snow.

I whirled to the mirror.

Where I had been standing . . . that beast now sat, scaled tail idly swishing through the snow.

Watching me.

No—not watching.

Gazing back at me. My reflection.

Of what lurked beneath my skin.

My knife clattered to the stones and snow. And I looked into the mirror.

⳩

The Bone Carver was sitting against the wall as I entered his cell.

"No escort this time?"

I only stared at him—that boy. My son.

And for once, the Carver seemed to go very still and quiet.

He whispered, "You retrieved it."

I looked toward a corner of his cell. The Ouroboros appeared, snow and ice still crusting it. Mine to summon, wherever and whenever I wished.

"How."

Words were still foreign, strange things.

This body that I had returned to . . . it was strange, too.

My tongue was dry as paper as I said, "I looked."

"What did you see?" The Carver got to his feet.

I sank a little further back into my body. Just enough to smile slightly. "That is none of your concern." For the mirror . . . it had shown me. So many things.

I did not know how long had passed. Time—it had been different inside the mirror.

But even a few hours might have been too many—

I pointed to the door. "You have your mirror. Now uphold your end. Battle awaits."

The Bone Carver glanced between me and the mirror. And he smiled. "It would be my pleasure."

And the way he said it . . . I was wrung dry, my soul new and trembling, and yet I asked, "What do you mean?"

The Carver simply straightened his clothes. "I have little need for that thing," he said, gesturing to the mirror. "But you did."

I blinked slowly.

"I wanted to see if you were worth helping," the Carver went on. "It's a rare person to face who they truly are and not run from it—not be broken by it. That's what the Ouroboros shows all who look into it: who they are, every despicable and unholy inch. Some gaze upon it and don't even realize that the horror they're seeing is *them*—even as the terror of it drives them mad. Some swagger in and are shattered by the small, sorry creature they find instead. But you . . . Yes, rare indeed. I could risk leaving here for nothing less."

Rage—blistering rage started to fill in the holes left by what I'd beheld in that mirror. "You wanted to see if I was *worthy*?" That innocent people were *worthy* of being helped.

A nod. "I did. And you are. And now I shall help you."

I debated slamming that cell door in his face.

But I only said quietly, "Good." I walked over to him. And I was not afraid as I grabbed the Bone Carver's cold hand. "Then let's begin."

CHAPTER 69

Dawn broke, gilding the low-lying mists snaking over the plains of the mortal land.

Hybern had razed everything from the Spring Court down to the few miles before the sea.

Including my village.

There was nothing left but smoking cinders and crumbled stone as we marched past.

And my father's estate . . . One-third of the house remained standing, the rest wrecked. Windows shattered, walls cracked down to the foundation.

Elain's garden was trampled, little more than a mud pit. That proud oak near the edge of the property—where Nesta had liked to stand in the shade and overlook our lands . . . It had been burned into a skeletal husk.

It was a personal attack. I knew it. We all did. The king had ordered our livestock killed. I'd gotten the dogs and horses out the night before—along with the servants and their families. But the riches, the personal touches . . . Looted or destroyed.

That Hybern had not lingered to decimate what was left standing of the house, Cassian told me, suggested he did not want us gaining too much on him. He'd establish his advantage—pick the right battlefield. We had no doubt that finding the empty villages along the way whetted the king's rage. And there were enough towns and villages that we had not reached in time that we hurried.

An easier feat in theory than in practice, with an army of our size and made up of so many differently trained soldiers, with so many leaders giving orders about what to do.

The Illyrians were testy—yanking at the leash, even under Lord Devlon's strict command. Annoyed that we had to wait for the others, that we couldn't just fly ahead and intercept Hybern, stop them before they could select the battlefield.

I watched Cassian lay into two different captains within the span of three hours—watched him reassign the grumbling soldiers to hauling carts and wagons of supplies, pulling some off the honor of being on the front lines. As soon as the others saw that he meant every word, every threat . . . the complaining ceased.

Keir and his Darkbringers watched Cassian, too—and were wise enough to keep any discontent off their tongues, their faces. To keep marching, their dark armor growing muddier with every passing mile.

During the brief midday break in a large meadow, Nesta and I climbed inside one of the supply caravan's covered wagons to change into Illyrian fighting leathers. When we emerged, Nesta even buckled a knife at her side. Cassian had insisted, yet he'd admitted that since she was untrained, she was just as likely to hurt herself as she was to hurt someone else.

Elain . . . She'd taken one look at us in the swaying grasses outside that wagon, the legs and assets on display, and turned crimson. Viviane stepped in, offering a Winter Court fashion that was far less scandalous: leather pants, but paired with a thigh-length blue surcoat, white fur trimming the collar. In the heat, it'd be miserable, but Elain was thankful enough that she didn't complain when we again emerged from the covered wagon and found our companions waiting. She refused the knife Cassian handed her, though.

Went white as death at the sight of it.

Azriel, still limping, merely nudged aside Cassian and extended another option.

"This is Truth-Teller," he told her softly. "I won't be using it today—so I want you to."

His wings had healed—though long, thin scars now raked down them. Still not strong enough, Madja had warned him, to fly today.

The argument with Rhys this morning had been swift and brutal: Azriel insisted he *could* fly—fight with the legions, as they'd planned. Rhys refused. Cassian refused. Azriel threatened to slip into shadow and fight anyway. Rhys merely said that if he so much as tried, he'd chain Azriel to a tree.

And Azriel . . . It was only when Mor had entered the tent and begged him—*begged* him with tears in her eyes—that he relented. Agreed to be eyes and ears and nothing else.

And now, standing amongst the sighing meadow grasses in his Illyrian armor, all seven Siphons gleaming . . .

Elain's eyes widened at the obsidian-hilted blade in Azriel's scarred hand. The runes on the dark scabbard.

"It has never failed me once," the shadowsinger said, the midday sun devoured by the dark blade. "Some people say it is magic and will always strike true." He gently took her hand and pressed the hilt of the legendary blade into it. "It will serve you well."

"I—I don't know how to use it—"

"I'll make sure you don't have to," I said, grass crunching as I stepped closer.

Elain weighed my words . . . and slowly closed her fingers around the blade.

Cassian gawked at Azriel, and I wondered how often Azriel had lent out that blade—

Never, Rhys said from where he finished buckling on his own weapons against the side of the wagon. *I have never once seen Azriel let another person touch that knife.*

Elain looked up at Azriel, their eyes meeting, his hand still lingering on the hilt of the blade.

I saw the painting in my mind: the lovely fawn, blooming spring vibrant behind her. Standing before Death, shadows and terrors lurking over his shoulder. Light and dark, the space between their bodies a blend of the two. The only bridge of connection . . . that knife.

Paint that when we get home.

Busybody.

I peered over my shoulder to Rhys, who stepped up to our little circle in the grass. His face remained more haggard than usual, lines of strain bracketing his mouth. And I realized . . . I would not get that last night with him. Last night—*that* had been the final night. We'd spent it winnowing—

Don't think like that. Don't go into this battle thinking you won't walk off again. His gaze was sharp. Unyielding.

Breathing became difficult. *This break is the last time we'll all be here—talking.*

For this final leg of the march we were about to embark on . . . It would take us right to the battlefield.

Rhys lifted a brow. *Would you like to go into that wagon for a few minutes, then? It's a little cramped between the weapons and supplies, but I can make it work.*

The humor—as much for me as it was for him. I took his hand, realizing the others were talking quietly, Mor having sauntered over in full, dark armor, Amren . . . Amren was in Illyrian leathers, too. So small—they must have been built for a child.

Don't tell her, but they were.

My lips tugged toward a smile. But Rhys stared at all of us, somehow assembled here in the sun-drenched open grasses without being given the order. Our family—our court. The Court of Dreams.

They all quieted.

Rhys looked them each in the eye, even my sisters, his hand brushing the back of my own.

"Do you want the inspiring talk or the bleak one?" he asked.

"We want the real one," Amren said.

Rhys pushed his shoulders back, elegantly folding his wings behind him. "I believe everything happens for a reason. Whether it is decided by the Mother, or the Cauldron, or some sort of tapestry of Fate, I don't know. I don't really care. But I am grateful for it, whatever it is. Grateful that it brought you all into my life. If it hadn't . . . I might have become as awful as that prick we're going to face today. If I had not met an Illyrian warrior-in-training," he said to Cassian, "I would not have known the true depths of strength, of resilience, of honor and loyalty." Cassian's eyes gleamed bright. Rhys said to Azriel, "If I had not met a shadowsinger, I would not have known that it is the family you make, not the one you are born into, that matters. I would not have known what it is to truly hope, even when the world tells you to despair." Azriel bowed his head in thanks.

Mor was already crying when Rhys spoke to her. "If I had not met my cousin, I would never have learned that light can be found in even the darkest of hells. That kindness can thrive even amongst cruelty." She wiped away her tears as she nodded.

I waited for Amren to offer a retort. But she was only waiting.

Rhys bowed his head to her. "If I had not met a tiny monster who hoards jewels more fiercely than a firedrake . . ." A quiet laugh from all of us at that. Rhys smiled softly. "My own power would have consumed me long ago."

Rhys squeezed my hand as he looked to me at last. "And if I had not met my mate . . ." His words failed him as silver lined his eyes.

He said down the bond, *I would have waited five hundred more years for you. A thousand years. And if this was all the time we were allowed to have . . . The wait was worth it.*

He wiped away the tears sliding down my face. "I believe that everything happened, exactly the way it had to . . . so I could find you." He kissed another tear away.

And then he said to my sisters, "We have not known each other for long. But I have to believe that you were brought here, into our family, for a reason, too. And maybe today we'll find out why."

He surveyed them all again—and held out his hand to Cassian. Cassian took it, and held out his other for Mor. Then Mor extended her other to Azriel. Azriel to Amren. Amren to Nesta. Nesta to Elain. And Elain to me. Until we were all linked, all bound together.

Rhys said, "We will walk onto that field and only accept Death when it comes to haul us away to the Otherworld. We will fight for life, for survival, for our futures. But if it is decided by that tapestry of Fate or the Cauldron or the Mother that we do not walk off that field today . . ." His chin lifted. "The great joy and honor of my life has been to know you. To call you my family. And I am grateful—more than I can possibly say—that I was given this time with you all."

"We are grateful, Rhysand," Amren said quietly. "More than you know."

Rhys gave her a small smile as the others murmured their agreement.

He squeezed my hand again as he said, "Then let's go make Hybern very *un*grateful to have known us, too."

✠

I could smell the sea long before we beheld the battlefield. Hybern had chosen well.

A vast, grassy plain stretched to the shore. A mile inland, he had planted his army.

It rippled away, a dark mass spreading to the eastern horizon. Rocky foothills arose at his back—some of his army also stationed atop them. Indeed, even the plain seemed to slope upward to the east.

I lingered at Rhysand's side atop a broad knoll overlooking the plain, my sisters, Azriel, and Amren close behind. At the distant front lines far ahead, Helion, resplendent in golden armor and a rippling red cape, gave the order to halt. Armies obeyed, shifting into the positions they'd sorted out.

The host we faced, though . . . they were waiting. Poised.

So many. I knew without counting that we were vastly outnumbered.

Cassian landed from the skies, stone-faced, all of his Siphons smoldering as he crossed the flat-topped knoll in a few steps. "The prick took every inch of high ground and advantage he could find. If we want to rout them, we'll have to chase them up into those hills. Which I have no doubt he's already calculated. Likely set with all kinds of surprises." In the distance, those naga-hounds began snarling and howling. With hunger.

Rhys only asked, "How long do you think we have?"

Cassian clenched his jaw, glancing at my sisters. Nesta was watching him keenly; Elain monitored the army from our minor elevation, face white with dread. "We have five High Lords, and there's only one of him. You all could shield us for a while. But it might not be in our interest to drain every one of you like that. He'll have shields, too—and the Cauldron. He's been careful not to let us see the full extent of his power. I have no doubt we're about to, though."

"He'll likely be using spells," I said, remembering that he'd trained Amarantha.

"Make sure Helion is on alert," Azriel offered, limping to Rhys's side. "And Thesan."

"You didn't answer my question," Rhys said to Cassian.

Cassian sized up Hybern's unending army, then our own. "Let's say it goes badly. Shields shattered, disarray, he uses the Cauldron . . . A few hours."

I closed my eyes. During that time, I'd have to get across the battlefield before us, find wherever he kept the Cauldron, and stop it.

"My shadows are hunting for it," Azriel said to me, reading my face as I opened my eyes. His jaw clenched at the words. He was supposed to have been searching for it himself. He flared and settled his wings, as if testing them. "But the wards are strong—no doubt reinforced by the king after you shredded through his at the camp. You might have to go on foot. Wait until the slaughter starts getting sloppy."

Cassian dipped his head and said to Amren, "You'll know when."

She nodded sharply, crossing her arms. I wondered if she'd said good-bye to Varian.

Cassian clapped Rhys on the shoulder. "On your command, I'll get the Illyrians into the skies. We advance on your signal after that."

Rhys nodded distantly, attention still fixed on that overwhelming army.

Cassian took a step away, but looked back at Nesta. Her face was hard as granite. He opened his mouth, but seemed to decide against whatever he was about to say. My sister said nothing as Cassian shot into the sky with a powerful thrust of his wings. Yet she tracked his flight until he was hardly more than a dark speck.

"I can fight on foot," Azriel said to Rhys.

"No." There was no arguing with that tone.

Azriel seemed like he was debating it, but Amren shook her head in warning and he backed down, shadows coiling at his fingers.

In silence, we watched our army settle into neat, solid lines. Watched the Illyrians lift into the skies at whatever silent command Rhys sent to Cassian, forming mirror lines above. Siphons glinted with color, and shields locked into place, both magical and metal. The ground itself shook with each step toward that demarcation line.

Rhys said into my mind, *If Hybern has a lock on my power, he will sense me sneaking across the battlefield.*

I knew what he was implying. *You're needed here. If we both disappear, he'll know.*

A pause. *Are you afraid?*

Are you?

His violet eyes caught mine. So few stars now shone within them. "Yes," he breathed. *Not for myself. For all of you.*

Tarquin barked an order far ahead, and our unified army came to a halt, like some mighty beast pausing. Summer, Winter, Day, Dawn, and Night—each court's forces clearly marked by the alterations in color and armor. In the faeries who fought alongside the High Fae, ethereal and deadly. A legion of Thesan's Peregryns flapped into rank beside the Illyrians, their golden armor gleaming against the solid black of our own.

No sign of Beron or Eris—not a whisper of Autumn coming to assist us. Or Tamlin.

But Hybern's army did not advance. They might as well have been statues. The stillness, I knew, was more to unnerve us.

"Magic first," Amren was explaining to Nesta. "Both sides will try to bring down the shields around the armies."

As if in answer, they did. My magic writhed in response to the High Lords unleashing their might—all but Rhysand.

He was saving his power for once the shields came down. I had no doubt Hybern himself was doing the same across the plain.

Shields faltered on either side. Some died. Not many, but a few. Magic against magic, the earth shuddering, the grass between the armies withering and turning to ash.

"I forgot how boring this part is," Amren muttered.

Rhys shot her a dry look. But he prowled to the edge of our little outlook, as if sensing the stalemate was soon to break. He'd deliver a mighty, devastating blow to the army the moment their shield buckled. A veritable tidal wave of night-kissed power. His fingers curled at his sides.

To my left, Azriel's Siphons glowed—readying to unleash blasts to echo Rhysand's. He might not be able to fight, but he would wield his power from here.

I came to Rhys's side. Ahead, both shields were wobbling at last.

"I never got you a mating present," I said.

Rhys monitored the battle ahead. His power rumbled beneath us, surging from the shadowy heart of the world.

Soon. A matter of moments. My heart thundered, sweat beading my brow—not just from the summer heat now thick across the field.

"I've been thinking and thinking," I went on, "about what to get you."

Slowly, so slowly, Rhys's eyes slid to mine. Only a chasm of power lay within them—blotting out those stars.

I smiled at him, bathing in that power, and sent an image into his mind.

Of the column of my spine, now inked from my base to my nape with four phases of the moon. And a small star in the middle of them.

"But, I'll admit," I said as his eyes flared, "this mating gift is probably for *both* of us."

Hybern's shield came crashing down. My magic snapped from me, cleaving through the world. Revealing the glamour I'd had in place for hours.

Before our front line . . . A cloud of darkness appeared, writhing and whirling on itself.

"Mother above," Azriel breathed. Right as a male figure appeared beside that swirling ebony smoke.

Both armies seemed to pause with surprise.

"You retrieved the Ouroboros," Rhys whispered.

For standing before Hybern were the Bone Carver and the living nest of shadows that was Bryaxis, the former contained and freed in a Fae body by myself last night. Both bound to obey by the simple bargain now inked onto my spine. "I did."

He scanned me from head to toe, the wind stirring his blue-black hair as he asked softly, "What did you see?"

Hybern was stirring, frantically assessing what and who now stood before them. The Carver had chosen the form of an Illyrian soldier in his prime. Bryaxis remained within the darkness roiling around it, the living tapestry it would use to reveal the nightmares of its victims.

"Myself," I said at last. "I saw myself."

It was, perhaps, the one thing I would never show him. Anyone. How I had cowered and raged and wept. How I had vomited, and screamed, and clawed at the mirror. Slammed my fists into it. And then curled up, trembling at every horrific and cruel and selfish thing I'd beheld within that monster—within me. But I had kept watching. I did not turn from it.

And when my shaking stopped, I studied it. All of those wretched things. The pride and the hypocrisy and the shame. The rage and the cowardice and the hurt.

Then I began to see other things. More important things—more vital.

"And what I saw," I said quietly to him as the Carver raised a hand. "I think—I think I loved it. Forgave it—me. All of it." It was only in that moment when I knew—I'd understood what the Suriel had meant. Only I could allow the bad to break me. Only I could own it, embrace it. And when I'd learned that . . . the Ouroboros had yielded to me.

Rhys arched a brow, even as awe crept across his face. "You loved all of it—the good and the bad?"

I smiled a bit. "Especially the bad." The two figures seemed to take a breath—a mighty inhale that had Bryaxis's dark cloud contracting. Readying to spring. I inclined my head to my mate. "Here's to a long, happy mating, Rhys."

"Seems like you beat me to it."

"To what?"

With a wink, Rhys pointed toward Bryaxis and the Carver. Another figure appeared.

The Carver stumbled back a step. And I knew—from the slim, female figure, the dark, flowing hair, the once-again beautiful face . . . I knew who she was.

Stryga—the Weaver.

And atop the Weaver's dark hair . . . A pale blue jewel glittered.

Ianthe's jewel. A blood trophy as the Weaver smiled at her twin, gave him a mocking bow, and faced the host before them. The Carver halted his slow retreat, stared at his sister for a long moment, then turned to the army once more.

"You're not the only one who can offer bargains, you know," Rhys drawled with a wicked smile.

The Weaver. Rhys had gotten the *Weaver* to join us— "How?"

He angled his neck, revealing a small, curling tattoo behind his ear. "I sent Helion to bargain on my behalf—that was why he was in the Middle that day he found you. To offer to break the containment spell on the Weaver . . . in exchange for her services today."

I blinked at my mate. Then grinned, not bothering to hide the savagery within it. "Hybern has no idea about the hell that's about to rain down upon them, do they."

"Here's to family reunions," was all Rhys said.

Then the Weaver, the Carver, and Bryaxis unleashed themselves upon Hybern.

CHAPTER 70

"You actually did it," Amren murmured, gaping as the three immortals slammed into Hybern's lines, and the screaming began.

Bodies fell before them; bodies were left in their wake—some mere husks encased in armor. Drained by the Carver and Stryga. Some fled from what they beheld in Bryaxis—the face of their deepest fears.

Rhys was still smiling at me as he extended a hand toward Hybern's army, now trying to adjust to the rampant havoc.

His fingers pointed.

Obsidian power erupted from him.

A massive chunk of Hybern's army just . . .

Misted.

Red mist, and metal shavings lay where they had been.

Rhys panted, his eyes a bit wild. The hit had been well placed. Splitting the army in two.

Azriel unleashed a second blast—blue light slamming into the now-exposed flank. Driving them farther apart.

The Illyrians moved. That had been Rhys's signal.

They shot down from the skies—just as a legion rose up from Hybern teeming with things like the Attor. Hidden amongst Hybern's ranks. Siphons flared, locking shields into place—and the Illyrians rained arrows with deadly accuracy.

But the Attor legion was well prepared. And when they answered with a volley of their own . . . Ash shafts, but arrowheads made from faebane. Even with Nuan's antidote in our soldiers' veins, it did not extend to their magic—and it was no defense against the stone itself. Faebane arrows pierced Siphon-shields as easily as butter. The king had adapted—improved—his arsenal.

Some Illyrians went down quickly. The others realized the threat and used their metal shields, unhooking them from across their backs.

On land, Tarquin's, Helion's, and Kallias's soldiers began to charge. Hybern unleashed its hounds—and other beasts.

And as those two sides barreled for each other . . . Rhys sent another blast, followed by a wave of power from Tarquin. Splitting and shoving Hybern's lines into uneven groups.

And through it all, Bryaxis . . . All I could make of it was a blur of ever-changing claws and fangs and wings and muscle, shifting and whirling within that dark cloud that struck and smothered. Blood sprayed wherever it plunged into screaming soldiers. Some seemed to die of pure terror.

The Bone Carver fought near Bryaxis. No weapons to be seen beyond a scimitar of ivory—of bone—in that male's hands. He swept it before himself, as if he were threshing wheat.

Soldiers dropped dead before it—with barely a blow laid upon them. Even that Fae body of his could not contain that lethal power—stifle it.

Hybern fled before him. Before the Weaver. For on the other side of the Carver, leaving husks of corpses in her wake . . . Stryga shredded through Hybern in a tangle of black hair and white limbs.

Our own soldiers, mercifully, did not balk as they ran for the enemy lines. And I sent a roaring order down that two-pronged bond that now linked me to the Carver and Bryaxis, reminding them, my teeth gritted, that our soldiers were *not* fair game. Only Hybern and its allies.

Both raged against the order, yanking at the leash.

I rallied every scrap of night and starlight and snarled at them to *obey*.

I could have sworn an otherworldly, ungodly sense of *self* grumbled about it in response.

But they listened. And did not turn on our soldiers who at last intercepted Hybern's lines.

The sound as both armies collided . . . I didn't have words for it. Elain covered her ears, cringing.

My friends were down there. Mor fought with Viviane, keeping an eye on her as she'd promised Kallias, while he released his power in sprays of skin-shredding ice. Cassian—I couldn't even spot him beyond the blazing flare of his Siphons near the front lines, crimson glowing amid the vicious shadows of Keir's Darkbringers as they wielded them to their advantage: blinding swaths of Hybern soldiers in sudden darkness . . . then blinding them doubly when they ripped those shadows away and left nothing but glaring sunlight. Left nothing but their awaiting blades.

"It's already getting messy," Amren said, even though our lines—especially the Illyrians and Thesan's Peregryns—held.

"Not yet," Rhys said. "Much of the army isn't yet engaged past the front lines. We need Hybern's focus elsewhere."

Starting with Rhys setting foot on that battlefield.

My guts twisted up. Hybern's army began to move, pressing ahead. The Weaver, Carver, and Bryaxis plunged deep into the ranks, but Hybern's soldiers quickly stepped up to staunch the holes in the lines.

Helion bellowed at our front lines to hold steady. Arrows rose and fell on either side. The ones tipped in faebane found their mark. Over and over again. As if the king had spelled them to hunt their targets.

"This will be over before we can even walk down this hill," Amren snapped.

Rhys growled at her. "*Not yet*—"

A horn sounded—to the north.

Both armies seemed to pause to look.

And Rhys only breathed to me, "Now. You have to go *now*."

Because the army that broke over the northern horizon . . .

Three armies. One bearing the burnt-orange flag of Beron.

The other the grass-green flag of the Spring Court.

And one . . . one of mortal men in iron armor. Bearing a cobalt flag with a striking badger. Graysen's crest.

Out of a rip in the world, Eris appeared atop our knoll, clad head to toe in silver armor, a red cape spilling from his shoulders. Rhys snarled a warning, too far gone in his power to bother controlling himself.

Eris just rested a hand on the pommel of his fine sword and said, "We thought you might need some help."

Because Tamlin's small army, and Beron's, and Graysen's . . . Now they were running and winnowing and blasting for Hybern's ranks. And leading that human army . . .

Jurian.

But Beron. *Beron* had come.

Eris registered our shock at that, too, and said, "Tamlin made him. Dragged my father out by his neck." A half smile. "It was delightful."

They had come—and Tamlin had managed to rally that force I'd so gleefully destroyed—

"Tamlin wants orders," Eris said. "Jurian does, too."

Rhys's voice was rough—low. "And what of your father?"

"We're taking care of a problem," was all Eris said, and pointed toward his father's army.

For those were his brothers approaching the front line, winnowing in bursts through the host. Right past the front lines and to the enemy wagons scattered throughout Hybern's ranks.

Wagons full of faebane, I realized as they crackled with blue fire and then turned to ash without even a trace of smoke. His brothers winnowed to every cache, every arsenal. Flames exploded in their path.

Destroying that supply of deadly faebane. Burning it into nothing.

As if someone—Jurian or Tamlin—had told them precisely where each would be.

Rhys blinked, his only sign of surprise. He looked to me, then Amren, and nodded. *Go. Now.*

While Hybern was focused on the approaching army—trying to calculate the risks, to staunch the chaos Beron and his sons unleashed with their targeted attacks. Trying to figure out what the hell Jurian was doing there, and how many weaknesses Jurian had learned. And would now exploit.

Amren ushered my sisters forward, even as Elain let out a low sob at the sight of the Graysen coat of arms. "Now. Quick and quiet as shadows."

We were going down—into *that*. Bryaxis and the Carver were still shredding, still slaughtering in their little pockets past the enemy lines. And the Weaver . . . Where was the Weaver—

There. Slowly plowing a slim path of carnage. As Rhys had instructed her moments before.

"This way," I said to them, keeping an eye on Stryga's path of horror. Elain was shaking, still gazing toward that human army and her betrothed in it. Nesta monitored the Illyrian legions soaring past overhead, their lines unfaltering.

"I assume we'll be following the path of bodies," Amren muttered to me. "How does the Weaver know how to find the Cauldron?"

Rhys seemed to be listening, even as we turned away, his fingers brushing mine in silent farewell. I just said, "Because she appears to have an unnaturally good sense of smell."

Amren snorted, and we fell into flanking positions around my sisters. A glamour of invisibility would hopefully allow us to skirt the southern edge of the battlefield—along with Azriel's shadows as he monitored from behind. But once we got behind enemy lines . . .

I looked back as we neared the edge of the knoll. Just once. At Rhys, where he now stood talking to Azriel and Eris, explaining the plan to relay to Tamlin, Beron, and Jurian. Eris's brothers made it back behind their father's lines—fires now burning throughout Hybern's army. Not enough to stop them, but . . . at least the faebane had been dealt with. For now.

Rhys's attention slid to me. And even with the battle around us, hell unleashing everywhere . . . For a heartbeat, we were the only two people on this plain.

I opened up my mental barriers to speak to him. Just one more farewell, one more—

Nesta inhaled a shuddering gasp. Stumbled, and took down Amren with her when she tried to keep her upright.

Rhys was instantly there, before the understanding dawned upon me. The Cauldron.

Hybern was rousing the Cauldron.

Amren squirmed out from beneath Nesta, whirling toward the battlefield. "*Shields—*"

Eris winnowed away—to warn his father, no doubt.

Nesta pushed herself onto her elbows, hair shaking free of her braid, lips bloodless. She heaved into the grass.

Rhys's magic shot out of him, arcing around our entire army, his breathing a wet rasp—

Nesta's hands grappled into the grass as she lifted her head, scanning the horizon.

Like she could see right to where the Cauldron was now about to be unleashed.

Rhys's power flowed and flowed out of him, bracing for impact. Azriel's Siphons flashed, a sprawling shield of cobalt locking over Rhysand's, his breathing just as heavy as my mate's—

And then Nesta began screaming. Not in pain. But a name. Over and over.

"*CASSIAN.*"

Amren reached for her, but Nesta roared, "*CASSIAN!*"

She scrambled to her feet, as if she'd leap into the skies.

Her body lurched, and she went down, heaving again.

A figure shot from the Illyrian ranks, spearing for us, flapping hard, red Siphons blazing—

Nesta moaned, writhing on the ground.

The earth seemed to shudder in response.

No—not in response to her. In terror of the thing that erupted from Hybern's army.

I understood why the king had claimed those rocky foothills. Not to make us charge uphill if we should push them so far. But to position the Cauldron.

For it was from the rocky outcropping that a battering ram of death-white light hurled for our army. Just about level with the Illyrian legion in the sky—as the Attor's legion dropped to the earth, and ducked for cover. Leaving the Illyrians exposed.

Cassian was halfway to us when the Cauldron's blast hit the Illyrian forces.

I saw him scream—but heard nothing. The force of that power . . .

It shredded Azriel's shield. Then Rhysand's. And then shredded any Siphon-made ones.

It hollowed out my ears and seared my face.

And where a thousand soldiers had been a heartbeat before . . .

Ashes rained down upon our foot soldiers.

Nesta had known. She gaped up at me, terror and agony on her face, then scanned the sky for Cassian, who flapped in place, as if torn between coming for us and charging back to the scattering Illyrian and Peregryn ranks. She'd known where that blast was about to hit.

Cassian had been right in the center of it.

Or would have been, if she hadn't called him away.

Rhys was looking at her like he knew, too. Like he didn't know whether to scold her for the guilt Cassian would no doubt feel, or thank her for saving him.

Nesta's body went stiff again, a low moan breaking from her.

I felt Rhys cast out his power—a silent warning signal.

The other High Lords raised shields this time, backing the one he rallied.

But the Cauldron did not hit the same spot twice. And Hybern was willing to incinerate part of his own army if it meant wiping out a strength of ours.

Cassian was again hurtling for us, for Nesta sprawled on the ground, as the light and unholy heat of the Cauldron were unleashed again.

Right into its own lines. Where the Bone Carver was gleefully shredding apart soldiers, draining the life from them in sweeps and gusts of that deadly wind.

An unearthly, female shriek broke from deep in the Hybern forces. A sister's warning—and pain. Just as that white light slammed into the Bone Carver.

But the Carver . . . I could have sworn he looked toward me as the Cauldron's power crashed into him. Could have sworn he smiled—and it was not a hideous thing at all.

There—and gone.

The Cauldron wiped him away without any sign of effort.

CHAPTER 71

I could barely hear, barely think in the wake of the Cauldron's power.

In the wake of the empty, blasted bit of plain where the Carver had been. The sudden cold that shuddered down my spine—as if erasing the tattoo inked upon it.

And then the silence—silence in some pocket of my mind as a section of that two-pronged leash of control faded into darkness without end. Leaving nothing behind.

I wondered who would carve his death in the Prison.

If he had perhaps already carved it for himself on the walls of that cell. If he had wanted to make sure I was worthy not to taunt me, but because he wanted his end . . . he wanted his end to be worth carving.

And as I gazed at that decimated part of the plain, the ashes of the Illyrians still raining down . . . I wondered if the Carver had made it. To wherever he had been so curious about going.

I sent up a quiet prayer for him—for all the soldiers who had been there and were now ash on the wind . . . sent up a prayer that they found it everything they'd hoped it would be.

It was the Illyrians who drew me out of the quiet, the ringing in my ears. Even as our army began to panic in the wake of the Cauldron's might, the remaining bulk of the Illyrian legions re-formed their lines and charged ahead, Thesan's Peregryns wholly interspersed with them now.

Jurian's human army, made up of Graysen's men and others . . . To their credit, they did not falter. Did not break, even as they went down one by one.

If the Cauldron dealt another blow . . .

Nesta had her brow in the grass as Cassian landed so hard the ground shuddered. He was reaching for her as he panted, "What is it, what—"

"It's gone quiet again," Nesta breathed, letting Cassian haul her into a sitting position as he scanned her face. Devastation and rage lay in his own. Did he know? That she had screamed for him, knowing he'd come . . . That she'd done it to save him?

Rhys only ordered him, "Get back in line. The soldiers need you there."

Cassian bared his teeth. "What the *hell* can we do against that?"

"I'm going in," Azriel said.

"No," Rhys snapped. But Azriel was spreading his wings, the sunlight so stark on the new, slashing scars down the membrane.

"Chain me to a tree, Rhys," Azriel said softly. "Go ahead." He began checking the buckles on his weapons. "I'll rip it out of the ground and fly with it on my damned back."

Rhys just stared at him—the wings. Then the decimated Illyrian forces.

Any chance we had of victory . . .

Nesta wasn't going anywhere. She could barely stay sitting. And Elain . . . Amren was holding Elain upright as she vomited in the grass. Not from the Cauldron. But pure terror.

But if we did not stop the Cauldron before it refilled again . . . We'd be gone within a few more strikes. I met Amren's gaze. *Can it be done—with just me?*

Her eyes narrowed. *Maybe.* A pause. *Maybe. It never specified how many. Between the two of us . . . it could be enough.*

I eased to my feet. The view of the battle was so much worse standing.

Helion, Tarquin, and Kallias struggled to hold our lines. Jurian, Tamlin, and Beron still battered the northern flank, while the Illyrians and Peregryns slammed back the aerial legion; Keir's Darkbringers now little more than wisps of shadow amid the chaos, but . . .

But it was not enough. And Hybern's sheer size . . . It was beginning to push us back.

Beginning to overwhelm us.

Even by the time Amren and I crossed the miles of battlefield . . . What would be left?

Who would be left?

There was another horn, then.

I knew it did not belong to any ally.

Just as I knew Hybern had not only picked this battlefield for its physical advantages . . . but geographical ones.

Because toward the sea, sailing out of the west, out of Hybern . . .

An armada appeared.

So many ships. All teeming with soldiers.

I caught the look between Cassian, Azriel, and Rhys as they beheld the other army sailing in—at our backs.

Not another army. The *rest* of Hybern's army.

We were trapped between them.

Amren swore. "We might need to run, Rhysand. Before they make landfall."

We could not fight both armies. Couldn't even fight one.

Rhys turned to me. *If you can get across that battlefield in time, then do it. Try to stop the army. The king. But if you can't, when it all goes to hell . . . When there are none of us left . . .*

Don't, I begged him. *Don't say it.*

I want you to run. I don't care what it costs. You run. Get far away, and live to fight another day. You don't look back.

I began to shake my head. *You said no good-byes.*

"Azriel," Rhys said quietly. Hoarsely. "You lead the remaining Illyrians on the northern flank." Guilt—guilt and fear rippled in my mate's eyes at the command. Knowing that Azriel was not fully healed—

Azriel didn't give Rhys a chance to reconsider. Didn't say good-bye to any of us. He shot into the sky, those still-healing wings beating hard as they carried him toward the scrambling northern flank.

That armada sailed nearer. Hybern, sensing their reinforcements were soon to make landfall, cheered and pushed. Hard. So hard the Illyrian lines buckled. Azriel sailed closer and closer to them, Siphons trailing tendrils of blue flame in his wake.

Rhys watched him for a moment, throat bobbing, before he said, "Cassian, you take the southern flank."

This was it. The last moments . . . the last time I would see them all.

I wouldn't run. If it all went to hell, I would make it count and use my own last breath to get that army and king wiped off the earth. But right now . . .

Hybern's armada sailed directly for the distant beach. If I didn't go now, I'd have to charge right through them. The Weaver was already slowing on the eastern front, her death-dance hindered by too many enemies. Bryaxis continued to shred through the lines, swaths of the dead in its wake. But it was still not enough. All that planning . . . it was still not enough.

Cassian said to Rhys, to me, to Nesta, "I'll see you on the other side."

I knew he didn't mean the battlefield.

His wings shifted, readying to lift him.

A horn blast cleaved the world.

A dozen horns, lifted in perfect, mighty harmony.

Rhys went still.

Utterly still at the sound of those horns from the distance. From the east—from the sea.

He whipped his head to me, grabbed me by the waist, and hauled me into the sky. A heartbeat later, Cassian was beside us, Nesta in his arms—as if she'd demanded to see.

And there . . . sailing over the eastern horizon . . .

I did not know where to look.

At the winged soldiers—thousands upon thousands of them—flying straight toward us, high above the ocean. Or the armada of ships stretching away beneath them. More than Hybern's armada. Far, far more.

I knew who they were the moment the aerial host's white, feathered wings became clear.

The Seraphim.

Drakon's legion.

And in those ships below . . . So many different ships. A thousand ships from countless nations, it seemed. Miryam's people. But the other ships . . .

Out of the clouds, a tan-skinned, dark-haired Seraphim warrior soared for us. And Rhys's choked laugh was enough to tell me who it was. Who now flapped before us, grinning broadly.

"You could have asked for aid, you know," drawled the male—*Drakon*. "Instead of letting us hear of all this through the rumor mill. Seems we arrived just in time."

"We came looking for you—and found you gone," Rhys said—but those were tears in his eyes. "Makes it hard to ask someone for aid."

Drakon snorted. "Yes, we realized that. Miryam figured it out—why we hadn't heard from you yet." His white wings were almost blindingly bright in the sun. "Three centuries ago, we had some trouble on our borders and set up a glamour to keep the island shielded. Tied to—you know. So that anyone who approached would only see a ruin and be inclined to turn around." He winked at Rhys. "Miryam's idea—she got it from you and your city." Drakon winced a bit. "Turns out, it worked *too* well, if it kept out both enemies *and* friends."

"You mean to tell me," Rhys said softly, "that you've been on Cretea this entire time."

Drakon grimaced. "Yes. Until . . . we heard about Hybern. About Miryam being . . . hunted again." By Jurian. The prince's face tightened with rage, but he surveyed me, then Nesta and Cassian, with a sharp-eyed scrutiny. "Shall we assist you, or just flap here, talking?"

Rhys inclined his head. "At your leisure, Prince." He glanced to the armada now aiming for Hybern's forces. "Friends of yours?"

Drakon's mouth quirked to the side. "Friends of yours, I think." My heart stopped. "Some of Miryam's boats are down there, she with them, but most of that came for you."

"What," Nesta said sharply, not quite a question.

Drakon pointed to the ships. "We met up with them on the flight here. Saw them crossing the channel and decided to join ranks. It's why we're a little late—though we gave them a bit of a push across." Indeed, wind was now whipping at their white sails, propelling those boats faster and faster toward that Hybern armada.

Drakon rubbed his jaw. "I can't even begin to explain the convoluted story they told me, but . . ." He shook his head. "They're led by a queen named Vassa."

I began crying.

"Who apparently was found by—"

"Lucien," I breathed.

"Who?" Drakon's brows narrowed. "Oh, the male with the eye. No. He met up with them later on—told them where to go. To come *now*, actually. So pushy, you Prythian males. Good thing we, at least, were already on our way to see if you needed help."

"Who found Vassa," Nesta said with that same flat tone. As if she somehow already knew.

Closer, those human ships sailed. So many—so, so many, bearing a variety of different flags that I could just start to make out, thanks to my Fae sight.

"He calls himself the Prince of Merchants," Drakon said. "Apparently, he discovered the human queens were traitors months ago, and has been gathering an independent human army to face Hybern ever since. He managed to find Queen Vassa—and together they rallied this army." Drakon shrugged. "He told me that he's got three daughters who live here. And that he failed them for many years. But he would not fail them this time."

The ships at the front of the human armada became clear, along with the gold lettering on their sides.

"He named his three personal ships after them," Drakon said with a smile.

And there, sailing at the front . . . I beheld the names of those ships.

The *Feyre*.

The *Elain*.

And leading the charge against Hybern, flying over the waves, unyielding and without an ounce of fear . . .

The *Nesta*.

With my father . . . our father at the helm.

CHAPTER 72

The wind whipped away the tears rolling down Nesta's face at the sight of our father's ships.

At the sight of the ship he'd chosen to sail into battle, for the daughter who had hated him for not fighting for us, who had hated him for our mother dying, for the poverty and the despair and years lost.

Drakon said drily, "I take it you're acquainted?"

Our father—gone for months and months with no word.

He had left, my sisters had once said, to attend a meeting regarding the threat above the wall. At that meeting, had it become clear that we had been betrayed by our own kind? And had he then departed, under such secrecy he would not risk the messages to us falling into the wrong hands, to find help?

For us. For me, and my sisters.

Rhys said to Drakon, "Meet Nesta. And my mate, Feyre."

Neither of us looked to the prince. Only at our father's fleet—at the ships he'd named in honor of us.

"Speaking of Vassa," Rhys said to Drakon, "was her curse—ended?"

The human armada and the Hybern host neared, and I knew the

impact would be lethal. Saw Hybern's magic shields go up. Saw the Seraphim raise their own. "See for yourself," Drakon said.

I blinked at what began to shoot between the human boats. What soared over the water, fast as a shooting star. Spearing for Hybern. Red and gold and white—vibrant as molten metal.

I could have sworn Hybern's fleet began to panic as it broke from the lines of the human armada and closed the gap between them.

As it spread its wings wide, trailing sparks and embers across the waves, and I realized what—*who*—now flew at that enemy host.

A firebird. Burning as hot and furious as the heart of a forge.

Vassa—the lost queen.

✣

Rhys kissed away the tears sliding down my own face as that firebird queen slammed into Hybern's fleet. Burning husks of ships were left in her wake.

Our father and the human army spread wide. To pick off the others.

Rhys said to Drakon, "Get your legion on land."

A slim chance—a fool's chance of winning this thing. Or staunching the slaughter.

Drakon's eyes went glazed in a way that told me he was conveying orders to someone far away. I wondered if Nephelle and her wife were in that legion—if the last time they had drawn swords was that long-ago battle at the bottom of the sea.

Rhys seemed to be thinking of the past, too. Because he muttered to Drakon over the din exploding off the sea and the battle below, "Jurian is here."

The casual, cocky grace of the prince vanished. Cold rage hardened his features into something terrifying. And his brown eyes . . . they went wholly black.

"He fights for us."

Drakon didn't look convinced, but he nodded. He jerked his chin to

Cassian. "I assume you're Cassian." The general's chin dipped. I could already see the shadows in his eyes—at the loss of those soldiers. "My legion is yours. Command them as you like."

Cassian scanned our foundering host, the northern flank that Azriel was reassembling, and gave Drakon a few terse orders. Drakon flapped those white wings, so stark against his honey-brown skin, and said to Rhys, "Miryam's furious with you, by the way. Three hundred fifty-one years since you last visited. If we survive, expect to do some groveling."

Rhys rasped a laugh. "Tell that witch it goes both ways."

Drakon grinned, and with a powerful sweep of his wings, he was gone.

Rhys and Cassian looked after him, then at the armadas now engaged in outright bloodshed. Our father was down there—our father, who I had never seen wield a weapon in his *life*—

The firebird rained hell upon the ships. Literally. Burning, molten hell as she slammed into them and sent their panicking soldiers to the bottom of the sea.

"Now," I said to Rhys. "Amren and I need to go *now*."

The chaos was complete. With a battle raging in every direction . . . Amren and I could make it. Perhaps the king would be preoccupied.

Rhys made to shoot me back down to the ground, where Amren and Elain were still waiting. Nesta said, "Wait."

Rhys obeyed.

Nesta stared toward that armada, toward our father fighting in it. "Use me. As bait."

I blinked at the same moment Cassian said, "No."

Nesta ignored him. "The king is probably waiting beside that Cauldron. Even if you get there, you'll have him to contend with. Draw him out. Draw him far away. To me."

"How," Rhys said softly.

"It goes both ways," Nesta murmured, as if my mate's words

moments before had triggered the idea. "He doesn't know how much I took. And if . . . if I make it seem like I'm about to use his power . . . He'll come running. Just to kill me."

"He *will* kill you," Cassian snarled.

Her hand clenched on his arm. "That's—that's where you come in."

To guard her. Protect her. To lay a trap for the king.

"No," Rhys said.

Nesta snorted. "You're not my High Lord. I may do as I wish. And since he'll sense that you're with me . . . You need to go far away, too."

Rhys said to Cassian, "I'm not letting you throw your life away for this."

I was inclined to agree.

Cassian surveyed the depleted Illyrian lines, now holding strong as Azriel rallied them. "Az has control of the lines."

"I said *no*," Rhys snapped. I'd never heard him use that tone with Cassian, with any of them.

Cassian said steadily, "It's the only shot we have of a diversion. Luring him away from that Cauldron." His hands tightened on Nesta. "You gave everything, Rhys. You went through that *hell* for us, for *fifty years*." He'd never addressed it—not fully. "You think I don't know what happened? I know, Rhys. We all do. And we know you did it to save us, spare us." He shook his head, sunlight glinting off that dark, winged helmet. "Let us return the favor. Let us repay the debt."

"There is no debt to repay." Rhys's voice broke. The sound of it cracked my heart.

Cassian's own voice broke as he said, "I never got to repay your mother—for her kindness. Let me do it this way. Let me buy you time."

"I can't."

I wasn't sure if in the entire history of Illyria, there had ever been such a discussion.

"You can," Cassian said gently. "You can, Rhys." He gave a lazy grin. "Save some of the glory for the rest of us."

"Cassian—"

But Cassian asked Nesta, "Do you have what you need?"

Nesta nodded. "Amren showed me enough. What to do to rally the power to me."

And if Amren and I could control the Cauldron between us . . . That distraction they'd offer . . .

Nesta looked down to Elain—our sister monitoring the bloodbath ahead. Then to me. She said quietly, "Tell Father—thank you."

She wrapped her arms tightly around Cassian, those gray-blue eyes bright, then they were gone.

Rhys's body strained with the effort of not going after them as they soared for a copse of trees far behind the battlefield. "He might survive," I said softly.

"No," Rhys said, flying us down to Amren and Elain. "He won't."

I had Rhys move Elain to the farthest reaches of our camp. And when he returned, my mate only pressed a kiss to my mouth before he took to the skies, spearing for the heart of the battle—the heaviest fighting. I could barely stand to look—to see where he landed.

Alone with Amren, she said to me, "Shield us from sight, and run as fast as you can. Don't stop; try not to kill. It'll leave a trail."

I nodded, checking my weapons. The Seraphim were soaring overhead now, wings bright as the sun on snow. I settled a glamour around us, veiling us and muffling our sounds.

"Quickly," Amren repeated, silver eyes churning like thunderclouds. "Don't look back."

So I didn't.

CHAPTER 73

The Cauldron had been nestled in a craggy overlook.

The Weaver had done her job well. Key guards and posts were little more than wet, red piles of bone and sinew. And I knew that when I saw her again . . . she would be even more blindingly beautiful.

Amren's power flared again and again, breaking through wards in our path until we reached Stryga's wake. Whatever spells the king had laid . . . Amren was prepared for them. *Hungry* for them. She shattered them all with a savage smile.

But the gray hill was crawling with Hybern commanders, content to let their underlings fight. Waiting until the killing field had sorted the grunts from the true warriors. I could hear them hissing about who on our side they wanted to personally take on.

Helion and Tarquin were two of the most frequent wishes.

Tamlin was the other. Tamlin, for his two-faced lying. And Jurian. How they would suffer.

Varian. Azriel. Cassian. Kallias and Viviane. Mor. They said the names of my friends like they were horses at a race. Who would last long enough for them to face off. Who would haul the pretty mate of the Lord of Winter back here. Who would break the Morrigan at last.

Who would bring home Illyrian wings to pin on the wall. My blood was boiling, even as my bones quaked. I hoped Bryaxis devoured them all—and made them wet themselves in terror before it did.

But I dared look behind us once.

Mor and Viviane weren't coming to this camp anytime soon. They held off an entire cluster of Hybern soldiers, flanked by that white-haired female I'd seen in the Winter camp and a unit of those mighty bears that shredded apart soldiers with swipes of their enormous paws.

Amren hissed in warning, and I faced forward as we began to scale the quiet side of the gray hill. No sign of Stryga, though she had stopped here, at the base of the hill atop which the Cauldron squatted. I could already feel its terrible presence—the beckoning.

Amren and I climbed slowly. Listening after every step.

The battle raged behind us. In the skies and on the earth and in the sea.

I did not think . . . even with Drakon and the human army . . . I did not think it was going well.

My hands bit into the sharp gray rock of the hill's cliff face, body straining as I hauled myself up, Amren climbing with ease. Nesta had to lure the king away soon, or we'd be face-to-face with him.

Movement at the base of the rock caught my attention.

I went still as death.

A beautiful, dark-haired young woman stood there. Staring up at us, squinting and sniffing.

A smile bloomed on her red—her *bloody* mouth. She smiled in my general direction. Revealing blood-coated teeth.

Stryga. The Weaver had waited. Hiding here. Until we arrived.

She brushed a snow-white hand over the tattoo of a crescent moon now on her forearm. Rhys's bargain-mark. A reminder—and warning.

To go. To hurry.

She faced the rocky path half-visible to our left, Ianthe's jewel splattered with blood where it sat atop her head. Strode right to the guards stationed there, who we'd been climbing the cliff face to avoid. Some of them jolted. Stryga smiled once—a hateful, awful smile—and leaped upon them.

A diversion.

Amren shuddered, but we launched into motion once more. The guards were focused on her slaughtering, sprinting from their posts up the hill to meet her.

Faster—we didn't have much time. I could feel the Cauldron rallying—

No. Not the Cauldron.

That power . . . it came from *behind*.

Nesta.

"Good girl," Amren muttered under her breath. Just before she grabbed me by the back of my jacket and slammed me face-first into the stone, ducking low.

Right as a pair of boots strolled down the narrow path. I knew the sound of his footsteps. They haunted my dreams.

The King of Hybern walked right past us. Focused on Stryga, on Nesta's distant rumble of power.

The Weaver paused as she beheld who approached. Smiled, blood dripping off her chin.

"How beautiful you are," he murmured, his voice a seductive croon. "How magnificent, ancient one."

She brushed her dark hair over a slim shoulder. "You may bow, king. As it was once done."

The King of Hybern walked right up to her. Smiled down at Stryga's exquisite face.

Then he took that face in his broad hands, faster than she could move, and snapped her neck.

It might not have killed her. The Weaver was a death-god—her very existence defied our own. So it might not have killed her, that cracking of her spine. Had the king not tossed her body down to the two naga-hounds snarling at the foot of the hill.

They ripped into the Weaver's limp body without hesitation.

Even Amren let out a sound of dismay.

But the king was staring northward. Toward Nesta.

That power—*her* power—surged again. Beckoning, as the Cauldron atop this rock now called to me.

He gazed toward the sea—the battle raging there.

I could have sworn he was smiling as he winnowed away.

"Now," Amren breathed.

I couldn't move. Cassian and Nesta—even Rhys thought there was no shot of survival.

"You make it count," Amren snapped, and that was true grief shining in her eyes. She knew what was about to happen. The window that we'd been bought.

I swallowed my despair, my terror, and charged up the hill—to the crag.

To where the Cauldron sat. Unguarded. Waiting for us.

The Book appeared in Amren's small hands. The Cauldron was nearly as tall as she was. A looming black pit of hate and power.

I could stop this. Right now. Stop this army—and the king before he killed Nesta and Cassian. Amren opened the Book. Looked at me expectantly.

"Put your hand on the Cauldron," she said quietly. I obeyed.

The Cauldron's endless power slammed into me, a wave threatening to sweep me under, a storm with no end.

I could barely keep one foot in this world, barely remember my name. I clung to what I had seen in the Ouroboros—clung to every reflection and memory I had faced and owned, the good and wicked and the gray. Who I was, who I was, who I was—

Amren watched me for a long moment. And did not read from the Book. Did not put it in my hands. She shut the gold pages and shoved it behind her with a kick.

Amren had lied. She did not plan to leash the king or his army with the Cauldron and the Book.

And whatever trap she had set . . . I had fallen right into it.

CHAPTER 74

I gripped my sense of self in the face of the black maw of the Cauldron. Gripped it with everything I had.

Amren only said, "I'm sorry I lied to you."

I could not remove my hand. Could not pry my fingers away. I was being shredded apart, slowly, thoroughly.

I flung my magic out, desperate for any chain to this world to save me, keep me from being devoured by the eternal, awful *thing* that now tried to drag me into its embrace.

Fire and water and light and wind and ice and night. All rallied. All failed me.

Some tether slipped, and my mind slid closer to the Cauldron's outstretched arms.

I felt it *touch* me.

And then I was half gone.

Half there, standing silently next to the Cauldron, hand glued to the black rim.

Half . . . elsewhere.

Flying through the world. Searching. The Cauldron now hunted for that power that had come so close . . . And now taunted it.

Nesta.

The Cauldron searched for her, searched for her as the king now sought her.

It skimmed across the battlefield like an insect over the surface of a pond.

We were losing. Badly. Seraphim and Illyrians were bloodied and being hauled out of the sky. Azriel had been forced to the ground, his wings dragging in the bloody mud as he fought sword to sword against the endless onslaught. Our foot soldiers had broken the lines in places, Keir screaming at his Darkbringers to get back into position, plumes of shadows flaring from him.

I saw Rhysand. In the thick of those breaking lines. Blood-splattered, fighting beautifully.

I saw him assess the field ahead—and transform.

The talons came first. Replacing fingers and feet. Then dark scales or perhaps feathers, I couldn't get a look at them, covered his legs, his arms, his chest. His body contorted, bones and muscles growing and shifting.

The beast form Rhys had kept hidden. Never liked to unleash.

Unless it was dire enough to do so.

Before the Cauldron swept me away, I beheld what happened to his head, his face.

It was a thing of nightmares. Nothing human or Fae in it. It was a creature that lived in black pits and only emerged at night to hunt and feast. The face . . . it was those creatures that had been carved into the rock of the Court of Nightmares. That made up his throne. The throne not only a representation of his power . . . but of what lurked within. And with the wings . . .

Hybern soldiers began fleeing.

Helion beheld what happened and ran, too—but toward Rhys.

Shifting as well.

If Rhys was a flying terror crafted from shadows and cold moonlight, Helion was his daytime equivalent.

Gold feathers and shredding claws and feathered wings—

Together, my mate and the High Lord of Day unleashed themselves upon Hybern.

Until they paused. Until a slim, short male walked out of the ranks toward them—one of Hybern's commanders, no doubt. Rhys's snarl shook the earth. But it was Helion, glowing with white light, who stepped forward to face the male, claws sinking deep into the mud.

The commander didn't so much as wear a sword. Only fine gray clothes and a vaguely amused expression on his face. Amethyst light swirled around him. Helion growled at Rhys—an order.

And my mate nodded, gore dripping from his maw, before he lunged back into the fray.

Leaving the commander and Helion Spell-Cleaver to go head-to-head. Spell to spell.

Soldiers on either side began fleeing.

But the Cauldron whipped me away as Helion unleashed a blast of light toward the commander, its quarry not to be found on that battlefield.

Come, Nesta's power seemed to sing. *Come*.

The Cauldron caught her scent and hurtled us onward.

We arrived before the king did.

The Cauldron seemed to skid to a halt at the clearing. Seemed to coil and reel back, a snake poised to strike.

Nesta and Cassian stood there, his sword out, Nesta's eyes blazing with that inner, unholy fire. "Get ready," she breathed. "He's coming."

The power Nesta was holding back . . .

She'd kill the King of Hybern.

Cassian was the distraction—while her blow found its mark.

Time seemed to slow and warp. The dark power of the king speared toward us. Toward that clearing where I was neither seen nor heard, where I was nothing but a scrap of soul carried on a black wind.

The King of Hybern winnowed right in front of them.

Nesta's power rallied—then vanished.

Cassian did not move. Did not dare.

For the King of Hybern held my father before him, a sword to his throat.

✢

That was why he had looked to the sea. He'd known Nesta would land that killing blow the moment he appeared, and the only way to stop it . . .

A human shield. One she'd think twice about allowing to die.

Our father was blood-splattered, leaner than the last time I'd seen him. "Nesta," he breathed, noting the ears, the Fae grace. The power sputtering out in her eyes.

The king smiled. "What a loving father—to bring an entire *army* to save his daughters."

Nesta did not say anything. Cassian's attention darted through the clearing, sizing up every advantage, every angle.

Save him, I begged the Cauldron of my father. *Help him*.

The Cauldron did not answer. It had no voice, no consciousness save some base need to take back that which had been stolen.

The King of Hybern tilted his head to peer at my father's bearded and weather-tanned face. "So many things have changed since you were last home. Three daughters, now Fae. One of them married *quite* well."

My father only gazed at my sister. Ignored the monster behind him and said to her, "I loved you from the first moment I held you in my arms. And I am . . . I am so sorry, Nesta—my Nesta. I am so sorry, for all of it."

"Please," Nesta said to the king. Her only word, guttural and hoarse. "Please."

"What will you give me, Nesta Archeron?"

Nesta stared and stared at my father, who was shaking his head. Cassian's hand twitched, the blade rising. Trying to get a good shot.

"Will you give back what you took?"

"Yes."

"Even if I have to carve it out of you?"

Our father snarled, "Don't you lay your filthy hands on my daughter—"

I heard the crack before I realized what happened.

Before I saw the way my father's head twisted. Saw the light freeze in his eyes.

Nesta made no sound. Showed no reaction as the King of Hybern snapped our father's neck.

I began screaming. Screaming and thrashing inside the Cauldron's grip. Begging it to stop it—to bring him back, to end it—

Nesta looked down at my father's body as it crumpled to the forest floor.

And as the king had predicted . . . Nesta's power flickered out.

But Cassian's had not.

Arrows of blinding red shot for the King of Hybern, a shield locking around Nesta as Cassian launched himself forward.

And as Cassian took on the king, who laughed and seemed willing to engage in a bit of swordplay . . . I stared at my father on that ground. At his open, unseeing eyes.

Cassian pushed the king away from my father's body, swords and magics clashing. Not for long. Only long enough to hold him off—for Nesta to perhaps run.

For me to finish what I had let my family give their lives for. But the Cauldron still held me there.

Even as I tried to come back to that hill where Amren had betrayed me, had used me for whatever purpose of her own—

Nesta knelt before our father, her face a void. She gazed into his still-open eyes.

Closed them gently. Hands steady as stone.

Cassian had shoved the king deeper into the trees. His shouts rang out.

Nesta leaned forward to press a kiss to our father's blood-splattered brow.

And when she lifted her head . . .

The Cauldron thrashed and roiled.

For in Nesta's eyes, limning her skin . . . Uncut power.

She gazed toward the king and Cassian. Just as Cassian's bark of pain cut toward us.

The power around her shuddered. Nesta got to her feet.

Then Cassian screamed. I looked toward him. Away from my father.

Not twenty feet away, Cassian was on the ground. Wings—snapped in spots. Blood leaking from them.

Bone jutted from his thigh. His Siphons were dull. Empty.

He'd already drained them before coming here. Was exhausted.

But he had come—for her. For us.

He was panting, blood dribbling from his nose. Arms buckling as he tried to rise.

The King of Hybern stood over him, and extended a hand.

Cassian arched off the ground, bellowing in pain. A bone cracked somewhere in his body.

"Stop."

The king looked over a shoulder as Nesta stepped forward. Cassian mouthed at her to run, blood escaping from his lips and onto the moss beneath him.

Nesta took in his broken body, the pain in Cassian's eyes, and angled her head.

The movement was not human. Not Fae.

Purely animal.

Purely predator.

And when her eyes lifted to the king again . . . "I am going to kill you," she said quietly.

"Really?" the king asked, lifting a brow. "Because I can think of *far* more interesting things to do with you."

Not again. I could not watch this play out again. Standing by, idle, while those I loved suffered.

The Cauldron crept along with Nesta, a hound at her side.

Nesta's fingers curled.

The king snorted. And brought his foot down upon Cassian's nearest wing.

Bone snapped. And his scream—

I thrashed against the Cauldron's grip. Thrashed and clawed.

Nesta exploded.

All of that power, all at once—

The king winnowed out of the way.

Her power blasted the trees behind him to cinders. Blasted across the battlefield in a low arc, then landed right in the Hybern ranks. Taking out hundreds before they knew what happened.

The king appeared perhaps thirty feet away and laughed at the smoking ruins behind him. "Magnificent," he said. "Barely trained, brash, but magnificent."

Nesta's fingers curled again, as if rallying that power.

But she'd spent it all in one blow. Her eyes were blue-gray once more.

"Go," Cassian managed to breathe. "*Go.*"

"This seems familiar," the king mused. "Was it him or the other bastard who crawled toward you that day?"

Cassian was indeed now crawling toward her, broken wings and leg dragging, leaving a trail of blood over the grass and roots.

Nesta rushed to him, kneeling.

Not to comfort.

But to pick up his Illyrian blade.

Cassian tried to stop her as she stood. As Nesta lifted that sword before the King of Hybern.

She said nothing. Only held her ground.

The king chuckled and angled his own blade. "Shall I see what the Illyrians taught you?"

He was upon her before she could lift the sword higher.

Nesta jumped back, clipping his sword with her own, eyes flaring wide. The king lunged again, and Nesta again dodged and retreated through the trees.

Leading him away—away from Cassian.

She managed to draw him another few feet before the king grew bored.

In two movements, he had her disarmed. In another, he struck her across the face, so hard she went down.

Cassian cried out her name, trying again to crawl to her.

The king only sheathed his sword, towering over her as she pushed off the ground. "Well? What else do you have?"

Nesta turned over, and threw out a hand.

White, burning power shot out of her palm and slammed into his chest.

A ploy. To get him close. To lower his guard.

Her power sent him flying back, trees snapping under him. One after another after another.

The Cauldron seemed to settle. All that was left—that was it. All that was left of her power.

Nesta surged to her feet, staggering across the clearing, blood at her mouth from where he'd hit her, and threw herself to her knees before Cassian. "Get up," she sobbed, hauling at his shoulder. "*Get up*."

He tried—and failed.

"You're too heavy," she pleaded, but still tried to raise him, fingers scrabbling in his black, bloodied armor. "I can't—he's coming—"

"Go," Cassian groaned.

Her power had stopped hurling the king across the forest. He now stalked toward them, brushing off splinters and leaves from his jacket—taking his time. Knowing she would not leave. Savoring the awaiting slaughter.

Nesta gritted her teeth, trying to haul Cassian up once more. A broken sound of pain ripped from him. "*Go!*" he barked at her.

"I can't," she breathed, voice breaking. "I *can't*."

The same words Rhys had given him.

Cassian grunted in pain, but lifted his bloodied hands—to cup her face. "I have no regrets in my life, but this." His voice shook with every word. "That we did not have time. That I did not have time with *you*, Nesta."

She didn't stop him as he leaned up and kissed her—lightly. As much as he could manage.

Cassian said softly, brushing away the tear that streaked down her face, "I will find you again in the next world—the next life. And we will have that time. I promise."

The King of Hybern stepped into that clearing, dark power wafting from his fingertips.

And even the Cauldron seemed to pause in surprise—surprise or some . . . *feeling* as Nesta looked at the king with death twining around his hands, then down at Cassian.

And covered Cassian's body with her own.

Cassian went still—then his hand slid over her back.

Together. They'd go together.

I will offer you a bargain, I said to the Cauldron. *I will offer you my soul. Save them.*

"Romantic," the king said, "but ill-advised."

Nesta did not move from where she shielded Cassian's body.

The king raised his hand, power whirling like a dark galaxy in his palm.

I knew they'd both die the moment that power hit them.

Anything, I begged the Cauldron. *Anything*—

The king's hand began to drop.

And then halted. A choking noise came out of him.

For a moment, I thought the Cauldron had answered my pleas.

But as a black blade broke through the king's throat, spraying blood, I realized someone else had.

Elain stepped out of a shadow behind him, and rammed Truth-Teller to the hilt through the back of the king's neck as she snarled in his ear, "*Don't you touch my sister.*"

CHAPTER 75

The Cauldron purred in Elain's presence as the King of Hybern slumped to his knees, clawing at the knife jutting through his throat. Elain backed away a step.

Choking, blood dribbling from his lips, the king gaped at Nesta. My sister lunged to her feet.

Not to go to Elain. But to the king.

Nesta wrapped her hand around Truth-Teller's obsidian hilt.

And slowly, as if savoring every bit of effort it took . . . Nesta began to twist the blade. Not a rotation of the blade itself—but a rotation *into* his neck.

Elain rushed to Cassian, but the warrior was panting—smiling grimly and panting—as Nesta twisted and twisted the blade into the king's neck. Severing flesh and bone and tendon.

Nesta looked down at the king before she made the final pass, his hands still trying to rise, to claw the blade free.

And in Nesta's eyes . . . it was the same look, the same gleam that she'd had that day in Hybern. When she pointed her finger at him in a death-promise. She smiled a little—as if she remembered, too.

And then she pushed the blade, like a worker heaving the spoke of a mighty, grinding wheel.

The king's eyes flared—then his head tumbled off his shoulders.

"Nesta," Cassian groaned, trying to reach for her.

The king's blood sprayed her leathers, her face.

Nesta didn't seem to care as she bent over. As she took up his fallen head and lifted it. Lifted it in the air and stared at it—into Hybern's dead eyes, his gaping mouth.

She did not smile. She only stared and stared and stared.

Savage. Unyielding. Brutal.

"Nesta," Elain whispered.

Nesta blinked, and seemed to realize it, then—whose head she was holding.

What she and Elain had done.

The king's head rolled from her bloodied hands.

The Cauldron seemed to realize what she'd done, too, as his head thumped onto the mossy ground. That Elain . . . Elain had defended this thief. Elain, who it had gifted with such powers, found her so lovely it had wanted to give her *something* . . . It would not harm Elain, even in its hunt to reclaim what had been taken.

It retreated the moment Elain's eyes fell on our dead father lying in the adjacent clearing.

The moment the scream came out of her.

No. I lunged for them, but the Cauldron was too fast. Too strong.

It whipped me back, back, back—across the battlefield.

No one seemed to know the king was dead. And our armies . . .

Rhys and the other High Lords had given themselves wholly to the monsters that lurked under their skins, swaths of enemy soldiers dying in their wake, shredded or gutted or rent in two. And Helion—

The High Lord of Day was bloodied, his golden fur singed and torn, but he still battled against the Hybern commander. The commander remained unmarred. His face unruffled. As if he knew—he might very well win against Helion Spell-Cleaver today.

We arced away, across the field. To Bryaxis—still fighting. Holding the line for Graysen's men. A black cloud that cut a path for them, shielded them. Bryaxis, Fear itself, guarding the mortals.

We passed Drakon and a black-haired woman with skin like dark honey, both squaring off against—

Jurian. They were fighting Jurian. Drakon had an ancient score to settle—and so did Miryam.

We whisked by so quickly I couldn't hear what was said, couldn't see if Jurian was indeed fighting back or trying to fend them off while he explained. Mor joined the fray, bloodied and limping, shouting at them—it was the least of our problems.

Because our armies . . .

Hybern was overwhelming us. Without the king, without the Cauldron, they'd still do it. The fervor the king had roused in them, their belief that they had been wronged and forgotten . . . They'd keep fighting. No solution would ever appease them beyond the complete reclaiming of what they still believed they were entitled to—*deserved*.

There were too many. So many. And we were all drained.

The Cauldron hurtled away, withdrawing toward itself.

There was a roar of pain—a roar I recognized, even with the different, harrowing form.

Rhys. *Rhys*—

He was faltering, he needed *help*—

The Cauldron sucked back into itself, and I was again atop that rock.

Again staring at Amren, who was slapping my face, shouting my name.

"*Stupid girl*," she barked. "*Fight it!*"

Rhys was hurt. Rhys was being overwhelmed—

I snapped back into my body. My hand remained atop the Cauldron.

A living bond. But with the Cauldron settled into itself . . . I blinked. I *could* blink.

Amren blew out a breath. "What in *hell*—"

"The king is dead," I said, my voice cold and foreign. "And you're going to be soon, too."

I'd kill her for this, for betraying us for whatever reason—

"I know," Amren said quietly. "And I need you to help me do it."

I almost let go of the Cauldron at the words, but she shook her head. "Don't break it—the contact. I need you to be . . . a conduit."

"I don't understand."

"The Suriel—it gave you a message. For me. Only me."

My brows narrowed.

Amren said, "The answer in the Book was no spell of control. I lied about that. It was . . . an unbinding spell. For me."

"What?"

Amren looked to the carnage, the screams of the dying ringing us. "I thought I'd need your sisters to help you control the Cauldron, but after you faced the Ouroboros . . . I knew you could do it. Just you. And just me. Because when you unbind me with the Cauldron's power, in my real form . . . I will wipe that army away. Every last one of them."

"Amren—"

But a male voice pleaded from behind, "*Don't.*"

Varian appeared from the rocky path, gasping for breath, splattered with blood.

Amren smirked. "Like a hound on a scent."

"Don't," was all Varian said.

"Unleash me," Amren said, ignoring him. "Let me end this."

I began shaking my head. "You—you will be *gone*. You said you won't remember us, won't be *you* anymore if you're freed."

Amren smiled slightly—at me, at Varian. "I watched them for so many eons. Humans—in my world, there were humans, too. And I watched them love, and hate—wage senseless war and find precious peace. Watched them build lives, build *worlds*. I was . . . I was never allowed such things. I had not been designed that way, had not been ordered to do so. So I watched. And that day I came here . . . it was the first selfish thing I had done. For a long, long while I thought it was punishment for disobeying my Father's orders, for *wanting*. I thought this world was some hell he'd locked me into for disobedience."

Amren swallowed.

"But I think . . . I wonder if my Father knew. If he saw how I watched them love and hate and build, and opened that rip in the world not as punishment . . . but as a gift." Her eyes gleamed. "For it has been a gift. This time—with you. With all of you. It has been a gift."

"Amren," Varian said, and sank onto his knees. "I am *begging* you—"

"Tell the High Lord," she said softly, "to leave out a cup for me."

I did not think I had it in my heart for another ounce of sorrow. I gripped the Cauldron a little harder my throat thick. "I will."

She looked to Varian, a wry smile on her red mouth. "I watched them most—the humans who loved. I never understood it—*how* it happened. *Why* it happened." She paused a step away from the Cauldron. "I think I might have learned with you, though. Perhaps that was a last gift, too."

Varian's face twisted with anguish. But he made no further move to stop her.

She turned to me. And spoke the words into my head—the spell I must think and feel and *do*. I nodded.

"When I am free," Amren said to us, "do not run. It will attract my attention."

She lifted a steady hand toward my arm.

"I am glad we met, Feyre."

I smiled at her, bowing my head. "Me too, Amren. Me too."

Amren grabbed my wrist. And swung herself into the Cauldron.

⁜

I fought. I fought with every breath to get through the spell, my arm half-submerged in the Cauldron as Amren went under the dark water that had filled it. I said the words with my tongue, said them with my heart and blood and bones. Screamed them.

Her hand vanished from my arm, melting away like dew under the morning sun.

The spell ended, shuddering out of me, and I snapped back, losing my hold on the Cauldron. Varian caught me before I fell, and gripped me hard as we gazed at the black mass of the Cauldron, the still surface.

He breathed, "Is she—"

It started far, far beneath us. As if she had gone to the earth's core.

I let Varian haul me a few steps away as the ripple thundered up through the ground, spearing for us, the Cauldron.

We had only enough time to throw ourselves behind the nearest rock when it hit us.

The Cauldron shattered into three pieces, peeling apart like a blossoming flower—and then she came.

She exploded from that mortal shell, light blinding us. Light and fire.

She was roaring—in victory and rage and pain.

And I could have sworn I saw great, burning wings, each feather a simmering ember, spread wide. Could have sworn a crown of incandescent light floated just above her flaming hair.

She paused. The thing that was inside Amren paused.

Looked at us—at the battlefield and all of our friends, our family still fighting on it.

As if to say, *I remember you.*

And then she was gone.

She spread those wings, flame and light rippling to encompass her, no more than a burning behemoth that swept down upon Hybern's armies.

They began running.

Amren came down on them like a hammer, raining fire and brimstone.

She swept through them, burning them, drinking in their death. Some died at the mere whisper of her passing.

I heard Rhys bellowing—and the sound was the same as hers. Victory and rage and pain. And warning. A warning not to run from her.

Bit by bit, she destroyed that endless Hybern army. Bit by bit, she wiped away their taint, their threat. The suffering they had brought.

She shattered through that Hybern commander, poised to strike Helion a deathblow. Shattered through that commander as if he were made of glass. She left only ashes behind.

But that power—it was fading. Vanishing ember by ember.

Yet Amren went to the sea, where my father and Vassa's army battled alongside Miryam's people. Entire boats full of Hybern soldiers fell still after she passed.

As if she had inhaled the life right out of them. Even while her own life sputtered out.

Amren reached the final boat—the very last ship of our enemy—and was no more than a flame on the breeze.

And when that ship, too, fell silent . . .

There was only light. Bright, clean light, dancing on the waves.

CHAPTER 76

Tears slid down Varian's blood-flecked skin as we watched that spot on the sea where Amren had vanished.

Below, beyond, our forces were beginning to cry out with victory—with joy.

Up on the rock . . . utter quiet.

I looked at last toward the broken thirds of the Cauldron.

Perhaps I had done it. In unbinding her, I had unbound the Cauldron. Or perhaps Amren in her unleashed power . . . even that had been too great for the Cauldron.

"We should go," I said to Varian. The others would be looking for us.

I had to get my father. Had to bury him. Help Cassian.

Had to see who else was among the dead—or living.

Hollow—I was so tired and hollow.

I managed to stand. To take one step before I felt it.

The . . . *thing* in the Cauldron. Or lack of it.

It was lack and substance, absence and presence. And . . . it was leaking into the world.

I dared a step toward it. And what I beheld in those ruins of the Cauldron . . .

It was a void. But also *not* a void—a growth.

It did not belong here. Belong anywhere.

There were hands at my face, turning me, touching me. "Are you hurt, are you—"

Rhys's face was battered—bloody. His hands were still tipped in talons, his canines still elongated. Barely out of that beast form. "You—you freed her—"

He was stammering. Shaking. I wasn't entirely sure how he was even standing.

I didn't know where to begin. How to explain.

I let him into my mind, his presence gentle—and as exhausted as I was, I let him see my father. Nesta and Cassian. The king. And Amren.

All of it.

Including that *thing* behind us. That hole.

Rhys folded me into his arms—just for a moment.

"We have a problem," Varian murmured, pointing behind us.

We followed the line of his finger. To where that fissure in the world within the shards of the Cauldron . . . It was growing.

The Cauldron could never be destroyed, we had been warned. Because our very *world* was bound to it.

If the Cauldron were destroyed . . . we would be, too.

"What have I done," I breathed. I had saved our friends—only to damn us all.

Made. Made and un-Made.

I had broken it. I could remake it again.

I ran for the Book, flinging open the pages.

But the gold was engraved with symbols only one being on this earth knew how to read, and she was gone. I hurled the damn thing into the void inside the Cauldron.

It vanished and did not appear again.

"Well, that's one way to try," Rhys said.

I whirled at the humor, but his face was hard. Grim.

"I don't know what to do," I whispered.

Rhys studied the ruins. "Amren said you were a conduit." I nodded. "So be one again."

"What?"

He looked at me like *I* was the insane one as he said, "Remake the Cauldron. Forge it anew."

"With *what* power?"

"My own."

"You're—you're drained, Rhys. So am I. We all are."

"Try. Humor me."

I blinked, that edge of panic dulling a bit. Yes—yes, with him, with my mate . . .

I thought through the spell Amren had shown me. If I changed one small thing . . . It was a gamble. But it might work.

"Better than nothing," I said, blowing out a breath.

"That's the spirit." Humor danced in his eyes.

The dead lay around us for miles, cries of the wounded and grieving starting to rise up, but . . . We had stopped Hybern. Stopped the king.

Perhaps in this . . . in this we would be lucky, too.

I reached for him—with my hand, my mind.

His shields were up—solid walls he'd erected during battle. I brushed a hand along one, but it remained. Rhys smiled down at me, kissed me once. "Remind me to never get on Nesta's bad side."

That he could even *joke*—no, it was a form of enduring. For both of us. Because the alternative to laughter . . . Varian's devastated face, watching us silently, was the alternative. And with this thing before us, this final task . . .

So I managed a laugh.

And I was still smiling, just a bit, when I again laid my hand on the broken shards of the Cauldron.

It was a hole. Airless. No life could exist here. No light.

It was . . . it was what had existed at the beginning. Before all things had exploded from it.

It did not belong here. Maybe one day, when the earth had grown old and died, when the stars had vanished, too . . . maybe then, we would return to this place.

Not today. Not now.

I was both form and nothing.

And behind me . . . Rhys's power was a tether. An unending lightning strike that surged from me into this . . . place. To be shaped as I willed it.

Made and un-Made.

From a distant corner of my memory, my human mind . . . I remembered a mural I had seen at the Spring Court. Tucked away in a dusty, unused library. It told the story of Prythian.

It told the story of a Cauldron. *This* Cauldron.

And when it was held by female hands . . . All life flowed from it.

I reached mine out, Rhys's power rippling through me.

United. Joined as one. Ask and answer.

I was not afraid. Not with him there.

I cupped my hands as if the cracked thirds of the Cauldron could fit into them. The entire universe into the palm of my hand.

I began to speak that last spell Amren had found us. Speak and think and feel it. Word and breath and blood.

Rhys's power flowed through me, out of me. The Cauldron appeared.

Light danced along the fissures where the broken thirds had come together. There—there I would need to forge. To weld. To *bind*.

I put a hand against the side of the Cauldron. Raw, brutal power cascaded out of me.

I leaned back into him, unafraid of that power, of the male who held me.

It flowed and flowed, a burst dam of night.

The cracks fizzled and blurred.

That void began to slither back in.

More. We needed more.

He gave it to me. Rhys handed over everything.

I was a bearer, a vessel, a link.

I love you, he whispered into my mind.

I only leaned back into him, savoring his warmth, even in this non-place.

Power shuddered through him. Wrapped around the Cauldron. I recited the spell over and over and over.

The first crack healed.

Then the second.

I felt him tremble behind me, heard his wet rasp of breath. I tried to turn—

I love you, he said again.

The third and final crack began to heal over.

His power began to sputter. But it kept flowing out.

I threw mine into it, sparks and snow and light and water. Together, we threw everything in. We gave every last drop.

Until that Cauldron was whole. Until the thing it contained . . . it was in there. Locked away.

Until I could feel the sun again warming my face. And saw that Cauldron squatting before me—beneath my hand.

I eased my fingers from the icy iron rim. Gazed down into the inky depths.

No cracks. Whole.

I loosed a shuddering breath. We had done it. We had done—

I turned.

It took me a moment to grasp it. What I saw.

Rhys was sprawled on the rocky ground, wings draped behind him.

He looked like he was sleeping.

But as I breathed in—

It wasn't there.

That thing that rose and fell with each breath. That echoed each heartbeat.

The mating bond.

It wasn't there. It was gone.

Because his own chest . . . it was not moving.

And Rhys was dead.

CHAPTER 77

I had only silence in my head. Only silence, as I began screaming.

Screaming and screaming and screaming.

The emptiness in my chest, my *soul* at the lack of that bond, that *life*—

I was shaking him, screaming his name and shaking him, and my body stopped being my body and just became this *thing* that held me and this *lack* of him, and I could not stop screaming and screaming—

Then Mor was there. And Azriel, swaying on his feet, an arm hooked around Cassian—just as bloody and barely standing thanks to the blue, webbed Siphon-patches all over him. Over them both.

They were saying things, but all I could hear was that last *I love you*, which had not been a declaration but a good-bye.

And he had known. He had *known* he had nothing left, and stopping it would take everything. It would *cost* him everything. He'd kept his shields up so I wouldn't see, because I wouldn't have said yes, I would have rather the world *ended* than this, this *thing* he had done and this *emptiness* where he was, where we were—

Someone was trying to haul me away from him, and I let out a sound that might have been a snarl or another scream, and they let go.

I couldn't live with this, couldn't endure this, couldn't *breathe*—

There were hands—unknown hands on his throat. Touching him—

I lunged for them, but someone held me back. "He's seeing if there's anything to be done," Mor said, voice raw.

He—him. Thesan. High Lord of the Dawn. And of healing. I lunged again, to beg him, to plead—

But he shook his head. At Mor. At the others.

Tarquin was there. Helion. Panting and battered. "He . . . ," Helion rasped, then shook his head, closing his eyes. "Of course he did," he said, more to himself than anyone.

"Please," I said, and wasn't sure who I was speaking to. My fingers scraped against Rhys's armor, trying to get to the heart beneath.

The Cauldron—maybe the Cauldron—

I did not know those spells. How to put him in and make sure *he* came back out—

Hands wrapped around my own. They were blood-splattered and cut up, but gentle. I tried to pull away, but they held firm as Tarquin knelt beside me and said, "I'm sorry."

It was those two words that shattered me. Shattered me in a way I didn't know I could still be broken, a rending of every tether and leash.

Stay with the High Lord. The Suriel's last warning. *Stay . . . and live to see everything righted.*

A lie. A *lie*, as Rhys had lied to me. *Stay with the High Lord.*

Stay.

For there . . . the torn scraps of the mating bond. Floating on a phantom wind inside me. I grasped at them—tugged at them, as if he'd answer.

Stay. Stay, stay, stay.

I clung to those scraps and remnants, clawing at the void that lurked beyond.

Stay.

I looked up at Tarquin, lip curling back from my teeth. Looked at

Helion. And Thesan. And Beron and Kallias, Viviane weeping at his side. And I snarled, "*Bring him back.*"

Blank faces.

I screamed at them, "*BRING HIM BACK.*"

Nothing.

"You did it for me," I said, breathing hard. "*Now do it for him.*"

"You were a human," Helion said carefully. "It is not the same—"

"I don't care. Do it." When they didn't move, I rallied the dregs of my power, readying to rip into their minds and force them, not caring what rules or laws it broke. I wouldn't care, only if—

Tarquin stepped forward. He slowly extended his hand toward me.

"For what he gave," Tarquin said quietly. "Today and for many years before."

And as that seed of light appeared in his palm . . . I began crying again. Watched it drop onto Rhys's bare throat and vanish into the skin beneath, an echo of light flaring once.

Helion stepped forward. That kernel of light in his hand flickered as it fell onto Rhys's skin.

Then Kallias. And Thesan.

Until only Beron stood there.

Mor drew her sword and laid it on his throat. He jerked, having not even seen her move. "I do not mind making one more kill today," she said.

Beron gave her a withering glare, but shoved off the sword and strode forward. He practically chucked that fleck of light onto Rhys. I didn't care about that, either.

I didn't know the spell, the power it came from. But I was High Lady.

I held out my palm. Willing that spark of life to appear. Nothing happened.

I took a steadying breath, remembering how it had looked. "Tell me how," I growled to no one.

Thesan coughed and stepped forward. Explaining the core of power and on and on and I didn't care, but I listened, until—

There. Small as a sunflower seed, it appeared in my palm. A bit of me—my life.

I laid it gently on Rhys's blood-crusted throat.

And I realized, just as he appeared, what was missing.

Tamlin stood there, summoned by either the death of a fellow High Lord or one of the others around me. He was splattered in mud and gore, his new bandolier of knives mostly empty.

He studied Rhys, lifeless before me. Studied all of us—the palms still out.

There was no kindness on his face. No mercy.

"Please," was all I said to him.

Then Tamlin glanced between us—me and my mate. His face did not change.

"*Please*," I wept. "I will—I will give you *anything*—"

Something shifted in his eyes at that. But not kindness. No emotion at all.

I laid my head on Rhysand's chest, listening for any kind of heartbeat through that armor.

"Anything," I breathed to no one in particular. "Anything."

Steps scuffed on the rocky ground. I braced myself for another set of hands trying to pull me away, and dug my fingers in harder.

The steps remained behind me for long enough that I looked.

Tamlin stood there. Staring down at me. Those green eyes swimming with some emotion I couldn't place.

"Be happy, Feyre," he said quietly.

And dropped that final kernel of light onto Rhysand.

I had not witnessed it—when it had been done to me.

So all I did was hold on to him. To his body, to the tatters of that bond.

Stay, I begged. *Stay*.

Light glowed beyond my shut eyelids.

Stay.

And in the silence . . . I began to tell him.

About that first night I'd seen him. When I'd heard that voice beckoning me to the hills. When I couldn't resist its summons, and now . . . now I wondered if I had heard him calling for me on Calanmai. If it had been his voice that brought me there that night.

I told him how I had fallen in love with him—every glance and passed note and croak of laughter he coaxed from me. I told him of everything we'd done, and what it had meant to me, and all that I still wanted to do. All the *life* still left before us.

And in return . . . a thud sounded.

I opened my eyes. Another thud.

And then his chest rose, lifting my head with it.

I couldn't move, couldn't breathe—

A hand brushed my back.

Then Rhys groaned, "If we're all here, either things went very, very wrong or very right."

Cassian's broken laugh cracked out of him.

I couldn't lift my head, couldn't do anything but hold him, savoring every heartbeat and breath and the rumble of his voice as Rhys rasped, "You lot will be pleased to know . . . My power remains my own. No thieving here."

"You do know how to make an entrance," Helion drawled. "Or should I say exit?"

"You're horrible," Viviane snapped. "That's not even remotely funny—"

I didn't hear what else they said. Rhys sat up, lifting me off him. He brushed away the hair clinging to my damp cheeks.

"*Stay with the High Lord*," he murmured.

I hadn't believed it—until I looked into that face. Those star-flecked eyes.

Hadn't let myself believe it wasn't anything but some delusion—

"It's real," he said, kissing my brow. "And—there's another surprise."

He pointed with a healed hand toward the Cauldron. "Someone fish out dear Amren before she catches a cold."

Varian whirled toward us. But Mor was sprinting for the Cauldron, and her cry as she reached in—

"How?" I breathed.

Azriel and Varian were there, helping Mor heave a waterlogged form out of the dark water.

Her chest rose and fell, her features the same, but . . .

"She was there," Rhys said. "When the Cauldron was sealing. Going . . . wherever we go."

Amren sputtered water, vomiting onto the rocky ground. Mor thumped her back, coaxing her through it.

"So I reached out a hand," Rhys went on quietly. "To see if she might want to come back."

And as Amren opened her eyes, as Varian let out a choked sound of relief and joy—

I knew—what she had given up to come back. High Fae—and just that.

For her silver eyes were solid. Unmoving. No smoke, no burning mist in them.

A normal life, no trace of her powers to be seen.

And as Amren smiled at me . . . I wondered if that had been her last gift.

If it all . . . if it all had been a gift.

CHAPTER 78

Amongst the sprawling field of corpses and wounded, there was one body I wanted to bury.

Only Nesta, Elain, and I returned to that clearing, once Azriel had given the all-clear that the battle was well and truly over.

Letting Rhys out of my sight to wrangle our scattered armies, sort through the living and dead, and figure out some semblance of order was an effort in self-control.

I nearly begged Rhys to come with us, so I didn't have to let go of his hand, which I had not stopped clutching since those moments I'd heard his beautiful, solid heartbeat echoing into his body once more.

But this task, this farewell . . . I knew, deep down, that it was only for my sisters and me.

So I released Rhys's hand, kissing him once, twice, and left him in the war-camp to help Mor haul a barely standing Cassian to the nearest healer.

Nesta was watching them when I reached her and Elain at the tree-lined outskirts. Had she done some healing, somehow, in those moments after she'd severed the king's head? Or had it been Cassian's immortal blood and Azriel's battlefield patching that had already healed him enough to manage to stand, even with the wing and leg? I didn't ask my sister, and she supplied no answer as she took the water bucket dangling from Elain's still-bloody hands, and I followed them both through the trees.

The King of Hybern's corpse lay in the clearing, crows already picking at it.

Nesta spat on it before we approached our father. The crows barely scattered in time.

The screams and moaning of the wounded was a distant wall of sound—another world away from the sun-dappled clearing. From the blood still fresh on the moss and grass. I blocked out the coppery tang of it—Cassian's blood, the king's blood, Nesta's blood.

Only our father had not bled. He hadn't been given the chance to. And through whatever small mercy of the Mother, the crows hadn't started on him.

Elain quietly washed his face. Combed out his hair and beard. Straightened his clothes.

She found flowers—somewhere. She laid them at his head, on his chest.

We stared down at him in silence.

"I love you," Elain whispered, voice breaking.

Nesta said nothing, face unreadable. There were such shadows in her eyes. I had not told her what I'd seen—had let them tell me what they wanted.

Elain breathed, "Should we—say a prayer?"

We did not have such things in the human world, I remembered. My sisters had no prayers to offer him. But in Prythian . . .

"Mother hold you," I whispered, reciting words I had not heard since that day Under the Mountain. "May you pass through the gates; may you smell that immortal land of milk and honey." Flame ignited at my fingertips. All I could muster. All that was left. "Fear no evil. Feel no pain." My mouth trembled as I breathed, "May you enter eternity."

Tears slid down Elain's pallid cheeks as she adjusted an errant flower on our father's chest, white-petaled and delicate, and then backed away to my side with a nod.

Nesta's face did not shift as I sent that fire to ignite our father's body.

He was ash on the wind in a matter of moments.

We stared at the burned slab of earth for long minutes, the sun shifting overhead.

Steps crunched on the grass behind us.

Nesta whirled, but—

Lucien. It was Lucien.

Lucien, haggard and bloody, panting for breath. As if he'd run from the shore.

His gaze settled on Elain, and he sagged a little. But Elain only wrapped her arms around herself and remained at my side.

"Are you hurt?" he asked, coming toward us. Spying the blood speckling Elain's hands.

He halted short as he noticed the King of Hybern's decapitated head on the other side of the clearing. Nesta was still showered with his blood.

"I'm fine," Elain said quietly. And then asked, noticing the gore on him, the torn clothes and still-bloody weapons, "Are you—"

"Well, I never want to fight in another battle as long as I live, but . . . yes, I'm in one piece."

A faint smile bloomed on Elain's lips. But Lucien noticed that scorched patch of grass behind us and said, "I heard—what happened. I'm sorry for your loss. All of you."

I just strode to him and threw my arms around his neck, even if it wasn't the embrace he was hoping for. "Thank you—for coming. With the battle, I mean."

"I've got one hell of a story to tell you," he said, squeezing me tightly. "And don't be surprised if Vassa corners you as soon as the ships are sorted. And the sun sets."

"Is she really—"

"Yes. But your father, ever the negotiator . . ." A sad, small smile toward that burnt grass. "He managed to cut a deal with Vassa's *keeper* to come here. Temporarily, but . . . better than nothing. But yes—queen by night, firebird by day." He blew out a breath. "Nasty curse."

"The human queens are still out there," I said. Maybe I'd hunt them down.

"Not for long—not if Vassa has anything to do with it."

"You sound like an acolyte."

Lucien blushed, glancing at Elain. "She's got a foul temper and a fouler mouth." He cut me a wry look. "You'll get along just fine."

I nudged him in the ribs.

But Lucien again looked at that singed grass, and his blood-splattered face turned solemn. "He was a good man," he said. "He loved you all very much."

I nodded, unable to form the words. The thoughts. Nesta didn't so much as blink to indicate she'd heard. Elain just wrapped her arms tighter around herself, a few more tears streaking free.

I spared Lucien the torment of debating whether to touch her, and linked my arm through his as I began to walk away, letting my sisters decide to follow or remain—if they wanted a moment alone with that burnt grass.

Elain came.

Nesta stayed.

Elain fell into step beside me, peering at Lucien. He noticed it. "I heard you made the killing blow," he said.

Elain studied the trees ahead. "Nesta did. I just stabbed him."

Lucien seemed to fumble for a response, but I said to him, "So where now? Off with Vassa?" I wondered if he'd heard of Tamlin's role—the help he'd given us. A look at my friend showed me he had. Someone, perhaps my mate, had informed him.

Lucien shrugged. "First—here. To help. Then . . ." Another glance at Elain. "Who knows?"

I nudged Elain, who blinked at me, then blurted, "You could come to Velaris."

He saw all of it, but nodded graciously. "It would be my pleasure."

As we strode back to the camp, Lucien told us of his time away—how he'd hunted for Vassa, how he'd found her already with my father, an army marching westward. How Miryam and Drakon had found them on their own journey to help us.

I was still mulling over all he said when I slipped into my tent to finally change out of my leathers, leaving him and Elain to go find a place to wash up. And talk—perhaps.

But as I strode through the flaps, sound greeted me within—talking. Many voices, one of them belonging to my mate.

I got one step inside and knew I wouldn't be changing my clothes anytime soon.

For seated in a chair before the brazier was Prince Drakon, Rhys sprawled and still bloody on the cushions across from him. And on the pillows beside Rhys sat a lovely female, her dark hair tumbling down her back in luscious curls, already smiling at me.

Miryam.

CHAPTER 79

Miryam's smiling face was more human than High Fae. But Miryam, I remembered as she and Drakon rose to their feet to greet me, was only half Fae. She bore the delicately pointed ears, but . . . there was something still human about her. In that broad smile that lit up her brown eyes.

I instantly liked her. Mud splattered her own leathers—a different make than the Illyrians', but obviously designed by another aerial people to keep warm in the skies—and a few speckles of blood coated the honey-brown skin along her neck and hands, but she didn't seem to notice. Or care. She held out her hands to me. "High Lady," Miryam said, her accent the same as Drakon's. Rolling and rich.

I took her hands, surprised to find them dry and warm. She squeezed my fingers tightly while I managed to say, "I've heard so much about you—thank you for coming." I cast a look at where Rhys still remained sprawled on the cushions, watching us with raised brows. "For someone who was just dead," I said tightly, "you seem remarkably relaxed."

Rhys smirked. "I'm glad you're bouncing back to your usual spirits, Feyre darling."

Drakon snorted, and took my hands, squeezing them as tightly as his mate had. "What he doesn't want to tell you, my lady, is that he's so damn old he *can't* stand up right now."

I whirled to Rhys. "Are you—"

"Fine, fine," Rhys said, waving a hand, even as he groaned a bit. "Though perhaps now you see why I didn't bother visiting these two for so long. They're terribly cruel to me."

Miryam laughed, plopping down on the cushions again. "Your mate was in the middle of telling us *your* story, as it seems you've already heard ours."

I had, but even as Prince Drakon gracefully returned to his seat and I slid into the chair beside his, just watching the two of them . . . I wanted to know the entire thing. One day—not tomorrow or the day after, but . . . one day, I wanted to hear their tale in full. But for now . . .

"I—saw you two. Battling Jurian." Drakon instantly stiffened, Miryam's eyes going shuttered as I asked, "Is he . . . Is he dead?"

"No," was all Drakon said.

"Mor," Miryam cut in, frowning, "wound up convincing us not to . . . settle things."

They would have. From the expression on Drakon's face, the prince still didn't seem convinced. And from the haunted gleam in Miryam's eyes, it seemed as if far more had occurred during that fight than they let on. But I still asked, "Where is he?"

Drakon shrugged. "After we didn't kill him, I have no idea where he slithered off to."

Rhys gave me a half smile. "He's with Lord Graysen's men—seeing to the wounded."

Miryam asked carefully, "Are you—friends with Jurian?"

"No," I said. "I mean—I don't think so. But . . . every word he said was true. And he did help me. A great deal."

Neither of them so much as nodded as they exchanged a long glance, unspoken words passing between them.

Rhys asked, "I thought I saw Nephelle during the battle—any

chance I'll get to say hello, or is she too important now to bother with me?" Laughter—beautiful laughter—danced in his eyes.

I straightened, smiling. "She's here?"

Drakon lifted a dark brow. "You know Nephelle?"

"Know *of* her," I said, and glanced toward the tent flaps as if she'd come striding right in. "I—it's a long story."

"We have time to hear it," Miryam said, then added, "Or . . . a bit of time, I suppose."

For there were indeed many, many things to sort out. Including—

I shook my head. "Later," I said to Miryam, to her mate. The proof that a world could exist without a wall, without a Treaty. "There's something . . ." I relayed my thought down the bond to Rhys, earning a nod of approval before I said, "Is your island still secret?"

Miryam and Drakon exchanged a guilty look. "We do apologize for that," Miryam offered. "It seems that the glamour worked *too* well, if it kept well-meaning messengers away." She shook her head, those beautiful curls moving with her. "We would have come sooner—we left the moment we realized what trouble you all were in."

"No," I said, shaking my own head, scrambling for the words. "No—I don't blame you. Mother above, we owe you . . ." I blew out a breath. "We are in your debt." Drakon and Miryam objected to that, but I went on, "What I mean is . . . If there was an object of terrible power that now needed to be hidden . . . Would Cretea remain a good place to conceal it?"

Again that look between them, a look between mates. "Yes," Drakon said.

Miryam breathed, "You mean the Cauldron."

I nodded. It had been hauled into our camp, guarded by whatever Illyrians could still stand. None of the other High Lords had asked—for now. But I could see the debate that would rage, the war we might start internally over who, exactly, got to keep the Cauldron. "It needs to disappear," I said softly. "Permanently." I added, "Before anyone remembers to lay claim to it."

Drakon and Miryam considered, some unspoken conversation passing between them, perhaps down their own mating bond. "When we leave," Drakon said at last, "one of our ships might find itself a little heavier in the water."

I smiled. "Thank you."

"When are you, exactly, planning to leave?" Rhys asked, lifting a brow.

"Kicking us out already?" Drakon said with a half smile.

"A few days," Miryam cut in wryly. "As soon as the injured are ready."

"Good," I said.

They all looked to me. I swallowed. "I mean . . . Not that I'm glad for you to go . . ." The amusement in Miryam's eyes spread, twinkling. I smiled myself. "I want you here. Because I'd like to call a meeting."

A day later . . . I didn't know how it'd come together so quickly. I'd merely explained what I wanted, what we *needed* to do, and . . . Rhys and Drakon made it happen.

There was no proper space to do it—not with the camps in disarray. But there was one place—a few miles off.

And as the sun set and my family's half-ruined estate became filled with High Lords and princes, generals and commanders, humans and Fae . . . I still didn't have the words to really express it. How we could all gather in the giant sitting room, the only usable space in my family's old estate, and actually have . . . this meeting.

I'd slept through the night, deep and undisturbed, Rhys in bed beside me. I hadn't let go of him until dawn had leaked into our tent. And then . . . the war-camps were too full of blood and injured and the dead. And there was this meeting to arrange between various armies and camps and peoples.

It took all day, but by the end of it, I found myself in the wrecked foyer, Rhys and the others beside me, the chandelier a broken mass behind us on the cracked marble floor.

The High Lords arrived first. Starting with Beron.

Beron, who did not so much as glance at his son-who-was-not-his-son. Lucien, standing on my other side, didn't acknowledge Beron's existence, either. Or Eris's, as he strode a step behind his father.

Eris was bruised and cut up enough to indicate he must have been in terrible shape after the fighting ceased yesterday, sporting a brutal slice down his cheek and neck—barely healed. Mor let out a satisfied grunt at the sight of it—or perhaps a sound of disappointment that the wound had not been fatal.

Eris continued by as if he hadn't heard it, but didn't sneer at least. Rather—he just nodded at Rhys.

It was silent promise enough: soon. Soon, perhaps, Eris would finally take what he desired—and call in our debt.

We did not bother to nod back. None of us.

Especially not Lucien, who continued dutifully ignoring his eldest brother.

But as Eris strode by . . . I could have sworn there was something like sadness—like regret, as he glanced to Lucien.

Tamlin crossed the threshold moments later.

He had a bandage over his neck, and one over his arm. He came, as he had to that first meeting, with no one in tow.

I wondered if he knew that this wrecked house had been purchased with the money he'd given my father. With the kindness he'd shown them.

But Tamlin's attention didn't go to me.

It went to the person just to my left. To Lucien.

Lucien stepped forward, head high, even as that metal eye whirred. My sisters were already within the sitting room, ready to guide our guests to their predetermined spots. We'd planned those carefully, too.

Tamlin paused a few feet away. None of us said a word. Not as Lucien opened his mouth.

"Tamlin—"

But Tamlin's attention had gone to the clothes Lucien now wore. The Illyrian leathers.

He might as well have been wearing Night Court black.

It was an effort to keep my mouth shut, to not explain that Lucien didn't have any other clothes with him, and that they weren't a sign of his allegiance—

Tamlin just shook his head, loathing simmering in his green eyes, and walked past. Not a word.

I looked at Lucien in time to see the guilt, the devastation, flicker in that russet eye. Rhys had indeed told Lucien everything about Tamlin's covert assistance. His help in dragging Beron here. Saving me at the camp. But Lucien remained standing with us as Tamlin found his place in the sitting room to our right. Did not glance at his friend even once.

Lucien wasn't foolish enough to beg for forgiveness.

That conversation, that confrontation—it would take place at another time. Another day, or week, or month.

I lost track of who filed in afterward. Drakon and Miryam, along with a host of their people. Including—

I started at the slight, dark-haired female who entered on Miryam's right, her wings much smaller than the other Seraphim.

I glanced to where Azriel stood on Rhys's other side, bandaged all over and wings in splints after he'd worked them too hard yesterday. The shadowsinger nodded in confirmation. Nephelle.

I smiled at the legendary warrior-scribe when she noticed my stare as she passed by. She grinned right back at me.

Kallias and Viviane flowed in, along with that female who was indeed her sister. Then Tarquin and Varian. Thesan and his battered Peregryn captain—whose hand he tightly held.

Helion was the last of the High Lords to arrive. I didn't dare look through the ruined doorway to where Lucien now stood in the sitting room, close to Elain's side as she and my sister silently kept against the wall by the intact bay of windows.

Beron, wisely, didn't approach—and Eris only looked over every now and then. To watch.

Helion was limping, flanked by a few of his captains and generals, but still managed a grim smile. "Better enjoy this while it lasts," he said to me and Rhys. "I doubt we'll be so unified when we walk out of here."

"Thank you for the words of encouragement," I said tightly, and Helion chuckled as he eased inside.

More and more people filled that room, the tense conversation broken up by bursts of laughter or greeting. Rhys at last told our family to head into the room—while he and I waited.

Waited and waited, long minutes.

It'd take them longer to arrive, I realized. Since they could not winnow or move as quickly through the world.

I was about to turn into the room to begin without them when two male figures filled the night-darkened doorway.

Jurian. And Graysen.

And behind them . . . a small contingent of other humans.

I swallowed hard. Now the difficult part would begin.

Graysen looked inclined to turn around, the fresh cut down his cheek crinkling as he scowled, but Jurian nudged him in. A black eye bloomed on the left side of Jurian's face. I wondered if Miryam or Drakon had given it to him. My money was on the former.

Graysen only gave us a tight nod. Jurian smirked at me.

"I put you on opposite ends of the room," I said.

From both Miryam and Drakon. And from Elain.

Neither man responded, and only strode, proud and tall, into that room full of Fae.

Rhys kissed my cheek and strode in behind them. Which left—

As Lucien had promised, with darkness now overhead, Vassa found me.

The last to arrive—the last piece of this meeting. She stormed over the threshold, breathless and unfaltering, and paused only a foot away.

Her unbound hair was a reddish gold, thick dark lashes and brows framing the most stunningly blue eyes I'd ever seen. Beautiful, her freckled skin golden-brown and gleaming. Only a few years older than me, but . . . young-feeling. Coltish. Fierce and untamed, despite her curse.

Vassa said in a lilting accent, "Are you Feyre Cursebreaker?"

"Yes," I said, sensing Rhys listening wryly from the other room, where the rest were now beginning to quiet themselves. To wait for me.

Vassa's full mouth tightened. "I am sorry—about your father. He was a great man."

Nesta, striding out of the sitting room, halted at the words. Looked Vassa up and down.

Vassa returned the favor. "You are Nesta," Vassa declared, and I wondered how my father had described her so that Vassa would know. "I am sorry for your loss, too."

Nesta simply regarded her with that cool indifference.

"I heard you slew the King of Hybern," Vassa said, those dark brows narrowing as she again surveyed Nesta, searching for any sign of a warrior beneath the blue dress she wore. Vassa only shrugged to herself when Nesta didn't reply and said to me, "He was a better father to me than my own. I owe much to him, and will honor his memory as long as I live."

The look Nesta was giving the queen was enough to wither the grass beyond the shattered front door. It didn't get any better as Vassa said, "Can you break the curse on me, Feyre Archeron?"

"Is that why you agreed to come so quickly?"

A half smile. "Partly. Lucien suggested you had gifts. And other High Lords do as well."

Like his father—his true one. Helion.

She went on before I could answer. "I do not have much time left—before I must return to the lake. To him."

To the death-lord who held her leash. "Who is he?" I breathed.

Vassa only shook her head, waving a hand as her eyes darkened, and repeated, "Can you break my curse?"

"I—I don't know how to break those kinds of spells," I admitted. Her face fell. I added, "But . . . we can try."

She considered. "With the healing of our armies, I won't be able to leave for some time. Perhaps it will give me a . . . loophole, as Lucien called it, to remain longer." Another shake of the head. "We shall discuss this later," she declared. "Along with the threat my fellow queens pose."

My heart stumbled a beat.

A cruel smile curved Vassa's mouth. "They will try to intervene," she said. "With any sort of peace talks. Hybern sent them back before this battle, but I have no doubt they were smart enough to encourage that. Not to waste their armies here."

"But they will elsewhere?" Nesta demanded.

Vassa tossed her smooth sheet of hair over a shoulder. "We shall see. And you will think of ways to help me."

I waited until she headed for the sitting room before I flicked my brows up at the order. Either she didn't know or didn't care that I was *also* a queen in my right.

Nesta smirked. "Good luck with *that*."

I scowled, shoving down the worry already blooming in my gut, and said, "Where are you going? The meeting is starting."

"Why should I be in there?"

"You're the guest of honor. You killed the king."

Shadows flickered in her face. "So what."

I blinked. "You're our emissary as well. You should be here for this."

Nesta looked toward the stairs, and I noticed the object she clutched in her fist.

The small, wooden carving. I couldn't make out what manner of animal it was, but I knew the wood. Knew the work.

One of the little carvings our father had crafted during those years he—he hadn't done much of anything at all. I looked at her face before she could notice my attention.

Nesta said, "Do you think it will work—this meeting?"

With so many Fae ears in the room beyond, I didn't dare give any answer but the truth. "I don't know. But I'm willing to try." I offered my hand to my sister. "I want you here for this. With me."

Nesta considered that outstretched hand. For a moment, I thought she'd walk away.

But she slid her hand into mine, and together we walked into that room crammed with humans and Fae. Both parts of this world. *All* parts of this world.

High Fae from every court. Miryam and Drakon and their retinue. Humans from many territories.

All watching me and Nesta as we entered, as we strode to where Rhys and the others waited, facing the gathered room. I tried not to cringe at the shattered furniture that had been sorted through for any possible seats. At the ripped wallpaper, the half-dangling curtains. But it was better than nothing.

I supposed the same could be said of our world.

Silence settled. Rhys nudged me forward, a hand brushing the small of my back as I took a step past him. I lifted my chin, scanning the room. And I smiled at them, the humans and Fae assembled here—in peace.

My voice was clear and unwavering. "My name is Feyre Archeron. I was once human—and now I am Fae. I call both worlds my home. And I would like to discuss renegotiating the Treaty."

CHAPTER 80

A world divided was not a world that could thrive.

That first meeting went on for hours, many of us short-tempered with exhaustion, but . . . channels were made. Stories were exchanged. Tales narrated of either side of the wall.

I told them my story.

All of it.

I told it to the strangers who did not know me, I told it to my friends, and I told it to Tamlin, hard-faced by the distant wall. I explained the years of poverty, the trials Under the Mountain, the love I had found and let go, the love that had healed and saved me. My voice did not quaver. My voice did not break. Nearly everything I had seen in the Ouroboros—I let them see it, too. Told them.

And when I was done, Miryam and Drakon stepped forward to tell their own story.

Another glimmer of proof—that humans and Fae could not only work together, live together, but become so much more. I listened to every word of it—and did not bother to brush away my tears at times. I only clutched Rhys's hand, and did not let go.

There were several others with tales. Some that went counter to our own. Relations that had not gone so well. Crimes committed. Hurts that could not be forgiven.

But it was a start.

There was still much work to be done, trust to build, but the matter of crafting a new wall . . .

It remained to be seen whether we could agree on that. Many of us were against it. Many of the humans, rightfully so, were wary. There were still other Fae territories to contend with—those who had found Hybern's promises appealing. Seductive.

The High Lords quarreled the most about the possibility of a new wall. And with every word of it, just as Helion said, that temporary allegiance frayed and snapped. Court lines were redrawn.

But at least they stayed until the end—until the early hours of the morning when we finally decided that the rest would be discussed on another day. At another place.

It would take time. Time, and healing, and trust.

And I wondered if the road ahead—the road to true peace—would perhaps be the hardest and longest one yet.

The others left, winnowing or flying or striding off into the darkness, already peeling back into their groups and courts and war-bands. I watched them go from the open doorway of the estate until they were only shadows against the night.

I'd seen Elain staring out the window earlier—watching Graysen leave with his men without so much as a look back at her. He had meant every word that day at his keep. Whether he noticed that Elain still wore his engagement ring, that Elain stared and stared at him as he walked off into the night . . . I didn't know. Let Lucien deal with that—for now.

I sighed, leaning my head against the cracked stone door frame. The grand wooden door had been shattered completely, the splinters still scattered on the marble entry behind me.

I recognized his scent before I heard his easy steps approach.

"Where do you go now?" I asked without looking over my shoulder as Jurian paused beside me and stared into the darkness. Miryam and Drakon had left quickly, needing to tend to their wounded—and to spirit away the Cauldron to one of their ships before the other High Lords had a moment to consider its whereabouts.

Jurian leaned against the opposite door frame. "Queen Vassa offered me a place within her court." Indeed, Vassa still remained inside, chatting with Lucien animatedly. I supposed that if she only had until dawn before turning back into that firebird, she wanted to make every minute count. Lucien, surprisingly, was chuckling, his shoulders loose and his head angled while he listened.

"Are you going to accept?"

Jurian's face was solemn—tired. "What sort of court can a cursed queen have? She's bound to that death-lord—she has to go back to his lake on the continent at some point." He shook his head. "Too bad the king was so spectacularly beheaded by your sister. I bet he could have found a way to break that curse of hers."

"Too bad indeed," I muttered.

Jurian grunted his amusement.

"Do you think we stand a chance?" I asked, motioning to the human figures still walking, far away, back toward the camp. "Of peace between all of us?"

Jurian was silent for a long moment. "Yes," he said softly. "I do."

And I didn't know why, but it gave me comfort.

I was still mulling over Jurian's words days later, when that war-camp was at last dismantled. When we said our final good-byes, and made promises—some more sincere than others—to see each other again.

When my court, my family, winnowed back to Velaris.

Sunlight still leaked in through the windows of the town house. The scent of citrus and the sea and baked bread still filled every room.

And distantly . . . Children were still laughing in the streets.

Home. Home was the same—home was untouched.

I squeezed Rhys's hand so tightly I thought he'd complain, but he only squeezed right back.

And even though we had all bathed, as we stood there . . . there was a grime to us. Like the blood hadn't entirely washed off.

And I realized that home was indeed the same, but we . . . perhaps we were not.

Amren muttered, "I suppose I shall have to eat real food now."

"A monumental sacrifice," Cassian quipped.

She gave him a vulgar gesture, but her eyes narrowed at the sight of his still-bandaged wings. Her eyes—normal silver eyes—slid to Nesta, holding herself by the stair rail, as if she'd retreat to her room.

My sister had barely spoken, barely eaten these past few days. Had not visited Cassian in his healing bed. Still had not talked to me about what had happened.

Amren said to her, "I'm surprised you didn't take the king's head back to have stuffed and hung on your wall."

Nesta's eyes shot to her.

Mor clicked her tongue. "Some would consider that joke to be in bad taste, Amren."

"I saved your asses. I'm entitled to say what I want."

And with that Amren stalked out of the house and into the city streets.

"The new Amren is even crankier than the old one," Elain said softly.

I burst out laughing. The others joined me, and even Elain smiled—broadly.

All but Nesta, who stared at nothing.

When the Cauldron had broken . . . I didn't know if it had broken that power in her, too. Severed its bond. Or if it still lived, somewhere within her.

"Come on," Mor said, slinging her arm around Azriel's shoulders, then one carefully around Cassian's and leading them toward the sitting room. "We need a drink."

"We're opening the fancy bottles," Cassian called over his shoulder to Rhys, still limping on that barely healed leg.

My mate sketched a subservient bow. "Save a bit for me, at least."

Rhys glanced at my sisters, then winked at me. The shadows of battle still lingered, but that wink . . . I was still shaky with terror that it wasn't real. That it was all some fever dream inside the Cauldron.

It is real, he purred into my mind. *I'll prove it to you later. For hours.*

I snorted, and watched as he made an excuse to no one in particular about finding food and sauntered down the hall, hands in his pockets.

Alone in the foyer with my sisters, Elain still smiling a bit, Nesta stone-faced, I took a breath.

Lucien had remained behind to help with any of the human wounded still needing Fae healing, but had promised to come here when he finished. And as for Tamlin . . .

I had not spoken to him. Had barely seen him after he'd told me to be happy, and given me back my mate. He'd left the meeting before I could say anything.

So I gave Lucien a note to hand to him if he saw him. Which I knew—I knew he would. There was a stop that Lucien had to make before he came here, he'd said. I knew where he meant.

My note to Tamlin was short. It conveyed everything I needed to say.

Thank you.

I hope you find happiness, too.

And I did. Not just for what he'd done for Rhys, but . . . Even for an immortal, there was not enough *time* in life to waste it on hatred. On feeling it and putting it into the world.

So I wished him well—I truly did, and hoped that one day . . . One day, perhaps he would face those insidious fears, that destructive rage rotting away inside him.

"So," I said to my sisters. "What now?"

Nesta just turned and went up the stairs, each step slow and stiff. She shut her door with a decisive click once she got to her bedroom.

"With Father," Elain whispered, still staring up those steps, "I don't think Nesta—"

"I know," I murmured. "I think Nesta needs to sort through . . . a lot of it."

Too much of it.

Elain faced me. "Do we help her?"

I fiddled with the end of my braid. "Yes—but not today. Not tomorrow." I loosed a breath. "When—when she's ready." When *we* were ready, too.

Elain nodded, smiling up at me, and it was tentative joy—and *life* that shone in her eyes. A promise of the future, gleaming and sweet.

I led her into the sitting room, where Cassian had a bottle of amber-colored liquor in each hand, Azriel was already rubbing his temples, and Mor was grabbing fine-cut crystal glasses off a shelf.

"What now?" Elain mused, at last answering my question from moments ago as her attention drifted to the windows facing the sunny street. That smile grew, bright enough that it lit up even Azriel's shadows across the room. "I would like to build a garden," she declared. "After all of this . . . I think the world needs more gardens."

My throat was too tight to immediately reply, so I just kissed my sister's cheek before I said, "Yes—I think it does."

CHAPTER 81

Rhysand

Even from the kitchen, I could hear all of them. The lapping of what was surely the oldest bottle of liquor I owned, then the clink of those equally ancient crystal glasses against each other.

Then the laughter. The deep rumble—that was Azriel. Laughing at whatever Mor had said that prompted her into a fit of it as well, the sound cackling and merry.

And then another laugh—silvery and bright. More beautiful than any music played at one of Velaris's countless halls and theaters.

I stood at the kitchen window, staring at the garden in full summer splendor, not quite seeing the blooms Elain Archeron had tended these weeks. Just staring—and listening to that beautiful laugh. My mate's laugh.

I rubbed a hand over my chest at that sound—the joy in it.

Their conversation flitted past, falling back into old rhythms and yet . . . Close. We had all come so close to not seeing it again. This place. Each other. And I knew that the laughter . . . it was in part because of that, too. In defiance and gratitude.

"You coming to drink, or are you just going to stare at the flowers all day?" Cassian's voice cut through the melody of sounds.

I turned, finding him and Azriel in the kitchen doorway, each with a drink in hand. A second lay in Azriel's other scarred hand—he floated it over to me on a blue-tinged breeze.

I clasped the cool, heavy crystal tumbler. "Sneaking up on your High Lord is ill-advised," I told them, drinking deeply. The liquor burned its way down my throat, warming my stomach.

"It's good to keep you on edge in your old age," Cassian said, drinking himself. He leaned against the doorway. "Why are you hiding in here?"

Azriel shot him a look, but I snorted, taking another sip. "You really did open the fancy bottles."

They waited. But Feyre's laugh sounded again, followed by Elain's and Mor's. And when I dragged my gaze back to my brothers, I saw the understanding on their faces.

"It's real," Azriel said softly.

Neither laughed or commented on the burning in my eyes. I took another drink to wash away the tightness in my throat, and approached them. "Let's not do this again for another five hundred years," I said a bit hoarsely, and clinked my glass against theirs.

Azriel cracked a smile as Cassian lifted a brow. "And what are we going to do until then?"

Beyond brokering peace, beyond those queens who were sure to be a problem, beyond healing our fractured world . . .

Mor called for us, demanding we bring them a spread of food. An *impressive* one, she added. *With extra bread.*

I smiled. Smiled wider as Feyre's laugh sounded again—as I *felt* it down the bond, sparkling brighter than the entirety of Starfall.

"Until then," I said to my brothers, slinging my arms around their shoulders and leading them back to the sitting room. I looked ahead, toward that laugh, that light—and that vision of the future Feyre had shown me, more beautiful than anything I could have ever wished for—anything I *had* wished for, on those long-ago, solitary nights with only the stars for company. A dream still unanswered—but not forever. "Until then, we enjoy every heartbeat of it."

CHAPTER 82

Feyre

Rhysand was on the roof, the stars bright and low, the tiles beneath my bare feet still warm from the day's sun.

He sat in one of those small iron chairs, no light, no bottle of liquor—just him, and the stars, and the city.

I slid into his lap and let him wrap his arms around me.

We sat in silence for a long time. We'd barely had a moment alone in the aftermath of the battle, and had been too tired to do anything but sleep. But tonight . . . His hand ran down my thigh, bared with the way my nightgown had hitched.

He startled when he actually looked at me, then huffed a laugh against my shoulder.

"I should have known."

"The shop ladies gave it to me for free. As thanks for saving them from Hybern. Maybe I should do it more often, if it gets me free lingerie."

For I indeed wore that pair of red, lacy underthings—beneath a matching red nightgown that was so scandalously sheer it showed them off.

"Hasn't anyone told you? You're disgustingly rich."

"Just because I have money doesn't mean I need to spend it."

He squeezed my knee. "Good. We need someone with a head for money around here. I've been bleeding out gold left and right thanks to our Court of Dreams taking advantage of my ridiculous generosity."

A laugh rumbled deep in my throat as I leaned my head back against his shoulder. "Is Amren still your Second?"

"Our Second."

"Semantics."

Rhys traced idle circles on my bare skin, along my knee and lower thigh. "If she wants it, it's hers."

"Even if she doesn't have her powers anymore?"

"She's now High Fae. I'm sure she'll discover some hidden talent to terrorize us with."

I laughed again, savoring the feel of his hand on my skin, the warmth of his body around me.

"I heard you," he said softly. "When I was—gone."

I began to tense at the lingering terror that had driven me from sleep these past few nights—the terror I doubted I'd soon recover from. "Those minutes," I said once he began making long, soothing strokes down my thigh. "Rhys . . . I never want to feel that again."

"Now you know how I felt Under the Mountain."

I craned my neck to look up at him. "*Never* lie to me again. Not about that."

"But about other things?"

I pinched his arm hard enough that he laughed and batted away my hand. "I couldn't let all you *ladies* take the credit for saving us. Some male had to claim a bit of glory so you don't trample us until the end of time with your bragging."

I punched his arm this time.

But he wrapped his arm around my waist and squeezed, breathing me in. "I heard you, even in death. It made me look back. Made me stay—a little longer."

Before going to that place I had once tried to describe to the Carver.

"When it's time to go there," I said quietly, "we go together."

"It's a bargain," he said, and kissed me gently.

I murmured back onto his lips, "Yes, it is."

The skin on my left arm tingled. A lick of warmth snaked down it.

I looked down to find another tattoo there—the twin to the one that had once graced it, save for that black band of the bargain I'd made with Bryaxis. He'd modified this one to fit around it, to be seamlessly integrated amid the whorls and swirls.

"I missed the old one," he said innocently.

On his own left arm, the same tattoo flowed. Not to his fingers the way mine did, but rather from his wrist to his elbow.

"Copycat," I said tartly. "It looks better on me."

"Hmmm." He traced a line down my spine, then poked two spots along it. "Sweet Bryaxis has vanished. Do you know what that means?"

"That I have to go hunt it down and put it back in the library?"

"Oh, you most certainly do."

I twisted in his lap, looping my arms around his neck as I said, "And will you come with me? On this adventure—and all the rest?"

Rhys leaned forward and kissed me. "Always."

The stars seemed to burn brighter in response, creeping closer to watch. His wings rustled as he shifted us in the chair and deepened the kiss until I was breathless.

And then I was flying.

Rhys gathered me up in his arms, shooting us high into the starry night, the city a glimmering reflection beneath.

Music flitted out from the riverfront cafés. People laughed as they walked arm in arm down the streets and across the bridges spanning the Sidra. Dark spots still stained some of the glimmering expanse—piles of rubble and ruined buildings—but even some of those had been lit up with small lights. Candles. Defiant and lovely against the blackness.

We would need more of that in the days to come—on the long road ahead. To a new world. One I would leave a better place than how I'd found it.

But for now . . . this moment, with the city below us, the world around us, savoring that hard-won peace . . . I savored it, too. Every heartbeat. Every sound and smell and image that planted itself in my mind, so many that it would take me a lifetime—several of them—to paint.

Rhys leveled out, sent a thought into my mind, and grinned broadly as I summoned wings.

He let go of me and I swept smoothly out of his arms, basking in the warm wind caressing every inch of me, drinking in the air laced with salt and citrus. It took me a few flaps to get it right—the feel and rhythm. But then I was steady, even.

Then I was flying. Soaring.

Rhys fell into flight beside me, and when he smiled at me again as we sailed through the stars and the lights and the sea-kissed breeze, when he showed me all the wonders of Velaris, the glittering Rainbow a living river of color beneath us . . . When he brushed his wing against mine, just because he could, because he wanted to and we'd have an eternity of nights to do this, to see everything together . . .

A gift.

All of it.

ACKNOWLEDGMENTS

Even after nine books, it never gets any easier to express my tremendous gratitude to the people in my life, both personally and professionally, who make my world brighter just by being in it.

To Josh: Every moment with you is a gift. Long ago, when I looked up at the stars and wished, it was for someone like you to be in my life. I truly believe those stars listened, because getting to share this wild adventure with you has been a dream answered. I love you more than words can convey.

To Annie: Thank you for the cuddles, the sass, and the constant demands for more treats that keep me on my toes. I love you forever and ever and ever, baby pup (and no matter what anyone says, I swear you *can* read this).

To my agent, Tamar, who works so tirelessly and is the fiercest badass I know: none of this would be possible without you, and I will never stop being grateful for it. Thank you for everything.

To Cat Onder: Working with you was such an enormous privilege and joy. Thank you for being such a creative, caring, and insightful editor, and for all the years of friendship.

To the genius team at Bloomsbury worldwide: Cindy Loh, Cristina Gilbert, Kathleen Farrar, Nigel Newton, Rebecca McNally, Sonia Palmisano, Emma Hopkin, Ian Lamb, Emma Bradshaw, Lizzy Mason, Courtney Griffin, Erica Barmash, Emily Ritter, Grace Whooley, Eshani Agrawal, Emily Klopfer, Alice Grigg, Elise Burns, Jenny Collins, Beth Eller, Kerry Johnson, Kelly de Groot, Ashley Poston, Lucy Mackay-Sim, Hali Baumstein, Melissa Kavonic, Diane Aronson, Linda Minton, Christine Ma, Donna Mark, John Candell, Nicholas Church, and the entire foreign rights team—thank you for the hard work to make these books a reality and for being the best damn global publishing team *ever*. To Jon Cassir and the team at CAA: thank you for championing me and my books.

To Cassie Homer, assistant extraordinaire: thank you for all of your help and for being such a delight to work with!

To my parents: thank you for the fairy tales and folklore, for the adventures around the world, and for the weekend mornings with bagels and lox from Murray's. To Linda and Dennis: you raised such a spectacular son, and I will be forever grateful for it. To my family: I'm so lucky to have all of you in my life.

To Roshani Chokshi, Lynette Noni, and Jennifer Armentrout: thank you for being such bright lights and wonderful friends—and for all your invaluable feedback with this book. To Renée Ahdieh, Steph Brown, and Alice Fanchiang: I adore you.

A massive thank-you to Sasha Alsberg, Vilma Gonzalez, Alexa Santiago, Rachel Domingo, Jessica Reigle, Kelly Grabowski, Jennifer Kelly, Laura Ashforth, and Diyana Wan for being supremely awesome and lovely people. To the marvelous Caitie Flum: thank you *so* much for taking the time to read this book and for providing such valuable feedback. To Louisse Ang: thank you, thank you, thank you for all of your remarkable kindness, infectious joy, and astounding generosity.

To Charlie Bowater, who is not only a brilliant artist, but also a magnificent human being: thank you for the art that has moved and inspired me, and for all of your hard and phenomenal work on the coloring book. It's an honor to work with you.

And lastly, to *you*, dear reader: thank you from the bottom of my heart for coming with me and Feyre on this journey. Your heartfelt letters and incredible art, your lovely music and clever cosplays . . . all of it means more than I can possibly say. I'm truly blessed to have you as readers, and can't wait to share more of this world with you in the next book!

FEYRE NAVIGATES HER FIRST WINTER SOLSTICE AS HIGH LADY IN . . .

READ ON FOR A SNEAK PEEK AT THE NEXT BOOK IN THIS ELECTRIFYING SERIES.

Feyre

The first snow of winter had begun whipping through Velaris an hour earlier.

The ground had finally frozen solid last week, and by the time I'd finished devouring my breakfast of toast and bacon, washed down with a heady cup of tea, the pale cobblestones were dusted with fine, white powder.

I had no idea where Rhys was. He hadn't been in bed when I'd awoken, the mattress on his side already cold. Nothing unusual, as we were both busy to the point of exhaustion these days.

Seated at the long cherrywood dining table at the town house, I frowned at the whirling snow beyond the leaded glass windows.

Once, I had dreaded that first snow, had lived in terror of long, brutal winters.

But it had been a long, brutal winter that had brought me so deep into the woods that day nearly two years ago. A long, brutal winter that had made me desperate enough to kill a wolf, that had eventually led me here—to this life, this . . . happiness.

The snow fell, thick clumps plopping onto the dried grass of the tiny front lawn, crusting the spikes and arches of the decorative fence beyond it.

Deep inside me, rising with every swirling flake, a sparkling, crisp power stirred. I was High Lady of the Night Court, yes, but also one blessed with the gifts of all the courts. It seemed Winter now wanted to play.

Finally awake enough to be coherent, I lowered the shield of black adamant guarding my mind and cast a thought down the soul-bridge between me and Rhys. *Where'd you fly off to so early?*

My question faded into blackness. A sure sign that Rhys was nowhere near Velaris. Likely not even within the borders of the Night Court. Also not unusual—he'd been visiting our war allies these months to solidify our relationships, build trade, and keep tabs on their post-wall intentions. When my own work allowed it, I often joined him.

I scooped up my plate, draining my tea to the dregs, and padded toward the kitchen. Playing with ice and snow could wait.

Nuala was already preparing for lunch at the worktable, no sign of her twin, Cerridwen, but I waved her off as she made to take my dishes. "I can wash them," I said by way of greeting.

Up to the elbows in making some sort of meat pie, the half-wraith gave me a grateful smile and let me do it. A female of few words, though neither twin could be considered shy. Certainly not when they worked—spied—for both Rhys and Azriel.

"It's still snowing," I observed rather pointlessly, peering out the kitchen window at the garden beyond as I rinsed off the plate, fork, and cup. Elain had already readied the garden for winter, veiling the more delicate bushes and beds with burlap. "I wonder if it'll let up at all."

Nuala laid the ornate lattice crust atop the pie and began pinching the edges together, her shadowy fingers making quick, deft work of it. "It'll be nice to have a white Solstice," she said, voice lilting and yet hushed. Full of whispers and shadows. "Some years, it can be fairly mild."

Right. The Winter Solstice. In a week. I was still new enough to being High Lady that I had no idea what my formal role was to be. If we'd have a High Priestess do some odious ceremony, as Ianthe had done the year before—

A year. Gods, nearly a year since Rhys had called in his bargain, desperate to get me away from the poison of the Spring Court, to save me from my despair. Had he been only a minute later, the Mother knew what would have happened. Where I'd now be.

Snow swirled and eddied in the garden, catching in the brown fibers of the burlap covering the shrubs.

My mate—who had worked so hard and so selflessly, all without hope that I would ever be with him.

We had both fought for that love, bled for it. Rhys had died for it.

I still saw that moment, in my sleeping and waking dreams. How his face had looked, how his chest had not risen, how the bond between us had shredded into ribbons. I still felt it, that hollowness in my chest where the bond had been, where *he* had been. Even now, with that bond again flowing between us like a river of star-flecked night, the echo of its vanishing lingered. Drew me from sleep; drew me from a conversation, a painting, a meal.

Rhys knew exactly why there were nights when I would cling tighter to him, why there were moments in the bright, clear sunshine that I would grip his hand. He knew, because *I* knew why his eyes sometimes turned distant, why he occasionally just blinked at all of us as if not quite believing it and rubbed his chest as if to ease an ache.

Working had helped. Both of us. Keeping busy, keeping focused—I sometimes dreaded the quiet, idle days when all those thoughts snared me at last. When there was nothing but me and my mind, and that memory of Rhys lying dead on the rocky ground, the King of Hybern snapping my father's neck, all those Illyrians blasted out of the sky and falling to earth as ashes.

Perhaps one day, even the work wouldn't be a battlement to keep the memories out.

Mercifully, plenty of work remained for the foreseeable future. Rebuilding Velaris after the attacks from Hybern being only one of many monumental tasks. For other tasks required doing as well—both in Velaris and beyond it: in the Illyrian Mountains, in the Hewn City, in the vastness of the entire Night Court. And then there were the other courts of Prythian. And the new, emerging world beyond.

But for now: Solstice. The longest night of the year. I turned from the window to Nuala, who was still fussing over the edges of her pie. "It's a special holiday here as well, right?" I asked casually. "Not just in Winter and Day." And Spring.

"Oh, yes," Nuala said, stooping over the worktable to examine her pie. Skilled spy—trained by Azriel himself—and master cook. "We love it dearly. It's intimate, warm, lovely. Presents and music and food, sometimes feasting under the starlight . . ." The opposite of the enormous, wild, days-long party I'd been subjected to last year. But—presents.

I had to buy presents for all of them. Not had to, but *wanted* to.

Because all my friends, now my family, had fought and bled and nearly died as well.

I shut out the image that tore through my mind: Nesta, leaning over a wounded Cassian, the two of them prepared to die together against the King of Hybern. My father's corpse behind them.

I rolled my neck. We could use something to celebrate. It had become so rare for all of us to be gathered for more than an hour or two.

Nuala went on, "It's a time of rest, too. And a time to reflect on the darkness—how it lets the light shine."

"Is there a ceremony?"

The half-wraith shrugged. "Yes, but none of us go. It's more for those who wish to honor the light's rebirth, usually by spending the entire night sitting in absolute darkness." A ghost of a smirk. "It's not quite such a novelty for my sister and me. Or for the High Lord."

I tried not to look too relieved that I wouldn't be dragged to a temple for hours as I nodded.

Setting my clean dishes to dry on the little wooden rack beside the sink, I wished Nuala luck on lunch, and headed upstairs to dress. Cerridwen had already laid out clothes, but there was still no sign of Nuala's twin as I donned the heavy charcoal sweater, the tight black leggings, and fleece-lined boots before loosely braiding back my hair.

A year ago, I'd been stuffed into fine gowns and jewels, made to parade in front of a preening court who'd gawked at me like a prized breeding mare.

Here . . . I smiled at the silver-and-sapphire band on my left hand. The ring I'd won for myself from the Weaver in the Wood.

My smile faded a bit.

I could see her, too. See Stryga standing before the King of

Hybern, covered in the blood of her prey, as he took her head in his hands and snapped her neck. Then threw her to his beasts.

I clenched my fingers into a fist, breathing in through my nose, out through my mouth, until the lightness in my limbs faded, until the walls of the room stopped pressing on me.

Until I could survey the blend of personal objects in Rhys's room—our room. It was by no means a small bedroom, but it had lately started to feel . . . tight. The rosewood desk against one wall was covered in papers and books from both of our own dealings; my jewelry and clothes now had to be divided between here and my old bedroom. And then there were the weapons.

Daggers and blades, quivers and bows. I scratched my head at the heavy, wicked-looking *mace* that Rhys had somehow dumped beside the desk without my noticing.

I didn't even want to know. Though I had no doubt Cassian was somehow behind it.

We could, of course, store everything in the pocket between realms, but . . . I frowned at my own set of Illyrian blades, leaning against the towering armoire.

If we got snowed in, perhaps I'd use the day to organize things. Find room for everything. Especially that mace.

It would be a challenge, since Elain still occupied a bedroom down the hall. Nesta had chosen her own home across the city, one that I opted to not think about for too long. Lucien, at least, had taken up residence in an elegant apartment down by the river the day after he'd returned from the battlefields. And the Spring Court.

I hadn't asked Lucien any questions about that visit—to Tamlin.

Lucien hadn't explained the black eye and cut lip, either. He'd only asked Rhys and me if we knew of a place to stay in Velaris, since he did not wish to inconvenience us further by staying at the town house, and did not wish to be isolated at the House of Wind.

He hadn't mentioned Elain, or his proximity to her. Elain had not asked him to stay, or to go. And whether she cared about the bruises on his face, she certainly hadn't let on.

But Lucien had remained, and found ways to keep busy, often gone for days or weeks at a time.

Yet even with Lucien and Nesta staying in their own apartments, the town house was a bit small these days. Even more so if Mor, Cassian, and Azriel stayed over. And the House of Wind was too big, too formal, too far from the city proper. Nice for a night or two, but . . . I loved this house.

It was my home. The first I'd really had in the ways that counted.

And it'd be nice to celebrate the Solstice here. With all of them, crowded as it might be.

I scowled at the pile of papers I had to sort through: letters from other courts, priestesses angling for positions, and kingdoms both human and faerie. I'd put them off for weeks now, and had finally set aside this morning to wade through them.

High Lady of the Night Court, Defender of the Rainbow and the . . . Desk.

I snorted, flicking my braid over a shoulder. Perhaps my Solstice gift to myself would be to hire a personal secretary. Someone to read and answer those things, to sort out what was vital and what could be put aside. Because a little extra time to myself, for *Rhys* . . .

I'd look through the court budget that Rhys never really cared to follow and see what could be moved around for the possibility of such a thing. For him and for me.

I knew our coffers ran deep, knew we could easily afford it and not make so much as a dent in our fortune, but I didn't mind the work. I loved the work, actually. This territory, its people—they were as much my heart as my mate. Until yesterday, nearly every waking hour had been packed with helping them. Until I'd been politely, graciously, told to *go home and enjoy the holiday*.

In the wake of the war, the people of Velaris had risen to the challenge of rebuilding and helping their own. Before I'd even come up with an idea of *how* to help them, multiple societies had been created to assist the city. So I'd volunteered with a handful of them for tasks ranging from finding homes for those displaced by the destruction to visiting families affected during the war to helping those without shelter or belongings ready for winter with new coats and supplies.

All of it was vital; all of it was good, satisfying work. And yet . . . there was more. There was *more* that I could do to help. Personally. I just hadn't figured it out yet.

It seemed I wasn't the only one eager to assist those who'd lost so much. With the holiday, a surge of fresh volunteers had arrived, cramming the public hall near the Palace of Thread and Jewels, where so many of the societies were headquartered. *Your help has been crucial, Lady*, one charity matron had said to me yesterday. *You have been here nearly every day—you have worked yourself to the bone. Take the week off. You've earned it. Celebrate with your mate.*

I'd tried to object, insisting that there were still more coats to hand out, more firewood to be distributed, but the faerie had just motioned to the crowded public hall around us, filled to the brim with volunteers. *We have more help than we know what to do with.*

When I'd tried objecting again, she'd shooed me out the front door. And shut it behind me.

Point taken. The story had been the same at every other organization I'd stopped by yesterday afternoon. *Go home and enjoy the holiday*.

So I had. At least, the first part. The *enjoying* bit, however . . .

Rhys's answer to my earlier inquiry about his whereabouts finally flickered down the bond, carried on a rumble of dark, glittering power. *I'm at Devlon's camp*.

It took you this long to respond? It was a long distance to the Illyrian Mountains, yes, but it shouldn't have taken minutes to hear back.

A sensual huff of laughter. *Cassian was ranting. He didn't take a breath.*

My poor Illyrian baby. We certainly do torment you, don't we?

Rhys's amusement rippled toward me, caressing my innermost self with night-veiled hands. But it halted, vanishing as quickly as it had come. *Cassian's getting into it with Devlon. I'll check in later.* With a loving brush against my senses, he was gone.

I'd get a full report about it soon, but for now . . .

I smiled at the snow waltzing outside the windows.

Rhysand

It was barely nine in the morning, and Cassian was already pissed.

The watery winter sun tried and failed to bleed through the clouds looming over the Illyrian Mountains, the wind a boom across the gray peaks. Snow already lay inches deep over the bustling camp, a vision of what would soon befall Velaris.

It had been snowing when I departed at dawn—perhaps there would be a good coating already on the ground by the time I returned. I hadn't had a chance to ask Feyre about it during our brief conversation down the bond minutes ago, but perhaps she would go for a walk with me through it. Let me show her how the City of Starlight glistened under fresh snow.

Indeed, my mate and city seemed a world away from the hive of activity in the Windhaven camp, nestled in a wide, high mountain pass. Even the bracing wind that swept between the peaks, belying the camp's very name by whipping up dervishes of snow, didn't deter the Illyrians from going about their daily chores.

For the warriors: training in the various rings that opened onto a sheer drop to the small valley floor below, those not present out on patrol. For the males who hadn't made the cut: tending to various trades, whether merchants or blacksmiths or cobblers. And for the females: drudgery.

They didn't see it as such. None of them did. But their required tasks, whether old or young, remained the same: cooking, cleaning, child-rearing, clothes-making, laundry . . . There was honor in such tasks—pride and good work to be found in them. But not when every single one of the females here was *expected* to do it. And if they shirked those duties, either one of the half-dozen camp-mothers or whatever males controlled their lives would punish them.

So it had been, as long as I'd known this place, for my mother's people. The world had been reborn during the war months before, the wall blasted to nothingness, and yet some things did not alter. Especially here, where change was slower than the melting glaciers scattered amongst these mountains. Traditions going back thousands of years, left mostly unchallenged.

Until us. Until now.

Drawing my attention away from the bustling camp beyond the edge of the chalk-lined training rings where we stood, I schooled my face into neutrality as Cassian squared off against Devlon.

"The girls are busy with preparations for the Solstice," the camp-lord was saying, his arms crossed over his barrel chest. "The wives need all the help they can get, if all's to be ready in time. They can practice next week."

I'd lost count of how many variations of this conversation we'd had during the decades Cassian had been pushing Devlon on this.

The wind whipped Cassian's dark hair, but his face remained hard as granite as he said to the warrior who had begrudgingly trained us, "The girls can help their mothers *after* training is done for the day. We'll cut practice down to two hours. The rest of the day will be enough to assist in the preparations."

Devlon slid his hazel eyes to where I lingered a few feet away. "Is it an order?"

I held that gaze. And despite my crown, my power, I tried not to fall back into the trembling child I'd been five centuries ago, that first day Devlon had towered over me and then hurled me into the sparring ring. "If Cassian says it's an order, then it is."

It had occurred to me, during the years we'd been waging this same battle with Devlon and the Illyrians, that I could simply rip into his mind, all their minds, and make them agree. Yet there were some lines I could not, would not cross. And Cassian would never forgive me.

Devlon grunted, his breath a curl of steam. "An hour."

"Two hours," Cassian countered, wings flaring slightly as he held a hard line that I'd been called in this morning to help him maintain.

It had to be bad, then, if my brother had asked me to come. Really damn bad. Perhaps we needed a permanent presence out here, until the Illyrians remembered things like consequences.

PRAISE FOR SARAH J. MAAS'S COURT OF THORNS AND ROSES SERIES

A COURT OF THORNS AND ROSES

"Simply dazzles." —*Booklist*, starred review

"Passionate, violent, sexy and daring. . . . A true page-turner." —*USA Today*

"Suspense, romance, intrigue and action. This is not a book to be missed!" —HuffPost

"Vicious and intoxicating. . . . A dazzling world, complex characters and sizzling romance." —*RT Book Reviews*, Top Pick

"A sexy, action-packed fairytale." —Bustle

A COURT OF MIST AND FURY

"Fiercely romantic, irresistibly sexy and hypnotically magical. A veritable feast for the senses." —*USA Today*

"Hits the spot for fans of dark, lush, sexy fantasy." —*Kirkus Reviews*

"An immersive, satisfying read." —*Publishers Weekly*

"Darkly sexy and thrilling." —Bustle

A COURT OF WINGS AND RUIN

"Fast-paced and explosively action-packed." —*Booklist*

"The plot manages to seduce you with its alluring characters, irresistible world and never-ending action, leaving you craving more." —*RT Book Reviews*

BOOKS BY SARAH J. MAAS

THE COURT OF THORNS AND ROSES SERIES

A Court of Thorns and Roses
A Court of Mist and Fury
A Court of Wings and Ruin
A Court of Frost and Starlight

A Court of Thorns and Roses Colouring Book

THE CRESCENT CITY SERIES

House of Earth and Blood

THE THRONE OF GLASS SERIES

The Assassin's Blade
Throne of Glass
Crown of Midnight
Heir of Fire
Queen of Shadows
Empire of Storms
Tower of Dawn
Kingdom of Ash

The Throne of Glass Colouring Book

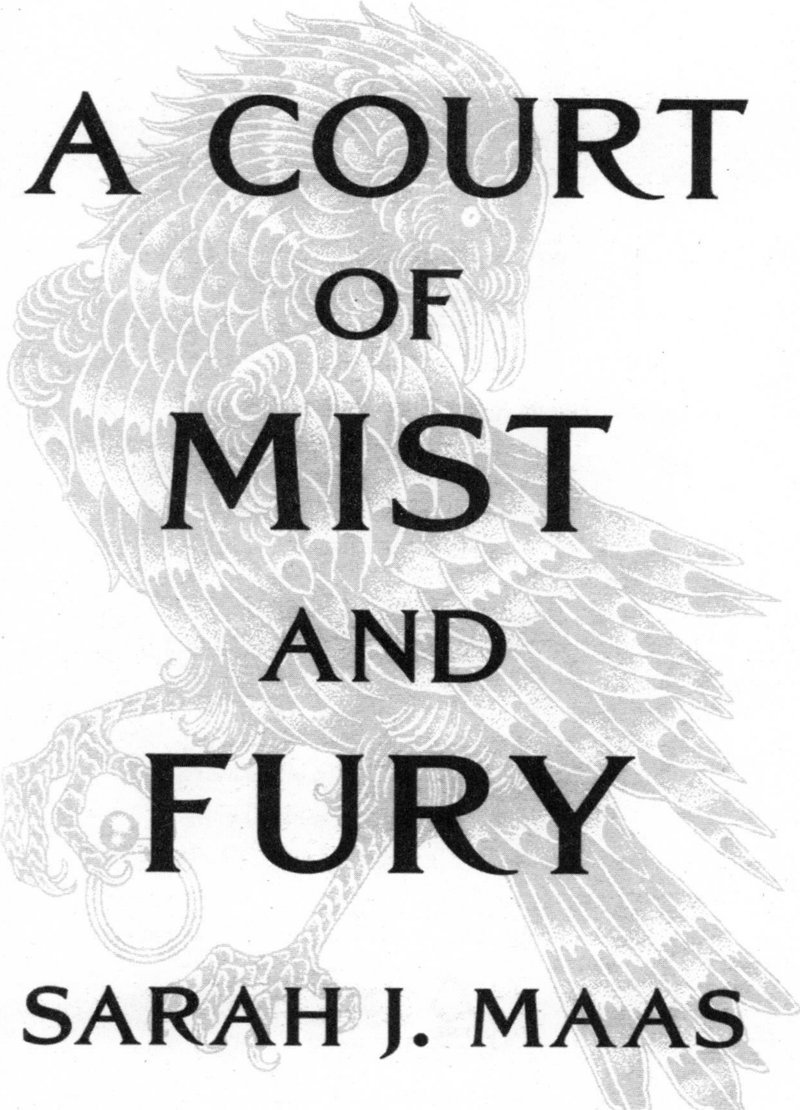

A COURT OF MIST AND FURY

SARAH J. MAAS

BLOOMSBURY PUBLISHING
LONDON • OXFORD • NEW YORK • NEW DELHI • SYDNEY

BLOOMSBURY PUBLISHING
Bloomsbury Publishing Plc
50 Bedford Square, London, WC1B 3DP, UK
29 Earlsfort Terrace, Dublin 2, Ireland

BLOOMSBURY, BLOOMSBURY PUBLISHING and the Diana logo are trademarks of Bloomsbury Publishing Plc

First published in Great Britain 2016
This edition published 2020

A catalogue record for this book is available from the British Library

ISBN: PB: 978-1-5266-1716-3; eBook: 978-1-4088-5789-2

19 20

Typeset by Westchester Publishing Services
Printed and bound in Great Britain by CPI Group (UK) Ltd, Croydon CR0 4YY

MIX
Paper from responsible sources
FSC® C020471
FSC www.fsc.org

For Josh and Annie—
my own Court of Dreams

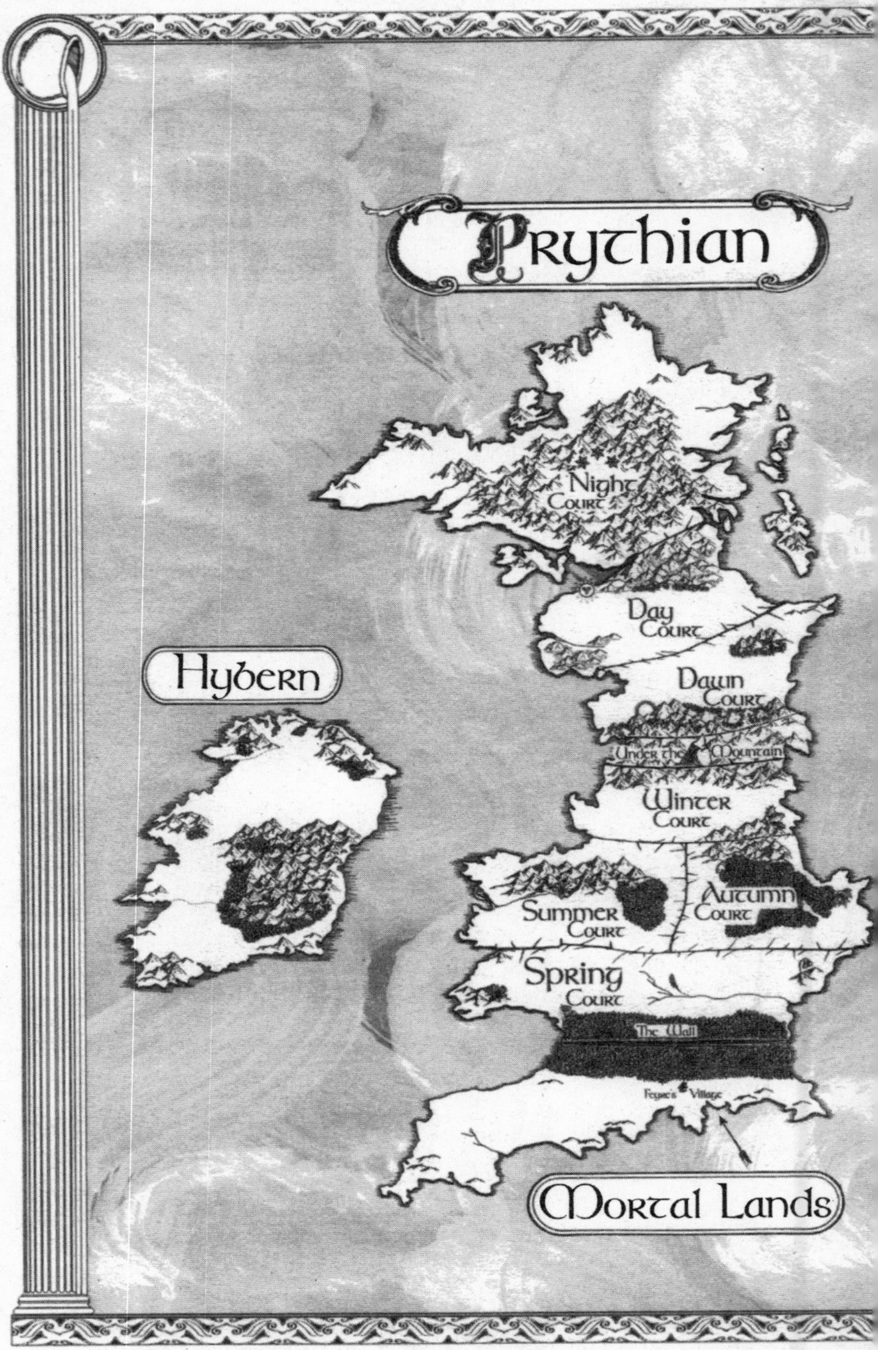
Prythian
Night Court
Day Court
Dawn Court
Under the Mountain
Winter Court
Summer Court
Autumn Court
Spring Court
The Wall
Feyre's Village
Hybern
Mortal Lands

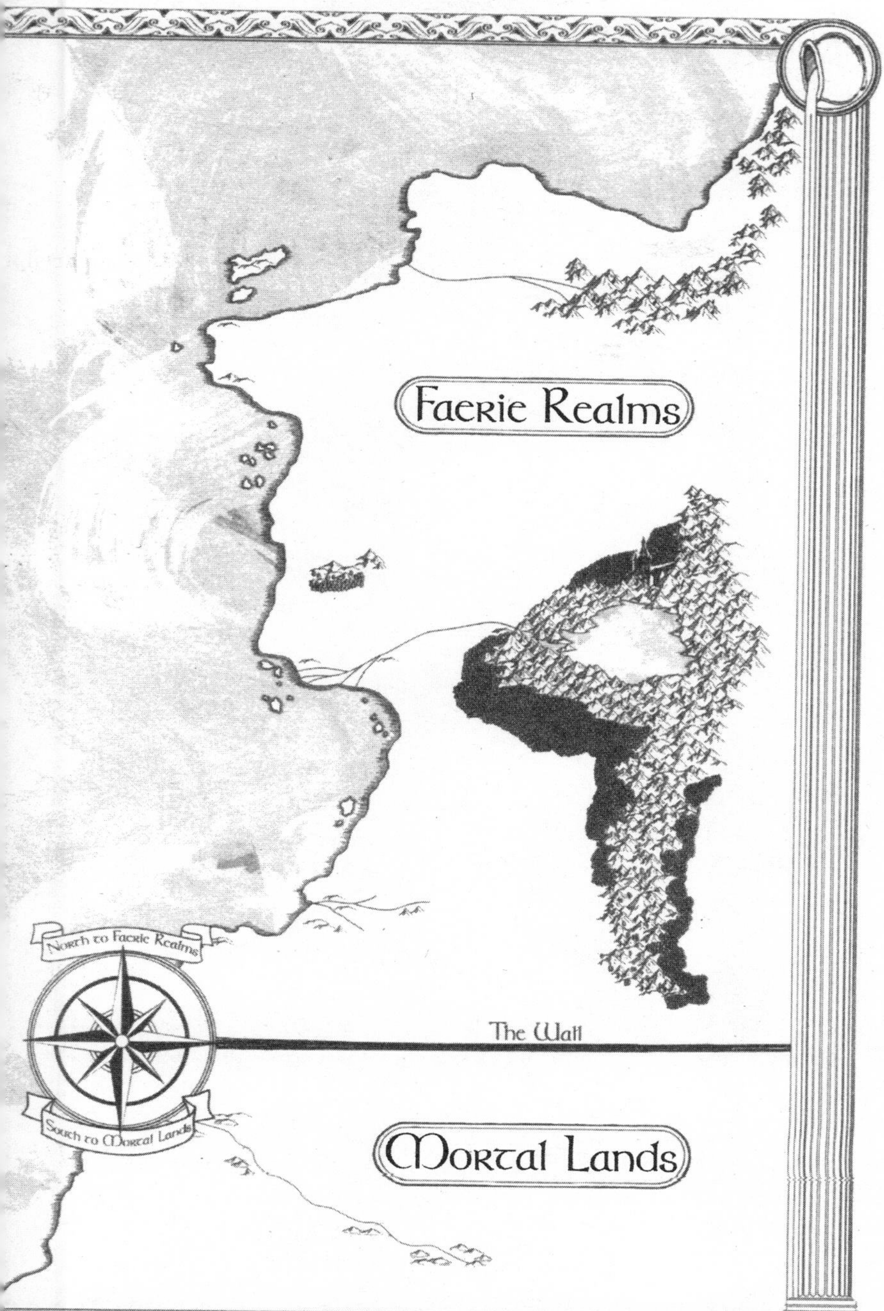
Faerie Realms
North to Faerie Realms
The Wall
South to Mortal Lands
Mortal Lands

A COURT
OF
MIST
AND
FURY

Maybe I'd always been broken and dark inside.

Maybe someone who'd been born whole and good would have put down the ash dagger and embraced death rather than what lay before me.

There was blood everywhere.

It was an effort to keep a grip on the dagger as my blood-soaked hand trembled. As I fractured bit by bit while the sprawled corpse of the High Fae youth cooled on the marble floor.

I couldn't let go of the blade, couldn't move from my place before him.

"Good," Amarantha purred from her throne. "Again."

There was another ash dagger waiting, and another Fae kneeling. Female.

I knew the words she'd say. The prayer she'd recite.

I knew I'd slaughter her, as I'd slaughtered the youth before me.

To free them all, to free Tamlin, I would do it.

I was the butcher of innocents, and the savior of a land.

"Whenever you're ready, lovely Feyre," Amarantha drawled, her deep red hair as bright as the blood on my hands. On the marble.

Murderer. Butcher. Monster. Liar. Deceiver.

I didn't know who I meant. The lines between me and the queen had long since blurred.

My fingers loosened on the dagger, and it clattered to the ground, splattering the spreading pool of blood. Flecks splashed onto my worn boots—remnants of a mortal life so far behind me it might as well have been one of my fever-dreams these few last months.

I faced the female waiting for death, that hood sagging over her head, her lithe body steady. Braced for the end I was to give her, the sacrifice she was to become.

I reached for the second ash dagger atop a black velvet pillow, its hilt icy in my warm, damp hand. The guards yanked off her hood.

I knew the face that stared up at me.

Knew the blue-gray eyes, the brown-gold hair, the full mouth and sharp cheekbones. Knew the ears that had now become delicately arched, the limbs that had been streamlined, limned with power, any human imperfections smoothed into a subtle immortal glow.

Knew the hollowness, the despair, the corruption that leaked from that face.

My hands didn't tremble as I angled the dagger.

As I gripped the fine-boned shoulder, and gazed into that hated face—*my* face.

And plunged the ash dagger into my awaiting heart.

PART ONE

THE HOUSE OF BEASTS

CHAPTER 1

I vomited into the toilet, hugging the cool sides, trying to contain the sounds of my retching.

Moonlight leaked into the massive marble bathing room, providing the only illumination as I was quietly, thoroughly sick.

Tamlin hadn't stirred as I'd jolted awake. And when I hadn't been able to tell the darkness of my chamber from the endless night of Amarantha's dungeons, when the cold sweat coating me felt like the blood of those faeries, I'd hurtled for the bathing room.

I'd been here for fifteen minutes now, waiting for the retching to subside, for the lingering tremors to spread apart and fade, like ripples in a pool.

Panting, I braced myself over the bowl, counting each breath.

Only a nightmare. One of many, asleep and waking, that haunted me these days.

It had been three months since Under the Mountain. Three months of adjusting to my immortal body, to a world struggling to piece itself together after Amarantha had fractured it apart.

I focused on my breathing—in through my nose, out through my mouth. Over and over.

When it seemed like I was done heaving, I eased from the toilet—but didn't go far. Just to the adjacent wall, near the cracked window, where I could see the night sky, where the breeze could caress my sticky face. I leaned my head against the wall, flattening my hands against the chill marble floor. Real.

This was real. I had survived; I'd made it out.

Unless it was a dream—just a fever-dream in Amarantha's dungeons, and I'd awaken back in that cell, and—

I curled my knees to my chest. Real. *Real.*

I mouthed the words.

I kept mouthing them until I could loosen my grip on my legs and lift my head. Pain splintered through my hands—

I'd somehow curled them into fists so tight my nails were close to puncturing my skin.

Immortal strength—more a curse than a gift. I'd dented and folded every piece of silverware I'd touched for three days upon returning here, had tripped over my longer, faster legs so often that Alis had removed any irreplaceable valuables from my rooms (she'd been particularly grumpy about me knocking over a table with an eight-hundred-year-old vase), and had shattered not one, not two, but *five* glass doors merely by accidentally closing them too hard.

Sighing through my nose, I unfolded my fingers.

My right hand was plain, smooth. Perfectly Fae.

I tilted my left hand over, the whorls of dark ink coating my fingers, my wrist, my forearm all the way to the elbow, soaking up the darkness of the room. The eye etched into the center of my palm seemed to watch me, calm and cunning as a cat, its slitted pupil wider than it'd been earlier that day. As if it adjusted to the light, as any ordinary eye would.

I scowled at it.

At whoever might be watching through that tattoo.

I hadn't heard from Rhys in the three months I'd been here. Not a whisper. I hadn't dared ask Tamlin, or Lucien, or anyone—lest it'd somehow summon the High Lord of the Night Court, somehow remind him of the fool's bargain I'd struck Under the Mountain: one week with him every month in exchange for his saving me from the brink of death.

But even if Rhys had miraculously forgotten, I never could. Nor could Tamlin, Lucien, or anyone else. Not with the tattoo.

Even if Rhys, at the end . . . even if he hadn't been exactly an enemy.

To Tamlin, yes. To every other court out there, yes. So few went over the borders of the Night Court and lived to tell. No one really knew what *existed* in the northernmost part of Prythian.

Mountains and darkness and stars and death.

But I hadn't felt like Rhysand's enemy the last time I'd spoken to him, in the hours after Amarantha's defeat. I'd told no one about that meeting, what he'd said to me, what I'd confessed to him.

Be glad of your human heart, Feyre. Pity those who don't feel anything at all.

I squeezed my fingers into a fist, blocking out that eye, the tattoo. I uncoiled to my feet, and flushed the toilet before padding to the sink to rinse out my mouth, then wash my face.

I wished I felt nothing.

I wished my human heart had been changed with the rest of me, made into immortal marble. Instead of the shredded bit of blackness that it now was, leaking its ichor into me.

Tamlin remained asleep as I crept back into my darkened bedroom, his naked body sprawled across the mattress. For a moment, I just admired the powerful muscles of his back, so lovingly traced by the moonlight, his golden hair, mussed with sleep and the fingers I'd run through it while we made love earlier.

For him, I had done this—for him, I'd gladly wrecked myself and my immortal soul.

And now I had eternity to live with it.

I continued to the bed, each step heavier, harder. The sheets were now cool and dry, and I slipped in, curling my back to him, wrapping my arms around myself. His breathing was deep—even. But with my Fae ears . . . sometimes I wondered if I heard his breath catch, only for a heartbeat. I never had the nerve to ask if he was awake.

He never woke when the nightmares dragged me from sleep; never woke when I vomited my guts up night after night. If he knew or heard, he said nothing about it.

I knew similar dreams chased him from his slumber as often as I fled from mine. The first time it had happened, I'd awoken—tried to speak to him. But he'd shaken off my touch, his skin clammy, and had shifted into that beast of fur and claws and horns and fangs. He'd spent the rest of the night sprawled across the foot of the bed, monitoring the door, the wall of windows.

He'd since spent many nights like that.

Curled in the bed, I pulled the blanket higher, craving its warmth against the chill night. It had become our unspoken agreement—not to let Amarantha win by acknowledging that she still tormented us in our dreams and waking hours.

It was easier to not have to explain, anyway. To not have to tell him that though I'd freed him, saved his people and all of Prythian from Amarantha . . . I'd broken myself apart.

And I didn't think even eternity would be long enough to fix me.

CHAPTER 2

"I want to go."

"No."

I crossed my arms, tucking my tattooed hand under my right bicep, and spread my feet slightly further apart on the dirt floor of the stables. "It's been three months. Nothing's happened, and the village isn't even five miles—"

"No." The midmorning sun streaming through the stable doors burnished Tamlin's golden hair as he finished buckling the bandolier of daggers across his chest. His face—ruggedly handsome, exactly as I'd dreamed it during those long months he'd worn a mask—was set, his lips a thin line.

Behind him, already atop his dapple-gray horse, along with three other Fae lord-sentries, Lucien silently shook his head in warning, his metal eye narrowing. *Don't push him*, he seemed to say.

But as Tamlin strode toward where his black stallion had already been saddled, I gritted my teeth and stormed after him. "The village needs all the help it can get."

"And we're still hunting down Amarantha's beasts," he said,

mounting his horse in one fluid motion. Sometimes, I wondered if the horses were just to maintain an appearance of civility—of normalcy. To pretend that he couldn't run faster than them, didn't live with one foot in the forest. His green eyes were like chips of ice as the stallion started into a walk. "I don't have the sentries to spare to escort you."

I lunged for the bridle. "I don't need an escort." My grip tightened on the leather as I tugged the horse to a stop, and the golden ring on my finger—along with the square-cut emerald glittering atop it—flashed in the sun.

It had been two months since Tamlin had proposed—two months of enduring presentations about flowers and clothes and seating arrangements and food. I'd had a small reprieve a week ago, thanks to the Winter Solstice, though I'd traded contemplating lace and silk for selecting evergreen wreaths and garlands. But at least it had been a break.

Three days of feasting and drinking and exchanging small presents, culminating in a long, rather odious ceremony atop the foothills on the longest night to escort us from one year to another as the sun died and was born anew. Or something like that. Celebrating a winter holiday in a place that was permanently entrenched in spring hadn't done much to improve my general lack of festive cheer.

I hadn't particularly listened to the explanations of its origins—and the Fae themselves debated whether it had emerged from the Winter Court or Day Court. Both now claimed it as their holiest holiday. All I really knew was that I'd had to endure two ceremonies: one at sunset to begin that endless night of presents and dancing and drinking in honor of the old sun's death; and one at the following dawn, bleary-eyed and feet aching, to welcome the sun's rebirth.

It was bad enough that I'd been required to stand before the gathered courtiers and lesser faeries while Tamlin made his many toasts and salutes. Mentioning that my birthday had also fallen on that longest night of the year was a fact I'd conveniently forgotten to tell anyone. I'd received enough presents, anyway—and would no doubt receive many, many more on my wedding day. I had little use for so many *things*.

Now, only two weeks stood between me and the ceremony. If I didn't get out of the manor, if I didn't have a day to do *something* other than spend Tamlin's money and be groveled to—

"Please. The recovery efforts are so slow. I could hunt for the villagers, get them food—"

"It's not safe," Tamlin said, again nudging his stallion into a walk. The horse's coat shone like a dark mirror, even in the shade of the stables. "Especially not for you."

He'd said that every time we had this argument; every time I begged him to let me go to the nearby village of High Fae to help rebuild what Amarantha had burned years ago.

I followed him into the bright, cloudless day beyond the stables, the grasses coating the nearby foothills undulating in the soft breeze. "People want to come back, they want a place to *live*—"

"Those same people see you as a blessing—a marker of stability. If something happened to you . . . " He cut himself off as he halted his horse at the edge of the dirt path that would take him toward the eastern woods, Lucien now waiting a few yards down it. "There's no point in rebuilding anything if Amarantha's creatures tear through the lands and destroy it again."

"The wards are up—"

"Some slipped in before the wards were repaired. Lucien hunted down five naga yesterday."

I whipped my head toward Lucien, who winced. He hadn't told me that at dinner last night. He'd *lied* when I'd asked him why he was limping. My stomach turned over—not just at the lie, but . . . naga. Sometimes I dreamed of their blood showering me as I killed them, of their leering serpentine faces while they tried to fillet me in the woods.

Tamlin said softly, "I can't do what I need to if I'm worrying about whether you're safe."

"Of course I'll be safe." As a High Fae, with my strength and speed, I'd stand a good chance of getting away if something happened.

"Please—please just do this for me," Tamlin said, stroking his stallion's thick neck as the beast nickered with impatience. The others had already moved their horses into easy canters, the first of them nearly within the shade of the woods. Tamlin jerked his chin toward the alabaster estate looming behind me. "I'm sure there are things to help with around the house. Or you could paint. Try out that new set I gave you for Winter Solstice."

There was nothing but wedding planning waiting for me in the house, since Alis refused to let me lift a finger to do anything. Not because of who I was to Tamlin, what I was about to become to Tamlin, but . . . because of what I'd done for her, for her boys, for Prythian. All the servants were the same; some still cried with gratitude when they passed me in the halls. And as for painting . . .

"Fine," I breathed. I made myself look him in the eye, made myself smile. "Be careful," I said, and meant it. The thought of him going out there, hunting the monsters that had once served Amarantha . . .

"I love you," Tamlin said quietly.

I nodded, murmuring it back as he trotted to where Lucien still waited, the emissary now frowning slightly. I didn't watch them go.

I took my time retreating through the hedges of the gardens, the spring birds chirping merrily, gravel crunching under my flimsy shoes.

I hated the bright dresses that had become my daily uniform, but didn't have the heart to tell Tamlin—not when he'd bought so many, not when he looked so happy to see me wear them. Not when his words weren't far from the truth. The day I put on my pants and tunics, the day I strapped weapons to myself like fine jewelry, it would send a message far and clear across the lands. So I wore the gowns, and let Alis arrange my hair—if only so it would buy these people a measure of peace and comfort.

At least Tamlin didn't object to the dagger I kept at my side, hanging from a jeweled belt. Lucien had gifted both to me—the dagger during the months before Amarantha, the belt in the weeks after her downfall, when I'd carried the dagger, along with many others, everywhere I went. *You might as well look good if you're going to arm yourself to the teeth*, he'd said.

But even if stability reigned for a hundred years, I doubted I'd ever awaken one morning and not put on the knife.

A hundred years.

I had that—I had centuries ahead of me. Centuries with Tamlin, centuries in this beautiful, quiet place. Perhaps I'd sort myself out sometime along the way. Perhaps not.

I paused before the stairs leading up into the rose-and-ivy-covered house, and peeked toward the right—toward the formal rose garden and the windows just beyond it.

I'd only set foot in that room—my old painting studio—once, when I'd first returned.

And all those paintings, all the supplies, all that blank canvas waiting for me to pour out stories and feelings and dreams . . . I'd hated it.

I'd walked out moments later and hadn't returned since.

I'd stopped cataloging color and feeling and texture, stopped noticing it. I could barely look at the paintings hanging inside the manor.

A sweet, female voice trilled my name from inside the open doors of the manor, and the tightness in my shoulders eased a bit.

Ianthe. The High Priestess, as well as a High Fae noble and childhood friend of Tamlin's, who had taken it upon herself to help plan the wedding festivities.

And who had taken it upon herself to worship me and Tamlin as if we were newly minted gods, blessed and chosen by the Cauldron itself.

But I didn't complain—not when Ianthe knew everyone in the court and outside of it. She'd linger by my side at events and dinners, feeding me details about those in attendance, and was the main reason why I'd survived the merry whirlwind of Winter Solstice. She'd been the one presiding over the various ceremonies, after all—and I'd been more than happy to let her choose what manner of wreaths and garlands should adorn the manor and grounds, what silverware complemented each meal.

Beyond that . . . while Tamlin was the one who paid for my everyday clothes, it was Ianthe's eye that selected them. She was the heart of her people, ordained by the Hand of the Goddess to lead them from despair and darkness.

I was in no position to doubt. She hadn't led me astray yet—and I'd learned to dread the days when she was busy at her own temple on the grounds, overseeing pilgrims and her acolytes. Today, though—yes, spending time with Ianthe was better than the alternative.

I bunched the gauzy skirts of my dawn-pink gown in a hand and ascended the marble steps into the house.

Next time, I promised myself. Next time, I'd convince Tamlin to let me go to the village.

"Oh, we can't let *her* sit next to him. They'd rip each other to shreds, and then we'd have blood ruining the table linens." Beneath her pale, blue-gray hood, Ianthe furrowed her brow, crinkling the tattoo of the various stages of a moon's cycle stamped across it. She scribbled out the name she'd dashed onto one of the seating charts moments before.

The day had turned warm, the room a bit stuffy even with the breeze through the open windows. And yet the heavy hooded robe remained on.

All the High Priestesses wore the billowing, artfully twisted and layered robes—though they certainly were far from matronly. Ianthe's slim waist was on display with a fine belt of sky-blue, limpid stones, each perfectly oval and held in shining silver. And atop her hood sat a matching circlet—a delicate band of silver, with a large stone at its center. A panel of cloth had been folded up beneath the circlet, a built-in swath meant to be pulled over the brow and eyes when she needed to pray, beseech the Cauldron and Mother, or just think.

Ianthe had shown me once what the panel looked like when down: only her nose and full, sensuous mouth visible. The Voice of the Cauldron. I'd found the image unsettling—that merely covering the upper part of her face had somehow turned the bright, cunning female into an effigy, into something Other. Mercifully, she kept it folded back most of the time. Occasionally, she even took the hood off entirely to let the sun play in her long, gently curling golden hair.

Ianthe's silver rings gleamed atop her manicured fingers as she wrote another name down. "It's like a game," she said, sighing through her pert nose. "All these pieces, vying for power or dominance, willing to shed blood, if need be. It must be a strange adjustment for you."

Such elegance and wealth—yet the savagery remained. The High Fae weren't the tittering nobility of the mortal world. No, if they feuded, it *would* end with someone being ripped to bloody ribbons. Literally.

Once, I'd trembled to share breathing space with them.

I flexed my fingers, stretching and contorting the tattoos etched into my skin.

Now I could fight alongside them, against them. Not that I'd tried.

I was too watched—too monitored and judged. Why should the bride of the High Lord learn to fight if peace had returned? That had been Ianthe's reasoning when I'd made the mistake of mentioning it at dinner. Tamlin, to his credit, had seen both sides: I'd learn to protect myself . . . but the rumors would spread.

"Humans aren't much better," I told her at last. And because Ianthe was about the only one of my new companions who didn't look particularly stunned or frightened by me, I tried to make conversation and said, "My sister Nesta would likely fit right in."

Ianthe cocked her head, the sunlight setting the blue stone atop her hood glimmering. "*Will* your mortal kin be joining us?"

"No." I hadn't thought to invite them—hadn't wanted to expose them to Prythian. Or to what I'd become.

She tapped a long, slender finger on the table. "But they live so close to the wall, don't they? If it was important for you to have them here, Tamlin and I could ensure their safe journey." In the hours we'd spent together, I'd told her about the village, and the house my sisters now lived in, about Isaac Hale and Tomas Mandray. I hadn't been able to mention Clare Beddor—or what had happened to her family.

"For all that she'd hold her own," I said, fighting past the memory of that human girl, and what had been done to her, "my sister Nesta detests your kind."

"*Our* kind," Ianthe corrected quietly. "We've discussed this."

I just nodded.

But she went on, "We are old, and cunning, and enjoy using words like blades and claws. Every word from your mouth, every turn of phrase, will be judged—and possibly used against you." As if to soften the warning, she added, "Be on your guard, Lady."

Lady. A nonsense name. No one knew what to call me. I wasn't born High Fae.

I'd been Made—resurrected and given this new body by the seven High Lords of Prythian. I wasn't Tamlin's mate, as far as I knew. There was no mating bond between us—yet.

Honestly . . . Honestly, Ianthe, with her bright gold hair, those teal eyes, elegant features, and supple body, looked more like Tamlin's mate. His equal. A union with Tamlin—a High Lord and a High Priestess—would send a clear message of strength to any possible threats to our lands. And secure the power Ianthe was no doubt keen on building for herself.

Among the High Fae, the priestesses oversaw their ceremonies and rituals, recorded their histories and legends, and advised their lords and ladies in matters great and trivial. I hadn't witnessed any magic from her, but when I'd asked Lucien, he'd frowned and said their magic was drawn from their ceremonies, and could be utterly lethal should they choose it. I'd watched her on the Winter Solstice for any signs of it, marking the way she'd positioned herself so that the rising sun filled her uplifted arms, but there had been no ripple or thrum of power. From her, or the earth beneath us.

I didn't know what I'd really expected from Ianthe—one of the twelve High Priestesses who together governed their sisters across every territory in Prythian. Ancient, celibate, and quiet had been the extent of my expectations, thanks to those whispered mortal legends, when Tamlin had announced that an old friend was soon to occupy and renovate the crumbling temple complex on our lands. But Ianthe had breezed into our house the next morning and those expectations had immediately been trampled. Especially the celibate part.

Priestesses could marry, bear children, and dally as they would. It would dishonor the Cauldron's gift of fertility to lock up their instincts, their inherent female magic in bearing life, Ianthe had once told me.

So while the seven High Lords ruled Prythian from thrones, the twelve High Priestesses reigned from the altars, their children as powerful and respected as any lord's offspring. And Ianthe, the youngest High Priestess in three centuries, remained unmarried, childless, and keen to *enjoy the finest males the land has to offer*.

I often wondered what it was like to be that free and so settled within yourself.

When I didn't respond to her gentle reprimand, she said, "Have you given any thought to what color roses? White? Pink? Yellow? Red—"

"Not red."

I hated that color. More than anything. Amarantha's hair, all that blood, the welts on Clare Beddor's broken body, spiked to the walls of Under the Mountain—

"Russet could be pretty, with all the green . . . But maybe that's too Autumn Court." Again, that finger tapped on the table.

"Whatever color you want." If I were being blunt with myself, I'd admit that Ianthe had become a crutch. But she seemed willing to do it—caring when I couldn't bring myself to.

Yet Ianthe's brows lifted slightly.

Despite being a High Priestess, she and her family had escaped the horrors of Under the Mountain by running. Her father, one of Tamlin's strongest allies amongst the Spring Court and a captain in his forces, had sensed trouble coming and packed off Ianthe, her mother, and two younger sisters to Vallahan, one of the countless faerie territories across the ocean. For fifty years, they'd lived in the foreign court, biding their time while their people were butchered and enslaved.

She hadn't once mentioned it. I knew better than to ask.

"Every element of this wedding sends a message to not only Prythian, but the world beyond," she said. I stifled a sigh. I knew—she'd told me this before. "I know you are not fond of the dress—"

Understatement. I hated the monstrosity of tulle she'd selected. Tamlin had, too—though he'd laughed himself hoarse when I showed him in the privacy of my room. But he'd promised me that though the dress was absurd, the priestess knew what she was doing. I'd wanted to push back about it, hating that though he agreed with me, he had sided with her, but . . . it took more energy than it was worth.

Ianthe went on, "But it makes the right statement. I've spent time amongst enough courts to know how they operate. Trust me in this."

"I do trust you," I said, and waved a hand toward the papers before us. "You know how to do these things. I don't."

Silver tinkled at Ianthe's wrists, so like the bracelets the Children of the Blessed wore on the other side of the wall. I sometimes wondered if those foolish humans had stolen the idea from the High Priestesses of Prythian—if it had been a priestess like Ianthe who had spread such nonsense among humans.

"It's an important moment for me as well," Ianthe said carefully, adjusting the circlet atop her hood. Teal eyes met mine. "You and I are so alike—young, untested amongst these . . . wolves. I am grateful to you, and to Tamlin, to allow me to preside over the ceremony, to be invited to work with this court, be a part of this court. The other High Priestesses do not particularly care for me, nor I for them, but . . . " She shook her head, the hood swaying with her. "Together," she murmured, "the three of us make a formidable unit. Four, if you count Lucien." She snorted. "Not that he particularly wants anything to do with me."

A leading statement.

She often found ways to bring him up, to corner him at events, to touch his elbow or shoulder. He ignored it all. Last week, I'd finally asked him if she'd set her sights on him, and Lucien had merely given me a look, snarling softly, before stalking off. I took that as a yes.

But a match with Lucien would be nearly as beneficial as one with Tamlin: the right hand of a High Lord *and* another High Lord's son . . . Any offspring would be powerful, coveted.

"You know it's . . . hard for him, where females are involved," I said neutrally.

"He has been with *many* females since the death of his lover."

"Perhaps it's different with you—perhaps it'd mean something he's not ready for." I shrugged, searching for the right words. "Perhaps he stays away because of it."

She considered, and I prayed she bought my half lie. Ianthe was ambitious, clever, beautiful, and bold—but I did not think Lucien forgave her, or would ever forgive her, for fleeing during Amarantha's reign. Sometimes I honestly wondered if my friend might rip her throat out for it.

Ianthe nodded at last. "Are you at least excited for the wedding?"

I fiddled with my emerald ring. "It'll be the happiest day of my life."

The day Tamlin had asked me to marry him, I'd certainly felt that way. I'd wept with joy as I told him yes, yes, a thousand times yes, and made love to him in the field of wildflowers where he'd brought me for the occasion.

Ianthe nodded. "The union is Cauldron-blessed. Your survival of the horrors Under the Mountain only proves it."

I caught her glance then—toward my left hand, the tattoos.

It was an effort not to tuck my hand beneath the table.

The tattoo on her brow was of midnight-blue ink—but somehow still fit, still accented the feminine dresses, the bright silver jewelry. Unlike the elegant brutality of mine.

"We could get you gloves," she offered casually.

And that would send another message—perhaps to the person I so desperately hoped had forgotten I existed.

"I'll consider it," I said with a bland smile.

It was all I could do to keep from bolting before the hour was up and Ianthe floated to her own personal prayer room—a gift from Tamlin upon her return—to offer midday thanks to the Cauldron for our land's liberation, my triumph, and Tamlin's ensured dominance over this land.

I sometimes debated asking her to pray for me as well.

To pray that I'd one day learn to love the dresses, and the parties, and my role as a blushing, pretty bride.

I was already in bed when Tamlin entered my room, silent as a stag through a wood. I lifted my head, going for the dagger I kept on the nightstand, but relaxed at the broad shoulders, at the hallway candlelight gilding his tan skin and veiling his face in shadow.

"You're awake?" he murmured. I could hear the frown in his voice. He'd been in his study since dinner, sorting through the pile of paperwork Lucien had dumped on his desk.

"I couldn't sleep," I said, watching his muscles shift as he moved to the bathing room to wash up. I'd been trying to sleep for an hour now—but each time I closed my eyes, my body locked up, the walls of the room pushed in. I'd gone so far as to throw open the windows, but . . . It was going to be a long night.

I lay back on the pillows, listening to the steady, efficient sounds of him preparing for bed. He kept his own quarters, deeming it vital for me to have my own space.

But he slept in here every night. I'd yet to visit his bed, though I wondered if our wedding night would change that. I prayed I wouldn't thrash awake and vomit on the sheets when I didn't recognize where I was, when I didn't know if the darkness was permanent.

Maybe that was why he hadn't pushed the issue yet.

He emerged from the bathing room, slinging off his tunic and shirt, and I propped myself on my elbows to watch as he paused at the edge of the bed.

My attention went right to the strong, clever fingers that unfastened his pants.

Tamlin let out a low snarl of approval, and I bit my bottom lip as he removed his pants, along with his undergarments, revealing the proud, thick length of him. My mouth went dry, and I dragged my gaze up his muscled torso, over the panes of his chest, and then—

"Come here," he growled, so roughly the words were barely discernable.

I pushed back the blankets, revealing my already naked body, and he hissed.

His features turned ravenous while I crawled across the bed and rose up on my knees. I took his face in my hands, the golden skin framed on either side by fingers of ivory and of swirling black, and kissed him.

He held my gaze through the kiss, even as I pushed myself closer, biting back a small noise when he brushed against my stomach.

His callused hands grazed my hips, my waist, then held me there as he lowered his head, seizing the kiss. A brush of his tongue against the seam of my lips had me opening fully for him, and he swept in, claiming me, branding me.

I moaned then, tilting my head back to give him better access. His hands clamped on my waist, then moved—one going to cup my rear, the other sliding between us.

This—this moment, when it was him and me and nothing between our bodies . . .

His tongue scraped the roof of my mouth as he dragged a finger down the center of me, and I gasped, my back arching. "Feyre," he said against my lips, my name like a prayer more devout than any Ianthe had offered up to the Cauldron on that dark solstice morning.

His tongue swept my mouth again, in time to the finger that he slipped inside of me. My hips undulated, demanding more, craving the fullness of him, and his growl reverberated in my chest as he added another finger.

I moved on him. Lightning lashed through my veins, and my focus narrowed to his fingers, his mouth, his body on mine. His palm pushed against the bundle of nerves at the apex of my thighs, and I groaned his name as I shattered.

My head thrown back, I gulped down night-cool air, and then I was being lowered to the bed, gently, delicately, lovingly.

He stretched out above me, his head lowering to my breast, and all it took was one press of his teeth against my nipple before I was clawing at his back, before I hooked my legs around him and he settled between them. This—I needed *this*.

He paused, arms trembling as he held himself over me.

"Please," I gasped out.

He just brushed his lips against my jaw, my neck, my mouth.

"Tamlin," I begged. He palmed my breast, his thumb flicking over my nipple. I cried out, and he buried himself in me with a mighty stroke.

For a moment, I was nothing, no one.

Then we were fused, two hearts beating as one, and I promised myself it always would be that way as he pulled out a few inches, the muscles of his back flexing beneath my hands, and then slammed back into me. Again and again.

I broke and broke against him as he moved, as he murmured my name and told me he loved me. And when that lightning once more filled my veins, my head, when I gasped out his name, his own release found him. I gripped him through each shuddering wave, savoring the weight of him, the feel of his skin, his strength.

For a while, only the rasp of our breathing filled the room.

I frowned as he withdrew at last—but he didn't go far. He stretched out on his side, head propped on a fist, and traced idle circles on my stomach, along my breasts.

"I'm sorry about earlier," he murmured.

"It's fine," I breathed. "I understand."

Not a lie, but not quite true.

His fingers grazed lower, circling my belly button. "You are—you're everything to me," he said thickly. "I need . . . I need you to be all right. To know they can't get to you—can't hurt you anymore."

"I know." Those fingers drifted lower. I swallowed hard and said again, "I know." I brushed his hair back from his face. "But what about you? Who gets to keep you safe?"

His mouth tightened. With his powers returned, he didn't need anyone to protect him, shield him. I could almost see invisible hackles raising—not at me, but at the thought of what he'd been mere months ago: prone to Amarantha's whims, his power barely a trickle compared to the cascade now coursing through him. He took a steadying breath, and leaned to kiss my heart, right between my breasts. It was answer enough.

"Soon," he murmured, and those fingers traveled back to my waist. I almost groaned. "Soon you'll be my wife, and it'll be fine. We'll leave all this behind us."

I arched my back, urging his hand lower, and he chuckled roughly. I didn't quite hear myself speak as I focused on the fingers that obeyed my silent command. "What will everyone call me, then?" He grazed my belly button as he leaned down, sucking the tip of my breast into his mouth.

"Hmm?" he said, and the rumble against my nipple made me writhe.

"Is everyone just going to call me 'Tamlin's wife'? Do I get a . . . title?"

He lifted his head long enough to look at me. "Do you want a title?"

Before I could answer, he nipped at my breast, then licked over the small hurt—licked as his fingers at last dipped between my legs. He stroked lazy, taunting circles. "No," I gasped out. "But I don't want people . . . " Cauldron boil me, his damned *fingers*— "I don't know if I can handle them calling me High Lady."

His fingers slid into me again, and he growled in approval at the wetness between my thighs, both from me and him. "They won't," he said against my skin, positioning himself over me again and sliding down my body, trailing kisses as he went. "There is no such thing as a High Lady."

He gripped my thighs to spread my legs wide, lowering his mouth, and—

"What do you mean, there's no such thing as a High Lady?"

The heat, his touch—all of it stopped.

He looked up from between my legs, and I almost climaxed at the sight of it. But what he said, what he'd implied . . . He kissed the inside of my thigh. "High Lords only take wives. Consorts. There has never been a High Lady."

"But Lucien's mother—"

"She's Lady of the Autumn Court. Not High Lady. Just as you will be Lady of the Spring Court. They will address you as they address her. They will respect you as they respect her." He lowered his gaze back to what was inches away from his mouth.

"So Lucien's—"

"I don't want to hear another male's name on your lips right now," he growled, and lowered his mouth to me.

At the first stroke of his tongue, I stopped arguing.

CHAPTER 3

Tamlin's guilt must have hit him hard, because although he was gone the next day, Lucien was waiting with an offer to inspect the progress on the nearby village.

I hadn't visited in well over a month—I couldn't remember the last time I'd even left the grounds. A few of the villagers had been invited to our Winter Solstice celebrations, but I'd barely managed to do more than greet them, thanks to the size of the crowd.

The horses were already saddled outside the front doors of the stables, and I counted the sentries by the distant gates (four), on either side of the house (two at each corner), and the ones now by the garden through which I'd just exited (two). Though none spoke, their eyes pressed on me.

Lucien made to mount his dapple-gray mare but I cut off his path. "A tumble off your damned horse?" I hissed, shoving his shoulder.

Lucien actually staggered back, the mare nickering in alarm, and I blinked at my outstretched hand. I didn't let myself contemplate what the guards made of it. Before he could say anything, I demanded, "Why did you lie about the naga?"

Lucien crossed his arms, his metal eye narrowing, and shook the red hair from his face.

I had to look away for a moment.

Amarantha's hair had been darker—and her face a creamy white, not at all like the sun-kissed gold of Lucien's skin.

I studied the stables behind him instead. At least it was big, open, the stable hands now off in another wing. I usually had little issue with being inside, which was mostly whenever I was bored enough to visit the horses housed within. Plenty of space to move, to escape. The walls didn't feel too . . . permanent.

Not like the kitchens, which were too low, the walls too thick, the windows not big enough to climb through. Not like the study, with not enough natural light or easy exits. I had a long list in my head of what places I could and couldn't endure at the manor, ranked by precisely how much they made my body lock up and sweat.

"I didn't *lie*," Lucien said tightly. "I technically *did* fall off my horse." He patted his mount's flank. "After one of them tackled me off her."

Such a faerie way of thinking, of lying. "Why?"

Lucien clamped his mouth shut.

"*Why*?"

He just twisted back to the patient mare. But I caught the expression on his face—the . . . *pity* in his eye.

I blurted, "Can we walk instead?"

He slowly turned. "It's three miles."

"And you could run that in a few minutes. I'd like to see if I can keep up."

His metal eye whirred, and I knew what he'd say before he opened his mouth.

"Never mind," I said, heading for my white mare, a sweet-tempered beast, if not a bit lazy and spoiled. Lucien didn't try to convince me otherwise, and kept quiet as we rode from the estate and onto the forest road. Spring, as always, was in full bloom, the breeze laden with lilac, the brush flanking the path rustling with life. No hint of the Bogge, of the naga, of any of the creatures who had once cast such stillness over the wood.

I said to him at last, "I don't want your damn pity."

"It's not pity. Tamlin said I shouldn't tell you—" He winced a bit.

"I'm not made of glass. If the naga attacked you, I *deserve* to know—"

"Tamlin is my High Lord. He gives an order, I follow it."

"You didn't have that mentality when you worked around his commands to send me to see the Suriel." And I'd nearly died.

"I was desperate then. We all were. But now—now we need order, Feyre. We need rules, and rankings, and *order*, if we're going to stand a chance of rebuilding. So what he says goes. I am the *first* one the others look to—I set the example. Don't ask me to risk the stability of this court by pushing back. Not right now. He's giving you as much free rein as he can."

I forced a steady breath to fill my too-tight lungs. "For all that you refuse to interact with Ianthe, you certainly sound a great deal like her."

He hissed, "You have *no idea* how hard it is for him to even let you off the estate grounds. He's under more pressure than you realize."

"I know exactly how much pressure he endures. And I didn't realize I'd become a prisoner."

"You're not—" He clenched his jaw. "That's not how it is and you know it."

"He didn't have any trouble letting me hunt and wander on my own when I was a mere human. When the borders were far less safe."

"He didn't care for you the way he does now. And after what happened Under the Mountain . . . " The words clanged in my head, along my too-tense muscles. "He's terrified. *Terrified* of seeing you in his enemies' hands. And they know it, too—they know all they have to do to own him would be to get ahold of you."

"You think I don't know that? But does he honestly expect me to spend the rest of my life in that manor, overseeing servants and wearing pretty clothes?"

Lucien watched the ever-young forest. "Isn't that what all human women wish for? A handsome faerie lord to wed and shower them with riches for the rest of their lives?"

I gripped the reins of my horse hard enough that she tossed her head. "Good to know you're still a prick, Lucien."

His metal eye narrowed. "Tamlin is a High Lord. You will be his wife. There are traditions and expectations you must uphold. *We* must uphold, in order to present a solid front that is healed from Amarantha and willing to destroy any foes who try to take what is ours again." Ianthe had given me almost the same speech yesterday. "The Tithe is happening soon," he continued, shaking his head, "the first he's called in since . . . her curse." His cringe was barely perceptible. "He gave our people three months to get their affairs in order, and he wanted to wait until the new year had started, but next month, he will demand the Tithe. Ianthe told him it's time—that the people are ready."

He waited, and I wanted to spit at him, because he knew—he *knew* that I didn't know what it was, and wanted me to admit to it. "Tell me," I said flatly.

"Twice a year, usually around the Summer and Winter Solstices, each member of the Spring Court, whether they're High Fae or lesser faerie, must pay a Tithe, dependent on their income and status. It's how we keep the estate running, how we pay for things like sentries and food and servants. In exchange, Tamlin protects them, rules them, helps them when he can. It's a give or take. This year, he pushed the Tithe back by a month—just to grant them that extra time to gather funds, to celebrate. But soon, emissaries from every group, village, or clan will be arriving to pay their Tithes. As Tamlin's wife, you will be expected to sit with him. And if they can't pay . . . You will be expected to sit there while he metes out judgment. It can get ugly. I'll be keeping track of who does and doesn't show up, who doesn't pay. And afterward, if they fail to pay their Tithe within the three days' grace he will officially offer them, he'll be expected to hunt them down. The High Priestesses themselves—Ianthe—grant him sacred hunting rights for this."

Horrible—brutal. I wanted to say it, but the look Lucien was giving me . . . I'd had enough of people judging me.

"So give him time, Feyre," Lucien said. "Let's get through the wedding, then the Tithe next month, and then . . . then we can see about the rest."

"I've given him time," I said. "I can't stay cooped up in the house forever."

"He knows that—he doesn't say it, but he knows it. Trust me. You will forgive him if his family's own slaughter keeps him from being so . . . liberal with your safety. He's lost those he cares for too many times. We all have."

Every word was like fuel added to the simmering pit in my gut. "I don't want to marry a High Lord. I just want to marry *him*."

"One doesn't exist without the other. He is what he is. He will always, *always* seek to protect you, whether you like it or not. Talk to him about it—really talk to him, Feyre. You'll figure it out." Our gazes met. A muscle feathered in Lucien's jaw. "Don't ask me to pick."

"But you're deliberately *not* telling me things."

"He is my High Lord. His word is *law*. We have this one chance, Feyre, to rebuild and make the world as it should be. I will not begin that new world by breaking his trust. Even if you . . ."

"Even if I what?"

His face paled, and he stroked a hand down the mare's cobweb-colored mane. "I was forced to watch as my father butchered the female I loved. My brothers *forced me* to watch."

My heart tightened for him—for the pain that haunted him.

"There was no magic spell, no miracle to bring her back. There were no gathered High Lords to resurrect her. I watched, and she died, and I will *never* forget that moment when I *heard* her heart stop beating."

My eyes burned.

"Tamlin got what I didn't," Lucien said softly, his breathing ragged. "We all heard your neck break. But you got to come back. And I doubt that he will ever forget that sound, either. And he will do everything in his power to protect you from that danger again, even if it means keeping secrets, even if it means sticking to rules you don't like. In this, he will not bend. So don't ask him to—not yet."

I had no words in my head, my heart. Giving Tamlin time, letting him adjust . . . It was the least I could do.

The clamor of construction overtook the chittering of forest birds long before we set foot in the village: hammers on nails, people barking orders, livestock braying.

We cleared the woods to find a village halfway toward being built: pretty little buildings of stone and wood, makeshift structures over the supplies and livestock . . . The only things that seemed absolutely finished were the large well in the center of the town and what looked to be a tavern.

Sometimes, the normalcy of Prythian, the utter similarities between it and the mortal lands, still surprised me. I might as well have been in my own village back home. A much nicer, newer village, but the layout, the focal points . . . All the same.

And I felt like just as much an outsider when Lucien and I rode into the heart of the chaos and everyone paused their laboring or selling or milling about to look at us.

At me.

Like a ripple of silence, the sounds of activity died in even the farthest reaches of the village.

"Feyre Cursebreaker," someone whispered.

Well, that was a new name.

I was grateful for the long sleeves of my riding habit, and the matching gloves I'd tugged on before we'd entered the village border.

Lucien pulled up his mare to a High Fae male who looked like he was in charge of building a house bordering the well fountain. "We came to see if any help was needed," he said, loud enough for everyone to hear. "Our services are yours for the day."

The male blanched. "Gratitude, my lord, but none is needed." His eyes gobbled me up, widening. "The debt is paid."

The sweat on my palms felt thicker, warmer. My mare stomped a hoof on the ruddy dirt street.

"Please," Lucien said, bowing his head gracefully. "The effort to rebuild is our burden to share. It would be our honor."

The male shook his head. "The debt is paid."

And so it went at every place we stopped in the village: Lucien dismounting, asking to help, and polite, reverent rejections.

Within twenty minutes, we were already riding back into the shadows and rustle of the woods.

"Did he let you take me today," I said hoarsely, "so that I'd stop asking to help rebuild?"

"No. I decided to take you myself. For that exact reason. They don't want or need your help. Your presence is a distraction and a reminder of what they went through."

I flinched. "They weren't Under the Mountain, though. I recognized none of them."

Lucien shuddered. "No. Amarantha had . . . camps for them. The nobles and favored faeries were allowed to dwell Under the Mountain. But if the people of a court weren't working to bring in goods and food, they were locked in camps in a network of tunnels beneath the Mountain. Thousands of them, crammed into chambers and tunnels with no light, no air. For fifty years."

"No one ever said—"

"It was forbidden to speak of it. Some of them went mad, started preying on the others when Amarantha forgot to order her guards to feed them. Some formed bands that prowled the camps and did—" He rubbed his brows with a thumb and forefinger. "They did horrible things. Right now, they're trying to remember what it is to be normal—how to *live*."

Bile burned my throat. But this wedding . . . yes, perhaps it would be the start of that healing.

Still, a blanket seemed to smother my senses, drowning out sound, taste, feeling.

"I know you wanted to help," Lucien offered. "I'm sorry."

So was I.

The vastness of my now-unending existence yawned open before me.

I let it swallow me whole.

CHAPTER 4

A few days before the wedding ceremony, guests began arriving, and I was grateful that I'd never be High Lady, never be Tamlin's equal in responsibility and power.

A small, forgotten part of me roared and screamed at that, but . . .

Dinner after dinner, luncheons and picnics and hunts.

I was introduced and passed around, and my face hurt from the smile I kept plastered there day and night. I began looking forward to the wedding just knowing that once it was over, I wouldn't have to be pleasant or talk to anyone or *do* anything for a week. A month. A year.

Tamlin endured it all—in that quiet, near-feral way of his—and told me again and again that the parties were a way to introduce me to his court, to give his people something to celebrate. He assured me that he hated the gatherings as much as I did, and that Lucien was the only one who really enjoyed himself, but . . . I caught Tamlin grinning sometimes. And truthfully, he deserved it, had earned it. And these people deserved it, too.

So I weathered it, clinging to Ianthe when Tamlin wasn't at my side, or, if they were together, letting the two of them lead conversations while I counted down the hours until everyone would leave.

"You should head to bed," Ianthe said, both of us watching the assembled revelers packing the great hall. I'd spotted her by the open doors thirty minutes ago, and was grateful for the excuse to leave the gaggle of Tamlin's friends I'd been stuck talking to. Or *not* talking to. Either they outright stared at me, or they tried so damn hard to come up with common topics. Hunting, mostly. Conversation usually stalled after three minutes.

"I've another hour before I need to sleep," I said. Ianthe was in her usual pale robe, hood up and that circlet of silver with its blue stone atop it.

High Fae males eyed her as they meandered past where we stood by the wood-paneled wall near the main doors, either from awe or lust or perhaps both, their gazes occasionally snagging on me. I knew the wide eyes had nothing to do with my bright green gown or pretty face (fairly bland compared to Ianthe's). I tried to ignore them.

"Are you ready for tomorrow? Is there anything I can do for you?" Ianthe sipped from her glass of sparkling wine. The gown I wore tonight was a gift from her, actually—Spring Court green, she'd called it. Alis had merely lingered while I dressed, unnervingly silent, letting Ianthe claim her usual duties.

"I'm fine." I'd already contemplated how pathetic it would be if I asked her to permanently stay after the wedding. If I revealed that I dreaded her leaving me to this court, these people, until Nynsar—a minor spring holiday to celebrate the end of seeding the fields and to pass out the first flower clippings of the season. Months and months from now. Even having her live at her own temple felt too removed.

Two males that had circled past twice already finally worked up the courage to approach us—her.

I leaned against the wall, the wood digging into my back, as they flanked Ianthe. Handsome, in the way that most of them were handsome, armed with weapons that marked them as two of the High Fae who guarded Tamlin's lands. Perhaps they even worked under Ianthe's father. "Priestess," one said, bowing deep.

By now, I'd become accustomed to people kissing her silver rings and beseeching her for prayers for themselves, their families, or their lovers. Ianthe received it all without that beautiful face shifting in the slightest.

"Bron," she said to the one on her left, brown-haired and tall. "And Hart," she said to the one on her right, black-haired and built a bit more powerfully than his friend. She gave a coy, pretty tilt of her lips that I'd learned meant she was now on the hunt for nighttime companionship. "I haven't seen you two troublemakers in a while."

They parried with flirtatious comments, until the two males began glancing my way.

"Oh," Ianthe said, hood shifting as she turned. "Allow me to introduce Lady Feyre." She lowered her eyes, angling her head in a deep nod. "Savior of Prythian."

"We know," Hart said quietly, bowing with his friend at the waist. "We were Under the Mountain with you."

I managed to incline my head a bit as they straightened. "Congratulations on tomorrow," Bron said, grinning. "A fitting end, eh?"

A fitting end would have been me in a grave, burning in hell.

"The Cauldron," Ianthe said, "has blessed all of us with such a union." The males murmured their agreement, bowing their heads again. I ignored it.

"I have to say," Bron went on, "that trial—with the Middengard Wyrm? Brilliant. One of the most brilliant things I ever saw."

It was an effort not to push myself wholly flat against the wall, not to think about the reek of that mud, the gnashing of those flesh-shredding teeth bearing down upon me. "Thank you."

"Oh, it sounded terrible," Ianthe said, stepping closer as she noted I was no longer wearing that bland smile. She put a hand on my arm. "Such bravery is awe-inspiring."

I was grateful, so pathetically grateful, for the steadying touch. For the squeeze. I knew then that she'd inspire hordes of young Fae females to join her order—not for worshipping their Mother and Cauldron, but to learn how she *lived*, how she could shine so brightly and love herself, move from male to male as if they were dishes at a banquet.

"We missed the hunt the other day," Hart said casually, "so we haven't had a chance to see your talents up close, but I think the High Lord will be stationing us near the estate next month—it'd be an honor to ride with you."

Tamlin wouldn't allow me out with them in a thousand years. And I had no desire to tell them that I had no interest in ever using a bow and arrow again, or hunting anything at all. The hunt I'd been dragged on two days ago had almost been too much. Even with everyone watching me, I hadn't drawn an arrow.

They were still waiting for a reply, so I said, "The honor would be mine."

"Does my father have you two on duty tomorrow, or will you be attending the ceremony?" Ianthe said, putting a distracting hand on Bron's arm. Precisely why I sought her out at events.

Bron answered her, but Hart's eyes lingered on me—on my crossed arms. On my tattooed fingers. He said, "Have you heard from the High Lord at all?"

Ianthe stiffened, and Bron immediately cut his gaze toward my inked flesh.

"No," I said, holding Hart's gaze.

"He's probably running scared now that Tamlin's got his powers back."

"Then you don't know Rhysand very well at all."

Hart blinked, and even Ianthe kept silent. It was probably the most assertive thing I'd said to anyone during these parties.

"Well, we'll take care of him if need be," Hart said, shifting on his feet as I continued to hold his gaze, not bothering to soften my expression.

Ianthe said to him, to me, "The High Priestesses are taking care of it. We will not allow our savior to be treated so ill."

I schooled my face into neutrality. Was *that* why Tamlin had initially sought out Ianthe? To make an alliance? My chest tightened a bit. I turned to her. "I'm going up. Tell Tamlin I'll see him tomorrow."

Tomorrow, because tonight, Ianthe had told me, we'd spend apart. As dictated by their long-held traditions.

Ianthe kissed my cheek, her hood shielding me from the room for a heartbeat. "I'm at your disposal, Lady. Send word if you need anything."

I wouldn't, but I nodded.

As I slipped from the room, I peered toward the front—where Tamlin and Lucien were surrounded by a circle of High Fae males and females. Perhaps not as refined as some of the others, but . . . They had the look of people who had been together a long time, fought at each other's sides. Tamlin's friends. He'd introduced me to them, and I'd immediately forgotten their names. I hadn't tried to learn them again.

Tamlin tipped his head back and laughed, the others howling with him.

I left before he could spot me, easing through the crowded halls until I was in the dim, empty upstairs of the residential wing.

Alone in my bedroom, I realized I couldn't remember the last time I'd truly laughed.

✠

The ceiling pushed down, the large, blunt spikes so hot I could see the heat rippling off them even from where I was chained to the floor. Chained, because I was illiterate and couldn't read the riddle written on the wall, and Amarantha was glad to let me be impaled.

Closer and closer. There was no one coming to save me from this horrible death.

It'd hurt. It'd hurt and be slow, and I'd cry—I might even cry for my mother, who had never cared for me, anyway. I might beg her to save me—

⁜

My limbs flailed as I shot upright in bed, yanking against invisible chains.

I would have lurched for the bathing room had my legs and arms not shook so badly, had I been able to breathe, breathe, *breathe*—

I scanned the bedroom, shuddering. Real—this was real. The horrors, those were nightmares. I was out; I was alive; I was safe.

A night breeze floated through the open windows, ruffling my hair, drying the cold sweat on me. The dark sky beckoned, the stars so dim and small, like speckles of frost.

Bron had sounded as if watching my encounter with the Middengard Wyrm was a sporting match. As if I hadn't been one mistake away from being devoured whole and my bones spat out.

Savior and jester, apparently.

I stumbled to the open window, and pushed it wider, clearing my view of the star-flecked darkness.

I rested my head against the wall, savoring the cool stones.

In a few hours, I'd be married. I'd have my happy ending, whether I deserved it or not. But this land, these people—*they* would have their happy ending, too. The first few steps toward healing. Toward peace. And then things would be fine.

Then I'd be fine.

⁜

I really, truly hated my wedding gown.

It was a monstrosity of tulle and chiffon and gossamer, so unlike the loose gowns I usually wore: the bodice fitted, the neckline curved to plump my breasts, and the skirts . . . The skirts were a sparkling tent, practically floating in the balmy spring air.

No wonder Tamlin had laughed. Even Alis, as she'd dressed me, had hummed to herself, but said nothing. Most likely because Ianthe had personally selected the gown to complement whatever tale she'd weave today—the legend she'd proclaim to the world.

I might have dealt with it all if it weren't for the puffy capped sleeves, so big I could almost see them glinting from the periphery of my vision. My hair had been curled, half up, half down, entwined with pearls and jewels and the Cauldron knew what, and it had taken all my self-control to keep from cringing at the mirror before descending the sweeping stairs into the main hall. My dress hissed and swished with each step.

Beyond the shut patio doors where I paused, the garden had been bedecked in ribbons and lanterns in shades of cream, blush, and sky blue. Three hundred chairs were assembled in the largest courtyard, each seat occupied by Tamlin's court. I'd make my way down the main aisle, enduring their stares, before I reached the dais at the other end—where Tamlin would be waiting.

Then Ianthe would sanction and bless our union right before sundown, as a representative of *all* twelve High Priestesses. She'd hinted that they'd pushed to be present—but through whatever cunning, she'd managed to keep the other eleven away. Either to claim the attention for herself, or to spare me from being hounded by the pack of them. I couldn't tell. Perhaps both.

My mouth went paper-dry as Alis fluffed out the sparkling train of my gown in the shadow of the garden doors. Silk and gossamer rustled and sighed, and I gripped the pale bouquet in my gloved hands, nearly snapping the stems.

Elbow-length silk gloves—to hide the markings. Ianthe had delivered them herself this morning in a velvet-lined box.

"Don't be nervous," Alis clucked, her tree-bark skin rich and flushed in the honey-gold evening light.

"I'm not," I rasped.

"You're fidgeting like my youngest nephew during a haircut." She finished fussing over my dress, shooing away some servants who'd come to spy on me before the ceremony. I pretended I didn't see them, or the glittering, sunset-gilded crowd seated in the courtyard ahead, and toyed with some invisible fleck of dust on my skirts.

"You look beautiful," Alis said quietly. I was fairly certain her thoughts on the dress were the same as my own, but I believed her.

"Thank you."

"And you sound like you're going to your funeral."

I plastered a grin on my face. Alis rolled her eyes. But she nudged me toward the doors as they opened on some immortal wind, lilting music streaming in. "It'll be over faster than you can blink," she promised, and gently pushed me into the last of the sunlight.

Three hundred people rose to their feet and pivoted toward me.

Not since my last trial had so many gathered to watch me, judge me. All in finery so similar to what they'd worn Under the Mountain. Their faces blurred, melded.

Alis coughed from the shadows of the house, and I remembered to start walking, to look toward the dais—

At Tamlin.

The breath knocked from me, and it was an effort to keep going down the stairs, to keep my knees from buckling. He was resplendent in a tunic of green and gold, a crown of burnished laurel leaves gleaming on his head. He'd loosened the grip on his glamour, letting that immortal light and beauty shine through—for me.

My vision narrowed on him, on my High Lord, his wide eyes glistening as I stepped onto the soft grass, white rose petals scattered down it—

And red ones.

Like drops of blood amongst the white, red petals had been sprayed across the path ahead.

I forced my gaze up, to Tamlin, his shoulders back, head high.

So unaware of the true extent of how broken and dark I was inside. How unfit I was to be clothed in white when my hands were so filthy.

Everyone else was thinking it. They had to be.

Every step was too fast, propelling me toward the dais and Tamlin. And toward Ianthe, clothed in dark blue robes tonight, beaming beneath that hood and silver crown.

As if I were good—as if I hadn't murdered two of their kind.

I was a murderer and a liar.

A cluster of red petals loomed ahead—just like that Fae youth's blood had pooled at my feet.

Ten steps from the dais, at the edge of that splatter of red, I slowed.

Then stopped.

Everyone was watching, exactly as they had when I'd nearly died, spectators to my torment.

Tamlin extended a broad hand, brows narrowing slightly. My heart beat so fast, too fast.

I was going to vomit.

Right over those rose petals; right over the grass and ribbons trailing into the aisle from the chairs flanking it.

And between my skin and bones, something thrummed and pounded, rising and pushing, lashing through my blood—

So many eyes, too many eyes, pressed on me, witnesses to every crime I'd committed, every humiliation—

I don't know why I'd even bothered to wear gloves, why I'd let Ianthe convince me.

The fading sun was too hot, the garden too hedged in. As inescapable as the vow I was about to make, binding me to him forever, shackling him to my broken and weary soul. The thing inside me was roiling now, my body shaking with the building force of it as it hunted for a way out—

Forever—I would never get better, never get free of myself, of that dungeon where I'd spent three months—

"Feyre," Tamlin said, his hand steady as he continued to reach for mine. The sun sank past the lip of the western garden wall; shadows pooled, chilling the air.

If I turned away, they'd start talking, but I couldn't make the last few steps, couldn't, couldn't, couldn't—

I was going to fall apart, right there, right then—and they'd see precisely how ruined I was.

Help me, help me, help me, I begged someone, anyone. Begged Lucien, standing in the front row, his metal eye fixed on me. Begged Ianthe, face serene and patient and lovely within that hood. *Save me—please, save me. Get me out. End this.*

Tamlin took a step toward me—concern shading those eyes.

I retreated a step. *No.*

Tamlin's mouth tightened. The crowd murmured. Silk streamers laden with globes of gold faelight twinkled into life above and around us.

Ianthe said smoothly, "Come, Bride, and be joined with your true love. Come, Bride, and let good triumph at last."

Good. I was not good. I was *nothing*, and my soul, my eternal soul, was damned—

I tried to get my traitorous lungs to draw air so I could voice the word. *No—no.*

But I didn't have to say it.

Thunder cracked behind me, as if two boulders had been hurled against each other.

People screamed, falling back, a few vanishing outright as darkness erupted.

I whirled, and through the night drifting away like smoke on a wind, I found Rhysand straightening the lapels of his black jacket.

"Hello, Feyre darling," he purred.

CHAPTER 5

I shouldn't have been surprised. Not when Rhysand liked to make a spectacle of everything. And found pissing off Tamlin to be an art form.

But there he was.

Rhysand, High Lord of the Night Court, now stood beside me, darkness leaking from him like ink in water.

He angled his head, his blue-black hair shifting with the movement. Those violet eyes sparkled in the golden faelight as they fixed on Tamlin, as he held up a hand to where Tamlin and Lucien and their sentries had their swords half-drawn, sizing up how to get me out of the way, how to bring him down—

But at the lift of that hand, they froze.

Ianthe, however, was backing away slowly, face drained of color.

"What a pretty little wedding," Rhysand said, stuffing his hands into his pockets as those many swords remained in their sheaths. The remaining crowd was pressing back, some climbing over seats to get away.

Rhys looked me over slowly, and clicked his tongue at my silk gloves. Whatever had been building beneath my skin went still and cold.

"Get the hell out," growled Tamlin, stalking toward us. Claws ripped from his knuckles.

Rhys clicked his tongue again. "Oh, I don't think so. Not when I need to call in my bargain with Feyre darling."

My stomach hollowed out. No—no, not now.

"You try to break the bargain, and you know what will happen," Rhys went on, chuckling a bit at the crowd still falling over themselves to get away from him. He jerked his chin toward me. "I gave you three months of freedom. You could at least look happy to see me."

I was shaking too badly to say anything. Rhys's eyes flickered with distaste.

The expression was gone when he faced Tamlin again. "I'll be taking her now."

"Don't you dare," Tamlin snarled. Behind him, the dais was empty; Ianthe had vanished entirely. Along with most of those in attendance.

"Was I interrupting? I thought it was over." Rhys gave me a smile dripping with venom. He knew—through that bond, through whatever magic was between us, he'd known I was about to say no. "At least, Feyre seemed to think so."

Tamlin snarled, "Let us finish the ceremony—"

"Your High Priestess," Rhys said, "seems to think it's over, too."

Tamlin stiffened as he looked over a shoulder to find the altar empty. When he faced us again, the claws had eased halfway back into his hands. "Rhysand—"

"I'm in no mood to bargain," Rhys said, "even though I could work it to my advantage, I'm sure." I jolted at the caress of his hand on my elbow. "Let's go."

I didn't move.

"Tamlin," I breathed.

Tamlin took a single step toward me, his golden face turning sallow, but remained focused on Rhys. "Name your price."

"Don't bother," Rhys crooned, linking elbows with me. Every spot of contact was abhorrent, unbearable.

He'd take me back to the Night Court, the place Amarantha had supposedly modeled Under the Mountain after, full of depravity and torture and death—

"Tamlin, please."

"Such dramatics," Rhysand said, tugging me closer.

But Tamlin didn't move—and those claws were wholly replaced by smooth skin. He fixed his gaze on Rhys, his lips pulling back in a snarl. "If you hurt her—"

"I know, I know," Rhysand drawled. "I'll return her in a week."

No—no, Tamlin couldn't be making those kinds of threats, not when they meant he was letting me go. Even Lucien was gaping at Tamlin, his face white with fury and shock.

Rhys released my elbow only to slip a hand around my waist, pressing me into his side as he whispered in my ear, "Hold on."

Then darkness roared, a wind tearing me this way and that, the ground falling away beneath me, the world gone around me. Only Rhys remained, and I hated him as I clung to him, I hated him with my entire heart—

Then the darkness vanished.

I smelled jasmine first—then saw stars. A sea of stars flickering beyond glowing pillars of moonstone that framed the sweeping view of endless snowcapped mountains.

"Welcome to the Night Court," was all Rhys said.

It was the most beautiful place I'd ever seen.

Whatever building we were in had been perched atop one of the gray-stoned mountains. The hall around us was open to the elements, no windows to be found, just towering pillars and gossamer curtains, swaying in that jasmine-scented breeze.

It must be some magic, to keep the air warm in the dead of winter. Not to mention the altitude, or the snow coating the mountains, mighty winds sending veils of it drifting off the peaks like wandering mist.

Little seating, dining, and work areas dotted the hall, sectioned off with those curtains or lush plants or thick rugs scattered over the moonstone floor. A few balls of light bobbed on the breeze, along with colored-glass lanterns dangling from the arches of the ceiling.

Not a scream, not a shout, not a plea to be heard.

Behind me, a wall of white marble arose, broken occasionally by open doorways leading into dim stairwells. The rest of the Night Court had to be through there. No wonder I couldn't hear anyone screaming, if they were all inside.

"This is my private residence," Rhys said casually. His skin was darker than I'd remembered—golden now, rather than pale.

Pale, from being locked Under the Mountain for fifty years. I scanned him, searching for any sign of the massive, membranous wings—the ones he'd admitted he loved flying with. But there was none. Just the male, smirking at me.

And that too-familiar expression— "How *dare* you—"

Rhys snorted. "I certainly missed *that* look on your face." He stalked closer, his movements feline, those violet eyes turning subdued—lethal. "You're welcome, you know."

"For *what*?"

Rhys paused less than a foot away, sliding his hands into his pockets. The night didn't seem to ripple from him here—and he appeared, despite his perfection, almost normal. "For saving you when asked."

I stiffened. "I didn't ask for anything."

His stare dipped to my left hand.

Rhys gave no warning as he gripped my arm, snarling softly, and tore off the glove. His touch was like a brand, and I flinched, yielding a step, but he held firm until he'd gotten both gloves off. "I heard you begging someone, *anyone*, to rescue you, to get you out. I heard you say *no*."

"I didn't say anything."

He turned my bare hand over, his hold tightening as he examined the eye he'd tattooed. He tapped the pupil. Once. Twice. "I heard it loud and clear."

I wrenched my hand away. "Take me back. *Now.* I didn't want to be stolen away."

He shrugged. "What better time to take you here? Maybe Tamlin didn't notice you were about to reject him in front of his entire court—maybe you can now simply blame it on me."

"You're a bastard. You made it clear enough that I had . . . reservations."

"Such gratitude, as always."

I struggled to get down a single, deep breath. "What do you want from me?"

"*Want*? I want you to say thank you, first of all. Then I want you to take off that hideous dress. You look . . . " His mouth cut a cruel line. "You look exactly like the doe-eyed damsel he and that simpering priestess want you to be."

"You don't know anything about me. Or us."

Rhys gave me a knowing smile. "Does Tamlin? Does he ever ask you why you hurl your guts up every night, or why you can't go into certain rooms or see certain colors?"

I froze. He might as well have stripped me naked. "Get the hell out of my head."

Tamlin had horrors of his own to endure, to face down.

"Likewise." He stalked a few steps away. "You think I enjoy being awoken every night by visions of you puking? You send everything right down that bond, and I don't appreciate having a front-row seat when I'm trying to sleep."

"Prick."

Another chuckle. But I wouldn't ask about what he meant—about the bond between us. I wouldn't give him the satisfaction of looking curious. "As for what else I want from you . . . " He gestured to the house behind us. "I'll tell you tomorrow at breakfast. For now, clean yourself up. Rest." That rage flickered in his eyes again at the dress, the hair. "Take the stairs on the right, one level down. Your room is the first door."

"Not a dungeon cell?" Perhaps it was foolish to reveal that fear, to suggest it to him.

But Rhys half turned, brows lifting. "You are not a prisoner, Feyre. You made a bargain, and I am calling it in. You will be my guest here, with the privileges of a member of my household. None of my subjects are going to touch you, hurt you, or so much as think ill of you here."

My tongue was dry and heavy as I said, "And where might those subjects be?"

"Some dwell here—in the mountain beneath us." He angled his head. "They're forbidden to set foot in this residence. They know they'd be signing their death warrant." His eyes met mine, stark and clear, as if he could sense the panic, the shadows creeping in. "Amarantha wasn't very creative," he said with quiet wrath. "My court beneath this mountain has long been feared, and she chose to replicate it by violating the space of Prythian's sacred mountain. So, yes: there's a court beneath this mountain—the court your Tamlin now expects me to be subjecting you to. I preside over it every now and then, but it mostly rules itself."

"When—when are you taking me there?" If I had to go underground, had to see those kinds of horrors again . . . I'd beg him—*beg* him not to take me. I didn't care how pathetic it made me. I'd lost any sort of qualms about what lines I'd cross to survive.

"I'm not." He rolled his shoulders. "This is my home, and the court beneath it is my . . . occupation, as you mortals call it. I do not like for the two to overlap very often."

My brows rose slightly. "'You mortals'?"

Starlight danced along the planes of his face. "Should I consider you something different?"

A challenge. I shoved away my irritation at the amusement again tugging at the corners of his lips, and instead said, "And the other denizens of your court?" The Night Court territory was enormous—bigger than any other in Prythian. And all around us were those empty, snow-blasted mountains. No sign of towns, cities, or anything.

"Scattered throughout, dwelling as they wish. Just as *you* are now free to roam where you wish."

"I wish to roam home."

Rhys laughed, finally sauntering toward the other end of the hall, which ended in a veranda open to the stars. "I'm willing to accept your thanks at any time, you know," he called to me without looking back.

Red exploded in my vision, and I couldn't breathe fast enough, couldn't *think* above the roar in my head. One heartbeat, I was staring after him—the next, I had my shoe in a hand.

I hurled it at him with all my strength.

All my considerable, immortal strength.

I barely saw my silk slipper as it flew through the air, fast as a shooting star, so fast that even a High Lord couldn't detect it as it neared—

And slammed into his head.

Rhys whirled, a hand rising to the back of his head, his eyes wide.

I already had the other shoe in my hand.

Rhys's lip pulled back from his teeth. "*I dare you.*" Temper—he had to be in some mood today to let his temper show this much.

Good. That made two of us.

I flung my other shoe right at his head, as swift and hard as the first one.

His hand snatched up, grabbing the shoe mere inches from his face.

Rhys hissed and lowered the shoe, his eyes meeting mine as the silk dissolved to glittering black dust in his fist. His fingers unfurled, the last of the sparkling ashes blowing into oblivion, and he surveyed my hand, my body, my face.

"Interesting," he murmured, and continued on his way.

I debated tackling him and pummeling that face with my fists, but I wasn't stupid. I was in his home, on top of a mountain in the middle of absolutely nowhere, it seemed. No one would be coming to rescue me—no one was even here to witness my screaming.

So I turned toward the doorway he'd indicated, heading for the dim stairwell beyond.

I'd nearly reached it, not daring to breathe too loudly, when a bright, amused female voice said behind me—far away, from wherever Rhys had gone to at the opposite end of the hall, "So, *that* went well."

Rhys's answering snarl sent my footsteps hurrying.

My room was . . . a dream.

After scouring it for any sign of danger, after learning every exit and entrance and hiding place, I paused in the center to contemplate where, exactly, I'd be staying for the next week.

Like the upstairs living area, its windows were open to the brutal world beyond—no glass, no shutters—and sheer amethyst curtains fluttered in that unnatural, soft breeze. The large bed was a creamy white-and-ivory concoction, with pillows and blankets and throws for days, made more inviting by the twin golden lamps beside it. An armoire and dressing table occupied a wall, framed by those glass-less windows. Across the room, a chamber with a porcelain sink and toilet lay behind an arched wooden door, but the bath . . .

The bath.

Occupying the other half of the bedroom, my bathtub was actually a pool, hanging right off the mountain itself. A pool for soaking or enjoying myself. Its far edge seemed to disappear into nothing, the water flowing silently off the side and into the night beyond. A narrow ledge on the adjacent wall was lined with fat, guttering candles whose glow gilded the dark, glassy surface and wafting tendrils of steam.

Open, airy, plush, and . . . calm.

This room was fit for an empress. With the marble floors, silks, velvets, and elegant details, only an empress could have afforded it. I tried not to think what Rhys's chamber was like, if this was how he treated his guests.

Guest—not prisoner.

Well . . . the room proved it.

I didn't bother barricading the door. Rhys could likely fly in if he felt like it. And I'd seen him shatter a faerie's mind without so much as blinking. I doubted a bit of wood would keep out that horrible power.

I again surveyed the room, my wedding gown hissing on the warm marble floors.

I peered down at myself.

You look ridiculous.

Heat itched along my cheeks and neck.

It didn't excuse what he'd done. Even if he'd . . . saved me—I choked on the word—from having to refuse Tamlin. Having to explain.

Slowly, I tugged the pins and baubles from my curled hair, piling them onto the dressing table. The sight was enough for me to grit my teeth, and I swept them into an empty drawer instead, slamming it shut so hard the mirror above the table rattled. I rubbed at my scalp, aching from the weight of the curls and prodding pins. This afternoon, I'd imagined Tamlin pulling them each from my hair, a kiss for every pin, but now—

I swallowed against the burning in my throat.

Rhys was the least of my concerns. Tamlin had seen the hesitation, but had he understood that I was about to say no? Had Ianthe? I had to tell him. Had to explain that there couldn't be a wedding, not for a while yet. Maybe I'd wait until the mating bond snapped into place, until I knew for sure it couldn't be some mistake, that . . . that I was worthy of him.

Maybe wait until he, too, had faced the nightmares stalking him. Relaxed his grip on things a bit. On me. Even if I understood his need to protect, that fear of losing me . . . Perhaps I should explain everything when I returned.

But—so many people had seen it, seen *me* hesitate—

My lower lip trembled, and I began unbuttoning my gown, then tugged it off my shoulders.

I let it slide to the ground in a sigh of silk and tulle and beading, a deflated soufflé on the marble floor, and took a large step out of it. Even my undergarments were ridiculous: frothy scraps of lace, intended solely for Tamlin to admire—and then tear into ribbons.

I snatched up the gown, storming to the armoire and shoving it inside. Then I stripped off the undergarments and chucked them in as well.

My tattoo was stark against the pile of white silk and lace. My breath came faster and faster. I didn't realize I was weeping until I grabbed the first bit of fabric within the armoire I could find—a set of turquoise nightclothes—and shoved my feet into the ankle-length pants, then pulled the short-sleeved matching shirt over my head, the hem grazing the top of my navel. I didn't care that it had to be some Night Court fashion, didn't care that they were soft and warm.

I climbed into that big, fluffy bed, the sheets smooth and welcoming, and could barely draw a breath steady enough to blow out the lamps on either side.

But as soon as darkness enveloped the room, my sobs hit in full—great, gasping pants that shuddered through me, flowing out the open windows, and into the starry, snow-kissed night.

Rhys hadn't been lying when he said I was to join him for breakfast.

My old handmaidens from Under the Mountain appeared at my door just past dawn, and I might not have recognized the pretty, dark-haired twins had they not acted like they knew me. I had never seen them as anything but shadows, their faces always concealed in impenetrable night. But here—or perhaps without Amarantha—they were fully corporeal.

Nuala and Cerridwen were their names, and I wondered if they'd ever told me. If I had been too far gone Under the Mountain to even care.

Their gentle knock hurled me awake—not that I'd slept much during the night. For a heartbeat, I wondered why my bed felt so much softer, why mountains flowed into the distance and not spring grasses and hills . . . and then it all poured back in. Along with a throbbing, relentless headache.

After the second, patient knock, followed by a muffled explanation through the door of who they were, I scrambled out of bed to let them in. And after a miserably awkward greeting, they informed me that breakfast would be served in thirty minutes, and I was to bathe and dress.

I didn't bother to ask if Rhys was behind that last order, or if it was their recommendation based on how grim I no doubt looked, but they laid out some clothes on the bed before leaving me to wash in private.

I was tempted to linger in the luxurious heat of the bathtub for the rest of the day, but a faint, endlessly amused *tug* cleaved through my headache. I knew that tug—had been called by it once before, in those hours after Amarantha's downfall.

I ducked to my neck in the water, scanning the clear winter sky, the fierce wind whipping the snow off those nearby peaks . . . No sign of him, no pound of beating wings. But the tug yanked again in my mind, my gut—a summoning. Like some servant's bell.

Cursing him soundly, I scrubbed myself down and dressed in the clothes they'd left.

And now, striding across the sunny upper level as I blindly followed the source of that insufferable tug, my magenta silk shoes near-silent on the moonstone floors, I wanted to shred the clothes off me, if only for the fact that they belonged to this place, to *him*.

My high-waisted peach pants were loose and billowing, gathered at the ankles with velvet cuffs of bright gold. The long sleeves of the matching top were made of gossamer, also gathered at the wrists, and the top itself hung just to my navel, revealing a sliver of skin as I walked.

Comfortable, easy to move in—to run. Feminine. Exotic. Thin enough that, unless Rhysand planned to torment me by casting me into the winter wasteland around us, I could assume I wasn't leaving the borders of whatever warming magic kept the palace so balmy.

At least the tattoo, visible through the sheer sleeve, wouldn't be out of place here. But—the clothes were still a part of this court.

And no doubt part of some game he intended to play with me.

At the very end of the upper level, a small glass table gleamed like quicksilver in the heart of a stone veranda, set with three chairs and laden with fruits, juices, pastries, and breakfast meats. And in one of those chairs . . . Though Rhys stared out at the sweeping view, the snowy mountains near-blinding in the sunlight, I knew he'd sensed my arrival from the moment I cleared the stairwell at the other side of the hall. Maybe since I'd awoken, if that tug was any indication.

I paused between the last two pillars, studying the High Lord lounging at the breakfast table and the view he surveyed.

"I'm not a dog to be summoned," I said by way of greeting.

Slowly, Rhys looked over his shoulder. Those violet eyes were vibrant in the light, and I curled my fingers into fists as they swept from my head to my toes and back up again. He frowned at whatever he found lacking. "I didn't want you to get lost," he said blandly.

My head throbbed, and I eyed the silver teapot steaming in the center of the table. A cup of tea . . . "I thought it'd always be dark here," I said, if only to not look quite as desperate for that life-giving tea so early in the morning.

"We're one of the three Solar Courts," he said, motioning for me to sit with a graceful twist of his wrist. "Our nights are far more beautiful, and our sunsets and dawns are exquisite, but we do adhere to the laws of nature."

I slid into the upholstered chair across from him. His tunic was unbuttoned at the neck, revealing a hint of the tanned chest beneath. "And do the other courts choose not to?"

"The nature of the Seasonal Courts," he said, "is linked to their High Lords, whose magic and will keeps them in eternal spring, or winter, or fall, or summer. It has always been like that—some sort of strange stagnation. But the Solar Courts—Day, Dawn, and Night—are of a more . . . symbolic nature. We might be powerful, but even we cannot alter the sun's path or strength. Tea?"

The sunlight danced along the curve of the silver teapot. I kept my eager nod to a restrained dip of my chin. "But you will find," Rhysand went on, pouring a cup for me, "that our nights are more spectacular—so spectacular that some in my territory even awaken at sunset and go to bed at dawn, just to live under the starlight."

I splashed some milk in the tea, watching the light and dark eddy together. "Why is it so warm in here, when winter is in full blast out there?"

"Magic."

"Obviously." I set down my teaspoon and sipped, nearly sighing at the rush of heat and smoky, rich flavor. "But *why*?"

Rhys scanned the wind tearing through the peaks. "You heat a house in the winter—why shouldn't I heat this place as well? I'll admit I don't know *why* my predecessors built a palace fit for the Summer Court in the middle of a mountain range that's mildly warm at best, but who am I to question?"

I took a few more sips, that headache already lessening, and dared to scoop some fruit onto my plate from a glass bowl nearby.

He watched every movement. Then he said quietly, "You've lost weight."

"You're prone to digging through my head whenever you please," I said, stabbing a piece of melon with my fork. "I don't see why you're surprised by it."

His gaze didn't lighten, though that smile again played about his sensuous mouth, no doubt his favorite mask. "Only occasionally will I do that. And I can't help it if *you* send things down the bond."

I contemplated refusing to ask as I had done last night, but . . . "How does it work—this *bond* that allows you to see into my head?"

He sipped from his own tea. "Think of the bargain's bond as a bridge between us—and at either end is a door to our respective minds. A shield. My innate talents allow me to slip through the mental shields of anyone I wish, with or without that bridge—unless they're very, very strong, or have trained extensively to keep those shields tight. As a human, the gates to your mind were flung open for me to stroll through. As Fae . . . " A little shrug. "Sometimes, you unwittingly have a shield up—sometimes, when emotion seems to be running strong, that shield vanishes. And sometimes, when those shields are open, you might as well be standing at the gates to your mind, shouting your thoughts across the bridge to me. Sometimes I hear them; sometimes I don't."

I scowled, clenching my fork harder. "And how often do you just rifle through my mind when my shields are down?"

All amusement faded from his face. "When I can't tell if your nightmares are real threats or imagined. When you're about to be married and you silently beg anyone to help you. Only when you drop your mental shields and unknowingly blast those things down the bridge. And to answer your question before you ask, yes. Even with your shields up, I could get through them if I wished. You could train, though—learn how to shield against someone like me, even with the bond bridging our minds and my own abilities."

I ignored the offer. Agreeing to do anything with him felt too permanent, too accepting of the bargain between us. "What do you want with me? You said you'd tell me here. So tell me."

Rhys leaned back in his chair, folding powerful arms that even the fine clothes couldn't hide. "For this week? I want you to learn how to read."

CHAPTER 6

Rhysand had mocked me about it once—had asked me while we were Under the Mountain if forcing me to learn how to read would be my personal idea of torture.

"No, thank you," I said, gripping my fork to keep from chucking it at his head.

"You're going to be a High Lord's wife," Rhys said. "You'll be expected to maintain your own correspondences, perhaps even give a speech or two. And the Cauldron knows what else he and Ianthe will deem appropriate for you. Make menus for dinner parties, write thank-you letters for all those wedding gifts, embroider sweet phrases on pillows . . . It's a necessary skill. And, you know what? Why don't we throw in shielding while we're at it. Reading and shielding—fortunately, you can practice them together."

"They are *both* necessary skills," I said through my teeth, "but *you* are not going to teach me."

"What else are you going to do with yourself? Paint? How's that going these days, Feyre?"

"What the hell does it even matter to you?"

"It serves various purposes of mine, of course."

"What. Purposes."

"You'll have to agree to work with me to find out, I'm afraid."

Something sharp poked into my hand.

I'd folded the fork into a tangle of metal.

When I set it down on the table, Rhys chuckled. "Interesting."

"You said that last night."

"Am I not allowed to say it twice?"

"That's not what I was implying and you know it."

His gaze raked over me again, as if he could see beneath the peach fabric, through the skin, to the shredded soul beneath. Then it drifted to the mangled fork. "Has anyone ever told you that you're rather strong for a High Fae?"

"Am I?"

"I'll take that as a no." He popped a piece of melon into his mouth. "Have you tested yourself against anyone?"

"Why would I?" I was enough of a wreck as it was.

"Because you were resurrected and reborn by the combined powers of the seven High Lords. If I were you, I'd be curious to see if anything else transferred to me during that process."

My blood chilled. "Nothing else *transferred* to me."

"It'd just be rather . . . interesting," he smirked at the word, "if it did."

"It didn't, and I'm not going to learn to read or shield with you."

"Why? From spite? I thought you and I got past that Under the Mountain."

"Don't get me started on what you did to me Under the Mountain."

Rhys went still.

As still as I'd ever seen him, as still as the death now beckoning in those eyes. Then his chest began to move, faster and faster.

Across the pillars towering behind him, I could have sworn the shadow of great wings spread.

He opened his mouth, leaning forward, and then stopped. Instantly, the shadows, the ragged breathing, the intensity were gone, the lazy grin returning. "We have company. We'll discuss this later."

"No, we won't." But quick, light footsteps sounded down the hall, and then she appeared.

If Rhysand was the most beautiful male I'd ever seen, she was his female equivalent.

Her bright, golden hair was tied back in a casual braid, and the turquoise of her clothes—fashioned like my own—offset her sun-kissed skin, making her practically glow in the morning light.

"Hello, hello," she chirped, her full lips parting in a dazzling smile as her rich brown eyes fixed on me.

"Feyre," Rhys said smoothly, "meet my cousin, Morrigan. Mor, meet the lovely, charming, and open-minded Feyre."

I debated splashing my tea in his face, but Mor strode toward me. Each step was assured and steady, graceful, and . . . grounded. Merry but alert. Someone who didn't need weapons—or at least bother to sheath them at her side. "I've heard so much about you," she said, and I got to my feet, awkwardly jutting out my hand.

She ignored it and grabbed me into a bone-crushing hug. She smelled like citrus and cinnamon. I tried to relax my taut muscles as she pulled away and grinned rather fiendishly. "You look like you were getting under Rhys's skin," she said, strutting to her seat between us. "Good thing I came along. Though I'd enjoy seeing Rhys's balls nailed to the wall."

Rhys slid incredulous eyes at her, his brows lifting.

I hid the smile that tugged on my lips. "It's—nice to meet you."

"Liar," Mor said, pouring herself some tea and loading her plate. "You want nothing to do with us, do you? And wicked Rhys is making you sit here."

"You're . . . perky today, Mor," Rhys said.

Mor's stunning eyes lifted to her cousin's face. "Forgive me for being excited about having company *for once*."

"You could be attending your own duties," he said testily. I clamped my lips tighter together. I'd never seen Rhys . . . irked.

"I needed a break, and you told me to come here whenever I liked, so what better time than now, when you brought my new friend to finally meet me?"

I blinked, realizing two things at once: one, she actually meant what she said; two, hers was the female voice I'd heard speak last night, mocking Rhys for our squabble. *So,* that *went well*, she'd teased. As if there were any other alternative, any chance of pleasantness, where he and I were concerned.

A new fork had appeared beside my plate, and I picked it up, only to spear a piece of melon. "You two look nothing alike," I said at last.

"Mor is my cousin in the *loosest* definition," he said. She grinned at him, devouring slices of tomato and pale cheese. "But we were raised together. She's my only surviving family."

I didn't have the nerve to ask what happened to everyone else. Or remind myself whose father was responsible for the lack of family at my own court.

"And as my only remaining relative," Rhys went on, "Mor believes she is entitled to breeze in and out of my life as she sees fit."

"So grumpy this morning," Mor said, plopping two muffins onto her plate.

"I didn't see you Under the Mountain," I found myself saying, hating those last three words more than anything.

"Oh, I wasn't there," she said. "I was in—"

"Enough, Mor," he said, his voice laced with quiet thunder.

It was a trial in itself not to sit up at the interruption, not to study them too closely.

Rhysand set his napkin on the table and rose. "Mor will be here for the rest of the week, but by all means, do not feel that you have to oblige her with your presence." Mor stuck out her tongue at him. He rolled his eyes, the most human gesture I'd ever seen him make. He examined my plate. "Did you eat enough?" I nodded. "Good. Then let's go." He inclined his head toward the pillars and swaying curtains behind him. "Your first lesson awaits."

Mor sliced one of the muffins in two in a steady sweep of her knife. The angle of her fingers, her wrist, indeed confirmed my suspicions that weapons weren't at all foreign to her. "If he pisses you off, Feyre, feel free to shove him over the rail of the nearest balcony."

Rhys gave her a smooth, filthy gesture as he strode down the hall.

I eased to my feet when he was a good distance ahead. "Enjoy your breakfast."

"Whenever you want company," she said as I edged around the table, "give a shout." She probably meant that literally.

I merely nodded and trailed after the High Lord.

I agreed to sit at the long, wooden table in a curtained-off alcove only because he had a point. Not being able to read had almost cost me my life Under the Mountain. I'd be damned if I let it become a weakness again, his personal agenda or no. And as for shielding . . . I'd be a damned fool not to take up the offer to learn from him. The thought of anyone, especially Rhys, sifting through the mess in my mind, taking information about the Spring Court, about the people I loved . . . I'd never allow it. Not willingly.

But it didn't make it any easier to endure Rhysand's presence at the wooden table. Or the stack of books piled atop it.

"I know my alphabet," I said sharply as he laid a piece of paper in front of me. "I'm not that stupid." I twisted my fingers in my lap, then pinned my restless hands under my thighs.

"I didn't say you were stupid," he said. "I'm just trying to determine where we should begin." I leaned back in the cushioned seat. "Since you've refused to tell me a thing about how much you know."

My face warmed. "Can't you hire a tutor?"

He lifted a brow. "Is it that hard for you to even try in front of me?"

"You're a High Lord—don't you have better things to do?"

"Of course. But none as enjoyable as seeing you squirm."

"You're a real bastard, you know that?"

Rhys huffed a laugh. "I've been called worse. In fact, I think you've called me worse." He tapped the paper in front of him. "Read that."

A blur of letters. My throat tightened. "I can't."

"Try."

The sentence had been written in elegant, concise print. His writing, no doubt. I tried to open my mouth, but my spine locked up. "What, *exactly*, is your stake in all this? You said you'd tell me if I worked with you."

"I didn't specify *when* I'd tell you." I peeled back from him as my lip curled. He shrugged. "Maybe I resent the idea of you letting those sycophants and war-mongering fools in the Spring Court make you feel inadequate. Maybe I indeed enjoy seeing you squirm. Or maybe—"

"I get it."

Rhys snorted. "Try to read it, Feyre."

Prick. I snatched the paper to me, nearly ripping it in half in the process. I looked at the first word, sounding it out in my head. "Y-you . . ." The next I figured out with a combination of my silent pronunciation and logic. "Look . . ."

"Good," he murmured.

"I didn't ask for your approval."

Rhys chuckled.

"Ab . . . Absolutely." It took me longer than I wanted to admit to figure that out. The next word was even worse. "De . . . Del . . . "

I deigned to glance at him, brows raised.

"Delicious," he purred.

My brows now knotted. I read the next two words, then whipped my face toward him. "*You look absolutely delicious today, Feyre*?! That's what you wrote?"

He leaned back in his seat. As our eyes met, sharp claws caressed my mind and his voice whispered inside my head: *It's true, isn't it?*

I jolted back, my chair groaning. "*Stop that*!"

But those claws now dug in—and my entire body, my heart, my lungs, my *blood* yielded to his grip, utterly at his command as he said, *The fashion of the Night Court suits you.*

I couldn't move in my seat, couldn't even blink.

This is what happens when you leave your mental shields down. Someone with my sort of powers could slip inside, see what they want, and take your mind for themselves. Or they could shatter it. I'm currently standing on the threshold of your mind . . . but if I were to go deeper, all it would take would be half a thought from me and who you are, your very self, would be wiped away.

Distantly, sweat slid down my temple.

You should be afraid. You should be afraid of this, and you should be thanking the gods-damned Cauldron that in the past three months, no one with my sorts of gifts has run into you. Now shove me out.

I couldn't. Those claws were everywhere—digging into every thought, every piece of self. He pushed a little harder.

Shove. Me. Out.

I didn't know where to begin. I blindly pushed and slammed myself into him, into those claws that were everywhere, as if I were a top loosed in a circle of mirrors.

His laughter, low and soft, filled my mind, my ears. *That way, Feyre.*

In answer, a little open path gleamed inside my mind. The road out.

It'd take me forever to unhook each claw and shove the mass of his presence out that narrow opening. If I could wash it away—

A wave. A wave of self, of *me*, to sweep all of him out—

I didn't let him see the plan take form as I rallied myself into a cresting wave and struck.

The claws loosened—reluctantly. As if letting me win this round. He merely said, "Good."

My bones, my breath and blood, they were mine again. I slumped in my seat.

"Not yet," he said. "Shield. Block me out so I can't get back in."

I already wanted to go somewhere quiet and sleep for a while—

Claws at that outer layer of my mind, stroking—

I imagined a wall of adamant snapping down, black as night and a foot thick. The claws retracted a breath before the wall sliced them in two.

Rhys was grinning. "Very nice. Blunt, but nice."

I couldn't help myself. I grabbed the piece of paper and shredded it in two, then four. "You're a pig."

"Oh, most definitely. But look at you—you read that whole sentence, kicked me out of your mind, *and* shielded. Excellent work."

"Don't condescend to me."

"I'm not. You're reading at a level far higher than I anticipated."

That burning returned to my cheeks. "But mostly illiterate."

"At this point, it's about practice, spelling, and more practice. You could be reading novels by Nynsar. And if you keep adding to those shields, you might very well keep me out entirely by then, too."

Nynsar. It'd be the first Tamlin and his court would celebrate in nearly fifty years. Amarantha had banned it on a whim, along with a few other small, but beloved Fae holidays that she had deemed *unnecessary*. But Nynsar was months from now. "Is it even possible—to truly keep you out?"

"Not likely, but who knows how deep that power goes? Keep practicing and we'll see what happens."

"And will I still be bound by this bargain at Nynsar, too?"

Silence.

I pushed, "After—after what happened—" I couldn't mention specifics on what had occurred Under the Mountain, what he'd done for me during that fight with Amarantha, what he'd done after— "I think we can agree that I owe you nothing, and you owe *me* nothing."

His gaze was unflinching.

I blazed on, "Isn't it enough that we're all free?" I splayed my tattooed hand on the table. "By the end, I thought you were different, thought that it was all a mask, but taking me away, *keeping* me here . . . " I shook my head, unable to find the words vicious enough, clever enough to convince him to end this bargain.

His eyes darkened. "I'm not your enemy, Feyre."

"Tamlin says you are." I curled the fingers of my tattooed hand into a fist. "Everyone else says you are."

"And what do *you* think?" He leaned back in his chair again, but his face was grave.

"You're doing a damned good job of making me agree with them."

"Liar," he purred. "Did you even tell your friends about *what I did to you* Under the Mountain?"

So that comment at breakfast *had* gotten under his skin. "I don't want to talk about anything related to that. With you or them."

"No, because it's so much easier to pretend it never happened and let them coddle you."

"I don't *let* them coddle me—"

"They had you wrapped up like a present yesterday. Like you were *his* reward."

"So?"

"So?" A flicker of rage, then it was gone.

"I'm ready to be taken home," I merely said.

"Where you'll be cloistered for the rest of your life, especially once you start punching out heirs. I can't wait to see what Ianthe does when she gets her hands on *them*."

"You don't seem to have a particularly high opinion of her."

Something cold and predatory crept into his eyes. "No, I can't say that I do." He pointed to a blank piece of paper. "Start copying the alphabet. Until your letters are perfect. And every time you get through a round, lower and raise your shield. Until *that* is second nature. I'll be back in an hour."

"What?"

"Copy. The. Alphabet. Until—"

"I heard what you said." Prick. Prick, prick, *prick*.

"Then get to work." Rhys uncoiled to his feet. "And at least have the decency to only call me a prick when your shields are back up."

He vanished into a ripple of darkness before I realized that I'd let the wall of adamant fade again.

✢

By the time Rhys returned, my mind felt like a mud puddle.

I spent the entire hour doing as I'd been ordered, though I'd flinched at every sound from the nearby stairwell: quiet steps of servants, the flapping of sheets being changed, someone humming a beautiful and winding melody. And beyond that, the chatter of birds that dwelled in the unnatural warmth of the mountain or in the many potted citrus trees. No sign of my impending torment. No sentries, even, to monitor me. I might as well have had the entire place to myself.

Which was good, as my attempts to lower and raise that mental shield often resulted in my face being twisted or strained or pinched.

"Not bad," Rhys said, peering over my shoulder.

He'd appeared moments before, a healthy distance away, and if I hadn't known better, I might have thought it was because he didn't want to startle me. As if he'd known about the time Tamlin had crept up behind me, and panic had hit me so hard I'd knocked him on his ass with a punch to his stomach. I'd blocked it out—the shock on Tam's face, how *easy* it had been to take him off his feet, the humiliation of having my stupid terror so out in the open . . .

Rhys scanned the pages I'd scribbled on, sorting through them, tracking my progress.

Then, a scrape of claws inside my mind—that only sliced against black, glittering adamant.

I threw my lingering will into that wall as the claws pushed, testing for weak spots . . .

"Well, well," Rhysand purred, those mental claws withdrawing. "Hopefully I'll be getting a good night's rest at last, if you can manage to keep the wall up while you sleep."

I dropped the shield, sent a word blasting down that mental bridge between us, and hauled the walls back up. Behind it, my mind wobbled like jelly. I needed a nap. Desperately.

"Prick I might be, but look at you. Maybe we'll get to have some fun with our lessons after all."

I was still scowling at Rhys's muscled back as I kept a healthy ten steps behind him while he led me through the halls of the main building, the sweeping mountains and blisteringly blue sky the only witnesses to our silent trek.

I was too drained to demand where we were now going, and he didn't bother explaining as he led me up, up—until we entered a round chamber at the top of a tower.

A circular table of black stone occupied the center, while the largest stretch of uninterrupted gray stone wall was covered in a massive map of our world. It had been marked and flagged and pinned, for whatever reasons I couldn't tell, but my gaze drifted to the windows throughout the room—so many that it felt utterly exposed, breathable. The perfect home, I supposed, for a High Lord blessed with wings.

Rhys stalked to the table, where there was another map spread, figurines dotting its surface. A map of Prythian—and Hybern.

Every court in our land had been marked, along with villages and cities and rivers and mountain passes. Every court . . . but the Night Court.

The vast, northern territory was utterly blank. Not even a mountain range had been etched in. Strange, likely part of some strategy I didn't understand.

I found Rhysand watching me—his raised brows enough to make me shut my mouth against the forming question.

"Nothing to ask?"

"No."

A feline smirk danced on his lips, but Rhys jerked his chin toward the map on the wall. "What do you see?"

"Is this some sort of way of convincing me to embrace my reading lessons?" Indeed, I couldn't decipher any of the writing, only the shapes of things. Like the wall, its massive line bisecting our world.

"Tell me what you see."

"A world divided in two."

"And do you think it should remain that way?"

I whipped my head toward him. "My family—" I halted on the word. I should have known better than to admit to having a family, that I cared for them—

"Your human family," Rhys finished, "would be deeply impacted if the wall came down, wouldn't they? So close to its border . . . If they're lucky, they'll flee across the ocean before it happens."

"*Will* it happen?"

Rhysand didn't break my stare. "Maybe."

"Why?"

"Because war is coming, Feyre."

CHAPTER 7

War.

The word clanged through me, freezing my veins.

"Don't invade," I breathed. I'd get on my knees for this. I'd crawl if I had to. "Don't invade—please."

Rhys cocked his head, his mouth tightening. "You truly think I'm a monster, even after everything."

"Please," I gasped out. "They're defenseless, they won't stand a chance—"

"I'm not going to invade the mortal lands," he said too quietly.

I waited for him to go on, glad for the spacious room, the bright air, as the ground started to slide out from beneath me.

"Put your damn shield up," he growled.

I looked inward, finding that invisible wall had dropped again. But I was so tired, and if war was coming, if my family—

"Shield. *Now*."

The raw command in his voice—the voice of the High Lord of the Night Court—had me acting on instinct, my exhausted mind building the wall brick by brick. Only when it'd ensconced my mind once more did he speak, his eyes softening almost imperceptibly. "Did you think it would end with Amarantha?"

"Tamlin hasn't said . . . " And why would he tell me? But there were so many patrols, so many meetings I wasn't allowed to attend, such . . . tension. He had to know. I needed to ask him—demand why he hadn't told me—

"The King of Hybern has been planning his campaign to reclaim the world south of the wall for over a hundred years," Rhys said. "Amarantha was an experiment—a forty-nine-year test, to see how easily and how long a territory might fall and be controlled by one of his commanders."

For an immortal, forty-nine years was nothing. I wouldn't have been surprised to hear he'd been planning this for far longer than a century. "Will he attack Prythian first?"

"Prythian," Rhys said, pointing to the map of our massive island on the table, "is all that stands between the King of Hybern and the continent. He wants to reclaim the human lands there—perhaps seize the faerie lands, too. If anyone is to intercept his conquering fleet before it reaches the continent, it would be us."

I slid into one of the chairs, my knees wobbling so badly I could hardly keep upright.

"He will seek to remove Prythian from his way swiftly and thoroughly," Rhys continued. "And shatter the wall at some point in the process. There are already holes in it, though mercifully small enough to make it difficult to swiftly pass his armies through. He'll want to bring the whole thing down—and likely use the ensuing panic to his advantage."

Each breath was like swallowing glass. "When—when is he going to attack?" The wall had held steady for five centuries, and even then, those damned holes had allowed the foulest, hungriest Fae beasts to sneak through and prey on humans. Without that wall, if Hybern was indeed to launch an assault on the human world . . . I wished I hadn't eaten such a large breakfast.

"That is the question," he said. "And why I brought you here."

I lifted my head to meet his stare. His face was drawn, but calm.

"I don't know when or where he plans to attack Prythian," Rhys went on. "I don't know who his allies here might be."

"He'd have allies here?"

A slow nod. "Cowards who would bow and join him, rather than fight his armies again."

I could have sworn a whisper of darkness spread along the floor behind him. "Did . . . did you fight in the War?"

For a moment, I thought he wouldn't answer. But then Rhys nodded. "I was young—by our standards, at least. But my father had sent aid to the mortal-faerie alliance on the continent, and I convinced him to let me take a legion of our soldiers." He sat in the chair beside mine, gazing vacantly at the map. "I was stationed in the south, right where the fighting was thickest. The slaughter was . . . " He chewed on the inside of his cheek. "I have no interest in ever seeing full-scale slaughter like that again."

He blinked, as if clearing the horrors from his mind. "But I don't think the King of Hybern will strike that way—not at first. He's too smart to waste his forces here, to give the continent time to rally while we fight him. If he makes his move to destroy Prythian and the wall, it'll be through stealth and trickery. To weaken us. Amarantha was the first part of that plan. We now have several untested High Lords, broken courts with High Priestesses angling for control like wolves around a carcass, and a people who have realized how powerless they might truly be."

"Why are you telling me this?" I said, my voice thin, scratchy. It made no sense—none—that he would reveal his suspicions, his fears.

And Ianthe—she might be ambitious, but she was Tamlin's friend. *My* friend, of sorts. Perhaps the only ally we'd have against the other High Priestesses, Rhys's personal dislike for her or no . . .

"I am telling you for two reasons," he said, his face so cold, so calm, that it unnerved me as much as the news he was delivering. "One, you're . . . close to Tamlin. He has men—but he also has long-existing ties to Hybern—"

"He'd *never* help the king—"

Rhys held up a hand. "I want to know if Tamlin is willing to fight with us. If he can use those connections to our advantage. As he and I have strained relations, you have the pleasure of being the go-between."

"He doesn't inform me of those things."

"Perhaps it's time he did. Perhaps it's time you insisted." He examined the map, and I followed where his gaze landed. On the wall within Prythian—on the small, vulnerable mortal territory. My mouth went dry.

"What is your other reason?"

Rhys looked me up and down, assessing, weighing. "You have a skill set that I need. Rumor has it you caught a Suriel."

"It wasn't that hard."

"I've tried and failed. Twice. But that's a discussion for another day. I saw you trap the Middengard Wyrm like a rabbit." His eyes twinkled. "I need you to help me. To use those skills of yours to track down what I need."

"What *do* you need? Whatever was tied to my reading and shielding, I'm guessing?"

"You'll learn of that later."

I didn't know why I'd even bothered to ask. "There have to be at least a dozen other hunters more experienced and skilled—"

"Maybe there are. But you're the only one I trust."

I blinked. "I could betray you whenever I feel like it."

"You could. But you won't." I gritted my teeth, and was about to say something vicious when he added, "And then there's the matter of your powers."

"I don't have any powers." It came out so fast that there was no chance of it sounding like anything but denial.

Rhys crossed his legs. "Don't you? The strength, the speed . . . If I didn't know better, I'd say you and Tamlin were doing a very good job of pretending you're normal. That the powers you're displaying aren't usually the first indications among our kind that a High Lord's son might become his Heir."

"I'm not a High Lord."

"No, but you were given life by all seven of us. Your very essence is tied to us, born of us. What if we gave you more than we expected?" Again, that gaze raked over me. "What if you could stand against us—hold your own, a High Lady?"

"There are no High Ladies."

His brows furrowed, but he shook his head. "We'll talk about *that* later, too. But yes, Feyre—there *can* be High Ladies. And perhaps you aren't one of them, but . . . what if you were something similar? What if you were able to wield the power of seven High Lords at once? What if you could blend into darkness, or shape-shift, or freeze over an entire room—an entire army?"

The winter wind on the nearby peaks seemed to howl in answer. That thing I'd felt under my skin . . .

"Do you understand what that might mean in an oncoming war? Do you understand how it might destroy you if you don't learn to control it?"

"One, stop asking so many rhetorical questions. Two, we don't know if I *do* have these powers—"

"You do. But you need to start mastering them. To learn what you inherited from us."

"And I suppose you're the one to teach me, too? Reading and shielding aren't enough?"

"While you hunt with me for what I need, yes."

I began shaking my head. "Tamlin won't allow it."

"Tamlin isn't your keeper, and you know it."

"I'm his subject, and he is my High Lord—"

"You are *no one's subject.*"

I went rigid at the flash of teeth, the smoke-like wings that flared out.

"I will say this once—and only once," Rhysand purred, stalking to the map on the wall. "You can be a pawn, be someone's reward, and spend the rest of your immortal life bowing and scraping and pretending you're less than him, than Ianthe, than any of us. If you want to pick that road, then fine. A shame, but it's your choice." The shadow of wings rippled again. "But I know you—more than you realize, I think—and I don't believe for one damn minute that you're remotely fine with being a pretty trophy for someone who sat on his ass for nearly fifty years, then sat on his ass while you were shredded apart—"

"Stop it—"

"Or," he plowed ahead, "you've got another choice. You can master whatever powers we gave to you, and make it count. You can play a role in this war. Because war is coming one way or another, and do not try to delude yourself that any of the Fae will give a shit about your family across the wall when our whole territory is likely to become a charnel house."

I stared at the map—at Prythian, and that sliver of land at its southern base.

"You want to save the mortal realm?" he asked. "Then become someone Prythian listens to. Become vital. Become a weapon. Because there might be a day, Feyre, when only you stand between the King of Hybern and your human family. And you do not want to be unprepared."

I lifted my gaze to him, my breath tight, aching.

As if he hadn't just knocked the world from beneath my feet, Rhysand said, "Think it over. Take the week. Ask Tamlin, if it'll make you sleep better. See what charming Ianthe says about it. But it's your choice to make—no one else's."

I didn't see Rhysand for the rest of the week. Or Mor.

The only people I encountered were Nuala and Cerridwen, who delivered my meals, made my bed, and occasionally asked how I was faring.

The only evidence I had at all that Rhys remained on the premises were the blank copies of the alphabet, along with several sentences I was to write every day, swapping out words, each one more obnoxious than the last:

Rhysand is the most handsome High Lord.
Rhysand is the most delightful High Lord.
Rhysand is the most cunning High Lord.

Every day, one miserable sentence—with one changing word of varying arrogance and vanity. And every day, another simple set of instructions: shield up, shield down; shield up, shield down. Over and over and over.

How he knew if I obeyed or not, I didn't care—but I threw myself into my lessons, I raised and lowered and thickened those mental shields. If only because it was all I had to do.

My nightmares left me groggy, sweaty—but the room was so open, the starlight so bright that when I'd jerk awake, I didn't rush to the toilet. No walls pushing in around me, no inky darkness. I knew where I was. Even if I resented being there.

The day before our week finally finished, I was trudging to my usual little table, already grimacing at what delightful sentences I'd find waiting and all the mental acrobatics ahead, when Rhys's and Mor's voices floated toward me.

It was a public space, so I didn't bother masking my footsteps as I neared where they spoke in one of the sitting areas, Rhys pacing before the open plunge off the mountain, Mor lounging in a cream-colored armchair.

"Azriel would want to know that," Mor was saying.

"Azriel can go to hell," Rhys sniped back. "He likely already knows, anyway."

"We played games the last time," Mor said with a seriousness that made me pause a healthy distance away, "and we lost. Badly. We're not going to do that again."

"You should be working," was Rhysand's only response. "I gave you control for a reason, you know."

Mor's jaw tightened, and she at last faced me. She gave me a smile that was more of a cringe.

Rhys turned, frowning at me. "Say what it is you came here to say, Mor," he said tightly, resuming his pacing.

Mor rolled her eyes for my benefit, but her face turned solemn as she said, "There was another attack—at a temple in Cesere. Almost every priestess slain, the trove looted."

Rhys halted. And I didn't know what to process: her news, or the utter rage conveyed in one word as Rhys said, "Who."

"We don't know," Mor said. "Same tracks as last time: small group, bodies that showed signs of wounds from large blades, and no trace of where they came from and how they disappeared. No survivors. The bodies weren't even found until a day later, when a group of pilgrims came by."

By the Cauldron. I must have made some tiny noise, because Mor gave me a strained, but sympathetic look.

Rhys, though . . . First the shadows started—plumes of them from his back.

And then, as if his rage had loosened his grip on that beast he'd once told me he hated to yield to, those wings became flesh.

Great, beautiful, brutal wings, membranous and clawed like a bat's, dark as night and strong as hell. Even the way he stood seemed altered—steadier, grounded. Like some final piece of him had clicked into place. But Rhysand's voice was still midnight-soft and he said, "What did Azriel have to say about it?"

Again, that glance from Mor, as if unsure I should be present for whatever this conversation was. "He's pissed. Cassian even more so—he's convinced it must be one of the rogue Illyrian war-bands, intent on winning new territory."

"It's something to consider," Rhys mused. "Some of the Illyrian clans gleefully bowed to Amarantha during those years. Trying to expand their borders could be their way of seeing how far they can push me and get away with it." I hated the sound of her name, focused on it more than the information he was allowing me to glean.

"Cassian and Az are waiting—" She cut herself off and gave me an apologetic wince. "They're waiting in the usual spot for your orders."

Fine—that was fine. I'd seen that blank map on the wall. I was an enemy's bride. Even mentioning where his forces were stationed, what they were up to, might be dangerous. I had no idea where Cesere even *was*—what it was, actually.

Rhys studied the open air again, the howling wind that shoved dark, roiling clouds over the distant peaks. Good weather, I realized, for flying.

"Winnowing in would be easier," Mor said, following the High Lord's gaze.

"Tell the pricks I'll be there in a few hours," he merely said.

Mor gave me a wary grin, and vanished.

I studied the empty space where she'd been, not a trace of her left behind.

"How does that . . . vanishing work?" I said softly. I'd seen only a few High Fae do it—and no one had ever explained.

Rhys didn't look at me, but he said, "Winnowing? Think of it as . . . two different points on a piece of cloth. One point is your current place in the world. The other one across the cloth is where you want to go. Winnowing . . . it's like folding that cloth so the two spots align.

The magic does the folding—and all we do is take a step to get from one place to another. Sometimes it's a long step, and you can feel the dark fabric of the world as you pass through it. A shorter step, let's say from one end of the room to the other, would barely register. It's a rare gift, and a helpful one. Though only the stronger Fae can do it. The more powerful you are, the farther you can jump between places in one go."

I knew the explanation was as much for my benefit as it was to distract himself. But I found myself saying, "I'm sorry about the temple—and the priestesses."

The wrath still glimmered in those eyes as he at last turned to me. "Plenty more people are going to die soon enough, anyway."

Maybe that was why he'd allowed me to get close, to overhear this conversation. To remind me of what might very well happen with Hybern.

"What are . . . ," I tried. "What are Illyrian war-bands?"

"Arrogant bastards, that's what," he muttered.

I crossed my arms, waiting.

Rhys stretched his wings, the sunlight setting the leathery texture glowing with subtle color. "They're a warrior-race within my lands. And general pains in my ass."

"Some of them supported Amarantha?"

Darkness danced in the hall as that distant storm grew close enough to smother the sun. "Some. But me and mine have enjoyed ourselves hunting them down these past few months. And ending them."

Slowly was the word he didn't need to add.

"That's why you stayed away—you were busy with that?"

"I was busy with many things."

Not an answer. But it seemed he was done talking to me, and whoever Cassian and Azriel were, meeting with them was far more important.

So Rhys didn't as much as say good-bye before he simply walked off the edge of the veranda—into thin air.

My heart stopped dead, but before I could cry out, he swept past, swift as the wicked wind between the peaks. A few booming wing beats had him vanishing into the storm clouds.

"Good-bye to you, too," I grumbled, giving him a vulgar gesture, and started my work for the day, with only the storm raging beyond the house's shield for company.

Even as snow lashed the protective magic of the hall, even as I toiled over the sentences—*Rhysand is interesting; Rhysand is gorgeous; Rhysand is flawless*—and raised and lowered my mental shield until my mind was limping, I thought of what I'd heard, what they'd said.

I wondered what Ianthe would know about the murders, if she knew any of the victims. Knew what Cesere was. If temples were being targeted, she should know. Tamlin should know.

That final night, I could barely sleep—half from relief, half from terror that perhaps Rhysand really did have some final, nasty surprise in store. But the night and the storm passed, and when dawn broke, I was dressed before the sun had fully risen.

I'd taken to eating in my rooms, but I swept up the stairs, heading across that massive open area, to the table at the far veranda.

Sprawled in his usual chair, Rhys was in the same clothes as yesterday, the collar of his black jacket unbuttoned, the shirt as rumpled as his hair. No wings, fortunately. I wondered if he'd just returned from wherever he'd met Mor and the others. Wondered what he'd learned.

"It's been a week," I said by way of greeting. "Take me home."

Rhys took a long sip of whatever was in his cup. It didn't look like tea. "Good morning, Feyre."

"Take me home."

He studied my teal and gold clothes, a variation of my daily attire. If I had to admit, I didn't mind them. "That color suits you."

"Do you want me to say please? Is that it?"

"I want you to talk to me like a person. Start with 'good morning' and let's see where it gets us."

"Good morning."

A faint smile. Bastard. "Are you ready to face the consequences of your departure?"

I straightened. I hadn't thought about the wedding. All week, yes, but today . . . today I'd only thought of Tamlin, of wanting to see him, hold him, ask him about everything Rhys had claimed. During the past several days, I hadn't shown any signs of the power Rhysand believed I had, hadn't *felt* anything stirring beneath my skin—and thank the Cauldron.

"It's none of your business."

"Right. You'll probably ignore it, anyway. Sweep it under the rug, like everything else."

"No one asked for your opinion, Rhysand."

"Rhysand?" He chuckled, low and soft. "I give you a week of luxury and you call me Rhysand?"

"I didn't ask to be here, or be given that week."

"And yet look at you. Your face has some color—and those marks under your eyes are almost gone. Your mental shield is stellar, by the way."

"Please take me home."

He shrugged and rose. "I'll tell Mor you said good-bye."

"I barely saw her all week." Just that first meeting—then that conversation yesterday. When we hadn't exchanged two words.

"She was waiting for an invitation—she didn't want to pester you. I wish she extended me the same courtesy."

"No one told me." I didn't particularly care. No doubt she had better things to do, anyway.

"You didn't ask. And why bother? Better to be miserable and alone." He approached, each step smooth, graceful. His hair was definitely ruffled, as if he'd been dragging his hands through it. Or just flying for hours to whatever secret spot. "Have you thought about my offer?"

"I'll let you know next month."

He stopped a hand's breadth away, his golden face tight. "I told you once, and I'll tell you again," he said. "I am not your enemy."

"And I told you once, so I'll tell you again. You're *Tamlin*'s enemy. So I suppose that makes you mine."

"Does it?"

"Free me from my bargain and let's find out."

"I can't do that."

"Can't, or won't?"

He just extended his hand. "Shall we go?"

I nearly lunged for it. His fingers were cool, sturdy—callused from weapons I'd never seen on him.

Darkness gobbled us up, and it was instinct to grab him as the world vanished from beneath my feet. Winnowing indeed. Wind tore at me, and his arm was a warm, heavy weight across my back while we tumbled through realms, Rhys snickering at my terror.

But then solid ground—flagstones—were under me, then blinding sunshine above, greenery, little birds chirping—

I shoved away from him, blinking at the brightness, at the massive oak hunched over us. An oak at the edge of the formal gardens—of *home*.

I made to bolt for the manor house, but Rhys gripped my wrist. His eyes flashed between me and the manor. "Good luck," he crooned.

"Get your hand off me."

He chuckled, letting go.

"I'll see you next month," he said, and before I could spit on him, he vanished.

I found Tamlin in his study, Lucien and two other sentries standing around the map-covered worktable.

Lucien was the first to turn to where I lurked in the doorway, falling silent mid-sentence. But then Tamlin's head snapped up, and he was racing across the room, so fast that I hardly had time to draw breath before he was crushing me against him.

I murmured his name as my throat burned, and then—

Then he was holding me at arm's length, scanning me from head to toe. "Are you all right? Are you hurt?"

"I'm fine," I said, noticing the exact moment when he realized the Night Court clothes I was wearing, the strip of bare skin exposed at my midriff. "No one touched me."

But he kept scouring my face, my neck. And then he rotated me, examining my back, as if he could discern through the clothes. I tore out of his grip. "I said no one touched me."

He was breathing hard, his eyes wild. "You're all right," he said. And then said it again. And again.

My heart cracked, and I reached to cup his cheek. "Tamlin," I murmured. Lucien and the other sentries, wisely, made their exit. My friend caught my gaze as he left, giving me a relieved smile.

"He can harm you in other ways," Tamlin croaked, closing his eyes against my touch.

"I know—but I'm all right. I truly am," I said as gently as I could. And then noticed the study walls—the claw marks raked down them. All over them. And the table they'd been using . . . that was new. "You trashed the study."

"I trashed half the house," he said, leaning forward to press his brow to mine. "He took you away, he stole you—"

"And left me alone."

Tamlin pulled back, growling. "Probably to get you to drop your guard. You have no idea what games he plays, what he's capable of doing—"

"I know," I said, even as it tasted like ash on my tongue. "And the next time, I'll be careful—"

"There won't be a next time."

I blinked. "You found a way out?" Or perhaps Ianthe had.

"I'm not letting you go."

"He said there were consequences for breaking a magical bargain."

"Damn the consequences." But I heard it for the empty threat it was—and how much it destroyed him. That was who he was, what he was: protector, defender. I couldn't ask him to stop being that way—to stop worrying about me.

I rose onto my toes and kissed him. There was so much I wanted to ask him, but—later. "Let's go upstairs," I said onto his lips, and he slid his arms around me.

"I missed you," he said between kisses. "I went out of my mind."

That was all I needed to hear. Until—

"I need to ask you some questions."

I let out a low sound of affirmation, but angled my head further. "Later." His body was so warm, so hard against mine, his scent so familiar—

Tamlin gripped my waist, pressing his brow to my own. "No—now," he said, but groaned softly as I slid my tongue against his teeth. "While . . . " He pulled back, ripping his mouth from mine. "While it's all fresh in your mind."

I froze, one hand tangled in his hair, the other gripping the back of his tunic. "What?"

Tamlin stepped back, shaking his head as if to clear the desire addling his senses. We hadn't been apart for so long since Amarantha, and he wanted to press me for information about the Night Court? "Tamlin."

But he held up a hand, his eyes locked on mine as he called for Lucien.

In the moments that it took for his emissary to appear, I straightened my clothes—the top that had ridden up my torso—and finger-combed my hair. Tamlin just strode to his desk and plopped down, motioning for me to take a seat in front of it. "I'm sorry," he said quietly, as Lucien's strolling footsteps neared again. "This is for our own good. Our safety."

I took in the shredded walls, the scuffed and chipped furniture. What nightmares had he suffered, waking and asleep, while I was away? What had it been like, to imagine me in his enemy's hands, after seeing what Amarantha had done to me?

"I know," I murmured at last. "I know, Tamlin." Or I was trying to know.

I'd just slid into the low-backed chair when Lucien strode in, shutting the door behind him. "Glad to see you in one piece, Feyre," he said, claiming the seat beside me. "I could do without the Night Court attire, though."

Tamlin gave a low growl of agreement. I said nothing. Yet I understood—I really did—why it'd be an affront to them.

Tamlin and Lucien exchanged glances, speaking without uttering a word in that way only people who had been partners for centuries could do. Lucien gave a slight nod and leaned back in his chair—to listen, to observe.

"We need you to tell us everything," Tamlin said. "The layout of the Night Court, who you saw, what weapons and powers they bore, what Rhys did, who he spoke to, any and every detail you can recall."

"I didn't realize I was a spy."

Lucien shifted in his seat, but Tamlin said, "As much as I hate your bargain, you've been granted access into the Night Court. Outsiders rarely get to go in—and if they do, they rarely come out in one piece. And if they can function, their memories are usually . . . scrambled. Whatever Rhysand is hiding in there, he doesn't want us knowing about it."

A chill slithered down my spine. "Why do you want to know? What are you going to do?"

"Knowing my enemy's plans, his lifestyle, is vital. As for what we're going to do . . . That's neither here nor there." His green eyes pinned me. "Start with the layout of the court. Is it true it's under a mountain?"

"This feels an awful lot like an interrogation."

Lucien sucked in a breath, but remained silent.

Tamlin spread his hands on the desk. "We need to know these things, Feyre. Or—or can you not remember?" Claws glinted at his knuckles.

"I can remember everything," I said. "He didn't damage my mind." And before he could question me further, I began to speak of all that I had seen.

Because I trust you, Rhysand had said. And maybe—maybe he had scrambled my mind, even with the lessons in shielding, because describing the layout of his home, his court, the mountains around them, felt like bathing in oil and mud. He *was* my enemy, he was holding me to a bargain I'd made from pure desperation—

I kept talking, describing that tower room. Tamlin grilled me on the figures on the maps, making me turn over every word Rhysand had uttered, until I mentioned what had weighed on me the most this past week: the powers Rhys believed I now possessed . . . and Hybern's plans. I told him about that conversation with Mor—about that temple being sacked (Cesere, Tamlin explained, was a northern outpost in the Night Court, and one of the few known towns), and Rhysand mentioning two people named Cassian and Azriel. Both of their faces had tightened at that, but they didn't mention if they knew them, or of them. So I told him about whatever the Illyrians were—and how Rhys had hunted down and killed the traitors amongst them. When I finished, Tamlin was silent, Lucien practically buzzing with whatever repressed words he was dying to spew.

"Do you think I might have those abilities?" I said, willing myself to hold his gaze.

"It's possible," Tamlin said with equal quiet. "And if it's true . . . "

Lucien said at last, "It's a power other High Lords might kill for." It was an effort not to fidget while his metal eye whirred, as if detecting whatever power ran through my blood. "My father, for one, would not be pleased to learn a drop of his power is missing—or that Tamlin's bride now has it. He'd do anything to make sure you *don't* possess it—including kill you. There are other High Lords who would agree."

That *thing* beneath my skin began roiling. "I'd never use it against anyone—"

"It's not about using it against them; it's about having an edge when you shouldn't," Tamlin said. "And the moment word gets out about it, you will have a target on your back."

"Did you know?" I demanded. Lucien wouldn't meet my eyes. "Did you suspect?"

"I'd hoped it wasn't true," Tamlin said carefully. "And now that Rhys suspects, there's no telling what he'll do with the information—"

"He wants me to train." I wasn't stupid enough to mention the mental shield training—not right now.

"Training would draw too much attention," Tamlin said. "You don't *need* to train. I can guard you from whatever comes our way."

For there had been a time when he could not. When he had been vulnerable, and when he had watched me be tortured to death. And could do nothing to stop Amarantha from—

I would not allow another Amarantha. I would not allow the King of Hybern to bring his beasts and minions here to hurt more people. To hurt me and mine. And bring down that wall to hurt countless others across it. "I could use my powers against Hybern."

"That's out of the question," Tamlin said, "especially as there will be no war against Hybern."

"Rhys says war is inevitable, and we'll be hit hard."

Lucien said drily, "And Rhys knows everything?"

"No—but . . . He was concerned. He thinks I can make a difference in any upcoming conflict."

Tamlin flexed his fingers—keeping those claws contained. "You have no training in battle or weaponry. And even if I started training you today, it'd be years before you could hold your own on an immortal battlefield." He took a tight breath. "So despite what he thinks you might be able to do, Feyre, I'm not going to have you anywhere *near* a battlefield. Especially if it means revealing whatever powers you have to our enemies. You'd be fighting Hybern at your front, and have foes with friendly faces at your back."

"I don't care—"

"*I* care," Tamlin snarled. Lucien whooshed out a breath. "*I* care if you die, if you're hurt, if you will be in danger every moment for the rest of our lives. So there will be no training, and we're going to keep this between us."

"But Hybern—"

Lucien intervened calmly, "I already have my sources looking into it."

I gave him a beseeching look.

Lucien sighed a bit and said to Tamlin, "If we perhaps trained her in secret—"

"Too many risks, too many variables," Tamlin countered. "And there will be no conflict with Hybern, no war."

I snapped, "That's wishful thinking."

Lucien muttered something that sounded like a plea to the Cauldron.

Tamlin stiffened. "Describe his map room for me again," was his only response.

End of discussion. No room for debate.

We stared each other down for a moment, and my stomach twisted further.

He was the High Lord—*my* High Lord. He was the shield and defender of his people. Of me. And if keeping me safe meant that his people could continue to hope, to build a new life, that he could do the same . . . I could bow to him on this one thing.

I could do it.

You are no one's subject.

Maybe Rhysand *had* altered my mind, shields or no.

The thought alone was enough for me to begin feeding Tamlin details once more.

CHAPTER 8

A week later, the Tithe arrived.

I'd had all of one day with Tamlin—one day spent wandering the grounds, making love in the high grasses of a sunny field, and a quiet, private dinner—before he was called to the border. He didn't tell me why or where. Only that I was to keep to the grounds, and that I'd have sentries guarding me at all times.

So I spent the week alone, waking in the middle of the night to hurl up my guts, to sob through the nightmares. Ianthe, if she'd learned of her sisters' massacre in the north, said nothing about it the few times I saw her. And given how little *I* liked to be pushed into talking about the things that plagued me, I opted not to bring it up during the hours she spent visiting, helping select my clothes, my hair, my jewelry, for the Tithe.

When I'd asked her to explain what to anticipate, she merely said that Tamlin would take care of everything. I should watch from his side, and observe.

Easy enough—and perhaps a relief, to not be expected to speak or act.

But it had been an effort not to look at the eye tattooed into my palm—to remember what Rhys had snarled at me.

Tamlin had only returned the night before to oversee today's Tithe. I tried not to take it personally, not when he had so much on his shoulders. Even if he wouldn't tell me much about it beyond what Ianthe had mentioned.

Seated beside Tamlin atop a dais in the manor's great hall of marble and gold, I endured the endless stream of eyes, of tears, of gratitude and blessings for what I'd done.

In her usual pale blue hooded robe, Ianthe was stationed near the doors, offering benedictions to those that departed, comforting words to those who fell apart entirely in my presence, promises that the world was better now, that good had won out over evil.

After twenty minutes, I was near fidgeting. After four hours, I stopped hearing entirely.

They kept coming, the emissaries representing every town and people in the Spring Court, bearing their payments in the form of gold or jewels or chickens or crops or clothes. It didn't matter what it was, so long as it equated to what they owed. Lucien stood at the foot of the dais, tallying every amount, armed to the teeth like the ten other sentries stationed through the hall. The receiving room, Lucien had called it, but it felt a hell of a lot like a throne room to me. I wondered if he'd called it that because the other words . . .

I'd spent too much time in another throne room. So had Tamlin.

And I hadn't been seated on a dais like him, but kneeling before it. Approaching it like the slender, gray-skinned faerie slinking from the front of the endless line full of lesser and High Fae.

She wore no clothes. Her long, dark hair hung limp over her high, firm breasts—and her massive eyes were wholly black. Like a stagnant pond. And as she moved, the afternoon light shimmered on her iridescent skin.

Lucien's face tightened with disapproval, but he made no comment as the lesser faerie lowered her delicate, pointed face, and clasped her spindly, webbed fingers over her breasts.

"On behalf of the water-wraiths, I greet thee, High Lord," she said, her voice strange and hissing, her full, sensuous lips revealing teeth as sharp and jagged as a pike's. The sharp angles of her face accentuated those coal-black eyes.

I'd seen her kind before. In the pond just past the edge of the manor. There were five of them who lived amongst the reeds and lilypads. I'd rarely glimpsed more than their shining heads peeking through the glassy surface—had never known how horrific they were up close. Thank the Cauldron I'd never gone swimming in that pond. I had a feeling she'd grab me with those webbed fingers—those jagged nails digging in deep—and drag me beneath the surface before I could scream.

"Welcome," Tamlin said. Five hours in, and he looked as fresh as he'd been that morning.

I supposed that with his powers returned, few things tired him now.

The water-wraith stepped closer, her webbed, clawed foot a mottled gray. Lucien took a casual step between us.

That was why he'd been stationed on my side of the dais.

I gritted my teeth. Who did they think would attack us in our own home, on our own land, if they weren't convinced Hybern might be launching an assault? Even Ianthe had paused her quiet murmurings in the back of the hall to monitor the encounter.

Apparently, this conversation was not the same as all the others.

"Please, High Lord," the faerie was saying, bowing so low that her inky hair grazed the marble. "There are no fish left in the lake."

Tamlin's face was like granite. "Regardless, you are expected to pay." The crown atop his head gleamed in the afternoon light. Crafted with emeralds, sapphires, and amethyst, the gold had been molded into a wreath of spring's first flowers. One of five crowns belonging to his bloodline.

The faerie exposed her palms, but Tamlin interrupted her. "There are no exceptions. You have three days to present what is owed—or offer double next Tithe."

It was an effort to keep from gaping at the immovable face, and the pitiless words. In the back, Ianthe gave a nod of confirmation to no one in particular.

The water-wraith had nothing to eat—how could he expect her to give *him* food?

"Please," she whispered through her pointed teeth, her silvery, mottled skin glistening as she began trembling. "There is nothing left in the lake."

Tamlin's face didn't change. "You have three days—"

"But we have no gold!"

"Do *not* interrupt me," he said. I looked away, unable to stomach that merciless face.

She ducked her head even lower. "Apologies, my lord."

"You have three days to pay, or bring double next month," he repeated. "If you fail to do so, you know the consequences." Tamlin waved a hand in dismissal. Conversation over.

After a final, hopeless look at Tamlin, she walked from the chamber. As the next faerie—a goat-legged fawn bearing what looked to be a basket of mushrooms—patiently waited to be invited to approach the dais, I twisted to Tamlin.

"We don't need a basket of fish," I murmured. "Why make her suffer like that?"

He flicked his eyes to where Ianthe had stepped aside to let the creature pass, a hand on the jewels of her belt. As if the female would snatch them right off her to use as payment. Tamlin frowned. "I cannot make exceptions. Once you do, everyone will demand the same treatment."

I clutched the arms of my chair, a small seat of oak beside his giant throne of carved roses. "But we don't *need* these things. Why do we need a golden fleece, or a jar of jam? If she has no fish left, three days won't make a difference. Why make her starve? Why not help her replenish the pond?" I'd spent enough years with an aching belly to not be able to drop it, to want to scream at the unfairness of it.

His emerald eyes softened as if he read each thought on my face, but he said: "Because that's the way it is. That's the way my father did it, and his father, and the way my son shall do it." He offered a smile, and reached for my hand. "Someday."

Someday. If we ever got married. If I ever became less of a burden, and we both escaped the shadows haunting us. We hadn't broached the subject at all. Ianthe, mercifully, had not said anything, either. "We could still help her—find some way to keep that pond stocked."

"We have enough to deal with as it is. Giving handouts won't help her in the long run."

I opened my mouth, but shut it. Now wasn't the time for debate.

So I pulled my hand from his as he motioned the goat-legged fawn to approach at last. "I need some fresh air," I said, and slid from my chair. I didn't give Tamlin a chance to object before I stalked off the dais. I tried not to notice the three sentries Tamlin sent after me, or the line of emissaries who gaped and whispered as I crossed the hall.

Ianthe tried to catch me as I stormed by, but I ignored her.

I cleared the front doors and walked as fast as I dared past the gathered line snaking down the steps and onto the gravel of the main drive. Through the latticework of various bodies, High Fae and lesser faeries alike, I spotted the retreating form of the wraith heading around the corner of our house—toward the pond beyond the grounds. She trudged along, wiping at her eyes.

"Excuse me," I called, catching up to her, the sentries on my trail keeping a respectful distance behind.

She paused at the edge of the house, whirling with preternatural smoothness. I avoided the urge to take a step back as those unearthly features devoured me. Keeping only a few paces away, the guards monitored us with hands on their blades.

Her nose was little more than two slits, and delicate gills flared beneath her ears.

She inclined her head slightly. Not a full bow—because I was no one, but recognition that I was the High Lord's plaything.

"Yes?" she hissed, her pike's teeth gleaming.

"How much is your Tithe?"

My heart beat faster as I beheld the webbed fingers and razor-sharp teeth. Tamlin had once told me that the water-wraiths ate anything. And if there were no fish left . . . "How much gold does he want—what is your fish worth in gold?"

"Far more than you have in your pocket."

"Then here," I said, unfastening a ruby-studded gold bracelet from my wrist, one Ianthe had told me better suited my coloring than the silver I'd almost worn. I offered it to her. "Take this." Before she could grasp it, I ripped the gold necklace from my throat, and the diamond teardrops from my ears. "And these." I extended my hands, glittering with gold and jewels. "Give him what you owe, then buy yourself some food," I said, swallowing as her eyes widened. The nearby village had a small market every week—a fledgling gathering of vendors for now, and one I'd hoped to help thrive. Somehow.

"And what payment do you require?"

"Nothing. It's—it's not a bargain. Just take it." I extended my hands further. "Please."

She frowned at the jewels draping from my hands. "You desire nothing in return?"

"Nothing." The faeries in the line were now staring unabashedly. "Please, just take them."

With a final assessing look, her cold, clammy fingers brushed mine, gathering up the jewelry. It glimmered like light on water in her webbed hands.

"Thank you," she said, and bowed deeply this time. "I will not forget this kindness." Her voice slithered over the words, and I shivered again as her black eyes threatened to swallow me whole. "Nor will any of my sisters."

She stalked back toward the manor, the faces of my three sentries tight with reproach.

I sat at the dinner table with Lucien and Tamlin. Neither of them spoke, but Lucien's gaze kept bouncing from me, to Tamlin, then to his plate.

After ten minutes of silence, I set down my fork and said to Tamlin, "What is it?"

Tamlin didn't hesitate. "You know what it is."

I didn't reply.

"You gave that water-wraith your jewelry. Jewelry *I* gave you."

"We have a damned house full of gold and jewels."

Lucien took a deep breath that sounded a lot like: "Here we go."

"Why shouldn't I give them to her?" I demanded. "Those things don't mean anything to me. I've never worn the same piece of jewelry twice! Who cares about any of it?"

Tamlin's lips thinned. "Because you *undermine* the laws of this court when you behave like that. Because this is how things are *done* here, and when you hand that gluttonous faerie the money she needs, it makes me—it makes this entire court—look *weak*."

"Don't you talk to me like that," I said, baring my teeth. He slammed his hand on the table, claws poking through his flesh, but I leaned forward, bracing my own hands on the wood. "You still have no idea what it was like for me—to be on the verge of starvation for months at a time. And you can call her a glutton all you like, but I have sisters, too, and I remember what it felt like to return home without any food." I calmed my heaving chest, and that force beneath my skin stirred, undulating along my bones. "So maybe she'll spend all that money on stupid things—maybe she and her sisters have no self-control. But I'm not going to take that chance and let them starve, because of some *ridiculous* rule that your ancestors invented."

Lucien cleared his throat. "She meant no harm, Tam."

"I know she meant no harm," he snapped.

Lucien held his gaze. "Worse things have happened, worse things *can* happen. Just relax."

Tamlin's emerald eyes were feral as he snarled at Lucien, "Did I ask for your opinion?"

Those words, the *look* he gave Lucien and the way Lucien lowered his head—my temper was a burning river in my veins. *Look up*, I silently beseeched him. *Push back. He's wrong, and we're right*. Lucien's jaw tightened. That force thrummed in me again, seeping out, spearing for Lucien. *Do* not *back down*—

Then I was gone.

Still there, still seeing through my eyes, but also half looking through another angle in the room, another person's vantage point—

Thoughts slammed into me, images and memories, a pattern of thinking and feeling that was old, and clever, and sad, so endlessly sad and guilt-ridden, hopeless—

Then I was back, blinking, no more than a heartbeat passing as I gaped at Lucien.

His head. I had been *inside* his head, had slid through his mental walls—

I stood, chucking my napkin on the table with hands that were unnervingly steady.

I knew who *that* gift had come from. My dinner rose in my throat, but I willed it down.

"We're not finished with this meal," Tamlin growled.

"Oh, get over yourself," I barked, and left.

I could have sworn I beheld two burned handprints on the wood, peeking out from beneath my napkin. I prayed neither of them noticed.

And that Lucien remained ignorant to the violation I'd just committed.

CHAPTER 9

I paced my room for a good while. Maybe I'd been mistaken when I'd spotted those burns—maybe they'd been there before. Maybe I hadn't somehow summoned heat and branded the wood. Maybe I hadn't slid into Lucien's mind as if I were moving from one room to another.

Just as she always did, Alis appeared to help me change for bed. As I sat before the vanity, letting her comb my hair, I cringed at my reflection. The purple beneath my eyes seemed permanent now—my face wan. Even my lips were a bit pale, and I sighed as I closed my eyes.

"You gave your jewels to a water-wraith," Alis mused, and I found her reflection in the mirror. Her brown skin looked like crushed leather, and her dark eyes gleamed for a moment before she focused on my hair. "They're a slippery sort."

"She said they were starving—that they had no food," I murmured.

Alis gently coaxed out a tangle. "Not one faerie in that line today would have given her the money. Not one would have dared. Too many have gone to a watery grave because of their hunger. Insatiable appetite—it is their curse. Your jewels won't last her a week."

I tapped a foot on the floor.

"But," Alis went on, setting down the brush to braid my hair into a single plait. Her long, spindly fingers scratched against my scalp. "She will never forget it. So long as she lives, no matter what you said, she is in your debt." Alis finished the braid and patted my shoulder. "Too many faeries have tasted hunger these past fifty years. Don't think word of this won't spread."

I was afraid of that perhaps more than anything.

It was after midnight when I gave up waiting, walked down the dark, silent corridors, and found him in his study, alone for once.

A wooden box wrapped with a fat pink bow sat on the small table between the twin armchairs. "I was just about to come up," he said, lifting his head to do a quick scan over my body to make sure all was right, all was fine. "You should be asleep."

I shut the door behind me. I knew I wouldn't be able to sleep—not with the words we'd shouted ringing in my ears. "So should you," I said, my voice as tenuous as the peace between us. "You work too hard." I crossed the room to lean against the armchair, eyeing the present as Tamlin had eyed me.

"Why do you think I had such little interest in being High Lord?" he said, rising from his seat to round the desk. He kissed my brow, the tip of my nose, my mouth. "So much paperwork," he grumbled onto my lips. I chuckled, but he pressed his mouth to the bare spot between my neck and shoulder. "I'm sorry," he murmured, and my spine tingled. He kissed my neck again. "I'm sorry."

I ran a hand down his arm. "Tamlin," I started.

"I shouldn't have said those things," he breathed onto my skin. "To you or Lucien. I didn't mean any of them."

"I know," I said, and his body relaxed against mine. "I'm sorry I snapped at you."

"You had every right," he said, though I technically didn't. "I was wrong."

What he said had been true—if he made exceptions, then other faeries would demand the same treatment. And what I had done *could* be construed as undermining. "Maybe I was—"

"No. You were right. I don't understand what it's like to be starving—or any of it."

I pulled back a bit to incline my head toward the present waiting there, more than willing to let this be the last of it. I gave a small, wry smile. "For you?"

He nipped at my ear in answer. "For you. From me." An apology.

Feeling lighter than I had in days, I tugged the ribbon loose, and examined the pale wood box beneath. It was perhaps two feet high and three feet wide, a solid iron handle anchored in the top—no crest or lettering to indicate what might be within. Certainly not a dress, but . . .

Please not a crown.

Though surely, a crown or diadem would be in something less . . . rudimentary.

I unlatched the small brass lock and flipped open the broad lid.

It was worse than a crown, actually.

Built into the box were compartments and sleeves and holders, all full of brushes and paints and charcoal and sheets of paper. A traveling painting kit.

Red—the red paint inside the glass vial was so bright, the blue as stunning as the eyes of that faerie woman I'd slaughtered—

"I thought you might want it to take around the grounds with you. Rather than lug all those bags like you always do."

The brushes were fresh, gleaming—the bristles soft and clean.

Looking at that box, at what was inside, felt like examining a crow-picked corpse.

I tried to smile. Tried to will some brightness to my eyes.

He said, "You don't like it."

"No," I managed to say. "No—it's wonderful." And it was. It really was.

"I thought if you started painting again . . . " I waited for him to finish.

He didn't.

My face heated.

"And what about you?" I asked quietly. "Will the paperwork help with anything at all?"

I dared meet his eyes. Temper flared in them. But he said, "We're not talking about me. We're talking—about you."

I studied the box and its contents again. "Will I even be allowed to roam where I wish to paint? Or will there be an escort, too?"

Silence.

A no—and a yes, then.

I began shaking, but for me, for *us*, I made myself say, "Tamlin—Tamlin, I can't . . . I can't live my life with guards around me day and night. I can't live with that . . . suffocation. Just let me help you—let me work with you."

"You've given enough, Feyre."

"I know. But . . . " I faced him. Met his stare—the full power of the High Lord of the Spring Court. "I'm harder to kill now. I'm faster, stronger—"

"My family was faster and stronger than you. And they were murdered quite easily."

"*Then marry someone who can put up with this.*"

He blinked. Slowly. Then he said with terrible softness, "Do you not want to marry me, then?"

I tried not to look at the ring on my finger, at that emerald. "Of course I do. *Of course I do.*" My voice broke. "But you . . . Tamlin . . . " The walls pushed in on me. The quiet, the guards, the stares. What I'd seen at the Tithe today. "I'm drowning," I managed to say. "I am *drowning*. And the more you do this, the more guards . . . You might as well be shoving my head under the water."

Nothing in those eyes, that face.

But then—

I cried out, instinct taking over as his power blasted through the room.

The windows shattered.

The furniture splintered.

And that box of paints and brushes and paper . . .

It exploded into dust and glass and wood.

CHAPTER 10

One breath, the study was intact.

The next, it was shards of nothing, a shell of a room.

None of it had touched me from where I had dropped to the floor, my hands over my head.

Tamlin was panting, the ragged breaths almost like sobs.

I was shaking—shaking so hard I thought my bones would splinter as the furniture had—but I made myself lower my arms and look at him.

There was devastation on that face. And pain. And fear. And grief.

Around me, no debris had fallen—as if he had shielded me.

Tamlin took a step toward me, over that invisible demarcation.

He recoiled as if he'd hit something solid.

"Feyre," he rasped.

He stepped again—and that line held.

"Feyre, please," he breathed.

And I realized that the line, that bubble of protection . . .

It was from me.

A shield. Not just a mental one—but a physical one, too.

I didn't know what High Lord it had come from, who controlled air or wind or any of that. Perhaps one of the Solar Courts. I didn't care.

"Feyre," Tamlin groaned a third time, pushing a hand against what indeed looked like an invisible, curved wall of hardened air. "*Please. Please.*"

Those words cracked something in me. Cracked me open.

Perhaps they cracked that shield of solid wind as well, for his hand shot through it.

Then he stepped over that line between chaos and order, danger and safety.

He dropped to his knees, taking my face in his hands. "I'm sorry, I'm sorry."

I couldn't stop trembling.

"I'll try," he breathed. "I'll try to be better. I don't . . . I can't control it sometimes. The rage. Today was just . . . today was bad. With the Tithe, with all of it. Today—let's forget it, let's just move past it. Please."

I didn't fight as he slid his arms around me, tucking me in tightly enough that his warmth soaked through me. He buried his face in my neck and said onto my nape, as if the words would be absorbed by my body, as if he could only say it the way we'd always been good at communicating—skin to skin, "I couldn't save you before. I couldn't protect you from them. And when you said that, about . . . about me drowning you . . . Am I any better than they were?"

I should have told him it wasn't true, but . . . I had spoken with my heart. Or what was left of it.

"I'll try to be better," he said again. "Please—give me more time. Let me . . . let me get through this. Please."

Get through what? I wanted to ask. But words had abandoned me. I realized I hadn't spoken yet.

Realized he was waiting for an answer—and that I didn't have one.

So I put my arms around him, because body to body was the only way I could speak, too.

It was answer enough. "I'm sorry," he said again. He didn't stop murmuring it for minutes.

You've given enough, Feyre.

Perhaps he was right. And perhaps I didn't have anything left to give, anyway.

I looked over his shoulder as I held him.

The red paint had splattered on the wall behind us. And as I watched it slide down the cracked wood paneling, I thought it looked like blood.

Tamlin didn't stop apologizing for days. He made love to me, morning and night. He worshipped my body with his hands, his tongue, his teeth. But that had never been the hard part. We just got tripped up with the rest.

But he was good for his word.

There were fewer guards as I walked the grounds. Some remained, but no one haunted my steps. I even went on a ride through the wood without an escort.

Though I knew the stable hands had reported to Tamlin the moment I'd left—and returned.

Tamlin never mentioned that shield of solid wind I'd used against him. And things were good enough that I didn't dare bring it up, either.

The days passed in a blur. Tamlin was away more often than not, and whenever he returned, he didn't tell me anything. I'd long since stopped pestering him for answers. A protector—that's who he was, and would always be. What *I* had wanted when I was cold and hard and joyless; what *I* had needed to melt the ice of bitter years on the cusp of starvation.

I didn't have the nerve to wonder what I wanted or needed now. Who I had become.

So with idleness my only option, I spent my days in the library.

Practicing my reading and writing. Adding to that mental shield, brick by brick, layer by layer. Sometimes seeing if I could summon that physical wall of solid air, too. Savoring the silence, even as it crept into my veins, my head.

Some days, I didn't speak to anyone at all. Even Alis.

I awoke each night, shaking and panting. And became glad when Tamlin wasn't there to witness it. When I, too, didn't witness him being yanked from his dreams, cold sweat coating his body. Or shifting into that beast and staying awake until dawn, monitoring the estate for threats. What could I say to calm those fears, when I was the source of so many of them?

But he returned for an extended stay about two weeks after the Tithe—and I'd decided to try to talk, to interact. I owed it to him to try. Owed it to myself.

He seemed to have the same idea. And the first time in a while . . . things felt normal. Or as normal as they could be.

I awoke one morning to the sound of low, deep voices in the hallway outside my bedroom. Closing my eyes, I nestled into the pillow and pulled the blankets higher. Despite our morning roll in the sheets, I'd been rising later every day—sometimes not bothering to get out of bed until lunch.

A growl cut through the walls, and I opened my eyes again.

"Get out," Tamlin warned.

There was a quiet response—too soft for me to make out beyond basic mumbling.

"I'll say it one last time—"

He was interrupted by that voice, and the hair on my arms rose. I studied the tattoo on my forearm as I did a tally. No—no, today couldn't have come so quickly.

Kicking back the covers, I rushed to the door, realizing halfway there that I was naked. Thanks to Tamlin, my clothes had been shredded and flung across the other side of the room, and I had no robe in sight. I grabbed a blanket from a nearby chair and wrapped it around me before opening the door a crack.

Sure enough, Tamlin and Rhysand stood in the hallway. Upon hearing the door open, Rhys turned toward me. The grin that had been on his face faltered.

"Feyre." Rhys's eyes lingered, taking in every detail. "Are you running low on food here?"

"What?" Tamlin demanded.

Those violet eyes had gone cold. Rhys extended a hand toward me. "Let's go."

Tamlin was in Rhysand's face in an instant, and I flinched. "*Get out.*" He pointed toward the staircase. "She'll come to you when she's ready."

Rhysand just brushed an invisible fleck of dust off Tamlin's sleeve. Part of me admired the sheer nerve it must have taken. Had Tamlin's teeth been inches from my throat, I would have bleated in panic.

Rhys cut a glance at me. "No, you wouldn't have. As far as your memory serves me, the last time Tamlin's teeth were near your throat, you slapped him across the face." I snapped up my forgotten shields, scowling.

"*Shut your mouth,*" Tamlin said, stepping further between us. "*And get out.*"

The High Lord conceded a step toward the stairs and slid his hands into his pockets. "You really should have your wards inspected. Cauldron knows what other sort of riffraff might stroll in here as easily as I did." Again, Rhys assessed me, his gaze hard. "Put some clothes on."

I bared my teeth at him as I stepped back into my room. Tamlin followed after me, slamming the door hard enough that the chandeliers shuddered, sending shards of light shivering over the walls.

I dropped the blanket and strode for the armoire across the room, the mattress groaning behind me as Tamlin sank onto the bed. "How did he get in here?" I asked, throwing open the doors and rifling through the clothes until I found the turquoise Night Court attire I'd asked Alis to keep. I knew she'd wanted to burn them, but I told her I'd wind up coming home with another set anyway.

"I don't know," Tamlin said. I slipped on my pants, twisting to find him running a hand through his hair. I felt the lie beneath his words. "He just—it's just part of whatever game he's playing."

I tugged the short shirt over my head. "If war is coming, maybe we'd be better served trying to mend things." We hadn't spoken of that subject since my first day back. I dug through the bottom of the armoire for the matching silk shoes, and turned to him as I slid them on.

"I'll start mending things the day he releases you from your bargain."

"Maybe he's keeping the bargain so that you'll attempt to listen to him." I strode to where he sat on the bed, my pants a bit looser around the waist than last month.

"Feyre," he said, reaching for me, but I stepped out of range. "Why do you need to know these things? Is it not enough for you to recover in peace? You earned that for yourself. You *earned* it. I relaxed the number of sentries here; I've been trying . . . trying to be better about it. So leave the rest of it—" He took a steadying breath. "This isn't the time for this conversation."

It was never the time for *this* conversation, or *that* conversation. But I didn't say it. I didn't have the energy to say it, and all the words dried up and blew away. So I memorized the lines of Tamlin's face, and didn't fight him as he pulled me to his chest and held me tightly.

Someone coughed from the hall, and Tamlin's body seized up around me.

But I'd had enough fighting, and snarling, and going back to that open, serene place atop that mountain . . . It seemed better than hiding in the library.

I pulled away, and Tamlin lingered as I walked back into the hall.

Rhys frowned at me. I debated barking something nasty at him, but it would have required more fire than I had—and would have required caring what he thought.

Rhys's face became unreadable as he extended a hand.

Only for Tamlin to appear behind me, and shove that hand down. "You end her bargain right here, right now, and I'll give you anything you want. Anything."

My heart stopped dead. "Are you out of your mind?"

Tamlin didn't so much as blink in my direction.

Rhysand merely raised a brow. "I already have everything I want." He stepped around Tamlin as if he were a piece of furniture and took my hand. Before I could say good-bye, a black wind gathered us up, and we were gone.

CHAPTER 11

"What the hell happened to you?" Rhysand said before the Night Court had fully appeared around us.

"Why don't you just look inside my head?" Even as I said it, the words had no bite. I didn't bother to shove him as I stepped out of his hold.

He gave me a wink. "Where's the fun in that?"

I didn't smile.

"No shoe throwing this time?" I could almost see the other words in his eyes. *Come on. Play with me.*

I headed for the stairs that would take me to my room.

"Eat breakfast with me," he said.

There was a note in those words that made me pause. A note of what I could have sworn was desperation. Worry.

I twisted, my loose clothes sliding over my shoulders, my waist. I hadn't realized how much weight I'd lost. Despite things creeping back to normal.

I said, "Don't you have other things to deal with?"

"Of course I do," he said, shrugging. "I have so many things to deal with that I'm sometimes tempted to unleash my power across the world and wipe the board clean. Just to buy me some damned peace." He grinned, bowing at the waist. Even that casual mention of his power failed to chill me, awe me. "But I'll always make time for you."

I was hungry—I hadn't yet eaten. And that was indeed worry glimmering behind the cocky, insufferable grin.

So I motioned him to lead the way to that familiar glass table at the end of the hall.

We walked a casual distance apart. Tired. I was so—tired.

When we were almost to the table, Rhys said, "I felt a spike of fear this month through our lovely bond. Anything exciting happen at the wondrous Spring Court?"

"It was nothing," I said. Because it was. And it was none of his business.

I glanced sidelong at him—and rage, not worry—flickered in those eyes.

I could have sworn the mountain beneath us trembled in response.

"If you know," I said coldly, "why even ask about it?" I dropped into my chair as he slid into his.

He said quietly, "Because these days, all I hear through that bond is nothing. Silence. Even with your shields up rather impressively most of the time, I should be able to *feel* you. And yet I don't. Sometimes I'll tug on the bond only to make sure you're still alive." Darkness guttered. "And then one day, I'm in the middle of an important meeting when terror blasts through the bond. All I get are glimpses of you and him—and then nothing. Back to silence. I'd like to know what caused such a disruption."

I served myself from the platters of food, barely caring what had been laid on the table. "It was an argument, and the rest is none of your concern."

"Is it why you look like your grief and guilt and rage are eating you alive, bit by bit?"

I didn't want to talk about it. "Get out of my head."

"Make me. *Push* me out. You dropped your shield this morning—anyone could have walked right in."

I held his stare. Another challenge. And I just . . . I didn't care. I didn't care about whatever smoldered in my body, about how I'd slipped into Lucien's head as easily as Rhys could slip into mine, shield or no shield. "Where's Mor?" I asked instead.

He tensed, and I braced myself for him to push, to provoke, but he said, "Away. She has duties to attend to." Shadows swirled around him again and I dug into my food. "Is the wedding on hold, then?"

I paused eating barely long enough to mumble, "Yes."

"I expected an answer more along the lines of, '*Don't ask stupid questions you already know the answer to*,' or my timeless favorite, '*Go to hell.*'"

I only reached for a platter of tartlets. His hands were flat on the table—and a whisper of black smoke curled over his fingers. Like talons.

He said, "Did you give my offer any thought?"

I didn't answer until my plate was empty and I was heaping more food onto it. "I'm not going to work with you."

I almost felt the dark calm that settled over him. "And why, Feyre, are you refusing me?"

I pushed around the fruit on my plate. "I'm not going to be a part of this war you think is coming. You say I should be a weapon, not a pawn—they seem like the same to me. The only difference is who's wielding it."

"I want your help, not to manipulate you," he snapped.

His flare of temper made me at last lift my head. "You want my help because it'll piss off Tamlin."

Shadows danced around his shoulders—as if the wings were trying to take form.

"Fine," he breathed. "I dug that grave myself, with all I did Under the Mountain. But I need your help."

Again, I could feel the other unspoken words: *Ask me why; push me about it.*

And again, I didn't want to. Didn't have the energy to.

Rhys said quietly, "I was a prisoner in her court for nearly fifty years. I was tortured and beaten and fucked until only telling myself who I was, what I had to protect, kept me from trying to find a way to end it. Please—help me keep that from happening again. To Prythian."

Some distant part of my heart ached and bled at the words, at what he'd laid bare.

But Tamlin had made exceptions—he'd lightened the guards' presence, allowed me to roam a bit more freely. He was trying. We were trying. I wouldn't jeopardize that.

So I went back to eating.

Rhys didn't say another word.

I didn't join him for dinner.

I didn't rise in time for breakfast, either.

But when I emerged at noon, he was waiting upstairs, that faint, amused smile on his face. He nudged me toward the table he'd arranged with books and paper and ink.

"Copy these sentences," he drawled from across the table, handing me a piece of paper.

I looked at them and read perfectly:

"*Rhysand is a spectacular person. Rhysand is the center of my world. Rhysand is the best lover a female can ever dream of.*" I set down the paper, wrote out the three sentences, and handed it to him.

The claws slammed into my mind a moment later.

And bounced harmlessly off a black, glimmering shield of adamant.

He blinked. "You practiced."

I rose from the table and walked away. "I had nothing better to do."

That night, he left a pile of books by my door with a note.

I have business elsewhere. The house is yours. Send word if you need me.

Days passed—and I didn't.

Rhys returned at the end of the week. I'd taken to situating myself in one of the little lounges overlooking the mountains, and had almost read an entire book in the deep-cushioned armchair, going slowly as I learned new words. But it had filled my time—given me quiet, steadfast company with those characters, who did not exist and never would, but somehow made me feel less . . . alone.

The woman who'd hurled a bone-spear at Amarantha . . . I didn't know where she was anymore. Perhaps she'd vanished that day her neck had snapped and faerie immortality had filled her veins.

I was just finishing up a particularly good chapter—the second-to-last in the book—a shaft of buttery afternoon sunlight warming my feet, when Rhysand slid between two of the oversized armchairs, twin plates of food in his hands, and set them on the low-lying table before me. "Since you seem hell-bent on a sedentary lifestyle," he said, "I thought I'd go one step further and bring your food to you."

My stomach was already twisting with hunger, and I lowered the book into my lap. "Thank you."

A short laugh. "*Thank you*? Not '*High lord and servant?*' Or: '*Whatever it is you want, you can go shove it up your ass, Rhysand.*'?" He clicked his tongue. "How disappointing."

I set down the book and extended a hand for the plate. He could listen to himself talk all day if he wished, but I wanted to eat. Now.

My fingers had almost grazed the rim of the plate when it just *slid* away.

I reached again. Once more, a tendril of his power yanked the plate further back.

"Tell me what to do," he said. "Tell me what to do to help you."

Rhys kept the plate beyond reach. He spoke again, and as if the words tumbling out loosened his grip on his power, talons of smoke curled over his fingers and great wings of shadow spread from his back. "Months and months, and you're still a ghost. Does no one there ask what the hell is happening? Does your High Lord simply not care?"

He did care. Tamlin *did* care. Perhaps too much. "He's giving me space to sort it out," I said, with enough of a bite that I barely recognized my voice.

"Let me help you," Rhys said. "We went through enough Under the Mountain—"

I flinched.

"She wins," Rhys breathed. "That bitch wins if you let yourself fall apart."

I wondered if he'd been telling himself that for months now, wondered if he, too, had moments when his own memories sometimes suffocated him deep in the night.

But I lifted the book, firing two words down the bond between us before I blasted my shields up again.

Conversation over.

"Like hell it is," he snarled. A thrum of power caressed my fingers, and then the book sealed shut between my hands. My nails dug into the leather and paper—to no avail.

Bastard. Arrogant, presuming *bastard.*

Slowly, I lifted my eyes to him. And I felt . . . not hot temper—but icy, glittering rage.

I could almost *feel* that ice at my fingertips, kissing my palms. And I swore there was frost coating the book before I hurled it at his head.

He shielded fast enough that it bounced away and slid across the marble floor behind us.

"Good," he said, his breathing a bit uneven. "What else do you have, Feyre?"

Ice melted to flame, and my fingers curled into fists.

And the High Lord of the Night Court honestly looked relieved at the sight of it—of that wrath that made me want to rage and burn.

A feeling, for once. Not like that hollow cold and silence.

And the thought of returning to that manor with the sentries and the patrols and the secrets . . . I sank back into my chair. Frozen once more.

"Any time you need someone to play with," Rhys said, pushing the plate toward me on a star-flecked wind, "whether it's during our marvelous week together or otherwise, you let me know."

I couldn't muster up a response, exhausted from the bit of temper I'd shown.

And I realized I was in a free fall with no end. I had been for a while. From the moment I'd stabbed that Fae youth in the heart.

I didn't look up at him again as I devoured the food.

The next morning, Tamlin was waiting in the shade of the gnarled, mighty oak tree in the garden.

A murderous expression twisted his face, directed solely at Rhys. Yet there was nothing amused in Rhys's smile as he stepped back from me—only a cold, cunning predator gazing out.

Tamlin growled at me, "Get inside."

I looked between the two High Lords. And seeing that fury in Tamlin's face . . . I knew there would be no more solitary rides or walks through the grounds.

Rhys just said to me, "Fight it."

And then he was gone.

"I'm fine," I said to Tamlin, as his shoulders slumped, his head bowing.

"I will find a way to end this," he swore.

I wanted to believe him. I knew he'd do anything to achieve it.

He made me again walk through every detail I had learned at Rhys's home. Every conversation, however brief. I told him everything, each word quieter than the last.

Protect, protect, protect—I could see the word in his eyes, feel it in every thrust he made into my body that night. I had been taken from him once in the most permanent of ways, but never again.

The sentries returned in full force the next morning.

CHAPTER 12

During that first week back, I wasn't allowed out of sight of the house.

Some nameless threat had broken onto the lands, and Tamlin and Lucien were called away to deal with it. I asked my friend to tell me what it was, yet . . . Lucien had that look he always did when he wanted to, but his loyalty to Tamlin got in the way. So I didn't ask again.

While they were gone, Ianthe returned—to keep me company, protect me, I don't know.

She was the only one allowed in. The semi-permanent gaggle of Spring Court lords and ladies at the manor had been dismissed, along with their personal servants. I was grateful for it, that I no longer would run into them while walking the halls of the manor, or the gardens, and have to dredge up a memory of their names, personal histories, no longer have to endure them trying not to stare at the tattoo, but . . . I knew Tamlin had liked having them around. Knew some of them were indeed old friends, knew he liked the manor being full of sound and laughter and chatter. Yet I'd found they all talked to each other like they were sparring partners. Pretty words masking sharp-edged insults.

I was glad for the silence—even as it became a weight on me, even as it filled my head until there was nothing inside of it beyond . . . emptiness.

Eternity. Was this to be my eternity?

I was burning through books every day—stories about people and places I'd never heard of. They were perhaps the only thing that kept me from teetering into utter despair.

Tamlin returned eight days later, brushing a kiss over my brow and looking me over, and then headed into the study. Where Ianthe had news for him.

That I was also not to hear.

Alone in the hall, watching as the hooded priestess led him toward the double doors at its other end, a glimmer of red—

My body tensed, instinct roaring through me as I whirled—

Not Amarantha.

Lucien.

The red hair was his, not hers. I was here, not in that dungeon—

My friend's eyes—both metal and flesh—were fixed on my hands.

Where my nails were growing, curving. Not into talons of shadow, but claws that had shredded through my undergarments time and again—

Stop stop stop stop stop—

It did.

Like blowing out a candle, the claws vanished into a wisp of shadow.

Lucien's gaze slid to Tamlin and Ianthe, unaware of what had happened, and then he silently inclined his head, motioning for me to follow.

We took the sweeping stairs to the second level, the halls deserted. I didn't look at the paintings flanking either side. Didn't look beyond the towering windows to the bright gardens.

We passed my bedroom door, passed his own—until we entered a small study on the second level, mostly left unused.

He shut the door after I'd entered the room, and leaned against the wood panel.

"How long have the claws been appearing?" he said softly.

"That was the first time." My voice rang hollow and dull in my ears.

Lucien surveyed me—the vibrant fuchsia gown Ianthe had selected that morning, the face I didn't bother to set into a pleasant expression . . .

"There's only so much I can do," he said hoarsely. "But I'll ask him tonight. About the training. The powers will manifest whether we train you or not, no matter who is around. I'll ask him tonight," he repeated.

I already knew what the answer would be, though.

Lucien didn't stop me as I opened the door he'd been leaning against and left without another word. I slept until dinner, roused myself enough to eat—and when I went downstairs, the raised voices of Tamlin, Lucien, and Ianthe sent me right back to the steps.

They will hunt her, and kill her, Ianthe had hissed at Lucien.

Lucien had growled back, *They'll do it anyway, so what's the difference?*

The difference, Ianthe had seethed, *lies in us having the advantage of this knowledge—it won't be Feyre alone who is targeted for the gifts stolen from those High Lords. Your children*, she then said to Tamlin, *will also have such power. Other High Lords will know that. And if they do not kill Feyre outright, then they might realize what* they *stand to gain if gifted with offspring from her, too.*

My stomach had turned over at the implication. That I might be stolen—and kept—for . . . breeding. Surely . . . surely no High Lord would go so far.

If they were to do that, Lucien had countered, *none of the other High Lords would stand with them. They would face the wrath of six courts bearing down on them. No one is that stupid.*

Rhysand is that stupid, Ianthe had spat. *And with that power of his, he could potentially withstand it. Imagine*, she said, voice softening as she had no doubt turned to Tamlin, *a day might come when he does not return her. You hear the poisoned lies he whispers in her ear. There are other ways around it*, she had added with such quiet venom. *We might not be able to deal with him, but there are some friends that I made across the sea . . .*

We are not assassins, Lucien had cut in. *Rhys is what he is, but who would take his place—*

My blood went cold, and I could have sworn ice frosted my fingertips.

Lucien had gone on, his tone pleading, *Tamlin. Tam. Just let her train, let her master this—if the other High Lords* do *come for her, let her stand a chance . . .*

Silence fell as they let Tamlin consider.

My feet began moving the moment I heard the first word out of his mouth, barely more than a growl. *No.*

With each step up the stairs, I heard the rest.

We give them no reason to suspect she might have any abilities, which training will surely do. Don't give me that look, Lucien.

Silence again.

Then a vicious snarl, and a shudder of magic rocked the house.

Tamlin's voice had been low, deadly. *Do not push me on this.*

I didn't want to know what was happening in that room, what he'd done to Lucien, what Lucien had even looked like to cause that pulse of power.

I locked the door to my bedroom and did not bother to eat dinner at all.

Tamlin didn't seek me out that night. I wondered if he, Ianthe, and Lucien were still debating my future and the threats against me.

There were sentries outside of my bedroom the following afternoon—when I finally dragged myself from bed.

According to them, Tamlin and Lucien were already holed up in his study. Without Tamlin's courtiers poking around, the manor was again silent as I, without anything else to do, headed to walk the garden paths I'd followed so many times I was surprised the pale dirt wasn't permanently etched with my footprints.

Only my steps sounded in the shining halls as I passed guard after guard, armed to the teeth and trying their best not to gawk at me. Not one spoke to me. Even the servants had taken to keeping to their quarters unless absolutely necessary.

Maybe I'd become too slothful; maybe my lazing about made me more prone to these outbursts. *Anyone* might have seen me yesterday.

And though we'd never spoken of it . . . Ianthe knew. About the powers. How long had she been aware? The thought of Tamlin telling her . . .

My silk slippers scuffed on the marble stairs, the chiffon trail of my green gown slithering behind me.

Such silence. Too much silence.

I needed to get out of this house. Needed to *do* something. If the villagers didn't want my help, then fine. I could do other things. Whatever they were.

I was about to turn down the hall that led to the study, determined to ask Tamlin if there was *any* task that I might perform, ready to beg him, when the study doors flung open and Tamlin and Lucien emerged, both heavily armed. No sign of Ianthe.

"You're going so soon?" I said, waiting for them to reach the foyer.

Tamlin's face was a grim mask as they approached. "There's activity on the western sea border. I have to go." The one closest to Hybern.

"Can I come with you?" I'd never asked it outright, but—

Tamlin paused. Lucien continued past, through the open front doors of the house, barely able to hide his wince. "I'm sorry," Tamlin said, reaching for me. I stepped out of his grip. "It's too dangerous."

"I know how to remain hidden. Just—take me with you."

"I won't risk our enemies getting their hands on you." *What enemies? Tell me—tell me* something.

I stared over his shoulder, toward where Lucien lingered in the gravel beyond the house entrance. No horses. I supposed they weren't necessary this time, when they were faster without them. But maybe I could keep up. Maybe I'd wait until they left and—

"Don't even think about it," Tamlin warned.

My attention snapped to his face.

He growled, "Don't even try to come after us."

"I can fight," I tried again. A half-truth. A knack for survival wasn't the same as trained skill. "Please."

I'd never hated a word more.

He shook his head, crossing the foyer to the front doors.

I followed him, blurting, "There will *always* be some threat. There will always be some conflict or enemy or *something* that keeps me in here."

He slowed to a stop just inside the towering oak doors, so lovingly restored after Amarantha's cronies had trashed them. "You can barely sleep through the night," he said carefully.

I retorted, "Neither can you."

But he just plowed ahead, "You can barely handle being around other people—"

"You *promised.*" My voice cracked. And I didn't care that I was begging. "I need to get out of this house."

"Have Bron take you and Ianthe on a ride—"

"I don't want to go for a ride!" I splayed my arms. "I don't want to go for a ride, or a picnic, or pick wildflowers. I want to *do* something. So take me with you."

That girl who had needed to be protected, who had craved stability and comfort . . . she had died Under the Mountain. *I* had died, and there had been no one to protect me from those horrors before my neck snapped. So I had done it myself. And I would not, *could not*, yield that part of me that had awoken and transformed Under the Mountain. Tamlin had gotten his powers back, had become whole again—become that protector and provider he wished to be.

I was not the human girl who needed coddling and pampering, who wanted luxury and easiness. I didn't know how to go back to craving those things. To being docile.

Tamlin's claws punched out. "Even if I risked it, your untrained abilities render your presence more of a liability than anything."

It was like being hit with stones—so hard I could feel myself cracking. But I lifted my chin and said, "I'm coming along whether you want me to or not."

"No, you aren't." He strode right through the door, his claws slashing the air at his sides, and was halfway down the steps before I reached the threshold.

Where I slammed into an invisible wall.

I staggered back, trying to reorder my mind around the impossibility of it. It was identical to the one I'd built that day in the study, and I searched inside the shards of my soul, my heart, for a tether to that shield, wondering if I'd blocked *myself*, but—there was no power emanating from me.

I reached a hand to the open air of the doorway. And met solid resistance.

"Tamlin," I rasped.

But he was already down the front drive, walking toward the looming iron gates. Lucien remained at the foot of the stairs, his face so, so pale.

"*Tamlin*," I said again, pushing against the wall.

He didn't turn.

I slammed my hand into the invisible barrier. No movement—nothing but hardened air. And I had not learned about my own powers enough to try to push through, to shatter it . . . I had *let* him convince me not to learn those things for *his* sake—

"Don't bother trying," Lucien said softly, as Tamlin cleared the gates and vanished—winnowed. "He shielded the entire house around you. Others can go in and out, but you can't. Not until he lifts the shield."

He'd locked me in here.

I hit the shield again. Again.

Nothing.

"Just—be patient, Feyre," Lucien tried, wincing as he followed after Tamlin. "Please. I'll see what I can do. I'll try again."

I barely heard him over the roar in my ears. Didn't wait to see him pass the gates and winnow, too.

He'd locked me in. He'd sealed me inside this house.

I hurtled for the nearest window in the foyer and shoved it open. A cool spring breeze rushed in—and I shoved my hand through it—only for my fingers to bounce off an invisible wall. Smooth, hard air pushed against my skin.

Breathing became difficult.

I was trapped.

I was trapped inside this house. I might as well have been Under the Mountain; I might as well have been inside that cell again—

I backed away, my steps too light, too fast, and slammed into the oak table in the center of the foyer. None of the nearby sentries came to investigate.

He'd trapped me in here; he'd *locked me up*.

I stopped seeing the marble floor, or the paintings on the walls, or the sweeping staircase looming behind me. I stopped hearing the chirping of the spring birds, or the sighing of the breeze through the curtains.

And then crushing black pounded down and rose up from beneath, devouring and roaring and shredding.

It was all I could do to keep from screaming, to keep from shattering into ten thousand pieces as I sank onto the marble floor, bowing over my knees, and wrapped my arms around myself.

He'd trapped me; he'd trapped me; he'd trapped me—

I had to get *out*, because I'd barely escaped from another prison once before, and this time, this time—

Winnowing. I could vanish into nothing but air and appear somewhere else, somewhere open and free. I fumbled for my power, for anything, *something* that might show me the way to do it, the way out. Nothing. There was nothing and I had become *nothing*, and I couldn't ever get out—

Someone was shouting my name from far away.

Alis—Alis.

But I was ensconced in a cocoon of darkness and fire and ice and wind, a cocoon that melted the ring off my finger until the golden ore dripped away into the void, the emerald tumbling after it. I wrapped that raging force around myself as if it could keep the walls from crushing me entirely, and maybe, maybe buy me the tiniest sip of air—

I couldn't get out; I couldn't get out; I couldn't get out—

Slender, strong hands gripped me under the shoulders.

I didn't have the strength to fight them off.

One of those hands moved to my knees, the other to my back, and then I was being lifted, held against what was unmistakably a female body.

I couldn't see her, didn't want to see her.

Amarantha.

Come to take me away again; come to kill me at last.

There were words being spoken around me. Two women.

Neither of them . . . neither of them was Amarantha.

"Please—please take care of her." Alis.

From right by my ear, the other replied, "Consider yourselves very, very lucky that your High Lord was not here when we arrived. Your guards will have one hell of a headache when they wake up, but they're alive. Be grateful." Mor.

Mor held me—carried me.

The darkness guttered long enough that I could draw breath, that I could see the garden door she walked toward. I opened my mouth, but she peered down at me and said, "Did you think his shield would keep us from you? Rhys shattered it with half a thought."

But I didn't spy Rhys anywhere—not as the darkness swirled back in. I clung to her, trying to breathe, to think.

"You're free," Mor said tightly. "You're free."

Not safe. Not protected.

Free.

She carried me beyond the garden, into the fields, up a hill, down it, and into—into a cave—

I must have started bucking and thrashing in her arms, because she said, "You're out; you're *free*," again and again and again as true darkness swallowed us.

Half a heartbeat later, she emerged into sunlight—bright, strawberry-and-grass-scented sunlight. I had a thought that this might be Summer, then—

Then a low, vicious growl split the air before us, cleaving even my darkness.

"I did everything by the book," Mor said to the owner of that growl.

I was passed from her arms to someone else's, and I struggled to breathe, fought for any trickle of air down my lungs. Until Rhysand said, "Then we're done here."

Wind tore at me, along with ancient darkness.

But a sweeter, softer shade of night caressed me, stroking my nerves, my lungs, until I could at last get air inside, until it seduced me into sleep.

CHAPTER 13

I woke to sunlight, and open space—nothing but clear sky and snow-capped mountains around me.

And Rhysand lounging in an armchair across from the couch where I was sprawled, gazing at the mountains, his face uncharacteristically solemn.

I swallowed, and his head whipped toward me.

No kindness in his eyes. Nothing but unending, icy rage.

But he blinked, and it was gone. Replaced by perhaps relief. Exhaustion.

And the pale sunlight warming the moonstone floors . . . dawn. It was dawn. I didn't want to think about how long I'd been unconscious.

"What happened?" I said. My voice was hoarse. As if I'd been screaming.

"You *were* screaming," he said. I didn't care if my mental shield was up or down or completely shattered. "You also managed to scare the shit out of every servant and sentry in Tamlin's manor when you wrapped yourself in darkness and they couldn't see you."

My stomach hollowed out. "Did I hurt any—"

"No. Whatever you did, it was contained to you."

"You weren't—"

"By law and protocol," he said, stretching out his long legs, "things would have become very complicated and very messy if I had been the one to walk into that house and take you. Smashing that shield was fine, but Mor had to go in on her own two feet, render the sentries unconscious through her own power, and carry you over the border to another court before I could bring you here. Or else Tamlin would have free rein to march his forces into my lands to reclaim you. And as I have no interest in an internal war, we had to do everything by the book."

That's what Mor had said—that she did everything by the book.

But— "When I go back . . ."

"As your presence here isn't part of our monthly requirement, you are under no obligation to go back." He rubbed at his temple. "Unless you wish to."

The question settled in me like a stone sinking to the bottom of a pool. There was such quiet in me, such . . . nothingness.

"He locked me in that house," I managed to say.

A shadow of mighty wings spread behind Rhys's chair. But his face was calm as he said, "I know. I felt you. Even with your shields up—for once."

I made myself meet his stare. "I have nowhere else to go."

It was both a question and a plea.

He waved a hand, the wings fading. "Stay here for however long you want. Stay here forever, if you feel like it."

"I—I need to go back at some point."

"Say the word, and it's done." He meant it, too. Even if I could tell from the ire in his eyes that he didn't like it. He'd bring me back to the Spring Court the moment I asked.

Bring me back to silence, and those sentries, and a life of doing nothing but dressing and dining and planning parties.

He crossed his ankle over a knee. "I made you an offer when you first came here: help me, and food, shelter, clothing . . . All of it is yours."

I'd been a beggar in the past. The thought of doing it now . . .

"Work for me," Rhysand said. "I owe you, anyway. And we'll figure out the rest day by day, if need be."

I looked toward the mountains, as if I could see all the way to the Spring Court in the south. Tamlin would be furious. He'd shred the manor apart.

But he'd . . . he'd locked me up. Either he so deeply misunderstood me or he'd been so broken by what went on Under the Mountain, but . . . he'd locked me up.

"I'm not going back." The words rang in me like a death knell. "Not—not until I figure things out." I shoved against the wall of anger and sorrow and outright despair as my thumb brushed over the vacant band of skin where that ring had once sat.

One day at a time. Maybe—maybe Tamlin would come around. Heal himself, that jagged wound of festering fear. Maybe I'd sort myself out. I didn't know.

But I did know that if I stayed in that manor, if I was locked up one more time . . . It might finish the breaking that Amarantha had started.

Rhysand summoned a mug of hot tea from nowhere and handed it to me. "Drink it."

I took the mug, letting its warmth soak into my stiff fingers. He watched me until I took a sip, and then went back to monitoring the mountains. I took another sip—peppermint and . . . licorice and another herb or spice.

I wasn't going back. Maybe I'd never even . . . gotten to come back. Not from Under the Mountain.

When the mug was half-finished, I fished for something, anything, to say to keep the crushing silence at bay. "The darkness—is that . . . part of the power *you* gave me?"

"One would assume so."

I drained the rest of the mug. "No wings?"

"If you inherited some of Tamlin's shape-shifting, perhaps you can make wings of your own."

A shiver went down my spine at the thought, at the claws I'd grown that day with Lucien. "And the other High Lords? Ice—that's Winter. That shield I once made of hardened wind—who did that come from? What might the others have given me? Is—is winnowing tied to any one of you in particular?"

He considered. "Wind? The Day Court, likely. And winnowing—it's not confined to any court. It's wholly dependent on your own reserve of power—and training." I didn't feel like mentioning how spectacularly I'd failed to even move an inch. "And as for the gifts you got from everyone else . . . That's for you to find out, I suppose."

"I should have known your goodwill would wear off after a minute."

Rhys let out a low chuckle and got to his feet, stretching his muscled arms over his head and rolling his neck. As if he'd been sitting there for a long, long while. For the entirety of the night. "Rest a day or two, Feyre," he said. "Then take on the task of figuring out everything else. I have business in another part of my lands; I'll be back by the end of the week."

Despite how long I'd slept, I was so tired—tired in my bones, in my crumpled heart. When I didn't reply, Rhys strode off between the moonstone pillars.

And I saw how I would spend the next few days: in solitude, with nothing to do and only my own, horrible thoughts for company. I began speaking before I could reconsider. "Take me with you."

Rhys halted as he pushed through two purple gossamer curtains. And slowly, he turned back. "You should rest."

"I've rested enough," I said, setting down the empty mug and standing. My head spun slightly. When had I last eaten? "Wherever you're going, whatever you're doing—take me along. I'll stay out of trouble. Just . . . Please." I hated the last word; choked on it. It hadn't done anything to sway Tamlin.

For a long moment, Rhys said nothing. Then he prowled toward me, his long stride eating up the distance and his face set like stone. "If you come with me, there is no going back. You will not be allowed to speak of what you see to anyone outside of my court. Because if you do, people will die—*my* people will die. So if you come, you will have to lie about it forever; if you return to the Spring Court, you *cannot* tell anyone there what you see, and who you meet, and what you will witness. If you would rather not have that between you and—your friends, then stay here."

Stay here, stay locked up in the Spring Court . . . My chest was a gaping, open wound. I wondered if I'd bleed out from it—if a spirit could bleed out and die. Maybe that had already happened. "Take me with you," I breathed. "I won't tell anyone what I see. Even—them." I couldn't bear to say his name.

Rhys studied me for a few heartbeats. And finally he gave me a half smile. "We leave in ten minutes. If you want to freshen up, go ahead."

An unusually polite reminder that I probably looked like the dead. I felt like it. But I said, "Where are we going?"

Rhys's smile widened into a grin. "To Velaris—the City of Starlight."

✢

The moment I entered my room, the hollow quiet returned, washing away with it any questions I might have had about—about a city.

Everything had been destroyed by Amarantha. If there were a city in Prythian, I would no doubt be visiting a ruin.

I jumped into the bath, scrubbing down as swiftly as I could, then hurried into the Night Court clothes that had been left for me. My motions were mindless, each one some feeble attempt to keep from thinking about what had happened, what—what Tamlin had tried to do and had done, what *I* had done—

By the time I returned to the main atrium, Rhys was leaning against a moonstone pillar, picking at his nails. He merely said, "That was fifteen minutes," before extending his hand.

I had no glimmering ember to even try to look like I cared about his taunting before we were swallowed by the roaring darkness.

Wind and night and stars wheeled by as he winnowed us through the world, and the calluses of his hand scratched against my own fading ones before—

Before sunlight, not starlight, greeted me. Squinting at the brightness, I found myself standing in what was unmistakably a foyer of someone's house.

The ornate red carpet cushioned the one step I staggered away from him as I surveyed the warm, wood-paneled walls, the artwork, the straight, wide oak staircase ahead.

Flanking us were two rooms: on my left, a sitting room with a black marble fireplace, lots of comfortable, elegant, but worn furniture, and bookshelves built into every wall. On my right: a dining room with a long, cherrywood table big enough for ten people—small, compared to the dining room at the manor. Down the slender hallway ahead were a few more doors, ending in one that I assumed would lead to a kitchen. A town house.

I'd visited one once, when I was a child and my father had brought me along to the largest town in our territory: it'd belonged to a fantastically wealthy client, and had smelled like coffee and mothballs. A pretty place, but stuffy—formal.

This house . . . this house was a *home* that had been lived in and enjoyed and cherished.

And it was in a city.

PART TWO

THE HOUSE OF WIND

CHAPTER 14

"Welcome to my home," Rhysand said.

A city—a world lay out there.

Morning sunlight streamed through the windows lining the front of the town house. The ornately carved wood door before me was inset with fogged glass that peeked into a small antechamber and the actual front door beyond it, shut and solid against whatever city lurked beyond.

And the thought of setting foot out into it, into the leering crowds, seeing the destruction Amarantha had likely wreaked upon them . . . A heavy weight pressed into my chest.

I hadn't dredged up the focus to ask until now, hadn't given an ounce of room to consider that this might be a mistake, but . . . "What is this place?"

Rhys leaned a broad shoulder against the carved oak threshold that led into the sitting room and crossed his arms. "This is my house. Well, I have two homes in the city. One is for more . . . official business, but this is only for me and my family."

I listened for any servants but heard none. Good—maybe that was good, rather than have people weeping and gawking.

"Nuala and Cerridwen are here," he said, reading my glance down the hall behind us. "But other than that, it'll just be the two of us."

I tensed. It wasn't that things had been any different at the Night Court itself, but—this house was much, much smaller. There would be no escaping him. Save for the city outside.

There were no cities left in our mortal territory. Though some had sprung up on the main continent, full of art and learning and trade. Elain had once wanted to go with me. I didn't suppose I'd ever get that chance now.

Rhysand opened his mouth, but then the silhouettes of two tall, powerful bodies appeared on the other side of the front door's fogged glass. One of them banged on it with a fist.

"Hurry up, you lazy ass," a deep male voice drawled from the antechamber beyond. Exhaustion drugged me so heavily that I didn't particularly care that there were wings peeking over their two shadowy forms.

Rhys didn't so much as blink toward the door. "Two things, Feyre darling."

The pounding continued, followed by the second male murmuring to his companion, "If you're going to pick a fight with him, do it after breakfast." That voice—like shadows given form, dark and smooth and . . . cold.

"*I* wasn't the one who hauled me out of bed just now to fly down here," the first one said. Then added, "Busybody."

I could have sworn a smile tugged on Rhys's lips as he went on, "One, no one—*no one*—but Mor and I are able to winnow directly inside this house. It is warded, shielded, and then warded some more. Only those I wish—and *you* wish—may enter. You are safe here; and safe anywhere in this city, for that matter. Velaris's walls are well protected and have not been breached in five thousand years. No one with ill intent enters this city unless I allow it. So go where you wish, do what you wish, and see who you wish. Those two in the antechamber," he added, eyes sparkling, "might not be on that list of people you should bother knowing, if they keep banging on the door like children."

Another pound, emphasized by the first male voice saying, "You know we can hear you, prick."

"*Secondly*," Rhys went on, "in regard to the two bastards at my door, it's up to you whether you want to meet them now, or head upstairs like a wise person, take a nap since you're still looking a little peaky, and then change into city-appropriate clothing while I beat the hell out of one of them for talking to his High Lord like that."

There was such light in his eyes. It made him look . . . younger, somehow. More mortal. So at odds with the icy rage I'd seen earlier when I'd awoken . . .

Awoken on that couch, and then decided I wasn't returning home.

Decided that, perhaps, the Spring Court might not be my home.

I was drowning in that old heaviness, clawing my way up to a surface that might not ever exist. I'd slept for the Mother knew how long, and yet . . . "Just come get me when they're gone."

That joy dimmed, and Rhys looked like he might say something else, but a female voice—crisp and edged—now sounded behind the two males in the antechamber. "You Illyrians are worse than cats yowling to be let in the back door." The knob jangled. She sighed sharply. "Really, Rhysand? You locked us out?"

Fighting to keep that immense heaviness at bay a bit longer, I made for the stairs—at the top of which now stood Nuala and Cerridwen, wincing at the front door. I could have sworn Cerridwen subtly gestured me to hurry up. And I might have kissed both twins for that bit of normalcy.

I might have kissed Rhys, too, for waiting to open the front door until I was halfway down the cerulean-blue hallway on the second level.

All I heard was that first male voice declare, "Welcome home, bastard," followed by the shadowy male voice saying, "I sensed you were back. Mor filled me in, but I—"

That strange female voice cut him off. "Send your dogs out in the yard to play, Rhysand. You and I have matters to discuss."

That midnight voice said with quiet cold that licked down my spine, "As do I."

Then the cocky one drawled to her, "We were here first. Wait your turn, Tiny Ancient One."

On either side of me, Nuala and Cerridwen flinched, either from holding in laughter or some vestige of fear, or perhaps both. Definitely both as a feminine snarl sliced through the house—albeit a bit halfheartedly.

The upstairs hall was punctuated with chandeliers of swirled, colored glass, illuminating the few polished doors on either side. I wondered which belonged to Rhysand—and then wondered which one belonged to Mor as I heard her yawn amid the fray below:

"Why is everyone here so *early*? I thought we were meeting tonight at the House."

Below, Rhysand grumbled—*grumbled*—"Trust me, there's no party. Only a massacre, if Cassian doesn't shut his mouth."

"We're hungry," that first male—Cassian—complained. "Feed us. *Someone* told me there'd be breakfast."

"Pathetic," that strange female voice quipped. "You idiots are pathetic."

Mor said, "We know that's true. But *is* there food?"

I heard the words—heard and processed them. And then they floated into the blackness of my mind.

Nuala and Cerridwen opened a door, leading to a fire-warmed, sunlit room. It faced a walled, winter-kissed garden in the back of the town house, the large windows peering over the sleeping stone fountain in its center, drained for the season. Everything in the bedroom itself was of rich wood and soft white, with touches of subtle sage. It felt, strangely enough, almost human.

And the bed—massive, plush, adorned in quilts and duvets of cream and ivory to keep out the winter chill—that looked the most welcoming of all.

But I wasn't so far gone that I couldn't ask a few basic questions—to at least give myself the illusion of caring a bit about my own welfare.

"Who was that?" I managed to say as they shut the door behind us.

Nuala headed for the small attached bathing room—white marble, a claw-foot tub, more sunny windows that overlooked the garden wall and the thick line of cypress trees that stood watch behind it. Cerridwen, already stalking for the armoire, cringed a bit and said over a shoulder, "They're Rhysand's Inner Circle."

The ones I'd heard mentioned that day at the Night Court—who Rhys kept going to meet. "I wasn't aware that High Lords kept things so casual," I admitted.

"They don't," Nuala said, returning from the bathing room with a brush. "But Rhysand does."

Apparently, my hair was a mess, because Nuala brushed it as Cerridwen pulled out some ivory sleeping clothes—a warm and soft lace-trimmed top and pants.

I took in the clothes, then the room, then the winter garden and the slumbering fountain beyond, and Rhysand's earlier words clicked into place.

The walls of this city have not been breached for five thousand years.

Meaning Amarantha . . .

"How is this city here?" I met Nuala's gaze in the mirror. "How—how did it survive?"

Nuala's face tightened, and her dark eyes flicked to her twin, who slowly rose from a dresser drawer, fleece-lined slippers for me in hand. Cerridwen's throat bobbed as she swallowed.

"The High Lord is very powerful," Cerridwen said—carefully. "And was devoted to his people long before his father's mantle passed to him."

"*How* did it survive?" I pushed. A city—a lovely one, if the sounds from my window, the garden beyond it, were any indication—lay all around me. Untouched, whole. Safe. While the rest of the world had been left to ruin.

The twins exchanged looks again, some silent language they'd learned in the womb passing between them. Nuala set down the brush on the vanity. "It is not for us to tell."

"He *asked* you not to—"

"No," Cerridwen interrupted, folding back the covers of the bed. "The High Lord made no such demand. But what he did to shield this city is his story to tell, not ours. We would be more comfortable if he told you, lest we get any of it wrong."

I glared between them. Fine. Fair enough.

Cerridwen moved to shut the curtains, sealing the room in darkness.

My heart stumbled, taking my anger with it, and I blurted, "Leave them open."

I couldn't be sealed up and shut in darkness—not yet.

Cerridwen nodded and left the curtains open, both of the twins telling me to send word if I needed anything before they departed.

Alone, I slid into the bed, hardly feeling the softness, the smoothness of the sheets.

I listened to the crackling fire, the chirp of birds in the garden's potted evergreens—so different from the spring-sweet melodies I was used to. That I might never hear or be able to endure again.

Maybe Amarantha had won after all.

And some strange, new part of me wondered if my never returning might be a fitting punishment for him. For what *he* had done to me.

Sleep claimed me, swift and brutal and deep.

CHAPTER 15

I awoke four hours later.

It took me minutes to remember where I was, what had happened. And each tick of the little clock on the rosewood writing desk was a shove back-back-back into that heavy dark. But at least I wasn't tired. Weary, but no longer on the cusp of feeling like sleeping forever.

I'd think about what happened at the Spring Court later. Tomorrow. Never.

Mercifully, Rhysand's Inner Circle left before I'd finished dressing.

Rhys was waiting at the front door—which was open to the small wood-and-marble antechamber, which in turn was open to the street beyond. He ran an eye over me, from the suede navy shoes—practical and comfortably made—to the knee-length sky-blue overcoat, to the braid that began on one side of my head and curved around the back. Beneath the coat, my usual flimsy attire had been replaced by thicker, warmer brown pants, and a pretty cream sweater that was so soft I could have slept in it. Knitted gloves that matched my shoes had already been stuffed into the coat's deep pockets.

"Those two certainly like to fuss," Rhysand said, though something about it was strained as we headed out the front door.

Each step toward that bright threshold was both an eternity and an invitation.

For a moment, the weight in me vanished as I gobbled down the details of the emerging city:

Buttery sunlight that softened the already mild winter day, a small, manicured front lawn—its dried grass near-white—bordered with a waist-high wrought iron fence and empty flower beds, all leading toward a clean street of pale cobblestones. High Fae in various forms of dress meandered by: some in coats like mine to ward against the crisp air, some wearing mortal fashions with layers and poofy skirts and lace, some in riding leathers—all unhurried as they breathed in the salt-and-lemon-verbena breeze that even winter couldn't chase away. Not one of them looked toward the house. As if they either didn't know or weren't worried that their own High Lord dwelled in one of the many marble town houses lining either side of the street, each capped with a green copper roof and pale chimneys that puffed tendrils of smoke into the brisk sky.

In the distance, children shrieked with laughter.

I staggered to the front gate, unlatching it with fumbling fingers that hardly registered the ice-cold metal, and took all of three steps into the street before I halted at the sight at the other end.

The street sloped down, revealing more pretty town houses and puffing chimneys, more well-fed, unconcerned people. And at the very bottom of the hill curved a broad, winding river, sparkling like deepest sapphire, snaking toward a vast expanse of water beyond.

The sea.

The city had been built like a crust atop the rolling, steep hills that flanked the river, the buildings crafted from white marble or warm sandstone. Ships with sails of varying shapes loitered in the river, the white wings of birds shining brightly above them in the midday sun.

No monsters. No darkness. Not a hint of fear, of despair.

Untouched.

The city has not been breached in five thousand years.

Even during the height of her dominance over Prythian, whatever Rhys had done, whatever he'd sold or bartered . . . Amarantha truly had not touched this place.

The rest of Prythian had been shredded, then left to bleed out over the course of fifty years, yet Velaris . . . My fingers curled into fists.

I sensed something looming and gazed down the other end of the street.

There, like eternal guardians of the city, towered a wall of flat-topped mountains of red stone—the same stone that had been used to build some of the structures. They curved around the northern edge of Velaris, to where the river bent toward them and flowed into their shadow. To the north, different mountains surrounded the city across the river—a range of sharp peaks like fish's teeth cleaved the city's merry hills from the sea beyond. But these mountains behind me . . . They were sleeping giants. Somehow alive, awake.

As if in answer, that undulating, slithering power slid along my bones, like a cat brushing against my legs for attention. I ignored it.

"The middle peak," Rhys said from behind me, and I whirled, remembering he was there. He just pointed toward the largest of the plateaus. Holes and—*windows* seemed to have been built into the uppermost part of it. And flying toward it, borne on large, dark wings, were two figures. "That's my other home in this city. The House of Wind."

Sure enough, the flying figures swerved on what looked to be a wicked, fast current.

"We'll be dining there tonight," he added, and I couldn't tell if he sounded irritated or resigned about it.

And I didn't quite care. I turned toward the city again and said, "How?"

He understood what I meant. "Luck."

"Luck? Yes, how lucky for you," I said quietly, but not weakly, "that the rest of Prythian was ravaged while your people, your city, remained safe."

The wind ruffled Rhys's dark hair, his face unreadable.

"Did you even think for one moment," I said, my voice like gravel, "to extend that *luck* to anywhere else? Anyone else?"

"Other cities," he said calmly, "are known to the world. Velaris has remained secret beyond the borders of these lands for millennia. Amarantha did not touch it, because she did not know it existed. None of her beasts did. No one in the other courts knows of its existence, either."

"*How*?"

"Spells and wards and my ruthless, ruthless ancestors, who were willing to do anything to preserve a piece of goodness in our wretched world."

"And when Amarantha came," I said, nearly spitting her name, "you didn't *think* to open this place as a refuge?"

"When Amarantha came," he said, his temper slipping the leash a bit as his eyes flashed, "I had to make some very hard choices, very quickly."

I rolled my eyes, twisting away to scan the rolling, steep hills, the sea far beyond. "I'm assuming you *won't* tell me about it." But I had to know—how he'd managed to save this slice of peace and beauty.

"Now's not the time for that conversation."

Fine. I'd heard that sort of thing a thousand times before at the Spring Court, anyway. It wasn't worth dredging up the effort to push about it.

But I wouldn't sit in my room, *couldn't* allow myself to mourn and mope and weep and sleep. So I would venture out, even if it was an agony, even if the size of this place . . . Cauldron, it was enormous. I jerked my chin toward the city sloping down toward the river. "So what is there that was worth saving at the cost of everyone else?"

When I faced him, his blue eyes were as ruthless as the churning winter sea in the distance. "Everything," he said.

Rhysand wasn't exaggerating.

There was everything to see in Velaris: tea shops with delicate tables and chairs scattered outside their cheery fronts, surely heated by some warming spell, all full of chattering, laughing High Fae—and a few strange, beautiful faeries. There were four main market squares; Palaces, they were called: two on this side—the southern side—of the Sidra River, two on the northern.

In the hours that we wandered, I only made it to two of them: great, white-stoned squares flanked by the pillars supporting the carved and painted buildings that watched over them and provided a covered walkway beneath for the shops built into the street level.

The first market we entered, the Palace of Thread and Jewels, sold clothes, shoes, supplies for making both, and jewelry—endless, sparkling jeweler's shops. Yet nothing inside me stirred at the glimmer of sunlight on the undoubtedly rare fabrics swaying in the chill river breeze, at the clothes displayed in the broad glass windows, or the luster of gold and ruby and emerald and pearl nestled on velvet beds. I didn't dare glance at the now-empty finger on my left hand.

Rhys entered a few of the jewelry shops, looking for a present for a friend, he said. I chose to wait outside each time, hiding in the shadows beneath the Palace buildings. Walking around today was enough. Introducing myself, enduring the gawking and tears and judgment . . . If I had to deal with that, I might very well climb into bed and never get out.

But no one on the streets looked twice at me, even at Rhysand's side. Perhaps they had no idea who I was—perhaps city-dwellers didn't care who was in their midst.

The second market, the Palace of Bone and Salt, was one of the Twin Squares: one on this side of the river, the other one—the Palace of Hoof and Leaf—across it, both crammed with vendors selling meat, produce, prepared foods, livestock, confections, spices . . . So many spices, scents familiar and forgotten from those precious years when I had known the comfort of an invincible father and bottomless wealth.

Rhysand kept a few steps away, hands in his pockets as he offered bits of information every now and then. Yes, he told me, many stores and homes used magic to warm them, especially popular outdoor spaces. I didn't inquire further about it.

No one avoided him—no one whispered about him or spat on him or stroked him as they had Under the Mountain.

Rather, the people that spotted him offered warm, broad smiles. Some approached, gripping his hand to welcome him back. He knew each of them by name—and they addressed him by his.

But Rhys grew ever quieter as the afternoon pressed on. We paused at the edge of a brightly painted pocket of the city, built atop one of the hills that flowed right to the river's edge. I took one look at the first storefront and my bones turned brittle.

The cheery door was cracked open to reveal art and paints and brushes and little sculptures.

Rhys said, "This is what Velaris is known for: the artists' quarter. You'll find a hundred galleries, supply stores, potters' compounds, sculpture gardens, and anything in between. They call it the Rainbow of Velaris. The performing artists—the musicians, the dancers, the actors—dwell on that hill right across the Sidra. You see the bit of gold glinting near the top? That's one of the main theaters. There are five notable ones in the city, but that's the most famous. And then there are the smaller theaters, and the amphitheater on the sea cliffs . . . " He trailed off as he noticed my gaze drifting back to the assortment of bright buildings ahead.

High Fae and various lesser faeries I'd never encountered and didn't know the names of wandered the streets. It was the latter that I noticed more than the others: some long-limbed, hairless, and glowing as if an inner moon dwelled beneath their night-dark skin, some covered in opalescent scales that shifted color with each graceful step of their clawed, webbed feet, some elegant, wild puzzles of horns and hooves and striped fur. Some were bundled in heavy overcoats, scarves, and mittens—others strode about in nothing but their scales and fur and talons and didn't seem to think twice about it. Neither did anyone else. All of them, however, were preoccupied with taking in the sights, some shopping, some splattered with clay and dust and—and paint.

Artists. I'd never called myself an artist, never thought that far or that grandly, but . . .

Where all that color and light and texture had once dwelled, there was only a filthy prison cell. "I'm tired," I managed to say.

I could feel Rhys's gaze, didn't care if my shield was up or down to ward against him reading my thoughts. But he only said, "We can come back another day. It's almost time for dinner, anyway."

Indeed, the sun was sinking toward where the river met the sea beyond the hills, staining the city pink and gold.

I didn't feel like painting that, either. Even as people stopped to admire the approaching sunset—as if the residents of this place, this court, had the freedom, the safety of enjoying the sights whenever they wished. And had never known otherwise.

I wanted to scream at them, wanted to pick up a loose piece of cobblestone and shatter the nearest window, wanted to unleash that power again boiling beneath my skin and tell them, *show* them, what had been done to me, to the rest of the world, while they admired sunsets and painted and drank tea by the river.

"Easy," Rhys murmured.

I whipped my head to him, my breathing a bit jagged.

His face had again become unreadable. "My people are blameless."

That easily, my rage vanished, as if it had slipped a rung of the ladder it had been steadily climbing inside me and splattered on the pale stone street.

Yes—yes, of course they were blameless. But I didn't feel like thinking more on it. On anything. I said again, "I'm tired."

His throat bobbed, but he nodded, turning from the Rainbow. "Tomorrow night, we'll go for a walk. Velaris is lovely in the day, but it was built to be viewed after dark."

I'd expect nothing less from the City of Starlight, but words had again become difficult.

But—dinner. With him. At that House of Wind. I mustered enough focus to say, "Who, exactly, is going to be at this dinner?"

Rhys led us up a steep street, my thighs burning with the movement. Had I become so out of shape, so weakened? "My Inner Circle," he said. "I want you to meet them before you decide if this is a place you'd like to stay. If you'd like to work with me, and thus work with them. Mor, you've met, but the three others—"

"The ones who came this afternoon."

A nod. "Cassian, Azriel, and Amren."

"Who are they?" He'd said something about Illyrians, but Amren—the female voice I'd heard—hadn't possessed wings. At least ones I'd glimpsed through the fogged glass.

"There are tiers," he said neutrally, "within our circle. Amren is my Second in command."

A female? The surprise must have been written on my face because Rhys said, "Yes. And Mor is my Third. Only a fool would think my Illyrian warriors were the apex predators in our circle." Irreverent, cheerful Mor—was Third to the High Lord of the Night Court. Rhys went on, "You'll see what I mean when you meet Amren. She looks High Fae, but something different prowls beneath her skin." Rhys nodded to a passing couple, who bowed their heads in merry greeting. "She might be older than this city, but she's vain, and likes to hoard her baubles and belongings like a firedrake in a cave. So . . . be on your guard. You both have tempers when provoked, and I don't want you to have any surprises tonight."

Some part of me didn't want to know what manner of creature, exactly, she was. "So if we get into a brawl and I rip off her necklace, she'll roast and eat me?"

He chuckled. "No—Amren would do far, far worse things than that. The last time Amren and Mor got into it, they left my favorite mountain retreat in cinders." He lifted a brow. "For what it's worth, I'm the most powerful High Lord in Prythian's history, and merely interrupting Amren is something *I've* only done once in the past century."

The most powerful High Lord in history.

In the countless millennia they had existed here in Prythian, Rhys—*Rhys* with his smirking and sarcasm and bedroom eyes . . .

And Amren was worse. And older than *five thousand years*.

I waited for the fear to hit; waited for my body to shriek to find a way to get out of this dinner, but . . . nothing. Maybe it'd be a mercy to be ended—

A broad hand gripped my face—gently enough not to hurt, but hard enough to make me look at him. "Don't you *ever* think that," Rhysand hissed, his eyes livid. "*Not for one damned moment.*"

That bond between us went taut, and my lingering mental shields collapsed. And for a heartbeat, just as it had happened Under the Mountain, I flashed from my body to his—from my eyes to his own.

I had not realized . . . how I looked . . .

My face was gaunt, my cheekbones sharp, my blue-gray eyes dull and smudged with purple beneath. The full lips—my father's mouth—were wan, and my collarbones jutted above the thick wool neckline of my sweater. I looked as if . . . as if rage and grief and despair had eaten me alive, as if I was again starved. Not for food, but . . . but for joy and life—

Then I was back in my body, seething at him. "Was that a trick?"

His voice was hoarse as he lowered his hand from my face. "No." He angled his head to the side. "How did you get through it? My shield."

I didn't know what he was talking about. I hadn't *done* anything. Just . . . slipped. And I didn't want to talk about it, not here, not with him. I stormed into a walk, my legs—so damn thin, so *useless*—burning with every step up the steep hill.

He gripped my elbow, again with that considerate gentleness, but strong enough to make me pause. "How many other minds have you accidentally slipped into?"

Lucien—

"*Lucien?*" A short laugh. "What a miserable place to be."

A low snarl rippled from me. "*Do not* go into my head."

"Your shield is down." I hauled it back up. "You might as well have been shouting his name at me." Again, that contemplative angling of his head. "Perhaps you having my power . . . " He chewed on his bottom lip, then snorted. "It'd make sense, of course, if the power came from *me*—if my own shield sometimes mistook *you* for me and let you slip past. Fascinating."

I debated spitting on his boots. "Take your power back. I don't want it."

A sly smile. "It doesn't work that way. The power is bound to your life. The only way to get it back would be to kill you. And since I like your company, I'll pass on the offer." We walked a few steps before he said, "You need to be vigilant about keeping your mental wards up. Especially now that you've seen Velaris. If you ever go somewhere else, beyond these lands, and someone slipped into your mind and saw this place . . ." A muscle quivered in his jaw. "We're called daemati—those of us who can walk into another person's mind as if we were going from one room to another. We're rare, and the trait appears as the Mother wills it, but there are enough of us scattered throughout the world that many—mostly those in positions of influence—extensively train against our skill set. If you were to ever encounter a daemati without those shields up, Feyre, they'd take whatever they wanted. A more powerful one could make you their unwitting slave, make you do whatever they wanted and you'd never know it. My lands remain mystery enough to outsiders that some would find you, among other things, a highly valuable source of information."

Daemati—was I now one if I, too, could do such things? Yet another damned title for people to whisper as I passed. "I take it that in a potential war with Hybern, the king's armies wouldn't even know to strike here?" I waved a hand to the city around us. "So, what—your pampered people . . . those who can't shield their minds—they get your protection *and* don't have to fight while the rest of us will bleed?"

I didn't let him answer, and just increased my pace. A cheap shot, and childish, but . . . Inside, inside I had become like that distant sea, relentlessly churning, tossed about by squalls that tore away any sense of where the surface might be.

Rhys kept a step behind for the rest of the walk to the town house.

Some small part of me whispered that I could survive Amarantha; I could survive leaving Tamlin; I could survive transitioning into this new, strange body . . . But that empty, cold hole in my chest . . . I wasn't sure I could survive that.

Even in the years I'd been one bad week away from starvation, that part of me had been full of color, of light. Maybe becoming a faerie had broken it. Maybe Amarantha had broken it.

Or maybe I had broken it, when I shoved that dagger into the hearts of two innocent faeries and their blood had warmed my hands.

✢

"Absolutely not," I said atop the town house's small rooftop garden, my hands shoved deep into the pockets of my overcoat to warm them against the bite in the night air. There was room enough for a few boxed shrubs and a round iron table with two chairs—and me and Rhysand.

Around us, the city twinkled, the stars themselves seeming to hang lower, pulsing with ruby and amethyst and pearl. Above, the full moon set the marble of the buildings and bridges glowing as if they were all lit from within. Music played, strings and gentle drums, and on either side of the Sidra, golden lights bobbed over riverside walkways dotted with cafés and shops, all open for the night, already packed.

Life—so full of life. I could nearly taste it crackling on my tongue.

Clothed in black accented with silver thread, Rhysand crossed his arms. And rustled his massive wings as I said, "No."

"The House of Wind is warded against people winnowing inside—exactly like this house. Even against High Lords. Don't ask me why, or who did it. But the option is either walk up the ten thousand steps, which I *really* do not feel like doing, Feyre, or fly in." Moonlight glazed the talon at the apex of each wing. He gave me a slow grin that I hadn't seen all afternoon. "I promise I won't drop you."

I frowned at the midnight-blue dress I'd selected—even with the long sleeves and heavy, luxurious fabric, the plunging vee of the neckline did nothing against the cold. I'd debated wearing the sweater and thicker pants, but had opted for finery over comfort. I already regretted it, even with the coat. But if his Inner Circle was anything like Tamlin's court . . . better to wear the more formal attire. I winced at the swath of night between the roof and the mountain-residence. "The wind will rip the gown right off."

His grin became feline.

"I'll take the stairs," I seethed, the anger welcome from the past few hours of numbness as I headed for the door at the end of the roof.

Rhys snapped out a wing, blocking my path.

Smooth membrane—flecked with a hint of iridescence. I peeled back. "Nuala spent an hour on my hair."

An exaggeration, but she had fussed while I'd sat there in hollow silence, letting her tease the ends into soft curls and pin a section along the top of my head with pretty gold barrettes. But maybe staying inside tonight, alone and quiet . . . maybe it'd be better than facing these people. Than interacting.

Rhys's wing curved around me, herding me closer to where I could nearly feel the heat of his powerful body. "I promise I won't let the wind destroy your hair." He lifted a hand as if he might tug on one of those loose curls, then lowered it.

"If I'm to decide whether I want to work against Hybern with you—with your Inner Circle, can't we just . . . meet here?"

"They're all up there already. And besides, the House of Wind has enough space that I won't feel like chucking them all off the mountain."

I swallowed. Sure enough, curving along the top of the center mountain behind us, floors of lights glinted, as if the mountain had been crowned in gold. And between me and that crown of light was a long, *long* stretch of open air. "You mean," I said, because it might have been the only weapon in my arsenal, "that this town house is too small, and their personalities are too big, and you're worried I might lose it again."

His wing pushed me closer, a whisper of warmth on my shoulder. "So what if I am?"

"I'm not some broken doll." Even if this afternoon, that conversation we'd had, what I'd glimpsed through his eyes, said otherwise. But I yielded another step.

"I know you're not. But that doesn't mean I'll throw you to the wolves. If you meant what you said about wanting to work with me to keep Hybern from these lands, keep the wall intact, I want you to meet my friends first. Decide on your own if it's something you can handle. And I want this meeting to be on *my* terms, not whenever they decide to ambush this house again."

"I didn't know you even had friends." Yes—anger, sharpness . . . It felt good. Better than feeling nothing.

A cold smile. "You didn't ask."

Rhysand was close enough now that he slid a hand around my waist, both of his wings encircling me. My spine locked up. A cage—

The wings swept back.

But he tightened his arm. Bracing me for takeoff. Mother save me. "You say the word tonight, and we come back here, no questions asked. And if you can't stomach working with me, with them, then no questions asked on that, either. We can find some other way for you to live here, be fulfilled, regardless of what I need. It's your choice, Feyre."

I debated pushing him on it—on insisting I stay. But stay for what? To sleep? To avoid a meeting I should most certainly have before deciding *what* I wanted to do with myself? And to fly . . .

I studied the wings, the arm around my waist. "Please don't drop me. And please don't—"

We shot into the sky, fast as a shooting star.

Before my yelp finished echoing, the city had yawned wide beneath us. Rhys's hand slid under my knees while the other wrapped around my back and ribs, and we flapped up, up, up into the star-freckled night, into the liquid dark and singing wind.

The city lights dropped away until Velaris was a rippling velvet blanket littered with jewels, until the music no longer reached even our pointed ears. The air was chill, but no wind other than a gentle breeze brushed my face—even as we soared with magnificent precision for the House of Wind.

Rhys's body was hard and warm against mine, a solid force of nature crafted and honed for this. Even the smell of him reminded me of the wind—rain and salt and something citrus-y I couldn't name.

We swerved into an updraft, rising so fast it was instinct to clutch his black tunic as my stomach clenched. I scowled at the soft laugh that tickled my ear. "I expected more screaming from you. I must not be trying hard enough."

"*Do not*," I hissed, focusing on the approaching tiara of lights in the eternal wall of the mountain.

With the sky wheeling overhead and the lights shooting past below, up and down became mirrors—until we were sailing through a sea of stars. Something tight in my chest eased a fraction of its grip.

"When I was a boy," Rhys said in my ear, "I'd sneak out of the House of Wind by leaping out my window—and I'd fly and fly all night, just making loops around the city, the river, the sea. Sometimes I still do."

"Your parents must have been thrilled."

"My father never knew—and my mother . . ." A pause. "She was Illyrian. Some nights, when she caught me right as I leaped out the window, she'd scold me . . . and then jump out herself to fly with me until dawn."

"She sounds lovely," I admitted.

"She was," he said. And those two words told me enough about his past that I didn't pry.

A maneuver had us rising higher, until we were in direct line with a broad balcony, gilded by the light of golden lanterns. At the far end, built into the red mountain itself, two glass doors were already open, revealing a large, but surprisingly casual dining room carved from the stone, and accented with rich wood. Each chair fashioned, I noted, to accommodate wings.

Rhys's landing was as smooth as his takeoff, though he kept an arm beneath my shoulders as my knees buckled at the adjustment. I shook off his touch, and faced the city behind us.

I'd spent so much time squatting in trees that heights had lost their primal terror long ago. But the sprawl of the city . . . worse, the vast expanse of dark beyond—the sea . . . Maybe I remained a human fool to feel that way, but I had not realized the size of the world. The size of Prythian, if a city this large could remain hidden from Amarantha, from the other courts.

Rhysand was silent beside me. Yet after a moment, he said, "Out with it."

I lifted a brow.

"You say what's on your mind—one thing. And I'll say one, too."

I shook my head and turned back to the city.

But Rhys said, "I'm thinking that I spent fifty years locked Under the Mountain, and I'd sometimes let myself dream of this place, but I never expected to see it again. I'm thinking that I wish I had been the one who slaughtered her. I'm thinking that if war comes, it might be a long while yet before I get to have a night like this."

He slid his eyes to me, expectant.

I didn't bother asking again how he'd kept this place from her, not when he was likely to refuse to answer. So I said, "Do you think war will be here that soon?"

"This was a no-questions-asked invitation. I told you . . . three things. Tell me one."

I stared toward the open world, the city and the restless sea and the dry winter night.

Maybe it was some shred of courage, or recklessness, or I was so high above everything that no one save Rhys and the wind could hear, but I said, "I'm thinking that I must have been a fool in love to allow myself to be shown so little of the Spring Court. I'm thinking there's a great deal of that territory I was never allowed to see or hear about and maybe I would have lived in ignorance forever like some pet. I'm thinking . . . " The words became choked. I shook my head as if I could clear the remaining ones away. But I still spoke them. "I'm thinking that I was a lonely, hopeless person, and I might have fallen in love with the first thing that showed me a hint of kindness and safety. And I'm thinking maybe he knew that—maybe not actively, but maybe *he* wanted to be that person for someone. And maybe that worked for who I was before. Maybe it doesn't work for who—what I am now."

There.

The words, hateful and selfish and ungrateful. For all Tamlin had done—

The thought of his name clanged through me. Only yesterday afternoon, I had been there. No—no, I wouldn't think about it. Not yet.

Rhysand said, "That was five. Looks like I owe you two thoughts." He glanced behind us. "Later."

Because the two winged males from earlier were standing in the doorway.

Grinning.

CHAPTER 16

Rhys sauntered toward the two males standing by the dining room doors, giving me the option to stay or join.

One word, he'd promised, and we could go.

Both of them were tall, their wings tucked in tight to powerful, muscled bodies covered in plated, dark leather that reminded me of the worn scales of some serpentine beast. Identical long swords were each strapped down the column of their spines—the blades beautiful in their simplicity. Perhaps I needn't have bothered with the fine clothes after all.

The slightly larger of the two, his face masked in shadow, chuckled and said, "Come on, Feyre. We don't bite. Unless you ask us to."

Surprise sparked through me, setting my feet moving.

Rhys slid his hands into his pockets. "The last I heard, Cassian, no one has ever taken you up on that offer."

The second one snorted, the faces of both males at last illuminated as they turned toward the golden light of the dining room, and I honestly wondered why no one hadn't: if Rhysand's mother had also been Illyrian, then its people were blessed with unnatural good looks.

Like their High Lord, the males—warriors—were dark-haired, tan-skinned. But unlike Rhys, their eyes were hazel and fixed on me as I at last stepped close—to the waiting House of Wind behind them.

That was where any similarities between the three of them halted.

Cassian surveyed Rhys from head to foot, his shoulder-length black hair shifting with the movement. "So fancy tonight, brother. And you made poor Feyre dress up, too." He winked at me. There was something rough-hewn about his features—like he'd been made of wind and earth and flame and all these civilized trappings were little more than an inconvenience.

But the second male, the more classically beautiful of the two . . . Even the light shied from the elegant planes of his face. With good reason. Beautiful, but near-unreadable. He'd be the one to look out for—the knife in the dark. Indeed, an obsidian-hilted hunting knife was sheathed at his thigh, its dark scabbard embossed with a line of silver runes I'd never seen before.

Rhys said, "This is Azriel—my spymaster." Not surprising. Some buried instinct had me checking that my mental shields were intact. Just in case.

"Welcome," was all Azriel said, his voice low, almost flat, as he extended a brutally scarred hand to me. The shape of it was normal—but the skin . . . It looked like it had been swirled and smudged and rippled. Burns. They must have been horrific if even their immortal blood had not been able to heal them.

The leather plates of his light armor flowed over most of it, held by a loop around his middle finger. Not to conceal, I realized as his hand breached the chill night air between us. No, it was to hold in place the large, depthless cobalt stone that graced the back of the gauntlet. A matching one lay atop his left hand; and twin red stones adorned Cassian's gauntlets, their color like the slumbering heart of a flame.

I took Azriel's hand, and his rough fingers squeezed mine. His skin was as cold as his face.

But the word Cassian had used a moment ago snagged my attention as I released his hand and tried not to look too eager to step back to Rhys's side. "You're brothers?" The Illyrians looked similar, but only in the way that people who had come from the same place did.

Rhysand clarified, "Brothers in the sense that all bastards are brothers of a sort."

I'd never thought of it that way. "And—you?" I asked Cassian.

Cassian shrugged, wings tucking in tighter. "I command Rhys's armies."

As if such a position were something that one shrugged off. And—armies. Rhys had armies. I shifted on my feet. Cassian's hazel eyes tracked the movement, his mouth twitching to the side, and I honestly thought he was about to give me his professional opinion on how doing so would make me unsteady against an opponent when Azriel clarified, "Cassian also excels at pissing everyone off. Especially amongst our friends. So, as a friend of Rhysand . . . good luck."

A friend of Rhysand—not savior of their land, not murderer, not human-faerie-*thing*. Maybe they didn't know—

But Cassian nudged his bastard-brother-whatever out of the way, Azriel's mighty wings flaring slightly as he balanced himself. "How the hell did you make that bone ladder in the Middengard Wyrm's lair when you look like your own bones can snap at any moment?"

Well, that settled that. And the question of whether he'd been Under the Mountain. But where he'd been instead . . . Another mystery. Perhaps here—with these people. Safe and coddled.

I met Cassian's gaze, if only because having Rhysand defend me might very well make me crumble a bit more. And maybe it made me as mean as an adder, maybe I relished being one, but I said, "How the hell did *you* manage to survive this long without anyone killing you?"

Cassian tipped back his head and laughed, a full, rich sound that bounced off the ruddy stones of the House. Azriel's brows flicked up with approval as the shadows seemed to wrap tighter around him. As if he were the dark hive from which they flew and returned.

I tried not to shudder and faced Rhys, hoping for an explanation about his spymaster's dark gifts.

Rhys's face was blank, but his eyes were wary. Assessing. I almost demanded what the hell he was looking at, until Mor breezed onto the balcony with, "If Cassian's howling, I hope it means Feyre told him to shut his fat mouth."

Both Illyrians turned toward her, Cassian bracing his feet slightly farther apart on the floor in a fighting stance I knew all too well.

It was almost enough to distract me from noticing Azriel as those shadows lightened, and his gaze slid over Mor's body: a red, flowing gown of chiffon accented with gold cuffs, and combs fashioned like gilded leaves swept back the waves of her unbound hair.

A wisp of shadow curled around Azriel's ear, and his eyes snapped to mine. I schooled my face into bland innocence.

"I don't know why I ever forget you two are related," Cassian told Mor, jerking his chin at Rhys, who rolled his eyes. "You two and your clothes."

Mor sketched a bow to Cassian. Indeed, I tried not to slump with relief at the sight of the fine clothes. At least I wouldn't look overdressed now. "I wanted to impress Feyre. You could have at least bothered to comb your hair."

"Unlike some people," Cassian said, proving my suspicions correct about that fighting stance, "I have better things to do with my time than sit in front of the mirror for hours."

"Yes," Mor said, tossing her long hair over a shoulder, "since swaggering around Velaris—"

"We have company," was Azriel's soft warning, wings again spreading a bit as he herded them through the open balcony doors to the dining room. I could have sworn tendrils of darkness swirled in their wake.

Mor patted Azriel on the shoulder as she dodged his outstretched wing. "Relax, Az—no fighting tonight. We promised Rhys."

The lurking shadows vanished entirely as Azriel's head dipped a bit—his night-dark hair sliding over his handsome face as if to shield him from that mercilessly beautiful grin.

Mor gave no indication that she noticed and curved her fingers toward me. "Come sit with me while they drink." I had enough dignity remaining not to look to Rhys for confirmation it was safe. So I obeyed, falling into step beside her as the two Illyrians drifted back to walk the few steps with their High Lord. "Unless you'd rather drink," Mor offered as we entered the warmth and red stone of the dining room. "But I want you to myself before Amren hogs you—"

The interior dining room doors opened on a whispering wind, revealing the shadowed, crimson halls of the mountain beyond.

And maybe part of me remained mortal, because even though the short, delicate woman *looked* like High Fae . . . as Rhys had warned me, every instinct was roaring to run. To hide.

She was several inches shorter than me, her chin-length black hair glossy and straight, her skin tan and smooth, and her face—pretty, bordering on plain—was bored, if not mildly irritated. But Amren's eyes . . .

Her silver eyes were unlike anything I'd ever seen; a glimpse into the creature that I knew in my bones wasn't High Fae. Or hadn't been born that way.

The silver in Amren's eyes seemed to swirl like smoke under glass.

She wore pants and a top like those I'd worn at the other mountain-palace, both in shades of pewter and storm cloud, and pearls—white and gray and black—adorned her ears, fingers, and wrists. Even the High Lord at my side felt like a wisp of shadow compared to the power thrumming from her.

Mor groaned, slumping into a chair near the end of the table, and poured herself a glass of wine. Cassian took a seat across from her, wiggling his fingers for the wine bottle. But Rhysand and Azriel just stood there, watching—maybe monitoring—as the female approached me, then halted three feet away.

"Your taste remains excellent, High Lord. Thank you." Her voice was soft—but honed sharper than any blade I'd encountered. Her slim, small fingers grazed a delicate silver-and-pearl brooch pinned above her right breast.

So that's who he'd bought the jewelry for. The jewelry I was to never, under any circumstances, try to steal.

I studied Rhys and Amren, as if I might be able to read what further bond lay between them, but Rhysand waved a hand and bowed his head. "It suits you, Amren."

"Everything suits me," she said, and those horrible, enchanting eyes again met my own. Like leashed lightning.

She took a step closer, sniffing delicately, and though I stood half a foot taller, I'd never felt meeker. But I held my chin up. I didn't know why, but I did.

Amren said, "So there are two of us now."

My brows nudged toward each other.

Amren's lips were a slash of red. "We who were born something else—and found ourselves trapped in new, strange bodies."

I decided I *really* didn't want to know what she'd been before.

Amren jerked her chin at me to sit in the empty chair beside Mor, her hair shifting like molten night. She claimed the seat across from me, Azriel on her other side as Rhys took the one across from him—on my right.

No one at the head of the table.

"Though there *is* a third," Amren said, now looking at Rhysand. "I don't think you've heard from Miryam in . . . centuries. Interesting."

Cassian rolled his eyes. "Please just get to the point, Amren. I'm hungry."

Mor choked on her wine. Amren slid her attention to the warrior to her right. Azriel, on her other side, monitored the two of them very, very carefully. "No one warming your bed right now, Cassian? It must be *so* hard to be an Illyrian and have no thoughts in your head save for those about your favorite part."

"You know I'm always happy to tangle in the sheets with you, Amren," Cassian said, utterly unfazed by the silver eyes, the power radiating from her every pore. "I know how much you enjoy Illyrian—"

"Miryam," Rhysand said, as Amren's smile became serpentine, "and Drakon are doing well, as far as I've heard. And what, exactly, is interesting?"

Amren's head tilted to the side as she studied me. I tried not to shrink from it. "Only once before was a human Made into an immortal. Interesting that it should happen again right as all the ancient players have returned. But Miryam was gifted long life—not a new body. And you, girl . . ." She sniffed again, and I'd never felt so laid bare. Surprise lit Amren's eyes. Rhys just nodded. Whatever that meant. I was tired already. Tired of being assessed and evaluated. "Your very blood, your veins, your bones were Made. A mortal soul in an immortal body."

"I'm hungry," Mor said nudging me with a thigh. She snapped a finger, and plates piled high with roast chicken, greens, and bread appeared. Simple, but . . . elegant. Not formal at all. Perhaps the sweater and pants wouldn't have been out of place for such a meal. "Amren and Rhys can talk all night and bore us to tears, so don't bother waiting for them to dig in." She picked up her fork, clicking her tongue. "I asked Rhys if *I* could take you to dinner, just the two of us, and he said you wouldn't want to. But honestly—would you rather spend time with those two ancient bores, or me?"

"For someone who is the same age as me," Rhys drawled, "you seem to forget—"

"Everyone wants to talk-talk-talk," Mor said, giving a warning glare at Cassian, who had indeed opened his mouth. "Can't we eat-eat-eat, and *then* talk?"

An interesting balance between Rhys's terrifying Second and his disarmingly chipper Third. If Mor's rank was higher than that of the two warriors at this table, then there had to be some other reason beyond that irreverent charm. Some power to allow her to get into the fight with Amren that Rhys had mentioned—and walk away from it.

Azriel chuckled softly at Mor, but picked up his fork. I followed suit, waiting until he'd taken a bite before doing so. Just in case—

Good. So good. And the wine—

I hadn't even realized Mor had poured me a glass until I finished my first sip, and she clinked her own against mine. "Don't let these old busybodies boss you around."

Cassian said, "Pot. Kettle. Black." Then he frowned at Amren, who had hardly touched her plate. "I always forget how bizarre that is." He unceremoniously took her plate, dumping half the contents on his own before passing the rest to Azriel.

Azriel said to Amren as he slid the food onto his plate, "I keep telling him to ask before he does that."

Amren flicked her fingers and the empty plate vanished from Azriel's scarred hands. "If you haven't been able to train him after all these centuries, boy, I don't think you'll make any progress now." She straightened the silverware on the vacant place setting before her.

"You don't—eat?" I said to her. The first words I'd spoken since sitting.

Amren's teeth were unnervingly white. "Not this sort of food."

"Cauldron boil me," Mor said, gulping from her wine. "Can we *not*?"

I decided I didn't want to know what Amren ate, either.

Rhys chuckled from my other side. "Remind me to have family dinners more often."

Family dinners—not official court gatherings. And tonight . . . either they didn't know that I was here to decide if I truly wished to work with Rhys, or they didn't feel like pretending to be anything but what they were. They'd no doubt worn whatever they felt like—I had the rising feeling that I could have shown up in my nightgown and they wouldn't have cared. A unique group indeed. And against Hybern . . . who would they be, what could they do, as allies or opponents?

Across from me, a cocoon of silence seemed to pulse around Azriel, even as the others dug into their food. I again peered at that oval of blue stone on his gauntlet as he sipped from his glass of wine. Azriel noted the look, swift as it had been—as I had a feeling he'd been noticing and cataloging all of my movements, words, and breaths. He held up his hands, the backs to me so both jewels were on full display. "They're called Siphons. They concentrate and focus our power in battle."

Only he and Cassian wore them.

Rhys set down his fork, and clarified for me, "The power of stronger Illyrians tends toward 'incinerate now, ask questions later.' They have little magical gifts beyond that—the killing power."

"The gift of a violent, warmongering people," Amren added. Azriel nodded, shadows wreathing his neck, his wrists. Cassian gave him a sharp look, face tightening, but Azriel ignored him.

Rhys went on, though I knew he was aware of every glance between the spymaster and army commander, "The Illyrians bred the power to give them advantage in battle, yes. The Siphons filter that raw power and allow Cassian and Azriel to transform it into something more subtle and varied—into shields and weapons, arrows and spears. Imagine the difference between hurling a bucket of paint against the wall and using a brush. The Siphons allow for the magic to be nimble, precise on the battlefield—when its natural state lends itself toward something far messier and unrefined, and potentially dangerous when you're fighting in tight quarters."

I wondered how much of that any of them had needed to do. If those scars on Azriel's hands had come from it.

Cassian flexed his fingers, admiring the clear red stones adorning the backs of his own broad hands. "Doesn't hurt that they also look damn good."

Amren muttered, "Illyrians."

Cassian bared his teeth in feral amusement, and took a drink of his wine.

Get to know them, try to envision how I might work with them, rely on them, if this conflict with Hybern exploded . . . I scrambled for something to ask and said to Azriel, those shadows gone again, "How did you—I mean, how do you and Lord Cassian—"

Cassian spewed his wine across the table, causing Mor to leap up, swearing at him as she used a napkin to mop her dress.

But Cassian was howling, and Azriel had a faint, wary smile on his face as Mor waved a hand at her dress and the spots of wine appeared on Cassian's fighting—or perhaps flying, I realized—leathers. My cheeks heated. Some court protocol that I'd unknowingly broken and—

"Cassian," Rhys drawled, "is not a lord. Though I'm sure he appreciates you thinking he is." He surveyed his Inner Circle. "While we're on the subject, neither is Azriel. Nor Amren. Mor, believe it or not, is the only pure-blooded, titled person in this room." Not him? Rhys must have seen the question on my face because he said, "I'm half-Illyrian. As good as a bastard where the thoroughbred High Fae are concerned."

"So you—you three aren't High Fae?" I said to him and the two males.

Cassian finished his laughing. "Illyrians are certainly not High Fae. And glad of it." He hooked his black hair behind an ear—rounded; as mine had once been. "And we're not lesser faeries, though some try to call us that. We're just—Illyrians. Considered expendable aerial cavalry for the Night Court at the best of times, mindless soldier grunts at the worst."

"Which is most of the time," Azriel clarified. I didn't dare ask if those shadows were a part of being Illyrian, too.

"I didn't see you Under the Mountain," I said instead. I had to know without a doubt—if they were there, if they'd seen me, if it'd impact how I interacted while working with—

Silence fell. None of them, even Amren, looked at Rhysand.

It was Mor who said, "Because none of us were."

Rhys's face was a mask of cold. "Amarantha didn't know they existed. And when someone tried to tell her, they usually found themselves without the mind to do so."

A shudder went down my spine. Not at the cold killer, but—but . . . "You truly kept this city, and all these people, hidden from her for fifty years?"

Cassian was staring hard at his plate, as if he might burst out of his skin.

Amren said, "We will continue to keep this city and these people hidden from our enemies for a great many more."

Not an answer.

Rhys hadn't expected to see them again when he'd been dragged Under the Mountain. Yet he had kept them safe, somehow.

And it killed them—the four people at this table. It killed them all that he'd done it, however he'd done it. Even Amren.

Perhaps not only for the fact that Rhys had endured Amarantha while they had been here. Perhaps it was also for those left outside of the city, too. Perhaps picking one city, one place, to shield was better than nothing. Perhaps . . . perhaps it was a comforting thing, to have a spot in Prythian that remained untouched. Unsullied.

Mor's voice was a bit raw as she explained to me, her golden combs glinting in the light, "There is not one person in this city who is unaware of what went on outside these borders. Or of the cost."

I didn't want to ask what price had been demanded. The pain that laced the heavy silence told me enough.

Yet if they might all live through their pain, might still laugh . . . I cleared my throat, straightening, and said to Azriel, who, shadows or no, seemed the safest and therefore was probably the least so, "How did you meet?" A harmless question to feel them out, learn who they were. Wasn't it?

Azriel merely turned to Cassian, who was staring at Rhys with guilt and love on his face, so deep and agonized that some now-splintered instinct had me almost reaching across the table to grip his hand.

But Cassian seemed to process what I'd asked and his friend's silent request that he tell the story instead, and a grin ghosted across his face. "We all hated each other at first."

Beside me, the light had winked out of Rhys's eyes. What I'd asked about Amarantha, what horrors I'd made him remember . . .

A confession for a confession—I thought he'd done it for my sake. Maybe he had things he needed to voice, *couldn't* voice to these people, not without causing them more pain and guilt.

Cassian went on, drawing my attention from the silent High Lord at my right, "We *are* bastards, you know. Az and I. The Illyrians . . . We love our people, and our traditions, but they dwell in clans and camps deep in the mountains of the North, and do not like outsiders. Especially High Fae who try to tell them what to do. But they're just as obsessed with lineage, and have their own princes and lords among them. Az," he said, pointing a thumb in his direction, his red Siphon catching the light, "was the bastard of one of the local lords. And if you think the bastard son of a lord is hated, then you can't imagine how hated the bastard is of a war-camp laundress and a warrior she couldn't or wouldn't remember." His casual shrug didn't match the vicious glint in his hazel eyes. "Az's father sent him to our camp for training once he and his charming wife realized he was a shadowsinger."

Shadowsinger. Yes—the title, whatever it meant, seemed to fit.

"Like the daemati," Rhys said to me, "shadowsingers are rare—coveted by courts and territories across the world for their stealth and predisposition to hear and feel things others can't."

Perhaps those shadows were indeed whispering to him, then. Azriel's cold face yielded nothing.

Cassian said, "The camp lord practically shit himself with excitement the day Az was dumped in our camp. But me . . . once my mother weaned me and I was able to walk, they flew me to a distant camp, and chucked me into the mud to see if I would live or die."

"They would have been smarter throwing you off a cliff," Mor said, snorting.

"Oh, definitely," Cassian said, that grin going razor-sharp. "Especially because when I was old and strong enough to go back to the camp I'd been born in, I learned those pricks worked my mother until she died."

Again that silence fell—different this time. The tension and simmering anger of a unit who had endured so much, survived so much . . . and felt each other's pain keenly.

"The Illyrians," Rhys smoothly cut in, that light finally returning to his gaze, "are unparalleled warriors, and are rich with stories and traditions. But they are also brutal and backward, particularly in regard to how they treat their females."

Azriel's eyes had gone near-vacant as he stared at the wall of windows behind me.

"They're barbarians," Amren said, and neither Illyrian male objected. Mor nodded emphatically, even as she noted Azriel's posture and bit her lip. "They cripple their females so they can keep them for breeding more flawless warriors."

Rhys cringed. "My mother was low-born," he told me, "and worked as a seamstress in one of their many mountain war-camps. When females come of age in the camps—when they have their first bleeding—their wings are . . . clipped. Just an incision in the right place, left to improperly heal, can cripple you forever. And my mother—she was gentle and wild and loved to fly. So she did everything in her power to keep herself from maturing. She starved herself, gathered illegal herbs—anything to halt the natural course of her body. She turned eighteen and hadn't yet bled, to the mortification of her parents. But her bleeding finally arrived, and all it took was for her to be in the wrong place, at the wrong time, before a male scented it on her and told the camp's lord. She tried to flee—took right to the skies. But she was young, and the warriors were faster, and they dragged her back. They were about to tie her to the posts in the center of camp when my father winnowed in for a meeting with the camp's lord about readying for the War. He saw my mother thrashing and fighting like a wildcat, and . . ." He swallowed. "The mating bond between them clicked into place. One look at her, and he knew what she was. He misted the guards holding her."

My brows narrowed. "Misted?"

Cassian let out a wicked chuckle as Rhys floated a lemon wedge that had been garnishing his chicken into the air above the table. With a flick of his finger, it turned to citrus-scented mist.

"Through the blood-rain," Rhys went on as I shut out the image of what it'd do to a body, what *he* could do, "my mother looked at him. And the bond fell into place for her. My father took her back to the Night Court that evening and made her his bride. She loved her people, and missed them, but never forgot what they had tried to do to her—what they did to the females among them. She tried for decades to get my father to ban it, but the War was coming, and he wouldn't risk isolating the Illyrians when he needed them to lead his armies. And to die for him."

"A real prize, your father," Mor grumbled.

"At least he liked you," Rhys countered, then clarified for me, "my father and mother, despite being mates, were wrong for each other. My father was cold and calculating, and could be vicious, as he had been trained to be since birth. My mother was soft and fiery and beloved by everyone she met. She hated him after a time—but never stopped being grateful that he had saved her wings, that he allowed her to fly whenever and wherever she wished. And when I was born, and could summon the Illyrian wings as I pleased . . . She wanted me to know her people's culture."

"She wanted to keep you out of your father's claws," Mor said, swirling her wine, her shoulders loosening as Azriel at last blinked, and seemed to shake off whatever memory had frozen him.

"That, too," Rhys added drily. "When I turned eight, my mother brought me to one of the Illyrian war-camps. To be trained, as all Illyrian males were trained. And like all Illyrian mothers, she shoved me toward the sparring ring on the first day, and walked away without looking back."

"She abandoned you?" I found myself saying.

"No—never," Rhys said with a ferocity I'd heard only a few times, one of them being this afternoon. "She was staying at the camp as well. But it is considered an embarrassment for a mother to coddle her son when he goes to train."

My brows lifted and Cassian laughed. "Backward, like he said," the warrior told me.

"I was scared out of my mind," Rhys admitted, not a shade of shame to be found. "I'd been learning to wield my powers, but Illyrian magic was a mere fraction of it. And it's rare amongst them—usually possessed only by the most powerful, pure-bred warriors." Again, I looked at the slumbering Siphons atop the warriors' hands. "I tried to use a Siphon during those years," Rhys said. "And shattered about a dozen before I realized it wasn't compatible—the stones couldn't hold it. My power flows and is honed in other ways."

"So difficult, being such a powerful High Lord," Mor teased.

Rhys rolled his eyes. "The camp-lord banned me from using my magic. For all our sakes. But I had no idea how to fight when I set foot into that training ring that day. The other boys in my age group knew it, too. Especially one in particular, who took a look at me, and beat me into a bloody mess."

"You were so *clean*," Cassian said, shaking his head. "The pretty half-breed son of the High Lord—how fancy you were in your new training clothes."

"Cassian," Azriel told me with that voice like darkness given sound, "resorted to getting new clothes over the years by challenging other boys to fights, with the prize being the clothes off their backs." There was no pride in the words—not for his people's brutality. I didn't blame the shadowsinger, though. To treat *anyone* that way . . .

Cassian, however, chuckled. But I was now taking in the broad, strong shoulders, the light in his eyes.

I'd never met anyone else in Prythian who had ever been hungry, desperate—not like I'd been.

Cassian blinked, and the way he looked at me shifted—more assessing, more . . . sincere. I could have sworn I saw the words in his eyes: *You know what it is like. You know the mark it leaves.*

"I'd beaten every boy in our age group twice over already," Cassian went on. "But then Rhys arrived, in his clean clothes, and he smelled . . . different. Like a true opponent. So I attacked. We both got three lashings apiece for the fight."

I flinched. Hitting children—

"They do worse, girl," Amren cut in, "in those camps. Three lashings is practically an encouragement to fight again. When they do something truly bad, bones are broken. Repeatedly. Over weeks."

I said to Rhys, "Your mother willingly sent you into that?" Soft fire indeed.

"My mother didn't want me to rely on my power," Rhysand said. "She knew from the moment she conceived me that I'd be hunted my entire life. Where one strength failed, she wanted others to save me.

"My education was another weapon—which was why she went with me: to tutor me after lessons were done for the day. And when she took me home that first night to our new house at the edge of the camp, she made me read by the window. It was there that I saw Cassian trudging through the mud—toward the few ramshackle tents outside of the camp. I asked her where he was going, and she told me that bastards are given nothing: they find their own shelter, own food. If they survive and get picked to be in a war-band, they'll be bottom-ranking forever, but receive their own tents and supplies. But until then, he'd stay in the cold."

"Those mountains," Azriel added, his face hard as ice, "offer some of the harshest conditions you can imagine."

I'd spent enough time in frozen woods to get it.

"After my lessons," Rhys went on, "my mother cleaned my lashings, and as she did, I realized for the first time what it was to be warm, and safe, and cared for. And it didn't sit well."

"Apparently not," Cassian said. "Because in the dead of night, that little prick woke me up in my piss-poor tent and told me to keep my mouth shut and come with him. And maybe the cold made me stupid, but I did. His mother was *livid*. But I'll never forget the look on her beautiful face when she saw me and said, 'There is a bathtub with hot running water. Get in it or you can go back into the cold.' Being a smart lad, I obeyed. When I got out, she had clean nightclothes and ordered me into bed. I'd spent my life sleeping on the ground—and when I balked, she said she understood because she had felt the same once, and that it would feel as if I was being swallowed up, but the bed was mine for as long as I wanted it."

"And you were friends after that?"

"No—Cauldron no," Rhysand said. "We hated each other, and only behaved because if one of us got into trouble or provoked the other, then neither of us ate that night. My mother started tutoring Cassian, but it wasn't until Azriel arrived a year later that we decided to be allies."

Cassian's grin grew as he reached around Amren to clap his friend on the shoulder. Azriel sighed—the sound of the long-suffering. The warmest expression I'd seen him make. "A new bastard in the camp—and an untrained shadowsinger to boot. Not to mention he couldn't even *fly* thanks to—"

Mor cut in lazily, "Stay on track, Cassian."

Indeed, any warmth had vanished from Azriel's face. But I quieted my own curiosity as Cassian again shrugged, not even bothering to take note of the silence that seemed to leak from the shadowsinger. Mor saw, though—even if Azriel didn't bother to acknowledge her concerned stare, the hand that she kept looking at as if she'd touch, but thought better of it.

Cassian went on, "Rhys and I made his life a living hell, shadow-singer or no. But Rhys's mother had known Az's mother, and took him in. As we grew older, and the other males around us did, too, we realized everyone else hated us enough that we had better odds of survival sticking together."

"Do you have any gifts?" I asked him. "Like—them?" I jerked my chin to Azriel and Rhys.

"A volatile temper doesn't count," Mor said as Cassian opened his mouth.

He gave her that grin I realized likely meant trouble was coming, but said to me, "No. I don't—not beyond a heaping pile of the killing power. Bastard-born nobody, through and through." Rhys sat forward like he'd object, but Cassian forged ahead, "Even so, the other males knew that we were different. And not because we were two bastards and a half-breed. We were stronger, faster—like the Cauldron knew we'd been set apart and wanted us to find each other. Rhys's mother saw it, too. Especially as we reached the age of maturity, and all we wanted to do was fuck and fight."

"Males are horrible creatures, aren't they?" Amren said.

"Repulsive," Mor said, clicking her tongue

Some surviving, small part of my heart wanted to . . . laugh at that.

Cassian shrugged. "Rhys's power grew every day—and everyone, even the camp-lords, knew he could mist *everyone* if he felt like it. And the two of us . . . we weren't far behind." He tapped his crimson Siphon with a finger. "A bastard Illyrian had never received one of these. Ever. For Az and me to both be appointed them, albeit begrudgingly, had every warrior in every camp across those mountains sizing us up. Only pure-blood pricks get Siphons—born and bred *for* the killing power. It still keeps them up at night, puzzling over where the hell we got it from."

"Then the War came," Azriel took over. Just the way he said the words made me sit up. Listen. "And Rhys's father visited our camp to see how his son had fared after twenty years."

"My father," Rhys said, swirling his wine once—twice, "saw that his son had not only started to rival him for power, but had allied himself with perhaps the two deadliest Illyrians in history. He got it into his head that if we were given a legion in the War, we might very well turn it against him when we returned."

Cassian snickered. "So the prick separated us. He gave Rhys command of a legion of Illyrians who hated him for being a half-breed, and threw me into a different legion to be a common foot soldier, even when my power outranked any of the war-leaders. Az, he kept for himself as his personal shadowsinger—mostly for spying and his dirty work. We only saw each other on battlefields for the seven years the War raged. They'd send around casualty lists amongst the Illyrians, and I read each one, wondering if I'd see their names on it. But then Rhys was captured—"

"*That* is a story for another time," Rhys said, sharply enough that Cassian lifted his brows, but nodded. Rhys's violet eyes met mine, and I wondered if it was true starlight that flickered so intensely in them as he spoke. "Once I became High Lord, I appointed these four to my Inner Circle, and told the rest of my father's old court that if they had a problem with my friends, they could leave. They all did. Turns out, having a half-breed High Lord was made worse by his appointment of two females and two Illyrian bastards."

As bad as humans, in some ways. "What—what happened to them, then?"

Rhys shrugged, those great wings shifting with the movement. "The nobility of the Night Court fall into one of three categories: those who hated me enough that when Amarantha took over, they joined her court and later found themselves dead; those who hated me enough to try to overthrow me and faced the consequences; and those who hated me, but not enough to be stupid and have since tolerated a half-breed's rule, especially when it so rarely interferes with their miserable lives."

"Are they—are they the ones who live beneath the mountain?"

A nod. "In the Hewn City, yes. I gave it to them, for not being fools. They're happy to stay there, rarely leaving, ruling themselves and being as wicked as they please, for all eternity."

That was the court he must have shown Amarantha when she first arrived—and its wickedness must have pleased her enough that she modeled her own after it.

"The Court of Nightmares," Mor said, sucking on a tooth.

"And what is this court?" I asked, gesturing to them. The most important question.

It was Cassian, eyes clear and bright as his Siphon, who said, "The Court of Dreams."

The Court of Dreams—the dreams of a half-breed High Lord, two bastard warriors, and . . . the two females. "And you?" I said to Mor and Amren.

Amren merely said, "Rhys offered to make me his Second. No one had ever asked me before, so I said yes, to see what it might be like. I found I enjoyed it."

Mor leaned back in her seat, Azriel now watching every movement she made with subtle, relentless focus.

"I was a dreamer born into the Court of Nightmares," Mor said. She twirled a curl around a finger, and I wondered if her story might be the worst of all of them as she said simply, "So I got out."

"What's your story, then?" Cassian said to me with a jerk of his chin.

I'd assumed Rhysand had told them everything. Rhys merely shrugged at me.

So I straightened. "I was born to a wealthy merchant family, with two older sisters and parents who only cared about their money and social standing. My mother died when I was eight; my father lost his fortune three years later. He sold everything to pay off his debts, moved us into a hovel, and didn't bother to find work while he let us slowly starve for years. I was fourteen when the last of the money ran out, along with the food. He wouldn't work—couldn't, because the debtors came and shattered his leg in front of us. So I went into the forest and taught myself to hunt. And I kept us all alive, if not near starvation at times, for five years. Until . . . everything happened."

They fell quiet again, Azriel's gaze now considering. He hadn't told his story. Did it ever come up? Or did they never discuss those burns on his hands? And what did the shadows whisper to him—did they speak in a language at all?

But Cassian said, "You taught yourself to hunt. What about to fight?" I shook my head. Cassian braced his arms on the table. "Lucky for you, you've just found yourself a teacher."

I opened my mouth, protesting, but— Rhysand's mother had given him an arsenal of weapons to use if the other failed. What did I have in my own beyond a good shot with a bow and brute stubbornness? And if I had this new power—these *other* powers . . .

I would not be weak again. I would not be dependent on anyone else. I would never have to endure the touch of the Attor as it dragged me because I was too helpless to know where and how to hit. Never again.

But what Ianthe and Tamlin had said . . . "You don't think it sends a bad message if people see me learning to fight—using weapons?"

The moment the words were out, I realized the stupidity of them. The stupidity of—of what had been shoved down my throat these past few months.

Silence. Then Mor said with a soft venom that made me understand the High Lord's Third had received training of her own in that Court of Nightmares, "Let me tell you two things. As someone who has perhaps been in your shoes before." Again, that shared bond of anger, of pain throbbed between them all, save for Amren, who was giving me a look dripping with distaste. "One," Mor said, "you have left the Spring Court." I tried not to let the full weight of those words sink in. "If that does not send a message, for good or bad, then your training will not, either. Two," she continued, laying her palm flat on the table, "I once lived in a place where the opinion of others mattered. It suffocated me, nearly broke me. So you'll understand me, Feyre, when I say that I know what you feel, and I know what they tried to do to you, and that with enough courage, you can say to hell with a reputation." Her voice gentled, and the tension between them all faded with it. "You do what you love, what *you* need."

Mor would not tell me what to wear or not wear. She would not allow me to step aside while she spoke for me. She would not . . . would not do any of the things that I had so willingly, desperately, allowed Ianthe to do.

I had never had a female friend before. Ianthe . . . she had not been one. Not in the way that mattered, I realized. And Nesta and Elain, in those few weeks I'd been at home before Amarantha, had started to fill that role, but . . . but looking at Mor, I couldn't explain it, couldn't understand it, but . . . I felt it. Like I could indeed go to dinner with her. Talk to her.

Not that I had much of anything to offer her in return.

But what she'd said . . . what they'd all said . . . Yes, Rhys had been wise to bring me here. To let me decide if I could handle them—the teasing and intensity and power. If I *wanted* to be a part of a group who would likely push me, and overwhelm me, and maybe frighten me, but . . . If they were willing to stand against Hybern, after already fighting them five hundred years ago . . .

I met Cassian's gaze. And though his eyes danced, there was nothing amused in them. "I'll think about it."

Through the bond in my hand, I could have sworn I felt a glimmer of pleased surprise. I checked my mental shields—but they were intact. And Rhysand's calm face revealed no hint of its origin.

So I said clearly, steadily to him, "I accept your offer—to work with you. To earn my keep. And help with Hybern in whatever way I can."

"Good," Rhys merely replied. Even as the others raised their brows. Yes, they'd obviously *not* been told this was an interview of sorts. "Because we start tomorrow."

"Where? And what?" I sputtered.

Rhys interlaced his fingers and rested them on the table, and I realized there was another point to this dinner beyond my decision as he announced to all of us, "Because the King of Hybern is indeed about to launch a war, and he wants to resurrect Jurian to do it."

Jurian—the ancient warrior whose soul Amarantha had imprisoned within that hideous ring as punishment for killing her sister. The ring that contained his eye . . .

"Bullshit," Cassian spat. "There's no way to do that."

Amren had gone still, and it was she whom Azriel was observing, marking.

Amarantha was just the beginning, Rhys had once told me. Had he known this even then? Had those months Under the Mountain merely been a prelude to whatever hell was about to be unleashed? Resurrecting the dead. What sort of unholy power—

Mor groaned, "Why would the king want to resurrect *Jurian*? He was so odious. All he liked to do was talk about himself."

The age of these people hit me like a brick, despite all they'd told me minutes earlier. The War—they had all . . . they had all fought *in* the War five hundred years ago.

"That's what I want to find out," Rhysand said. "And how the king plans to do it."

Amren at last said, "Word will have reached him about Feyre's Making. He knows it's possible for the dead to be remade."

I shifted in my seat. I'd expected brute armies, pure bloodshed. But this—

"All seven High Lords would have to agree to that," Mor countered.

"There's not a chance it happens. He'll take another route." Her eyes narrowed to slits as she faced Rhys. "All the slaughtering—the massacres at temples. You think it's tied to this?"

"I know it's tied to this. I didn't want to tell you until I knew for certain. But Azriel confirmed that they'd raided the memorial in Sangravah three days ago. They're looking for something—or found it." Azriel nodded in confirmation, even as Mor cast a surprised look in his direction. Azriel gave her an apologetic shrug back.

I breathed, "That—that's why the ring and the finger bone vanished after Amarantha died. For this. But who . . ." My mouth went dry. "They never caught the Attor, did they?"

Rhys said too quietly, "No. No, they didn't." The food in my stomach turned leaden. He said to Amren, "How does one take an eye and a finger bone and make it into a man again? And how do we stop it?"

Amren frowned at her untouched wine. "You already know how to find the answer. Go to the Prison. Talk to the Bone Carver."

"Shit," Mor and Cassian both said.

Rhys said calmly, "Perhaps you would be more effective, Amren."

I was grateful for the table separating us as Amren hissed, "I will not set foot in the Prison, Rhysand, and you know it. So go yourself, or send one of these dogs to do it for you."

Cassian grinned, showing his white, straight teeth—perfect for biting. Amren snapped hers once in return.

Azriel just shook his head. "I'll go. The Prison sentries know me—what I am."

I wondered if the shadowsinger was usually the first to throw himself into danger. Mor's fingers stilled on the stem of her wineglass, her eyes narrowing on Amren. The jewels, the red gown—all perhaps a way to downplay whatever dark power roiled in her veins—

"If anyone's going to the Prison," Rhys said before Mor opened her mouth, "it's me. And Feyre."

"What?" Mor demanded, palms now flat on the table.

"He won't talk to Rhys," Amren said to the others, "or to Azriel. Or to any of us. We've got nothing to offer him. But an immortal with a mortal soul . . ." She stared at my chest as if she could see the heart pounding beneath . . . And I contemplated yet again what she ate. "The Bone Carver might be willing indeed to talk to her."

They stared at me. As if waiting for me to beg not to go, to curl up and cower. Their quick, brutal interview to see if they wanted to work with *me*, I supposed.

But the Bone Carver, the naga, the Attor, the Suriel, the Bogge, the Middengard Wyrm . . . Maybe they'd broken whatever part of me truly feared. Or maybe fear was only something I now felt in my dreams.

"Your choice, Feyre," Rhys said casually.

To shirk and mourn or face some unknown horror—the choice was easy. "How bad can it be?" was my response.

"Bad," Cassian said. None of them bothered to contradict him.

CHAPTER 17

Jurian.

The name clanged through me, even after we finished dinner, even after Mor and Cassian and Azriel and Amren had stopped debating and snarling about who would do what and be where while Rhys and I went to the Prison—whatever that was—tomorrow.

Rhys flew me back over the city, plunging into the lights and darkness. I quickly found I much preferred ascending, and couldn't bring myself to watch for too long without feeling my dinner rise up. Not fear—just some reaction of my body.

We flew in silence, the whistling winter wind the only sound, despite his cocoon of warmth blocking it from freezing me entirely. Only when the music of the streets welcomed us did I peer into his face, his features unreadable as he focused on flying. "Tonight—I felt you again. Through the bond. Did I get past your shields?"

"No," he said, scanning the cobblestone streets below. "This bond is . . . a living thing. An open channel between us, shaped by my powers, shaped . . . by what you needed when we made the bargain."

"I needed not to be dead when I agreed."

"You needed not to be alone."

Our eyes met. It was too dark to read whatever was in his gaze. I was the one who looked away first.

"I'm still learning how and why we can sometimes feel things the other doesn't want known," he admitted. "So I don't have an explanation for what you felt tonight."

You needed not to be alone. . . .

But what about him? Fifty years he'd been separated from his friends, his family . . .

I said, "You let Amarantha and the entire world think you rule and delight in a Court of Nightmares. It's all a front—to keep what matters most safe."

The city lights gilded his face. "I love my people, and my family. Do not think I wouldn't become a monster to keep them protected."

"You already did that Under the Mountain." The words were out before I could stop them.

The wind rustled his hair. "And I suspect I'll have to do it again soon enough."

"What was the cost?" I dared ask. "Of keeping this place secret and free?"

He shot straight down, wings beating to keep us smooth as we landed on the roof of the town house. I made to step away, but he gripped my chin. "You know the cost already."

Amarantha's whore.

He nodded, and I think I might have said the two vile words aloud.

"When she tricked me out of my powers and left the scraps, it was still more than the others. And I decided to use it to tap into the mind of every Night Court citizen she captured, and anyone who might know the truth. I made a web between all of them, actively controlling their minds every second of every day, every decade, to forget about Velaris, to forget about Mor, and Amren, and Cassian, and Azriel. Amarantha wanted to know who was close to me—who to kill and torture. But my true court was here, ruling this city and the others. And I used the remainder of my power to shield them all from sight and sound. I had only enough for one city—one place. I chose the one that had been hidden from history already. *I* chose, and now must live with the consequences of knowing there were more left outside who suffered. But for those here . . . anyone flying or traveling near Velaris would see nothing but barren rock, and if they tried to walk through it, they'd find themselves suddenly deciding otherwise. Sea travel and merchant trading were halted—sailors became farmers, working the earth around Velaris instead. And because my powers were focused on shielding them all, Feyre, I had very little to use against Amarantha. So I decided that to keep her from asking questions about the people who mattered, I would be her whore."

He'd done all of that, had done such horrible things . . . done *everything* for his people, his friends. And the only piece of himself that he'd hidden and managed to keep her from tainting, destroying, even if it meant fifty years trapped in a cage of rock . . .

Those wings now flared wide. How many knew about those wings outside of Velaris or the Illyrian war-camps? Or had he wiped all memory of them from Prythian long before Amarantha?

Rhys released my chin. But as he lowered his hand, I gripped his wrist, feeling the solid strength. "It's a shame," I said, the words nearly gobbled up by the sound of the city music. "That others in Prythian don't know. A shame that you let them think the worst."

He took a step back, his wings beating the air like mighty drums. "As long as the people who matter most know the truth, I don't care about the rest. Get some sleep."

Then he shot into the sky, and was swallowed by the darkness between the stars.

I tumbled into a sleep so heavy my dreams were an undertow that dragged me down, down, down until I couldn't escape them.

I lay naked and prone on a familiar red marble floor while Amarantha slid a knife along my bare ribs, the steel scraping softly against my skin. "Lying, traitorous human," she purred, "with your filthy, lying heart."

The knife scratched, a cool caress. I struggled to get up, but my body wouldn't work.

She pressed a kiss to the hollow of my throat. "You're as much a monster as me." She curved the knife over my breast, angling it toward my peaked nipple, as if she could see the heart beating beneath. I started sobbing. "Don't waste your tears."

Someone far away was roaring my name; begging for me.

"I'm going to make eternity a hell for you," she promised, the tip of the dagger piercing the sensitive flesh beneath my breast, her lips hovering a breath above mine as she pushed—

✣

Hands—there were hands on my shoulders, shaking me, squeezing me. I thrashed against them, screaming, screaming—

"*FEYRE.*"

The voice was at once the night and the dawn and the stars and the earth, and every inch of my body calmed at the primal dominance in it.

"Open your eyes," the voice ordered.

I did.

My throat was raw, my mouth full of ash, my face soaked and sticky, and Rhysand—Rhysand was hovering above me, his eyes wide.

"It was a dream," he said, his breathing as hard as mine.

The moonlight trickling through the windows illuminated the dark lines of swirling tattoos down his arm, his shoulders, across his sculpted chest. Like the ones I bore on my arm. He scanned my face. "A dream," he said again.

Velaris. I was in Velaris, at his house. And I had—my dream—

The sheets, the blankets were ripped. Shredded. But not with a knife. And that ashy, smoky taste coating my mouth . . .

My hand was unnervingly steady as I lifted it to find my fingers ending in simmering embers. Living claws of flame that had sliced through my bed linens like they were cauterizing wounds—

I shoved him off with a hard shoulder, falling out of bed and slamming into a small chest before I hurtled into the bathing room, fell to my knees before the toilet, and was sick to my stomach. Again. Again. My fingertips hissed against the cool porcelain.

Large, warm hands pulled my hair back a moment later.

"Breathe," Rhys said. "Imagine them winking out like candles, one by one."

I heaved into the toilet again, shuddering as light and heat crested and rushed out of me, and savored the empty, cool dark that pooled in their wake.

"Well, that's one way to do it," he said.

When I dared to look at my hands, braced on the bowl, the embers had been extinguished. Even that power in my veins, along my bones, slumbered once more.

"I have this dream," Rhys said as I retched again, holding my hair. "Where it's not me stuck under her, but Cassian or Azriel. And she's pinned their wings to the bed with spikes, and there's nothing I can do to stop it. She's commanded me to watch, and I have no choice but to see how I failed them."

I clung to the toilet, spitting once, and reached up to flush. I watched the water swirl away entirely before I twisted my head to look at him.

His fingers were gentle, but firm where he'd fisted them in my hair. "You never failed them," I rasped.

"I did . . . horrible things to ensure that." Those violet eyes near-glowed in the dim light.

"So did I." My sweat clung like blood—the blood of those two faeries—

I pivoted, barely turning in time. His other hand stroked long, soothing lines down the curve of my back, as over and over I yielded my dinner. When the latest wave had ebbed, I breathed, "The flames?"

"Autumn Court."

I couldn't muster a response. At some point, I leaned against the coolness of the nearby bathtub and closed my eyes.

When I awoke, sun streamed through the windows, and I was in my bed—tucked in tightly to the fresh, clean sheets.

I stared up at the sharp grassy slope of the small mountain, shivering at the veils of mist that wafted past. Behind us, the land swept away to brutal cliffs and a violent pewter sea. Ahead, nothing but a wide, flat-topped mountain of gray stone and moss.

Rhys stood at my side, a double-edged sword sheathed down his spine, knives strapped to his legs, clothed in what I could only assume were Illyrian fighting leathers, based on what Cassian and Azriel had worn the night before. The dark pants were tight, the scale-like plates of leather worn and scarred, and sculpted to legs I hadn't noticed were quite that muscled. His close-fitting jacket had been built around the wings that were now fully out, bits of dark, scratched armor added at the shoulders and forearms.

If his attire hadn't told me enough about what we might be facing today—if my *own*, similar attire hadn't told me enough—all I needed was to take one look at the rock before us and know it wouldn't be pleasant. I'd been so distracted in the study an hour ago by what Rhys had been writing as he drafted a careful request to visit the Summer Court that I hadn't thought to ask what to expect *here*. Not that Rhys had really bothered explaining why he wanted to visit the Summer Court beyond "improving diplomatic relations."

"Where are we?" I said, our first words since winnowing in a moment ago. Velaris had been brisk, sunny. This place, wherever it was, was freezing, deserted, barren. Only rock and grass and mist and sea.

"On an island in the heart of the Western Isles," Rhysand said, staring up at the mammoth mountain. "And that," he said, pointing to it, "is the Prison."

There was nothing—no one around.

"I don't see anything."

"The rock is the Prison. And inside it are the foulest, most dangerous creatures and criminals you can imagine."

Go inside—inside the stone, under another mountain—

"This place," he said, "was made before High Lords existed. Before Prythian was Prythian. Some of the inmates remember those days. Remember a time when it was Mor's family, not mine, that ruled the North."

"Why won't Amren go in here?"

"Because she was once a prisoner."

"Not in that body, I take it."

A cruel smile. "No. Not at all."

I shivered.

"The hike will get your blood warming," Rhys said. "Since we can't winnow inside or fly to the entrance—the wards demand that visitors walk in. The long way."

I didn't move. "I—" The word lodged in my throat. Go under another mountain—

"It helps the panic," he said quietly, "to remind myself that I got out. That we all got out."

"Barely." I tried to breathe. I couldn't, I couldn't—

"We got out. And it might happen again if we don't go inside."

The chill mist bit at my face. And I tried—I did—to take a step toward it.

My body refused to obey.

I tried to take a step again; I tried for Elain and Nesta and the human world that might be wrecked, but . . . I couldn't.

"Please," I whispered. I didn't care if it meant that I'd failed my first day of work.

Rhysand, as promised, didn't ask any questions as he gripped my hand and brought us back to the winter sun and rich colors of Velaris.

I didn't get out of bed for the rest of the day.

CHAPTER 18

Amren was standing at the foot of my bed.

I jolted back, slamming into the headboard, blinded by the morning light blazing in, fumbling for a weapon, anything to use—

"No wonder you're so thin if you vomit up your guts every night." She sniffed, her lip curling. "You reek of it."

The bedroom door was shut. Rhys had said no one entered without his permission, but—

She chucked something onto the bed. A little gold amulet of pearl and cloudy blue stone. "This got me out of the Prison. Wear it in, and they can never keep you."

I didn't touch the amulet.

"Allow me to make one thing clear," Amren said, bracing both hands on the carved wooden footboard. "I do not give that amulet lightly. But you may borrow it, while you do what needs to be done, and return it to me when you are finished. If you keep it, I will find you, and the results won't be pleasant. But it is yours to use in the Prison."

By the time my fingers brushed the cool metal and stone, she'd walked out the door.

Rhys hadn't been wrong about the firedrake comparison.

✢

Rhys kept frowning at the amulet as we hiked the slope of the Prison, so steep that at times we had to crawl on our hands and knees. Higher and higher we climbed, and I drank from the countless little streams that gurgled through the bumps and hollows in the moss-and-grass slopes. All around the mist drifted by, whipped by the wind, whose hollow moaning drowned out our crunching footsteps.

When I caught Rhys looking at the necklace for the tenth time, I said, "What?"

"She gave you that."

Not a question.

"It must be serious, then," I said. "The risk with—"

"Don't say anything you don't want others hearing." He pointed to the stone beneath us. "The inmates have nothing better to do than to listen through the earth and rock for gossip. They'll sell any bit of information for food, sex, maybe a breath of air."

I could do this; I could master this fear.

Amren had gotten out. And stayed out. And the amulet—it'd keep me free, too.

"I'm sorry," I said. "About yesterday." I'd stayed in bed for hours, unable to move or think.

Rhys held out a hand to help me climb a particularly steep rock, easily hauling me up to where he perched at its top. It had been so long—too long—since I'd been outdoors, using my body, relying on it. My breathing was ragged, even with my new immortality. "You've got nothing to be sorry for," he said. "You're here now." But enough of a coward that I never would have gone without that amulet. He added with a wink, "I won't dock your pay."

I was too winded to even scowl. We climbed until the upper face of the mountain became a wall before us, nothing but grassy slopes sweeping behind, far below, to where they flowed to the restless gray sea. Rhys drew the sword from his back in a swift movement.

"Don't look so surprised," he said.

"I've—never seen you with a weapon." Aside from the dagger he'd grabbed to slit Amarantha's throat at the end—to spare me from agony.

"Cassian would laugh himself hoarse hearing that. And then make me go into the sparring ring with him."

"Can he beat you?"

"Hand-to-hand combat? Yes. He'd have to earn it for a change, but he'd win." No arrogance, no pride. "Cassian is the best warrior I've encountered in any court, any land. He leads my armies because of it."

I didn't doubt his claim. And the other Illyrian . . . "Azriel—his hands. The scars, I mean," I said. "Where did they come from?"

Rhys was quiet a moment. Then he said too softly, "His father had two legitimate sons, both older than Azriel. Both cruel and spoiled. They learned it from their mother, the lord's wife. For the eleven years that Azriel lived in his father's keep, she saw to it he was kept in a cell with no window, no light. They let him out for an hour every day—let him see his mother for an hour once a week. He wasn't permitted to train, or fly, or any of the things his Illyrian instincts roared at him to do. When he was eight, his brothers decided it'd be fun to see what happened when you mixed an Illyrian's quick healing gifts with oil—and fire. The warriors heard Azriel's screaming. But not quick enough to save his hands."

Nausea swamped me. But that still left him with three more years living with them. What other horrors had he endured before he was sent to that mountain-camp? "Were—were his brothers punished?"

Rhys's face was as unfeeling as the rock and wind and sea around us as he said with lethal quiet, "Eventually."

There was enough rawness in the words that I instead asked, "And Mor—what does she do for you?"

"Mor is who I'll call in when the armies fail and Cassian and Azriel are both dead."

My blood chilled. "So she's supposed to wait until then?"

"No. As my Third, Mor is my . . . court overseer. She looks after the dynamics between the Court of Nightmares and the Court of Dreams, and runs both Velaris and the Hewn City. I suppose in the mortal realm, she might be considered a queen."

"And Amren?"

"Her duties as my Second make her my political adviser, walking library, and doer of my dirty work. I appointed her upon gaining my throne. But she was my ally, maybe my friend, long before that."

"I mean—in that war where your armies fail and Cassian and Azriel are dead, and even Mor is gone." Each word was like ice on my tongue.

Rhys paused his reach for the bald rock face before us. "If that day comes, I'll find a way to break the spell on Amren and unleash her on the world. And ask her to end me first."

By the Mother. "What *is* she?" After our chat this morning, perhaps it was stupid to ask.

"Something else. Something worse than us. And if she ever finds a way to shed her prison of flesh and bone . . . Cauldron save us all."

I shivered again and stared up at the sheer stone wall. "I can't climb bare rock like that."

"You don't need to," Rhys said, laying a hand flat on the stone. Like a mirage, it vanished in a ripple of light.

Pale, carved gates stood in its place, so high their tops were lost to the mist.

Gates of bone.

✠

The bone-gates swung open silently, revealing a cavern of black so inky I had never seen its like, even Under the Mountain.

I gripped the amulet at my throat, the metal warm under my palm. Amren got out. I would walk out, too.

Rhys put a warm hand on my back and guided me inside, three balls of moonlight bobbing before us.

No—no, no, no, no—

"Breathe," he said in my ear. "One breath."

"Where are the guards?" I managed to get out past the tightness in my lungs.

"They dwell within the rock of the mountain," he murmured, his hand finding mine and wrapping around it as he tugged me into the immortal gloom. "They only emerge at feeding time, or to deal with restless prisoners. They are nothing but shadows of thought and an ancient spell."

With the small lights floating ahead, I tried not to look too long at the gray walls. Especially when they were so rough-hewn that the jagged bits could have been a nose, or a craggy brow, or a set of sneering lips.

The dry ground was clear of anything but pebbles. And there was silence. Utter silence as we rounded a bend, and the last of the light from the misty world faded into inky black.

I focused on my breathing. I couldn't be trapped here; I couldn't be locked in this horrible, dead place.

The path plunged deep into the belly of the mountain, and I clutched Rhys's fingers to keep from losing my footing. He still had his sword gripped in his other hand.

"Do all the High Lords have access?" My words were so soft they were devoured by the dark. Even that thrumming power in my veins had vanished, burrowing somewhere in my bones.

"No. The Prison is law unto itself; the island may be even an eighth court. But it falls under my jurisdiction, and my blood is keyed to the gates."

"Could you free the inmates?"

"No. Once the sentence is given and a prisoner passes those gates . . . They belong to the Prison. It will never let them out. I take sentencing people here very, very seriously."

"Have you ever—"

"Yes. And now is not the time to speak of it." He squeezed my hand in emphasis.

We wound down through the gloom.

There were no doors. No lights.

No sounds. Not even a trickle of water.

But I could feel them.

I could feel them sleeping, pacing, running hands and claws over the other side of the walls.

They were ancient, and cruel in a way I had never known, not even with Amarantha. They were infinite, and patient, and had learned the language of darkness, of stone.

"How long," I breathed. "How long was she in here?" I didn't dare say her name.

"Azriel looked once. Into archives in our oldest temples and libraries. All he found was a vague mention that she went in before Prythian was split into the courts—and emerged once they had been established. Her imprisonment predates our written word. I don't know how long she was in here—a few millennia seems like a fair guess."

Horror roiled in my gut. "You never asked?"

"Why bother? She'll tell me when it's necessary."

"Where did she come from?" The brooch he'd given her—such a small gift, for a monster who had once dwelled here.

"I don't know. Though there are legends that claim when the world was born, there were . . . rips in the fabric of the realms. That in the chaos of Forming, creatures from other worlds could walk through one of those rips and enter another world. But the rips closed at will, and the creatures could become trapped, with no way home."

It was more horrifying than I could fathom—both that monsters had walked between worlds, and the terror of being trapped in another realm. "You think she was one of them?"

"I think that she is the only one of her kind, and there is no record of others ever having existed. Even the Suriel have numbers, however small. But she—and some of those in the Prison . . . I think they came from somewhere else. And they have been looking for a way home for a long, long time."

I was shivering beneath the fur-lined leather, my breath clouding in front of me.

Down and down we went, and time lost its grip. It could have been hours or days, and we paused only when my useless, wasted body demanded water. Even while I drank, he didn't let go of my hand. As if the rock would swallow me up forever. I made sure those breaks were swift and rare.

And still we went onward, deeper. Only the lights and his hand kept me from feeling as if I were about to free-fall into darkness. For a heartbeat, the reek of my own dungeon cell cloyed in my nose, and the crunch of moldy hay tickled my cheek—

Rhys's hand tightened on my own. "Just a bit farther."

"We must be near the bottom by now."

"Past it. The Bone Carver is caged beneath the roots of the mountain."

"Who is he? What is he?" I'd only been briefed in what I was to say—nothing of what to expect. No doubt to keep me from panicking too thoroughly.

"No one knows. He'll appear as he wants to appear."

"Shape-shifter?"

"Yes and no. He'll appear to you as one thing, and I might be standing right beside you and see another."

I tried not to start bleating like cattle. "And the bone carving?"

"You'll see." Rhys stopped before a smooth slab of stone. The hall continued down—down into the ageless dark. The air here was tight, compact. Even my puffs of breath on the chill air seemed short-lived.

Rhysand at last released my hand, only to lay his once more on the bare stone. It rippled beneath his palm, forming—a door.

Like the gates above, it was of ivory—bone. And in its surface were etched countless images: flora and fauna, seas and clouds, stars and moons, infants and skeletons, creatures fair and foul—

It swung away. The cell was pitch-black, hardly distinguishable from the hall—

"I have carved the doors for every prisoner in this place," said a small voice within, "but my own remains my favorite."

"I'd have to agree," Rhysand said. He stepped inside, the light bobbing ahead to illuminate a dark-haired boy sitting against the far wall, eyes of crushing blue taking in Rhysand, then sliding to where I lurked in the doorway.

Rhys reached into a bag I hadn't realized he'd been carrying—no, one he'd summoned from whatever pocket between realms he used for storage. He chucked an object toward the boy, who looked no more than eight. White gleamed as it clacked on the rough stone floor. Another bone, long and sturdy—and jagged on one end.

"The calf-bone that made the final kill when Feyre slew the Middengard Wyrm," Rhys said.

My very blood stilled. There had been many bones that I'd laid in my trap—I hadn't noticed which had ended the Wyrm. Or thought anyone would.

"Come inside," was all the Bone Carver said, and there was no innocence, no kindness in that child's voice.

I took one step in and no more.

"It has been an age," the boy said, gobbling down the sight of me, "since something new came into this world."

"Hello," I breathed.

The boy's smile was a mockery of innocence. "Are you frightened?"

"Yes," I said. *Never lie*—that had been Rhys's first command.

The boy stood, but kept to the other side of the cell. "Feyre," he murmured, cocking his head. The orb of faelight glazed the inky hair in silver. "Fay-ruh," he said again, drawing out the syllables as if he could taste them. At last, he straightened his head. "Where did you go when you died?"

"A question for a question," I replied, as I'd been instructed over breakfast.

The Bone Carver inclined his head to Rhysand. "You were always smarter than your forefathers." But those eyes alighted on me. "Tell me where you went, what you saw—and I will answer your question."

Rhys gave me a subtle nod, but his eyes were wary. Because what the boy had asked . . .

I had to calm my breathing to think—to remember.

But there was blood and death and pain and screaming—and she was breaking me, killing me so slowly, and Rhys was there, roaring in fury as I died, Tamlin begging for my life on his knees before her throne . . . But there was so much agony, and I wanted it to be over, wanted it all to stop—

Rhys had gone rigid while he monitored the Bone Carver, as if those memories were freely flowing past the mental shields I'd made sure were intact this morning. And I wondered if he thought I'd give up then and there.

I bunched my hands into fists.

I had lived; I had gotten out. I would get out today.

"I heard the crack," I said. Rhys's head whipped toward me. "I heard the crack when she broke my neck. It was in my ears, but also inside my skull. I was gone before I felt anything more than the first lash of pain."

The Bone Carver's violet eyes seemed to glow brighter.

"And then it was dark. A different sort of dark than this place. But there was a . . . thread," I said. "A tether. And I yanked on it—and suddenly I could see. Not through my eyes, but—but his," I said, inclining my head toward Rhys. I uncurled the fingers of my tattooed hand. "And I knew I was dead, and this tiny scrap of spirit was all that was left of me, clinging to the thread of our bargain."

"But was there anyone there—were you seeing anything beyond?"

"There was only that bond in the darkness."

Rhysand's face had gone pale, his mouth a tight line. "And when I was Made anew," I said, "I followed that bond back—to me. I knew that home was on the other end of it. There was light then. Like swimming up through sparkling wine—"

"Were you afraid?"

"All I wanted was to return to—to the people around me. I wanted it badly enough I didn't have room for fear. The worst had happened, and the darkness was calm and quiet. It did not seem like a bad thing to fade into. But I wanted to go home. So I followed the bond home."

"There was no other world," the Bone Carver pushed.

"If there was or is, I did not see it."

"No light, no portal?"

Where is it that you want to go? The question almost leaped off my tongue. "It was only peace and darkness."

"Did you have a body?"

"No."

"Did—"

"That's enough from you," Rhysand purred—the sound like velvet over sharpest steel. "You said a question for a question. Now you've asked . . . " He did a tally on his fingers. "Six."

The Bone Carver leaned back against the wall and slid to a sitting position. "It is a rare day when I meet someone who comes back from true death. Forgive me for wanting to peer behind the curtain." He waved a delicate hand in my direction. "Ask it, girl."

"If there was no body—nothing but perhaps a bit of bone," I said as solidly as I could, "would there be a way to resurrect that person? To grow them a new body, put their soul into it."

Those eyes flashed. "Was the soul somehow preserved? Contained?"

I tried not to think about the eye ring Amarantha had worn, the soul she'd trapped inside to witness her every horror and depravity. "Yes."

"There is no way."

I almost sighed in relief.

"Unless . . . " The boy bounced each finger off his thumb, his hand like some pale, twitchy insect. "Long ago, before the High Fae, before man, there was a Cauldron . . . They say all the magic was contained inside it, that the world was born in it. But it fell into the wrong hands. And great and horrible things were done with it. Things were *forged* with it. Such wicked things that the Cauldron was eventually stolen back at great cost. It could not be destroyed, for it had Made all things, and if it were broken, then life would cease to be. So it was hidden. And forgotten. Only with that Cauldron could something that is dead be reforged like that."

Rhysand's face was again a mask of calm. "Where did they hide it?"

"Tell me a secret no one knows, Lord of Night, and I'll tell you mine."

I braced myself for whatever horrible truth was about to come my way. But Rhysand said, "My right knee gets a twinge of pain when it rains. I wrecked it during the War, and it's hurt ever since."

The Bone Carver bit out a harsh laugh, even as I gaped at Rhys. "You always were my favorite," he said, giving a smile I would never for a moment think was childlike. "Very well. The Cauldron was hidden at the bottom of a frozen lake in Lapplund—" Rhys began to turn for me, as if he'd head there right now, but the Bone Carver added, "And vanished a long, long time ago." Rhys halted. "I don't know where it went to—or where it is now. Millennia before you were born, the three feet on which it stands were successfully cleaved from its base in an attempt to fracture *some* of its power. It worked—barely. Removing the feet was like cutting off the first knuckle of a finger. Irksome, but you could still use the rest with some difficulty. The feet were hidden at three different temples—Cesere, Sangravah, and Itica. If *they* have gone missing, it is likely the Cauldron is active once more—and that the wielder wants it at full power and not a wisp of it missing."

That was why the temples had been ransacked. To get the feet on which the Cauldron stood and restore it to its full power. Rhys merely said, "I don't suppose you know *who* now has the Cauldron."

The Bone Carver pointed a small finger at me. "Promise that you'll give me her bones when she dies and I'll think about it." I stiffened, but the boy laughed. "No—I don't think even you would promise that, Rhysand."

I might have called the look on Rhys's face a warning. "Thank you for your help," he said, placing a hand on my back to guide me out.

But if he knew . . . I turned again to the boy-creature. "There was a choice—in Death," I said.

Those eyes guttered with cobalt fire.

Rhys's hand contracted on my back, but remained. Warm, steady. And I wondered if the touch was more to reassure him that I was there, still breathing.

"I knew," I went on, "that I could drift away into the dark. And I chose to fight—to hold on for a bit longer. Yet I knew if I wanted, I could have faded. And maybe it would be a new world, a realm of rest and peace. But I wasn't ready for it—not to go there alone. I knew there was something else waiting beyond that dark. Something good."

For a moment, those blue eyes flared brighter. Then the boy said, "You know who has the Cauldron, Rhysand. Who has been pillaging the temples. You only came here to confirm what you have long guessed."

"The King of Hybern."

Dread sluiced through my veins and pooled in my stomach. I shouldn't have been surprised, should have known, but . . .

The Carver said nothing more. Waiting for another truth.

So I offered up another shattered piece of me. "When Amarantha made me kill those two faeries, if the third hadn't been Tamlin, I would have put the dagger in my own heart at the end."

Rhys went still.

"I knew there was no coming back from what I'd done," I said, wondering if the blue flame in the Carver's eyes might burn my ruined soul to ash. "And once I broke their curse, once I knew I'd saved them, I just wanted enough time to turn that dagger on myself. I only decided I wanted to live when she killed me, and I knew I had not finished whatever . . . whatever it was I'd been born to do."

I dared a glance at Rhys, and there was something like devastation on his beautiful face. It was gone in a blink.

Even the Bone Carver said gently, "With the Cauldron, you could do other things than raise the dead. You could shatter the wall."

The only thing keeping human lands—my family—safe from not just Hybern, but any other faeries.

"It is likely that Hybern has been quiet for so many years because he was hunting the Cauldron, learning its secrets. Resurrection of a specific individual might very well have been his first test once the feet were reunited—and now he finds that the Cauldron is pure energy, pure power. And like any magic, it can be depleted. So he will let it rest, let it gather strength—learn its secrets to feed it more energy, more power."

"Is there a way to stop it," I breathed.

Silence. Expectant, waiting silence.

Rhys's voice was hoarse as he said, "Don't offer him one more—"

"When the Cauldron was made," the Carver interrupted, "its dark maker used the last of the molten ore to forge a book. The Book of Breathings. In it, written between the carved words, are the spells to negate the Cauldron's power—or control it wholly. But after the War, it was split into two pieces. One went to the Fae, one to the six human queens. It was part of the Treaty, purely symbolic, as the Cauldron had been lost for millennia and considered mere myth. The Book was believed harmless, because like calls to like—and only that which was Made can speak those spells and summon its power. No creature born of the earth may wield it, so the High Lords and humans dismissed it as little more than a historical heirloom, but if the Book were in the hands of something reforged . . . You would have to test such a theory, of course—but . . . it might be possible." His eyes narrowed to amused slits as I realized . . . realized . . .

"So now the High Lord of Summer possesses our piece, and the reigning mortal queens have the other entombed in their shining palace by the sea. Prythian's half is guarded, protected with blood-spells keyed to Summer himself. The one belonging to the mortal queens . . . They were crafty, when they received their gift. They used our own kind to spell the Book, to bind it—so that if it were ever stolen, if, let's say, a High Lord were to winnow into their castle to steal it . . . the Book would melt into ore and be lost. It must be freely given by a mortal queen, with no trickery, no magic involved." A little laugh. "Such clever, lovely creatures, humans."

The Carver seemed lost in ancient memory—then shook his head. "Reunite both halves of the Book of Breathings and you will be able to nullify the powers of the Cauldron. Hopefully before it returns to full strength and shatters that wall."

I didn't bother saying thank you. Not with the information he'd told us. Not when I'd been forced to say those things—and could still feel Rhys's lingering attention. As if he'd suspected, but never believed just how badly I'd broken in that moment with Amarantha.

We turned away, his hand sliding from my back to grip my hand.

The touch was light—gentle. And I suddenly had no strength to even grip it back.

The Carver picked up the bone Rhysand had brought him and weighed it in those child's hands. "I shall carve your death in here, Feyre."

Up and up into the darkness we walked, through the sleeping stone and the monsters who dwelled within it. At last I said to Rhys, "What did you see?"

"You first."

"A boy—around eight; dark-haired and blue-eyed."

Rhys shuddered—the most human gesture I'd seen him make.

"What did you see?" I pushed.

"Jurian," Rhys said. "He appeared exactly as Jurian looked the last time I saw him: facing Amarantha when they fought to the death."

I didn't want to learn how the Bone Carver knew who we'd come to ask about.

CHAPTER 19

"Amren's right," Rhys drawled, leaning against the threshold of the town house sitting room. "You *are* like dogs, waiting for me to come home. Maybe I should buy treats."

Cassian gave him a vulgar gesture from where he lounged on the couch before the hearth, an arm slung over the back behind Mor. Though everything about his powerful, muscled body suggested someone at ease, there was a tightness in his jaw, a coiled-up energy that told me they'd been waiting here for a while.

Azriel lingered by the window, comfortably ensconced in shadows, a light flurry of snow dusting the lawn and street behind him. And Amren . . .

Nowhere to be seen. I couldn't tell if I was relieved or not. I'd have to hunt her down to give her back the necklace soon—if Rhys's warnings and her own words were to be believed.

Damp and cold from the mist and wind that chased us down from the Prison, I strode for the armchair across from the couch, which had been shaped, like so much of the furniture here, to accommodate Illyrian wings. I stretched my stiff limbs toward the fire, and stifled a groan at the delicious heat.

"How'd it go?" Mor said, straightening beside Cassian. No gown today—just practical black pants and a thick blue sweater.

"The Bone Carver," Rhys said, "is a busybody gossip who likes to pry into other people's business far too much."

"But?" Cassian demanded, bracing his arms on his knees, wings tucked in tight.

"But," Rhys said, "he can also be helpful, when he chooses. And it seems we need to start doing what we do best."

I flexed my numbed fingers, content to let them discuss, needing a moment to reel myself back in, to shut out what I'd revealed to the Bone Carver.

And what the Bone Carver suggested I might actually be asked to do with that book. The abilities I might have.

So Rhys told them of the Cauldron, and the reason behind the temple pillagings, to no shortage of swearing and questions—and revealed nothing of what I had admitted in exchange for the information. Azriel emerged from his wreathing shadows to ask the most questions; his face and voice remained unreadable. Cassian, surprisingly, kept quiet—as if the general understood that the shadowsinger would know what information was necessary, and was busy assessing it for his own forces.

When Rhys was done, his spymaster said, "I'll contact my sources in the Summer Court about where the half of the Book of Breathings is hidden. I can fly into the human world myself to figure out where they're keeping their part of the Book before we ask them for it."

"No need," Rhys said. "And I don't trust this information, even with your sources, with anyone outside of this room. Save for Amren."

"They can be trusted," Azriel said with quiet steel, his scarred hands clenching at his leather-clad sides.

"We're not taking risks where this is concerned," Rhys merely said. He held Azriel's stare, and I could almost hear the silent words Rhys added, *It is no judgment or reflection on you, Az. Not at all.*

But Azriel yielded no tinge of emotion as he nodded, his hands unfurling.

"So what *do* you have planned?" Mor cut in—perhaps for Az's sake.

Rhys picked an invisible piece of dirt off his fighting leathers. When he lifted his head, those violet eyes were glacial. "The King of Hybern sacked one of our temples to get a missing piece of the Cauldron. As far as I'm concerned, it's an act of war—an indication that His Majesty has no interest in wooing me."

"He likely remembers our allegiance to the humans in the War, anyway," Cassian said. "He wouldn't jeopardize revealing his plans while trying to sway you, and I bet some of Amarantha's cronies reported to him about Under the Mountain. About how it all ended, I mean." Cassian's throat bobbed.

When Rhys had tried to kill her. I lowered my hands from the fire.

Rhys said, "Indeed. But this means Hybern's forces have already successfully infiltrated our lands—without detection. I plan to return the favor."

Mother above. Cassian and Mor just grinned with feral delight. "How?" Mor asked.

Rhys crossed his arms. "It will require careful planning. But if the Cauldron is in Hybern, then to Hybern we must go. Either to take it back . . . or use the Book to nullify it."

Some cowardly, pathetic part of me was already trembling.

"Hybern likely has as many wards and shields around it as we have here," Azriel countered. "We'd need to find a way to get through them undetected first."

A slight nod. "Which is why we start now. While we hunt for the Book. So when we get both halves, we can move swiftly—before word can spread that we even possess it."

Cassian nodded, but asked, "How are you going to retrieve the Book, then?"

I braced myself as Rhys said, "Since these objects are spelled to the individual High Lords, and can only be found by them—through their power . . . Then, in addition to her uses regarding the handling of the Book of Breathings itself, it seems we possibly have our own detector."

Now they all looked at me.

I cringed. "*Perhaps* was what the Bone Carver said in regard to me being able to track things. You don't know . . . " My words faded as Rhys smirked.

"You have a kernel of all our power—like having seven thumbprints. If we've hidden something, if we've made or protected it with our power, no matter where it has been concealed, you will be able to track it through that very magic."

"You can't know that for sure," I tried again.

"No—but there is a way to test it." Rhys was still smiling.

"Here we go," Cassian grumbled. Mor gave Azriel a warning glare to tell him *not* to volunteer this time. The spymaster just gave her an incredulous look in return.

I might have lounged in my chair to watch their battle of wills had Rhys not said, "With your abilities, Feyre, you might be able to find the half of the Book at the Summer Court—and break the wards around it. But I'm not going to take the Carver's word for it, or bring you there without testing you first. To make sure that when it counts, when we need to get that book, you—*we* do not fail. So we're going on another little trip. To see if you can find a valuable object of mine that I've been missing for a considerably long time."

"Shit," Mor said, plunging her hands into the thick folds of her sweater.

"Where?" I managed to say.

It was Azriel who answered. "To the Weaver."

Rhys held up a hand as Cassian opened his mouth. "The test," he said, "will be to see if Feyre can identify the object of mine in the Weaver's trove. When we get to the Summer Court, Tarquin might have spelled his half of the Book to look different, feel different."

"By the Cauldron, Rhys," Mor snapped, setting both feet on the carpet. "Are you out of your—"

"Who is the Weaver?" I pushed.

"An ancient, wicked creature," Azriel said, and I surveyed the faint scars on his wings, his neck, and wondered how many such things he'd encountered in his immortal life. If they were any worse than the people who shared blood ties with him. "Who should remain unbothered," he added in Rhys's direction. "Find another way to test her abilities."

Rhys merely shrugged and looked to me. To let me choose. Always—it was always my choice with him these days. Yet he hadn't let me go back to the Spring Court during those two visits—because he knew how badly I needed to get away from it?

I gnawed on my lower lip, weighing the risks, waiting to feel any kernel of fear, of emotion. But this afternoon had drained any reserve of such things. "The Bone Carver, the Weaver . . . Can't you ever just call someone by a given name?"

Cassian chuckled, and Mor settled back in the sofa cushions.

Only Rhys, it seemed, understood that it hadn't entirely been a joke. His face was tight. Like he knew precisely how tired I was—how I knew I should be quaking at the thought of this Weaver, but after the Bone Carver, what I'd revealed to it . . . I could feel nothing at all.

Rhys said to me, "What about adding one more name to that list?"

I didn't particularly like the sound of that. Mor said as much.

"Emissary," Rhysand said, ignoring his cousin. "Emissary to the Night Court—for the human realm."

Azriel said, "There hasn't been one for five hundred years, Rhys."

"There also hasn't been a human-turned-immortal since then, either." Rhys met my gaze. "The human world must be as prepared as we are—especially if the King of Hybern plans to shatter the wall and unleash his forces upon them. We need the other half of the Book from those mortal queens—and if we can't use magic to influence them, then they're going to have to bring it to us."

More silence. On the street beyond the bay of windows, wisps of snow brushed past, dusting the cobblestones.

Rhys jerked his chin at me. "You are an immortal faerie—with a human heart. Even as such, you might very well set foot on the continent and be . . . hunted for it. So we set up a base in neutral territory. In a place where humans trust us—trust *you*, Feyre. And where other humans might risk going to meet with you. To hear the voice of Prythian after five centuries."

"My family's estate," I said.

"Mother's tits, Rhys," Cassian cut in, wings flaring wide enough to nearly knock over the ceramic vase on the side table next to him. "You think we can just take over her family's house, demand that of them?"

Nesta hadn't wanted any dealings with the Fae, and Elain was so gentle, so sweet . . . how could I bring them into this?

"The land," Mor said, reaching over to return the vase to its place, "will run red with blood, Cassian, regardless of what we do with her family. It is now a matter of where that blood will flow—and how much will spill. How much human blood we can save."

And maybe it made me a cowardly fool, but I said, "The Spring Court borders the wall—"

"The wall stretches across the sea. We'll fly in offshore," Rhys said without so much as a blink. "I won't risk discovery from any court, though word might spread quickly enough once we're there. I know it won't be easy, Feyre, but if there's any way you could convince those queens—"

"I'll do it." I said. Clare Beddor's broken and nailed body flashed in my vision. Amarantha had been one of his commanders. Just one—of many. The King of Hybern had to be horrible beyond reckoning to be her master. If these people got their hands on my sisters . . . "They might not be happy about it, but I'll make Elain and Nesta do it."

I didn't have the nerve to ask Rhys if he could simply force my family to agree to help us if they refused. I wondered if his powers would work on Nesta when even Tamlin's glamour had failed against her steel mind.

"Then it's settled," Rhys said. None of them looked particularly happy. "Once Feyre darling returns from the Weaver, we'll bring Hybern to its knees."

Rhys and the others were gone that night—where, no one told me. But after the events of the day, I barely finished devouring the food Nuala and Cerridwen brought to my room before I tumbled into sleep.

I dreamed of a long, white bone, carved with horrifying accuracy: my face, twisted in agony and despair; the ash knife in my hand; a pool of blood leaking away from two corpses—

But I awoke to the watery light of winter dawn—my stomach full from the night before.

A mere minute after I'd risen to consciousness, Rhys knocked on my door. I'd barely granted him permission to enter before he stalked inside like a midnight wind, and chucked a belt hung with knives onto the foot of the bed.

"Hurry," he said, flinging open the doors of the armoire and yanking out my fighting leathers. He tossed them onto the bed, too. "I want to be gone before the sun is fully up."

"Why?" I said, pushing back the covers. No wings today.

"Because time is of the essence." He dug out my socks and boots. "Once the King of Hybern realizes that someone is searching for the Book of Breathings to nullify the powers of the Cauldron, then his agents will begin hunting for it, too."

"You suspected this for a while, though." I hadn't had the chance to discuss it with him last night. "The Cauldron, the king, the Book . . . You wanted it confirmed, but you were waiting for me."

"Had you agreed to work with me two months ago, I would have taken you right to the Bone Carver to see if he confirmed my suspicions about your talents. But things didn't go as planned."

No, they most certainly hadn't.

"The reading," I said, sliding my feet into fleece-lined, thick-soled slippers. "That's why you insisted on the lessons. So if your suspicions were true and I could harness the Book . . . I could actually read it—or any translation of whatever is inside." A book that old might very well be written in an entirely different language. A different alphabet.

"Again," he said, now striding for the dresser, "had you started to work with me, I would have told you why. I couldn't risk discovery otherwise." He paused with a hand on the knob. "You should have learned to read no matter what. But yes, when I told you it served my own purposes—it was because of this. Do you blame me for it?"

"No," I said, and meant it. "But I'd prefer to be notified of any future schemes."

"Duly noted." Rhys yanked open the drawers and pulled out my undergarments. He dangled the bits of midnight lace and chuckled. "I'm surprised you didn't demand Nuala and Cerridwen buy you something else."

I stalked to him, snatching the lace away. "You're drooling on the carpet." I slammed the bathing room door before he could respond.

He was waiting as I emerged, already warm within the fur-lined leather. He held up the belt of knives, and I studied the loops and straps. "No swords, no bow or arrows," he said. He'd worn his own Illyrian fighting leathers—that simple, brutal sword strapped down his spine.

"But knives are fine?"

Rhys knelt and spread wide the web of leather and steel, beckoning for me to stick a leg through one loop.

I did as instructed, ignoring the brush of his steady hands on my thighs as I stepped through the other loop, and he began tightening and buckling things. "She will not notice a knife, as she has knives in her cottage for eating and her work. But things that are out of place—objects that have not been there . . . A sword, a bow and arrow . . . She might sense those things."

"What about me?"

He tightened a strap. Strong, capable hands—so at odds with the finery he usually wore to dazzle the rest of the world into thinking he was something else entirely. "Do not make a sound, do not touch *anything* but the object she took from me."

Rhys looked up, hands braced on my thighs.

Bow, he'd once ordered Tamlin. And now here he was, on his knees before me. His eyes glinted as if he remembered it, too. Had that been a part of his game—that façade? Or had it been vengeance for the horrible blood feud between them?

"If we're correct about your powers," he said, "if the Bone Carver wasn't lying to us, then you and the object will have the same . . . imprint, thanks to the preserving spells I placed on it long ago. You are one and the same. She will not notice your presence so long as you touch *only* it. You will be invisible to her."

"She's blind?"

A nod. "But her other senses are lethal. So be quick, and quiet. Find the object and run out, Feyre." His hands lingered on my legs, wrapping around the back of them.

"And if she notices me?"

His hands tightened slightly. "Then we'll learn precisely how skilled you are."

Cruel, conniving bastard. I glared at him.

Rhys shrugged. "Would you rather I locked you in the House of Wind and stuffed you with food and made you wear fine clothes and plan my parties?"

"Go to hell. Why not get this object yourself, if it's so important?"

"Because the Weaver knows me—and if I am caught, there would be a steep price. High Lords are not to interfere with her, no matter the direness of the situation. There are many treasures in her hoard, some she has kept for millennia. Most will never be retrieved—because the High Lords do not dare be caught, thanks to the laws that protect her, thanks to her wrath. Any thieves on their behalf . . . Either they do not return, or they are never sent, for fear of it leading back to their High Lord. But you . . . She does not know you. You belong to every court."

"So I'm your huntress and thief?"

His hands slid down to cup the backs of my knees as he said with a roguish grin, "You are my salvation, Feyre."

CHAPTER 20

Rhysand winnowed us into a wood that was older, more aware, than any place I'd been.

The gnarled beech trees were tightly woven together, splattered and draped so thoroughly with moss and lichen that it was nearly impossible to see the bark beneath.

"Where are we?" I breathed, hardly daring to whisper.

Rhys kept his hands within casual reach of his weapons. "In the heart of Prythian, there is a large, empty territory that divides the North and South. At the center of it is our sacred mountain."

My heart stumbled, and I focused on my steps through the ferns and moss and roots. "This forest," Rhys went on, "is on the eastern edge of that neutral territory. Here, there is no High Lord. Here, the law is made by who is strongest, meanest, most cunning. And the Weaver of the Wood is at the top of their food chain."

The trees groaned—though there was no breeze to shift them. No, the air here was tight and stale. "Amarantha didn't wipe them out?"

"Amarantha was no fool," Rhys said, his face dark. "She did not touch these creatures or disturb the wood. For years, I tried to find ways to manipulate her to make that foolish mistake, but she never bought it."

"And now we're disturbing her—for a mere test."

He chuckled, the sound bouncing off the gray stones strewn across the forest floor like scattered marbles. "Cassian tried to convince me last night not to take you. I thought he might even punch me."

"Why?" I barely knew him.

"Who knows? With Cassian, he's probably more interested in fucking you than protecting you."

"You're a pig."

"You could, you know," Rhys said, holding up the branch of a scrawny beech for me to slip under. "If you needed to move on in a physical sense, I'm sure Cassian would be more than happy to oblige."

It felt like a test in itself. And it pissed me off enough that I crooned, "Then tell him to come to my room tonight."

"If you survive this test."

I paused atop a little lichen-crusted rock. "You seem pleased by the idea that I won't."

"Quite the opposite, Feyre." He prowled to where I stood on the stone. I was almost eye level with him. The forest went even quieter—the trees seeming to lean closer, as if to catch every word. "I'll let Cassian know you're . . . open to his advances."

"Good," I said. A bit of hollowed-out air pushed against me, like a flicker of night. That power along my bones and blood stirred in answer.

I made to jump off the stone, but he gripped my chin, the movement too fast to detect. His words were a lethal caress as he said, "Did you enjoy the sight of me kneeling before you?"

I knew he could hear my heart as it ratcheted into a thunderous beat. I gave him a hateful little smirk, anyway, yanking my chin out of his touch and leaping off the stone. I might have aimed for his feet. And he might have shifted out of the way just enough to avoid it. "Isn't that all you males are good for, anyway?" But the words were tight, near-breathless.

His answering smile evoked silken sheets and jasmine-scented breezes at midnight.

A dangerous line—one Rhys was forcing me to walk to keep me from thinking about what I was about to face, about what a wreck I was inside.

Anger, this . . . flirtation, annoyance . . . He knew those were my crutches.

What I was about to encounter, then, must be truly harrowing if he wanted me going in there mad—thinking about sex, about anything but the Weaver of the Wood.

"Nice try," I said hoarsely. Rhysand just shrugged and swaggered off into the trees ahead.

Bastard. Yes, it had been to distract me, but—

I stormed after him as silently as I could, intent on tackling him and slamming my fist into his spine, but he held up a hand as he stopped before a clearing.

A small, whitewashed cottage with a thatched roof and half-crumbling chimney sat in the center. Ordinary—almost mortal. There was even a well, its bucket perched on the stone lip, and a wood pile beneath one of the round windows of the cottage. No sound or light within—not even smoke puffed from the chimney.

The few birds in the forest fell quiet. Not entirely, but to keep their chatter to a minimum. And—there.

Faint, coming from inside the cottage, was a pretty, steady humming.

It might have been the sort of place I would have stopped if I were thirsty, or hungry, or in need of shelter for the night.

Maybe that was the trap.

The trees around the clearing, so close that their branches nearly clawed at the thatched roof, might very well have been the bars of a cage.

Rhys inclined his head toward the cottage, bowing with dramatic grace.

In, out—don't make a sound. Find whatever object it was and snatch it from beneath a blind person's nose.

And then run like hell.

Mossy earth paved the way to the front door, already cracked slightly. A bit of cheese. And I was the foolish mouse about to fall for it.

Eyes twinkling, Rhys mouthed, *Good luck*.

I gave him a vulgar gesture and slowly, silently made my way toward the front door.

The woods seemed to monitor each of my steps. When I glanced behind, Rhys was gone.

He hadn't said if he'd interfere if I were in mortal peril. I probably should have asked.

I avoided any leaves and stones, falling into a pattern of movement that some part of my body—some part that was not born of the High Lords—remembered.

Like waking up. That's what it felt like.

I passed the well. Not a speck of dirt, not a stone out of place. A perfect, pretty trap, that mortal part of me warned. A trap designed from a time when humans were prey; now laid for a smarter, immortal sort of game.

I was not prey any longer, I decided as I eased up to that door.

And I was not a mouse.

I was a wolf.

I listened on the threshold, the rock worn as if many, many boots had passed through—and perhaps never passed back over again. The words of her song became clear now, her voice sweet and beautiful, like sunlight on a stream:

"There were two sisters, they went playing,
To see their father's ships come sailing . . .
And when they came unto the sea-brim
The elder did push the younger in."

A honeyed voice, for an ancient, horrible song. I'd heard it before—slightly different, but sung by humans who had no idea that it had come from faerie throats.

I listened for another moment, trying to hear anyone else. But there was only a clatter and thrum of some sort of device, and the Weaver's song.

"Sometimes she sank, and sometimes she swam,
'Til her corpse came to the miller's dam."

My breath was tight in my chest, but I kept it even—directing it through my mouth in silent breaths. I eased open the front door, just an inch.

No squeak—no whine of rusty hinges. Another piece of the pretty trap: practically inviting thieves in. I peered inside when the door had opened wide enough.

A large main room, with a small, shut door in the back. Floor-to-ceiling shelves lined the walls, crammed with bric-a-brac: books, shells, dolls, herbs, pottery, shoes, crystals, more books, jewels . . . From the ceiling and wood rafters hung all manner of chains, dead birds, dresses, ribbons, gnarled bits of wood, strands of pearls . . .

A junk shop—of some immortal hoarder.

And that hoarder . . .

In the gloom of the cottage, there sat a large spinning wheel, cracked and dulled with age.

And before that ancient spinning wheel, her back to me, sat the Weaver.

Her thick hair was of richest onyx, tumbling down to her slender waist as she worked the wheel, snow-white hands feeding and pulling the thread around a thorn-sharp spindle.

She looked young—her gray gown simple but elegant, sparkling faintly in the dim forest light through the windows as she sang in a voice of glittering gold:

"But what did he do with her breastbone?
He made him a viol to play on.
What'd he do with her fingers so small?
He made pegs to his viol withall."

The fiber she fed into the wheel was white—soft. Like wool, but . . . I knew, in that lingering human part of me, it was not wool. I knew that I did not want to learn what creature it had come from, *who* she was spinning into thread.

Because on the shelf directly beyond her were cones upon cones of threads—of every color and texture. And on the shelf adjacent to her were swaths and yards of that woven thread—woven, I realized, on the massive loom nearly hidden in the darkness near the hearth. The Weaver's loom.

I had come on spinning day—would she have been singing if I had come on weaving day instead? From the strange, fear-drenched scent that came from those bolts of fabric, I already knew the answer.

A wolf. I was a wolf.

I stepped into the cottage, careful of the scattered debris on the earthen floor. She kept working, the wheel clattering so merrily, so at odds with her horrible song:

"And what did he do with her nose-ridge?
Unto his viol he made a bridge.
What did he do with her veins so blue?
He made strings to his viol thereto."

I scanned the room, trying not to listen to the lyrics.

Nothing. I felt . . . nothing that might pull me toward one object in particular. Perhaps it would be a blessing if I were indeed *not* the one to track the Book—if today was not the start of what was sure to be a slew of miseries.

The Weaver perched there, working.

I scanned the shelves, the ceiling. Borrowed time. I was on borrowed time, and I was almost out of it.

Had Rhys sent me on a fool's errand? Maybe there was nothing here. Maybe this *object* had been taken. It would be just like him to do that. To tease me in the woods, to see what sort of things might make my body react.

And maybe I resented Tamlin enough in that moment to enjoy that deadly bit of flirtation. Maybe I was as much a monster as the female spinning before me.

But if I was a monster, then I supposed Rhys was as well.

Rhys and I were one in the same—beyond the power that he'd given me. It'd be fitting if Tamlin hated me, too, once he realized I'd truly left.

I felt it, then—like a tap on my shoulder.

I pivoted, keeping one eye on the Weaver and the other on the room as I wove through the maze of tables and junk. Like a beacon, a bit of light laced with his half smile, it tugged me.

Hello, it seemed to say. *Have you come to claim me at last?*

Yes—yes, I wanted to say. Even as part of me wished it were otherwise.

The Weaver sang behind me,

"What did he do with her eyes so bright?
On his viol he set at first light.
What did he do with her tongue so rough?
'Twas the new till and it spoke enough."

I followed that pulse—toward the shelf lining the wall beside the hearth. Nothing. And nothing on the second. But the third, right above my eyeline . . . There.

I could almost smell his salt-and-citrus scent. The Bone Carver had been correct.

I rose on my toes to examine the shelf. An old letter knife, books in leather that I did not want to touch or smell; a handful of acorns, a tarnished crown of ruby and jasper, and—

A ring.

A ring of twisted strands of gold and silver, flecked with pearl, and set with a stone of deepest, solid blue. Sapphire—but different. I'd never seen a sapphire like that, even at my father's offices. This one . . . I could have sworn that in the pale light, the lines of a six-pointed star radiated across the round, opaque surface.

Rhys—this had Rhys written all over it.

He'd sent me here for a *ring*?

The Weaver sang,

"Then bespake the treble string,
'O yonder is my father the king.'"

I watched her for another heartbeat, gauging the distance between the shelf and the open door. Grab the ring, and I could be gone in a heartbeat. Quick, quiet, calm.

"Then bespake the second string,
'O yonder sits my mother the queen.'"

I dropped a hand toward one of the knives strapped to my thighs. When I got back to Rhys, maybe I'd stab him in the gut.

That fast, the memory of phantom blood covered my hands. I knew how it'd feel to slide my dagger through his skin and bones and flesh. Knew how the blood would dribble out, how he'd groan in pain—

I shut out the thought, even as I could feel the blood of those faeries soaking that human part of me that hadn't died and belonged to no one but my miserable self.

"Then bespake the strings all three,
'Yonder is my sister that drowned me.'"

My hand was quiet as a final, dying breath as I plucked the ring from the shelf.

The Weaver stopped singing.

CHAPTER 21

I froze, the ring now in the pocket of my jacket. She'd finished the last song—maybe she'd start another.

Maybe.

The spinning wheel slowed.

I backed a step toward the door. Then another.

Slower and slower, each rotation of the ancient wheel longer than the last.

Only ten steps to the door.

Five.

The wheel went round, one last time, so slow I could see each of the spokes.

Two.

I turned for the door as she lashed out with a white hand, gripping the wheel and stopping it wholly.

The door before me snicked shut.

I lunged for the handle, but there was none.

Window. Get to the window—

"Who is in my house?" she said softly.

Fear—undiluted, unbroken fear—slammed into me, and I remembered. I remembered what it was to be human and helpless and weak. I remembered what it was to want to *fight* to live, to be willing to do anything to stay breathing—

I reached the window beside the door. Sealed. No latch, no opening. Just glass that was not glass. Solid and impenetrable.

The Weaver turned her face toward me.

Wolf or mouse, it made no difference, because I became no more than an animal, sizing up my chance of survival.

Above her young, supple body, beneath her black, beautiful hair, her skin was gray—wrinkled and sagging and dry. And where eyes should have gleamed instead lay rotting black pits. Her lips had withered to nothing but deep, dark lines around a hole full of jagged stumps of teeth—like she had gnawed on too many bones.

And I knew she would be gnawing on my bones soon if I did not get out.

Her nose—perhaps once pert and pretty, now half-caved in—flared as she sniffed in my direction.

"What are you?" she said in a voice that was so young and lovely.

Out—out, I had to get *out*—

There was another way.

One suicidal, reckless way.

I did not want to die.

I did not want to be eaten.

I did not want to go into that sweet darkness.

The Weaver rose from her little stool.

And I knew my borrowed time had run out.

"What is like all," she mused, taking one graceful step toward me, "but unlike all?"

I *was* a wolf.

And I bit when cornered.

I lunged for the sole candle burning on the table in the center of the room. And hurled it against the wall of woven thread—against all those miserable, dark bolts of fabric. Woven bodies, skins, lives. Let them be free.

Fire erupted, and the Weaver's shriek was so piercing I thought my head might shatter; thought my blood might boil in its veins.

She dashed for the flames, as if she'd put them out with those flawless white hands, her mouth of rotted teeth open and screaming like there was nothing but black hell inside her.

I hurtled for the darkened hearth. For the fireplace and chimney above.

A tight squeeze, but wide—wide enough for me.

I didn't hesitate as I grabbed onto the ledge and hauled myself up, arms buckling. Immortal strength—it got me only so far, and I'd become so weak, so malnourished.

I had *let them* make me weak. Bent to it like some wild horse broken to the bit.

The soot-stained bricks were loose, uneven. Perfect for climbing.

Faster—I had to go faster.

But my shoulders scraped against the brick, and it *reeked* in here, like carrion and burned hair, and there was an oily sheen on the stone, like cooked fat—

The Weaver's screaming was cut short as I was halfway up her chimney, sunlight and trees almost visible, every breath a near-sob.

I reached for the next brick, fingernails breaking as I hauled myself up so violently that my arms barked in protest against the squeezing of the stone around me, and—

And I was stuck.

Stuck, as the Weaver hissed from within her house, "What little mouse is climbing about in my chimney?"

I had just enough room to look down as the Weaver's rotted face appeared below.

She put that milk-white hand on the ledge, and I realized how little room there was between us.

My head emptied out.

I pushed against the grip of the chimney, but couldn't budge.

I was going to die here. I was going to be dragged down by those beautiful hands and ripped apart and eaten. Maybe while I was still alive, she'd set that hideous mouth on my flesh and gnaw and tear and bite and—

Black panic crushed in, and I was again trapped under a nearby mountain, in a muddy trench, the Middengard Wyrm barreling for me. I'd barely escaped, barely—

I couldn't breathe, couldn't breathe, couldn't breathe—

The Weaver's nails scratched against the brick as she took a step up.

No, no, no, no, no—

I kicked and kicked against the bricks.

"Did you think you could steal and flee, thief?"

I would have preferred the Middengard Wyrm. Would have preferred those massive, sharp teeth to her jagged stumps—

Stop.

The word came out of the darkness of my mind.

And the voice was my own.

Stop, it said—*I* said.

Breathe.

Think.

The Weaver came closer, brick crumbling under her hands. She'd climb up like a spider—like I was a fly in her web—

Stop.

And that word quieted everything.

I mouthed it.

Stop, stop, stop.

Think.

I had survived the Wyrm—survived Amarantha. And I had been granted gifts. Considerable gifts.

Like strength.

I *was* strong.

I slammed a hand against the chimney wall, as low as I could get. The Weaver hissed at the debris that rained down. I smashed my fist again, rallying that strength.

I was not a pet, not a doll, not an animal.

I was a survivor, and I was strong.

I would not be weak, or helpless again. I would not, *could not* be broken. Tamed.

I pounded my fist into the bricks over and over, and the Weaver paused.

Paused long enough for the brick I'd loosened to slide free into my waiting palm.

And for me to hurl it at her hideous, horrible face as hard as I could.

Bone crunched and she roared, black blood spraying. But I rammed my shoulders into the sides of the chimney, skin tearing beneath my leather. I kept going, going, going, until I was stone breaking stone, until nothing and no one held me back and I was scaling the chimney.

I didn't dare stop, not as I reached the lip and hauled myself out, tumbling onto the thatched roof. Which was not thatched with hay at all.

But hair.

And with all that fat lining the chimney—all that fat now gleaming on my skin . . . the hair clung to me. In clumps and strands and tufts. Bile rose, but the front door banged open—a shriek following it.

No—not that way. Not to the ground.

Up, up, up.

A tree branch hung low and close by, and I scrambled across that heinous roof, trying not to think about who and what I was stepping on, what clung to my skin, my clothes. A heartbeat later, I'd jumped onto the waiting branch, scrambling into the leaves and moss as the Weaver screamed, "*WHERE ARE YOU*?"

But I was running through the tree—running toward another one nearby. I leaped from branch to branch, bare hands tearing on the wood. Where was Rhysand?

Farther and farther I fled, her screams chasing me, though they grew ever-distant.

Where are you, where are you, where are you—

And then, lounging on a branch in a tree before me, one arm draped over the edge, Rhysand drawled, "What the hell did you *do*?"

I skidded to a stop, breathing raw. I thought my lungs might actually be bleeding.

"*You*," I hissed.

But he raised a finger to his lips and winnowed to me—grabbing my waist with one hand and cupping the back of my neck with his other as he spirited us away—

To Velaris. To just above the House of Wind.

We free-fell, and I didn't have breath to scream as his wings appeared, spreading wide, and he curved us into a steady glide . . . right through the open windows of what had to be a war room. Cassian was there—in the middle of arguing with Amren about something.

Both froze as we landed on the red floor.

There was a mirror on the wall behind them, and I glimpsed myself long enough to know why they were gaping.

My face was scratched and bloody, and I was covered in dirt and grease—*boiled fat*—and mortar dust, the hair stuck to me, and I smelled—

"You smell like barbecue," Amren said, cringing a bit.

Cassian loosened the hand he'd wrapped around the fighting knife at his thigh.

I was still panting, still trying to gobble down breath. The hair clinging to me scratched and tickled, and—

"You kill her?" Cassian said.

"No," Rhys answered for me, loosely folding his wings. "But given how much the Weaver was screaming, I'm dying to know what Feyre darling did."

Grease—I had the grease and hair of *people* on me—

I vomited all over the floor.

Cassian swore, but Amren waved a hand and it was instantly gone—along with the mess on me. But I could feel the ghost of it there, the remnants of people, the mortar of those bricks . . .

"She . . . detected me somehow," I managed to say, slumping against the large black table and wiping my mouth against the shoulder of my leathers. "And locked the doors and windows. So I had to climb out through the chimney. I got stuck," I added as Cassian's brows rose, "and when she tried to climb up, I threw a brick at her face."

Silence.

Amren looked to Rhysand. "And where were you?"

"Waiting, far enough away that she couldn't detect me."

I snarled at him, "I could have used some help."

"You survived," he said. "And found a way to help yourself." From the hard glimmer in his eye, I knew he was aware of the panic that had almost gotten me killed, either through mental shields I'd forgotten to raise or whatever anomaly in our bond. He'd been aware of it—and let me endure it.

Because it *had* almost gotten me killed, and I'd be no use to him if it happened when it mattered—with the Book. Exactly like he'd said.

"That's what this was also about," I spat. "Not just this *stupid ring*," I reached into my pocket, slamming the ring down on the table, "or my *abilities*, but if I can master my panic."

Cassian swore again, his eyes on that ring.

Amren shook her head, sheet of dark hair swaying. "Brutal, but effective."

Rhys only said, "Now you know. That you can use your abilities to hunt our objects, and thus track the Book at the Summer Court, *and* master yourself."

"You're a prick, Rhysand," Cassian said quietly.

Rhys merely tucked his wings in with a graceful snap. "You'd do the same."

Cassian shrugged, as if to say fine, he would.

I looked at my hands, my nails bloody and cracked. And I said to Cassian, "I want you to teach me—how to fight. To get strong. If the offer to train still stands."

Cassian's brows rose, and he didn't bother looking to Rhys for approval. "You'll be calling *me* a prick pretty damn fast if we train. And I don't know anything about training humans—how breakable your bodies are. Were, I mean," he added with a wince. "We'll figure it out."

"I don't want my only option to be running," I said.

"Running," Amren cut in, "kept you alive today."

I ignored her. "I want to know how to fight my way out. I don't want to have to wait on anyone to rescue me." I faced Rhys, crossing my arms. "Well? Have I proved myself?"

But he merely picked up the ring and gave me a nod of thanks. "It was my mother's ring." As if that were all the explanation and answers owed.

"How'd you lose it?" I demanded.

"I didn't. My mother gave it to me as a keepsake, then took it back when I reached maturity—and gave it to the Weaver for safekeeping."

"Why?"

"So I wouldn't waste it."

Nonsense and idiocy and—I wanted a bath. I wanted *quiet* and a bath. The need for those things hit me strong enough that my knees buckled.

I'd barely looked at Rhys before he grabbed my hand, flared his wings, and had us soaring back through the windows. We free-fell for five thunderous, wild heartbeats before he winnowed to my bedroom in the town house. A hot bath was already running. I staggered to it, exhaustion hitting me like a physical blow, when Rhys said, "And what about training your other . . . gifts?"

Through the rising steam from the tub, I said, "I think you and I would shred each other to bits."

"Oh, we most definitely will." He leaned against the bathing room threshold. "But it wouldn't be fun otherwise. Consider *our* training now officially part of your work requirements with me." A jerk of the chin. "Go ahead—try to get past my shields."

I knew which ones he was talking about. "I'm tired. The bath will go cold."

"I promise it'll be just as hot in a few moments. Or, if you mastered your gifts, you might be able to take care of that yourself."

I frowned. But took a step toward him, then another—making him yield a step, two, into the bedroom. The phantom grease and hair clung to me, reminded me what he'd done—

I held his stare, those violet eyes twinkling.

"You feel it, don't you," he said over the burbling and chittering garden birds. "Your power, stalking under your skin, purring in your ear."

"So what if I do?"

A shrug. "I'm surprised Ianthe didn't carve you up on an altar to see what that power looks like inside you."

"What, precisely, is your issue with her?"

"I find the High Priestesses to be a perversion of what they once were—once promised to be. Ianthe among the worst of them."

A knot twisted in my stomach. "Why do you say that?"

"Get past my shields and I'll *show* you."

So that explained the turn in conversation. A taunt. Bait.

Holding his stare . . . I let myself fall for it. I let myself imagine that line between us—a bit of braided light . . . And there was his mental shield at the other end of the bond. Black and solid and impenetrable. No way in. However I'd slipped through before . . . I had no idea. "I've had enough tests for the day."

Rhys crossed the two feet between us. "The High Priestesses have burrowed into a few of the courts—Dawn, Day, and Winter, mostly. They've entrenched themselves so thoroughly that their spies are everywhere, their followers near-fanatic with devotion. And yet, during those fifty years, they escaped. They remained hidden. I would not be surprised if Ianthe sought to establish a foothold in the Spring Court."

"You mean to tell me they're all black-hearted villains?"

"No. Some, yes. Some are compassionate and selfless and wise. But there are some who are merely self-righteous . . . Though those are the ones that always seem the most dangerous to me."

"And Ianthe?"

A knowing sparkle in his eyes.

He really wouldn't tell me. He'd dangle it before me like a piece of meat—

I lunged. Blindly, wildly, but I sent my power lashing down that line between us.

And yelped as it slammed against his inner shields, the reverberations echoing in me as surely as if I'd hit something with my body.

Rhys chuckled, and I saw fire. "Admirable—sloppy, but an admirable effort."

Panting a bit, I seethed.

But he said, "Just for trying . . . ," and took my hand in his. The bond went taut, that thing under my skin pulsing, and—

There was dark, and the colossal sense of *him* on the other side of his mental barricade of black adamant. That shield went on forever, the product of half a millennia of being hunted, attacked, hated. I brushed a mental hand against that wall.

Like a mountain cat arching into a touch, it seemed to purr—and then relaxed its guard.

His mind opened for me. An antechamber, at least. A single space he'd carved out, to allow me to see—

A bedroom carved from obsidian; a mammoth bed of ebony sheets, large enough to accommodate wings.

And on it, sprawled in nothing but her skin, lay Ianthe.

I reeled back, realizing it was a memory, and Ianthe was in *his* bed, in *his* court beneath that mountain, her full breasts peaked against the chill—

"There is more," Rhys's voice said from far away as I struggled to pull out. But my mind slammed into the shield—the other side of it. He'd trapped me in here—

"You kept me waiting," Ianthe sulked.

The sensation of hard, carved wood digging into my back—Rhysand's back—as he leaned against the bedroom door. "Get out."

Ianthe gave a little pout, bending her knee and shifting her legs wider, baring herself to him. "I see the way you look at me, High Lord."

"You see what you want to see," he—we—said. The door opened beside him. "Get out."

A coy tilt of her lips. "I heard you like to play games." Her slender hand drifted low, trailing past her belly button. "I think you'll find me a diverting playmate."

Icy wrath crept through me—him—as he debated the merits of splattering her on the walls, and how much of an inconvenience it'd cause. She'd hounded him relentlessly—stalked the other males, too. Azriel had left last night because of it. And Mor was about one more comment away from snapping her neck.

"I thought your allegiance lay with other courts." His voice was so cold. The voice of the High Lord.

"My allegiance lies with the future of Prythian, with the true power in this land." Her fingers slid between her legs—and halted. Her gasp cleaved the room as he sent a tendril of power blasting for her, pinning that arm to the bed—away from herself. "Do you know what a union

between us could do for Prythian, for the world?" she said, eyes devouring him still.

"You mean yourself."

"Our offspring could rule Prythian."

Cruel amusement danced through him. "So you want my crown—and for me to play stud?"

She tried to writhe her body, but his power held her. "I don't see anyone else worthy of the position."

She'd be a problem—now, and later. He knew it. Kill her now, end the threat before it began, face the wrath of the other High Priestesses, or . . . see what happened. "Get out of my bed. Get out of my room. And get out of my court."

He released his power's grip to allow her to do so.

Ianthe's eyes darkened, and she slithered to her feet, not bothering with her clothes, draped over his favorite chair. Each step toward him had her generous breasts bobbing. She stopped barely a foot away. "You have no idea what I can make you feel, High Lord."

She reached a hand for him, right between his legs.

His power lashed around her fingers before she could grab him.

He crunched the power down, twisting.

Ianthe screamed. She tried backing away, but his power froze her in place—so much power, so easily controlled, roiling around her, contemplating ending her existence like an asp surveying a mouse.

Rhys leaned close to breathe into her ear, "Don't ever touch me. Don't ever touch another male in my court." His power snapped bones and tendons, and she screamed again. "Your hand will heal," he said, stepping back. "The next time you touch me or anyone in my lands, you will find that the rest of you will not fare so well."

Tears of agony ran down her face—the effect wasted by the hatred lighting her eyes. "You will regret this," she hissed.

He laughed softly, a lover's laugh, and a flicker of power had her thrown onto her ass in the hallway. Her clothes followed a heartbeat later. Then the door slammed.

Like a pair of scissors through a taut ribbon, the memory was severed, the shield behind me fell, and I stumbled back, blinking.

"Rule one," Rhys told me, his eyes glazed with the rage of that memory, "don't go into someone's mind unless you hold the way open. A daemati might leave their minds spread wide for you—and then shut you inside, turn you into their willing slave."

A chill went down my spine at the thought. But what he'd shown me . . .

"Rule two," he said, his face hard as stone, "when—"

"When was that," I blurted. I knew him well enough not to doubt its truth. "When did that happen between you?"

The ice remained in his eyes. "A hundred years ago. At the Court of Nightmares. I allowed her to visit after she'd begged for years, insisting she wanted to build ties between the Night Court and the priestesses. I'd heard rumors about her nature, but she was young and untried, and I hoped that perhaps a new High Priestess might indeed be the change her order needed. It turned out that she was already well trained by some of her less-benevolent sisters."

I swallowed hard, my heart thundering. "She—she didn't act that way at . . ."

Lucien.

Lucien had hated her. Had made vague, vicious allusions to not liking her, to being approached by her—

I was going to throw up. Had she . . . had she pursued him like that? Had he . . . had he been forced to say yes because of her position?

And if I went back to the Spring Court one day . . . How would I ever convince Tamlin to dismiss her? What if, now that I was gone, she was—

"Rule two," Rhys finally went on, "be prepared to see things you might not like."

Only fifty years later, Amarantha had come. And done exactly to Rhys what he'd wanted to kill Ianthe for. He'd let it happen to him. To keep them safe. To keep Azriel and Cassian from the nightmares that would haunt him forever, from enduring any more pain than what they'd suffered as children . . .

I lifted my head to ask him more. But Rhys had vanished.

Alone, I peeled off my clothes, struggling with the buckles and straps he'd put on me—when had it been? An hour or two ago?

It felt as if a lifetime had passed. And I was now a certified Book-tracker, it seemed.

Better than a party-planning wife for breeding little High Lords. What Ianthe had wanted to make me—to serve whatever agenda she had.

The bath was indeed hot, as he'd promised. And I mulled over what he'd shown me, seeing that hand again and again reach between his legs, the ownership and arrogance in that gesture—

I shut out the memory, the bath water suddenly cold.

CHAPTER 22

Word still hadn't come from the Summer Court the following morning, so Rhysand made good on his decision to bring us to the mortal realm.

"What does one wear, exactly, in the human lands?" Mor said from where she sprawled across the foot of my bed. For someone who claimed to have been out drinking and dancing until the Mother knew when, she appeared unfairly perky. Cassian and Azriel, grumbling and wincing over breakfast, had looked like they'd been run over by wagons. Repeatedly. Some small part of me wondered what it would be like to go out with them—to see what Velaris might offer at night.

I rifled through the clothes in my armoire. "Layers," I said. "They . . . cover everything up. The décolletage might be a little daring depending on the event, but . . . everything else gets hidden beneath skirts and petticoats and nonsense."

"Sounds like the women are used to not having to run—or fight. I don't remember it being that way five hundred years ago."

I paused on an ensemble of turquoise with accents of gold—rich, bright, regal. "Even with the wall, the threat of faeries remained, so . . . surely practical clothes would have been necessary to run, to fight any that crept through. I wonder what changed." I pulled out the top and pants for her approval.

Mor merely nodded—no commentary like Ianthe might have provided, no beatific *intervention*.

I shoved away the thought, and the memory of what she'd tried to do to Rhys, and went on, "Nowadays, most women wed, bear children, and then plan their children's marriages. Some of the poor might work in the fields, and a rare few are mercenaries or hired soldiers, but . . . the wealthier they are, the more restricted their freedoms and roles become. You'd think that money would buy you the ability to do whatever you pleased."

"Some of the High Fae," Mor said, pulling at an embroidered thread in my blanket, "are the same."

I slipped behind the dressing screen to untie the robe I'd donned moments before she'd entered to keep me company while I prepared for our journey today.

"In the Court of Nightmares," she went on, that voice falling soft and a bit cold once more, "females are . . . prized. Our virginity is guarded, then sold off to the highest bidder—whatever male will be of the most advantage to our families."

I kept dressing, if only to give myself something to do while the horror of what I began to suspect slithered through my bones and blood.

"I was born stronger than anyone in my family. Even the males. And I couldn't hide it, because they could smell it—the same way you can smell a High Lord's Heir before he comes to power. The power leaves a mark, an . . . echo. When I was twelve, before I bled, I prayed it meant no male would take me as a wife, that I would escape what my elder cousins had endured: loveless, sometimes brutal, marriages."

I tugged my blouse over my head, and buttoned the velvet cuffs at my wrists before adjusting the sheer, turquoise sleeves into place.

"But then I began bleeding a few days after I turned seventeen. And the moment my first blood came, my power awoke in full force, and even that gods-damned mountain trembled around us. But instead of being horrified, every single ruling family in the Hewn City saw me as a prize mare. Saw that power and wanted it bred into their bloodline, over and over again."

"What about your parents?" I managed to say, slipping my feet into the midnight-blue shoes. It'd be the end of winter in the mortal lands—most shoes would be useless. Actually, my current ensemble would be useless, but only for the moments I'd be outside—bundled up.

"My family was beside themselves with glee. They could have their pick of an alliance with any of the other ruling families. My pleas for choice in the matter went unheard."

She got out, I reminded myself. Mor got out, and now lived with people who cared for her, who loved her.

"The rest of the story," Mor said as I emerged, "is long, and awful, and I'll tell you some other time. I came in here to say I'm not going with you—to the mortal realm."

"Because of how they treat women?"

Her rich brown eyes were bright, but calm. "When the queens come, I will be there. I wish to see if I recognize any of my long-dead friends in their faces. But . . . I don't think I would be able to . . . behave with any others."

"Did Rhys tell you not to go?" I said tightly.

"No," she said, snorting. "He tried to convince me to come, actually. He said I was being ridiculous. But Cassian . . . he gets it. The two of us wore him down last night."

My brows rose a bit. Why they'd gone out and gotten drunk, no doubt. To ply their High Lord with alcohol.

Mor shrugged at the unasked question in my eyes. "Cassian helped Rhys get me out. Before either had the real rank to do so. For Rhys, getting caught would have been a mild punishment, perhaps a bit of social shunning. But Cassian . . . he risked everything to make sure I stayed out of that court. And he laughs about it, but he believes he's a low-born bastard, not worthy of his rank or life here. He has no idea that he's worth more than any other male I met in that court—and outside of it. Him and Azriel, that is."

Yes—Azriel, who kept a step away, whose shadows trailed him and seemed to fade in her presence. I opened my mouth to ask about her history with him, but the clock chimed ten. Time to go.

My hair had been arranged before breakfast in a braided coronet atop my head, a small diadem of gold—flecked with lapis lazuli—set before it. Matching earrings dangled low enough to brush the sides of my neck, and I picked up the twisting gold bracelets that had been left out on the dresser, sliding one onto either wrist.

Mor made no comment—and I knew that if I had worn nothing but my undergarments, she would have told me to own every inch of it. I turned to her. "I'd like my sisters to meet you. Maybe not today. But if you ever feel like it . . ."

She cocked her head.

I rubbed the back of my bare neck. "I want them to hear your story. And know that there is a special strength . . . " As I spoke I realized I needed to hear it, know it, too. "A special strength in enduring such dark trials and hardships . . . And still remaining warm, and kind. Still willing to trust—and reach out."

Mor's mouth tightened and she blinked a few times.

I went for the door, but paused with my hand on the knob. "I'm sorry if I was not as welcoming to you as you were to me when I arrived at the Night Court. I was . . . I'm trying to learn how to adjust."

A pathetic, inarticulate way of explaining how ruined I'd become.

But Mor hopped off the bed, opened the door for me, and said, "There are good days and hard days for me—even now. Don't let the hard days win."

✢

Today, it seemed, would indeed be yet another hard day.

With Rhys, Cassian, and Azriel ready to go—Amren and Mor remaining in Velaris to run the city and plan our inevitable trip to Hybern—I was left with only one choice: who to fly with.

Rhys would winnow us off the coast, right to the invisible line where the wall bisected our world. There was a tear in its magic about half a mile offshore—which we'd fly through.

But standing in that hallway, all of them in their fighting leathers and me bundled in a heavy, fur-lined cloak, I took one look at Rhys and felt those hands on my thighs again. Felt how it'd been to look inside his mind, felt his cold rage, felt him . . . defend himself, his people, his friends, using the power and masks in his arsenal. He'd seen and endured such . . . such unspeakable things, and yet . . . his hands on my thighs had been gentle, the touch like—

I didn't let myself finish the thought as I said, "I'll fly with Azriel."

Rhys and Cassian looked as if I'd declared I wanted to parade through Velaris in nothing but my skin, but the shadowsinger merely bowed his head and said, "Of course." And that, thankfully, was that.

Rhys winnowed in Cassian first, returning a heartbeat later for me and Azriel.

The spymaster had waited in silence. I tried not to look too uncomfortable as he scooped me into his arms, those shadows that whispered to him stroking my neck, my cheek. Rhys was frowning a bit, and I just gave him a sharp look and said, "Don't let the wind ruin my hair."

He snorted, gripped Azriel's arm, and we all vanished into a dark wind.

Stars and blackness, Azriel's scarred hands clenching tightly around me, my arms entwined around his neck, bracing, waiting, counting—

Then blinding sunlight, roaring wind, a plunge down, down—

Then we tilted, shooting straight. Azriel's body was warm and hard, though those brutalized hands were considerate as he gripped me. No shadows trailed us, as if he'd left them in Velaris.

Below, ahead, behind, the vast, blue sea stretched. Above, fortresses of clouds plodded along, and to my left . . . A dark smudge on the horizon. Land.

Spring Court land.

I wondered if Tamlin was on the western sea border. He'd once hinted about trouble there. Could he sense me, sense us, now?

I didn't let myself think about it. Not as I *felt* the wall.

As a human, it had been nothing but an invisible shield.

As a faerie . . . I couldn't see it, but I could hear it crackling with power—the tang of it coating my tongue.

"It's abhorrent, isn't it," Azriel said, his low voice nearly swallowed up by the wind.

"I can see why you—*we* were deterred for all these centuries," I admitted. Every heartbeat had us racing closer to that gargantuan, nauseating sense of power.

"You'll get used to it—the wording," he said. Clinging to him so tightly, I couldn't see his face. I watched the light shift inside the sapphire Siphon instead, as if it were the great eye of some half-slumbering beast from a frozen wasteland.

"I don't really know where I fit in anymore," I admitted, perhaps only because the wind was screeching around us and Rhys had already winnowed ahead to where Cassian's dark form flew—beyond the wall.

"I've been alive almost five and a half centuries, and I'm not sure of that, either," Azriel said.

I tried to pull back to read the beautiful, icy face, but he tightened his grip, a silent warning to brace myself.

How Azriel knew where the cleft was, I had no idea. It all looked the same to me: invisible, open sky.

But I felt the wall as we swept through. Felt it lunge for me, as if enraged we'd slipped past, felt the power flare and try to close that gap but failing—

Then we were out.

The wind was biting, the temperature so cold it snatched the breath from me. That bitter wind seemed somehow less alive than the spring air we'd left behind.

Azriel banked, veering toward the coastline, where Rhys and Cassian were now sweeping over the land. I shivered in my fur-lined cloak, clinging to Azriel's warmth.

We cleared a sandy beach at the base of white cliffs, and flat, snowy land dotted with winter-ravaged forests spread beyond them.

The human lands.

My home.

CHAPTER 23

It had been a year since I had stalked through that labyrinth of snow and ice and killed a faerie with hate in my heart.

My family's emerald-roofed estate was as lovely at the end of winter as it had been in the summer. A different sort of beauty, though—the pale marble seemed warm against the stark snow piled high across the land, and bits of evergreen and holly adorned the windows, the archways, and the lampposts. The only bit of decoration, of celebration, humans bothered with. Not when they'd banned and condemned every holiday after the War, all a reminder of their immortal overseers.

Three months with Amarantha had destroyed me. I couldn't begin to imagine what millennia with High Fae like her might do—the scars it'd leave on a culture, a people.

My people—or so they had once been.

Hood up, fingers tucked into the fur-lined pockets of my cloak, I stood before the double doors of the house, listening to the clear ringing of the bell I'd pulled a heartbeat before.

Behind me, hidden by Rhys's glamours, my three companions waited, unseen.

I'd told them it would be best if I spoke to my family first. Alone.

I shivered, craving the moderate winter of Velaris, wondering how it could be so temperate in the far north, but . . . everything in Prythian was strange. Perhaps when the wall hadn't existed, when magic had flowed freely between realms, the seasonal differences hadn't been so vast.

The door opened, and a merry-faced, round housekeeper—Mrs. Laurent, I recalled—squinted at me. "May I help . . . " The words trailed off as she noticed my face.

With the hood on, my ears and crown were hidden, but that glow, that preternatural stillness . . . She didn't open the door wider.

"I'm here to see my family," I choked out.

"Your—your father is away on business, but your sisters . . . " She didn't move.

She knew. She could tell there was something different, something *off*—

Her eyes darted around me. No carriage, no horse.

No footprints through the snow.

Her face blanched, and I cursed myself for not thinking of it—

"Mrs. Laurent?"

Something in my chest broke at Elain's voice from the hall behind her.

At the sweetness and youth and kindness, untouched by Prythian, unaware of what I'd done, become—

I backed away a step. I couldn't do this. Couldn't bring this upon them.

Then Elain's face appeared over Mrs. Laurent's round shoulder.

Beautiful—she'd always been the most beautiful of us. Soft and lovely, like a summer dawn.

Elain was exactly as I'd remembered her, the way I'd made myself remember her in those dungeons, when I told myself that if I failed, if Amarantha crossed the wall, she'd be next. The way she'd be next if the King of Hybern shattered the wall, if I didn't get the Book of Breathings.

Elain's golden-brown hair was half up, her pale skin creamy and flushed with color, and her eyes, like molten chocolate, were wide as they took me in.

They filled with tears and silently overran, spilling down those lovely cheeks.

Mrs. Laurent didn't yield an inch. She'd shut this door in my face the moment I so much as breathed wrong.

Elain lifted a slender hand to her mouth as her body shook with a sob.

"Elain," I said hoarsely.

Footsteps on the sweeping stairs behind them, then—

"Mrs. Laurent, draw up some tea and bring it to the drawing room."

The housekeeper looked to the stairs, then to Elain, then to me.

A phantom in the snow.

The woman merely gave me a look that promised death if I harmed my sisters as she turned into the house, leaving me before Elain, still quietly crying.

But I took a step over the threshold and looked up the staircase.

To where Nesta stood, a hand braced on the rail, staring as if I were a ghost.

✢

The house was beautiful, but there was something untouched about it. Something new, compared to the age and worn love of Rhys's homes in Velaris.

And seated before the carved marble sitting room hearth, my hood on, hands outstretched toward the roaring fire, I felt . . . felt like they had let in a wolf.

A wraith.

I had become too big for these rooms, for this fragile mortal life, too stained and wild and . . . powerful. And I was about to bring that permanently into their lives as well.

Where Rhys, Cassian, and Azriel were, I didn't know. Perhaps they stood as shadows in the corner, watching. Perhaps they'd remained outside in the snow. I wouldn't put it past Cassian and Azriel to be now flying the grounds, inspecting the layout, making wider circles until they reached the village, my ramshackle old cottage, or maybe even the forest itself.

Nesta looked the same. But older. Not in her face, which was as grave and stunning as before, but . . . in her eyes, in the way she carried herself.

Seated across from me on a small sofa, my sisters stared—and waited.

I said, "Where is Father?" It felt like the only safe thing to say.

"In Neva," Nesta said, naming one of the largest cities on the continent. "Trading with some merchants from the other half of the world. And attending a summit about the threat above the wall. A threat I wonder if you've come back to warn us about."

No words of relief, of love—never from her.

Elain lifted her teacup. "Whatever the reason, Feyre, we are happy to see you. Alive. We thought you were—"

I pulled my hood back before she could go on.

Elain's teacup rattled in its saucer as she noticed my ears. My longer, slender hands—the face that was undeniably Fae.

"I *was* dead," I said roughly. "I was dead, and then I was reborn—remade."

Elain set her shivering teacup onto the low-lying table between us. Amber liquid splashed over the side, pooling in the saucer.

And as she moved, Nesta angled herself—ever so slightly. Between me and Elain.

It was Nesta's gaze I held as I said, "I need you to listen."

They were both wide-eyed.

But they did.

I told them my story. In as much detail as I could endure, I told them of Under the Mountain. Of my trials. And Amarantha. I told them about death. And rebirth.

Explaining the last few months, however, was harder.

So I kept it brief.

But I explained what needed to happen here—the threat Hybern posed. I explained what this house needed to be, what we needed to be, and what I needed from them.

And when I finished, they remained wide-eyed. Silent.

It was Elain who at last said, "You—you want other High Fae to come . . . *here*. And . . . and the Queens of the Realm."

I nodded slowly.

"Find somewhere else," Nesta said.

I turned to her, already pleading, bracing for a fight.

"Find somewhere else," Nesta said again, straight-backed. "I don't want them in my house. Or near Elain."

"Nesta, please," I breathed. "There is nowhere else; nowhere I can go without someone hunting me, crucifying me—"

"And what of us? When the people around here learn we're Fae sympathizers? Are we any better than the Children of the Blessed, then? Any standing, any influence we have—gone. And Elain's wedding—"

"Wedding," I blurted.

I hadn't noticed the pearl-and-diamond ring on her finger, the dark metal band glinting in the firelight.

Elain's face was pale, though, as she looked at it.

"In five months," Nesta said. "She's marrying a lord's son. And his father has devoted his life to hunting down *your kind* when they cross the wall."

Your kind.

"So there will be no meeting here," Nesta said, shoulders stiff. "There will be no Fae in this house."

"Do you include me in that declaration?" I said quietly.

Nesta's silence was answer enough.

But Elain said, "Nesta."

Slowly, my eldest sister looked at her.

"Nesta," Elain said again, twisting her hands. "If . . . if we do not help Feyre, there won't *be* a wedding. Even Lord Nolan's battlements and all his men, couldn't save me from . . . from them." Nesta didn't so much as flinch. Elain pushed, "We keep it secret—we send the servants away. With the spring approaching, they'll be glad to go home. And if Feyre needs to be in and out for meetings, she'll send word ahead, and we'll clear them out. Make up excuses to send them on holidays. Father won't be back until the summer, anyway. No one will know." She put a hand on Nesta's knee, the purple of my sister's gown nearly swallowing up the ivory hand. "Feyre gave and gave—for years. Let us now help her. Help . . . others."

My throat was tight, and my eyes burned.

Nesta studied the dark ring on Elain's finger, the way she still seemed to cradle it. A lady—that's what Elain would become. What she was risking for this.

I met Nesta's gaze. "There is no other way."

Her chin lifted slightly. "We'll send the servants away tomorrow."

"Today," I pushed. "We don't have any time to lose. Order them to leave now."

"I'll do it," Elain said, taking a deep breath and squaring her shoulders. She didn't wait for either of us before she strode out, graceful as a doe.

Alone with Nesta, I said, "Is he good—the lord's son she's to marry?"

"She thinks he is. She loves him like he is."

"And what do you think?"

Nesta's eyes—my eyes, our mother's eyes—met mine. "His father built a wall of stone around their estate so high even the trees can't reach over it. I think it looks like a prison."

"Have you said anything to her?"

"No. The son, Graysen, is kind enough. As smitten with Elain as she is with him. It's the father I don't like. He sees the money she has to offer their estate—and his crusade against the Fae. But the man is old. He'll die soon enough."

"Hopefully."

A shrug. Then Nesta asked, "Your High Lord . . . You went through all that"—she waved a hand at me, my ears, my body—"and it still did not end well?"

I was heavy in my veins again. "That lord built a wall to keep the Fae out. My High Lord wanted to keep me caged in."

"Why? He let you come back here all those months ago."

"To save me—protect me. And I think . . . I think what happened to him, to us, Under the Mountain broke him." Perhaps more than it had broken me. "The drive to protect at all costs, even my own well-being . . . I think he wanted to stifle it, but he couldn't. He couldn't let go of it." There was . . . there was much I still had to do, I realized. To settle things. Settle myself.

"And now you are at a new court."

Not quite a question, but I said, "Would you like to meet them?"

CHAPTER 24

It took hours for Elain to work her charm on the staff to swiftly pack their bags and leave, each with a purse of money to hasten the process. Mrs. Laurent, though the last to depart, promised to keep what she'd seen to herself.

I didn't know where Rhys, Cassian, and Azriel had been waiting, but when Mrs. Laurent had hauled herself into the carriage crammed with the last of the staff, heading down to the village to catch transportation to wherever they all had family, there was a knock on the door.

The light was already fading, and the world outside was thick with shades of blue and white and gray, stained golden as I opened the front door and found them waiting.

Nesta and Elain were in the large dining room—the most open space in the house.

Looking at Rhys, Cassian, and Azriel, I knew I'd been right to select it as the meeting spot.

They were enormous—wild and rough and ancient.

Rhys's brows lifted. "You'd think they'd been told plague had befallen the house."

I pulled the door open wide enough to let them in, then quickly shut it against the bitter cold. "My sister Elain can convince anyone to do anything with a few smiles."

Cassian let out a low whistle as he turned in place, surveying the grand entry hall, the ornate furniture, the paintings. All of it paid for by Tamlin—initially. He'd taken such care of my family, yet his own . . . I didn't want to think about his family, murdered by a rival court for whatever reason no one had ever explained to me. Not now that I was living amongst them—

He'd been good—there was a part of Tamlin that was good—

Yes. He'd given me everything I needed to become myself, to feel safe. And when he got what he wanted . . . He'd stopped. Had tried, but not really. He'd let himself remain blind to what I needed after Amarantha.

"Your father must be a fine merchant," Cassian said. "I've seen castles with less wealth."

I found Rhys studying me, a silent question written across his face. I answered, "My father is away on business—and attending a meeting in Neva about the threat of Prythian."

"Prythian?" Cassian said, twisting toward us. "Not Hybern?"

"It's possible my sisters were mistaken—your lands are foreign to them. They merely said 'above the wall.' I assumed they thought it was Prythian."

Azriel came forward on feet as silent as a cat's. "If humans are aware of the threat, rallying against it, then that might give us an advantage when contacting the queens."

Rhys was still watching me, as if he could see the weight that had pressed into me since arriving here. The last time I'd been in this house, I'd been a woman in love—such frantic, desperate love that I went back into Prythian, I went Under the Mountain, as a mere human. As fragile as my sisters now seemed to me.

"Come," Rhys said, offering me a subtle, understanding nod before motioning to lead the way. "Let's make this introduction."

My sisters were standing by the window, the light of the chandeliers coaxing the gold in their hair to glisten. So beautiful, and young, and alive—but when would that change? How would it be to speak to them when I remained this way while their skin had grown paper-thin and wrinkled, their backs curved with the weight of years, their white hands speckled?

I would be barely into my immortal existence when theirs was wiped out like a candle before a cold breath.

But I could give them a few good years—safe years—until then.

I crossed the room, the three males a step behind, the wooden floors as shining and polished as a mirror beneath us. I had removed my cloak now that the servants were gone, and it was to me—not the Illyrians—that my sisters first looked. At the Fae clothes, the crown, the jewelry.

A stranger—this part of me was now a stranger to them.

Then they took in the winged males—or two of them. Rhys's wings had vanished, his leathers replaced with his fine black jacket and pants.

My sisters both stiffened at Cassian and Azriel, at those mighty wings tucked in tight to powerful bodies, at the weapons, and then at the devastatingly beautiful faces of all three males.

Elain, to her credit, did not faint.

And Nesta, to hers, did not hiss at them. She just took a not-so-subtle step in front of Elain, and ducked her fisted hand behind her simple, elegant amethyst gown. The movement did not go unnoticed by my companions.

I halted a good four feet away, giving my sisters breathing space in a room that had suddenly been deprived of all air. I said to the males, "My sisters, Nesta and Elain Archeron."

I had not thought of my family name, had not used it, for years and years. Because even when I had sacrificed and hunted for them, I had not wanted my father's name—not when he sat before that little fire and let us starve. Let me walk into the woods alone. I'd stopped using it the day I'd killed that rabbit, and felt its blood stain my hands, the same way the blood of those faeries had marred it years later like an invisible tattoo.

My sisters did not curtsy. Their hearts wildly pounded, even Nesta's, and the tang of their terror coated my tongue—

"Cassian," I said, inclining my head to the left. Then I shifted to the right, grateful those shadows were nowhere to be found as I said, "Azriel." I half turned. "And Rhysand, High Lord of the Night Court."

Rhys had dimmed it, too, I realized. The night rippling off him, the otherworldly grace and thrum of power. But looking in those star-flecked violet eyes, no one would ever mistake him for anything but extraordinary.

He bowed to my sisters. "Thank you for your hospitality—and generosity," he said with a warm smile. But there was something strained in it.

Elain tried to return the smile but failed.

And Nesta just looked at the three of them, then at me, and said, "The cook left dinner on the table. We should eat before it goes cold." She didn't wait for my agreement before striding off—right to the head of the polished cherry table.

Elain rasped, "Nice to meet you," before hustling after her, the silk skirts of her cobalt dress whispering over the parquet floor.

Cassian was grimacing as we trailed them, Rhys's brows were raised, and Azriel looked more inclined to blend into the nearest shadow and avoid this conversation all together.

Nesta was waiting at the head of the table, a queen ready to hold court. Elain trembled in the upholstered, carved wood chair to her left.

I did them all a favor and took the one to Nesta's right. Cassian claimed the spot beside Elain, who clenched her fork as if she might wield it against him, and Rhys slid into the seat beside me, Azriel on his other side. A faint smile bloomed upon Azriel's mouth as he noticed Elain's fingers white-knuckled on that fork, but he kept silent, focusing instead, as Cassian was subtly trying to do, on adjusting his wings around a human chair. Cauldron damn me. I should have remembered. Though I doubted either would appreciate it if I now brought in two stools.

I sighed through my nose and yanked the lids off the various dishes and casseroles. Poached salmon with dill and lemon from the hothouse, whipped potatoes, roast chicken with beets and turnips from the root cellar, and some casserole of egg, game meat, and leeks. Seasonal food—whatever they had left at the end of the winter.

I scooped food onto my plate, the sounds of my sisters and companions doing the same filling the silence. I took a bite and fought my cringe.

Once, this food would have been rich and flavorful.

Now it was ash in my mouth.

Rhys was digging into his chicken without hesitation. Cassian and Azriel ate as if they hadn't had a meal in months. Perhaps being warriors, fighting in wars, had given them the ability to see food as strength—and put taste aside.

I found Nesta watching me. "Is there something wrong with our food?" she said flatly.

I made myself take another bite, each movement of my jaw an effort. "No." I swallowed and gulped down a healthy drink of water.

"So you can't eat normal food anymore—or are you too good for it?" A question and a challenge.

Rhys's fork clanked on his plate. Elain made a small, distressed noise.

And though Nesta had let me use this house, though she'd tried to cross the wall for me and we'd worked out a tentative truce, the *tone*, the disgust and disapproval . . .

I laid my hand flat on the table. "I can eat, drink, fuck, and fight just as well as I did before. Better, even."

Cassian choked on his water. Azriel shifted on his seat, angling to spring between us if need be.

Nesta let out a low laugh.

But I could taste fire in my mouth, hear it roaring in my veins, and—

A blind, solid *tug* on the bond, cooling darkness sweeping into me, my temper, my senses, calming that fire—

I scrambled to throw my mental shields up. But they were intact.

Rhys didn't so much as blink at me before he said evenly to Nesta, "If you ever come to Prythian, you will discover why your food tastes so different."

Nesta looked down her nose at him. "I have little interest in ever setting foot in your land, so I'll have to take your word on it."

"Nesta, please," Elain murmured.

Cassian was sizing up Nesta, a gleam in his eyes that I could only interpret as a warrior finding himself faced with a new, interesting opponent.

Then, Mother above, Nesta shifted her attention to Cassian, noticing that gleam—what it meant. She snarled softly, "What are you looking at?"

Cassian's brows rose—little amusement to be found now. "Someone who let her youngest sister risk her life every day in the woods while she did nothing. Someone who let a fourteen-year-old child go out into that forest, so close to the wall." My face began heating, and I opened my mouth. To say what, I didn't know. "Your sister died—*died* to save my people. She is willing to do so again to protect you from war. So don't expect me to sit here with my mouth shut while you sneer at her for a choice she did not get to make—and insult *my* people in the process."

Nesta didn't bat an eyelash as she studied the handsome features, the muscled torso. Then turned to me. Dismissing him entirely.

Cassian's face went almost feral. A wolf who had been circling a doe . . . only to find a mountain cat wearing its hide instead.

Elain's voice wobbled as she noted the same thing and quickly said to him, "It . . . it is very hard, you understand, to . . . accept it." I realized the dark metal of her ring . . . it was iron. Even though I had told them about iron being useless, there it was. The gift from her Fae-hating soon-to-be-husband's family. Elain cast pleading eyes on Rhys, then Azriel, such mortal fear coating her features, her scent. "We are raised this way. We hear stories of your kind crossing the wall to hurt us. Our own neighbor, Clare Beddor, was taken, her family murdered . . ."

A naked body spiked to a wall. Broken. Dead. Nailed there for months.

Rhys was staring at his plate. Unmoving. Unblinking.

He had given Amarantha Clare's name—given it, despite knowing I'd lied to him about it.

Elain said, "It's all very disorienting."

"I can imagine," Azriel said. Cassian flashed him a glare. But Azriel's attention was on my sister, a polite, bland smile on his face. Her shoulders loosened a bit. I wondered if Rhys's spymaster often got his information through stone-cold manners as much as stealth and shadows.

Elain sat a little higher as she said to Cassian, "And as for Feyre's hunting during those years, it was not Nesta's neglect alone that is to blame. We were scared, and had received no training, and everything had been taken, and we failed her. Both of us."

Nesta said nothing, her back rigid.

Rhys gave me a warning look. I gripped Nesta's arm, drawing her attention to me. "Can we just . . . start over?"

I could almost taste her pride roiling in her veins, barking to not back down.

Cassian, damn him, gave her a taunting grin.

But Nesta merely hissed, "Fine." And went back to eating.

Cassian watched every bite she took, every bob of her throat as she swallowed.

I forced myself to clean my plate, aware of Nesta's own attention on *my* eating.

Elain said to Azriel, perhaps the only two civilized ones here, "Can you truly fly?"

He set down his fork, blinking. I might have even called him self-conscious. He said, "Yes. Cassian and I hail from a race of faeries called Illyrians. We're born hearing the song of the wind."

"That's very beautiful," she said. "Is it not—frightening, though? To fly so high?"

"It is sometimes," Azriel said. Cassian tore his relentless attention from Nesta long enough to nod his agreement. "If you are caught in a storm, if the current drops away. But we are trained so thoroughly that the fear is gone before we're out of swaddling." And yet, Azriel had not been trained until long after that. *You get used to the wording*, he'd told me earlier. How often did he have to remind himself to use such words? Did "we" and "our" and "us" taste as foreign on his tongue as they did on mine?

"You look like High Fae," Nesta cut in, her voice like a honed blade. "But you are not?"

"Only the High Fae who look like *them*," Cassian drawled, waving a hand to me and Rhys, "are High Fae. Everyone else, any other differences, mark you as what they like to call 'lesser' faeries."

Rhysand at last said, "It's become a term used for ease, but masks a long, bloody history of injustices. Many lesser faeries resent the term—and wish for us all to be called one thing."

"Rightly so," Cassian said, drinking from his water.

Nesta surveyed me. "But you were not High Fae—not to begin. So what do they call you?" I couldn't tell if it was a jab or not.

Rhys said, "Feyre is whoever she chooses to be."

Nesta now examined us all, raising her eyes to that crown. But she said, "Write your letter to the queens tonight. Tomorrow, Elain and I will go to the village to dispatch it. If the queens do come here," she added, casting a frozen glare at Cassian, "I'd suggest bracing yourselves for prejudices far deeper than ours. And contemplating how you plan to get us *all* out of this mess should things go sour."

"We'll take that into account," Rhys said smoothly.

Nesta went on, utterly unimpressed by any of us, "I assume you'll want to stay the night."

Rhys glanced at me in silent question. We could easily leave, the males finding the way home in the dark, but . . . Too soon, perhaps, the world would go to hell. I said, "If it's not too much trouble, then yes. We'll leave after breakfast tomorrow."

Nesta didn't smile, but Elain beamed. "Good. I think there are a few bedrooms ready—"

"We'll need two," Rhys interrupted quietly. "Next to each other, with two beds each."

I narrowed my brows at him.

Rhys explained to me, "Magic is different across the wall. So our shields, our senses, might not work right. I'm taking no chances. Especially in a house with a woman betrothed to a man who gave her an iron engagement ring."

Elain flushed a bit. "The—the bedrooms that have two beds aren't next to each other," she murmured.

I sighed. "We'll move things around. It's fine. This one," I added with a glare in Rhys's direction, "is only cranky because he's old and it's past his bedtime."

Rhys chuckled, Cassian's wrath slipping enough that he grinned, and Elain, noticing Azriel's ease as proof that things weren't indeed about to go badly, offered one of her own as well.

Nesta just rose to her feet, a slim pillar of steel, and said to no one in particular, "If we're done eating, then this meal is over."

And that was that.

Rhys wrote the letter for me, Cassian and Azriel chiming in with corrections, and it took us until midnight before we had a draft we all thought sounded impressive, welcoming, and threatening enough.

My sisters cleaned the dishes while we worked, and had excused themselves to bed hours before, mentioning where to find our rooms.

Cassian and Azriel were to share one, Rhys and I the other.

I frowned at the large guest bedroom as Rhys shut the door behind us. The bed was large enough for two, but I wasn't sharing it. I whirled to him, "I'm not—"

Wood thumped on carpet, and a small bed appeared by the door. Rhys plopped onto it, tugging off his boots. "Nesta is a delight, by the way."

"She's . . . her own creature," I said. It was perhaps the kindest thing I could say about her.

"It's been a few centuries since someone got under Cassian's skin that easily. Too bad they're both inclined to kill the other."

Part of me shuddered at the havoc the two would wreak if they decided to stop fighting.

"And Elain," Rhys said, sighing as he removed his other boot, "should not be marrying that lord's son, not for about a dozen reasons, the least of which being the fact that you won't be invited to the wedding. Though maybe that's a good thing."

I hissed. "That's not funny."

"At least you won't have to send a gift, either. I doubt her father-in-law would deign to accept it."

"You have a lot of nerve mocking my sisters when your own friends have equally as much melodrama." His brows lifted in silent question. I snorted. "Oh, so you haven't noticed the way Azriel looks at Mor? Or how she sometimes watches *him*, defends him? And how both of them do *such* a good job letting Cassian be a buffer between them most of the time?"

Rhys leveled a look at me. "I'd suggest keeping those observations to yourself."

"You think I'm some busybody gossip? My life is miserable enough as it is—why would I want to spread that misery to those around me as well?"

"Is it miserable? Your life, I mean." A careful question.

"I don't know. Everything is happening so quickly that I don't know what to feel." It was more honest than I'd been in a while.

"Hmmm. Perhaps once we return home, I should give you the day off."

"How considerate of you, *my lord.*"

He snorted, unbuttoning his jacket. I realized I stood in all my finery—with nothing to wear to sleep.

A snap of Rhys's fingers, and my nightclothes—and some flimsy underthings—appeared on the bed. "I couldn't decide which scrap of lace I wanted you to wear, so I brought you a few to choose from."

"Pig," I barked, snatching the clothes and heading to the adjoining bathing room.

The room was toasty when I emerged, Rhys in the bed he'd summoned from wherever, all light gone save for the murmuring embers in the hearth. Even the sheets were warm as I slid between them.

"Thank you for warming the bed," I said into the dimness.

His back was to me, but I heard him clearly as he said, "Amarantha never once thanked me for that."

Any warmth leeched away. "She didn't suffer enough."

Not even close, for what she had done. To me, to him, to Clare, to so many others.

Rhys didn't answer. Instead he said, "I didn't think I could get through that dinner."

"What do you mean?" He'd been rather . . . calm. Contained.

"Your sisters mean well, or one of them does. But seeing them, sitting at that table . . . I hadn't realized it would hit me as strongly. How young you were. How they didn't protect you."

"I managed just fine."

"We owe them our gratitude for letting us use this house," he said quietly, "but it will be a long while yet before I can look at your sisters without wanting to roar at them."

"A part of me feels the same way," I admitted, nestling down into the blankets. "But if I hadn't gone into those woods, if they hadn't let me go out there alone . . . You would still be enslaved. And perhaps Amarantha would now be readying her forces to wipe out these lands."

Silence. Then, "I am paying you a wage, you know. For all of this."

"You don't need to." Even if . . . even if I had no money of my own.

"Every member of my court receives one. There's already a bank account in Velaris for you, where your wages will be deposited. And you have lines of credit at most stores. So if you don't have enough on you when you're shopping, you can have the bill sent to the House."

"I—you didn't have to do that." I swallowed hard. "And how much, exactly, am I getting paid each month?"

"The same amount the others receive." No doubt a generous—likely *too* generous—salary. But he suddenly asked, "When is your birthday?"

"Do I even need to count them anymore?" He merely waited. I sighed. "It's the Winter Solstice."

He paused. "That was months ago."

"Mmmhmm."

"You didn't . . . I don't remember seeing you celebrate it."

Through the bond, through my unshielded, mess of a mind. "I didn't tell anyone. I didn't want a party when there was already all that celebrating going on. Birthdays seem meaningless now, anyway."

He was quiet for a long minute. "You were truly born on the Winter Solstice?"

"Is that so hard to believe? My mother claimed I was so withdrawn and strange because I was born on the longest night of the year. She tried one year to have my birthday on another day, but forgot to do it the next time—there was probably a more advantageous party she had to plan."

"Now I know where Nesta gets it. Honestly, it's a shame we can't stay longer—if only to see who'll be left standing: her or Cassian."

"My money's on Nesta."

A soft chuckle that snaked along my bones—a reminder that he'd once bet on me. Had been the only one Under the Mountain who had put money on me defeating the Middengard Wyrm. He said, "So's mine."

CHAPTER 25

Standing beneath the latticework of snow-heavy trees, I took in the slumbering forest and wondered if the birds had gone quiet because of my presence. Or that of the High Lord beside me.

"Freezing my ass off first thing in the morning isn't how I intended to spend our day off," Rhysand said, frowning at the wood. "I should take you to the Illyrian Steppes when we return—the forest there is far more interesting. And warmer."

"I have no idea where those are." Snow crunched under the boots Rhys had summoned when I declared I wanted to train with him. And not physically, but—with the powers I had. Whatever they were. "You showed me a blank map that one time, remember?"

"Precautions."

"Am I ever going to see a proper one, or will I be left to guess about where everything is?"

"You're in a lovely mood today," Rhys said, and lifted a hand in the air between us. A folded map appeared, which he took his sweet time opening. "Lest you think I don't trust you, Feyre darling . . . " He pointed to just south of the Northern Isles. "These are the Steppes. Four days that way on foot," he dragged a finger upward and into the mountains along the isles, "will take you into Illyrian territory."

I took in the map, noted the peninsula jutting out about halfway up the western coast of the Night Court and the name marked there. *Velaris*. He'd once shown me a blank one—when I had belonged to Tamlin and been little more than a spy and prisoner. Because he'd known I'd tell Tamlin about the cities, their locations.

That Ianthe might learn about it, too.

I pushed back against that weight in my chest, my gut.

"Here," Rhys said, pocketing the map and gesturing to the forest around us. "We'll train here. We're far enough now."

Far enough from the house, from anyone else, to avoid detection. Or casualties.

Rhys held out a hand, and a thick, stumpy candle appeared in his palm. He set it on the snowy ground. "Light it, douse it with water, and dry the wick."

I knew he meant without my hands.

"I can't do a single one of those things," I said. "What about physical shielding?" At least I'd been able to do *some* of that.

"That's for another time. Today, I suggest you start trying some *other* facet of your power. What about shape-shifting?"

I glared at him. "Fire, water, and air it is." Bastard—insufferable bastard.

He didn't push the matter, thankfully—didn't ask *why* shape-shifting might be the one power I'd never bother to pull apart and master. Perhaps for the same reason I didn't particularly want to ask about one key piece of his history, didn't want to know if Azriel and Cassian had helped when the Spring Court's ruling family had been killed.

I looked Rhys over from head to toe: the Illyrian warrior garb, the sword over his shoulder, the wings, and that general sense of overwhelming power that always radiated from him. "Maybe you should . . . go."

"Why? You seemed so insistent that *I* train you."

"I can't concentrate with you around," I admitted. "And go . . . far. I can feel you from a room away."

A suggestive curve shaped his lips.

I rolled my eyes. "Why don't you just hide in one of those pocket-realms for a bit?"

"It doesn't work like that. There's no air there." I gave him a look to say he should definitely do it then, and he laughed. "Fine. Practice all you want in privacy." He jerked his chin at my tattoo. "Give a shout down the bond if you get anything accomplished before breakfast."

I frowned at the eye in my palm. "What—literally shout at the tattoo?"

"You could try rubbing it on certain body parts and I might come faster."

He vanished into nothing before I could hurl the candle at him.

Alone in the frost-gilded forest, I replayed his words and a quiet chuckle rasped out of me.

I wondered if I should have tested out the bow and arrows I'd been given before asking him to leave. I hadn't yet tried out the Illyrian bow—hadn't shot anything in months, actually.

I stared at the candle. Nothing happened.

An hour passed.

I thought of everything that enraged me, sickened me; thought of Ianthe and her entitlement, her demands. Not even a wisp of smoke emerged.

When my eyes were on the verge of bleeding, I took a break to scrounge through the pack I'd brought. I found fresh bread, a magically warmed canister of stew, and a note from Rhysand that said:

I'm bored. Any sparks yet?

Not surprisingly, a pen clattered in the bottom of the bag.

I grabbed the pen and scribbled my response atop the canister before watching the letter vanish right out of my palm: *No, you snoop. Don't you have important things to do?*

The letter flitted back a moment later.

I'm watching Cassian and Nesta get into it again over their tea. Something you subjected me to when you kicked me off training. I thought this was our day off.

I snorted and wrote back, *Poor baby High Lord. Life is so hard.*

Paper vanished, then reappeared, his scribble now near the top of the paper, the only bit of clear space left. *Life is better when you're around. And look at how lovely your handwriting is.*

I could almost feel him waiting on the other side, in the sunny breakfast room, half paying attention to my eldest sister and the Illyrian warrior's sparring. A faint smile curved my lips. *You're a shameless flirt,* I wrote back.

The page vanished. I watched my open palm, waiting for it to return.

And I was so focused on it that I didn't notice anyone was behind me until the hand covered my mouth and yanked me clean off my feet.

I thrashed, biting and clawing, shrieking as whoever it was hauled me up.

I tried to shove away, snow churning around us like dust on a road, but the arms that gripped me were immovable, like bands of iron and—

A rasping voice sounded in my ear, "Stop, or I snap your neck."

I knew that voice. It prowled through my nightmares.

The Attor.

CHAPTER 26

The Attor had vanished in the moments after Amarantha died, suspected to have fled for the King of Hybern. And if it was here, in the mortal lands—

I went pliant in its arms, buying a wisp of time to scan for something, anything to use against it.

"Good," it hissed in my ear. "Now tell me—"

Night exploded around us.

The Attor screamed—*screamed*—as that darkness swallowed us, and I was wrenched from its spindly, hard arms, its nails slicing into my leather. I collided face-first with packed, icy snow.

I rolled, flipping back, whirling to get my feet under me—

The light returned as I rose into a crouch, knife angled.

And there was Rhysand, binding the Attor to a snow-shrouded oak with nothing but twisting bands of night. Like the ones that had crushed Ianthe's hand. Rhysand's own hands were in his pockets, his face cold and beautiful as death. "I'd been wondering where you slithered off to."

The Attor panted as it struggled against the bonds.

Rhysand merely sent two spears of night shooting into its wings.

The Attor shrieked as those spears met flesh—and sank deep into the bark behind it.

"Answer my questions, and you can crawl back to your master," Rhys said, as if he were inquiring about the weather.

"Whore," the Attor spat. Silvery blood leaked from its wings, hissing as it hit the snow.

Rhys smiled. "You forget that I rather enjoy these things." He lifted a finger.

The Attor screamed, "*No!*" Rhys's finger paused. "I was sent," it panted, "to get her."

"Why?" Rhys asked with that casual, terrifying calm.

"That was my order. I am not to question. The king wants her."

My blood went as cold as the woods around us.

"Why?" Rhys said again. The Attor began screaming—this time beneath the force of a power I could not see. I flinched.

"*Don't know, don't know, don't know.*" I believed it.

"Where is the king currently?"

"Hybern."

"Army?"

"Coming soon."

"How large?"

"Endless. We have allies in every territory, all waiting."

Rhys cocked his head as if contemplating what to ask next. But he straightened, and Azriel slammed into the snow, sending it flying like water from a puddle. He'd flown in so silently, I hadn't even heard the beat of his wings. Cassian must have stayed at the house to defend my sisters.

There was no kindness on Azriel's face as the snow settled—the immovable mask of the High Lord's shadowsinger.

The Attor began trembling, and I almost felt bad for it as Azriel stalked for him. Almost—but didn't. Not when these woods were so close to the chateau. To my sisters.

Rhys came to my side as Azriel reached the Attor. "The next time you try to take her," Rhys said to the Attor, "I kill first; ask questions later."

Azriel caught his eye. Rhys nodded. The Siphons atop his scarred hands flickered like rippling blue fire as he reached for the Attor. Before the Attor could scream, it and the spymaster vanished.

I didn't want to think about where they'd go, what Azriel would do. I hadn't even known Azriel possessed the ability to winnow, or whatever power he'd channeled through his Siphons. He'd let Rhys winnow us both in the other day—unless the power was too draining to be used so lightly.

"Will he kill him?" I said, my puffs of breath uneven.

"No." I shivered at the raw power glazing his taut body. "We'll use him to send a message to Hybern that if they want to hunt the members of my court, they'll have to do better than that."

I started—at the claim he'd made of me, and at the words. "You knew—you knew he was hunting me?"

"I was curious who wanted to snatch you the first moment you were alone."

I didn't know where to start. So Tamlin was right—about my safety. To some degree. It didn't excuse anything. "So you never planned to stay with me while I trained. You used me as *bait*—"

"Yes, and I'd do it again. You were safe the entire time."

"*You should have told me!*"

"Maybe next time."

"*There will be no next time!*" I slammed a hand into his chest, and he staggered back a step from the strength of the blow. I blinked. I'd forgotten—forgotten that strength in my panic. Just like with the Weaver. I'd forgotten how strong I was.

"Yes, you did," Rhysand snarled, reading the surprise on my face, that icy calm shattering. "You forgot that strength, and that you can burn and become darkness, and grow claws. You *forgot*. *You stopped fighting*."

He didn't just mean the Attor. Or the Weaver.

And the rage rose up in me in such a mighty wave that I had no thought in my head but wrath: at myself, what I'd been forced to do, what had been done to me, to him.

"So what if I did?" I hissed, and shoved him again. "So *what* if I did?"

I went to shove him again, but Rhys winnowed away a few feet.

I stormed for him, snow crunching underfoot. "It's not easy." The rage ran me over, obliterated me. I lifted my arms to slam my palms into his chest—

And he vanished again.

He appeared behind me, so close that his breath tickled my ear as he said, "You have no idea how *not* easy it is."

I whirled, grappling for him. He vanished before I could strike him, pound him.

Rhys appeared across the clearing, chuckling. "Try harder."

I couldn't fold myself into darkness and pockets. And if I could—if I could turn myself into smoke, into air and night and stars, I'd use it to appear right in front of him and smack that smile off his face.

I moved, even if it was futile, even as he rippled into darkness, and I hated him for it—for the wings and ability to move like mist on the wind. He appeared a step away, and I pounced, hands out—*talons* out—

And slammed into a tree.

He laughed as I bounced back, teeth singing, talons barking as they shredded through wood. But I was already lunging as he vanished, lunging like I could disappear into the folds of the world as well, track him across eternity—

And so I did.

Time slowed and curled, and I could see the darkness of him turn to smoke and veer, as if it were running for another spot in the clearing. I hurtled for that spot, even as I felt my own lightness, folding my very self into wind and shadow and dust, the looseness of it radiating out of me, all while I aimed for where he was headed—

Rhysand appeared, a solid figure in my world of smoke and stars.

And his eyes were wide, his mouth split in a grin of wicked delight, as I winnowed in front of him and tackled him into the snow.

CHAPTER 27

I panted, sprawled on top of Rhys in the snow while he laughed hoarsely. "*Don't*," I snarled into his face, "*ever*," I pushed his rock-hard shoulders, talons curving at my fingertips, "*use me as bait again*."

He stopped laughing.

I pushed harder, those nails digging in through his leather. "You said I could be a weapon—teach me to become one. *Don't* use me like a pawn. And if being one is part of my *work* for you, then I'm done. *Done*."

Despite the snow, his body was warm beneath me, and I wasn't sure I'd realized just how much bigger he was until our bodies were flush—too close. Much, much too close.

Rhys cocked his head, loosening a chunk of snow clinging to his hair. "Fair enough."

I shoved off him, snow crunching as I backed away. My talons were gone.

He hoisted himself up onto his elbows. "Do it again. Show me how you did it."

"No." The candle he'd brought now lay in pieces, half-buried under the snow. "I want to go back to the chateau." I was cold, and tired, and he'd . . .

His face turned grave. "I'm sorry."

I wondered how often he said those two words. I didn't care.

I waited while he uncoiled to his feet, brushing the snow off him, and held out a hand.

It wasn't just an offer.

You forgot, he'd said. I had.

"Why does the King of Hybern want me? Because he knows I can nullify the Cauldron's power with the Book?"

Darkness flickered, the only sign of the temper Rhysand had once again leashed. "That's what I'm going to find out."

You stopped fighting.

"I'm sorry," he repeated, hand still outstretched. "Let's eat breakfast, then go home."

"Velaris isn't my home."

I could have sworn hurt flashed in his eyes before he spirited us back to my family's house.

CHAPTER 28

My sisters ate breakfast with Rhys and me, Azriel gone to wherever he'd taken the Attor. Cassian had flown off to join him the moment we returned. He'd given Nesta a mocking bow, and she'd given him a vulgar gesture I hadn't realized she knew how to make.

Cassian had merely laughed, his eyes snaking over Nesta's ice-blue gown with a predatory intent that, given her hiss of rage, he knew would set her spitting. Then he was gone, leaving my sister on the broad doorstep, her brown-gold hair ruffled by the chill wind stirred by his mighty wings.

We brought my sisters to the village to mail our letter, Rhys glamouring us so we were invisible while they went into the little shop to post them. After we returned home, our good-byes were quick. I knew Rhys wanted to return to Velaris—if only to learn what the Attor was up to.

I'd said as much to Rhys while he flew us through the wall, into the warmth of Prythian, then winnowed us to Velaris.

Morning mist still twined through the city and the mountains around it. The chill also remained—but not nearly as unforgiving as the cold of the mortal world. Rhys left me in the foyer, huffing hot air into my frozen palms, without so much as a good-bye.

Hungry again, I found Nuala and Cerridwen, and I gobbled down cheese-and-chive scones while thinking through what I'd seen, what I'd done.

Not an hour later, Rhys found me in the living room, my feet propped on the couch before the fire, a book in my lap, a cup of rose tea steaming on the low table before me. I stood as he entered, scanning him for any sign of injury. Something tight in my chest eased when I found nothing amiss.

"It's done," he said, dragging a hand through his blue-black hair. "We learned what we needed to." I braced myself to be shut out, to be told it'd be taken care of, but Rhys added, "It's up to you, Feyre, to decide how much of our methods you want to know about. What you can handle. What we did to the Attor wasn't pretty."

"I want to know everything," I said. "Take me there."

"The Attor isn't in Velaris. He was in the Hewn City, in the Court of Nightmares—where it took Azriel less than an hour to break him." I waited for more, and as if deciding I wasn't about to crumple, Rhys stalked closer, until less than a foot of the ornate red carpet lay between us. His boots, usually impeccably polished . . . that was silver blood speckled on them. Only when I met his gaze did he say, "I'll show you."

I knew what he meant, and steadied myself, blocking out the murmuring fire and the boots and the lingering cold around my heart.

Immediately, I was in that antechamber of his mind—a pocket of memory he'd carved for me.

Darkness flowed through me, soft and seductive, echoing up from an abyss of power so great it had no end and no beginning.

"Tell me how you tracked her," Azriel said in the quiet voice that had broken countless enemies.

I—Rhys—leaned against the far wall of the holding cell, arms crossed. Azriel crouched before where the Attor was chained to a chair in the center of the room. A few levels above, the Court of Nightmares reveled on, unaware their High Lord had come.

I'd have to pay them a visit soon. Remind them who held their leash.

Soon. But not today. Not when Feyre had winnowed.

And she was still pissed as hell at me.

Rightly so, if I was being honest. But Azriel had learned that a small enemy force had infiltrated the North two days ago, and my suspicions were confirmed. Either to get at Tamlin or at me, they wanted her. Maybe for their own experimenting.

The Attor let out a low laugh. "I received word from the king that's where you were. I don't know how he knew. I got the order, flew to the wall as fast as I could."

Azriel's knife was out, balanced on a knee. Truth-Teller—the name stamped in silver Illyrian runes on the scabbard. He'd already learned that the Attor and a few others had been stationed on the outskirts of the Illyrian territory. I was half tempted to dump the Attor in one of the war-camps and see what the Illyrians did to it.

The Attor's eyes shifted toward me, glowing with a hatred I'd become well accustomed to. "Good luck trying to keep her, High Lord."

Azriel said, "Why?"

People often made the mistake of assuming Cassian was the wilder one; the one who couldn't be tamed. But Cassian was all hot temper—temper that could be used to forge and weld. There was an icy rage in Azriel I had never been able to thaw. In the centuries I'd known him, he'd said little about his life, those years in his father's keep, locked in darkness. Perhaps the shadow-singer gift had come to him then, perhaps he'd taught himself the language of shadow and wind and stone. His half-brothers hadn't been forthcoming, either. I knew because I'd met them, asked them, and had shattered their legs when they'd spat on Azriel instead.

They'd walked again—eventually.

The Attor said, "Do you think it is not common knowledge that you took her from Tamlin?"

I knew that already. That had been Azriel's task these days: monitor the situation with the Spring Court, and prepare for our own attack on Hybern.

But Tamlin had shut down his borders—sealed them so tightly that even flying overhead at night was impossible. And any ears and eyes Azriel had once possessed in the court had gone deaf and blind.

"The king could help you keep her—consider sparing you, if you worked with him . . ."

As the Attor spoke, I rummaged through its mind, each thought more vile and hideous than the next. It didn't even know I'd slipped inside, but—there: images of the army that had been built, the twin to the one I'd fought against five centuries ago; of Hybern's shores full of ships, readying for an assault; of the king, lounging on his throne in his crumbling castle. No sign of Jurian sulking about or the Cauldron. Not a whisper of the Book being on their minds. Everything the Attor had confessed was true. And it had no more value.

Az looked over his shoulder. The Attor had given him everything. Now it was just babbling to buy time.

I pushed off the wall. "Break its legs, shred its wings, and dump it off the coast of Hybern. See if it survives." The Attor began thrashing, begging. I paused by the door and said to it, "I remember every moment of it. Be grateful I'm letting you live. For now."

I hadn't let myself see the memories from Under the Mountain: of me, of the others . . . of what it had done to that human girl I'd given Amarantha in Feyre's place. I didn't let myself see what it had been like to beat Feyre—to torment and torture her.

I might have splattered him on the walls. And I needed him to send a message more than I needed my own vengeance.

The Attor was already screaming beneath Truth-Teller's honed edge when I left the cell.

Then it was done. I staggered back, spooling myself into my body.

Tamlin had closed his borders. "What *situation* with the Spring Court?"

"None. As of right now. But you know how far Tamlin can be driven to . . . protect what he thinks is his."

The image of paint sliding down the ruined study wall flashed in my mind.

"I should have sent Mor that day," Rhys said with quiet menace.

I snapped up my mental shields. I didn't want to talk about it. "Thank you for telling me," I said, and took my book and tea up to my room.

"Feyre," he said. I didn't stop. "I am sorry—about deceiving you earlier."

And this, letting me into his mind . . . a peace offering. "I need to write a letter."

✢

The letter was quick, simple. But each word was a battle.

Not because of my former illiteracy. No, I could now read and write just fine.

It was because of the message that Rhys, standing in the foyer, now read:

I left of my own free will.

I am cared for and safe. I am grateful for all that you did for me, all that you gave.

Please don't come looking for me. I'm not coming back.

He swiftly folded it in two and it vanished. "Are you sure?"

Perhaps it would help with whatever *situation* was going on at the Spring Court. I glanced to the windows beyond him. The mist wreathing the city had wandered off, revealing a bright, cloudless sky. And somehow, my head felt clearer than it had in days—months.

A city lay out there, that I had barely observed or cared about.

I wanted it—life, people. I wanted to see it, feel its rush through my blood. No boundaries, no limits to what I might encounter or do.

"I am no one's pet," I said. Rhys's face was contemplative, and I wondered if he remembered that he'd told me the same thing once, when I was too lost in my own guilt and despair to understand. "What next?"

"For what it's worth, I did actually want to give you a day to rest—"

"Don't coddle me."

"I'm not. And I'd hardly call our encounter this morning *rest.* But you will forgive me if I make assessments based on your current physical condition."

"I'll be the person who decides that. What about the Book of Breathings?"

"Once Azriel returns from dealing with the Attor, he's to put his other skill set to use and infiltrate the mortal queens' courts to learn where they're keeping it—and what their plans might be. And as for the half in Prythian . . . We'll go to the Summer Court within a few days, if my request to visit is approved. High Lords visiting other courts makes everyone jumpy. We'll deal with the Book then."

He shut his mouth, no doubt waiting for me to trudge upstairs, to brood and sleep.

Enough—I'd had enough of sleeping.

I said, "You told me that this city was better seen at night. Are you all talk, or will you ever bother to show me?"

A low laugh as he looked me over. I didn't recoil from his gaze.

When his eyes found mine again, his mouth twisted in a smile so few saw. Real amusement—perhaps a bit of happiness edged with relief. The male behind the High Lord's mask. "Dinner," he said. "Tonight. Let's find out if *you*, Feyre darling, are all talk—or if you'll allow a Lord of Night to take you out on the town."

Amren came to my room before dinner. Apparently, we were *all* going out tonight.

Downstairs, Cassian and Mor were sniping at each other about whether Cassian could fly faster short-distance than Mor could winnow to the same spot. I assumed Azriel was nearby, seeking sanctuary in the shadows. Hopefully, he'd gotten some rest after dealing with the Attor—and would rest a bit more before heading into the mortal realm to spy on those queens.

Amren, at least, knocked this time before entering. Nuala and Cerridwen, who had finished setting combs of mother-of-pearl into my hair, took one look at the delicate female and vanished into puffs of smoke.

"Skittish things," Amren said, her red lips cutting a cruel line. "Wraiths always are."

"Wraiths?" I twisted in the seat before the vanity. "I thought they were High Fae."

"Half," Amren said, surveying my turquoise, cobalt, and white clothes. "Wraiths are nothing but shadow and mist, able to walk through walls, stone—you name it. I don't even want to know how those two were conceived. High Fae will stick their cocks anywhere."

I choked on what could have been a laugh or a cough. "They make good spies."

"Why do you think they're now whispering in Azriel's ear that I'm in here?"

"I thought they answered to Rhys."

"They answer to both, but they were trained by Azriel first."

"Are they spying on me?"

"No." She frowned at a loose thread in her rain cloud–colored shirt. Her chin-length dark hair swayed as she lifted her head. "Rhys has told them time and again not to, but I don't think Azriel will ever trust me fully. So they're reporting on my movements. And with good reason."

"Why?"

"Why not? I'd be disappointed if Rhysand's spymaster didn't keep tabs on me. Even go against orders to do so."

"Rhys doesn't punish him for disobeying?"

Those silver eyes glowed. "The Court of Dreams is founded on three things: to defend, to honor, and to cherish. Were you expecting brute strength and obedience? Many of Rhysand's top officials have little to no power. He values loyalty, cunning, compassion. And Azriel, despite his disobedience, is acting to defend his court, his people. So, no. Rhysand does not punish that. There are rules, but they are flexible."

"What about the Tithe?"

"What Tithe?"

I stood from the little bench. "The Tithe—taxes, whatever. Twice a year."

"There are taxes on city dwellers, but there is no Tithe." She clicked her tongue. "But the High Lord of Spring enacts one."

I didn't want to think about it entirely, not yet—not with that letter now on its way to him, if not already delivered. So I reached for the small box on the vanity and pulled out her amulet. "Here." I handed over the gold-and-jewel-encrusted thing. "Thank you."

Amren's brows rose as I dropped it into her waiting palm. "You gave it back."

"I didn't realize it was a test."

She set it back into the case. "Keep it. There's no magic to it."

I blinked. "You lied—"

She shrugged, heading for the door. "I found it at the bottom of my jewelry box. You needed something to believe you could get out of the Prison again."

"But Rhys kept looking at it—"

"Because *he* gave it to me two hundred years ago. He was probably surprised to see it again, and wondered why I'd given it to you. Likely *worried* why I might have given it to you."

I clenched my teeth, but Amren was already breezing through the door with a cheerful, "You're welcome."

CHAPTER 29

Despite the chill night, every shop was open as we walked through the city. Musicians played in the little squares, and the Palace of Thread and Jewels was packed with shoppers and performers, High Fae and lesser faeries alike. But we continued past, down to the river itself, the water so smooth that the stars and lights blended on its dark surface like a living ribbon of eternity.

The five of them were unhurried as we strolled across one of the wide marble bridges spanning the Sidra, often moving forward or dropping back to chat with one another. From the ornate lanterns that lined either side of the bridge, faelight cast golden shadows on the wings of the three males, gilding the talons at the apex of each.

The conversation ranged from the people they knew, matches and teams for sports I'd never heard of (apparently, Amren was a vicious, obsessive supporter of one), new shops, music they'd heard, clubs they favored . . . Not a mention of Hybern or the threats we faced—no doubt from secrecy, but I had a feeling it was also because tonight, this time together . . . they did not want that terrible, hideous presence intruding. As if they were all just ordinary citizens—even Rhys. As if they weren't the most powerful people in this court, maybe in all of Prythian. And no one, absolutely no one, on the street balked or paled or ran.

Awed, perhaps a little intimidated, but . . . no fear. It was so unusual that I kept silent, merely observing them—their world. The normalcy that they each fought so hard to preserve. That I had once raged against, resented.

But there was no place like this in the world. Not so serene. So loved by its people and its rulers.

The other side of the city was even more crowded, with patrons in finery out to attend the many theaters we passed. I'd never seen a theater before—never seen a play, or a concert, or a symphony. In our ramshackle village, we'd gotten mummers and minstrels at best—herds of beggars yowling on makeshift instruments at worst.

We strolled along the riverside walkway, past shops and cafés, music spilling from them. And I thought—even as I hung back from the others, my gloved hands stuffed into the pockets of my heavy blue overcoat—that the sounds of it all might have been the most beautiful thing I'd ever heard: the people, and the river, and the music; the clank of silverware on plates; the scrape of chairs being pulled out and pushed in; the shouts of vendors selling their wares as they ambled past.

How much had I missed in these months of despair and numbness?

But no longer. The lifeblood of Velaris thrummed through me, and in rare moments of quiet, I could have sworn I heard the clash of the sea, clawing at the distant cliffs.

Eventually, we entered a small restaurant beside the river, built into the lower level of a two-story building, the whole space bedecked in greens and golds and barely big enough to fit all of us. And three sets of Illyrian wings.

But the owner knew them, and kissed them each on the cheek, even Rhysand. Well, except for Amren, whom the owner bowed to before she hustled back into her kitchen and bade us sit at the large table that was half in, half out of the open storefront. The starry night was crisp, the wind rustling the potted palms placed with loving care along the riverside walkway railing. No doubt spelled to keep from dying in the winter—just as the warmth of the restaurant kept the chill from disturbing us or any of those dining in the open air at the river's edge.

Then the food platters began pouring out, along with the wine and the conversation, and we dined under the stars beside the river. I'd never had such food—warm and rich and savory and spicy. Like it filled not only my stomach, but that lingering hole in my chest, too.

The owner—a slim, dark-skinned female with lovely brown eyes—was standing behind my chair, chatting with Rhys about the latest shipment of spices that had come to the Palaces. "The traders were saying the prices might rise, High Lord, especially if rumors about Hybern awakening are correct."

Down the table, I felt the others' attention slide to us, even as they kept talking.

Rhys leaned back in his seat, swirling his goblet of wine. "We'll find a way to keep the prices from skyrocketing."

"Don't trouble yourself, of course," the owner said, wringing her fingers a bit. "It's just . . . so lovely to have such spices available again—now that . . . that things are better."

Rhys gave her a gentle smile, the one that made him seem younger. "I wouldn't be troubling myself—not when I like your cooking so much."

The owner beamed, flushing, and looked to where I'd half twisted in my seat to watch her. "Is it to your liking?"

The happiness on her face, the satisfaction that only a day of hard work doing something you love could bring, hit me like a stone.

I—I remembered feeling that way. After painting from morning until night. Once, that was all I had wanted for myself. I looked to the dishes, then back at her, and said, "I've lived in the mortal realm, and lived in other courts, but I've never had food like this. Food that makes me . . . feel awake."

It sounded about as stupid as it felt coming out, but I couldn't think of another way to say it. But the owner nodded like she understood and squeezed my shoulder. "Then I'll bring you a special dessert," she said, and strode into her kitchen.

I turned back to my plate, but found Rhysand's eyes on me. His face was softer, more contemplative than I'd ever seen it, his mouth slightly open.

I lifted my brows. *What?*

He gave me a cocky grin and leaned in to hear the story Mor was telling about—

I forgot what she was talking about as the owner emerged with a metal goblet full of dark liquid and placed it before Amren.

Rhys's Second hadn't touched her plate, but pushed the food around like she might actually be trying to be polite. When she saw the goblet laid before her, she flicked her brows up. "You didn't have to do that."

The owner shrugged her slim shoulders. "It's fresh and hot, and we needed the beast for tomorrow's roast, anyway."

I had a horrible feeling I knew what was inside.

Amren swirled the goblet, the dark liquid lapping at the sides like wine, then sipped from it. "You spiced it nicely." Blood gleamed on her teeth.

The owner bowed. "No one leaves my place hungry," she said before walking away.

Indeed, I almost asked Mor to roll me out of the restaurant by the time we were done and Rhys had paid the tab, despite the owner's protests. My muscles were barking thanks to my earlier *training* in the mortal forest, and at some point during the meal, every part of me I'd used while tackling Rhys into the snow had started to ache.

Mor rubbed her stomach in lazy circles as we paused beside the river.

"I want to go dancing. I won't be able to fall asleep when I'm this full. Rita's is right up the street."

Dancing. My body groaned in protest and I glanced about for an ally to shoot down this ridiculous idea.

But Azriel—*Azriel* said, his eyes wholly on Mor, "I'm in."

"Of course you are," Cassian grumbled, frowning at him. "Don't you have to be off at dawn?"

Mor's frown now mirrored Cassian's—as if she realized where and what he'd be doing tomorrow. She said to Azriel, "We don't have to—"

"I want to," Azriel said, holding her gaze long enough that Mor dropped it, twisted toward Cassian, and said, "Will you deign to join us, or do you have plans to ogle your muscles in the mirror?"

Cassian snorted, looping his elbow through hers and leading her up the street. "I'll go—for the drinks, you ass. No dancing."

"Thank the Mother. You nearly shattered my foot the last time you tried."

It was an effort not to stare at Azriel as he watched them head up the steep street, arm in arm and bickering with every step. The shadows gathered around his shoulders, like they were indeed whispering to him, shielding him, perhaps. His broad chest expanded with a deep breath that sent them skittering, and then he set into an easy, graceful stroll after them. If Azriel was going with them, then any excuse I might make *not* to—

I turned pleading eyes to Amren, but she'd vanished.

"She's getting more blood in the back to take home with her," Rhys said in my ear, and I nearly jumped out of my skin. His chuckle was warm against my neck. "And then she'll be going right to her apartment to gorge herself."

I tried not to shudder as I faced him. "Why blood?"

"It doesn't seem polite to ask."

I frowned up at him. "Are *you* going dancing?"

He peered over my shoulder at his friends, who had almost scaled the steep street, some people pausing to greet them. "I'd rather walk home," Rhys said at last. "It's been a long day."

Mor turned back at the top of the hill, her purple clothes floating around her in the winter wind, and raised a dark gold brow. Rhys shook his head, and she waved, followed by short waves from Azriel and Cassian, who'd dropped back to talk with his brother-in-arms.

Rhys gestured forward. "Shall we? Or are you too cold?"

Consuming blood with Amren in the back of the restaurant sounded more appealing, but I shook my head and fell into step beside him as we walked along the river toward the bridge.

I drank in the city as greedily as Amren had gobbled down the spiced blood, and I almost stumbled as I spied the glimmer of color across the water.

The Rainbow of Velaris glowed like a fistful of jewels, as if the paint they used on their houses came alive in the moonlight.

"This is my favorite view in the city," Rhys said, stopping at the metal railing along the river walkway and gazing toward the artists' quarter. "It was my sister's favorite, too. My father used to have to drag her kicking and screaming out of Velaris, she loved it so much."

I fumbled for the right response to the quiet sorrow in those words. But like a useless fool, I merely asked, "Then why are both your houses on the other side of the river?" I leaned against the railing, watching the reflections of the Rainbow wobble on the river surface like bright fishes struggling in the current.

"Because I wanted a quiet street—so I could visit this clamor whenever I wished and then have a home to retreat to."

"You could have just reordered the city."

"Why the hell would I change one thing about this place?"

"Isn't that what High Lords do?" My breath clouded in front of me in the brisk night. "Whatever they please?"

He studied my face. "There are a great many things that I wish to do, and don't get to."

I hadn't realized how close we were standing. "So when you buy jewelry for Amren, is it to keep yourself in her good graces or because you're—together?"

Rhys barked a laugh. "When I was young and stupid, I once invited her to my bed. She laughed herself hoarse. The jewelry is just because I enjoy buying it for a friend who works hard for me, and has my back when I need it. Staying in her good graces is an added bonus."

None of it surprised me. "And you didn't marry anyone."

"So many questions tonight." I stared at him until he sighed. "I've had lovers, but I never felt tempted to invite one of them to share a life with me. And I honestly think that if I'd asked, they all would have said no."

"I would have thought they'd be fighting each other to win your hand." Like Ianthe.

"Marrying me means a life with a target on your back—and if there were offspring, then a life of knowing they'd be hunted from the moment they were conceived. Everyone knows what happened to my family—and my people know that beyond our borders, we are hated."

I still didn't know the full story, but I asked, "Why? Why are you hated? Why keep the truth of this place secret? It's a shame no one knows about it—what good you do here."

"There was a time when the Night Court *was* a Court of Nightmares and was ruled from the Hewn City. Long ago. But an ancient High Lord had a different vision, and rather than allowing the world to see his territory vulnerable at a time of change, he sealed the borders and staged a coup, eliminating the worst of the courtiers and predators, building Velaris for the dreamers, establishing trade and peace."

His eyes blazed, as if he could peer all the way back in time to see it. With those remarkable gifts of his, it wouldn't surprise me.

"To preserve it," Rhys continued, "he kept it a secret, and so did his offspring, and their offspring. There are many spells on the city itself—laid by him, and his Heirs, that make those who trade here unable to spill our secrets, and grant them adept skills at lying in order to keep the origin of their goods, their ships, hidden from the rest of the world. Rumor has it that ancient High Lord cast his very life's blood upon the stones and river to keep that spell eternal.

"But along the way, despite his best intentions, darkness grew again—not as bad as it had once been . . . But bad enough that there is a permanent divide within my court. We allow the world to see the other half, to fear them—so that they might never guess this place thrives here. And we allow the Court of Nightmares to continue, blind to Velaris's existence, because we know that without them, there are some courts and kingdoms that might strike us. And invade our borders to discover the many, many secrets we've kept from the other High Lords and courts these millennia."

"So truly none of the others know? In the other courts?"

"Not a soul. You will not find it on a single map, or mentioned in any book beyond those written here. Perhaps it is our loss to be so contained and isolated, but . . . " He gestured to the city around us. "My people do not seem to be suffering much for it."

Indeed, they did not. Thanks to Rhys—and his Inner Circle. "Are you worried about Az going to the mortal lands tomorrow?"

He tapped a finger against the rail. "Of course I am. But Azriel has infiltrated places far more harrowing than a few mortal courts. He'd find my worrying insulting."

"Does he mind what he does? Not the spying, I mean. What he did to the Attor today."

Rhys loosed a breath. "It's hard to tell with him—and he'd never tell me. I've witnessed Cassian rip apart opponents and then puke his guts up once the carnage stopped, sometimes even mourn them. But Azriel . . . Cassian tries, I try—but I think the only person who ever gets him to admit to any sort of feeling is Mor. And that's only when she's pestered him to the point where even his infinite patience has run out."

I smiled a bit. "But he and Mor—they never . . . ?"

"That's between them—and Cassian. I'm not stupid or arrogant enough to get in the middle of it." Which I would certainly be if I shoved my nose in their business.

We walked in silence across the packed bridge to the other side of the river. My muscles quivered at the steep hills between us and the town house.

I was about to beg Rhys to fly me home when I caught the strands of music pouring from a group of performers outside a restaurant.

My hands slackened at my sides. A reduced version of the symphony I'd heard in a chill dungeon, when I had been so lost to terror and despair that I had hallucinated—hallucinated as this music poured into my cell . . . and kept me from shattering.

And once more, the beauty of it hit me, the layering and swaying, the joy and peace.

They had never played a piece like it Under the Mountain—never this sort of music. And I'd never heard music in my cell save for that one time.

"You," I breathed, not taking my eyes from the musicians playing so skillfully that even the diners had set down their forks in the cafés nearby. "You sent that music into my cell. Why?"

Rhysand's voice was hoarse. "Because you were breaking. And I couldn't find another way to save you."

The music swelled and built. I'd seen a palace in the sky when I'd hallucinated—a place between sunset and dawn . . . a house of moonstone pillars. "I saw the Night Court."

He glanced sidelong at me. "I didn't send those images to you."

I didn't care. "Thank you. For everything—for what you did. Then . . . and now."

"Even after the Weaver? After this morning with my trap for the Attor?"

My nostrils flared. "You ruin everything."

Rhys grinned, and I didn't notice if people were staring as he slid an arm under my legs, and shot us both into the sky.

I could learn to love it, I realized. The flying.

I was reading in bed, listening to the merry chatter of the toasty birch fire across the room, when I turned the page of my book and a piece of paper fell out.

I took one look at the cream stationery and the handwriting and sat up straight.

On it, Rhysand had written,

I might be a shameless flirt, but at least I don't have a horrible temper. You should come tend to my wounds from our squabble in the snow. I'm bruised all over thanks to you.

Something clicked against the nightstand, and a pen rolled across the polished mahogany. Hissing, I snatched it up and scribbled:

Go lick your wounds and leave me be.

The paper vanished.

It was gone for a while—far longer than it should have taken to write the few words that appeared on the paper when it returned.

I'd much rather you licked my wounds for me.

My heart pounded, faster and faster, and a strange sort of rush went through my veins as I read the sentence again and again. A challenge.

I clamped my lips shut to keep from smiling as I wrote,

Lick you where, exactly?

The paper vanished before I'd even completed the final mark.

His reply was a long time coming. Then,

Wherever you want to lick me, Feyre.

I'd like to start with "Everywhere," but I can choose, if necessary.

I wrote back,

Let's hope my licking is better than yours. I remember how horrible you were at it Under the Mountain.

Lie. He'd licked away my tears when I'd been a moment away from shattering.

He'd done it to keep me distracted—keep me angry. Because anger was better than feeling nothing; because anger and hatred were the long-lasting fuel in the endless dark of my despair. The same way that music had kept me from breaking.

Lucien had come to patch me up a few times, but no one risked quite so much in keeping me not only alive, but as mentally intact as I could be considering the circumstances. Just as he'd been doing these past few weeks—taunting and teasing me to keep the hollowness at bay. Just as he was doing now.

I was under duress, his next note read. *If you want, I'd be more than happy to prove you wrong. I've been told I'm very, very good at licking.*

I clenched my knees together and wrote back, *Good night.*

A heartbeat later, his note said, *Try not to moan too loudly when you dream about me. I need my beauty rest.*

I got up, chucked the letter in the burbling fire, and gave it a vulgar gesture.

I could have sworn laughter rumbled down the hall.

I didn't dream about Rhys.

I dreamed about the Attor, its claws on me, gripping me as I was punched. I dreamed about its hissing laughter and foul stench.

But I slept through the night. And did not wake once.

CHAPTER 30

Cassian might have been cocky grins and vulgarity most of the time, but in the sparring ring in a rock-carved courtyard atop the House of Wind the next afternoon, he was a stone-cold killer.

And when those lethal instincts were turned on me . . .

Beneath the fighting leathers, even with the brisk temperature, my skin was slick with sweat. Each breath ravaged my throat, and my arms trembled so badly that any time I so much as tried to use my fingers, my pinkie would start shaking uncontrollably.

I was watching it wobble of its own accord when Cassian closed the gap between us, gripped my hand, and said, "This is because you're hitting on the wrong knuckles. Top two—pointer and middle finger—that's where the punches should connect. Hitting here," he said, tapping a callused finger on the already-bruised bit of skin in the vee between my pinkie and ring finger, "will do more damage to you than to your opponent. You're lucky the Attor didn't want to get into a fistfight."

We'd been going at it for an hour now, walking through the basic steps of hand-to-hand combat. And it turned out that I might have been good at hunting, at archery, but using my left side? Pathetic. I was as uncoordinated as a newborn fawn attempting to walk. Punching *and* stepping with the left side of my body at once had been nearly impossible, and I'd stumbled into Cassian more often than I'd hit him. The right punches—those were easy.

"Get a drink," he said. "Then we're working on your core. No point in learning to punch if you can't even hold your stance."

I frowned toward the sound of clashing blades in the open sparring ring across from us.

Azriel, surprisingly, had returned from the mortal realm by lunch. Mor had intercepted him first, but I'd gotten a secondhand report from Rhys that he'd found some sort of barrier around the queens' palace, and had needed to return to assess what might be done about it.

Assess—and brood, it seemed, since Azriel had barely managed a polite hello to me before launching into sparring with Rhysand, his face grim and tight. They'd been at it now for an hour straight, their slender blades like flashes of quicksilver as they moved around and around. I wondered if it was as much for practice as it was for Rhys to help his spymaster work off his frustration.

At some point since I'd last looked, despite the sunny winter day, they'd removed their leather jackets and shirts.

Their tan, muscled arms were both covered in the same manner of tattoos that adorned my own hand and forearm, the ink flowing across their shoulders and over their sculpted pectoral muscles. Between their wings, a line of them ran down the column of their spine, right beneath where they typically strapped their blades.

"We get the tattoos when we're initiated as Illyrian warriors—for luck and glory on the battlefield," Cassian said, following my stare. I doubted Cassian was drinking in the rest of the image, though: the stomach muscles gleaming with sweat in the bright sun, the bunching of their powerful thighs, the rippling strength in their backs, surrounding those mighty, beautiful wings.

Death on swift wings.

The title came out of nowhere, and for a moment, I saw the painting I'd create: the darkness of those wings, faintly illuminated with lines of red and gold by the radiant winter sun, the glare off their blades, the harshness of the tattoos against the beauty of their faces—

I blinked, and the image was gone, like a cloud of hot breath on a cold night.

Cassian jerked his chin toward his brothers. "Rhys is out of shape and won't admit it, but Azriel is too polite to beat him into the dirt."

Rhys looked anything but out of shape. Cauldron boil me, what the hell did they *eat* to look like that?

My knees wobbled a bit as I strode to the stool where Cassian had brought a pitcher of water and two glasses. I poured one for myself, my pinkie trembling uncontrollably again.

My tattoo, I realized, had been made with Illyrian markings. Perhaps Rhys's own way of wishing me luck and glory while facing Amarantha.

Luck and glory. I wouldn't mind a little of either of those things these days.

Cassian filled a glass for himself and clinked it against mine, so at odds from the brutal taskmaster who, moments ago, had me walking through punches, hitting his sparring pads, and trying not to crumple on the ground to beg for death. So at odds from the male who had gone head to head with my sister, unable to resist matching himself against Nesta's spirit of steel and flame.

"So," Cassian said, gulping down the water. Behind us, Rhys and Azriel clashed, separated, and clashed again. "When are you going to talk about how you wrote a letter to Tamlin, telling him you've left for good?"

The question hit me so viciously that I sniped, "How about when you talk about how you tease and taunt Mor to hide whatever it is you feel for her?" Because I had no doubt that he was well aware of the role he played in their little tangled web.

The beat of crunching steps and clashing blades behind us stumbled—then resumed.

Cassian let out a startled, rough laugh. "Old news."

"I have a feeling that's what she probably says about you."

"Get back in the ring," Cassian said, setting down his empty glass. "No core exercises. Just fists. You want to mouth off, then back it up."

But the question he'd asked swarmed in my skull. *You've left for good; you've left for good; you've left for good.*

I had—I'd meant it. But without knowing what he thought, if he'd even care that much . . . No, I knew he'd care. He'd probably trashed the manor in his rage.

If my mere mention of him suffocating me had caused him to destroy his study, then this . . . I had been frightened by those fits of pure rage, cowed by them. And it had been love—I had loved him so deeply, so greatly, but . . .

"Rhys told you?" I said.

Cassian had the wisdom to look a bit nervous at the expression on my face. "He informed Azriel, who is . . . monitoring things and needs to know. Az told me."

"I assume it was while you were out drinking and dancing." I drained the last of my water and walked back into the ring.

"Hey," Cassian said, catching my arm. His hazel eyes were more green than brown today. "I'm sorry. I didn't mean to hit a nerve. Az only told me because I told him *I* needed to know for my own forces; to know what to expect. None of us . . . we don't think it's a joke. What you did was a hard call. A really damn hard call. It was just my shitty way of trying to see if you needed to talk about it. I'm sorry," he repeated, letting go.

The stumbling words, the earnestness in his eyes . . . I nodded as I resumed my place. "All right."

Though Rhysand kept at it with Azriel, I could have sworn his eyes were on me—had been on me from the moment Cassian had asked me that question.

Cassian shoved his hands into the sparring pads and held them up. "Thirty one-two punches; then forty; then fifty." I winced at him over his gloves as I wrapped my hands. "You didn't answer my question," he said with a tentative smile—one I doubted his soldiers or Illyrian brethren ever saw.

It had been love, and I'd meant it—the happiness, the lust, the peace . . . I'd felt all of those things. Once.

I positioned my legs at twelve and five and lifted my hands up toward my face.

But maybe those things had blinded me, too.

Maybe they'd been a blanket over my eyes about the temper. The need for control, the need to protect that ran so deep he'd locked me up. Like a prisoner.

"I'm fine," I said, stepping and jabbing with my left side. Fluid—smooth like silk, as if my immortal body at last aligned.

My fist slammed into Cassian's sparring pad, snatching back as fast as a snake's bite as I struck with my right, shoulder and foot twisting.

"One," Cassian counted. Again, I struck, one-two. "Two. And fine is good—fine is great."

Again, again, again.

We both knew "fine" was a lie.

I had done everything—*everything* for that love. I had ripped myself to shreds, I had killed innocents and debased myself, and he had *sat* beside Amarantha on that throne. And he couldn't do anything, hadn't risked it—hadn't risked being caught until there was one night left, and all he'd wanted to do wasn't free me, but fuck me, and—

Again, again, again. One-two; one-two; one-two—

And when Amarantha had broken me, when she had snapped my bones and made my blood boil in its veins, he'd just knelt and begged her. He hadn't tried to kill her, hadn't crawled for me. Yes, he'd fought for me—but I'd fought harder for him.

Again, again, again, each pound of my fists on the sparring pads a question and an answer.

And he had the nerve once his powers were back to shove me into a cage. The *nerve* to say I was no longer useful; I was to be cloistered for *his* peace of mind. He'd given me everything I needed to become myself, to feel safe, and when he got what he wanted—when he got his power back, his lands back . . . he stopped trying. He was still good, still Tamlin, but he was just . . . wrong.

And then I was sobbing through my clenched teeth, the tears washing away that infected wound, and I didn't care that Cassian was there, or Rhys or Azriel.

The clashing steel stopped.

And then my fists connected with bare skin, and I realized I'd punched through the sparring pads—no, *burned* through them, and—

And I stopped, too.

The wrappings around my hands were now mere smudges of soot. Cassian's upraised palms remained before me—ready to take the blow, if I needed to make it. "I'm all right," he said quietly. Gently.

And maybe I was exhausted and broken, but I breathed, "I killed them."

I hadn't said the words aloud since it had happened.

Cassian's lips tightened. "I know." Not condemnation, not praise. But grim understanding.

My hands slackened as another shuddering sob worked its way through me. "It should have been me."

And there it was.

Standing there under the cloudless sky, the winter sun beating on my head, nothing around me save for rock, no shadows in which to hide, nothing to cling to . . . There it was.

Then darkness swept in, soothing, gentle darkness—no, shade—and a sweat-slick male body halted before me. Gentle fingers lifted my chin until I looked up . . . at Rhysand's face.

His wings had wrapped around us, cocooned us, the sunlight casting the membrane in gold and red. Beyond us, outside, in another world, maybe, the sounds of steel on steel—Cassian and Azriel sparring—began.

"You will feel that way every day for the rest of your life," Rhysand said. This close, I could smell the sweat on him, the sea-and-citrus scent beneath it. His eyes were soft. I tried to look away, but he held my chin firm. "And I know this because I have felt that way every day since my mother and sister were slaughtered and I had to bury them myself, and even retribution didn't fix it." He wiped away the tears on one cheek, then another. "You can either let it wreck you, let it get you killed like it nearly did with the Weaver, or you can learn to live with it."

For a long moment, I just stared at the open, calm face—maybe his true face, the one beneath all the masks he wore to keep his people safe. "I'm sorry—about your family," I rasped.

"I'm sorry I didn't find a way to spare you from what happened Under the Mountain," Rhys said with equal quiet. "From dying. From *wanting* to die." I began to shake my head, but he said, "I have two kinds of nightmares: the ones where I'm again Amarantha's whore or my friends are . . . And the ones where I hear your neck snap and see the light leave your eyes."

I had no answer to that—to the tenor in his rich, deep voice. So I examined the tattoos on his chest and arms, the glow of his tan skin, so golden now that he was no longer caged inside that mountain.

I stopped my perusal when I got to the vee of muscles that flowed beneath the waist of his leather pants. Instead, I flexed my hand in front of me, my skin warm from the heat that had burned through those pads.

"Ah," he said, wings sweeping back as he folded them gracefully behind him. "That."

I squinted at the flood of sunlight. "Autumn Court, right?"

He took my hand, examining it, the skin already bruised from sparring. "Right. A gift from its High Lord, Beron."

Lucien's father. Lucien—I wondered what he made of all this. If he missed me. If Ianthe continued to . . . prey on him.

Still sparring, Cassian and Azriel were trying their best not to look like they were eavesdropping.

"I'm not well versed in the complexities of the other High Lords' elemental gifts," Rhys said, "but we can figure it out—day by day, if need be."

"If you're the most powerful High Lord in history . . . does that mean the drop I got from you holds more sway over the others?" Why I'd been able to break into his head that one time?

"Give it a try." He jerked his chin toward me. "See if you can summon darkness. I won't ask you to try to winnow," he added with a grin.

"I don't know how I did it to begin with."

"Will it into being."

I gave him a flat stare.

He shrugged. "Try thinking of me—how good-looking I am. How talented—"

"How arrogant."

"That, too." He crossed his arms over his bare chest, the movement making the muscles in his stomach flicker.

"Put a shirt on while you're at it," I quipped.

A feline smile. "Does it make you uncomfortable?"

"I'm surprised there aren't more mirrors in this house, since you seem to love looking at yourself so much."

Azriel launched into a coughing fit. Cassian just turned away, a hand clamped over his mouth.

Rhys's lips twitched. "There's the Feyre I adore."

I scowled, but closed my eyes and tried to look inward—toward any dark corner of myself I could find. There were too many.

Far too many.

And right now—right now they each contained that letter I'd written yesterday.

A good-bye.

For my own sanity, my *own* safety . . .

"There are different kinds of darkness," Rhys said. I kept my eyes shut. "There is the darkness that frightens, the darkness that soothes, the darkness that is restful." I pictured each. "There is the darkness of lovers, and the darkness of assassins. It becomes what the bearer wishes it to be, needs it to be. It is not wholly bad or good."

I only saw the darkness of that dungeon cell; the darkness of the Bone Carver's lair.

Cassian swore, but Azriel murmured a soft challenge that had their blades striking again.

"Open your eyes." I did.

And found darkness all around me. Not from me—but from Rhys. As if the sparring ring had been wiped away, as if the world had yet to begin.

Quiet.

Soft.

Peaceful.

Lights began twinkling—little stars, blooming irises of blue and purple and white. I reached out a hand toward one, and starlight danced on my fingertips. Far away, in another world perhaps, Azriel and Cassian sparred in the dark, no doubt using it as a training exercise.

I shifted the star between my fingers like a coin on the hand of a magician. Here in the soothing, sparkling dark, a steady breath filled my lungs.

I couldn't remember the last time I'd done such a thing. Breathed easily.

Then the darkness splintered and vanished, swifter than smoke on a wind. I found myself blinking back the blinding sun, arm still out, Rhysand still before me.

Still without a shirt.

He said, "We can work on it later. For now." He sniffed. "Go take a bath."

I gave him a particularly vulgar gesture—and asked Cassian to fly me home instead.

CHAPTER 31

"Don't dance so much on your toes," Cassian said to me four days later, as we spent the unusually warm afternoon in the sparring ring. "Feet planted, daggers up. Eyes on mine. If you were on a battlefield, you would have been dead with that maneuver."

Amren snorted, picking at her nails while she lounged in a chaise. "She heard you the first ten times you said it, Cassian."

"Keep talking, Amren, and I'll drag you into the ring and see how much practice you've actually been doing."

Amren just continued cleaning her nails—with a tiny bone, I realized. "Touch me, Cassian, and I'll remove your favorite part. Small as it might be."

He let out a low chuckle. Standing between them in the sparring ring atop the House of Wind, a dagger in each hand, sweat sliding down my body, I wondered if I should find a way to slip out. Perhaps winnow—though I hadn't been able to do it again since that morning in the mortal realm, despite my quiet efforts in the privacy of my own bedroom.

Four days of this—training with him, working with Rhys afterward on trying to summon flame or darkness. Unsurprisingly, I made more progress with the former.

Word had not yet arrived from the Summer Court. Or from the Spring Court, regarding my letter. I hadn't decided if that was a good thing. Azriel continued his attempt to infiltrate the human queens' courts, his network of spies now seeking a foothold to get inside. That he hadn't managed to do so yet had made him quieter than usual—colder.

Amren's silver eyes flicked up from her nails. "Good. You can play with her."

"Play with who?" said Mor, stepping from the stairwell shadows.

Cassian's nostrils flared. "Where'd you go the other night?" he asked Mor without so much as a nod of greeting. "I didn't see you leave Rita's." Their usual dance hall for drinking and revelry.

They'd dragged me out two nights ago—and I'd spent most of the time sitting in their booth, nursing my wine, talking over the music with Azriel, who had arrived content to brood, but reluctantly joined me in observing Rhys holding court at the bar. Females and males watched Rhysand throughout the hall—and the shadowsinger and I made a game of betting on who, exactly, would work up the nerve to invite the High Lord home.

Unsurprisingly, Az won every round. But at least he was smiling by the end of the night—to Mor's delight when she'd stumbled back to our table to chug another drink before prancing onto the dance floor again.

Rhys didn't accept any offers that came his way, no matter how beautiful they were, no matter how they smiled and laughed. And his refusals were polite—firm, but polite.

Had he been with anyone since Amarantha? Did he *want* another person in his bed after Amarantha? Even the wine hadn't given me the nerve to ask Azriel about it.

Mor, it seemed, went to Rita's more than anyone else—practically lived there, actually. She shrugged at Cassian's demand and another chaise like Amren's appeared. "I just went . . . out," she said, plopping down.

"With whom?" Cassian pushed.

"Last I was aware," Mor said, leaning back in the chair, "I didn't take orders from you, Cassian. Or report to you. So where I was, and who I was with, is none of your damn concern."

"You didn't tell Azriel, either."

I paused, weighing those words, Cassian's stiff shoulders. Yes, there was some tension between him and Mor that resulted in that bickering, but . . . perhaps . . . perhaps Cassian accepted the role of buffer not to keep them apart, but to keep the shadowsinger from hurt. From being *old news*, as I'd called him.

Cassian finally remembered I'd been standing in front of him, noted the look of understanding on my face, and gave me a warning one in return. Fair enough.

I shrugged and took a moment to set down the daggers and catch my breath. For a heartbeat, I wished Nesta were there, if only to see *them* go head to head. We hadn't heard from my sisters—or the mortal queens. I wondered when we'd send another letter or try another route.

"Why, exactly," Cassian said to Amren and Mor, not even bothering to try to sound pleasant, "are you two *ladies* here?"

Mor closed her eyes as she tipped back her head, sunning her golden face with the same irreverence that Cassian perhaps sought to shield Azriel from—and Mor herself perhaps tried to shield Azriel from as well. "Rhys is coming in a few moments to give us some news, apparently. Didn't Amren tell you?"

"I forgot," Amren said, still picking at her nails. "I was having too much fun watching Feyre evade Cassian's tried-and-true techniques to get people to do what he wants."

Cassian's brows rose. "You've been here for an *hour*."

"Oops," Amren said.

Cassian threw up his hands. "Get off your ass and give me twenty lunges—"

A vicious, unearthly snarl cut him off.

But Rhys strolled out of the stairwell, and I couldn't decide if I should be relieved or disappointed that Cassian versus Amren was put to a sudden stop.

He was in his fine clothes, not fighting leathers, his wings nowhere in sight. Rhys looked at them, at me, the daggers I'd left in the dirt, and then said, "Sorry to interrupt while things were getting interesting."

"Fortunately for Cassian's balls," Amren said, nestling back in her chaise, "you arrived at the right time."

Cassian snarled halfheartedly at her.

Rhys laughed, and said to none of us in particular, "Ready to go on a summer holiday?"

Mor said, "The Summer Court invited you?"

"Of course they did. Feyre, Amren, and I are going tomorrow."

Only the three of us? Cassian seemed to have the same thought, his wings rustling as he crossed his arms and faced Rhys. "The Summer Court is full of hotheaded fools and arrogant pricks," he warned. "I should join you."

"You'd fit right in," Amren crooned. "Too bad you still aren't going."

Cassian pointed a finger at her. "Watch it, Amren."

She bared her teeth in a wicked smile. "Believe me, I'd prefer not to go, either."

I clamped my lips shut to keep from smiling or grimacing, I didn't know.

Rhys rubbed his temples. "Cassian, considering the fact that the last time you visited, it didn't end well—"

"I wrecked *one* building—"

"*And*," Rhys cut him off. "Considering the fact that they are utterly terrified of sweet Amren, *she* is the wiser choice."

I didn't know if there was anyone alive who *wasn't* utterly terrified of her.

"It could easily be a trap," Cassian pushed. "Who's to say the delay in replying wasn't because they're contacting our enemies to ambush you?"

"That is *also* why Amren is coming," Rhys said simply.

Amren was frowning—bored and annoyed.

Rhys said too casually, "There is also a great deal of treasure to be found in the Summer Court. If the Book is hidden, Amren, you might find other objects to your liking."

"Shit," Cassian said, throwing up his hands again. "Really, Rhys? It's bad enough we're stealing from them, but robbing them blind—"

"Rhysand *does* have a point," Amren said. "Their High Lord is young and untested. I doubt he's had much time to catalog his inherited hoard since he was appointed Under the Mountain. I doubt he'll know anything is missing. Very well, Rhysand—I'm in."

No better than a firedrake guarding its trove indeed. Mor gave me a secret, subtle look that conveyed the same thing, and I swallowed a chuckle.

Cassian started to object again, but Rhys said quietly, "I will need you—not Amren—in the human realm. The Summer Court has banned you for eternity, and though your presence would be a good distraction while Feyre does what she has to, it could lead to more trouble than it's worth."

I stiffened. What I had to do—meaning track down that Book of Breathings and steal it. Feyre Cursebreaker . . . and thief.

"Just cool your heels, Cassian," Amren said, eyes a bit glazed—as she no doubt imagined the treasure she might steal from the Summer Court. "We'll be fine without your swaggering and growling at everyone. Their High Lord owes Rhys a favor for saving his life Under the Mountain—and keeping his secrets."

Cassian's wings twitched, but Mor chimed in, "And the High Lord also probably wants to figure out where we stand in regard to any upcoming conflict."

Cassian's wings settled again. He jerked his chin at me. "Feyre, though. It's one thing to have her here—even when everyone knows it. It's another to bring her to a different court, and introduce her as a member of our own."

The message it'd send to Tamlin. If my letter wasn't enough.

But Rhys was done. He inclined his head to Amren and strolled for the open archway. Cassian lurched a step, but Mor lifted a hand. "Leave it," she murmured. Cassian glared, but obeyed.

I took that as a chance to follow after Rhys, the warm darkness inside the House of Wind blinding me. My Fae eyes adjusted swiftly, but for the first few steps down the narrow hallway, I trailed after Rhys on memory alone.

"Any more traps I should know about before we go tomorrow?" I said to his back.

Rhys looked over a shoulder, pausing atop the stair landing. "Here I was, thinking your notes the other night indicated you'd forgiven me."

I took in that half grin, the chest I might have suggested I'd lick and had avoided looking at for the past four days, and halted a healthy distance away. "One would think a High Lord would have more important things to do than pass notes back and forth at night."

"I do have more important things to do," he purred. "But I find myself unable to resist the temptation. The same way you can't resist watching me whenever we're out. So territorial."

My mouth went a bit dry. But—flirting with him, fighting with him . . . It was easy. Fun.

Maybe I deserved both of those things.

So I closed the distance between us, smoothly stepped past him, and said, "*You* haven't been able to keep away from me since Calanmai, it seems."

Something rippled in his eyes that I couldn't place, but he flicked my nose—hard enough that I hissed and batted his hand away.

"I can't wait to see what that sharp tongue of yours can do at the Summer Court," he said, gaze fixed on my mouth, and vanished into shadow.

CHAPTER 32

In the end, only Amren and I joined Rhys, Cassian having failed to sway his High Lord, Azriel still off overseeing his network of spies and investigating the human realm, and Mor tasked with guarding Velaris. Rhys would winnow us directly into Adriata, the castle-city of the Summer Court—and there we would stay, for however long it took me to detect and then steal the first half of the Book.

As Rhys's newest pet, I would be granted tours of the city and the High Lord's personal residence. If we were lucky, none of them would realize that Rhys's lapdog was actually a bloodhound.

And it was a very, very good disguise.

Rhys and Amren stood in the town house foyer the next day, the rich morning sunlight streaming through the windows and pooling on the ornate carpet. Amren wore her usual shades of gray—her loose pants cut to just beneath her navel, the billowing top cropped to show the barest slice of skin along her midriff. Alluring as a calm sea under a cloudy sky.

Rhys was in head-to-toe black accented with silver thread—no wings. The cool, cultured male I'd first met. His favorite mask.

For my own, I'd selected a flowing lilac dress, its skirts floating on a phantom wind beneath the silver-and-pearl-crusted belt at my waist. Matching night-blooming silver flowers had been embroidered to climb from the hem to brush my thighs, and a few more twined down the folds at my shoulders. The perfect gown to combat the warmth of the Summer Court.

It swished and sighed as I descended the last two stairs into the foyer. Rhys surveyed me with a long, unreadable sweep from my silver-slippered feet to my half-up hair. Nuala had curled the strands that had been left down—soft, supple curls that brought out the gold in my hair.

Rhys simply said, "Good. Let's go."

My mouth popped open, but Amren explained with a broad, feline smile, "He's pissy this morning."

"Why?" I asked, watching Amren take Rhys's hand, her delicate fingers dwarfed by his. He held out the other to me.

"Because," Rhys answered for her, "I stayed out late with Cassian and Azriel, and they took me for all I was worth in cards."

"Sore loser?" I gripped his hand. His calluses scraped against my own—the only reminder of the trained warrior beneath the clothes and veneer.

"I am when my brothers tag-team me," he grumbled. He offered no warning before we vanished on a midnight wind, and then—

Then I was squinting at the glaring sun off a turquoise sea, just as I was trying to reorder my body around the dry, suffocating heat, even with the cooling breeze off the water.

I blinked a few times—and that was as much reaction as I let myself show as I yanked my hand from Rhys's grip.

We seemed to be standing on a landing platform at the base of a tan stone palace, the building itself perched atop a mountain-island in the heart of a half-moon bay. The city spread around and below us, toward that sparkling sea—the buildings all from that stone, or glimmering white material that might have been coral or pearl. Gulls flapped over the many turrets and spires, no clouds above them, nothing on the breeze with them but salty air and the clatter of the city below.

Various bridges connected the bustling island to the larger landmass that circled it on three sides, one of them currently raising itself so a many-masted ship could cruise through. Indeed, there were more ships than I could count—some merchant vessels, some fishing ones, and some, it seemed, ferrying people from the island-city to the mainland, whose sloping shores were crammed full of more buildings, more people.

More people like the half dozen before us, framed by a pair of sea glass doors that opened into the palace itself. On our little balcony, there was no option to escape—no path out but winnowing away . . . or going through those doors. Or, I supposed, the plunge awaiting us to the red roofs of the fine houses a hundred feet below.

"Welcome to Adriata," said the tall male in the center of the group.

And I knew him—remembered him.

Not from memory. I'd already remembered that the handsome High Lord of Summer had rich brown skin, white hair, and eyes of crushing, turquoise blue. I'd already remembered he'd been forced to watch as his courtier's mind was invaded and then his life snuffed out by Rhysand. As Rhysand lied to Amarantha about what he'd learned, and spared the male from a fate perhaps worse than death.

No—I now remembered the High Lord of Summer in a way I couldn't quite explain, like some fragment of me knew it had come from him, from here. Like some piece of me said, *I remember, I remember, I remember. We are one and the same, you and I.*

Rhys merely drawled, "Good to see you again, Tarquin."

The five other people behind the High Lord of Summer swapped frowns of varying severity. Like their lord, their skin was dark, their hair in shades of white or silver, as if they had lived under the bright sun their entire lives. Their eyes, however, were of every color. And they now shifted between me and Amren.

Rhys slid one hand into a pocket and gestured with the other to

Amren. "Amren, I think you know. Though you haven't met her since your . . . promotion." Cool, calculating grace, edged with steel.

Tarquin gave Amren the briefest of nods. "Welcome back to the city, lady."

Amren didn't nod, or bow, or so much as curtsy. She looked over Tarquin, tall and muscled, his clothes of sea-green and blue and gold, and said, "At least you are far more handsome than your cousin. He was an eyesore." A female behind Tarquin outright glared. Amren's red lips stretched wide. "Condolences, of course," she added with as much sincerity as a snake.

Wicked, cruel—that's what Amren and Rhys were . . . what *I* was to be to these people.

Rhys gestured to me. "I don't believe you two were ever formally introduced Under the Mountain. Tarquin, Feyre. Feyre, Tarquin." No titles here—either to unnerve them or because Rhys found them a waste of breath.

Tarquin's eyes—such stunning, crystal blue—fixed on me.

I remember you, I remember you, I remember you.

The High Lord did not smile.

I kept my face neutral, vaguely bored.

His gaze drifted to my chest, the bare skin revealed by the sweeping vee of my gown, as if he could see where that spark of life, his power, had gone.

Rhys followed that gaze. "Her breasts *are* rather spectacular, aren't they? Delicious as ripe apples."

I fought the urge to scowl, and instead slid my attention to him, as indolently as he'd looked at me, at the others. "Here I was, thinking you had a fascination with my mouth."

Delighted surprise lit Rhys's eyes, there and gone in a heartbeat.

We both looked back to our hosts, still stone-faced and stiff-backed.

Tarquin seemed to weigh the air between my companions and me, then said carefully, "You have a tale to tell, it seems."

"We have many tales to tell," Rhys said, jerking his chin toward the glass doors behind them. "So why not get comfortable?"

The female a half-step behind Tarquin inched closer. "We have refreshments prepared."

Tarquin seemed to remember her and put a hand on her slim shoulder. "Cresseida—Princess of Adriata."

The ruler of his capital—or wife? There was no ring on either of their fingers, and I didn't recognize her from Under the Mountain. Her long, silver hair blew across her pretty face in the briny breeze, and I didn't mistake the light in her brown eyes for anything but razor-sharp cunning. "A pleasure," she murmured huskily to me. "And an honor."

My breakfast turned to lead in my gut, but I didn't let her see what the groveling did to me; let her realize it was ammunition. Instead I gave her my best imitation of Rhysand's shrug. "The honor's mine, princess."

The others were hastily introduced: three advisers who oversaw the city, the court, and the trade. And then a broad-shouldered, handsome male named Varian, Cresseida's younger brother, captain of Tarquin's guard, and Prince of Adriata. His attention was fixed wholly on Amren—as if he knew where the biggest threat lay. And would be happy to kill her, if given the chance.

In the brief time I'd known her, Amren had never looked more delighted.

We were led into a palace crafted of shell-flecked walkways and walls, countless windows looking out to the bay and mainland or the open sea beyond. Sea glass chandeliers swayed on the warm breeze over gurgling streams and fountains of fresh water. High fae—servants and courtiers—hurried across and around them, most brown-skinned and clad in loose, light clothing, all far too preoccupied with their own matters to take note or interest in our presence. No lesser faeries crossed our path—not one.

I kept a step behind Rhysand as he walked at Tarquin's side, that mighty power of his leashed and dimmed, the others flowing behind us. Amren remained within reach, and I wondered if she was also to be my bodyguard. Tarquin and Rhys had been talking lightly, both already sounding bored, of the approaching Nynsar—of the native flowers that both courts would display for the minor, brief holiday.

Calanmai wouldn't be too long after that.

My stomach twisted. If Tamlin was intent on upholding tradition, if I was no longer with him . . . I didn't let myself get that far down the road. It wouldn't be fair. To me—to him.

"We have four main cities in my territory," Tarquin said to me, looking over his muscled shoulder. "We spend the last month of winter and first spring months in Adriata—it's finest at this time of year."

Indeed, I supposed that with endless summer, there was no limit to how one might enjoy one's time. In the country, by the sea, in a city under the stars . . . I nodded. "It's very beautiful."

Tarquin stared at me long enough that Rhys said, "The repairs have been going well, I take it."

That hauled Tarquin's attention back. "Mostly. There remains much to be done. The back half of the castle is a wreck. But, as you can see, we've finished most of the inside. We focused on the city first—and those repairs are ongoing."

Amarantha had sacked the city? Rhys said, "I hope no valuables were lost during its occupation."

"Not the most important things, thank the Mother," Tarquin said.

Behind me, Cresseida tensed. The three advisers peeled off to attend to other duties, murmuring farewell—with wary looks in Tarquin's direction. As if this might very well be the first time he'd needed to play host and *they* were watching their High Lord's every move.

He gave them a smile that didn't reach his eyes, and said nothing more as he led us into a vaulted room of white oak and green glass—overlooking the mouth of the bay and the sea that stretched on forever.

I had never seen water so vibrant. Green and cobalt and midnight. And for a heartbeat, a palette of paint flashed in my mind, along with the blue and yellow and white and black I might need to paint it . . .

"This is my favorite view," Tarquin said beside me, and I realized I'd gone to the wide windows while the others had seated themselves around the mother-of-pearl table. A handful of servants were heaping fruits, leafy greens, and steamed shellfish onto their plates.

"You must be very proud," I said, "to have such stunning lands."

Tarquin's eyes—so like the sea beyond us—slid to me. "How do they compare to the ones you have seen?" Such a carefully crafted question.

I said dully, "Everything in Prythian is lovely, when compared to the mortal realm."

"And is being immortal lovelier than being human?"

I could feel everyone's attention on us, even as Rhys engaged Cresseida and Varian in bland, edged discussion about the status of their fish markets. So I looked the High Lord of Summer up and down, as he had examined me, brazenly and without a shred of politeness, and then said, "You tell me."

Tarquin's eyes crinkled. "You are a pearl. Though I knew that the day you threw that bone at Amarantha and splattered mud on her favorite dress."

I shut out the memories, the blind terror of that first trial.

What did he make of that tug between us—did he realize it was his own power, or think it was a bond of its own, some sort of strange allure?

And if I had to steal from him . . . perhaps that meant getting closer. "I do not remember you being quite so handsome Under the Mountain. The sunlight and sea suit you."

A lesser male might have preened. But Tarquin knew better—knew that I had been with Tamlin, and was now with Rhys, and had now been brought here. Perhaps he thought me no better than Ianthe. "How, exactly, do you fit within Rhysand's court?"

A direct question, after such roundabout ones—to no doubt get me on uneven footing.

It almost worked—I nearly admitted, "*I don't know*," but Rhys said from the table, as if he'd heard every word, "Feyre is a member of my Inner Circle. And is my Emissary to the Mortal Lands."

Cresseida, seated beside him, said, "Do you have much contact with the mortal realm?"

I took that as an invitation to sit—and get away from the too-heavy stare of Tarquin. A seat had been left open for me at Amren's side, across from Rhys.

The High Lord of the Night Court sniffed at his wine—white, sparkling—and I wondered if he was trying to piss them off by implying they'd poisoned it as he said, "I prefer to be prepared for every potential situation. And, given that Hybern seems set on making themselves a nuisance, striking up a conversation with the humans might be in our best interest."

Varian drew his focus away from Amren long enough to say roughly, "So it's been confirmed, then? Hybern is readying for war."

"They're done readying," Rhys drawled, at last sipping from his wine. Amren didn't touch her plate, though she pushed things around as she always did. I wondered what—who—she'd eat while here. Varian seemed like a good guess. "War is imminent."

"Yes, you mentioned that in your letter," Tarquin said, claiming the seat at the head of the table between Rhys and Amren. A bold move, to situate himself between two such powerful beings. Arrogance—or an attempt at friendship? Tarquin's gaze again drifted to me before focusing on Rhys. "And you know that against Hybern, we will fight. We lost enough good people Under the Mountain. I have no interest in being slaves again. But if you are here to ask me to fight in another war, Rhysand—"

"That is not a possibility," Rhys smoothly cut in, "and had not even entered my mind."

My glimmer of confusion must have shown, because Cresseida crooned to me, "High Lords have gone to war for less, you know. Doing it over such an *unusual* female would be nothing unexpected."

Which was likely why they had accepted this invitation, favor or no. To feel us out.

If—if Tamlin went to war to get me back. No. No, that wouldn't be an option.

I'd written to him, told him to stay away. And he wasn't foolish enough to start a war he could not win. Not when he wouldn't be fighting other High Fae, but Illyrian warriors, led by Cassian and Azriel. It would be slaughter.

So I said, bored and flat and dull, "Try not to look too excited, princess. The High Lord of Spring has no plans to go to war with the Night Court."

"And are you in contact with Tamlin, then?" A saccharine smile.

My next words were quiet, slow, and I decided I did not mind stealing from them, not one bit. "There are things that are public knowledge, and things that are not. My relationship with him is well known. Its current standing, however, is none of your concern. Or anyone else's. But I do know Tamlin, and I know that there will be no internal war between courts—at least not over me, or *my* decisions."

"What a relief, then," Cresseida said, sipping from her white wine before cracking a large crab claw, pink and white and orange. "To know we are not harboring a stolen bride—and that we need not bother returning her to her master, as the law demands. And as any wise person might do, to keep trouble from their doorstep."

Amren had gone utterly still.

"I left of my own free will," I said. "And no one is my master."

Cresseida shrugged. "Think that all you want, lady, but the law is the law. You are—were his bride. Swearing fealty to another High Lord does not change that. So it is a very good thing that he respects your decisions. Otherwise, all it would take would be one letter from him to Tarquin, requesting your return, and we would have to obey. Or risk war ourselves."

Rhysand sighed. "You are always a joy, Cresseida."

Varian said, "Careful, High Lord. My sister speaks the truth."

Tarquin laid a hand on the pale table. "Rhysand is our guest—his courtiers are our guests. And we will treat them as such. We will treat them, Cresseida, as we treat people who saved our necks when all it would have taken was one word from them for us to be very, very dead."

Tarquin studied me and Rhysand—whose face was gloriously disinterested. The High Lord of Summer shook his head and said to Rhys, "We have more to discuss later, you and I. Tonight, I'm throwing a party for you all on my pleasure barge in the bay. After that, you're free to roam in this city wherever you wish. You will forgive its princess if she is protective of her people. Rebuilding these months has been long and hard. We do not wish to do it again any time soon."

Cresseida's eyes grew dark, haunted.

"Cresseida made many sacrifices on behalf of her people," Tarquin offered gently—to me. "Do not take her caution personally."

"We all made sacrifices," Rhysand said, the icy boredom now shifting into something razor-sharp. "And you now sit at this table with your family because of the ones Feyre made. So you will forgive *me*, Tarquin, if I tell your princess that if she sends word to Tamlin, or if any of your people try to bring her to him, their lives will be forfeit."

Even the sea breeze died.

"Do not threaten me in my own home, Rhysand," Tarquin said. "My gratitude goes only so far."

"It's not a threat," Rhys countered, the crab claws on his plate cracking open beneath invisible hands. "It's a promise."

They all looked at me, waiting for any response.

So I lifted my glass of wine, looked them each in the eye, holding Tarquin's gaze the longest, and said, "No wonder immortality never gets dull."

Tarquin chuckled—and I wondered if his loosed breath was one of profound relief.

And through that bond between us, I felt Rhysand's flicker of approval.

CHAPTER 33

We were given a suite of connecting rooms, all centered on a large, lavish lounge that was open to the sea and city below. My bedroom was appointed in seafoam and softest blue with pops of gold—like the gilded clamshell atop my pale wood dresser. I had just set it down when the white door behind me clicked open and Rhys slid in.

He leaned against the door once he shut it, the top of his black tunic unbuttoned to reveal the upper whorls of the tattoo spanning his chest.

"The problem, I've realized, will be that I like Tarquin," he said by way of greeting. "I even like Cresseida. Varian, I could live without, but I bet a few weeks with Cassian and Azriel, and he'd be thick as thieves with them and I'd have to learn to like him. Or he'd be wrapped around Amren's finger, and I'd have to leave him alone entirely or risk her wrath."

"And?" I took up a spot against the dresser, where clothes that I had not packed but were clearly of Night Court origin had been already waiting for me.

The space of the room—the large bed, the windows, the sunlight—filled the silence between us.

"And," Rhys said, "I want you to find a way to do what you have to do without making enemies of them."

"So you're telling me don't get caught."

A nod. Then, "Do you like that Tarquin can't stop looking at you? I can't tell if it's because he wants you, or because he knows you have his power and wants to see how much."

"Can't it be both?"

"Of course. But having a High Lord lusting after you is a dangerous game."

"First you taunt me with Cassian, now Tarquin? Can't you find other ways to annoy me?"

Rhys prowled closer, and I steadied myself for his scent, his warmth, the impact of his power. He braced a hand on either side of me, gripping the dresser. I refused to shrink away. "You have one task here, Feyre. One task that no one can know about. So do anything you have to in order to accomplish it. But get that book. And do not get caught."

I wasn't some simpering fool. I knew the risks. And that *tone*, that *look* he always gave me . . . "*Anything*?" His brows rose. I breathed, "If I fucked him for it, what would you do?"

His pupils flared, and his gaze dropped to my mouth. The wood dresser groaned beneath his hands. "You say such atrocious things." I waited, my heart an uneven beat. He at last met my eyes again. "You are always free to do what you want, with whomever you want. So if you want to ride him, go ahead."

"Maybe I will." Though a part of me wanted to retort, *Liar*.

"Fine." His breath caressed my mouth.

"Fine," I said, aware of every inch between us, the distance smaller and smaller, the challenge heightening with each second neither of us moved.

"Do not," he said softly, his eyes like stars, "jeopardize this mission."

"I know the cost." The sheer power of him enveloped me, shaking me awake.

The salt and the sea and the breeze tugged on me, sang to me.

And as if Rhys heard them, too, he inclined his head toward the unlit candle on the dresser. "Light it."

I debated arguing, but looked at the candle, summoning fire, summoning that hot anger he managed to rile—

The candle was knocked off the dresser by a violent splash of water, as if someone had chucked a bucketful.

I gaped at the water drenching the dresser, its dripping on the marble floor the only sound.

Rhys, hands still braced on either side of me, laughed quietly. "Can't you ever follow orders?"

But whatever it was—being here, close to Tarquin and his power . . . I could feel that water answering me. Feel it coating the floor, feel the sea churning and idling in the bay, taste the salt on the breeze. I held Rhys's gaze.

No one was my master—but I might be master of everything, if I wished. If I dared.

Like a strange rain, the water rose from the floor as I willed it to become like those stars Rhys had summoned in his blanket of darkness. I willed the droplets to separate until they hung around us, catching the light and sparkling like crystals on a chandelier.

Rhys broke my stare to study them. "I suggest," he murmured, "you not show Tarquin that little trick in the bedroom."

I sent each and every one of those droplets shooting for the High Lord's face.

Too fast, too swiftly for him to shield. Some of them sprayed me as they ricocheted off him.

Both of us now soaking, Rhys gaped a bit—then smiled. "Good work," he said, at last pushing off the dresser. He didn't bother to wipe away the water gleaming on his skin. "Keep practicing."

But I said, "Will he go to war? Over me?"

He knew who I meant. The hot temper that had been on Rhys's face moments before turned to lethal calm. "I don't know."

"I—I would go back. If it came to that, Rhysand. I'd go back, rather than make you fight."

He slid a still-wet hand into his pocket. "Would you *want* to go back? Would going to war on your behalf make you love him again? Would that be a grand gesture to win you?"

I swallowed hard. "I'm tired of death. I wouldn't want to see anyone else die—least of all for me."

"That doesn't answer my question."

"No. I wouldn't want to go back. But I would. Pain and killing wouldn't win me."

Rhys stared at me for a moment longer, his face unreadable, before he strode to the door. He stopped with his fingers on the sea urchin–shaped handle. "He locked you up because he knew—the bastard knew what a treasure you are. That you are worth more than land or gold or jewels. He knew, and wanted to keep you all to himself."

The words hit me, even as they soothed some jagged piece in my soul. "He did—does love me, Rhysand."

"The issue isn't whether he loved you, it's how much. Too much. Love can be a poison."

And then he was gone.

The bay was calm enough—perhaps willed to flatness by its lord and master—that the pleasure barge hardly rocked throughout the hours we dined and drank aboard it.

Crafted of richest wood and gold, the enormous boat was amply sized for the hundred or so High Fae trying their best not to observe every movement Rhys, Amren, and I made.

The main deck was full of low tables and couches for eating and relaxing, and on the upper level, beneath a canopy of tiles set with mother-of-pearl, our long table had been set. Tarquin was summer incarnate in turquoise and gold, bits of emerald shining at his buttons and fingers. A crown of sapphire and white gold fashioned like cresting waves sat atop his seafoam-colored hair—so exquisite that I often caught myself staring at it.

As I was now, when he turned to where I sat on his right and noticed my stare.

"You'd think with our skilled jewelers, they could make a crown a bit more comfortable. This one digs in horribly."

A pleasant enough attempt at conversation, when I'd stayed quiet throughout the first hour, instead watching the island-city, the water, the mainland—casting a net of awareness, of blind power, toward it, to see if anything answered. If the Book slumbered somewhere out there.

Nothing had answered my silent call. So I figured it was as good a time as any as I said, "How did you keep it out of her hands?"

Saying Amarantha's name here, amongst such happy, celebrating people, felt like inviting in a rain cloud.

Seated at his left, deep in conversation with Cresseida, Rhys didn't so much as look over at me. Indeed, he'd barely spoken to me earlier, not even noting my clothes.

Unusual, given that even *I* had been pleased with how I looked, and had again selected it for myself: my hair unbound and swept off my face with a headband of braided rose gold, my sleeveless, dusk-pink chiffon gown—tight in the chest and waist—the near-twin to the purple one I'd worn that morning. Feminine, soft, pretty. I hadn't felt like those things in a long, long while. Hadn't wanted to.

But here, being those things wouldn't earn me a ticket to a life of party planning. Here, I could be soft and lovely at sunset, and awaken in the morning to slide into Illyrian fighting leathers.

Tarquin said, "We managed to smuggle out most of our treasure when the territory fell. Nostrus—my predecessor—was my cousin. I served as prince of another city. So I got the order to hide the trove in the dead of night, fast as we could."

Amarantha had killed Nostrus when he'd rebelled—and executed his entire family for spite. Tarquin must have been one of the few surviving members, if the power had passed to him.

"I didn't know the Summer Court valued treasure so much," I said.

Tarquin huffed a laugh. "The earliest High Lords did. We do now out of tradition, mostly."

I said carefully, casually, "So is it gold and jewels you value, then?"

"Among other things."

I sipped my wine to buy time to think of a way to ask without raising suspicions. But maybe being direct about it would be better. "Are outsiders allowed to see the collection? My father was a merchant—I spent most of my childhood in his office, helping him with his goods. It would be interesting to compare mortal riches to those made by Fae hands."

Rhys kept talking to Cresseida, not even a hint of approval or amusement going through our bond.

Tarquin cocked his head, the jewels in his crown glinting. "Of course. Tomorrow—after lunch, perhaps?"

He wasn't stupid, and he might have been aware of the game, but . . . the offer was genuine. I smiled a bit, nodding. I looked toward the crowd milling about on the deck below, the lantern-lit water beyond, even as I felt Tarquin's gaze linger.

He said, "What was it like? The mortal world?"

I picked at the strawberry salad on my plate. "I only saw a very small slice of it. My father was called the Prince of Merchants—but I was too young to be taken on his voyages to other parts of the mortal world. When I was eleven, he lost our fortune on a shipment to Bharat. We spent the next eight years in poverty, in a backwater village near the wall. So I can't speak for the entirety of the mortal world when I say that what I saw there was . . . hard. Brutal. Here, class lines are far more blurred, it seems. There, it's defined by money. Either you have it and you don't share it, or you are left to starve and fight for your survival.

My father . . . He regained his wealth once I went to Prythian." My heart tightened, then dropped into my stomach. "And the very people who had been content to let us starve were once again our friends. I would rather face every creature in Prythian than the monsters on the other side of the wall. Without magic, without power, money has become the only thing that matters."

Tarquin's lips were pursed, but his eyes were considering. "Would you spare them if war came?"

Such a dangerous, loaded question. I wouldn't tell him what we were doing over the wall—not until Rhys had indicated we should.

"My sisters dwell with my father on his estate. For them, I would fight. But for those sycophants and peacocks . . . I would not mind to see their order disrupted." Like the hate-mongering family of Elain's betrothed.

Tarquin said very quietly, "There are some in Prythian who would think the same of the courts."

"What—get rid of the High Lords?"

"Perhaps. But mostly eliminate the inherent privileges of High Fae over the lesser faeries. Even the terms imply a level of unfairness. Maybe it is more like the human realm than you realize, not as blurred as it might seem. In some courts, the lowest of High Fae servants has more rights than the wealthiest of lesser faeries."

I became aware that we were not the only people on the barge, at this table. And that we were surrounded by High Fae with animal-keen hearing. "Do you agree with them? That it should change?"

"I am a young High Lord," he said. "Barely eighty years old." So he'd been thirty when Amarantha took over. "Perhaps others might call me inexperienced or foolish, but I have seen those cruelties firsthand, and known many good lesser faeries who suffered for merely being born on the wrong side of power. Even within my own residences, the confines of tradition pressure me to enforce the rules of my predecessors: the lesser faeries are neither to be seen nor heard as they work. I would like to one day see a Prythian in which they have a voice, both in my home and in the world beyond it."

I scanned him for any deceit, manipulation. I found none.

Steal from him—I *would* steal from him. But what if I asked instead? Would he give it to me, or would the traditions of his ancestors run too deep?

"Tell me what that look means," Tarquin said, bracing his muscled arms on the gold tablecloth.

I said baldly, "I'm thinking it would be very easy to love you. And easier to call you my friend."

He smiled at me—broad and without restraint. "I would not object to either."

Easy—very easy to fall in love with a kind, considerate male.

But I glanced over at Cresseida, who was now almost in Rhysand's lap. And Rhysand was smiling like a cat, one finger tracing circles on the back of her hand while she bit her lip and beamed. I faced Tarquin, my brows high in silent question.

He made a face and shook his head.

I hoped they went to her room.

Because if I had to listen to Rhys bed her . . . I didn't let myself finish the thought.

Tarquin mused, "It has been many years since I saw her look like that."

My cheeks heated—shame. Shame for what? Wanting to throttle her for no good reason? Rhysand teased and taunted me—he never . . . seduced me, with those long, intent stares, the half smiles that were pure Illyrian arrogance.

I supposed I'd been granted that gift once—and had used it up and fought for it and broken it. And I supposed that Rhysand, for all he had sacrificed and done . . . He deserved it as much as Cresseida.

Even if . . . even if for a moment, I wanted it.

I wanted to feel like that again.

And . . . I was lonely.

I had been lonely, I realized, for a very, very long time.

Rhys leaned in to hear something Cresseida was saying, her lips brushing his ear, her hand now entwining with his.

And it wasn't sorrow, or despair, or terror that hit me, but . . . unhappiness. Such bleak, sharp unhappiness that I got to my feet.

Rhys's eyes shifted toward me, at last remembering I existed, and there was nothing on his face—no hint that he felt any of what I did through our bond. I didn't care if I had no shield, if my thoughts were wide open and he read them like a book. He didn't seem to care, either. He went back to chuckling at whatever Cresseida was telling him, sliding closer.

Tarquin had risen to his feet, scanning me and Rhys.

I was unhappy—not just broken. But unhappy.

An emotion, I realized. It was an emotion, rather than the unending emptiness or survival-driven terror.

"I need some fresh air," I said, even though we were in the open. But with the golden lights, the people up and down the table . . . I needed to find a spot on this barge where I could be alone, just for a moment, mission or no.

"Would you like me to join you?"

I looked at the High Lord of Summer. I hadn't lied. It would be easy to fall in love with a male like him. But I wasn't entirely sure that even with the hardships he'd encountered Under the Mountain, Tarquin could understand the darkness that might always be in me. Not only from Amarantha, but from years spent being hungry, and desperate.

That I might always be a little bit vicious or restless. That I might crave peace, but never a cage of comfort.

"I'm fine, thank you," I said, and headed for the sweeping staircase that led down onto the stern of the ship—brightly lit, but quieter than the main areas at the prow. Rhys didn't so much as look in my direction as I walked away. Good riddance.

I was halfway down the wood steps when I spotted Amren and Varian—both leaning against adjacent pillars, both drinking wine, both ignoring each other. Even as they spoke to no one else.

Perhaps that was another reason why she'd come: to distract Tarquin's watchdog.

I reached the main deck, found a spot by the wooden railing that was a bit more shadowed than the rest, and leaned against it. Magic propelled the boat—no oars, no sails. So we moved through the bay, silent and smooth, hardly a ripple in our wake.

I didn't realize I'd been waiting for him until the barge docked at the base of the island-city, and I'd somehow spent the entire final hour alone.

When I filed onto land with the rest of the crowd, Amren, Varian, and Tarquin were waiting for me at the docks, all a bit stiff-backed.

Rhysand and Cresseida were nowhere to be seen.

CHAPTER 34

Mercifully, there was no sound from his closed bedroom. And no sounds came out of it during that night, when I jolted awake from a nightmare of being turned over a spit, and couldn't remember where I was.

Moonlight danced on the sea beyond my open windows, and there was silence—such silence.

A weapon. I was a weapon to find that book, to stop the king from breaking the wall, to stop whatever he had planned for Jurian and the war that might destroy my world. That might destroy this place—and a High Lord who might very well overturn the order of things.

For a heartbeat, I missed Velaris, missed the lights and the music and the Rainbow. I missed the cozy warmth of the town house to welcome me in from the crisp winter, missed . . . what it had been like to be a part of their little unit.

Maybe wrapping his wings around me, writing me notes, had been Rhys's way of ensuring his weapon didn't break beyond repair.

That was fine—fair enough. We owed each other nothing beyond our promises to work and fight together.

He could still be my friend. Companion—whatever this thing was between us. His taking someone to his bed didn't change those things.

It'd just been a relief to think that for a moment, he might have been as lonely as me.

I didn't have the nerve to come out of my room for breakfast, to see if Rhys had returned.

To see whom he came to breakfast with.

I had nothing else to do, I told myself as I lay in bed, until my lunch-time visit with Tarquin. So I stayed there until the servants came in, apologized for disturbing me, and started to leave. I stopped them, saying I'd bathe while they cleaned the room. They were polite—if nervous—and merely nodded as I did as I'd claimed.

I took my time in the bath. And behind the locked door, I let that kernel of Tarquin's power come out, first making the water rise from the tub, then shaping little animals and creatures out of it.

It was about as close to transformation as I'd let myself go. Contemplating how I might give myself animalistic features only made me shaky, sick. I could ignore it, ignore that occasional scrape of claws in my blood for a while yet.

I was on to water-butterflies flitting through the room when I realized I'd been in the tub long enough that the bath had gone cold.

Like the night before, Nuala walked through the walls from wherever *she* was staying in the palace, and dressed me, somehow attuned to when I'd be ready. Cerridwen, she told me, had drawn the short stick and was seeing to Amren. I didn't have the nerve to ask about Rhys, either.

Nuala selected seafoam green accented with rose gold, curling and then braiding back my hair in a thick, loose plait glimmering with bits of pearl. Whether Nuala knew why I was there, what I'd be doing, she didn't say. But she took extra care of my face, brightening my lips with raspberry pink, dusting my cheeks with the faintest blush. I might have looked innocent, charming—were it not for my gray-blue eyes. More hollow than they'd been last night, when I'd admired myself in the mirror.

I'd seen enough of the palace to navigate to where Tarquin had said to meet before we bid good night. The main hall was situated on a level about halfway up—the perfect meeting place for those who dwelled in the spires above and those who worked unseen and unheard below.

This level held all the various council rooms, ballrooms, dining rooms, and whatever other rooms might be needed for visitors, events, gatherings. Access to the residential levels from which I'd come was guarded by four soldiers at each stairwell—all of whom watched me carefully as I waited against a seashell pillar for their High Lord. I wondered if he could sense that I'd been playing with his power in the bathtub, that the piece of him he'd yielded was now here and answering to me.

Tarquin emerged from one of the adjacent rooms as the clock struck two—followed by my own companions.

Rhysand's gaze swept over me, noting the clothes that were obviously in honor of my host and his people. Noting the way I did not meet his eyes, or Cresseida's, as I looked solely at Tarquin and Amren beside him—Varian now striding off to the soldiers at the stairs—and gave them both a bland, close-lipped smile.

"You're looking well today," Tarquin said, inclining his head.

Nuala, it seemed, was a spectacularly good spy. Tarquin's pewter tunic was accented with the same shade of seafoam green as my clothes. We might as well have been a matching set. I supposed with my brown-gold hair and pale skin, I was his mirror opposite.

I could feel Rhys still assessing me.

I shut him out. Maybe I'd send a water-dog barking after him later—let it bite him in the ass.

"I hope I'm not interrupting," I said to Amren.

Amren shrugged her slim shoulders, clad in flagstone gray today. "We were finishing up a rather lively debate about armadas and who might be in charge of a unified front. Did you know," she said, "that before they became so big and powerful, Tarquin and Varian led Nostrus's fleet?"

Varian, several feet away, stiffened, but did not turn.

I met Tarquin's eye. "You didn't mention you were a sailor." It was an effort to sound intrigued, like I had nothing at all bothering me.

Tarquin rubbed his neck. "I had planned to tell you during our tour." He held out an arm. "Shall we?"

Not one word—I had not uttered one word to Rhysand. And I wasn't about to start as I looped my arm through Tarquin's, and said to none of them in particular, "See you later."

Something brushed against my mental shield, a rumble of something dark—powerful.

Perhaps a warning to be careful.

Though it felt an awful lot like the dark, flickering emotion that had haunted me—so much like it that I stepped a bit closer to Tarquin. And then I gave the High Lord of Summer a pretty, mindless smile that I had not given to *anyone* in a long, long time.

That brush of emotion went silent on the other side of my shields.

Good.

⸸

Tarquin brought me to a hall of jewels and treasure so vast that I gawked for a good minute. A minute that I used to scan the shelves for any twinkle of feeling—anything that *felt* like the male at my side, like the power I'd summoned in the bathtub.

"And this is—this is just *one* of the troves?" The room had been carved deep beneath the castle, behind a heavy lead door that had only opened when Tarquin placed his hand on it. I didn't dare get close enough to the lock to see if it might work under my touch—*his* feigned signature.

A fox in the chicken coop. That's what I was.

Tarquin loosed a chuckle. "My ancestors were greedy bastards."

I shook my head, striding to the shelves built into the wall. Solid stone—no way to break in, unless I tunneled through the mountain itself. Or if someone winnowed me. Though there were likely wards similar to those on the town house and the House of Wind.

Boxes overflowed with jewels and pearls and uncut gems, gold heaped in trunks so high it spilled onto the cobblestone floor. Suits of ornate armor stood guard against one wall; dresses woven of cobwebs and starlight leaned against another. There were swords and daggers of every sort. But no books. Not one.

"Do you know the history behind each piece?"

"Some," he said. "I haven't had much time to learn about it all."

Good—maybe he wouldn't know about the Book, wouldn't miss it.

I turned in a circle. "What's the most valuable thing in here?"

"Thinking of stealing?"

I choked on a laugh. "Wouldn't asking that question make me a lousy thief?"

Lying, two-faced wretch—that's what asking *that* question made me.

Tarquin studied me. "I'd say I'm looking at the most valuable thing in here."

I didn't fake the blush. "You're—very kind."

His smile was soft. As if his position had not yet broken the compassion in him. I hoped it never did. "Honestly, I don't know what's the most valuable thing. These are all priceless heirlooms of my house."

I walked up to a shelf, scanning. A necklace of rubies was splayed on a velvet pillow—each of them the size of a robin's egg. It'd take a tremendous female to wear that necklace, to dominate the gems and not the other way around.

On another shelf, a necklace of pearls. Then sapphires.

And on another . . . a necklace of black diamonds.

Each of the dark stones was a mystery—and an answer. Each of them slumbered.

Tarquin came up behind me, peering over my shoulder at what had snagged my interest. His gaze drifted to my face. "Take it."

"What?" I whirled to him.

He rubbed the back of his neck. "As a thank-you. For Under the Mountain."

Ask it now—ask him for the Book instead.

But that would require trust, and . . . kind as he was, he was a High Lord.

He pulled the box from its resting spot and shut the lid before handing it to me. "You were the first person who didn't laugh at my idea to break down class barriers. Even Cresseida snickered when I told her. If you won't accept the necklace for saving us, then take it for that."

"It is a good idea, Tarquin. Appreciating it doesn't mean you have to reward me."

He shook his head. "Just take it."

It would insult him if I refused—so I closed my hands around the box.

Tarquin said, "It will suit you in the Night Court."

"Perhaps I'll stay here and help you revolutionize the world."

His mouth twisted to the side. "I could use an ally in the North."

Was that why he had brought me? Why he'd given me the gift? I hadn't realized how alone we were down here, that I was beneath ground, in a place that could be easily sealed—

"You have nothing to fear from me," he said, and I wondered if my scent was that readable. "But I meant it—you have . . . sway with Rhysand. And he is notoriously difficult to deal with. He gets what he wants, has plans he does not tell anyone about until after he's completed them, and does not apologize for any of it. Be his emissary to the human realm—but also be ours. You've seen my city. I have three others like it. Amarantha wrecked them almost immediately after she took over. All my people want now is peace, and safety, and to never have to look over their shoulders again. Other High Lords have told me about Rhys—and warned me about him. But he spared me Under the Mountain. Brutius was my cousin, and we had forces gathering in all of our cities to storm Under the Mountain. They caught him sneaking out through the tunnels to meet with them. Rhys saw that in Brutius's mind—I know he did. And yet he lied to her face, and defied her when she gave the order to turn him into a living ghost. Maybe it was for his own schemes, but I know it was a mercy. He knows that I am young—and inexperienced, and he spared me." Tarquin shook his head, mostly at himself. "Sometimes, I think Rhysand . . . I think he might have been her whore to spare us all from her full attention."

I would betray nothing of what I knew. But I suspected he could see it in my eyes—the sorrow at the thought.

"I know I'm supposed to look at you," Tarquin said, "and see that he's made you into a pet, into a monster. But I see the kindness in you. And I think that reflects more on him than anything. I think it shows that you and he might have many secrets—"

"Stop," I blurted. "Just—stop. You know I can't tell you anything. And I can't promise you anything. Rhysand is High Lord. I only serve in his court."

Tarquin glanced at the ground. "Forgive me if I've been forward. I'm still learning how to play the games of these courts—to my advisers' chagrin."

"I hope you never learn how to play the games of these courts."

Tarquin held my gaze, face wary, but a bit bleak. "Then allow me to ask you a blunt question. Is it true you left Tamlin because he locked you up in his house?"

I tried to block out the memory, the terror and agony of my heart breaking apart. But I nodded.

"And is it true that you were saved from confinement by the Night Court?"

I nodded again.

Tarquin said, "The Spring Court is my southern neighbor. I have tenuous ties with them. But unless asked, I will not mention that you were here."

Thief, liar, manipulator. I didn't deserve his alliance.

But I bowed my head in thanks. "Any other treasure troves to show me?"

"Are gold and jewels not impressive enough? What of your merchant's eye?"

I tapped the box. "Oh, I got what I wanted. Now I'm curious to see how much your alliance is worth."

Tarquin laughed, the sound bouncing off the stone and wealth around us. "I didn't feel like going to my meetings this afternoon, anyway."

"What a reckless, wild young High Lord."

Tarquin linked elbows with me again, patting my arm as he led me from the chamber. "You know, I think it might be very easy to love you, too, Feyre. Easier to be your friend."

I made myself look away shyly as he sealed the door shut behind us, placing a palm flat on the space above the handle. I listened to the click of locks sliding into place.

He took me to other rooms beneath his palace, some full of jewels, others weapons, others clothes from eras long since past. He showed me one full of books, and my heart leaped—but there was nothing in there. Nothing but leather and dust and quiet. No trickle of power that felt like the male beside me—no hint of the book I needed.

Tarquin brought me to one last room, full of crates and stacks covered in sheets. And as I beheld all the artwork looming beyond the open door I said, "I think I've seen enough for today."

He asked no questions as he resealed the chamber and escorted me back to the busy, sunny upper levels.

There had to be other places where it might be stored. Unless it was in another city.

I had to find it. Soon. There was only so long Rhys and Amren could draw out their political debates before we had to go home. I just prayed I'd find it fast enough—and not hate myself any more than I currently did.

Rhysand was lounging on my bed as if he owned it.

I took one look at the hands crossed behind his head, the long legs draped over the edge of the mattress, and ground my teeth. "What do you want?" I shut the door loud enough to emphasize the bite in my words.

"Flirting and giggling with Tarquin did you no good, I take it?"

I chucked the box onto the bed beside him. "You tell me."

The smile faltered as he sat up, flipping open the lid. "This isn't the Book."

"No, but it's a beautiful gift."

"You want me to buy you jewelry, Feyre, then say the word. Though given your wardrobe, I thought you were aware that it was *all* bought for you."

I hadn't realized, but I said, "Tarquin is a good male—a good High Lord. You should just *ask* him for the damned Book."

Rhys snapped shut the lid. "So he plies you with jewels and pours honey in your ear, and now you feel bad?"

"He wants your alliance—desperately. He wants to trust you, rely on you."

"Well, Cresseida is under the impression that her cousin is rather ambitious, so I'd be careful to read between his words."

"Oh? Did she tell you that before, during, or after you took her to bed?"

Rhys stood in a graceful, slow movement. "Is that why you wouldn't look at me? Because you think I fucked her for information?"

"Information or your own pleasure, I don't care."

He came around the bed, and I stood my ground, even as he stopped with hardly a hand's breadth between us. "Jealous, Feyre?"

"If I'm jealous, then you're jealous about Tarquin and his honey pouring."

Rhysand's teeth flashed. "Do you think I particularly like having to flirt with a lonely female to get information about her court, her High Lord? Do you think I feel good about myself, doing that? Do you think I enjoy doing it just so you have the space to ply Tarquin with your smiles and pretty eyes, so we can get the Book and go home?"

"You seemed to enjoy yourself plenty last night."

His snarl was soft—vicious. "I didn't take her to bed. She wanted to, but I didn't so much as kiss her. I took her out for a drink in the city, let her talk about her life, her pressures, and brought her back to her room, and went no farther than the door. I waited for you at breakfast, but you slept in. Or avoided me, apparently. And I tried to catch your eye this afternoon, but you were *so good* at shutting me out completely."

"Is that what got under your skin? That I shut you out, or that it was so easy for Tarquin to get in?"

"What got under my skin," Rhys said, his breathing a bit uneven, "is that you *smiled* at him."

The rest of the world faded to mist as the words sank in. "You are jealous."

He shook his head, stalking to the little table against the far wall and knocking back a glass of amber liquid. He braced his hands on the table, the powerful muscles of his back quivering beneath his shirt as the shadow of those wings struggled to take form.

"I heard what you told him," he said. "That you thought it would be easy to fall in love with him. You meant it, too."

"So?" It was the only thing I could think of to say.

"I was jealous—of that. That I'm not . . . that sort of person. For anyone. The Summer Court has always been neutral; they only showed backbone during those years Under the Mountain. I spared Tarquin's life because I'd heard how he wanted to even out the playing field between High Fae and lesser faeries. I've been trying to do that for years. Unsuccessfully, but . . . I spared him for that alone. And Tarquin, with his neutral court . . . he will never have to worry about someone walking away because the threat against their life, their children's lives, will always be there. So, yes, I was jealous of him—because it will always be easy for him. And he will never know what it is to look up at the night sky and wish."

The Court of Dreams.

The people who knew that there was a price, and one worth paying, for that dream. The bastard-born warriors, the Illyrian half-breed, the monster trapped in a beautiful body, the dreamer born into a court of nightmares . . . And the huntress with an artist's soul.

And perhaps because it was the most vulnerable thing he'd said to me, perhaps it was the burning in my eyes, but I walked to where he stood over the little bar. I didn't look at him as I took the decanter of amber liquid and poured myself a knuckle's length, then refilled his.

But I met his stare as I clinked my glass against his, the crystal ringing clear and bright over the crashing sea far below, and said, "To the people who look at the stars and wish, Rhys."

He picked up his glass, his gaze so piercing that I wondered why I had bothered blushing at all for Tarquin.

Rhys clinked his glass against mine. "To the stars who listen—and the dreams that are answered."

CHAPTER 35

Two days passed. Every moment of it was a balancing act of truth and lies. Rhys saw to it that I was not invited to the meetings he and Amren held to distract my kind host, granting me time to scour the city for any hint of the Book.

But not too eagerly; not too intently. I could not look too intrigued as I wandered the streets and docks, could not ask too many leading questions of the people I encountered about the treasures and legends of Adriata. Even when I awoke at dawn, I made myself wait until a reasonable hour before setting out into the city, made myself take an extended bath to secretly practice that water-magic. And while crafting water-animals grew tedious after an hour . . . it came to me easily. Perhaps because of my proximity to Tarquin, perhaps because of whatever affinity for water was already in my blood, my soul—though I certainly was in no position to ask.

Once breakfast had finally been served and consumed, I made sure to look a bit bored and aimless when I finally strode through the shining halls of the palace on my way out into the awakening city.

Hardly anyone recognized me as I casually examined shops and houses and bridges for any glimmer of a spell that *felt* like Tarquin, though I doubted they had reason to. It had been the High Fae—the nobility—that had been kept Under the Mountain. These people had been left here . . . to be tormented.

Scars littered the buildings, the streets, from what had been done in retaliation for their rebellion: burn marks, gouged bits of stone, entire buildings turned to rubble. The back of the castle, as Tarquin had claimed, was indeed in the middle of being repaired. Three turrets were half shattered, the tan stone charred and crumbling. No sign of the Book. Workers toiled there—and throughout the city—to fix those broken areas.

Just as the people I saw—High Fae and faeries with scales and gills and long, spindly webbed fingers—all seemed to be slowly healing. There were scars and missing limbs on more than I could count. But in their eyes . . . in their eyes, light gleamed.

I had saved them, too.

Freed them from whatever horrors had occurred during those five decades.

I had done a terrible thing to save them . . . but I had saved them.

And it would never be enough to atone, but . . . I did not feel quite so heavy, despite not finding a glimmer of the Book's presence, when I returned to the palace atop the hill on the third night to await Rhysand's report on the day's meetings—and learn if he'd managed to discover anything, too.

As I strode up the steps of the palace, cursing myself for remaining so out of shape even with Cassian's lessons, I spied Amren perched on the ledge of a turret balcony, cleaning her nails.

Varian leaned against the threshold of another tower balcony within jumping range—and I wondered if he was debating if he could clear the distance fast enough to push her off.

A cat playing with a dog—that's what it was. Amren was practically washing herself, silently daring him to get close enough to sniff. I doubted Varian would like her claws.

Unless that was why he hounded her day and night.

I shook my head, continuing up the steps—watching as the tide swept out.

The sunset-stained sky caught on the water and tidal muck. A little night breeze whispered past, and I leaned into it, letting it cool the sweat on me. There had once been a time when I'd dreaded the end of summer, had prayed it would hold out for as long as possible. Now the thought of endless warmth and sun made me . . . bored. Restless.

I was about to turn back to the stairs when I beheld the bit of land that had been revealed near the tidal causeway. The small building.

No wonder I hadn't seen it, as I'd never been up this high in the day when the tide was out . . . And during the rest of the day, from the muck and seaweed now gleaming on it, it would have been utterly covered.

Even now, it was half submerged. But I couldn't tear my eyes from it.

Like it was a little piece of home, wet and miserable-looking as it was, and I need only hurry along the muddy causeway between the quieter part of the city and the mainland—fast, fast, fast, so I might catch it before it vanished beneath the waves again.

But the site was too visible, and from the distance, I couldn't definitively tell if it *was* the Book contained within.

We'd have to be absolutely certain before we went in—to warrant the risks in searching. Absolutely certain.

I wished I didn't, but I realized I already had a plan for that, too.

⁂

We dined with Tarquin, Cresseida, and Varian in their family dining room—a sure sign that the High Lord did indeed want that alliance, ambition or no.

Varian was studying Amren as if he was trying to solve a riddle she'd posed to him, and she paid him no heed whatsoever as she debated with

Cresseida about the various translations of some ancient text. I'd been leading up to my question, telling Tarquin of the things I'd seen in his city that day—the fresh fish I'd bought for myself on the docks.

"You ate it right there," Tarquin said, lifting his brows.

Rhys had propped his head on a fist as I said, "They fried it with the other fishermen's lunches. Didn't charge me extra for it."

Tarquin let out an impressed laugh. "I can't say I've ever done that—sailor or no."

"You should," I said, meaning every word. "It was delicious."

I'd worn the necklace he'd given me, and Nuala and I planned my clothes around it. We'd decided on gray—a soft, dove shade—to show off the glittering black. I had worn nothing else—no earrings, no bracelets, no rings. Tarquin had seemed pleased by it, even though Varian had choked when he beheld me in an heirloom of his household. Cresseida, surprisingly, had told me it suited me and it didn't fit in here, anyway. A backhanded compliment—but praise enough.

"Well, maybe I'll go tomorrow. If you'll join me."

I grinned at Tarquin—aware of every one I offered him, now that Rhys had mentioned it. Beyond his giving me brief, nightly updates on their lack of progress with discovering anything about the Book, we hadn't really spoken since that evening I'd filled his glass—though it had been because of our own full days, not awkwardness.

"I'd like that," I said. "Perhaps we could go for a walk in the morning down the causeway when the tide is out. There's that little building along the way—it looks fascinating."

Cresseida stopped speaking, but I went on, sipping from my wine. "I figure since I've seen most of the city now, I could see it on my way to visit some of the mainland, too."

Tarquin's glance at Cresseida was all the confirmation I needed.

That stone building indeed guarded what we sought.

"It's a temple ruin," Tarquin said blandly—the lie smooth as silk. "Just mud and seaweed at this point. We've been meaning to repair it for years."

"Maybe we'll take the bridge then. I've had enough of mud for a while."

Remember that I saved you, that I fought the Middengard Wyrm—forget the threat . . .

Tarquin's eyes held mine—for a moment too long.

In the span of a blink, I hurled my silent, hidden power toward him, a spear aimed toward his mind, those wary eyes.

There was a shield in place—a shield of sea glass and coral and the undulating sea.

I became that sea, became the whisper of waves against stone, the glimmer of sunlight on a gull's white wings. I became *him*—became that mental shield.

And then I was through it, a clear, dark tether showing me the way back should I need it. I let instinct, no doubt granted from Rhys, guide me forward. To what I needed to see.

Tarquin's thoughts hit me like pebbles. *Why does she ask about the temple? Of all the things to bring up . . .* Around me, they continued eating. *I* continued eating. I willed my own face, in a different body, a different world, to smile pleasantly.

Why did they want to come here so badly? Why ask about my trove?

Like lapping waves, I sent my thoughts washing over his.

She is harmless. She is kind, and sad, and broken. You saw her with your people—-you saw how she treated them. How she treats you. Amarantha did not break that kindness.

I poured my thoughts into him, tinting them with brine and the cries of terns—wrapping them in the essence that was Tarquin, the essence he'd given to me.

Take her to the mainland tomorrow. That'll keep her from asking about the temple. She saved Prythian. She is your friend.

My thoughts settled in him like a stone dropped into a pool. And as the wariness faded in his eyes, I knew my work was done.

I hauled myself back, back, back, slipping through that ocean-and-pearl wall, reeling inward until my body was a cage around me.

Tarquin smiled. "We'll meet after breakfast. Unless Rhysand wants me for more meetings." Neither Cresseida nor Varian so much as glanced at him. Had Rhys taken care of their own suspicions?

Lightning shot through my blood, even as my blood chilled to realize what I'd done—

Rhys waved a lazy hand. "By all means, Tarquin, spend the day with my lady."

My lady. I ignored the two words. But I shut out my own marveling at what I'd accomplished, the slow-building horror at the invisible violation Tarquin would never know about.

I leaned forward, bracing my bare forearms on the cool wood table. "Tell me what there is to see on the mainland," I asked Tarquin, and steered him away from the temple on the tidal causeway.

✢

Rhys and Amren waited until the household lights dimmed before coming into my room.

I'd been sitting in bed, counting down the minutes, forming my plan. None of the guest rooms looked out on the causeway—as if they wanted no one to notice it.

Rhys arrived first, leaning against the closed door. "What a fast learner you are. It takes most daemati years to master that sort of infiltration."

My nails bit into my palms. "You knew—that I did it?" Speaking the words aloud felt too much, too . . . real.

A shallow nod. "And what expert work you did, using the essence of *him* to trick his shields, to get past them . . . Clever lady."

"He'll never forgive me," I breathed.

"He'll never know." Rhys angled his head, silky dark hair sliding over his brow. "You get used to it. The sense that you're crossing a boundary, that you're violating them. For what it's worth, I didn't particularly enjoy convincing Varian and Cresseida to find other matters more interesting."

I dropped my gaze to the pale marble floor.

"If you hadn't taken care of Tarquin," he went on, "the odds are we'd be knee-deep in shit right now."

"It was my fault, anyway—I was the one who asked about the temple. I was only cleaning up my own mess." I shook my head. "It doesn't feel right."

"It never does. Or it shouldn't. Far too many daemati lose that sense. But here—tonight . . . the benefits outweighed the costs."

"Is that also what you told yourself when you went into my mind? What was the benefit then?"

Rhys pushed off the door, crossing to where I sat on the bed. "There are parts of your mind I left undisturbed, things that belong solely to you, and always will. And as for the rest . . . " His jaw clenched. "You scared the shit out of me for a long while, Feyre. Checking in that way . . . I couldn't very well stroll into the Spring Court and ask how you were doing, could I?" Light footsteps sounded in the hall—Amren. Rhys held my gaze though as he said, "I'll explain the rest some other time."

The door opened. "It seems like a stupid place to hide a book," Amren said by way of greeting as she entered, plopping onto the bed.

"And the last place one would look," Rhys said, prowling away from me to take a seat on the vanity stool before the window. "They could spell it easily enough against wet and decay. A place only visible for brief moments throughout the day—when the land around it is exposed for all to see? You could not ask for a better place. We have the eyes of thousands watching us."

"So how do we get in?" I said.

"It's likely warded against winnowing," Rhys said, bracing his forearms on his thighs. "I won't risk tripping any alarms by trying. So we go in at night, the old-fashioned way. I can carry you both, then keep watch," he added when I lifted my brows.

"Such gallantry," Amren said, "to do the easy part, then leave us helpless females to dig through mud and seaweed."

"Someone needs to be circling high enough to see anyone approaching—or sounding the alarm. And masking you from sight."

I frowned. "The locks respond to his touch; let's hope they respond to mine."

Amren said, "When do we move?"

"Tomorrow night," I said. "We note the guard's rotations tonight at low tide—figure out where the watchers are. Who we might need to take out before we make our move."

"You think like an Illyrian," Rhys murmured.

"I believe that's supposed to be a compliment," Amren confided.

Rhys snorted, and shadows gathered around him as he loosened his grip on his power. "Nuala and Cerridwen are already on the move inside the castle. I'll take to the skies. The two of you should go for a midnight walk—considering how hot it is." Then he was gone with a rustle of invisible wings and a warm, dark breeze.

Amren's lips were bloodred in the moonlight. I knew who would have the task of taking out any spying eyes—and wind up with a meal. My mouth dried out a bit. "Care for a stroll?"

CHAPTER 36

The following day was torture. Slow, unending, hot-as-hell torture.

Feigning interest in the mainland as I walked with Tarquin, met his people, smiled at them, grew harder as the sun meandered across the sky, then finally began inching toward the sea. Liar, thief, deceiver—that's what they'd call me soon.

I hoped they'd know—that Tarquin would know—that we'd done it for their sake.

Supreme arrogance, perhaps, to think that way, but . . . it was true. Given how quickly Tarquin and Cresseida had glanced at each other, guided me away from that temple . . . I'd bet that they wouldn't have handed over that book. For whatever reasons of their own, they wanted it.

Maybe this new world of Tarquin's could only be built on trust . . . But he wouldn't get a chance to build it if it was all wiped away beneath the King of Hybern's armies.

That's what I told myself over and over as we walked through his city—as I endured the greetings of his people. Perhaps not as joyous as those in Velaris, but . . . a tentative hard-won warmth. People who had endured the worst and tried now to move beyond it.

As I should be moving beyond my own darkness.

When the sun was at last sliding into the horizon, I confessed to Tarquin that I was tired and hungry—and, being kind and accommodating, he took me back, buying me a baked fish pie on the way home. He'd even eaten a fried fish at the docks that afternoon.

Dinner was worse.

We'd be gone before breakfast—but they didn't know that. Rhys mentioned returning to the Night Court tomorrow afternoon, so perhaps an early departure wouldn't be so suspicious. He'd leave a note about urgent business, thanking Tarquin for his hospitality, and then we'd vanish home—to Velaris. If it went according to plan.

We'd learned where the guards were stationed, how their rotations operated, and where their posts were on the mainland, too.

And when Tarquin kissed my cheek good night, saying he wished that it was not my last evening and perhaps he would see about visiting the Night Court soon . . . I almost fell to my knees to beg his forgiveness.

Rhysand's hand on my back was a solid warning to keep it together—even as his face held nothing but that cool amusement.

I went to my room. And found Illyrian fighting leathers waiting for me. Along with that belt of Illyrian knives.

So I dressed for battle once again.

Rhys flew us in close to low tide, dropping us off before taking to the skies, where he'd circle, monitoring the guards on the island and mainland, while we hunted.

The muck reeked, squelching and squeezing us with every step from the narrow causeway road to the little temple ruin. Barnacles, seaweed, and limpets clung to the dark gray stones—and every step into the sole interior chamber had that *thing* in my chest saying *where are you, where are you, where are you?*

Rhys and Amren had checked for wards around the site—but found none. Odd, but fortunate. Thanks to the open doorway, we didn't dare risk a light, but with the cracks in the stone overhead, the moonlight provided enough illumination.

Knee-deep in muck, the tidal water slinking out over the stones, Amren and I surveyed the chamber, barely more than forty feet wide.

"I can feel it," I breathed. "Like a clawed hand running down my spine." Indeed, my skin tingled, hair standing on end beneath my warm leathers. "It's—sleeping."

"No wonder they hid it beneath stone and mud and sea," Amren muttered, the muck squelching as she turned in place.

I shivered, the Illyrian knives on me now feeling as useful as toothpicks, and again turned in place. "I don't feel anything in the walls. But it's here."

Indeed, we both looked down at the same moment and cringed.

"We should have brought a shovel," she said.

"No time to get one." The tide was fully out now. Every minute counted. Not just for the returning water—but the sunrise that was not too far off.

Every step an effort through the firm grip of the mud, I honed in on that feeling, that call. I stopped in the center of the room—dead center. *Here, here, here,* it whispered.

I leaned down, shuddering at the icy muck, at the bits of shell and debris that scraped my bare hands as I began hauling it away. "Hurry."

Amren hissed, but stooped to claw at the heavy, dense mud. Crabs and skittering things tickled my fingers. I refused to think about them.

So we dug, and dug, until we were covered in salty mud that burned our countless little cuts as we panted at a stone floor. And a lead door.

Amren swore. "Lead to keep its full force in, to preserve it. They used to line the sarcophagi of the great rulers with it—because they thought they'd one day awaken."

"If the King of Hybern goes unchecked with that Cauldron, they might very well."

Amren shuddered, and pointed. "The door is sealed."

I wiped my hand on the only clean part of me—my neck—and used the other to scrape away the last bit of mud from the round door. Every brush against the lead sent pangs of cold through me. But there—a carved whorl in the center of the door. "This has been here for a very long time," I murmured.

Amren nodded. "I would not be surprised if, despite the imprint of the High Lord's power, Tarquin and his predecessors had never set foot here—if the blood-spell to ward this place instantly transferred to them once they assumed power."

"Why covet the Book, then?"

"Wouldn't you want to lock away an object of terrible power? So no one could use it for evil—or their own gain? Or perhaps they locked it away for their own bargaining chip if it ever became necessary. I had no idea why they, of all courts, was granted the half of the Book in the first place."

I shook my head and laid my hand flat on the whorl in the lead.

A jolt went through me like lightning, and I grunted, bearing down on the door.

My fingers froze to it, as if the power were leeching my essence, drinking as Amren drank, and I felt it hesitate, question—

I am Tarquin. I am summer; I am warmth; I am sea and sky and planted field.

I became every smile he'd given me, became the crystalline blue of his eyes, the brown of his skin. I felt my own skin shift, felt my bones stretch and change. Until I *was* him, and it was a set of male hands I now possessed, now pushed against the door. Until the essence of me became what I had tasted in that inner, mental shield of his—sea and sun and brine. I did not give myself a moment to think of what power I might have just used. Did not allow any part of me that *wasn't* Tarquin to shine through.

I am your master, and you will let me pass.

The lock pulled harder and harder, and I could barely breathe—

Then a click and groan.

I shifted back into my own skin, and scrambled into the piled mud right as the door sank and swung away, tucking beneath the stones to reveal a spiral staircase drifting into a primordial gloom. And on a wet, salty breeze from below came the tendrils of power.

Across the open stair, Amren's face had gone paler than usual, her silver eyes glowing bright. "I never saw the Cauldron," she said, "but it must be terrible indeed if even a grain of its power feels . . . like this."

Indeed, that power was filling the chamber, my head, my lungs—smothering and drowning and seducing—

"Quickly," I said, and a small ball of faelight shot down the curve of the stairs, illuminating gray, worn steps slick with slime.

I drew my hunting knife and descended, one hand braced on the freezing stone wall to keep from slipping.

I made it one rotation down, Amren close behind, before faelight danced on waist-deep, putrid water. I scanned the passage at the foot of the stairs. "There's a hall, and a chamber beyond that. All clear."

"Then hurry the hell up," Amren said.

Bracing myself, I stepped into the dark water, biting down my yelp at the near-freezing temperature, the oiliness of it. Amren gagged, the water nearly up to her chest.

"This place no doubt fills up swiftly once the tide comes back in," she observed as we sloshed through the water, frowning at the many drainage holes in the walls.

We went only slow enough for her to detect any sort of ward or trap, but—there was none. Nothing at all. Though who would ever come down here, to such a place?

Fools—desperate fools, that's who.

The long stone hall ended in a second lead door. Behind it, that power coiled, overlaying Tarquin's imprint. "It's in there."

"Obviously."

I scowled at her, both of us shivering. The cold was deep enough that I wondered if I might have already been dead in my human body. Or well on my way to it.

I laid my palm flat on the door. The sucking and questioning and draining were worse this time. So much worse, and I had to brace my tattooed hand on the door to keep from falling to my knees and crying out as it ransacked me.

I am summer, I am summer, I am summer.

I didn't shift into Tarquin this time—didn't need to. A click and groan, and the lead door rolled into the wall, water merging and splashing as I stumbled back into Amren's waiting arms. "Nasty, nasty lock," she hissed, shuddering not just from the water.

My head was spinning. Another lock and I might very well pass out.

But the faelight bobbed into the chamber beyond us, and we both halted.

The water had not merged with another source—but rather halted against an invisible threshold. The dry chamber beyond was empty save for a round dais and pedestal.

And a small, lead box atop it.

Amren waved a tentative hand over the air where the water just—stopped. Then, satisfied there were no waiting wards or tricks, she stepped beyond, dripping onto the gray stones as she stood in the chamber, wincing a bit, and beckoned.

Wading as fast as I could, I followed her, half falling onto the floor as my body adjusted to sudden air. I turned—and sure enough, the water was a black wall, as if there were a pane of glass keeping it in place.

"Let's be quick about it," she said, and I didn't disagree.

We both carefully surveyed the chamber: floors, walls, ceilings. No signs of hidden mechanisms or triggers.

Though no larger than an ordinary book, the lead box seemed to gobble up the faelight—and inside it, whispering . . . The seal of Tarquin's power, and the Book.

And now I heard, clear as if Amren herself whispered it:

Who are you—what are you? Come closer—let me smell you, let me see you . . .

We paused on opposite sides of the pedestal, the faelight hovering over the lid. "No wards," Amren said, her voice barely more than the scrape of her boots on the stone. "No spells. You have to remove it—carry it out." The thought of touching that box, getting close to that thing inside it— "The tide is coming back in," Amren added, surveying the ceiling.

"That soon?"

"Perhaps the sea knows. Perhaps the sea is the High Lord's servant."

And if we were caught down here when the water came in—

I did not think my little water-animals would help. Panic writhed in my gut, but I pushed it away and steeled myself, lifting my chin.

The box would be heavy—and cold.

Who are you, who are you, who are you—

I flexed my fingers and cracked my neck. *I am summer; I am sea and sun and green things.*

"Come on, come on," Amren murmured. Above, water trickled over the stones.

Who are you, who are you, who are you—

I am Tarquin; I am High Lord; I am your master.

The box quieted. As if that were answer enough.

I snatched the box off the pedestal, the metal biting into my hands, the power an oily smear through my blood.

An ancient, cruel voice hissed:

Liar.

And the door slammed shut.

CHAPTER 37

"*No!*" Amren screamed, at the door in an instant, her fist a radiant forge as she slammed it into the lead—once, twice.

And above—the rush and gargle of water tumbling downstairs, filling the chamber—

No, no, no—

I reached the door, sliding the box into the wide inside pocket of my leather jacket while Amren's blazing palm flattened against the door, burning, heating the metal, swirls and whorls radiating out through it as if they were a language all her own, and then—

The door burst open.

Only for a flood to come crashing in.

I grappled for the threshold, but missed as the water slammed me back, sweeping me under the dark, icy surface. The cold stole the breath from my lungs. Find the floor, find the floor—

My feet connected and I pushed up, gulping down air, scanning the dim chamber for Amren. She was clutching the threshold, eyes on me, hand out—glowing bright.

The water already flowed up to my breasts, and I rushed to her, fighting the onslaught flooding the chamber, willing that new strength into my body, my arms—

The water became easier, as if that kernel of power soothed its current, its wrath, but Amren was now climbing up the threshold. "You have it?" she shouted over the roaring water.

I nodded, and I realized her outstretched hand wasn't for me—but for the door she'd forced back into the wall. Holding it away until I could get out.

I shoved through the archway, Amren slipping around the threshold—just as the door rolled shut again, so violently that I wondered at the power she'd used to push it back.

The only downside was that the water in the hall now had much less space to fill.

"Go," she said, but I didn't wait for her approval before I grabbed her, hooking her feet around my stomach as I hoisted her onto my back.

"Just—do what you have to," I gritted out, neck craned above the rising water. Not too much farther to the stairs—the stairs that were now a cascade. Where the hell was Rhysand?

But Amren held out a palm in front of us, and the water buckled and trembled. Not a clear path, but a break in the current. I directed that kernel of Tarquin's power—*my* power now—toward it. The water calmed further, straining to obey my command.

I ran, gripping her thighs probably hard enough to bruise. Step by step, water now raging down, now at my jaw, now at my mouth—

But I hit the stairs, almost slipping on the slick step, and Amren's gasp stopped me cold.

Not a gasp of shock, but a gasp for air as a wall of water poured down the stairs. As if a mighty wave had swept over the entire site. Even my own mastery over the element could do nothing against it.

I had enough time to gulp down air, to grab Amren's legs and brace myself—

And watch as that door atop the stairs slid shut, sealing us in a watery tomb.

I was dead. I knew I was dead, and there was no way out of it.

I had consumed my last breath, and I would be aware for every second until my lungs gave out and my body betrayed me and I swallowed that fatal mouthful of water.

Amren beat at my hands until I let go, until I swam after her, trying to calm my panicking heart, my lungs, trying to convince them to make each second count as Amren reached the door and slammed her palm into it. Symbols flared—again and again. But the door held.

I reached her, shoving my body into the door, over and over, and the lead dented beneath my shoulders. Then I had talons, talons not claws, and I was slicing and punching at the metal—

My lungs were on fire. My lungs were seizing—

Amren pounded on the door, that bit of faelight guttering, as if it were counting down her heartbeats—

I had to take a breath, had to open my mouth and take a breath, had to ease the burning—

Then the door was ripped away.

And the faelight remained bright enough for me to see the three beautiful, ethereal faces hissing through fish's teeth as their spindly webbed fingers snatched us out of the stairs, and into their frogskin arms.

Water-wraiths.

But I couldn't stand it.

And as those spiny hands grabbed my arm, I opened my mouth, water shoving in, cutting off thought and sound and breath. My body seized, those talons vanishing—

Debris and seaweed and water shot past me, and I had the vague sense of being hurtled through the water, so fast the water burned beneath my eyelids.

And then hot air—air, air, air, but my lungs were full of water as—

A fist slammed into my stomach and I vomited water across the waves. I gulped down air, blinking at the bruised purple and blushing pink of the morning sky.

A sputter and gasp not too far from me, and I treaded water as I turned in the bay to see Amren vomiting as well—but alive.

And in the waves between us, onyx hair plastered to their strange heads like helmets, the water-wraiths floated, staring with dark, large eyes.

The sun was rising beyond them—the city encircling us stirring.

The one in the center said, "Our sister's debt is paid."

And then they were gone.

Amren was already swimming for the distant mainland shore.

Praying they didn't come back and make a meal of us, I hurried after her, trying to keep my movements small to avoid detection.

We both reached a quiet, sandy cove and collapsed.

✣

A shadow blocked out the sun, and a boot toed my calf. "What," said Rhysand, still in battle-black, "are you two doing?"

I opened my eyes to find Amren hoisting herself up on her elbows. "Where the *hell* were you?" she demanded.

"You two set off every damned trigger in the place. I was hunting down each guard who went to sound the alarm." My throat was ravaged—and sand tickled my cheeks, my bare hands. "I thought you had it covered," he said to her.

Amren hissed, "That *place*, or that damned book, nearly nullified my powers. We almost drowned."

His gaze shot to me. "I didn't feel it through the bond—"

"It probably nullified that, too, you stupid bastard," Amren snapped.

His eyes flickered. "Did you get it?" Not at all concerned that we were half-drowned and had very nearly been dead.

I touched my jacket—the heavy metal lump within.

"Good," Rhys said, and I looked behind him at the sudden urgency in his tone.

Sure enough, in the castle across the bay, people were darting about.

"I missed some guards," he gritted out, grabbed both our arms, and we vanished.

The dark wind was cold and roaring, and I had barely enough strength to cling to him.

It gave out entirely, along with Amren's, as we landed in the town house foyer—and we both collapsed to the wood floor, spraying sand and water on the carpet.

Cassian shouted from the dining room behind us, "What the hell?"

I glared up at Rhysand, who merely stepped toward the breakfast table. "I'm waiting for an explanation, too," he merely said to wide-eyed Cassian, Azriel, and Mor.

But I turned to Amren, who was still hissing on the floor. Her red-rimmed eyes narrowed. "How?"

"During the Tithe, the water-wraith emissary said they had no gold, no food to pay. They were starving." Every word ached, and I thought I might vomit again. He'd deserve it, if I puked all over the carpet. Though he'd probably take it from my wages. "So I gave her some of my jewelry to pay her dues. She swore that she and her sisters would never forget the kindness."

"Can someone explain, please?" Mor called from the room beyond.

We remained on the floor as Amren began quietly laughing, her small body shaking.

"What?" I demanded.

"Only an immortal with a mortal heart would have given one of those horrible beasts the money. It's so . . . " Amren laughed again, her dark hair plastered with sand and seaweed. For a moment, she even looked human. "Whatever luck you live by, girl . . . thank the Cauldron for it."

The others were all watching, but I felt a chuckle whisper out of me.

Followed by a laugh, as rasping and raw as my lungs. But a real laugh, perhaps edged by hysteria—and profound relief.

We looked at each other, and laughed again.

"Ladies," Rhysand purred—a silent order.

I groaned as I got to my feet, sand falling everywhere, and offered a hand to Amren to rise. Her grip was firm, but her quicksilver eyes were surprisingly tender as she squeezed it before snapping her fingers.

We were both instantly clean and warm, our clothes dry. Save for a wet patch around my breast—where that box waited.

My companions were solemn-faced as I approached and reached inside that pocket. The metal bit into my fingers, so cold it burned.

I dropped it onto the table.

It thudded, and they all recoiled, swearing.

Rhys crooked a finger at me. "One last task, Feyre. Unlock it, please."

My knees were buckling—my head spinning and mouth bone-dry and full of salt and grit, but . . . I wanted to be rid of it.

So I slid into a chair, tugging that hateful box to me, and placed a hand on top.

Hello, liar, it purred.

"Hello," I said softly.

Will you read me?

"No."

The others didn't say a word—though I felt their confusion shimmering in the room. Only Rhys and Amren watched me closely.

Open, I said silently.

Say please.

"Please," I said.

The box—the Book—was silent. Then it said, *Like calls to like.*

"Open," I gritted out.

Unmade and Made; Made and Unmade—that is the cycle. Like calls to like.

I pushed my hand harder, so tired I didn't care about the thoughts tumbling out, the bits and pieces that were a part of and not part of me: heat and water and ice and light and shadow.

Cursebreaker, it called to me, and the box clicked open.

I sagged back in my chair, grateful for the roaring fire in the nearby fireplace.

Cassian's hazel eyes were dark. "I never want to hear that voice again."

"Well, you will," Rhysand said blandly, lifting the lid. "Because you're coming with us to see those mortal queens as soon as they deign to visit."

I was too tired to think about that—about what we had left to do. I peered into the box.

It was not a book—not with paper and leather.

It had been formed of dark metal plates bound on three rings of gold, silver, and bronze, each word carved with painstaking precision, in an alphabet I could not recognize. Yes, it indeed turned out my reading lessons were unnecessary.

Rhys left it inside the box as we all peered in—then recoiled.

Only Amren remained staring at it. The blood drained from her face entirely.

"What language is that?" Mor asked.

I thought Amren's hands might have been shaking, but she shoved them into her pockets. "It is no language of this world."

Only Rhys was unfazed by the shock on her face. As if he'd suspected what the language might be. Why he had picked her to be a part of this hunt.

"What is it, then?" Azriel asked.

She stared and stared at the Book—as if it were a ghost, as if it were a miracle—and said, "It is the Leshon Hakodesh. The Holy Tongue." Those quicksilver eyes shifted to Rhysand, and I realized she'd understood, too, why she'd gone.

Rhysand said, "I heard a legend that it was written in a tongue of mighty beings who feared the Cauldron's power and made the Book to combat it. Mighty beings who were here . . . and then vanished. You are the only one who can uncode it."

It was Mor who warned, "Don't play those sorts of games, Rhysand."

But he shook his head. "Not a game. It was a gamble that Amren would be able to read it—and a lucky one."

Amren's nostrils flared delicately, and for a moment, I wondered if she might throttle him for not telling her his suspicions, that the Book might indeed be more than the key to our own salvation.

Rhys smiled at her in a way that said he'd be willing to let her try.

Even Cassian slid a hand toward his fighting knife.

But then Rhysand said, "I thought, too, that the Book might also contain the spell to free you—and send you home. If they were the ones who wrote it in the first place."

Amren's throat bobbed—slightly.

Cassian said, "Shit."

Rhys went on, "I did not tell you my suspicions, because I did not want to get your hopes up. But if the legends about the language were indeed right . . . Perhaps you might find what you've been looking for, Amren."

"I need the other piece before I can begin decoding it." Her voice was raw.

"Hopefully our request to the mortal queens will be answered soon," he said, frowning at the sand and water staining the foyer. "And hopefully the next encounter will go better than this one."

Her mouth tightened, yet her eyes were blazing bright. "Thank you."

Ten thousand years in exile—alone.

Mor sighed—a loud, dramatic sound no doubt meant to break the heavy silence—and complained about wanting the full story of what happened.

But Azriel said, "Even if the book can nullify the Cauldron . . . there's Jurian to contend with."

We all looked at him. "That's the piece that doesn't fit," Azriel clarified, tapping a scarred finger on the table. "Why resurrect him in the first place? And how does the king keep him bound? What does the king have over Jurian to keep him loyal?"

"I'd considered that," Rhys said, taking a seat across from me at the table, right between his two brothers. Of course he had considered it. Rhys shrugged. "Jurian was . . . obsessive in his pursuits of things. He died with many of those goals left unfinished."

Mor's face paled a bit. "If he suspects Miryam is alive—"

"Odds are, Jurian believes Miryam is gone," Rhys said. "And who better to raise his former lover than a king with a Cauldron able to resurrect the dead?"

"Would Jurian ally with Hybern just because he thinks Miryam is dead and wants her back?" Cassian said, bracing his arms on the table.

"He'd do it to get revenge on Drakon for winning her heart," Rhys said. He shook his head. "We'll discuss this later." And I made a note to ask him who these people were, what their history was—to ask Rhys why he'd never hinted Under the Mountain that he *knew* the man behind the eye on Amarantha's ring. After I'd had a bath. And water. And a nap.

But they all looked to me and Amren again—still waiting for the story. Brushing a few grains of sand off, I let Amren launch into the tale, each word more unbelievable than the last.

Across the table, I lifted my gaze from my clothes and found Rhys's eyes already on me.

I inclined my head slightly, and lowered my shield only long enough to say down the bond: *To the dreams that are answered.*

A heartbeat later, a sensual caress trailed along my mental shields—a polite request. I let it drop, let him in, and his voice filled my head. *To the huntresses who remember to reach back for those less fortunate—and water-wraiths who swim very, very fast.*

CHAPTER 38

Amren took the Book to wherever it was she lived in Velaris, leaving the five of us to eat. While Rhys told them of our visit to the Summer Court, I managed to scarf down breakfast before the exhaustion of staying up all night, unlocking those doors, and very nearly dying hit me. When I awoke, the house was empty, the afternoon sunlight warm and golden, and the day so unusually warm and lovely that I brought a book down to the small garden in the back.

The sun eventually shifted, shading the garden to the point of frigidness again. Not quite willing to give up the sun yet, I trudged the three levels to the rooftop patio to watch it set.

Of course—*of course*—Rhysand was already lounging in one of the white-painted iron chairs, an arm slung over the back while his other hand idly gripped a glass of some sort of liquor, a crystal decanter full of it set on the table before him.

His wings were draped behind him on the tile floor, and I wondered if he was also taking advantage of the unusually mild day to sun them as I cleared my throat.

"I know you're there," he said without turning from the view of the Sidra and the red-gold sea beyond.

I scowled. "If you want to be alone, I can go."

He jerked his chin toward the empty seat at the iron table. Not a glowing invitation, but . . . I sat down.

There was a wood box beside the decanter—and I might have thought it was something for whatever he was drinking had I not noticed the dagger fashioned of mother-of-pearl in the lid.

Had I not sworn I could smell the sea and heat and soil that was Tarquin. "What is that?"

Rhys drained his glass, held up a hand—the decanter floating to him on a phantom wind—and poured himself another knuckle's length before he spoke.

"I debated it for a good while, you know," he said, staring out at his city. "Whether I should just ask Tarquin for the Book. But I thought that he might very well say no, then sell the information to the highest bidder. I thought he might say yes, and it'd still wind up with too many people knowing our plans and the potential for that information to get out. And at the end of the day, I needed the *why* of our mission to remain secret for as long as possible." He drank again, and dragged a hand through his blue-black hair. "I didn't like stealing from him. I didn't like hurting his guards. I didn't like vanishing without a word, when, ambition or no, he did truly want an alliance. Maybe even friendship. No other High Lords have ever bothered—or dared. But I think Tarquin wanted to be my friend."

I glanced between him and the box and repeated, "What is that?"

"Open it."

I gingerly flipped back the lid.

Inside, nestled on a bed of white velvet, three rubies glimmered, each the size of a chicken egg. Each so pure and richly colored that they seemed crafted of—

"Blood rubies," he said.

I pulled back the fingers that had been inching toward the stones.

"In the Summer Court, when a grave insult has been committed, they send a blood ruby to the offender. An official declaration that there is a price on their head—that they are now hunted, and will soon be dead. The box arrived at the Court of Nightmares an hour ago."

Mother above. "I take it one of these has my name on it. And yours. And Amren's."

The lid flipped shut on a dark wind. "I made a mistake," he said. I opened my mouth, but he went on, "I should have wiped the minds of the guards and let them continue on. Instead, I knocked them out. It's been a while since I had to do any sort of physical . . . defending like that, and I was so focused on my Illyrian training that I forgot the other arsenal at my disposal. They probably awoke and went right to him."

"He would have noticed the Book was missing soon enough."

"We could have denied that we stole it and chalked it up to coincidence." He drained his glass. "I made a mistake."

"It's not the end of the world if you do that every now and then."

"You've been told you are now public enemy number one of the Summer Court and you're fine with it?"

"No. But I don't blame you."

He loosed a breath, staring out at his city as the warmth of the day succumbed to winter's bite once more. It didn't matter to him.

"Perhaps you could return the Book once we've neutralized the Cauldron—apologize."

Rhys snorted. "No. Amren will get that book for as long as she needs it."

"Then make it up to him in some way. Clearly, *you* wanted to be his friend as much as he wanted to be yours. You wouldn't be so upset otherwise."

"I'm not upset. I'm pissed off."

"Semantics."

He gave me a half smile. "Feuds like the one we just started can last centuries—millennia. If that's the cost of stopping this war, helping Amren . . . I'll pay it."

He'd pay with everything he had, I realized. Any hopes for himself, his own happiness.

"Do the others know—about the blood rubies?"

"Azriel was the one who brought them to me. I'm debating how I'll tell Amren."

"Why?"

Darkness filled those remarkable eyes. "Because her answer would be to go to Adriata and wipe the city off the map."

I shuddered.

"Exactly," he said.

I stared out at Velaris with him, listening to the sounds of the day wrapping up—and the night unfolding. Adriata felt rudimentary by comparison.

"I understand," I said, rubbing some warmth into my now-chilled hands, "why you did what you had to in order to protect this city." Imagining the destruction that had been wreaked upon Adriata here in Velaris made my blood run cold. His eyes slid to me, wary and dull. I swallowed. "And I understand why you will do anything to keep it safe during the times ahead."

"And your point is?"

A bad day—this was a bad day, I realized, for him. I didn't scowl at the bite in his words. "Get through this war, Rhysand, and then worry about Tarquin and the blood rubies. Nullify the Cauldron, stop the king from shattering the wall and enslaving the human realm again, and then we'll figure out the rest after."

"You sound as if you plan to stay here for a while." A bland, but edged question.

"I can find my own lodging, if that's what you're referring to. Maybe I'll use that generous paycheck to get myself something lavish."

Come on. Wink at me. Play with me. Just—stop looking like that.

He only said, "Spare your paycheck. Your name has already been added to the list of those approved to use my household credit. Buy whatever you wish. Buy yourself a whole damn house if you want."

I ground my teeth, and maybe it was panic or desperation, but I said sweetly, "I saw a pretty shop across the Sidra the other day. It sold what looked to be lots of lacy little things. Am I allowed to buy that on your credit, too, or does that come out of my personal funds?"

Those violet eyes again drifted to me. "I'm not in the mood."

There was no humor, no mischief. I could go warm myself by a fire inside, but . . .

He had stayed. And fought for me.

Week after week, he'd fought for me, even when I had no reaction, even when I had barely been able to speak or bring myself to care if I lived or died or ate or starved. I couldn't leave him to his own dark thoughts, his own guilt. He'd shouldered them alone long enough.

So I held his gaze. "I never knew Illyrians were such morose drunks."

"I'm not drunk—I'm drinking," he said, his teeth flashing a bit.

"Again, semantics." I leaned back in my seat, wishing I'd brought my coat. "Maybe you should have slept with Cresseida after all—so you could both be sad and lonely together."

"So you're entitled to have as many bad days as you want, but I can't get a few hours?"

"Oh, take however long you want to mope. I was going to invite you to come shopping with me for said lacy little unmentionables, but . . . sit up here forever, if you have to."

He didn't respond.

I went on, "Maybe I'll send a few to Tarquin—with an offer to wear them for him if he forgives us. Maybe he'll take those blood rubies right back."

His mouth barely, barely tugged up at the corners. "He'd see that as a taunt."

"I gave him a few smiles and he handed over a family heirloom. I bet he'd give me the keys to his territory if I showed up wearing those undergarments."

"Someone thinks mighty highly of herself."

"Why shouldn't I? You seem to have difficulty *not* staring at me day and night."

There it was—a kernel of truth and a question.

"Am I supposed to deny," he drawled, but something sparked in those eyes, "that I find you attractive?"

"You've never said it."

"I've told you many times, and quite frequently, how attractive I find you."

I shrugged, even as I thought of all those times—when I'd dismissed them as teasing compliments, nothing more. "Well, maybe you should do a better job of it."

The gleam in his eyes turned into something predatory. A thrill went through me as he braced his powerful arms on the table and purred, "Is that a challenge, Feyre?"

I held that predator's gaze—the gaze of the most powerful male in Prythian. "*Is* it?"

His pupils flared. Gone was the quiet sadness, the isolated guilt. Only that lethal focus—on me. On my mouth. On the bob of my throat as I tried to keep my breathing even. He said, slow and soft, "Why don't we go down to that store right now, Feyre, so you can try on those lacy little things—so I can help you pick which one to send to Tarquin."

My toes curled inside my fleece-lined slippers. Such a dangerous line we walked together. The ice-kissed night wind rustled our hair.

But Rhys's gaze cut skyward—and a heartbeat later, Azriel shot from the clouds like a spear of darkness.

I wasn't sure whether I should be relieved or not, but I left before Azriel could land, giving the High Lord and his spymaster some privacy.

As soon as I entered the dimness of the stairwell, the heat rushed from me, leaving a sick, cold feeling in my stomach.

There was flirting, and then there was . . . this.

I had loved Tamlin. Loved him so much I had not minded destroying myself for it—for him. And then everything had happened, and now I was here, and . . . and I might have very well gone to that pretty shop with Rhysand.

I could almost see what would have happened:

The shop ladies would have been polite—a bit nervous—and given us privacy as Rhys sat on the settee in the back of the shop while I went behind the curtained-off chamber to try on the red lace set I'd eyed thrice now. And when I emerged, mustering up more bravado than I felt, Rhys would have looked me up and down. Twice.

And he would have kept staring at me as he informed the shop ladies that the store was closed and they should all come back tomorrow, and we'd leave the tab on the counter.

I would have stood there, naked save for scraps of red lace, while we listened to the quick, discreet sounds of them closing up and leaving.

And he would have looked at me the entire time—at my breasts, visible through the lace; at the plane of my stomach, now finally looking less starved and taut. At the sweep of my hips and thighs—between them. Then he would have met my gaze again, and crooked a finger with a single murmured, "Come here."

And I would have walked to him, aware of every step, as I at last stopped in front of where he sat. Between his legs.

His hands would have slid to my waist, the calluses scraping my skin. Then he'd have tugged me a bit closer before leaning in to brush a kiss to my navel, his tongue—

I swore as I slammed into the post of the stairwell landing.

And I blinked—blinked as the world returned and I realized . . .

I glared at the eye tattooed in my hand and hissed both with my tongue and that silent voice within the bond itself, "*Prick.*"

In the back of my mind, a sensual male voice chuckled with midnight laughter.

My face burning, cursing him for the vision he'd slipped past my mental shields, I reinforced them as I entered my room. And took a very, very cold bath.

I ate with Mor that night beside the crackling fire in the town house dining room, Rhys and the others off somewhere, and when she finally asked why I kept scowling every time Rhysand's name was mentioned, I told her about the vision he'd sent into my mind. She'd laughed until wine came out of her nose, and when I scowled at *her*, she told me I should be proud: when Rhys was prepared to brood, it took nothing short of a miracle to get him out of it.

I tried to ignore the slight sense of triumph—even as I climbed into bed.

I was just starting to drift off, well past two in the morning thanks to chatting with Mor on the couch in the living room for hours and hours about all the great and terrible places she'd seen, when the house let out a groan.

Like the wood itself was being warped, the house began to moan and shudder—the colored glass lights in my room tinkling.

I jolted upright, twisting to the open window. Clear skies, nothing—

Nothing but the darkness leaking into my room from the hall door.

I knew that darkness. A kernel of it lived in me.

It rushed in from the cracks of the door like a flood. The house shuddered again.

I vaulted from bed, yanked the door open, and darkness swept past me on a phantom wind, full of stars and flapping wings and—pain.

So much pain, and despair, and guilt and fear.

I hurtled into the hall, utterly blind in the impenetrable dark. But there was a thread between us, and I followed it—to where I knew his room was. I fumbled for the handle, then—

More night and stars and wind poured out, my hair whipping around me, and I lifted an arm to shield my face as I edged into the room. "Rhysand."

No response. But I could feel him there—feel that lifeline between us.

I followed it until my shins banged into what had to be his bed. "*Rhysand*," I said over the wind and dark. The house shook, the floorboards clattering under my feet. I patted the bed, feeling sheets and blankets and down, and then—

Then a hard, taut male body. But the bed was enormous, and I couldn't get a grip on him. "*Rhysand!*"

Around and around the darkness swirled, the beginning and end of the world.

I scrambled onto the bed, lunging for him, feeling what was his arm, then his stomach, then his shoulders. His skin was freezing as I gripped his shoulders and shouted his name.

No response, and I slid a hand up his neck, to his mouth—to make sure he was still breathing, that this wasn't his power floating away from him—

Icy breath hit my palm. And, bracing myself, I rose up on my knees, aiming blindly, and slapped him.

My palm stung—but he didn't move. I hit him again, *pulling* on that bond between us, shouting his name down it like it was a tunnel, banging on that wall of ebony adamant within his mind, roaring at it.

A crack in the dark.

And then his hands were on me, flipping me, pinning me with expert skill to the mattress, a taloned hand at my throat.

I went still. "Rhysand." I breathed. *Rhys*, I said through the bond, putting a hand against that inner shield.

The dark shuddered.

I threw my own power out—black to black, soothing his darkness, the rough edges, willing it to calm, to soften. My darkness sang his own a lullaby, a song my wet nurse had hummed when my mother had shoved me into her arms to go back to attending parties.

"It was a dream," I said. His hand was so cold. "It was a dream."

Again, the dark paused. I sent my own veils of night brushing up against it, running star-flecked hands down it.

And for a heartbeat, the inky blackness cleared enough that I saw his face above me: drawn, lips pale, violet eyes wide—scanning.

"Feyre," I said. "I'm Feyre." His breathing was jagged, uneven. I gripped the wrist that held my throat—held, but didn't hurt. "You were dreaming."

I willed that darkness inside myself to echo it, to sing those raging fears to sleep, to brush up against that ebony wall within his mind, gentle and soft . . .

Then, like snow shaken from a tree, his darkness fell away, taking mine with it.

Moonlight poured in—and the sounds of the city.

His room was similar to mine, the bed so big it must have been built to accommodate wings, but all tastefully, comfortably appointed. And he was naked above me—utterly naked. I didn't dare look lower than the tattooed panes of his chest.

"Feyre," he said, his voice hoarse. As if he'd been screaming.

"Yes," I said. He studied my face—the taloned hand at my throat. And released me immediately.

I lay there, staring up at where he now knelt on the bed, rubbing his hands over his face. My traitorous eyes indeed dared to look lower than his chest—but my attention snagged on the twin tattoos on each of his knees: a towering mountain crowned by three stars. Beautiful—but brutal, somehow.

"You were having a nightmare," I said, easing into a sitting position. Like some dam had been cracked open inside me, I glanced at my hand—and willed it to vanish into shadow. It did.

Half a thought scattered the darkness again.

His hands, however, still ended in long, black talons—and his feet . . . they ended in claws, too. The wings were out, slumped down behind him. And I wondered how close he'd been to fully shifting into that beast he'd once told me he hated.

He lowered his hands, talons fading into fingers. "I'm sorry."

"That's why you're staying here, not at the House. You don't want the others seeing this."

"I normally keep it contained to my room. I'm sorry it woke you."

I fisted my hands in my lap to keep from touching him. "How often does it happen?"

Rhys's violet eyes met mine, and I knew the answer before he said, "As often as you."

I swallowed hard. "What did you dream of tonight?"

He shook his head, looking toward the window—to where snow had dusted the nearby rooftops. "There are memories from Under the Mountain, Feyre, that are best left unshared. Even with you."

He'd shared enough horrific things with me that they had to be . . . beyond nightmares, then. But I put a hand on his elbow, naked body and all. "When you want to talk, let me know. I won't tell the others."

I made to slither off the bed, but he grabbed my hand, keeping it against his arm. "Thank you."

I studied the hand, the ravaged face. Such pain lingered there—and exhaustion. The face he never let anyone see.

I pushed up onto my knees and kissed his cheek, his skin warm and soft beneath my mouth. It was over before it started, but—but how many nights had I wanted someone to do the same for me?

His eyes were a bit wide as I pulled away, and he didn't stop me as I eased off the bed. I was almost out the door when I turned back to him.

Rhys still knelt, wings drooping across the white sheets, head bowed, his tattoos stark against his golden skin. A dark, fallen prince.

The painting flashed into my mind.

Flashed—and stayed there, glimmering, before it faded.

But it remained, shining faintly, in that hole inside my chest.

The hole that was slowly starting to heal over.

CHAPTER 39

"Do you think you can decode it once we get the other half?" I said to Amren, lingering by the front door of her apartment the next afternoon.

She owned the top floor of a three-story building, the sloped ceiling ending on either side in a massive window. One looked out on the Sidra; the other on a tree-lined city square. The entire apartment consisted of one giant room: the faded oak floors were covered in equally worn carpets, furniture was scattered about as if she constantly moved it for whatever purpose.

Only her bed, a large, four-poster monstrosity canopied in gossamer, seemed set in a permanent place against the wall. There was no kitchen—only a long table and a hearth burning hot enough to make the room near-stifling. The dusting of snow from the night before had vanished in the dry winter sun by midmorning, the temperature crisp but mild enough that the walk here had been invigorating.

Seated on the floor before a low-lying table scattered with papers, Amren looked up from the gleaming metal of the book. Her face was paler than usual, her lips wan. "It's been a long while since I used this language—I want to master it again before tackling the Book. Hopefully by then, those haughty queens will have given us their share."

"And how long will relearning the language take?"

"Didn't His Darkness fill you in?" She went back to the Book.

I strode for the long wooden table and set the package I'd brought on the scratched surface. A few pints of hot blood—straight from the butcher. I'd nearly run here to keep them from going cold. "No," I said, taking out the containers. "He didn't." Rhys had already been gone by breakfast, though one of his notes had been on a bedside table.

Thank you—for last night, was all it had said. No pen to write a response.

But I'd hunted down one anyway, and had written back, *What do the tattooed stars and mountain on your knees mean?*

The paper had vanished a heartbeat later. When it hadn't returned, I'd dressed and gone to breakfast. I was halfway through my eggs and toast when the paper appeared beside my plate, neatly folded.

That I will bow before no one and nothing but my crown.

This time, a pen had appeared. I'd merely written back, *So dramatic.* And through our bond, on the other side of my mental shields, I could have sworn I heard his laugh.

Smiling at the memory, I unscrewed the lid on the first jar, the tang of blood filling my nostrils. Amren sniffed, then whipped her head to the glass pints. "You—oh, I like you."

"It's lamb, if that makes a difference. Do you want me to heat it up?"

She rushed from the Book, and I just watched as she clutched the jar in both hands and gulped it down like water.

Well, at least I wouldn't have to bother finding a pot in this place.

Amren drank half in one go. A trickle of blood ran down her chin, and she let it drip onto her gray shirt—rumpled in a way I'd never seen. Smacking her lips, she set the jar on the table with a great sigh. Blood gleamed on her teeth. "Thank you."

"Do you have a favorite?"

She jerked her bloody chin, then wiped it with a napkin as she realized she'd made a mess. "Lamb has always been my favorite. Horrible as it is."

"Not—human?"

She made a face. "Watery, and often tastes like what they last ate. And since most humans have piss-poor palates, it's too much of a gamble. But lamb . . . I'll take goat, too. The blood's purer. Richer. Reminds me of—another time. And place."

"Interesting," I said, and meant it. I wondered what world, exactly, she meant.

She drained the rest, color already blooming on her face, and placed the jar in the small sink along the wall.

"I thought you'd live somewhere more . . . ornate," I admitted.

Indeed, all her fine clothes were hanging on racks near the bed, her jewelry scattered on a few armoires and tables. There was enough of the latter to provide an emperor's ransom.

She shrugged, plopping down beside the Book once more. "I tried that once. It bored me. And I didn't like having servants. Too nosy. I've lived in palaces and cottages and in the mountains and on the beach, but I somehow like this apartment by the river the best." She frowned at the skylights that dotted the ceiling. "It also means I never have to host parties or guests. Both of which I abhor."

I chuckled. "Then I'll keep my visit short."

She let out an amused huff, crossing her legs beneath her. "Why *are* you here?"

"Cassian said you'd been holed up in here night and day since we got back, and I thought you might be hungry. And—I had nothing else to do."

"Cassian is a busybody."

"He cares about you. All of you. You're the only family he has." They were *all* the only family they each had.

"Ach," she said, studying a piece of paper. But it seemed to please her nonetheless. A gleam of color caught my attention on the floor near her.

She was using her blood ruby as a paperweight.

"Rhys convinced you not to destroy Adriata for the blood ruby?"

Amren's eyes flicked up, full of storms and violent seas. "He did no such thing. *That* convinced me not to destroy Adriata." She pointed to her dresser.

Sprawled across the top like a snake lay a familiar necklace of diamonds and rubies. I'd seen it before—in Tarquin's trove. "How . . . what?"

Amren smiled to herself. "Varian sent it to me. To soften Tarquin's declaration of our blood feud."

I'd thought the rubies would need to be worn by a mighty female—and could think of no mightier female than the one before me. "Did you and Varian . . . ?"

"Tempting, but no. The prick can't decide if he hates or wants me."

"Why can't it be both?"

A low chuckle. "Indeed."

Thus began weeks of waiting. Waiting for Amren to relearn a language spoken by no other in our world. Waiting for the mortal queens to answer our request to meet.

Azriel continued his attempt to infiltrate their courts—still to no avail. I heard about it mostly from Mor, who always knew when he'd return to the House of Wind, and always made a point to be there the moment he touched down.

She told me little of the specifics—even less about how the frustration of *not* being able to get his spies *or* himself into those courts took a toll on him. The standards to which he held himself, she confided in me, bordered on sadistic.

Getting Azriel to take *any* time for himself that didn't involve work or training was nearly impossible. And when I pointed out that he *did* go to Rita's with her whenever she asked, Mor simply informed me that it had taken her *four centuries* to get him to do that. I sometimes wondered what went on up at the House of Wind while Rhys and I stayed at the town house.

I only really visited in the mornings, when I filled the first half of my day training with Cassian—who, along with Mor, had decided to point out what foods I should be eating to gain back the weight I'd lost, to become strong and swift again. And as the days passed, I went from physical defense to learning to wield an Illyrian blade, the weapon so fine, I'd nearly taken Cassian's arm off.

But I was learning to use it—slowly. Painfully. I'd had one break from Cassian's brutal training—just one morning, when he'd flown to the human realm to see if my sisters had heard from the queens and deliver *another* letter from Rhys to be sent to them.

I assumed seeing Nesta went about as poorly as could be imagined, because my lesson the following morning was longer and harder than it'd been in previous days. I'd asked what, exactly, Nesta had said to him to get under his skin so easily. But Cassian had only snarled and told me to mind my own business, and that my family was full of bossy, know-it-all females.

Part of me had wondered if Cassian and Varian might need to compare notes.

Most afternoons . . . if Rhys was around, I'd train with him. Mind to mind, power to power. We slowly worked through the gifts I'd been given—flame and water, ice and darkness. There were others, we knew, that had gone undiscovered, undelved. Winnowing still remained impossible. I hadn't been able to do it since that snowy morning with the Attor.

It'd take time, Rhys told me each day, when I'd inevitably snap at him—time, to learn and master each one.

He infused each lesson with information about the High Lords whose power I'd stolen: about Beron, the cruel and vain High Lord of the Autumn Court; about Kallias, the quiet and cunning High Lord of Winter; about Helion Spell-Cleaver, the High Lord of Day, whose one thousand libraries had been personally looted by Amarantha, and whose clever people excelled at spell work and archived the knowledge of Prythian.

Knowing *who* my power had come from, Rhys said, was as important as learning the nature of the power itself. We never spoke of shapeshifting—of the talons I could sometimes summon. The threads that went along with us looking at that gift were too tangled, the unspoken history too violent and bloody.

So I learned the other courts' politics and histories, and learned their masters' powers, until my waking and sleeping hours were spent with flame singeing my mouth and hoarfrost cracking between my fingers. And each night, exhausted from a day of training my body and powers, I tumbled into a heavy sleep, laced with jasmine-scented darkness.

Even my nightmares were too tired to hound me.

On the days when Rhys was called elsewhere, to deal with the inner workings of his own court, to remind them who ruled them or mete out judgment, to prepare for our inevitable visit to Hybern, I would read, or sit with Amren while she worked on the Book, or stroll through Velaris with Mor. The latter was perhaps my favorite, and the female certainly excelled at finding ways to spend money. I'd peeked only once at the account Rhys had set up for me—just once, and realized he was grossly, *grossly* overpaying me.

I tried not to be disappointed on those afternoons that he was gone, tried not to admit that I'd begun looking forward to it—mastering my powers, and . . . bantering with him. But even when he was gone, he would talk to me, in the notes that had become our own strange secret.

One day, he'd written to me from Cesere, a small city in the northeast where he was meeting with the few surviving priestesses to discuss rebuilding after their temple had been wrecked by Hybern's forces. None of the priestesses were like Ianthe, he'd promised.

Tell me about the painting.

I'd written back from my seat in the garden, the fountain finally revived with the return of milder weather, *There's not much to say.*

Tell me about it anyway.

It had taken me a while to craft the response, to think through that little hole in me and what it had once meant and felt like. But then I said, *There was a time when all I wanted was enough money to keep me and my family fed so that I could spend my days painting. That was all I wanted. Ever.*

A pause. Then he'd written, *And now?*

Now, I'd replied, *I don't know what I want. I can't paint anymore.*

Why?

Because that part of me is empty. Though maybe that night I'd seen him kneeling in the bed . . . maybe that had changed a bit. I had contemplated the next sentence, then written, *Did you always want to be High Lord?*

A lengthy pause again. *Yes. And no. I saw how my father ruled and knew from a young age that I did not want to be like him. So I decided to be a different sort of High Lord; I wanted to protect my people, change the perceptions of the Illyrians, and eliminate the corruption that plagued the land.*

For a moment, I hadn't been able to stop myself from comparing: Tamlin hadn't wanted to be High Lord. He resented being High Lord—and maybe . . . maybe that was part of why the court had become what it was. But Rhysand, with a vision, with the will and desire and passion to do it . . . He'd built something.

And then gone to the mat to defend it.

It was what he'd seen in Tarquin, why those blood rubies had hit him so hard. Another High Lord with vision—a radical vision for the future of Prythian.

So I wrote back, *At least you make up for your shameless flirting by being one hell of a High Lord.*

He'd returned that evening, smirking like a cat, and had merely said "One hell of a High Lord?" by way of greeting.

I'd sent a bucket's worth of water splashing into his face.

Rhys hadn't bothered to shield against it. And instead shook his wet hair like a dog, spraying me until I yelped and darted away. His laughter had chased me up the stairs.

Winter was slowly loosening its grip when I awoke one morning and found another letter from Rhys beside my bed. No pen.

No training with your second-favorite Illyrian this morning. The queens finally deigned to write back. They're coming to your family's estate tomorrow.

I didn't have time for nerves. We left after dinner, soaring into the thawing human lands under cover of darkness, the brisk wind screaming as Rhys held me tightly.

ᚔ

My sisters were ready the following morning, both dressed in finery fit for any queen, Fae or mortal.

I supposed I was, too.

I wore a white gown of chiffon and silk, cut in typical Night Court fashion to reveal my skin, the gold accents on the dress glittering in the midmorning light streaming through the sitting room windows. My father, thankfully, would remain on the continent for another two months—due to whatever vital trade he'd been seeking across the kingdoms.

Near the fireplace, I stood beside Rhys, who was clad in his usual black, his wings gone, his face a calm mask. Only the dark crown atop his head—the metal shaped like raven's feathers—was different. The crown that was the sibling to my gold diadem.

Cassian and Azriel monitored everything from the far wall, no weapons in sight.

But their Siphons gleamed, and I wondered what manner of weapon, exactly, they could craft with it, if the need demanded it. For that had been one of the demands the queens had issued for this meeting: no weapons. No matter that the Illyrian warriors themselves were weapons enough.

Mor, in a red gown similar to mine, frowned at the clock atop the white mantel, her foot tapping on the ornate carpet. Despite my wishes for her to get to know my sisters, Nesta and Elain had been so tense and pale when we'd arrived that I'd immediately decided now was not the time for such an encounter.

One day—one day, I'd bring them all together. If we didn't die in this war first. If these queens chose to help us.

Eleven o'clock struck.

There had been two other demands.

The meeting was to begin at eleven. No earlier. No later.

And they had wanted the exact geographical location of the house. The layout and size of each room. Where the furniture was. Where the windows and doors were. What room, likely, we would greet them in.

Azriel had provided it all, with my sisters' help.

The chiming of the clock atop the mantel was the only sound.

And I realized, as it finished its last strike, that the third demand wasn't just for security.

No, as a wind brushed through the room, and five figures appeared, flanked by two guards apiece, I realized it was because the queens could winnow.

CHAPTER 40

The mortal queens were a mixture of age, coloring, height, and temperament. The eldest of them, clad in an embroidered wool dress of deepest blue, was brown-skinned, her eyes sharp and cold, and unbent despite the heavy wrinkles carved into her face.

The two who appeared middle-aged were opposites: one dark, one light; one sweet-faced, one hewn from granite; one smiling and one frowning. They even wore gowns of black and white—and seemed to move in question and answer to each other. I wondered what their kingdoms were like, what relations they had. If the matching silver rings they each wore bound them in other ways.

And the youngest two queens . . . One was perhaps a few years older than me, black-haired and black-eyed, careful cunning oozing from every pore as she surveyed us.

And the final queen, the one who spoke first, was the most beautiful—the only beautiful one of them. These were women who, despite their finery, did not care if they were young or old, fat or thin, short or tall. Those things were secondary; those things were a sleight of hand.

But this one, this beautiful queen, perhaps no older than thirty . . .

Her riotously curly hair was as golden as Mor's, her eyes of purest amber. Even her brown, freckled skin seemed dusted with gold. Her body was supple where she'd probably learned men found it distracting, lithe where it showed grace. A lion in human flesh.

"Well met," Rhysand said, remaining still as their stone-faced guards scanned us, the room. As the queens now took our measure.

The sitting room was enormous enough that one nod from the golden queen had the guards peeling off to hold positions by the walls, the doors. My sisters, silent before the bay window, shuffled aside to make room.

Rhys stepped forward. The queens all sucked in a little breath, as if bracing themselves. Their guards casually, perhaps foolishly, rested a hand on the hilt of their broadswords—so large and clunky compared to Illyrian blades. As if they stood a chance—against any of us. Myself included, I realized with a bit of a start.

But it was Cassian and Azriel who would play the role of mere guards today—distractions.

But Rhys bowed his head slightly and said to the assembled queens, "We are grateful you accepted our invitation." He lifted a brow. "Where is the sixth?"

The ancient queen, her blue gown heavy and rich, merely said, "She is unwell, and could not make the journey." She surveyed me. "You are the emissary."

My back stiffened. Beneath her gaze, my crown felt like a joke, like a bauble, but— "Yes," I said. "I am Feyre."

A cutting glance toward Rhysand. "And you are the High Lord who wrote us such an interesting letter after your first few were dispatched."

I didn't dare look at him. He'd sent many letters through my sisters by now.

You didn't ask what was inside them, he said mind to mind with me, laughter dancing along the bond. I'd left my mental shields down—just in case we needed to silently communicate.

"I am," Rhysand said with a hint of a nod. "And this is my cousin, Morrigan."

Mor stalked toward us, her crimson gown floating on a phantom wind. The golden queen sized her up with each step, each breath. A threat—for beauty and power and dominance. Mor bowed at my side. "It has been a long time since I met with a mortal queen."

The black-clad queen placed a moon-white hand on her lower bodice. "Morrigan—*the* Morrigan from the War."

They all paused as if in surprise. And a bit of awe and fear.

Mor bowed again. "Please—sit." She gestured to the chairs we'd laid out a comfortable distance from each other, all far enough apart that the guards could flank their queens as they saw fit.

Almost as one, the queens sat. Their guards, however, remained at their posts around the room.

The golden-haired queen smoothed her voluminous skirts and said, "I assume those are our hosts." A cutting look at my sisters.

Nesta had gone straight-backed, but Elain bobbed a curtsy, flushing rose pink.

"My sisters," I clarified.

Amber eyes slid to me. To my crown. Then Rhys's. "An emissary wears a golden crown. Is that a tradition in Prythian?"

"No," Rhysand said smoothly, "but she certainly looks good enough in one that I can't resist."

The golden queen didn't smile as she mused, "A human turned into a High Fae . . . and who is now standing beside a High Lord at the place of honor. Interesting."

I kept my shoulders back, chin high. Cassian had been teaching me these weeks about how to feel out an opponent—what were her words but the opening movements in another sort of battle?

The eldest declared to Rhys, "You have an hour of our time. Make it count."

"How is it that you can winnow?" Mor asked from her seat beside me.

The golden queen now gave a smile—a small, mocking one—and replied, "It is our secret, and our gift from your kind."

Fine. Rhys looked to me, and I swallowed as I inched forward on my seat. "War is coming. We called you here to warn you—and to beg a boon."

There would be no tricks, no stealing, no seduction. Rhys could not even risk looking inside their heads for fear of triggering the inherent wards around the Book and destroying it.

"We know war is coming," the oldest said, her voice like crackling leaves. "We have been preparing for it for many years."

It seemed the three others were positioned as observers while the eldest and the golden-haired one led the charge.

I said as calmly and clearly as I could, "The humans in this territory seem unaware of the larger threat. We've seen no signs of preparation." Indeed, Azriel had gleaned as much these weeks, to my dismay.

"This territory," the golden one explained coolly, "is a slip of land compared to the vastness of the continent. It is not in our interests to defend it. It would be a waste of resources."

No. *No*, that—

Rhys drawled, "Surely the loss of even one innocent life would be abhorrent."

The eldest queen folded her withered hands in her lap. "Yes. To lose one life is always a horror. But war is war. If we must sacrifice this tiny territory to save the majority, then we shall do it."

I didn't dare look at my sisters. Look at this house, that might very well be turned to rubble. I rasped, "There are good people here."

The golden queen sweetly parried with, "Then let the High Fae of Prythian defend them."

Silence.

And it was Nesta who hissed from behind us, "We have servants here. With families. There are *children* in these lands. And you mean to leave us all in the hands of the Fae?"

The eldest one's face softened. "It is no easy choice, girl—"

"It is the choice of *cowards*," Nesta snapped.

I interrupted before Nesta could dig us a deeper grave, "For all that your kind hate ours . . . You'd leave the Fae to defend your people?"

"Shouldn't they?" the golden one asked, sending that cascade of curls sliding over a shoulder as she angled her head to the side. "Shouldn't they defend against a threat of their own making?" A snort. "Should Fae blood not be spilled for their crimes over the years?"

"Neither side is innocent," Rhys countered calmly. "But we might protect those who are. Together."

"Oh?" said the eldest, her wrinkles seeming to harden, deepen. "The High Lord of the Night Court asks us to join with him, save lives with him. To fight for peace. And what of the lives you have taken during your long, hideous existence? What of the High Lord who walks with darkness in his wake, and shatters minds as he sees fit?" A crow's laugh. "We have heard of you, even on the continent, Rhysand. We have heard what the Night Court does, what you do to your enemies. *Peace?* For a male who melts minds and tortures for sport, I did not think you knew the word."

Wrath began simmering in my blood; embers crackled in my ears. But I cooled that fire I'd slowly been stoking these past weeks and tried, "If you will not send forces here to defend your people, then the artifact we requested—"

"Our half of the Book, child," the crone cut me off, "does not leave our sacred palace. It has not left those white walls since the day it was gifted as part of the Treaty. It will never leave those walls, not while we stand against the terrors in the North."

"Please," was all I said.

Silence again.

"Please," I repeated. Emissary—I was their emissary, and Rhys had chosen me for this. To be the voice of both worlds. "I was turned into *this*—into a faerie—because one of the commanders from Hybern *killed* me."

Through our bond, I could have sworn I felt Rhys flinch.

"For fifty years," I pushed on, "she terrorized Prythian, and when I defeated her, when I freed its people, she *killed* me. And before she did, I witnessed the horrors that she unleashed on human and faerie alike. One of them—just *one* of them was able to cause such destruction and suffering. Imagine what an army like her might do. And now their king plans to use a weapon to shatter the wall, to destroy *all* of you. The war will be swift, and brutal. And you will not win. *We* will not win. Survivors will be slaves, and their children's children will be slaves. Please . . . Please, give us the other half of the Book."

The eldest queen swapped a glance with the golden one before saying gently, placatingly, "You are young, child. You have much to learn about the ways of the world—"

"Do not," Rhys said with deadly quiet, "condescend to her." The eldest queen—who was but a child to *him*, to his centuries of existence—had the good sense to look nervous at that tone. Rhys's eyes were glazed, his face as unforgiving as his voice as he went on, "Do not insult Feyre for speaking with her heart, with compassion for those who cannot defend themselves, when you speak from only selfishness and cowardice."

The eldest stiffened. "For the greater good—"

"Many atrocities," Rhys purred, "have been done in the name of the greater good."

No small part of me was impressed that she held his gaze. She said simply, "The Book will remain with us. We will weather this storm—"

"That's enough," Mor interrupted.

She got to her feet.

And Mor looked each and every one of those queens in the eye as she said, "I am the Morrigan. You know me. What I am. You know that my gift is truth. So you will hear my words now, and know them as truth—as your ancestors once did."

Not a word.

Mor gestured behind her—to me. "Do you think it is any simple coincidence that a human has been made immortal again, at the very moment when our old enemy resurfaces? I fought side by side with Miryam in the War, fought beside her as Jurian's ambition and bloodlust drove him mad, and drove them apart. Drove him to torture Clythia to death, then battle Amarantha until his own." She took a sharp breath, and I could have sworn Azriel inched closer at the sound. But Mor blazed on, "I marched back into the Black Land with Miryam to free the slaves left in that burning sand, the slavery she had herself escaped. The slaves Miryam had promised to return to free. I marched with her—my friend. Along with Prince Drakon's legion. Miryam was my *friend*, as Feyre is now. And your ancestors, those queens who signed that Treaty . . . They were my friends, too. And when I look at you . . . " She bared her teeth. "I see *nothing* of those women in you. When I look at you, I know that your ancestors would be *ashamed*.

"You laugh at the idea of peace? That we can have it between our peoples?" Mor's voice cracked, and again Azriel subtly shifted nearer to her, though his face revealed nothing. "There is an island in a forgotten, stormy part of the sea. A vast, lush island, shielded from time and spying eyes. And on that island, Miryam and Drakon still live. With their children. With *both* of their peoples. Fae and human and those in between. Side by side. For five hundred years, they have prospered on that island, letting the world believe them dead—"

"Mor," Rhys said—a quiet reprimand.

A secret, I realized, that perhaps had remained hidden for five centuries.

A secret that had fueled the dreams of Rhysand, of his court.

A land where two dreamers had found peace between their peoples.

Where there was no wall. No iron wards. No ash arrows.

The golden queen and ancient queen looked to each other again.

The ancient one's eyes were bright as she declared, "Give us proof. If you are not the High Lord that rumor claims, give us one shred of proof that you are as you say—a male of peace."

There was one way. Only one way to show them, prove it to them.

Velaris.

My very bones cried out at the thought of revealing that gem to these . . . spiders.

Rhys rose in a fluid motion. The queens did the same. His voice was like a moonless night as he said, "You desire proof?" I held my breath, praying . . . praying he wouldn't tell them. He shrugged, the silver thread in his jacket catching the sunlight. "I shall get it for you. Await my word, and return when we summon you."

"We are summoned by no one, human or faerie," the golden queen simpered.

Perhaps that was why they'd taken so long to reply. To play some power game.

"Then come at your leisure," Rhys said, with enough of a bite that the queens' guards stepped forward. Cassian only grinned at them—and the wisest among them instantly paled.

Rhys barely inclined his head as he added, "Perhaps then you'll comprehend how vital the Book is to *both* our efforts."

"We will consider it once we have your *proof*." The ancient one nearly spat the word. Some part of me reminded myself that she was old, and royal, and smacking that sneer off her face would *not* be in our best interests. "That book has been ours to protect for five hundred years. We will not hand it over without due consideration."

The guards flanked them—as if the words had been some predetermined signal. The golden queen smirked at me, and said, "Good luck."

Then they were gone. The sitting room was suddenly too big, too quiet.

And it was Elain—*Elain*—who sighed and murmured, "I hope they all burn in hell."

CHAPTER 41

We were mostly silent during the flight and winnowing to Velaris. Amren was already waiting in the town house, her clothes rumpled, face unnervingly pale. I made a note to get her more blood immediately.

But rather than gather in the dining or sitting room, Rhys strolled down the hall, hands in his pockets, past the kitchen, and out into the courtyard garden in the back.

The rest of us lingered in the foyer, staring after him—the silence radiating from him. Like the calm before a storm.

"It went well, I take it," Amren said. Cassian gave her a look, and trailed after his friend.

The sun and arid day had warmed the garden, bits of green now poking their heads out here and there in the countless beds and pots. Rhys sat on the rim of the fountain, forearms braced on his knees, staring at the moss-flecked flagstone between his feet.

We all found our seats in the white-painted iron chairs throughout. If only humans could see them: faeries, sitting on iron. They'd throw away those ridiculous baubles and jewelry. Perhaps even Elain would receive an engagement ring that hadn't been forged with hate and fear.

"If you're out here to brood, Rhys," Amren said from her perch on a little bench, "then just say so and let me go back to my work."

Violet eyes lifted to hers. Cold, humorless. "The humans wish for proof of our good intentions. That we can be trusted."

Amren's attention cut to me. "Feyre was not enough?"

I tried not to let the words sting. No, I had not been enough; perhaps I'd even failed in my role as emissary—

"She is more than enough," Rhys said with that deadly calm, and I wondered if I'd sent my own pathetic thoughts down the bond. I snapped my shield up once more. "They're fools.. Worse—frightened fools." He studied the ground again, as if the dried moss and stone made up some pattern no one but him could see.

Cassian said, "We could . . . depose them. Get newer, smarter queens on their thrones. Who might be willing to bargain."

Rhys shook his head. "One, it'd take too long. We don't have that time." I thought of the past few wasted weeks, how hard Azriel had tried to get into those courts. If even his shadows and spies could not breach their inner workings, then I doubted an assassin would. The confirming shake of the head Azriel gave Cassian said as much. "Two," Rhys continued, "who knows if that would somehow impact the magic of their half of the Book. It must be given freely. It's possible the magic is strong enough to see our scheming." He sucked on his teeth. "We are stuck with them."

"We could try again," Mor said. "Let me speak to them, let me go to their palace—"

"No," Azriel said. Mor raised her brows, and a faint color stained Azriel's tan face. But his features were set, his hazel eyes solid. "You're not setting foot in that human realm."

"I fought in the War, you will do well to remember—"

"No," Azriel said again, refusing to break her stare. His shifting wings rasped against the back of his chair. "They would string you up and make an example of you."

"They'd have to catch me first."

"That palace is a death trap for our kind," Azriel countered, his voice low and rough. "Built by Fae hands to protect the humans from us. You set foot inside it, Mor, and you won't walk out again. Why do you think we've had such trouble getting a foothold in there?"

"If going into their territory isn't an option," I cut in before Mor could say whatever the temper limning her features hissed at her to retort and surely wound the shadowsinger more than she intended, "and deceit or any mental manipulation might make the magic wreck the Book . . . What proof can be offered?" Rhys lifted his head. "Who is—who is this Miryam? Who was she to Jurian, and who was that prince you spoke of—Drakon? Perhaps we . . . perhaps they could be used as proof. If only to vouch for you."

The heat died from Mor's eyes as she shifted a foot against the moss and flagstone.

But Rhys interlocked his fingers in the space between his knees before he said, "Five hundred years ago, in the years leading up to the War, there was a Fae kingdom in the southern part of the continent. It was a realm of sand surrounding a lush river delta. The Black Land. There was no crueler place to be born a human—for no humans were born free. They were all of them slaves, forced to build great temples and palaces for the High Fae who ruled. There was no escape; no chance of having their freedom purchased. And the queen of the Black Land . . . " Memory stirred in his face.

"She made Amarantha seem as sweet as Elain," Mor explained with soft venom.

"Miryam," Rhys continued, "was a half-Fae female born of a human mother. And as her mother was a slave, as the conception was . . . against her mother's will, so, too, was Miryam born in shackles, and deemed human—denied any rights to her Fae heritage."

"Tell the full story another time," Amren cut in. "The gist of it, girl," she said to me, "is that Miryam was given as a wedding gift by the queen to her betrothed, a foreign Fae prince named Drakon. He was horrified, and let Miryam escape. Fearing the queen's wrath, she fled through the desert, across the sea, into more desert . . . and was found by Jurian. She fell in with his rebel armies, became his lover, and was a healer amongst the warriors. Until a devastating battle found her tending to Jurian's new Fae allies—including Prince Drakon. Turns out, Miryam had opened his eyes to the monster he planned to wed. He'd broken the engagement, allied his armies with the humans, and had been looking for the beautiful slave-girl for three years. Jurian had no idea that his new ally coveted his lover. He was too focused on winning the War, on destroying Amarantha in the North. As his obsession took over, he was blind to witnessing Miryam and Drakon falling in love behind his back."

"It wasn't behind his back," Mor snapped. "Miryam ended it with Jurian before she ever laid a finger on Drakon."

Amren shrugged. "Long story short, girl, when Jurian was slaughtered by Amarantha, and during the long centuries after, she told him what had happened to his lover. That she'd betrayed him for a Fae male. Everyone believed Miryam and Drakon perished while liberating her people from the Black Land at the end of the War—even Amarantha."

"And they didn't," I said. Rhys and Mor nodded. "It was all a way to escape, wasn't it? To start over somewhere else, with both their peoples?" Another set of nods. "So why not show the queens that? You started to tell them—"

"Because," Rhys cut in, "in addition to it not proving a thing about *my* character, which seemed to be their biggest gripe, it would be a grave betrayal of our friends. Their only wish was to remain hidden—to live in peace with their peoples. They fought and bled and suffered enough for it. I will not bring them into this conflict."

"Drakon's aerial army," Cassian mused, "was as good as ours. We might need to call upon him by the end."

Rhys merely shook his head. Conversation over. And perhaps he was right: revealing Drakon and Miryam's peaceful existence explained nothing about his own intentions. About his own merits and character.

"So, what do we offer them instead?" I asked. "What do we show them?"

Rhys's face was bleak. "We show them Velaris."

"What?" Mor barked. But Amren shushed her.

"You can't mean to bring them here," I said.

"Of course not. The risks are too great, entertaining them for even a night would likely result in bloodshed." Rhys said. "So I plan to merely show them."

"They'll dismiss it as mind tricks," Azriel countered.

"No," Rhys said, getting to his feet. "I mean to *show* them—playing by their own rules."

Amren clicked her nails against each other. "What do you mean, High Lord?"

But Rhys only said to Mor, "Send word to your father. We're going to pay him and my other court a visit."

My blood iced over. The Court of Nightmares.

There was an orb, it turned out, that had belonged to Mor's family for millennia: the Veritas. It was rife with the truth-magic she'd claimed to possess—that many in her bloodline also bore. And the Veritas was one of their most valued and guarded talismans.

Rhys wasted no time planning. We'd go to the Court of Nightmares within the Hewn City tomorrow afternoon, winnowing near the massive mountain it was built within, and then flying the rest of the way.

Mor, Cassian, and I were mere distractions to make Rhys's sudden visit less suspicious—while Azriel stole the orb from Mor's father's chambers.

The orb was known amongst the humans, had been wielded by them in the War, Rhys told me over a quiet dinner that night. The queens would know it. And would know it was absolute truth, not illusion or a trick, when we used it to show them—like peering into a living painting—that this city and its good people existed.

The others had suggested other places within his territory to prove he wasn't some warmongering sadist, but none had the same impact as Velaris, Rhys claimed. For his people, for the *world*, he'd offer the queens this slice of truth.

After dinner, I wandered into the streets, and found myself eventually standing at the edge of the Rainbow, the night in full swing, patrons and artists and everyday citizens bustling from shop to shop, peering in the galleries, buying supplies.

Compared to the sparkling lights and bright colors of the little hill sloping down to the river ahead, the streets behind me were shadowed, sleeping.

I'd been here nearly two months and hadn't worked up the courage to walk through the artists' quarter.

But this place . . . Rhys would risk this beautiful city, these lovely people, all for a shot at peace. Perhaps the guilt of leaving it protected while the rest of Prythian had suffered drove him; perhaps offering up Velaris on a silver platter was his own attempt to ease the weight. I rubbed at my chest, an ache building in there.

I took a step toward the quarter—and halted.

Maybe I should have asked Mor to come. But she'd left after dinner, pale-faced and jumpy, ignoring Cassian's attempt to speak with her. Azriel had taken to the clouds to contact his spies. He'd quietly promised the pacing Cassian to find Mor when he was done.

And Rhys . . . He had enough going on. And he hadn't objected when I stated I was going for a walk. He hadn't even warned me to be careful. If it was trust, or absolute faith in the safety of his city, or just that he knew how badly I'd react if he tried to tell me not to go or warn me, I didn't know.

I shook my head, clearing my thoughts as I again stared down the main street of the Rainbow.

I'd felt flickers these past few weeks in that hole inside my chest—flickers of images, but nothing solid. Nothing roaring with life and demand. Not in the way it had that night, seeing him kneel on that bed, naked and tattooed and winged.

It'd be stupid to venture into the quarter, anyway, when it might very well be ruined in any upcoming conflict. It'd be stupid to fall in love with it, when it might be torn from me.

So, like a coward, I turned and went home.

Rhys was waiting in the foyer, leaning against the post of the stair banister. His face was grim.

I halted in the middle of the entry carpet. "What's wrong?"

His wings were nowhere to be seen, not even the shadow of them. "I'm debating asking you to stay tomorrow."

I crossed my arms. "I thought I was going." *Don't lock me up in this house, don't shove me aside*—

He ran a hand through his hair. "What I have to be tomorrow, who I have to become, is not . . . it's not something I want you to see. How I will treat you, treat others . . ."

"The mask of the High Lord," I said quietly.

"Yes." He took a seat on the bottom step of the stairs.

I remained in the center of the foyer as I asked carefully, "Why don't you want me to see that?"

"Because you've only started to look at me like I'm not a monster, and I can't stomach the idea of anything you see tomorrow, being beneath that mountain, putting you back into that place where I found you."

Beneath that mountain—underground. Yes, I'd forgotten that. Forgotten I'd see the court that Amarantha had modeled her own after, that I'd be trapped beneath the earth . . .

But with Cassian, and Azriel, and Mor. With . . . him.

I waited for the panic, the cold sweat. Neither came. "Let me help. In whatever way I can."

Bleakness shaded the starlight in those eyes. "The role you will have to play is not a pleasant one."

"I trust you." I sat beside him on the stairs, close enough that the heat of his body warmed the chill night air clinging to my overcoat. "Why did Mor look so disturbed when she left?"

His throat bobbed. I could tell it was rage, and pain, that kept him from telling me outright—not mistrust. After a moment, he said, "I was there, in the Hewn City, the day her father declared she was to be sold in marriage to Eris, eldest son of the High Lord of the Autumn Court." Lucien's brother. "Eris had a reputation for cruelty, and Mor . . . begged me not to let it happen. For all her power, all her wildness, she had no voice, no rights with those people. And my father didn't particularly care if his cousins used their offspring as breeding stock."

"What happened?" I breathed.

"I brought Mor to the Illyrian camp for a few days. And she saw Cassian, and decided she'd do the one thing that would ruin her value to these people. I didn't know until after, and . . . it was a mess. With Cassian, with her, with our families. And it's another long story, but the short of it is that Eris refused to marry her. Said she'd been sullied by a bastard-born lesser faerie, and he'd now sooner fuck a sow. Her family . . . they . . . " I'd never seen him at such a loss for words. Rhys cleared his throat. "When they were done, they dumped her on the Autumn Court border, with a note nailed to her body that said she was Eris's problem."

Nailed—*nailed* to her.

Rhys said with soft wrath, "Eris left her for dead in the middle of their woods. Azriel found her a day later. It was all I could do to keep him from going to either court and slaughtering them all."

I thought of that merry face, the flippant laughter, the female that did not care who approved. Perhaps because she had seen the ugliest her kind had to offer. And had survived.

And I understood—why Rhys could not endure Nesta for more

than a few moments, why he could not let go of that anger where her failings were concerned, even if I had.

Beron's fire began crackling in my veins. *My* fire, not his. Not his son's, either.

I took Rhys's hand, and his thumb brushed against the back of my palm. I tried not to think about the ease of that stroke as I said in a hard, calm voice I barely recognized, "Tell me what I need to do tomorrow."

CHAPTER 42

I was not frightened.

Not of the role that Rhys had asked me to play today. Not of the roaring wind as we winnowed into a familiar, snow-capped mountain range refusing to yield to spring's awakening kiss. Not of the punishing drop as Rhys flew us between the peaks and valleys, swift and sleek. Cassian and Azriel flanked us; Mor would meet us at the gates to the mountain base.

Rhys's face was drawn, his shoulders tense as I gripped them. I knew what to expect, but . . . even after he'd told me what he needed me to do, even after I had agreed, he'd been . . . aloof. Haunted.

Worried for me, I realized.

And just because of that worry, just to get that tightness off his face, even for these few minutes before we faced his unholy realm beneath that mountain, I said over the wind, "Amren and Mor told me that the span of an Illyrian male's wings says a lot about the size of . . . other parts."

His eyes shot to mine, then to pine-tree-coated slopes below. "Did they now."

I shrugged in his arms, trying not to think about the naked body that night all those weeks ago—though I hadn't glimpsed much. "They also said Azriel's wings are the biggest."

Mischief danced in those violet eyes, washing away the cold distance, the strain. The spymaster was a black blur against the pale blue sky. "When we return home, let's get out the measuring stick, shall we?"

I pinched the rock-hard muscle of his forearm. Rhys flashed me a wicked grin before he tilted down—

Mountains and snow and trees and sun and utter free fall through wisps of cloud—

A breathless scream came out of me as we plummeted. Throwing my arms around his neck was instinct. His low laugh tickled my nape. "You're willing to brave my brand of darkness and put up one of your own, willing to go to a watery grave and take on the Weaver, but a little free fall makes you scream?"

"I'll leave you to rot the next time you have a nightmare," I hissed, my eyes still shut and body locked as he snapped out his wings to ease us into a steady glide.

"No, you won't," he crooned. "You liked seeing me naked too much."

"Prick."

His laugh rumbled against me. Eyes closed, the wind roaring like a wild animal, I adjusted my position, gripping him tighter. My knuckles brushed one of his wings—smooth and cool like silk, but hard as stone with it stretched taut.

Fascinating. I blindly reached again . . . and dared to run a fingertip along some inner edge.

Rhysand shuddered, a soft groan slipping past my ear. "That," he said tightly, "is very sensitive."

I snatched my finger back, pulling away far enough to see his face. With the wind, I had to squint, and my braided hair ripped this way and that, but—he was entirely focused on the mountains around us. "Does it tickle?"

He flicked his gaze to me, then to the snow and pine that went on forever. "It feels like this," he said, and leaned in so close that his lips brushed the shell of my ear as he sent a gentle breath into it. My back arched on instinct, my chin tipping up at the caress of that breath.

"Oh," I managed to say. I felt him smile against my ear and pull away.

"If you want an Illyrian male's attention, you'd be better off grabbing him by the balls. We're trained to protect our wings at all costs. Some males attack first, ask questions later, if their wings are touched without invitation."

"And during sex?" The question blurted out.

Rhys's face was nothing but feline amusement as he monitored the mountains. "During sex, an Illyrian male can find completion just by having someone touch his wings in the right spot."

My blood thrummed. Dangerous territory; more lethal than the drop below. "Have *you* found that to be true?"

His eyes stripped me bare. "I've never allowed anyone to see or touch my wings during sex. It makes you vulnerable in a way that I'm not . . . comfortable with."

"Too bad," I said, staring out too casually toward the mighty mountain that now appeared on the horizon, towering over the others. And capped, I noted, with that glimmering palace of moonstone.

"Why?" he asked warily.

I shrugged, fighting the upward tugging of my lips. "Because I bet you could get into some interesting positions with those wings."

Rhys loosed a barking laugh, and his nose grazed my ear. I felt him open his mouth to whisper something, but—

Something dark and fast and sleek shot for us, and he plunged down and away, swearing.

But another one, and another, kept coming.

Not just ordinary arrows, I realized as Rhys veered, snatching one out of the air. Others bounced harmlessly off a shield he blasted up.

He studied the wood in his palm and dropped it with a hiss. Ash arrows. To kill faeries.

And now that I was one . . .

Faster than the wind, faster than death, Rhys shot for the ground. Flew, not winnowed, because he wanted to know where our enemies were, didn't want to lose them. The wind bit my face, screeched in my ears, ripped at my hair with brutal claws.

Azriel and Cassian were already hurtling for us. Shields of translucent blue and red encircled them—sending those arrows bouncing off. Their Siphons at work.

The arrows shot from the pine forest coating the mountains, then vanished.

Rhys slammed into the ground, snow flying in his wake, and fury like I hadn't seen since that day in Amarantha's court twisted his features. I could feel it thrumming against me, roiling through the clearing we now stood in.

Azriel and Cassian were there in an instant, their colored shields shrinking back into their Siphons. The three of them forces of nature in the pine forest, Rhysand didn't even look at me as he ordered Cassian, "Take her to the palace, and stay there until I'm back. Az, you're with me."

Cassian reached for me, but I stepped away. "No."

"What?" Rhys snarled, the word near-guttural.

"Take me with you," I said. I didn't want to go to that moonstone palace to pace and wait and wring my fingers.

Cassian and Azriel, wisely, kept their mouths shut. And Rhys, Mother bless him, only tucked in his wings and crossed his arms—waiting to hear my reasons.

"I've seen ash arrows," I said a bit breathlessly. "I might recognize where they were made. And if they came from the hand of another High Lord . . . I can detect that, too." If they'd come from Tarquin . . . "And I can track just as well on the ground as any of you." Except for Azriel, maybe. "So you and Cassian take the skies," I said, still waiting for the rejection, the order to lock me up. "And I'll hunt on the ground with Azriel."

The wrath radiating through the snowy clearing ebbed into frozen, too-calm rage. But Rhys said, "Cassian—I want aerial patrols on the sea borders, stationed in two-mile rings, all the way out toward Hybern. I want foot soldiers in the mountain passes along the southern border; make sure those warning fires are ready on every peak. We're not going to rely on magic." He turned to Azriel. "When you're done, warn your spies that they might be compromised, and prepare to get them out. And put fresh ones in. We keep this contained. We don't tell anyone inside that court what happened. If anyone mentions it, say it was a training exercise."

Because we couldn't afford to let that weakness show, even amongst his subjects.

His eyes at last found mine. "We've got an hour until we're expected at court. Make it count."

We searched, but the missed arrows had been snatched up by our attackers—and even the shadows and wind told Azriel nothing, as if our enemy had been hidden from them as well.

But that was twice now that they'd known where Rhys and I would be.

Mor found Azriel and me after twenty minutes, wanting to know what the hell had happened. We'd explained—and she'd winnowed away, to spin whatever excuse would keep her horrible family from suspecting anything was amiss.

But at the end of the hour, we hadn't found a single track. And we could delay our meeting no longer.

The Court of Nightmares lay behind a mammoth set of doors carved into the mountain itself. And from the base, the mountain rose so high I couldn't see the palace I had once stayed in atop it. Only snow, and rock, and birds circling above. There was no one outside—no village, no signs of life. Nothing to indicate a whole city of people dwelled within.

But I did not let my curiosity or any lingering trepidation show as Mor and I entered. Rhys, Cassian, and Azriel would arrive minutes later.

There were sentries at the stone gates, clothed not in black, as I might have suspected, but in gray and white—armor meant to blend into the mountain face. Mor didn't so much as look at them as she led me silently inside the mountain-city.

My body clenched as soon as the darkness, the scent of rock and fire and roasting meat, hit me. I had been here before, suffered here—

Not Under the Mountain. This was not Under the Mountain.

Indeed, Amarantha's court had been the work of a child.

The Court of Nightmares was the work of a god.

While Under the Mountain had been a series of halls and rooms and levels, this . . . this was truly a city.

The walkway that Mor led us down was an avenue, and around us, rising high into gloom, were buildings and spires, homes and bridges. A metropolis carved from the dark stone of the mountain itself, no inch of it left unmarked or without some lovely, hideous artwork etched into it. Figures danced and fornicated; begged and reveled. Pillars were carved to look like curving vines of night-blooming flowers. Water ran throughout in little streams and rivers tapped from the heart of the mountain itself.

The Hewn City. A place of such terrible beauty that it was an effort to keep the wonder and dread off my face. Music was already playing somewhere, and our hosts still did not come out to greet us. The people we passed—only High Fae—were clothed in finery, their faces deathly pale and cold. Not one stopped us, not one smiled or bowed.

Mor ignored them all. Neither of us had said one word. Rhys had told me not to—that the walls had ears here.

Mor led me down the avenue toward another set of stone gates, thrown open at the base of what looked to be a castle *within* the mountain. The official seat of the High Lord of the Night Court.

Great, scaled black beasts were carved into those gates, all coiled together in a nest of claws and fangs, sleeping and fighting, some locked in an endless cycle of devouring each other. Between them flowed vines of jasmine and moonflowers. I could have sworn the beasts seemed to writhe in the silvery glow of the bobbing faelights throughout the mountain-city. The Gates of Eternity—that's what I'd call the painting that flickered in my mind.

Mor continued through them, a flash of color and life in this strange, cold place.

She wore deepest red, the gossamer and gauze of her sleeveless gown clinging to her breasts and hips, while carefully placed shafts left much of her stomach and back exposed. Her hair was down in rippling waves, and cuffs of solid gold glinted around her wrists. A queen—a queen who bowed to no one, a queen who had faced them all down and triumphed. A queen who owned her body, her life, her destiny, and never apologized for it.

My clothes, which she had taken a moment in the pine wood to shift me into, were of a similar ilk, nearly identical to those I had been forced to wear Under the Mountain. Two shafts of fabric that hardly covered my breasts flowed to below my navel, where a belt across my hips joined them into one long shaft that draped between my legs and barely covered my backside.

But unlike the chiffon and bright colors I had worn then, this one was fashioned of black, glittering fabric that sparkled with every swish of my hips.

Mor had fashioned my hair onto a crown atop my head—right behind the black diadem that had been set before it, accented with flecks of diamond that made it glisten like the night sky. She'd darkened and lengthened my eyelashes, sweeping out an elegant, vicious line of kohl at the outer corner of each. My lips she'd painted bloodred.

Into the castle beneath the mountain we strode. There were more people here, milling about the endless halls, watching our every breath. Some looked like Mor, with their gold hair and beautiful faces. They even hissed at her.

Mor smirked at them. Part of me wished she'd rip their throats out instead.

We at last came to a throne room of polished ebony. More of the serpents from the front gates were carved here—this time, wrapped around the countless columns supporting the onyx ceiling. It was so high up that gloom hid its finer details, but I knew more had been carved there, too. Great beasts to monitor the manipulations and scheming within this room. The throne itself had been fashioned out of a few of them, a head snaking around either side of the back—as if they watched over the High Lord's shoulder.

A crowd had gathered—and for a moment, I was again in Amarantha's throne room, so similar was the atmosphere, the malice. So similar was the dais at the other end.

A golden-haired, beautiful man stepped into our path toward that ebony throne, and Mor smoothly halted. I knew he was her father without him saying a word.

He was clothed in black, a silver circlet atop his head. His brown eyes were like old soil as he said to her, "Where is he?"

No greeting, no formality. He ignored me wholly.

Mor shrugged. "He arrives when he wishes to." She continued on.

Her father looked at me then. And I willed my face into a mask like hers. Disinterested. Aloof.

Her father surveyed my face, my body—and where I thought he'd sneer and ogle . . . there was nothing. No emotion. Just heartless cold.

I followed Mor before disgust wrecked my own icy mask.

Banquet tables against the black walls were covered with fat, succulent fruits and wreaths of golden bread, interrupted with roast meats, kegs of cider and ale, and pies and tarts and little cakes of every size and variety.

It might have made my mouth water . . . Were it not for the High Fae in their finery. Were it not for the fact that no one touched the food—the power and wealth lying in letting it go to waste.

Mor went right up to the obsidian dais, and I halted at the foot of the steps as she took up a place beside the throne and said to the crowd in a voice that was clear and cruel and cunning, "Your High Lord approaches. He is in a foul mood, so I suggest being on your best behavior—unless you wish to be the evening entertainment."

And before the crowd could begin murmuring, I felt it. Felt—him.

The very rock beneath my feet seemed to tremble—a pulsing, steady beat.

His footsteps. As if the mountain shuddered at each touch.

Everyone in that room went still as death. As if petrified that their very breathing would draw the attention of the predator now strolling toward us.

Mor's shoulders were back, her chin high—feral, wanton pride at her master's arrival.

Remembering my role, I kept my own chin lowered, watching beneath my brows.

First Cassian and Azriel appeared in the doorway. The High Lord's general and shadowsinger—and the most powerful Illyrians in history.

They were not the males I had come to know.

Clad in battle-black that hugged their muscled forms, their armor was intricate, scaled—their shoulders impossibly broader, their faces a portrait of unfeeling brutality. They reminded me, somehow, of the ebony beasts carved into the pillars they passed.

More Siphons, I realized, glimmered in addition to the ones atop each of their hands. A Siphon in the center of their chest. One on either shoulder. One on either knee.

For a moment, my knees quaked, and I understood what the camp-lords had feared in them. If one Siphon was what most Illyrians needed to handle their killing power . . . Cassian and Azriel had seven each. *Seven.*

The courtiers had the good sense to back away a step as Cassian and Azriel strolled through the crowd, toward the dais. Their wings gleamed, the talons at the apex sharp enough to pierce air—like they'd honed them.

Cassian's focus had gone right to Mor, Azriel indulging in all of a glance before scanning the people around them. Most shirked from the spymaster's eyes—though they trembled as they beheld Truth-Teller at his side, the Illyrian blade peeking above his left shoulder.

Azriel, his face a mask of beautiful death, silently promised them all endless, unyielding torment, even the shadows shuddering in his wake. I knew why; knew for whom he'd gladly do it.

They had tried to sell a seventeen-year-old girl into marriage with a sadist—and then brutalized her in ways I couldn't, wouldn't, let myself consider. And these people now lived in utter terror of the three companions who stood at the dais.

Good. They should be afraid of them.

Afraid of me.

And then Rhysand appeared.

He had released the damper on his power, on who he was. His power filled the throne room, the castle, the mountain. The world. It had no end and no beginning.

No wings. No weapons. No sign of the warrior. Nothing but the elegant, cruel High Lord the world believed him to be. His hands were in his pockets, his black tunic seeming to gobble up the light. And on his head sat a crown of stars.

No sign of the male who had been drinking on the roof; no sign of the fallen prince kneeling on his bed. The full impact of him threatened to sweep me away.

Here—here was the most powerful High Lord ever born.

The face of dreams and nightmares.

Rhys's eyes met mine briefly from across the room as he strolled between the pillars. To the throne that was his by blood and sacrifice and might. My own blood sang at the power that thrummed from him, at the sheer beauty of him.

Mor stepped off the dais, dropping to one knee in a smooth bow. Cassian and Azriel followed suit.

So did everyone in that room.

Including me.

The ebony floor was so polished I could see my red-painted lips in it; see my own expressionless face. The room was so silent I could hear each of Rhys's footsteps toward us.

"Well, well," he said to no one in particular. "Looks like you're all on time for once."

Raising his head as he continued kneeling, Cassian gave Rhys a half grin—the High Lord's commander incarnate, eager to do his bloodletting.

Rhys's boots stopped in my line of sight.

His fingers were icy on my chin as he lifted my face.

The entire room, still on the floor, watched. But this was the role he needed me to play. To be a distraction and novelty. Rhys's lips curved upward. "Welcome to my home, Feyre Cursebreaker."

I lowered my eyes, my kohl-thick lashes tickling my cheek. He clicked his tongue, his grip on my chin tightening. Everyone noticed the push of his fingers, the predatory angle of his head as he said, "Come with me."

A tug on my chin, and I rose to my feet. Rhys dragged his eyes over me and I wondered if it wasn't entirely for show as they glazed a bit.

He led me the few steps onto the dais—to the throne. He sat, smiling faintly at his monstrous court. He owned every inch of the throne. These people.

And with a tug on my waist, he perched me on his lap.

The High Lord's whore. Who I'd become Under the Mountain—who the world expected me to be. The dangerous new pet that Mor's father would now seek to feel out.

Rhys's hand slid along my bare waist, the other running down my exposed thigh. Cold—his hands were so cold I almost yelped.

He must have felt the silent flinch. A heartbeat later, his hands had warmed. His thumb, curving around the inside of my thigh, gave a slow, long stroke as if to say *Sorry*.

Rhys indeed leaned in to bring his mouth near my ear, well aware his subjects had not yet risen from the floor. As if they had once done so before they were bidden, long ago, and had learned the consequences. Rhysand whispered to me, his other hand now stroking the bare skin of my ribs in lazy, indolent circles, "Try not to let it go to your head."

I knew they could all hear it. So did he.

I stared at their bowed heads, my heart hammering, but said with midnight smoothness, "What?"

Rhys's breath caressed my ear, the twin to the breath he'd brushed against it merely an hour ago in the skies. "That every male in here is contemplating what they'd be willing to give up in order to get that pretty, red mouth of yours on them."

I waited for the blush, the shyness, to creep in.

But I *was* beautiful. I was strong.

I had survived—triumphed. As Mor had survived in this horrible, poisoned house . . .

So I smiled a bit, the first smile of my new mask. Let them see that pretty, red mouth, and my white, straight teeth.

His hand slid higher up my thigh, the proprietary touch of a male who knew he owned someone body and soul. He'd apologized in advance for it—for this game, these roles we'd have to play.

But I leaned into that touch, leaned back into his hard, warm body. I was pressed so closely against him that I could feel the deep rumble of his voice as he at last said to his court, "Rise."

As one, they did. I smirked at some of them, gloriously bored and infinitely amused.

Rhys brushed a knuckle along the inside of my knee, and every nerve in my body narrowed to that touch.

"Go play," he said to them all.

They obeyed, the crowd dispersing, music striking up from a distant corner.

"Keir," Rhys said, his voice cutting through the room like lightning on a stormy night.

It was all he needed to summon Mor's father to the foot of the dais. Keir bowed again, his face lined with icy resentment as he took in Rhys, then me—glancing once at Mor and the Illyrians. Cassian gave Keir a slow nod that told him he remembered—and would never forget—what the Steward of the Hewn City had done to his own daughter.

But it was from Azriel that Keir cringed. From the sight of Truth-Teller.

One day, I realized, Azriel would use that blade on Mor's father. And take a long, long while to carve him up.

"Report," Rhys said, stroking a knuckle down my ribs. He gave a dismissive nod to Cassian, Mor, and Azriel, and the trio faded away into the crowd. Within a heartbeat, Azriel had vanished into shadows and was gone. Keir didn't even turn.

Before Rhys, Keir was nothing more than a sullen child. Yet I knew Mor's father was older. Far older. The Steward clung to power, it seemed.

Rhys *was* power.

"Greetings, milord," Keir said, his deep voice polished smooth. "And greetings to your . . . guest."

Rhys's hand flattened on my thigh as he angled his head to look at me. "She is lovely, isn't she?"

"Indeed," Keir said, lowering his eyes. "There is little to report, milord. All has been quiet since your last visit."

"No one for me to punish?" A cat playing with his food.

"Unless you'd like for me to select someone here, no, milord."

Rhys clicked his tongue. "Pity." He again surveyed me, then leaned to tug my earlobe with his teeth.

And damn me to hell, but I leaned farther back as his teeth pressed down at the same moment his thumb drifted high on the side of my thigh, sweeping across sensitive skin in a long, luxurious touch. My body went loose and tight, and my breathing . . . Cauldron damn me again, the scent of him, the citrus and the sea, the power roiling off him . . . my breathing hitched a bit.

I knew he noticed; knew he felt that shift in me.

His fingers stilled on my leg.

Keir began mentioning people I didn't know in the court, bland reports on marriages and alliances, blood-feuds, and Rhys let him talk.

His thumb stroked again—this time joined with his pointer finger.

A dull roaring was filling my ears, drowning out everything but that touch on the inside of my leg. The music was throbbing, ancient, wild, and people ground against each other to it.

His eyes on the Steward, Rhys made vague nods every now and then. While his fingers continued their slow, steady stroking on my thighs, rising higher with every pass.

People were watching. Even as they drank and ate, even as some danced in small circles, people were watching. I was sitting in his lap, his own personal plaything, his every touch visible to them . . . and yet it might as well have been only the two of us.

Keir listed the expenses and costs of running the court, and Rhys gave another vague nod. This time, his nose brushed the spot between my neck and shoulder, followed by a passing graze of his mouth.

My breasts tightened, becoming full and heavy, aching—aching like what was now pooling in my core. Heat filled my face, my blood.

But Keir said at last, as if his own self-control slipped the leash, "I had heard the rumors, and I didn't quite believe them." His gaze settled on me, on my breasts, peaked through the folds of my dress, of my legs, spread wider than they'd been minutes before, and Rhys's hand in dangerous territory. "But it seems true: Tamlin's pet is now owned by another master."

"You should see how I make her beg," Rhys murmured, nudging my neck with his nose.

Keir clasped his hands behind his back. "I assume you brought her to make a statement."

"You know everything I do is a statement."

"Of course. This one, it seems, you enjoy putting in cobwebs and crowns."

Rhys's hand paused, and I sat straighter at the tone, the disgust. And I said to Keir in a voice that belonged to another woman, "Perhaps I'll put a leash on *you*."

Rhys's approval tapped against my mental shield, the hand at my ribs now making lazy circles. "She does enjoy playing," he mused onto my shoulder. He jerked his chin toward the Steward. "Get her some wine."

Pure command. No politeness.

Keir stiffened, but strode off.

Rhys didn't dare break from his mask, but the light kiss he pressed beneath my ear told me enough. Apology and gratitude—and more apologies. He didn't like this any more than I did. And yet to get what we needed, to buy Azriel time . . . He'd do it. And so would I.

I wondered, then, with his hands beneath my breasts and between my legs, what Rhys *wouldn't* give of himself. Wondered if . . . if perhaps the arrogance and swagger . . . if they masked a male who perhaps thought he wasn't worth very much at all.

A new song began, like dripping honey—and edged into a swift-moving wind, punctuated with driving, relentless drums.

I twisted, studying his face. There was nothing warm in his eyes, nothing of the friend I'd made. I opened my shield enough to let him in. *What?* His voice floated into my mind.

I reached down the bond between us, caressing that wall of ebony adamant. A small sliver cracked—just for me. And I said into it, *You are good, Rhys. You are kind. This mask does not scare me. I see you beneath it.*

His hands tightened on me, and his eyes held mine as he leaned forward to brush his mouth against my cheek. It was answer enough—and . . . an unleashing.

I leaned a bit more against him, my legs widening ever so slightly. *Why'd you stop?* I said into his mind, into him.

A near-silent growl reverberated against me. He stroked my ribs again, in time to the beat of the music, his thumb rising nearly high enough to graze the underside of my breasts.

I let my head drop back against his shoulder.

I let go of the part of me that heard their words—*whore, whore, whore*—

Let go of the part that said those words alongside them—*traitor, liar, whore*—

And I just *became*.

I became the music, and the drums, and the wild, dark thing in the High Lord's arms.

His eyes were wholly glazed—and not with power or rage. Something red-hot and edged with glittering darkness exploded in my mind.

I dragged a hand down his thigh, feeling the hidden warrior's strength there. Dragged it back up again in a long, idle stroke, needing to touch him, feel him.

I was going to catch fire and burn. I was going to start burning right here—

Easy, he said with wicked amusement through the open sliver in my shield. *If you become a living candle, poor Keir will throw a hissy fit. And then you'd ruin the party for everyone.*

Because the fire would let them all know I wasn't normal—and no doubt Keir would inform his almost-allies in the Autumn Court. Or one of these other monsters would.

Rhys shifted his hips, rubbing against me with enough pressure that for a second, I didn't care about Keir, or the Autumn Court, or what Azriel might be doing right now to steal the orb.

I had been so cold, so lonely, for so long, and my body cried out at the contact, at the joy of being touched and held and *alive*.

The hand that had been on my waist slid across my abdomen, hooking into the low-slung belt there. I rested my head between his shoulder and neck, staring at the crowd as they stared at me, savoring every place where Rhys and I connected and wanting *more more more*.

At last, when my blood had begun to boil, when Rhys skimmed the underside of my breast with his knuckle, I looked to where I knew Keir was standing, watching us, my wine forgotten in his hand.

We both did.

The Steward was staring unabashedly as he leaned against the wall. Unsure whether to interrupt. Half terrified to. *We* were his distraction. *We* were the sleight of hand while Az stole the orb.

I knew Rhys was still holding Keir's gaze as the tip of his tongue slid up my neck.

I arched my back, eyes heavy-lidded, breathing uneven. I'd burn and burn and burn—

I think he's so disgusted that he might have given me the orb just to get out of here, Rhys said in my mind, that other hand drifting dangerously south. But there was such a growing ache there, and I wore nothing beneath that would conceal the damning evidence if he slid his hand a fraction higher.

You and I put on a good show, I said back. The person who said that, husky and sultry—I'd never heard that voice come out of me before. Even in my mind.

His hand slid to my upper thigh, fingers curving in.

I ground against him, trying to shift those hands away from what he'd learn—

To find him hard against my backside.

Every thought eddied from my head. Only a thrill of power remained as I writhed along that impressive length. Rhys let out a low, rough laugh.

Keir just watched and watched and watched. Rigid. Horrified. Stuck here, until Rhys released him—and not thinking twice about why. Or where the spymaster had gone.

So I turned around again, meeting Rhysand's now-blazing eyes, and then licked up the column of his throat. Wind and sea and citrus and sweat. It almost undid me.

I faced forward, and Rhys dragged his mouth along the back of my neck, right over my spine, just as I shifted against the hardness pushing into me, insistent and dominating. Precisely as his hand slid a bit too high on my inner thigh.

I felt the predatory focus go right to the slickness he'd felt there. Proof of my traitorous body. His arms tightened around me, and my face burned—perhaps a bit from shame, but—

Rhys sensed my focus, my fire slip. *It's fine,* he said, but that mental voice sounded breathless. *It means nothing. It's just your body reacting—*

Because you're so irresistible? My attempt to deflect sounded strained, even in my mind.

But he laughed, probably for my benefit.

We'd danced around and teased and taunted each other for months. And maybe it was my body's reaction, maybe it was *his* body's reaction, but the taste of him threatened to destroy me, consume me, and—

Another male. I'd had another male's hands all over me, when Tamlin and I were barely—

Fighting my nausea, I pasted a sleepy, lust-fogged smile on my face. Right as Azriel returned and gave Rhys a subtle nod. He'd gotten the orb.

Mor slid up to the spymaster, running a proprietary hand over his shoulders, his chest, as she circled to look into his face. Az's scar-mottled hand wrapped around her bare waist—squeezing once. The confirmation she also needed.

She offered him a little grin that would no doubt spread rumors, and sauntered into the crowd again. Dazzling, distracting, leaving them thinking Az had been here the whole time, leaving them pondering if she'd extend Azriel an invitation to her bed.

Azriel just stared after Mor, distant and bored. I wondered if he was as much of a mess inside as I was.

Rhys crooked a finger to Keir, who, scowling a bit in his daughter's direction, stumbled forward with my wine. He'd barely reached the dais before Rhys's power took it from him, floating the goblet to us.

Rhys set it on the ground beside the throne, a stupid task he'd thought up for the Steward to remind him of his powerlessness, that this throne was not his.

"Should I test it for poison?" Rhys drawled even as he said into my mind, *Cassian's waiting. Go.*

Rhys had the same, sex-addled expression on his perfect face—but his eyes . . . I couldn't read the shadows in his eyes.

Maybe—maybe for all our teasing, after Amarantha, he didn't *want* to be touched by a woman like that. Didn't even enjoy being wanted like that.

I had been tortured and tormented, but his horrors had gone to another level.

"No, milord," Keir groveled. "I would never dare harm you." Another distraction, this conversation. I took that as my cue to stride to Cassian, who was snarling by a pillar at anyone who came too close.

I felt the eyes of the court slide to me, felt them all sniff delicately at what was so clearly written over my body. But as I passed Keir, even with the High Lord at my back, he hissed almost too quietly to hear, "You'll get what's coming to you, whore."

Night exploded into the room.

People cried out. And when the darkness cleared, Keir was on his knees.

Rhys still lounged on the throne. His face a mask of frozen rage.

The music stopped. Mor appeared at the edge of the crowd—her own features set in smug satisfaction. Even as Azriel approached her side, standing too close to be casual.

"Apologize," Rhys said. My heart thundered at the pure command, the utter wrath.

Keir's neck muscles strained, and sweat broke out on his lip.

"I said," Rhys intoned with such horrible calm, "apologize."

The Steward groaned. And when another heartbeat passed—

Bone cracked. Keir screamed.

And I watched—I watched as his arm fractured into not two, not three, but *four* different pieces, the skin going taut and loose in all the wrong spots—

Another crack. His elbow disintegrated. My stomach churned.

Keir began sobbing, the tears half from rage, judging by the hatred in his eyes as he looked at me, then Rhys. But his lips formed the words, *I'm sorry*.

The bones of his other arm splintered, and it was an effort not to cringe.

Rhys smiled as Keir screamed again and said to the room, "Should I kill him for it?"

No one answered.

Rhys chuckled. He said to his Steward, "When you wake up, you're not to see a healer. If I hear that you do . . . " Another crack—Keir's pinkie finger went saggy. The male shrieked. The heat that had boiled my blood turned to ice. "If I hear that you do, I'll carve you into pieces and bury them where no one can stand a chance of putting you together again."

Keir's eyes widened in true terror now. Then, as if an invisible hand had struck the consciousness from him, he collapsed to the floor.

Rhys said to no one in particular, "Dump him in his room."

Two males who looked like they could be Mor's cousins or brothers rushed forward, gathering up the Steward. Mor watched them, sneering faintly—though her skin was pale.

He'd wake up. That's what Rhys had said.

I made myself keep walking as Rhys summoned another courtier to give him reports on whatever trivial matters.

But my attention remained on the throne behind me, even as I slipped beside Cassian, daring the court to approach, to play with me. None did.

And for the long hour afterward, my focus half remained on the High Lord whose hands and mouth and body had suddenly made me feel awake—burning. It didn't make me forget, didn't make me obliterate hurts or grievances, it just made me . . . alive. Made me feel as if I'd been asleep for a year, slumbering inside a glass coffin, and he had just shattered through it and shaken me to consciousness.

The High Lord whose power had not scared me. Whose wrath did not wreck me.

And now—now I didn't know where that put me.

Knee-deep in trouble seemed like a good place to start.

CHAPTER 43

The wind roared around Rhys and me as he winnowed from the skies above his court. But Velaris didn't greet us.

Rather, we were standing by a moonlit mountain lake ringed in pine trees, high above the world. We'd left the court as we'd come in—with swagger and menace. Where Cassian, Azriel, and Mor had gone with the orb, I had no idea.

Alone at the edge of the lake, Rhys said hoarsely, "I'm sorry."

I blinked. "What do you possibly have to be sorry for?"

His hands were shaking—as if in the aftermath of that fury at what Keir had called me, what he'd threatened. Perhaps he'd brought us here before heading home in order to have some privacy before his friends could interrupt. "I shouldn't have let you go. Let you see that part of us. Of me." I'd never seen him so raw, so . . . stumbling.

"I'm fine." I didn't know what to make of what had been done. Both between us and to Keir. But it had been my choice. To play that role, to wear these clothes. To let him touch me. But . . . I said slowly, "We knew what tonight would require of us. Please—please don't start . . . protecting me. Not like that." He knew what I meant. He'd protected me

Under the Mountain, but that primal, male rage he'd just shown Keir . . . A shattered study splattered in paint flashed through my memory.

Rhys rasped, "I will never—*never* lock you up, force you to stay behind. But when he threatened you tonight, when he called you . . . " Whore. That's what they'd called *him*. For fifty years, they'd hissed it. I'd listened to Lucien spit the words in his face. Rhys released a jagged breath. "It's hard to shut down my instincts."

Instincts. Just like . . . like someone *else* had instincts to protect, to hide me away. "Then you should have prepared yourself better," I snapped. "You seemed to be going along *just fine* with it, until Keir said—"

"I will *kill* anyone who harms you," Rhys snarled. "I will *kill* them, and take a damn long time doing it." He panted. "Go ahead. Hate me—despise me for it."

"You are my *friend*," I said, and my voice broke on the word. I hated the tears that slipped down my face. I didn't even know why I was crying. Perhaps for the fact that it had felt real on that throne with him, even for a moment, and . . . and it likely hadn't been. Not for him. "You're my friend—and I understand that you're High Lord. I understand that you will defend your true court, and punish threats against it. But I can't . . . I don't want you to stop telling me things, inviting me to do things, because of the threats against me."

Darkness rippled, and wings tore from his back. "I am not him," Rhys breathed. "I will *never* be him, act like him. He locked you up and let you wither, and die."

"He tried—"

"Stop comparing. *Stop* comparing me to him."

The words cut me short. I blinked.

"You think I don't know how stories get written—how *this* story will be written?" Rhys put his hands on his chest, his face more open, more anguished than I'd seen it. "I am the dark lord, who stole away the bride of spring. I am a demon, and a nightmare, and I will meet a bad end. He is the golden prince—the hero who will get to keep you as his reward for not dying of stupidity and arrogance."

The things I love have a tendency to be taken from me. He'd admitted that to me Under the Mountain.

But his words were kindling to my temper, to whatever pit of fear was yawning open inside of me. "And what about my story?" I hissed. "What about *my* reward? What about what *I* want?"

"What is it that you want, Feyre?"

I had no answer. I didn't know. Not anymore.

"What is it that you *want*, Feyre?"

I stayed silent.

His laugh was bitter, soft. "I thought so. Perhaps you should take some time to figure that out one of these days."

"Perhaps I don't know what I want, but at least I don't hide what I am behind a mask," I seethed. "At least I let them see who I am, broken bits and all. Yes—it's to save your people. But what about the other masks, Rhys? What about letting your friends see your real face? But maybe it's easier not to. Because what if you did let someone in? And what if they saw *everything*, and still walked away? Who could blame them—who would want to bother with that sort of mess?"

He flinched.

The most powerful High Lord in history flinched. And I knew I'd hit hard—and deep.

Too hard. Too deep.

"Rhys," I said.

"Let's go home."

The word hung between us, and I wondered if he'd take it back—even as I waited for my own mouth to bark that it wasn't home. But the thought of the clear, crisp blue skies of Velaris at sunset, the sparkle of the city lights . . .

Before I could say yes, he grabbed my hand, not meeting my stare, and winnowed us away.

The wind was hollow as it roared around us, the darkness cold and foreign.

Cassian, Azriel, and Mor were indeed waiting at the town house. I bid them good night while they ambushed Rhysand for answers about what Keir had said to provoke him.

I was still in my dress—which felt vulgar in the light of Velaris—but found myself heading into the garden, as if the moonlight and chill might cleanse my mind.

Though, if I was being honest . . . I was waiting for him. What I'd said . . .

I had been awful. He'd told me those secrets, those vulnerabilities in confidence. And I'd thrown them in his face.

Because I knew it'd hurt him. And I knew I hadn't been talking about him, not really.

Minutes passed, the night still cool enough to remind me that spring had not fully dawned, and I shivered, rubbing my arms as the moon drifted. I listened to the fountain, and the city music . . . he didn't come. I wasn't sure what I'd even tell him.

I knew he and Tamlin were different. Knew that Rhysand's protective anger tonight had been justified, that I would have had a similar reaction. I'd been bloodthirsty at the barest details of Mor's suffering, had wanted to *punish* them for it.

I had known the risks. I had known I'd be sitting in his lap, touching him, using him. I'd been using him for a while now. And maybe I should tell him I didn't . . . I didn't want or expect anything from him.

Maybe Rhysand needed to flirt with me, taunt me, as much for a distraction and sense of normalcy as I did.

And maybe I'd said what I had to him because . . . because I'd realized that I might very well be the person who wouldn't let anyone in.

And tonight, when he'd recoiled after he'd seen how he affected me . . . It had crumpled something in my chest.

I had been jealous—of Cresseida. I had been so profoundly unhappy on that barge because I'd wanted to be the one he smiled at like that.

And I knew it was wrong, but . . . I did not think Rhys would call me a whore if I wanted it—wanted . . . *him*. No matter how soon it was after Tamlin.

Neither would his friends. Not when they had been called the same and worse.

And learned to live—and love—beyond it. Despite it.

So maybe it was time to tell Rhys that. To explain that I didn't want to pretend. I didn't want to write it off as a joke, or a plan, or a distraction.

And it'd be hard, and I was scared and might be difficult to deal with, but . . . I was willing to try—with him. To try to . . . be something. Together. Whether it was purely sex, or more, or something between or beyond them, I didn't know. We'd find out.

I was healed—or healing—enough to want to try.

If he was willing to try, too.

If he didn't walk away when I voiced what I wanted: him.

Not the High Lord, not the most powerful male in Prythian's history.

Just . . . him. The person who had sent music into that cell; who had picked up that knife in Amarantha's throne room to fight for me when no one else dared, and who had kept fighting for me every day since, refusing to let me crumble and disappear into nothing.

So I waited for him in the chilled, moonlit garden.

But he didn't come.

Rhys wasn't at breakfast. Or lunch. He wasn't in the town house at all.

I'd even written him a note on the last piece of paper we'd used.

I want to talk to you.

I'd waited thirty minutes for the paper to vanish.

But it'd stayed in my palm—until I threw it in the fire.

I was pissed enough that I stalked into the streets, barely remarking that the day was balmy, sunny, that the very air now seemed laced with citrus and wildflowers and new grass. Now that we had the orb, he'd no doubt be in touch with the queens. Who would no doubt waste our time, just to remind us they were important; that they, too, had power.

Part of me wished Rhys could crush their bones the way he'd done with Keir's the night before.

I headed for Amren's apartment across the river, needing the walk to clear my head.

Winter had indeed yielded to spring. By the time I was halfway there, my overcoat was slung over my arm, and my body was slick with sweat beneath my heavy cream sweater.

I found Amren the same way I'd seen her the last time: hunched over the Book, papers strewn around her. I set the blood on the counter.

She said without looking up, "Ah. The reason why Rhys bit my head off this morning."

I leaned against the counter, frowning. "Where's he gone off to?"

"To hunt whoever attacked you yesterday."

If they had ash arrows in their arsenal . . . I tried to soothe the worry that bit deep. "Do you think it was the Summer Court?" The blood ruby still sat on the floor, still used as a paperweight against the river breeze blowing in from the open windows. Varian's necklace was now beside her bed. As if she fell asleep looking at it.

"Maybe," Amren said, dragging a finger along a line of text. She must be truly absorbed to not even bother with the blood. I debated leaving her to it. But she went on, "Regardless, it seems that our enemies have a track on Rhys's magic. Which means they're able to find him when he winnows anywhere or if he uses his powers." She at last looked up. "You lot are leaving Velaris in two days. Rhys wants you stationed at one of the Illyrian war-camps—where you'll fly down to the human lands once the queens send word."

"Why not today?"

Amren said, "Because Starfall is tomorrow night—the first we've had together in fifty years. Rhys is expected to be here, amongst his people."

"What's Starfall?"

Amren's eyes twinkled. "Outside of these borders, the rest of the world celebrates tomorrow as Nynsar—the Day of Seeds and Flowers." I almost flinched at that. I hadn't realized just how much time had passed since I'd come here. "But Starfall," Amren said, "only at the Night Court can you witness it—only within this territory is Starfall celebrated in lieu of the Nynsar revelry. The rest, and the why of it, you'll find out. It's better left as a surprise."

Well, that explained why people had seemed to already be preparing for a celebration of sorts: High Fae and faeries hustling home with arms full of vibrant wildflower bouquets and streamers and food. The streets were being swept and washed, storefronts patched up with quick, skilled hands.

I asked, "Will we come back here once we leave?"

She returned to the Book. "Not for a while."

Something in my chest started sinking. To an immortal, a while must be . . . a long, long time.

I took that as an invitation to leave, and headed for the door in the back of the loft. But Amren said, "When Rhys came back, after Amarantha, he was a ghost. He pretended he wasn't, but he was. You made him come alive again."

Words stalled, and I didn't want to think about it, not when whatever good I'd done—whatever good we'd done for *each other*—might have been wiped away by what I'd said to him.

So I said, "He is lucky to have all of you."

"No," she said softly—more gently than I'd ever heard. "*We* are lucky to have him, Feyre." I turned from the door. "I have known many High Lords," Amren continued, studying her paper. "Cruel ones, cunning ones, weak ones, powerful ones. But never one that dreamed. Not as he does."

"Dreams of what?" I breathed.

"Of peace. Of freedom. Of a world united, a world thriving. Of something better—for all of us."

"He thinks he'll be remembered as the villain in the story."

She snorted.

"But I forgot to tell him," I said quietly, opening the door, "that the villain is usually the person who locks up the maiden and throws away the key."

"Oh?"

I shrugged. "He was the one who let me out."

If you've moved elsewhere, I wrote after getting home from Amren's apartment, *you could have at least given me the keys to this house. I keep leaving the door unlocked when I go out. It's getting to be too tempting for the neighborhood burglars.*

No response. The letter didn't even vanish.

I tried after breakfast the next day—the morning of Starfall. *Cassian says you're sulking in the House of Wind. What un-High-Lord-like behavior. What of my training?*

Again, no reply.

My guilt and—and whatever else it was—started to shift. I could barely keep from shredding the paper as I wrote my third one after lunch.

Is this punishment? Or do people in your Inner Circle not get second chances if they piss you off? You're a hateful coward.

I was climbing out of the bath, the city abuzz with preparations for the festivities at sundown, when I looked at the desk where I'd left the letter.

And watched it vanish.

Nuala and Cerridwen arrived to help me dress, and I tried not to stare at the desk as I waited—waited and waited for the response.

It didn't come.

CHAPTER 44

But despite the letter, despite the mess between us, as I gaped at the mirror an hour later, I couldn't quite believe what stared back.

I had been so relieved these past few weeks to be sleeping at all that I'd forgotten to be grateful that I was keeping down my food.

The fullness had come back to my face, my body. What should have taken weeks longer as a human had been hurried along by the miracle of my immortal blood. And the dress . . .

I'd never worn anything like it, and doubted I'd ever wear anything like it again.

Crafted of tiny blue gems so pale they were almost white, it clung to every curve and hollow before draping to the floor and pooling like liquid starlight. The long sleeves were tight, capped at the wrists with cuffs of pure diamond. The neckline grazed my collarbones, the modesty of it undone by how the gown hugged areas I supposed a female might enjoy showing off. My hair had been swept off my face with two combs of silver and diamond, then left to drape down my back. And I thought, as I stood alone in my bedroom, that I might have looked like a fallen star.

Rhysand was nowhere to be found when I worked up the courage to go to the rooftop garden. The beading on the dress clinked and hissed against the floors as I walked through the nearly dark house, all the lights softened or extinguished.

In fact, the whole city had blown out its lights.

A winged, muscled figure stood atop the roof, and my heart stumbled.

But then he turned, just as the scent hit me. And something in my chest sank a bit as Cassian let out a low whistle. "I should have let Nuala and Cerridwen dress me."

I didn't know whether to smile or wince. "You look rather good despite it." He did. He was out of his fighting clothes and armor, sporting a black tunic cut to show off that warrior's body. His black hair had been brushed and smoothed, and even his wings looked cleaner.

Cassian held his arms out. His Siphons remained—a metal, fingerless gauntlet that stretched beneath the tailored sleeves of his jacket. "Ready?"

He'd kept me company the past two days, training me each morning. While he'd shown me more particulars on how to use an Illyrian blade—mostly how to disembowel someone with it—we'd chatted about everything: our equally miserable lives as children, hunting, food . . . Everything, that is, except for the subject of Rhysand.

Cassian had mentioned only once that Rhys was up at the House, and I supposed my expression had told him enough about not wanting to hear anything else. He grinned at me now. "With all those gems and beads, you might be too heavy to carry. I hope you've been practicing your winnowing in case I drop you."

"Funny." I allowed him to scoop me into his arms before we shot into the sky. Winnowing might still evade me, but I wished I had wings, I realized. Great, powerful wings so I might fly as they did; so I might see the world and all it had to offer.

Below us, every lingering light winked out. There was no moon; no music flitted through the streets. Silence—as if waiting for something.

Cassian soared through the quiet dark to where the House of Wind loomed. I could make out crowds gathered on the many balconies and patios only from the faint gleam of starlight on their hair, then the clink of their glasses and low chatter as we neared.

Cassian set me down on the crowded patio off the dining room, only a few revelers bothering to look at us. Dim bowls of faelight inside the House illuminated spreads of food and endless rows of green bottles of sparkling wine atop the tables. Cassian was gone and returned before I missed him, pressing a glass of the latter into my hand. No sign of Rhysand.

Maybe he'd avoid me the entire party.

Someone called Cassian's name from down the patio, and he clapped me on the shoulder before striding off. A tall male, his face in shadow, clasped forearms with Cassian, his white teeth gleaming in the darkness. Azriel stood with the stranger already, his wings tucked in tight to keep revelers from knocking into them. He, Cassian, and Mor had all been quiet today—understandably so. I scanned for signs of my other—

Friends.

The word sounded in my head. Was that what they were?

Amren was nowhere in sight, but I spotted a golden head at the same moment she spied me, and Mor breezed to my side. She wore a gown of pure white, little more than a slip of silk that showed off her generous curves. Indeed, a glance over her shoulder revealed Azriel staring blatantly at the back view of it, Cassian and the stranger already too deep in conversation to notice what had drawn the spymaster's attention. For a moment, the ravenous hunger on Azriel's face made my stomach tighten.

I'd remembered feeling like that. Remembered how it felt to yield to it. How I'd come close to doing that the other night.

Mor said, "It won't be long now."

"Until *what*?" No one had told me what to expect, as they hadn't wanted to ruin the *surprise* of Starfall.

"Until the fun."

I surveyed the party around us—"This isn't the fun?"

Mor lifted an eyebrow. "None of us really care about this part. Once it starts, you'll see." She took a sip of her sparkling wine. "That's some dress. You're lucky Amren is hiding in her little attic, or she'd probably steal it right off you. The vain drake."

"She won't take time off from decoding?"

"Yes, and no. Something about Starfall disturbs her, she claims. Who knows? She probably does it to be contrary."

Even as she spoke, her words were distant—her face a bit tight. I said quietly, "Are you . . . ready for tomorrow?" Tomorrow, when we'd leave Velaris to keep anyone from noticing our movements in this area. Mor, Azriel had told me tightly over breakfast that morning, would return to the Court of Nightmares. To check in on her father's . . . recovery.

Probably not the best place to discuss our plans, but Mor shrugged. "I don't have any choice but to be ready. I'll come with you to the camp, then go my way afterward."

"Cassian will be happy about that," I said. Even if Azriel was the one trying his best *not* to stare at her.

Mor snorted. "Maybe."

I lifted a brow. "So you two . . . ?"

Another shrug. "Once. Well, not even. I was seventeen, he wasn't even a year older."

When everything had happened.

But there was no darkness on her face as she sighed. "Cauldron, that was a long time ago. I visited Rhys for two weeks when he was training in the war-camp, and Cassian, Azriel, and I became friends. One night, Rhys and his mother had to go back to the Night Court, and Azriel went with them, so Cassian and I were left alone. And that night, one thing led to another, and . . . I wanted Cassian to be the one who did it. I wanted to choose." A third shrug. I wondered if Azriel had wished to be the one she chose instead. If he'd ever admitted to it to Mor—or Rhys.

If he resented that he'd been away that night, that Mor hadn't considered him.

"Rhys came back the next morning, and when he learned what had happened . . . " She laughed under her breath. "We try not to talk about the Incident. He and Cassian . . . I've never seen them fight like that. Hopefully I never will again. I know Rhys wasn't pissed about my virginity, but rather the danger that losing it had put me in. *Azriel* was even angrier about it—though he let Rhys do the walloping. They knew what my family would do for *debasing* myself with a bastard-born lesser faerie." She brushed a hand over her abdomen, as if she could feel that nail they'd spiked through it. "They were right."

"So you and Cassian," I said, wanting to move on from it, that darkness, "you were never together again after that?"

"No," Mor said, laughing quietly. "I was desperate, reckless that night. I'd picked him not just for his kindness, but also because I wanted my first time to be with one of the legendary Illyrian warriors. I wanted to lie with the greatest of Illyrian warriors, actually. And I'd taken one look at Cassian and known. After I got what I wanted, after . . . everything, I didn't like that it caused a rift with him and Rhys, or even him and Az, so . . . never again."

"And you were never with anyone after it?" Not the cold, beautiful shadowsinger who tried so hard not to watch her with longing on his face?

"I've had lovers," Mor clarified, "but . . . I get bored. And Cassian has had them, too, so don't get that unrequited-love, moony-woo-woo look. He just wants what he can't have, and it's irritated him for centuries that I walked away and never looked back."

"Oh, it drives him insane," Rhys said from behind me, and I jumped. But the High Lord was circling me. I crossed my arms as he paused and smirked. "You look like a woman again."

"You really know how to compliment females, cousin," Mor said, and patted him on the shoulder as she spotted an acquaintance and went to say hello.

I tried not to look at Rhys, who was in a black jacket, casually unbuttoned at the top so that the white shirt beneath—also unbuttoned at the neck—showed the tattoos on his chest peeking through. Tried not to look—and failed.

"Do you plan to ignore me some more?" I said coolly.

"I'm here now, aren't I? I wouldn't want you to call me a hateful coward again."

I opened my mouth, but felt all the wrong words start to come out. So I shut it and looked for Azriel or Cassian or anyone who might talk to me. Going up to a stranger was starting to sound appealing when Rhys said a bit hoarsely, "I wasn't punishing you. I just . . . I needed time."

I didn't want to have this conversation here—with so many people listening. So I gestured to the party and said, "Will you please tell me what this . . . gathering is about?"

Rhysand stepped up behind me, snorting as he said into my ear, "Look up."

Indeed, as I did so, the crowd hushed.

"No speech for your guests?" I murmured. Easy—I just wanted it to be easy between us again.

"Tonight's not about me, though my presence is appreciated and noted," he said. "Tonight's about that."

As he pointed . . .

A star vaulted across the sky, brighter and closer than any I'd seen before. The crowd and city below cheered, raising their glasses as it passed right overhead, and only when it had disappeared over the curve of the horizon did they drink deeply.

I leaned back a step into Rhys—and quickly stepped away, out of his heat and power and scent. We'd done enough damage in a similar position at the Court of Nightmares.

Another star crossed the sky, twirling and twisting over itself, as if it were reveling in its own sparkling beauty. It was chased by another, and another, until a brigade of them were unleashed from the edge of the horizon, like a thousand archers had loosed them from mighty bows.

The stars cascaded over us, filling the world with white and blue light. They were like living fireworks, and my breath lodged in my throat as the stars kept on falling and falling.

I'd never seen anything so beautiful.

And when the sky was full with them, when the stars raced and danced and flowed across the world, the music began.

Wherever they were, people began dancing, swaying and twirling, some grabbing hands and spinning, spinning, spinning to the drums, the strings, the glittering harps. Not like the grinding and thrusting of the Court of Nightmares, but—joyous, peaceful dancing. For the love of sound and movement and life.

I lingered with Rhysand at the edge of it, caught between watching the people dancing on the patio, hands upraised, and the stars streaming past, closer and closer until I swore I could have touched them if I'd leaned out.

And there were Mor and Azriel—and Cassian. The three of them dancing together, Mor's head tipped back to the sky, arms up, the starlight gleaming on the pure white of her gown. Dancing as if it might be her last time, flowing between Azriel and Cassian like the three of them were one unit, one being.

I looked behind me to find Rhys watching them, his face soft. Sad.

Separated for fifty years, and reunited—only to be cleaved apart so soon to fight again for their freedom.

Rhys caught my gaze and said, "Come. There's a better view. Quieter." He held a hand out to me.

That sorrow, that weight, lingered in his eyes. And I couldn't bear to see it—just as I couldn't bear to see my three friends dancing together as if it was the last time they'd ever do it.

⳩

Rhys led me to a small private balcony jutting from the upper level of the House of Wind. On the patios below, the music still played, the people still danced, the stars wheeling by, close and swift.

He let go as I took a seat on the balcony rail. I immediately decided against it as I beheld the drop, and backed away a healthy step.

Rhys chuckled. "If you fell, you know I'd bother to save you before you hit the ground."

"But not until I was close to death?"

"Maybe."

I leaned a hand against the rail, peering at the stars whizzing past. "As punishment for what I said to you?"

"I said some horrible things, too," he murmured.

"I didn't mean it," I blurted. "I meant it more about myself than you. And I'm sorry."

He watched the stars for a moment before he replied. "You were right, though. I stayed away because you were right. Though I'm glad to hear my absence felt like a punishment."

I snorted, but was grateful for the humor—for the way he'd always been able to amuse me. "Any news with the orb or the queens?"

"Nothing yet. We're waiting for them to deign to reply."

We were silent again, and I studied the stars. "They're not—they're not stars at all."

"No." Rhys came up beside me at the rail. "Our ancestors thought they were, but . . . They're just spirits, on a yearly migration to somewhere. Why they pick this day to appear here, no one knows."

I felt his eyes upon me, and tore my gaze from the shooting stars. Light and shadow passed over his face. The cheers and music of the city far, far below were barely audible over the crowd gathered at the House.

"There must be hundreds of them," I managed to say, dragging my stare back to the stars whizzing past.

"Thousands," he said. "They'll keep coming until dawn. Or, I hope they will. There were less and less of them the last time I witnessed Starfall."

Before Amarantha had locked him away.

"What's happening to them?" I looked in time to see him shrug. Something twanged in my chest.

"I wish I knew. But they keep coming back despite it."

"Why?"

"Why does anything cling to something? Maybe they love wherever they're going so much that it's worth it. Maybe they'll keep coming back, until there's only one star left. Maybe that one star will make the trip forever, out of the hope that someday—if it keeps coming back often enough—another star will find it again."

I frowned at the wine in my hand. "That's . . . a very sad thought."

"Indeed." Rhys rested his forearms on the balcony edge, close enough for my fingers to touch if I dared.

A calm, full silence enveloped us. Too many words—I still had too many words in me.

I don't know how much time passed, but it must have been a while, because when he spoke again, I jolted. "Every year that I was Under the Mountain and Starfall came around, Amarantha made sure that I . . . serviced her. The entire night. Starfall is no secret, even to outsiders—even the Court of Nightmares crawls out of the Hewn City to look up at the sky. So she knew . . . She knew what it meant to me."

I stopped hearing the celebrations around us. "I'm sorry." It was all I could offer.

"I got through it by reminding myself that my friends were safe; that Velaris was safe. Nothing else mattered, so long as I had that. She could use my body however she wanted. I didn't care."

"So why aren't you down there with them?" I asked, even as I tucked the horror of what had been done to him into my heart.

"They don't know—what she did to me on Starfall. I don't want it to ruin their night."

"I don't think it would. They'd be happy if you let them shoulder the burden."

"The same way you rely on others to help with your own troubles?"

We stared at each other, close enough to share breath.

And maybe all those words bottled up in me . . . Maybe I didn't need them right now.

My fingers grazed his. Warm and sturdy—patient, as if waiting to see what else I might do. Maybe it was the wine, but I stroked a finger down his.

And as I turned to him more fully, something blinding and tinkling slammed into my face.

I reeled back, crying out as I bent over, shielding my face against the light that I could still see against my shut eyes.

Rhys let out a startled laugh.

A *laugh*.

And when I realized that my eyes hadn't been singed out of their sockets, I whirled on him. "I could have been blinded!" I hissed, shoving him. He took a look at my face and burst out laughing again. Real laughter, open and delighted and lovely.

I wiped at my face, and when I pulled my hands down, I gaped. Pale green light—like drops of paint—glowed in flecks on my hand.

Splattered star-spirit. I didn't know if I should be horrified or amused. Or disgusted.

When I went to rub it off, Rhys caught my hands. "Don't," he said, still laughing. "It looks like your freckles are glowing."

My nostrils flared, and I went to shove him again, not caring if my new strength knocked him off the balcony. He could summon wings; he could deal with it.

He sidestepped me, veering toward the balcony rail, but not fast enough to avoid the careening star that collided with the side of his face.

He leaped back with a curse. I laughed, the sound rasping out of me. Not a chuckle or snort, but a cackling laugh.

And I laughed again, and again, as he lowered his hands from his eyes.

The entire left side of his face had been hit.

Like heavenly war paint, that's what it looked like. I could see why he didn't want me to wipe mine away.

Rhys was examining his hands, covered in the dust, and I stepped toward him, peering at the way it glowed and glittered.

He went still as death as I took one of his hands in my own and traced a star shape on the top of his palm, playing with the glimmer and shadows, until it looked like one of the stars that had hit us.

His fingers tightened on mine, and I looked up. He was smiling at me. And looked so un-High-Lord-like with the glowing dust on the side of his face that I grinned back.

I hadn't even realized what I'd done until his own smile faded, and his mouth parted slightly.

"Smile again," he whispered.

I hadn't smiled for him. Ever. Or laughed. Under the Mountain, I had never grinned, never chuckled. And afterward . . .

And this male before me . . . my friend . . .

For all that he had done, I had never given him either. Even when I had just . . . I had just painted something. On him. For him.

I'd—painted again.

So I smiled at him, broad and without restraint.

"You're exquisite," he breathed.

The air was too tight, too close between our bodies, between our joined hands. But I said, "You owe me two thoughts—back from when I first came here. Tell me what you're thinking."

Rhys rubbed his neck. "You want to know why I didn't speak or see you? Because I was so convinced you'd throw me out on my ass. I just . . . " He dragged a hand through his hair, and huffed a laugh. "I figured hiding was a better alternative."

"Who would have thought the High Lord of the Night Court could be afraid of an illiterate human?" I purred. He grinned, nudging me with an elbow. "That's one," I pushed. "Tell me another thought."

His eyes fell on my mouth. "I'm wishing I could take back that kiss Under the Mountain."

I sometimes forgot that kiss, when he'd done it to keep Amarantha from knowing that Tamlin and I had been in the forgotten hall, tangled up together. Rhysand's kiss had been brutal, demanding, and yet . . . "Why?"

His gaze settled on the hand I'd painted instead, as if it were easier to face. "Because I didn't make it pleasant for you, and I was jealous and pissed off, and I knew you hated me."

Dangerous territory, I warned myself.

No. Honesty, that's what it was. Honesty, and trust. I'd never had that with anyone.

Rhys looked up, meeting my gaze. And whatever was on my face—I think it might have been mirrored on his: the hunger and longing and surprise.

I swallowed hard, traced another line of stardust along the inside of his powerful wrist. I didn't think he was breathing. "Do you—do you want to dance with me?" I whispered.

He was silent for long enough that I lifted my head to scan his face. But his eyes were bright—silver-lined. "You want to dance?" he rasped, his fingers curling around mine.

I pointed with my chin toward the celebration below. "Down there—with them." Where the music beckoned, where *life* beckoned. Where he should spend the night with his friends, and where I wanted to spend it with them, too. Even with the strangers in attendance.

I did not mind stepping out of the shadows, did not mind even *being* in the shadows to begin with, so long as he was with me. My friend through so many dangers—who had fought for me when no one else would, even myself.

"Of course I'll dance with you," Rhys said, his voice still raw. "All night, if you wish."

"Even if I step on your toes?"

"Even then."

He leaned in, brushing his mouth against my heated cheek. I closed my eyes at the whisper of a kiss, at the hunger that ravaged me in its wake, that might ravage Prythian. And all around us, as if the world itself were indeed falling apart, stars rained down.

Bits of stardust glowed on his lips as he pulled away, as I stared up at him, breathless, while he smiled. The smile the world would likely never see, the smile he'd given up for the sake of his people, his lands. He said softly, "I am . . . very glad I met you, Feyre."

I blinked away the burning in my eyes. "Come on," I said, tugging on his hand. "Let's go join the dance."

CHAPTER 45

The Illyrian war-camp deep in the northern mountains was freezing. Apparently, spring was still little more than a whisper in the region.

Mor winnowed us all in, Rhysand and Cassian flanking us.

We had danced. All of us together. And I had never seen Rhys so happy, laughing with Azriel, drinking with Mor, bickering with Cassian. I'd danced with each of them, and when the night had shifted toward dawn and the music became soft and honeyed, I had let Rhys take me in his arms and dance with me, slowly, until the other guests had left, until Mor was asleep on a settee in the dining room, until the gold disc of the sun gilded Velaris.

He'd flown me back to the town house through the pink and purple and gray of the dawn, both of us silent, and had kissed my brow once before walking down the hall to his own room.

I didn't lie to myself about why I waited for thirty minutes to see if my door would open. Or to at least hear a knock. But nothing.

We were bleary-eyed but polite at the lunch table hours later, Mor and Cassian unusually quiet, talking mostly to Amren and Azriel, who had come to bid us farewell. Amren would continue working on the Book until we received the second half—if we received it; the shadowsinger was heading out to gather information and manage his spies stationed at the other courts and attempting to break into the human one. I managed to speak to them, but most of my energy went into *not* looking at Rhysand, or thinking about the feeling of his body pressed to mine as we'd danced for hours, that brush of his mouth on my skin.

I'd barely been able to fall asleep because of it.

Traitor. Even if I'd left Tamlin, I was a traitor. I'd been gone for two months—just two. In faerie terms, it was probably considered less than a day.

Tamlin had given me so much, done so many kind things for me and my family. And here I was, wanting another male, even as I hated Tamlin for what he'd done, how he'd failed me. *Traitor.*

The word continued echoing in my head as I stood at Mor's side, Rhys and Cassian a few steps ahead, and peered out at the wind-blown camp. Mor had barely given Azriel more than a brief embrace before bidding him good-bye. And for all the world, the spymaster looked like he didn't care—until he gave me a swift, warning look. I was still torn between amusement and outrage at the assumption I'd stick my nose into *his* business. Indeed.

Built near the top of a forested mountain, the Illyrian camp was all bare rock and mud, interrupted only by crude, easy-to-pack tents centered around large fire pits. Near the tree line, a dozen permanent buildings had been erected of the gray mountain stone. Smoke puffed from their chimneys against the brisk cloudy morning, occasionally swirled by the passing wings overhead.

So many winged males soaring past on their way to other camps or in training.

Indeed, on the opposite end of the camp, in a rocky area that ended in a sheer plunge off the mountain, were the sparring and training rings. Racks of weapons were left out to the elements; in the chalk-painted rings males of all ages now trained with sticks and swords and shields and spears. Fast, lethal, brutal. No complaints, no shouts of pain.

There was no warmth here, no joy. Even the houses at the other end of the camp had no personal touches, as if they were used only for shelter or storage.

And this was where Rhys, Azriel, and Cassian had grown up—where Cassian had been cast out to survive on his own. It was so cold that even bundled in my fur-lined leather, I was shivering. I couldn't imagine a child going without adequate clothing—or shelter—for a night, much less eight years.

Mor's face was pale, tight. "I hate this place," she said under her breath, the heat of it clouding the air in front of us. "It should be burned to the ground."

Cassian and Rhys were silent as a tall, broad-shouldered older male approached, flanked by five other Illyrian warriors, wings all tucked in, hands within casual reach of their weapons.

No matter that Rhys could rip their minds apart without lifting a finger.

They each wore Siphons of varying colors on the backs of their hands, the stones smaller than Azriel and Cassian's. And only one. Not like the seven apiece that my two friends wore to manage their tremendous power.

The male in front said, "Another camp inspection? Your dog," he jerked his chin at Cassian, "was here just the other week. The girls are training."

Cassian crossed his arms. "I don't see them in the ring."

"They do chores first," the male said, shoulders pushing back and wings flaring slightly, "then when they've finished, they get to train."

A low snarl slipped past Mor's mouth, and the male turned our way. He stiffened. Mor flashed him a wicked smile. "Hello, Lord Devlon."

The leader of the camp, then.

He gave her a dismissive once-over and looked back to Rhys. Cassian's warning growl rumbled in my stomach.

Rhys said at last, "Pleasant as it always is to see you, Devlon, there are two matters at hand: First, the girls, as you were clearly told by Cassian, are to train *before* chores, not after. Get them out on the pitch. Now." I shuddered at the pure command in that tone. He continued, "Second, we'll be staying here for the time being. Clear out my mother's old house. No need for a housekeeper. We'll look after ourselves."

"The house is occupied by my top warriors."

"Then un-occupy it," Rhysand said simply. "And have them clean it before they do."

The voice of the High Lord of the Night Court—who delighted in pain, and made his enemies tremble.

Devlon sniffed at me. I poured every bit of cranky exhaustion into holding his narrowed gaze. "Another like that . . . creature you bring here? I thought she was the only one of her ilk."

"Amren," Rhys drawled, "sends her regards. And as for *this* one . . . " I tried not to flinch away from meeting his stare. "She's mine," he said quietly, but viciously enough that Devlon and his warriors nearby heard. "And if any of you lay a hand on her, you lose that hand. And then you lose your head." I tried not to shiver, as Cassian and Mor showed no reaction at all. "And once Feyre is done killing you," Rhys smirked, "then I'll grind your bones to dust."

I almost laughed. But the warriors were now assessing the threat Rhys had established me as—and coming up short with answers. I gave them all a small smile, anyway, one I'd seen Amren make a hundred times. Let them wonder what I could do if provoked.

"We're heading out," Rhys said to Cassian and Mor, not even bothering to dismiss Devlon before walking toward the tree line. "We'll be back at nightfall." He gave his cousin a look. "Try to stay out of trouble, please. Devlon hates us the least of the war-lords and I don't feel like finding another camp."

Mother above, the others must be . . . unpleasant, if Devlon was the mildest of them.

Mor winked at us both. "I'll try."

Rhys just shook his head and said to Cassian, "Check on the forces, then make sure those girls are practicing like they should be. If Devlon or the others object, do what you have to."

Cassian grinned in a way that showed he'd be more than happy to do exactly that. He was the High Lord's general . . . and yet Devlon called him a dog. I didn't want to imagine what it had been like for Cassian without that title growing up.

Then finally Rhys looked at me again, his eyes shuttered. "Let's go."

"You heard from my sisters?"

A shake of the head. "No. Azriel is checking today if they received a response. You and I . . . " The wind rustled his hair as he smirked. "We're going to train."

"Where?"

He gestured to the sweeping land beyond—to the forested steppes he'd once mentioned. "Away from any potential casualties." He offered his hand as his wings flared, his body preparing for flight.

But all I heard were those two words he'd said, echoing against the steady beat of *traitor, traitor*:

She's mine.

Being in Rhys's arms again, against his body, was a test of stubbornness. For both of us. To see who'd speak about it first.

We'd been flying over the most beautiful mountains I'd ever seen—snowy and flecked with pines—heading toward rolling steppes beyond them when I said, "You're training female Illyrian warriors?"

"Trying to." Rhys gazed across the brutal landscape. "I banned wing-clipping a long, long time ago, but . . . at the more zealous camps, deep within the mountains, they do it. And when Amarantha took over, even the milder camps started doing it again. To keep their women safe, they claimed. For the past hundred years, Cassian has been trying to build an aerial fighting unit amongst the females, trying to prove that they have a place on the battlefield. So far, he's managed to train a few dedicated warriors, but the males make life so miserable that many of them left. And for the girls in training . . . " A hiss of breath. "It's a long road. But Devlon is one of the few who even lets the girls train without a tantrum."

"I'd hardly call disobeying orders 'without a tantrum.' "

"Some camps issued decrees that if a female was caught training, she was to be deemed unmarriageable. I can't fight against things like that, not without slaughtering the leaders of each camp and personally raising each and every one of their offspring."

"And yet your mother loved them—and you three wear their tattoos."

"I got the tattoos in part for my mother, in part to honor my brothers, who fought every day of their lives for the right to wear them."

"Why do you let Devlon speak to Cassian like that?"

"Because I know when to pick my fights with Devlon, and I know Cassian would be pissed if I stepped in to crush Devlon's mind like a grape when he could handle it himself."

A whisper of cold went through me. "Have you thought about doing it?"

"I did just now. But most camp-lords never would have given the three of us a shot at the Blood Rite. Devlon let a half-breed and two bastards take it—and did not deny us our victory."

Pines dusted with fresh snow blurred beneath us.

"What's the Blood Rite?"

"So many questions today." I squeezed his shoulder hard enough to hurt, and he chuckled. "You go unarmed into the mountains, magic banned, no Siphons, wings bound, with no supplies or clothes beyond what you have on you. You, and every other Illyrian male who wants to move from novice to true warrior. A few hundred head into the mountains at the start of the week—not all come out at the end."

The frost-kissed landscape rolled on forever, unyielding as the warriors who ruled over it. "Do you—kill each other?"

"Most try to. For food and clothes, for vengeance, for glory between feuding clans. Devlon allowed us to take the Rite—but also made sure Cassian, Azriel, and I were dumped in different locations."

"What happened?"

"We found each other. Killed our way across the mountains to get to each other. Turns out, a good number of Illyrian males wanted to prove they were stronger, smarter than us. Turns out they were wrong."

I dared a look at his face. For a heartbeat, I could see it: blood-splattered, savage, fighting and slaughtering to get to his friends, to protect and save them.

Rhys set us down in a clearing, the pine trees towering so high they seemed to caress the underside of the heavy, gray clouds passing on the swift wind.

"So, you're not using magic—but I am?" I said, taking a few steps from him.

"Our enemy is keyed in on my powers. You, however, remain invisible." He waved his hand. "Let's see what all your practicing has amounted to."

I didn't feel like it. I just said, "When—when did you meet Tamlin?"

I knew what Rhysand's father had done. I hadn't let myself think too much about it.

About how he'd killed Tamlin's father and brothers. And mother.

But now, after last night, after the Court of Nightmares . . . I had to know.

Rhys's face was a mask of patience. "Show me something impressive, and I'll tell you. Magic—for answers."

"I know what sort of game you're playing—" I cut myself off at the hint of a smirk. "Very well."

I held out my hand before me, palm cupped, and willed silence into my veins, my mind.

Silence and calm and weight, like being underwater.

In my hand, a butterfly of water flapped and danced.

Rhys smiled a bit, but the amusement died as he said, "Tamlin was younger than me—born when the War started. But after the War, when he'd matured, we got to know each other at various court functions. He . . . " Rhys clenched his jaw. "He seemed decent for a High Lord's son. Better than Beron's brood at the Autumn Court. Tamlin's brothers were equally as bad, though. Worse. And they knew Tamlin would take the title one day. And to a half-breed Illyrian who'd had to prove himself, defend his power, I saw what Tamlin went through . . . I befriended him. Sought him out whenever I was able to get away from the war-camps or court. Maybe it was pity, but . . . I taught him some Illyrian techniques."

"Did anyone know?"

He raised his brows—giving a pointed look to my hand.

I scowled at him and summoned songbirds of water, letting them flap around the clearing as they'd flown around my bathing room at the Summer Court.

"Cassian and Azriel knew," Rhys went on. "My family knew. And disapproved." His eyes were chips of ice. "But Tamlin's father was threatened by it. By me. And because he was weaker than both me and Tamlin, he wanted to prove to the world that he wasn't. My mother and sister were to travel to the Illyrian war-camp to see me. I was supposed to meet them halfway, but I was busy training a new unit and decided to stay."

My stomach turned over and over and over, and I wished I had something to lean against as Rhys said, "Tamlin's father, brothers, and Tamlin himself set out into the Illyrian wilderness, having heard from Tamlin—*from me*—where my mother and sister would be, that I had plans to see them. I was supposed to be there. I wasn't. And they slaughtered my mother and sister anyway."

I began shaking my head, eyes burning. I didn't know what I was trying to deny, or erase, or condemn.

"It should have been me," he said, and I understood—understood what he'd said that day I'd wept before Cassian in the training pit.

"They put their heads in boxes and sent them down the river—to the nearest camp. Tamlin's father kept their wings as trophies. I'm surprised you didn't see them pinned in the study."

I was going to vomit; I was going to fall to my knees and weep.

But Rhys looked at the menagerie of water-animals I'd crafted and said, "What else?"

Perhaps it was the cold, perhaps it was his story, but hoarfrost cracked in my veins, and the wild song of a winter wind howled in my heart. I felt it then—how easy it would be to jump between them, *join* them together, my powers.

Each one of my animals halted mid-air . . . and froze into perfectly carved bits of ice.

One by one, they dropped to the earth. And shattered.

They were one. They had come from the same, dark origin, the same eternal well of power. Once, long ago—before language was invented and the world was new.

Rhys merely continued, "When I heard, when my father heard . . . I wasn't wholly truthful to you when I told you Under the Mountain that my father killed Tamlin's father and brothers. I went with him. Helped him. We winnowed to the edge of the Spring Court that night, then went the rest of the way on foot—to the manor. I slew Tamlin's brothers on sight. I held their minds, and rendered them helpless while I cut them into pieces, then melted their brains inside their skulls. And when I got to the High Lord's bedroom—he was dead. And my father . . . my father had killed Tamlin's mother as well."

I couldn't stop shaking my head.

"My father had promised not to touch her. That we weren't the kind of males who would do that. But he lied to me, and he did it, anyway. And then he went for Tamlin's room."

I couldn't breathe—couldn't breathe as Rhys said, "I tried to stop him. He didn't listen. He was going to kill him, too. And I couldn't . . . After all the death, I was done. I didn't care that Tamlin had been there, had allowed them to kill my mother and sister, that he'd come to kill me because he didn't want to risk standing against them. I was done with death. So I stopped my father before the door. He tried to go through me. Tamlin opened the door, saw us—smelled the blood already leaking into the hallway. And I didn't even get to say a word before Tamlin killed my father in one blow.

"I felt the power shift to me, even as I saw it shift to him. And we just looked at each other, as we were both suddenly crowned High Lord—and then I ran."

He'd murdered Rhysand's family. The High Lord I'd loved—he'd murdered his friend's family, and when I'd asked how *his* family died, he'd merely told me a rival court had done it. *Rhysand* had done it, and—

"He didn't tell you any of that."

"I—I'm sorry," I breathed, my voice hoarse.

"What do you possibly have to be sorry for?"

"I didn't know. I didn't know that he'd done that—"

And Rhys thought I'd been comparing him—comparing *him* against Tamlin, as if I held him to be some paragon . . .

"Why did you stop?" he said, motioning to the ice shards on the pine-needle carpet.

The people he'd loved most—gone. Slaughtered in cold blood. Slaughtered by *Tamlin*.

The clearing exploded in flame.

The pine needles vanished, the trees groaned, and even Rhys swore as fire swept through the clearing, my heart, and devoured everything in its path.

No wonder he'd made Tamlin beg that day I'd been formally introduced to him. No wonder he'd relished every chance to taunt Tamlin. Maybe my presence here was just to—

No. I knew that wasn't true. I knew my being here had nothing to do with what was between him and Tamlin, though he no doubt enjoyed interrupting our wedding day. Saved me from that wedding day, actually.

"Feyre," Rhys said as the fire died.

But there it was—crackling inside my veins. Crackling beside veins of ice, and water.

And darkness.

Embers flared around us, floating in the air, and I sent out a breath of soothing dark, a breath of ice and water, as if it were a wind—a wind at dawn, sweeping clean the world.

The power did not belong to the High Lords. Not any longer.

It belonged to me—as I belonged *only* to me, as my future was *mine* to decide, to forge.

Once I discovered and mastered what the others had given me, I could weave them together—into something new, something of every court and none of them.

Flame hissed as it was extinguished so thoroughly that no smoke remained.

But I met Rhys's stare, his eyes a bit wide as he watched me work. I rasped, "Why didn't you tell me sooner?"

The sight of him in his Illyrian fighting gear, wings spread across the entire width of the clearing, his blade peeking over his shoulder . . .

There, in that hole in my chest—I saw the image there. At first interpretation, he'd look terrifying, vengeance and wrath incarnate. But if you came closer . . . the painting would show the beauty on his face, the wings flared not to hurt, but to carry me from danger, to shield me.

"I didn't want you to think I was trying to turn you against him," he said.

The painting—I could see it; *feel* it. I wanted to paint it.

I wanted to paint.

I didn't wait for him to stretch out his hand before I went to him. And looking up into his face I said, "I want to paint you."

He gently lifted me into his arms. "Nude would be best," he said in my ear.

CHAPTER 46

I was so cold I might never be warm again. Even during winter in the mortal realm, I'd managed to find some kernel of heat, but after nearly emptying my cache of magic that afternoon, even the roaring hearth fire couldn't thaw the chill around my bones. Did spring *ever* come to this blasted place?

"They pick these locations," Cassian said across from me as we dined on mutton stew around the table tucked into the corner of the front of the stone house. "Just to ensure the strongest among us survive."

"Horrible people," Mor grumbled into her earthenware bowl. "I don't blame Az for never wanting to come here."

"I take it training the girls went well," Rhys drawled from beside me, his thigh so close its warmth brushed my own.

Cassian drained his mug of ale. "I got one of them to confess they hadn't received a lesson in ten days. They'd all been too busy with 'chores,' apparently."

"No born fighters in this lot?"

"Three, actually," Mor said. "Three out of ten isn't bad at all. The others, I'd be happy if they just learned to defend themselves. But those three . . . They've got the instinct—the claws. It's their stupid families that want them clipped and breeding."

I rose from the table, taking my bowl to the sink tucked into the wall. The house was simple, but still bigger and in better condition than our old cottage. The front room served as kitchen, living area, and dining room, with three doors in the back: one for the cramped bathing room, one for the storage room, and one being a back door, because no true Illyrian, according to Rhys, ever made a home with only one exit.

"When do you head for the Hewn City tomorrow?" Cassian said to her—quietly enough that I knew it was probably time to head upstairs.

Mor scraped the bottom of her bowl. Apparently, Cassian had made the stew—it hadn't been half-bad. "After breakfast. Before. I don't know. Maybe in the afternoon, when they're all just waking up."

Rhys was a step behind me, bowl in hand, and motioned to leave my dirty dish in the sink. He inclined his head toward the steep, narrow stairs at the back of the house. They were wide enough to fit only one Illyrian warrior—another safety measure—and I glanced at the table one last time before disappearing upstairs.

Mor and Cassian both stared at their empty bowls of food, softly talking for once.

Every step upward, I could feel Rhys at my back, the heat of him, the ebb and flow of his power. And in this small space, the scent of him washed over me, beckoned to me.

Upstairs was dark, illuminated by the small window at the end of the hall, and the moonlight streaming in through a thin gap in the pines around us. There were only two doors up here, and Rhys pointed to one of them. "You and Mor can share tonight—just tell her to shut up if she babbles too much." I wouldn't, though. If she needed to talk, to distract herself and be ready for what was to come tomorrow, I'd listen until dawn.

He put a hand on his own doorknob, but I leaned against the wood of my door.

It'd be so easy to take the three steps to cross the hall.

To run my hands over that chest, trace those beautiful lips with my own.

I swallowed as he turned to me.

I didn't want to think what it meant, what I was doing. What this was—whatever it was—between us.

Because things between us had never been normal, not from the very first moment we'd met on Calanmai. I'd been unable to easily walk away from him then, when I'd thought he was deadly, dangerous. But now . . .

Traitor, traitor, traitor—

He opened his mouth, but I had already slipped inside my room and shut the door.

Freezing rain trickled through the pine boughs as I stalked through the mists in my Illyrian fighting leathers, armed with a bow, quiver, and knives, shivering like a wet dog.

Rhys was a few hundred feet behind, carrying our packs. We'd flown deep into the forest steppes, far enough that we'd have to spend the night out here. Far enough that no one and nothing might see another "glorious explosion of flame and temper," as Rhys had put it. Azriel hadn't brought word from my sisters of the queens' status, so we had time to spare. Though Rhys certainly hadn't looked like it when he informed me that morning. But at least we wouldn't have to camp out here. Rhys had promised there was some sort of wayfarer's inn nearby.

I turned toward where Rhys trailed behind me, spotting his massive wings first. Mor had set off before I'd even been awake, and Cassian had been pissy and on edge during breakfast . . . So much so that I'd been glad to leave as soon as I'd finished my porridge. And felt slightly bad for the Illyrians who had to deal with him that day.

Rhys paused once he caught up, and even with the trees and rain between us, I could see his brows lift in silent question of why I'd paused. We hadn't spoken of Starfall or the Court of Nightmares—and last night, as I twisted and turned in the tiny bed, I'd decided: fun and distraction. It didn't need to be complicated. Keeping things purely physical . . . well, it didn't feel like as much of a betrayal.

I lifted a hand, signaling Rhys to stay where he was. After yesterday, I didn't want him too close, lest I burn him. Or worse. He sketched a dramatic bow, and I rolled my eyes as I stalked to the stream ahead, contemplating where I might indeed try to play with Beron's fire. *My* fire.

Every step away, I could feel Rhys's stare devouring me. Or maybe that was through the bond, brushing against my mental shields—flashes of hunger so insatiable that it was an effort to focus on the task ahead and not on the feeling of what his hands had been like, stroking my thighs, pushing me against him.

I could have sworn I felt a trickle of amusement on the other side of my mental shield, too. I hissed and made a vulgar gesture over my shoulder, even as I let my shield drop, just a bit.

That amusement turned into full delight—and then a lick of pleasure that went straight down my spine. Lower.

My face heated, and a twig cracked under my boot, as loud as lightning. I gritted my teeth. The ground sloped toward a gray, gushing stream, fast enough that it had to be fed by the towering snow-blasted mountains in the distance.

Good—this spot was good. An extra supply of water to drown any flames that might escape, plenty of open space. The wind blew away from me, tugging my scent southward, deeper into the forest as I opened my mouth to tell Rhys to stay back.

With that wind, and the roaring stream, it was no surprise that I didn't hear them until they had surrounded me.

"Feyre."

I whirled, arrow nocked and aimed at the source of the voice—

Four Spring Court sentinels stalked from the trees behind me like wraiths, armed to the teeth and wide-eyed. Two, I knew: Bron and Hart.

And between them stood Lucien.

CHAPTER 47

If I wanted to escape, I could either face the stream or face them. But Lucien . . .

His red hair was tied back, and there wasn't a hint of finery on him: just armored leather, swords, knives . . . His metal eye roamed over me, his golden skin pale. "We've been hunting for you for over two months," he breathed, now scanning the woods, the stream, the sky.

Rhys. Cauldron save me. Rhys was too far back, and—

"How did you find me?" My steady, cold voice wasn't one I recognized. But—*hunting* for me. As if I were indeed prey.

If Tamlin was here . . . My blood went icier than the freezing rain now sluicing down my face, into my clothes.

"Someone tipped us off you'd been out here, but it was luck that we caught your scent on the wind, and—" Lucien took a step toward me.

I stepped back. Only three feet between me and the stream.

Lucien's eye widened slightly. "We need to get out of here. Tamlin's been—he hasn't been himself. I'll take you right to—"

"No," I breathed.

The word rasped through the rain, the stream, the pine forest.

The four sentinels glanced between each other, then to the arrow I kept aimed.

Lucien took me in again.

And I could see what he was now gleaning: the Illyrian fighting leathers. The color and fullness that had returned to my face, my body.

And the silent steel of my eyes.

"Feyre," he said, holding out a hand. "Let's go home."

I didn't move. "That stopped being my home the day you let him lock me up inside of it."

Lucien's mouth tightened. "It was a mistake. We *all* made mistakes. He's sorry—more sorry than you realize. So am I." He stepped toward me, and I backed up another few inches.

Not much space remained between me and the gushing waters below.

Cassian's training crashed into me, as if all the lessons he'd been drilling into me each morning were a net that caught me as I free-fell into my rising panic. Once Lucien touched me, he'd winnow us out. Not far—he wasn't that powerful—but he was fast. He'd jump miles away, then farther, and farther, until Rhys couldn't reach me. He *knew* Rhys was here.

"Feyre," Lucien pleaded, and dared another step, his hand outraised.

My arrow angled toward him, my bowstring groaning.

I'd never realized that while Lucien had been trained as a warrior, Cassian, Azriel, Mor, and Rhys were Warriors. Cassian could wipe Lucien off the face of the earth in a single blow.

"Put the arrow down," Lucien murmured, like he was soothing a wild animal.

Behind him, the four sentinels closed in. Herding me.

The High Lord's pet and possession.

"Don't," I breathed. "Touch. Me."

"You don't understand the mess we're in, Feyre. We—*I* need you home. Now."

I didn't want to hear it. Peering at the stream below, I calculated my odds.

The look cost me. Lucien lunged, hand out. One touch, that was all it'd take—

I was not the High Lord's pet any longer.

And maybe the world should learn that I did indeed have fangs.

Lucien's finger grazed the sleeve of my leather jacket.

And I became smoke and ash and night.

The world stilled and bent, and there was Lucien, lunging so slowly for what was now blank space as I stepped around him, as I hurtled for the trees behind the sentinels.

I stopped, and time resumed its natural flow. Lucien staggered, catching himself before he went over the cliff—and whirled, eye wide to discover me now standing behind his sentinels. Bron and Hart flinched and backed away. From me.

And from Rhysand at my side.

Lucien froze. I made my face a mirror of ice; the unfeeling twin to the cruel amusement on Rhysand's features as he picked at a fleck of lint on his dark tunic.

Dark, elegant clothes—no wings, no fighting leathers.

The unruffled, fine clothes . . . Another weapon. To hide just how skilled and powerful he was; to hide where he came from and what he loved. A weapon worth the cost of the magic he'd used to hide it—even if it put us at risk of being tracked.

"Little Lucien," Rhys purred. "Didn't the Lady of the Autumn Court ever tell you that when a woman says no, she means it?"

"Prick," Lucien snarled, storming past his sentinels, but not daring to touch his weapons. "You filthy, whoring prick."

I loosed a growl.

Lucien's eyes sliced to me and he said with quiet horror, "What have you done, Feyre?"

"Don't come looking for me again," I said with equal softness.

"He'll never stop looking for you; never stop waiting for you to come home."

The words hit me in the gut—like they were meant to. It must have shown in my face because Lucien pressed, "What did he do to you? Did he take your mind and—"

"Enough," Rhys said, angling his head with that casual grace. "Feyre and I are busy. Go back to your lands before I send your heads as a reminder to my old friend about what happens when Spring Court flunkies set foot in my territory."

The freezing rain slid down the neck of my clothes, down my back. Lucien's face was deathly pale. "You made your point, Feyre—now come home."

"I'm not a child playing games," I said through my teeth. That's how they'd seen me: in need of coddling, explaining, defending . . .

"Careful, Lucien," Rhysand drawled. "Or Feyre darling will send you back in pieces, too."

"We are not your enemies, Feyre," Lucien pleaded. "Things got bad, Ianthe got out of hand, but it doesn't mean you give up—"

"You gave up," I breathed.

I felt even Rhys go still.

"*You* gave up on me," I said a bit more loudly. "You were my friend. And you picked *him*—picked obeying him, even when you saw what his orders and his rules did to me. Even when you saw me wasting away *day by day*."

"You have *no idea* how volatile those first few months were," Lucien snapped. "We *needed* to present a unified, obedient front, and I was supposed to be the example to which all others in our court were held."

"You *saw* what was happening to me. But you were too afraid of him to truly do anything about it."

It was fear. Lucien had pushed Tamlin, but to a point. He'd always yielded at the end.

"I begged you," I said, the words sharp and breathless. "I begged you so many times to help me, to get me out of the house, even for an hour. And you left me alone, or shoved me into a room with Ianthe, or told me to stick it out."

Lucien said too quietly, "And I suppose the Night Court is so much better?"

I remembered—remembered what I was supposed to know, to have experienced. What Lucien and the others could never know, not even if it meant forfeiting my own life.

And I would. To keep Velaris safe, to keep Mor and Amren and Cassian and Azriel and . . . *Rhys* safe.

I said to Lucien, low and quiet and as vicious as the talons that formed at the tips of my fingers, as vicious as the wondrous weight between my shoulder blades, "When you spend so long trapped in darkness, Lucien, you find that the darkness begins to stare back."

A pulse of surprise, of wicked delight against my mental shields, at the dark, membranous wings I knew were now poking over my shoulders. Every icy kiss of rain sent jolts of cold through me. Sensitive—so sensitive, these Illryian wings.

Lucien backed up a step. "What did you do to yourself?"

I gave him a little smile. "The human girl you knew died Under the Mountain. I have no interest in spending immortality as a High Lord's pet."

Lucien started shaking his head. "Feyre—"

"Tell Tamlin," I said, choking on his name, on the thought of what he'd done to Rhys, to his family, "if he sends anyone else into these lands, I will hunt each and every one of you down. And I will demonstrate exactly what the darkness taught me."

There was something like genuine pain on his face.

I didn't care. I just watched him, unyielding and cold and dark. The creature I might one day have become if I had stayed at the Spring Court, if I had remained broken for decades, centuries . . . until I learned to quietly direct those shards of pain outward, learned to savor the pain of others.

Lucien nodded to his sentinels. Bron and Hart, wide-eyed and shaking, vanished with the other two.

Lucien lingered for a moment, nothing but air and rain between us. He said softly to Rhysand, "You're dead. You, and your entire cursed court."

Then he was gone. I stared at the empty space where he'd been, waiting, waiting, not letting that expression off my face until a warm, strong finger traced a line down the edge of my right wing.

It felt like—like having my ear breathed into.

I shuddered, arching as a gasp came out of me.

And then Rhys was in front of me, scanning my face, the wings behind me. "How?"

"Shape-shifting," I managed to say, watching the rain slide down his golden-tan face. And it was distracting enough that the talons, the wings, the rippling darkness faded, and I was left light and cold in my own skin.

Shape-shifting . . . at the sight of part of the history, the male I had not really let myself remember. Shape-shifting—a gift from Tamlin that I had not wanted, or needed . . . until now.

Rhys's eyes softened. "That was a very convincing performance."

"I gave him what he wanted to see," I murmured. "We should find another spot."

He nodded, and his tunic and pants vanished, replaced by those familiar fighting leathers, the wings, the sword. My warrior—

Not *my* anything.

"Are you all right?" he said as he scooped me into his arms to fly us to another location.

I nestled into his warmth, savoring it. "The fact that it was so easy, that I felt so little, upsets me more than the encounter itself."

Perhaps that had been my problem all along. Why I hadn't dared take that final step at Starfall. I was guilty that I *didn't* feel awful, not truly. Not for wanting him.

A few mighty flaps had us soaring up through the trees and sailing low over the forest, rain slicing into my face.

"I knew things were bad," Rhysand said with quiet rage, barely audible over the freezing bite of the wind and rain, "but I thought Lucien, at least, would have stepped in."

"I thought so, too," I said, my voice smaller than I intended.

He squeezed me gently, and I blinked at him through the rain. For once, his eyes were on me, not the landscape below. "You look good with wings," he said, and kissed my brow.

Even the rain stopped feeling so cold.

CHAPTER 48

Apparently, the nearby "inn" was little more than a raucous tavern with a few rooms for rent—usually by the hour. And, as it was, there were no vacancies. Save for a tiny, *tiny* room in what had once been part of the attic.

Rhys didn't want anyone knowing who, exactly, was amongst the High Fae, faeries, Illyrians, and whoever else was packed in the inn below. Even I barely recognized him as he—without magic, without anything but adjusting his posture—muted that sense of otherworldly power until he was nothing but a common, very good-looking Illyrian warrior, pissy about having to take the last available room, so high up that there was only a narrow staircase leading to it: no hall, no other rooms. If I needed to use the bathing room, I'd have to venture to the level below, which . . . given the smells and sounds of the half dozen rooms on that level, I made a point to use quickly on our way up and then vow not to visit again until morning.

A day of playing with water and fire and ice and darkness in the freezing rain had wrecked me so thoroughly that no one looked my way, not even the drunkest and loneliest of patrons in the town's tavern. The small town was barely that: a collection of an inn, an outfitter's store, supply store, and a brothel. All geared toward the hunters, warriors, and travelers passing through this part of the forest either on their way to the Illyrian lands or out of them. Or just for the faeries who dwelled here, solitary and glad to be that way. Too small and too remote for Amarantha or her cronies to have ever bothered with.

Honestly, I didn't care where we were, so long as it was dry and warm. Rhys opened the door to our attic room and stood aside to let me pass.

Well, at least it was one of those things.

The ceiling was so slanted that to get to the other side of the bed, I'd have to crawl across the mattress; the room so cramped it was nearly impossible to walk around the bed to the tiny armoire shoved against the other wall. I could sit on the bed and open the armoire easily.

The bed.

"I asked for two," Rhys said, hands already up.

His breath clouded in front of him. Not even a fireplace. And not enough space to even demand he sleep on the floor. I didn't trust my mastery over flame to attempt warming the room. I'd likely burn this whole filthy place to the ground.

"If you can't risk using magic, then we'll have to warm each other," I said, and instantly regretted it. "Body heat," I clarified. And, just to wipe that look off his face I added, "My sisters and I had to share a bed—I'm used to it."

"I'll try to keep my hands to myself."

My mouth went a bit dry. "I'm hungry."

He stopped smiling at that. "I'll go down and get us food while you change." I lifted a brow. He said, "Remarkable as my own abilities are to blend in, my face is recognizable. I'd rather not be down there long enough to be noticed." Indeed, he fished a cloak from his pack and slid it on, the panels fitting over his wings—which he wouldn't risk vanishing again. He'd used power earlier in the day—small enough, he said, that it might not be noticed, but we wouldn't be returning to that part of the forest anytime soon.

He tugged on the hood, and I savored the shadows and menace and wings.

Death on swift wings. That's what I'd call the painting.

He said softly, "I love it when you look at me like that."

The purr in his voice heated my blood. "Like what?"

"Like my power isn't something to run from. Like you see me."

And to a male who had grown up knowing he was the most powerful High Lord in Prythian's history, that he could shred minds if he wasn't careful, that he was alone—alone in his power, in his burden, but that fear was his mightiest weapon against the threats to his people . . . I'd hit home when we'd fought after the Court of Nightmares.

"I was afraid of you at first."

His white teeth flashed in the shadows of his hood. "No, you weren't. Nervous, maybe, but never afraid. I've felt the genuine terror of enough people to know the difference. Maybe that's why I couldn't keep away."

When? Before I could ask, he walked downstairs, shutting the door behind him.

My half-frozen clothes were a misery to peel off as they clung to my rain-swollen skin, and I knocked into the slanted ceiling, nearby walls, and slammed my knee into the brass bedpost as I changed. The room was so cold I had to get undressed in segments: replacing a freezing shirt for a dry one, pants for fleece-lined leggings, sodden socks for thick, hand-knit lovelies that went up to my calves. When I'd tucked myself into an oversized sweater that smelled faintly of Rhys, I sat cross-legged on the bed and waited.

The bed wasn't small, but certainly not large enough for me to pretend I wouldn't be sleeping next to him. Especially with the wings.

The rain tinkled on the roof mere inches away, a steady beat to the thoughts that now pulsed in my head.

The Cauldron knew what Lucien was reporting to Tamlin, likely at this very moment, if not hours ago.

I'd sent that note to Tamlin . . . and he'd chosen to ignore it. Just as he'd ignored or rejected nearly all of my requests, acted out of his deluded sense of what *he* believed was right for my well-being and safety. And Lucien had been prepared to take me against my will.

Fae males were territorial, dominant, arrogant—but the ones in the Spring Court . . . something had festered in their training. Because I knew—deep in my bones—that Cassian might push and test my limits, but the moment I said no, he'd back off. And I knew that if . . . that if I had been wasting away and Rhys had done nothing to stop it, Cassian or Azriel would have pulled me out. They would have taken me somewhere—wherever I needed to be—and dealt with Rhys later.

But Rhys . . . Rhys would never have *not* seen what was happening to me; would never have been so misguided and arrogant and self-absorbed. He'd known what Ianthe was from the moment he met her. And he'd understood what it was like to be a prisoner, and helpless, and to struggle—every day—with the horrors of both.

I had loved the High Lord who had shown me the comforts and wonders of Prythian; I had loved the High Lord who let me have the time and food and safety to paint. Maybe a small part of me might always care for him, but . . . Amarantha had broken us both. Or broken me so that who he was and what I now was no longer fit.

And I could let that go. I could accept that. Maybe it would be hard for a while, but . . . maybe it'd get better.

Rhys's feet were near-silent, given away only by the slight groan of the stairs. I rose to open the door before he could knock, and found him standing there, tray in his hands. Two stacks of covered dishes sat on it, along with two glasses and a bottle of wine, and—

"Tell me that's stew I smell." I breathed in, stepping aside and shutting the door while he set the tray on the bed. Right—not even room for a table up here.

"Rabbit stew, if the cook's to be believed."

"I could have lived without hearing that," I said, and Rhys grinned. That smile tugged on something low in my gut, and I looked away, sitting down beside the food, careful not to jostle the tray. I opened the lid of the top dishes: two bowls of stew. "What's the other one beneath?"

"Meat pie. I didn't dare ask what kind of meat." I shot him a glare, but he was already edging around the bed to the armoire, his pack in hand. "Go ahead and eat," he said, "I'm changing first."

Indeed, he was soaked—and had to be freezing and sore.

"You should have changed before going downstairs." I picked up the spoon and swirled the stew, sighing at the warm tendrils of steam that rose to kiss my chilled face.

The rasp and slurp of wet clothes being shucked off filled the room. I tried not to think about that bare, golden chest, the tattoos. The hard muscles. "You were the one training all day. Getting you a hot meal was the least I could do."

I took a sip. Bland, but edible and, most importantly, *hot*. I ate in silence, listening to the rustle of his clothes being donned, trying to think of ice baths, of infected wounds, of toe fungus—anything but his naked body, so close . . . and the bed I was sitting on. I poured myself a glass of wine—then filled his.

At last, Rhys squeezed between the bed and jutting corner of the wall, his wings tucked in close. He wore loose, thin pants, and a tight-fitting shirt of what looked to be softest cotton. "How do you get it over the wings?" I asked while he dug into his own stew.

"The back is made of slats that close with hidden buttons . . . But in normal circumstances, I just use magic to seal it shut."

"It seems like you have a great deal of magic constantly in use at once."

A shrug. "It helps me work off the strain of my power. The magic needs release—draining—or else it'll build up and drive me insane.

That's why we call the Illyrian stones Siphons—they help them channel the power, empty it when necessary."

"Actually insane?" I set aside the empty stew bowl and removed the lid from the meat pie.

"Actually insane. Or so I was warned. I can feel it, though—the pull of it, if I go too long without releasing it."

"That's horrible."

Another shrug. "Everything has its cost, Feyre. If the price of being strong enough to shield my people is that I have to struggle with that same power, then I don't mind. Amren taught me enough about controlling it. Enough that I owe a great deal to her. Including the current shield around my city while we're here."

Everyone around him had some use, some mighty skill. And yet there I was . . . nothing more than a strange hybrid. More trouble than I was worth.

"You're not," he said.

"Don't read my thoughts."

"I can't help what you sometimes shout down the bond. And besides, everything is usually written on your face, if you know where to look. Which made your performance today so much more impressive."

He set aside his stew just as I finished devouring my meat pie, and I slid back on the bed to the pillows, cupping my glass of wine between my chilled hands. I watched him eat while I drank. "Did you think I would go with him?"

He paused mid-bite, then lowered his fork. "I heard every word between you. I knew you could take care of yourself, and yet . . . " He went back to his pie, swallowing a bite before continuing. "And yet I found myself deciding that if you took his hand, I would find a way to live with it. It would be your choice."

I sipped from my wine. "And if he had grabbed me?"

There was nothing but uncompromising will in his eyes. "Then I would have torn apart the world to get you back."

A shiver went down my spine, and I couldn't look away from him. "I would have fired at him," I breathed, "if he had tried to hurt you."

I hadn't even admitted that to myself.

His eyes flickered. "I know."

He finished eating, placed the empty tray in the corner, and faced me on the bed, refilling my glass before tending to his. He was so tall he had to stoop to keep from hitting his head on the slanted ceiling.

"One thought in exchange for another," I said. "No training involved, please."

A chuckle rasped out of him, and he drained his glass, setting it on the tray.

He watched me take a long drink from mine. "I'm thinking," he said, following the flick of my tongue over my bottom lip, "that I look at you and feel like I'm dying. Like I can't breathe. I'm thinking that I want you so badly I can't concentrate half the time I'm around you, and this room is too small for me to properly bed you. Especially with the wings."

My heart stumbled a beat. I didn't know what to do with my arms, my legs, my face. I gulped down the rest of my wine and discarded the glass beside the bed, steeling my spine as I said, "I'm thinking that I can't stop thinking about you. And that it's been that way for a long while. Even before I left the Spring Court. And maybe that makes me a traitorous, lying piece of trash, but—"

"It doesn't," he said, his face solemn.

But it did. I'd wanted to see Rhysand during those weeks between visits. And hadn't cared when Tamlin stopped visiting my bedroom. Tamlin had given up on me, but I'd also given up on him. And I was a lying piece of trash for it.

I murmured, "We should go to sleep."

The patter of the rain was the only sound for a long moment before he said, "All right."

I crawled over the bed to the side tucked almost against the slanted ceiling and shimmied beneath the quilt. Cool, crisp sheets wrapped around me like an icy hand. But my shiver was from something else entirely as the mattress shifted, the blanket moved, and then the two candles beside the bed went out.

Darkness hit me at the same moment the warmth from his body did. It was an effort not to nudge toward it. Neither one of us moved, though.

I stared into the dark, listening to that icy rain, trying to steal the warmth from him.

"You're shivering so hard the bed is shaking," he said.

"My hair is wet," I said. It wasn't a lie.

Rhys was silent, then the mattress groaned, sinking directly behind me as his warmth poured over me. "No expectations," he said. "Just body heat." I scowled at the laughter in his voice.

But his broad hands slid under and over me: one flattening against my stomach and tugging me against the hard warmth of him, the other sliding under my ribs and arms to band around my chest, pressing his front into me. He tangled his legs with mine, and then a heavier, warmer darkness settled over us, smelling of citrus and the sea.

I lifted a hand toward that darkness, and met with a soft, silky material—his wing, cocooning and warming me. I traced my finger along it, and he shuddered, his arms tightening around me.

"Your finger . . . is very cold," he gritted out, the words hot on my neck.

I tried not to smile, even as I tilted my neck a bit more, hoping the heat of his breath might caress it again. I dragged my finger along his wing, the nail scraping gently against the smooth surface. Rhys tensed, his hand splaying across my stomach.

"You cruel, wicked thing," he purred, his nose grazing the exposed bit of neck I'd arched beneath him. "Didn't anyone ever teach you manners?"

"I never knew Illyrians were such sensitive babies," I said, sliding another finger down the inside of his wing.

Something hard pushed against my behind. Heat flooded me, and

I went taut and loose all at once. I stroked his wing again, two fingers now, and he twitched against my backside in time with the caress.

The fingers he'd spread over my stomach began to make idle, lazy strokes. He swirled one around my navel, and I inched imperceptibly closer, grinding up against him, arching a bit more to give that other hand access to my breasts.

"Greedy," he murmured, his lips hovering over my neck. "First you terrorize me with your cold hands, now you want . . . what is it you want, Feyre?"

More, more, more, I almost begged him as his fingers traveled down the slope of my breasts, while his other hand continued its idle stroking along my stomach, my abdomen, slowly—so slowly—heading toward the low band of my pants and the building ache beneath it.

Rhysand's teeth scraped against my neck in a lazy caress. "What is it you want, Feyre?" He nipped at my earlobe.

I cried out just a little, arching fully against him, as if I could get that hand to slip exactly to where I wanted it. I knew what he wanted me to say. I wouldn't give him the satisfaction of it. Not yet.

So I said, "I want a distraction." It was breathless. "I want—fun."

His body again tensed behind mine.

And I wondered if he somehow didn't see it for the lie it was; if he thought . . . if he thought that was all I indeed wanted.

But his hands resumed their roaming. "Then allow me the pleasure of distracting you."

He slipped a hand beneath the top of my sweater, diving clean under my shirt. Skin to skin, the calluses of his hands made me groan as they scraped the top of my breast and circled around my peaked nipple. "I love these," he breathed onto my neck, his hand sliding to my other breast. "You have no idea how much I love these."

I groaned as he caressed a knuckle against my nipple, and I bowed into the touch, silently begging him. He was hard as granite behind me, and I ground against him, eliciting a soft, wicked hiss from him. "Stop that," he snarled onto my skin. "You'll ruin *my* fun."

I would do no such thing. I began twisting, reaching for him, needing to just *feel* him, but he clicked his tongue and pushed himself harder against me, until there was no room for my hand to even slide in.

"I want to touch you first," he said, his voice so guttural I barely recognized it. "Just—let me touch you." He palmed my breast for emphasis.

It was enough of a broken plea that I paused, yielding as his other hand again trailed lazy lines on my stomach.

I can't breathe when I look at you.

Let me touch you.

Because I was jealous, and pissed off . . .

She's mine.

I shut out the thoughts, the bits and pieces he'd given me.

Rhys slid his finger along the band of my pants again, a cat playing with its dinner.

Again.

Again.

"Please," I managed to say.

He smiled against my neck. "There are those missing manners." His hand at last trailed beneath my pants. The first brush of him against me dragged a groan from deep in my throat.

He snarled in satisfaction at the wetness he found waiting for him, and his thumb circled that spot at the apex of my thighs, teasing, brushing up against it, but never quite—

His other hand gently squeezed my breast at the same moment his thumb pushed down exactly where I wanted. I bucked my hips, my head fully back against his shoulder now, panting as his thumb flicked—

I cried out, and he laughed, low and soft. "Like that?"

A moan was my only reply. *More more more.*

His fingers slid down, slow and brazen, straight through the core of me, and every point in my body, my mind, my soul, narrowed to the feeling of his fingers poised there like he had all the time in the world.

Bastard. "*Please*," I said again, and ground my ass against him for emphasis.

He hissed at the contact and slid a finger inside me. He swore. "Feyre—"

But I'd already started to move on him, and he swore again in a long exhale. His lips pressed into my neck, kissing up, up toward my ear.

I let out a moan so loud it drowned out the rain as he slid in a second finger, filling me so much I couldn't think around it, couldn't breathe. "That's it," he murmured, his lips tracing my ear.

I was sick of my neck and ear getting such attention. I twisted as much as I could, and found him staring at me, at the hand down the front of my pants, watching me move on him.

He was still staring at me when I captured his mouth with my own, biting on his lower lip.

Rhys groaned, plunging his fingers in deeper. Harder.

I didn't care—I didn't care one bit about what I was and who I was and where I'd been as I yielded fully to him, opening my mouth. His tongue swept in, moving in a way that I knew exactly what he'd do if he got between my legs.

His fingers plunged in and out, slow and hard, and my very existence narrowed to the feel of them, to the tightness in me ratcheting up with every deep stroke, every echoing thrust of his tongue in my mouth.

"You have no idea how much I—" He cut himself off, and groaned again. "*Feyre*."

The sound of my name on his lips was my undoing. Release barreled down my spine, and I cried out, only to have his lips cover mine, as if he could devour the sound. His tongue flicked the roof of my mouth while I shuddered around him, clenching tight. He swore again, breathing hard, fingers stroking me through the last throes of it, until I was limp and trembling in his arms.

I couldn't breathe hard enough, fast enough, as Rhys withdrew his fingers, pulling back so I could meet his stare. He said, "I wanted to do that when I felt how drenched you were at the Court of Nightmares. I wanted to have you right there in the middle of everyone. But mostly I just wanted to do this." His eyes held mine as he brought those fingers to his mouth and sucked on them.

On the taste of me.

I was going to eat him alive. I slid a hand up to his chest to pin him down, but he gripped my wrist. "When you lick me," he said roughly, "I want to be alone—far away from everyone. Because when you lick me, Feyre," he said, pressing nipping kisses to my jaw, my neck, "I'm going to let myself roar loud enough to bring down a mountain."

I was instantly liquid again, and he laughed under his breath. "And when I lick *you*," he said, sliding his arms around me and tucking me in tight to him, "I want you splayed out on a table like my own personal feast."

I whimpered.

"I've had a long, long time to think about how and where I want you," Rhys said onto the skin of my neck, his fingers sliding under the band of my pants, but stopping just beneath. Their home for the evening. "I have no intention of doing it all in one night. Or in a room where I can't even fuck you against the wall."

I shuddered. He remained long and hard against me. I had to feel him, had to get that considerable length inside of me—

"Sleep," he said. He might as well have commanded me to breathe underwater.

But he began stroking my body again—not to arouse, but to soothe—long, luxurious strokes down my stomach, my sides.

Sleep found me faster than I'd thought.

And maybe it was the wine, or the aftermath of the pleasure he'd wrung from me, but I didn't have a single nightmare.

CHAPTER 49

I awoke, warm and rested and calm.

Safe.

Sunlight streamed through the filthy window, illuminating the reds and golds in the wall of wing before me—where it had been all night, shielding me from the cold.

Rhysand's arms were banded around me, his breathing deep and even. And I knew it was just as rare for him to sleep that soundly, peacefully.

What we'd done last night . . .

Carefully, I twisted to face him, his arms tightening slightly, as if to keep me from vanishing with the morning mist.

His eyes were open when I nestled my head against his arm. Within the shelter of his wing, we watched each other.

And I realized I might very well be content to do exactly that forever.

I said quietly, "Why did you make that bargain with me? Why demand a week from me every month?"

His violet eyes shuttered.

And I didn't dare admit what I expected, but it was not, "Because I wanted to make a statement to Amarantha; because I wanted to piss off Tamlin, and I needed to keep you alive in a way that wouldn't be seen as merciful."

"Oh."

His mouth tightened. "You know—you know there is nothing I wouldn't do for my people, for my family."

And I'd been a pawn in that game.

His wing folded back, and I blinked at the watery light. "Bath or no bath?" he said.

I cringed at the memory of the grimy, reeking bathing room a level below. Using it to see to my needs would be bad enough. "I'd rather bathe in a stream," I said, pushing past the sinking in my gut.

Rhys let out a low laugh and rolled out of bed. "Then let's get out of here."

For a heartbeat, I wondered if I'd dreamed up everything that had happened the night before. From the slight, pleasant soreness between my legs, I knew I hadn't, but . . .

Maybe it'd be easier to pretend that nothing had happened.

The alternative might be more than I could endure.

We flew for most of the day, far and wide, close to where the forested steppes rose up to meet the Illyrian Mountains. We didn't speak of the night before—we barely spoke at all.

Another clearing. Another day of playing with my power. Summoning wings, winnowing, fire and ice and water and—now wind. The wind and breezes that rippled across the sweeping valleys and wheat fields of the Day Court, then whipped up the snow capping their highest peaks.

I could feel the words rising in him as the hours passed. I'd catch him watching me whenever I paused for a break—catch him opening up his mouth . . . and then shutting it.

It rained at one point, and then turned colder and colder with the cloud cover. We had yet to stay in the woods past dark, and I wondered what sort of creatures might prowl through them.

The sun was indeed sinking by the time Rhys gathered me in his arms and took to the skies.

There was only the wind, and his warmth, and the boom of his powerful wings.

I ventured, "What is it?"

His attention remained on the dark pines sweeping past. "There is one more story I need to tell you."

I waited. He didn't continue.

I put my hand against his cheek, the first intimate touch we'd had all day. His skin was chilled, his eyes bleak as they slid to me. "I don't walk away—not from you," I swore quietly.

His gaze softened. "Feyre—"

Rhys roared in pain, arching against me.

I felt the impact—felt blinding pain through the bond that ripped through my own mental shields, felt the shudder of the dozen places the arrows struck him as they shot from bows hidden beneath the forest canopy.

And then we were falling.

Rhys gripped me, and his magic twisted around us in a dark wind, readying to winnow us out—and failed.

Failed, because those were ash arrows through him. Through his wings. They'd tracked us—yesterday, the little magic he'd used with Lucien, they'd somehow *tracked* it and found us even so far away—

More arrows—

Rhys flung out his power. Too late.

Arrows shredded his wings. Struck his legs.

And I think I was screaming. Not for fear as we plummeted, but for him—for the blood and the greenish sheen on those arrows. Not just ash, but poison—

A dark wind—his power—slammed into me, and then I was being

thrown far and wide as he sent me tumbling beyond the arrows' range, tumbling through the air—

Rhys's roar of wrath shook the forest, the mountains beyond. Birds rose up in waves, taking to the skies, fleeing that bellow.

I slammed into the dense canopy, my body barking in agony as I shattered through wood and pine and leaf. Down and down—

Focus focus focus

I flung out a wave of that hard air that had once shielded me from Tamlin's temper. Threw it out beneath me like a net.

I collided with an invisible wall so solid I thought my right arm might snap.

But—I stopped falling through the branches.

Thirty feet below, the ground was nearly impossible to see in the growing darkness.

I did not trust that shield to hold my weight for long.

I scrambled across it, trying not to look down, and leaped the last few feet onto a wide pine bough. Hurtling over the wood, I reached the trunk and clung to it, panting, reordering my mind around the pain, the steadiness of being on ground.

I listened—for Rhys, for his wings, for his next roar. Nothing.

No sign of the archers who he'd been falling to meet. Who he'd thrown me far, far away from.Trembling, I dug my nails into the bark as I listened for him.

Ash arrows. Poisoned ash arrows.

The forest grew ever darker, the trees seeming to wither into skeletal husks. Even the birds hushed themselves.

I stared at my palm—at the eye inked there—and sent a blind thought through it, down that bond. *Where are you? Tell me and I'll come to you. I'll find you.*

There was no wall of onyx adamant at the end of the bond. Only endless shadow.

Things—great, enormous things—were rustling in the forest.

Rhysand. No response.

The last of the light slipped away.

Rhysand, please.

No sound. And the bond between us . . . silent. I'd always felt it protecting me, seducing me, laughing at me on the other side of my shields. And now . . . it had vanished.

A guttural howl rippled from the distance, like rocks scraping against each other.

Every hair on my body rose. We never stayed out here past sunset.

I took steadying breaths, nocking one of my few remaining arrows into my bow.

On the ground, something sleek and dark slithered past, the leaves crunching under what looked to be enormous paws tipped in needle-like claws.

Something began screaming. High, panicked screeches. As if it were being torn apart. Not Rhys—something else.

I began shaking again, the tip of my arrow gleaming as it shuddered with me.

Where are you where are you where are you

Let me find you let me find you let me find you

I unstrung my bow. Any bit of light might give me away.

Darkness was my ally; darkness might shield me.

It had been anger the first time I'd winnowed—and anger the second time I'd done it.

Rhys was hurt. They had *hurt* him. Targeted him. And now . . . Now . . .

It was not hot anger that poured through me.

But something ancient, and frozen, and so vicious that it honed my focus into razor-sharpness.

And if I wanted to track him, if I wanted to get to the spot I'd last seen him . . . I'd become a figment of darkness, too.

I was running down the branch just as something crashed through the brush nearby, snarling and hissing. But I folded myself into smoke and starlight, and winnowed from the edge of my branch and into the tree across from me. The creature below loosed a cry, but I paid it no heed.

I was night; I was wind.

Tree to tree, I winnowed, so fast the beasts roaming the forest floor barely registered my presence. And if I could grow claws and wings . . . I could change my eyes, too.

I'd hunted at dusk often enough to see how animal eyes worked, how they glowed.

Cool command had my own eyes widening, shifting—a temporary blindness as I winnowed between trees again, running down a wide branch and winnowing through the air for the next—

I landed, and the night forest became bright. And the things prowling on the forest floor below . . . I didn't look at them.

No, I kept my attention on winnowing through the trees until I was on the outskirts of the spot where we'd been attacked, all the while tugging on that bond, searching for that familiar wall on the other side of it. Then—

An arrow was stuck in the branches high above me. I winnowed onto the broad bough.

And when I yanked out that length of ash wood, when I felt my immortal body quail in its presence, a low snarl slipped out of me.

I hadn't been able to count how many arrows Rhys had taken. How many he'd shielded me from, using his own body.

I shoved the arrow into my quiver, and continued on, circling the area until I spotted another—down by the pine-needle carpet.

I thought frost might have gleamed in my wake as I winnowed in the direction the arrow would have been shot, finding another, and another. I kept them all.

Until I discovered the place where the pine branches were broken and shattered. Finally I smelled Rhys, and the trees around me glimmered with ice as I spied his blood splattered on the branches, the ground.

And ash arrows all around the site.

As if an ambush had been waiting, and unleashed a hail of hundreds, too fast for him to detect or avoid. Especially if he'd been distracted with me. Distracted all day.

I winnowed in bursts through the site, careful not to stay on the ground too long lest the creatures roaming nearby scent me.

He'd fallen hard, the tracks told me. And they'd had to drag him away. Quickly.

They'd tried to hide the blood trail, but even without his mind speaking to me, I could find that scent anywhere. I *would* find that scent anywhere.

They might have been good at concealing their tracks, but I was better.

I continued my hunt, an ash arrow now nocked into my bow as I read the signs.

Two dozen at least had taken him away, though more had been there for the initial assault. The others had winnowed out, leaving limited numbers to haul him toward the mountains—toward whoever might be waiting.

They were moving swiftly. Deeper and deeper into the woods, toward the slumbering giants of the Illyrian Mountains. His blood had flowed all the way.

Alive, it told me. He was alive—though if the wounds weren't clotting . . . The ash arrows were doing their work.

I'd brought down one of Tamlin's sentinels with a single well-placed ash arrow. I tried not to think about what a barrage of them could do. His roar of pain echoed in my ears.

And through that merciless, unyielding rage, I decided that if Rhys was not alive, if he was harmed beyond repair . . . I didn't care who they were and why they had done it.

They were all dead.

Tracks veered from the main group—scouts probably sent to find a spot for the night. I slowed my winnowing, carefully tracing their steps now. Two groups had split, as if trying to hide where they'd gone. Rhys's scent clung to both.

They'd taken his clothes, then. Because they'd known I'd track them, seen me with him. They'd known I'd come for him. A trap—it was likely a trap.

I paused at the top branches of a tree overlooking where the two groups had cleaved, scanning the ground. One headed deeper into the mountains. One headed along them.

Mountains were Illyrian territory—mountains would run the risk of being discovered by a patrol. They'd assume that's where *I* would doubt they would be stupid enough to go. They'd assume I'd think they'd keep to the unguarded, unpatrolled forest.

I weighed my options, smelling the two paths.

They hadn't counted on the small, second scent that clung there, entwined with his.

And I didn't let myself think about it as I winnowed toward the mountain tracks, outracing the wind. I didn't let myself think about the fact that *my* scent was on Rhys, clinging to him after last night. He'd changed his clothes that morning—but the smell on his body . . . Without taking a bath, I was all over him.

So I winnowed toward him, toward *me*. And when the narrow cave appeared at the foot of a mountain, the faintest glimmer of light escaping from its mouth . . . I halted.

A whip cracked.

And every word, every thought and feeling, went out of me. Another whip—and another.

I slung my bow over my shoulder and pulled out a second ash arrow. It was quick work to bind the two arrows together, so that a tip gleamed on either end—and to do the same for two more. And when I was done, when I looked at the twin makeshift daggers in either hand, when that whip sounded again . . . I winnowed into the cave.

They'd picked one with a narrow entrance that opened into a wide, curving tunnel, setting up their little camp around the bend to avoid detection.

The scouts at the front—two High Fae males with unmarked armor who I didn't recognize—didn't notice as I went past.

Two other scouts patrolled just inside the cave mouth, watching those at the front. I was there and vanished before they could spot me. I rounded the corner, time slipping and bending, and my night-dark eyes burned at the light. I changed them, winnowing between one blink and the next, past the other two guards.

And when I beheld the four others in that cave, beheld the tiny fire they'd built and what they'd already done to him . . . I pushed against the bond between us—almost sobbing as I felt that adamant wall . . . But there was nothing behind it. Only silence.

They'd found strange chains of bluish stone to spread his arms, suspending him from either wall of the cave. His body sagged from them, his back a ravaged slab of meat. And his wings . . .

They'd left the ash arrows through his wings. Seven of them.

His back to me, only the sight of the blood running down his skin told me he was alive.

And it was enough—it was enough that I detonated.

I winnowed to the two guards holding twin whips.

The others around them shouted as I dragged my ash arrows across their throats, deep and vicious, just like I'd done countless times while hunting. One, two—then they were on the ground, whips limp. Before the guards could attack, I winnowed again to the ones nearest.

Blood sprayed.

Winnow, strike; winnow, strike.

Those wings—those beautiful, powerful wings—

The guards at the mouth of the cave had come rushing in.

They were the last to die.

And the blood on my hands felt different from what it had been like Under the Mountain. This blood . . . I savored. Blood for blood. Blood for every drop they'd spilled of his.

Silence fell in the cave as their final shouts finished echoing, and I winnowed in front of Rhys, shoving the bloody ash daggers into my belt. I gripped his face. Pale—too pale.

But his eyes opened to slits and he groaned.

I didn't say anything as I lunged for the chains holding him, trying not to notice the bloody handprints I'd left on him. The chains were like ice—worse than ice. They felt *wrong*. I pushed past the pain and strangeness of them, and the weakness that barreled down my spine, and unlatched him.

His knees slammed into the rock so hard I winced, but I rushed to the other arm, still upraised. Blood flowed down his back, his front, pooling in the dips between his muscles.

"Rhys," I breathed. I almost dropped to my own knees as I felt a flicker of *him* behind his mental shields, as if the pain and exhaustion had reduced it to window-thinness. His wings, peppered with those arrows, remained spread—so painfully taut that I winced. "Rhys—we need to winnow home."

His eyes opened again, and he gasped, "Can't."

Whatever poison was on those arrows, then his magic, his strength . . .

But we couldn't stay here, not when the other group was nearby. So I said, "Hold on," and gripped his hand before I threw us into night and smoke.

Winnowing was so heavy, as if all the weight of him, all that power, dragged me back. It was like wading through mud, but I focused on the forest, on a moss-shrouded cave I'd seen earlier that day while slaking my thirst, tucked into the side of the riverbank. I'd peeked into it, and nothing but leaves had been within. At least it was safe, if not a bit damp. Better than being in the open—and it was our only option.

Every mile was an effort. But I kept my grip on his hand, terrified that if I let go, I'd leave him somewhere I might never be able to find, and—

And then we were there, in that cave, and he grunted in agony as we slammed into the wet, cold stone floor.

"Rhys," I pleaded, stumbling in the dark—such impenetrable dark, and with those creatures around us, I didn't risk a fire—

But he was so cold, and still bleeding.

I willed my eyes to shift again, and my throat tightened at the damage. The lashings across his back kept dribbling blood, but the wings . . . "I have to get these arrows out."

He grunted again, hands braced on the floor. And the sight of him like that, unable to even make a sly comment or half smile . . .

I went up to his wing. "This is going to hurt." I clenched my jaw as I studied the way they'd pierced the beautiful membrane. I'd have to snap the arrows in two and slide each end out.

No—not snapping. I'd have to cut it—slowly, carefully, smoothly, to keep any shards and rough bits from causing further damage. Who knew what an ash splinter might do if it got stuck in there?

"Do it," he panted, his voice hoarse.

There were seven arrows in total: three in this wing, four in the other. They'd removed the ones from his legs, for whatever reason—the wounds already half-clotted.

Blood dripped on the floor.

I took the knife from where it was strapped to my thigh, studied the entry wound, and gently gripped the shaft. He hissed. I paused.

"Do it," Rhys repeated, his knuckles white as he fisted his hands on the ground.

I set the small bit of serrated edge against the arrow and began sawing as gently as I could. The blood-soaked muscles of his back shifted and tensed, and his breathing turned sharp, uneven. Too slow—I was going too slowly.

But any faster and it might hurt him more, might damage the sensitive wing.

"Did you know," I said over the sound of my sawing, "that one summer, when I was seventeen, Elain bought me some paint? We'd had just enough to spend on extra things, and she bought me and Nesta presents. She didn't have enough for a full set, but bought me red and blue and yellow. I used them to the last drop, stretching them as much as I could, and painted little decorations in our cottage."

His breath heaved out of him, and I finally sawed through the shaft. I didn't let him know what I was doing before I yanked out the arrowhead in a smooth pull.

He swore, body locking up, and blood gushed out—then stopped.

I almost loosed a sigh of relief. I set to work on the next arrow.

"I painted the table, the cabinets, the doorway . . . And we had this old, black dresser in our room—one drawer for each of us. We didn't have much clothing to put in there, anyway." I got through the second arrow faster, and he braced himself as I tugged it out. Blood flowed, then clotted. I started on the third. "I painted flowers for Elain on her drawer," I said, sawing and sawing. "Little roses and begonias and irises. And for Nesta . . . " The arrow clattered to the ground and I ripped out the other end.

I watched the blood flow and stop—watched him slowly lower the wing to the ground, his body trembling.

"Nesta," I said, starting on the other wing, "I painted flames for her. She was always angry, always burning. I think she and Amren would be fast friends. I think she would like Velaris, despite herself. And I think Elain—Elain would like it, too. Though she'd probably cling to Azriel, just to have some peace and quiet."

I smiled at the thought—at how handsome they would be together. If the warrior ever stopped quietly loving Mor. I doubted it. Azriel would likely love Mor until he was a whisper of darkness between the stars.

I finished the fourth arrow and started on the fifth.

Rhys's voice was raw as he said to the floor, "What did you paint for yourself?"

I drew out the fifth, moving to the sixth before saying, "I painted the night sky."

He stilled. I went on, "I painted stars and the moon and clouds and just endless, dark sky." I finished the sixth, and was well on my way sawing through the seventh before I said, "I never knew why. I rarely went outside at night—usually, I was so tired from hunting that I just wanted to sleep. But I wonder . . . " I pulled out the seventh and final arrow. "I wonder if some part of me knew what was waiting for me. That I would never be a gentle grower of things, or someone who burned like fire—but that I would be quiet and enduring and as faceted as the night. That I would have beauty, for those who knew where to look, and if people didn't bother to look, but to only fear it . . . Then I didn't particularly care for them, anyway. I wonder if, even in my despair and hopelessness, I was never truly alone. I wonder if I was looking for this place—looking for you all."

The blood stopped flowing, and his other wing lowered to the ground. Slowly, the lashes on his back began to clot. I walked around to where he was bowed over the floor, hands braced on the rock, and knelt.

His head lifted. Pain-filled eyes, bloodless lips. "You saved me," he rasped.

"You can explain who they were later."

"Ambush," Rhys said anyway, his eyes scanning my face for signs of hurt. "Hybern soldiers with ancient chains from the king himself, to nullify my power. They must have traced the magic I used yesterday . . . I'm sorry." The words tumbled out of him. I brushed back his dark hair. That was why I hadn't been able to use the bond, to speak mind to mind.

"Rest," I said, and moved to retrieve the blanket from my pack. It'd have to do. He gripped my wrist before I could rise. His eyelids lowered. Consciousness ripped from him—too fast. Much too fast and too heavy.

"I was looking for you, too," Rhys murmured.

And passed out.

CHAPTER 50

I slept beside him, offering what warmth I could, monitoring the cave entrance the entirety of the night. The beasts in the forest prowled past in an endless parade, and only in the gray light before dawn did their snarls and hissing fade.

Rhys was unconscious as watery sunlight painted the stone walls, his skin clammy. I checked his wounds and found them barely healed, an oily sheen oozing from them.

And when I put a hand on his brow, I swore at the heat.

Poison had coated those arrows. And that poison remained in his body.

The Illyrian camp was so distant that my own powers, feeble from the night before, wouldn't get us far.

But if they had those horrible chains to nullify his powers, had ash arrows to bring him down, then that poison . . .

An hour passed. He didn't get better. No, his golden skin was pale—paling. His breaths were shallow. "Rhys," I said softly.

He didn't move. I tried shaking him. If he could tell me what the poison was, maybe I could try to find something to help him . . . He did not awaken.

Around midday, panic gripped me in a tight fist.

I didn't know anything about poisons or remedies. And out here, so far from anyone . . . Would Cassian track us down in time? Would Mor winnow in? I tried to rouse Rhys over and over.

The poison had dragged him down deep. I would not risk waiting for help to arrive.

I would not risk him.

So I bundled him in as many layers as I could spare, yet took my cloak, kissed his brow, and left.

We were only a few hundred yards from where I'd been hunting the night before, and as I emerged from the cave, I tried not to look at the tracks of the beasts who had passed through, right above us. Enormous, horrible tracks.

What I was to hunt would be worse.

We were already near running water—so I made my trap close by, building my snare with hands that I refused to let shake.

I placed the cloak—mostly new, rich, lovely—in the center of my snare. And I waited.

An hour. Two.

I was about to start bargaining with the Cauldron, with the Mother, when a creeping, familiar silence fell over the wood.

Rippling toward me, the birds stopped chirping, the wind stopped sighing in the pines.

And when a crack sounded through the forest, followed by a screech that hollowed out my ears, I nocked an arrow into my bow and set off to see the Suriel.

It was as horrific as I remembered:

Tattered robes barely concealing a body made of not skin, but what looked to be solid, worn bone. Its lipless mouth held too-large teeth, and its fingers—long, spindly—clicked against each other while it weighed the fine cloak I'd laid in the center of my snare, as if the cloth had been blown in on a wind.

"Feyre Cursebreaker," it said, turning toward me, in a voice that was both one and many.

I lowered my bow. "I have need of you."

Time—I was running out of time. I could feel it, that urgency begging me to hurry through the bond.

"What fascinating changes a year has wrought on you—on the world," it said.

A year. Yes, it had been over a year now since I'd first crossed the wall.

"I have questions," I said.

It smiled, each of those stained, too-large brown teeth visible. "You have two questions."

An answer and an order.

I didn't waste time; not with Rhys, not when this wood might be full of enemies hunting for us.

"What poison was used on those arrows?"

"Bloodbane," it said.

I didn't know that poison—had never heard of it.

"Where do I find the cure?"

The Suriel clicked its bone fingers against each other, as if the answer lay inside the sound. "In the forest."

I hissed, my brows flattening. "Please—please don't be cryptic. *What* is the cure?"

The Suriel cocked its head, the bone gleaming in the light. "Your blood. Give him your blood, Cursebreaker. It is rich with the healing gift of the High Lord of the Dawn. It shall spare him from the bloodbane's wrath."

"That's it?" I pushed. "*How much* blood?"

"A few mouthfuls will do." A hollow, dry wind—not at all like the misty, cold veils that usually drifted past—brushed my face. "I helped you before. I have helped you now. And you will free me before I lose my patience, Cursebreaker."

Some primal, lingering human part of me trembled as I took in the snare around its legs, pinning it to the ground. Perhaps this time, the Suriel had let itself be caught. And knew how to free itself—had learned it the moment I'd spared it from the naga.

A test—of honor. And a favor. For the arrow I'd shot to save it last year.

But I nocked an ash arrow into my bow, cringing at the sheen of poison coating it. "Thank you for your help," I said, bracing myself for flight should it charge at me.

The Suriel's stained teeth clacked against each other. "If you wish to speed your mate's healing, in addition to your blood, a pink-flowered weed sprouts by the river. Make him chew it."

I fired my arrow at the snare before I finished hearing its words.

The trap sprang free. And the word clicked through me.

Mate.

"What did you say?"

The Suriel rose to its full height, towering over me even from across the clearing. I had not realized that despite the bone, it was muscled—powerful.

"If you wish to . . ." The Suriel paused, and grinned, showing nearly all of those brown, thick teeth. "You did not know, then."

"Say it," I gritted out.

"The High Lord of the Night Court is your mate."

I wasn't entirely sure I was breathing.

"Interesting," the Suriel said.

Mate.

Mate.

Mate.

Rhysand was my mate.

Not lover, not husband, but more than that. A bond so deep, so permanent that it was honored over all others. Rare, cherished.

Not Tamlin's mate.

Rhysand's.

I was jealous, and pissed off . . .

You're mine.

The words slipped out of me, low and twisted, "Does he know?"

The Suriel clenched the robes of its new cloak in its bone-fingers. "Yes."

"For a long while?"

"Yes. Since—"

"No. He can tell me—I want to hear it from his lips."

The Suriel cocked its head. "You are—you are feeling too much, too fast. I cannot read it."

"How can I possibly be his mate?" Mates were equals—matched, at least in some ways.

"He is the most powerful High Lord to ever walk this earth. You are . . . new. You are made of all seven High Lords. Unlike anything. Are you two not similar in that? Are you not matched?"

Mate. And he knew—he'd *known*.

I glanced toward the river, as if I could see all the way to the cave, to where Rhysand slept.

When I looked back at the Suriel, it was gone.

✣

I found the pink weed, and ripped it out of the ground as I stalked back to the cave.

Mercifully, Rhys was half-awake, the layers I'd thrown on him now scattered across the blanket, and he gave me a strained smile as I entered.

I chucked the weed at him, showering his bare chest with soil. "Chew on that."

He blinked blearily at me.

Mate.

But he obeyed, frowning at the plant before he plucked off a few leaves and started chewing. He grimaced as he swallowed. I tore off my jacket, shoved up my sleeve, and strode to him. He'd known, and kept it from me.

Had the others known? Had they guessed?

He'd—he'd promised not to lie, not to keep things from me.

And this—this *most important thing in my immortal existence* . . .

I drew a dagger across my forearm, the cut long and deep, and dropped to my knees before him. I didn't feel the pain. "Drink this. *Now.*"

Rhys blinked again, brows raising, but I didn't give him the chance to object before I gripped the back of his head, lifted my arm to his mouth, and shoved him against my skin.

He paused as my blood touched his lips. Then his mouth opened wider, his tongue brushing my arm as he sucked in my blood. One mouthful. Two. Three.

I yanked back my arm, the wound already healing, and shoved down my sleeve.

"You don't get to ask questions," I said, and he looked up at me, exhaustion and pain lining his face, my blood shining on his lips. Part of me hated the words, for acting like this while he was wounded, but I didn't care. "You only get to answer them. And nothing more."

Wariness flooded his eyes, but he nodded, biting off another mouthful of the weed and chewing.

I stared down at him, the half-Illyrian warrior who was my soul-bonded partner.

"How long have you known that I'm your mate?"

Rhys stilled. The entire world stilled.

He swallowed. "Feyre."

"How long have you known that I'm your mate?"

"You . . . You ensnared the Suriel?" How he'd pieced it together, I didn't give a shit.

"I said you don't get to ask questions."

I thought something like panic might have flashed over his features. He chewed again on the plant—as if it instantly helped, as if he knew that he wanted to be at his full strength to face this, face me. Color was already blooming on his cheeks, perhaps from whatever healing was in my blood.

"I suspected for a while," Rhys said, swallowing once more. "I knew for certain when Amarantha was killing you. And when we stood on the balcony Under the Mountain—right after we were freed, I *felt* it snap into place between us. I think when you were Made, it . . . it heightened the smell of the bond. I looked at you then and the strength of it hit me like a blow."

He'd gone wide-eyed, had stumbled back as if shocked—terrified. And had vanished.

That had been over half a year ago.

My blood pounded in my ears. "When were you going to tell me?"

"Feyre."

"*When were you going to tell me?*"

"I don't know. I wanted to yesterday. Or whenever you'd noticed that it wasn't just a bargain between us. I hoped you might realize when I took you to bed, and—"

"Do the others know?"

"Amren and Mor do. Azriel and Cassian suspect."

My face burned. They knew—they— "Why didn't you tell me?"

"You were in love with him; you were going to marry him. And then you . . . you were enduring everything and it didn't feel right to tell you."

"I deserved to know."

"The other night you told me you wanted a distraction, you wanted *fun*. Not a mating bond. And not to someone like me—a mess." So the words I'd spat after the Court of Nightmares had haunted him.

"You promised—you promised no secrets, no games. You *promised*."

Something in my chest was caving in on itself. Some part of me I'd thought long gone.

"I know I did," Rhys said, the glow returning to his face. "You think

I didn't want to tell you? You think I liked hearing you wanted me only for amusement and release? You think it didn't drive me out of my mind so completely that those bastards shot me out of the sky because I was too busy wondering if I should just tell you, or wait—or maybe take whatever pieces that you offered me and be happy with it? Or that maybe I should let you go so you don't have a lifetime of assassins and High Lords hunting you down for being with me?"

"I don't want to hear this. I don't want to hear you explain how you assumed that you knew best, that I couldn't handle it—"

"I didn't do that—"

"I don't want to hear you tell me that you decided I was to be kept in the dark while your friends knew, while *you all* decided what was right for me—"

"Feyre—"

"Take me back to the Illyrian camp. Now."

He was panting in great, rattling gulps. "Please."

But I stormed to him and grabbed his hand. "*Take me back now.*"

And I saw the pain and sorrow in his eyes. Saw it and didn't care, not as that thing in my chest was twisting and breaking. Not as my heart—my *heart*—ached, so viciously that I realized it'd somehow been repaired in these past few months. Repaired by him.

And now it hurt.

Rhys saw all that and more on my face, and I saw nothing but agony in his as he rallied his strength and, grunting in pain, winnowed us into the Illyrian camp.

CHAPTER 51

We slammed into freezing mud right outside the little stone house.

I think he'd meant to winnow us into it, but his powers had given out. Across the yard, I spied Cassian—and Mor—at the window of the house, eating breakfast. Their eyes went wide, and then they were rushing for the door.

"Feyre," Rhys groaned, bare arms buckling as he tried to rise.

I left him lying in the mud and stormed toward the house.

The door flung open, and Cassian and Mor were sprinting for us, scanning every inch of our bodies. Cassian realized I was in one piece and hurtled for Rhys, who was struggling to rise, mud covering his bare skin, but Mor—Mor saw my face.

I went up to her, cold and hollow. "I want you to take me somewhere far away," I said. "Right now." I needed to get away—needed to think, to have space and quiet and calm.

Mor looked between us, biting her lip.

"Please," I said, and my voice broke on the word.

Behind me, Rhys moaned my name again.

Mor scanned my face once more, and gripped my hand.

We vanished into wind and night.

Brightness assaulted me, and I gobbled up my surroundings: mountains and snow all around, fresh and gleaming in the midday light, so clean against the dirt on me.

We were high up on the peaks, and about a hundred yards away, a log cabin stood tucked between two upper fangs of the mountains, shielding it from the wind. The house was dark—there was nothing around it for as far as I could see.

"The house is warded, so no one can winnow in. No one can get beyond this point, actually, without our family's permission." Mor stepped ahead, snow crunching under her boots. Without the wind, the day was mild enough to remind me that spring had dawned in the world, though I'd bet it would be freezing once the sun vanished. I trailed after her, something zinging against my skin. "You're—allowed in," Mor said.

"Because I'm his mate?"

She kept wading through the knee-high snow. "Did you guess, or did he tell you?"

"The Suriel told me. After I went to hunt it for information on how to heal him."

She swore. "Is he—is he all right?"

"He'll live," I said. She didn't ask any other questions. And I wasn't feeling generous enough to supply further information. We reached the door to the cabin, which she unlocked with a wave of her hand.

A main, wood-paneled room consisting of a kitchen to the right, a living area with a leather sofa covered in furs to the left; a small hall in the back that led to two bedrooms and a shared bathing room, and nothing else.

"We got sent up here for 'reflection' when we were younger," Mor said. "Rhys used to smuggle in books and booze for me."

I cringed at the sound of his name. "It's perfect," I said tightly. Mor waved a hand, and a fire sprang to life in the hearth, heat flooding the room. Food landed on the counters of the kitchen, and something in the pipes groaned. "No need for firewood," she said. "It'll burn until you leave." She lifted a brow as if to ask when that would be.

I looked away. "Please don't tell him where I am."

"He'll try to find you."

"Tell him I don't want to be found. Not for a while."

Mor bit her lip. "It's not my business—"

"Then don't say anything."

She did, anyway. "He wanted to tell you. And it killed him not to. But . . . I've never seen him so happy as he is when he's with you. And I don't think that has anything to do with you being his mate."

"I don't care." She fell silent, and I could feel the words she wanted to say building up. So I said, "Thank you for bringing me here." A polite dismissal.

Mor bowed her head. "I'll check back in three days. There are clothes in the bedrooms, and all the hot water you want. The house is spelled to take care of you—merely wish or speak for things, and it'll be done."

I only wanted solitude and quiet, but . . . a hot bath sounded like a nice way to start.

She left the cottage before I could say anything else.

Alone, no one around for miles, I stood in the silent cabin and stared at nothing.

PART THREE

THE HOUSE OF MIST

CHAPTER 52

There was a deep, sunken tub in the floor of the mountain cabin—large enough to accommodate Illyrian wings. I filled it with water near-scalding, not caring how the magic of this house operated, only that it worked. Hissing and wincing, I climbed in.

Three days without a bath and I could have wept at the warmth and cleanliness of it.

No matter that I'd once gone weeks without one—not when drawing hot water for it in my family's cottage had been more trouble than it was worth. Not when we didn't even have a bathtub and it required buckets and buckets to get clean.

I washed with dark soap that smelled of smoke and pine, and when I was done, I sat there, watching the steam slither amongst the few candles.

Mate.

The word chased me from the bath sooner than I wanted, and hounded me as I pulled on the clothes I'd found in a drawer of the bedroom: dark leggings, a large, cream-colored sweater that hung to mid-thigh, and thick socks. My stomach grumbled, and I realized I hadn't eaten since the day before, because—

Because he'd been injured, and I'd gone out of my mind—absolutely insane—when he'd been taken from me, shot out of the sky like a bird.

I'd acted on instinct, on a drive to protect him that had come from so deep in me . . .

So deep in me—

I found a container of soup on the wood counter that Mor must have brought in, and scrounged up a cast iron pot to heat it. Fresh, crusty bread sat near the stove, and I ate half of it while waiting for the soup to warm.

He'd suspected it before I'd even freed us from Amarantha.

My wedding day . . . Had he interrupted to spare me from a horrible mistake or for his own ends? Because I was his mate, and letting me bind myself to someone else was unacceptable?

I ate my dinner in silence, with only the murmuring fire for company.

And beneath the barrage of my thoughts, a throb of relief.

My relationship with Tamlin had been doomed from the start. I had left—only to find my mate. To go to my mate.

If I were looking to spare us both from embarrassment, from rumor, only that—only that I had found my true mate—would do the trick.

I was not a lying piece of traitorous filth. Not even close. Even if Rhys . . . Rhys had known I was his mate.

While I'd shared a bed with Tamlin. For months and months. He'd known I was sharing a bed with him, and hadn't let it show. Or maybe he didn't care.

Maybe he didn't want the bond. Had hoped it'd vanish.

I'd owed nothing to Rhys then—had nothing to apologize for.

But he'd known I'd react badly. That it'd hurt me more than help me.

And what if I had known?

What if I *had* known that Rhys was my mate while I'd loved Tamlin?

It didn't excuse his not telling me. Didn't excuse the recent weeks, when I'd hated myself so much for wanting him so badly—when he should have told me. But . . . I understood.

I washed the dishes, swept the crumbs off the small dining table between the kitchen and living area, and climbed into one of the beds.

Just last night, I'd been curled beside him, counting his breaths to make sure he didn't stop making them. The night before, I'd been in his arms, his fingers between my legs, his tongue in my mouth. And now . . . though the cabin was warm, the sheets were cold. The bed was large—empty.

Through the small glass window, the snow-blasted land around me glowed blue in the moonlight. The wind was a hollow moan, brushing great, sparkling drifts of snow past the cabin.

I wondered if Mor had told him where I was.

Wondered if he'd indeed come looking for me.

Mate.

My mate.

Sunlight on snow awoke me, and I squinted at the brightness, cursing myself for not closing the curtains. It took me a moment to remember where I was; why I was in this isolated cabin, deep in the mountains of—I didn't know what mountains these were.

Rhys had once mentioned a favorite retreat that Mor and Amren had burned to cinders in a fight. I wondered if this was it; if it had been rebuilt. Everything was comfortable, worn, but in relatively good shape.

Mor and Amren had known.

I couldn't decide if I hated them for it.

No doubt, Rhys had ordered them to keep quiet, and they'd respected his wishes, but . . .

I made the bed, fixed breakfast, washed the dishes, and then stood in the center of the main living space.

I'd run away.

Precisely how Rhys expected me to run—how I'd told him anyone in their right mind *would* run from him. Like a coward, like a fool, I'd left him injured in the freezing mud.

I'd walked away from him—a day after I'd told him he was the only thing I'd never walk away from.

I'd demanded honesty, and at the first true test, I hadn't even let him give it to me. I hadn't granted him the consideration of hearing him out.

You see me.

Well, I'd refused to see him. Maybe I'd refused to see what was right in front of me.

I'd walked away.

And maybe . . . maybe I shouldn't have.

Boredom hit me halfway through the day.

Supreme, unrelenting boredom, thanks to being trapped inside while the snow slowly melted under the mild spring day, listening to it drip-drip-dripping off the roof.

It made me nosy—and once I'd finished going through the drawers and closets of both bedrooms (clothes, old bits of ribbon, knives and weapons tucked between as if one of them had chucked them in and just forgotten), the kitchen cabinets (food, preserved goods, pots and pans, a stained cookbook), and the living area (blankets, some books, more weapons hidden *everywhere*), I ventured into the supply closet.

For a High Lord's retreat, the cabin was . . . not common, because everything had been made and appointed with care, but . . . casual. As if this were the sole place where they might all come, and pile into beds and on the couch, and not be anyone but themselves, taking turns with who cooked that night and who hunted and who cleaned and—

A family.

It felt like a family—the one I'd never quite had, had never dared really hope for. Had stopped expecting when I'd grown used to the space and formality of living in a manor. To being a symbol for a broken people, a High Priestess's golden idol and puppet.

I opened the storeroom door, a blast of cold greeting me, but candles sputtered to life, thanks to the magic that kept the place hospitable. Shelves free of dust (another magical perk, no doubt) gleamed with more food stores. Books, sporting equipment, packs and ropes and, big surprise, more weapons. I sorted through it all, these remnants of adventures past and future, and almost missed them as I walked past.

Half a dozen cans of paint.

Paper, and a few canvases. Brushes, old and flecked with paint from lazy hands.

There were other art supplies—pastels and watercolors, what looked to be charcoal for sketching, but . . . I stared at the paint, the brushes.

Which of them had tried to paint while stuck here—or enjoying a holiday with them all?

I told myself my hands were trembling with the cold as I reached for the paint and pried open the lid.

Still fresh. Probably from the magic preserving this place.

I peered into the dark, gleaming interior of the can I'd opened: blue.

And then I started gathering supplies.

I painted all day.

And when the sun vanished, I painted all through the night.

The moon had set by the time I washed my hands and face and neck and stumbled into bed, not even bothering to undress before unconsciousness swept me away.

I was up, brush in hand, before the spring sun could resume its work thawing the mountains around me.

I paused only long enough to eat. The sun was setting again, exhausted from the dent it'd made in the layer of snow outside, when a knock sounded on the front door.

Splattered in paint—the cream-colored sweater utterly wrecked—I froze.

Another knock, light, but insistent. Then—"Please don't be dead."

I didn't know whether it was relief or disappointment that sank in my chest as I opened the door and found Mor huffing hot air into her cupped hands.

She looked at the paint on my skin, in my hair. At the brush in my hand.

And then at what I had done.

Mor stepped in from the brisk spring night and let out a low whistle as she shut the door. "Well, you've certainly been busy."

Indeed.

I'd painted nearly every surface in the main room.

And not with just broad swaths of color, but with decorations—little images. Some were basic: clusters of icicles drooping down the sides of the threshold. They melted into the first shoots of spring, then burst into full blooms of summer, before brightening and deepening into fall leaves. I'd painted a ring of flowers round the card table by the window; leaves and crackling flames around the dining table.

But in between the intricate decorations, I'd painted them. Bits and pieces of Mor, and Cassian, and Azriel, and Amren . . . and Rhys.

Mor went up to the large hearth, where I'd painted the mantel in black shimmering with veins of gold and red. Up close, it was a solid, pretty bit of paint. But from the couch . . . "Illyrian wings," she said. "Ugh, they'll never stop gloating about it."

But she went to the window, which I'd framed in tumbling strands of gold and brass and bronze. Mor fingered her hair, cocking her head. "Nice," she said, surveying the room again.

Her eyes fell on the open threshold to the bedroom hallway, and she grimaced. "Why," she said, "are Amren's eyes there?"

Indeed, right above the door, in the center of the archway, I'd painted a pair of glowing silver eyes. "Because she's always watching."

Mor snorted. "That simply won't do. Paint my eyes next to hers. So the males of this family will know we're *both* watching them the next time they come up here to get drunk for a week straight."

"They do that?"

"They used to." *Before Amarantha.* "Every autumn, the three of them would lock themselves in this house for five days and drink and drink and hunt and hunt, and they'd come back to Velaris looking halfway to death but grinning like fools. It warms my heart to know that from now on, they'll have to do it with me and Amren staring at them."

A smile tugged on my lips. "Who does this paint belong to?"

"Amren," Mor said, rolling her eyes. "We were all here one summer, and she wanted to teach herself to paint. She did it for about two days before she got bored and decided to start hunting poor creatures instead."

A quiet chuckle rasped out of me. I strode to the table, which I'd used as my main surface for blending and organizing paints. And maybe I was a coward, but I kept my back to her as I said, "Any news from my sisters?"

Mor started rifling through the cabinets, either to look for food or assess what I needed. She said over a shoulder, "No. Not yet."

"Is he . . . hurt?" I'd left him in the freezing mud, injured and working the poison out of his system. I'd tried not to dwell on it while I'd painted.

"Still recovering, but fine. Pissed at me, of course, but he can shove it."

I combined Mor's yellow gold with the red I'd used for the Illyrian wings, and blended until vibrant orange emerged. "Thank you—for not telling him I was here."

A shrug. Food began popping onto the counter: fresh bread, fruit, containers of something that I could smell from across the kitchen and made me nearly groan with hunger. "You should talk to him, though. Make him stew over it, of course, but . . . hear him out." She didn't look at me as she spoke. "Rhys always has his reasons, and he might be arrogant as all hell, but he's usually right about his instincts. He makes mistakes, but . . . You should hear him out."

I'd already decided that I would, but I said, "How was your visit to the Court of Nightmares?"

She paused, her face going uncharacteristically pale. "Fine. It's always a delight to see my parents. As you might guess."

"Is your father healing?" I added the cobalt of Azriel's Siphons to the orange and mixed until a rich brown appeared.

A small, grim smile. "Slowly. I might have snapped some more bones when I visited. My mother has since banished me from their private quarters. Such a shame."

Some feral part of me beamed in savage delight at that. "A pity indeed," I said. I added a bit of frost white to lighten the brown, checked it against the gaze she slid to me, and grabbed a stool to stand on as I began painting the threshold. "Rhys really makes you do this often? Endure visiting them?"

Mor leaned against the counter. "Rhys gave me permission the day he became High Lord to kill them all whenever I pleased. I attend these meetings, go to the Court of Nightmares, to . . . remind them of that sometimes. And to keep communication between our two courts flowing, however strained it might be. If I were to march in there tomorrow and slaughter my parents, he wouldn't blink. Perhaps be inconvenienced by it, but . . . he would be pleased."

I focused on the speck of caramel brown I painted beside Amren's eyes. "I'm sorry—for all that you endured."

"Thank you," she said, coming over to watch me. "Visiting them always leaves me raw."

"Cassian seemed concerned." Another prying question.

She shrugged. "Cassian, I think, would also savor the opportunity to shred that entire court to pieces. Starting with my parents. Maybe I'll let him do it one year as a present. Him and Azriel both. It'd make a perfect solstice gift."

I asked perhaps a bit too casually. "You told me about the time with Cassian, but did you and Azriel ever . . . ?"

A sharp laugh. "No. Azriel? After that time with Cassian, I swore off any of Rhys's friends. Azriel's got no shortage of lovers, though, don't worry. He's better at keeping them secret than we are, but . . . he has them."

"So if he were ever interested would you . . . ?"

"The issue, actually, wouldn't be me. It'd be him. I could peel off my clothes right in front of him and he wouldn't move an inch. He might have defied and proved those Illyrian pricks wrong at every turn, but it won't matter if Rhys makes him Prince of Velaris—he'll see himself as a bastard-born nobody, and not good enough for anyone. Especially me."

"But . . . *are* you interested?"

"Why are you asking such things?" Her voice became tight, sharp. More wary than I'd ever heard.

"I'm still trying to figure out how you all work together."

A snort, that wariness gone. I tried not to look too relieved. "We have five centuries of tangled history for you to sort through. Good luck."

Indeed. I finished her eyes—honey brown to Amren's quicksilver. But almost in answer, Mor declared, "Paint Azriel's. Next to mine. And Cassian's next to Amren's."

I lifted my brows.

Mor gave me an innocent smile. "So we can all watch over you."

I just shook my head and hopped off the stool to start figuring out how to paint hazel eyes.

Mor said quietly, "Is it so bad—to be his mate? To be a part of our court, our family, tangled history and all?"

I blended the paint in the small dish, the colors swirling together like so many entwined lives. "No," I breathed. "No, it's not."

And I had my answer.

CHAPTER 53

Mor stayed overnight, even going so far as to paint some rudimentary stick figures on the wall beside the storeroom door. Three females with absurdly long, flowing hair that all resembled hers; and three winged males, who she somehow managed to make look puffed up on their own sense of importance. I laughed every time I saw it.

She left after breakfast, having to walk out to where the no-winnowing shield ended, and I waved to her distant, shivering figure before she vanished into nothing.

I stared across the glittering white expanse, thawed enough that bald patches peppered it—revealing bits of winter-white grass reaching toward the blue sky and mountains. I knew summer had to eventually reach even this melting dreamland, for I'd found fishing poles and sporting equipment that suggested warm-weather usage, but it was hard to imagine snow and ice becoming soft grass and wildflowers.

Brief as a glimmering spindrift, I saw myself there: running through the meadow that slumbered beneath the thin crust of snow, splashing through the little streams already littering the floor, feasting on fat summer berries as the sun set over the mountains . . .

And then I would go home to Velaris, where I would finally walk through the artists' quarter, and enter those shops and galleries and learn what they knew, and maybe—maybe one day—I would open my own shop. Not to sell my work, but to teach others.

Maybe teach the others who were like me: broken in places and trying to fight it—trying to learn who they were around the dark and pain. And I would go home at the end of every day exhausted but content—fulfilled.

Happy.

I'd go home every day to the town house, to my friends, chock full of stories of their own days, and we'd sit around that table and eat together.

And Rhysand . . .

Rhysand . . .

He would be there. He'd give me the money to open my own shop; and because I wouldn't charge anyone, I'd sell my paintings to pay him back. Because I would pay him back, mate or no.

And he'd be here during the summer, flying over the meadow, chasing me across the little streams and up the sloped, grassy mountainside. He would sit with me under the stars, feeding me fat summer berries. And he would be at that table in the town house, roaring with laughter—never again cold and cruel and solemn. Never again anyone's slave or whore.

And at night . . . At night we'd go upstairs together, and he would whisper stories of his adventures, and I'd whisper about my day, and . . .

And there it was.

A future.

The future I saw for myself, bright as the sunrise over the Sidra.

A direction, and a goal, and an invitation to see what else immortality might offer me. It did not seem so listless, so empty, anymore.

And I would fight until my last breath to attain it—to defend it.

So I knew what I had to do.

⁜

Five days passed, and I painted every room in the cottage. Mor had winnowed in extra paint before she'd left, along with more food than I could possibly eat.

But after five days, I was sick of my own thoughts for company—sick of waiting, sick of the thawing, dripping snow.

Thankfully, Mor returned that night, banging on the door, thunderous and impatient.

I'd taken a bath an hour before, scrubbing off paint in places I hadn't even known it was possible to smear it, and my hair was still drying as I flung open the door to the blast of cool air.

But Mor wasn't leaning against the threshold.

CHAPTER 54

I stared at Rhys.

He stared at me.

His cheeks were tinged pink with cold, his dark hair ruffled, and he honestly looked *freezing* as he stood there, wings tucked in tight.

And I knew that one word from me, and he'd go flying off into the crisp night. That if I shut the door, he'd go and not push it.

His nostrils flared, scenting the paint behind me, but he didn't break his stare. Waiting.

Mate.

My—mate.

This beautiful, strong, selfless male . . . Who had sacrificed and wrecked himself for his family, his people, and didn't feel it was enough, that *he* wasn't enough for anyone . . . Azriel thought he didn't deserve someone like Mor. And I wondered if Rhys . . . if he somehow felt the same about me. I stepped aside, holding the door open for him.

I could have sworn I felt a pulse of knee-wobbling relief through the bond.

But Rhys took in the painting I'd done, gobbling down the bright colors that now made the cottage come alive, and said, "You painted us."

"I hope you don't mind."

He studied the threshold to the bedroom hallway. "Azriel, Mor, Amren, and Cassian," he said, marking the eyes I'd painted. "You do know that one of them is going to paint a moustache under the eyes of whoever pisses them off that day."

I clamped my lips to keep the smile in. "Oh, Mor already promised to do that."

"And what about my eyes?"

I swallowed. All right, then. No dancing around it.

My heart was pounding so wildly I knew he could hear it. "I was afraid to paint them."

Rhys faced me fully. "Why?"

No more games, no more banter. "At first, because I was so mad at you for not telling me. Then because I was worried I'd like them too much and find that you . . . didn't feel the same. Then because I was scared that if I painted them, I'd start wishing you were here so much that I'd just stare at them all day. And it seemed like a pathetic way to spend my time."

A twitch of his lips. "Indeed."

I glanced at the shut door. "You flew here."

He nodded. "Mor wouldn't tell me where you'd gone, and there are only so many places that are as secure as this one. Since I didn't want our Hybern friends tracking me to you, I had to do it the old-fashioned way. It took . . . a while."

"You're—better?"

"Healed completely. Quickly, considering the bloodbane. Thanks to you."

I avoided his stare, turning for the kitchen. "You must be hungry. I'll heat something up."

Rhys straightened. "You'd—make me food?"

"Heat," I said. "I can't cook."

It didn't seem to make a difference. But whatever it was, the act of offering him food . . . I dumped some cold soup into a pan and lit the burner. "I don't know the rules," I said, my back to him. "So you need to explain them to me."

He lingered in the center of the cabin, watching my every move. He said hoarsely, "It's an . . . important moment when a female offers her mate food. It goes back to whatever beasts we were a long, long time ago. But it still matters. The first time matters. Some mated pairs will make an occasion of it—throwing a party just so the female can formally offer her mate food . . . That's usually done amongst the wealthy. But it means that the female . . . accepts the bond."

I stared into the soup. "Tell me the story—tell me everything."

He understood my offer: tell me while I cooked, and I'd decide at the end whether or not to offer him that food.

A chair scraped against the wood floor as he sat at the table. For a moment, there was only silence, interrupted by the clack of my spoon against the pot.

Then Rhys said, "I was captured during the War. By Amarantha's army."

I paused my stirring, my gut twisting.

"Cassian and Azriel were in different legions, so they had no idea that my forces and I had been taken prisoner. And that Amarantha's captains held us for weeks, torturing and slaughtering my warriors. They put ash bolts through my wings, and they had those same chains from the other night to keep me down. Those chains are one of Hybern's greatest assets—stone delved from deep in their land, capable of nullifying a High Fae's powers. Even mine. So they chained me up between two trees, beating me when they felt like it, trying to get me to tell them where the Night Court forces were, using my warriors—their deaths and pain—to break me.

"Only I didn't break," he said roughly, "and they were too dumb to know that I was an Illyrian, and all they had to do to get me to yield would have been to try to cut off my wings. And maybe it was luck, but they never did. And Amarantha . . . She didn't care that I was there. I was yet another High Lord's son, and Jurian had just slaughtered her sister. All she cared about was getting to him—*killing* him. She had no idea that every second, every breath, I plotted her death. I was willing to make it my last stand: to kill her at any cost, even if it meant shredding my wings to break free. I'd watched the guards and learned her schedule, so I knew where she'd be. I set a day, and a time. And I was ready—I was so damned ready to make an end of it, and wait for Cassian and Azriel and Mor on the other side. There was nothing but my rage, and my relief that my friends weren't there. But the day before I was to kill Amarantha, to make my final stand and meet my end, she and Jurian faced each other on the battlefield."

He paused, swallowing.

"I was chained in the mud, forced to watch as they battled. To watch as Jurian took my killing blow. Only—she slaughtered him. I watched her rip out his eye, then rip off his finger, and when he was prone, I watched her drag him back to the camp. Then I listened to her slowly, over days and days, tear him apart. His screaming was endless. She was so focused on torturing him that she didn't detect my father's arrival. In the panic, she killed Jurian rather than see him liberated, and fled. So my father rescued me—and told his men, told Azriel, to leave the ash spikes in my wings as punishment for getting caught. I was so injured that the healers informed me if I tried to fight before my wings healed, I'd never fly again. So I was forced to return home to recover—while the final battles were waged.

"They made the Treaty, and the wall was built. We'd long ago freed our slaves in the Night Court. We didn't trust the humans to keep our secrets, not when they bred so quickly and frequently that my forefathers couldn't hold all their minds at once. But our world was changed nonetheless. We were all changed by the War. Cassian and Azriel came back different; I came back different. We came here—to this cabin. I was still so injured that they carried me here between them.

We were here when the messages arrived about the final terms of the Treaty.

"They stayed with me when I roared at the stars that Amarantha, for all she had done, for every crime committed, would go unpunished. That the King of Hybern would go unpunished. Too much killing had occurred on either side for everyone to be brought to justice, they said. Even my father gave me an order to let it go—to build toward a future of co-existence. But I never forgave what Amarantha had done to my warriors. And I never forgot it, either. Tamlin's father—he was her friend. And when my father slaughtered him, I was so damn smug that perhaps she'd feel an inkling of what I'd felt when she murdered my soldiers."

My hands were shaking as I stirred the soup. I'd never known . . . never thought . . .

"When Amarantha returned to these shores centuries later, I still wanted to kill her. The worst part was, she didn't even know who I was. Didn't even remember that I was the High Lord's son that she'd held captive. To her, I was merely the son of the man who had killed her friend—I was just the High Lord of the Night Court. The other High Lords were convinced she wanted peace and trade. Only Tamlin mistrusted her. I hated him, but he'd known Amarantha personally—and if he didn't trust her . . . I knew she hadn't changed.

"So I planned to kill her. I told no one. Not even Amren. I'd let Amarantha think I was interested in trade, in alliance. I decided I'd go to the party thrown Under the Mountain for all the courts to celebrate our trade agreement with Hybern . . . And when she was drunk, I'd slip into her mind, make her reveal every lie and crime she'd committed, and then I'd turn her brain to liquid before anyone could react. I was prepared to go to war for it."

I turned, leaning against the counter. Rhys was looking at his hands, as if the story were a book he could read between them.

"But she thought faster—acted faster. She had been trained against my particular skill set, and had extensive mental shields. I was so busy working to tunnel through them that I didn't think about the drink in my hand. I hadn't wanted Cassian or Azriel or anyone else there that night to witness what I was to do—so no one bothered to sniff my drink.

"And as I felt my powers being ripped away by that spell she'd put on it at the toast, I flung them out one last time, wiping Velaris, the wards, all that was good, from the minds of the Court of Nightmares—the only ones I'd allowed to come with me. I threw the shield around Velaris, binding it to my friends so that they had to remain or risk that protection collapsing, and used the last dregs to tell them mind to mind what was happening, and to stay away. Within a few seconds, my power belonged wholly to Amarantha."

His eyes lifted to mine. Haunted, bleak.

"She slaughtered half the Court of Nightmares right then and there. To prove to me that she could. As vengeance for Tamlin's father. And I knew . . . I knew in that moment there was nothing I wouldn't do to keep her from looking at my court again. From looking too long at who I was and what I loved. So I told myself that it was a new war, a different sort of battle. And that night, when she kept turning her attention to me, I knew what she wanted. I knew it wasn't about fucking me so much as it was about getting revenge at my father's ghost. But if that was what she wanted, then that was what she would get. I made her beg, and scream, and used my lingering powers to make it so good for her that she wanted more. Craved more."

I gripped the counter to keep from sliding to the ground.

"Then she cursed Tamlin. And my other great enemy became the one loophole that might free us all. Every night that I spent with Amarantha, I knew that she was half wondering if I'd try to kill her. I couldn't use my powers to harm her, and she had shielded herself against physical attacks. But for fifty years—whenever I was inside her, I'd think about killing her. She had no idea. None. Because I was so good at my job that she thought I enjoyed it, too. So she began to trust me—more than the others. Especially when I proved what I could do to her enemies. But I was glad to do it. I hated myself, but I was glad to do it. After a decade, I stopped expecting to see my friends or my people again. I forgot what their faces looked like. And I stopped hoping."

Silver gleamed in his eyes, and he blinked it away. "Three years ago," he said quietly, "I began to have these . . . dreams. At first, they were glimpses, as if I were staring through someone else's eyes. A crackling hearth in a dark home. A bale of hay in a barn. A warren of rabbits. The images were foggy, like looking through cloudy glass. They were brief—a flash here and there, every few months. I thought nothing of them, until one of the images was of a hand . . . This beautiful, human hand. Holding a brush. Painting—flowers on a table."

My heart stopped beating.

"And that time, I pushed a thought back. Of the night sky—of the image that brought me joy when I needed it most. Open night sky, stars, and the moon. I didn't know if it was received, but I tried, anyway."

I wasn't sure I was breathing.

"Those dreams—the flashes of that person, that woman . . . I treasured them. They were a reminder that there was some peace out there in the world, some light. That there was a place, and a person, who had enough safety to paint flowers on a table. They went on for years, until . . . a year ago. I was sleeping next to Amarantha, and I jolted awake from this dream . . . this dream that was clearer and brighter, like that fog had been wiped away. She—you were dreaming. I was in your dream, watching as you had a nightmare about some woman slitting your throat, while you were chased by the Bogge . . . I couldn't reach you, speak to you. But you were seeing our kind. And I realized that the fog had probably been the wall, and that you . . . you were now in Prythian.

"I saw you through your dreams—and I hoarded the images, sorting through them over and over again, trying to place where you were, who you were. But you had such horrible nightmares, and the creatures belonged to all courts. I'd wake up with your scent in my nose, and it would haunt me all day, every step. But then one night, you dreamed of standing amongst green hills, seeing unlit bonfires for Calanmai."

There was such silence in my head.

"I knew there was only one celebration that large; I knew those hills—and I knew you'd probably be there. So I told Amarantha . . ." Rhys swallowed. "I told her that I wanted to go to the Spring Court for the celebration, to spy on Tamlin and see if anyone showed up wishing to conspire with him. We were so close to the deadline for the curse that she was paranoid—restless. She told me to bring back traitors. I promised her I would."

His eyes lifted to mine again.

"I got there, and I could smell you. So I tracked that scent, and . . . And there you were. Human—utterly human, and being dragged away by those piece-of-shit picts, who wanted to . . ." He shook his head. "I debated slaughtering them then and there, but then they shoved you, and I just . . . moved. I started speaking without knowing what I was saying, only that you were there, and I was touching you, and . . ." He loosed a shuddering breath.

There you are. I've been looking for you.

His first words to me—not a lie at all, not a threat to keep those faeries away.

Thank you for finding her for me.

I had the vague feeling of the world slipping out from under my feet like sand washing away from the shore.

"You looked at me," Rhys said, "and I knew you had no idea who I was. That I might have seen your dreams, but you hadn't seen mine. And you were just . . . human. You were so young, and breakable, and had no interest in me whatsoever, and I knew that if I stayed too long, someone would see and report back, and she'd find you. So I started walking away, thinking you'd be glad to get rid of me. But then you called after me, like you couldn't let go of me just yet, whether you knew it or not. And I knew . . . I knew we were on dangerous ground, somehow. I knew that I could never speak to you, or see you, or think of you again.

"I didn't want to know why you were in Prythian; I didn't even want to know your name. Because seeing you in my dreams had been one thing, but in person . . . Right then, deep down, I think I knew what you were. And I didn't let myself admit it, because if there was the slightest chance that you were my mate . . . They would have done such unspeakable things to you, Feyre.

"So I let you walk away. I told myself after you were gone that maybe . . . maybe the Cauldron had been kind, and not cruel, for letting me see you. Just once. A gift for what I was enduring. And when you were gone, I found those three picts. I broke into their minds, reshaping their lives, their histories, and dragged them before Amarantha. I made them confess to conspiring to find other rebels that night. I made them lie and claim that they hated her. I watched her carve them up while they were still alive, protesting their innocence. I enjoyed it—because I knew what they had wanted to do to you. And knew that it would have paled in comparison to what Amarantha would have done if she'd found you."

I wrapped a hand around my throat. *I had my reasons to be out then*, he'd once said to me Under the Mountain. *Do not think, Feyre, that it did not cost me.*

Rhys kept staring at the table as he said, "I didn't know. That you were with Tamlin. That you were staying at the Spring Court. Amarantha sent me that day after the Summer Solstice because I'd been so successful on Calanmai. I was prepared to mock him, maybe pick a fight. But then I got into that room, and the scent was familiar, but hidden . . . And then I saw the plate, and felt the glamour, and . . . There you were. Living in my second-most enemy's house. Dining with him. Reeking of his scent. Looking at him like . . . Like you loved him."

The whites of his knuckles showed.

"And I decided that I had to scare Tamlin. I had to scare you, and Lucien, but mostly Tamlin. Because I saw how he looked at you, too. So what I did that day . . . " His lips were pale, tight. "I broke into your mind and held it enough that you felt it, that it terrified you, hurt you. I made Tamlin beg—as Amarantha had made me beg, to show him how powerless he was to save you. And I prayed my performance was enough to get him to send you away. Back to the human realm, away from Amarantha. Because she was going to find you. If you broke that curse, she was going to find you and kill you.

"But I was so selfish—I was so stupidly selfish that I couldn't walk away without knowing your name. And you were looking at me like I was a monster, so I told myself it didn't matter, anyway. But you lied when I asked. I knew you did. I had your mind in my hands, and you had the defiance and foresight to lie to my face. So I walked away from you again. I vomited my guts up as soon as I left."

My lips wobbled, and I pressed them together.

"I checked back once. To ensure you were gone. I went with them the day they sacked the manor—to make my performance complete. I told Amarantha the name of that girl, thinking you'd invented it. I had no idea . . . I had no idea she'd send her cronies to retrieve Clare. But if I admitted my lie . . . " He swallowed hard. "I broke into Clare's head when they brought her Under the Mountain. I took away her pain, and told her to scream when expected to. So they . . . they did those things to her, and I tried to make it right, but . . . After a week, I couldn't let them do it. Hurt her like that anymore. So while they tortured her, I slipped into her mind again and ended it. She didn't feel any pain. She felt none of what they did to her, even at the end. But . . . But I still see her. And my men. And the others that I killed for Amarantha."

Two tears slid down his cheeks, swift and cold.

He didn't wipe them away as he said, "I thought it was done after that. With Clare's death, Amarantha believed you were dead. So you were safe, and far away, and my people were safe, and Tamlin had lost, so . . . it was done. We were done. But then . . . I was in the back of the throne room that day the Attor brought you in. And I have never known such horror, Feyre, as I did when I watched you make that bargain. Irrational, stupid terror—I didn't know you. I didn't even know your name. But I thought of those painter's hands, the flowers I'd seen you create. And how she'd delight in breaking your fingers apart. I had to stand and watch as the Attor and its cronies beat you. I had to watch the disgust and hatred on your face as you looked at me, watched me threaten to shatter Lucien's mind. And then—then I learned your name. Hearing you say it . . . it was like an answer to a question I'd been asking for five hundred years.

"I decided, then and there, that I was going to fight. And I would fight dirty, and kill and torture and manipulate, but I was going to fight. If there was a shot of freeing us from Amarantha, you were it. I thought . . . I thought the Cauldron had been sending me these dreams to tell me that you would be the one to save us. Save my people.

"So I watched your first trial. Pretending—always pretending to be that person you hated. When you were hurt so badly against the Wyrm . . . I found my way in with you. A way to defy Amarantha, to spread the seeds of hope to those who knew how to read the message, and a way to keep you alive without seeming too suspicious. And a way to get back at Tamlin . . . To use him against Amarantha, yes, but . . . To get back at him for my mother and sister, and for . . . having you. When we made that bargain, you were so hateful that I knew I'd done my job well.

"So we endured it. I made you dress like that so Amarantha wouldn't suspect, and made you drink the wine so you would not remember the nightly horrors in that mountain. And that last night, when I found you two in the hall . . . I was jealous. I was jealous of him, and pissed off that he'd used that one shot of being unnoticed not to get you out, but to be with you, and . . . Amarantha saw that jealousy. She saw me kissing you to hide the evidence, but she saw why. For the first time, she saw why. So that night, after I left you, I had to . . . service her. She kept me there longer than usual, trying to squeeze the answers out of me. But I gave her what she wanted to hear: that you were nothing, that you were human garbage, that I'd use and discard you. Afterward . . . I wanted to see you. One last time. Alone. I thought about telling you everything—but who I'd become, who you thought I was . . . I didn't dare shatter that deception.

"But your final trial came, and . . . When she started torturing you, something snapped in a way I couldn't explain, only that seeing you bleeding and screaming undid me. It broke me at last. And I knew as I picked up that knife to kill her . . . I knew right then what you were. I knew that you were my mate, and you were in love with another male, and had destroyed yourself to save him, and that . . . that I didn't care. If you were going to die, I was going to die with you. I couldn't stop thinking it over and over as you screamed, as I tried to kill her: you were my mate, my mate, my mate.

"But then she snapped your neck."

Tears rolled down his face.

"And I felt you die," he whispered.

Tears were sliding down my own cheeks.

"And this beautiful, wonderful thing that had come into my life, this gift from the Cauldron . . . It was gone. In my desperation, I clung to that bond. Not the bargain—the bargain was nothing, the bargain was like a cobweb. But I grabbed that bond between us and I *tugged*, I willed you to hold on, to stay with me, because if we could get free . . . If we could get free, then all seven of us were there. We could bring you back. And I didn't care if I had to slice into all of their minds to do it. I'd *make* them save you." His hands were shaking. "You'd freed us with your last breath, and my power—I wrapped my power around the bond. The mating bond. I could feel you flickering there, holding on."

Home. Home had been at the end of the bond, I'd told the Bone Carver. Not Tamlin, not the Spring Court, but . . . Rhysand.

"So Amarantha died, and I spoke to the High Lords mind to mind, convincing them to come forward, to offer that spark of power. None of them disagreed. I think they were too stunned to think of saying no.

And . . . I again had to watch as Tamlin held you. Kissed you. I wanted to go home, to Velaris, but I had to stay, to make sure things were set in motion, that you were all right. So I waited as long as I could, then I sent a tug through the bond. Then you came to find me.

"I almost told you then, but . . . You were so sad. And tired. And for once, you looked at me like . . . like I was worth something. So I promised myself that the next time I saw you, I'd free you of the bargain. Because I was selfish, and knew that if I let go right then, he'd lock you up and I'd never get to see you again. When I went to leave you . . . I think transforming you into Fae made the bond lock into place permanently. I'd known it existed, but it *hit* me then—hit me so strong that I panicked. I knew if I stayed a second longer, I'd damn the consequences and take you with me. And you'd hate me forever.

"I landed at the Night Court, right as Mor was waiting for me, and I was so frantic, so . . . unhinged, that I told her everything. I hadn't seen her in fifty years, and my first words to her were, 'She's my mate.' And for three months . . . for three months I tried to convince myself that you were better off without me. I tried to convince myself that everything I'd done had made you hate me. But I felt you through the bond, through your open mental shields. I felt your pain, and sadness, and loneliness. I felt you struggling to escape the darkness of Amarantha the same way I was. I heard you were going to marry him, and I told myself you were happy. I should let you be happy, even if it killed me. Even if you were my mate, you'd earned that happiness.

"The day of your wedding, I'd planned to get rip-roaring drunk with Cassian, who had no idea why, but . . . But then I felt you again. I felt your panic, and despair, and heard you beg someone—anyone—to save you. I lost it. I winnowed to the wedding, and barely remembered who I was supposed to be, the part I was supposed to play. All I could see was you, in your stupid wedding dress—so thin. So, so thin, and pale. And I wanted to kill him for it, but I had to get you out. Had to call in that bargain, just once, to get you away, to see if you were all right."

Rhys looked up at me, eyes desolate. "It killed me, Feyre, to send you back. To see you waste away, month by month. It killed me to know he was sharing your bed. Not just because you were my mate, but because I . . . " He glanced down, then up at me again. "I knew . . . I knew I was in love with you that moment I picked up the knife to kill Amarantha.

"When you finally came here . . . I decided I wouldn't tell you. Any of it. I wouldn't let you out of the bargain, because your hatred was better than facing the two alternatives: that you felt nothing for me, or that you . . . you might feel something similar, and if I let myself love you, you would be taken from me. The way my family was—the way my friends were. So I didn't tell you. I watched as you faded away. Until that day . . . that day he locked you up.

"I would have killed him if he'd been there. But I broke some very, very fundamental rules in taking you away. Amren said if I got you to admit that we were mates, it would keep any trouble from our door, but . . . I couldn't force the bond on you. I couldn't try to seduce you into accepting the bond, either. Even if it gave Tamlin license to wage war on me. You had been through so much already. I didn't want you to think that everything I did was to win you, just to keep my lands safe. But I couldn't . . . I couldn't stop being around you, and loving you, and wanting you. I still can't stay away."

He leaned back, loosing a long breath.

Slowly, I turned around, to where the soup was now boiling, and ladled it into a bowl.

He watched every step I took to the table, the steaming bowl in my hands.

I stopped before him, staring down.

And I said, "You love me?"

Rhys nodded.

And I wondered if love was too weak a word for what he felt, what he'd done for me. For what I felt for him.

I set the bowl down before him. "Then eat."

CHAPTER 55

I watched him consume every spoonful, his eyes darting between where I stood and the soup.

When he was done, he set down his spoon.

"Aren't you going to say anything?" he said at last.

"I was going to tell you what I'd decided the moment I saw you on the threshold."

Rhys twisted in his seat toward me. "And now?"

Aware of every breath, every movement, I sat in his lap. His hands gently braced my hips as I studied his face. "And now I want you to know, Rhysand, that I love you. I want you to know . . . " His lips trembled, and I brushed away the tear that escaped down his cheek. "I want you to know," I whispered, "that I am broken and healing, but every piece of my heart belongs to you. And I am honored—*honored* to be your mate."

His arms wrapped around me and he pressed his forehead to my shoulder, his body shaking. I stroked a hand through his silken hair.

"I love you," I said again. I hadn't dared say the words in my head. "And I'd endure every second of it over again so I could find you. And if war comes, we'll face it. Together. I won't let them take me from you. And I won't let them take you from me, either."

Rhys looked up, his face gleaming with tears. He went still as I leaned in, kissing away one tear. Then the other. As he had once kissed away mine.

When my lips were wet and salty with them, I pulled back far enough to see his eyes. "You're mine," I breathed.

His body shuddered with what might have been a sob, but his lips found my own.

It was gentle—soft. The kiss he might have given me if we'd been granted time and peace to meet across our two separate worlds. To court each other. I slid my arms around his shoulders, opening my mouth to him, and his tongue slipped in, caressing my own. Mate—my mate.

He hardened against me, and I groaned into his mouth.

The sound snapped whatever leash he'd had on himself, and Rhysand scooped me up in a smooth movement before laying me flat on the table—amongst and on top of all the paints.

He deepened the kiss, and I wrapped my legs around his back, hooking him closer. He tore his lips from my mouth to my neck, where he dragged his teeth and tongue down my skin as his hands slid under my sweater and went up, up, to cup my breasts. I arched into the touch, and lifted my arms as he peeled away my sweater in one easy motion.

Rhys pulled back to survey me, my body naked from the waist up. Paint soaked into my hair, my arms. But all I could think of was his mouth as it lowered to my breast and sucked, his tongue flicking against my nipple.

I plunged my fingers into his hair, and he braced a hand beside my head—smack atop a palette of paint. He let out a low laugh, and I watched, breathless, as he took that hand and traced a circle around my breast, then lower, until he painted a downward arrow beneath my belly button.

"Lest you forget where this is going to end," he said.

I snarled at him, a silent order, and he laughed again, his mouth finding my other breast. He ground his hips against me, teasing—teasing me so horribly that I had to touch him, had to just feel *more* of him. There was paint all over my hands, my arms, but I didn't care as I grabbed at his clothes. He shifted enough to let me remove them, weapons and leather thudding to the ground, revealing that beautiful tattooed body, the powerful muscles and wings now peeking above them.

My mate—my mate.

His mouth crashed into mine, his bare skin so warm against my own, and I gripped his face, smearing paint there, too. Smearing it in his hair, until great streaks of blue and red and green ran through it. His hands found my waist, and I bucked my hips off the table to help him remove my socks, my leggings.

Rhys pulled back again, and I let out a bark of protest—that choked off into a gasp as he gripped my thighs and yanked me to the edge of the table, through paints and brushes and cups of water, hooked my legs over his shoulders to rest on either side of those beautiful wings, and knelt before me.

Knelt on those stars and mountains inked on his knees. He would bow for no one and nothing—

But his mate. His equal.

The first lick of Rhysand's tongue set me on fire.

I want you splayed out on the table like my own personal feast.

He growled his approval at my moan, my taste, and unleashed himself on me entirely.

A hand pinning my hips to the table, he worked me in great sweeping strokes. And when his tongue slid inside me, I reached up to grip the edge of the table, to grip the edge of the world that I was very near to falling off.

He licked and kissed his way to the apex of my thighs, just as his fingers replaced where his mouth had been, pumping inside me as he sucked, his teeth scraping ever so slightly—

I bowed off the table as my climax shattered through me, splintering my consciousness into a million pieces. He kept licking me, fingers still moving. "Rhys," I rasped.

Now. I wanted him now.

But he remained kneeling, feasting on me, that hand pinning me to the table.

I went over the edge again. And only when I was trembling, half sobbing, limp with pleasure, did Rhys rise from the floor.

He looked me over, naked, covered in paint, his own face and body smeared with it, and give me a slow, satisfied male smile. "You're *mine*," he snarled, and hefted me up into his arms.

I wanted the wall—I wanted him to just take me against the wall, but he carried me into the room I'd been using and set me down on the bed with heartbreaking gentleness.

Wholly naked, I watched as he unbuttoned his pants, and the considerable length of him sprang free. My mouth went dry at the sight of it. I wanted him, wanted every glorious inch of him in me, wanted to claw at him until our souls were forged together.

He didn't say anything as he came over me, wings tucked in tight. He'd never gone to bed with a female while his wings were out. But I was his mate. He would yield only for me.

And I wanted to touch him.

I leaned up, reaching over his shoulder to caress the powerful curve of his wing.

Rhys shuddered, and I watched his cock twitch.

"Play later," he ground out.

Indeed.

His mouth found mine, the kiss open and deep, a clash of tongues and teeth. He lay me down on the pillows, and I locked my legs around his back, careful of the wings.

Though I stopped caring as he nudged at my entrance. And paused.

"*Play later*," I snarled into his mouth.

Rhys laughed in a way that skittered along my bones, and slid in. And in. And in.

I could hardly breathe, hardly think beyond where our bodies were joined. He stilled inside me, letting me adjust, and I opened my eyes to find him staring down at me. "Say it again," he murmured.

I knew what he meant.

"You're mine," I breathed.

Rhys pulled out slightly and thrust back in slow. So torturously slow.

"You're mine," I gasped out.

Again, he pulled out, then thrust in.

"You're mine."

Again—faster, deeper this time.

I felt it then, the bond between us, like an unbreakable chain, like an undimmable ray of light.

With each pounding stroke, the bond glowed clearer and brighter and stronger. "You're mine," I whispered, dragging my hands through his hair, down his back, across his wings.

My friend through many dangers.

My lover who had healed my broken and weary soul.

My mate who had waited for me against all hope, despite all odds.

I moved my hips in time with his. He kissed me over and over, and both of our faces turned damp. Every inch of me burned and tightened, and my control slipped entirely as he whispered, "I love you."

Release tore through my body, and he pounded into me, hard and fast, drawing out my pleasure until I felt and saw and smelled that bond between us, until our scents *merged*, and I was his and he was mine, and we were the beginning and middle and end. We were a song that had been sung from the very first ember of light in the world.

Rhys roared as he came, slamming in to the hilt. Outside, the mountains trembled, the remaining snow rushing from them in a cascade of glittering white, only to be swallowed up by the waiting night below.

Silence fell, interrupted only by our panting breaths.

I took his paint-smeared face between my own colorful hands and made him look at me.

His eyes were radiant like the stars I'd painted once, long ago.

And I smiled at Rhys as I let that mating bond shine clear and luminous between us.

I don't know how long we lay there, lazily touching each other, as if we might indeed have all the time in the world.

"I think I fell in love with you," Rhys murmured, stroking a finger down my arm, "the moment I realized you were cleaving those bones to make a trap for the Middengard Wyrm. Or maybe the moment you flipped me off for mocking you. It reminded me so much of Cassian. For the first time in decades, I wanted to *laugh*."

"You fell in love with me," I said flatly, "because I reminded you of your friend?"

He flicked my nose. "I fell in love with you, smartass, because you were one of us—because you weren't afraid of me, and you decided to end your spectacular victory by throwing that piece of bone at Amarantha like a javelin. I felt Cassian's spirit beside me in that moment, and could have sworn I heard him say, '*If you don't marry her, you stupid prick, I will.*' "

I huffed a laugh, sliding my paint-covered hand over his tattooed chest. Paint—right.

We were both covered in it. So was the bed.

Rhys followed my eyes and gave me a grin that was positively wicked. "How convenient that the bathtub is large enough for two."

My blood heated, and I rose from the bed only to have him move faster—scooping me up in his arms. He was splattered with paint, his hair crusted with it, and his poor, beautiful wings . . . Those were my handprints on them. Naked, he carried me into the bath, where the water was already running, the magic of this cabin acting on our behalf.

He strode down the steps into the water, his hiss of pleasure a brush of air against my ear. And I might have moaned a little myself when the hot water hit me as he sat us both down in the tub.

A basket of soaps and oils appeared along the stone rim, and I pushed off him to sink further beneath the surface. The steam wafted between us, and Rhys picked up a bar of that pine tar–smelling soap and handed it to me, then passed a washrag. "Someone, it seems, got my wings dirty."

My face heated, but my gut tightened. Illyrian males and their wings—so sensitive.

I twirled my finger to motion him to turn around. He obeyed, spreading those magnificent wings enough for me to find the paint stains. Carefully, so carefully, I soaped up the washcloth and began wiping the red and blue and purple away.

The candlelight danced over his countless, faint scars—nearly invisible save for harder bits of membrane. He shuddered with each pass, hands braced on the lip of the tub. I peeked over his shoulder to see the evidence of that sensitivity, and said, "At least the rumors about wingspan correlating with the size of other parts were right."

His back muscles tensed as he choked out a laugh. "Such a dirty, wicked mouth."

I thought of all the places I wanted to put that mouth and blushed a bit.

"I think I was falling in love with you for a while," I said, the words barely audible over the trickle of water as I washed his beautiful wings. "But I knew on Starfall. Or came close to knowing and was so scared of it that I didn't want to look closer. I was a coward."

"You had perfectly good reasons to avoid it."

"No, I didn't. Maybe—thanks to Tamlin, yes. But it had nothing to do with you, Rhys. *Nothing* to do with you. I was never afraid of the consequences of being with you. Even if every assassin in the world hunts us . . . It's worth it. *You* are worth it."

His head dipped a bit. And he said hoarsely, "Thank you."

My heart broke for him then—for the years he'd spent thinking the opposite. I kissed his bare neck, and he reached back to drag a finger down my cheek.

I finished the wings and gripped his shoulder to turn him to face me. "What now?" Wordlessly, he took the soap from my hands and turned me, rubbing down my back, scrubbing lightly with the cloth.

"It's up to you," Rhys said. "We can go back to Velaris and have the bond verified by a priestess—no one like Ianthe, I promise—and be declared officially Mated. We could have a small party to celebrate—dinner with our . . . cohorts. Unless you'd rather have a large party, though I think you and I are in agreement about our aversion for them." His strong hands kneaded muscles that were tight and aching in my back, and I groaned. "We could also go before a priestess and be declared husband and wife as well as mates, if you want a more human thing to call me."

"What will *you* call me?"

"Mate," he said. "Though also calling you my wife sounds mighty appealing, too." His thumbs massaged the column of my spine. "Or if you want to wait, we can do none of those things. We're mated, whether it's shouted across the world or not. There's no rush to decide."

I turned. "I was asking about Jurian, the king, the queens, and the Cauldron, but I'm glad to know I have so many options where our relationship stands. And that you'll do whatever I want. I must have you wrapped completely around my finger."

His eyes danced with feline amusement. "Cruel, beautiful thing."

I snorted. The idea that he found me beautiful at all—

"You are," he said. "You're the most beautiful thing I've ever seen. I thought that from the first moment I saw you on Calanmai."

And it was stupid, stupid for beauty to mean anything at all, but . . . My eyes burned.

"Which is good," he added, "because you thought *I* was the most beautiful male you'd ever seen. So it makes us even."

I scowled, and he laughed, hands sliding to grip my waist and tug me to him. He sat down on the built-in bench of the tub, and I straddled him, idly stroking his muscled arms.

"Tomorrow," Rhys said, features becoming grave. "We're leaving tomorrow for your family's estate. The queens sent word. They return in three days."

I started. "You're telling me this *now*?"

"I got sidetracked," he said, his eyes twinkling.

And the light in those eyes, the quiet joy . . . They knocked the breath from me. A future—we would have a future together. *I* would have a future. A *life*.

His smile faded into something awed, something . . . reverent, and I reached out to cup his face in my hands—

To find my skin glowing.

Faintly, as if some inner light shone beneath my skin, leaking out into the world. Warm and white light, like the sun—like a star. Those wonder-filled eyes met mine, and Rhys ran a finger down my arm. "Well, at least now I can gloat that I literally make my mate glow with happiness."

I laughed, and the glow flared a little brighter. He leaned in, kissing me softly, and I melted for him, wrapping my arms around his neck. He was rock-hard against me, pushing against where I sat poised right above him. All it would take would be one smooth motion and he'd be inside me—

But Rhys stood from the water, both of us dripping wet, and I hooked my legs around him as he walked us back into the bedroom. The sheets had been changed by the domestic magic of the house, and they were warm and smooth against my naked body as he set me down and stared at me. Shining—I was shining bright and pure as a star. "Day Court?" I asked.

"I don't care," he said roughly, and removed the glamour from himself.

It was a small magic, he'd once told me, to keep the damper on who he was, what his power looked like.

As the full majesty of him was unleashed, he filled the room, the world, my soul, with glittering ebony power. Stars and wind and shadows; peace and dreams and the honed edge of nightmares. Darkness rippled from him like tendrils of steam as he reached out a hand and laid it flat against the glowing skin of my stomach.

That hand of night splayed, the light leaking through the wafting shadows, and I hoisted myself up on my elbows to kiss him.

Smoke and mist and dew.

I moaned at the taste of him, and he opened his mouth for me, letting me brush my tongue against his, scrape it against his teeth. Everything he was had been laid before me—one final question.

I wanted it all.

I gripped his shoulders, guiding him onto the bed. And when he lay flat on his back, I saw the flash of protest at the pinned wings. But I crooned, "Illyrian baby," and ran my hands down his muscled abdomen—farther. He stopped objecting.

He was enormous in my hand—so hard, yet so silken that I just ran a finger down him in wonder. He hissed, cock twitching as I brushed my thumb over the tip. I smirked as I did it again.

He reached for me, but I froze him with a look. "My turn," I told him.

Rhys gave me a lazy, male smile before he settled back, tucking a hand behind his head. Waiting.

Cocky bastard.

So I leaned down and put my mouth on him.

He jerked at the contact with a barked, "*Shit*," and I laughed around him, even as I took him deeper into my mouth.

His hands were now fisted in the sheets, white-knuckled as I slid my tongue over him, grazing slightly with my teeth. His groan was fire to my blood.

Honestly, I was surprised he waited the full minute before interrupting me.

Pouncing was a better word for what Rhys did.

One second, he was in my mouth, my tongue flicking over the broad head of him; the next, his hands were on my waist and I was being flipped onto my front. He nudged my legs apart with his knees, spreading me as he gripped my hips, tugging them up, up before he sheathed himself deep in me with a single stroke.

I moaned into the pillow at every glorious inch of him, rising onto my forearms as my fingers grappled into the sheets.

Rhys pulled out and plunged back in, eternity exploding around me in that instant, and I thought I might break apart from not being able to get enough of him.

"Look at you," he murmured as he moved in me, and kissed the length of my spine.

I managed to rise up enough to see where we were joined—to see the sunlight shimmer off me against the rippling night of him, merging and blending, enriching. And the sight of it wrecked me so thoroughly that I climaxed with his name on my lips.

Rhys hauled me up against him, one hand cupping my breast as the other rolled and stroked that bundle of nerves between my legs, and I couldn't tell where one climax ended and the second began as he thrust in again, and again, his lips on my neck, on my ear.

I could die from this, I decided. From wanting him, from the pleasure of being with him.

He twisted us, pulling out only long enough to lie on his back and haul me over him.

There was a glimmer in the darkness—a flash of lingering pain, a scar. And I understood why he wanted me like this, wanted to end it like this, with me astride him.

It broke my heart. I leaned forward to kiss him, softly, tenderly.

As our mouths met, I slid onto him, the fit so much deeper, and he murmured my name into my mouth. I kissed him again and again, and rode him gently. Later—there would be other times to go hard and fast. But right now . . . I wouldn't think of why this position was one he wanted to end in, to have me banish the stained dark with the light.

But I would glow—for him, I'd glow. For my own future, I'd glow.

So I sat up, hands braced on his broad chest, and unleashed that light in me, letting it drive out the darkness of what had been done to him, my mate, my friend.

Rhys barked my name, thrusting his hips up. Stars wheeled as he slammed deep.

I think the light pouring out of me might have been starlight, or maybe my own vision fractured as release barreled into me again and Rhys found his, gasping my name over and over as he spilled himself in me.

When we were done, I remained atop him, fingertips digging into his chest, and marveled at him. At us.

He tugged on my wet hair. "We'll have to find a way to put a damper on that light."

"I can keep the shadows hidden easily enough."

"Ah, but you only lose control of those when you're pissed. And since I have every intention of making you as happy as a person can be . . . I have a feeling we'll need to learn to control that wondrous glow."

"Always thinking; always calculating."

Rhys kissed the corner of my mouth. "You have no idea how many things I've thought up when it comes to you."

"I remember mention of a wall."

His laugh was a sensual promise. "Next time, Feyre, I'll fuck you against the wall."

"Hard enough to make the pictures fall off."

Rhys barked a laugh. "Show me again what you can do with that wicked mouth."

I obliged him.

It was wrong to compare, because I knew probably every High Lord could keep a woman from sleeping all night, but Rhysand was . . . ravenous. I got perhaps an hour total of sleep that night, though I supposed I was to equally share the blame.

I couldn't stop, couldn't get enough of the taste of him in my mouth, the feel of him inside of me. More, more, more—until I thought I might burst out of my skin from pleasure.

"It's normal," Rhys said around a mouthful of bread as we sat at the table for breakfast. We'd barely made it into the kitchen. He'd taken one step out of bed, giving me a full view of his glorious wings, muscled back, and that beautiful backside, and I'd leaped on him. We'd tumbled to the floor and he'd shredded the pretty little area rug beneath his talons as I rode him.

"What's normal?" I said. I could barely look at him without wanting to combust.

"The . . . frenzy," he said carefully, as if fearful the wrong word might send us both hurtling for each other before we could get sustenance into our bodies. "When a couple accepts the mating bond, it's . . . overwhelming. Again, harkening back to the beasts we once were. Probably something about ensuring the female was impregnated." My heart paused at that. "Some couples don't leave the house for a week. Males get so volatile that it can be dangerous for them to be in public, anyway. I've seen males of reason and education shatter a room because another male looked too long in their mate's direction, too soon after they'd been mated."

I hissed out a breath. Another shattered room flashed in my memory.

Rhys said softly, knowing what haunted me, "I'd like to believe I have more restraint than the average male, but . . . Be patient with me, Feyre, if I'm a little on edge."

That he'd admit that much . . . "You don't want to leave this house."

"I want to stay in that bedroom and fuck you until we're both hoarse."

That fast, I was ready for him, aching for him, but—but we had to go. Queens. Cauldron. Jurian. War. "About—pregnancy," I said.

And might as well have thrown a bucket of ice over both of us.

"We didn't—I'm not taking a tonic. I haven't been, I mean."

He set down his bread. "Do you want to start taking it again?"

If I did, if I started today, it'd negate what we'd done last night, but . . . "If I am a High Lord's mate, I'm expected to bear you offspring, aren't I? So perhaps I shouldn't."

"You are not expected to bear me *anything*," he snarled. "Children are rare, yes. So rare, and so precious. But I don't want you to have them unless you want to—unless we *both* want to. And right now, with this war coming, with Hybern . . . I'll admit that I'm terrified at the thought of my mate being pregnant with so many enemies around us. I'm terrified of what *I* might do if you're pregnant and threatened. Or harmed."

Something tight in my chest eased, even as a chill went down my back as I considered that power, that rage I'd seen at the Night Court, unleashed upon the earth. "Then I'll start taking it today, once we get back."

I rose from the table on shaky knees and headed for the bedroom. I had to bathe—I was covered in him, my mouth tasted of him, despite breakfast. Rhys said softly from behind me, "I would be happy beyond reason, though, if you one day did honor me with children. To share that with you."

I turned back to him. "I want to live first," I said. "With you. I want to see things and have adventures. I want to learn what it is to be immortal, to be your mate, to be part of your family. I want to be . . . ready for them. And I selfishly want to have you all to myself for a while."

His smile was gentle, sweet. "You take all the time you need. And if I get you all to myself for the rest of eternity, then I won't mind that at all."

I made it to the edge of the bath before Rhys caught me, carried me into the water, and made love to me, slow and deep, amid the billowing steam.

CHAPTER 56

Rhys winnowed us to the Illyrian camp. We wouldn't be staying long enough to be at risk—and with ten thousand Illyrian warriors surrounding us on the various peaks, Rhys doubted anyone would be stupid enough to attack.

We'd just appeared in the mud outside the little house when Cassian drawled from behind us, "Well, it's about time."

The savage, wild snarl that ripped out of Rhys was like nothing I'd heard, and I gripped his arm as he whirled on Cassian.

Cassian looked at him and laughed.

But the Illyrian warriors in the camp began shooting into the sky, hauling women and children with them.

"Hard ride?" Cassian tied back his dark hair with a worn strap of leather.

Preternatural quiet now leaked from Rhys where the snarl had erupted a moment before. And rather than see him turn the camp to rubble I said, "When he bashes your teeth in, Cassian, don't come crying to me."

Cassian crossed his arms. "Mating bond chafing a bit, Rhys?"

Rhys said nothing.

Cassian snickered. "Feyre doesn't look too tired. Maybe she could give me a ride—"

Rhys exploded.

Wings and muscles and snapping teeth, and they were rolling through the mud, fists flying, and—

And Cassian had known exactly what he was saying and doing, I realized as he kicked Rhys off him, as Rhys didn't touch that power that could have flattened these mountains.

He'd seen the edge in Rhys's eyes and known he had to dull it before we could go any further.

Rhys had known, too. Which was why we'd winnowed here first—and not Velaris.

They were a sight to behold, two Illyrian males fighting in the mud and stones, panting and spitting blood. None of the other Illyrians dared land.

Nor would they, I realized, until Rhys had worked off his temper—or left the camp entirely. If the average male needed a week to adjust . . . What was required of Rhysand? A month? Two? A year?

Cassian laughed as Rhys slammed a fist into his face, blood spraying. Cassian slung one right back at him, and I cringed as Rhys's head knocked to the side. I'd seen Rhys fight before, controlled and elegant, and I'd seen him mad, but never so . . . feral.

"They'll be at it for a while," Mor said, leaning against the threshold of the house. She held open the door. "Welcome to the family, Feyre."

And I thought those might have been the most beautiful words I'd ever heard.

Rhys and Cassian spent an hour pummeling each other into exhaustion, and when they trudged back into the house, bloody and filthy, one look at my mate was all it took for me to crave the smell and feel of him.

Cassian and Mor instantly found somewhere else to be, and Rhys didn't bother taking my clothes all the way off before he bent me over the kitchen table and made me moan his name loud enough for the Illyrians still circling high above to hear.

But when we finished, the tightness in his shoulders and the tension coiled in his eyes had vanished . . . And a knock on the door from Cassian had Rhys handing me a damp washcloth to clean myself. A moment later, the four of us had winnowed to the music and light of Velaris.

To home.

The sun had barely set as Rhys and I walked hand in hand into the dining room of the House of Wind, and found Mor, Azriel, Amren, and Cassian already seated. Waiting for us.

As one, they stood.

As one, they looked at me.

And as one, they bowed.

It was Amren who said, "We will serve and protect."

They each placed a hand over their heart.

Waiting—for my reply.

Rhys hadn't warned me, and I wondered if the words were supposed to come from my heart, spoken without agenda or guile. So I voiced them.

"Thank you," I said, willing my voice to be steady. "But I'd rather you were my friends before the serving and protecting."

Mor said with a wink, "We are. But we will serve and protect."

My face warmed, and I smiled at them. My—family.

"Now that we've settled that," Rhys drawled from behind me, "can we please eat? I'm famished." Amren opened her mouth with a wry smile, but he added, "Do *not* say what you were going to say, Amren." Rhys gave Cassian a sharp look. Both of them were still bruised—but healing fast. "Unless you want to have it out on the roof."

Amren clicked her tongue and instead jerked her chin at me. "I heard you grew fangs in the forest and killed some Hybern beasts. Good for you, girl."

"She saved his sorry ass is more like it," Mor said, filling her glass of wine. "Poor little Rhys got himself in a bind."

I held out my own glass for Mor to fill. "He does need unusual amounts of coddling."

Azriel choked on his wine, and I met his gaze—warm for once. Soft, even. I felt Rhys tense beside me and quickly looked away from the spymaster.

A glance at the guilt in Rhys's eyes told me he was sorry. And fighting it. So strange, the High Fae with their mating and primal instincts. So at odds with their ancient traditions and learning.

We left for the mortal lands soon after dinner. Mor carried the orb; Cassian carried her, Azriel flying close, and Rhys . . . Rhys held me tightly, his arms strong and unyielding around me. We were silent as we soared over the dark water.

As we went to show the queens the secret they'd all suffered so much, for so long, to keep.

CHAPTER 57

Spring had at last dawned on the human world, crocuses and daffodils poking their heads out of the thawed earth.

Only the eldest and the golden-haired queens came this time.

They were escorted by just as many guards, however.

I once again wore my flowing, ivory gown and crown of gold feathers, once again beside Rhysand as the queens and their sentries winnowed into the sitting room.

But now Rhys and I stood hand in hand—unflinching, a song without end or beginning.

The eldest queen slid her cunning eyes over us, our hands, our crowns, and merely sat without our bidding, adjusting the skirts of her emerald gown around her. The golden queen remained standing for a moment longer, her shining, curly head angling slightly. Her red lips twitched upward as she claimed the seat beside her companion.

Rhys did not so much as lower his head to them as he said, "We appreciate you taking the time to see us again."

The younger queen merely gave a little nod, her amber gaze leaping over to our friends behind us: Cassian and Azriel on either side of the bay of windows where Elain and Nesta stood in their finery, Elain's garden in bloom behind them. Nesta's shoulders were already locked. Elain bit her lip.

Mor stood on Rhys's other side, this time in blue-green that reminded me of the Sidra's calm waters, the onyx box containing the Veritas in her tan hands.

The ancient queen, surveying us all with narrowed eyes, let out a huff. "After being so gravely insulted the last time . . . " A simmering glare thrown at Nesta. My sister leveled a look of pure, unyielding flame right back at her. The old woman clicked her tongue. "We debated for many days whether we should return. As you can see, three of us found the insult to be unforgivable."

Liar. To blame it on Nesta, to try to sow discord between us for what Nesta had tried to defend . . . I said with surprising calm, "If that is the worst insult any of you have ever received in your lives, I'd say you're all in for quite a shock when war comes."

The younger one's lips twitched again, amber eyes alight—a lion incarnate. She purred to me, "So he won your heart after all, Cursebreaker."

I held her stare as Rhys and I both sat in our chairs, Mor sliding into one beside him. "I do not think," I said, "that it was mere coincidence that the Cauldron let us find each other on the eve of war returning between our two peoples."

"The Cauldron? And two peoples?" The golden one toyed with a ruby ring on her finger. "*Our* people do not invoke a Cauldron; *our* people do not have magic. The way I see it, there is *your* people—and ours. *You* are little better than those Children of the Blessed." She lifted a groomed brow. "What *does* happen to them when they cross the wall?" She angled her head at Rhys, at Cassian and Azriel. "Are they prey? Or are they used and discarded, and left to grow old and infirm while you remain young forever? Such a pity . . . so unfair that you, Cursebreaker, received what all those fools no doubt begged for. Immortality, eternal youth . . . What would Lord Rhysand have done if you had aged while he did not?"

Rhys said evenly, "Is there a point to your questions, other than to hear yourself talk?"

A low chuckle, and she turned to the ancient queen, her yellow dress rustling with the movement. The old woman simply extended a wrinkled hand to the box in Mor's slender fingers. "Is that the proof we asked for?"

Don't do it, my heart began bleating. *Don't show them.*

Before Mor could so much as nod, I said, "Is my love for the High Lord not proof enough of our good intentions? Does my sisters' presence here not speak to you? There is an iron engagement ring upon my sister's finger—and yet she stands with us."

Elain seemed to be fighting the urge to tuck her hand behind the skirts of her pale pink and blue dress, but stayed tall while the queens surveyed her.

"I would say that it is proof of her idiocy," the golden one sneered, "to be engaged to a Fae-hating man . . . and to risk the match by associating with you."

"Do not," Nesta hissed with quiet venom, "judge what you know *nothing* about."

The golden one folded her hands in her lap. "The viper speaks again." She raised her brows at me. "Surely the wise move would have been to have her sit this meeting out."

"She offers up her house and risks her social standing for us to have these meetings," I said. "She has the right to hear what is spoken in them. To stand as a representative of the people of these lands. They both do."

The crone interrupted the younger before she could reply, and again waved that wrinkled hand at Mor. "Show us, then. Prove us wrong."

Rhys gave Mor a subtle nod. No—no, it wasn't right. Not to show them, not to reveal the treasure that was Velaris, that was my home . . .

War is sacrifice, Rhys said into my mind, through the small sliver I now kept open for him. *If we do not gamble Velaris, we risk losing Prythian—and more.*

Mor opened the lid of the black box.

The silver orb inside glimmered like a star under glass. "This is the

Veritas," Mor said in a voice that was young and old. "The gift of my first ancestor to our bloodline. Only a few times in the history of Prythian have we used it—have we unleashed its truth upon the world."

She lifted the orb from its velvet nest. It was no larger than a ripe apple, and fit within her cupped palms as if her entire body, her entire being, had been molded for it.

"Truth is deadly. Truth is freedom. Truth can break and mend and bind. The Veritas holds in it the truth of the world. I am the Morrigan," she said, her eyes not wholly of this earth. The hair on my arms rose. "You know I speak truth."

She set the Veritas onto the carpet between us. Both queens leaned in.

But it was Rhys who said, "You desire proof of our goodness, our intentions, so that you may trust the Book in our hands?" The Veritas began pulsing, a web of light spreading with each throb. "There is a place within my lands. A city of peace. And art. And prosperity. As I doubt you or your guards will dare pass through the wall, then I will show it to you—show you the truth of these words, show you this place within the orb itself."

Mor stretched out a hand, and a pale cloud swirled from the orb, merging with its light as it drifted past our ankles.

The queens flinched, the guards edging forward with hands on their weapons. But the clouds continued roiling as the truth of it, of Velaris, leaked from the orb, from whatever it dragged up from Mor, from Rhys. From the truth of the world.

And in the gray gloom, a picture appeared.

It was Velaris, as seen from above—as seen by Rhys, flying in. A speck in the coast, but as he dropped down, the city and the river became clearer, vibrant.

Then the image banked and swerved, as if Rhys had flown through his city just this morning. It shot past boats and piers, past the homes and streets and theaters. Past the Rainbow of Velaris, so colorful and lovely in the new spring sun. People, happy and thoughtful, kind and welcoming, waved to him. Moment after moment, images of the Palaces, of the restaurants, of the House of Wind. All of it—all of that secret, wondrous city. My home.

And I could have sworn that there was love in that image. I could not explain how the Veritas conveyed it, but the colors . . . I understood the colors, and the light, what they conveyed, what the orb somehow picked up from whatever link it had to Rhys's memories.

The illusion faded, color and light and cloud sucked back into the orb.

"That is Velaris," Rhys said. "For five thousand years, we have kept it a secret from outsiders. And now you know. That is what I protect with the rumors, the whispers, the fear. Why I fought for your people in the War—only to begin my own supposed reign of terror once I ascended my throne, and ensured everyone heard the legends about it. But if the cost of protecting my city and people is the contempt of the world, then so be it."

The two queens were gaping at the carpet as if they could still see the city there. Mor cleared her throat. The golden one, as if Mor had barked, started and dropped an ornate lace handkerchief on the ground. She leaned to pick it up, cheeks a bit red.

But the crone raised her eyes to us. "Your trust is . . . appreciated."

We waited.

Both of their faces turned grave, unmoved. And I was glad I was sitting as the eldest added at last, "We will consider."

"There is no time to consider," Mor countered. "Every day lost is another day that Hybern gets closer to shattering the wall."

"We will discuss amongst our companions, and inform you at our leisure."

"Do you not understand the risks you take in doing so?" Rhys said, no hint of condescension. Only—only perhaps shock. "You need this alliance as much as we do."

The ancient queen shrugged her frail shoulders. "Did you think we would be moved by your letter, your plea?" She jerked her chin to the guard closest, and he reached into his armor to pull out a folded letter. The old woman read, "*I write to you not as a High Lord, but as a male in love with a woman who was once human. I write to you to beg you to act quickly. To save her people—to help save my own. I write to you so one day we might know true peace. So I might one day be able to live in a world where the woman I love may visit her family without fear of hatred and reprisal. A better world.*" She set down the letter.

Rhys had written that letter weeks ago . . . before we'd mated. Not a demand for the queens to meet—but a love letter. I reached across the space between us and took his hand, squeezing gently. Rhys's fingers tightened around my own.

But then the ancient one said, "Who is to say that this is not all some grand manipulation?"

"What?" Mor blurted.

The golden queen nodded her agreement and dared say to Mor, "A great many things have changed since the War. Since your so-called friendships with our ancestors. Perhaps you are not who you say you are. Perhaps the High Lord has crept into our minds to make us believe you are the Morrigan."

Rhys was silent—we all were. Until Nesta said too softly, "This is the talk of madwomen. Of arrogant, stupid *fools*."

Elain grabbed for Nesta's hand to silence her. But Nesta stalked forward a step, face white with rage. "Give them the Book."

The queens blinked, stiffening.

My sister snapped, "*Give them the Book.*"

And the eldest queen hissed, "*No.*"

The word clanged through me.

But Nesta went on, flinging out an arm to encompass us, the room, the world, "There are innocent people here. In these lands. If you will not risk your necks against the forces that threaten us, then grant those people a fighting chance. Give my sister the Book."

The crone sighed sharply through her nose. "An evacuation may be possible—"

"You would need ten thousand ships," Nesta said, her voice breaking. "You would need an armada. I have calculated the numbers. And if you are readying for war, you will not send your ships to us. We are stranded here."

The crone gripped the polished arms of her chair as she leaned forward a bit. "Then I suggest asking one of your winged males to carry you across the sea, girl."

Nesta's throat bobbed. "Please." I didn't think I'd ever heard that word from her mouth. "Please—do not leave us to face this alone."

The eldest queen remained unmoved. I had no words in my head.

We had shown them . . . we had . . . we had done everything. Even Rhys was silent, his face unreadable.

But then Cassian crossed to Nesta, the guards stiffening as the Illyrian moved through them as if they were stalks of wheat in a field.

He studied Nesta for a long moment. She was still glaring at the queens, her eyes lined with tears—*tears* of rage and despair, from that fire that burned her so violently from within. When she finally noticed Cassian, she looked up at him.

His voice was rough as he said, "Five hundred years ago, I fought on battlefields not far from this house. I fought beside human and faerie alike, bled beside them. I will stand on that battlefield again, Nesta Archeron, to protect this house—your people. I can think of no better way to end my existence than to defend those who need it most."

I watched a tear slide down Nesta's cheek. And I watched as Cassian reached up a hand to wipe it away.

She did not flinch from his touch.

I didn't know why, but I looked at Mor.

Her eyes were wide. Not with jealousy, or irritation, but . . . something perhaps like awe.

Nesta swallowed and at last turned away from Cassian. He stared at my sister a moment longer before facing the queens.

Without signal, the two women rose.

Mor demanded, on her feet as well, "Is it a sum you're after? Name your price, then."

The golden queen snorted as their guards closed in around them. "We have all the riches we need. We will now return to our palace to deliberate with our sisters."

"You're already going to say no," Mor pushed.

The golden queen smirked. "Perhaps." She took the crone's withered hand.

The ancient queen lifted her chin. "We appreciate the gesture of your trust."

Then they were gone.

Mor swore. And I looked at Rhys, my own heart breaking, about to demand why he hadn't pushed, why he hadn't said more—

But his eyes were on the chair where the golden queen had been seated.

Beneath it, somehow hidden by her voluminous skirts while she'd sat, was a box.

A box . . . that she must have removed from wherever she was hiding it when she'd leaned down to pick up her handkerchief.

Rhys had known it. Had stopped speaking to get them out as fast as possible.

How and where she'd smuggled in that lead box was the least of my concerns.

Not as the voice of the second and final piece of the Book filled the room, sang to me.

Life and death and rebirth

Sun and moon and dark

Rot and bloom and bones

Hello, sweet thing. Hello, lady of night, princess of decay. Hello, fanged beast and trembling fawn. Love me, touch me, sing me.

Madness. Where the first half had been cold cunning, this box . . . this was chaos, and disorder, and lawlessness, joy and despair.

Rhys smoothly picked it up and set it on the golden queen's chair. He did not need my power to open it—because no High Lord's spells had been keyed to it.

Rhys flipped back the lid. A note lay atop the golden metal of the book.

I read your letter. About the woman you love. I believe you. And I believe in peace.

I believe in a better world.

If anyone asks, you stole this during the meeting.

Do not trust the others. The sixth queen was not ill.

That was it.

Rhys picked up the Book of Breathings.

Light and dark and gray and light and dark and gray—

He said to my two sisters, Cassian sticking close to Nesta, "It is your choice, ladies, whether you wish to remain here, or come with us. You have heard the situation at hand. You have done the math about an evacuation." A nod of approval as he met Nesta's gray-blue stare. "Should you choose to remain, a unit of my soldiers will be here within the hour to guard this place. Should you wish to come live with us in that city we just showed them, I'd suggest packing now."

Nesta looked to Elain, still silent and wide-eyed. The tea she'd prepared—the finest, most exotic tea money could buy—sat undisturbed on the table.

Elain thumbed the iron ring on her finger.

"It is your choice," Nesta said with unusual gentleness. For her, Nesta would go to Prythian.

Elain swallowed, a doe caught in a snare. "I—I can't. I . . ."

But my mate nodded—kindly. With understanding. "The sentries will be here, and remain unseen and unfelt. They will look after themselves. Should you change your minds, one will be waiting in this room every day at noon and at midnight for you to speak. My home is your home. Its doors are always open to you."

Nesta looked between Rhys and Cassian, then to me. Despair still paled her face, but . . . she bowed her head. And said to me, "That was why you painted stars on your drawer."

CHAPTER 58

We immediately returned to Velaris, not trusting the queens to go long without noticing the Book's absence, especially if the vague mention of the sixth alluded to further foul play amongst them.

Amren had the second half within minutes, not even bothering to ask about the meeting before she vanished into the dining room of the town house and shut the doors behind her. So we waited.

And waited.

Two days passed.

Amren still hadn't cracked the code.

Rhys and Mor left in the early afternoon to visit the Court of Nightmares—to return the Veritas to Keir without his knowing, and ensure that the Steward was indeed readying his forces. Cassian had reports that the Illyrian legions were now camped across the mountains, waiting for the order to fly out to wherever our first battle might be.

There would be one, I realized. Even if we nullified the Cauldron using the Book, even if *I* was able to stop that Cauldron and the king from using it to shatter the wall and the world, he had armies gathered. Perhaps we'd take the fight to him once the Cauldron was disabled.

There was no word from my sisters, no report from Azriel's soldiers that they'd changed their minds. My father, I remembered, was still trading in the continent for the Mother knew what goods. Another variable in this.

And there was no word from the queens. It was of them that I most frequently thought. Of the two-faced, golden-eyed queen with not just a lion's coloring . . . but a lion's heart, too.

I hoped I saw her again.

With Rhys and Mor gone, Cassian and Azriel came to stay at the town house as they continued to plan our inevitable visit to Hybern. After that first dinner, when Cassian had broken out one of Rhys's *very* old bottles of wine so we could celebrate my mating in style, I'd realized they'd come to stay for company, to dine with me, and . . . the Illyrians had taken it upon themselves to look after me.

Rhys said as much that night when I'd written him a letter and watched it vanish. Apparently, he didn't mind his enemies knowing he was at the Court of Nightmares. If Hybern's forces tracked him there . . . good luck to them.

I'd written to Rhys, *How do I tell Cassian and Azriel I don't need them here to protect me? Company is fine, but I don't need sentries.*

He'd written back, *You* don't *tell them. You set boundaries if they cross a line, but you are their friend—and my mate. They will protect you on instinct. If you kick their asses out of the house, they'll just sit on the roof.*

I scribbled, *You Illyrian males are insufferable.*

Rhys had just said, *Good thing we make up for it with impressive wingspans.*

Even with him across the territory, my blood had heated, my toes curling. I'd barely been able to hold the pen long enough to write, *I'm missing that impressive wingspan in my bed. Inside me.*

He'd replied, *Of course you are.*

I'd hissed, jotting down, *Prick*.

I'd almost felt his laughter down the bond—our mating bond. Rhys wrote back, *When I return, we're going to that shop across the Sidra and you're going to try on all those lacy little underthings for me*.

I fell asleep thinking about it, wishing my hand was his, praying he'd finish at the Court of Nightmares and return to me soon. Spring was bursting all across the hills and peaks around Velaris. I wanted to sail over the yellow and purple blooms with him.

The next afternoon, Rhys was still gone, Amren was still buried in the book, Azriel off on a patrol of the city and nearby shoreline, and Cassian and I were—of all things—just finishing up an early afternoon performance of some ancient, revered Fae symphony. The amphitheater was on the other side of the Sidra, and though he'd offered to fly me, I'd wanted to walk. Even if my muscles were barking in protest after his brutal lesson that morning.

The music had been lovely—strange, but lovely, written at a time, Cassian had told me, when humans had not even walked the earth. He found the music puzzling, off-kilter, but . . . I'd been entranced.

Walking back across one of the main bridges spanning the river, we remained in companionable silence. We'd dropped off more blood for Amren—who said thank you and get the hell out—and were now headed toward the Palace of Thread and Jewels, where I wanted to buy both of my sisters presents for helping us. Cassian had promised to send them down with the next scout dispatched to retrieve the latest report. I wondered if he'd send anything to Nesta while he was at it.

I paused at the center of the marble bridge, Cassian halting beside me as I peered down at the blue-green water idling past. I could feel the threads of the current far below, the strains of salt and fresh water twining together, the swaying weeds coating the mussel-flecked floor, the tickling of small, skittering creatures over rock and mud. Could Tarquin sense such things? Did he sleep in his island-palace on the sea and swim through the dreams of fishes?

Cassian braced his forearms on the broad stone railing, his red Siphons like living pools of flame.

I said, perhaps because I was a busybody who liked to stick my nose in other people's affairs, "It meant a great deal to me—what you promised my sister the other day."

Cassian shrugged, his wings rustling. "I'd do it for anyone."

"It meant a lot to her, too." Hazel eyes narrowed slightly. But I casually watched the river. "Nesta is different from most people," I explained. "She comes across as rigid and vicious, but I think it's a wall. A shield—like the ones Rhys has in his mind."

"Against what?"

"Feeling. I think Nesta feels everything—sees too much; sees and feels it all. And she burns with it. Keeping that wall up helps from being overwhelmed, from caring too greatly."

"She barely seems to care about anyone other than Elain."

I met his stare, scanning that handsome, tan face. "She will never be like Mor," I said. "She will never love freely and gift it to everyone who crosses her path. But the few she does care for . . . I think Nesta would shred the world apart for them. Shred herself apart for them. She and I have our . . . issues. But Elain . . . " My mouth quirked to the side. "She will never forget, Cassian, that you offered to defend Elain. Defend her people. As long as she lives, she will remember that kindness."

He straightened, rapping his knuckles against the smooth marble. "Why are you telling me this?"

"I just—thought you should know. For whenever you see her again and she pisses you off. Which I'm certain will happen. But know that deep down, she is grateful, and perhaps does not possess the ability to say so. Yet the feeling—the heart—is there."

I paused, debating pushing him, but the river flowing beneath us shifted.

Not a physical shifting. But . . . a tremor in the current, in the bedrock, in the skittering things crawling on it. Like ink dropped in water.

Cassian instantly went on alert as I scanned the river, the banks on either side.

"What the hell is that?" he murmured. He tapped the Siphon on each hand with a finger.

I gaped as scaled black armor began unfolding and slithering up his wrists, his arms, replacing the tunic that had been there. Layer after layer, coating him like a second skin, flowing up to his shoulders. The additional Siphons appeared, and more armor spread across his neck, his shoulders, down his chest and waist. I blinked, and it had covered his legs—then his feet.

The sky was cloudless, the streets full of chatter and life.

Cassian kept scanning, a slow rotation over Velaris.

The river beneath me remained steady, but I could feel it roiling, as if trying to flee from— "From the sea," I breathed. Cassian's gaze shot straight ahead, to the river before us, to the towering cliffs in the distance that marked the raging waves where it met the ocean.

And there, on the horizon, a smear of black. Swift-moving—spreading wider as it grew closer.

"Tell me those are birds," I said. My power flooded my veins, and I curled my fingers into fists, willing it to calm, to steady—

"There's no Illyrian patrol that's supposed to know about this place . . . ," he said, as if it were an answer. His gaze cut to me. "We're going back to the town house right now."

The smear of black separated, fracturing into countless figures. Too big for birds. Far too big. I said, "You have to sound the alarm—"

But people were. Some were pointing, some were shouting.

Cassian reached for me, but I jumped back. Ice danced at my fingertips, wind howled in my blood. I'd pick them off one by one— "Get Azriel and Amren—"

They'd reached the sea cliffs. Countless, long-limbed flying creatures, some bearing soldiers in their arms . . . An invading host. "Cassian."

But an Illyrian blade had appeared in Cassian's hand, twin to the one across his back. A fighting knife now shone in the other. He held them both out to me. "Get back to the town house—right now."

I most certainly would not go. If they were flying, I could use my power to my advantage: freeze their wings, burn them, break them. Even if there were so many, even if—

So fast, as if they were carried on a fell wind, the force reached the outer edges of the city. And unleashed arrows upon the shrieking people rushing for cover in the streets. I grabbed his outstretched weapons, the cool metal hilts hissing beneath my forge-hot palms.

Cassian lifted his hand into the air. Red light exploded from his Siphon, blasting up and away—forming a hard wall in the sky above the city, directly in the path of that oncoming force.

He ground his teeth, grunting as the winged legion slammed into his shield. As if he felt every impact.

The translucent red shield shoved out farther, knocking them back—

We both watched in mute horror as the creatures lunged for the shield, arms out—

They were not just any manner of faerie. Any rising magic in me sputtered and went out at the sight of them.

They were all like the Attor.

All long-limbed, gray-skinned, with serpentine snouts and razor-sharp teeth. And as the legion of its ilk punched through Cassian's shield as if it were a cobweb, I beheld on their spindly gray arms gauntlets of that bluish stone I'd seen on Rhys, glimmering in the sun.

Stone that broke and repelled magic. Straight from the unholy trove of the King of Hybern.

One after one after one, they punched through his shield.

Cassian sent another wall barreling for them. Some of the creatures peeled away and launched themselves upon the outskirts of the city, vulnerable outside of his shield. The heat that had been building in my palms faded to clammy sweat.

People were shrieking, fleeing. And I knew his shields would not hold—

"*GO!*" Cassian roared. I lurched into motion, knowing he likely lingered because I stayed, that he needed Azriel and Amren and—

High above us, three of them slammed into the dome of the red shield. Clawing at it, ripping through layer after layer with those stone gauntlets.

That's what had delayed the king these months: gathering his arsenal. Weapons to fight magic, to fight High Fae who would rely on it—

A hole ripped open, and Cassian threw me to the ground, shoving me against the marble railing, his wings spreading wide over me, his legs as solid as the bands of carved rock at my back—

Screams on the bridge, hissing laughter, and then—

A wet, crunching thud.

"Shit," Cassian said. "*Shit*—"

He moved a step, and I lunged from under him to see what it was, who it was—

Blood shone on the white marble bridge, sparkling like rubies in the sun.

There, on one of those towering, elegant lampposts flanking the bridge . . .

Her body was bent, her back arched on the impact, as if she were in the throes of passion.

Her golden hair had been shorn to the skull. Her golden eyes had been plucked out.

She was twitching where she had been impaled on the post, the metal pole straight through her slim torso, gore clinging to the metal above her.

Someone on the bridge vomited, then kept running.

But I could not break my stare from the golden queen. Or from the Attor, who swept through the hole it had made and alighted atop the blood-soaked lamppost.

"Regards," it hissed, "of the mortal queens. And Jurian." Then the Attor leaped into flight, fast and sleek—heading right for the theater district we'd left.

Cassian had pressed me back down against the bridge—and he surged toward the Attor. He halted, remembering me, but I rasped, "*Go.*"

"Run home. *Now.*"

That was the final order—and his good-bye as he shot into the sky after the Attor, who had already disappeared into the screaming streets.

Around me, hole after hole was punched through that red shield, those winged creatures pouring in, dumping the Hybern soldiers they had carried across the sea.

Soldiers of every shape and size—lesser faeries.

The golden queen's gaping mouth was opening and closing like a fish on land. Save her, help her—

My blood. I could—

I took a step. Her body slumped.

And from wherever in me that power originated, I felt her death whisper past.

The screams, the beating wings, the whoosh and thud of arrows erupted in the sudden silence.

I ran. I ran for my side of the Sidra, for the town house. I didn't trust myself to winnow—could barely think around the panic barking through my head. I had minutes, perhaps, before they hit my street. Minutes to get there and bring as many inside with me as I could. The house was warded. No one would get in, not even these things.

Faeries were rushing past, racing for shelter, for friends and family. I hit the end of the bridge, the steep hills rising up—

Hybern soldiers were already atop the hill, at the two Palaces, laughing at the screams, the pleading as they broke into buildings, dragging people out. Blood dribbled down the cobblestones in little rivers.

They had done this. Those queens had . . . had given this city of art and music and food over to these . . . monsters. The king must have used the Cauldron to break its wards.

A thunderous *boom* rocked the other side of the city, and I went down at the impact, blades flying, hands ripping open on the cobblestones. I whirled toward the river, scrambling up, lunging for my weapons.

Cassian and Azriel were both in the skies now. And where they flew, those winged creatures died. Arrows of red and blue light shot from them, and those shields—

Twin shields of red and blue merged, sizzling, and slammed into the rest of the aerial forces. Flesh and wings tore, bone melted—

Until hands encased in stone tumbled from the sky. Only hands. Clattering on rooftops, splashing into the river. All that was left of them—what two Illyrian warriors had worked their way around.

But there were countless more who had already landed. Too many. Roofs were wrenched apart, doors shattered, screaming rising and then silenced—

This was not an attack to sack the city. It was an extermination.

And rising up before me, merely a few blocks down, the Rainbow of Velaris was bathed in blood.

The Attor and his ilk had converged there.

As if the queens had told him where to strike; where in Velaris would be the most defenseless. The beating heart of the city.

Fire was rippling, black smoke staining the sky—

Where was Rhys, where was my mate—

Across the river, thunder boomed again.

And it was not Cassian, or Azriel, who held the other side of the river. But Amren.

Her slim hands had only to point, and soldiers would fall—fall as if their own wings failed them. They slammed into the streets, thrashing, choking, clawing, shrieking, just as the people of Velaris had shrieked.

I whipped my head to the Rainbow a few blocks away—left unprotected. Defenseless.

The street before me was clear, the lone safe passage through hell.

A female screamed inside the artists' quarter. And I knew my path.

I flipped my Illyrian blade in my hand and winnowed into the burning and bloody Rainbow.

This was my home. These were my people.

If I died defending them, defending that small place in the world where art thrived . . .

Then so be it.

And I became darkness, and shadow, and wind.

I winnowed into the edge of the Rainbow as the first of the Hybern soldiers rounded its farthest corner, spilling onto the river avenue, shredding the cafés where I had lounged and laughed. They did not see me until I was upon them.

Until my Illyrian blade cleaved through their heads, one after another.

Six went down in my wake, and as I halted at the foot of the Rainbow, staring up into the fire and blood and death . . . Too many. Too many soldiers.

I'd never make it, never kill them all—

But there was a young female, green-skinned and lithe, an ancient, rusted bit of pipe raised above her shoulder. Standing her ground in front of her storefront—a gallery. People crouched inside the shop were sobbing.

Before them, laughing at the faerie, at her raised scrap of metal, circled five winged soldiers. Playing with her, taunting her.

Still she held the line. Still her face did not crumple. Paintings and pottery were shattered around her. And more soldiers were landing, spilling down, butchering—

Across the river, thunder boomed—Amren or Cassian or Azriel, I didn't know.

The river.

Three soldiers spotted me from up the hill. Raced for me.

But I ran faster, back for the river at the foot of the hill, for the singing Sidra.

I hit the edge of the quay, the water already stained with blood, and slammed my foot down in a mighty stomp.

And as if in answer, the Sidra rose.

I yielded to that thrumming power inside my bones and blood and breath. I became the Sidra, ancient and deep. And I bent it to my will.

I lifted my blades, willing the river higher, shaping it, forging it.

Those Hybern soldiers stopped dead in their tracks as I turned toward them.

And wolves of water broke from behind me.

The soldiers whirled, fleeing.

But my wolves were faster. *I* was faster as I ran with them, in the heart of the pack.

Wolf after wolf roared out of the Sidra, as colossal as the one I had once killed, pouring into the streets, racing upward.

I made it five steps before the pack was upon the soldiers taunting the shop owner.

I made it seven steps before the wolves brought them down, water shoving down their throats, drowning them—

I reached the soldiers, and my blade sang as I severed their choking heads from their bodies.

The shopkeeper was sobbing as she recognized me, her rusted bar still raised. But she nodded—only once.

I ran again, losing myself amongst my water-wolves. Some of the soldiers were taking to the sky, flapping upward, backtracking.

So my wolves grew wings, and talons, and became falcons and hawks and eagles.

They slammed into their bodies, their armor, drenching them. The airborne soldiers, realizing they hadn't been drowned, halted their flight and laughed—sneering.

I lifted a hand skyward, and clenched my fingers into a fist.

The water soaking them, their wings, their armor, their faces . . . It turned to ice.

Ice that was so cold it had existed before light, before the sun had warmed the earth. Ice of a land cloaked in winter, ice from the parts of me that felt no mercy, no sympathy for what these creatures had done and were doing to my people.

Frozen solid, dozens of the winged soldiers fell to the earth as one. And shattered upon the cobblestones.

My wolves raged around me, tearing and drowning and hunting. And those that fled them, those that took to the skies—they froze and shattered; froze and shattered. Until the streets were laden with ice and gore and broken bits of wing and stone.

Until the screaming of my people stopped, and the screams of the soldiers became a song in my blood. One of the soldiers rose up above the brightly painted buildings . . . I knew him.

The Attor was flapping, frantic, blood of the innocent coating his gray skin, his stone gauntlets. I sent an eagle of water shooting for him, but he was quicker, nimble.

He evaded my eagle, and my hawk, and my falcon, soaring high, clawing his way through the air. Away from me, my power—from Cassian and Azriel, holding the river and the majority of the city, away from Amren, using whatever dark power she possessed to send so many droves of them crashing down without visible injury.

None of my friends saw the Attor sailing up, sailing free.

It would fly back to Hybern—to the king. It had chosen to come here, to lead them. For spite. And I had no doubt that the golden, lioness-queen had suffered at its hands. As Clare had.

Where are you?

Rhys's voice sounded distantly in my head, through the sliver in my shield.

WHERE ARE YOU?

The Attor was getting away. With each heartbeat, it flew higher and higher—

WHERE—

I sheathed the Illyrian blade and fighting knife through my belt and scrambled to pick up the arrows that had fallen on the street. Shot at my people. Ash arrows, coated in familiar greenish poison. Bloodbane.

I'm exactly where I need to be, I said to Rhys.

And then I winnowed into the sky.

CHAPTER 59

I winnowed to a nearby rooftop, an ash arrow clenched in either hand, scanning where the Attor was high above, flapping—

FEYRE.

I slammed a mental shield of adamant up against that voice; against him.

Not now. Not this moment.

I could vaguely feel him pounding against that shield. Roaring at it. But even he could not get in.

The Attor was *mine*.

In the distance, rushing toward me, toward Velaris, a mighty darkness devoured the world. Soldiers in its path did not emerge again.

My mate. Death incarnate. Night triumphant.

I spotted the Attor again, veering toward the sea, toward Hybern, still over the city.

I winnowed, throwing my awareness toward it like a net, spearing mind to mind, using the tether like a rope, leading me through time and distance and wind—

I latched onto the oily smear of its malice, pinpointing my being, my focus onto the core of it. A beacon of corruption and filth.

When I emerged from wind and shadow, I was right atop the Attor.

It shrieked, wings curving as I slammed into it. As I plunged those poisoned ash arrows through each wing. Right through the main muscle.

The Attor arched in pain, its forked tongue cleaving the air between us. The city was a blur below, the Sidra a mere stream from the height.

In the span of a heartbeat, I wrapped myself around the Attor. I became a living flame that burned everywhere I touched, became unbreakable as the adamant wall inside my mind.

Shrieking, the Attor thrashed against me—but its wings, with those arrows, with my grip . . .

Free fall.

Down into the world. Into blood and pain. The wind tore at us.

The Attor could not break free of my flaming grasp. Or from my poisoned arrows skewering its wings. Laming him. Its burning skin stung my nose.

As we fell, my dagger found its way into my hand.

The darkness consuming the horizon shot closer—as if spotting me.

Not yet.

Not yet.

I angled my dagger over the Attor's bony, elongated rib cage. "This is for Rhys," I hissed in its pointed ear.

The reverberation of steel on bone barked into my hand.

Silvery blood warmed my fingers. The Attor screamed.

I yanked out my dagger, blood flying up, splattering my face.

"This is for Clare."

I plunged my blade in again, twisting.

Buildings took form. The Sidra ran red, but the sky was empty—free of soldiers. So were the streets.

The Attor was screaming and hissing, cursing and begging, as I ripped free the blade.

I could make out people; make out their shapes. The ground swelled up to meet us. The Attor was bucking so violently it was all I could do to keep it in my forge-hot grip. Burning skin ripped away, carried above us.

"And this," I breathed, leaning close to say the words into its ear, into its rotted soul. I slid my dagger in a third time, relishing the splintering of bones and flesh. "This is for *me*."

I could count the cobblestones. See Death beckoning with open arms.

I kept my mouth beside its ear, close as a lover, as our reflection in a pool of blood became clear. "I'll see you in hell," I whispered, and left my blade in its side.

Wind rippled the blood upon the cobblestones mere inches away.

And I winnowed out, leaving the Attor behind.

I heard the crack and splatter, even as I sifted through the world, propelled by my own power and the velocity of my plummet. I emerged a few feet away—my body taking longer than my mind to catch up.

My feet and legs gave out, and I rocked back into the wall of a pink-painted building behind me. So hard the plaster dented and cracked against my spine, my shoulders.

I panted, trembling. And on the street ahead—what lay broken and oozing on the cobblestones . . . The Attor's wings were a twisted ruin. Beyond that, scraps of armor, splintered bone, and burned flesh were all that remained.

That wave of darkness, Rhysand's power, at last hit my side of the river.

No one cried out at the star-flecked cascade of night that cut off all light.

I thought I heard vague grunting and scraping—as if it had sought out hidden soldiers lingering in the Rainbow, but then . . .

The wave vanished. Sunlight.

A crunch of boots before me, the beat and whisper of mighty wings.

A hand on my face, tilting up my chin as I stared and stared at the splattered ruin of the Attor. Violet eyes met mine.

Rhys. Rhys was here.

And . . . and I had . . .

He leaned forward, his brow sweat-coated, his breathing uneven. He gently pressed a kiss to my mouth.

To remind us both. Who we were, what we were. My icy heart thawed, the fire in my gut was soothed by a tendril of dark, and the water trickled out of my veins and back into the Sidra.

Rhys pulled back, his thumb stroking my cheek. People were weeping. Keening.

But no more screams of terror. No more bloodshed and destruction.

My mate murmured, "Feyre Cursebreaker, the Defender of the Rainbow."

I slid my arms around his waist and sobbed.

And even as his city wailed, the High Lord of the Night Court held me until I could at last face this blood-drenched new world.

CHAPTER 60

"Velaris is secure," Rhys said in the black hours of the night. "The wards the Cauldron took out have been remade."

We had not stopped to rest until now. For hours we'd worked, along with the rest of the city, to heal, to patch up, to hunt down answers any way we could. And now we were all again gathered, the clock chiming three in the morning.

I didn't know how Rhys was standing as he leaned against the mantel in the sitting room. I was near-limp on the couch beside Mor, both of us coated in dirt and blood. Like the rest of them.

Sprawled in an armchair built for Illyrian wings, Cassian's face was battered and healing slowly enough that I knew he'd drained his power during those long minutes when he'd defended the city alone. But his hazel eyes still glowed with the embers of rage.

Amren was hardly better off. The tiny female's gray clothes hung mostly in strips, her skin beneath pale as snow. Half-asleep on the couch across from mine, she leaned against Azriel, who kept casting alarmed glances at her, even as his own wounds leaked a bit. Atop his scarred hands, Azriel's blue Siphons were dull, muted. Utterly empty.

As I had helped the survivors in the Rainbow tend to their wounded, count their dead, and begin repairs, Rhys had checked in every now and then while he'd rebuilt the wards with whatever power lingered in his arsenal. During one of our brief breaks, he'd told me what Amren had done on her side of the river.

With her dark power, she had spun illusions straight into the soldiers' minds. They believed they had fallen into the Sidra and were drowning; they believed they were flying a thousand feet above and had dived, fast and swift, for the city—only to find the street mere feet away, and the crunch of their skulls. The crueler ones, the wickedest ones, she had unleashed their own nightmares upon them—until they died from terror, their hearts giving out.

Some had fallen into the river, drinking their own spreading blood as they drowned. Some had disappeared wholly.

"Velaris might be secure," Cassian replied, not even bothering to lift his head from where it rested against the back of the chair, "but for how long? Hybern knows about this place, thanks to those wyrm-queens. Who else will they sell the information to? How long until the other courts come sniffing? Or Hybern uses that Cauldron again to take down our defenses?"

Rhys closed his eyes, his shoulders tight. I could already see the weight pushing down on that dark head.

I hated to add to that burden, but I said, "If we all go to Hybern to destroy the Cauldron . . . who will defend the city?"

Silence. Rhys's throat bobbed.

Amren said, "I'll stay." Cassian opened his mouth to object, but Rhys slowly looked at his Second. Amren held his gaze as she added, "If Rhys must go to Hybern, then I am the only one of you who might hold the city until help arrives. Today was a surprise. A bad one. When you leave, we will be better prepared. The new wards we built today will not fall so easily."

Mor loosed a sigh. "So what do we do now?"

Amren simply said, "We sleep. We eat."

And it was Azriel who added, his voice raw with the aftermath of battle-rage, "And then we retaliate."

Rhys did not come to bed.

And when I emerged from the bath, the water clouded with dirt and blood, he was nowhere to be found.

But I felt for the bond between us and trudged upstairs, my stiff legs barking in pain. He was sitting on the roof—in the dark. His great wings were spread behind him, draped over the tiles.

I slid into his lap, looping my arms around his neck.

He stared at the city around us. "So few lights. So few lights left tonight."

I did not look. I only traced the lines of his face, then brushed my thumb over his mouth. "It is not your fault," I said quietly.

His eyes shifted to mine, barely visible in the dark. "Isn't it? I handed this city over to them. I said I would be willing to risk it, but . . . I don't know who I hate more: the king, those queens, or myself."

I brushed the hair out of his face. He gripped my hand, halting my fingers. "You shut me out," he breathed. "You—shielded against me. Completely. I couldn't find a way in."

"I'm sorry."

Rhys let out a bitter laugh. "Sorry? Be impressed. That shield . . . What you did to the Attor . . . " He shook his head. "You could have been killed."

"Are you going to scold me for it?"

His brows furrowed. Then he buried his face in my shoulder. "How could I scold you for defending my people? I want to throttle you, yes, for not going back to the town house, but . . . You chose to fight for them. For Velaris." He kissed my neck. "I don't deserve you."

My heart strained. He meant it—truly felt that way. I stroked his hair again. And I said to him, the words the only sounds in the silent, dark city, "We deserve each other. And we deserve to be happy."

Rhys shuddered against me. And when his lips found mine, I let him lay me down upon the roof tiles and make love to me under the stars.

Amren cracked the code the next afternoon. The news was not good.

"To nullify the Cauldron's power," she said by way of greeting as we crowded around the dining table in the town house, having rushed in from the repairs we'd all been making on very little sleep, "you must touch the Cauldron—and speak these words." She had written them all down for me on a piece of paper.

"You know this for certain?" Rhys said. He was still bleak-eyed from the attack, from healing and helping his people all day.

Amren hissed. "I'm trying not to be insulted, Rhysand."

Mor elbowed her way between them, staring at the two assembled pieces of the Book of Breathings. "What happens if we put both halves together?"

"Don't put them together," Amren simply said.

With either piece laid out, their voices blended and sang and hissed—evil and good and madness; dark and light and chaos.

"You put the pieces together," she clarified when Rhys gave her a questioning look, "and the blast of power will be felt in every corner and hole in the earth. You won't just attract the King of Hybern. You'll draw enemies far older and more wretched. Things that have long been asleep—and should remain so."

I cringed a bit. Rhys put a hand on my back.

"Then we move in now," Cassian said. His face had healed, but he limped a bit from an injury I couldn't see beneath his fighting leathers. He jerked his chin to Rhys. "Since you can't winnow without being tracked, Mor and Az will winnow us all in, Feyre breaks the Cauldron, and we get out. We'll be there and gone before anyone notices and the King of Hybern will have a new piece of cookware."

I swallowed. "It could be anywhere in his castle."

"We know where it is," Cassian countered.

I blinked. Azriel said to me, "We've been able to narrow it down to the lower levels." Through his spying, their planning for this *trip* all these months. "Every inch of the castle and surrounding lands is heavily guarded, but not impossible to get through. We've worked out the timing of it—for a small group of us to get in and out, quick and silent, and be gone before they know what's happening."

Mor said to him, "*But* the King of Hybern could notice Rhys's presence the moment he arrives. And if Feyre needs time to nullify the Cauldron, and we don't know *how* much time, that's a risky variable."

Cassian said, "We've considered that. So you and Rhys will winnow us in off the coast; we fly in while he stays." They'd have to winnow me, I realized, since I still had not yet mastered doing it over long distances. At least, not with many stops in between. "As for the spell," Cassian continued, "it's a risk we'll have to take."

Silence fell as they waited for Rhys's answer. My mate scanned my face, eyes wide.

Azriel pushed, "It's a solid plan. The king doesn't know our scents. We wreck the Cauldron and vanish before he notices . . . It'll be a graver insult than the bloodier, direct route we'd been considering, Rhys. We beat them yesterday, so when we go into that castle . . ." Vengeance indeed danced in that normally placid face. "We'll leave a few reminders that we won the last damn war for a reason."

Cassian nodded grimly. Even Mor smiled a bit.

"Are you asking me," Rhys finally said, far too calmly, "to *stay outside* while my mate goes into his stronghold?"

"Yes," Azriel said with equal calm, Cassian shifting himself slightly between them. "If Feyre can't nullify the Cauldron easily or quickly, we steal it—send the pieces back to the bastard when we're done breaking it apart. Either way, Feyre calls you through the bond when we're done—you and Mor winnow us out. They won't be able to track you fast enough if you only come to retrieve us."

Rhysand dropped onto the couch beside me at last, loosing a breath. His eyes slid to me. "If you want to go, then you go, Feyre."

If I hadn't been already in love with him, I might have loved him for that—for not insisting I stay, even if it drove his instincts mad, for not locking me away in the aftermath of what had happened yesterday.

And I realized—I realized how badly I'd been treated before, if my standards had become so low. If the freedom I'd been granted felt like a privilege and not an inherent right.

Rhys's eyes darkened, and I knew he read what I thought, felt. "You might be my mate," he said, "but you remain your own person. You decide your fate—your choices. Not me. You chose yesterday. You choose every day. Forever."

And maybe he only understood because he, too, had been helpless and without choices, had been forced to do such horrible things, and locked up. I threaded my fingers through his and squeezed. Together—together we'd find our peace, our future. Together we'd fight for it.

"Let's go to Hybern," I said.

I was halfway up the stairs an hour later when I realized that I still had no idea what room to go to. I'd gone to my bedroom since we'd returned from the cabin, but . . . what of his?

With Tamlin, he'd kept his own rooms and slept in mine. And I supposed—I supposed it'd be the same.

I was almost to my bedroom door when Rhysand drawled from behind me, "We can use your room if you like, but . . . " He was leaning against his open bedroom door. "Either your room or mine—but we're sharing one from now on. Just tell me whether I should move my clothes or yours. If that's all right with you."

"Don't you—you don't want your own space?"

"No," he said baldly. "Unless you do. I need you protecting me from our enemies with your water-wolves."

I snorted. He'd made me tell him that part of my tale over and over. I jerked my chin toward his bedroom. "Your bed is bigger."

And that was that.

I walked in to find my clothes already there, a second armoire now beside his. I stared at the massive bed, then at all the open space around us.

Rhys shut the door and went to a small box on the desk—then silently handed it to me.

My heart thundered as I opened the lid. The star sapphire gleamed in the candlelight, as if it were one of the Starfall spirits trapped in stone. "Your mother's ring?"

"My mother gave me that ring to remind me she was always with me, even during the worst of my training. And when I reached my majority, she took it away. It was an heirloom of her family—had been handed down from female to female over many, many years. My sister wasn't yet born, so she wouldn't have known to give it to her, but . . . My mother gave it to the Weaver. And then she told me that if I were to marry or mate, then the female would either have to be smart or strong enough to get it back. And if the female wasn't either of those things, then she wouldn't survive the marriage. I promised my mother that any potential bride or mate would have the test . . . And so it sat there for centuries."

My face heated. "You said this was something of value—"

"It is. To me, and my family."

"So my trip to the Weaver—"

"It was vital that we learn if you could detect those objects. But . . . I picked the object out of pure selfishness."

"So I won my wedding ring without even being asked if I wanted to marry you."

"Perhaps."

I cocked my head. "Do—do you want me to wear it?"

"Only if you want to."

"When we go to Hybern . . . Let's say things go badly. Will anyone be able to tell that we're mated? Could they use that against you?"

Rage flickered in his eyes. "If they see us together and can scent us both, they'll know."

"And if I show up alone, wearing a Night Court wedding ring—"

He snarled softly.

I closed the box, leaving the ring inside. "After we nullify the Cauldron, I want to do it all. Get the bond declared, get married, throw a stupid party and invite everyone in Velaris—all of it."

Rhys took the box from my hands and set it down on the nightstand before herding me toward the bed. "And if I wanted to go one step beyond that?"

"I'm listening," I purred as he laid me on the sheets.

CHAPTER 61

I'd never worn so much steel. Blades had been strapped all over me, hidden in my boots, my inside pockets. And then there was the Illyrian blade down my back.

Just a few hours ago, I'd known such overwhelming happiness after such horror and sorrow. Just a few hours ago, I'd been in his arms while he made love to me.

And now Rhysand, my mate and High Lord and partner, stood beside me in the foyer, Mor and Azriel and Cassian armed and ready in their scale-like armor, all of us too quiet.

Amren said, "The King of Hybern is old, Rhys—very old. Do not linger."

A voice near my chest whispered, *Hello lovely, wicked liar.*

The two halves of the Book of Breathings, each part tucked into a different pocket. In one of them, the spell I was to say had been written out clearly. I hadn't dared speak it, though I had read it a dozen times.

"We'll be in and out before you miss us," Rhysand said. "Guard Velaris well."

Amren studied my gloved hands and weapons. "That Cauldron," she said, "makes the Book seem harmless. If the spell fails, or if you cannot move it, then *leave*." I nodded. She surveyed us all again. "Fly well." I supposed that was as much concern as she'd show.

We turned to Mor—whose arms were out, waiting for me. Cassian and Rhys would winnow with Azriel, my mate dropped off a few miles from the coast before the Illyrians found Mor and me seconds later.

I moved toward her, but Rhys stepped in front of me, his face tense. I rose up on my toes and kissed him. "I'll be fine—we'll all be fine." His eyes held mine through the kiss, and when I broke away, his gaze went right to Cassian.

Cassian bowed. "With my life, High Lord. I'll protect her with my life."

Rhys looked to Azriel. He nodded, bowing, and said, "With both of our lives."

It was satisfactory enough to my mate—who at last looked at Mor.

She nodded once, but said, "I know my orders."

I wondered what those might be—why I hadn't been told—but she gripped my hand.

Before I could say good-bye to Amren, we were gone.

⁜

Gone—and plunging through open air, toward a night-dark sea—

A warm body slammed into mine, catching me before I could panic and perhaps winnow myself somewhere. "Easy," Cassian said, banking right. I looked below to see Mor still plummeting, then winnow again into nothing.

No sign or glimmer of Rhys's presence near or behind us. A few yards ahead, Azriel was a swift shadow over the black water. Toward the landmass we were now approaching.

Hybern.

No lights burned on it. But it felt . . . old. As if it were a spider that had been waiting in its web for a long, long time.

"I've been here twice," Cassian murmured. "Both times, I was counting down the minutes until I could leave."

I could see why. A wall of bone-white cliffs arose, their tops flat and grassy, leading away to a terrain of sloping, barren hills. And an overwhelming sense of nothingness.

Amarantha had slaughtered all her slaves rather than free them. She had been a commander here—one of many. If that force that had attacked Velaris was a vanguard . . . I swallowed, flexing my hands beneath my gloves.

"That's his castle ahead," Cassian said through clenched teeth, swerving.

Around a bend in the coast, built into the cliffs and perched above the sea, was a lean, crumbling castle of white stone.

Not imperious marble, not elegant limestone, but . . . off-white. Bone-colored. Perhaps a dozen spires clawed at the night sky. A few lights flickered in the windows and balconies. No one outside—no patrol. "Where is everyone?"

"Guard shift." They'd planned this around it. "There's a small sea door at the bottom. Mor will be waiting for us there—it's the closest entrance to the lower levels."

"I'm assuming she can't winnow us in."

"Too many wards to risk the time it'd cost for her to break through them. Rhys might be able to. But we'll meet him at the door on the way out."

My mouth went a bit dry. Over my heart, the Book said, *Home—take me home*.

And indeed I could feel it. With every foot we flew in, faster and faster, dipping down so the spray from the ocean chilled me to my bones, I could feel it.

Ancient—cruel. Without allegiance to anyone but itself.

The Cauldron. They needn't have bothered learning where it was held inside this castle. I had no doubt I'd be drawn right to it. I shuddered.

"Easy," Cassian said again. We swept in toward the base of the cliffs to the sea door before a platform. Mor was waiting, sword out, the door open.

Cassian loosed a breath, but Azriel reached her first, landing swiftly and silently, and immediately prowled into the castle to scout the hall ahead.

Mor waited for us—her eyes on Cassian as we landed. They didn't speak, but their glance was too long to be anything but casual. I wondered what their training, their honed senses, detected.

The passage ahead was dark, silent. Azriel appeared a heartbeat later. "Guards are down." There was blood on his knife—an ash knife. Az's cold eyes met mine. "Hurry."

I didn't need to focus to track the Cauldron to its hiding place. It tugged on my every breath, hauling me to its dark embrace.

Any time we reached a crossroads, Cassian and Azriel would branch out, usually returning with bloodied blades, faces grim, silently warning me to hurry.

They'd been working these weeks, through whatever sources Azriel had, to get this encounter down to an exact schedule. If I needed more time than they'd allotted, if the Cauldron couldn't be moved . . . it might all be for nothing. But not these deaths. No, those I did not mind at all.

These people—these people had hurt Rhys. They'd brought *tools* with them to incapacitate him. They had sent that legion to wreck and butcher my city.

I descended through an ancient dungeon, the stones dark and stained. Mor kept at my side, constantly monitoring. The last line of defense.

If Cassian and Azriel were hurt, I realized, she was to make sure I got out by whatever means. Then return.

But there was no one in the dungeon—not that I encountered, once the Illyrians were done with them. They had executed this masterfully. We found another stairwell, leading down, down, down—

I pointed, nausea roiling. "There. It's down there."

Cassian took the stairs, Illyrian blade stained with dark blood.

Neither Mor nor Azriel seemed to breathe until Cassian's low whistle bounced off the stairwell stones from below.

Mor put a hand on my back, and we descended into the dark.

Home, the Book of Breathings sighed. *Home.*

Cassian was standing in a round chamber beneath the castle—a ball of faelight floating above his shoulder.

And in the center of the room, atop a small dais, sat the Cauldron.

CHAPTER 62

The Cauldron was absence and presence. Darkness and . . . whatever the darkness had come from.

But not life. Not joy or light or hope.

It was perhaps the size of a bathtub, forged of dark iron, its three legs—those three legs the king had ransacked those temples to find—crafted like creeping branches covered in thorns.

I had never seen something so hideous—and alluring.

Mor's face had drained of color. "Hurry," she said to me. "We've got a few minutes."

Azriel scanned the room, the stairs we'd strode down, the Cauldron, its legs. I made to approach the dais, but he extended an arm into my path. "Listen."

So we did.

Not words. But a throbbing.

Like blood pulsed through the room. Like the Cauldron had a heartbeat.

Like calls to like. I moved toward it. Mor was at my back, but didn't stop me as I stepped up onto the dais.

Inside the Cauldron was nothing but inky, swirling black.

Perhaps the entire universe had come from it.

Azriel and Cassian tensed as I laid a hand on the lip. Pain—pain and ecstasy and power and weakness flowed into me. Everything that was and wasn't, fire and ice, light and dark, deluge and drought.

The map for creation.

Reeling back into myself, I readied to read that spell.

The paper trembled as I pulled it from my pocket. As my fingers brushed the half of the Book inside.

Sweet-tongued liar, lady of many faces—

One hand on half of the Book of Breathings, the other on the Cauldron, I took a step outside myself, a jolt passing through my blood as if I were no more than a lightning rod.

Yes, you see now, princess of carrion—you see what you must do . . .

"Feyre," Mor murmured in warning.

But my mouth was foreign, my lips might as well have been as far away as Velaris while the Cauldron and the Book flowed through me, communing.

The other one, the Book hissed. *Bring the other one . . . let us be joined, let us be free.*

I slid the Book from my pocket, tucking it into the crook of my arm as I tugged the second half free. *Lovely girl, beautiful bird—so sweet, so generous . . .*

Together together together

"Feyre." Mor's voice cut through the song of both halves.

Amren had been wrong. Separate, their power was cleaved—not enough to take on the abyss of the Cauldron's might. But together . . . Yes, together, the spell would work when I spoke it.

Whole, I would become not a conduit between them, but rather their master. There was no moving the Cauldron—it had to be now.

Realizing what I was about to do, Mor lunged for me with a curse.

Too slow.

I laid the second half of the Book atop the other.

A silent ripple of power hollowed out my ears, buckled my bones.

Then nothing.

From far away, Mor said, "We can't risk—"

"Give her a minute," Cassian cut her off.

I was the Book and the Cauldron and sound and silence.

I was a living river through which one flowed into the other, eddying and ebbing, over and over, a tide with no end or beginning.

The spell—the words—

I looked to the paper in my hand, but my eyes did not see, my lips did not move.

I was not a tool, not a pawn. I would not be a conduit, not be the lackey of these *things*—

I'd memorized the spell. I would say it, breathe it, think it—

From the pit of my memory the first word formed. I slogged toward it, reaching for that one word, that one word that would be a tether back into myself, into who I was—

Strong hands tugged me back, wrenching me away.

Murky light and moldy stone poured into me, the room spinning as I gasped down breath, finding Azriel shaking me, eyes so wide I could see the white around them. What had happened, what—

Steps sounded above. Azriel instantly shoved me behind him, bloodied blade lifting.

The movement cleared my head enough to feel something wet and warm trickle down my lip and chin. Blood—my nose had been bleeding.

But those steps grew louder, and my friends had their weapons angled as a handsome brown-haired male swaggered down the steps. Human—his ears were round. But his eyes . . .

I knew the color of those eyes. I'd stared at one, encased in crystal, for three months.

"Stupid fool," he said to me.

"Jurian," I breathed.

CHAPTER 63

I gauged the distance between my friends and Jurian, weighed my sword against the twin ones crossed over his back. Cassian took a step toward the descending warrior and snarled, "*You.*"

Jurian snickered. "Worked your way up the ranks, did you? Congratulations."

I felt him sweep toward us. Like a ripple of night and wrath, Rhys appeared at my side. The Book was instantly gone, his movement so slick as he took it from me and tucked it into his own jacket that I barely registered it had happened.

But the moment that metal left my hands . . . Mother above, what had happened? I'd failed, failed so completely, been so pathetically overwhelmed by it—

"You look good, Jurian," Rhys said, strolling to Cassian's side—casually positioning himself between me and the ancient warrior. "For a corpse."

"Last time I saw you," Jurian sneered, "you were warming Amarantha's sheets."

"So you remember," Rhysand mused, even as my rage flared. "Interesting."

Jurian's eyes sliced to Mor. "Where is Miryam?"

"She's dead," Mor said flatly. The lie that had been told for five hundred years. "She and Drakon drowned in the Erythrian Sea." The impassive face of the princess of nightmares.

"Liar," Jurian crooned. "You were always such a liar, Morrigan."

Azriel growled, the sound unlike any I'd heard from him before.

Jurian ignored him, chest starting to heave. "*Where did you take Miryam?*"

"Away from you," Mor breathed. "I took her to Prince Drakon. They were mated and married that night you slaughtered Clythia. And she never thought of you again."

Wrath twisted his tan face. Jurian—hero of the human legions . . . who along the way had turned himself into a monster as awful as those he'd fought.

Rhys reached back to grab my hand. We'd seen enough. I gripped the rim of the Cauldron again, willing it to obey, to come with us. I braced for the wind and darkness.

Only they didn't come.

Mor gripped Cassian and Azriel's hands—and stayed still.

Jurian smiled.

Rhysand drawled, hand tightening in mine, "New trick?"

Jurian shrugged. "I was sent to distract you—while he worked his spell." His smile turned lupine. "You won't leave this castle unless he allows you to. Or in pieces."

My blood ran cold. Cassian and Azriel crouched into fighting stances, but Rhys cocked his head. I felt his dark power rise and rise, as if he'd splatter Jurian then and there.

But nothing happened. Not even a brush of night-flecked wind.

"Then there's that," Jurian said. "Didn't you remember? Perhaps you forgot. It was a good thing I was there, awake for every moment, Rhysand. She stole *his* book of spells—to take your powers."

Inside me, like a key clicking in a lock, that molten core of power just . . . halted. Whatever tether to it between my mind and soul was snipped—no, squeezed so tight by some invisible hand that nothing could flow.

I reached for Rhys's mind, for the bond—

I slammed into a hard wall. Not of adamant, but of foreign, unfeeling stone.

"He made sure," Jurian went on as I banged against that internal wall, tried to summon my own gifts to no avail, "that particular book was returned to him. She didn't know how to use half of the nastier spells. Do you know what it is like to be unable to sleep, to drink or eat or breathe or *feel* for five hundred years? Do you understand what it is like to be constantly awake, forced to watch everything she did?"

It had made him insane—tortured his soul until he went insane. That's what the sharp gleam was in his eyes.

"It couldn't have been so bad," Rhys said, even as I knew he was unleashing every ounce of will on that spell that contained us, bound us, "if you're now working for her master."

A flash of too-white teeth. "Your suffering will be long, and thorough."

"Sounds delightful," Rhys said, now turning us from the room. A silent shout to *run*.

But someone appeared atop the stairs.

I knew him—in my bones. The shoulder-length black hair, the ruddy skin, the clothes that edged more toward practicality than finery. He was of surprisingly average height, but muscled like a young man.

But his face—which looked perhaps like a human man in his forties . . . Blandly handsome. To hide the depthless, hateful black eyes that burned there.

The King of Hybern said, "The trap was so easy, I'm honestly a bit disappointed you didn't see it coming."

Faster than any of us could see, Jurian fired a hidden ash bolt through Azriel's chest.

Mor screamed.

We had no choice but to go with the king.

The ash bolt was coated in bloodbane that the King of Hybern claimed flowed where he willed it. If we fought, if we did not come with him upstairs, the poison would shoot to his heart. And with our magic locked down, without the ability to winnow . . .

If I could somehow get to Azriel, give him a mouthful of my blood . . . But it'd take too long, require too many moving parts.

Cassian and Rhys hauled Azriel between them, his blood splattering on the floor behind us as we went up the twisting stairways of the king's castle.

I tried not to step in it as Mor and I followed behind, Jurian at our backs. Mor was shaking—trying hard not to, but shaking as she stared at the protruding end of that arrow, visible between the gap in Azriel's wings.

None of us dared strike the King of Hybern where he stalked ahead, leading the way. He'd taken the Cauldron with him, vanishing it with a snap of his fingers and a wry look at me.

We knew the king wasn't bluffing. It'd take one move on their part for Azriel to die.

The guards were out now. And courtiers. High Fae and creatures—I didn't know where they fit in—who smiled like we were their next meal. Their eyes were all dead. Empty.

No furniture, no art. As if this castle were the skeleton of some mighty creature.

The throne room doors were open, and I balked. A throne room—*the* throne room that had honed Amarantha's penchant for public displays of cruelty. Faelights slithered along the bone-white walls, the windows looking out to the crashing sea far below.

The king mounted a dais carved of a single block of dark emerald—his throne assembled from the bones of . . . I felt the blood drain from my face. Human bones. Brown and smooth with age.

We stopped before it, Jurian leering at our backs. The throne room doors shut.

The king said to no one in particular, "Now that I've upheld my end of the bargain, I expect you to uphold yours." From the shadows near a side door, two figures emerged.

I began shaking my head as if I could unsee it as Lucien and Tamlin stepped into the light.

CHAPTER 64

Rhysand went still as death. Cassian snarled. Hanging between them, Azriel tried and failed to lift his head.

But I was staring at Tamlin—at that face I had loved and hated so deeply—as he halted a good twenty feet away from us.

He wore his bandolier of knives—Illyrian hunting-blades, I realized.

His golden hair was cut shorter, his face more gaunt than I'd last seen it. And his green eyes . . . Wide as they scanned me from head to toe. Wide as they took in my fighting leathers, the Illyrian sword and knives, the way I stood within my group of friends—my family.

He'd been working with the King of Hybern. "No," I breathed.

But Tamlin dared one more step closer, staring at me as if I were a ghost. Lucien, metal eye whirring, stopped him with a hand on his shoulder.

"No," I said again, this time louder.

"What was the cost," Rhysand said softly from my side. I clawed and tore at the wall separating our minds; heaved and pulled against that fist stifling my magic.

Tamlin ignored him, looking at the king at last. "You have my word."

The king smiled.

I took a step toward Tamlin. "*What have you done*?"

The King of Hybern said from his throne, "We made a bargain. I give you over, and he agrees to let my forces enter Prythian through his territory. And then use it as a base as we remove that ridiculous wall."

I shook my head. Lucien refused to meet the pleading stare I threw his way.

"You're insane," Cassian hissed.

Tamlin held out a hand. "Feyre." An order—like I was no better than a summoned dog.

I made no movement. I had to get free; had to get that damn power free—

"You," the king said, pointing a thick finger at me, "are a very difficult female to get ahold of. Of course, we've also agreed that you'll work for me once you've been returned home to your husband, but . . . Is it husband-to-be, or husband? I can't remember."

Lucien glanced between us all, face paling. "Tamlin," he murmured.

But Tamlin didn't lower the hand stretched toward me. "I'm taking you home."

I backed up a step—toward where Rhysand still held Azriel with Cassian.

"There's that other bit, too. The other thing I wanted," the king went on. "Well, Jurian wanted. Two birds with one stone, really. The High Lord of Night dead—and to learn who his friends were. It drove Jurian quite mad, honestly, that you never revealed it during those fifty years. So now you know, Jurian. And now you can do what you please with them."

Around me, my friends were tense—taut. Even Azriel was subtly moving a bloody, scarred hand closer to his blades. His blood pooled at the edge of my boots.

I said steadily, clearly, to Tamlin, "I'm not going anywhere with you."

"You'll say differently, my dear," the king countered, "when I complete the final part of my bargain."

Horror coiled in my gut.

The king jerked his chin at my left arm. "Break that bond between you two."

"Please," I whispered.

"How else is Tamlin to have his bride? He can't very well have a wife who runs off to another male once a month."

Rhys remained silent, though his grip tightened on Azriel. Observing—weighing, sorting through the lock on his power. The thought of that silence between our souls being permanent . . .

My voice cracked as I said to Tamlin, still at the opposite end of the crude half circle we'd formed before the dais, "Don't. Don't let him. I told you—I *told you* that I was fine. That I left—"

"You weren't well," Tamlin snarled. "He *used* that bond to manipulate you. Why do you think I was gone so often? I was looking for a way to get you *free*. And you *left*."

"I left because I was going to *die* in that house!"

The King of Hybern clicked his tongue. "Not what you expected, is it?"

Tamlin growled at him, but again held out his hand toward me. "Come home with me. Now."

"No."

"Feyre." An unflinching command.

Rhys was barely breathing—barely moving.

And I realized . . . realized it was to keep his scent from becoming apparent. Our scent. Our mating bond.

Jurian's sword was already out—and he was looking at Mor as if he was going to kill her first. Azriel's blood-drained face twisted with rage as he noticed that stare. Cassian, still holding him upright, took them all in, assessing, readying himself to fight, to defend.

I stopped beating at the fist on my power. Stroked it gently—lovingly.

I am Fae and not-Fae, all and none, I told the spell that gripped me. *You do not hold me. I am as you are—real and not, little more than gathered wisps of power. You do not hold me.*

"I'll come with you," I said softly to Tamlin, to Lucien, shifting on his feet, "if you leave them alone. Let them go."

You do not hold me.

Tamlin's face contorted with wrath. "They're monsters. They're—" He didn't finish as he stalked across the floor to grab me. To drag me out of here, then no doubt winnow away.

You do not hold me.

The fist gripping my power relaxed. Vanished.

Tamlin lunged for me over the few feet that remained. So fast—too fast—

I became mist and shadow.

I winnowed beyond his reach. The king let out a low laugh as Tamlin stumbled.

And went sprawling as Rhysand's fist connected with his face.

Panting, I retreated right into Rhysand's arms as one looped around my waist, as Azriel's blood on him soaked into my back. Behind us, Mor leaped in to fill the space Rhys had vacated, slinging Azriel's arm over her shoulders.

But that wall of hideous stone remained in my mind, and still blocked Rhys's own power.

Tamlin rose, wiping the blood now trickling from his nose as he backed to where Lucien held his position with a hand on his sword.

But just as Tamlin neared his Emissary, he staggered a step. His face went white with rage.

And I knew Tamlin understood a moment before the king laughed. "I don't believe it. Your bride left you only to find her mate. The Mother has a warped sense of humor, it seems. And what a talent—tell me, girl: how did you unravel that spell?"

I ignored him. But the hatred in Tamlin's eyes made my knees buckle. "I'm sorry," I said, and meant it.

Tamlin's eyes were on Rhysand, his face near-feral. "*You*," he snarled, the sound more animal than Fae. "*What did you do to her?*"

Behind us, the doors opened and soldiers poured in. Some looked like the Attor. Some looked worse. More and more, filling up the room, the exits, armor and weapons clanking.

Mor and Cassian, Azriel sagging and heavy-lidded between them, scanned each soldier and weapon, sizing up our best odds of escape. I left them to it as Rhys and I faced Tamlin.

"I'm not going with you," I spat at Tamlin. "And even if I did . . . You spineless, *stupid* fool for selling us out to *him*! Do you know what he wants to do with that Cauldron?"

"Oh, I'm going to do many, many things with it," the king said.

And the Cauldron appeared again between us.

"Starting now."

Kill him kill him kill him

I could not tell if the voice was mine or the Cauldron's. I didn't care. I unleashed myself.

Talons and wings and shadows were instantly around me, surrounded by water and fire—

Then they vanished, stifled as that invisible hand gripped my power again, so hard I gasped.

"Ah," the king said to me, clicking his tongue, "that. Look at you. A child of all seven courts—like and unlike all. How the Cauldron purrs in your presence. Did you plan to use it? Destroy it? With that book, you could do anything you wished."

I didn't say anything. The king shrugged. "You'll tell me soon enough."

"I made no bargain with you."

"No, but your master did, so you will obey."

Molten rage poured into me. I hissed at Tamlin, "If you bring me from here, if you take me from my mate, I will *destroy* you. I will destroy your court, and everything you hold dear."

Tamlin's lips thinned. But he said simply, "You don't know what you're talking about."

Lucien cringed.

The king jerked his chin to the guards by the side door through which Tamlin and Lucien had appeared. "No—she doesn't." The doors opened again. "There will be no destroying," the king went on as people—as *women* walked through those doors.

Four women. Four humans. The four remaining queens.

"Because," the king said, the queens' guards falling into rank behind them, hauling something in the core of their formation, "you will find, Feyre Archeron, that it is in your best interest to behave."

The four queens sneered at us with hate in their eyes. Hate.

And parted to let their personal guards through.

Fear like I had never known entered my heart as the men dragged my sisters, gagged and bound, before the King of Hybern.

CHAPTER 65

This was some new hell. Some new level of nightmare. I even went so far as to try to wake myself up.

But there they were—in their nightgowns, the silk and lace dirty, torn.

Elain was quietly sobbing, the gag soaked with her tears. Nesta, hair disheveled as if she'd fought like a wildcat, was panting as she took us in. Took in the Cauldron.

"You made a very big mistake," the king said to Rhysand, my mate's arms banded around me, "the day you went after the Book. I had no need of it. I was content to let it lie hidden. But the moment your forces started sniffing around . . . I decided who better than to be my liaison to the human realm than my newly reborn friend, Jurian? He'd just finished all those months of recovering from the process, and longed to see what his former home had become, so he was more than happy to visit the continent for an extended visit."

Indeed the queens smiled at him—bowed their heads. Rhys's arms tightened in silent warning.

"The brave, cunning Jurian, who suffered so badly at the end of the

War—now my ally. Here to help me convince these queens to aid in my cause. For a price of his own, of course, but it has no bearing here. And wiser to work with me, my men, than to allow you monsters in the Night Court to rule and attack. Jurian was right to warn their Majesties that you'd try to take the Book—that you would feed them lies of love and goodness, when *he* had seen what the High Lord of the Night Court was capable of. The hero of the human forces, reborn as a gesture to the human world of my good faith. I do not wish to invade the continent—but to work with them. My powers ensconced their court from *prying* eyes, just to show them the benefits." A smirk at Azriel, who could hardly lift his head to snarl back. "Such impressive attempts to infiltrate their sacred palace, Shadowsinger—and utter proof to their Majesties, of course, that your court is not as benevolent as you seem."

"Liar," I hissed, and whirled on the queens, daring only a step away from Rhys. "They are *liars*, and if you do not let my sisters go, I will *slaughter*—"

"Do you hear the threats, the language they use in the Night Court?" the king said to the mortal queens, their guards now around us in a half circle. "Slaughter, ultimatums . . . They wish to end life. I desire to give it."

The eldest queen said to him, refusing to acknowledge me, my words, "Then show us—prove this gift you mentioned."

Rhysand tugged me back against him. He said quietly to the queen, "You're a fool."

The king cut in, "Is she? Why submit to old age and ailments when what I offer is so much better?" He waved a hand toward me. "Eternal youth. Do you deny the benefits? A mortal queen becomes one who might reign forever. Of course, there are risks—the transition can be . . . difficult. But a strong-willed individual could survive."

The youngest queen, the dark-haired one, smiled slightly. Arrogant youth—and bitter old age. Only the two others, the ones who wore white and black, seemed to hesitate, stepping closer to each other—and their towering guards.

The ancient queen lifted her chin, "Show us. Demonstrate it can be done, that it is safe." She had spoken of eternal youth that day, had spat in my face about it. Two-faced *bitch*.

The king nodded. "Why did you think I asked my dear friend Ianthe to see who Feyre Archeron would appreciate having with her for eternity?" Even as horror filled my ears with roaring silence, I glanced at the queens, the question no doubt written on my face. The king explained, "Oh, I asked them first. They deemed it too . . . uncouth to betray two young, misguided women. Ianthe had no such qualms. Consider it my wedding present for you both," he added to Tamlin.

But Tamlin's face tightened. "What?"

The king cocked his head, savoring every word. "I think the High Priestess was waiting until your return to tell you, but didn't you ever ask *why* she believed I might be able to break the bargain? Why she had so many musings on the idea? So many millennia have the High Priestesses been forced to their knees for the High Lords. And during those years she dwelled in that foreign court . . . such an open mind, she has. Once we met, once I painted for her a portrait of a Prythian free of High Lords, where the High Priestesses might rule with grace and wisdom . . . She didn't take much convincing."

I was going to vomit. Tamlin, to his credit, looked like he might, too.

Lucien's face had slackened. "She sold out—she sold out Feyre's family. To you."

I had told Ianthe everything about my sisters. She had asked. Asked who they were, where they lived. And I had been so stupid, so broken . . . I had fed her every detail.

"Sold out?" The king snorted. "Or saved from the shackles of mortal death? Ianthe suggested they were both strong-willed women, like their sister. No doubt they'll survive. And prove to our queens it *can* be done. If one has the strength."

My heart stopped. "*Don't you—*

The king cut me off, "I would suggest bracing yourselves."

And then hell exploded in the hall.

Power, white and unending and hideous, barreled into us.

All I knew was Rhysand's body covering mine as we were all thrown to the floor, the shout of pain as he took the brunt of the king's power.

Cassian twisted, wings flaring wide as he shielded Azriel.

His wings—his wings—

Cassian's scream as his wings shredded under talons of pure magic was the most horrific sound I'd ever heard. Mor surged for him, but too late.

Rhys was moving in an instant, as if he'd lunge for the king, but power hit us again, and again. Rhys slammed to his knees.

My sisters were shrieking over their gags. But Elain's cry—a warning. A warning to—

To my right, now exposed, Tamlin ran for me. To grab me at last.

I hurled a knife at him—as hard as I could.

He had to dive to miss it. And he backed away at the second one I had ready, gaping at me, at Rhys, as if he could indeed see the mating bond between us.

But I whirled as soldiers pressed in, cutting us off. Whirled, and saw Cassian and Azriel on the ground, Jurian laughing softly at the blood gushing from Cassian's ravaged wings—

Shreds of them remained.

I scrambled for him. My blood. It might be enough, be—

Mor, on her knees beside Cassian, hurtled for the king with a cry of pure wrath.

He sent a punch of power to her. She dodged, a knife angled in her hand, and—

Azriel cried out in pain.

She froze. Stopped a foot from the throne. Her knife clattered to the floor.

The king rose. "What a mighty queen you are," he breathed.

And Mor backed away. Step by step.

"What a prize," the king said, that black gaze devouring her.

Azriel's head lifted from where he was sprawled in his own blood, eyes full of rage and pain as he snarled at the king, "*Don't you touch her*."

Mor looked at Azriel—and there was real fear there. Fear—and something else. She didn't stop moving until she again kneeled beside him and pressed a hand to his wound. Azriel hissed—but covered her bloody fingers with his own.

Rhys positioned himself between me and the king as I dropped to my knees before Cassian. I ripped at the leather covering my forearm—

"Put the prettier one in first," the king said, Mor already forgotten.

I twisted—only to have the king's guards grab me from behind. Rhys was instantly there, but Azriel shouted, back arching as the king's poison worked its way in.

"Please refrain," the king said, "from getting any stupid ideas, Rhysand." He smiled at me. "If any of you interfere, the shadowsinger dies. Pity about the other brute's wings." He gave my sisters a mockery of a bow. "Ladies, eternity awaits. Prove to their Majesties the Cauldron is safe for . . . strong-willed individuals."

I shook my head, unable to breathe, to think a way out of it—

Elain was shaking, sobbing, as she was hauled forward. Toward the Cauldron.

Nesta began thrashing against the men that held her.

Tamlin said, "Stop."

The king did no such thing.

Lucien, beside Tamlin, again put a hand on his sword. "Stop this."

Nesta was bellowing at the guards, at the king, as Elain yielded step after step toward that Cauldron. As the king waved his hand, and liquid filled it to the brim. *No, no*—

The queens only watched, stone-faced. And Rhys and Mor, separated from me by those guards, did not dare to even shift a muscle.

Tamlin spat at the king, "This is not part of our deal. *Stop this now*."

"I don't care," the king said simply.

Tamlin launched himself at the throne, as if he'd rip him to shreds.

That white-hot magic slammed into him, shoving him to the ground. Leashing him.

Tamlin strained against the collar of light on his neck, around his wrists. His golden power flared—to no avail. I tore at the fist still gripping my own, sliced at it, over and over—

Lucien staggered a step forward as Elain was gripped between two guards and hoisted up. She began kicking then, weeping while her feet slammed into the sides of the Cauldron as if she'd push off it, as if she'd knock it down—

"*That is enough.*" Lucien surged for Elain, for the Cauldron.

And the king's power leashed him, too. On the ground beside Tamlin, his single eye wide, Lucien had the good sense to look horrified as he glanced between Elain and the High Lord.

"Please," I begged the king, who motioned Elain to be shoved into the water. "Please, I will do anything, I will give you anything." I shot to my feet, stepping away from where Cassian lay prostrate, and looked to the queens. "Please—you do not need proof, I am proof that it works. Jurian is proof it is safe."

The ancient queen said, "You are a thief, and a liar. You conspired with our sister. Your punishment should be the same as hers. Consider this a gift instead."

Elain's foot hit the water, and she screamed—screamed in terror that hit me so deep I began sobbing. "Please," I said to none of them.

Nesta was still fighting, still roaring through her gag.

Elain, who Nesta would have killed and whored and stolen for. Elain, who had been gentle and sweet. Elain, who was to marry a lord's son who hated faeries . . .

The guards shoved my sister into the Cauldron in a single movement.

My cry hadn't finished sounding before Elain's head went under.

She did not come up.

Nesta's screaming was the only sound. Cassian blindly lurched toward it—toward her, moaning in pain.

The King of Hybern bowed slightly to the queens. "Behold."

Rhys, a wall of guards still cleaving us, curled his fingers into a fist. But he did not move, as Mor and I did not dare move, not with Azriel's life dangling in the king's grasp.

And as if it had been tipped by invisible hands, the Cauldron turned on its side.

More water than seemed possible dumped out in a cascade. Black, smoke-coated water.

And Elain, as if she'd been thrown by a wave, washed onto the stones facedown.

Her legs were so pale—so delicate. I couldn't remember the last time I'd seen them bare.

The queens pushed forward. Alive, she had to be *alive*, had to have wanted to live—

Elain sucked in a breath, her fine-boned back rising, her wet nightgown nearly sheer.

And as she rose from the ground onto her elbows, the gag in place, as she twisted to look at me—

Nesta began roaring again.

Pale skin started to glow. Her face had somehow become more beautiful—infinitely beautiful, and her ears . . . Elain's ears were now pointed beneath her sodden hair.

The queens gasped. And for a moment, all I could think of was my father. What he would do, what he would say, when his most beloved daughter looked at him with a Fae face.

"So we can survive," the dark-haired youngest breathed, eyes bright.

I fell to my knees, the guards not bothering to grab me as I sobbed. What he'd done, what he'd done—

"The hellcat now, if you'll be so kind," the King of Hybern said.

I whipped my head to Nesta as she went silent. The Cauldron righted itself.

Cassian again stirred, slumping on the floor—but his hand twitched. Toward Nesta.

Elain was still shivering on the wet stones, her nightgown shoved up to her thighs, her small breasts fully visible beneath the soaked fabric. Guards snickered.

Lucien snarled at the king over the bite of the magic at his throat, "*Don't just leave her on the damned floor—*"

There was a flare of light, and a scrape, and then Lucien was stalking toward Elain, freed of his restraints. Tamlin remained leashed on the ground, a gag of white, iridescent magic in his mouth now. But his eyes were on Lucien as—

As Lucien took off his jacket, kneeling before Elain. She cringed away from the coat, from him—

The guards hauled Nesta toward the Cauldron.

There were different kinds of torture, I realized.

There was the torture that I had endured, that Rhys had endured.

And then there was this.

The torture that Rhys had worked so hard those fifty years to avoid; the nightmares that haunted him. To be unable to move, to fight . . . while our loved ones were broken. My eyes met with those of my mate. Agony rippled in that violet stare—rage and guilt and utter agony. The mirror to my own.

Nesta fought every step of the way.

She did not make it easy for them. She clawed and kicked and bucked.

And it was not enough.

And we were not enough to save her.

I watched as she was hoisted up. Elain remained shuddering on the ground, Lucien's coat draped around her. She did not look at the Cauldron behind her, not as Nesta's thrashing feet slammed into the water.

Cassian stirred again, his shredded wings twitching and spraying blood, his muscles quivering. At Nesta's shouts, her raging, his eyes fluttered open, glazed and unseeing, an answer to some call in his blood, a promise he'd made her. But pain knocked him under again.

Nesta was shoved into the water up to her shoulders. She bucked even as the water sprayed. She clawed and screamed her rage, her defiance.

"*Put her under*," the king hissed.

The guards, straining, shoved her slender shoulders. Her brown-gold head.

And as they pushed her head down, she thrashed one last time, freeing her long, pale arm.

Teeth bared, Nesta pointed one finger at the King of Hybern.

One finger, a curse and a damning.

A promise.

And as Nesta's head was forced under the water, as that hand was violently shoved down, the King of Hybern had the good sense to look somewhat unnerved.

Dark water lapped for a moment. The surface went flat.

I vomited on the floor.

The guards at last let Rhysand kneel beside me in the growing pool of Cassian's blood—let him tuck me into him as the Cauldron again tilted.

Water poured forth, Lucien hoisting Elain in his arms and out of the way. The bonds on Tamlin vanished, along with the gag. He was instantly on his feet, snarling at the king. Even the fist on my mind lightened to a mere caress. As if he knew he'd won.

I didn't care. Not as Nesta was sprawled upon the stones.

I knew that she was different.

From however Elain had been Made . . . Nesta was different.

Even before she took her first breath, I felt it.

As if the Cauldron in making her . . . had been forced to give more than it wanted. As if Nesta had fought even after she went under, and had decided that if she was to be dragged into hell, she was taking that Cauldron with her.

As if that finger she'd pointed was now a death-promise to the King of Hybern.

Nesta took a breath. And when I beheld my sister, with her somehow magnified beauty, her ears . . . When Nesta looked to me . . .

Rage. Power. Cunning.

Then it was gone, horror and shock crumpling her face, but she didn't pause, didn't halt. She was free—she was loose.

She was on her feet, tripping over her slightly longer, leaner limbs, ripping the gag from her mouth—

Nesta slammed into Lucien, grabbing Elain from his arms, and screamed at him as he fell back, "*Get off her!*"

Elain's feet slipped against the floor, but Nesta gripped her upright, running her hands over Elain's face, her shoulders, her hair— "*Elain, Elain, Elain*," she sobbed.

Cassian again stirred—trying to rise, to answer Nesta's voice as she held my sister and cried her name again and again.

But Elain was staring over Nesta's shoulder.

At Lucien—whose face she had finally taken in.

Dark brown eyes met one eye of russet and one of metal.

Nesta was still weeping, still raging, still inspecting Elain—

Lucien's hands slackened at his sides.

His voice broke as he whispered to Elain, "You're my mate."

CHAPTER 66

I didn't let Lucien's declaration sink in.

Nesta, however, whirled on him. "She is *no such thing*," she said, and shoved him again.

Lucien didn't move an inch. His face was pale as death as he stared at Elain. My sister said nothing, the iron ring glinting dully on her finger.

The King of Hybern murmured, "Interesting. So very interesting." He turned to the queens. "See? I showed you not once, but twice that it is safe. Who should like to be Made first? Perhaps you'll get a handsome Fae lord as your mate, too."

The youngest queen stepped forward, her eyes indeed darting between all the Fae men assembled. As if they were hers for the picking.

The king chuckled. "Very well, then."

Hate flooded me, so violent I had no control over it, no song in my heart but its war-cry. I was going to kill them. I was going to kill *all* of them—

"If you're so willing to hand out bargains," Rhys suddenly said, rising to his feet and tugging me with him, "perhaps I'll make one with you."

"Oh?"

Rhys shrugged.

No. No more bargains—no more sacrifices. No more giving himself away piece by piece.

No more.

And if the king refused, if there was nothing to do but watch my friends die . . .

I could not accept it. I could not endure it—not that.

And for Rhys, for the family I'd found . . . They had not needed me—not really. Only to nullify the Cauldron.

I had failed them. Just as I had failed my sisters, whose lives I'd now shattered . . .

I thought of that ring waiting for me at home. I thought of the ring on Elain's finger, from a man who would now likely hunt her down and kill her. If Lucien let her leave at all.

I thought of all the things I wanted to paint—and never would.

But for them—for my family both of blood and my own choosing, for my mate . . . The idea that hit me did not seem so frightening.

And so I was not afraid.

I dropped to my knees in a spasm, gripping my head as I gnashed my teeth and sobbed, sobbed and panted, pulling at my hair—

The fist of that spell didn't have time to seize me again as I exploded past it.

Rhys reached for me, but I unleashed my power, a flash of that white, pure light, all that could escape with the damper from the king's spell. A flash of the light that was only for Rhys, only because of Rhys. I hoped he understood.

It erupted through the room, the gathered force hissing and dropping back.

Even Rhys had frozen—the king and queens openmouthed. My sisters and Lucien had whirled, too.

But there, deep within Day's light . . . I gleaned it. A purifying, clear power. Cursebreaker—spellbreaker. The light wiped through every physical trapping, showing me the snarls of spells and glamours, showing me the way through . . . I burned brighter, looking, looking—

Buried inside the bone-walls of the castle, the wards were woven strong.

I sent that blinding light flaring once more—a distraction and sleight of hand as I severed the wards at their ancient arteries.

Now I only had to play my part.

The light faded, and I was curled on the floor, head in my hands.

Silence. Silence as they all gawked at me.

Even Jurian had stopped gloating from where he now leaned against the wall.

But my eyes were only on Tamlin as I lowered my hands, gulping down air, and blinked. I looked at the host and the blood and the Night Court, and then finally back at him as I breathed, "Tamlin?"

He didn't move an inch. Beyond him, the king gaped at me. Whether he knew I'd ripped his wards wide open, whether he knew it was intentional, was not my concern—not yet.

I blinked again, as if clearing my head. "Tamlin?" I peered at my hands, the blood, and when I beheld Rhys, when I saw my grim-faced friends, and my drenched, immortal sisters—

There was nothing but shock and confusion on Rhys's face as I scrambled back from him.

Away from them. Toward Tamlin. "Tamlin," I managed to say again. Lucien's eye widened as he stepped between me and Elain. I whirled on the King of Hybern. "Where—" I again faced Rhysand. "What did you do to me," I breathed, low and guttural. Backing toward Tamlin. "*What did you do?*"

Get them out. Get my sisters out.

Play—please play along. Please—

There was no sound, no shield, no glimmer of feeling in our bond. The king's power had blocked it out too thoroughly. There was nothing I could do against it, Cursebreaker or no.

But Rhys slid his hands into his pockets as he purred, "How did you get free?"

"What?" Jurian seethed, pushing off the wall and storming toward us.

But I turned toward Tamlin and ignored the features and smell and clothes that were all wrong. He watched me warily. "Don't let him take me again, don't let him—don't—" I couldn't keep the sobs from shuddering out, not as the full force of what I was doing hit me.

"Feyre," Tamlin said softly. And I knew I had won.

I sobbed harder.

Get my sisters out, I begged Rhys through the silent bond. *I ripped the wards open for you—all of you. Get them out.*

"Don't let him take me," I sobbed again. "I don't want to go back."

And when I looked at Mor, at the tears streaming down her face as she helped Cassian get upright, I knew she realized what I meant. But the tears vanished—became sorrow for Cassian as she turned a hateful, horrified face to Rhysand and spat, "What did you do to that girl?"

Rhys cocked his head. "How did you do it, Feyre?" There was so much blood on him. One last game—this was one last game we were to play together.

I shook my head. The queens had fallen back, their guards forming a wall between us.

Tamlin watched me carefully. So did Lucien.

So I turned to the king. He was smiling. Like he knew.

But I said, "Break the bond."

Rhysand went still as death.

I stormed to the king, knees barking as I dropped to the floor before his throne. "Break the bond. The bargain, the—the mating bond. He—he made me do it, made me swear it—"

"No," Rhysand said.

I ignored him, even as my heart broke, even as I knew that he hadn't meant to say it— "Do it," I begged the king, even as I silently prayed he wouldn't notice his ruined wards, the door I'd left wide open. "I know you can. Just—free me. Free me from it."

"*No*," Rhysand said.

But Tamlin was staring between us. And I looked at him, the High Lord I had once loved, and I breathed, "No more. No more death—no more killing." I sobbed through my clenched teeth. Made myself look at my sisters. "*No more.* Take me *home* and let them go. Tell him it's part of the bargain and let them go. But no more—please."

Cassian slowly, every movement pained, stirred enough to look over a shredded wing at me. And in his pain-glazed eyes, I saw it—the understanding.

The Court of Dreams. I had belonged to a court of dreams. And dreamers.

And for their dreams . . . for what they had worked for, sacrificed for . . . I could do it.

Get my sisters out, I said to Rhys one last time, sending it into that stone wall between us.

I looked to Tamlin. "No more." Those green eyes met mine—and the sorrow and tenderness in them was the most hideous thing I'd ever seen. "Take me home."

Tamlin said flatly to the king, "Let them go, break her bond, and let's be done with it. Her sisters come with us. You've already crossed too many lines."

Jurian began objecting, but the king said, "Very well."

"No," was all Rhys said again.

Tamlin snarled at him, "I don't give a *shit* if she's your mate. I don't give a shit if you think you're entitled to her. She is *mine*—and one day, I am going to repay every bit of pain she felt, every bit of suffering and despair. One day, perhaps when she decides she wants to end you, I'll be happy to oblige her."

Walk away—just go. Take my sisters with you.

Rhys was only staring at me. "Don't."

But I backed away—until I hit Tamlin's chest, until his hands, warm and heavy, landed on my shoulders. "Do it," he said to the king.

"No," Rhys said again, his voice breaking.

But the king pointed at me. And I screamed.

Tamlin gripped my arms as I screamed and screamed at the pain that tore through my chest, my left arm.

Rhysand was on the ground, roaring, and I thought he might have said my name, might have bellowed it as I thrashed and sobbed. I was being shredded, I was dying, I was dying—

No. No, I didn't want it, I didn't want to—

A crack sounded in my ears.

And the world cleaved in two as the bond snapped.

CHAPTER 67

I fainted.

When I opened my eyes, mere seconds had passed. Mor was now hauling away Rhys, who was panting on the floor, eyes wild, fingers clenching and unclenching—

Tamlin yanked off the glove on my left hand.

Pure, bare skin greeted him. No tattoo.

I was sobbing and sobbing, and his arms came around me. Every inch of them felt wrong. I nearly gagged on his scent.

Mor let go of Rhysand's jacket collar, and he crawled—*crawled* back toward Azriel and Cassian, their blood splashing on his hands, on his neck, as he hauled himself through it. His rasping breaths sliced into me, my soul—

The king merely waved a hand at him. "You are free to go, Rhysand. Your friend's poison is gone. The wings on the other, I'm afraid, are a bit of a mess."

Don't fight it—don't say anything, I begged him as Rhys reached his brothers. *Take my sisters. The wards are down.*

Silence.

So I looked—just once—at Rhysand, and Cassian, and Mor, and Azriel.

They were already looking at me. Faces bloody and cold and enraged. But beneath them . . . I knew it was love beneath them. They understood the tears that rolled down my face as I silently said good-bye.

Then Mor, swift as an adder, winnowed to Lucien. To my sisters. To show Rhys, I realized, what I'd done, the hole I'd blasted for them to escape—

She slammed Lucien away with a palm to the chest, and his roar shook the halls as Mor grabbed my sisters by the arm and vanished.

Lucien's bellow was still sounding as Rhys lunged, gripping Azriel and Cassian, and did not even turn toward me as they winnowed out.

The king shot to his feet, spewing his wrath at his guards, at Jurian, for not grabbing my sisters. Demanding to know what had happened to the castle wards—

I barely heard him. There was only silence in my head. Such silence where there had once been dark laughter and wicked amusement. A wind-blasted wasteland.

Lucien was shaking his head, panting, and whirled to us. "*Get her back*," he snarled at Tamlin over the ranting of the king. A mate—a mate already going wild to defend what was his.

Tamlin ignored him. So I did, too. I could barely stand, but I faced the king as he slumped into his throne, gripping the arms so tightly the whites of his knuckles showed. "Thank you," I breathed, a hand on my chest—the skin so pale, so white. "Thank you."

He merely said to the gathered queens, now a healthy distance away, "Begin."

The queens looked at each other, then their wide-eyed guards, and snaked toward the Cauldron, their smiles growing. Wolves circling prey. One of them sniped at another for pushing her—the king murmured something to them all that I didn't bother to hear.

Jurian stalked over to Lucien amid the rising squabble, laughing under his breath. "Do you know what Illyrian bastards do to pretty females? You won't have a mate left—at least not one that's useful to you in any way."

Lucien's answering growl was nothing short of feral.

I spat at Jurian's feet. "You can go to hell, you hideous prick."

Tamlin's hands tightened on my shoulders. Lucien spun toward me, and that metal eye whirred and narrowed. Centuries of cultivated reason clicked into place.

I was not panicking at my sisters being taken.

I said quietly, "We will get her back."

But Lucien was watching me warily. Too warily.

I said to Tamlin, "Take me home."

But the king cut in over the bickering of the queens, "Where is it."

I preferred the amused, arrogant voice to the flat, brutal one that sliced through the hall.

"You—*you* were to wield the Book of Breathings," the king said. "I could feel it in here, with . . ."

The entire castle shuddered as he realized I had not been holding it in my jacket.

I just said to him, "Your mistake."

His nostrils flared. Even the sea far below seemed to recoil in terror at the wrath that whitened his ruddy face. But he blinked and it was gone. He said tightly to Tamlin, "When the Book is retrieved, I expect your presence here."

Power, smelling of lilac and cedar and the first bits of green, swirled around me. Readying us to winnow away—through the wards they had no inkling I'd smashed apart.

So I said to the king, and Jurian, and the queens assembled, already at the lip of the Cauldron and hissing over who would go in first, "I will light your pyres myself for what you did to my sisters."

Then we were gone.

CHAPTER 68

Rhysand

I slammed into the floor of the town house, and Amren was instantly there, hands on Cassian's wings, swearing at the damage. Then at the hole in Azriel's chest.

Even her healing couldn't fix both. No, we'd need a real healer for each of them, and fast, because if Cassian lost those wings . . . I knew he'd prefer death. Any Illyrian would.

"Where is she?" Amren demanded.

Where is she where is she where is she

"Get the Book out of here," I said, dumping the pieces onto the ground. I hated the touch of them, their madness and despair and joy. Amren ignored the order.

Mor hadn't appeared—dropping off or hiding Nesta and Elain wherever she deemed safest.

"Where is she?" Amren said again, pressing a hand to Cassian's ravaged back. I knew she didn't mean Mor.

As if my thoughts had summoned her, my cousin appeared—panting, haggard. She dropped to the floor before Azriel, her blood-caked hands shaking as she ripped the arrow free of his chest, blood showering the carpet. She shoved her fingers over the wound, light flaring as her power knit bone and flesh and vein together.

"*Where is she?*" Amren snapped one more time.

I couldn't bring myself to say the words.

So Mor said them for me as she knelt over Azriel, both of my brothers mercifully unconscious. "Tamlin offered passage through his lands and our heads on platters to the king in exchange for trapping Feyre, breaking her bond, and getting to bring her back to the Spring Court. But Ianthe betrayed Tamlin—told the king where to find Feyre's sisters. So the king had Feyre's sisters brought with the queens—to prove he could make them immortal. He put them in the Cauldron. We could do nothing as they were turned. He had us by the balls."

Those quicksilver eyes shot to me. "Rhysand."

I managed to say, "We were out of options, and Feyre knew it. So she pretended to free herself from the control Tamlin thought I'd kept on her mind. Pretended that she . . . hated us. And told him she'd go home—but only if the killing stopped. If we went free."

"And the bond," Amren breathed, Cassian's blood shining on her hands as she slowed its dribbling.

Mor said, "She asked the king to break the bond. He obliged."

I thought I might be dying—thought my chest might actually be cleaved in two.

"That's impossible," Amren said. "That sort of bond cannot be broken."

"The king said he could do it."

"The king is a fool," Amren barked. "That sort of bond *cannot* be broken."

"No, it can't," I said.

They both looked at me.

I cleared my head, my shattering heart—breaking for what my mate had done, sacrificed for me and my family. For her sisters. Because she hadn't thought . . . hadn't thought she was essential. Even after all she had done. "The king broke the bargain between us. Hard to do, but he couldn't tell that it wasn't the mating bond."

Mor started. "Does—does Feyre know—"

"Yes," I breathed. "And now my mate is in our enemy's hands."

"Go get her," Amren hissed. "*Right now*."

"*No*," I said, and hated the word.

They gaped at me, and I wanted to roar at the sight of the blood coating them, at my unconscious and suffering brothers on the carpet before them.

But I managed to say to my cousin, "Weren't you listening to what Feyre said to him? She promised to destroy him—from within."

Mor's face paled, her magic flaring on Azriel's chest. "She's going into that house to take him down. To take them all down."

I nodded. "She is now a spy—with a direct line to me. What the King of Hybern does, where he goes, what his plans are, she will know. And report back."

For between us, faint and soft, hidden so none might find it . . . between us lay a whisper of color, and joy, of light and shadow—a whisper of *her*. Our bond.

"She's your mate," Amren bit at me. "Not your spy. *Go get her*."

"She is my mate. And my spy," I said too quietly. "And she is the High Lady of the Night Court."

"What?" Mor whispered.

I caressed a mental finger down that bond now hidden deep, deep within us, and said, "If they had removed her other glove, they would have seen a second tattoo on her right arm. The twin to the other. Inked last night, when we crept out, found a priestess, and I swore her in as my High Lady."

"Not—not consort," Amren blurted, blinking. I hadn't seen her surprised in . . . centuries.

"Not consort, not wife. Feyre is High Lady of the Night Court." My equal in every way; she would wear my crown, sit on a throne beside mine. Never sidelined, never designated to breeding and parties and child-rearing. My queen.

As if in answer, a glimmer of love shuddered down the bond. I clamped down on the relief that threatened to shatter any calm I feigned having.

"You mean to tell me," Mor breathed, "that my High Lady is now surrounded by enemies?" A lethal sort of calm crept over her tear-stained face.

"I mean to tell you," I said, watching the blood clot on Cassian's wings with Amren's tending. Beneath Mor's own hands, Azriel's bleeding at last eased. Enough to keep them alive until the healer got here. "I mean to tell you," I said again, my power building and rubbing itself against my skin, my bones, desperate to be unleashed upon the world, "that your High Lady made a sacrifice for her court—and we will move when the time is right."

Perhaps Lucien being Elain's mate would help—somehow. I'd find a way.

And then I'd assist my mate in ripping the Spring Court, Ianthe, those mortal queens, and the King of Hybern to shreds. Slowly.

"Until then?" Amren demanded. "What of the Cauldron—of the Book?"

"Until then," I said, staring toward the door as if I might see her walk through it, laughing and vibrant and beautiful, "we go to war."

CHAPTER 69

Feyre

Tamlin landed us in the gravel of the front drive.

I had forgotten how quiet it was here.

How small. Empty.

Spring bloomed—the air gentle and scented with roses.

Still lovely. But there were the front doors he'd sealed me behind. There was the window I'd banged on, trying to get out. A pretty, rose-covered prison.

But I smiled, head throbbing, and said through my tears, "I thought I'd never see it again."

Tamlin was just staring at me, as if not quite believing it. "I thought you would never, either."

And you sold us out—sold out every innocent in this land for that. All so you could have me back.

Love—love was a balm as much as it was a poison.

But it was love that burned in my chest. Right alongside the bond that the King of Hybern hadn't so much as touched, because he hadn't known how deep and far he'd have to delve to cleave it. To cleave me and Rhysand apart.

It had hurt—hurt like hell to have the bargain between us ended—and Rhys had done his job perfectly, his horror flawless. We had always been so good at playing together.

I had not doubted him, had not said anything but *Yes* when he'd taken me down to the temple the night before, and I'd sworn my vows. To him, to Velaris, to the Night Court.

And now . . . a gentle, loving stroke down that bond, concealed beneath that wasteland where the bargain had been. I sent a glimmer of feeling back down the line, wishing I could touch him, hold him, laugh with him.

But I kept those thoughts clear from my face. Kept anything but quiet relief from it as I leaned into Tamlin, sighing. "It feels—feels as if some of it was a dream, or a nightmare. But . . . But I remembered you. And when I saw you there today, I started clawing at it, fighting, because I knew it might be my only chance, and—"

"How did you break free of his control," Lucien said flatly from behind us.

Tamlin gave him a warning growl.

I'd forgotten he was there. My sister's mate. The Mother, I decided, did have a sense of humor. "I wanted it—I don't know how. I just wanted to break free of him, so I did."

We stared each other down, but Tamlin brushed a thumb over my shoulder. "Are—are you hurt?"

I tried not to bristle. I knew what he meant. That he thought Rhysand would do anything like that to anyone— "I—I don't know," I stammered. "I don't . . . I don't remember those things."

Lucien's metal eye narrowed, as if he could sense the lie.

But I looked up at Tamlin, and brushed my hand over his mouth. My bare, empty skin. "You're real," I said. "You freed me."

It was an effort not to turn my hands into claws and rip out his eyes. Traitor—liar. Murderer.

"You freed yourself," Tamlin breathed. He gestured to the house.

"Rest—and then we'll talk. I . . . need to find Ianthe. And make some things very, very clear."

"I—I want to be a part of it this time," I said, halting when he tried to herd me back into that beautiful prison. "No more . . . No more shutting me out. No more guards. Please. I have so much to tell you about them—bits and pieces, but . . . I can help. We can get my sisters back. Let me help."

Help lead you in the wrong direction. Help bring you and your court to your knees, and take down Jurian and those conniving, traitorous queens. And then tear Ianthe into tiny, tiny pieces and bury them in a pit no one can find.

Tamlin scanned my face, and finally nodded. "We'll start over. Do things differently. When you were gone, I realized . . . I'd been wrong. So wrong, Feyre. And I'm sorry."

Too late. Too damned late. But I rested my head on his arm as he slipped it around me and led me toward the house. "It doesn't matter. I'm home now."

"Forever," he promised.

"Forever," I parroted, glancing behind—to where Lucien stood in the gravel drive.

His gaze on me. Face hard. As if he'd seen through every lie.

As if he knew of the second tattoo beneath my glove, and the glamour I now kept on it.

As if he knew that they had let a fox into a chicken coop—and he could do nothing.

Not unless he never wanted to see his mate—Elain—again.

I gave Lucien a sweet, sleepy smile. So our game began.

We hit the sweeping marble stairs to the front doors of the manor.

And so Tamlin unwittingly led the High Lady of the Night Court into the heart of his territory.

ACKNOWLEDGMENTS

Thank you to the following people who make my life blessed beyond all measure:

To my husband, Josh: You got me through this year. (Through many years before it, but this one in particular.) I don't have the words to describe how much I love you, and how grateful I am for all that you do. For the countless meals you cooked so I didn't have to stop writing; for the hundreds of dishes you washed afterward so I could run back into my office and keep working; for the hours of dog-walking, especially those early mornings, just so I could get some sleep . . . This book is now a *real* book because of you. Thank you for carrying me when I was too weary, for wiping away my tears when my heart was heavy, and for coming with me on so many adventures around the world.

To Annie, who can't read this, but who deserves credit, anyway: Every second with you is a gift. Thank you for making a fairly solitary job not the slightest bit lonely—and for the laughter and joy and love you've brought into my life. Love you, baby pup.

To Susan Dennard, my Threadsister and *anam cara*: Pretty sure I'm a broken record at this point, but *thank you* for being a friend worth waiting for, and for the fun, truly epic times we've had together. To Alex Bracken, Erin Bowman, Lauren Billings, Christina Hobbs, Victoria Aveyard, Jennifer L. Armentrout, Gena Showalter, and Claire Legrand: I'm so lucky to call you guys my friends. I adore you all.

To my agent, Tamar Rydzinski: What would I do without you? You've been my rock, my guiding star, and my fairy godmother from the very beginning. Seven books later, I still don't have the words to express my gratitude. To my editor, Cat Onder: Working with you on these books has been a highlight of my career. Thank you for your wisdom, your kindness, and your editorial brilliance.

To my phenomenal teams at Bloomsbury worldwide and CAA—Cindy Loh, Cristina Gilbert, Jon Cassir, Kathleen Farrar, Nigel Newton, Rebecca McNally, Natalie Hamilton, Sonia Palmisano, Emma Hopkin, Ian Lamb, Emma Bradshaw, Lizzy Mason, Courtney Griffin, Erica Barmash, Emily Ritter, Grace Whooley, Eshani Agrawal, Nick Thomas, Alice Grigg, Elise Burns, Jenny Collins, Linette Kim, Beth Eller, Diane Aronson, Emily Klopfer, Melissa Kavonic, Donna Mark, John Candell, Nicholas Church, Adiba Oemar, Hermione Lawton, Kelly de Groot, and the entire foreign rights team—it's an honor to know and work with you. Thank you for making my dreams come true. To Cassie Homer: Thank you for *everything*. You are an absolute delight.

To my family (especially my parents): I love you to the moon and back.

To Louisse Ang, Nicola Wilksinson, Elena Yip, Sasha Alsberg, Vilma Gonzalez, Damaris Cardinali, Alexa Santiago, Rachel Domingo, Jamie Miller, Alice Fanchiang, and the Maas Thirteen: your generosity, friendship, and support mean the world to me.

And, lastly, to my readers: You guys are the greatest. The actual greatest. None of this would have been possible without *you*. Thank you from the very bottom of my heart for all that you do for me and my books.

Feyre's story continues in . . .

Read on for a sneak peek at the next book in this electrifying series.

The painting was a lie.

A bright, pretty lie, bursting with pale pink blooms and fat beams of sunshine.

I'd begun it yesterday, an idle study of the rose garden lurking beyond the open windows of the studio. Through the tangle of thorns and satiny leaves, the brighter green of the hills rolled away into the distance.

Incessant, unrelenting spring.

If I'd painted this glimpse into the court the way my gut had urged me, it would have been flesh-shredding thorns, flowers that choked off the sunlight for any plants smaller than them, and rolling hills stained red.

But each brushstroke on the wide canvas was calculated; each dab and swirl of blending colors meant to portray not just idyllic spring, but a sunny disposition as well. Not too happy, but gladly, finally healing from horrors I carefully divulged.

I supposed that in the past weeks, I had crafted my demeanor as intricately as one of these paintings. I supposed that if I had also chosen to show myself as I truly wished, I would have been adorned with flesh-shredding talons, and hands that choked the life out of those now in my company. I would have left the gilded halls stained red.

But not yet.

Not yet, I told myself with every brushstroke, with every move I'd made these weeks. Swift revenge helped no one and nothing but my own, roiling rage.

Even if every time I spoke to them, I heard Elain's sobbing as she was forced into the Cauldron. Even if every time I looked at them, I saw Nesta fling that finger at the King of Hybern in a death-promise. Even if every time I scented them, my nostrils were again full of the tang of Cassian's blood as it pooled on the dark stones of that bone-castle.

The paintbrush snapped between my fingers.

I'd cleaved it in two, the pale handle damaged beyond repair.

Cursing under my breath, I glanced to the windows, the doors. This place was too full of watching eyes to risk throwing it in the rubbish bin.

I cast my mind around me like a net, trawling for any others near enough to witness, to be spying. I found none.

I held my hands before me, one half of the brush in each palm.

For a moment, I let myself see past the glamour that concealed the tattoo on my right hand and forearm. The markings of my true heart. My true title.

High Lady of the Night Court.

Half a thought had the broken paintbrush going up in flames.

The fire did not burn me, even as it devoured wood and brush and paint.

When it was nothing but smoke and ash, I invited in a wind that swept them from my palms and out the open windows.

For good measure, I summoned a breeze from the garden to snake through the room, wiping away any lingering tendril of smoke, filling it with the musty, suffocating smell of roses.

Perhaps when my task here was done, I'd burn this manor to the ground, too. Starting with those roses.

Two approaching presences tapped against the back of my mind, and I snatched up another brush, dipping it in the closest swirl of paint, and lowered the invisible, dark snares I'd erected around this room to alert me of any visitors.

I was working on the way the sunlight illuminated the delicate veins in a rose petal, trying not to think of how I'd once seen it do the same to Illyrian wings, when the doors opened.

I made a good show of appearing lost in my work, hunching my shoulders a bit, angling my head. And made an even better show of slowly looking over my shoulder, as if the struggle to part myself from the painting was a true effort.

But the battle was the smile I forced to my mouth. To my eyes—the real tell of a smile's genuine nature. I'd practiced in the mirror. Over and over.

So my eyes easily crinkled as I gave a subdued yet happy smile to Tamlin.

To Lucien.

"Sorry to interrupt," Tamlin said, scanning my face for any sign of the shadows I remembered to occasionally fall prey to, the ones I wielded to keep him at bay when the sun sank beyond those foothills. "But I thought you might want to get ready for the meeting."

I made myself swallow. Lower the paintbrush. No more than the nervous, unsure girl I'd been long ago. "Is—you talked it over with Ianthe? She's truly coming?"

I hadn't seen her yet. The High Priestess who had betrayed my sisters to Hybern, betrayed *us* to Hybern.

And even if Rhysand's murky, swift reports through the mating bond had soothed some of my dread and terror . . . She was responsible for it. What had happened weeks ago.

It was Lucien who answered, studying my painting as if it held the proof I knew he was searching for. "Yes. She . . . had her reasons. She is willing to explain them to you."

Perhaps along with her reasons for laying her hands on whatever males she pleased, whether they wished her to or not. For doing it to Rhys, and Lucien.

I wondered what Lucien truly made of it. And the fact that the collateral in her friendship with Hybern had wound up being *his* mate. Elain.

We had not spoken of Elain save for once, the day after I'd returned.

Despite what Jurian implied regarding how my sisters will be treated by Rhysand, I had told him, *despite what the Night Court is like, they won't hurt Elain or Nesta like that—not yet. Rhysand has more creative ways to harm them.*

Lucien still seemed to doubt it.

But then again, I had also implied, in my own "gaps" of memory, that perhaps I had not received the same creativity or courtesy.

That they believed it so easily, that they thought Rhysand would ever force someone . . . I added the insult to the long, long list of things to repay them for.

I set down the brush and pulled off the paint-flecked smock, carefully laying it on the stool I'd been perched on for two hours now.

"I'll go change," I murmured, flicking my loose braid over a shoulder.

Tamlin nodded, monitoring my every movement as I neared them. "The painting looks beautiful."

"It's nowhere near done," I said, dredging up that girl who had shunned praise and compliments, who had wanted to go unnoticed. "It's still a mess."

Frankly, it was some of my best work, even if its soullessness was only apparent to me.

"I think we all are," Tamlin offered with a tentative smile.

I reined in the urge to roll my eyes, and returned his smile, brushing my hand over his shoulder as I passed.

Lucien was waiting outside my new bedroom when I emerged ten minutes later.

It had taken me two days to stop going to the old one—to turn right at the top of the stairs and not left. But there was nothing in that old bedroom.

I'd looked into it once, the day after I returned.

Shattered furniture; shredded bedding; clothes strewn about as if he'd gone looking for me inside the armoire. No one, it seemed, had been allowed in to clean.

But it was the vines—the thorns—that had made it unlivable. My old bedroom had been overrun with them. They'd curved and slithered over the walls, entwined themselves amongst the debris. As if they'd crawled off the trellises beneath my windows, as if a hundred years had passed and not months.

That bedroom was now a tomb.

I gathered the soft pink skirts of my gauzy dress in a hand and shut the bedroom door behind me. Lucien remained leaning against the door across from mine.

His room.

I didn't doubt he'd ensured I now stayed across from him. Didn't doubt that the metal eye he possessed was always turned toward my own chambers, even while he slept.

"I'm surprised you're so calm, given your promises in Hybern," Lucien said by way of greeting.

The promise I'd made to kill the human queens, the King of Hybern, Jurian, and Ianthe for what they'd done to my sisters. To my friends.

"You yourself said Ianthe had her reasons. Furious as I might be, I can hear her out."

I had not told Lucien of what I knew regarding her true nature. It would mean explaining that Rhys had thrown her out of his own home, that Rhys had done it to defend himself and the members of his court, and it would raise too many questions, undermine too many carefully crafted lies that had kept him and his court—*my* court—safe.

Though I wondered if, after Velaris, it was even necessary. Our enemies knew of the city, knew it was a place of good and peace. And had tried to destroy it at the first opportunity.

The guilt for the attack on Velaris after Rhys had revealed it to those human queens would haunt my mate for the rest of our immortal lives.

"She's going to spin a story that you'll want to hear," Lucien warned.

I shrugged, heading down the carpeted, empty hall. "I can decide for myself. Though it sounds like you've already chosen not to believe her."

He fell into step beside me. "She dragged two innocent women into this."

"She was working to ensure Hybern's alliance held strong."

Lucien halted me with a hand around my elbow.

I allowed it because *not* allowing it, winnowing the way I'd done in the woods those months ago, or using an Illyrian defensive maneuver to knock him on his ass, would ruin my ruse. "You're smarter than that."

I studied the broad, tan hand wrapped around my elbow. Then I met one eye of russet and one of whirring gold.

Lucien breathed, "Where is he keeping her?"

I knew who he meant.

I shook my head. "I don't know. Rhysand has a hundred places where they could be, but I doubt he'd use any of them to hide Elain, knowing that I'm aware of them."

"Tell me anyway. List all of them."

"You'll die the moment you set foot in his territory."

"I survived well enough when I found you."

"You couldn't see that he had me in thrall. You let him take me back." Lie, lie, lie.

But the hurt and guilt I expected weren't there. Lucien slowly released his grip. "I need to find her."

"You don't even know Elain. The mating bond is just a physical reaction overriding your good sense."

"Is that what it did to you and Rhys?"

A quiet, dangerous question. But I made fear enter my eyes, let myself drag up memories of the Weaver, the Carver, the Middengard Wyrm so that old terror drenched my scent. "I don't want to talk about that," I said, my voice a rasping wobble.

A clock chimed on the main level. I sent a silent prayer of thanks to the Mother and launched into a quick walk. "We'll be late."

Lucien only nodded. But I felt his gaze on my back, fixed right on my spine, as I headed downstairs. To see Ianthe.

And at last decide how I was going to shred her into pieces.

The High Priestess looked exactly as I remembered, both in those memories Rhys had shown me and in my own daydreamings of using the talons hidden beneath my nails to carve out her eyes, then her tongue, then open up her throat.

My rage had become a living thing inside my chest, an echoing heartbeat that soothed me to sleep and stirred me to waking. I quieted it as I stared at Ianthe across the formal dining table, Tamlin and Lucien flanking me.

She still wore the pale hood and silver circlet set with its limpid blue stone.

Like a Siphon—the jewel in its center reminded me of Azriel's and Cassian's Siphons. And I wondered if, like the Illyrian warriors', the jewel somehow helped shape an unwieldy gift of magic into something more refined, deadlier. She had never removed it—but then again, I had never seen Ianthe summon any greater power than igniting a ball of faelight in a room.

The High Priestess lowered her teal eyes to the dark wood table, the hood casting shadows on her perfect face. "I wish to begin by saying how truly sorry I am. I acted out of a desire to . . . to grant what I believed you perhaps yearned for but did not dare voice, while also keeping our allies in Hybern satisfied with our allegiance."

Pretty, poisoned lies. But finding her true motive . . . I'd been waiting these weeks for this meeting. Had spent these weeks pretending to convalesce, pretending to *heal* from the horrors I'd survived at Rhysand's hands.

"Why would I ever wish for my sisters to endure that?" My voice came out trembling, cold.

Ianthe lifted her head, scanning my unsure, if not a bit aloof, face. "So you could be with them forever. And if Lucien had discovered that Elain was his mate beforehand, it would have been . . . devastating to realize he'd only have a few decades."

The sound of Elain's name on her lips sent a snarl rumbling up my throat. But I leashed it, falling into that mask of pained quiet, the newest in my arsenal.

Lucien answered, "If you expect our gratitude, you'll be waiting a while, Ianthe."

Tamlin shot him a warning look—both at the words and the tone. Perhaps Lucien would kill Ianthe before I had the chance, just for the horror she'd put his mate through that day.

"No," Ianthe breathed, eyes wide, the perfect picture of remorse and guilt. "No, I don't expect gratitude in the least. Or forgiveness. But understanding . . . This is my home, too." She lifted a slender hand clad in silver rings and bracelets to encompass the room, the manor. "We have all had to make alliances we didn't believe we'd ever forge—perhaps unsavory ones, yes, but . . . Hybern's force is too great to stop. It now can only be weathered like any other storm." A glance toward Tamlin. "We have worked so hard to prepare ourselves for Hybern's inevitable arrival—all these months. I made a grave mistake, and I will always regret any pain I caused, but let us continue this good work together. Let us find a way to ensure our lands and people survive."

"At the cost of how many others?" Lucien demanded.

Again, that warning look from Tamlin. But Lucien ignored him.

"What I saw in Hybern," Lucien said, gripping the arms of his chair hard enough that the carved wood groaned. "Any promises he made of peace and immunity . . ." He halted, as if remembering that Ianthe might very well feed this back to the king. He loosened his grip on the chair, his long fingers flexing before settling on the arms again. "We have to be careful."

"We will be," Tamlin promised. "But we've already agreed to certain conditions. Sacrifices. If we break apart now . . . even with Hybern as our ally, we have to present a solid front. Together."

He still trusted her. Still thought that Ianthe had merely made a bad call. Had no idea what lurked beneath the beauty, the clothes, and the pious incantations.

But then again, that same blindness kept him from realizing what prowled beneath my skin as well. Ianthe bowed her head again. "I will endeavor to be worthy of my friends."

Lucien seemed to be trying very, very hard not to roll his eyes.

But Tamlin said, "We'll all try."

That was his new favorite word: *try*.

I only swallowed, making sure he heard it, and nodded slowly, keeping my eyes on Ianthe. "Don't ever do anything like that again."

A fool's command—one she'd expected me to make, from the quickness with which she nodded. Lucien leaned back in his seat, refusing to say anything else.

"Lucien is right, though," I blurted, the portrait of concern. "What of the people in this court during this conflict?" I frowned at Tamlin. "They were brutalized by Amarantha—I'm not sure how well they will endure living beside Hybern. They have suffered enough."

Tamlin's jaw tightened. "Hybern has promised that our people shall remain untouched and undisturbed." *Our* people. I nearly scowled—even as I nodded again in understanding. "It was a part of our . . . bargain." When he'd sold out all of Prythian, sold out everything decent and good in himself, to *retrieve* me. "Our people will be safe when Hybern arrives. Though I've sent out word that families should . . . relocate to the eastern part of the territory. For the time being."

Good. At least he'd considered those potential casualties—at least he cared that much about his people, understood what sorts of sick games Hybern liked to play and that he might swear one thing but mean another. If he was already moving those most at risk during this conflict out of the way . . . It made my work here all the easier. And east—a bit of information I tucked away. If east was safe, then the west . . . Hybern would indeed be coming from that direction. Arriving there.

Tamlin blew out a breath. "That brings me to the other reason behind this meeting."

I braced myself, schooling my face into bland curiosity, as he declared, "The first delegation from Hybern arrives tomorrow." Lucien's golden skin paled. Tamlin added, "Jurian will be here by noon."

I'd barely heard a whisper of Jurian these past weeks—hadn't seen the resurrected human commander since that night in Hybern.

Jurian had been reborn through the Cauldron using the hideous remnants of him that Amarantha had hoarded as trophies for five hundred years, his soul trapped and aware within his own magically preserved eye. He was mad—had gone mad long before the King of Hybern had resurrected him to lead the human queens down a path of ignorant submission.

Tamlin and Lucien had to know. Had to have seen that gleam in Jurian's eyes.

But . . . they also did not seem to entirely mind that the King of Hybern possessed the Cauldron—that it was capable of cleaving this world apart. Starting with the wall. The only thing standing between the gathering, lethal Fae armies and the vulnerable human lands below.

No, that threat certainly didn't seem to keep Lucien or Tamlin awake at night. Or from inviting these monsters into their home.

Tamlin had promised upon my return that I was to be included in the planning, in every meeting. And he was true to his word when he explained that Jurian would arrive with two other commanders from Hybern, and I would be present for it. They indeed wished to survey the wall, to test for the perfect spot to rend it once the Cauldron had recovered its strength.

Turning my sisters into Fae, apparently, had drained it.

My smugness at the fact was short-lived.

My first task: learn where they planned to strike, and how long the Cauldron required to return to its full capacity. And then smuggle that information to Rhysand and the others.

I took extra care dressing the next day, after sleeping fitfully thanks to a dinner with a guilt-ridden Ianthe, who went to excessive lengths to kiss my ass and Lucien's. The priestess apparently wished to wait until the Hybern commanders were settled before making her appearance. She'd cooed about wanting to ensure they had the chance to get to know us before she intruded, but one look at Lucien told me that he and I, for once, agreed: she had likely planned some sort of grand entrance.

It made little difference to me—to my plans.

Plans that I sent down the mating bond the next morning, words and images tumbling along a night-filled corridor.

I did not dare risk using the bond too often. I had communicated with Rhysand only once since I'd arrived. Just once, in the hours after I'd walked into my old bedroom and spied the thorns that had conquered it.

It had been like shouting across a great distance, like speaking underwater. *I am safe and well*, I'd fired down the bond. *I'll tell you what I know soon*. I'd waited, letting the words travel into the dark. Then I'd asked, *Are they alive? Hurt?*

I didn't remember the bond between us being so hard to hear, even when I'd dwelled on this estate and he'd used it to see if I was still breathing, to make sure my despair hadn't swallowed me whole.

But Rhysand's response had come a minute later. *I love you. They are alive. They are healing.*

'Think *Game of Thrones* meets *Buffy the Vampire Slayer* with a drizzle of E.L. James' *Telegraph*
SARAH J. MAAS
'Devour with relish' *Daily Mail*
HOUSE of EARTH and BLOOD
A CRESCENT CITY NOVEL
BLOOMSBURY

PRAISE FOR SARAH J. MAAS'S COURT OF THORNS AND ROSES SERIES

A COURT OF THORNS AND ROSES

"Simply dazzles." —*Booklist*, starred review

"Passionate, violent, sexy and daring. . . .
A true page-turner." —*USA Today*

"Suspense, romance, intrigue and action. This is
not a book to be missed!" —HuffPost

"Vicious and intoxicating. . . . A dazzling world, complex characters
and sizzling romance." —*RT Book Reviews*, Top Pick

"A sexy, action-packed fairytale." —Bustle

A COURT OF MIST AND FURY

"Fiercely romantic, irresistibly sexy and hypnotically magical.
A veritable feast for the senses." —*USA Today*

"Hits the spot for fans of dark, lush, sexy fantasy." —*Kirkus Reviews*

"An immersive, satisfying read." —*Publishers Weekly*

"Darkly sexy and thrilling." —Bustle

A COURT OF WINGS AND RUIN

"Fast-paced and explosively action-packed." —*Booklist*

"The plot manages to seduce you with its alluring
characters, irresistible world and never-ending action,
leaving you craving more." —*RT Book Reviews*

BOOKS BY SARAH J. MAAS

THE COURT OF THORNS AND ROSES SERIES

A Court of Thorns and Roses

A Court of Mist and Fury

A Court of Wings and Ruin

A Court of Frost and Starlight

A Court of Thorns and Roses Colouring Book

THE CRESCENT CITY SERIES

House of Earth and Blood

THE THRONE OF GLASS SERIES

The Assassin's Blade

Throne of Glass

Crown of Midnight

Heir of Fire

Queen of Shadows

Empire of Storms

Tower of Dawn

Kingdom of Ash

The Throne of Glass Colouring Book

A COURT OF THORNS AND ROSES

SARAH J. MAAS

BLOOMSBURY PUBLISHING
LONDON • OXFORD • NEW YORK • NEW DELHI • SYDNEY

BLOOMSBURY PUBLISHING
Bloomsbury Publishing Plc
50 Bedford Square, London, WC1B 3DP, UK
29 Earlsfort Terrace, Dublin 2, Ireland

BLOOMSBURY, BLOOMSBURY PUBLISHING and the Diana logo are trademarks of Bloomsbury Publishing Plc

First published in Great Britain 2015
This edition published 2020

A catalogue record for this book is available from the British Library

ISBN: PB: 978-1-5266-0539-9; eBook: 978-1-4088-5787-8

22

Typeset by Westchester Publishing Services
Printed and bound in Great Britain by CPI Group (UK) Ltd, Croydon CR0 4YY

MIX
Paper from responsible sources
FSC® C020471

To find out more about our authors and books visit www.bloomsbury.com and sign up for our newsletters, including news about Sarah J. Maas.

For Josh—

Because you would go Under the Mountain for me.

I love you.

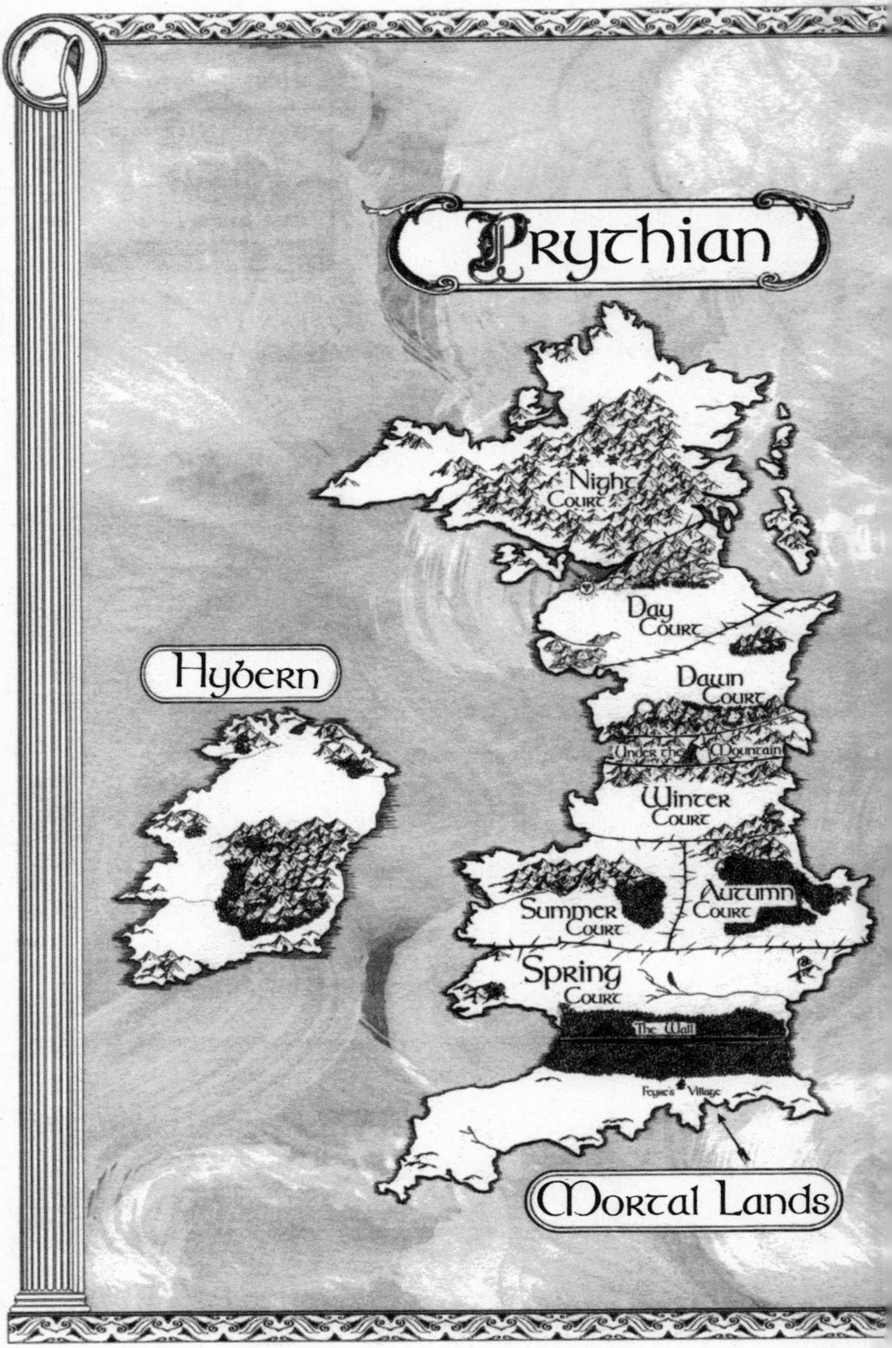
Prythian
Night Court
Day Court
Dawn Court
Under the Mountain
Winter Court
Summer Court
Autumn Court
Spring Court
The Wall
Feyre's Village
Hybern
Mortal Lands

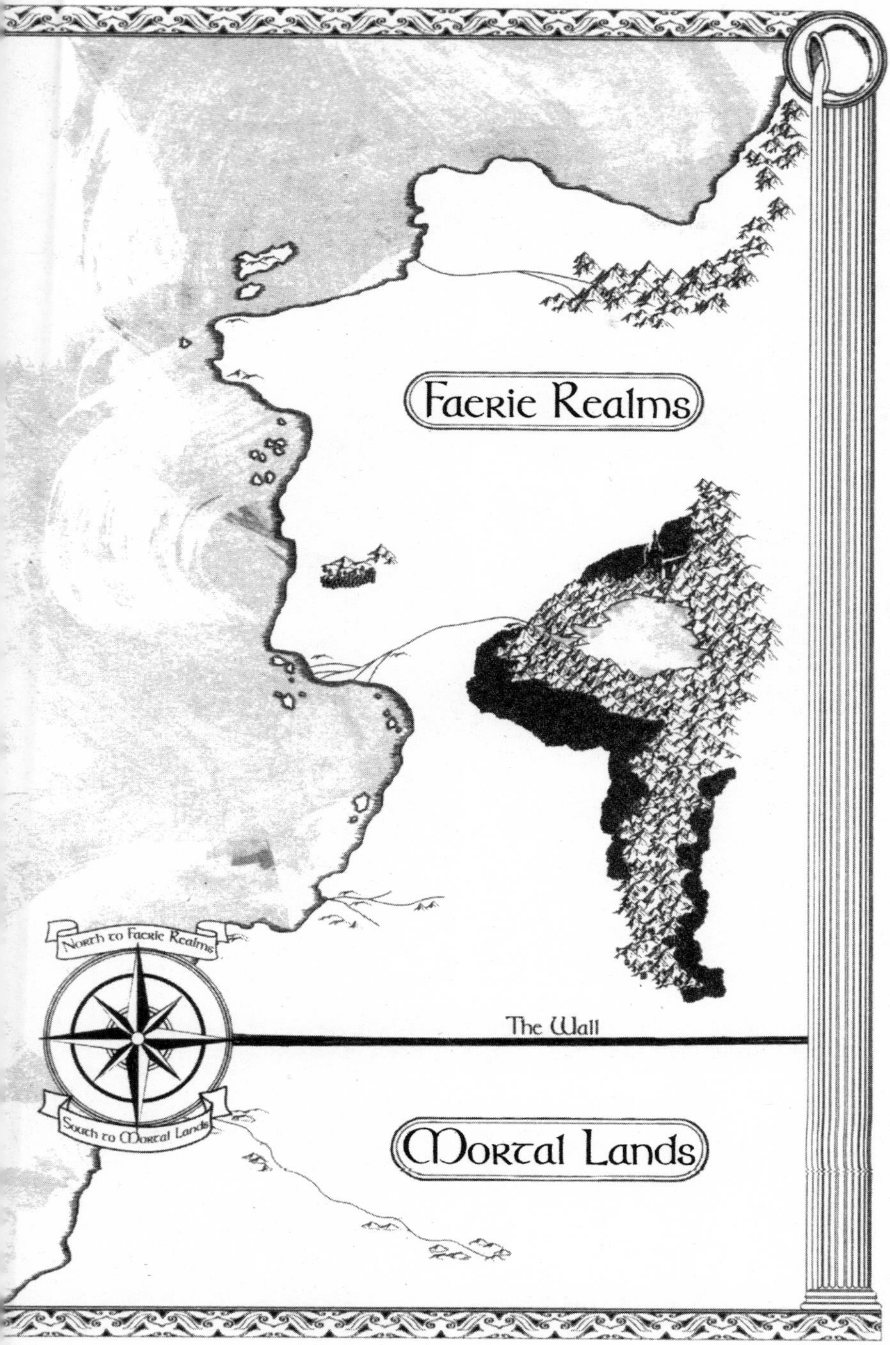

Faerie Realms
The Wall
Mortal Lands
North to Faerie Realms
South to Mortal Lands

A COURT
OF
THORNS
AND
ROSES

CHAPTER 1

The forest had become a labyrinth of snow and ice.

I'd been monitoring the parameters of the thicket for an hour, and my vantage point in the crook of a tree branch had turned useless. The gusting wind blew thick flurries to sweep away my tracks, but buried along with them any signs of potential quarry.

Hunger had brought me farther from home than I usually risked, but winter was the hard time. The animals had pulled in, going deeper into the woods than I could follow, leaving me to pick off stragglers one by one, praying they'd last until spring.

They hadn't.

I wiped my numb fingers over my eyes, brushing away the flakes clinging to my lashes. Here there were no telltale trees stripped of bark to mark the deer's passing—they hadn't yet moved on. They would remain until the bark ran out, then travel north past the wolves' territory and perhaps into the faerie lands of Prythian—where no mortals would dare go, not unless they had a death wish.

A shudder skittered down my spine at the thought, and I shoved it away, focusing on my surroundings, on the task ahead. That was all I could do, all I'd been able to do for years: focus on surviving the week, the day, the hour ahead. And now, with the snow, I'd be lucky to spot anything—especially from my position up in the tree, scarcely able to see fifteen feet ahead. Stifling a groan as my stiff limbs protested at the movement, I unstrung my bow before easing off the tree.

The icy snow crunched under my fraying boots, and I ground my teeth. Low visibility, unnecessary noise—I was well on my way to yet another fruitless hunt.

Only a few hours of daylight remained. If I didn't leave soon, I'd have to navigate my way home in the dark, and the warnings of the town hunters still rang fresh in my mind: giant wolves were on the prowl, and in numbers. Not to mention whispers of strange folk spotted in the area, tall and eerie and deadly.

Anything but faeries, the hunters had beseeched our long-forgotten gods—and I had secretly prayed alongside them. In the eight years we'd been living in our village, two days' journey from the immortal border of Prythian, we'd been spared an attack—though traveling peddlers sometimes brought stories of distant border towns left in splinters and bones and ashes. These accounts, once rare enough to be dismissed by the village elders as hearsay, had in recent months become commonplace whisperings on every market day.

I had risked much in coming so far into the forest, but we'd finished our last loaf of bread yesterday, and the remainder of our dried meat the day before. Still, I would have rather spent another night with a hungry belly than found myself satisfying the appetite of a wolf. Or a faerie.

Not that there was much of me to feast on. I'd turned gangly by this time of the year, and could count a good number of my ribs. Moving as nimbly and quietly as I could between the trees, I pushed a hand against my hollow and aching stomach. I knew the expression that would be on my two elder sisters' faces when I returned to our cottage empty-handed yet again.

After a few minutes of careful searching, I crouched in a cluster of snow-heavy brambles. Through the thorns, I had a half-decent view of a clearing and the small brook flowing through it. A few holes in the ice suggested it was still frequently used. Hopefully something would come by. Hopefully.

I sighed through my nose, digging the tip of my bow into the ground, and leaned my forehead against the crude curve of wood. We wouldn't last another week without food. And too many families had already started begging for me to hope for handouts from the wealthier townsfolk. I'd witnessed firsthand exactly how far their charity went.

I eased into a more comfortable position and calmed my breathing, straining to listen to the forest over the wind. The snow fell and fell, dancing and curling like sparkling spindrifts, the white fresh and clean against the brown and gray of the world. And despite myself, despite my numb limbs, I quieted that relentless, vicious part of my mind to take in the snow-veiled woods.

Once it had been second nature to savor the contrast of new grass against dark, tilled soil, or an amethyst brooch nestled in folds of emerald silk; once I'd dreamed and breathed and thought in color and light and shape. Sometimes I would even indulge in envisioning a day when my sisters were married and it was only me and Father, with enough food to go around, enough money to buy some paint, and enough time to put those colors and shapes down on paper or canvas or the cottage walls.

Not likely to happen anytime soon—perhaps ever. So I was left with moments like this, admiring the glint of pale winter light on snow. I couldn't remember the last time I'd done it—bothered to notice anything lovely or interesting.

Stolen hours in a decrepit barn with Isaac Hale didn't count; those times were hungry and empty and sometimes cruel, but never lovely.

The howling wind calmed into a soft sighing. The snow fell lazily now, in big, fat clumps that gathered along every nook and bump of the trees.

Mesmerizing—the lethal, gentle beauty of the snow. I'd soon have to return to the muddy, frozen roads of the village, to the cramped heat of our cottage. Some small, fragmented part of me recoiled at the thought.

Bushes rustled across the clearing.

Drawing my bow was a matter of instinct. I peered through the thorns, and my breath caught.

Less than thirty paces away stood a small doe, not yet too scrawny from winter, but desperate enough to wrench bark from a tree in the clearing.

A deer like that could feed my family for a week or more.

My mouth watered. Quiet as the wind hissing through dead leaves, I took aim.

She continued tearing off strips of bark, chewing slowly, utterly unaware that her death waited yards away.

I could dry half the meat, and we could immediately eat the rest—stews, pies . . . Her skin could be sold, or perhaps turned into clothing for one of us. I needed new boots, but Elain needed a new cloak, and Nesta was prone to crave anything someone else possessed.

My fingers trembled. So much food—such salvation. I took a steadying breath, double-checking my aim.

But there was a pair of golden eyes shining from the brush adjacent to mine.

The forest went silent. The wind died. Even the snow paused.

We mortals no longer kept gods to worship, but if I had known their lost names, I would have prayed to them. All of them. Concealed in the thicket, the wolf inched closer, its gaze set on the oblivious doe.

He was enormous—the size of a pony—and though I'd been warned about their presence, my mouth turned bone-dry.

But worse than his size was his unnatural stealth: even as he inched closer in the brush, he remained unheard, unspotted by the doe. No animal that massive could be so quiet. But if he was no ordinary animal, if he was of Prythian origin, if he was somehow a faerie, then being eaten was the least of my concerns.

If he was a faerie, I should already be running.

Yet maybe . . . maybe it would be a favor to the world, to my village, to myself, to kill him while I remained undetected. Putting an arrow through his eye would be no burden.

But despite his size, he *looked* like a wolf, moved like a wolf. *Animal*, I reassured myself. *Just an animal.* I didn't let myself consider the alternative—not when I needed my head clear, my breathing steady.

I had a hunting knife and three arrows. The first two were ordinary arrows—simple and efficient, and likely no more than bee stings to a wolf that size. But the third arrow, the longest and heaviest one, I'd bought from a traveling peddler during a summer when we'd had enough coppers for extra luxuries. An arrow carved from mountain ash, armed with an iron head.

From songs sung to us as lullabies over our cradles, we all knew from infancy that faeries hated iron. But it was the ash wood that made their immortal, healing magic falter long enough for a human to make a killing blow. Or so legend and rumor claimed. The only proof we had of the ash's effectiveness was its sheer rarity. I'd seen drawings of the trees, but never one with my own eyes—not after the High Fae had burned them all long ago. So few remained, most of them small and sickly and hidden by the nobility within high-walled groves. I'd spent weeks after my purchase debating whether that overpriced bit of wood had been a waste of money, or a fake, and for three years, the ash arrow had sat unused in my quiver.

Now I drew it, keeping my movements minimal, efficient—anything to avoid that monstrous wolf looking in my direction. The arrow was long and heavy enough to inflict damage—possibly kill him, if I aimed right.

My chest became so tight it ached. And in that moment, I realized my life boiled down to one question: Was the wolf alone?

I gripped my bow and drew the string farther back. I was a decent shot, but I'd never faced a wolf. I'd thought it made me lucky—even blessed. But now . . . I didn't know where to hit or how fast they moved. I couldn't afford to miss. Not when I had only one ash arrow.

And if it was indeed a faerie's heart pounding under that fur, then good riddance. Good riddance, after all their kind had done to us. I wouldn't risk this one later creeping into our village to slaughter and maim and torment. Let him die here and now. I'd be glad to end him.

The wolf crept closer, and a twig snapped beneath one of his paws—each bigger than my hand. The doe went rigid. She glanced to either side, ears straining toward the gray sky. With the wolf's downwind position, she couldn't see or smell him.

His head lowered, and his massive silver body—so perfectly blended into the snow and shadows—sank onto its haunches. The doe was still staring in the wrong direction.

I glanced from the doe to the wolf and back again. At least he was alone—at least I'd been spared that much. But if the wolf scared the doe off, I was left with nothing but a starving, oversize wolf—possibly a faerie—looking for the next-best meal. And if he killed her, destroying precious amounts of hide and fat . . .

If I judged wrongly, my life wasn't the only one that would be lost. But my life had been reduced to nothing but risks these past eight years that I'd been hunting in the woods, and I'd picked correctly most of the time. Most of the time.

The wolf shot from the brush in a flash of gray and white and black, his yellow fangs gleaming. He was even more gargantuan in the open, a marvel of muscle and speed and brute strength. The doe didn't stand a chance.

I fired the ash arrow before he destroyed much else of her.

The arrow found its mark in his side, and I could have sworn the ground itself shuddered. He barked in pain, releasing the doe's neck as his blood sprayed on the snow—so ruby bright.

He whirled toward me, those yellow eyes wide, hackles raised. His low growl reverberated in the empty pit of my stomach as I surged to my feet, snow churning around me, another arrow drawn.

But the wolf merely looked at me, his maw stained with blood, my ash arrow protruding so vulgarly from his side. The snow began falling again. He *looked*, and with a sort of awareness and surprise that made me fire the second arrow. Just in case—just in case that intelligence was of the immortal, wicked sort.

He didn't try to dodge the arrow as it went clean through his wide yellow eye.

He collapsed to the ground.

Color and darkness whirled, eddying in my vision, mixing with the snow.

His legs were twitching as a low whine sliced through the wind. Impossible—he should be dead, not dying. The arrow was through his eye almost to the goose fletching.

But wolf or faerie, it didn't matter. Not with that ash arrow buried in his side. He'd be dead soon enough. Still, my hands shook as I brushed off snow and edged closer, still keeping a good distance. Blood gushed from the wounds I'd given him, staining the snow crimson.

He pawed at the ground, his breathing already slowing. Was he in much pain, or was his whimper just his attempt to shove death away? I wasn't sure I wanted to know.

The snow swirled around us. I stared at him until that coat of charcoal and obsidian and ivory ceased rising and falling. Wolf—definitely just a wolf, despite his size.

The tightness in my chest eased, and I loosed a sigh, my breath clouding in front of me. At least the ash arrow had proved itself to be lethal, regardless of who or what it took down.

A rapid examination of the doe told me I could carry only one animal—and even that would be a struggle. But it was a shame to leave the wolf.

Though it wasted precious minutes—minutes during which any predator could smell the fresh blood—I skinned him and cleaned my arrows as best I could.

If anything, it warmed my hands. I wrapped the bloody side of his pelt around the doe's death-wound before I hoisted her across my shoulders. It was several miles back to our cottage, and I didn't need a trail of blood leading every animal with fangs and claws straight to me.

Grunting against the weight, I grasped the legs of the deer and spared a final glance at the steaming carcass of the wolf. His remaining golden eye now stared at the snow-heavy sky, and for a moment, I wished I had it in me to feel remorse for the dead thing.

But this was the forest, and it was winter.

CHAPTER 2

The sun had set by the time I exited the forest, my knees shaking. My hands, stiff from clenching the legs of the deer, had gone utterly numb miles ago. Not even the carcass could ward off the deepening chill.

The world was awash in hues of dark blue, interrupted only by shafts of buttery light escaping from the shuttered windows of our dilapidated cottage. It was like striding through a living painting—a fleeting moment of stillness, the blues swiftly shifting to solid darkness.

As I trudged up the path, each step fueled only by near-dizzying hunger, my sisters' voices fluttered out to meet me. I didn't need to discern their words to know they most likely were chattering about some young man or the ribbons they'd spotted in the village when they should have been chopping wood, but I smiled a bit nonetheless.

I kicked my boots against the stone door frame, knocking the snow from them. Bits of ice came free from the gray stones of the cottage, revealing the faded ward-markings etched around the threshold. My father had once convinced a passing charlatan to trade the engravings against faerie harm in exchange for one of his wood carvings. There was so little that my father was ever able to do for us that I hadn't possessed the heart to tell him the engravings were useless . . . and undoubtedly fake. Mortals didn't possess magic—didn't possess any of the superior strength and speed of the faeries or High Fae. The man, claiming some High Fae blood in his ancestry, had just carved the whorls and swirls and runes around the door and windows, muttered a few nonsense words, and ambled on his way.

I yanked open the wooden door, the frozen iron handle biting my skin like an asp. Heat and light blinded me as I slipped inside.

"Feyre!" Elain's soft gasp scraped past my ears, and I blinked back the brightness of the fire to find my second-eldest sister before me. Though she was bundled in a threadbare blanket, her gold-brown hair—the hair all three of us had—was coiled perfectly about her head. Eight years of poverty hadn't stripped from her the desire to look lovely. "Where did you get that?" The undercurrent of hunger honed her words into a sharpness that had become too common in recent weeks. No mention of the blood on me. I'd long since given up hope of them actually noticing whether I came back from the woods every evening. At least until they got hungry again. But then again, my mother hadn't made *them* swear anything when they stood beside her deathbed.

I took a calming breath as I slung the doe off my shoulders. She hit the wooden table with a thud, rattling a ceramic cup on its other end.

"Where do you think I got it?" My voice had turned hoarse, each word burning as it came out. My father and Nesta still silently warmed their hands by the hearth, my eldest sister ignoring him, as usual. I peeled the wolf pelt from the doe's body, and after removing my boots and setting them by the door, I turned to Elain.

Her brown eyes—my father's eyes—remained pinned on the doe. "Will it take you long to clean it?" Me. Not her, not the others. I'd never once seen their hands sticky with blood and fur. I'd only learned to prepare and harvest my kills thanks to the instruction of others.

Elain pushed her hand against her belly, probably as empty and aching as my own. It wasn't that Elain was cruel. She wasn't like Nesta, who had been born with a sneer on her face. Elain sometimes just . . . didn't grasp things. It wasn't meanness that kept her from offering to help; it simply never occurred to her that she might be capable of getting her hands dirty. I'd never been able to decide whether she actually didn't understand that we were truly poor or if she just refused to accept it. It still hadn't stopped me from buying her seeds for the flower garden she tended in the milder months, whenever I could afford it.

And it hadn't stopped her from buying me three small tins of paint—red, yellow, and blue—during that same summer I'd had enough to buy the ash arrow. It was the only gift she'd ever given me, and our house still bore the marks of it, even if the paint was now fading and chipped: little vines and flowers along the windows and thresholds and edges of things, tiny curls of flame on the stones bordering the hearth. Any spare minutes I'd had that bountiful summer I used to bedeck our house in color, sometimes hiding clever decorations inside drawers, behind the threadbare curtains, underneath the chairs and table.

We hadn't had a summer that easy since.

"Feyre." My father's deep rumble came from the fire. His dark beard was neatly trimmed, his face spotless—like my sisters'. "What luck you had today—in bringing us such a feast."

From beside my father, Nesta snorted. Not surprising. Any bit of praise for anyone—me, Elain, other villagers—usually resulted in her dismissal. And any word from our father usually resulted in her ridicule as well.

I straightened, almost too tired to stand, but braced a hand on the table beside the doe as I shot Nesta a glare. Of us, Nesta had taken the loss of our fortune the hardest. She had quietly resented my father from the moment we'd fled our manor, even after that awful day one of the creditors had come to show just how displeased he was at the loss of his investment.

But at least Nesta didn't fill our heads with useless talk of regaining our wealth, like my father. No, she just spent whatever money I didn't hide from her, and rarely bothered to acknowledge my father's limping presence at all. Some days, I couldn't tell which of us was the most wretched and bitter.

"We can eat half the meat this week," I said, shifting my gaze to the doe. The deer took up the entirety of the rickety table that served as our dining area, workspace, and kitchen. "We can dry the other half," I went on, knowing that no matter how nicely I phrased it, I'd still do the bulk of it. "And I'll go to the market tomorrow to see how much I can get for the hides," I finished, more to myself than to them. No one bothered to confirm they'd heard me, anyway.

My father's ruined leg was stretched out before him, as close to the fire's heat as it could get. The cold, or the rain, or a change in temperature always aggravated the vicious, twisted wounds around his knee. His simply carved cane was propped up against his chair—a cane he'd made for himself . . . and that Nesta was sometimes prone to leaving far out of his reach.

He could find work if he wasn't so ashamed, Nesta always said when I hissed about it. She hated him for the injury, too—for not fighting back when that creditor and his thugs had burst into the cottage and smashed his knee again and again. Nesta and Elain had fled into the bedroom, barricading the door. I had stayed, begging and weeping through every scream of my father, every crunch of bone. I'd soiled myself—and then vomited right on the stones before the hearth. Only then did the men leave. We never saw them again.

We'd used a massive chunk of our remaining money to pay for the healer. It had taken my father six months to even walk, a year before he could go a mile. The coppers he brought in when someone pitied him enough to buy his wood carvings weren't enough to keep us fed. Five years ago, when the money was well and truly gone, when my father still couldn't—wouldn't—move much about, he hadn't argued when I announced that I was going hunting.

He hadn't bothered to attempt to stand from his seat by the fire, hadn't bothered to look up from his wood carving. He just let me walk into those deadly, eerie woods that even the most seasoned hunters were wary of. He'd become a little more aware now—sometimes offered signs of gratitude, sometimes hobbled all the way into town to sell his carvings—but not much.

"I'd love a new cloak," Elain said at last with a sigh, at the same moment Nesta rose and declared: "I need a new pair of boots."

I kept quiet, knowing better than to get in the middle of one of their arguments, but I glanced at Nesta's still-shiny pair by the door. Beside hers, my too-small boots were falling apart at the seams, held together only by fraying laces.

"But I'm freezing with my raggedy old cloak," Elain pleaded. "I'll shiver to death." She fixed her wide eyes on me and said, "Please, Feyre." She drew out the two syllables of my name—*fay-ruh*—into the most hideous whine I'd ever endured, and Nesta loudly clicked her tongue before ordering her to shut up.

I drowned them out as they began quarreling over who would get the money the hide would fetch tomorrow and found my father now standing at the table, one hand braced against it to support his weight as he inspected the deer. His attention slid to the giant wolf pelt. His fingers, still smooth and gentlemanly, turned over the pelt and traced a line through the bloody underside. I tensed.

His dark eyes flicked to mine. "Feyre," he murmured, and his mouth became a tight line. "Where did you get this?"

"The same place I got the deer," I replied with equal quiet, my words cool and sharp.

His gaze traveled over the bow and quiver strapped to my back, the wooden-hilted hunting knife at my side. His eyes turned damp. "Feyre . . . the risk . . ."

I jerked my chin at the pelt, unable to keep the snap from my voice as I said, "I had no other choice."

What I really wanted to say was: *You don't even bother to attempt to leave the house most days. Were it not for me, we would starve. Were it not for me, we'd be dead.*

"Feyre," he repeated, and closed his eyes.

My sisters had gone quiet, and I looked up in time to see Nesta crinkle her nose with a sniff. She picked at my cloak. "You stink like a pig covered in its own filth. Can't you at least *try* to pretend that you're not an ignorant peasant?"

I didn't let the sting and ache show. I'd been too young to learn more than the basics of manners and reading and writing when our family had fallen into misfortune, and she'd never let me forget it.

She stepped back to run a finger over the braided coils of her gold-brown hair. "Take those disgusting clothes off."

I took my time, swallowing the words I wanted to bark back at her. Older than me by three years, she somehow looked younger than I did, her golden cheeks always flushed with a delicate, vibrant pink. "Can you make a pot of hot water and add wood to the fire?" But even as I asked, I noticed the woodpile. There were only five logs left. "I thought you were going to chop wood today."

Nesta picked at her long, neat nails. "I hate chopping wood. I always get splinters." She glanced up from beneath her dark lashes. Of all of us, Nesta looked the most like our mother—especially when she wanted something. "Besides, Feyre," she said with a pout, "you're so much better at it! It takes you half the time it takes me. Your hands are suited for it—they're already so rough."

My jaw clenched. "Please," I asked, calming my breathing, knowing an argument was the last thing I needed or wanted. "Please get up at dawn to chop that wood." I unbuttoned the top of my tunic. "Or we'll be eating a cold breakfast."

Her brows narrowed. "I will do no such thing!"

But I was already walking toward the small second room where my sisters and I slept. Elain murmured a soft plea to Nesta, which earned her a hiss in response. I glanced over my shoulder at my father and pointed to the deer. "Get the knives ready," I said, not bothering to sound pleasant. "I'll be out soon." Without waiting for an answer, I shut the door behind me.

The room was large enough for a rickety dresser and the enormous ironwood bed we slept in. The sole remnant of our former wealth, it had been ordered as a wedding gift from my father to my mother. It was the bed in which we'd been born, and the bed in which my mother died. In all the painting I'd done to our house these past few years, I'd never touched it.

I slung off my outer clothes onto the sagging dresser—frowning at the violets and roses I'd painted around the knobs of Elain's drawer, the crackling flames I'd painted around Nesta's, and the night sky—whorls of yellow stars standing in for white—around mine. I'd done it to brighten the otherwise dark room. They'd never commented on it. I don't know why I'd ever expected them to.

Groaning, it was all I could do to keep from collapsing onto the bed.

We dined on roasted venison that night. Though I knew it was foolish, I didn't object when each of us had a small second helping until I declared the meat off-limits. I'd spend tomorrow preparing the deer's remaining parts for consumption, then I'd allot a few hours to currying up both hides before taking them to the market. I knew a few vendors who might be interested in such a purchase—though neither was likely to give me the fee I deserved. But money was money, and I didn't have the time or the funds to travel to the nearest large town to find a better offer.

I sucked on the tines of my fork, savoring the remnants of fat coating the metal. My tongue slipped over the crooked prongs—the fork was part of a shabby set my father had salvaged from the servants' quarters while the creditors ransacked our manor home. None of our utensils matched, but it was better than using our fingers. My mother's dowry flatware had long since been sold.

My mother. Imperious and cold with her children, joyous and dazzling among the peerage who frequented our former estate, doting on my father—the one person whom she truly loved and respected. But she also had truly loved parties—so much so that she didn't have time to do anything with me at all save contemplate how my budding abilities to sketch and paint might secure me a future husband. Had she lived long enough to see our wealth crumble, she would have been shattered by it—more so than my father. Perhaps it was a merciful thing that she died.

If anything, it left more food for us.

There was nothing left of her in the cottage beyond the ironwood bed—and the vow I'd made.

Every time I looked toward a horizon or wondered if I should just walk and walk and never look back, I'd hear that promise I made eleven years ago as she wasted away on her deathbed. *Stay together, and look after them.* I'd agreed, too young to ask why she hadn't begged my elder sisters, or my father. But I'd sworn it to her, and then she'd died, and in our miserable human world—shielded only by the promise made by the High Fae five centuries ago—in our world where we'd forgotten the names of our gods, a promise was law; a promise was currency; a promise was your bond.

There were times when I hated her for asking that vow of me. Perhaps, delirious with fever, she hadn't even known what she was demanding. Or maybe impending death had given her some clarity about the true nature of her children, her husband.

I set down the fork and watched the flames of our meager fire dance along the remaining logs, stretching out my aching legs beneath the table.

I turned to my sisters. As usual, Nesta was complaining about the villagers—they had no manners, they had no social graces, they had no idea just how shoddy the fabric of their clothes was, even though they pretended that it was as fine as silk or chiffon. Since we had lost our fortune, their former friends dutifully ignored them, so my sisters paraded about as though the young peasants of the town made up a second-rate social circle.

I took a sip from my cup of hot water—we couldn't even afford tea these days—as Nesta continued her story to Elain.

"Well, I said to *him*, 'If you think you can just ask me so nonchalantly, sir, I'm going to decline!' And you know what Tomas said?" Arms braced on the table and eyes wide, Elain shook her head.

"Tomas Mandray?" I interrupted. "The woodcutter's second son?"

Nesta's blue-gray eyes narrowed. "Yes," she said, and shifted to address Elain again.

"What does he want?" I glanced at my father. No reaction—no hint of alarm or sign that he was even listening. Lost to whatever fog of memory had crept over him, he was smiling mildly at his beloved Elain, the only one of us who bothered to really speak to him at all.

"He wants to marry her," Elain said dreamily. I blinked.

Nesta cocked her head. I'd seen predators use that movement before. I sometimes wondered if her unrelenting steel would have helped us better survive—thrive, even—if she hadn't been so preoccupied with our lost status. "Is there a problem, *Feyre*?" She flung my name like an insult, and my jaw ached from clenching it so hard.

My father shifted in his seat, blinking, and though I knew it was foolish to react to her taunts, I said, "You can't chop wood for us, but you want to marry a *woodcutter's* son?"

Nesta squared her shoulders. "I thought all you wanted was for us to get out of the house—to marry off me and Elain so you can have enough time to paint your glorious masterpieces." She sneered at the pillar of foxglove I'd painted along the edge of the table—the colors too dark and too blue, with none of the white freckling inside the trumpets, but I'd made do, even if it had killed me not to have white paint, to make something so flawed and lasting.

I drowned the urge to cover up the painting with my hand. Maybe tomorrow I'd just scrape it off the table altogether. "Believe me," I said to her, "the day you want to marry someone worthy, I'll march up to his house and hand you over. But you're not going to marry Tomas."

Nesta's nostrils delicately flared. "There's nothing you can do. Clare Beddor told me this afternoon that Tomas *is* going to propose to me any day now. And then I'll never have to eat these scraps again." She added with a small smile, "At least I don't have to resort to rutting in the hay with Isaac Hale like an animal."

My father let out an embarrassed cough, looking to his cot by the fire. He'd never said a word against Nesta, from either fear or guilt, and apparently he wasn't going to start now, even if this was the first he was hearing of Isaac.

I laid my palms flat on the table as I stared her down. Elain removed her hand from where it lay nearby, as if the dirt and blood beneath my fingernails would somehow jump onto her porcelain skin. "Tomas's family is barely better off than ours," I said, trying to keep from growling. "You'd be just another mouth to feed. If he doesn't know this, then his parents must."

But Tomas knew—we'd run into each other in the forest before. I'd seen the gleam of desperate hunger in his eyes when he spotted me sporting a brace of rabbits. I'd never killed another human, but that day, my hunting knife had felt like a weight at my side. I'd kept out of his way ever since.

"We can't afford a dowry," I continued, and though my tone was firm, my voice quieted. "For either of you." If Nesta wanted to leave, then fine. Good. I'd be one step closer to attaining that glorious, peaceful future, to attaining a quiet house and enough food and time to paint. But we had nothing—absolutely nothing—to entice any suitor to take my sisters off my hands.

"We're in love," Nesta declared, and Elain nodded her agreement. I almost laughed—when had they gone from mooning over aristos to making doe-eyes at peasants?

"Love won't feed a hungry belly," I countered, keeping my gaze as sturdy as possible.

As if I'd struck her, Nesta leaped from her seat on the bench. "You're just jealous. I heard them saying how Isaac is going to marry some Greenfield village girl for a handsome dowry."

So had I; Isaac had ranted about it the last time we'd met. "Jealous?" I said slowly, digging down deep to bury my fury. "We have nothing to offer them—no dowry; no livestock, even. While Tomas might want to marry you . . . you're a burden."

"What do you know?" Nesta breathed. "You're just a half-wild beast with the nerve to bark orders at all hours of the day and night. Keep it up, and someday—someday, Feyre, you'll have no one left to remember you, or to care that you ever existed." She stormed off, Elain darting after her, cooing her sympathy. They slammed the door to the bedroom hard enough to rattle the dishes.

I'd heard the words before—and knew she only repeated them because I'd flinched that first time she spat them. They still burned anyway.

I took a long sip from the chipped mug. The wooden bench beneath my father groaned as he shifted. I took another swallow and said, "You should talk some sense into her."

He examined a burn mark on the table. "What can I say? If it's love—"

"It *can't* be love, not on his part. Not with his wretched family. I've seen the way he acts around the village—there's one thing he wants from her, and it's *not* her hand in—"

"We need hope as much as we need bread and meat," he interrupted, his eyes clear for a rare moment. "We need hope, or else we cannot endure.

So let her keep this hope, Feyre. Let her imagine a better life. A better world."

I stood from the table, fingers curling into fists, but there was nowhere to run in our two-room cottage. I looked at the discolored foxglove painting at the edge of the table. The outer trumpets were already chipped and faded, the lower bit of the stem rubbed off entirely. Within a few years, it would be gone—leaving no mark that it had ever been there. That I'd ever been there.

When I looked at my father, my gaze was hard. "There is no such thing."

CHAPTER 3

The trampled snow coating the road into our village was speckled with brown and black from passing carts and horses. Elain and Nesta clicked their tongues and grimaced as we made our way along it, dodging the particularly disgusting parts. I knew why they'd come—they'd taken one look at the hides I'd folded into my satchel and grabbed their cloaks.

I didn't bother talking to them, as they hadn't deigned to speak to me after last night, though Nesta had awoken at dawn to chop wood. Probably because she knew I'd be selling the hides at the market today and would go home with money in my pocket. They trailed me down the lone road wending through the snow-covered fields, all the way into our ramshackle village.

The stone houses of the village were ordinary and dull, made grimmer by the bleakness of winter. But it was market day, which meant the tiny square in the center of town would be full of whatever vendors had braved the brisk morning.

From a block away, the scent of hot food wafted by—spices that tugged on the edge of my memory, beckoning. Elain let out a low moan behind me. Spices, salt, sugar—rare commodities for most of our village, impossible for us to afford.

If I did well at the market, perhaps I'd have enough to buy us something delicious. I opened my mouth to suggest it, but we turned the corner and nearly stumbled into one another as we all halted.

"May the Immortal Light shine upon thee, sisters," said the pale-robed young woman directly in our path.

Nesta and Elain clicked their tongues; I stifled a groan. Perfect. Exactly what I needed, to have the Children of the Blessed in town on market day, distracting and riling everyone. The village elders usually allowed them to stay for only a few hours, but the sheer presence of the fanatic fools who still worshipped the High Fae made people edgy. Made *me* edgy. Long ago, the High Fae had been our overlords—not gods. And they certainly hadn't been kind.

The young woman extended her moon-white hands in a gesture of greeting, a bracelet of silver bells—*real* silver—tinkling at her wrist. "Have you a moment to spare so that you might hear the Word of the Blessed?"

"No," Nesta sneered, ignoring the girl's hands and nudging Elain into a walk. "We don't."

The young woman's unbound dark hair gleamed in the morning light, and her clean, fresh face glowed as she smiled prettily. There were five other acolytes behind her, young men and women both, their hair long, uncut—all scanning the market beyond for young folk to pester. "It would take but a minute," the woman said, stepping into Nesta's path.

It was impressive—truly impressive—to see Nesta go ramrod straight, to square her shoulders and look down her nose at the young acolyte, a queen without a throne. "Go spew your fanatic nonsense to some ninny. You'll find no converts here."

The girl shrank back, a shadow flickering in her brown eyes. I reined in my wince. Perhaps not the best way to deal with them, since they could become a true nuisance if agitated—

Nesta lifted a hand, pushing down the sleeve of her coat to show the iron bracelet there. The same one Elain wore; they'd bought matching adornments years ago. The acolyte gasped, eyes wide. "You see this?" Nesta hissed, taking a step forward. The acolyte retreated a step. "This is what you *should* be wearing. Not some silver bells to attract those faerie monsters."

"How *dare* you wear that vile affront to our immortal friends—"

"Go preach in another town," Nesta spat.

Two plump and pretty farmers' wives strolled past on their way to the market, arm in arm. As they neared the acolytes, their faces twisted with identical expressions of disgust. "*Faerie-loving whore*," one of them hurled at the young woman. I couldn't disagree.

The acolytes kept silent. The other villager—wealthy enough to have a full necklace of braided iron around her throat—narrowed her eyes, her upper lip curling back from her teeth. "Don't you idiots understand what those monsters did to us for all those centuries? What they still do for sport, when they can get away with it? You deserve the end you'll meet at faerie hands. Fools and whores, all of you."

Nesta nodded her agreement to the women as they continued on their way. We turned back to the young woman still lingering before us, and even Elain frowned in distaste.

But the young woman took a breath, her face again becoming serene, and said, "I lived in such ignorance, too, until I heard the Word of the Blessed. I grew up in a village so similar to this—so bleak and grim. But not one month ago, a friend of my cousin went to the border as our offering to Prythian—and she has not been sent back. Now she dwells in riches and comfort as a High Fae's bride, and so might you, if you were to take a moment to—"

"She was likely eaten," Nesta said. "That's why she hasn't returned."

Or worse, I thought, if a High Fae truly was involved in spiriting a human into Prythian. I'd never encountered the cruel, human-looking High Fae who ruled Prythian itself, or the faeries who occupied their lands, with their scales and wings and long, spindly arms that could drag you deep, deep beneath the surface of a forgotten pond. I didn't know which would be worse to face.

The acolyte's face tightened. "Our benevolent masters would never harm us. Prythian is a land of peace and plenty. Should they bless you with their attention, you would be glad to live amongst them."

Nesta rolled her eyes. Elain was shooting glances between us and the market ahead—to the villagers now watching, too. Time to go.

Nesta opened her mouth again, but I stepped between them and ran an eye along the girl's pale blue robes, the silver jewelry on her, the utter cleanness of her skin. Not a mark or smudge to be found. "You're fighting an uphill battle," I said to her.

"A worthy cause." The girl beamed beatifically.

I gave Nesta a gentle push to get her walking and said to the acolyte, "No, it's not."

I could feel the acolytes' attention still fixed on us as we strode into the busy market square, but I didn't look back. They'd be gone soon enough, off to preach in another town. We'd have to take the long way out of the village to avoid them. When we were far enough away, I glanced over a shoulder at my sisters. Elain's face remained set in a wince, but Nesta's eyes were stormy, her lips thin. I wondered if she'd stomp back to the girl and pick a fight.

Not my problem—not right now. "I'll meet you here in an hour," I said, and didn't give them time to cling to me before slipping into the crowded square.

It took me ten minutes to contemplate my three options. There were my usual buyers: the weathered cobbler and the sharp-eyed clothier who came to our market from a nearby town. And then the unknown: a mountain of a woman sitting on the lip of our broken square fountain, without any cart or stall, but looking like she was holding court nonetheless. The scars and weapons on her marked her easily enough. A mercenary.

I could feel the eyes of the cobbler and clothier on me, sense their feigned disinterest as they took in the satchel I bore. Fine—it would be that sort of day, then.

I approached the mercenary, whose thick, dark hair was shorn to her chin. Her tan face seemed hewn of granite, and her black eyes narrowed slightly at the sight of me. Such interesting eyes—not just one shade of black, but . . . many, with hints of brown that glimmered amongst the shadows. I pushed against that useless part of my mind, the instincts that had me thinking about color and light and shape, and kept my shoulders back as she assessed me as a potential threat or employer. The weapons on her—gleaming and wicked—were enough to make me swallow. And stop a good two feet away.

"I don't barter goods for my services," she said, her voice clipped with an accent I'd never heard before. "I only accept coin."

A few passing villagers tried their best not to look too interested in our conversation, especially as I said, "Then you'll be out of luck in this sort of place."

She was massive even sitting down. "What is your business with me, girl?"

She could have been aged anywhere from twenty-five to thirty, but I supposed I looked like a girl to her in my layers, gangly from hunger. "I have a wolf pelt and a doe hide for sale. I thought you might be interested in purchasing them."

"You steal them?"

"No." I held her stare. "I hunted them myself. I swear it."

She ran those dark eyes down me again. "How." Not a question—a command. Perhaps someone who had encountered others who did not see vows as sacred, words as bonds. And had punished them accordingly.

So I told her how I'd brought them down, and when I finished, she flicked a hand toward my satchel. "Let me see." I pulled out both carefully folded hides. "You weren't lying about the wolf's size," she murmured. "Doesn't seem like a faerie, though." She examined them with an expert eye, running her hands over and under. She named her price.

I blinked—but stifled the urge to blink a second time. She was overpaying—by a lot.

She looked beyond me—past me. "I'm assuming those two girls watching from across the square are your sisters. You all have that brassy hair—and that hungry look about you." Indeed, they were still trying their best to eavesdrop without being spotted.

"I don't need your pity."

"No, but you need my money, and the other traders have been cheap all morning. Everyone's too distracted by those calf-eyed zealots bleating across the square." She jerked her chin toward the Children of the Blessed, still ringing their silver bells and jumping into the path of anyone who tried to walk by.

The mercenary was smiling faintly when I turned back to her. "Up to you, girl."

"Why?"

She shrugged. "Someone once did the same for me and mine, at a time when we needed it most. Figure it's time to repay what's due."

I watched her again, weighing. "My father has some wood carvings that I could give you as well—to make it more fair."

"I travel light and have no need for them. These, however"—she patted the pelts in her hands—"save me the trouble of killing them myself."

I nodded, my cheeks heating as she reached for the coin purse inside her heavy coat. It was full—and weighed down with at least silver, possibly gold, if the clinking was any indication. Mercenaries tended to be well paid in our territory.

Our territory was too small and poor to maintain a standing army to monitor the wall with Prythian, and we villagers could rely only on the strength of the Treaty forged five hundred years ago. But the upper class could afford hired swords, like this woman, to guard their lands bordering the immortal realm. It was an illusion of comfort, just as the markings on our threshold were. We all knew, deep down, that there was nothing to be done against the faeries. We'd all been told it, regardless of class or rank, from the moment we were born, the warnings sung to us while we rocked in cradles, the rhymes chanted in schoolyards. One of the High Fae could turn your bones to dust from a hundred yards away. Not that my sisters or I had ever seen it.

But we still tried to believe that something—anything—might work against them, if we ever were to encounter them. There were two stalls in the market catering to those fears, offering up charms and baubles and incantations and bits of iron. I couldn't afford them—and if they did indeed work, they would buy us only a few minutes to prepare ourselves. Running was futile; so was fighting. But Nesta and Elain still wore their iron bracelets whenever they left the cottage. Even Isaac had an iron cuff around one wrist, always tucked under his sleeve. He'd once offered to buy me one, but I'd refused. It had felt too personal, too much like payment, too . . . permanent a reminder of whatever we were and weren't to each other.

The mercenary transferred the coins to my waiting palm, and I tucked them into my pocket, their weight as heavy as a millstone. There was no possible chance that my sisters hadn't spotted the money—no chance they weren't already wondering how they might persuade me to give them some.

"Thank you," I said to the mercenary, trying and failing to keep the bite from my voice as I felt my sisters sweep closer, like vultures circling a carcass.

The mercenary stroked the wolf pelt. "A word of advice, from one hunter to another."

I lifted my brows.

"Don't go far into the woods. I wouldn't even get close to where you were yesterday. A wolf this size would be the least of your problems. More and more, I've been hearing stories about those *things* slipping through the wall."

A chill spider-walked down my spine. "Are they—are they going to attack?" If it were true, I'd find a way to get my family off our miserable, damp territory and head south—head far from the invisible wall that bisected our world before they could cross it.

Once—long ago and for millennia before that—we had been slaves to High Fae overlords. Once, we had built them glorious, sprawling civilizations from our blood and sweat, built them temples to their feral gods. Once, we had rebelled, across every land and territory. The War had been so bloody, so destructive, that it took six mortal queens crafting the Treaty for the slaughter to cease on both sides and for the wall to be constructed: the North of our world conceded to the High Fae and faeries, who took their magic with them; the South to we cowering mortals, forever forced to scratch out a living from the earth.

"No one knows what the Fae are planning," the mercenary said, her face like stone. "We don't know if the High Lords' leash on their beasts is slipping, or if these are targeted attacks. I guarded for an old nobleman who claimed it had been getting worse these past fifty years. He got on a boat south two weeks ago and told me I should leave if I was smart. Before he sailed off, he admitted that he'd had word from one of his friends that in the dead of night, a pack of martax crossed the wall and tore half his village apart."

"Martax?" I breathed. I knew there were different types of faeries, that they varied as much as any other species of animal, but I knew only a few by name.

The mercenary's night-dark eyes flickered. "Body big as a bear's, head something like a lion's—and three rows of teeth sharper than a shark's. And mean—meaner than all three put together. They left the villagers in literal ribbons, the nobleman said."

My stomach turned. Behind us, my sisters seemed so fragile—their pale skin so infinitely delicate and shredable. Against something like the martax, we'd never stand a chance. Those Children of the Blessed were fools—fanatic fools.

"So we don't know what all these attacks mean," the mercenary went on, "other than more hires for me, and you keeping well away from the wall. Especially if the High Fae start turning up—or worse, one of the High Lords. They would make the martax seem like dogs."

I studied her scarred hands, chapped from the cold. "Have you ever faced another type of faerie?"

Her eyes shuttered. "You don't want to know, girl—not unless you want to be hurling up your breakfast."

I was indeed feeling ill—ill and jumpy. "Was it deadlier than the martax?" I dared ask.

The woman pulled back the sleeve of her heavy jacket, revealing a tanned, muscled forearm flecked with gruesome, twisted scars. The arc of them so similar to—"Didn't have the brute force or size of a martax," she said, "but its bite was full of poison. Two months—that's how long I was down; four months until I had the strength to walk again." She pulled up the leg of her trousers. Beautiful, I thought, even as the horror of it writhed in my gut. Against her tanned skin, the veins were black—solid black, spiderwebbed, and creeping like frost. "Healer said there was nothing to be done for it—that I'm lucky to be walking with the poison still in my legs. Maybe it'll kill me one day, maybe it'll cripple me. But at least I'll go knowing I killed it first."

The blood in my own veins seemed to chill as she lowered the cuff of her pants. If anyone in the square had seen, no one dared speak about it—or to come closer. And I'd had enough for one day. So I took a step back, steadying myself against what she'd told me and shown me. "Thanks for the warnings," I said.

Her attention flicked behind me, and she gave a faintly amused smile. "Good luck."

Then a slender hand clamped onto my forearm, dragging me away. I knew it was Nesta before I even looked at her.

"They're dangerous," Nesta hissed, her fingers digging into my arm as she continued to pull me from the mercenary. "Don't go near them again."

I stared at her for a moment, then at Elain, whose face had gone pale and tight. "Is there something I need to know?" I asked quietly. I couldn't remember the last time Nesta had tried to warn me about anything; Elain was the only one she bothered to really look after.

"They're brutes, and will take any copper they can get, even if it's by force."

I glanced at the mercenary, who was still examining her new pelts. "She robbed you?"

"Not her," Elain murmured. "Some other one who passed through. We had only a few coins, and he got mad, but—"

"Why didn't you report him—or tell me?"

"What could you have done?" Nesta sneered. "Challenged him to a fight with your bow and arrows? And who in this sewer of a town would even care if we reported anything?"

"What about your Tomas Mandray?" I said coolly.

Nesta's eyes flashed, but a movement behind me caught her eye, and she gave me what I supposed was her attempt at a sweet smile—probably as she remembered the money I now carried. "Your friend is waiting for you."

I turned. Indeed, Isaac was watching from across the square, arms crossed as he leaned against a building. Though the eldest son of the only well-off farmer in our village, he was still lean from the winter, and his brown hair had turned shaggy. Relatively handsome, soft-spoken, and reserved, but with a sort of darkness running beneath it all that had drawn us to each other, that shared understanding of how wretched our lives were and would always be.

We'd vaguely known each other for years—since my family had moved to the village—but I had never thought much about him until we'd wound up walking down the main road together one afternoon. We'd only talked about the eggs he was bringing to market—and I'd admired the variation in colors within the basket he bore—browns and tans and the palest blues and greens. Simple, easy, perhaps a bit awkward, but he'd left me at my cottage feeling not quite so . . . alone. A week later, I pulled him into that decrepit barn.

He'd been my first and only lover in the two years since. Sometimes we'd meet every night for a week, others we'd go a month without setting eyes on each other. But every time was the same: a rush of shedding clothes and shared breaths and tongues and teeth. Occasionally we'd talk—or, rather, *he*'d talk about the pressures and burdens his father placed on him. Often, we wouldn't say a word the entire time. I couldn't say our lovemaking was particularly skilled, but it was still a release, a reprieve, a bit of selfishness.

There was no love between us, and never had been—at least what I assumed people meant when they talked about love—yet part of me had sunk when he'd said he would soon be married. I wasn't yet desperate enough to ask him to see me after he was wed.

Isaac inclined his head in a familiar gesture and then ambled off down the street—out of town and to the ancient barn, where he would be waiting. We were never inconspicuous about our dealings with each other, but we did take measures to keep it from being too obvious.

Nesta clicked her tongue, crossing her arms. "I do hope you two are taking precautions."

"It's a bit late to pretend to care," I said. But we were careful. Since I couldn't afford it, Isaac himself took the contraceptive brew. He knew I wouldn't have touched him otherwise. I reached into my pocket, drawing out a twenty-mark copper. Elain sucked in a breath, and I didn't bother to look at either of my sisters as I pushed it into her palm and said, "I'll see you at home."

Later, after another dinner of venison, when we were all gathered around the fire for the quiet hour before bed, I watched my sisters whispering and laughing together. They'd spent every copper I'd given them—on what, I didn't know, though Elain had brought back a new chisel for our father's wood carving. The cloak and boots they'd whined about the night before had been too expensive. But I hadn't scolded them for it, not when Nesta went out a second time to chop more wood without my asking. Mercifully, they'd avoided another confrontation with the Children of the Blessed.

My father was dozing in his chair, his cane laid across his gnarled knee. As good a time as any to broach the subject of Tomas Mandray with Nesta. I turned to her, opening my mouth.

But there was a roar that half deafened me, and my sisters screamed as snow burst into the room and an enormous, growling shape appeared in the doorway.

CHAPTER 4

I didn't know how the wooden hilt of my hunting knife had gotten into my hand. The first few moments were a blur of the snarling of a gigantic beast with golden fur, the shrieking of my sisters, the blistering cold cascading into the room, and my father's terror-stricken face.

Not a martax, I realized—though the relief was short-lived. The beast had to be as large as a horse, and while his body was somewhat feline, his head was distinctly wolfish. I didn't know what to make of the curled, elk-like horns that protruded from his head. But lion or hound or elk, there was no doubting the damage his black, daggerlike claws and yellow fangs could inflict.

Had I been alone in the woods, I might have let myself be swallowed by fear, might have fallen to my knees and wept for a clean, quick death. But I didn't have room for terror, wouldn't give it an inch of space, despite my heart's wild pounding in my ears. Somehow, I wound up in front of my sisters, even as the creature reared onto its hind legs and bellowed through a maw full of fangs: "*MURDERERS!*"

But it was another word that echoed through me:

Faerie.

Those ridiculous wards on our threshold were as good as cobwebs against him. I should have asked the mercenary how she'd killed that faerie. But the beast's thick neck—that looked like a good home for my knife.

I dared a glance over my shoulder. My sisters screamed, kneeling against the wall of the hearth, my father crouched in front of them. Another body for me to defend. Stupidly, I took another step toward the faerie, keeping the table between us, fighting the shaking in my hand. My bow and quiver were across the room—past the beast. I'd have to get around him to reach the ash arrow. And buy myself enough time to fire it.

"*MURDERERS!*" the beast roared again, hackles raised.

"P-please," my father babbled from behind me, failing to find it in himself to come to my side. "Whatever we have done, we did so unknowingly, and—"

"W-w-we didn't kill anyone," Nesta added, choking on her sobs, arm lifted over her head, as if that tiny iron bracelet would do anything against the creature.

I snatched another dinner knife off the table, the best I could do unless I found a way to get to the quiver. "Get out," I snapped at the creature, brandishing the knives before me. No iron in sight that I could use as a weapon—unless I chucked my sisters' bracelets at him. "Get out, and begone." With my trembling hands, I could barely keep my grip on the hilts. A nail—I'd take a damned iron nail, if it were available.

He bellowed at me in response, and the entire cottage shook, the plates and cups rattling against one another. But it left his massive neck exposed. I hurled my hunting knife.

Fast—so fast I could barely see it—he slashed out with a paw, sending it skittering away as he snapped for my face with his teeth.

I leaped back, almost stumbling over my cowering father. The faerie could have killed me—could have, yet the lunge had been a warning.

Nesta and Elain, weeping, prayed to whatever long-forgotten gods might still be skulking about.

"WHO KILLED HIM?" The creature stalked toward us. He set a paw on the table, and it groaned beneath him. His claws thudded as they embedded in the wood, one by one.

I dared another step forward as the beast stretched his snout over the table to sniff at us. His eyes were green and flecked with amber. Not animal eyes, not with their shape and coloring. My voice was surprisingly even as I challenged: "Killed who?"

He growled, low and vicious. "The wolf," he said, and my heart stumbled a beat. The roar was gone, but the wrath lingered—perhaps even traced with sorrow.

Elain's wail reached a high-pitched shriek. I kept my chin up. "A wolf?"

"A large wolf with a gray coat," he snarled in response. Would he know if I lied? Faeries couldn't lie—all mortals knew that—but could they smell the lies on human tongues? We had no chance of escaping this through fighting, but there might be other ways.

"If it was *mistakenly* killed," I said to the beast as calmly as I could, "what payment could we offer in exchange?" This was all a nightmare, and I'd awaken in a moment beside the fire, exhausted from my day at the market and my afternoon with Isaac.

The beast let out a bark that could have been a bitter laugh. He pushed off the table to pace in a small circle before the shattered door. The cold was so intense that I shivered. "The payment you must offer is the one demanded by the Treaty between our realms."

"For a wolf?" I retorted, and my father murmured my name in warning. I had vague memories of being read the Treaty during my childhood lessons, but could recall nothing about wolves.

The beast whirled on me. "Who killed the wolf?"

I stared into those jade eyes. "I did."

He blinked and glanced at my sisters, then back at me, at my thinness—no doubt seeing only frailness instead. "Surely you lie to save them."

"We didn't kill anything!" Elain wept. "Please . . . *please*, spare us!" Nesta hushed her sharply through her own sobbing, but pushed Elain farther behind her. My chest caved in at the sight of it.

My father climbed to his feet, grunting at the pain in his leg as he bobbled, but before he could limp toward me, I repeated: "I killed it." The beast, who had been sniffing at my sisters, studied me. I squared my shoulders. "I sold its hide at the market today. If I had known it was a faerie, I wouldn't have touched it."

"Liar," he snarled. "You knew. You would have been more tempted to slaughter it had you known it was one of my kind."

True, true, true. "Can you blame me?"

"Did it attack you? Were you provoked?"

I opened my mouth to say yes, but—"No," I said, letting out a snarl of my own. "But considering all that your kind has done to us, considering what your kind still likes to *do* to us, even if I *had* known beyond a doubt, it was deserved." Better to die with my chin held high than groveling like a cowering worm.

Even if his answering growl was the definition of wrath and rage.

The firelight shone upon his exposed fangs, and I wondered how they'd feel on my throat, and how loudly my sisters would scream before they, too, died. But I knew—with a sudden, uncoiling clarity—that Nesta would buy Elain time to run. Not my father, whom she resented with her entire steely heart. Not me, because Nesta had always known and hated that she and I were two sides of the same coin, and that I could fight my own battles. But Elain, the flower-grower, the gentle heart . . . Nesta would go down swinging for her.

It was that flash of understanding that had me angling my remaining knife at the beast. "What is the payment the Treaty requires?"

His eyes didn't leave my face as he said, "A life for a life. Any unprovoked attacks on faerie-kind by humans are to be paid only by a human life in exchange."

My sisters quieted their weeping. The mercenary in town had killed a faerie—but had attacked her first. "I didn't know," I said. "Didn't know about that part of the Treaty."

Faeries couldn't lie—and he spoke plainly enough, no word-twisting.

"Most of you mortals have chosen to forget that part of the Treaty," he said, "which makes punishing you far more enjoyable."

My knees quaked. I couldn't escape this, couldn't outrun this. Couldn't even try to run, since he blocked the way to the door. "Do it outside," I whispered, my voice trembling. "Not . . . here." Not where my family would have to wash away my blood and gore. If he even let them live.

The faerie huffed a vicious laugh. "Willing to accept your fate so easily?" When I just stared at him, he said, "For having the nerve to request *where* I slaughter you, I'll let you in on a secret, human: Prythian must claim your life in some way, for the life you took from it. So as a representative of the immortal realm, I can either gut you like swine, or . . . you can cross the wall and live out the remainder of your days in Prythian."

I blinked. "What?"

He said slowly, as if I were indeed as stupid as a swine, "You can either die tonight or offer your life to Prythian by living in it forever, forsaking the human realm."

"Do it, Feyre," my father whispered from behind me. "Go."

I didn't look at him as I said, "Live *where*? Every inch of Prythian is lethal to us." I'd be better off dying tonight than living in pure terror across the wall until I met my end in doubtlessly an even more awful way.

"I have lands," the faerie said quietly—almost reluctantly. "I will grant you permission to live there."

"Why bother?" Perhaps a fool's question, but—

"You murdered my friend," the beast snarled. "Murdered him, skinned his corpse, sold it at the market, and then said he *deserved* it, and yet you have the nerve to question my generosity?" *How typically human*, he seemed to silently add.

"You didn't need to mention the loophole." I stepped so close the faerie's breath heated my face. Faeries couldn't lie, but they could omit information.

The beast snarled again. "Foolish of me to forget that humans have such low opinions of us. Do you humans no longer understand mercy?" he said, his fangs inches from my throat. "Let me make this clear for you, girl: you can either come live at my home in Prythian—offer your life for the wolf's in that way—or you can walk outside right now and be shredded to ribbons. Your choice."

My father's hobbling steps sounded before he gripped my shoulder. "Please, good sir—Feyre is my youngest. I beseech you to spare her. She is all . . . she is all . . ." But whatever he meant to say died in his throat as the beast roared again. But hearing those few words he'd managed to get out, the effort he'd made . . . it was like a blade to my belly. My father cringed as he said, "Please—"

"*Silence*," the creature snapped, and rage boiled up in me so blistering it was an effort to keep from lunging to stab my dagger in his eye. But by the time I had so much as raised my arm, I knew he would have his maw around my neck.

"I can get gold—" my father said, and my rage guttered. The only way he would get money was by begging. Even then, he'd be lucky to get a few coppers. I'd seen how pitiless the well-off were in our village. The monsters in our mortal realm were just as bad as those across the wall.

The beast sneered. "How much is your daughter's life worth to you? Do you think it equates to a sum?"

Nesta still had Elain held behind her, Elain's face so pale it matched the snow drifting in from the open door. But Nesta monitored every move the beast made, her brows lowered. She didn't bother to look at my father—as if she knew his answer already.

When my father didn't reply, I dared another step toward the beast, drawing his attention to me. I had to get him out—get him away from my family. From the way he'd brushed away my knife, any hope of escaping lay in somehow sneaking up on him. With his hearing, I doubted I'd get a chance anytime soon, at least until he believed I was docile. If I tried to attack him or fled before then, he would destroy my family for the sheer enjoyment of it. Then he would find me again. I had no choice but to go. And then, later, I might find an opportunity to slit the beast's throat. Or at least disable him long enough to flee.

As long as the faeries couldn't find me again, they couldn't hold me to the Treaty. Even if it made me a cursed oath-breaker. But in going with him, I would be breaking the most important promise I'd ever made. Surely it trumped an ancient treaty that I hadn't even signed.

I loosened my grip on the hilt of my remaining dagger and stared into those green eyes for a long, silent while before I said, "When do we go?"

Those lupine features remained fierce—vicious. Any lingering hope I had of fighting died as he moved to the door—no, to the quiver I'd left behind it. He pulled out the ash arrow, sniffed, and snarled at it. With two movements, he snapped it in half and chucked it into the fire behind my sisters before turning back to me. I could smell my doom on his breath as he said, "Now."

Now.

Even Elain lifted her head to gape at me in mute horror. But I couldn't look at her, couldn't look at Nesta—not when they were still crouched there, still silent. I turned to my father. His eyes glistened, so I glanced to the few cabinets we had, faded too-yellow daffodils curving over the handles. *Now.*

The beast paced in the doorway. I didn't want to contemplate where

I was going or what he would do with me. Running would be foolish until it was the right time.

"The venison should hold you for two weeks," I said to my father as I gathered my clothes to bulk up against the cold. "Start on the fresh meat, then work your way through to the jerky—you know how to make it."

"Feyre—" my father breathed, but I continued as I fastened my cloak.

"I left the money from the pelts on the dresser," I said. "It will last you for a time, if you're careful." I finally looked at my father again and allowed myself to memorize the lines of his face. My eyes stung, but I blinked the moisture away as I stuffed my hands into my worn gloves. "When spring comes, hunt in the grove just south of the big bend in Silverspring Creek—the rabbits make their warrens there. Ask . . . ask Isaac Hale to show you how to make snares. I taught him last year."

My father nodded, covering his mouth with a hand. The beast growled his warning and prowled out into the night. I made to follow him but paused to look at my sisters, still crouched by the fire, as if they wouldn't dare to move until I was gone.

Elain mouthed my name but kept cowering, kept her head down. So I turned to Nesta, whose face was so similar to my mother's, so cold and unrelenting.

"Whatever you do," I said quietly, "don't marry Tomas Mandray. His father beats his wife, and none of his sons do anything to stop it." Nesta's eyes widened, but I added, "Bruises are harder to conceal than poverty."

Nesta stiffened but said nothing—both of my sisters said absolutely nothing—as I turned toward the open door. But a hand wrapped around my arm, tugging me into a stop.

Turning me around to face him, my father opened and closed his mouth. Outside, the beast, sensing I'd been detained, sent a snarl rumbling into the cottage.

"Feyre," my father said. His fingers trembled as he grasped my gloved hands, but his eyes became clearer and bolder than I'd seen them in years. "You were always too good for here, Feyre. Too good for us, too good for everyone." He squeezed my hands. "If you ever escape, ever convince them that you've paid the debt, don't return."

I hadn't expected a heart-wrenching good-bye, but I hadn't imagined *this*, either.

"Don't *ever* come back," my father said, releasing my hands to shake me by the shoulders. "Feyre." He stumbled over my name, his throat bobbing. "You go somewhere new—and you make a name for yourself."

Beyond, the beast was just a shadow. A life for a life—but what if the life offered as payment also meant losing three others? The thought alone was enough to steel me, anchor me.

I'd never told my father of the promise I'd made my mother, and there was no use explaining it now. So I shrugged off his grip and left.

I let the sounds of the snow crunching underfoot drive out my father's words as I followed the beast to the night-shrouded woods.

CHAPTER 5

Every step toward the line of trees was too swift, too light, too soon carrying me to whatever torment and misery awaited. I didn't dare look back at the cottage.

We entered the line of trees. Darkness beckoned beyond.

But a white mare was patiently waiting—unbound—beside a tree, her coat like fresh snow in the moonlight. She only lowered her head—as if in *respect*, of all things—as the beast lumbered up to her.

He motioned with a giant paw for me to mount. Still the horse remained calm, even as he passed close enough to gut her in one swipe. It had been years since I'd ridden, and I'd only ridden a pony at that, but I savored the warmth of the horse against my half-frozen body as I climbed into the saddle and she set into a walk. Without light to guide me, I let her trail the beast. They were nearly the same size. I wasn't surprised when we headed northward—toward faerie territory—though my stomach clenched so tightly it ached.

Live with him. I could live out the rest of my mortal life on his lands. Perhaps this was merciful—but then, he hadn't specified in what manner, exactly, I would live. The Treaty forbade faeries from taking us as slaves, but—perhaps that excluded humans who'd murdered faeries.

We'd likely go to whatever rift in the wall he'd used to get here, to steal me. And once we went through the invisible wall, once we were in Prythian, there was no way for my family to ever find me. I'd be little more than a lamb in a kingdom of wolves. Wolves—wolf.

Murdered a faerie. That was what I'd done.

My throat went dry. I'd killed a faerie. I couldn't bring myself to feel badly about it. Not with my family left behind me to surely starve; not when it meant one less wicked, awful creature in the world. The beast had burned my ash arrow—so I'd have to rely on luck to get even a splinter of the wood again, if I was to stand a chance of killing him. Or slowing him down.

Knowledge of that weakness, of their susceptibility to ash, was the only reason we'd ever survived against the High Fae during the ancient uprising, a secret betrayed by one of their own.

My blood chilled further as I uselessly scanned for any signs of the narrow trunk and explosion of branches that I'd learned marked ash trees. I'd never seen the forest so still. Whatever was out there had to be tame compared to the beast beside me, despite the horse's ease around him. Hopefully he would keep other faeries away after we entered his realm.

Prythian. The word was a death knell that echoed through me again and again.

Lands—he'd said he had lands, but what kind of dwelling? My horse was beautiful and its saddle was crafted of rich leather, which meant he had some sort of contact with civilized life. I'd never heard the specifics of what the lives of faeries or High Fae were like—never heard much about anything other than their deadly abilities and appetites. I clenched the reins to keep my hands from shaking.

There were few firsthand accounts of Prythian itself. The mortals who went over the wall—either willingly as tributes from the Children of the

Blessed or stolen—never came back. I'd learned most of the legends from villagers, though my father had occasionally offered up a milder tale or two on the nights he made an attempt to remember we existed.

As far as we knew, the High Fae still governed the northern parts of our world—from our enormous island over the narrow sea separating us from the massive continent, across depthless fjords and frozen wastelands and sandblasted deserts, all the way to the great ocean on the other side. Some faerie territories were empires; some were overseen by kings and queens. Then there were places like Prythian, divided and ruled by seven High Lords—beings of such unyielding power that legend claimed they could level buildings, break apart armies, and butcher you before you could blink. I didn't doubt it.

No one had ever told me why humans chose to linger in our territory, when so little space had been granted to us and we remained in such close proximity to Prythian. Fools—whatever humans had stayed here after the War must have been suicidal fools to live so close. Even with the centuries-old Treaty between the mortal and faerie realms, there were rifts in the warded wall separating our lands, holes big enough for those lethal creatures to slip into our territory to amuse themselves with tormenting us.

That was the side of Prythian that the Children of the Blessed never deigned to acknowledge—perhaps a side of Prythian I'd soon witness. My stomach turned. *Live with him*, I reminded myself, again and again and again. *Live*, not die.

Though I supposed I could also *live* in a dungeon. He would likely lock me up and forget that I was there, forget that humans needed things like food and water and warmth.

Prowling ahead of me, the beast's horns spiraled toward the night sky, and tendrils of hot breath curled from his snout. We had to make camp at some point; the border of Prythian was days away. Once we stopped, I would keep awake for the entirety of the night and never let him out of my sight. Even though he'd burned my ash arrow, I'd smuggled my remaining knife in my cloak. Maybe tonight would grant me an opportunity to use it.

But it was not my own doom I contemplated as I let myself tumble into dread and rage and despair. As we rode on—the only sounds snow crunching beneath paws and hooves—I alternated between a wretched smugness at the thought of my family starving and thus realizing how important I was, and a blinding agony at the thought of my father begging in the streets, his ruined leg giving out on him as he stumbled from person to person. Every time I looked at the beast, I could see my father limping through town, pleading for coppers to keep my sisters alive. Worse—what Nesta might resort to in order to keep Elain alive. She wouldn't mind my father's death. But she would lie and steal and sell anything for Elain's sake—and her own as well.

I took in the way the beast moved, trying to find any—*any*—weakness. I could detect none. "What manner of faerie are you?" I asked, the words nearly swallowed up by the snow and trees and star-heavy sky.

He didn't bother to turn around. He didn't bother to say anything at all. Fair enough. I'd killed his friend, after all.

I tried again. "Do you have a name?" Or anything to curse him by.

A huff of air that could have been a bitter laugh. "Does it even matter to you, human?"

I didn't answer. He might very well change his mind about sparing me.

But perhaps I would escape before he decided to gut me. I would grab my family and we'd stow away on a ship and sail far, far away. Perhaps I would try to kill him, regardless of the futility, regardless of whether it constituted another unprovoked attack, just for being the one who came to claim my life—my *life*, when these faeries valued ours so little. The mercenary had survived; maybe I could, too. Maybe.

I opened my mouth to again ask him for his name, but a growl of annoyance rippled out of him. I didn't have a chance to struggle, to fight back, when a charged, metallic tang stung my nose. Exhaustion slammed down upon me and blackness swallowed me whole.

I awoke with a jolt atop the horse, secured by invisible bonds. The sun was already high.

Magic—that's what the tang had been, what was keeping my limbs tucked in tight, preventing me from going for my knife. I recognized the power deep in my bones, from some collective mortal memory and terror. How long had it kept me unconscious? How long had *he* kept me unconscious, rather than have to speak to me?

Gritting my teeth, I might have demanded answers from him—might have shouted to where he still lumbered ahead, heedless of me. But then chirping birds flitted past me, and a mild breeze kissed my face. I spied a hedge-bordered metal gate ahead.

My prison or my salvation—I couldn't decide which.

Two days—it took two days from my cottage to reach the wall and enter the southernmost border of Prythian. Had I been held in an enchanted sleep for that long? Bastard.

The gate swung open without porter or sentry, and the beast continued through. Whether I wanted to or not, my horse followed after him.

CHAPTER 6

The estate sprawled across a rolling green land. I'd never seen anything like it; even our former manor couldn't compare. It was veiled in roses and ivy, with patios and balconies and staircases sprouting from its alabaster sides. The grounds were encased by woods, but stretched so far that I could barely see the distant line of the forest. So much color, so much sunlight and movement and texture . . . I could hardly drink it in fast enough. To paint it would be useless, would never do it justice.

My awe might have subdued my fear had the place not been so wholly empty and silent. Even the garden through which we walked, following a gravel path to the main doors of the house, seemed hushed and sleeping. Above the array of amethyst irises and pale snowdrops and butter-yellow daffodils swaying in the balmy breeze, the faint stench of metal ticked my nostrils.

Of course it would be magic, because it was spring here. What wretched power did they possess to make their lands so different from ours, to control the seasons and weather as if they owned them? Sweat trickled down my spine as my layers of clothes turned suffocating. I rotated my wrists and shifted in the saddle. Whatever bonds had held me were gone.

The faerie meandered on ahead, leaping nimbly up the grand marble staircase that led to the giant oak doors in one mighty, fluid movement. The doors swung open for him on silent hinges, and he prowled inside. He'd planned this entire arrival, no doubt—keeping me unconscious so I didn't know where I was, didn't know the way home or what other deadly faerie territories might be lurking between me and the wall. I felt for my knife, but found only layers of frayed clothes.

The thought of those claws pawing through my cloak to find my knife made my mouth go dry. I shoved away the fury and terror and disgust as my horse came to a stop of her own accord at the foot of the stairs. The message was clear enough. The towering estate house seemed to be watching, waiting.

I glanced over my shoulder toward the still-open gates. If I were to bolt, it would have to be now.

South—all I had to do was go south, and I would eventually make it to the wall. If I didn't encounter anything before then. I tugged on the reins, but the mare remained stationary—even as I dug my heels into her sides. I let out a low, sharp hiss. Fine. On foot.

My knees buckled as I hit the ground, bits of light flashing in my vision. I grasped the saddle and winced as soreness and hunger racked my senses. Now—I had to go *now*. I made to move, but the world was still spinning and flashing.

Only a fool would run with no food, no strength.

I wouldn't get half a mile like this. I wouldn't get half a mile before he caught me and tore me to ribbons, as he'd promised.

I took a long, shuddering breath. Food—getting food, *then* running at the next opportune moment. It sounded like a solid plan.

When I was steady enough to walk, I left the horse at the bottom of the stairs, taking the steps one at a time. My breath tight in my chest, I passed through the open doors and into the shadows of the house.

Inside, it was even more opulent. Black-and-white checkered marble shone at my feet, flowing to countless doors and a sweeping staircase. A long hall stretched ahead to the giant glass doors at the other end of the house, and through them I glimpsed a second garden, grander than the one out front. No sign of a dungeon—no shouts or pleas rising up from hidden chambers below. No, just the low growl from a nearby room, so deep that it rattled the vases overflowing with fat clusters of hydrangea atop the scattered hall tables. As if in response, an open set of polished wooden doors swung wider to my left. A command to follow.

My fingers shook as I rubbed my eyes. I'd known the High Fae had once built themselves palaces and temples around the world—buildings that my mortal ancestors had destroyed after the War out of spite—but I'd never considered how they might live today, the elegance and wealth they might possess. Never contemplated that the faeries, these feral monsters, might own estates grander than any mortal dwelling.

I tensed as I entered the room.

A long table—longer than any we'd ever possessed at our manor—filled most of the space. It was laden with food and wine—so much food, some of it wafting tendrils of steam, that my mouth watered. At least it was familiar, and not some strange faerie delicacy: chicken, bread, peas, fish, asparagus, lamb . . . it could have been a feast at any mortal manor. Another surprise. The beast padded to the oversized chair at the head of the table.

I lingered by the threshold, gazing at the food—all that hot, glorious food—that I couldn't eat. That was the first rule we were taught as children, usually in songs or chants: If misfortune forced you to keep company with a faerie, you never drank their wine, never ate their food. Ever. Unless you wanted to wind up enslaved to them in mind and soul—unless you wanted to wind up dragged back to Prythian. Well, the second part had already happened, but I might stand a chance at avoiding the first.

The beast plopped into the chair, the wood groaning, and, in a flash of white light, turned into a golden-haired man.

I stifled a cry and pushed myself against the paneled wall beside the door, feeling for the molding of the threshold, trying to gauge the distance between me and escape. This beast was not a man, not a lesser faerie. He was one of the High Fae, one of their ruling nobility: beautiful, lethal, and merciless.

He was young—or at least what I could see of his face seemed young. His nose, cheeks, and brows were covered by an exquisite golden mask embedded with emeralds shaped like whorls of leaves. Some absurd High Fae fashion, no doubt. It left only his eyes—looking the same as they had in his beast form, strong jaw, and mouth for me to see, and the latter tightened into a thin line.

"You should eat something," he said. Unlike the elegance of his mask, the dark green tunic he wore was rather plain, accented only with a leather baldric across his broad chest. It was more for fighting than style, even though he bore no weapons I could detect. Not just one of the High Fae, but . . . a warrior, too.

I didn't want to consider what might require him to wear a warrior's attire and tried not to look too hard at the leather of the baldric gleaming in the sunlight streaming in through the bank of windows behind him. I hadn't seen a cloudless sky like that in months. He filled a glass of wine from an exquisitely cut crystal decanter and drank deeply. As if he needed it.

I inched toward the door, my heart beating so fast I thought I'd vomit. The cool metal of the door's hinges bit into my fingers. If I moved fast, I could be out of the house and sprinting for the gate within seconds. He was undoubtedly faster—but chucking some of those pretty pieces of hallway furniture in his path might slow him down. Though his Fae ears—with their delicate, pointed arches—would pick up any whisper of movement from me.

"Who are you?" I managed to say. His light golden hair was so similar to the color of his beast form's pelt. Those giant claws undoubtedly still lurked just below the surface of his skin.

"Sit," he said gruffly, waving a broad hand to encompass the table. "Eat."

I ran through the chants in my head, again and again. Not worth it—easing my ravenous hunger was definitely not worth the risk of being enslaved to him in mind and soul.

He let out a low growl. "Unless you'd rather faint?"

"It's not safe for humans," I managed to say, offense be damned.

He huffed a laugh—more feral than anything. "The food is fine for you to eat, human." Those strange green eyes pinned me to the spot, as if he could detect every muscle in my body that was priming to bolt. "Leave, if you want," he added with a flash of teeth. "I'm not your jailer. The gates are open—you can live anywhere in Prythian."

And no doubt be eaten or tormented by a wretched faerie. But while every inch of this place was civilized and clean and beautiful, I had to get out, had to get back. That promise to my mother, cold and vain as she was, was all I had. I made no move toward the food.

"Fine," he said, the word laced with a growl, and began serving himself.

I didn't have to face the consequences of refusing him another time, as someone strode past me, heading right for the head of the table.

"Well?" the stranger said—another High Fae: red-haired and finely dressed in a tunic of muted silver. He, too, wore a mask. He sketched a bow to the seated male and then crossed his arms. Somehow, he hadn't spotted me where I was still pressed against the wall.

"Well, *what*?" My captor cocked his head, the movement more animal than human.

"Is Andras dead, then?"

A nod from my captor—savior, whatever he was. "I'm sorry," he said quietly.

"How?" the stranger demanded, his knuckles white as he gripped his muscled arms.

"An ash arrow," said the other. His red-haired companion hissed. "The Treaty's summons led me to the mortal. I gave her safe haven."

"A girl—a mortal girl actually killed Andras." Not a question so much as a venom-coated string of words. He glanced at the end of the table, where my empty chair stood. "And the summons found the girl responsible."

The golden-masked one gave a low, bitter laugh and pointed at me. "The Treaty's magic brought me right to her doorstep."

The stranger whirled with fluid grace. His mask was bronze and fashioned after a fox's features, concealing all but the lower half of his face—along with most of what looked like a wicked, slashing scar from his brow down to his jaw. It didn't hide the eye that was missing—or the carved golden orb that had replaced it and *moved* as though he could use it. It fixed on me.

Even from across the room, I could see his remaining russet eye widen. He sniffed once, his lips curling a bit to reveal straight white teeth, and then he turned to the other faerie. "You're joking," he said quietly. "That scrawny thing brought down *Andras* with a single ash arrow?"

Bastard—an absolute bastard. A pity I didn't have the arrow now—so I could shoot him instead.

"She admitted to it," the golden-haired one said tightly, tracing the rim of his goblet with a finger. A long, lethal claw slid out, scraping against the metal. I fought to keep my breathing steady. Especially as he added, "She didn't try to deny it."

The fox-masked faerie sank onto the edge of the table, the light catching in his long fire-red hair. I could understand his mask, with that brutal scar and missing eye, but the other High Fae seemed fine. Perhaps he wore it out of solidarity. Maybe that explained the absurd fashion. "Well," the red-haired one seethed, "now we're stuck with *that*, thanks to your useless mercy, and you've ruined—"

I stepped forward—only a step. I wasn't sure what I was going to say, but being spoken about that way . . . I kept my mouth shut, but it was enough.

"Did you enjoy killing my friend, human?" the red-haired one said. "Did you hesitate, or was the hatred in your heart riding you too hard to consider sparing him? It must have been so satisfying for a small mortal thing like you to take him down."

The golden-haired one said nothing, but his jaw tightened. As they studied me, I reached for a knife that wasn't there.

"Anyway," the fox-masked one continued, facing his companion again with a sneer. He would likely laugh if I ever drew a weapon on him. "Perhaps there's a way to—"

"Lucien," my captor said quietly, the name echoing with a hint of a snarl. "Behave."

Lucien went rigid, but he hopped off the edge of the table and bowed deeply to me. "My apologies, lady." Another joke at my expense. "I'm Lucien. Courtier and emissary." He gestured to me with a flourish. "Your eyes are like stars, and your hair like burnished gold."

He cocked his head—waiting for me to give him my name. But telling him anything about me, about my family and where I came from—

"Her name is Feyre," said the one in charge—the beast. He must have learned my name at my cottage. Those striking green eyes met mine again and then flicked to the door. "Alis will take you to your room. You could use a bath and fresh clothes."

I couldn't decide whether it was an insult or not. There was a firm hand at my elbow, and I flinched. A rotund brown-haired woman in a simple brass bird mask tugged on my arm and inclined her head toward the open door behind us. Her white apron was crisp above her homespun brown dress—a servant. The masks had to be some sort of trend, then.

If they cared so much about their clothes, about what even their servants wore, maybe they were shallow and vain enough for me to deceive, despite their master's warrior clothes. Still, they were High Fae. I would have to be clever and quiet and bide my time until I could escape. So I let Alis lead me away. *Room*—not *cell*. A small relief, then.

I'd barely made it a few steps before Lucien growled, "That's the hand the Cauldron thought to deal us? *She* brought Andras down? We never should have sent him out there—none of them should have been out there. It was a fool's mission." His growl was more bitter than threatening. Could he shape-shift as well? "Maybe we should just take a stand—maybe it's time to say *enough*. Dump the girl somewhere, kill her, I don't care—she's nothing but a burden here. She'd sooner put a knife in your back than talk to you—or any of us." I kept my breathing calm, my spine locking, and—

"No," the other bit out. "Not until we know for certain that there is no other way will we make a move. And as for the girl, she stays. Unharmed. End of discussion. Her life in that hovel was Hell enough." My cheeks heated, even while I loosed a tight breath, and I avoided looking at Alis as I felt her eyes slide to me. A hovel—I suppose that's what our cottage was when compared to this place.

"Then you've got your work cut out for you, old son," Lucien said. "I'm sure her life will be a fine replacement for Andras's—maybe she can even train with the others on the border."

A snarl of irritation resonated through the air.

The shining, spotless halls swallowed me up before I could hear more.

Alis led me through halls of gold and silver until we came to a lavish bedroom on the second level. I'll admit I didn't fight that hard when Alis and two other servants—also masked—bathed me, cut my hair, and then plucked me until I felt like a chicken being prepared for dinner. For all I knew, I might very well be their next meal.

It was only the High Fae's promise—to live out my days in Prythian instead of dying—that kept me from being sick at the thought. While these faeries also looked human, save for their ears, I'd never learned what the High Fae called their servants. But I didn't dare to ask, or to speak to them at all, not when just having their hands on me, having them so *close* was enough to make me focus solely on not trembling.

Still, I took one look at the velvet turquoise dress Alis had placed on the bed and wrapped my white dressing gown tightly around me, sinking into a chair and pleading for my old clothes to be returned. Alis refused, and when I begged again, trying my best to sound pathetic and sad and pitiful, she stormed out. I hadn't worn a dress in years. I wasn't about to start, not when escape was my main priority. I wouldn't be able to move freely in a gown.

Bundled in my robe, I sat for minute after minute, the chattering of small birds in the garden beyond the windows the only sounds. No screaming, no clashing weapons, no hint of any slaughter or torture.

The bedroom was larger than our entire cottage. Its walls were pale green, delicately sketched with patterns of gold, and the moldings were golden as well. I might have thought it tacky had the ivory furniture and rugs not complemented it so well. The gigantic bed was of a similar color scheme, and the curtains that hung from the towering headboard drifted in the faint breeze from the open windows. My dressing gown was of the finest silk, edged with lace—simple and exquisite enough that I ran a finger along the lapels.

The few stories I'd heard had been wrong—or five hundred years of separation had muddled them. Yes, I was still prey, still born weak and useless compared to them, but this place was . . . peaceful. Calm. Unless that was an illusion, too, and the loophole in the Treaty was a lie—a trick to set me at ease before they destroyed me. The High Fae liked to play with their food.

The door creaked, and Alis returned—a bundle of clothing in her hands. She lifted a sodden grayish shirt. "You want to wear this?" I gaped at the holes in the sides and sleeves. "It fell apart the moment the laundresses put it in water." She held up a few scraps of brown. "Here's what's left of your pants."

I clamped down on the curse building in my chest. She might be a servant, but she could easily kill me, too.

"Will you wear the dress now?" she demanded. I knew I should get up, should agree, but I slumped farther into my seat. Alis stared me down for a moment before leaving again.

She returned with trousers and a tunic that fit me well, both of them rich with color. A bit fancy, but I didn't complain when I donned the white shirt, nor when I buttoned the dark blue tunic and ran my hands over the scratchy, golden thread embroidered on the lapels. It had to cost a fortune in itself—and it tugged at that useless part of my mind that admired lovely and strange and colorful things.

I was too young to remember much before my father's downfall. He'd tolerated me enough to allow me to loiter about his offices, and sometimes even explained various goods and their worth, the details of which I'd long since forgotten. My time in his offices—full of the scents of exotic spices and the music of foreign tongues—made up the majority of my few happy memories. I didn't need to know the worth of everything in this room to understand that the emerald curtains alone—silk, with gold velvet—could have fed us for a lifetime.

A chill scuttled down my spine. It had been days since I'd left. The venison would be running low already.

Alis herded me into a low-backed chair before the darkened fireplace, and I didn't fight back as she ran a comb through my hair and began braiding it.

"You're hardly more than skin and bones," she said, her fingers luxurious against my scalp.

"Winter does that to poor mortals," I said, fighting to keep the sharpness from my tone.

She huffed a laugh. "If you're wise, you'll keep your mouth shut and your ears open. It'll do you more good here than a loose tongue. And keep your wits about you—even your senses will try to betray you here."

I tried not to cringe at the warning. Alis went on. "Some folk are bound to be upset about Andras. Yet if you ask me, Andras was a good sentinel, but he knew what he would face when he crossed the wall—knew he'd likely find trouble. And the others understand the terms of the Treaty, too—even if they might resent your presence here, thanks to the mercy of our master. So keep your head down, and none of them will bother you. Though Lucien—he could do with someone snapping at him, if you've the courage for it."

I didn't, and when I went to ask more about whom I should try to avoid, she had already finished with my hair and opened the door to the hall.

CHAPTER 7

The golden-haired High Fae and Lucien were lounging at the table when Alis returned me to the dining room. They no longer had plates before them, but still sipped from golden goblets. Real gold—not paint or foil. Our mismatched cutlery flashed through my mind as I paused in the middle of the room. Such wealth—such staggering wealth, when we had nothing.

A half-wild beast, Nesta had called me. But compared to him, compared to this place, compared to the elegant, easy way they held their goblets, the way the golden-haired one had called me *human* . . . we were all half-wild beasts to the High Fae. Even if they were the ones who could don fur and claws.

Food still remained on the table, the array of spices lingering in the air, beckoning. I was starving, my head unnervingly light.

The golden-haired High Fae's mask gleamed with the last rays of the afternoon sunshine. "Before you ask again: the food is safe for you to eat." He pointed to the chair at the other end of the table. No sign of his claws. When I didn't move, he sighed sharply. "What do you want, then?"

I said nothing. *To eat, flee, save my family* . . .

Lucien drawled from his seat along the length of the table, "I told you so, Tamlin." He flicked a glance toward his friend. "Your skills with females have definitely become rusty in recent decades."

Tamlin. He glowered at Lucien, shifting in his seat. I tried not to stiffen at the other bit of information Lucien had given away. *Decades*.

Tamlin didn't look much older than me, but his kind was immortal. He could be hundreds of years old. Thousands. My mouth dried up as I carefully studied their strange, masked faces—unearthly, primal, and imperious. Like immovable gods or feral courtiers.

"Well," Lucien said, his remaining russet eye fixed on me, "you don't look half as bad now. A relief, I suppose, since you're to live with us. Though the tunic isn't as pretty as a dress."

Wolves ready to pounce—that's what they were, just like their friend. I was all too aware of my diction, of the very breath I took as I said, "I'd prefer not to wear that dress."

"And why not?" Lucien crooned.

It was Tamlin who answered for me. "Because killing us is easier in pants."

I kept my face blank, willed my heart to calm as I said, "Now that I'm here, what . . . what do you plan to do with me?"

Lucien snorted, but Tamlin said with a snarl of annoyance, "Just sit down."

An empty seat had been pulled out at the end of the table. So many foods, piping hot and wafting those enticing spices. The servants had probably brought out new food while I'd washed. So much wasted. I clenched my hands into fists.

"We're not going to bite." Lucien's white teeth gleamed in a way that suggested otherwise. I avoided his gaze, avoided that strange, animated metal eye that focused on me as I inched to my seat and sat down.

Tamlin rose, stalking around the table—closer and closer, each movement smooth and lethal, a predator blooded with power. It was an effort to keep still—especially as he picked up a dish, brought it over to me, and piled some meat and sauce on my plate.

I said quietly, "I can serve myself." Anything, *anything* to keep him well away from me.

Tamlin paused, so close that one swipe of those claws lurking under his skin could rip my throat out. That was why the leather baldric bore no weapons: why use them when you were a weapon yourself? "It's an honor for a human to be served by a High Fae," he said roughly.

I swallowed hard. He continued piling various foods on my plate, stopping only when it was heaping with meat and sauce and bread, and then filled my glass with pale sparkling wine. I loosed a breath as he prowled back to his seat, though he could probably hear it.

I wanted nothing more than to bury my face in the plate and then eat my way down the table, but I pinned my hands beneath my thighs and stared at the two faeries.

They watched me, too closely to be casual. Tamlin straightened a bit and said, "You look . . . better than before."

Was that a compliment? I could have sworn Lucien gave Tamlin an encouraging nod.

"And your hair is . . . clean."

Perhaps it was my raging hunger making me hallucinate the piss-poor attempt at flattery. Still, I leaned back and kept my words calm and quiet, the way I might speak to any other predator. "You're High Fae—faerie nobility?"

Lucien coughed and looked to Tamlin. "You can take that question."

"Yes," Tamlin said, frowning—as if searching for anything to say to me. He settled on merely: "We are."

Fine. A man—faerie—of few words. I had killed his friend, was an unwanted guest. I wouldn't want to talk to me, either.

"What do you plan to do with me now that I'm here?"

Tamlin's eyes didn't leave my face. "Nothing. Do whatever you want."

"So I'm not to be your slave?" I dared ask.

Lucien choked on his wine. But Tamlin didn't smile. "I don't keep slaves."

I ignored the release of tightness in my chest at that. "But what am I to do with my *life* here?" I pressed. "Do you—do you wish me to earn my keep? To work?" A stupid question, if he hadn't considered it, but . . . but I had to know.

Tamlin stiffened. "What you do with your life isn't my problem."

Lucien pointedly cleared his throat, and Tamlin flashed him a glare. After an exchanged look I couldn't read, Tamlin sighed and said, "Don't you have any . . . interests?"

"No." Not entirely true, but I wasn't about to explain the painting to him. Not when he was apparently having a great deal of trouble just talking to me civilly.

Lucien muttered, "So typically human."

Tamlin's mouth quirked to the side. "Do whatever you want with your time. Just stay out of trouble."

"So you truly mean for me to stay here forever." What I meant was: *So I'm to stay in this luxury while my family starves to death?*

"I didn't make the rules," Tamlin said tersely.

"My family is *starving*," I said. I didn't mind begging—not for this. I'd given my word, and held to that word for so long that I was nothing and no one without it. "Please let me go. There must be—must be some other loophole out of the Treaty's rules—some other way to atone."

"Atone?" Lucien said. "Have you even apologized yet?"

Apparently, all attempts to flatter me were dead and gone. So I looked Lucien right in his remaining russet eye and said, "I'm sorry."

Lucien leaned back in his chair. "How did you kill him? Was it a bloody fight, or just cold-blooded murder?"

My spine stiffened. "I shot him with an ash arrow. And then an ordinary arrow through the eye. He didn't put up a fight. After the first shot, he just stared at me."

"Yet you killed him anyway—though he made no move to attack you. And then you *skinned* him," Lucien hissed.

"*Enough*, Lucien," Tamlin said to his courtier with a snarl. "I don't want to hear details." He turned to me, ancient and brutal and unyielding.

I spoke before he could say anything. "My family won't last a month without me." Lucien chuckled, and I gritted my teeth. "Do you know what it's like to be hungry?" I demanded, anger rising to devour any common sense. "Do you know what it's like to not know when your next meal will be?"

Tamlin's jaw tightened. "Your family is alive and well-cared for. You think so low of faeries that you believe I'd take their only source of income and nourishment and not replace it?"

I straightened. "You swear it?" Even if faeries couldn't lie, I had to hear it.

A low, incredulous laugh. "On everything that I am and possess."

"Why not tell me that when we left the cottage?"

"Would you have believed me? Do you even believe me now?" Tamlin's claws embedded in the arms of his chair.

"Why should I trust a word you say? You're all masters of spinning your truths to your own advantage."

"Some would say it's unwise to insult a Fae in his home," Tamlin ground out. "Some would say you should be grateful for me finding you before another one of my kind came to claim the debt, for sparing your life and then offering you the chance to live in comfort."

I shot to my feet, wisdom be damned, and was about to kick back my chair when invisible hands clapped on my arms and shoved me back into the seat.

"Do *not* do whatever it was you were contemplating," Tamlin said.

I went still as the tang of magic seared my nose. I tried to twist in the chair, testing the invisible bonds. But my arms were secured, and my back was pressed into the wood so hard that it ached. I glanced at the knife beside my plate. I should have gone for it first—futile effort or no.

"I'm going to warn you once," Tamlin said too softly. "Only once, and then it's on you, human. I don't care if you go live somewhere else in Prythian. But if you cross the wall, if you flee, your family will no longer be cared for."

His words were like a stone to the head. If I escaped, if I even *tried* to run, I might very well doom my family. And even if I dared risk it . . . even if I succeeded in reaching them, where would I take them? I couldn't stow my sisters away on a ship—and once we arrived somewhere else, somewhere safe, we'd have nowhere to live. But for him to hold my family's well-being against me, to throw away their survival if I stepped out of line . . .

I opened my mouth, but his snarl rattled the glasses. "Is that not a fair bargain? And if you flee, then you might not be so lucky with whoever comes to retrieve you next." His claws slipped back under his knuckles. "The food is not enchanted, or drugged, and it will be your own damn fault if you faint. So you're going to sit at this table and *eat*, Feyre. And *Lucien* will do his best to be polite." He threw a pointed look in his direction. Lucien shrugged.

The invisible bonds loosened, and I winced as I whacked my hands on the underside of the table. The bonds on my legs and middle remained intact. One glance at Tamlin's smoldering green eyes told me what I wanted to know: his guest or not, I wasn't going to get up from this table until I'd eaten something. I'd think about the sudden change in my plans to escape later. Now . . . for now I eyed the silver fork and carefully picked it up.

They still watched me—watched my every move, the flare of my nostrils as I sniffed the food on my plate. No metallic stench of magic.

And faeries couldn't lie. So he had to be right about the food, then. Stabbing a piece of chicken, I took a bite.

It was an effort to keep from grunting. I hadn't had food this good in years. Even the meals we'd had before our downfall were little more than ashes compared to this. I ate my entire plate in silence, too aware of the High Fae observing every bite, but as I reached for a second helping of chocolate torte, the food vanished. Just—vanished, as if it had never existed, not a crumb left behind.

Swallowing hard, I set my fork down so they wouldn't see my hand start to shake.

"One more bite and you'll hurl your guts up," Tamlin said, drinking deeply from his goblet.

The bonds holding me loosened. Silent permission to leave.

"Thank you for the meal," I said. It was all I could think of.

"Won't you stay for wine?" Lucien said with sweet venom from where he lounged in his seat.

I braced my hands on my chair to rise. "I'm tired. I'd like to sleep."

"It's been a few decades since I last saw one of you," Lucien drawled, "but you humans never change, so I don't think I'm wrong in asking *why* you find our company to be so unpleasant, when surely the men back home aren't much to look at."

At the other end of the table, Tamlin gave his emissary a long, warning look. Lucien ignored it.

"You're High Fae," I said tightly. "I'd ask why you'd even bother inviting me here at all—or dining with me." Fool—I really should have been killed ten times over already.

Lucien said, "True. But indulge me: you're a human woman, and yet you'd rather eat hot coals than sit here longer than necessary. Ignoring this"—he waved a hand at the metal eye and brutal scar on his face—"surely we're not so miserable to look at." Typical faerie vanity and arrogance. That, at least, the legends had been right about. I tucked the knowledge away. "Unless you have someone back home. Unless there's a line of suitors out the door of your hovel that makes us seem like worms in comparison."

There was enough dismissal there that I took a little bit of satisfaction in saying, "I was close with a man back in my village." *Before that Treaty ripped me away—before it became clear that* you *are allowed to do as you please to us, but we can hardly strike back against you.*

Tamlin and Lucien exchanged glances, but it was Tamlin who said, "Are you in love with this man?"

"No," I said as casually as I could. It wasn't a lie—but even if I'd felt anything like that for Isaac, my answer would have been the same. It was bad enough that High Fae now knew my family existed. I didn't need to add Isaac to that list.

Again, that shared look between the two males. "And do you . . . love anyone else?" Tamlin said through clenched teeth.

A laugh burst out of me, tinged with hysteria. "No." I looked between them. Nonsense. These lethal, immortal beings really had nothing better to do than this? "Is this really what you care to know about me? If I find you more handsome than human men, and if I have a man back home? Why bother to ask at all, when I'll be stuck here for the rest of my life?" A hot line of anger sliced through my senses.

"We wanted to learn more about you, since you'll be here for a good while," Tamlin said, his lips a thin line. "But Lucien's pride tends to get in the way of his manners." He sighed, as if ready to be done with me, and said, "Go rest. We're both busy most days, so if you need anything, ask the staff. They'll help you."

"Why?" I asked. "Why be so generous?" Lucien gave me a look that suggested he had no idea, either, given that I'd murdered their companion, but Tamlin stared at me for a long moment.

"I kill too often as it is," Tamlin said finally, shrugging his broad shoulders. "And you're insignificant enough to not ruffle this estate. Unless you decide to start killing us."

A faint warmth bloomed in my cheeks, my neck. Insignificant—yes, I was insignificant to their lives, their power. As insignificant as the fading, chipped designs I'd painted around the cottage. "Well . . . ," I said, not quite feeling grateful at all, "thank you."

He gave a distant nod and motioned for me to leave. Dismissed. Like the lowly human I was. Lucien propped his chin on a fist and gave me a lazy half smile.

Enough. I got to my feet and backed toward the door. Putting my back to them would have been like walking away from a wolf, sparing my life or no. They said nothing when I slipped out the door.

A moment later, Lucien's barking laugh echoed into the halls, followed by a sharp, vicious growl that shut him up.

I slept fitfully that night, and the lock on my bedroom door felt more like a joke than anything.

✢

I was wide awake before dawn, but I remained staring at the filigreed ceiling, watching the growing light creep between the drapes, savoring the softness of the down mattress. I was usually out of the cottage by first light—though my sisters hissed at me every morning for waking them so early. If I were home, I'd already be entering the woods, not wasting a moment of precious sunlight, listening to the drowsy chatter of the few winter birds. Instead, this bedroom and the house beyond were silent, the enormous bed foreign and empty. A small part of me missed the warmth of my sisters' bodies overlapping with mine.

Nesta must be stretching her legs and smiling at the extra room. She was probably content imagining me in the belly of a faerie—probably using the news as a chance to be fussed over by the villagers. Maybe my fate would prompt them to give my family some handouts. Or maybe Tamlin had given them enough money—or food, or whatever he thought "taking care" of them consisted of—to last through the winter. Or maybe the villagers would turn on my family, not wanting to be associated with people tied with Prythian, and run them out of town.

I buried my face in the pillow, pulling the blankets higher. If Tamlin had indeed provided for them, if those benefits would cease the moment I crossed the wall, then they'd likely resent my return more than celebrate it.

Your hair is . . . clean.

A pathetic compliment. I supposed that if he'd invited me to live here, to spare my life, he couldn't be completely . . . wicked. Perhaps he'd just been trying to smooth over our very, very rough beginning. Maybe there would be some way to persuade him to find some loophole, to get whatever magic that bound the Treaty to spare me. And if not some way, then some*one* . . .

I was drifting from one thought to another, trying to sort through the jumble, when the lock on the door clicked, and—

There was a screech and a thud, and I bolted upright to find Alis in a heap on the floor. The length of rope I'd made from the curtain trimmings now hung loosely from where I'd rigged it to snap into anyone's face. It had been the best I could do with what I had.

"I'm sorry, I'm sorry," I blurted, leaping from the bed, but Alis was already up, hissing at me as she brushed off her apron. She frowned at the rope dangling from the light fixture.

"What in the bottomless depths of the Cauldron is—"

"I didn't think anyone would be in here so early, and I meant to take it down, and—"

Alis looked me over from head to toe. "You think a bit of rope snapping in my face will keep me from breaking your bones?" My blood went cold. "You think that will do anything against one of us?"

I might have kept apologizing were it not for the sneer she gave me. I crossed my arms. "It was a warning bell to give me time to run. Not a trap."

She seemed poised to spit on me, but then her sharp brown eyes narrowed. "You can't outrun us, either, girl."

"I know," I said, my heart calming at last. "But at least I wouldn't face my death unaware."

Alis barked out a laugh. "My master gave his word that you could live here—*live*, not die. We will obey." She studied the hanging bit of rope. "But did you have to wreck those lovely curtains?"

I didn't want to—tried not to, but a hint of a smile tugged on my lips. Alis strode over to the remnants of the curtains and threw them open, revealing a sky that was still a deep periwinkle, splashed with hues of pumpkin and magenta from the rising dawn. "I am sorry," I said again.

Alis clicked her tongue. "At least you're willing to put up a fight, girl. I'll give you that."

I opened my mouth to speak, but another female servant with a bird mask entered, a breakfast tray in hand. She bid me a curt good morning, set the tray on a small table by the window, and disappeared into the attached bathing chamber. The sound of running water filled the room.

I sat at the table and studied the porridge and eggs and bacon—*bacon*. Again, such similar food to what we ate across the wall. I don't know why I'd expected otherwise. Alis poured me a cup of what looked and smelled like tea: full-bodied, aromatic tea, no doubt imported at great expense. Prythian and my adjoining homeland weren't exactly easy to reach. "What is this place?" I asked her quietly. "*Where* is this place?"

"It's safe, and that's all you need to know," Alis said, setting down the teapot. "At least the house is. If you go poking about the grounds, keep your wits about you."

Fine—if she wouldn't answer *that* . . . I tried again. "What sort of—faeries should I look out for?"

"All of them," Alis said. "My master's protection only goes so far. They'll want to hunt and kill you just for being a human—regardless of what you did to Andras."

Another useless answer. I dug into my breakfast, savoring each rich sip of tea, and she slipped into the bathing chamber. When I was done eating and bathing, I refused Alis's offer and dressed myself in another exquisite tunic—this one of purple so deep it could have been black. I wished I knew the name for the color, but cataloged it anyway. I pulled on the brown boots I'd worn the night before, and as I sat before a marble vanity letting Alis braid my wet hair, I cringed at my reflection.

It wasn't pleasing—though not for its actual appearance. While my nose was relatively straight, it was the other feature I'd inherited from my mother. I could still remember how her nose would crinkle with feigned amusement when one of her fabulously wealthy friends made some unfunny joke.

At least I had my father's soft mouth, though it made a mockery of my too-sharp cheekbones and hollow cheeks. I couldn't bring myself to look at my slightly uptilted eyes. I knew I'd see Nesta or my mother looking back at me. I'd sometimes wondered if that was why my sister had insulted me about my looks. I was a far cry from ugly, but . . . I bore too much of the people we'd hated and loved for Nesta to stand it. For me to stand it, too.

Though I supposed that for Tamlin—for High Fae used to ethereal, flawless beauty—it *had* been a struggle to find a compliment. Faerie bastard.

Alis finished my plait, and I jumped from the bench before she could weave in little flowers from the basket she'd brought. I would have lived up to my namesake were it not for the effects of poverty, but I'd never particularly cared. Beauty didn't mean anything in the forest.

When I asked Alis what I was to do now—*what I was to do with the entirety of my mortal life*—she shrugged and suggested a walk in the gardens. I almost laughed, but I kept my tongue still. I'd be foolish to push aside potential allies. I doubted she had Tamlin's ear, and I couldn't press her about it yet, but . . . At least a walk provided a chance to glean some sense of my surroundings—and whether there was anyone else who might plead my case to Tamlin.

The halls were silent and empty—strange for such a large estate. They'd mentioned others the night before, but I saw and heard no sign of them. A balmy breeze scented with . . . hyacinth, I realized—if only from Elain's small garden—floated down the halls, carrying with it the pleasant chirping of a bunting, a bird I wouldn't hear back home for months—if I ever heard them at all.

I was almost to the grand staircase when I noticed the paintings.

I hadn't let myself really *look* yesterday, but now, in the empty hall with no one to see me . . . a flash of color amid a shadowy, gloomy background made me stop, a riot of color and texture that compelled me to face the gilded frame.

I'd never—never—seen anything like it.

It's just a still life, a part of me said. And it was: a green glass vase with an assortment of flowers drooping over its narrow top, blossoms and leaves of every shape and size and color—roses, tulips, morning glory, goldenrod, maiden's lace, peonies . . .

The skill it must have taken to make them look so lifelike, to make them *more* than lifelike . . . Just a vase of flowers against a dark background—but more than that; the flowers seemed to be vibrant with their own light, as if in defiance of the shadows gathered around them. The mastery needed to make the glass vase hold that light, to bend the light with the water within, as if the vase did indeed have weight to it atop its stone pedestal . . . Remarkable.

I could have stared at it for hours—and the countless paintings along this hall alone could have occupied my entire day—but . . . garden. Plans.

Still, as I moved on, I couldn't deny that this place was far more . . . civilized than I'd thought. Peaceful, even, if I was willing to admit it.

And if the High Fae were indeed gentler than human legend and rumor had led me to believe, then maybe convincing Alis of my misery might not be too hard. If I could win over Alis, convince her that the Treaty had been wrong to demand such payment from me, she might indeed see if there was anything to get me out of this debt and—

"You," someone said, and I jumped back a step. In the light of the open glass doors to the garden, a towering male figure stood silhouetted before me.

Tamlin. He wore those warrior's clothes, cut close to show off his toned body, and three simple knives were now sheathed along his baldric—each long enough to look like it could gut me as easily as his beast's claws. His blond hair had been tied back from his face, revealing those pointed ears and that strange, beautiful mask. "Where are you going?" he said, gruffly enough that it almost sounded like a demand. *You*—I wondered if he even remembered my name.

It took a moment to will enough strength into my legs to rise from my half crouch. "Good morning," I said flatly. At least it was a better greeting than *You*. "You said my time was to be spent however I wanted. I didn't realize I was under house arrest."

His jaw tightened. "Of course you're not under house arrest." Even as he bit out the words, I couldn't ignore the sheer male beauty of that strong jaw, the richness of his golden-tan skin. He was probably handsome—if he ever took off that mask.

When he realized that I wasn't going to respond, he bared his teeth in what I supposed was an attempt at a smile and said, "Do you want a tour?"

"No, thank you," I managed to get out, conscious of every awkward motion of my body as I edged around him.

He stepped into my path—close enough that he conceded a step back. "I've been sitting inside all morning. I need some fresh air." *And you're insignificant enough that you wouldn't be a bother.*

"I'm fine," I said, casually dodging him. "You've . . . been generous enough." I tried to sound like I meant it.

A half smile, not so pleasant, no doubt unused to being denied. "Do you have some sort of problem with me?"

"No," I said quietly, and walked through the doors.

He let out a low snarl. "I'm not going to kill you, Feyre. I don't break my promises."

I almost stumbled down the garden steps as I glanced over my shoulder. He stood atop the stairs, as solid and ancient as the pale stones of the manor. "Kill—but not harm? Is that another loophole? One that Lucien might use against me—or anyone else here?"

"They're under orders not to even touch you."

"Yet I'm still trapped in your realm, for breaking a rule I didn't know existed. Why was your friend even in the woods that day? I thought the Treaty banned your kind from entering our lands."

He just stared at me. Perhaps I'd gone too far, questioned him too much. Perhaps he could tell why I'd really asked.

"That Treaty," he said quietly, "doesn't ban *us* from doing anything, except for enslaving you. The wall is an inconvenience. If we cared to, we could shatter it and march through to kill you all."

I might be forced to live in Prythian forever, but my family . . . I dared ask, "And do you care to destroy the wall?"

He looked me up and down, as if deciding whether I was worth the effort of explaining. "I have no interest in the mortal lands, though I can't speak for my kind."

But he still hadn't answered my question. "Then what was your friend doing there?"

Tamlin stilled. Such unearthly, primal grace, even to his breathing. "There is . . . a sickness in these lands. Across Prythian. There has been for almost fifty years now. It is why this house and these lands are so empty: most have left. The blight spreads slowly, but it has made magic act . . . strangely. My own powers are diminished due to it. These masks"—he tapped on his—"are the result of a surge of it that occurred during a masquerade forty-nine years ago. Even now, we can't remove them."

Stuck in masks—for nearly fifty years. I would have gone mad, would have peeled my skin off my face. "You didn't have a mask as a beast—and neither did your friend."

"The blight is cruel like that."

Either live as a beast, or live with the mask. "What—what sort of sickness is it?"

"It's not a disease—not a plague or illness. It's focused solely on magic, on those dwelling in Prythian. Andras was across the wall that day because I sent him to search for a cure."

"Can it hurt humans?" My stomach twisted. "Will it spread over the wall?"

"Yes," he said. "There is . . . a chance of it affecting mortals, and your territory. More than that, I don't know. It's slow-moving, and your kind is safe for now. We haven't had any progression in decades—magic seems to have stabilized, even though it's been weakened." That he'd even admitted so much spoke volumes about how he imagined my future: I was never going home, never going to encounter another human to whom I might spill this secret vulnerability.

"A mercenary told me she believed faeries might be thinking of attacking. Is it related?"

A hint of a smile, perhaps a bit surprised. "I don't know. Do you talk to mercenaries often?"

"I talk to whoever bothers to tell me anything useful."

He straightened, and it was only his promise not to kill me that kept me from cringing. Then he rolled his shoulders, as if shaking off his annoyance. "Was the trip wire you rigged in your room for me?"

I sucked on my teeth. "Can you blame me if it was?"

"I might take an animal form, but I am civilized, Feyre."

So he did remember my name, at least. But I looked pointedly at his hands, at the razor-sharp tips of those long, curved claws poking through his tanned skin.

Noticing my stare, he tucked his hands behind his back. He said sharply, "I'll see you at dinner."

It wasn't a request, but I still gave him a nod as I strode off between the hedges, not caring where I was going—only that he stayed far behind.

A sickness in their lands, affecting their magic, draining it from them . . . A magical blight that might one day spread to the human world. After so many centuries without magic, we'd be defenseless against it—against whatever it could do to humans.

I wondered if any of the High Fae would bother warning my kind.

It didn't take me long to know the answer.

CHAPTER 8

I pretended to meander through the exquisite and silent gardens, mentally marking the paths and clever places for hiding if I ever needed them. He'd taken my weapons, and I wasn't stupid enough to hope for an ash tree somewhere on the property with which to make my own. But his baldric had been laden with knives; there had to be an armory somewhere on the estate. And if not, I would find another weapon, then—steal it if I had to. Just in case.

Upon inspection the night before, I'd learned that there was no lock on my window. Sneaking out and rappelling down the wisteria vines wouldn't be difficult at all—I'd climbed enough trees to not mind the height. Not that I planned to escape, but . . . it was good to know, at least, how I might do so should I ever be desperate enough to risk it.

I didn't doubt Tamlin's claim that the rest of Prythian was deadly for a human—and if there was indeed some blight on these lands . . . I was better off here for the time being.

But not without trying to find someone who might plead my case to Tamlin.

Though Lucien—he could do with someone snapping at him, if you've the courage for it, Alis had said to me yesterday.

I chewed on my stubby nails as I walked, considering every possible plan and pitfall. I'd never been particularly good with words, had never learned the social warfare my sisters and mother had been so adept at, but . . . I'd been decent enough when selling hides at the village market.

So perhaps I'd seek out Tamlin's emissary, even if he detested me. He clearly had little interest in my living here—he'd suggested *killing me*. Perhaps he'd be eager to send me back, to persuade Tamlin to find some other way to fulfill the Treaty. If there even was one.

I approached a bench in an alcove blooming with foxglove when the sound of steps on shifting gravel filled the air. Two pairs of light, quick feet. I straightened, peering down the way I'd come, but the path was empty.

I lingered at the edge of an open field of lanky meadow buttercups. The vibrant green-and-yellow field was deserted. Behind me arose a gnarled crab apple tree in full, glorious bloom, the petals of its flowers littering the shaded bench on which I'd been about to sit. A breeze set the branches rustling, a waterfall of white petals flittering down like snow.

I scanned the garden, the field—carefully, carefully watching and listening for those two sets of feet.

There was nothing in the tree, or behind it.

A prickling sensation ran down my spine. I'd spent enough time in the woods to trust my instincts.

Someone stood behind me—perhaps two of them. A faint sniff and a quiet giggle issued from far too close. My heart leaped into my throat.

I cast a subtle glance over my shoulder. But only a shining silvery light flickered in the corner of my vision.

I had to turn around. I had to face it.

The gravel crunched, nearer now. The shimmering in the corner of my eye grew larger, separating into two small figures no taller than my waist. My hands clenched into fists.

"Feyre!" Alis's voice cut across the garden. I jumped out of my skin as she called me again. "Feyre, lunch!" she hollered. I whirled, a shout forming on my lips to alert her to whatever stood behind me, raising my fists, however futile it would be.

But the shining things had vanished, along with their sniffing and giggling, and I found myself facing a weathered statue of two merry, bounding lambs. I rubbed my neck.

Alis called me again, and I took a shuddering breath as I returned to the manor. But even as I strode through the hedges, carefully retracing my steps back to the house, I couldn't erase the creeping feeling that someone still watched me, curious and wanting to play.

I stole a knife from dinner that night. Just to have something—*anything*—to defend myself with.

It turned out that dinner was the only meal I was invited to attend, which was fine. Three meals a day with Tamlin and Lucien would have been torturous. I could endure an hour of sitting at their fancy table if it made them think I was docile and had no plans to change my fate.

While Lucien ranted to Tamlin about some malfunction of the magical, carved eye that indeed allowed him to see, I slipped my knife down the sleeve of my tunic. My heart beat so fast I thought they could hear it, but Lucien continued speaking, and Tamlin's focus remained on his courtier.

I supposed I should have pitied them for the masks they were forced to wear, for the blight that had infected their magic and people. But the less I interacted with them the better, especially when Lucien seemed to find everything I said to be hilariously human and uneducated. Snapping at him wouldn't help my plans. It would be an uphill battle to win his favor, if only for the fact that I was alive and his friend was not. I'd have to deal with him alone, or risk raising Tamlin's suspicions too soon.

Lucien's red hair shone in the firelight, the colors flickering with every movement he made, and the jewels in the hilt of his sword glinted—the ornate blade so unlike the baldric of knives still strapped across Tamlin's chest. But there was no one here to use a sword against. And while the sword was embedded with jewels and filigree, it was large enough to be more than decoration. Perhaps it had something to do with those invisible things in the garden. Maybe he'd lost his eye and earned that scar in battle. I fought against a shudder.

Alis had said the house was safe, but warned me to keep my wits about me. What might lurk beyond the house—or be able to use my human senses against me? Just how far would Tamlin's order not to harm me stretch? What kind of authority did he hold?

Lucien paused, and I found him smirking at me, making the scar even more brutal. "Were you admiring my sword, or just contemplating killing me, Feyre?"

"Of course not," I said softly, and glanced at Tamlin. The gold flecks in his eyes glowed, even from the other end of the table. My heart beat at a gallop. Had he somehow *heard* me take the knife, the whisper of metal on wood? I forced myself to look again at Lucien.

His lazy, vicious grin was still there. Act civilized, behave, possibly win him to my side . . . I could do that.

Tamlin broke the silence. "Feyre likes to hunt."

"I don't *like* to hunt." I should have probably used a more polite tone, but I went on. "I hunted out of necessity. And how did you know that?"

Tamlin's stare was bald, assessing. "Why else were you in the woods that day? You had a bow and arrows in your . . . house." I wondered whether he'd almost said *hovel*. "When I saw your father's hands, I knew he wasn't the one using them." He gestured to my scarred, callused hands. "You told him about the rations and money from pelts. Faeries might be many things, but we're not stupid. Unless your ridiculous legends claim that about us, too."

Ridiculous, *insignificant*.

I stared at the crumbs of bread and swirls of remaining sauce on my golden plate. Had I been at home, I would have licked my plate clean, desperate for any extra bit of nourishment. And the plates . . . I could have bought a team of horses, a plow, and a field for just one of them. Disgusting.

Lucien cleared his throat. "How old are you, anyway?"

"Nineteen." Pleasant, civilized . . .

Lucien tsked. "So young, and so grave. And a skilled killer already."

I tightened my hands into fists, the metal of the knife now warm against my skin. Docile, unthreatening, tame . . . I'd made my mother a promise, and I'd keep it. Tamlin's looking after my family wasn't the same as *my* looking after them. That wild, small dream could still come to pass: my sisters comfortably married off, and a lifetime with my father, with enough food for us both and enough time to maybe paint a little—or to maybe learn what *I* wanted. It could still happen—in a faraway land, perhaps—if I ever got out of this bargain. I could still cling to that scrap of a dream, though these High Fae would likely laugh at *how typically human* it was to think so small, to want so little.

Yet any bit of information might help, and if I showed interest in them, perhaps they would warm to me. What was this but another trap in the woods? So I said, "So is this what you do with your lives? Spare humans from the Treaty and have fine meals?" I gave a pointed glance toward Tamlin's baldric, the warrior's clothes, Lucien's sword.

Lucien smirked. "We also dance with the spirits under the full moon and snatch human babes from their cradles to replace them with changelings—"

"Didn't . . . ," Tamlin interrupted, his deep voice surprisingly gentle, "didn't your mother tell you anything about us?"

I prodded the table with my forefinger, digging my short nails into the wood. "My mother didn't have the time to tell me stories." I could reveal that part of my past, at least.

Lucien, for once, didn't laugh. After a rather stilted pause, Tamlin asked, "How did she die?" When I lifted my brows, he added a bit more softly, "I didn't see signs of an older woman in your house."

Predator or not, I didn't need his pity. But I said, "Typhus. When I was eight." I rose from my seat to leave.

"Feyre," Tamlin said, and I half turned. A muscle feathered in his cheek.

Lucien glanced between us, that metal eye roving, but kept silent. Then Tamlin shook his head, the movement more animal than anything, and murmured, "I'm sorry for your loss."

I tried to keep from grimacing as I turned on my heel and left. I didn't want or need his condolences—not for my mother, not when I hadn't missed her in years. Let Tamlin dismiss me as a rude, uncouth human not worth his careful watch.

I'd be better off persuading Lucien to speak to Tamlin on my behalf—and soon, before any of the others whom they'd mentioned appeared, or this blight of theirs grew. Tomorrow—I'd speak to Lucien then, test him out a bit.

In my room, I found a small satchel in the armoire and filled it with a spare set of clothes, along with my stolen knife. It was a pitiful blade, but a piece of cutlery was better than nothing. Just in case I was ever allowed to go—and had to leave at a moment's notice.

Just in case.

CHAPTER 9

The following morning, as Alis and the other servant woman prepared my bath, I contemplated my plan. Tamlin had mentioned that he and Lucien had various duties, and aside from running into him in the house yesterday, I'd seen neither of them around. So, locating Lucien—alone—would be the first order of business.

A casual question tossed in Alis's direction had her revealing that she believed Lucien was on border patrol today—and would be at the stables, preparing to leave.

I was halfway through the gardens, hurrying toward the outcropping of buildings I'd spied the day before, when Tamlin said from behind me, "No trip wires today?"

I froze midstep and looked over my shoulder. He was standing a few feet away.

How had he crept up so silently on the gravel? Faerie stealth, no doubt. I willed calm into my veins, my head. I said as politely as I could, "You said I was safe here. So I listened."

His eyes narrowed slightly, but he put on what I supposed was his attempt at a pleasant smile. "My morning work was postponed," he said.

Indeed, his usual tunic was off, the baldric gone, and the sleeves of his white shirt had been rolled up to the elbows to reveal tanned forearms corded with muscle. "If you want a ride across the grounds—if you're interested in your new . . . residence, I can take you."

Again, that effort to be accommodating, even when every word seemed to pain him. Maybe he could eventually be swayed by Lucien. And until then . . . how much could I get away with, if he was going to such lengths to make his people swear not to harm me, to shield me from the Treaty? I smiled blandly and said, "I'd prefer to spend today alone, I think. But thank you for the offer."

He tensed. "What about—"

"No, thank you," I interrupted, marveling a bit at my own audacity. But I had to catch Lucien alone, had to feel him out. He might already be gone.

Tamlin clenched his hands into fists, as if fighting against the claws itching to burst out. But he didn't reprimand me, didn't do anything other than prowl back into the house without another word.

Soon enough, if I was lucky, Tamlin wouldn't be my problem anymore. I hurried for the stables, tucking away the information. Maybe one day, if I was ever released, if there was an ocean and years between us, I would think back and wonder why he'd bothered.

I tried not to look too eager, too out of breath when I finally reached the pretty, painted stables. It didn't surprise me that the stableboys all wore horse masks. For them I felt a shred of pity at what the blight had done, the ridiculous masks they now had to wear until someone could figure out how to undo the magic binding them to their faces. But none of the stable hands even looked at me—either because I wasn't worth it or because they, too, resented me for the death of Andras. I didn't blame them.

Any attempt at casualness took a stumble when I finally found Lucien astride a black gelding, grinning down at me with too-white teeth.

"Morning, Feyre." I tried to hide the stiffening in my shoulders, tried to smile a bit. "Going for a ride, or merely reconsidering Tam's offer to live with us?" I tried to recall the words I'd come up with earlier, the words to win him, but he laughed—and not pleasantly. "Come now. I'm to patrol the southern woods today, and I'm curious about the . . . *abilities* you used to bring down my friend, whether accidental or not. It's been a while since I encountered a human, let alone a Fae-killer. Indulge me in a hunt."

Perfect—at least that part of this had gone well, even if it sounded as lovely as facing a bear in its den. So I stepped aside to let a stableboy pass. He moved with a fluid smoothness, like all of them here. And didn't look at me, either—no indication at all of what he thought of having a *Fae-killer* in his stable.

But my kind of hunting couldn't be done on horseback. Mine consisted of careful stalking and well-laid traps and snares. I didn't know how to give chase atop a horse. Lucien accepted a quiver of arrows from the returning stableboy with a nod of thanks. Lucien smiled in a way that didn't meet that metal eye—or the russet one. "No ash arrows today, unfortunately."

I clenched my jaw to keep a retort from slipping off my tongue. If he was forbidden from hurting me, I couldn't fathom why he would invite me along, save to mock me in whatever way he could. Perhaps he was truly that bored. Better for me.

So I shrugged, looking as bored as I could. "Well . . . I suppose I'm already dressed for a hunt."

"Perfect," Lucien said, his metal eye gleaming in the sunlight slanting in through the open stable doors. I prayed Tamlin wouldn't come prowling through them—prayed he wouldn't decide to go for a ride on his own and catch us here.

"Let's go, then," I said, and Lucien motioned for them to prepare a horse. I leaned against a wooden wall as I waited, keeping an eye on the doorway for signs of Tamlin, and offered my own bland replies to Lucien's remarks about the weather.

Mercifully, I was soon astride a white mare, riding with Lucien through the spring-shrouded woods beyond the gardens. I kept a healthy distance from the fox-masked faerie on the broad path, hoping that eye of his couldn't see through the back of his head.

The thought didn't sit well, and I shoved it away—along with the part of me that marveled at the way the sun illuminated the leaves, and the clusters of crocuses that grew like flashes of vibrant purple against the brown and green. Those were things that weren't necessary to my plans, useless details that only blocked out everything else: the shape and slope of the path, what trees were good for climbing, sounds of nearby water sources. *Those* things could help me survive if I ever needed to. But, like the rest of the grounds, the forest was utterly empty. No sign of faeries, nor any High Fae wandering around. Just as well.

"Well, you certainly have the *quiet* part of hunting down," Lucien said, falling back to ride beside me. Good—let him come to me, rather than me seeming too eager, too friendly.

I adjusted the weight of the quiver strap across my chest, then ran a finger along the smooth curve of the yew bow in my lap. The bow was larger than the one I used at home, the arrows heavier and heads thicker. I would probably miss whatever target I found until I adjusted to the weight and balance of the bow.

Five years ago I'd taken the very last of my father's coppers from our former fortune to purchase my bow and arrows. I'd since allotted a small sum every month for arrows and replacement strings.

"Well?" Lucien pressed. "No game good enough for you to slaughter? We've passed plenty of squirrels and birds." The canopy above cast shadows upon his fox mask—light and dark and gleaming metal.

"You seem to have enough food on your table that I don't need to add to it, especially when there's always plenty left over." I doubted squirrel would be good enough for their table.

Lucien snorted but didn't say anything else as we passed beneath a flowering lilac, its purple cones drooping low enough to graze my cheek like cool, velvety fingers. The sweet, crisp scent lingered in my nose even as we rode on. *Not useful*, I told myself. Although . . . the thick brush beyond it would be a good hiding spot, if I needed one.

"You said you were an emissary for Tamlin," I ventured. "Do emissaries usually patrol the grounds?" A casual, disinterested question.

Lucien clicked his tongue. "I'm Tamlin's emissary for formal uses, but this was Andras's shift. So someone needed to fill in. It's an honor to do it."

I swallowed hard. Andras had a place here, and *friends* here—he hadn't been just some nameless, faceless faerie. No doubt he was more missed than I was. "I'm . . . sorry," I said—and meant it. "I didn't know what—what he meant to you all."

Lucien shrugged. "Tamlin said as much, which was no doubt why he brought you here. Or maybe you looked so pathetic in those rags that he took pity on you."

"I wouldn't have joined you if I'd known you would use this ride as an excuse to insult me." Alis had mentioned that Lucien could use someone who snapped back at him. Easy enough.

Lucien smirked. "Apologies, Feyre."

I might have called him a liar for that apology had I not known he couldn't lie. Which made the apology . . . sincere? I couldn't sort it out.

"So," he said, "when are you going to start trying to persuade me to beseech Tamlin to find a way to free you from the Treaty's rules?"

I tried not to jolt. "What?"

"That's why you agreed to come out here, isn't it? Why you wound up at the stables exactly as I was leaving?" He shot me a sideways glance with that russet eye of his. "Honestly, I'm impressed—and flattered you think I have that kind of sway with Tamlin."

I wouldn't reveal my hand—not yet. "What are you talking—"

His cocked head was answer enough. He chuckled and said, "Before you waste one of your precious few human breaths, let me explain two things to you. One: if I had my way, you'd be gone, so it wouldn't take much convincing on your part. Two: I can't have my way, because there is no alternative to what the Treaty demands. There's no extra loophole."

"But—but there has to be something—"

"I admire your balls, Feyre—I really do. Or maybe it's stupidity. But since Tam won't gut you, which was *my* first choice, you're stuck here. Unless you want to rough it on your own in Prythian, which"—he looked me up and down—"I'd advise against."

No—no, I couldn't just . . . just *stay here*. Forever. Until I died. Maybe . . . maybe there was some other way, or someone else who could find a way out. I mastered my uneven breathing, shoving away the panicked, bleating thoughts.

"A valiant effort," Lucien said with a smirk.

I didn't bother hiding the glare I cut in his direction.

We rode on in silence, and aside from a few birds and squirrels, I saw nothing—heard nothing—unusual. After a few minutes I'd quieted my riotous thoughts enough to say, "Where is the rest of Tamlin's court? They all fled this blight on magic?"

"How'd you know about the court?" he asked so quickly that I realized he thought I meant something else.

I kept my face blank. "Do normal estates have emissaries? And servants chatter. Isn't that why you made them wear bird masks to that party?"

Lucien scowled, that scar stretching. "We each chose what to wear that night to honor Tamlin's shape-shifting gifts. The servants, too. But now, if we had the choice, we'd peel them off with our bare hands," he said, tugging on his own. It didn't move.

"What happened to the magic to make it act that way?"

Lucien let out a harsh laugh. "Something was sent from the shit-holes of Hell," he said, then glanced around and swore. "I shouldn't have said that. If word got back to her—"

"Who?"

The color had leeched from his sun-kissed skin. He dragged a hand through his hair. "Never mind. The less you know, the better. Tam might not find it troublesome to tell you about the blight, but I wouldn't put it past a human to sell the information to the highest bidder."

I bristled, but the few bits of information he'd released lay before me like glittering jewels. A *her* who scared Lucien enough to make him worry—to make him afraid someone might be listening, spying, monitoring his behavior. Even out here. I studied the shadows between the trees but found nothing.

Prythian was ruled by seven High Lords—perhaps this *she* was whoever governed this territory; if not a High Lord, then a High Lady. If that was even possible.

"How old are you?" I asked, hoping he'd keep divulging some more useful information. It was better than knowing nothing.

"Old," he said. He scanned the brush, but I had a feeling his darting eyes weren't looking for game. His shoulders were too tense.

"What sort of powers do you have? Can you shape-shift like Tamlin?"

He sighed, looking skyward before he studied me warily, that metal eye narrowing with unnerving focus. "Trying to figure out my weaknesses so you can—" I glowered at him. "Fine. No, I can't shape-shift. Only Tam can."

"But your friend—he appeared as a wolf. Unless that was his—"

"No, no. Andras was High Fae, too. Tam can shift us into other shapes if need be. He saves it for his sentries only, though. When Andras went across the wall, Tam changed him into a wolf so he wouldn't be spotted as a faerie. Though his size was probably indication enough."

A shudder went down my spine, violent enough that I didn't acknowledge the red-hot glare Lucien lobbed my way. I didn't have the nerve to ask if Tamlin could change me into another shape.

"Anyway," Lucien went on, "the High Fae don't have specific *powers* the way the lesser faeries do. I don't have a natural-born affinity, if that's what you're asking. I don't clean everything in sight or lure mortals to a watery death or grant you answers to whatever questions you might have if you trap me. We just exist—to rule."

I turned in the other direction so he couldn't see as I rolled my eyes. "I suppose if I were one of you, I'd be one of the faeries, not High Fae? A lesser faerie like Alis, waiting on you hand and foot?" He didn't reply, which amounted to a *yes*. With that arrogance, no wonder Lucien found my presence as a replacement for his friend to be abhorrent. And since he would probably loathe me forever, since he'd ended my scheming before it had even begun, I asked, "How'd you get that scar?"

"I didn't keep my mouth shut when I should have, and was punished for it."

"Tamlin did that to you?"

"Cauldron, no. He wasn't there. But he got me the replacement afterward."

More answers-that-weren't-answers. "So there are faeries who will actually answer any question if you trap them?" Maybe they'd know how to free me from the Treaty's terms.

"Yes," he said tightly. "The Suriel. But they're old and wicked, and not worth the danger of going out to find them. And if you're stupid enough to keep looking so intrigued, I'm going to become rather suspicious and tell Tam to put you under house arrest. Though I suppose you would deserve it if you were indeed stupid enough to seek one out."

They had to lurk nearby, then, if he was this concerned. Lucien whipped his head to the right, listening, his eye whirring softly. The hair on my neck stood, and I had my bow drawn in a heartbeat, pointing in the direction Lucien stared.

"Put your bow down," he whispered, his voice low and rough. "Put your damned bow down, human, and look straight ahead."

I did as he said, the hair on my arms rising as something rustled in the brush.

"Don't react," Lucien said, forcing his gaze ahead, too, the metal eye going still and silent. "No matter what you feel or see, don't react. *Don't look*. Just stare ahead."

I started trembling, gripping the reins in my sweaty hands. I might have wondered if this was some kind of horrible joke, but Lucien's face had gone so very, very pale. Our horses' ears flattened against their heads, but they continued walking, as if they'd also understood Lucien's command.

And then I felt it.

CHAPTER 10

My blood froze as a creeping, leeching cold lurched by. I couldn't see anything, just a vague shimmering in the corner of my vision, but my horse stiffened beneath me. I willed my face into blankness. Even the balmy spring woods seemed to recoil, to wither and freeze.

The cold thing whispered past, circling. I could see nothing, but I could *feel* it. And in the back of my mind, an ancient, hollow voice whispered:

I will grind your bones between my claws; I will drink your marrow; I will feast on your flesh. I am what you fear; I am what you dread . . . Look at me. Look at me.

I tried to swallow, but my throat had closed up. I kept my eyes on the trees, on the canopy, on anything but the cold mass circling us again and again.

Look at me.

I wanted to look—I needed to see what it was.

Look at me.

I stared at the coarse trunk of a distant elm, thinking of pleasant things. Like hot bread and full bellies—

I will fill my belly with you. I will devour you. Look at me.

A starry, unclouded night sky, peaceful and glittering and endless.

Summer sunrise. A refreshing bath in a forest pool. Meetings with Isaac, losing myself for an hour or two in his body, in our shared breaths.

It was all around us, so cold that my teeth chattered. *Look at me.*

I stared and stared at that ever-nearing tree trunk, not daring to blink. My eyes strained, filling with tears, and I let them fall, refusing to acknowledge the thing that lurked around us.

Look at me.

And just as I thought I would give in, when my eyes hurt so much from *not* looking, the cold disappeared into the brush, leaving a trail of still, recoiling plants behind it. Only after Lucien exhaled and our horses shook their heads did I dare sag in my seat. Even the crocuses seemed to straighten again.

"What was that?" I asked, brushing the tears from my face.

Lucien's face was still pale. "You don't want to know."

"Please. Was it that . . . Suriel you mentioned?"

Lucien's russet eye was dark as he answered hoarsely. "No. It was a creature that should not be in these lands. We call it the Bogge. You cannot hunt it, and you cannot kill it. Even with your beloved ash arrows."

"Why can't I look at it?"

"Because when you look at it—when you acknowledge it—that's when it becomes real. That's when it can kill you."

A shiver spider-walked down my spine. This was the Prythian I'd expected—the creatures that made humans speak of them in hushed tones even now. The reason I hadn't hesitated, not for a heartbeat, when I'd considered the possibility of that wolf being a faerie. "I heard its voice in my head. It told me to look."

Lucien rolled his shoulders. "Well, thank the Cauldron that you didn't. Cleaning up that mess would have ruined the rest of my day." He gave me a wan smile. I didn't return it.

I still heard the Bogge's voice whispering between the leaves, calling to me.

After an hour of meandering through the trees, hardly speaking to each other, I'd stopped trembling enough to turn to him.

"So you're old," I said. "And you carry around a sword, and go on border patrol. Did you fight in the War?" Fine—perhaps I hadn't quite let go of my curiosity about his eye.

He winced. "Shit, Feyre—I'm not that old."

"Are you a warrior, though?" *Would you be able to kill me if it ever came to that?*

Lucien huffed a laugh. "Not as good as Tam, but I know how to handle my weapons." He patted the hilt of his sword. "Would you like me to teach you how to wield a blade, or do you already know how, oh mighty mortal huntress? If you took down Andras, you probably don't need to learn anything. Only where to aim, right?" He tapped on his chest.

"I don't know how to use a sword. I only know how to hunt."

"Same thing, isn't it?"

"For me it's different."

Lucien fell silent, considering. "I suppose you humans are such hateful cowards that you would have wet yourself, curled up, and waited to die if you'd known beyond a doubt what Andras truly was." Insufferable. Lucien sighed as he looked me over. "Do you ever stop being *so* serious and dull?"

"Do you ever stop being such a prick?" I snapped back.

Dead—really, truly, I should have been dead for that.

But Lucien grinned at me. "Much better."

Alis, it seemed, had not been wrong.

✢

Whatever tentative truce we built that afternoon vanished at the dinner table.

Tamlin was lounging in his usual seat, a long claw out and circling his goblet. It paused on the lip as soon as I entered, Lucien on my heels. His green eyes pinned me to the spot.

Right. I'd brushed him off that morning, claiming I wanted to be alone.

Tamlin slowly looked at Lucien, whose face had turned grave. "We went on a hunt," Lucien said.

"I heard," Tamlin said roughly, glancing between us as we took our seats. "And did you have fun?" Slowly, his claw sank back into his flesh.

Lucien didn't answer, leaving it to me. *Coward*. I cleared my throat. "Sort of," I said.

"Did you catch anything?" Every word was clipped out.

"No." Lucien gave me a pointed cough, as if urging me to say more.

But I had nothing to say. Tamlin stared at me for a long moment, then dug into his food, not all that interested in talking to me, either.

Then Lucien quietly said, "Tam."

Tamlin looked up, more animal than fae in those green eyes. A demand for whatever it was Lucien had to say.

Lucien's throat bobbed. "The Bogge was in the forest today."

The fork in Tamlin's hand folded in on itself. He said with lethal calm, "You ran into it?"

Lucien nodded. "It moved past but came close. It must have snuck through the border."

Metal groaned as Tamlin's claws punched out, obliterating the fork. He rose to his feet with a powerful, brutal movement. I tried not to tremble at the contained fury, at how his canines seemed to lengthen as he said, "Where in the forest?"

Lucien told him. Tamlin threw a glance in my direction before stalking out of the room and shutting the door behind him with unnerving gentleness.

Lucien loosed a breath, pushing away his half-eaten food and rubbing at his temples.

"Where is he going?" I asked, staring toward the door.

"To hunt the Bogge."

"You said it couldn't be killed—that you can't face it."

"Tam can."

My breath caught a bit. The gruff High Fae halfheartedly flattering me was capable of killing a thing like the Bogge. And yet he'd served me himself that first night, offered me life rather than death. I'd known he was lethal, that he was a warrior of sorts, but . . .

"So he went to hunt the Bogge where we were earlier today?"

Lucien shrugged. "If he's going to pick up a trail, it would be there."

I had no idea how anyone could face that immortal horror, but . . . it wasn't my problem.

And just because Lucien wasn't going to eat anymore didn't mean I wouldn't. Lucien, lost in thought, didn't even notice the feast I downed.

I returned to my room, and—awake and with nothing else to do—began monitoring the garden beyond for any signs of Tamlin's return. He didn't come back.

I sharpened the knife I'd hidden away on a bit of stone I'd taken from the garden. An hour passed—and still Tamlin didn't return.

The moon showed her face, casting the garden below in silver and shadow.

Ridiculous. Utterly ridiculous to watch for his return, to see if he could indeed survive against the Bogge. I turned from the window, about to drag myself into bed.

But something moved out in the garden.

I lunged for the curtains beside the window, not wanting to be caught waiting for him, and peered out.

Not Tamlin—but someone lurked by the hedges, facing the house. Looking toward *me*.

Male, hunched, and—

The breath went out of me as the faerie hobbled closer—just two steps into the light leaking from the house.

Not a faerie, but a man.

My father.

CHAPTER 11

I didn't give myself a chance to panic, to doubt, to do anything but wish I had stolen some food from my breakfast table as I layered on tunic after tunic and bundled myself in a cloak, stuffing the knife I'd stolen into my boot. The extra clothes in the satchel would just be a burden to carry.

My father. My father had come to take me—to save me. Whatever benefits Tamlin had given him upon my departure couldn't be too tempting, then. Maybe he had a ship prepared to take us far, far away—maybe he had somehow sold the cottage and gotten enough money to set us up in a new place, a new continent.

My father—my crippled, broken father had come.

A quick survey of the ground beneath my window revealed no one outside—and the silent house told me no one had spotted my father yet. He was still waiting by the hedge, now beckoning to me. At least Tamlin had not returned.

With a final glance at my room, listening for anyone approaching from the hall, I grasped the nearby trellis of wisteria and eased down the building.

I winced at the crunch of gravel beneath my boots, but my father was already moving toward the outer gates, limping along with his cane. How had he even *gotten* here? There had to be horses nearby, then. He was hardly wearing enough clothing for the winter that would await us once we crossed the wall. But I'd layered on so much that I could spare him some items if need be.

Keeping my movements light and silent, carefully avoiding the light of the moon, I hurried after my father. He moved with surprising swiftness toward the darkened hedges and the gate beyond.

Only a few hall candles were burning inside the house. I didn't dare breathe too loudly—didn't dare call for my father as he limped toward the gate. If we left now, if he indeed had horses, we could be halfway home by the time they realized I was gone. Then we'd flee—flee Tamlin, flee the blight that could soon invade our lands.

My father reached the gates. They were already open, the dark forest beyond beckoning. He must have hidden the horses deeper in. He turned toward me, that familiar face drawn and tight, those brown eyes clear for once, and beckoned. *Hurry, hurry*, every movement of his hand seemed to shout.

My heart was a raging beat in my chest, in my throat. Only a few feet now—to him, to freedom, to a new life—

A massive hand wrapped around my arm. "Going somewhere?"

Shit, shit, *shit*.

Tamlin's claws poked through my layers of clothing as I looked up at him in unabashed terror.

I didn't dare move, not as his lips thinned and the muscles in his jaw quivered. Not as he opened his mouth and I glimpsed fangs—long, throat-tearing fangs shining in the moonlight.

He was going to kill me—kill me right there, and then kill my father. No more loopholes, no more flattery, no more mercy. He didn't care anymore. I was as good as dead.

"Please," I breathed. "My father—"

"Your *father*?" He lifted his stare to the gates behind me, and his growl rumbled through me as he bared his teeth. "Why don't you look again?" He released me.

I staggered back a step, whirling, sucking in a breath to tell my father to *run*, but—

But he wasn't there. Only a pale bow and a quiver of pale arrows remained, propped up against the gates. Mountain ash. They hadn't been there moments before, hadn't—

They rippled, as if they were nothing but water—and then the bow and quiver became a large pack, laden with supplies. Another ripple—and there were my sisters, huddled together, weeping.

My knees buckled. "What is . . ." I didn't finish the question. My father now stood there, still hunched and beckoning. A flawless rendering.

"Weren't you warned to keep your wits about you?" Tamlin snapped. "That your human senses would betray you?" He stepped beyond me and let out a snarl so vicious that whatever the thing was by the gates shimmered with light and darted out as fast as lightning streaking through the dark.

"Fool," he said to me, turning. "If you're ever going to run away, at least do it in the daytime." He stared me down, and the fangs slowly retracted. The claws remained. "There are worse things than the Bogge prowling these woods at night. That thing at the gates isn't one of them—and it still would have taken a good, long while devouring you."

Somehow, my mouth began working again. And of all the things to say, I blurted, "Can you blame me? My crippled father appears beneath my window, and you think I'm not going to run for him? Did you actually think I'd gladly stay here *forever*, even if you'd taken care of my family, all for some Treaty that had nothing to do with me and allows *your kind* to slaughter humans as you see fit?"

He flexed his fingers as if trying to get the claws back in, but they remained out, ready to slice through flesh and bone. "What do you want, Feyre?"

"I want to go *home*!"

"Home to what, exactly? You'd prefer that miserable human existence to this?"

"I made a promise," I said, my breathing ragged. "To my mother, when she died. That I'd look after my family. That I'd take care of them. All I have done, every single day, every hour, has been for that vow. And just because I was hunting to *save* my family, to put food in their bellies, I'm now forced to break it."

He stalked toward the house, and I gave him a wide berth before falling into step behind him. His claws slowly, slowly retracted. He didn't look at me as he said, "You are not breaking your vow—you are fulfilling it, and then some, by staying here. Your family is better cared for now than they were when you were there."

Those chipped, miscolored paintings inside the cottage flashed in my vision. Perhaps they would forget who had even painted them in the first place. Insignificant—that's what all those years I'd given them would be, as insignificant as I was to these High Fae. And that dream I'd had, of one day living with my father, with enough food and money and paint . . . it had been my dream—no one else's.

I rubbed at my chest. "I can't just give up on it, on them. No matter what you say."

Even if I had been a fool—a stupid, human fool—to believe my father would ever actually come for me.

Tamlin eyed me sidelong. "You're not giving up on them."

"Living in luxury, stuffing myself with food? How is that not—"

"They are cared for—they are fed and comfortable."

Fed and comfortable. If he couldn't lie, if it was true, then . . . then it was beyond anything I'd ever dared hope for.

Then . . . my vow to my mother was fulfilled.

It stunned me enough that I didn't say anything for a moment as we walked.

My life was now owned by the Treaty, but . . . perhaps I'd been freed in another sort of way.

We neared the sweeping stairs that led into the manor, and I finally asked, "Lucien goes on border patrol, and you've mentioned other sentries—yet I've never seen one here. Where are they all?"

"At the border," he said, as if that were a suitable answer. Then he added, "We don't need sentries if I'm here."

Because he was deadly enough. I tried not to think about it, but still I asked, "Were you trained as a warrior, then?"

"Yes." When I didn't reply, he added, "I spent most of my life in my father's war-band on the borders, training as a warrior to one day serve him—or others. Running these lands . . . was not supposed to fall to me." The flatness with which he said it told me enough about how he felt about his current title, about why the presence of his silver-tongued friend was necessary.

But it was too personal, too demanding, to ask what had occurred to change his circumstances so greatly. So I cleared my throat and said, "What manner of faeries prowl the woods beyond this gate, if the Bogge isn't the worst of them? What *was* that thing?"

What I'd meant to ask was, *What would have tormented and then eaten me? Who are you to be so powerful that they pose no threat to you?*

He paused on the bottom step, waiting for me to catch up. "A puca. They use your own desires to lure you to some remote place. Then they eat you. Slowly. It probably smelled your human scent in the woods and followed it to the house." I shivered and didn't bother to hide it. Tamlin went on. "These lands used to be well guarded. The deadlier faeries were contained within the borders of their native territories, monitored by the local Fae lords, or driven into hiding. Creatures like the puca never would have dared set foot here. But now, the sickness that infected Prythian has weakened the wards that kept them out." A long pause, like the words were choked out of him. "Things are different now. It's not safe to travel alone at night—especially if you're human."

Because humans were defenseless as babes compared to natural-born predators like Lucien—and Tamlin, who didn't need weapons to hunt. I glanced at his hands but found no trace of the claws. Only tanned, callused skin.

"What else is different now?" I asked, trailing him up the marble front steps.

He didn't stop this time, didn't even look over his shoulder to see me as he said, "Everything."

So I truly was to live there forever. As much as I longed to ensure that Tamlin's word about caring for my family was true, as much as his claim that I was taking better care of my family by staying away—even if I was truly fulfilling that vow to my mother by staying in Prythian . . . Without the weight of that promise, I was left hollow and empty.

Over the next three days, I found myself joining Lucien on Andras's old patrol while Tamlin hunted the grounds for the Bogge, unseen by us. Despite being an occasional bastard, Lucien didn't seem to mind my company, and he did most of the talking, which was fine; it left me to brood over the consequences of firing a single arrow.

An arrow. I never fired a single one during those three days we rode along the border. That very morning I'd spied a red doe in a glen and aimed out of instinct, my arrow poised to fly right into her eye as Lucien sneered that *she* was not a faerie, at least. But I'd stared at her—fat and healthy and content—and then slackened the bow, replaced the arrow in my quiver, and let the doe wander on.

I never saw Tamlin around the manor—off hunting the Bogge day and night, Lucien informed me. Even at dinner, he spoke little before leaving early—off to continue his hunt, night after night. I didn't mind his absence. It was a relief, if anything.

On the third night after my encounter with the puca, I'd scarcely sat down before Tamlin got up, giving an excuse about not wanting to waste hunting time.

Lucien and I stared after him for a moment.

What I could see of Lucien's face was pale and tight. "You worry about him," I said.

Lucien slumped in his seat, wholly undignified for a Fae lord. "Tamlin gets into . . . moods."

"He doesn't want your help hunting the Bogge?"

"He prefers being alone. And having the Bogge on our lands . . . I don't suppose you'd understand. The puca are minor enough not to bother him, but even after he's shredded the Bogge, he'll brood over it."

"And there's no one who can help him at all?"

"He would probably shred them for disobeying his order to stay away."

A brush of ice slithered across my nape. "He would be that brutal?"

Lucien studied the wine in his goblet. "You don't hold on to power by being everyone's friend. And among the faeries, lesser and High Fae alike, a firm hand is needed. We're too powerful, and too bored with immortality, to be checked by anything else."

It seemed like a cold, lonely position to have, especially when you didn't particularly want it. I wasn't sure why it bothered me so much.

The snow was falling, thick and merciless, already up to my knees as I pulled the bowstring back—farther and farther, until my arm trembled. Behind me, a shadow lurked—no, watched. *I didn't dare turn to look at it, to see who might be within that shadow, observing, not as the wolf stared at me across the clearing.*

Just staring. As if waiting, as if daring me to fire the ash arrow.

No—no, I didn't want to do it, not this time, not again, not—

But I had no control over my fingers, absolutely none, and he was still staring as I fired.

One shot—one shot straight through that golden eye.

A plume of blood splattering the snow, a thud of a heavy body, a sigh of wind. No.

It wasn't a wolf that hit the snow—no, it was a man, tall and well formed.

No—not a man. A High Fae, with those pointed ears.

I blinked, and then—then my hands were warm and sticky with blood, then his body was red and skinless, steaming in the cold, and it was his skin—his skin—*that I held in my hands, and—*

I threw myself awake, sweat slipping down my back, and forced myself to breathe, to open my eyes and note each detail of the night-dark bedroom. Real—this was real.

But I could still see that High Fae male facedown in the snow, my arrow through his eye, red and bloody all over from where I'd cut and peeled off his skin.

Bile stung my throat.

Not real. Just a dream. Even if what I'd done to Andras, even as a wolf, was . . . was . . .

I scrubbed at my face. Perhaps it was the quiet, the hollowness, of the past few days—perhaps it was only that I no longer had to think hour to hour about how to keep my family alive, but . . . It was regret, and maybe shame, that coated my tongue, my bones.

I shuddered as if I could fling it off, and kicked back the sheets to rise from the bed.

CHAPTER 12

I couldn't entirely shake the horror, the gore of my dream as I walked down the dark halls of the manor, the servants and Lucien long since asleep. But I had to do something—*anything*—after that nightmare. If only to avoid sleeping. A bit of paper in one hand and a pen gripped in the other, I carefully traced my steps, noting the windows and doors and exits, occasionally jotting down vague sketches and *X*s on the parchment.

It was the best I could do, and to any literate human, my markings would have made no sense. But I couldn't write or read more than my basic letters, and my makeshift map was better than nothing. If I were to remain here, it was essential to know the best hiding places, the easiest way out, should things ever go badly for me. I couldn't entirely let go of the instinct.

It was too dim to admire any of the paintings lining the walls, and I didn't dare risk a candle. These past three days, there had been servants in the halls when I'd worked up the nerve to look at the art—and the part of me that spoke with Nesta's voice had laughed at the idea of an ignorant human trying to admire faerie art. *Some other time, then*, I'd told myself. I would find another day, a quiet hour when no one was around, to look at them. I had plenty of hours now—a whole lifetime in front of me. Perhaps . . . perhaps I'd figure out what I wished to do with it.

I crept down the main staircase, moonlight flooding the black-and-white tiles of the entrance hall. I reached the bottom, my bare feet silent on the cold tiles, and listened. Nothing—no one.

I set my little map on the foyer table and drew a few *X*s and circles to signify the doors, the windows, the marble stairs of the front hall. I would become so familiar with the house that I could navigate it even if someone blinded me.

A breeze announced his arrival—and I turned from the table toward the long hall, to the open glass doors to the garden.

I'd forgotten how huge he was in this form—forgotten the curled horns and lupine face, the bearlike body that moved with a feline fluidity. His green eyes glowed in the darkness, fixing on me, and as the doors snicked shut behind him, the clicking of claws on marble filled the hall. I stood still—not daring to flinch, to move a muscle.

He limped slightly. And in the moonlight, dark, shining stains were left in his wake.

He continued toward me, stealing the air from the entire hall. He was so big that the space felt cramped, like a cage. The scrape of claw, a huff of uneven breathing, the dripping of blood.

Between one step and the next, he changed forms, and I squeezed my eyes shut at the blinding flash. When at last my eyes adjusted to the returning darkness, he was standing in front of me.

Standing, but—not quite there. No sign of the baldric, or his knives. His clothes were in shreds—long, vicious slashes that made me wonder how he wasn't gutted and dead. But the muscled skin peering out beneath his shirt was smooth, unharmed.

"Did you kill the Bogge?" My voice was hardly more than a whisper.

"Yes." A dull, empty answer. As if he couldn't be bothered to remember to be pleasant. As if I were at the very, very bottom of a long list of priorities.

"You're hurt," I said even more quietly.

Indeed, his hand was covered in blood, even more splattering on the floor beneath him. He looked at it blankly—as if it took some monumental effort to remember that he even had a hand, and that it was injured. What effort of will and strength had it taken to kill the Bogge, to face that wretched menace? How deep had he had to dig inside himself—to whatever immortal power and animal that lived there—to kill it?

He glanced down at the map on the table, and his voice was void of anything—any emotion, any anger or amusement—as he said, "What is that?"

I snatched up the map. "I thought I should learn my surroundings."

Drip, drip, drip.

I opened my mouth to point out his hand again, but he said, "You can't write, can you."

I didn't answer. I didn't know what to say. *Ignorant, insignificant human.*

"No wonder you became so adept at other things."

I supposed he was so far gone in thinking about his encounter with the Bogge that he hadn't realized the compliment he'd given me. If it was a compliment.

Another splatter of blood on the marble. "Where can we clean up your hand?"

He lifted his head to look at me again. Still and silent and weary. Then he said, "There's a small infirmary."

I wanted to tell myself that it was probably the most useful thing I'd learned all night. But as I followed him there, avoiding the blood he trailed, I thought of what Lucien had told me about his isolation, that burden, thought of what Tamlin had mentioned about how these estates should not have been his, and felt . . . sorry for him.

✣

The infirmary was well stocked, but was more of a supply closet with a worktable than an actual place to host sick faeries. I supposed that was all they needed when they could heal themselves with their immortal powers. But this wound—this wound wasn't healing.

Tamlin slumped against the edge of the table, gripping his injured hand at the wrist as he watched me sort through the supplies in the cabinets and drawers. When I'd gathered what I needed, I tried not to balk at the thought of touching him, but . . . I didn't let myself give in to my dread as I took his hand, the heat of his skin like an inferno against my cool fingers.

I cleaned off his bloody, dirty hand, bracing for the first flash of those claws. But his claws remained retracted, and he kept silent as I bound and wrapped his hand—surprisingly enough, there were no more than a few vicious cuts, none of them requiring stitching.

I secured the bandage in place and stepped away, bringing the bowl of bloody water to the deep sink in the back of the room. His eyes were a brand upon me as I finished cleaning, and the room became too small, too hot. He'd killed the Bogge and walked away relatively unscathed. If Tamlin was that powerful, then the High Lords of Prythian must be near-gods. Every mortal instinct in my body bleated in panic at the thought.

I was almost at the open door, stifling the urge to bolt back to my room, when he said, "You can't write, yet you learned to hunt, to survive. How?"

I paused with my foot on the threshold. "That's what happens when you're responsible for lives other than your own, isn't it? You do what you have to do."

He was still sitting on the table, still straddling that inner line between the here and now and wherever he'd had to go in his mind to endure the fight with the Bogge. I met his feral and glowing stare.

"You aren't what I expected—for a human," he said.

I didn't reply. And he didn't say good-bye as I walked out.

The next morning, as I made my way down the grand staircase, I tried not to think too much about the clean-washed marble tiles on the floor below—no sign of the blood Tamlin had lost. I tried not to think too much at all about our encounter, actually.

When I found the front hall empty, I almost smiled—felt a ripple in that hollow emptiness that had been hounding me. Perhaps now, perhaps in this moment of quiet, I could at last look through the art on the walls, take time to observe it, learn it, admire it.

Heart racing at the thought, I was about to head toward a hall I had noted was nearly covered in painting after painting when low male voices floated out from the dining room.

I paused. The voices were tense enough that I made my steps silent as I slid into the shadows behind the open door. A cowardly, wretched thing to do—but what they were saying had me shoving aside any guilt.

"I just want to know what you think you're doing." It was Lucien—that familiar lazy viciousness coating each word.

"What are *you* doing?" Tamlin snapped. Through the space between the hinge and the door I could glimpse the two of them standing almost face-to-face. On Tamlin's nonbandaged hand, his claws shone in the morning light.

"Me?" Lucien put a hand on his chest. "By the Cauldron, Tam—there isn't much time, and you're just sulking and glowering. You're not even trying to fake it anymore."

My brows rose. Tamlin turned away but whirled back a moment later, his teeth bared. "It was a mistake from the start. I can't stomach it, not after what my father did to their kind, to their lands. I won't follow in his footsteps—won't be that sort of person. So *back off*."

"Back off? Back off while you seal our fates and ruin everything? I stayed with you out of hope, not to watch you stumble. For someone with a heart of stone, yours is certainly soft these days. The Bogge was on our lands—the *Bogge*, Tamlin! The barriers between courts have vanished, and even our woods are teeming with filth like the puca. Are you just going to start living out there, slaughtering every bit of vermin that slinks in?"

"Watch your mouth," Tamlin said.

Lucien stepped toward him, exposing his teeth as well. A pulsing kind of air hit me in the stomach, and a metallic stench filled my nose. But I couldn't *see* any magic—only feel it. I couldn't tell if that made it worse.

"Don't push me, Lucien." Tamlin's tone became dangerously quiet, and the hair on the back of my neck stood as he emitted a growl that was pure animal. "You think I don't know what's happening on my own lands? What I've got to lose? What's lost already?"

The blight. Perhaps it was contained, but it seemed it was still wreaking havoc—still a threat, and perhaps one they truly didn't want me knowing about, either from lack of trust or because . . . because I was no one and nothing to them. I leaned forward, but as I did, my finger slipped and softly thudded against the door. A human might not have heard, but both High Fae whirled. My heart stumbled.

I stepped toward the threshold, clearing my throat as I came up with a dozen excuses to shield myself. I looked at Lucien and forced myself to smile. His eyes widened, and I had to wonder if it was because of that smile, or because I looked truly guilty. "Are you going out for a ride?" I said, feeling a bit sick as I gestured behind me with a thumb. I hadn't planned on riding with him today, but it sounded like a decent excuse.

Lucien's russet eye was bright, though the smile he gave me didn't meet it. The face of Tamlin's emissary—more court-trained and calculating than I'd seen him yet. "I'm unavailable today," he said. He jerked his chin to Tamlin. "He'll go with you."

Tamlin shot his friend a look of disdain that he took few pains to hide. His usual baldric was armed with more knives than I'd seen before, and their ornate metal handles glinted as he turned to me, his shoulders tight.

"Whenever you want to go, just say so." The claws of his free hand slipped back under his skin.

No. I almost said it aloud as I turned pleading eyes to Lucien. Lucien merely patted my shoulder as he passed by. "Perhaps tomorrow, human."

Alone with Tamlin, I swallowed hard.

He stood there, waiting.

"I don't want to go for a hunt," I finally said quietly. True. "I hate hunting."

He cocked his head. "Then what do you want to do?"

✠

Tamlin led me down the halls. A soft breeze laced with the scent of roses slipped in through the open windows to caress my face.

"You've been going for hunts," Tamlin said at last, "but you really don't have any interest in hunting." He cast me a sidelong glance. "No wonder you two never catch anything."

No trace of the hollow, cold warrior of the night before, or of the angry Fae noble of minutes before. Just Tamlin right now, it seemed.

I'd be a fool to let my guard down around Tamlin, to think that his acting naturally meant anything, especially when something was so clearly amiss at his estate. He'd taken down the Bogge—and that made him the most dangerous creature I'd ever encountered. I didn't quite know what to make of him, and said somewhat stiltedly, "How's your hand?"

He flexed his bandaged hand, studying the white bindings, stark and clean against his sun-kissed skin. "I didn't thank you."

"You don't need to."

But he shook his head, and his golden hair caught and held the morning light as if it were spun from the sun itself. "The Bogge's bite was crafted to slow the healing of High Fae long enough to kill us. You have my gratitude." When I shrugged it off, he added, "How did you learn to bind wounds like this? I can still use the hand, even with the wrappings."

"Trial and error. I had to be able to pull a bowstring the next day."

He was quiet as we turned down another sun-drenched marble hallway, and I dared to look at him. I found him carefully studying me, his lips in a thin line. "Has anyone ever taken care of you?" he asked quietly.

"No." I'd long since stopped feeling sorry for myself about it.

"Did you learn to hunt in a similar manner—trial and error?"

"I spied on hunters when I could get away with it, and then practiced until I hit something. When I missed, we didn't eat. So learning how to aim was the first thing I figured out."

"I'm curious," he said casually. The amber in his green eyes was glowing. Perhaps not all traces of that beast-warrior were gone. "Are you ever going to use that knife you stole from my table?"

I stiffened. "How did you know?"

Beneath the mask, I could have sworn his brows were raised. "I was trained to notice those things. But I could smell the fear on you, more than anything."

I grumbled, "I thought no one noticed."

He gave me a crooked smile, more genuine than all the faked smiles and flattery he'd given me before. "Regardless of the Treaty, if you want to stand a chance at escaping my kind, you'll need to think more creatively than stealing dinner knives. But with your affinity for eavesdropping, maybe you'll someday learn something valuable."

My ears flared with heat. "I—I wasn't . . . Sorry," I mumbled. But I ran through what I'd overheard. There was no point in pretending I hadn't eavesdropped. "Lucien said you didn't have much time. What did he mean? Are more creatures like the Bogge going to come here thanks to the blight?"

Tamlin went rigid, scanning the hall around us, taking in every sight and sound and scent. Then he shrugged, too stiff to be genuine. "I'm an immortal. I have nothing *but* time, Feyre."

He said my name with such . . . intimacy. As if he weren't a creature capable of killing monsters made from nightmares. I opened my mouth to demand more of an answer, but he cut me off. "The force plaguing our lands and powers—that, too, will pass someday, if we're Cauldron-blessed. But yes—now that the Bogge entered these lands, I'd say it's fair to assume others might follow it, especially if the puca was already so bold."

If the borders between the courts were gone, though, as I'd heard Lucien say—if everything in Prythian was different, as Tamlin had claimed, thanks to this blight . . . Well, I didn't want to be caught up in some brutal war or revolution. I doubted I'd survive very long.

Tamlin strode ahead and opened a set of double doors at the end of the hall. The powerful muscles of his back shifted beneath his clothes. I'd never forget what he was—what he was capable of. What he'd been trained to do, apparently.

"As requested," he said, "the study."

I saw what lay beyond him and my stomach twisted.

CHAPTER 13

Tamlin waved his hand, and a hundred candles sprang to life. Whatever Lucien had said about magic being drained and off-kilter thanks to the blight clearly hadn't affected Tamlin as dramatically, or perhaps he'd been far more powerful to start with, if he could transform his sentries into wolves whenever he pleased. The tang of magic stung my senses, but I kept my chin high. That is, until I peered inside.

My palms began sweating as I took in the enormous, opulent study. Tomes lined each wall like the soldiers of a silent army, and couches, desks, and rich rugs were scattered throughout the room. But . . . it had been over a week since I left my family. Though my father had said never to return, though my vow to my mother was fulfilled, I could at least let them know I was safe—relatively safe. And warn them about the sickness sweeping across Prythian that might someday soon cross the wall.

There was only one method to convey it.

"Do you need anything else?" Tamlin asked, and I jerked. He still stood behind me.

"No," I said, striding into the study. I couldn't think about the casual power he'd just shown—the graceful carelessness with which he'd brought so many flames to life. I had to focus on the task at hand.

It wasn't entirely my fault that I was scarcely able to read. Before our downfall, my mother had sorely neglected our education, not bothering to hire a governess. And after poverty struck and my elder sisters, who could read and write, deemed the village school beneath us, they didn't bother to teach me. I could read enough to function—enough to form my letters, but so poorly that even signing my name was mortifying.

It was bad enough that Tamlin knew. I would think about *how* to get the letter to them once it was finished; perhaps I could beg a favor of him, or Lucien.

Asking them to write it would be too humiliating. I could hear their words: *typical ignorant human*. And since Lucien seemed convinced that I would turn spy the moment I could, he would no doubt burn the letter, and any I tried to write after. So I'd have to learn myself.

"I'll leave you to it, then," Tamlin said as our silence became too prolonged, too tense.

I didn't move until he'd closed the doors, shutting me inside. My heartbeat pulsed throughout my body as I approached a shelf.

I had to take a break for dinner and to sleep, but I was back in the study before the dawn had fully risen. I'd found a small writing desk in a corner and gathered papers and ink. My finger traced a line of text, and I whispered the words.

"'*She grab-bed . . . grabbed her shoe, sta . . . nd . . . standing from her pos . . . po . . .*'" I sat back in my chair and pressed the heels of my palms into my eyes. When I felt less near to ripping out my hair, I took the quill and underlined the word: *position*.

With a shaking hand, I did my best to copy letter after letter onto the ever-growing list I kept beside the book. There were at least forty words on it, their letters malformed and barely legible. I would look up their pronunciations later.

I rose from the chair, needing to stretch my legs, my spine—or just to get away from that lengthy list of words I didn't know how to pronounce and the permanent heat that now warmed my face and neck.

I suppose the study was more of a library, as I couldn't see any of the walls thanks to the small labyrinths of stacks flanking the main area and a mezzanine dangling above, covered wall to wall in books. But *study* sounded less intimidating. I meandered through some of the stacks, following a trickle of sunlight to a bank of windows on the far side. I found myself overlooking a rose garden, filled with dozens of hues of crimson and pink and white and yellow.

I might have allowed myself a moment to take in the colors, gleaming with dew under the morning sun, had I not glimpsed the painting that stretched along the wall beside the windows.

Not a painting, I thought, blinking as I stepped back to view its massive expanse. No, it was . . . I searched for the word in that half-forgotten part of my mind. *Mural*. That's what it was.

At first I could do nothing but stare at its size, at the ambition of it, at the fact that this masterpiece was tucked back here for no one to ever see, as if it was nothing—absolutely nothing—to create something like this.

It told a story with the way colors and shapes and light flowed, the way the tone shifted across the mural. The story of . . . of Prythian.

It began with a cauldron.

A mighty black cauldron held by glowing, slender female hands in a starry, endless night. Those hands tipped it over, golden sparkling liquid pouring out over the lip. No—not sparkling, but . . . effervescent with small symbols, perhaps of some ancient faerie language. Whatever was written there, whatever it was, the contents of the cauldron were dumped into the void below, pooling on the earth to form our world . . .

The map spanned the entirety of our world—not just the land on which we stood, but also the seas and the larger continents beyond. Each territory was marked and colored, some with intricate, ornate depictions of the beings who had once ruled over lands that now belonged to humans. All of it, I remembered with a shudder, all of the world had once been theirs—at least as far as they believed, crafted for them by the bearer of the cauldron. There was no mention of humans—no sign of us here. I supposed we'd been as low as pigs to them.

It was hard to look at the next panel. It was so simple, yet so detailed that, for a moment, I stood there on that battlefield, feeling the texture of the bloodied mud beneath me, shoulder to shoulder with the thousands of other human soldiers lined up, facing the faerie hordes who charged at us. A moment of pause before the slaughter.

The humans' arrows and swords seemed so pointless against the High Fae in their glimmering armor, or the faeries bristling with claws and fangs. I knew—knew without another panel to explicitly show me—the humans hadn't survived that particular battle. The smear of black on the panel beside it, tinged with glimmers of red, said enough.

Then another map, of a much-reduced faerie realm. Northern territories had been cut up and divided to make room for the High Fae, who had lost their lands to the south of the wall. Everything north of the wall went to them; everything south was left as a blur of nothing. A decimated, forgotten world—as if the painter couldn't be bothered to render it.

I scanned the various lands and territories now given to the High Fae. Still so much territory—such monstrous power spread across the entire northern part of our world. I knew they were ruled by kings or queens or councils or empresses, but I'd never seen a representation of it, of how much they'd been forced to concede to the South, and how crammed their lands now were in comparison.

Our massive island had fared well for Prythian by comparison, with only the bottom tip given over to us miserable humans. The bulk of the sacrifice was borne by the southernmost of the seven territories: a territory painted with crocuses and lambs and roses. Spring lands.

I took a step closer, until I could see the dark, ugly smear that acted as the wall—another spiteful touch by the painter. No markers in the human realm, nothing to indicate any of the larger towns or centers, but . . . I found the rough area where our village was, and the woods that separated it from the wall. Those two days' journey seemed so small—too small—compared to the power lurking above us. I traced a line, my finger hovering over the paint, up over the wall, into these lands—the lands of the Spring Court. Again, no markers, but it was filled with touches of spring: trees in bloom, fickle storms, young animals . . . At least I was to live out my days in one of the more moderate courts, weather-wise. A small consolation.

I looked northward and stepped back again. The six other courts of Prythian occupied a patchwork of territories. Autumn, Summer, and Winter were easy enough to pick out. Then above them, two glowing courts: the southernmost one a softer, redder palate, the Dawn Court; above, in bright gold and yellow and blue, the Day Court. And above that, perched in a frozen mountainous spread of darkness and stars, the sprawling, massive territory of the Night Court.

There were things in the shadows between those mountains—little eyes, gleaming teeth. A land of lethal beauty. The hair on my arms rose.

I might have examined the other kingdoms across the seas that flanked our land, like the isolated faerie kingdom to the west that seemed to have gotten away with no territory loss and was still law unto itself, had I not looked to the heart of that beautiful, living map.

In the center of the land, as if it were the core around which everything else had spread, or perhaps the place where the cauldron's liquid had first touched, was a small, snowy mountain range. From it arose a mammoth, solitary peak. Bald of snow, bald of life—as if the elements refused to touch it. There were no more clues about what it might be; nothing to indicate its importance, and I supposed that the viewers were already supposed to know. This was not a mural for human eyes.

With that thought, I went back to my little table. At least I'd learned the layout of their lands—and I knew to never, ever go north.

I eased into my seat and found my place in the book, my face warming as I glanced at the illustrations scattered throughout. A children's book, and yet I could scarcely make it through its twenty or so pages. Why *did* Tamlin have children's books in his library? Were they from his own childhood, or in anticipation of children to come? It didn't matter. I couldn't even read them. I hated the smell of these books—the decaying rot of the pages, the mocking whisper of the paper, the rough skin of the binding. I looked at the piece of paper, at all those words I didn't know.

I bunched my list in my hand, crumpling the paper into a ball, and chucked it into the rubbish bin.

"I could help you write to them, if that's why you're in here."

I jerked back in my seat, almost knocking over the chair, and whirled to find Tamlin behind me, a stack of books in his arms. I pushed back against the heat rising in my cheeks and ears, the panic at the information he might be guessing I'd been trying to send. "Help? You mean a faerie is passing up the opportunity to mock an ignorant mortal?"

He set the books down on the table, his jaw tight. I couldn't read the titles glinting on the leather spines. "Why should I mock you for a shortcoming that isn't your fault? Let me help you. I owe you for the hand."

Shortcoming. It *was* a shortcoming.

Yet it was one thing to bandage his hand, to talk to him as if he wasn't a predator built to kill and destroy, but to reveal how little I truly knew, to let him see that part of me that was still a child, unfinished and raw . . . His face was unreadable. Though there had been no pity in his voice, I straightened. "I'm fine."

"You think I've got nothing better to do with my time than come up with elaborate ways to humiliate you?"

I thought of that smear of nothing that the painter had used to render the human lands, and didn't have an answer—at least, not one that was polite. I'd given enough already to them—to him.

Tamlin shook his head. "So you'll let Lucien take you on hunts and—"

"Lucien," I interrupted quietly but not softly, "doesn't pretend to be anything but what he is."

"What's that supposed to mean?" he growled, but his claws stayed retracted, even as he clenched his hands into fists at his sides.

I was definitely walking a dangerous line, but I didn't care. Even if he'd offered me sanctuary, I didn't have to fall at his feet. "It means," I said with that same cold quiet, "that I don't know you. I don't know who you are, or *what* you really are, or what you want."

"It means you don't trust me."

"How can I trust a faerie? Don't you delight in killing and tricking us?"

His snarl set the flames of the candles guttering. "You aren't what I had in mind for a *human*—believe me."

I could almost feel the wound deep in my chest as it ripped open and all those awful, silent words came pouring out. *Illiterate*, *ignorant*, *unremarkable*, *proud*, *cold*—all spoken from Nesta's mouth, all echoing in my head with her sneering voice.

I pinched my lips together.

He winced and lifted a hand slightly, as if about to reach for me. "Feyre," he began—softly enough that I just shook my head and left the room. He didn't stop me.

But that afternoon, when I went to retrieve my crumpled list from the wastebasket, it was gone. And my pile of books had been disturbed—the titles out of order. It had probably been a servant, I assured myself, calming the tightness in my chest. Just Alis or some other bird-masked faerie cleaning up. I hadn't written anything incriminating—there was no way he knew I'd been trying to warn my family. I doubted he would punish me for it, but . . . our conversation earlier had been bad enough.

Still, my hands were unsteady as I took my seat at the little desk and found my place in the book I'd used that morning. I knew it was shameful to mark the books with ink, but if Tamlin could afford gold plates, he could replace a book or two.

I stared at the book without seeing the jumble of letters.

Maybe I was a fool for not accepting his help, for not swallowing my pride and having him write the letter in a few moments. Not even a letter of warning, but just—just to let them know I was safe. If he had better things to do with his time than come up with ways to embarrass me, then surely he had better things to do than help me write letters to my family. And yet he'd offered.

A nearby clock chimed the hour.

Shortcoming—another one of my *shortcomings*. I rubbed my brows with my thumb and forefinger. I'd been equally foolish for feeling a shred of pity for him—for the lone, brooding faerie, for someone I had so *stupidly* thought would really care if he met someone who perhaps felt the same, perhaps understood—in my ignorant, insignificant human way—what it was like to bear the weight of caring for others. I should have let his hand bleed that night, should have known better than to think that maybe—maybe there would be someone, human or faerie or whatever, who could understand what my life—what *I*—had become these past few years.

A minute passed, then another.

Faeries might not be able to lie, but they could certainly withhold information; Tamlin, Lucien, and Alis had done their best not to answer my specific questions. Knowing more about the blight that threatened them—knowing *anything* about it, where it had come from, what else it could do, and especially what it could do to a *human*—was worth my time to learn.

And if there was a chance that they might also possess some knowledge about a forgotten loophole of that damned Treaty, if they knew some way to pay the debt I owed *and* return me to my family so I might warn them about the blight myself . . . I had to risk it.

Twenty minutes later I had tracked down Lucien in his bedroom. I'd marked on my little map where it was—in a separate wing on the second level, far from mine—and after searching in his usual haunts, it was the last place to look. I knocked on the white-painted double doors.

"Come in, human." He could probably detect me by my breathing patterns alone. Or maybe that eye of his could see through the door.

I eased open the door. The room was similar to mine in shape, but was bedecked in hues of orange and red and gold, with faint traces of green and brown. Like being in an autumn wood. But while my room was all softness and grace, his was marked with ruggedness. In lieu of a pretty breakfast table by the window, a worn worktable dominated the space, covered in various weapons. It was there he sat, wearing only a white shirt and trousers, his red hair unbound and gleaming like liquid fire. Tamlin's court-trained emissary, but a warrior in his own right.

"I haven't seen you around," I said, shutting the door and leaning against it.

"I had to go sort out some hotheads on the northern border—official emissary business," he said, setting down the hunting knife he'd been cleaning, a long, vicious blade. "I got back in time to hear your little spat with Tam, and decided I was safer up here. I'm glad to hear your human heart has warmed to me, though. At least I'm not on the top of your killing list."

I gave him a long look.

"Well," he went on, shrugging, "it seems that you managed to get under Tam's fur enough that he sought me out and nearly bit my head off. So I suppose I can thank you for ruining what should have been a peaceful lunch. Thankfully for me, there's been a disturbance out in the western forest, and my poor friend had to go deal with it in that way only he can. I'm surprised you didn't run into him on the stairs."

Thank the forgotten gods for some small mercies. "What sort of disturbance?"

Lucien shrugged, but the movement was too tense to be careless. "The usual sort: unwanted, nasty creatures raising hell."

Good—good that Tamlin was away and wouldn't be here to catch me in what I planned to do. Another bit of luck. "I'm impressed you answered me that much," I said as casually as I could, thinking through my words. "But it's too bad you're not like the Suriel, spouting any information I want if I'm clever enough to snare you."

For a moment, he blinked at me. Then his mouth twisted to the side, and that metal eye whizzed and narrowed on me. "I suppose you won't tell me what you want to know."

"You have your secrets, and I have mine," I said carefully. I couldn't tell whether he would try to convince me otherwise if I told him the truth. "But if you *were* a Suriel," I added with deliberate slowness, in case he hadn't caught my meaning, "how, exactly, would I trap you?"

Lucien set down the knife and picked at his nails. For a moment, I wondered if he would tell me anything at all. Wondered if he would go right to Tamlin and tattle.

But then he said, "I'd probably have a weakness for groves of young birch trees in the western woods, and freshly slaughtered chickens, and would probably be so greedy that I wouldn't notice the double-loop snare rigged around the grove to pin my legs in place."

"Hmm." I didn't dare ask why he had decided to be accommodating. There was still a good chance he wouldn't mind seeing me dead, but I would risk it. "I somehow prefer you as a High Fae."

He smirked, but the amusement was short-lived. "If I were insane and stupid enough to go after a Suriel, I'd also take a bow and quiver, and maybe a knife just like this one." He sheathed the knife he'd cleaned and set it down at the edge of the table—an offering. "And I'd be prepared to run like hell when I freed it—to the nearest running water, which they hate crossing."

"But you're not insane, so you'll be here, safe and sound?"

"I'll be conveniently hunting on the grounds, and with my superior hearing, I might be feeling generous enough to listen if someone screams from the western woods. But it's a good thing I had no role in telling you to go out today, since Tam would eviscerate anyone who told you how to trap a Suriel; and it's a good thing I had planned to hunt anyway, because if anyone caught me helping you, there would be trouble of a whole other hell awaiting us. I hope your secrets are worth it." He said it with his usual grin, but there was an edge to it—a warning I didn't miss.

Another riddle—and another bit of information. I said, "It's a good thing that while you have superior hearing, I possess superior abilities to keep my mouth shut."

He snorted as I took the knife from the table and turned to procure the bow from my room. "I think I'm starting to like you—for a murdering human."

CHAPTER 14

Western woods. Grove of young birch trees. Slaughtered chicken. Double-loop snare. Close to running water.

I repeated Lucien's instructions as I walked out of the manor, through the cultivated gardens, across the wild, rolling grassy hills beyond them, over clear streams, and into the spring woods beyond. No one had stopped me—no one had even been around to see me leave, bow and quiver across my back, Lucien's knife at my side. I lugged along a satchel stuffed with a freshly dead chicken courtesy of the baffled kitchen staff, and had tucked an extra blade into my boot.

The lands were as empty as the manor itself, though I occasionally glimpsed something shining in the corner of my eye. Every time I turned to look, the shimmering transformed into the sunlight dancing on a nearby stream, or the wind fluttering the leaves of a lone sycamore atop a knoll. As I passed a large pond nestled at the foot of a towering hill, I could have sworn I saw four shining female heads poking up from the bright water, watching me. I hurried my steps.

Only birds and the chittering and rustling of small animals sounded as I entered the still green western forest. I'd never ridden through these woods on my hunts with Lucien. There was no path here, nothing tame about it. Oaks, elms, and beeches intertwined in a thick weave, almost strangling the trickle of sunlight that crept in through the dense canopy. The moss-covered earth swallowed any sound I made.

Old—this forest was ancient. And alive, in a way that I couldn't describe but could only feel, deep in the marrow of my bones. Perhaps I was the first human in five hundred years to walk beneath those heavy, dark branches, to inhale the freshness of spring leaves masking the damp, thick rot.

Birch trees—running water. I made my way through the woods, breath tight in my throat. Night was the dangerous time, I reminded myself. I had only a few hours until sunset.

Even if the Bogge had stalked us in the daylight.

The Bogge was dead, and whatever horror Tamlin was now dealing with dwelled in another part of these lands. The Spring Court. I wondered in what ways Tamlin had to answer to its High Lord, or if it was his High Lord who had carved out Lucien's eye. Maybe it was the High Lord's consort—the *she* whom Lucien had mentioned—that instilled such fear in them. I pushed away the thought.

I kept my steps light, my eyes and ears open, and my heartbeat steady. Shortcomings or no, I could still hunt. And the answers I needed were worth it.

I found a glen of young, skinny birch trees, then stalked in ever-widening circles until I encountered the nearest stream. Not deep, but so wide that I'd have to take a running leap to cross it. Lucien had said to find running water, and this was close enough to make escape possible. If I needed to escape. Hopefully I wouldn't.

I traced and then retraced several different routes to the stream. And a few alternate routes, should my access to it somehow be blocked. And when I was sure of every root and rock and hollow in the surrounding area, I returned to the small clearing encircled by those white trees and laid my snare.

From my spot up a nearby tree—a sturdy, dense oak whose vibrant leaves hid me entirely from anyone below—I waited. And waited. The afternoon sun crept overhead, hot enough even through the canopy that I had to shrug off my cloak and roll up the sleeves of my tunic. My stomach grumbled, and I pulled a hunk of cheese out of my rucksack. Eating it would be quieter than the apple I'd also swiped from the kitchen on my way out. When I finished it off, I swigged water from the canteen I'd brought, parched from the heat.

Did Tamlin or Lucien ever grow tired of day after day of eternal spring, or ever venture into the other territories, if only to experience a different season? I wouldn't have minded endless, mild spring while looking after my family—winter brought us dangerously close to death every year—but if I were immortal, I might want a little variation to pass the time. I'd probably want to do more than lurk about a manor house, too. Though I still hadn't worked up the nerve to make the request that had crept into the back of my mind when I saw the mural.

I moved about as much as I dared on the branch, only to keep the blood flowing to my limbs. I'd just settled in again when a ripple of silence came toward me. As if the wood thrushes and squirrels and moths held their breath while something passed by.

My bow was already strung. Quietly, I loosely nocked an arrow. Closer and closer the silence crept.

The trees seemed to lean in, their entwined branches locking tighter, a living cage keeping even the smallest of birds from soaring out of the canopy.

Maybe this had been a very bad idea. Maybe Lucien had overestimated my abilities. Or maybe he had been waiting for the chance to lead me to my doom.

My muscles strained from holding still atop the branch, but I kept my balance and listened. Then I heard it: a whisper, as if cloth were dragging over root and stone, a hungry, wheezing sniffing from the nearby clearing.

I'd laid my snares carefully, making the chicken look as if it had wandered too far and snapped its own neck as it sought to free itself from a fallen branch. I'd taken care to keep my own scent off the bird as much as possible. But these faeries had such keen senses, and even though I'd covered my tracks—

There was a snap, a whoosh, and a hollowed-out, wicked scream that made my bones and muscles and breath lock up.

Another enraged shriek pierced the forest, and my snares groaned as they held, and held, and held.

I climbed out of the tree and went to meet the Suriel.

Lucien, I decided as I crept up to the faerie in the birch glen, really, truly wanted me dead.

I hadn't known what to expect as I entered the ring of white trees—tall and straight as pillars—but it was not the tall, thin veiled figure in dark tattered robes. Its hunched back facing me, I could count the hard knobs of its spine poking through the thin fabric. Spindly, scabby gray arms clawed at the snare with yellowed, cracked fingernails.

Run, some primal, intrinsically human part of me whispered. Begged. *Run and run and never look back.*

But I kept my arrow loosely nocked. I said quietly, "Are you one of the Suriel?"

The faerie went rigid. And sniffed. Once. Twice.

Then slowly, it turned to me, the dark veil draped over its bald head blowing in a phantom breeze.

A face that looked like it had been crafted from dried, weather-worn bone, its skin either forgotten or discarded, a lipless mouth and too-long teeth held by blackened gums, slitted holes for nostrils, and eyes . . . eyes that were nothing more than swirling pits of milky white—the white of death, the white of sickness, the white of clean-picked corpses.

Peeking above the ragged neck of its dark robes was a body of veins and bones, as dried and solid and horrific as the texture of its face. It let go of the snare, and its too-long fingers clicked against each other as it studied me.

"Human," it said, and its voice was at once one and many, old and young, beautiful and grotesque. My bowels turned watery. "Did you set this clever, wicked trap for me?"

"Are you one of the Suriel?" I asked again, my words scarcely more than a ragged breath.

"Indeed I am." *Click, click, click* went its fingers against each other, one for each word.

"Then the trap was for you," I managed. *Run, run, run.*

It remained sitting, its bare, gnarled feet caught in my snares. "I have not seen a human woman for an age. Come closer so I might look upon my captor."

I did no such thing.

It let out a huffing, awful laugh. "And which of my brethren betrayed my secrets to you?"

"None of them. My mother told me stories of you."

"Lies—I can smell the lies on your breath." It sniffed again, its fingers clacking together. It cocked its head to the side, an erratic, sharp movement, the dark veil snapping with it. "What would a human woman want from the Suriel?"

"You tell me," I said softly.

It let out another low laugh. "A test? A foolish and useless test, for if you dared to capture me, then you must want knowledge very badly." I said nothing, and it smiled with that lipless mouth, its grayed teeth horrifically large. "Ask me your questions, human, and then free me."

I swallowed hard. "Is there—is there truly no way for me to go home?"

"Not unless you seek to be killed, and your family with you. You must remain here."

Whatever last shred of hope I'd been clinging to, whatever foolish optimism, shriveled and died. This changed nothing. Before my fight with Tamlin that morning, I hadn't even entertained the idea, anyway. Perhaps I'd only come here out of spite. So, fine—if I was here, facing sure death, then I might as well learn something. "What do you know about Tamlin?"

"More specific, human. Be more specific. For I know a good many things about the High Lord of the Spring Court."

The earth tilted beneath me. "Tamlin is—Tamlin is a High Lord?"

Click, click, click. "You did not know. Interesting."

Not just some petty faerie lord of a manor, but . . . but a High Lord of one of the seven territories. A High Lord of Prythian.

"Did you also not know that this is the Spring Court, little human?"

"Yes—yes, I knew about that."

The Suriel settled on the ground. "Spring, Summer, Autumn, Winter, Dawn, Day, and Night," it mused, as if I hadn't even answered. "The seven Courts of Prythian, each ruled by a High Lord, all of them deadly in their own way. They are not merely powerful—they *are* Power." That was why Tamlin had been able to face the Bogge and live. High Lord.

I tucked away my fear. "Everyone at the Spring Court is stuck wearing a mask, and yet you aren't," I said cautiously. "Are you not a member of the Court?"

"I am a member of no Court. I am older than the High Lords, older than Prythian, older than the bones of this world."

Lucien had *definitely* overestimated my abilities. "And what can be done about this blight that has spread in Prythian, stealing and altering the magic? Where did it come from?"

"Stay with the High Lord, human," the Suriel said. "That's all you can do. You will be safe. Do not interfere; do not go looking for answers after today, or you will be devoured by the shadow over Prythian. He will shield you from it, so stay close to him, and all will be righted."

That wasn't exactly an answer. I repeated, "Where did the blight come from?"

Those milky eyes narrowed. "The High Lord does not know that you came here today, does he? He does not know that his human woman came to trap a Suriel, because he cannot give her the answers she seeks. But it is too late, human—for the High Lord, for you, perhaps for your realm as well . . ."

Despite all that it had said, despite its order to stop asking questions and stay with Tamlin, it was *his human woman* that echoed in my head. That made me clench my teeth.

But the Suriel went on. "Across the violent western sea, there is another faerie kingdom called Hybern, ruled by a wicked, powerful king. Yes, a king," he said when I raised a brow. "Not a High Lord—there, his territory is not divided into courts. There, he is law unto himself. Humans no longer exist in that realm—though his throne is made of their bones."

That large island I'd seen on the map, the one that hadn't yielded any lands to humans after the Treaty. And—a throne of bones. The cheese I'd eaten turned leaden in my stomach.

"For some time now, the King of Hybern has found himself unhappy with the Treaty the other ruling High Fae of the world made with you humans long ago. He resents that he was forced to sign it, to let his mortal slaves go and to remain confined to his damp green isle at the edge of the world. And so, a hundred years ago, he dispatched his most-trusted and loyal commanders, his deadliest warriors, remnants of the ancient armies that he once sailed to the continent to wage such a brutal war against you humans, all of them as hungry and vile as he. As spies and courtiers and lovers, they infiltrated the various High Fae courts and kingdoms and empires around the world for fifty years, and when they had gathered enough information, he made his plan. But nearly five decades ago, one of his commanders disobeyed him. The Deceiver. And—" The Suriel straightened. "We are not alone."

I drew my bow farther but kept it pointed at the ground as I scanned the trees. But everything had already gone silent in the presence of the Suriel.

"Human, you must free me and run," it said, those death-filled eyes widening. "Run for the High Lord's manor. Do not forget what I told you—*stay with the High Lord*, and live to see everything righted."

"What is it?" If I knew what came, I could stand a better chance of—

"The naga—faeries made of shadow and hate and rot. They heard my scream, and they smelled you. Free me, human. They will cage me if they catch me here. *Free me* and return to the High Lord's side."

Shit. *Shit*. I lunged for the snare, making to put away my bow and grab my knife.

But four shadowy figures slipped through the birch trees, so dark that they seemed made from a starless night.

CHAPTER 15

The naga were sprung from a nightmare. Covered in dark scales and nothing more, they were a horrendous combination of serpentine features and male humanoid bodies whose powerful arms ended in polished black, flesh-shredding talons.

Here were the creatures of the blood-filled legends, the ones that slipped through the wall to torment and slaughter mortals. The ones I would have been glad to kill that day in the snowy woods. Their huge, almond-shaped eyes greedily took in the Suriel and me.

The four of them paused across the clearing, the Suriel between us, and I trained my arrow toward the one in the center.

The creature smiled, a row of razor-sharp teeth greeting me as a silvery forked tongue darted out.

"The Dark Mother has sent us a gift today, brothers," he said, gazing at the Suriel, who was clawing at the snare now. The naga's amber eyes shifted toward me again. "And a meal."

"Not much to eat," another one said, flexing its claws.

I began backing away—toward the stream, toward the manor below, keeping my arrow pointed at them. One scream from me would notify

Lucien—but my breath was thin. And he might not come at all, if he'd sent me here. I kept every sense fixed on my retreating steps.

"*Human*," the Suriel begged.

I had ten arrows—nine, once I fired the one nocked in my bow. None of them ash, but maybe they'd keep the naga down long enough for me to flee.

I backed away another step. The four naga crept closer, as if savoring the slowness of the hunt, as if they already knew how I tasted.

I had three heartbeats to make up my mind. Three heartbeats to execute my plan.

I drew my bowstring back farther, my arm trembling.

And then I screamed. Sharp and loud and with every bit of air in my too-tight lungs.

With the naga now focused entirely on me, I fired at the tether holding the Suriel in place.

The snare shattered. Like a shadow on the wind, the Suriel was off, a blast of dark that set the four naga staggering back.

The one closest to me surged toward the Suriel, the strong column of its scaly neck stretching out. No chance of my movements being considered an unprovoked attack anymore—not now that they'd seen my aim. They still wanted to kill me.

So I let my arrow fly.

The tip glittered like a shooting star through the gloom of the forest. I had all of a blink before it struck home and blood sprayed.

The naga toppled back just as the remaining three whirled to me. I didn't know if it was a killing shot. I was already gone.

I raced for the stream using the path I'd calculated earlier, not daring to look back. Lucien had said he'd be nearby—but I was deep in the woods, too far from the manor and help.

Branches and twigs snapped behind me—too close—and snarls that sounded like nothing I'd heard from Tamlin or Lucien or the wolf or any animal filled the still woods.

My only hope of getting away alive lay in outrunning them long enough to reach Lucien, and then only if he was there as he'd promised to be. I didn't let myself think of all the hills I would have to climb once I cleared the forest itself. Or what I would do if Lucien had changed his mind.

The crashing through the brush became louder, closer, and I veered to the right, leaping over the stream. Running water might have stopped the Suriel, but a hiss and a thud close behind told me it did nothing to hold the naga at bay.

I careened through a thicket, and thorns ripped at my cheeks. I barely felt their stinging kisses or the warm blood sliding down my face. I didn't even have time to wince, not as two dark figures flanked me, closing in to cut me off.

My knees groaned as I pushed myself harder, focusing on the growing brightness of the woods' end. But the naga to my right rushed at me, so fast that I could only leap aside to avoid the slashing talons.

I stumbled but stayed upright just as the naga on my left pounced.

I hurled myself into a stop, swinging my bow up in a wide arc. I nearly lost my grip as it connected with that serpentine face, and bone crunched with a horrific screech. I hurdled over his enormous fallen body, not pausing to look for the others.

I made it three feet before the third naga stepped in front of me.

I swung my bow at his head. He dodged it. The other two hissed as they came up behind me, and I gripped the bow harder.

Surrounded.

I turned in a slow circle, bow ready to strike.

One of them sniffed at me, those slitted nostrils flaring. "Scrawny human thing," he spat to the others, whose smiles grew sharper. "Do you know what you've cost us?"

I wouldn't go down without a fight, without taking some of them with me. "Go to Hell," I said, but it came out in a gasp.

They laughed, stepping nearer. I swung the bow at the closest. He dodged it, chuckling. "We'll have our sport—though you might not find it as amusing."

I gritted my teeth as I swung again. I would not be hunted down like a deer among wolves. I would find a way out of this; I would—

A black-clawed hand closed around the shaft of my bow, and a resounding *snap* echoed through the too-silent woods.

The air left my chest in a whoosh, and I only had time to half turn before one of them grabbed me by the throat and hurled me to the ground. He pounded my arm so hard against the earth that my bones groaned and my fingers splayed, dropping the remnants of my bow.

"When we're done ripping off your skin, you'll wish you hadn't crossed into Prythian," he breathed into my face, the reek of carrion shoving down my throat. I gagged. "We'll cut you up so fine there won't be much for the crows to pick at."

A white-hot flame went through me. Rage or terror or wild instinct, I don't know. I didn't think. I grabbed the knife in my boot and slammed it into his leathery neck.

Blood rained down onto my face, into my mouth as I bellowed my fury, my terror.

The naga slumped back. I scrambled up before the remaining two could pin me, but something rock hard hit my face. I tasted blood and soil and grass as I hit the earth. Stars danced in my vision, and I stumbled to my feet again out of instinct, grabbing for Lucien's hunting knife.

Not like this, not like this, not like this.

One of them lunged for me, and I dodged aside. His talons caught in my cloak and yanked, ripping it into ribbons just as his companion threw me to the ground, my arms tearing beneath those claws.

"You'll bleed," one of them panted, laughing under his breath at the knife I lifted. "We'll bleed you nice and slow." He wiggled his talons—perfect for deep, brutal cutting. He opened his mouth again, and a bone-shattering roar sounded through the clearing.

Only it hadn't come from the creature's throat.

The noise hadn't finished echoing before the naga went flying off me, crashing into a tree so hard that the wood cracked. I made out the gleaming gold of his mask and hair and the long, deadly claws before Tamlin tore into the creature.

The naga holding me shrieked and released his grip, leaping to his feet as Tamlin's claws shredded through his companion's neck. Flesh and blood ripped away.

I kept low to the ground, knife at the ready, waiting.

Tamlin let out another roar that made the marrow of my bones go cold and revealed those lengthened canines.

The remaining creature darted for the woods.

He got only a few steps away before Tamlin tackled him, pinning him to the earth. And disemboweled the naga in one deep, long swipe.

I remained where I lay, my face half buried in leaves and twigs and moss. I didn't try to raise myself. I was shaking so badly that I thought I would fall apart at the seams. It was all I could do to keep holding the knife.

Tamlin got to his feet, wrenching his claws out of the creature's abdomen. Blood and gore dripped from them, staining the deep green moss.

High Lord. High Lord. High Lord.

Feral rage still smoldered in his gaze, and I flinched as he knelt beside me. He reached for me again, but I jerked back, away from the bloody claws that were still out. I raised myself into a sitting position before the shaking resumed. I knew I couldn't get to my feet.

"Feyre," he said. The wrath faded from his eyes, and the claws slipped back under his skin, but the roar still sounded in my ears. There had been nothing in that sound but primal fury.

"How?" It was all I could manage to say, but he understood me.

"I was tracking a pack of them—these four escaped, and must have followed your scent through the woods. I heard you scream."

So he didn't know about the Suriel. And he—he'd come to help me.

He reached a hand toward me, and I shuddered as he ran cool, wet fingers down my stinging, aching cheek. Blood—that was blood on them.

And from the stickiness on my face, I knew there was already enough blood splattered on me that it wouldn't make a difference.

The pain in my face and my arm faded, then vanished. His eyes darkened a bit at the bruise I knew was already blossoming on my cheekbone, but the throbbing quickly lessened. The metallic scent of magic wrapped around me, then floated away on a light breeze.

"I found one dead half a mile away," he went on, his hands leaving my face as he unbuckled his baldric, then shucked off his tunic and handed it to me. The front of my own had been ripped and torn by the talons of the naga. "I saw one of my arrows in his throat, so I followed their tracks here."

I pulled on Tamlin's tunic over my own, ignoring how easily I could see the cut of his muscles beneath his white shirt, the way the blood soaking it made them stand out even more. A purebred predator, honed to kill without a second thought, without remorse. I shivered again and savored the warmth that leaked from the cloth. *High Lord*. I should have known, should have guessed. Maybe I hadn't wanted to—maybe I'd been afraid.

"Here," he said, rising to his feet and offering me a bloodstained hand. I didn't dare look at the slaughtered naga as I gripped his extended hand and he pulled me to my feet. My knees buckled, but I stayed upright.

I stared at our linked hands, both coated in blood that wasn't our own.

No, he hadn't been the only one to spill blood just now. And it wasn't just my blood that still coated my tongue. Perhaps that made me as much of a beast as him. But he'd saved me. Killed for me. I spat onto the grass, wishing I hadn't lost my canteen.

"Do I want to know what you were doing out here?" he asked.

No. Definitely not. Not after he'd warned me plenty of times already. "I thought I wasn't confined to the house and garden. I didn't realize I'd come so far."

He dropped my hand. "On the days that I'm called away to deal with . . . trouble, stay close to the house."

I nodded a bit numbly. "Thank you," I mumbled, fighting past the shaking racking my body, my mind. The naga's blood on me became nearly unbearable. I spat again. "Not—not just for this. For saving my life, I mean." I wanted to tell him how much that meant—that the High Lord of the Spring Court thought I was *worth* saving—but couldn't find the words.

His fangs vanished. "It was . . . the least I could do. They shouldn't have gotten this far onto my lands." He shook his head, more at himself, his shoulders slumping. "Let's go home," he said, sparing me the effort of explaining why I'd been out here in the first place. I couldn't bring myself to tell him that the manor wasn't my home—that I might not even have a home at all anymore.

We walked back in silence, both of us blood-drenched and pale. I could still sense the carnage we'd left behind—the blood-soaked ground and trees. The pieces of the naga.

Well, I'd learned something from the Suriel, at least. Even if it wasn't entirely what I'd wanted to hear—or know.

Stay with the High Lord. Fine—easy enough. But as for the history lesson it had been in the middle of giving me, about wicked kings and their commanders and however they tied into the High Lord at my side and the blight . . . I still didn't have enough specifics to be able to thoroughly warn my family. But the Suriel had told me not to go looking for further answers.

I had a feeling I would surely be a fool to ignore his advice. My family would have to make do with the bare bones of my knowledge, then. Hopefully it would be enough.

I didn't ask Tamlin anything more about the naga—about how many he'd killed before those four slipped away—didn't ask him anything at all, because I didn't detect a trace of triumph in him, but rather a deep, unending sort of shame and defeat.

CHAPTER 16

After soaking in the bath for nearly an hour, I found myself sitting in a low-backed chair before my room's roaring fireplace, savoring the feel of Alis brushing out my damp hair. Though dinner was to be served soon, Alis had a cup of molten chocolate brought up and refused to do anything until I'd had a few sips.

It was the best thing I'd ever tasted. I drank from the thick mug as she brushed my hair, nearly purring at the feel of her thin fingers along my scalp.

But when the other maids had gone downstairs to help with the evening meal, I lowered my mug into my lap. "If more faeries keep crossing the court borders and attacking, is there going to be a war?" *Maybe we should just take a stand—maybe it's time to say* enough, Lucien had said to Tamlin that first night.

The brush stilled. "Don't ask such questions. You'll call down bad luck."

I twisted in my seat, glaring up into her masked face. "Why aren't the other High Lords keeping their subjects in line? Why are these awful creatures allowed to roam wherever they want?

Someone—someone began telling me a story about a king in Hybern—"

Alis grabbed my shoulder and pivoted me around. "It's none of your concern."

"Oh, I think it is." I turned around again, gripping the back of the wooden chair. "If this spills into the human world—if there's war, or this blight poisons our lands . . ." I pushed back against the crushing panic. I had to warn my family—*had* to write to them. Soon.

"The less you know, the better. Let Lord Tamlin deal with it—he's the only one who can." The Suriel had said as much. Alis's brown eyes were hard, unforgiving. "You think no one would tell me what you asked the kitchen to give you today, or realize what you went to trap? Foolish, stupid girl. Had the Suriel not been in a benevolent mood, you would have deserved the death it gave you. I don't know what's worse: this, or your idiocy with the puca."

"Would you have done anything else? If you had a family—"

"I do have a family."

I looked her up and down. There was no ring on her finger.

Alis noticed my stare and said, "My sister and her mate were murdered nigh on fifty years ago, leaving two younglings behind. Everything I do, everything I work for, is for those boys. So you don't get the right to give me that look and ask me if I would do anything different, girl."

"Where are they? Do they live here?" Perhaps that was why there were children's books in the study. Maybe those two small, shining figures in the garden . . . maybe that had been them.

"No, they don't live here," she said, too sharply. "They are somewhere else—far away."

I considered what she said, then cocked my head. "Do faerie children age differently?" If their parents had been killed almost fifty years ago, they could hardly be boys.

"Ah, some age like you and can breed as often as rabbits, but there are kinds—like me, like the High Fae—who are rarely able to produce younglings. The ones who are born age quite a bit slower. We all had a shock when my sister conceived the second one only five years later—and the eldest won't even reach adulthood until he's seventy-five. But they're so rare—all our young are—and more precious to us than jewels or gold." She clenched her jaw tightly enough that I knew that was all I would likely get from her.

"I didn't mean to question your dedication to them," I said quietly. When she didn't reply, I added, "I understand what you mean—about doing everything for them."

Alis's lips thinned, but she said, "The next time that fool Lucien gives you advice on how to trap the Suriel, you come to me. Dead chickens, my sagging ass. All you needed to do was offer it a new robe, and it would have groveled at your feet."

By the time I entered the dining room I'd stopped shaking, and some semblance of warmth had returned to my veins. High Lord of Prythian or no, I wouldn't cower—not after what I'd been through today.

Lucien and Tamlin were already waiting for me at the table. "Good evening," I said, moving to my usual seat. Lucien cocked his head in a silent inquiry, and I gave him a subtle nod as I sat. His secret was still safe, though he deserved to be walloped for sending me so unprepared to the Suriel.

Lucien slouched a bit in his chair. "I heard you two had a rather exciting afternoon. I wish I could have been there to help."

A hidden, perhaps halfhearted apology, but I gave him another little nod.

He said with forced lightness, "Well, you still look lovely, regardless of your Hell-sent afternoon."

I snorted. I'd never looked lovely a day in my life. "I thought faeries couldn't lie."

Tamlin choked on his wine, but Lucien grinned, that scar stark and brutal. "Who told you that?"

"Everyone knows it," I said, piling food on my plate even as I began wondering about everything they'd said to me so far, every statement I'd accepted as pure truth.

Lucien leaned back in his chair, smiling with feline delight. "Of course we can lie. We find lying to be an art. And we lied when we told those ancient mortals that we couldn't speak an untruth. How else would we get them to trust us and do our bidding?"

My mouth became a thin, tight line. He was telling the truth—because if he was lying . . . The logic of it made my head spin. "Iron?" I managed to say.

"Doesn't do us a lick of harm. Only ash, as you well know."

My face warmed. I'd taken everything they said as truth. Perhaps the Suriel had been lying today, too, with that long-winded explanation about the politics of the faerie realms. About staying with the High Lord, and everything being fixed in the end.

I looked to Tamlin. *High Lord*. That wasn't a lie—I could feel its truth in my bones. Even though he didn't act like the High Lords of legend who had sacrificed virgins and slaughtered humans at will. No—Tamlin was . . . exactly as those fanatic, calf-eyed Children of the Blessed had depicted the bounties and comforts of Prythian.

"Even though Lucien revealed some of our closely guarded *secrets*," Tamlin said, throwing the last word at his companion with a growl, "we've never used your misinformation against you." His gaze met mine. "We never willingly lied to you."

I managed a nod and took a long sip of water. I ate in silence, so busy trying to decipher every word I'd overheard since arriving that I didn't realize when Lucien excused himself before dessert. I was left alone with the most dangerous being I'd ever encountered.

The walls of the room pressed in on me.

"Are you feeling . . . better?" Though he had his chin propped on a fist, concern—and perhaps surprise at that concern—shone in his eyes.

I swallowed hard. "If I never encounter a naga again, I'll consider myself fortunate."

"What were you doing out in the western woods?"

Truth or lie, lie or truth . . . both. "I heard a legend once about a creature who answers your questions, if you can catch it."

Tamlin flinched as his claws shot out, slicing his face. But the wounds closed as soon as they opened, leaving only a smear of blood running down his golden skin—which he wiped away with the back of his sleeve. "You went to catch the Suriel."

"I caught the Suriel," I corrected.

"And did it tell you what you wanted to know?" I wasn't sure he was breathing.

"We were interrupted by the naga before it could tell me anything worthwhile."

His mouth tightened. "I'd start shouting, but I think today was punishment enough." He shook his head. "You actually snared the Suriel. A human girl."

Despite myself, despite the afternoon, my lips twitched upward. "Is it supposed to be hard?"

He chuckled, then fished something out of his pocket. "Well, if I'm lucky, I won't have to trap the Suriel to learn what this is about." He lifted my crumpled list of words.

My heart dropped to my stomach. "It's . . ." I couldn't think of a suitable lie—everything was absurd.

"*Unusual? Queue? Slaying? Conflagration?*" He read the list. I wanted to curl up and die. Words I couldn't recognize from the books—words that now seemed so simple, so absurdly easy as he was saying them aloud. "Is this a poem about murdering me and then burning my body?"

My throat closed up, and I had to clench my hands into fists to keep from hiding my face behind them. "Good night," I said, barely more than a whisper, and stood on shaking knees.

I was nearly to the door when he spoke again. "You love them very much, don't you?"

I half turned to him. His green eyes met mine as he rose from his chair to walk to me. He stopped a respectable distance away.

The list of malformed words was still clutched in his hand. "I wonder if your family realizes it," he murmured. "That everything you've done wasn't about that promise to your mother, or for your sake, but for theirs." I said nothing, not trusting my voice to keep my shame hidden. "I know—I know that when I said it earlier, it didn't come out well, but I could help you write—"

"Leave me alone," I said. I was almost through the door when I ran into someone—into him. I stumbled back a step. I'd forgotten how fast he was.

"I'm not insulting you." His quiet voice made it all the worse.

"I don't need your help."

"Clearly not," he said with a half smile. But the smile faded. "A human who can take down a faerie in a wolf's skin, who ensnared the Suriel and killed two naga on her own . . ." He choked on a laugh, and shook his head. The firelight danced along his mask. "They're fools. Fools for not seeing it." He winced. But his eyes held no mischief. "Here," he said, extending the list of words.

I shoved it into my pocket. I turned, but he gently grabbed my arm. "You gave up so much for them." He lifted his other hand as if to brush my cheek. I braced myself for the touch, but he lowered it before making contact. "Do you even know how to laugh?"

I shook off his arm, unable to stop the angry words. High Lord be damned. "I don't want your pity."

His jade eyes were so bright I couldn't look away. "What about a friend?"

"Can faeries be friends with mortals?"

"Five hundred years ago, enough faeries were friends with mortals that they went to war on their behalf."

"What?" I'd never heard that before. And it hadn't been in that mural in the study.

"How do you think the human armies survived as long as they did, and did such damage that my kind even came to agree to a treaty? With ash weapons alone? There were faeries who fought and died at the humans' sides for their freedom, and who mourned when the only solution was to separate our peoples."

"Were you one of them?"

"I was a child at the time, too young to understand what was happening—or even to be told," he said. *A child.* Which meant he had to be over . . . "But had I been old enough, I would have. Against slavery, against tyranny, I would gladly go to my death, no matter whose freedom I was defending."

I wasn't sure if I would do the same. My priority would be to protect my family—and I would have picked whatever side could keep them safest. I hadn't thought of it as a weakness until now.

"For what it's worth," Tamlin said, "your family knows you're safe. They have no memory of a beast bursting into their cottage, and think a long-lost, very wealthy aunt called you away to aid her on her deathbed. They know you're alive, and fed, and cared for. But they also know that there have been rumors of a . . . threat in Prythian, and are prepared to run should any of the warning signs about the wall faltering occur."

"You—you altered their memories?" I took a step back. Faerie arrogance, such faerie arrogance to change our minds, to implant thoughts as if it wasn't a violation—

"Glamoured their memories—like putting a veil over them. I was afraid your father might come after you, or persuade some villagers to cross the wall with him and further violate the Treaty."

And they all would have died anyway, once they ran into things like the puca or the Bogge or the naga. A silence blanketed my mind, until I was so exhausted I could barely think, and couldn't stop myself from saying, "You don't know him. My father wouldn't have bothered to do either."

Tamlin looked at me for a long moment. "Yes, he would have."

But he wouldn't—not with that twisted knee. Not with it as an excuse. I'd realized that the moment the puca's illusion had been ripped away.

Fed, comfortable, and safe—they'd even been warned about the blight, whether they understood that warning or not. His eyes were open, honest. He had gone farther than I would have ever guessed toward assuaging my every concern. "You truly warned them about—the possible threat?"

A grave nod. "Not an outright warning, but . . . it's woven into the glamour on their memories—along with an order to run at the first sign of something being amiss."

Faerie arrogance, but . . . but he had done more than I could. My family might have ignored my letter entirely. Had I known he possessed those abilities, I might have even asked the High Lord to glamour their memories if he hadn't done it himself.

I truly had nothing to fret about, save for the fact that they'd probably forget me sooner than expected. I couldn't entirely blame them. My vow fulfilled, my task complete—what was left for me?

The firelight danced on his mask, warming the gold, setting the emeralds glinting. Such color and variation—colors I didn't know the names of, colors I wanted to catalog and weave together. Colors I had no reason not to explore now.

"Paint," I said, barely more than a breath. He cocked his head and I swallowed, squaring my shoulders. "If—if it's not too much to ask, I'd like some paint. And brushes."

Tamlin blinked. "You like—art? You like to paint?"

His stumbling words weren't unkind. It was enough for me to say, "Yes. I'm not—not any good, but if it's not too much trouble . . . I'll paint outside, so I don't make a mess, but—"

"Outside, inside, on the roof—paint wherever you want. I don't care," he said. "But if you need paint and brushes, you'll also need paper and canvas."

"I can work—help around the kitchen or in the gardens—to pay for it."

"You'd be more of a hindrance. It might take a few days to track them down, but the paint, the brushes, the canvas, and the space are yours. Work wherever you want. This house is too clean, anyway."

"Thank you—I mean it, truly. Thank you."

"Of course." I turned, but he spoke again. "Have you seen the gallery?"

I blurted, "There's a gallery in this house?"

He grinned—actually grinned, the High Lord of the Spring Court. "I had it closed off when I inherited this place." When he inherited a title he seemed to have little joy in holding. "It seemed like a waste of time to have the servants keep it cleaned."

Of course it would, to a trained warrior.

He went on. "I'm busy tomorrow, and the gallery needs to be cleaned up, so . . . the next day—let me show it to you the next day." He rubbed at his neck, faint color creeping into those cheeks of his—more alive and warm than I'd yet seen them. "Please—it would be my pleasure." And I believed him that it would.

I nodded dumbly. If the paintings along the halls were exquisite, then the ones selected for the gallery had to be beyond my human imaginings. "I would like that—very much."

He smiled at me still, broadly and without restraint or hesitation. Isaac had never smiled at me like that. Isaac had never made my breath catch, just a little bit.

The feeling was startling enough that I walked out, grasping the crumpled paper in my pocket as if doing so could somehow keep that answering smile from tugging on my lips.

CHAPTER 17

I jerked awake in the middle of the night, panting. My dreams had been filled with the clicking of the Suriel's bone-fingers, the grinning naga, and a pale, faceless woman dragging her bloodred nails across my throat, splitting me open bit by bit. She kept asking for my name, but every time I tried to speak, my blood bubbled out of the shallow wounds on my neck, choking me.

I ran my hands through my sweat-damp hair. As my panting eased, a different sound filled the air, creeping in from the front hall through the crack beneath the door. Shouts, and someone's screams.

I was out of my bed in a heartbeat. The shouts weren't aggressive, but rather commanding—organizing. But the screaming . . .

Every hair on my body stood upright as I flung open the door. I might have stayed and cowered, but I'd heard screams like that before, in the forest at home, when I didn't make a clean kill and the animals suffered. I couldn't stand it. And I had to know.

I reached the top of the grand staircase in time to see the front doors of the manor bang open and Tamlin rush in, a screaming faerie slung over his shoulder.

The faerie was almost as big as Tamlin, and yet the High Lord carried him as if he were no more than a sack of grain. Another species of the lesser faeries, with his blue skin, gangly limbs, pointed ears, and long onyx hair. But even from atop the stairs, I could see the blood gushing down the faerie's back—blood from the black stumps protruding from his shoulder blades. Blood that now soaked into Tamlin's green tunic in deep, shining splotches. One of the knives from his baldric was missing.

Lucien rushed into the foyer below just as Tamlin shouted, "The table—clear it off!" Lucien shoved the vase of flowers off the long table in the center of the hall. Either Tamlin wasn't thinking straight, or he'd been afraid to waste the extra minutes bringing the faerie to the infirmary. Shattering glass set my feet moving, and I was halfway down the stairs before Tamlin eased the shrieking faerie face-first onto the table. The faerie wasn't wearing a mask; there was nothing to hide the agony contorting his long, unearthly features.

"Scouts found him dumped just over the borderline," Tamlin explained to Lucien, but his eyes darted to me. They flashed with warning, but I took another step down. He said to Lucien, "He's Summer Court."

"By the Cauldron," Lucien said, surveying the damage.

"My wings," the faerie choked out, his glossy black eyes wide and staring at nothing. "She took my wings."

Again, that nameless *she* who haunted their lives. If she wasn't ruling the Spring Court, then perhaps she ruled another. Tamlin flicked a hand, and steaming water and bandages just *appeared* on the table. My mouth dried up, but I reached the bottom of the stairs and kept walking toward the table and the death that was surely hovering in this hall.

"She took my wings," said the faerie. "She took my wings," he repeated, clutching the edge of the table with spindly blue fingers.

Tamlin murmured a soft, wordless sound—gentle in a way I hadn't heard before—and picked up a rag to dunk in the water. I took up a spot across the table from Tamlin, and the breath whooshed from my chest as I beheld the damage.

Whoever *she* was, she hadn't just taken his wings. She'd ripped them off.

Blood oozed from the black velvety stumps on the faerie's back. The wounds were jagged—cartilage and tissue severed in what looked like uneven cuts. As if she'd sawed off his wings bit by bit.

"She took my wings," the faerie said again, his voice breaking. As he trembled, shock taking over, his skin shimmered with veins of pure gold—iridescent, like a blue butterfly.

"Keep still," Tamlin ordered, wringing the rag. "You'll bleed out faster."

"N-n-no," the faerie started, and began to twist onto his back, away from Tamlin, from the pain that was surely coming when that rag touched those raw stumps.

It was instinct, or mercy, or desperation, perhaps, to grab the faerie's upper arms and shove him down again, pinning him to the table as gently as I could. He thrashed, strong enough that I had to concentrate solely on holding him. His skin was velvet-smooth and slippery, a texture I would never be able to paint, not even if I had eternity to master it. But I pushed against him, gritting my teeth and willing him to stop. I looked to Lucien, but the color had blanched from his face, leaving a sickly white-green in its wake.

"Lucien," Tamlin said—a quiet command. But Lucien kept gaping at the faerie's ruined back, at the stumps, his metal eye narrowing and widening, narrowing and widening. He backed up a step. And another. And then vomited in a potted plant before sprinting from the room.

The faerie twisted again and I held tight, my arms shaking with the effort. His injuries must have weakened him greatly if I could keep him pinned. "Please," I breathed. "Please hold still."

"She took my wings," the faerie sobbed. "She took them."

"I know," I murmured, my fingers aching. "I know."

Tamlin touched the rag to one of the stumps, and the faerie screamed so loudly that my senses guttered, sending me staggering back. He tried to rise but his arms buckled, and he collapsed face-first onto the table again.

Blood gushed—so fast and bright that it took me a heartbeat to realize that a wound like this required a tourniquet—and that the faerie had lost far too much blood for it to even make a difference. It poured down his back and onto the table, where it ran to the edge and *drip-drip-drip*ped to the floor near my feet.

I found Tamlin's eyes on me. "The wounds aren't clotting," he said under his breath as the faerie panted.

"Can't you use your magic?" I asked, wishing I could rip that mask off his face and see his full expression.

Tamlin swallowed hard. "No. Not for major damage. Once, but not any longer."

The faerie on the table whimpered, his panting slowing. "She took my wings," he whispered. Tamlin's green eyes flickered, and I knew, right then, that the faerie was going to die. Death wasn't just hovering in this hall; it was counting down the faerie's remaining heartbeats.

I took one of the faerie's hands in mine. The skin there was almost leathery, and, perhaps more out of reflex than anything, his long fingers wrapped around mine, covering them completely. "She took my wings," he said again, his shaking subsiding a bit.

I brushed the long, damp hair from the faerie's half-turned face, revealing a pointed nose and a mouth full of sharp teeth. His dark eyes shifted to mine, beseeching, pleading.

"It will be all right," I said, and hoped he couldn't smell lies the way the Suriel was able to. I stroked his limp hair, its texture like liquid night—another I would never be able to paint but would try to, perhaps forever.

"It will be all right." The faerie closed his eyes, and I tightened my grip on his hand.

Something wet touched my feet, and I didn't need to look down to see that his blood had pooled around me. "My wings," the faerie whispered.

"You'll get them back."

The faerie struggled to open his eyes. "You swear?"

"Yes," I breathed. The faerie managed a slight smile and closed his eyes again. My mouth trembled. I wished for something else to say, something more to offer him than my empty promises. The first false vow I'd ever sworn. But Tamlin began speaking, and I glanced up to see him take the faerie's other hand.

"Cauldron save you," he said, reciting the words of a prayer that was probably older than the mortal realm. "Mother hold you. Pass through the gates, and smell that immortal land of milk and honey. Fear no evil. Feel no pain." Tamlin's voice wavered, but he finished. "Go, and enter eternity."

The faerie heaved one final sigh, and his hand went limp in mine. I didn't let go, though, and kept stroking his hair, even when Tamlin released him and took a few steps from the table.

I could feel Tamlin's eyes on me, but I wouldn't let go. I didn't know how long it took for a soul to fade from the body. I stood in the puddle of blood until it grew cold, holding the faerie's spindly hand and stroking his hair, wondering if he knew I'd lied when I'd sworn he would get his wings back, wondering if, wherever he had now gone, he *had* gotten them back.

A clock chimed somewhere in the house, and Tamlin gripped my shoulder. I hadn't realized how cold I'd become until the heat of his hand warmed me through my nightgown. "He's gone. Let him go."

I studied the faerie's face—so unearthly, so inhuman. Who could be so cruel to hurt him like that?

"Feyre," Tamlin said, squeezing my shoulder. I brushed the faerie's hair behind his long, pointed ear, wishing I'd known his name, and let go.

Tamlin led me up the stairs, neither of us caring about the bloody footprints I left behind or the freezing blood soaking the front of my nightgown. I paused at the top of the steps, though, twisting out of his grip, and gazed at the table in the foyer below.

"We can't leave him there," I said, making to step down. Tamlin caught my elbow.

"I know," he said, the words so drained and weary. "I was going to walk you upstairs first."

Before he buried him. "I want to go with you."

"It's too deadly at night for you to—"

"I can hold my—"

"No," he said, his green eyes flashing. I straightened, but he sighed, his shoulders curving inward. "I must do this. Alone."

His head was bowed. No claws, no fangs—there was nothing to be done against this enemy, this fate. No one for him to fight. So I nodded, because I would have wanted to do it alone, too, and turned toward my bedroom. Tamlin remained at the top of the stairs.

"Feyre," he said—softly enough that I faced him again. "Why?" He tilted his head to the side. "You dislike our kind on a good day. And after Andras . . ." Even in the darkened hallway, his usually bright eyes were shadowed. "So why?"

I took a step closer to him, my blood-covered feet sticking to the rug. I glanced down the stairs to where I could still see the prone form of the faerie and the stumps of his wings.

"Because I wouldn't want to die alone," I said, and my voice wobbled as I looked at Tamlin again, forcing myself to meet his stare. "Because I'd want someone to hold my hand until the end, and awhile after that. That's something everyone deserves, human or faerie." I swallowed hard, my throat painfully tight. "I regret what I did to Andras," I said, the words so strangled they were no more than a whisper. "I regret that there was . . . such hate in my heart. I wish I could undo it—and . . . I'm sorry. So very sorry."

I couldn't remember the last time—if ever—I'd spoken to anyone like that. But he just nodded and turned away, and I wondered if I should say more, if I should kneel and beg for his forgiveness. If he felt such grief, such guilt, over a stranger, then Andras . . . By the time I opened my mouth, he was already down the steps.

I watched him—watched every movement he made, the muscles of his body visible through that blood-soaked tunic, watched that invisible weight bearing down on his shoulders. He didn't look at me as he scooped up the broken body and carried it to the garden doors beyond my line of sight. I went to the window at the top of the stairs, watching as Tamlin carried the faerie through the moonlit garden and into the rolling fields beyond. He never once glanced back.

CHAPTER 18

The next day, the blood of the faerie had been cleaned up by the time I ate, washed, and dressed. I'd taken my time in the morning, and it was nearly noon as I stood atop the staircase, peering down at the entry hall below. Just to make sure it was gone.

I'd been set on finding Tamlin and explaining—truly explaining—how sorry I was about Andras. If I was supposed to stay here, stay with him, then I could at least attempt to repair what I'd ruined. I glanced to the large window behind me, the view so sweeping that I could see all the way to the reflecting pool beyond the garden.

The water was still enough that the vibrant sky and fat, puffy clouds above were flawlessly reflected. Asking about them seemed vulgar after last night, but maybe—maybe once those paints and brushes *did* arrive, I could venture to the pool to capture it.

I might have remained staring out toward that smear of color and light and texture had Tamlin and Lucien not emerged from another wing of the manor, discussing some border patrol or another. They fell silent as I came down the stairs, and Lucien strode right out the front door without so much as a good morning—just a casual wave. Not a vicious gesture, but he clearly had no intention of joining the conversation that Tamlin and I were about to have.

I glanced around, hoping for any sign of those paints, but Tam pointed to the open front doors through which Lucien had exited. Beyond them, I could see both of our horses, already saddled and waiting. Lucien was already climbing into the saddle of a third horse. I turned to Tamlin.

Stay with him; he will keep me safe, and things will get better. Fine. I could do that.

"Where are we going?" My words were half-mumbled.

"Your supplies won't arrive until tomorrow, and the gallery's being cleaned, and my . . . meeting was postponed." Was he *rambling*? "I thought we'd go for a ride—no killing involved. Or naga to worry about." Even as he finished with a half smile, sorrow flickered in his eyes. Indeed, I'd had enough death in the past two days. Enough of killing faeries. Killing anything. No weapons were sheathed at his side or on his baldric—but a knife hilt glinted at his boot.

Where had he buried that faerie? A High Lord digging a grave for a stranger. I might not have believed it if I'd been told, might not have believed it if he hadn't offered me sanctuary rather than death.

"Where to?" I asked. He only smiled.

I couldn't come up with any words when we arrived—and knew that even if I had been able to paint it, nothing would have done it justice. It wasn't simply that it was the most beautiful place I'd ever been to, or that it filled me with both longing and mirth, but it just seemed . . . *right.* As if the colors and lights and patterns of the world had come together to form one perfect place—one true bit of beauty. After last night, it was exactly where I needed to be.

We sat atop a grassy knoll, overlooking a glade of oaks so wide and high they could have been the pillars and spires of an ancient castle. Shimmering tufts of dandelion fluff drifted by, and the floor of the clearing was carpeted with swaying crocuses and snowdrops and bluebells. It was an hour or two past noon by the time we arrived, but the light was thick and golden.

Though the three of us were alone, I could have sworn I heard singing. I hugged my knees and drank in the glen.

"We brought a blanket," Tamlin said, and I looked over my shoulder to see him jerk his chin to the purple blanket they'd laid out a few feet away. Lucien plopped down onto it and stretched his legs. Tamlin remained standing, waiting for my response.

I shook my head and faced forward, tracing my hand through the feather-soft grass, cataloging its color and texture. I'd never felt grass like it, and I certainly wasn't going to ruin the experience by sitting on a blanket.

Rushed whispers were exchanged behind me, and before I could turn around to investigate, Tamlin took a seat at my side. His jaw was clenched tight enough that I stared ahead. "What is this place?" I said, still running my fingers through the grass.

Out of the corner of my eye, Tamlin was no more than a glittering golden figure. "Just a glen." Behind us, Lucien snorted. "Do you like it?" Tamlin asked quickly. The green of his eyes matched the grass between my fingers, and the amber flecks were like the shafts of sunlight that streamed through the trees. Even his mask, odd and foreign, seemed to fit into the glen—as if this place had been fashioned for him alone. I could picture him here in his beast form, curled up in the grass, dozing.

"What?" I said. I'd forgotten his question.

"Do you like it?" he repeated, and his lips tugged into a smile.

I took an uneven breath and stared at the glen again. "Yes."

He chuckled. "That's it? '*Yes*'?"

"Would you like me to grovel with gratitude for bringing me here, High Lord?"

"Ah. The Suriel told you nothing important, did it?"

That smile of his sparked something bold in my chest. "He also said that you like being brushed, and if I'm a clever girl, I might train you with treats."

Tamlin tipped his head to the sky and roared with laughter. Despite myself, I let out a soft laugh.

"I might die of surprise," Lucien said behind me. "You made a joke, Feyre."

I turned to look at him with a cool smile. "You don't want to know what the Suriel said about *you*." I flicked my brows up, and Lucien lifted his hands in defeat.

"I'd pay good money to hear what the Suriel thinks of Lucien," Tamlin said.

A cork popped, followed by the sounds of Lucien chugging the bottle's contents and chuckling with a muttered "Brushed."

Tamlin's eyes were still bright with laughter as he put a hand at my elbow, pulling me to my feet. "Come on," he said, jerking his head down the hill to the little stream that ran along its base. "I want to show you something."

I got to my feet, but Lucien remained sitting on the blanket and lifted the bottle of wine in salute. He took a slug from it as he sprawled on his back and gazed at the green canopy.

Each of Tamlin's movements was precise and efficient, his powerfully muscled legs eating up the earth as we wove between the towering trees, hopped over tiny brooks, and clambered up steep knolls. We stopped atop a mound, and my hands slackened at my sides. There, in a clearing surrounded by towering trees, lay a sparkling silver pool. Even from a distance, I could tell that it wasn't water, but something more rare and infinitely more precious.

Tamlin grasped my wrist and tugged me down the hill, his callused fingers gently scraping against my skin. He let go of me to leap over the root of the tree in a single maneuver and prowled to the water's edge. I could only grind my teeth as I stumbled after him, heaving myself over the root.

He crouched by the pool and cupped his hand to fill it. He tilted his hand, letting the water fall. "Have a look."

The silvery sparkling water that dribbled from his hand set ripples dancing across the pool, each glimmering with various colors, and—

"That looks like starlight," I breathed.

He huffed a laugh, filling and emptying his hand again. I gaped at the glittering water. "It *is* starlight."

"That's impossible," I said, fighting the urge to take a step toward the water.

"This is Prythian. According to your legends, nothing is impossible."

"How?" I asked, unable to take my eyes from the pool—the silver, but also the blue and red and pink and yellow glinting beneath, the lightness of it . . .

"I don't know—I never asked, and no one ever explained."

When I continued gaping at the pool, he laughed, drawing away my attention—only for me to find him unbuttoning his tunic. "Jump in," he said, the invitation dancing in his eyes.

A swim—unclothed, alone. With a High Lord. I shook my head, falling back a step. His fingers paused at the second button from his collar.

"Don't you want to know what it's like?"

I didn't know what he meant: swimming in starlight, or swimming with him. "I—no."

"All right." He left his tunic unbuttoned. There was only bare, muscled, golden skin beneath.

"Why this place?" I asked, tearing my eyes away from his chest.

"This was my favorite haunt as a boy."

"Which was when?" I couldn't stop the question from coming out.

He cut a glance in my direction. "A very long time ago." He said it so quietly that it made me shift on my feet. A very long time ago indeed, if he'd been a boy during the War.

Well, I'd started down that road, so I ventured to ask, "Is Lucien all right? After last night, I mean." He seemed back to his usual snide, irreverent self, but he'd vomited at the sight of that dying faerie. "He . . . didn't react well."

Tamlin shrugged, but his words were soft as he said, "Lucien . . . Lucien has endured things that make times like last night . . . difficult. Not just the scar and the eye—though I bet last night brought back memories of that, too."

Tamlin rubbed at his neck, then met my stare. Such an ancient heaviness in his eyes, in the set of his jaw. "Lucien is the youngest son of the High Lord of the Autumn Court." I straightened. "The youngest of seven brothers. The Autumn Court is . . . cutthroat. Beautiful, but his brothers see each other only as competition, since the strongest of them will inherit the title, not the eldest. It is the same throughout Prythian, at every court. Lucien never cared about it, never expected to be crowned High Lord, so he spent his youth doing everything a High Lord's son probably shouldn't: wandering the courts, making friends with the sons of other High Lords"—a faint gleam in Tamlin's eyes at that—"and being with females who were a far cry from the nobility of the Autumn Court." Tamlin paused for a moment, and I could almost feel the sorrow before he said, "Lucien fell in love with a faerie whom his father considered to be grossly inappropriate for someone of his bloodline. Lucien said he didn't care that she wasn't one of the High Fae, that he was certain the mating bond would snap into place soon and that he was going to marry her and leave his father's court to his scheming brothers." A tight sigh. "His father had her put down. Executed, in front of Lucien, as his two eldest brothers held him and made him watch."

My stomach turned, and I pushed a hand against my chest. I couldn't imagine, couldn't comprehend that sort of loss.

"Lucien left. He cursed his father, abandoned his title and the Autumn Court, and walked out. And without his title protecting him, his brothers thought to eliminate one more contender to the High Lord's crown. Three of them went out to kill him; one came back."

"Lucien . . . killed them?"

"He killed one," Tamlin said. "I killed the other, as they had crossed into my territory, and I was now High Lord and could do what I wanted with trespassers threatening the peace of my lands." A cold, brutal statement. "I claimed Lucien as my own—named him emissary, since he'd already made many friends across the courts and had always been good at talking to people, while I . . . can find it difficult. He's been here ever since."

"As emissary," I began, "has he ever had dealings with his father? Or his brothers?"

"Yes. His father has never apologized, and his brothers are too frightened of me to risk harming him." No arrogance in those words, just icy truth. "But he has never forgotten what they did to her, or what his brothers tried to do to him. Even if he pretends that he has."

It didn't quite excuse everything Lucien had said and done to me, but . . . I understood now. I could understand the walls and barriers he had no doubt constructed around himself. My chest was too tight, too small to fit the ache building in it. I looked at the pool of glittering starlight and let out a heavy breath. I needed to change the subject. "What would happen if I were to drink the water?"

Tamlin straightened a bit—then relaxed, as if glad to release that old sadness. "Legend claims you'd be happy until your last breath." He added, "Perhaps we both need a glass."

"I don't think that entire pool would be enough for me," I said, and he laughed.

"Two jokes in one day—a miracle sent from the Cauldron," he said.

I cracked a smile. He came a step closer, as if forcibly leaving behind the dark, sad stain of what had happened to Lucien, and the starlight danced in his eyes as he said, "What *would* be enough to make you happy?"

I blushed from my neck to the top of my head. "I—I don't know." It was true—I'd never given that sort of thing any thought beyond getting my sisters safely married off and having enough food for me and my father, and time to learn to paint.

"Hmm," he said, not stepping away. "What about the ringing of bluebells? Or a ribbon of sunshine? Or a garland of moonlight?" He grinned wickedly.

High Lord of Prythian indeed. High Lord of Foolery was more like it. And he knew—he knew I'd say no, that I'd squirm a bit from merely being alone with him.

No. I wouldn't let him have the satisfaction of embarrassing me. I'd had enough of that lately, enough of . . . of that girl encased in ice and bitterness. So I gave him a sweet smile, doing my best to pretend that my stomach wasn't flipping over itself. "A swim sounds delightful."

I didn't allow myself room for second-guessing. And I took no small amount of pride in the fact that my fingers didn't tremble once as I removed my boots, then unbuttoned my tunic and pants and shucked them onto the grass. My undergarments were modest enough that I wasn't showing much, but I still looked straight at him as I stood on the grassy bank. The air was warm and mild, and a soft breeze kissed its way across my bare stomach.

Slowly, so slowly, his eyes roved down, then up. As if he were studying every inch, every curve of me. And even though I wore my ivory underthings, that gaze alone stripped me bare.

His eyes met mine and he gave me a lazy smile before removing his clothes. Button by button. I could have sworn the gleam in his eyes turned hungry and feral—enough so that I had to look anywhere but at his face.

I let myself indulge in the glimpse of a broad chest, arms corded with muscle, and long, strong legs before I walked right into that pool. He wasn't built like Isaac, whose body had very much still been in that gangly place between boy and man. No—Tamlin's glorious body was honed by centuries of fighting and brutality.

The liquid was delightfully warm, and I strode in until it was deep enough to swim out a few strokes and casually tread in place. Not water, but something smoother, thicker. Not oil, but something purer, thinner. Like being wrapped in warm silk. I was so busy savoring the tug of my fingers through the silvery substance that I didn't notice him until he was treading beside me.

"Who taught you to swim?" he asked, and dunked his head under the surface. When he came up, he was grinning, sparkling streams of starlight running along the contours of his mask.

I didn't go under, didn't quite know if he'd been joking about the water making me mirthful if I drank it. "When I was twelve, I watched the village children swimming at a pond and figured it out myself."

It had been one of the most terrifying experiences of my life, and I'd swallowed half the pond in the process, but I'd gotten the gist of it, managed to conquer my blind panic and terror and trust myself. Knowing how to swim had seemed like a vital ability—one that might someday mean the difference between life and death. I'd never expected it would lead to *this*, though.

He went under again, and when he emerged, he ran a hand through his golden hair. "How did your father lose his fortune?"

"How'd you know about that?"

Tamlin snorted. "I don't think born peasants have your kind of diction."

Some part of me wanted to come up with a comment about snobbery, but . . . well, he was right, and I couldn't blame him for being a skilled observer.

"My father was called the Prince of Merchants," I said plainly, treading that silky, strange water. I hardly had to put any effort into it—the water was so warm, so *light*, that it felt as if I were floating in air, every ache in my body oozing away into nothing. "But that title, which he'd inherited from his father, and his father before that, was a lie. We were just a good name that masked three generations of bad debts. My father had been trying to find a way to ease those debts for years, and when he found an opportunity to pay them off, he took it, regardless of the risks." I swallowed. "Eight years ago, he amassed our wealth on three ships to sail to Bharat for invaluable spices and cloth."

Tamlin frowned. "Risky indeed. Those waters are a death trap, unless you go the long way."

"Well, he didn't go the long way. It would have taken too much time, and our creditors were breathing down his neck. So he risked sending the ships directly to Bharat. They never reached Bharat's shores." I tipped my hair back in the water, clearing the memory of my father's face the day that news arrived of the sinking. "When the ships sank, the creditors circled him like wolves. They ripped him apart until there was nothing left of him but a broken name and a few gold pieces to purchase that cottage. I was eleven. My father . . . he just stopped trying after that." I couldn't bring myself to mention that final, ugly moment when that other creditor had come with his cronies to wreck my father's leg.

"That's when you started hunting?"

"No; even though we moved to the cottage, it took almost three years for the money to entirely run out," I said. "I started hunting when I was fourteen."

His eyes twinkled—no trace of the warrior forced to accept a High Lord's burden. "And here you are. What else did you figure out for yourself?"

Maybe it was the enchanted pool, or maybe it was the genuine interest behind the question, but I smiled and told him about those years in the woods.

Tired but surprisingly content from a few hours of swimming and eating and lounging in the glen, I eyed Lucien as we rode back to the manor that afternoon. We were crossing a broad meadow of new spring grass when he caught me glancing at him for the tenth time, and I braced myself as he fell back from Tamlin's side.

The metal eye narrowed on me while the other remained wary, unimpressed. "Yes?"

That was enough to persuade me not to say anything about his past. I would hate pity, too. And he didn't know me—not well enough to warrant anything but resentment if I brought it up, even if it weighed on *me* to know it, to grieve for him.

I waited until Tamlin was far enough ahead that even his High Fae hearing might not pick up on my words. "I never got to thank you for your advice with the Suriel."

Lucien tensed. "Oh?"

I looked ahead at the easy way Tamlin rode, the horse utterly unbothered by his mighty rider. "If you still want me dead," I said, "you might have to try a bit harder."

Lucien loosed a breath. "That's not what I intended." I gave him a long look. "I wouldn't shed any tears," he amended. I knew it was true. "But what happened to you—"

"I was joking," I said, and gave him a little smile.

"You can't possibly forgive me that easily for sending you into danger."

"No. And part of me would like nothing more than to wallop you for your lack of warning about the Suriel. But I understand: I'm a human who killed your friend, who now lives in your house, and you have to deal with me. I understand," I said again.

He was quiet for long enough that I thought he wouldn't reply. Just as I was about to move ahead, he spoke. "Tam told me that your first shot was to save the Suriel's life. Not your own."

"It seemed like the right thing to do."

The look he gave me was more contemplative than any he'd given me before. "I know far too many High Fae and lesser faeries who wouldn't have seen it that way—or bothered." He reached for something at his side and tossed it to me. I had to fight to stay in the saddle as I fumbled for it—a jeweled hunting knife.

"I heard you scream," he said as I examined the blade in my hands. I'd never held one so finely crafted, so perfectly balanced. "And I hesitated. Not long, but I hesitated before I came running. Even though Tam got there in time, I still broke my word in those seconds I waited." He jerked his chin at the knife. "It's yours. Don't bury it in my back, please."

CHAPTER 19

The next morning, my paint and supplies arrived from wherever Tamlin or the servants had dug them up, but before Tamlin let me see them, he brought me down hall after hall until we were in a wing of the house I'd never been to, even in my nocturnal exploring. I knew where we were going without his having to say. The marble floors shone so brightly that they had to have been freshly mopped, and that rose-scented breeze floated in through the opened windows. All this—he'd done this for me. As if I would have cared about cobwebs or dust.

When he paused before a set of wooden doors, the slight smile he gave me was enough to make me blurt, "Why do anything—anything this kind?"

The smile faltered. "It's been a long time since there was anyone here who appreciated these things. I like seeing them used again." Especially when there was such blood and death in every other part of his life.

He opened the gallery doors, and the breath was knocked from me.

The pale wooden floors gleamed in the clean, bright light pouring in from the windows. The room was empty save for a few large chairs and benches for viewing the . . . the . . .

I barely registered moving into the long gallery, one hand absentmindedly wrapping around my throat as I looked up at the paintings.

So many, so different, yet all arranged to flow together seamlessly . . . Such different views and snippets and angles of the world. Pastorals, portraits, still lifes . . . each a story and an experience, each a voice shouting or whispering or singing about what that moment, that feeling, had been like, each a cry into the void of time that they had been here, had existed. Some had been painted through eyes like mine, artists who saw in colors and shapes I understood. Some showcased colors I had not considered; these had a bend to the world that told me a different set of eyes had painted them. A portal into the mind of a creature so unlike me, and yet . . . and yet I looked at its work and understood, and felt, and cared.

"I never knew," Tamlin said from behind me, "that humans were capable of . . ." He trailed off as I turned, the hand I'd put on my throat sliding down to my chest, where my heart roared with a fierce sort of joy and grief and overwhelming humility—humility before that magnificent art.

He stood by the doors, head cocked in that animalistic way, the words still lost on his tongue.

I wiped at my damp cheeks. "It's . . ." *Perfect*, *wonderful*, *beyond my wildest imaginings* didn't cover it. I kept my hand over my heart. "Thank you," I said. It was all I could find to show him what these paintings—to be allowed into this room—meant.

"Come here whenever you want."

I smiled at him, hardly able to contain the brightness in my heart. His returning smile was tentative but shining, and then he left me to admire the gallery at my own leisure.

I stayed for hours—stayed until I was drunk on the art, until I was dizzy with hunger and wandered out to find food.

After lunch, Alis showed me to an empty room on the first floor with a table full of canvases of various sizes, brushes whose wooden handles gleamed in the perfect, clear light, and paints—so, so many paints, beyond the four basic ones I'd hoped for, that the breath was knocked from me again.

And when Alis was gone and the room was quiet and waiting and utterly mine . . .

Then I began to paint.

Weeks passed, the days melting together. I painted and painted, most of it awful and useless.

I never let anyone see it, no matter how much Tamlin prodded and Lucien smirked at my paint-splattered clothes; I never felt satisfied that my work matched the images burning in my mind. Often I painted from dawn until dusk, sometimes in that room, sometimes out in the garden. Occasionally I'd take a break to explore the Spring lands with Tamlin as my guide, coming back with fresh ideas that had me leaping out of bed the next morning to sketch or scribble down the scenes or colors as I'd glimpsed them.

But there were the days when Tamlin was called away to face the latest threat to his borders, and even painting couldn't distract me until he returned, covered in blood that wasn't his own, sometimes in his beast form, sometimes as the High Lord. He never gave me details, and I didn't presume to ask about them; his safe return was enough.

Around the manor itself, there was no sign of creatures like the naga or the Bogge, but I stayed well away from the western woods, even though I painted them often enough from memory. And though my dreams continued to be plagued by the deaths I'd witnessed, the deaths I'd caused, and that horrible pale woman ripping me to shreds—all watched over by a shadow I could never quite glimpse—I slowly stopped being so afraid. *Stay with the High Lord. You will be safe*. So I did.

The Spring Court was a land of rolling green hills and lush forests and clear, bottomless lakes. Magic didn't just abound in the bumps and the hollows—it *grew* there. Try as I might to paint it, I could never capture it—the feel of it. So sometimes I dared to paint the High Lord, who rode at my side when we wandered his grounds on lazy days—the High Lord, whom I was happy to talk to or spend hours in comfortable silence with.

It was probably the lulling of magic that clouded my thoughts, and I didn't think of my family until I passed the outer hedge wall one morning, scouting for a new spot to paint. A breeze from the south ruffled my hair—fresh and warm. Spring was now dawning on the mortal world.

My family, glamoured, cared for, safe, still had no idea where I was. The mortal world . . . it had moved on without me, as if I had never existed. A whisper of a miserable life—gone, unremembered by anyone whom I'd known or cared for.

I didn't paint, nor did I go riding with Tamlin that day. Instead, I sat before a blank canvas, no colors at all in my mind.

No one would remember me back home—I was as good as dead to them. And Tamlin had *let* me forget them. Maybe the paints had even been a distraction—a way to get me to stop complaining, to stop being a pain in his ass about wanting to see my family. Or maybe they were a distraction from whatever was happening with the blight and Prythian. I'd stopped asking, just as the Suriel had ordered—like a stupid, useless, obedient human.

It was an effort of stubborn will to make it through dinner. Tamlin and Lucien noticed my mood and kept conversation between themselves. It didn't do much for my growing rage, and when I had eaten my fill, I stalked into the moonlit garden and lost myself in its labyrinth of hedges and flower beds.

I didn't care where I was going. After a while, I paused in the rose garden. The moonlight stained the red petals a deep purple and cast a silvery sheen on the white blooms.

"My father had this garden planted for my mother," Tamlin said from behind me. I didn't bother to face him. I dug my nails into my palms as he stopped by my side. "It was a mating present."

I stared at the flowers without seeing anything. The flowers I'd painted on the table at home were probably crumbling or gone by now. Nesta might have even scraped them off.

My nails pricked the skin of my palms. Tamlin providing for them or no, glamouring their memories or no, I'd been . . . erased from their lives. Forgotten. I'd let him erase me. He'd offered me paints and the space and time to practice; he'd shown me pools of starlight; he'd saved my life like some kind of feral knight in a legend, and I'd gulped it down like faerie wine. I was no better than those zealot Children of the Blessed.

His mask was bronze in the darkness, and the emeralds glittered. "You seem . . . upset."

I stalked to the nearest rosebush and ripped off a rose, my fingers tearing on the thorns. I ignored the pain, the warmth of the blood that trickled down. I could never paint it accurately—never render it the way those artists had in the gallery pieces. I would never be able to paint Elain's little garden outside the cottage the way I remembered it, even if my family didn't remember me.

He didn't reprimand me for taking one of his parents' roses—parents who were as absent as my own, but who had probably loved each other and loved him better than mine cared for me. A family that would have offered to go in his place if someone had come to steal him away.

My fingers stung and ached, but I still held on to the rose as I said, "I don't know why I feel so tremendously ashamed of myself for leaving them. Why it feels so selfish and horrible to paint. I shouldn't—shouldn't feel that way, should I? I know I shouldn't, but I can't help it." The rose hung limply from my fingers. "All those years, what I did for them . . . And they didn't try to stop you from taking me." There it was, the giant pain that cracked me in two if I thought about it too long. "I don't know why I expected them to—why I believed that the puca's illusion was real that night. I don't know why I bother still thinking about it. Or still caring." He was silent long enough that I added, "Compared to you—to your borders and magic being weakened—I suppose my self-pity is absurd."

"If it grieves you," he said, the words caressing my bones, "then I don't think it's absurd at all."

"Why?" A flat question, and I chucked the rose into the bushes.

He took my hands. His callused fingers, strong and sturdy, were gentle as he lifted my bleeding hand to his mouth and kissed my palm. As if that were answer enough.

His lips were smooth against my skin, his breath warm, and my knees buckled as he lifted my other hand to his mouth and kissed it, too. Kissed it carefully—in a way that made heat begin pounding in my core, between my legs.

When he withdrew, my blood shone on his mouth. I glanced at my hands, which he still held, and found the wounds gone. I looked at his face again, at his gilded mask, the tanness of his skin, the red of his blood-covered lips as he murmured, "Don't feel bad for one moment about doing what brings you joy." He stepped closer, releasing one of my hands to tuck the rose I'd plucked behind my ear. I didn't know how it had gotten into his hand, or where the thorns had gone.

I couldn't stop myself from pushing. "Why—why do any of this?"

He leaned in closer, so close that I had to tip my head back to see him. "Because your human joy fascinates me—the way you experience things, in your life span, so wildly and deeply and all at once, is . . . entrancing. I'm drawn to it, even when I know I shouldn't be, even when I try not to be."

Because I was human, and I would grow old and—I didn't let myself get that far as he came closer still. Slowly, as if giving me time to pull away, he brushed his lips against my cheek. Soft and warm and heartbreakingly gentle. It was hardly more than a caress before he straightened. I hadn't moved from the moment his mouth had met my skin.

"One day—one day there will be answers for everything," he said, releasing my hand and stepping away. "But not until the time is right. Until it's safe." In the dark, his tone was enough to know that his eyes were flecked with bitterness.

He left me, and I took a gasping breath, not realizing I'd been holding it.

Not realizing that I craved his warmth, his nearness, until he was gone.

✥

Lingering mortification over what I'd admitted, what had . . . *changed* between us had me skulking out of the manor after breakfast, fleeing for the sanctuary of the woods for some fresh air—and to study the light and colors. I brought my bow and arrows, along with the jeweled hunting knife that Lucien had given me. Better to be armed than caught empty-handed.

I crept through the trees and brush for no more than an hour before I felt a presence behind me—coming ever closer, sending the animals running for cover. I smiled to myself, and twenty minutes later, I settled in the crook of a towering elm and waited.

Brush rustled—hardly more than a breeze's passing, but I knew what to expect, knew the signs.

A snap and roar of fury echoed across the lands, scattering the birds.

When I climbed out of the tree and walked into the little clearing, I merely crossed my arms and looked up at the High Lord, dangling by his legs from the snare I'd laid.

Even upside down, he smiled lazily at me as I approached. "Cruel human."

"That's what you get for stalking someone."

He chuckled, and I came close enough to dare stroke a finger along the silken golden hair dangling just above my face, admiring the many colors within it—the hues of yellow and brown and wheat. My heart thundered, and I knew he could probably hear it. But he leaned his head toward me, a silent invitation, and I ran my fingers through his hair—gently, carefully. He purred, the sound rumbling through my fingers, arms, legs, and core. I wondered how that sound would feel if he were fully pressed up against me, skin-to-skin. I stepped back.

He curled upward in a smooth, powerful motion and swiped with a single claw at the creeping vine I'd used for rope. I took a breath to shout, but he flipped as he fell, landing smoothly on his feet. It would be impossible for me to ever forget what he was, and what he was capable of. He took a step closer to me, the laughter still dancing on his face. "Feeling better today?"

I mumbled some noncommittal response.

"Good," he said, either ignoring or hiding his amusement. "But just in case, I wanted to give you this," he added, pulling some papers from his tunic and extending them to me.

I bit the inside of my cheek as I stared down at the three pieces of paper. It was a series of five-lined . . . *poems*. There were five of them altogether, and I began sweating at words I didn't recognize. It would take me an entire day just to figure out what these words meant.

"Before you bolt or start yelling . . . ," he said, coming around to peer over my shoulder. If I'd dared, I could have leaned back into his chest. His breath warmed my neck, the shell of my ear.

He cleared his throat and read the first poem.

There once was a lady most beautiful
Spirited, if a little unusual
Her friends were few
But how the men did queue
But to all she gave a refusal.

My brows rose so high I thought they'd touch my hairline, and I turned, blinking at him, our breath mingling as he finished the poem with a smile.

Without waiting for my response, Tamlin took the papers and stepped a pace away to read the second poem, which wasn't nearly as polite as the first. By the time he read the third poem, my face was burning. Tamlin paused before he read the fourth, then handed me back the papers.

"Final word in the second and fourth line of each poem," he said, jerking his chin toward the papers in my hands.

Unusual. Queue. I looked at the second poem. *Slaying. Conflagration.*

"These are—" I started.

"Your list of words was too interesting to pass up. And not good for love poems at all." When I lifted my brow in silent inquiry, he said, "We had contests to see who could write the dirtiest limericks while I was living with my father's war-band by the border. I don't particularly enjoy losing, so I took it upon myself to become good at them."

I didn't know how he'd remembered that long list I'd compiled—I didn't want to. Sensing I wasn't about to draw an arrow and shoot him, Tamlin took the papers and read the fifth poem, the dirtiest and foulest of them all.

When he finished, I tipped back my head and howled, my laughter like sunshine shattering age-hardened ice.

I was still smiling when we walked out of the park and toward the rolling hills, meandering back to the manor. "You said—that night in the rose garden . . ." I sucked on my teeth for a moment. "You said that your father had it planted for your parents upon their mating—not wedding?"

"High Fae mostly marry," he said, his golden skin flushing a bit. "But if they're blessed, they'll find their mate—their equal, their match in every way. High Fae wed without the mating bond, but if you find your mate, the bond is so deep that marriage is . . . insignificant in comparison."

I didn't have the nerve to ask if faeries had ever had mating bonds with humans, but instead dared to say, "Where are your parents? What happened to them?"

A muscle feathered in his jaw, and I regretted the question, if only for the pain that flickered in his eyes. "My father . . ." His claws gleamed at his knuckles but didn't go out any farther. I'd definitely asked the wrong question. "My father was as bad as Lucien's. Worse. My two older brothers were just like him. They kept slaves—all of them. And my brothers . . . I was young when the Treaty was forged, but I still remember what my brothers used to . . ." He trailed off. "It left a mark—enough of a mark that when I saw you, your house, I couldn't—wouldn't let myself be like them. Wouldn't bring harm to your family, or you, or subject you to faerie whims."

Slaves—there had been slaves *here*. I didn't want to know—had never looked for traces of them, even five hundred years later. I was still little better than chattel to most of his people, his world. That was why—why he'd offered the loophole, why he'd offered me the freedom to live wherever I wished in Prythian.

"Thank you," I said. He shrugged, as if that would dismiss his kindness, the weight of the guilt that still bore down on him. "What about your mother?"

Tamlin loosed a breath. "My mother—she loved my father deeply. Too deeply, but they were mated, and . . . Even if she saw what a tyrant he was, she wouldn't say an ill word against him. I never expected—never wanted—my father's title. My brothers would have never let me live to adolescence if they had suspected that I did. So the moment I was old enough, I joined my father's war-band and trained so that I might someday serve my father, or whichever of my brothers inherited his title." He flexed his hands, as if imagining the claws beneath. "I'd realized from an early age that fighting and killing were about the only things I was good at."

"I doubt that," I said.

He gave me a wry smile. "Oh, I can play a mean fiddle, but High Lords' sons don't become traveling minstrels. So I trained and fought for my father against whomever he told me to fight, and I would have been happy to leave the scheming to my brothers. But my power kept growing, and I couldn't hide it—not among our kind." He shook his head. "Fortunately or unfortunately, they were all killed by the High Lord of an enemy court. I was spared for whatever reason or Cauldron-granted luck. My mother, I mourned. The others . . ." A too-tight shrug. "My brothers would not have tried to save me from a fate like yours."

I looked up at him. Such a brutal, harsh world—with families killing each other for power, for revenge, for spite and control. Perhaps his generosity, his kindness, was a reaction to that—perhaps he'd seen me and found it to be like gazing into a mirror of sorts. "I'm sorry about your mother," I said, and it was all I could offer—all he'd once been able to offer me. He gave me a small smile. "So that's how you became High Lord."

"Most High Lords are trained from birth in manners and laws and court warfare. When the title fell to me, it was a . . . rough transition. Many of my father's courtiers defected to other courts rather than have a warrior-beast snarling at them."

A half-wild beast, Nesta had once called me. It was an effort to not take his hand, to not reach out to him and tell him that I understood. But I just said, "Then they're idiots. You've kept these lands protected from the blight, when it seems that others haven't fared so well. They're idiots," I said again.

But darkness flickered in Tamlin's eyes, and his shoulders seemed to curve inward ever so slightly. Before I could ask about it, we cleared the little wood, a spread of hills and knolls laid out ahead. In the distance, there were masked faeries atop many of them, building what seemed to be unlit fires. "What are those?" I asked, halting.

"They're setting up bonfires—for *Calanmai*. It's in two days."

"For what?"

"Fire Night?"

I shook my head. "We don't celebrate holidays in the human realm. Not after you—your people left. In some places, it's forbidden. We don't even remember the names of your gods. What does Cala—Fire Night celebrate?"

He rubbed his neck. "It's just a spring ceremony. We light bonfires, and . . . the magic that we create helps regenerate the land for the year ahead."

"How do you create the magic?"

"There's a ritual. But it's . . . very faerie." He clenched his jaw and continued walking, away from the unlit fires. "You might see more faeries around than usual—faeries from this court, and from other territories, who are free to wander across the borders that night."

"I thought the blight had scared many of them away."

"It has—but there will be a number of them. Just . . . stay away from them all. You'll be safe in the house, but if you run into one before we light the fires at sundown in two days, ignore them."

"And I'm not invited to your ceremony?"

"No. You're not." He clenched and loosened his fingers, again and again, as if trying to keep the claws contained.

Though I tried to ignore it, my chest caved a bit.

We walked back in the sort of tense silence we hadn't endured in weeks.

Tamlin went rigid the moment we entered the gardens. Not from me or our awkward conversation—it was quiet with that horrible stillness that usually meant one of the nastier faeries was around. Tamlin bared his teeth in a low snarl. "Stay hidden, and no matter what you overhear, don't come out."

Then he was gone.

Alone, I looked to either side of the gravel path, like some gawking idiot. If there was indeed something here, I'd be caught in the open. Perhaps it was shameful not to go to his aid, but—he was a High Lord. I would just get in the way.

I had just ducked behind a hedge when I heard Tamlin and Lucien approaching. I silently swore and froze. Maybe I could sneak across the fields to the stables. If there was something amiss, the stables not only had shelter but also a horse for me to flee on. I was about to make for the high grasses mere steps beyond the edge of the gardens when Tamlin's snarl rippled through the air on the other side of the hedge.

I turned—just enough to spy them through the dense leaves. *Stay hidden*, he'd said. If I moved now, I would surely be noticed.

"I know what day it is," Tamlin said—but not to Lucien. Rather, the two of them faced . . . nothing. Someone who wasn't *there*. Someone invisible. I would have thought they were playing a prank on me had I not heard a low, disembodied voice reply.

"Your continued behavior is garnering a lot of interest at court," the voice said, deep and sibilant. I shivered, despite the warmth of the day. "She has begun wondering—wondering why you haven't given up yet. And why four naga wound up dead not too long ago."

"Tamlin's not like the other fools," Lucien snapped, his shoulders pushed back to raise himself to his full height, more warrior-like than I'd yet seen him. No wonder he had all those weapons in his room. "If she expected bowed heads, then she's more of an idiot than I thought."

The voice hissed, and my blood went cold at the noise. "Speak you so ill of she who holds your fate in her hands? With one word, she could destroy this pathetic estate. She wasn't pleased when she heard of you dispatching your warriors." The voice now seemed turned toward Tamlin. "But, as nothing has come of it, she has chosen to ignore it."

There was a deep-throated growl from the High Lord, but his words were calm as he said, "Tell her I'm getting sick of cleaning up the trash she dumps on my borders."

The voice chuckled, the sound like sand shifting. "She sets them loose as gifts—and reminders of what will happen if she catches you trying to break the terms of—"

"He's not," Lucien snarled. "Now, *get out*. We have enough of your ilk swarming on the borders—we don't need you defiling our home, too. For that matter, stay the hell out of the cave. It's not some common road for filth like you to travel through as they please."

Tamlin loosed a growl of agreement.

The invisible thing laughed again, such a horrible, vicious sound. "Though you have a heart of stone, Tamlin," it said, and Tamlin went rigid, "you certainly keep a host of fear inside it." The voice sank into a croon. "Don't worry, *High Lord*." It spat the title like a joke. "All will be right as rain soon enough."

"Burn in Hell," Lucien replied for Tamlin, and the thing laughed again before a flap of leathery wings boomed, a foul wind bit my face, and everything went silent.

They breathed deeply after another moment. I closed my eyes, needing a steadying breath as well, but massive hands clamped onto my shoulders, and I yelped.

"It's gone," Tamlin said, releasing me. It was all I could do not to sag against the hedges.

"What did you hear?" Lucien demanded, coming around the corner and crossing his arms. I shifted my gaze to Tamlin's face, but found it to be so white with anger—anger at that *thing*—that I had to look again at Lucien.

"Nothing—I . . . well, nothing I understood," I said, and meant it. None of it made any sense. I couldn't stop shaking. Something about that voice had ripped away the warmth from me. "Who—*what* was that?"

Tamlin began pacing, the gravel churning beneath his boots.

"There are certain faeries in Prythian who inspired the legends that you humans are so afraid of. Some, like that one, are myth given flesh."

Inside that hissing voice I'd heard the screaming of human victims, the pleading of young maidens whose chests had been split open on sacrificial altars. Mentions of "court," seemingly different from Tamlin's own—was that *she* the one who had killed Tamlin's parents? A High Lady, perhaps, in lieu of a Lord. Considering how ruthless the High Fae were to their families, they had to be nightmarish to their enemies. And if there was to be warring between the courts, if the blight had left Tamlin already weakened . . .

"If the Attor saw her—" Lucien said, glancing around.

"It didn't," Tamlin said.

"Are you certain it—"

"*It didn't*," Tamlin growled over his shoulder, then looked at me, his face still pale with fury, lips tight. "I'll see you at dinner."

Understanding a dismissal, and craving the locked door of my bedroom, I trudged back to the house, contemplating who this *she* was to make Tamlin and Lucien so nervous and to command that *thing* as her messenger.

The spring breeze whispered that I didn't want to know.

CHAPTER 20

After a tense dinner during which Tamlin hardly spoke to Lucien or me, I lit all the candles in my room to chase away the shadows.

I didn't go outside the following day, and when I sat down to paint, what emerged on my canvas was a tall, skeletally thin gray creature with bat ears and giant, membranous wings. Its snout was open in a roar, revealing row after row of fangs as it leaped into flight. As I painted it, I could have sworn that I could smell breath that reeked of carrion, that the air beneath its wings whispered promises of death.

The finished product was chilling enough that I had to set aside the painting in the back of the room and go try to persuade Alis to let me help with the Fire Night food preparations in the kitchen. Anything to avoid going into the garden, where the Attor might appear.

The day of Fire Night—*Calanmai*, Tamlin had called it—dawned, and I didn't see Tamlin or Lucien all day. As the afternoon shifted into dusk, I found myself again at the main crossroads of the house. None of the bird-faced servants were to be found. The kitchen was empty of staff and the food they'd been preparing for two days. The sound of drums issued.

The drumbeats came from far away—beyond the garden, past the game park, into the forest that lay beyond. They were deep, probing. A single beat, echoed by two responding calls. Summoning.

I stood by the doors to the garden, staring out over the property as the sky became awash in hues of orange and red. In the distance, upon the sloping hills that led into the woods, a few fires flickered, plumes of dark smoke marring the ruby sky—the unlit bonfires I'd spotted two days ago. Not invited, I reminded myself. Not invited to whatever party had all the kitchen faeries tittering and laughing among one another.

The drums turned faster—louder. Though I'd grown accustomed to the smell of magic, my nose pricked with the rising tang of metal, stronger than I'd yet sensed it. I took a step forward, then halted on the threshold. I should go back in. Behind me, the setting sun stained the black-and-white tiles of the hall floor a shimmering shade of tangerine, and my long shadow seemed to pulse to the beat of the drums.

Even the garden, usually buzzing with the orchestra of its denizens, had quieted to hear the drums. There was a string—a string tied to my gut that pulled me toward those hills, commanding me to go, to hear the faerie drums . . .

I might have done just that had Tamlin not appeared from down the hall.

He was shirtless, with only the baldric across his muscled chest. The pommel of his sword glinted golden in the dying sunlight, and the feathered tops of arrows were stained red as they poked above his broad shoulder. I stared at him, and he watched me back. The warrior incarnate.

"Where are you going?" I managed to get out.

"It's *Calanmai*," he said flatly. "I have to go." He jerked his chin to the fires and drums.

"To do what?" I asked, glancing at the bow in his hand. My heart echoed the drums outside, building into a wilder beat.

His green eyes were shadowed beneath the gilded mask. "As a High Lord, I have to partake in the Great Rite."

"What's the Great—"

"Go to your chamber," he snarled, and glanced toward the fires. "Lock your doors, set up a snare, whatever you do."

"Why?" I demanded. The Attor's voice snaked through my memory. Tamlin had said something about a very faerie ritual—what the hell was it? From the weapons, it had to be brutal and violent—especially if Tamlin's beast form wasn't weapon enough.

"Just do it." His canines began to lengthen. My heart leaped into a gallop. "Don't come out until morning."

Stronger, faster, the drums beat, and the muscles in Tamlin's neck quivered, as if standing still were somehow painful to him.

"Are you going into battle?" I whispered, and he let out a breathy laugh.

He lifted a hand as if to touch my arm. But he lowered it before his fingers could graze the fabric of my tunic. "Stay in your chamber, Feyre."

"But I—"

"Please." Before I could ask him to reconsider bringing me along, he took off running. The muscles in his back shifted as he leaped down the short flight of stairs and bounded into the garden, as spry and swift as a stag. Within seconds he was gone.

I did as he commanded, though I soon realized that I'd locked myself in my room without having eaten dinner. And with the incessant drumming and dozens of bonfires that popped up along the far hills, I couldn't stop pacing up and down my room, gazing out toward the fires burning in the distance.

Stay in your chamber.

But a wild, wicked voice weaving in between the drumbeats whispered otherwise. *Go*, that voice said, tugging at me. *Go see.*

By ten o'clock, I could no longer stand it. I followed the drums.

The stables were empty, but Tamlin had taught me how to ride bareback these past few weeks, and my white mare was soon trotting along. I didn't need to guide her—she, too, followed the lure of the drums, and ascended the first of the foothills.

Smoke and magic hung thick in the air. Concealed in my hooded cloak, I gaped as I approached the first giant bonfire atop the hill. There were hundreds of High Fae milling about, but I couldn't discern any of their features beyond the various masks they wore. Where had they come from—where did they live, if they belonged to the Spring Court but did not dwell in the manor? When I tried to focus on a specific feature of their faces, it became a blur of color. They were more solid when I viewed them from the side of my vision, but if I turned to face them, I was met with shadows and swirling colors.

It was magic—some kind of glamour put on *me*, meant to prevent my viewing them properly, just as my family had been glamoured. I would have been furious, would have considered going back to the manor had the drums not echoed through my bones and that wild voice not beckoned to me.

I dismounted my mare but kept close to her as I made my way through the crowd, my telltale human features hidden in the shadows of my hood. I prayed that the smoke and countless scents of various High Fae and faeries were enough to cover my human smell, but I checked to ensure that my two knives were still at my sides anyway as I moved deeper into the celebration.

Though a cluster of drummers played on one side of the fire, the faeries flocked to a trench between two nearby hills. I left my horse tied to a solitary sycamore crowning a knoll and followed them, savoring the pulsing beat of the drums as it resonated through the earth and into the soles of my feet. No one looked twice in my direction.

I almost slid down the steep bank as I entered the hollow. At one end, a cave mouth opened into a soft hillside. Its exterior had been adorned with flowers and branches and leaves, and I could make out the beginnings of a pelt-covered floor just past the cave mouth. What lay inside was hidden from view as the chamber veered away from the entrance, but firelight danced upon the walls.

Whatever was occurring inside the cave—or whatever was about to happen—was the focus of the shadowy faeries as they lined either side of a long path leading to it. The path wended between the trenches among the hills, and the High Fae swayed in place, moving to the rhythm of the drumming, whose beats sounded in my stomach.

I watched them sway, then shifted on my feet. I'd been banned from *this*? I scanned the firelit area, trying to peer through the veil of night and smoke. I found nothing of interest, and none of the masked faeries paid me any heed. They remained along the path, more and more of them coming each minute. Something was definitely going to happen—whatever this Great Rite was.

I made my way back up the hillside and stood along the edge of a bonfire near the trees, watching the faeries. I was about to work up the courage to ask a lesser faerie who passed by—a bird-masked servant, like Alis—what sort of ritual was going to happen when someone grasped my arm and whirled me around.

I blinked at the three strangers, dumbfounded as I beheld their sharp-featured faces—free of masks. They looked like High Fae, but there was something slightly different about them, something taller and leaner than Tamlin or Lucien—something crueler in their pitch-black, depthless eyes. Faeries, then.

The one grasping my arm smiled down at me, revealing slightly pointed teeth. "Human woman," he murmured, running an eye over me. "We've not seen one of you for a while."

I tried yanking my arm back, but he held my elbow firm. "What do you want?" I demanded, keeping my voice steady and cold.

The two faeries who flanked him smiled at me, and one grabbed my other arm—just as I went for my knife. "Just some Fire Night fun," one of them said, reaching out a pale, too-long hand to brush back a lock of my hair. I twisted my head away and tried to step out of his touch, but he held firm. None of the faeries near the bonfire reacted—no one bothered to look.

If I cried for help, would someone answer? Would Tamlin answer? I couldn't be that lucky again; I'd probably used up my allotted portion of luck with the naga.

I yanked my arms in earnest. Their grip tightened until it hurt, and they kept my hands well away from my knives. The three of them stepped closer, sealing me off from the others. I glanced around, looking for any ally. There were more nonmasked faeries here now. The three faeries chuckled, a low hissing noise that ran along my body. I hadn't realized how far I stood from everyone else—how close I'd come to the forest's edge. "Leave me alone," I said, louder and angrier than I'd expected, given the shaking that was starting in my knees.

"Bold statement from a human on *Calanmai*," said the one holding my left arm. The fires didn't reflect in his eyes. It was as if they gobbled up the light. I thought of the naga, whose horrible exteriors matched their rotten hearts. Somehow, these beautiful, ethereal faeries were far worse. "Once the Rite's performed, we'll have some fun, won't we? A treat—such a treat—to find a human woman here."

I bared my teeth at him. "Get your hands off me," I said, loud enough for anyone to hear.

One of them ran a hand down my side, its bony fingers digging into my ribs, my hips. I jerked back, only to slam into the third one, who wove his long fingers through my hair and pressed close. No one looked; no one noticed.

"Stop it," I said, but the words came out in a strangled gasp as they began herding me toward the line of trees, toward the darkness. I pushed and thrashed against them; they only hissed. One of them shoved me and I staggered, falling out of their grasp. The ground welled up beneath me, and I reached for my knives, but sturdy hands grasped me under the shoulders before I could draw them or hit the grass.

They were strong hands—warm and broad. Not at all like the prodding, bony fingers of the three faeries who went utterly still as whoever caught me gently set me upright.

"There you are. I've been looking for you," said a deep, sensual male voice I'd never heard. But I kept my eyes on the three faeries, bracing myself for flight as the male behind me stepped to my side and slipped a casual arm around my shoulders.

The three lesser faeries paled, their dark eyes wide.

"Thank you for finding her for me," my savior said to them, smooth and polished. "Enjoy the Rite." There was enough of a bite beneath his last words that the faeries stiffened. Without further comment, they scuttled back to the bonfires.

I stepped out of the shelter of my savior's arm and turned to thank him.

Standing before me was the most beautiful man I'd ever seen.

CHAPTER 21

Everything about the stranger radiated sensual grace and ease. High Fae, no doubt. His short black hair gleamed like a raven's feathers, offsetting his pale skin and blue eyes so deep they were violet, even in the firelight. They twinkled with amusement as he beheld me.

For a moment, we said nothing. *Thank you* didn't seem to cover what he'd done for me, but something about the way he stood with absolute stillness, the night seeming to press in closer around him, made me hesitate to speak—made me want to run in the other direction.

He, too, wasn't wearing a mask. From another court, then.

A half smile played on his lips. "What's a mortal woman doing here on Fire Night?" His voice was a lover's purr that sent shivers through me, caressing every muscle and bone and nerve.

I took a step back. "My friends brought me."

The drumming was increasing in tempo, building to a climax I didn't understand. It had been so long since I'd seen a bare face that looked even vaguely human. His clothes—all black, all finely made—were cut close enough to his body that I could see how magnificent he was. As if he'd been molded from the night itself.

"And who are your friends?" He was still smiling at me—a predator sizing up prey.

"Two ladies," I lied again.

"Their names?" He prowled closer, slipping his hands into his pockets. I retreated a little more and kept my mouth shut. Had I just traded three monsters for something far worse?

When it became apparent I wouldn't answer, he chuckled. "You're welcome," he said. "For saving you."

I bristled at his arrogance but retreated another step. I was close enough to the bonfire, to that little hollow where the faeries were all gathered, that I could make it if I sprinted. Maybe someone would take pity on me—maybe Lucien or Alis were there.

"Strange for a mortal to be friends with two faeries," he mused, and began circling me. I could have sworn tendrils of star-kissed night trailed in his wake. "Aren't humans usually terrified of us? And aren't you, for that matter, supposed to keep to your side of the wall?"

I was terrified of *him*, but I wasn't about to let him know. "I've known them my whole life. I've never had anything to fear from them."

He paused his circling. He now stood between me and the bonfire—and my escape route. "And yet they brought you to the Great Rite and abandoned you."

"They went to get refreshments," I said, and his smile grew. Whatever I'd just said had given me away. I'd spotted the servants hauling off the food, but—maybe it wasn't here.

He smiled for a heartbeat longer. I had never seen anyone so handsome—and never had so many warning bells pealed in my head because of it.

"I'm afraid the refreshments are a long way off," he said, coming closer now. "It might be a while before they return. May I escort you somewhere in the meantime?" He removed a hand from his pocket to offer his arm.

He'd been able to scare off those faeries without lifting a finger. "No," I said, my tongue thick and heavy.

He waved his hand toward the hollow—toward the drums. "Enjoy the Rite, then. Try to stay out of trouble." His eyes gleamed in a way that suggested staying out of trouble meant staying far, far away from him.

Though it might have been the biggest risk I'd ever taken, I blurted, "So you're not a part of the Spring Court?"

He returned to me, every movement exquisite and laced with lethal power, but I held my ground as he gave me a lazy smile. "Do I look like I'm part of the Spring Court?" The words were tinged with an arrogance that only an immortal could achieve. He laughed under his breath. "No, I'm not a part of the noble Spring Court. And glad of it." He gestured to his face, where a mask might go.

I should have walked away, should have shut my mouth. "Why are you here, then?"

The man's remarkable eyes seemed to glow—with enough of a deadly edge that I backed up a step. "Because all the monsters have been let out of their cages tonight, no matter what court they belong to. So I may roam wherever I wish until the dawn."

More riddles and questions to be answered. But I'd had enough—especially as his smile turned cold and cruel. "Enjoy the Rite," I repeated as blandly as I could.

I hurried back to the hollow, too aware of the fact that I was putting my back to him. I was grateful to lose myself in the crowd milling along the path to the cave, still waiting for some moment to occur.

When I stopped shaking, I looked around at the gathered faeries. Most of them still wore masks, but there were some, like that lethal stranger and those three horrible faeries, who wore no masks at all—either faeries with no allegiance or members of other courts. I couldn't tell them apart. As I scanned the crowd, my eyes met with those of a masked faerie across the path. One was russet and shone as brightly as his red hair. The other was—metal. I blinked at the same moment he did, and then his eyes went wide. He vanished into nothing, and a second later, someone grabbed my elbow and yanked me out of the crowd.

"Have you lost your senses?" Lucien shouted above the drums. His face was ghostly pale. "What are you doing here?"

None of the faeries noticed us—they were all staring intensely down the path, away from the cave. "I wanted to—" I started, but Lucien cursed violently.

"Idiot!" he yelled at me, then glanced behind him toward where the other faeries stared. "Useless human fool." Without further word, he slung me over his shoulder as if I were a sack of potatoes.

Despite my wriggling and shouts of protest, despite my demands that he get my horse, he held firm, and when I looked up, I found that he was running—fast. Faster than anything should be able to move. It made me so nauseated that I shut my eyes. He didn't stop until the air was cooler and calmer, and the drumming was distant.

Lucien dropped me on the floor of the manor hallway, and when I steadied myself, I found his face just as pale as before. "You stupid mortal," he snapped. "Didn't he tell you to stay in your room?" Lucien looked over his shoulder, toward the hills, where the drumming became so loud and fast that it was like a rainstorm.

"That was hardly anything—"

"That wasn't even the ceremony!" It was only then that I saw the sweat on his face and the panicked gleam in his eyes. "By the Cauldron, if Tam found you there . . ."

"So what?" I said, shouting as well. I hated feeling like a disobedient child.

"It's the *Great Rite*, Cauldron boil me! Didn't anyone tell you what it is?" My silence was answer enough. I could almost see the drumbeats pulsing against his skin, beckoning him to rejoin the crowd. "Fire Night signals the official start of spring—in Prythian, as well as in the mortal world," Lucien said. While his words were calm, they trembled slightly. I leaned against the wall of the hallway, forcing myself into a casualness I didn't feel. "Here, our crops depend upon the magic we regenerate on *Calanmai*—tonight."

I stuffed my hands into the pockets of my pants. Tamlin had said something similar two days ago. Lucien shuddered, as if shaking off an invisible touch. "We do this by conducting the Great Rite. Each of the seven High Lords of Prythian performs this every year, since their magic comes from the earth and returns to it at the end—it's a give-and-take."

"But what is it?" I asked, and he clicked his tongue.

"Tonight, Tam will allow . . . great and terrible magic to enter his body," Lucien said, staring at the distant fires. "The magic will seize control of his mind, his body, his soul, and turn him into the Hunter. It will fill him with his sole purpose: to find the Maiden. From their coupling, magic will be released and spread to the earth, where it will regenerate life for the year to come."

My face became hot, and I fought the urge to fidget.

"Tonight, Tam won't be the faerie you know," Lucien said. "He won't even know his name. The magic will consume everything in him but that one basic command—and need."

"Who . . . who's the Maiden?" I got out.

Lucien snorted. "No one knows until it's time. After Tam hunts down the white stag and kills it for the sacrificial offering, he'll make his way to that sacred cave, where he'll find the path lined with faerie females waiting to be chosen as his mate for tonight."

"What?"

Lucien laughed. "Yes—all those female faeries around you were females for Tamlin to pick. It's an honor to be chosen, but it's his instincts that select her."

"But you were there—and other male faeries." My face burned so hot that I began sweating. That was why those three horrible faeries had been there—and they'd thought that just by my presence, I was happy to comply with their plans.

"Ah." Lucien chuckled. "Well, Tam's not the only one who gets to perform the rite tonight. Once he makes his choice, we're free to mingle. Though it's not the Great Rite, our own dalliances tonight will help the land, too." He shrugged off that invisible hand a second time, and his eyes fell upon the hills. "You're lucky I found you when I did, though," he said. "Because he would have smelled you, and claimed you, but it wouldn't have been Tamlin who brought you into that cave." His eyes met mine, and a chill went over me. "And I don't think you would have liked it. Tonight is not for lovemaking."

I swallowed my nausea.

"I should go," Lucien said, gazing at the hills. "I need to return before he arrives at the cave—at least to *try* to control him when he smells you and can't find you in the crowd."

It made me sick—the thought of Tamlin forcing me, that magic could strip away any sense of self, of right or wrong. But hearing that . . . that some feral part of him *wanted* me . . . My breath was painful.

"Stay in your room tonight, Feyre," Lucien said, walking to the garden doors. "No matter who comes knocking, keep the door locked. Don't come out until morning."

+

At some point, I dozed off while sitting at my vanity. I awoke the moment the drums stopped. A shuddering silence went through the house, and the hair on my arms arose as magic swept past me, rippling outward.

Though I tried not to, I thought about the probable source and blushed, even as my chest tightened. I glanced at the clock. It was past two in the morning.

Well, he'd certainly taken his time with the ritual, which meant the girl was probably beautiful and charming, and appealed to his *instincts*.

I wondered whether she was glad to be chosen. Probably. She'd come to the hill of her own free will. And after all, Tamlin was a High Lord, and it was a great honor. And I supposed Tamlin was handsome. Terribly handsome. Even though I couldn't see the upper part of his face, his eyes were fine, and his mouth beautifully curved and full. And then there was his body, which was . . . was . . . I hissed and stood.

I stared at my door, at the snare I'd rigged. How utterly absurd—as if bits of rope and wood could protect me from the demons in this land.

Needing to do something with my hands, I carefully disassembled the snare. Then I unlocked the door and strode into the hallway. What a ridiculous holiday. Absurd. It was good that humans had cast them aside.

I made it to the empty kitchen, gobbled down half a loaf of bread, an apple, and a lemon tart. I nibbled on a chocolate cookie as I walked to my little painting room. I needed to get some of the furious images out of my mind, even if I had to paint by candlelight.

I was about to turn down the hallway when a tall male figure appeared before me. The moonlight from the open window turned his mask silver, and his golden hair—unbound and crowned with laurel leaves—gleamed.

"Going somewhere?" Tamlin asked. His voice was not entirely of this world.

I suppressed a shudder. "Midnight snack," I said, and I was keenly aware of every movement, every breath I took as I neared him.

His bare chest was painted with whorls of dark blue woad, and from the smudges in the paint, I knew exactly where he'd been touched. I tried not to notice that they descended past his muscled midriff.

I was about to pass him when he grabbed me, so fast that I didn't see anything until he had me pinned against the wall. The cookie dropped from my hand as he grasped my wrists. "I smelled you," he breathed, his painted chest rising and falling so close to mine. "I searched for you, and you weren't there."

He reeked of magic. When I looked into his eyes, remnants of power flickered there. No kindness, none of the wry humor and gentle reprimands. The Tamlin I knew was gone.

"Let go," I said as evenly as I could, but his claws punched out, imbedding in the wood above my hands. Still riding the magic, he was half-wild.

"You drove me mad," he growled, and the sound trembled down my neck, along my breasts until they ached. "I searched for you, and you weren't there. When I didn't find you," he said, bringing his face closer to mine, until we shared breath, "it made me pick another."

I couldn't escape. I wasn't entirely sure that I wanted to.

"She asked me not to be gentle with her, either," he snarled, his teeth bright in the moonlight. He brought his lips to my ear. "I would have been gentle with you, though." I shuddered as I closed my eyes. Every inch of my body went taut as his words echoed through me. "I would have had you moaning my name throughout it all. And I would have taken a very, very long time, Feyre." He said my name like a caress, and his hot breath tickled my ear. My back arched slightly.

He ripped his claws free from the wall, and my knees buckled as he let go. I grasped the wall to keep from sinking to the floor, to keep from grabbing him—to strike or caress, I didn't know. I opened my eyes. He still smiled—smiled like an animal.

"Why should I want someone's leftovers?" I said, making to push him away. He grabbed my hands again and bit my neck.

I cried out as his teeth clamped onto the tender spot where my neck met my shoulder. I couldn't move—couldn't think, and my world narrowed to the feeling of his lips and teeth against my skin. He didn't pierce my flesh, but rather bit to keep me pinned. The push of his body against mine, the hard and the soft, made me see red—see lightning, made me grind my hips against his. I should hate him—hate him for his stupid ritual, for the female he'd been with tonight . . .

His bite lightened, and his tongue caressed the places his teeth had been. He didn't move—he just remained in that spot, kissing my neck. Intently, territorially, lazily. Heat pounded between my legs, and as he ground his body against me, against every aching spot, a moan slipped past my lips.

He jerked away. The air was bitingly cold against my freed skin, and I panted as he stared at me. "Don't ever disobey me again," he said, his voice a deep purr that ricocheted through me, awakening everything and lulling it into complicity.

Then I reconsidered his words and straightened. He grinned at me in that wild way, and my hand connected with his face.

"Don't tell me what to do," I breathed, my palm stinging. "And don't bite me like some enraged beast."

He chuckled bitterly. The moonlight turned his eyes to the color of leaves in shadow. More—I wanted the hardness of his body crushing against mine; I wanted his mouth and teeth and tongue on my bare skin, on my breasts, between my legs. Everywhere—I wanted him *everywhere*. I was drowning in that need.

His nostrils flared as he scented me—scented every burning, raging thought that was pounding through my body, my senses. The breath rushed from him in a mighty whoosh.

He growled once, low and frustrated and vicious, before prowling away.

CHAPTER 22

I awoke when the sun was high, after tossing and turning all night, empty and aching.

The servants were sleeping in after their night of celebrating, so I made myself a bath and took a good, long soak. Try as I might to forget the feel of Tamlin's lips on my neck, I had an enormous bruise where he'd bitten me. After bathing, I dressed and sat at the vanity to braid my hair.

I opened the drawers of the vanity, searching for a scarf or something to cover the bruise peeking over the collar of my blue tunic, but then paused and glared at myself in the mirror. He'd acted like a brute and a savage, and if he'd come to his senses by this morning, then seeing what he'd done would be minimal punishment.

Sniffing, I opened the collar of my tunic farther and tucked stray strands of my golden-brown hair behind my ears so there would be no concealing it. I was beyond cowering.

Humming to myself and swinging my hands, I strode downstairs and followed my nose to the dining room, where I knew lunch was usually served for Tamlin and Lucien. When I flung open the doors, I found them both sprawled in their chairs. I could have sworn that Lucien was sleeping upright, fork in hand.

"Good afternoon," I said cheerfully, with an especially saccharine smile for the High Lord. He blinked at me, and both of the faerie men murmured their greetings as I took a seat across from Lucien, not my usual place facing Tamlin.

I drank deeply from my goblet of water before piling food on my plate. I savored the tense silence as I consumed the meal before me.

"You look . . . refreshed," Lucien observed with a glance at Tamlin. I shrugged. "Sleep well?"

"Like a babe." I smiled at him and took another bite of food, and felt Lucien's eyes travel inexorably to my neck.

"What is that bruise?" Lucien demanded.

I pointed with my fork to Tamlin. "Ask him. He did it."

Lucien looked from Tamlin to me and then back again. "Why does Feyre have a bruise on her neck from you?" he asked with no small amount of amusement.

"I bit her," Tamlin said, not pausing as he cut his steak. "We ran into each other in the hall after the Rite."

I straightened in my chair.

"She seems to have a death wish," he went on, cutting his meat. The claws stayed retracted but pushed against the skin above his knuckles. My throat closed up. Oh, he was mad—furious at my foolishness for leaving my room—but somehow managed to keep his anger on a tight, tight leash. "So, if Feyre can't be bothered to listen to orders, then I can't be held accountable for the consequences."

"Accountable?" I sputtered, placing my hands flat on the table. "You cornered me in the hall like a wolf with a rabbit!"

Lucien propped an arm on the table and covered his mouth with his hand, his russet eye bright.

"While I might not have been myself, Lucien *and* I both told you to stay in your room," Tamlin said, so calmly that I wanted to rip out my hair.

I couldn't help it. Didn't even try to fight the red-hot temper that razed my senses. "Faerie pig!" I yelled, and Lucien howled, almost tipping back in his chair. At the sight of Tamlin's growing smile, I left.

It took me a couple of hours to stop painting little portraits of Tamlin and Lucien with pigs' features. But as I finished the last one—*Two faerie pigs wallowing in their own filth*, I would call it—I smiled into the clear, bright light of my private painting room. The Tamlin I knew had returned.

And it made me . . . happy.

✢

We apologized at dinner. He even brought me a bouquet of white roses from his parents' garden, and while I dismissed them as nothing, I made certain that Alis took good care of them when I returned to my room. She gave me only a wry nod before promising to set them in my painting room. I fell asleep with a smile still on my lips.

For the first time in a long, long while, I slept peacefully.

✢

"Don't know if I should be pleased or worried," Alis said the next night as she slid the golden underdress over my upraised arms, then tugged it down.

I smiled a bit, marveling at the intricate metallic lace that clung to my arms and torso like a second skin before falling loosely to the rug. "It's just a dress," I said, lifting my arms again as she brought over the gossamer turquoise overgown. It was sheer enough to see the gleaming gold mesh beneath, and light and airy and full of movement, as if it flowed on an invisible current.

Alis just chuckled to herself and guided me over to the vanity to work on my hair. I didn't have the courage to look at the mirror as she fussed over me.

"Does this mean you'll be wearing gowns from now on?" she asked, separating sections of my hair for whatever wonders she was doing to it.

"No," I said quickly. "I mean—I'll be wearing my usual clothes during the day, but I thought it might be nice to . . . try it out, at least for tonight."

"I see. Good that you aren't losing your common sense entirely, then."

I twisted my mouth to the side. "Who taught you how to do hair like this?"

Her fingers stilled, then continued their work. "My mother taught me and my sister, and her mother taught her before that."

"Have you always been at the Spring Court?"

"No," she said, pinning my hair in various, subtle places. "No, we were originally from the Summer Court—that's where my kin still dwells."

"How'd you wind up here?"

Alis met my eyes in the mirror, her lips a tight line. "I made a choice to come here—and my kin thought me mad. But my sister and her mate had been killed, and for her boys . . ." She coughed, as if choking on the words. "I came here to do what I could." She patted my shoulder. "Have a look."

I dared a glimpse at my reflection.

I hurried from the room before I could lose my nerve.

I had to keep my hands clenched at my sides to avoid wiping my sweaty palms on the skirts of my gown as I reached the dining room, and immediately contemplated bolting upstairs and changing into a tunic and pants. But I knew they'd already heard me, or smelled me, or used whatever heightened senses they had to detect my presence, and since fleeing would only make it worse, I found it in myself to push open the double doors.

Whatever discussion Tamlin and Lucien had been having stopped, and I tried not to look at their wide eyes as I strode to my usual place at the end of the table.

"Well, I'm late for something incredibly important," Lucien said, and before I could call him on his outright lie or beg him to stay, the fox-masked faerie vanished.

I could feel the full weight of Tamlin's undivided attention on me—on every breath and movement I took. I studied the candelabras atop the mantel beside the table. I had nothing to say that didn't sound absurd—yet for some reason, my mouth decided to start moving.

"You're so far away." I gestured to the expanse of table between us. "It's like you're in another room."

The quarters of the table vanished, leaving Tamlin not two feet away, sitting at an infinitely more intimate table. I yelped and almost tipped over in my chair. He laughed as I gaped at the small table that now stood between us. "Better?" he asked.

I ignored the metallic tang of magic as I said, "How . . . how did you *do* that? Where did it go?"

He cocked his head. "Between. Think of it as . . . a broom closet tucked between pockets of the world." He flexed his hands and rolled his neck, as if shaking off some pain.

"Does it tax you?" Sweat seemed to gleam on the strong column of his neck.

He stopped flexing his hands and set them flat on the table. "Once, it was as easy as breathing. But now . . . it requires concentration."

Because of the blight on Prythian and the toll it had taken on him. "You could have just taken a closer seat," I said.

Tamlin gave me a lazy grin. "And miss a chance to show off to a beautiful woman? Never." I smiled down at my plate.

"You do look beautiful," he said quietly. "I mean it," he added when my mouth twisted to the side. "Didn't you look in the mirror?"

Though his bruise still marred my neck, I *had* looked pretty.

Feminine. I wouldn't go so far as to call myself a beauty, but . . . I hadn't cringed. A few months here had done wonders for the awkward sharpness and angles of my face. And I dared say that some kind of light had crept into my eyes—*my* eyes, not my mother's eyes or Nesta's eyes. *Mine*.

"Thank you," I said, and was grateful to avoid saying anything else as he served me and then himself. When my stomach was full to bursting, I dared to look at him—really *look* at him—again.

Tamlin leaned back in his chair, yet his shoulders were tight, his mouth a thin line. He hadn't been called to the border in a few days—hadn't come back weary and covered in blood since before Fire Night. And yet . . . He'd grieved for that nameless Summer Court faerie with the hacked-off wings. What grief and burdens did he bear for whoever else had been lost in this conflict—lost to the blight, or to the attacks on the borders? High Lord—a position he hadn't wanted or expected, yet he'd been forced to bear its weight as best he could.

"Come," I said, rising from my chair and tugging on his hand. The calluses scraped against mine, but his fingers tightened as he looked up at me. "I have something for you."

"For me," he repeated carefully, but rose. I led him out of the dining room. When I went to drop his hand, he didn't let go. It was enough to keep me walking quickly, as if I could outrun my thundering heart or the sheer immortal presence of him at my side. I brought him down hall after hall until we got to my little painting room, and he finally released my hand as I reached for the key. Cold air bit into my skin without the warmth of his hand around mine.

"I knew you'd asked Alis for a key, but I didn't think you actually locked the room," he said behind me.

I gave him a narrowed glance over my shoulder as I pushed open the door. "Everyone snoops in this house. I didn't want you or Lucien coming in here until I was ready."

I stepped into the darkened room and cleared my throat, a silent request for him to light the candles. It took him longer than I'd seen him need before, and I wondered if shortening the table had somehow drained him more than he'd let on. The Suriel had said the High Lords *were* Power—and yet . . . yet something had to be truly, thoroughly wrong if this was all he could manage. The room gradually flared with light, and I pushed my worry aside as I stepped farther into the room. I took a deep breath and gestured to the easel and the painting I'd put there. I hoped he wouldn't notice the paintings I'd leaned against the walls.

He turned in place, staring around him at the room.

"I know they're strange," I said, my hands sweating again. I tucked them behind my back. "And I know they're not like—not as good as the ones you have here, but . . ." I walked to the painting on the easel. It was an impression, not a lifelike rendering. "I wanted you to see this one," I said, pointing to the smear of green and gold and silver and blue. "It's for you. A gift. For everything you've done."

Heat flared in my cheeks, my neck, my ears, as he silently approached the painting.

"It's the glen—with the pool of starlight," I said quickly.

"I know what it is," he murmured, studying the painting. I backed away a step, unable to bear watching him look at it, wishing I hadn't brought him in here, blaming it on the wine I'd had at dinner, on the stupid dress. He examined the painting for a miserable eternity, then looked away—to the nearest painting leaning against the wall.

My gut tightened. A hazy landscape of snow and skeletal trees and nothing else. It looked like . . . like nothing, I supposed, to anyone but me. I opened my mouth to explain, wishing I'd turned the others away from view, but he spoke.

"That was your forest. Where you hunted." He came closer to the painting, gazing at the bleak, empty cold, the white and gray and brown and black. "This was your life," he clarified.

I was too mortified, too stunned, to reply. He walked to the next painting I'd left against the wall. Darkness and dense brown, flickers of ruby red and orange squeezing out between them. "Your cottage at night."

I tried to move, to tell him to stop looking at those ones and look at the others I'd laid out, but I couldn't—couldn't even breathe properly as he moved to the next painting. A tanned, sturdy male hand fisted in the hay, the pale pieces of it entwined among strands of brown coated with gold—my hair. My gut twisted. "The man you used to see—in your village." He cocked his head again as he studied the picture, and a low growl slipped out. "While you made love." He stepped back, looking at the row of pictures. "This is the only one with any brightness."

Was that . . . jealousy? "It was the only escape I had." Truth. I wouldn't apologize for Isaac. Not when Tamlin had just been in the Great Rite. I didn't hold that against him—but if he was going to be jealous of *Isaac*—

Tamlin must have realized it, too, for he loosed a long, controlled breath before moving to the next painting. Tall shadows of men, bright red dripping off their fists, off their wooden clubs, hovering and filling the edges of the painting as they towered over the curled figure on the floor, the blood leaking from him, the leg at a wrong angle.

Tamlin swore. "You were there when they wrecked your father's leg."

"Someone had to beg them to stop."

Tamlin threw a too-knowing glance in my direction and turned to look at the rest of the paintings. There they were, all the wounds I'd slowly been leeching these few months. I blinked. A few months. Did my family believe that I would be forever away with this so-called dying aunt?

At last, Tamlin looked at the painting of the glen and the starlight. He nodded in appreciation. But he pointed to the painting of the snow-veiled woods. "That one. I want that one."

"It's cold and melancholy," I said, hiding my wince. "It doesn't suit this place at all."

He went up to it, and the smile he gave me was more beautiful than any enchanted meadow or pool of stars. "I want it nonetheless," he said softly.

I'd never yearned for anything more than to remove his mask and see the face beneath, to find out whether it matched how I'd dreamed he looked.

"Tell me there's some way to help you," I breathed. "With the masks, with whatever threat has taken so much of your power. Tell me—just tell me what I can do to help you."

"A human wishes to help a faerie?"

"Don't tease me," I said. "Please—just . . . tell me."

"There's nothing I want you to do, nothing you *can* do—or anyone. It's my burden to bear."

"You don't have to—"

"I do. What I have to face, what I endure, Feyre . . . you would not survive."

"So I'm to live here forever, in ignorance of the true scope of what's happening? If you don't want me to understand what's going on . . . would you rather . . ." I swallowed hard. "Rather I found someplace else to live? Where I'm not a distraction?"

"Didn't *Calanmai* teach you anything?"

"Only that magic makes you into a brute."

He laughed, though not entirely with amusement. When I remained silent, he sighed. "No, I don't want you to live somewhere else. I want you here, where I can look after you—where I can come home and know you're here, painting and safe."

I couldn't look away from him. "I thought about sending you away at first," he murmured. "Part of me still thinks I should have found somewhere else for you to live. But maybe I was selfish. Even when you made it so clear that you were more interested in ignoring the Treaty or finding a way out of it, I couldn't bring myself to let you go—to find someplace in Prythian where you'd be comfortable enough to not attempt to flee."

"Why?"

He picked up the small painting of the frozen forest and examined it again. "I've had many lovers," he admitted. "Females of noble birth, warriors, princesses . . ." Rage hit me, low and deep in the gut at the thought of them—rage at their titles, their undoubtedly good looks, at their closeness to him. "But they never understood. What it was like, what it *is* like, for me to care for my people, my lands. What scars are still there, what the bad days feel like." That wrathful jealousy faded away like morning dew as he smiled at my painting. "This reminds me of it."

"Of what?" I breathed.

He lowered the painting, looking right at me, right into me. "That I'm not alone."

I didn't lock my bedroom door that night.

CHAPTER 23

The next afternoon I lay on my back in the grass, savoring the warmth of the sunshine filtering through the canopy of leaves, noting how I might incorporate it into my next painting. Lucien, claiming that he had miserable emissary business to attend to, had left Tamlin and me to our own devices, and the High Lord had taken me to yet another beautiful spot in his enchanted forest.

But there were no enchantments here—no pools of starlight, no rainbow waterfalls. It was just a grassy glen watched over by a weeping willow, with a clear brook running through it. We lounged in comfortable silence, and I glanced at Tamlin, who dozed beside me. His golden hair and mask glistened bright against the emerald carpet. The delicate arch of his pointed ears made me pause.

He opened an eye and smiled lazily at me. "That willow's singing always puts me to sleep."

"The what of what?" I said, propping myself on my elbows to stare at the tree above us.

Tamlin pointed toward the willow. The branches sighed as they moved in the breeze. "It sings."

"I suppose it sings war-camp limericks, too?"

He smiled and half sat up, twisting to look at me. "You're human," he said, and I rolled my eyes. "Your senses are still sealed off from everything."

I made a face. "Just another of my many shortcomings." But the word—*shortcomings*—had somehow stopped finding its mark.

He plucked a strand of grass from my hair. Heat radiated from my face as his fingers grazed my cheek. "I could make you able to see it," he said. His fingers lingered at the end of my braid, twirling the curl of hair around. "See my world—hear it, smell it." My breathing became shallow as he sat up. "Taste it." His eyes flicked to the fading bruise on my neck.

"How?" I asked, heat blooming as he crouched before me.

"Every gift comes with a price." I frowned, and he grinned. "A kiss."

"Absolutely not!" But my blood raced, and I had to clench my hands in the grass to keep from touching him. "Don't you think it puts me at a disadvantage to not be able to see all this?"

"I'm one of the High Fae—we don't give anything without gaining something from it."

To my own surprise, I said, "Fine."

He blinked, probably expecting me to have fought a little harder. I hid my smile and sat up so that I faced him, our knees touching as we knelt in the grass. I licked my lips, my heart fluttering so quickly it felt as if I had a hummingbird inside my chest.

"Close your eyes," he said, and I obeyed, my fingers grappling onto the grass. The birds chattered, and the willow branches sighed. The grass crunched as Tamlin rose up on his knees. I braced myself at the brush of his mouth on one of my eyelids, then on the other. He pulled away, and I was left breathless, the kisses still lingering on my skin.

The singing of birds became an orchestra—a symphony of gossip and mirth. I'd never heard so many layers of music, never heard the variations and themes that wove between their arpeggios. And beyond the birdsong, there was an ethereal melody—a woman, melancholy and weary . . . the willow. Gasping, I opened my eyes.

The world had become richer, clearer. The brook was a near-invisible rainbow of water that flowed over stones as invitingly smooth as silk. The trees were clothed in a faint shimmer that radiated from their centers and danced along the edges of their leaves. There was no tangy metallic stench—no, the smell of magic had become like jasmine, like lilac, like roses. I would never be able to paint it, the richness, the feel . . . Maybe fractions of it, but not the whole thing.

Magic—*everything* was magic, and it broke my heart.

I looked to Tamlin, and my heart cracked entirely.

It was Tamlin, but not. Rather, it was the Tamlin I'd dreamed of. His skin gleamed with a golden sheen, and around his head glowed a circlet of sunshine. And his eyes—

Not merely green and gold, but every hue and variation that could be imagined, as though every leaf in the forest had bled into one shade. *This* was a High Lord of Prythian—devastatingly handsome, captivating, powerful beyond belief.

My breath caught in my throat as I touched the contours of his mask. The cool metal bit into my fingertips, and the emeralds slipped against my callused skin. I lifted my other hand and gently grasped either side of the mask. I pulled lightly.

It wouldn't move.

He began smiling as I pulled again, and I blinked, dropping my hands. Instantly, the golden, glowing Tamlin vanished, and the one I knew returned. I could still hear the singing of the willow and the birds, but . . .

"Why can't I see you anymore?"

"Because I willed my glamour back into place."

"Glamour for what?"

"To look normal. Or as normal as I can look with this damned thing," he added, gesturing to the mask. "Being a High Lord, even one with . . . limited powers, comes with physical markers, too. It's why I couldn't hide what I was becoming from my brothers—from anyone. It's still easier to blend in."

"But the mask truly can't come off—I mean, are you sure there's no one who knows how to fix what the magic did that night? Even someone in another court?" I don't know why the mask bothered me so greatly. I didn't need to see his entire face to know him.

"I'm sorry to disappoint you."

"I just . . . just want to know what you look like." I wondered when I'd grown so shallow.

"What do you think I look like?"

I tilted my head to the side. "A strong, straight nose," I said, drawing from what I'd once tried to paint. "High cheekbones that bring out your eyes. Slightly . . . slightly arched brows," I finished, blushing. He was grinning so broadly that I could almost see all of his teeth—those fangs nowhere in sight. I tried to think up an excuse for my forwardness, but a yawn crept from me as a sudden weight pressed on my eyes.

"What about your part of the bargain?"

"What?"

He leaned closer, his smile turning wicked. "What about my kiss?"

I grabbed his fingers. "Here," I said, and slammed my mouth against the back of his hand. "There's your kiss."

Tamlin roared with laughter, but the world blurred, lulling me to sleep. The willow beckoned me to lie down, and I obliged. From far off, I heard Tamlin curse. "Feyre?"

Sleep. I wanted sleep. And there was no better place to sleep than right here, listening to the willow and the birds and the brook. I curled on my side, using my arm for a pillow.

"I should bring you home," he murmured, but he didn't move to drag me to my feet. Instead, I felt a slight thud in the earth, and the spring rain and new grass scent of him cloyed in my nose as he lay beside me. I tingled with pleasure as he stroked my hair.

This was such a lovely dream. I'd never slept so wonderfully before. So warm, nestled beside him. Calm. Faintly, echoing into my world of slumber, he spoke again, his breath caressing my ear. "You're exactly as I dreamed you'd be, too." Darkness swallowed everything.

CHAPTER 24

It wasn't the dawn that awoke me, but rather a buzzing noise. I groaned as I sat up in bed and squinted at the squat woman with skin made from tree bark who fussed with my breakfast dishes.

"Where's Alis?" I asked, rubbing the sleep from my eyes. Tamlin must have carried me up here—must have carried me the whole way home.

"What?" She turned toward me. Her bird mask was familiar. But I would have remembered a faerie with skin like that. Would have painted it already.

"Is Alis unwell?" I said, sliding from the bed. This *was* my room, wasn't it? A quick glance told me yes.

"Are you out of your right mind?" the faerie said. I bit my lip. "I *am* Alis," she clucked, and with a shake of her head, she strode into the bathing room to start my bath.

It was impossible. The Alis I knew was fair and plump and looked like a High Fae.

I rubbed my eyes with my thumb and forefinger. A glamour—that's what Tamlin had said he wore. His faerie sight had stripped away the glamours I'd been seeing. But why bother to glamour everything?

Because I'd been a cowering human, that's why. Because Tamlin knew

I would have locked myself in this room and never come out if I'd seen them all for their true selves.

Things only got worse when I made my way downstairs to find the High Lord. The hallways were bustling with masked faeries I'd never seen before. Some were tall and humanoid—High Fae like Tamlin—others were . . . not. Faeries. I tried to avoid looking at those ones, as they seemed the most surprised to notice my attention.

I was almost shaking by the time I reached the dining room. Lucien, mercifully, appeared like Lucien. I didn't ask whether that was because Tamlin had informed him to put up a better glamour or because he didn't bother trying to be something he wasn't.

Tamlin lounged in his usual chair but straightened as I lingered in the doorway. "What's wrong?"

"There are . . . a lot of people—faeries—around. When did they arrive?"

I'd almost yelped when I looked out my bedroom window and spotted all the faeries in the garden. Many of them—all with insect masks—pruned the hedges and tended the flowers. Those faeries had been the strangest of all, with their iridescent, buzzing wings sprouting from their backs. And, of course, then there was the green-and-brown skin, and their unnaturally long limbs, and—

Tamlin bit his lip as if to keep from smiling. "They've been here all along."

"But . . . but I didn't *hear* anything."

"Of course you didn't," Lucien drawled, and twirled one of his daggers between his hands. "We made sure you couldn't see or hear anyone but those who were necessary."

I adjusted the lapels of my tunic. "So you mean that . . . that when I ran after the puca that night—"

"You had an audience," Lucien finished for me. I thought I'd been so stealthy. Meanwhile, I'd been tiptoeing past faeries who had probably laughed their heads off at the blind human following an illusion.

Fighting against my rising mortification, I turned to Tamlin. His lips twitched and he clamped them tightly together, but the amusement still danced in his eyes as he nodded. "It *was* a valiant effort."

"But I *could* see the naga—and the puca, and the Suriel. And—and that faerie whose wings were . . . ripped off," I said, wincing inwardly. "Why didn't the glamour apply to them?"

His eyes darkened. "They're not members of my court," Tamlin said, "so my glamour didn't keep a hold on them. The puca belongs to the wind and weather and everything that changes. And the naga . . . they belong to someone else."

"I see," I lied, not quite seeing at all. Lucien chuckled, sensing it, and I glared sidelong at him. "You've been noticeably absent again."

He used the dagger to clean his nails. "I've been busy. So have you, I take it."

"What's that supposed to mean?" I demanded.

"If I offer you the moon on a string, will you give me a kiss, too?"

"Don't be an ass," Tamlin said to him with a soft snarl, but Lucien continued laughing, and was still laughing when he left the room.

Alone with Tamlin, I shifted on my feet. "So if I were to encounter the Attor again," I said, mostly to avoid the heavy silence, "would I actually see it?"

"Yes, and it wouldn't be pleasant."

"You said it didn't see me that time, and it certainly doesn't seem like a member of your court," I ventured. "Why?"

"Because I threw a glamour over you when we entered the garden," he said simply. "The Attor couldn't see, hear, or smell you." His gaze went to the window beyond me, and he ran a hand through his hair. "I've done all I can to keep you invisible to creatures like the Attor—and worse. The blight is acting up again—and more of these creatures are being freed from their tethers."

My stomach turned over. "If you spot one," Tamlin continued, "even if it looks harmless but makes you feel uncomfortable, pretend you don't see it. Don't talk to it. If it hurts you, I . . . the results wouldn't be pleasant for it, or for me. You remember what happened with the naga."

This was for my own safety, not his amusement. He didn't want me hurt—he didn't want to punish them for hurting *me*. Even if the naga hadn't been part of his court, had it hurt him to kill them?

Realizing he waited for my answer, I nodded. "The . . . the blight is growing again?"

"So far, only in other territories. You're safe here."

"It's not my safety I'm worried about."

Tamlin's eyes softened, but his lips became a thin line as he said, "It'll be fine."

"Is it possible that the surge will be temporary?" A fool's hope.

Tamlin didn't reply, which was answer enough. If the blight was becoming active again . . . I didn't bother to offer my aid. I already knew he wouldn't allow me to help with whatever this conflict was.

But I thought of that painting I'd given him, and what he'd said about it . . . and wished he would let me in anyway.

The next morning, I found a head in the garden.

A bleeding male High Fae head—spiked atop a fountain statue of a great heron flapping its wings. The stone was soaked in enough blood to suggest that the head had been fresh when someone had impaled it on the heron's upraised bill.

I had been hauling my paints and easel out to the garden to paint one of the beds of irises when I stumbled across it. My tins and brushes had clattered to the gravel.

I didn't know where I went as I stared at that still-screaming head, the brown eyes bulging, the teeth broken and bloody. No mask—so he wasn't a part of the Spring Court. Anything else about him, I couldn't discern.

His blood was so bright on the gray stone—his mouth open so vulgarly. I backed away a step—and slammed into something warm and hard.

I whirled, hands rising out of instinct, but Tamlin's voice said, "It's me," and I stopped cold. Lucien stood beside him, pale and grim.

"Not Autumn Court," Lucien said. "I don't recognize him at all."

Tamlin's hands clamped on my shoulders as I turned back toward the head. "Neither do I." A soft, vicious growl laced his words, but no claws pricked my skin as he kept gripping me. His hands tightened, though, while Lucien stepped into the small pool in which the statue stood—striding through the red water until he peered up at the anguished face.

"They branded him behind the ear with a sigil," Lucien said, swearing. "A mountain with three stars—"

"Night Court," Tamlin said too quietly.

The Night Court—the northernmost bit of Prythian, if I recalled the mural's map correctly. A land of darkness and starlight. "Why . . . why would they do this?" I breathed.

Tamlin let go, coming to stand at my side as Lucien climbed the statue to remove the head. I looked toward a blossoming crab apple tree instead.

"The Night Court does what it wants," Tamlin said. "They live by their own codes, their own corrupt morals."

"They're all sadistic killers," Lucien said. I dared a glance at him; he was now perched on the heron's stone wing. I looked away again. "They delight in torture of every kind—and would find this sort of stunt to be amusing."

"Amusing, but not a message?" I scanned the garden.

"Oh, it's a message," Lucien said, and I cringed at the thick, wet sounds of flesh and bone on stone as he yanked the head off. I'd skinned enough animals, but this . . . Tamlin put another hand on my shoulder. "To get in and out of our defenses, to possibly commit the crime nearby, with the blood this fresh . . ." A splash as Lucien landed in the water again. "It's exactly what the High Lord of the Night Court would find amusing. The bastard."

I gauged the distance between the pool and the house. Sixty, maybe seventy feet. That's how close they'd come to us. Tamlin brushed a thumb against my shoulder. "You're still safe here. This was just their idea of a prank."

"This isn't connected to the blight?" I asked.

"Only in that they know the blight is again awakening—and want us to know they're circling the Spring Court like vultures, should our wards fall further." I must have looked as sick as I felt, because Tamlin added, "I won't let that happen."

I didn't have the heart to say that their masks made it fairly clear that nothing could be done against the blight.

Lucien splashed out of the fountain, but I couldn't look at him, not with the head he bore, the blood surely on his hands and clothes. "They'll get what's coming to them soon enough. Hopefully the blight will wreck them, too." Tamlin growled at Lucien to take care of the head, and the gravel crunched as Lucien departed.

I crouched to pick up my paints and brushes, my hands shaking as I fumbled for a large brush. Tamlin knelt next to me, but his hands closed around mine, squeezing.

"You're still safe," he said again. The Suriel's command echoed through my mind. *Stay with the High Lord, human. You will be safe.*

I nodded.

"It's court posturing," he said. "The Night Court is deadly, but this was only their lord's idea of a joke. Attacking anyone here—attacking you—would cause more trouble than it's worth for him. If the blight truly does harm these lands, and the Night Court enters our borders, we'll be ready."

My knees shook as I rose. Faerie politics, faerie courts . . . "Their idea of jokes must have been even more horrible when we were enslaved to you all." They must have tortured us whenever they liked—must have done such unspeakable, awful things to their human pets.

A shadow flickered in his eyes. "Some days, I'm very glad I was still a child when my father sent his slaves south of the wall. What I witnessed then was bad enough."

I didn't want to imagine. Even now, I still hadn't looked to see if any hints of those long-ago humans had been left behind. I did not think five centuries would be enough to cleanse the stain of the horrors that my people had endured. I should have let it go—should have, but couldn't. "Do you remember if they were happy to leave?"

Tamlin shrugged. "Yes. Yet they had never known freedom, or known the seasons as you do. They didn't know what to do in the mortal world. But yes—most of them were very, very happy to leave." Each word was more ground out than the next. "I was happy to see them go, even if my father wasn't." Despite the stillness with which he stood, his claws poked out from above his knuckles.

No wonder he'd been so awkward with me, had no idea what to do with me, when I'd first arrived. But I said quietly, "You're not your father, Tamlin. Or your brothers." He glanced away, and I added, "You never made me feel like a prisoner—never made me feel like little more than chattel."

The shadows that flickered in his eyes as he nodded his thanks told me there was more—still more that he had yet to tell me about his family, his life before they'd been killed and this title had been thrust upon him. I wouldn't ask, not with the blight pressing down on him—not until he was ready. He'd given me space and respect; I could offer him no less.

Still, I couldn't bring myself to paint that day.

CHAPTER 25

Tamlin was called away to one of the borders hours after I found that head—where and why, he wouldn't tell me. But I sensed enough from what he didn't say: the blight was indeed crawling from other courts, directly toward ours.

He stayed the night—the first he'd ever spent away—but sent Lucien to inform me that he was alive. Lucien had emphasized that last word enough that I slept terribly, even as a small part of me marveled that Tamlin had bothered to let me know about his well-being. I knew—I knew I was headed down a path that would likely end in my mortal heart being left in pieces, and yet . . . And yet I couldn't stop myself. I hadn't been able to since that day with the naga. But seeing that head . . . the games these courts played, with people's lives as tokens on a board . . . it was an effort to keep food down whenever I thought about it.

Yet despite the creeping malice, I awoke the next day to the sound of merry fiddling, and when I looked out the window I found the garden bedecked in ribbons and streamers. On the distant hills, I spied the makings of fires and maypoles being raised. When I asked Alis—whose people, I'd learned, were called the *urisk*—she simply said, "Summer Solstice. The main celebration used to be at the Summer Court, but . . . things are different. So now we have one here, too. You're going."

Summer—in the weeks that I'd been painting and dining with Tamlin and wandering the court lands at his side, summer had come. Did my family still truly believe me to be visiting some long-lost aunt? What were they doing with themselves? If it was the solstice, then there would be a small gathering in the village center—nothing religious, of course, though the Children of the Blessed might wander in to try to convert the young people; just some shared food, donated ale from the solitary tavern, and maybe some line dances. The only thing to celebrate was a day's break from the long summer days of planting and tilling. From the decorations around the estate, I could tell this would be something far grander—far more spirited.

Tamlin remained gone for most of the day. Worry gnawed at me even as I painted a quick, loose rendering of the streamers and ribbons in the garden. Perhaps it was petty and selfish, given the returning blight, but I also quietly hoped that the solstice didn't require the same rites as Fire Night. I didn't let myself think too much about what I would do if Tamlin had a flock of beautiful faeries lining up for him.

It wasn't until late afternoon that I heard Tamlin's deep voice and Lucien's braying laugh echo through the halls all the way to my painting room. Relief sent my chest caving in, but as I rushed to find them, Alis yanked me upstairs. She stripped off my paint-splattered clothes and insisted I change into a flowing, cornflower-blue chiffon gown. She left my hair unbound but wove a garland of pink, white, and blue wildflowers around the crown of my head.

I might have felt childish with it on, but in the months I'd been there, my sharp bones and skeletal form had filled out. A woman's body. I ran my hands over the sweeping, soft curves of my waist and hips. I had never thought I would feel anything but muscle and bone.

"Cauldron boil me," Lucien whistled as I came down the stairs. "She looks positively Fae."

I was too busy looking Tamlin over—scanning for any injury, any sign of blood or mark that the blight might have left—to thank Lucien for the compliment. But Tamlin was clean, almost glowing, completely unarmed—and smiling at me. Whatever he'd gone to deal with had left him unscathed. "You look lovely," Tamlin murmured, and something in his soft tone made me want to purr.

I squared my shoulders, disinclined to let him see how much his words or voice or sheer well-being impacted me. Not yet. "I'm surprised I'm even allowed to participate tonight."

"Unfortunately for you and your neck," Lucien countered, "tonight's just a party."

"Do you lie awake at night to come up with all your witty replies for the following day?"

Lucien winked at me, and Tamlin laughed and offered me his arm. "He's right," the High Lord said. I was aware of every inch where we touched, of the hard muscles beneath his green tunic. He led me into the garden, and Lucien followed. "Solstice celebrates when the sun outshines the night. As the longest day of the year, it's a time when everyone can take down their hair and simply enjoy being a faerie—not High Fae or faerie, just *us*, and nothing else."

"So there's singing and dancing and excessive drinking," Lucien chimed in, falling into step beside me. "And dallying," he added with a wicked grin.

Indeed, every brush of Tamlin's body against mine made it harder to avoid the urge to lean into him entirely, to smell him and touch him and taste him. Whether he noticed the heat singeing my neck and face, or heard my uneven heartbeat, he revealed nothing, holding my arm tighter as we walked out of the garden and into the fields beyond.

The sun was beginning its final descent when we reached the plateau on which the festivities were to be held. I tried not to gawk at the faeries gathered, even as I was in turn gawked at by them. I'd never seen so many in one place before, at least not without the glamour hiding them from me. Now that my eyes were open to the sight, the exquisite dresses and lithe forms that were shaped and colored and built so strangely and differently were a marvel to behold. Yet what little novelty my own presence by the High Lord's side offered soon wore off—helped by a low, warning growl from Tamlin that sent the others scattering to mind their own business.

Table after table of food had been lined up along the far edge of the plateau, and I lost Tamlin while I waited in line to fill a plate, leaving me to try my best not to look like I was some human plaything of his. Music started near the giant, smoking bonfire—fiddles and drums and merry instruments that had me tapping my feet in the grass. Light and joyous and open, the mirthful sister to the bloodthirsty Fire Night.

Lucien, of course, excelled at disappearing when I needed him, and so I ate my fill of strawberry shortcake, apple tart, and blueberry pie—no different from summer treats in the mortal realm—alone beneath a sycamore covered with silken lanterns and sparkling ribbons.

I didn't mind the solitude—not when I was busy contemplating the way the lanterns and ribbons shone, the shadows they cast; perhaps it would be my next painting. Or maybe I would paint the ethereal faeries beginning to dance. Such angles and colors to them. I wondered if any of them had been the subjects of the painters whose work was displayed in the gallery.

I moved only to get myself something to drink. The plateau became more crowded as the sun sank toward the horizon. Across the hills, other bonfires and parties began, their music filtering through the occasional pause in ours. I was pouring myself a goblet of golden sparkling wine when Lucien finally appeared behind me, peering over my shoulder. "I wouldn't drink that if I were you."

"Oh?" I said, frowning at the fizzing liquid.

"Faerie wine at the solstice," Lucien hinted.

"Hmm," I said, taking a sniff. It didn't reek of alcohol. In fact, it smelled like summers spent lying in the grass and bathing in cool pools. I'd never smelled anything so fantastic.

"I'm serious," Lucien said as I lifted the glass to my lips, my brows raised. "Remember the last time you ignored my warning?" He poked me in the neck, and I batted his hand away.

"I also remember you telling me how witchberries were harmless, and the next thing I knew, I was half-delirious and falling all over myself," I said, recalling the afternoon from a few weeks ago. I'd had hallucinations for hours afterward, and Lucien had laughed himself sick—enough so that Tamlin had chucked him into the reflection pool. I shook away the thought. Today—just for today—I would indeed let my hair down. Today, let caution be damned. Forget the blight hovering at the edges of the court, threatening my High Lord and his lands. Where *was* Tamlin, anyway? If there had been some threat, surely Lucien would have known—surely they would have called off the celebration.

"Well, I mean it this time," Lucien said, and I shifted my goblet out of his reach. "Tam would gut me if he caught you drinking that."

"Always looking after your best interests," I said, and pointedly chugged the contents of the glass.

It was like a million fireworks exploding inside me, filling my veins with starlight. I laughed aloud, and Lucien groaned.

"Human fool," he hissed. But his glamour had been ripped away. His auburn hair burned like hot metal, and his russet eye smoldered like a bottomless forge. *That* was what I would capture next.

"I'm going to paint you," I said, and giggled—actually *giggled*—as the words popped out.

"Cauldron boil and fry me," he muttered, and I laughed again. Before he could stop me, I'd downed another glass of faerie wine. It was the most glorious thing I'd ever tasted. It liberated me from bonds I hadn't known existed.

The music became a siren song. The melody was my lodestone, and

I was powerless against its lure. With each step, I savored the dampness of the grass beneath my bare feet. I didn't remember when I'd lost my shoes.

The sky was an eddy of molten amethyst, sapphire, and ruby, all bleeding into a final pool of onyx. I wanted to swim in it, wanted to bathe in its colors and feel the stars twinkling between my fingers.

I stumbled, blinking, and found myself standing at the edge of the ring of dancing. A cluster of musicians played their faerie instruments, and I swayed on my feet as I watched the faeries dancing, circling the bonfire. Not formal dancing. It was like they were as loose as I was. Free. I loved them for it.

"Damn it, Feyre," Lucien said, gripping my elbow. "Do you want me to kill myself trying to keep you from impaling your mortal hide on another rock?"

"What?" I said, turning to him. The whole world spun with me, delightful and entrancing.

"Idiot," he said when he looked at my face. "Drunken idiot."

The tempo increased. I wanted to be in the music, wanted to ride its speed and weave between its notes. I could *feel* the music around me, like a living, breathing thing of wonder and joy and beauty.

"Feyre, stop," Lucien said, and grabbed me again. I'd been dancing away, and my body was still swaying toward the pull of the sound.

"*You* stop. Stop being so serious," I said, shaking him off. I wanted to hear the music, wanted to hear it hot off the instruments. Lucien swore as I burst into movement.

I skipped between the dancers, twirling my skirts. The seated, masked musicians didn't look up at me as I leaped before them, dancing in place. No chains, no boundaries—just me and the music, dancing and dancing. I wasn't faerie, but I was a part of this earth, and the earth was a part of me, and I would be content to dance upon it for the rest of my life.

One of the musicians looked up from his fiddling, and I halted.

Sweat gleamed on the strong column of his neck as he rested his chin upon the dark wood of the fiddle. He'd rolled up the sleeves of his shirt, revealing the cords of muscle along his forearms. He had once mentioned that he would have liked to be a traveling minstrel if not a warrior or a High Lord—now, hearing him play, I knew he could have made a fortune from it.

"I'm sorry, Tam," Lucien panted, appearing from nowhere. "I left her alone for a little at one of the food tables, and when I caught up to her, she was drinking the wine, and—"

Tamlin didn't pause in his playing. His golden hair damp with sweat, he looked marvelously handsome—even though I couldn't see most of his face. He gave me a feral smile as I began to dance in place before him. "I'll look after her," Tamlin murmured above the music, and I glowed, my dancing becoming faster. "Go enjoy yourself." Lucien fled.

I shouted over the music, "I don't need a keeper!" I wanted to spin and spin and spin.

"No, you don't," Tamlin said, never once stumbling over his playing. How his bow did dance upon the strings, his fingers sturdy and strong, no signs of those claws that I had come to stop fearing . . . "Dance, Feyre," he whispered.

So I did.

I was loosened, a top whirling around and around, and I didn't know who I danced with or what they looked like, only that I had become the music and the fire and the night, and there was nothing that could slow me down.

Through it all, Tamlin and his musicians played such joyous music that I didn't think the world could contain it all. I sashayed over to him, my faerie lord, my protector and warrior, my friend, and danced before him. He grinned at me, and I didn't break my dancing as he rose from his seat and knelt before me in the grass, offering up a solo on his fiddle to me.

Music just for me—a gift. He played on, his fingers fast and hard upon the strings of his fiddle. My body slithering like a snake, I tipped my head back to the heavens and let Tamlin's music fill all of me.

There was a pressure at my waist, and I was swept away in someone's arms as they whisked me back into the ring of dancing. I laughed so hard I thought I'd combust, and when I opened my eyes, I found Tamlin there, spinning me round and round.

Everything became a blur of color and sound, and he was the only object in it, tethering me to sanity, to my body, which glowed and burned in every place he touched.

I was filled with sunshine. It was like I'd never experienced summer before, like I'd never known who was waiting to emerge from that forest of ice and snow. I didn't want it to end—I never wanted to leave this hilltop.

The music came to a close, and, gasping for breath, I glanced at the moon—it was near setting. Sweat slid down every part of my body.

Tamlin, panting as well, took my hand. "Time goes faster when you're drunk on faerie wine."

"I'm not drunk," I said, snorting. He only chuckled and led me from the dancing. I dug my heels into the ground as we neared the edge of the firelight. "They're starting again," I said, pointing to the dancers gathering before the refreshed musicians.

He leaned close, his breath caressing the shell of my ear as he whispered, "I want to show you something better."

I stopped objecting.

He led me off the hill, navigating his way by moonlight. Whatever path he chose, he did so out of consideration for my bare feet, for only soft grass cushioned my steps. Soon, even the music faded away, replaced by the sighing of trees in the night breeze.

"Here," Tamlin said, pausing at the edge of a vast meadow. His hand lingered on my shoulder as we looked out.

The high grasses moved like water as the last of the moonlight danced upon them.

"What is it?" I breathed, but he put a finger to his lips and beckoned me to look.

For a few minutes, there was nothing. Then, from the opposite side of the meadow, dozens of shimmering shapes floated out across the grass, little more than mirages of moonlight. That was when the singing began.

It was a collective voice, but in it existed both male and female—two sides of the same coin, singing to each other in a call and response. I raised a hand to my throat as their music rose and they danced. Ghostly and ethereal, they waltzed across the field, no more than slender slants of moonlight.

"What are they?"

"Will-o'-the-wisps—spirits of air and light," he said softly. "Come to celebrate the solstice."

"They're beautiful."

His lips grazed my neck as he murmured against my skin, "Dance with me, Feyre."

"Really?" I turned and found my face mere inches from his.

He cracked a lazy smile. "Really." As though I were nothing but air myself, he pulled me into a sweeping dance. I barely remembered any of the steps I'd learned in childhood, but he compensated for it with his feral grace, never faltering, always sensing any stumble before I made it as we danced across the spirit-riddled field.

I was as unburdened as a piece of dandelion fluff, and he was the wind that stirred me about the world.

He smiled at me, and I found myself smiling back. I didn't need to pretend, didn't need to be anything but what I was right then, being twirled about the meadow, the will-o'-the-wisps dancing around us like dozens of moons.

Our dancing slowed and we stood there, holding each other as we swayed to the songs of the spirits. He rested his chin upon my head and stroked my hair, his fingers grazing the bare skin of my neck.

"Feyre," he whispered onto my head. He made my name sound beautiful. "Feyre," he whispered again—not in question, but simply as if he enjoyed saying it.

As quickly as they'd appeared, the spirits vanished, taking their music with them. I blinked. The stars were fading, and the sky had turned grayish purple.

Tamlin's face was inches from my own. "It's almost dawn."

I nodded, mesmerized by the sight of him, the smell and feel of him holding me. I reached up to touch his mask. It was so cold, despite how flushed his skin was just beyond it. My hand shook, and my breathing became shallow as I grazed the skin of his jaw. It was smooth—and hot.

He wet his lips, his breathing as uneven as my own. His fingers contracted against the plane of my lower back, and I let him tug me closer to him—until our bodies were touching, and the warmth of him seeped into me.

I had to tilt my head back to see his face. His mouth was caught somewhere between a smile and a wince.

"What?" I asked, and put a hand on his chest, preparing to shove myself back. But his other hand slipped under my hair, resting at the base of my neck.

"I'm thinking I might kiss you," he said quietly, intently.

"Then do it." I blushed at my own boldness.

But Tamlin only gave that breathy laugh, and leaned in.

His lips brushed mine—testing, soft and warm. He pulled back a little. He was still staring at me, and I stared right back as he kissed me again, harder, but nothing like the way he'd kissed my neck. He withdrew more fully this time and watched me.

"That's it?" I demanded, and he laughed and kissed me fiercely.

My hands went around his neck, pulling him closer, crushing myself against him. His hands roved my back, playing in my hair, grasping my waist, as if he couldn't touch enough of me at once.

He let out a low groan. "Come," he said, kissing my brow. "We'll miss it if we don't go now."

"Better than will-o'-the-wisps?" I asked, but he kissed my cheeks, my neck, and finally my lips. I followed him into the trees, through the ever-lightening world. His hand was solid and unmovable around mine as we passed through the low-lying mists, and he helped me up a bare hill slick with dew.

We sat atop its crest, and I hid my smile as Tamlin put an arm around my shoulders, tucking me in close. I rested my head against his chest while he toyed with the flowers in my garland.

In silence, we stared out over the rolling green expanse.

The sky shifted into periwinkle, and the clouds filled with pink light. Then, like a shimmering disk too rich and clear to be described, the sun slipped over the horizon and lined everything with gold. It was like seeing the world being born, and we were the sole witnesses.

Tamlin's arm tightened around me, and he kissed the top of my head. I pulled back, looking up at him.

The gold in his eyes, bright with the rising sun, flickered. "What?"

"My father once told me that I should let my sisters imagine a better life—a better world. And I told him that there was no such thing." I ran my thumb over his mouth, marveling, and shook my head. "I never understood—because I couldn't . . . couldn't believe that it was even possible." I swallowed, lowering my hand. "Until now."

His throat bobbed. His kiss that time was deep and thorough, unhurried and intent.

I let the dawn creep inside me, let it grow with each movement of his lips and brush of his tongue against mine. Tears pricked beneath my closed eyes.

It was the happiest moment of my life.

CHAPTER 26

The next day, Lucien joined us for lunch—which was breakfast for all of us. Ever since I'd complained about the unnecessary size of the table, we'd taken to dining at a much-reduced version. Lucien kept rubbing at his temples as he ate, unusually silent, and I hid my smile as I asked him, "And where were you last night?"

Lucien's metal eye narrowed on me. "I'll have you know that while you two were dancing with the spirits, I was stuck on border patrol." Tamlin gave a pointed cough, and Lucien added, "With some company." He gave me a sly grin. "Rumor has it you two didn't come back until after dawn."

I glanced at Tamlin, biting my lip. I'd practically floated into my bedroom that morning. But Tamlin's gaze now roved my face as if searching for any tinge of regret, of fear. Ridiculous.

"You bit my neck on Fire Night," I said under my breath. "If I can face you after that, a few kisses are nothing."

He braced his forearms on the table as he leaned closer to me. "Nothing?" His eyes flicked to my lips. Lucien shifted in his seat, muttering to the Cauldron to spare him, but I ignored him.

"Nothing," I repeated a bit distantly, watching Tamlin's mouth move, so keenly aware of every movement he made, resenting the table between us. I could almost feel the warmth of his breath.

"Are you sure?" he murmured, intent and hungry enough that I was glad I was sitting. He could have had me right there, on top of that table. I wanted his broad hands running over my bare skin, wanted his teeth scraping against my neck, wanted his mouth all over me.

"I'm trying to eat," Lucien said, and I blinked, the air whooshing out of me. "But now that I have your attention, *Tamlin*," he snapped, though the High Lord was looking at me again—devouring me with his eyes. I could hardly sit still, could hardly stand the clothes scratching my too-hot skin. With some effort, Tamlin glanced back at his emissary.

Lucien shifted in his seat. "Not to be the bearer of truly bad tidings, but my contact at the Winter Court managed to get a letter to me." Lucien took a steadying breath, and I wondered—wondered if being emissary also meant being spymaster. And wondered why he was bothering to say this in my presence at all. The smile instantly faded from Tamlin's face. "The blight," Lucien said tightly, softly. "It took out two dozen of their younglings. *Two dozen*, all gone." He swallowed. "It just . . . burned through their magic, then broke apart their minds. No one in the Winter Court could do anything—no one could stop it once it turned its attention toward them. Their grief is . . . unfathomable. My contact says other courts are being hit hard—though the Night Court, of course, manages to remain unscathed. But the blight seems to be sending its wickedness this way—farther south with every attack."

All the warmth, all the sparkling joy, drained from me like blood down a drain. "The blight can . . . can truly kill people?" I managed to say. Younglings. It had killed children, like some storm of darkness and death. And if offspring were as rare as Alis had claimed, the loss of so many would be more devastating than I could imagine.

Tamlin's eyes were shadowed, and he slowly shook his head—as if trying to clear the grief and shock of those deaths from him. "The blight is capable of hurting us in ways you—" He shot to his feet so quickly that his chair flipped over. He unsheathed his claws and snarled at the open doorway, canines long and gleaming.

The house, usually full of the whispering skirts and chatter of servants, had gone silent.

Not the pregnant silence of Fire Night, but rather a trembling quiet that made me want to scramble under the table. Or just start running. Lucien swore and drew his sword.

"Get Feyre to the window—by the curtains," Tamlin growled to Lucien, not taking his eyes off the open doors. Lucien's hand gripped my elbow, dragging me out of my chair.

"What's—" I started, but Tamlin growled again, the sound echoing through the room. I snatched one of the knives off the table and let Lucien lead me to the window, where he pushed me against the velvet drapes. I wanted to ask why he didn't bother hiding me behind them, but the fox-masked faerie just pressed his back into me, pinning me between him and the wall.

The tang of magic shoved itself up my nostrils. Though his sword was pointed at the floor, Lucien's grip tightened on it until his knuckles turned white. Magic—a glamour. To conceal me, to make me a part of Lucien—invisible, hidden by the faerie's magic and scent. I peered over his shoulder at Tamlin, who took a long breath and sheathed his claws and fangs, his baldric of knives appearing from thin air across his chest. But he didn't draw any of the knives as he righted his chair and slouched in it, picking at his nails. As if nothing were happening.

But someone was coming, someone awful enough to frighten them—someone who would want to hurt me if they knew I was here.

The hissing voice of the Attor slithered through my memory. There were worse creatures than it, Tamlin had told me. Worse than the naga, and the Suriel, and the Bogge, too.

Footsteps sounded from the hall. Even, strolling, casual.

Tamlin continued cleaning his nails, and in front of me, Lucien assumed a position of appearing to be looking out the window. The footsteps grew louder—the scuff of boots on marble tiles.

And then he appeared.

No mask. He, like the Attor, belonged to something else. Some*one* else.

And worse . . . I'd met him before. He'd saved me from those three faeries on Fire Night.

With steps that were too graceful, too feline, he approached the dining table and stopped a few yards from the High Lord. He was exactly as I remembered him, with his fine, rich clothing cloaked in tendrils of night: an ebony tunic brocaded with gold and silver, dark pants, and black boots that went to his knees. I'd never dared to paint him—and now knew I would never have the nerve to.

"High Lord," the stranger crooned, inclining his head slightly. Not a bow.

Tamlin remained seated. With his back to me, I couldn't see his face, but Tamlin's voice was laced with the promise of violence as he said, "What do you want, Rhysand?"

Rhysand smiled—heartbreaking in its beauty—and put a hand on his chest. "Rhysand? Come now, Tamlin. I don't see you for forty-nine years, and you start calling me Rhysand? Only my prisoners and my enemies call me that." His grin widened as he finished, and something in his countenance turned feral and deadly, more so than I'd ever seen Tamlin look. Rhysand turned, and I held my breath as he ran an eye over Lucien. "A fox mask. Appropriate for you, Lucien."

"Go to Hell, Rhys," Lucien snapped.

"Always a pleasure dealing with the rabble," Rhysand said, and faced Tamlin again. I still didn't breathe. "I hope I wasn't interrupting."

"We were in the middle of lunch," Tamlin said—his voice void of the warmth to which I'd become accustomed. The voice of the High Lord. It turned my insides cold.

"Stimulating," Rhysand purred.

"What are you doing here, Rhys?" Tamlin demanded, still in his seat.

"I wanted to check up on you. I wanted to see how you were faring. If you got my little present."

"Your *present* was unnecessary."

"But a nice reminder of the fun days, wasn't it?" Rhysand clicked his tongue and surveyed the room. "Almost half a century holed up in a country estate. I don't know how you managed it. But," he said, facing Tamlin again, "you're such a stubborn bastard that this must have seemed like a paradise compared to Under the Mountain. I suppose it is. I'm surprised, though: forty-nine years, and no attempts to save yourself or your lands. Even now that things are getting interesting again."

"There's nothing to be done," conceded Tamlin, his voice low.

Rhysand approached Tamlin, each movement smooth as silk. His voice dropped into a whisper—an erotic caress of sound that brought heat to my cheeks. "What a pity that you must endure the brunt of it, Tamlin—and an even greater pity that you're so resigned to your fate. You might be stubborn, but this is pathetic. How different the High Lord is from the brutal war-band leader of centuries ago."

Lucien interrupted, "What do you know about anything? You're just Amarantha's whore."

"Her whore I might be, but not without my reasons." I flinched as his voice whetted itself into an edge. "At least I haven't bided my time among the hedges and flowers while the world has gone to Hell."

Lucien's sword rose slightly. "If you think that's all I've been doing, you'll soon learn otherwise."

"Little Lucien. You certainly gave them something to talk about when you switched to Spring. Such a sad thing, to see your lovely mother in perpetual mourning over losing you."

Lucien pointed his sword at Rhysand. "Watch your filthy mouth."

Rhysand laughed—a lover's laugh, low and soft and intimate. "Is that any way to speak to a High Lord of Prythian?"

My heart stopped dead. That was why those faeries had run off on Fire Night. To cross him would have been suicide. And from the way darkness seemed to ripple from him, from those violet eyes that burned like stars . . .

"Come now, Tamlin," Rhysand said. "Shouldn't you reprimand your lackey for speaking to me like that?"

"I don't enforce rank in my court," Tamlin said.

"Still?" Rhysand crossed his arms. "But it's so entertaining when they grovel. I suppose your father never bothered to show you."

"This isn't the Night Court," Lucien hissed. "And you have no power here—so clear out. Amarantha's bed is growing cold."

I tried not to breathe too loudly. Rhysand—*he'd* been the one to send that head. As a *gift*. I flinched. Was the Night Court where this woman—this Amarantha—was located, too?

Rhysand snickered, but then he was upon Lucien, too fast for me to follow with my human eyes, growling in his face. Lucien pressed me into the wall with his back, hard enough that I stifled a cry as I was squished against the wood.

"I was slaughtering on the battlefield before you were even born," Rhysand snarled. Then, as quickly as he had come, he withdrew, casual and careless. No, I would never dare to paint that dark, immortal grace—not in a hundred years. "Besides," he said, stuffing his hands into his pockets, "who do you think taught your beloved Tamlin the finer aspects of swords and females? You can't truly believe he learned everything in his father's little war-camps."

Tamlin rubbed his temples. "Save it for another time, Rhys. You'll see me soon enough."

Rhysand meandered toward the door. "She's already preparing for you. Given your current state, I think I can safely report that you've already been broken and will reconsider her offer." Lucien's breath hitched as Rhysand passed the table. The High Lord of the Night Court ran a finger along the back of my chair—a casual gesture. "I'm looking forward to seeing your face when you—"

Rhysand studied the table.

Lucien went stick-straight, pressing me harder against the wall. The table was still set for three, my half-eaten plate of food sitting right before him.

"Where's your guest?" Rhysand asked, lifting my goblet and sniffing it before setting it down again.

"I sent them off when I sensed your arrival," Tamlin lied coolly.

Rhysand now faced the High Lord, and his perfect face was void of emotion before his brows rose. A flicker of excitement—perhaps even disbelief—flashed across his features, but he whipped his head to Lucien. Magic seared my nostrils, and I stared at Rhysand in undiluted terror as his face contorted with rage.

"You *dare* glamour *me*?" he growled, his violet eyes burning as they bore into my own. Lucien just pressed me harder into the wall.

Tamlin's chair groaned as it was shoved back. He rose, claws at the ready, deadlier than any of the knives strapped to him.

Rhysand's face became a mask of calm fury as he stared and stared at me. "I remember you," he purred. "It seems like you ignored my warning to stay out of trouble." He turned to Tamlin. "Who, pray tell, is your guest?"

"My betrothed," Lucien answered.

"Oh? Here I was, thinking you still mourned your commoner lover after all these centuries," Rhysand said, stalking toward me. The sunlight didn't gleam on the metallic threads of his tunic, as if it balked from the darkness pulsing from him.

Lucien spat at Rhysand's feet and shoved his sword between us.

Rhysand's venom-coated smile grew. "You draw blood from me, Lucien, and you'll learn how quickly Amarantha's whore can make the entire Autumn Court bleed. Especially its darling Lady."

The color leeched from Lucien's face, but he held his ground. It was Tamlin who answered. "Put your sword down, Lucien."

Rhysand ran an eye over me. "I knew you liked to stoop low with your lovers, Lucien, but I never thought you'd actually dabble with mortal trash." My face burned. Lucien was trembling—with rage or fear or sorrow, I couldn't tell. "The Lady of the Autumn Court will be grieved indeed when she hears of her youngest son. If I were you, I'd keep your new pet well away from your father."

"Leave, Rhys," Tamlin commanded, standing a few feet behind the High Lord of the Night Court. And yet he didn't make a move to attack, despite the claws, despite Rhysand still approaching me. Perhaps a battle between two High Lords could tear this manor to its foundations—and leave only dust in its wake. Or perhaps, if Rhysand was indeed this woman's lover, the retaliation from hurting him would be too great. Especially with the added burden of facing the blight.

Rhysand brushed Lucien aside as if he were a curtain.

There was nothing between us now, and the air was sharp and cold. But Tamlin remained where he was, and Lucien didn't so much as blink as Rhysand, with horrific gentleness, pried the knife from my hands and sent it scattering across the room.

"That won't do you any good, anyway," Rhysand said to me. "If you were wise, you would be screaming and running from this place, from these people. It's a wonder that you're still here, actually." My confusion must have been written across my face, for Rhysand laughed loudly. "Oh, she doesn't know, does she?"

I trembled, unable to find words or courage.

"You have seconds, Rhys," Tamlin warned. "Seconds to get out."

"If I were you, I wouldn't speak to me like that."

Against my volition, my body straightened, every muscle going taut, my bones straining. Magic, but deeper than that. Power that seized everything inside me and took control: even my blood flowed where he willed it.

I couldn't move. An invisible, talon-tipped hand scraped against my mind. And I knew—one push, one swipe of those mental claws, and who I was would cease to exist.

"Let her go," Tamlin said, bristling, but didn't advance forward. A kind of panic had entered his eyes, and he glanced from me to Rhysand. *"Enough."*

"I'd forgotten that human minds are as easy to shatter as eggshells," Rhysand said, and ran a finger across the base of my throat. I shuddered, my eyes burning. "Look at how delightful she is—look how she's trying not to cry out in terror. It would be quick, I promise."

Had I retained any semblance of control over my body, I might have vomited.

"She has the most delicious thoughts about you, Tamlin," he said. "She's wondered about the feeling of your fingers on her thighs—between them, too." He chuckled. Even as he said my most private thoughts, even as I burned with outrage and shame, I trembled at the grip still on my mind. Rhysand turned to the High Lord. "I'm curious: Why did she wonder if it would feel good to have you bite her breast the way you bit her neck?"

"Let. Her. Go." Tamlin's face was twisted with such feral rage that it struck a different, deeper chord of terror in me.

"If it's any consolation," Rhysand confided to him, "she would have been the one for you—and you might have gotten away with it. A bit late, though. She's more stubborn than you are."

Those invisible claws lazily caressed my mind again—then vanished. I sank to the floor, curling over my knees as I reeled in everything that I was, as I tried to keep from sobbing, from screaming, from emptying my stomach onto the floor.

"Amarantha will enjoy breaking her," Rhysand observed to Tamlin. "Almost as much as she'll enjoy watching *you* as she shatters her bit by bit."

Tamlin was frozen, his arms—his claws—hanging limply at his side. I'd never seen him look like that. "Please" was all that Tamlin said.

"Please *what?*" Rhysand said—gently, coaxingly. Like a lover.

"Don't tell Amarantha about her," Tamlin said, his voice strained.

"And why not? As her *whore*," he said with a glance tossed in Lucien's direction, "I should tell her everything."

"Please," Tamlin managed, as if it were difficult to breathe.

Rhysand pointed at the ground, and his smile became vicious. "Beg, and I'll consider not telling Amarantha."

Tamlin dropped to his knees and bowed his head.

"Lower."

Tamlin pressed his forehead to the floor, his hands sliding along the floor toward Rhysand's boots. I could have wept with rage at the sight of Tamlin being forced to bow to someone, at the sight of my High Lord being put so low. Rhysand pointed at Lucien. "You too, fox-boy."

Lucien's face was dark, but he lowered himself to his knees, then touched his head to the ground. I wished for the knife Rhysand had chucked away, for anything with which to kill him.

I stopped shaking long enough to hear Rhys speak again. "Are you doing this for your sake, or for hers?" he pondered, then shrugged, as if he weren't forcing a High Lord of Prythian to grovel. "You're far too desperate, Tamlin. It's off-putting. Becoming High Lord made you so boring."

"Are you going to tell Amarantha?" Tamlin said, keeping his face on the floor.

Rhysand smirked. "Perhaps I'll tell her, perhaps I won't."

In a flash of motion too fast for me to detect, Tamlin was on his feet, fangs dangerously close to Rhysand's face.

"None of that," Rhysand said, clicking his tongue and lightly shoving Tamlin away with a single hand. "Not with a lady present." His eyes shifted to my face. "What's your name, love?"

Giving him my name—and my family name—would lead only to more pain and suffering. He might very well find my family and drag them into Prythian to torment, just to amuse himself. But he could steal my name from my mind if I hesitated for too long. Keeping my mind blank and calm, I blurted the first name that came to mind, a village friend of my sisters' whom I'd never spoken to and whose face I couldn't recall. "Clare Beddor." My voice was nothing more than a gasp.

Rhysand turned back to Tamlin, unfazed by the High Lord's proximity. "Well, this was entertaining. The most fun I've had in ages, actually. I'm looking forward to seeing you three Under the Mountain. I'll give Amarantha your regards."

Then Rhysand vanished into nothing—as if he'd stepped through a rip in the world—leaving us alone in horrible, trembling silence.

CHAPTER 27

I lay in bed, watching the pools of moonlight shift on the floor. It was an effort not to dwell on Tamlin's face as he ordered me and Lucien to leave and shut the door to the dining room. Had I not been so bent on piecing myself together, I might have stayed. Might have even asked Lucien about it—about everything. But, like the coward I was, I bolted to my room, where Alis was waiting with a cup of molten chocolate. It was even more of an effort not to recall the roaring that rattled the chandelier or the cracking of shattering furniture that echoed through the house.

I didn't go to dinner. I didn't want to know if there was a dining room to eat in. And I couldn't bring myself to paint.

The house had been quiet for some time now, but the ripples of Tamlin's rage echoed through it, reverberating in the wood and stone and glass.

I didn't want to think about all that Rhysand had said—didn't want to think about the looming storm of the blight, or Under the Mountain—whatever it was called—and why I might be forced to go there. And Amarantha—at last a name to go with the female presence that stalked their lives. I shuddered each time I considered how deadly she must be to command the High Lords of Prythian. To hold Rhysand's leash and to make Tamlin beg to keep me hidden from her.

The door creaked, and I jerked upright. Moonlight glimmered on gold, but my heart didn't ease as Tamlin shut the door and approached my bed. His steps were slow and heavy—and he didn't speak until he'd taken a seat on the edge of the mattress.

"I'm sorry," he said. His voice was hoarse and empty.

"It's fine," I lied, clenching the sheets in my hands. If I thought too long about it, I could still feel the claw-tipped caresses of Rhysand's power scraping against my mind.

"It's not fine," he growled, and grabbed one of my hands, wrenching my fingers from the sheets. "It's . . ." He hung his head, sighing deeply as his hand tightened on mine. "Feyre . . . I wish . . ." He shook his head and cleared his throat. "I'm sending you home, Feyre."

Something inside me splintered. "What?"

"I'm sending you home," he repeated, and though his words were stronger—louder—they trembled a bit.

"What about the terms of the Treaty—"

"I have taken on your life-debt. Should someone come inquiring after the broken laws, I'll take responsibility for Andras's death."

"But you once said that there was no other loophole. The Suriel said there was no—"

A snarl. "If they have a problem with it, they can tell me." And wind up in ribbons.

My chest caved in. Leaving—*free*. "Did I do something wrong—"

He lifted my hand to press it to his lower cheek. He was so invitingly warm. "You did nothing wrong." He turned his face to kiss my palm. "You were perfect," he murmured onto my skin, then lowered my hand.

"Then why do I have to go?" I yanked my hand away.

"Because there are . . . there are people who would hurt you, Feyre. Hurt you because of what you are to me. I thought I would be able to handle them, to shield you from it, but after today . . . I can't. So you need to go home—far from here. You'll be safe there."

"I can hold my own, and—"

"You *can't*," he said, and his voice wobbled. "Because *I* can't." He seized my face in both hands. "I can't even protect myself against them, against what's happening in Prythian." I felt every word as it passed from his mouth and onto my lips, a rush of hot, frantic air. "Even if we stood against the blight . . . they would hunt you down—she would find a way to kill you."

"Amarantha." He bristled at the name but nodded. "Who is—"

"When you get home," he cut in, "don't tell anyone the truth about where you were; let them believe the glamour. Don't tell them who I am; don't tell them where you stayed. Her spies will be looking for you."

"I don't understand." I grabbed his forearm and squeezed it tight. "*Tell me*—"

"You have to go *home*, Feyre."

Home. It wasn't my home—it was Hell. "I want to stay with you," I whispered, my voice breaking. "Treaty or no treaty, blight or no blight."

He ran a hand over his face. His fingers contracted when they met with his mask. "I know."

"So let me—"

"There's no debate," he snarled, and I glared at him. "Don't you understand?" He shot to his feet. "Rhys was the start of it. Do you want to be here when the Attor returns? Do you want to know what kind of creatures the Attor answers to? Things like the Bogge—and worse."

"Let me help you—"

"*No.*" He paced before the bed. "Didn't you read between the lines today?"

I hadn't, but I lifted my chin and crossed my arms. "So you're sending me away because I'm useless in a fight?"

"I'm sending you away because it makes me *sick* thinking about you in their hands!"

Silence fell, filled only by the sounds of his heavy breathing. He sank onto the bed and pressed the heels of his palms into his eyes.

His words echoed through me, melting my anger, turning everything inside me watery and frail. "How . . . how long do I have to go away for?"

He didn't reply.

"A week?" No answer. "A month?" He shook his head slowly. My upper lip curled, but I forced myself into neutrality. "A year?" That much time away from him . . .

"I don't know."

"But not forever, right?" Even if the blight spread to the Spring Court again, even if it could shred me apart . . . I would come back. He brushed the hair from my face. I shook him off. "I suppose it'll be easier if I'm gone," I said, looking away from him. "Who wants someone around who's so covered in thorns?"

"Thorns?"

"Thorny. Prickly. Sour. Contrary."

He leaned forward and kissed me lightly. "Not forever," he said onto my mouth.

And though I knew it was a lie, I put my arms around his neck and kissed him.

He pulled me onto his lap, holding me tightly against him as his lips parted mine. I became aware of every pore in my body when his tongue entered my mouth.

Though the horror of Rhysand's magic still tore at me, I pushed Tamlin onto the bed, straddling him, pinning him as if it would somehow keep me from leaving, as if it would make time stop entirely.

His hands rested on my hips, and their heat singed me through the thin silk of my nightgown. My hair fell around our faces like a curtain. I couldn't kiss him fast enough, hard enough to express the rushing need within me. He growled softly and deftly flipped us over, spreading me beneath him as he wrenched his lips from my mouth and made a trail of kisses down my neck.

My entire world constricted to the touch of his lips on my skin. Everything beyond them, beyond him, was a void of darkness and moonlight. My back arched as he reached the spot he'd once bitten, and I dragged my hands through his hair, savoring the silken smoothness.

He traced the arc of my hipbones, lingering at the edge of my undergarments. My nightgown had become hitched around my waist, but I didn't care. I hooked my bare legs around his, running my feet down the hard muscles of his calves.

He breathed my name onto my chest, one of his hands exploring the plane of my torso, rising up to the slope of my breast. I trembled, anticipating the feel of his hand there, and his mouth found mine again as his fingers stopped just below.

His kissing was slower this time—gentler. The fingertips of his other hand slipped beneath the waist of my undergarment, and I sucked in a breath.

He hesitated at the sound, pulling back slightly. But I bit his lip in a silent command that had him growling into my mouth. With one long claw, he shredded through silk and lace, and my undergarment fell away in pieces. The claw retracted, and his kiss deepened as his fingers slid between my legs, coaxing and teasing. I ground against his hand, yielding completely to the writhing wildness that had roared alive inside me, and breathed his name onto his skin.

He paused again—his fingers retracting—but I grabbed him, pulling him farther on top of me. I wanted him *now*—I wanted the barriers of our clothing to vanish, I wanted to taste his sweat, wanted to become full of him. "Don't stop," I gasped out.

"I—" he said thickly, resting his brow between my breasts as he shuddered. "If we keep going, I won't be able to stop at all."

I sat up and he watched me, hardly breathing. But I kept my eyes on his, my own breathing becoming steady as I raised my nightgown over my head and tossed it to the floor. Utterly naked before him, I watched his gaze travel to my bare breasts, peaked against the chill night, to my abdomen, to between my thighs. A ravenous, unyielding sort of hunger passed over his face. I bent a leg and slid it to the side, a silent invitation. He let out a low growl—and slowly, with predatory intent, raised his gaze to mine again.

The full force of that wild, unrelenting High Lord's power focused solely on me—and I felt the storm contained beneath his skin, so capable of sweeping away everything I was, even in its lessened state. But I could trust him, trust myself to weather that mighty power. I could throw all that I was at him and he wouldn't balk. "Give me everything," I breathed.

He lunged, a beast freed of its tether.

We were a tangle of limbs and teeth, and I tore at his clothes until they were on the floor, then tore at his skin until I marked him down his back, his arms. His claws were out, but devastatingly gentle on my hips as he slid down between my thighs and feasted on me, stopping only after I shuddered and fractured. I was moaning his name when he sheathed himself inside me in a powerful, slow thrust that had me splintering around him.

We moved together, unending and wild and burning, and when I went over the edge the next time, he roared and went with me.

I fell asleep in his arms, and when I awoke a few hours later, we made love again, lazily and intently, a slow-burning smolder to the wildfire of earlier. Once we were both spent, panting and sweat-slicked, we lay in silence for a time, and I breathed in the smell of him, earthy and crisp. I would never be able to capture that—never be able to paint the *feel* and taste of him, no matter how many times I tried, no matter how many colors I used.

Tamlin traced idle circles on the plane of my stomach and murmured, "We should sleep. You have a long journey tomorrow."

"Tomorrow?" I sat upright, not at all minding my nakedness, not after he'd seen everything, tasted everything.

His mouth was a hard line. "At dawn."

"But it's—"

He sat up in a smooth motion. "Please, Feyre."

Please. Tamlin had *bowed* before Rhysand. For my sake. He shifted toward the edge of the bed. "Where are you going?"

He looked over his shoulder at me. "If I stay, you won't get any sleep."

"Stay," I said. "I promise to keep my hands to myself." Lie—such an outright lie.

He gave me a half smile that told me he knew it, too, but nestled down, tugging me into his arms. I wrapped an arm around his waist and rested my head in the hollow of his shoulder.

He idly stroked my hair. I didn't want to sleep—didn't want to lose a minute with him—but an immense exhaustion was pulling me away from consciousness, until all I knew was the touch of his fingers in my hair and the sounds of his breathing.

I was leaving. Just when this place had become more than a sanctuary, when the command of the Suriel had become a blessing and Tamlin far, far more than a savior or friend, I was leaving. It could be years until I saw this house again, years until I smelled his rose garden, until I saw those gold-flecked eyes. Home—this was home.

As consciousness left me at last, I thought I heard him speak, his mouth close to my ear.

"I love you," he whispered, and kissed my brow. "Thorns and all."

He was gone when I awoke, and I was certain I had dreamed it.

CHAPTER 28

There wasn't much to my packing and farewells. I was somewhat surprised when Alis clothed me in an outfit very unlike my usual garb—frilly and confining and binding in all the wrong places. Some mortal fashion among the wealthy, no doubt. The dress was made up of layers of pale pink silk, accented with white and blue lace. Alis placed a short, lightweight jacket of white linen on me, and atop my head she angled an absurd little ivory hat, clearly for decoration. I half expected a parasol to go with it.

I said as much to Alis, who clicked her tongue. "Shouldn't you be giving me a weepy farewell?"

I tugged at the lace gloves—useless and flimsy. "I don't like goodbyes. If I could, I'd just walk out and not say anything."

Alis gave me a long look. "I don't like them, either."

I went to the door, but despite myself, I said, "I hope you get to be with your nephews again soon."

"Make the most of your freedom" was all she said.

Downstairs, Lucien snorted at the sight of me. "Those clothes are enough to convince me I never want to enter the human realm."

"I'm not sure the human realm would know what to do with you," I said.

Lucien's smile was edged, his shoulders tight as he gave a sharp look behind me to where Tam was waiting in front of a gilded carriage. When he turned back, that metal eye narrowed. "I thought you were smarter than this."

"Good-bye to you, too," I said. Friend indeed. It wasn't my choice, or my fault that they'd kept the bulk of their conflict from me. Even if I could do nothing against the blight, or against the creatures, or against Amarantha—whoever she was.

Lucien shook his head, his scar stark in the bright sun, and stalked toward Tamlin, despite the High Lord's warning growl. "You're not even going to give her a few more days? Just a few—before you send her back to that human cesspit?" Lucien demanded.

"This isn't up for debate," Tamlin snapped, pointing at the house. "I'll see you at lunch."

Lucien stared him down for a moment, spat on the ground, and stormed up the stairs. Tamlin didn't reprimand him.

I might have thought more on Lucien's words, might have shouted a retort after him, but . . . My chest hollowed out as I faced Tamlin in front of the gilded carriage, my hands sweaty within the gloves.

"Remember what I told you," he said. I nodded, too busy memorizing the lines of his face to reply. Had he meant what I thought he'd said last night—that he loved me? I shifted, already aching in the little white pumps into which Alis had stuffed my poor feet. "The mortal realm remains safe—for you, for your family." I nodded, wondering whether he might have tried to persuade me to leave our territory, to sail south, but understood that I would have refused to be so far from the wall, from him. That going back to my family was as far as I would allow to be sent from his side.

"My paintings—they're yours," I said, unable to come up with anything better to express how I felt, what it did to me to be sent away, and how terrified I was of the carriage looming behind me.

He lifted my chin with a finger. "I will see you again."

He kissed me, and pulled away too quickly. I swallowed hard, fighting the burning in my eyes. *I love you, Feyre.*

I turned before my vision blurred, but he was immediately there to help me into the opulent carriage. He watched me take my seat through the open door, his face a mask of calm. "Ready?"

No, no, I wasn't ready, not after last night, not after all these months. But I nodded. If Rhysand came back, if this Amarantha person was indeed such a threat that I would only be another body for Tamlin to defend . . . I needed to go.

He shut the door, sealing me inside with a click that sounded through me. He leaned through the open window to caress my cheek—and I could have sworn that I felt my heart crack. The footman snapped the whip.

Tamlin's fingers brushed my mouth. The carriage jolted as the six white horses started into a walk. I bit my lip to keep it from wobbling.

Tamlin smiled at me one last time. "I love you," he said, and stepped away.

I should say it—I should say those words, but they got stuck in my throat, because . . . because of what he had to face, because he might not find me again despite his promise, because . . . because beneath it all, he was an immortal, and I would grow old and die. And maybe he meant it now, and perhaps last night had been as altering for him as it had been for me, but . . . I would not become a burden to him. I would not become another weight pressing upon his shoulders.

So I said nothing as the carriage moved. And I did not look back as we passed through the manor gates and into the forest beyond.

+

Almost as soon as the carriage entered the woods, the sparkle of magic stuffed itself up my nose and I was dragged into a deep sleep. I was furious when I jerked awake, wondering why it had been at all necessary, but the air was full of the thunderous clopping of hooves against a flagstone path. Rubbing my eyes, I peered out the window to see a sloping drive lined with conical hedges and irises. I had never been here before.

I took in as many details as I could as the carriage came to a stop before a chateau of white marble and emerald roofs—nearly as large as Tamlin's manor.

The faces of the approaching servants were unfamiliar, and I kept my face blank as I gripped the footman's hand and stepped out of the carriage.

Human. He was utterly human, with his rounded ears, his ruddy face, his clothes.

The other servants were human, too—all of them restless, not at all like the utter stillness with which the High Fae held themselves. Unfinished, graceless creatures of earth and blood.

The servants were eyeing me but keeping back—shrinking away. Did I look so grand, then? I straightened at the flurry of motion and color that burst from the front doors.

I recognized my sisters before they saw me. They approached, smoothing their fine dresses, their brows rising at the gilded carriage.

That cracking, caved-in feeling in my chest worsened. Tamlin had said he'd taken care of my family, but *this* . . .

Nesta spoke first, curtsying low. Elain followed suit. "Welcome to our home," Nesta said a bit flatly, her eyes on the ground. "Lady . . ."

I let out a stark laugh. "Nesta," I said, and she went rigid. I laughed again. "Nesta, don't you recognize your own sister?"

Elain gasped. "Feyre?" She reached for me, but paused. "What of Aunt Ripleigh, then? Is she . . . dead?"

That was the story, I remembered—that I'd gone to care for a long-lost, wealthy aunt. I nodded slowly. Nesta took in my clothes and carriage, the pearls that were woven into her gold-brown hair gleaming in the sunlight. "She left you her fortune," Nesta stated flatly. It wasn't a question.

"Feyre, you should have told us!" Elain said, still gaping. "Oh, how awful—and you had to endure losing her all on your own, you poor thing. Father will be devastated that he didn't get to pay his respects."

Such . . . such simple things: relatives dying and fortunes being left and paying respect to the dead. And yet—yet . . . a weight I hadn't realized I'd still been carrying eased. These were the only things that worried them now.

"Why are you being so quiet?" Nesta said, keeping her distance.

I'd forgotten how cunning her eyes were, how cold. She'd been made differently, from something harder and stronger than bone and blood. She was as different from the humans around us as I had become.

"I'm . . . glad to see how well your own fortunes have improved," I managed. "What happened?" The driver—glamoured to look human, no mask in sight—began unloading trunks for the footmen. I hadn't known Tamlin had sent me off with belongings.

Elain beamed. "Didn't you get our letters?" She didn't remember—or maybe she'd never actually known, then, that I wouldn't have been able to read them, anyway. When I shook my head, she complained about the uselessness of the post and then said, "Oh, you'll never believe it! Almost a week after you went to care for Aunt Ripleigh, some stranger appeared at our door and asked Father to invest his money for him! Father was hesitant because the offer was so good, but the stranger insisted, so Father did it. He gave us a trunk of gold just for agreeing! Within a month, he'd doubled the man's investment, and then money started pouring in. And you know what? All those ships we lost were found in Bharat, complete with Father's profits!"

Tamlin—Tamlin had done that for them. I ignored the growing hollowness in my chest.

"Feyre, you look as dumbfounded as we were," Elain said, hooking elbows with me. "Come inside. We'll show you the house! We don't have a room decorated for you, because we thought you'd be with poor old Aunt Ripleigh for months yet, but we have so many bedrooms that you can sleep in a different one each night if you wish!"

I glanced over my shoulder at Nesta, who watched me with a carefully blank face. So she hadn't married Tomas Mandray after all.

"Father will likely faint when he sees you," Elain babbled on, patting my hand as she escorted me toward the main door. "Oh, maybe he'll throw a ball in your honor, too!"

Nesta fell into step behind us, a quiet, stalking presence. I didn't want to know what she was thinking. I wasn't certain whether I should be furious or relieved that they'd gotten on so well without me—and whether Nesta was wondering the same.

Horseshoes clopped, and the carriage began ambling down the driveway—away from me, back to my true home, back to Tamlin. It took all my will to keep from running after it.

He had said he loved me, and I'd felt the truth of it with our lovemaking, and he'd sent me away to keep me safe; he'd freed me from the Treaty to keep me safe. Because whatever storm was about to break in Prythian was brutal enough that even a High Lord couldn't stand against it.

I had to stay; it was wise to stay here. But I couldn't fight the sensation, like a darkening shadow within me, that I'd made a very, very big mistake in leaving, no matter Tamlin's orders. *Stay with the High Lord*, the Suriel had said. Its only command.

I shoved the thought from my mind as my father wept at the sight of me and did indeed order a ball in my honor. And though I knew that the promise I had once made to my mother was fulfilled—though I knew that I truly was free of it, and that my family was forever cared for . . . that growing, lengthening shadow blanketed my heart.

CHAPTER 29

Inventing stories about my time with Aunt Ripleigh required minimal effort: I read to her daily, she instructed me on deportment from her bedside, and I nursed her until she died in her sleep two weeks ago, leaving her fortune to me.

And what a tremendous fortune it was: the trunks that accompanied me hadn't contained just clothing—several of them had been filled with gold and jewels. Not cut jewels, either, but enormous, raw jewels that would pay for a thousand estates.

My father was currently taking inventory of those jewels; he'd holed himself up in the office that overlooked the garden in which I was sitting beside Elain in the grass. Through the window, I spied my father hunched over his desk, a little scale before him as he weighed an uncut ruby the size of a duck's egg. He was clear-eyed again, and moved with a sense of purpose, of vibrancy, that I hadn't seen since before the downfall. Even his limp was improved—made miraculously better by some tonic and a salve a strange, passing healer had given him for free. I would have been forever grateful to Tamlin for that kindness alone.

Gone were his hunched shoulders and downcast, misty eyes. My father smiled freely, laughed readily, and doted on Elain, who in turn doted on him. Nesta, though, had been quiet and watchful, only giving Elain answers not longer than a word or two.

"These bulbs," Elain said, pointing with a gloved hand to a cluster of purple-and-white flowers, "came all the way from the tulip fields of the continent. Father promised that next spring he'll take me to see them. He claims that for mile after mile, there's nothing but these flowers." She patted the rich, dark soil. The little garden beneath the window was hers: every bloom and shrub had been picked and planted by her hand; she would allow no one else to care for it. Even the weeding and watering she did on her own.

Though the servants *did* help her carry over the heavy watering cans, she admitted. She would have marveled—likely wept—at the gardens I'd become so accustomed to, at the flowers in perpetual bloom at the Spring Court.

"You should come with me," Elain went on. "Nesta won't go, because she says she doesn't want to risk the sea crossing, but you and I . . . Oh, we'd have fun, wouldn't we?"

I glanced sidelong at her. My sister was beaming, content—prettier than I'd ever seen her, even in her simple muslin gardening dress. Her cheeks were flushed beneath her large, floppy hat. "I think—I think I'd like to see the continent," I said.

And it was true, I realized. There was so much of the world that I hadn't seen, hadn't ever thought about visiting. Hadn't ever been *able* to dream of visiting.

"I'm surprised you're so eager to go next spring," I said. "Isn't that right in the middle of the season?" The socialite season, which had ended a few weeks ago, apparently, full of parties and balls and luncheons and gossip, gossip, gossip. Elain had told me all about it at dinner the night before, hardly noticing that it was an effort for me to get down my food. So much of it was the same—the meat, the bread, the vegetables, and yet . . . it was ash in my mouth compared to what I'd consumed in Prythian. "And I'm surprised you don't have a line of suitors out the door, begging for your hand."

Elain flushed but plunged her little shovel into the ground to dig out a weed. "Yes, well—there will always be other seasons. Nesta won't tell you, but this season was somewhat . . . strange."

"In what way?"

She shrugged her slim shoulders. "People acted as if we'd all just been ill for eight years, or had gone away to some distant country—not that we'd been a few villages over in that cottage. You'd think we dreamed it all up, what happened to us over those years. No one said a word about it."

"Did you think they would?" If we were as rich as this house suggested, there were surely plenty of families willing to overlook the stain of our poverty.

"No—but it made me . . . made me wish for those years again, even with the hunger and cold. This house feels so big sometimes, and father is always busy, and Nesta . . ." She looked over her shoulder to where my eldest sister stood by a gnarled mulberry tree, looking out over the flat expanse of our lands. She'd barely spoken to me the night before, and not at all during breakfast. I'd been surprised when she joined us outside, even if she'd stayed by the tree this whole time. "Nesta didn't finish the season. She wouldn't tell me why. She began refusing every invitation. She hardly talks to anyone, and I feel wretched when my friends pay a visit, because she makes them so uncomfortable when she stares at them in that way of hers . . ." Elain sighed. "Maybe you could talk to her."

I contemplated telling Elain that Nesta and I hadn't had a civil conversation in years, but then Elain added, "She went to see you, you know."

I blinked, my blood going a bit cold. "What?"

"Well, she was gone for only about a week, and she said that her carriage broke down not halfway there, and it was easier to come back. But you wouldn't know, since you never got any of our letters."

I looked over at Nesta, standing so still under the branches, the summer breeze rustling the skirts of her dress. Had she gone to see me, only to be turned back by whatever glamour magic Tamlin had cast on her?

I turned back to the garden and caught Elain staring at me. "What?"

Elain shook her head and went back to weeding. "You just look so . . . different. You sound so different, too."

Indeed, I hadn't quite believed my eyes when I'd passed a hall mirror last night. My face was still the same, but there was a . . . *glow* about me, a kind of shimmering light that was nearly undetectable. I knew without a doubt that it was because of my time in Prythian, that all that magic had somehow rubbed off on me. I dreaded the day it would forever fade.

"Did something happen at Aunt Ripleigh's house?" Elain asked. "Did you . . . meet someone?"

I shrugged and yanked at a weed nearby. "Just good food and rest."

Days passed. The shadow within me didn't lighten, and even the thought of painting was abhorrent. Instead I spent most of my time with Elain in her little garden. I was content to listen to her talk about every bud and bloom, about her plans to start another garden by the greenhouse, perhaps a vegetable garden, if she could learn enough about it over the next few months.

She had come alive here, and her joy was infectious. There wasn't a servant or gardener who didn't smile at her, and even the brusque head cook found excuses to bring her plates of cookies and tarts at various points in the day. I marveled at it, actually—that those years of poverty hadn't stripped away that light from Elain. Perhaps buried it a bit, but she was generous, loving, and kind—a woman I found myself proud to know, to call sister.

My father finished counting my jewels and gold; I was an extraordinarily wealthy woman. I invested a small percentage of it in his business, and when I looked at the remaining behemoth sum, I had him draw me up several bags of money and set out.

The manor was only three miles from our rundown cottage, and the road was familiar. I didn't mind when my hem became coated in mud from the sodden path. I savored hearing the wind in the trees and the sighing of the high grasses. If I drifted far enough into my memories, I could imagine myself walking alongside Tamlin through his woods.

I had no reason to believe that I would see him anytime soon, but I went to bed each night praying that I'd awaken to find myself in his manor, or that I'd receive a message summoning me to his side. Even worse than my disappointment that no such thing had happened was the creeping, nagging fear that he was in danger—that Amarantha, whoever she was, would somehow hurt him.

"*I love you.*" I could almost hear the words—almost hear him saying them, could almost see the sunlight glinting in his golden hair and the dazzling green of his eyes. I could almost feel his body pressed against mine, his fingers playing along my skin.

I reached a bend in the road that I could have navigated in the dark, and there it was.

So small—the cottage had been so small. Elain's old flower garden was a wild tangle of weeds and blooms, and the ward-markings were still etched on the stone threshold. The front door—shattered and broken the last time I'd seen it—had been replaced, but one of the circular windowpanes had become cracked. The interior was dark, the land undisturbed.

I traced the invisible path I'd taken across the tall grass every morning from our front door, over the road, and then across the rolling field, all the way to that line of trees. The forest—my forest.

It had seemed so terrifying once—so lethal and hungry and brutal. And now it just seemed . . . plain. Ordinary.

I gazed again at that sad, dark house—the place that had been a prison. Elain had said she missed it, and I wondered what she saw when she looked at the cottage. If she beheld not a prison but a shelter—a shelter from a world that had possessed so little good, but she tried to find it anyway, even if it had seemed foolish and useless to me.

She had looked at that cottage with hope; I had looked at it with nothing but hatred. And I knew which one of us had been stronger.

CHAPTER 30

I had one task left to do before I returned to my father's manor. The villagers who had once sneered at or ignored me instead gaped now, and a few stepped into my path to ask about my aunt, my fortune, on and on. I firmly but politely refused to fall into conversation with them, to give them anything to gossip over. But it still took me so long to reach the poor part of our village that I was fully drained by the time I knocked on the first dilapidated door.

The impoverished of our village didn't ask questions when I handed them the little bags of silver and gold. They tried to refuse, some of them not even recognizing me, but I left the money anyway. It was the least I could do.

As I walked back to my father's manor, I passed Tomas Mandray and his cronies lurking by the village fountain, chatting about some house that had burned down with its family trapped inside a week before and whether there was anything to loot from it. He gave me a too-long look, his eyes roving freely over my body, with a half smile I'd seen him give to the village girls a hundred times before. Why had Nesta changed her mind? I just stared him down and continued along.

I was almost out of town when a woman's laugh flitted over the stones, and I turned a corner to come face-to-face with Isaac Hale—and a pretty, plump young woman who could only be his new wife. They were arm in arm, both smiling—both lit up from within.

His smile faltered as he beheld me.

Human—he seemed so *human*, with his gangly limbs, his simple handsomeness, but that smile he'd had moments before had transformed him into something more.

His wife looked between us, perhaps a bit nervously. As if whatever she felt for him—the love I'd already seen shining—was so new, so unexpected, that she was still worried it would vanish. Carefully, Isaac inclined his head to me in greeting. He'd been a boy when I left, and yet this person who now approached me . . . whatever had blossomed with his wife, whatever was between them, it had made him into a man.

Nothing—there was nothing in my chest, my soul, for him beyond a vague sense of gratitude.

A few more steps had us passing each other. I smiled broadly at him, at them both, and bowed my head, wishing them well with my entire heart.

The ball my father was throwing in my honor was in two days, and the house was already a flurry of activity. Such money being thrown away on things we'd never dreamed of having again, even for a moment. I would have begged him not to host it, but Elain had taken charge of planning *and* finding me a last-minute dress, and . . . it would only be for an evening. An evening of enduring the people who had shunned us and let us starve for years.

The sun was near to setting as I stopped my work for the day: digging out a new square of earth for Elain's next garden. The gardeners had been slightly horrified that another one of us had taken up the activity—as if we'd soon be doing all their work ourselves and would get rid of them. I reassured them I had no green thumb and just wanted something to do with my day.

But I hadn't yet figured out what I would be doing with my week, or my month, or anything after that. If there was indeed a surge in the blight happening over the wall, if that Amarantha woman was sending out creatures to take advantage of it . . . It was hard not to dwell on that shadow in my heart, the shadow that trailed my every step. I hadn't felt like painting since I'd arrived—and that place inside me where all those colors and shapes and lights had come from had become still and quiet and dull. Soon, I told myself. Soon I would purchase some paints and start again.

I slid the shovel into the ground and set my foot atop it, resting for a moment. Perhaps the gardeners had just been horrified by the tunic and pants I'd scrounged up. One of them had even gone running to fetch me one of those big, floppy hats that Elain wore. I wore it for their sake; my skin had already become tan and freckled from months roaming the Spring Court lands.

I glanced at my hands, clutching the top of the shovel. Callused and flecked with scars, arcs of dirt under my nails. They'd surely be horrified when they beheld me splattered with paint.

"Even if you washed them, there'd be no hiding it," Nesta said behind me, coming over from that tree she liked to sit by. "To fit in, you'd have to wear gloves and never take them off."

She wore a simple, pale lavender muslin gown, her hair half-up and billowing behind her in a sheet of gold-brown. Beautiful, imperious, still as one of the High Fae.

"Maybe I don't want to fit in with your social circles," I said, turning back to the shovel.

"Then why are you bothering to stay here?" A sharp, cold question.

I plunged the shovel deeper, my arms and back straining as I heaved up a pile of dark soil and grass. "It's my home, isn't it?"

"No, it's not," she said flatly. I slammed the shovel back into the earth. "I think your home is somewhere very far away."

I paused.

I left the shovel in the ground and slowly turned to face her. "Aunt Ripleigh's house—"

"There is no Aunt Ripleigh." Nesta reached into her pocket and tossed something onto the churned-up earth.

It was a chunk of wood, as if it had been ripped from something. Painted on its smooth surface was a pretty tangle of vines and—foxglove. Foxglove painted in the wrong shade of blue.

My breath hitched. All this time, all these months . . .

"Your beast's little trick didn't work on me," she said with quiet steel. "Apparently, an iron will is all it takes to keep a glamour from digging in. So I had to watch as Father and Elain went from sobbing hysterics into *nothing*. I had to listen to them talk about how lucky it was for you to be taken to some made-up aunt's house, how some winter wind had shattered our door. And I thought I'd gone mad—but every time I did, I would look at that painted part of the table, then at the claw marks farther down, and know it wasn't in my head."

I'd never heard of a glamour not working. But Nesta's mind was so entirely her own; she had put up such strong walls—of steel and iron and ash wood—that even a High Lord's magic couldn't pierce them.

"Elain said—said you went to visit me, though. That you tried."

Nesta snorted, her face grave and full of that long-simmering anger that she could never master. "He stole you away into the night, claiming some nonsense about the Treaty. And then everything went on as if it had never happened. It wasn't right. None of it was right."

My hands slackened at my sides. "You went after me," I said. "You went after me—to Prythian."

"I got to the wall. I couldn't find a way through."

I raised a shaking hand to my throat. "You trekked two days there and two days back—through the winter woods?"

She shrugged, looking at the sliver she'd pried from the table. "I hired that mercenary from town to bring me a week after you were taken. With the money from your pelt. She was the only one who seemed like she would believe me."

"You did that—for me?"

Nesta's eyes—my eyes, our mother's eyes—met mine. "It wasn't right," she said again. Tamlin had been wrong when we'd discussed whether my father would have ever come after me—he didn't possess the courage, the anger. If anything, he would have hired someone to do it for him. But Nesta had gone with that mercenary. My hateful, cold sister had been willing to brave Prythian to rescue me.

"What happened to Tomas Mandray?" I asked, the words strangled.

"I realized he wouldn't have gone with me to save you from Prythian."

And for her, with that raging, unrelenting heart, it would have been a line in the sand.

I looked at my sister, really *looked* at her, at this woman who couldn't stomach the sycophants who now surrounded her, who had never spent a day in the forest but had gone into wolf territory . . . Who had shrouded the loss of our mother, then our downfall, in icy rage and bitterness, because the anger had been a lifeline, the cruelty a release. But she *had* cared—beneath it, she had cared, and perhaps loved more fiercely than I could comprehend, more deeply and loyally. "Tomas never deserved you anyway," I said softly.

My sister didn't smile, but a light shone in her blue-gray eyes. "Tell me everything that happened," she said—an order, not a request.

So I did.

And when I finished my story, Nesta merely stared at me for a long while before asking me to teach her how to paint.

Teaching Nesta to paint was about as pleasant as I had expected it to be, but at least it provided an excuse for us to avoid the busier parts of the house, which became more and more chaotic as my ball drew near. Supplies were easy enough to come by, but explaining how I painted, convincing Nesta to express what was in her mind, her heart . . . At the very least, she repeated my brushstrokes with a precise and solid hand.

When we emerged from the quiet room we'd commandeered, both of us splattered in paint and smeared with charcoal, the chateau was finishing up its preparations. Colored glass lanterns lined the long drive, and inside, wreaths and garlands of every flower and color decorated every rail, every surface, every archway. Beautiful. Elain had selected each flower herself and instructed the staff where to put them.

Nesta and I slipped up the stairs, but as we reached the landing, my father and Elain appeared below, arm in arm.

Nesta's face tightened. My father murmured his praises to Elain, who beamed at him and rested her head on his shoulder. And I was happy for them—for the comfort and ease of their lifestyle, for the contentment on both my father's and my sister's faces. Yes, they had their small sorrows, but both of them seemed so . . . relaxed.

Nesta walked down the hall, and I followed her. "There are days," Nesta said as she paused in front of the door to her room, across from mine, "when I want to ask him if he remembers the years he almost let us starve to death."

"You spent every copper I could get, too," I reminded her.

"I knew you could always get more. And if you couldn't, then I wanted to see if he would ever try to do it himself, instead of carving those bits of wood. If he would actually go out and fight for us. I couldn't take care of us, not the way you did. I hated you for that. But I hated him more. I still do."

"Does he know?"

"He's always known I hate him, even before we became poor. He let Mother die—he had a fleet of ships at his disposal to sail across the world for a cure, or he could have hired men to go into Prythian and beg them for help. But he let her waste away."

"He loved her—he grieved for her." I didn't know what the truth was—perhaps both.

"He let her die. You would have gone to the ends of the earth to save your High Lord."

My chest hollowed out again, but I merely said, "Yes, I would have," and slipped inside my room to get ready.

CHAPTER 31

The ball was a blur of waltzing and preening, of bejeweled aristos, of wine and toasts in my honor. I lingered at Nesta's side, because she seemed to do a good job of scaring off the too-curious suitors who wanted to know more about my fortune. But I tried to smile, if only for Elain, who flitted about the room, personally greeting each guest and dancing with all their important sons.

But I kept thinking about what Nesta had said—about saving Tamlin.

I'd known something was wrong. I'd known he was in trouble—not just with the blight on Prythian, but also that the forces gathering to destroy him were deadly, and yet . . . and yet I'd stopped looking for answers, stopped fighting it, glad—so selfishly *glad*—to be able to set down that savage, wild part of me that had only survived hour to hour. I'd let him send me home. I hadn't tried harder to piece together the information I'd gathered about the blight or Amarantha; I hadn't tried to save him. I hadn't even told him I loved him. And Lucien . . . Lucien had known it, too—and shown it in his bitter words on my last day, his disappointment in me.

Two in the morning, and yet the party was showing no signs of slowing. My father held court with several other merchants and aristo men to whom I had been introduced but whose names I'd instantly forgotten. Elain was laughing among a circle of beautiful friends, flushed and brilliant. Nesta had silently left at midnight, and I didn't bother to say good-bye as I finally slipped upstairs.

The following afternoon, bleary-eyed and quiet, we all gathered at the lunch table. I thanked my sister and father for the party, and dodged my father's inquiries regarding whether any of his friends' sons had caught my eye.

The summer heat had arrived, and I propped my chin on a fist as I fanned myself. I'd slept fitfully in the heat last night. It was never too hot or too cold at Tamlin's estate.

"I'm thinking of buying the Beddor land," my father was saying to Elain, who was the only one of us listening to him. "I heard a rumor it'll go up for sale soon, since none of the family survived, and it would be a good investment property. Perhaps one of you girls might build a house on it when you're ready."

Elain nodded interestedly, but I blinked. "What happened to the Beddors?"

"Oh, it was awful," Elain said. "Their house burned down, and everyone died. Well, they couldn't find Clare's body, but . . ." She looked down at her plate. "It happened in the dead of night—the family, their servants, everyone. The day before you came home to us, actually."

"Clare Beddor," I said slowly.

"Our friend, remember?" Elain said.

I nodded, feeling Nesta's eyes on me.

No—no, it couldn't be possible. It had to be a coincidence—*had* to be a coincidence, because the alternative . . .

I had given that name to Rhysand.

And he had not forgotten it.

My stomach turned over, and I fought against the nausea that roiled within me.

"Feyre?" my father asked.

I put a shaking hand over my eyes, breathing in. What had happened? Not just at the Beddors', but at home, in Prythian?

"Feyre," my father said again, and Nesta hissed at him, "Quiet."

I pushed back against the guilt, the disgust and terror. I had to get answers—had to know if it had been a coincidence, or if I might yet be able to save Clare. And if something had happened here, in the mortal realm, then the Spring Court . . . then those creatures Tamlin had been so frightened of . . . the blight that had infected magic, their lands . . .

Faeries. They had come over the wall and left no trace behind.

I lowered my hand and looked at Nesta. "You must listen very carefully," I said to her, swallowing hard. "Everything I have told you must remain a secret. You do not come looking for me. You do not speak my name again to anyone."

"What are you talking about, Feyre?" My father gaped at me from the end of the table. Elain glanced between us, shifting in her seat.

But Nesta held my gaze. Unflinching.

"I think something very bad might be happening in Prythian," I said softly. I'd never learned what warning signs Tamlin had instilled in their glamours to prod my family to run, but I wasn't going to risk relying solely on them. Not when Clare had been taken, her family murdered . . . because of me. Bile burned my throat.

"Prythian!" my father and Elain blurted. But Nesta held up a hand to silence them.

I went on, "If you won't leave, then hire guards—hire scouts to watch the wall, the forest. The village, too." I rose from my seat. "The first sign of danger, the first rumor you hear of the wall being breached or even something being *strange*, you get on a ship and go. You sail far away, as far south as you can get, to someplace the faeries would never desire."

My father and Elain began blinking, as if clearing some fog from their minds—as if emerging from a deep sleep. But Nesta followed me into the hall, up the stairs.

"The Beddors," she said. "That was meant to be us. But you gave them a fake name—those wicked faeries who threatened your High Lord." I nodded. I could see the plans calculating in her eyes. "Is there going to be an invasion?"

"I don't know. I don't know what's happening. I was told that there was a kind of sickness that had made their powers weaken or go wild, a blight on the land that had damaged the safety of their borders and could kill people if it struck badly enough. They—they said it was surging again . . . on the move. The last I heard, it wasn't near enough to harm our lands. But if the Spring Court is about to fall, then the blight has to be getting close, and Tamlin . . . Tamlin was one of the last bastions keeping the other courts in check—the deadly courts. And I think he's in danger."

I entered my room and began peeling off my gown. My sister helped me, then opened the wardrobe to pull out a heavy tunic and pants and boots. I slipped into them and was braiding back my hair when she said, "We don't need you here, Feyre. Do not look back."

I tugged on my boots and went for the hunting knives I'd discreetly acquired while here.

"Father once told you to never come back," Nesta said, "and I'm telling you now. We can take care of ourselves."

Once I might have thought it was an insult, but now I understood—understood what a gift she was offering me. I sheathed the knives at my side and slung a quiver of arrows across my back—none of them ash—before scooping up my bow. "They *can* lie," I said, giving her information I hoped she would never need. "Faeries can lie, and iron doesn't bother them one bit. But ash wood—that seems to work. Take my money and buy a damned grove of it for Elain to tend."

Nesta shook her head, clutching her wrist, the bracelet of iron still there. "What do you think you can even do to help? He's a High Lord—you're just a human." That wasn't an insult, either. A question from a coolly calculating mind.

"I don't care," I admitted, at the door now, which I flung open. "But I've got to try."

Nesta remained in my room. She would not say good-bye—she hated farewells as much as I did.

But I turned to my sister and said, "There is a better world, Nesta. There is a better world out there, waiting for you to find it. And if I ever get the chance, if things are ever better, safer . . . I will find you again."

It was all I could offer her.

But Nesta squared her shoulders. "Don't bother. I don't think I'd be particularly fond of faeries." I raised a brow. She went on with a slight shrug. "Try to send word once it's safe. And if it ever is . . . Father and Elain can have this place. I think I'd like to see what else is out there, what a woman might do with a fortune and a good name."

No limits, I thought. There were no limits to what Nesta might do, what she might make of herself once she found a place to call her own. I prayed I would be lucky enough to someday see it.

Elain, to my surprise, had a horse, a satchel of food, and supplies ready when I hurried down the stairs. My father was nowhere in sight. But Elain threw her arms around me, and, holding tightly, said, "I remember—I remember all of it now."

I wrapped my arms around her. "Be on your guard. All of you."

She nodded, tears in her eyes. "I would have liked to see the continent with you, Feyre."

I smiled at my sister, memorizing her lovely face, and wiped her tears away. "Maybe someday," I said. Another promise that I'd be lucky to keep.

Elain was still crying as I spurred my horse and galloped down the drive. I didn't have it in me to say good-bye to my father once more.

I rode all day and stopped only when it was too dark for me to see. Due north—that's where I would start and go until I hit the wall. I had to get back—had to see what had happened, had to tell Tamlin everything that was in my heart before it was too late.

I rode all of the second day, slept fitfully, and was off before first light.

On and on, through the summer forest, lush and dense and humming.

Until an absolute silence fell. I slowed my horse to a careful walk and scanned the brush and trees ahead for any sign, any ripple. There was nothing. Nothing, and then—

My horse bucked and shook her head, and it was all I could do to stay in the saddle as she refused to go forward. But still, there was nothing—no marker. Yet when I dismounted, hardly breathing as I put a hand out, I found that I could not pass.

There, cleaving through the forest, was an invisible wall.

But the faeries came and went through it—through holes, rumor claimed. So I led my horse down the line, tapping the wall every so often to make sure I hadn't veered away.

It took me two days—and the night between them was more terrifying than any I'd experienced at the Spring Court. Two days, before I spied the mossy stones placed across from each other, a faint whorl carved into them both. A gate.

This time, when I mounted my horse and steered her between them, she obeyed.

Magic stung my nostrils, zapping until my horse bucked again, but we were through.

I knew these trees.

I rode in silence, an arrow nocked and ready, the threats lurking in the forest far greater than those in the woods I'd just left.

Tamlin might be furious—he might command me to turn around and go home. But I would tell him that I was going to help, tell him that I loved him and would fight for him however I could, even if I had to tie him down to make him listen.

I became so intent on contemplating how I might convince him not to start roaring that I didn't immediately notice the quiet—how the birds didn't sing, even as I drew closer to the manor itself, how the hedges of the estate looked in need of a trim.

By the time I reached the gates, my mouth had gone dry. The gates were open, but the iron had been bent out of shape, as if mighty hands had wrenched them apart.

Every step of the horse's hooves was too loud on the gravel path, and my stomach dropped further when I beheld the wide-open front doors. One of them hung at an angle, ripped off its top hinge.

I dismounted, arrow still at the ready. But there was no need. Empty—it was utterly empty here. Like a tomb.

"Tam?" I called. I bounded up the front steps and into the house. I rushed inside, swearing as I slid on a piece of broken porcelain—the remnants of a vase. Slowly, I turned in the front hall.

It looked as if an army had marched through. Tapestries hung in shreds, the marble banister was fractured, and the chandeliers lay broken on the ground, reduced to mounds of shattered crystal.

"Tamlin?" I shouted. Nothing.

The windows had all been blown out. "Lucien?"

No one answered.

"Tam?" My voice echoed through the house, mocking me.

Alone in the wreckage of the manor, I sank to my knees.

He was gone.

CHAPTER 32

I gave myself a minute—just one minute—to kneel in the remnants of the entry hall.

Then I eased to my feet, careful not to disturb any of the shattered glass or wood or—blood. There were splatters of it everywhere, along with small puddles and smears down the gouged walls.

Another forest, I told myself. Another set of tracks.

Slowly, I moved across the floor, tracing the information left. It had been a vicious fight—and from the blood patterns, most of the damage to the house had been done during the fight, not afterward. The crushed glass and footprints came and went from the front and back of the house, as if the whole place had been surrounded. The intruders had needed to force their way in through the front door; they'd just completely shattered the doors to the garden.

No bodies, I kept repeating to myself. There were no bodies, and not much gore. They had to be alive. Tamlin *had* to be alive.

Because if he were dead . . .

I rubbed my face, taking a shuddering breath. I wouldn't let myself get that far. My hands shook as I paused before the dining room doors, both barely hanging on their hinges.

I couldn't tell if the damage was from his lashing out after Rhysand's arrival the day before my departure or if someone else had caused it. The giant table was in pieces, the windows smashed, the curtains in shreds. But no blood—there was no blood here. And from the prints in the shards of glass . . .

I studied the trail across the floor. It had been disturbed, but I could make out two sets—large and side by side—leading from where the table had been. As if Tamlin and Lucien had been sitting in here as the attack happened, and walked out without a fight.

If I was right . . . then they were alive. I traced the steps to the doorway, squatting for a moment to work through the churned-up shards, dirt, and blood. They'd been met here—by multiple sets of prints. And headed toward the garden—

Debris crunched from down the hall. I drew my hunting knife and ducked farther into the dining room, scanning for a place to hide. But everything was in pieces. With no other option, I lunged behind the open door. I pressed a hand over my mouth to keep from breathing too loudly and peered through the crack between the door and the wall.

Something limped into the room and sniffed. I could only see its back—cloaked in a plain cape, medium height . . . All it had to do to find me was shut the door. Perhaps if it came far enough into the dining room, I could slip out—but that would require leaving my hiding spot. Perhaps it would just look around and then leave.

The figure sniffed again, and my stomach clenched. It could smell me. I dared a better glance at it, hoping to find a weakness, a spot for my knife, if things came down to it.

The figure turned slightly toward me.

I cried out, and the figure screeched as I shoved away the door. *"Alis."*

She gaped at me, a hand on her heart, her usual brown dress torn and dirty, her apron gone entirely. Not bloodied, though—nothing save for the slight limp that favored her right ankle as she rushed for me, her tree-bark skin bleaching birch white. "You can't be here." She took in my knife, the bow and quiver. "You were told to stay away."

"Is he alive?"

"Yes, but—"

My knees buckled at the onslaught of relief. "And Lucien?"

"Alive as well. But—."

"Tell me what happened—tell me *everything*." I kept an eye on the window, listening to the manor and grounds around us. Not a sound.

Alis grasped my arm and pulled me from the room. She didn't speak as we hurried through the empty, too-quiet halls—all of them wrecked and bloodied, but . . . no bodies. Either they'd been hauled away, or—I didn't let myself consider it as we entered the kitchen.

A fire had scorched the giant room, and it was little more than cinders and blackened stone. After sniffing about and listening for any signs of danger, Alis released me. "What are you doing here?"

"I had to come back. I thought something had gone wrong—I couldn't stay away. I had to help."

"He told you not to come back," Alis snapped.

"Where is he?"

Alis covered her face with her long, bony hands, her fingertips grappling into the upper edge of her mask as if trying to tear it from her face. But the mask remained, and Alis sighed as she lowered her tree-bark hands. "She took him," she said, and my blood went cold. "She took him to her court Under the Mountain."

"Who?" But I already knew the answer.

"Amarantha," Alis whispered, and glanced again around the kitchen as if fearful that speaking her name would summon her.

"Why? And who is she—*what* is she? Please, *please* just tell me—just give me the truth."

Alis shuddered. "You want the truth, girl? Then here it is: she took him for the curse—because the seven times seven years were over, and he hadn't shattered her curse. She's summoned all the High Lords to her court this time—to make them watch her break him."

"What is she—*wh-what curse?*" A curse—the curse *she* had put on this place. A curse that I had failed to even see.

"Amarantha is High Queen of this land. The High Queen of Prythian," Alis breathed, her eyes wide with some memory of horror.

"But the seven High Lords rule Prythian—equally. There's no High Queen."

"That's how it used to be—how it's always been. Until a hundred years ago, when she appeared in these lands as an emissary from Hybern." Alis grabbed a large satchel that she must have left by the door. It was already half full of what looked like clothes and supplies.

As she began sifting through the ruined kitchen, gathering up knives and any food that had survived, I wondered at the information the Suriel had given me—of a wicked faerie king who had spent centuries resenting the Treaty he'd been forced to sign, and who had sent out his deadliest commanders to infiltrate the other faerie kingdoms and courts to see if they felt as he did—to see if they might consider reclaiming the human lands for themselves. I leaned against one of the soot-stained walls.

"She went from court to court," Alis went on, turning an apple over in her hands as she inspected it, deemed it good enough, and stuffed it into the bag, "charming the High Lords with talk of more trade between Hybern and Prythian, more communication, more sharing of assets. The Never-Fading Flower, they called her. And for fifty years, she lived here as a courtier bound to no court, making amends, she claimed, for her own actions and the actions of Hybern during the War."

"She fought in the War against mortals?"

Alis paused her gathering. "Her story is legend among our kind—legend, and nightmare. She was the King of Hybern's most lethal general—she fought on the front lines, slaughtering humans and any High Fae and faeries who dared defend them. But she had a younger sister,

Clythia, who fought at her side, as vicious and wretched as she . . . until Clythia fell in love with a mortal warrior. Jurian." Alis loosed a shaking sigh. "Jurian commanded mighty human armies, but Clythia still secretly sought him out, still loved him with an unrelenting madness. She was too blind to realize that Jurian was using her for information about Amarantha's forces. Amarantha suspected, but could not persuade Clythia to leave him—and could not bring herself to kill him, not when it would cause her sister such pain." Alis clicked her tongue and began opening the cabinets, scanning their ravaged insides. "Amarantha delighted in torture and killing, and yet she loved her sister enough to stay her hand."

"What happened?" I breathed.

"Oh, Jurian betrayed Clythia. After months of stomaching being her lover, he got the information he needed, then tortured and butchered her, crucifying her with ash wood so she couldn't move while he did it. He left the pieces of her for Amarantha to find. They say Amarantha's wrath could have brought down the skies themselves, had her king not ordered her to stand down. But she and Jurian had their final confrontation later—and since then, Amarantha has hated humans with a rage you cannot imagine." Alis found what looked to be a jar of preserves and added it to the satchel.

"After the two sides made the Treaty," Alis said, now going through the drawers, "she butchered her own slaves, rather than free them." I blanched. "But centuries later, the High Lords believed her when she told them that the death of her sister had changed her—especially when she opened trade lines between our two territories. The High Lords never knew that those same ships that brought over Hybernian goods also brought over her own personal forces. The King of Hybern didn't know, either. But we all soon learned that, in those fifty years she was here, she had decided she wanted Prythian for her own, to begin amassing power and use our lands as a launching point to one day destroy your world once and for all, with or without her king's blessing. So forty-nine years ago, she struck.

"She knew—knew that even with her personal army, she could never conquer the seven High Lords by numbers or power alone. But she was also cunning and cruel, and she waited until they absolutely trusted her, until they gathered at a ball in her honor, and that night she slipped a potion stolen from the King of Hybern's unholy spell book into their wine. Once they drank, the High Lords were prone, their magic laid bare—and she stole their powers from where they originated inside their bodies—plucked them out as if she were taking an apple from its branch, leaving them with only the basest elements of their magic. Your Tamlin—what you saw of him here was a shade of what he used to be, the power that he used to command. And with the High Lords' power so greatly decreased, Amarantha wrested control of Prythian from them in a matter of days. For forty-nine years, we have been her slaves. For forty-nine years, she has been biding her time, waiting for the right moment to break the Treaty and take your lands—and all human territories beyond it."

I wished there were a stool, a bench, a chair for me to slump into. Alis slammed shut the final drawer and limped for the pantry.

"Now they call her the Deceiver—she who trapped the seven High Lords and built her palace beneath the sacred Mountain in the heart of our land." Alis paused before the pantry door and covered her face again, taking a few steadying breaths.

The sacred mountain—that bald, monstrous peak I'd spotted in the mural in the library all those months ago. "But . . . the sickness in the lands . . . Tamlin said that the blight took their power—"

"*She* is the sickness in these lands," Alis snapped, lowering her hands and entering the pantry. "There is no blight but her. The borders were collapsing because she laid them to rubble. She found it amusing to send her creatures to attack our lands, to test whatever strength Tamlin had left."

If the blight was Amarantha, then the threat to the human realm . . . *She* was the threat to the human realm.

Alis emerged from the pantry, her arms full of various root vegetables. "You could have been the one to stop her." Her eyes were hard upon me, and she bared her teeth. They were alarmingly sharp. She shoved the turnips and beets into the bag. "You could have been the one to free him and his power, had you not been so blind to your own heart. Humans," she spat.

"I—I . . ." I lifted my hands, exposing my palms to her. "I didn't know."

"You couldn't know," Alis said bitterly, her laugh harsh as she entered the pantry again. "It was part of Tamlin's curse."

My head swam, and I pressed myself further against the wall. "What was?" I fought the rising hitch in my voice. "What was his curse? What did she do to him?"

Alis yanked remaining spice jars off the pantry shelf. "Tamlin and Amarantha knew each other before—his family had long been tied to Hybern. During the War, the Spring Court allied with Hybern to keep the humans enslaved. So his father—his father, who was a fickle and vicious Lord—was very close with the King of Hybern, to Amarantha. Tamlin as a child often accompanied him on trips to Hybern. And he met Amarantha in the process."

Tamlin had once said to me that he would fight to *protect* someone's freedom—that he would never allow slavery. Had it been solely because of shame for his own legacy, or because he . . . he'd come to somehow know what it was to be enslaved?

"Amarantha eventually grew to desire Tamlin—to lust for him with her entire wicked heart. But he'd heard the stories from others about the War, and knew what Amarantha and his father and the Hybern king had done to faeries and humans alike. What she did to Jurian as punishment for her sister's death. He was wary of her when she came here, despite her attempts to lure him into her bed—and kept his distance, right up until she stole his powers. Lucien . . . Lucien was sent to her as Tamlin's emissary, to try to treat for peace between them."

Bile rose in my throat.

"She refused, and . . . Lucien told her to go back to the shit-hole she'd crawled out of. She took his eye as punishment. Carved it out with her own fingernail, then scarred his face. She sent him back so bloody that Tamlin . . . The High Lord vomited when he saw his friend."

I couldn't let myself imagine what state Lucien had been in, then, if it had made Tamlin sick.

Alis tapped on her mask, the metal pinging beneath her nails. "After that, she hosted a masquerade Under the Mountain for herself. All the courts were present. A party, she said—to make amends for what she'd done to Lucien, and a masquerade so he didn't have to reveal the horrible scarring on his face. The entire Spring Court was to attend, even the servants, and to wear masks—to honor Tamlin's shape-shifting powers, she said. He was willing to try to end the conflict without slaughter, and he agreed to go—to bring all of us."

I pressed my hands against the stone wall behind me, savoring its coolness, its steadiness.

Pausing in the center of the kitchen, Alis set down her satchel, now full of food and supplies. "When all were assembled, she claimed that peace could be had—if Tamlin joined her as her lover and consort. But when she tried to touch him, he refused to let her near. Not after what she'd done to Lucien. He said—in front of everyone that night—that he would sooner take a human to his bed, sooner *marry* a human, than ever touch her. She might have let it go, had he not then said that her own sister had preferred a human's company to hers, that her own sister had chosen Jurian over her."

I winced, already knowing what Alis would say as she braced her hands on her hips and went on. "You can guess how well that went over with Amarantha. But she told Tamlin that she was in a generous mood—told him she'd give him a chance to break the spell she'd put upon him to steal his power.

"He spat in her face, and she laughed. She said he had seven times seven years before she claimed him, before he *had* to join her Under the Mountain. If he wanted to break her curse, he need only find a human girl willing to marry him. But not any girl—a human with ice in her heart, with hatred for our kind. A human girl willing to kill a faerie." The ground rocked beneath me, and I was grateful for the wall I leaned against. "Worse, the faerie she killed had to be one of *his* men, sent across the wall by him like lambs to slaughter. The girl could only be brought here to be courted if she killed one of his men in an unprovoked attack—killed him for hatred alone, just as Jurian had done to Clythia . . . So he could understand her sister's pain."

"The Treaty—"

"That was all a lie. There was no provision for that in the Treaty. You can kill as many innocent faeries as you want and never suffer the consequences. You just killed Andras, sent out by Tamlin as that day's sacrifice." *Andras was looking for a cure*, Tamlin had said. Not for some magical blight—but a cure to save Prythian from Amarantha, a cure for this curse.

The wolf—Andras had just . . . stared at me before I killed him. *Let* me kill him. So it could begin this chain of events, so that Tamlin might stand a chance of breaking the spell. And if Tamlin had sent Andras across the wall, knowing he might very well die . . . *Oh, Tamlin.*

Alis stooped to gather up a butter knife, twisted and bent, and carefully straightened out the blade. "It was all a cruel joke, a clever punishment, to Amarantha. You humans loathe and fear faeries so much it would be impossible—impossible for the same girl who slaughtered a faerie in cold blood to then fall in love with one. But the spell on Tamlin could only be broken if she did just that before the forty-nine years were over—if that girl said to his face that she loved him, and meant it with her entire heart. Amarantha knows humans are preoccupied with beauty, and thus bound the masks to all our faces, to his face, so it would be more difficult to find a girl willing to look beyond the mask, beyond his faerie nature, and to the soul beneath. Then she bound us so we couldn't say a word about the curse. Not a single word. We could hardly tell you a thing about our world, about our fate. He couldn't tell you—none of us properly could. The lies about the blight—that was the best he could do, the best we could all do. That I can tell you now . . . it means the game is over, to her." She pocketed the knife.

"When she first cursed him, Tamlin sent one of his men across the wall every day. To the woods, to farms, all disguised as wolves to make it more likely for one of your kind to want to kill them. If they came back, it was with stories of human girls who ran and screamed and begged, who didn't even lift a hand. When they didn't come back—Tamlin's bond with them as their Lord and master told him they'd been killed by others. Human hunters, older women, perhaps. For two years he sent them out, day after day, having to pick who crossed the wall. When all but a dozen of them were left, it broke him so badly he stopped. Called it all off. And since then, Tamlin has been here, defending his borders as chaos and disorder ruled in the other courts under Amarantha's thumb. The other High Lords fought back, too. Forty years ago, she executed three of them and most of their families for banding together against her."

"Open rebellion? What courts?" I straightened, taking a step away from the wall. Perhaps I might find allies among them to help me save Tamlin.

"The Day Court, Summer Court, and Winter Court. And no—it didn't even get far enough to be considered an open rebellion. She used the High Lords' powers to bind us to the land. So the rebel lords tried calling for aid from the other Fae territories using as messengers whatever humans were foolish enough to enter our lands—most of them young women who worshipped us like gods." The Children of the Blessed. They had indeed made it over the wall—but not to be brides. I was too battered by what I'd heard to grieve for them, rage for them.

"But Amarantha caught them all before they left these shores, and . . . you can imagine how it ended for those girls. Afterward, once Amarantha also butchered the rebellious High Lords, their successors were too terrified to tempt her wrath again."

"And where are they now? Are they allowed to live on their lands, like Tamlin was?"

"No. She keeps them and their entire courts Under the Mountain, where she can torment them as she pleases. Others—others, if they swear allegiance, if they grovel and serve her, she allows them a bit more freedom to come and go Under the Mountain as they will. Our court was only allowed to remain here until Tamlin's curse ran out, but . . ." Alis shivered.

"That's why you keep your nephews in hiding—to keep them away from this," I said, glancing at the full satchel at her feet.

Alis nodded, and as she went to right the overturned worktable, I moved to help her, both of us grunting at the weight. "My sister and I served in the Summer Court—and she and her mate were among those put down for spite when Amarantha first invaded. I took the boys and ran before Amarantha had everyone dragged Under the Mountain. I came here because it was the only place to go, and asked Tamlin to hide my boys. He did—and when I begged him to let me help, in whatever small way, he gave me a position here, days before the masque that put this wretched thing on my face. So I've been here for nearly fifty years, watching as Amarantha's noose grew tighter around his neck."

We set the table upright again, and both of us panted a bit as we slumped against it.

"He tried," Alis said. "Even with her spies, he tried finding ways to break the curse, to do anything against it, against having to send his men out again to be slaughtered by humans. He thought that if the human girl loved true, then bringing her here to free him was another form of slavery. And he thought that if he did indeed fall in love with her, Amarantha would do everything she could to destroy her, as her sister had been destroyed. So he spent decades refusing to do it, to even risk it. But this winter, with months to go, he just . . . snapped. He sent the last of his men out, one by one. And they were willing—they had begged him to go, all these years. Tamlin was desperate to save his people, desperate enough to risk the lives of his men, risk that human girl's life to save us. Three days in, Andras finally ran into a human girl in a clearing—and you killed him with hate in your heart."

But I had failed them. And in so doing, I'd damned them all.

I had damned each and every person on this estate, damned Prythian itself.

I was glad I was leaning against the table's edge—or else I might have slid to the floor.

"You could have broken it," Alis snarled, those sharp teeth mere inches from my face. "All you had to do was say that you loved him—say that you loved him and mean it with your whole useless human heart, and his power would have been freed. You stupid, *stupid* girl."

No wonder Lucien had resented me and yet still tolerated my presence—no wonder he'd been so bitterly disappointed when I left, had argued with Tamlin to let me stay longer. "I'm sorry," I said, my eyes burning.

Alis snorted. "Tell that to Tamlin. He had only three days after you left before the forty-nine years were over. *Three days*, and he let you go. She came here with her cronies at the exact moment the seven times seven years were over and seized him, along with most of the court, and brought them Under the Mountain to be her subjects. Creatures like me are too *lowly* for her—though she's not above murdering us for sport."

I tried not to visualize it. "But what of the King of Hybern—if she's conquered Prythian for herself and stolen his spells, then does he see her as insubordinate or as an ally?"

"If they are on bad terms, he has made no move to punish her. For forty-nine years now, she's held these lands in her grip. Worse, after the High Lords fell, all the wicked ones in our lands—the ones too awful even for the Night Court—flocked to her. They still do. She's offered them sanctuary. But we know—we know she's building her army, biding her time before launching an attack on your world, armed with the most lethal and vicious faeries in Prythian and Hybern."

"Like the Attor," I said, horror and dread twisting in my gut, and Alis nodded. "In the human territory," I said, "rumor claims more and more faeries have been sneaking over the wall to attack humans. And if no faeries can cross the wall without her permission, then that has to mean she's been sanctioning those attacks."

And if I was right about what had happened to Clare Beddor and her family, then Amarantha had given the order for that, too.

Alis swiped some dirt I couldn't see from the table we leaned against. "I would not be surprised if she has sent her minions into the human realm to investigate your strengths and weaknesses in anticipation of the destruction she one day hopes to cause."

This was worse—so much worse than I had thought when I warned Nesta and my family to stay on alert and leave at the slightest sign of trouble. I felt sick to think of what kind of company Tamlin was keeping—sick at the thought of him being so desperate, so stricken by guilt and grief over having to sacrifice his sentries and never being able to tell me . . . And he'd let me go. Let all their sacrifices, let Andras's sacrifice, be in vain.

He'd known that if I remained, I would be at risk of Amarantha's wrath, even if I freed him.

"I can't even protect myself against them, against what's happening in Prythian . . . Even if we stood against the blight, they would hunt you down—she would find a way to kill you."

I remembered that pathetic effort to flatter me upon my arrival—and then he'd given up on it, on any attempt to win me when I'd seemed so desperate to get away, to never talk to him. But he'd fallen in love with me despite all that—known I'd loved him, and let me go with days to spare. He had put me before his entire court, before all of Prythian.

"If Tamlin were freed—if he had his full powers," I said, staring at a blackened bit of wall, "would he be able to destroy Amarantha?"

"I don't know. She tricked the High Lords through cunning, not force. Magic's a specific kind of thing—it likes rules, and she manipulated them too well. She keeps their powers locked up inside herself, as if she can't use them, or can access very little of them, at least. She has her own deadly powers, yes, so if it came down to a fight—"

"But is he stronger?" I started wringing my hands.

"He's a High Lord," Alis replied, as if that were answer enough. "But none of that matters now. He's to be her slave, and we're all to wear these masks until he agrees to become her lover—even then, he'll never regain his full powers. And she'll never let those Under the Mountain go."

I pushed off the table and squared my shoulders. "How do I get Under the Mountain?"

She clicked her tongue. "You can't go Under the Mountain. No human who goes in ever comes out."

I squeezed my fists so hard that my nails bit into my flesh. "How. Do. I. Get. There."

"It's suicide—she'll kill you, even if you get close enough to see her."

Amarantha had tricked him—she had hurt him so badly. Hurt them all so badly.

"You're a human," Alis went on, standing as well. "Your flesh is paper-thin."

Amarantha must also have taken Lucien—she had carved out Lucien's eye and scarred him like that. Did his mother grieve for him?

"You were too blind to see Tamlin's curse," Alis continued. "How do you expect to face Amarantha? You'll make things worse."

Amarantha had taken everything I wanted, everything I finally dared desire. “Show me the way,” I said, my voice trembling, but not with tears.

“No.” Alis slung her satchel over a shoulder. “Go home. I’ll take you as far as the wall. There’s naught to be done now. Tamlin will remain her slave forever, and Prythian will stay under her rule. That’s what Fate dealt, that was what the Eddies of the Cauldron decided.”

“I don’t believe in Fate. Nor do I believe in some ridiculous *Cauldron*.”

She shook her head again, her wild brown hair like glistening mud in the dim light.

“Take me to her,” I insisted.

If Amarantha ripped out my throat, at least I would die doing something for him—at least I would die trying to fix the destruction I hadn’t prevented, trying to save the people I’d doomed. At least Tamlin would know it was for him, and that I loved him.

Alis studied me for a moment before her eyes softened. “As you wish.”

CHAPTER 33

I might have been going to my death, but I wouldn't arrive unarmed.

I tightened the strap of the quiver across my chest and then grazed my fingers over the arrow feathers peeking over my shoulder. Of course, there were no ash arrows. But I would make do with what I'd found scattered throughout the manor. I could have taken more, but weapons would only weigh me down, and I didn't know how to use most of them anyway. So I wore a full quiver, two daggers at my waist, and a bow slung over a shoulder. Better than nothing, even if I was up against faeries who'd been born knowing how to kill.

Alis led me through the silent woods and foothills, pausing every so often to listen, to alter our course. I didn't want to know what she heard or smelled out there, not when such stillness blanketed the lands. *Stay with the High Lord*, the Suriel had said. Stay with him, fall in love with him, and all would be righted. If I had stayed, if I had admitted what I'd felt . . . None of this would have happened.

The world steadily filled with night, and my legs ached from the steep slopes of the hills, but Alis pressed on—never once looking back to see that I followed.

I was beginning to wonder whether I should have brought more than a day's worth of food when she stopped in the hollow between two hills. The air was cold—far colder than the air at the top of the hill, and I shivered as my eyes fell upon a slender cave mouth. There was no way this was the entrance—not when that mural had painted Under the Mountain to be in the center of Prythian. It was weeks of travel away.

"All dark and miserable roads lead Under the Mountain," Alis said so quietly that her voice was nothing more than the rustling of leaves. She pointed to the cave. "It's an ancient shortcut—once considered sacred, but no more."

This was the cave Lucien had ordered the Attor not to use that day. I tried to master my trembling. I loved Tamlin, and I would go to the ends of the earth to make it right, to save him, but if Amarantha was worse than the Attor . . . if the Attor wasn't the wickedest of her cronies . . . if even Tamlin had been scared of her . . .

"I reckon you're regretting your hotheadedness right now."

I straightened. "I *will* free him."

"You'll be lucky if she gives you a clean death. You'll be lucky if you even get brought before her." I must have turned pale, because she pursed her lips and patted me on the shoulder. "A few rules to remember, girl," she said, and we both stared at the cave mouth. The darkness reeked from its maw to poison the fresh night air. "Don't drink the wine—it's not like what we had at the Solstice, and will do more harm than good. Don't make deals with anyone unless your life depends on it—and even then, consider whether it's worth it. And most of all: don't trust a soul in there—not even your Tamlin. Your senses are your greatest enemies; they will be waiting to betray you."

I fought the urge to touch one of my daggers and nodded my thanks instead.

"Do you have a plan?"

"No," I admitted.

"Don't expect that steel to do you any good," she said with a glance at my weapons.

"I don't." I faced her, biting the inside of my lip.

"There was one part of the curse. One part we can't tell you. Even now, my bones are crying out just for mentioning it. One part you have to figure out . . . on your own, one part she . . . she . . ." She swallowed loudly. "That she still doesn't want you to know, if I can't say it," she gasped out. "But keep—keep your ears open, girl. *Listen* to what you hear."

I touched her arm. "I will. Thank you for bringing me." For wasting precious hours, when that satchel of supplies—for herself, for her boys—said enough about where she was going.

"It's a rare day indeed when someone thanks you for bringing them to their death." If I thought about the danger too long, I might lose my nerve, Tamlin or no. She wasn't helping. "I'll wish you luck nonetheless," Alis added.

"Once you retrieve them, if you and your nephews need somewhere to flee," I said, "cross the wall. Go to my family's house." I told her the location. "Ask for Nesta—my eldest sister. She knows who you are, knows everything. She will shelter you in any way she can."

Nesta would do it, too, I knew now, even if Alis and her boys terrified her. She would keep them safe. Alis patted my hand. "Stay alive," she said.

I looked at her one last time, then at the night sky that was unfurling above us, and at the deep green of the hills. The color of Tamlin's eyes.

I walked into the cave.

⸸

The only sounds were my shallow breathing and the crunch of my boots on stone. Stumbling through the frigid dark, I inched onward. I kept close to the wall, and my hand soon turned numb as the cold, wet stone bit into my skin. I took small steps, fearful of some invisible pit that might send me tumbling to my doom.

After what felt like an eternity, a crack of orange light cleaved through the dark. And then came the voices.

Hissing and braying, eloquent and guttural—a cacophony bursting the silence like a firecracker. I pressed myself against the cave wall, but the sounds passed and faded.

I crept toward the light, blinking back my blindness when I found the source: a slight fissure in the rock. It opened onto a crudely carved, fire-lit subterranean passageway. I lingered in the shadows, my heart wild in my chest. The crack in the cave wall was large enough for one person to squeeze through—so jagged and rough that it was obviously not often used. A glance at the dirt revealed no tracks, no sign of anyone else using this entrance. The hallway beyond was clear, but it veered off, obscuring my view.

The passage was deathly quiet, but I remembered Alis's warning and didn't trust my ears, not when faeries could be silent as cats.

Still, I had to leave this cave. Tamlin had been here for weeks already. I had to find where Amarantha kept him. And hopefully not run into anyone in the process. Killing animals and the naga had been one thing, but killing any others . . .

I took several deep breaths, bracing myself. It was the same as hunting. Only this time the animals were faeries. Faeries who could torture me endlessly—torture me until I begged for death. Torture me the way they tormented that Summer Court faerie whose wings had been ripped off.

I didn't let myself think about those bleeding stumps as I eased toward the tiny opening, sucking in my stomach to squeeze through. My weapons scraped against the stone, and I winced at the hiss of falling pebbles. *Keep moving, keep moving.* Hurrying across the open hallway, I pressed into an alcove in the opposite wall. It didn't provide much cover.

I slunk along the wall, pausing at the bend in the hall. This was a mistake—only an idiot would come here. I could be anywhere in

Amarantha's court. Alis should have given me more information. I should have been smart enough to ask. Or smart enough to think of another way—*any* way but this.

I risked a glance around the corner and almost sobbed in frustration. Another hallway carved out of the mountain's pale stone, lined on either side by torches. No shadowy spots for concealment, and at its other end, my view was yet again obscured by a sharp turn. It was wide open. I was as good as a starving doe, ripping bark off a tree in a clearing.

But the halls were silent—the voices I'd heard earlier were gone. And if I heard anyone, I could sprint back to that cave mouth. I could do reconnaissance for a time, gather information, find out where Tamlin was—

No. A second opportunity might not arise for a while. I had to act *now*. If I stopped for too long, I'd never work up the nerve again. I made to slip around the corner.

Long, bony fingers wrapped around my arm, and I went rigid.

A pointed, leathery gray face came into view, and its silver fangs glistened as it smiled at me. "Hello," it hissed. "What's something like you doing here?"

I knew that voice. It still haunted my nightmares.

So it was all I could do to keep from screaming as its bat-like ears cocked, and I realized that I stood before the Attor.

CHAPTER 34

The Attor kept its icy grip on my upper arm as it half dragged me to the throne room. It didn't bother to strip me of my weapons. We both knew they were of little use.

Tamlin. Alis and her boys. My sisters. Lucien. I silently chanted their names again and again as the Attor loomed above me, a demon of malice. Its leathery wings rustled occasionally—and had I been able to speak without screaming, I might have asked why it hadn't killed me outright. The Attor just tugged me onward with that slithering gait, its clawed feet making leisurely scratches on the cave floor. It looked unnervingly identical to how I had painted it.

Leering faces—cruel and harsh—watched me go by, none of them looking remotely concerned or disturbed that I was in the claws of the Attor. Faeries—lots of them—but few High Fae to be seen.

We strode through two ancient, enormous stone doors—taller than Tamlin's manor—and into a vast chamber carved from pale rock, upheld by countless carved pillars. That small part of me that had again become trivial and useless noted that the carvings weren't just ornate designs, but actually depicted faeries and High Fae and animals in various environments and states of movement. Countless stories of Prythian were etched on them. Chandeliers of jewels hung between the pillars, staining the red marble floor with color. Here—here were the High Fae.

An assembled crowd took up most of the space, some of them dancing to strange, off-kilter music, some milling about chatting—a party of sorts. I thought I spied some glittering masks among the attendees, but everything was a blur of sharp teeth and fine clothing. The Attor hurled me forward, and the world spun.

The cold marble floor was unyielding as I slammed into it, my bones groaning and barking. I pushed myself up, sparks dancing in my eyes, but stayed on the ground, kept low, as I beheld the dais before me. A few steps led onto the platform. I lifted my head higher.

There, lounging on a black throne, was Amarantha.

Though lovely, she wasn't as devastatingly beautiful as I had imagined, wasn't some goddess of darkness and spite. It made her all the more petrifying. Her red-gold hair was neatly braided and woven through her golden crown, the deep color enriching her snow-white skin, which, in turn, set off her ruby lips. But while her ebony eyes shone, there was . . . *something* that sucked at her beauty, some kind of permanent sneer to her features that made her allure seem contrived and cold. To paint her would have driven me to madness.

The highest commander of the King of Hybern. She'd slaughtered human armies centuries ago, had murdered her slaves rather than free them. And she'd captured all of Prythian in a matter of days.

Then I looked to the black rock throne beside her, and my arms buckled beneath me.

He was still wearing that golden mask, still wearing his warrior's clothes, that baldric—even though there were no knives sheathed along it, not a single weapon anywhere on him. His eyes didn't widen; his mouth didn't tighten. No claws, no fangs. He just stared at me, unfeeling—unmoved. Unimpressed.

"What's this?" Amarantha said, her voice lilting despite the adder's smile she gave me. From her slender, creamy neck hung a long, thin chain—and from it dangled a single, age-worn bone the size of a finger. I didn't want to consider whom it might have belonged to as I remained on the floor. If I shifted my arm, I could draw my dagger—

"Just a human thing I found downstairs," the Attor hissed, and a forked tongue darted out between its razor-sharp teeth. It flapped its wings once, blasting foul-smelling air at me, and then neatly tucked them behind its skeletal body.

"Obviously," Amarantha purred. I avoided meeting her eyes, focusing on Tamlin's brown boots. He was ten feet from me—ten feet, and not saying a word, not even looking horrified or angry. "But why should I bother with her?"

The Attor chuckled, the sound like sizzling water on a griddle, and a taloned foot jabbed my side. "Tell Her Majesty why you were sneaking around the catacombs—why you came out of the old cave that leads to the Spring Court."

Would it be better to kill the Attor, or to try to make it to Amarantha? The Attor kicked me again, and I winced as its claws bit into my ribs. "Tell Her Majesty, you human filth."

I needed time—I needed to figure out my surroundings. If Tamlin was under some kind of spell, then I would have to worry about grabbing him. I eased to my feet, keeping my hands within casual reach of my daggers. I stared at Amarantha's glittering golden gown rather than meet her eyes.

"I came to claim the one I love," I said quietly. Perhaps the curse could still be broken. Again I looked at him, and the sight of those emerald eyes was a balm.

"Oh?" Amarantha said, leaning forward.

"I've come to claim Tamlin, High Lord of the Spring Court."

A gasp rippled through the assembled court. But Amarantha tipped back her head and laughed—a raven's caw.

The High Queen turned to Tamlin, and her lips pulled back in a wicked smile. "You certainly were busy all those years. Developed a taste for human beasts, did you?"

He said nothing, his face impassive. What had she done? He didn't move—her curse had worked, then. I was too late. I'd failed him, damned him.

"But," Amarantha said slowly. I could sense the Attor and the entire court looming behind me. "It makes me wonder—if only *one* human girl could be taken once she killed your sentinel . . ." Her eyes sparked. "Oh, you are *delicious*. You let me torture that innocent girl to keep *this* one safe? You lovely thing! You actually made a human worm love you. Marvelous." She clapped her hands, and Tamlin merely looked away from her, the only reaction I'd seen from him.

Tortured. She'd tortured—

"Let him go," I said, trying to keep my voice steady.

Amarantha laughed again. "Give me one reason why I shouldn't destroy you where you stand, human." Her teeth were so straight and white—almost glowing.

My blood pounded in my veins, but I kept my chin high as I said, "You tricked him—he is bound unfairly." Tamlin had gone very, very still.

Amarantha clicked her tongue and looked at one of her slender white hands—at the ring on her index finger. A ring, I noticed as she lowered her hand again, set with what looked like . . . like a human eye encased in crystal. I could have sworn it swiveled inside. "You human beasts are so uncreative. We spent years teaching you poetry and fine speech, and *that* is all you can come up with? I should rip out your tongue for letting it go to waste."

I clamped my teeth together.

"But I'm curious: What eloquence will pour from your lips when you behold what you should have been?" My brows narrowed as Amarantha pointed behind me, that hideous eye ring indeed looking with her, and I turned.

There, nailed high on the wall of the enormous cavern, was the mangled corpse of a young woman. Her skin was burned in places, her fingers were bent at odd angles, and garish red lines crisscrossed her naked body. I could hardly hear Amarantha over the roar in my ears.

"Perhaps I should have listened when she said she'd never seen Tamlin before," Amarantha mused. "Or when she insisted she'd never killed a faerie, never hunted a day in her life. Though her screaming was delightful. I haven't heard such lovely music in ages." Her next words were directed at me. "I should thank you for giving Rhysand her name instead of yours."

Clare Beddor.

This was where they'd taken her, what they'd done to her after they burned her family alive in their house. This was what *I'd* done to her, by giving Rhysand her name to protect my family.

My insides twisted; it was a concentrated effort not to empty my stomach onto the stones.

The Attor's talons dug into my shoulders as it shoved me around to face Amarantha, who was still giving me that snake's smile. I had as good as killed Clare. I'd saved my own life and damned her. That rotting body on the wall should be mine. Mine.

Mine.

"Come now, precious," Amarantha said. "What have you to say to that?"

I wanted to spit that she deserved to burn in Hell for eternity, but I could only see Clare's body nailed there, even as I stared blankly at Tamlin. He'd *let* them kill Clare like that—to keep them from knowing that I was alive. My eyes stung as bile burned my throat.

"Do you still wish to claim someone who would do that to an innocent?" Amarantha said softly—consolingly.

I snapped my gaze to her. I wouldn't let Clare's death be in vain. I wasn't going down without a fight. "Yes," I said. "Yes, I do."

Her lip curled back, revealing too-sharp canines. And as I stared into her black eyes, I realized I was going to die.

But Amarantha leaned back in her throne and crossed her legs. "Well, Tamlin," she said, putting a proprietary hand on his arm, "I don't suppose you ever expected *this* to occur." She waved a hand in my general direction. A murmur of laughter from those assembled echoed around me, hitting me like stones. "What do *you* have to say, High Lord?"

I looked at the face I loved so dearly, and his next words almost sent me to my knees. "I've never seen her before. Someone must have glamoured her as a joke. Probably Rhysand." Still trying to protect me, even now, even here.

"Oh, that's not even a halfway decent lie." Amarantha angled her head. "Could it be—could it be that *you*, despite your words so many years ago, return the human's feelings? A girl with hate in her heart for our kind has managed to fall in love with a faerie. And a faerie whose father once slaughtered the human masses by my side has actually fallen in love with her, too?" She let out that crow's laugh again. "Oh, this is too good—this is too fun." She fingered the bone hanging from her necklace and looked at the encased eye upon her hand. "I suppose if anyone can appreciate the moment," she said to the ring, "it would be you, Jurian." She smiled prettily. "A pity your human whore on the side never bothered to save you, though."

Jurian—that was *his* eye, his finger bone. Horror coiled in my gut. Through whatever evil, whatever power, she somehow held his soul, his consciousness, to the ring, the bone.

Tamlin still looked at me without recognition, without a flicker of feeling. Perhaps she had used that same power to glamour him; perhaps she'd taken all his memories.

The queen picked at her nails. "Things have been awfully boring since Clare decided to die on me. Killing you outright, human, would be dull." She flicked her gaze to me, then back to her nails—to the ring on her finger. "But Fate stirs the Cauldron in strange ways. Perhaps my darling Clare had to die in order for me to have some true amusement with you."

My bowels turned watery—I couldn't help it.

"You came to claim Tamlin?" Amarantha said—it wasn't a question, but a challenge. "Well, as it happens, I'm bored to tears of his sullen silence. I was worried when he didn't flinch while I played with darling Clare, when he didn't even show those lovely claws . . .

"But I'll make a bargain with you, human," she said, and warning bells pealed in my mind. *Unless your life depends on it*, Alis had said. "You complete three tasks of my choosing—three tasks to prove how deep that human sense of loyalty and love runs, and Tamlin is yours. Just three little challenges to prove your dedication, to prove to me, to darling Jurian, that your kind can indeed love true, and you can have your High Lord." She turned to Tamlin. "Consider it a favor, High Lord—these human dogs can make our kind so lust-blind that we lose all common sense. Better for you to see her true nature now."

"I want his curse broken, too," I blurted. She raised a brow, her smile growing, revealing far too many of those white teeth. "I complete all three of your tasks, and his curse is broken, and we—and all his court—can leave here. And remain free forever," I added. Magic was specific, Alis had said—that was how Amarantha had tricked them. I wouldn't let loopholes be my downfall.

"Of course," Amarantha purred. "I'll throw in another element, if you don't mind—just to see if you're worthy of one of our kind, if you're smart enough to deserve him." Jurian's eye swiveled wildly, and she clicked her tongue at it. The eye stopped moving. "I'll give you a way out, girl," she went on. "You'll complete all the tasks—*or*, when you can't stand it anymore, all you have to do is answer one question." I could barely hear her above the blood pounding in my ears. "A riddle. You solve the riddle, and his curse will be broken. *Instantaneously*. I won't even need to lift my finger and he'll be free. Say the right answer, and he's yours.

You can answer it at any time—but if you answer incorrectly . . ." She pointed, and I didn't need to turn to know she gestured to Clare.

I turned her words over, looking for traps and loopholes within her phrasing. But it all sounded right. "And what if I fail your tasks?"

Her smile became almost grotesque, and she rubbed a thumb across the dome of her ring. "If you fail a task, there won't be anything left of you for me to play with."

A chill slithered down my spine. Alis had warned me—warned me against bargains. But Amarantha would kill me in an instant if I said no. "What is the nature of my tasks?"

"Oh, revealing that would take all the fun out of it. But I'll tell you that you'll have one task every month—at the full moon."

"And in the meantime?" I dared a glance at Tamlin. The gold in his eyes was brighter than I remembered.

"In the meantime," Amarantha said a bit sharply, "you shall either remain in your cell or do whatever additional work I require."

"If you run me ragged, won't that put me at a disadvantage?" I knew she was losing interest—that she hadn't expected me to question her so much. But I had to try to gain some kind of edge.

"Nothing beyond basic housework. It's only fair for you to earn your keep." I could have strangled her for that, but I nodded. "Then we are agreed."

I knew she waited for me to echo her response, but I had to make sure. "If I complete your three tasks or solve your riddle, you'll do as I request?"

"Of course," Amarantha said. "Is it agreed?"

His face ghastly white, Tamlin's eyes met with mine, and they almost imperceptibly widened. *No.*

But it was either this or death—death like Clare's, slow and brutal. The Attor hissed behind me, a warning to reply. I didn't believe in Fate or the Cauldron—and I had no other choice.

Because when I looked into Tamlin's eyes, even now, seated beside

Amarantha as her slave or worse, I loved him with a fierceness that swept up my whole heart. Because when he had widened his eyes, I'd known he still loved me.

I had nothing left but that, but the shred of fool's hope that I might win—that I might outwit and defeat a Faerie Queen as ancient as the stone beneath me.

"Well?" Amarantha demanded. Behind me, I sensed the Attor preparing to pounce, to beat the answer from me, if need be. She'd tricked them all, but I hadn't survived poverty and years in the woods for naught. My best chance lay in revealing nothing about myself, or what I knew. What was her court but another forest, another hunting ground?

I glanced at Tamlin one last time before I said "Agreed."

Amarantha gave me a small, horrible smile, and magic sizzled in the air between us as she snapped her fingers. She nestled back in her throne. "Give her a greeting worthy of my hall," she said to someone behind me.

The Attor's hiss was my only warning as something rock-hard collided with my jaw.

I was thrown sideways, stunned from the pain, but another brutal blow to my face awaited. Bones crunched—*my* bones. My legs twisted beneath me, and the Attor's leathery skin grated against my cheek as it punched me again. I ricocheted away, but met with the fist of another—a twisted, lesser faerie whose face I didn't glimpse. It was like being slugged with a brick. *Crunch, crack*. I think there were three of them, and I became their punching bag—passed off from blow to blow, my bones screaming in agony. Maybe I was screaming in agony, too.

Blood sprayed from my mouth, and its metallic tang coated my tongue before I knew no more.

CHAPTER 35

My senses slowly returned to me, each one more painful than the last. The sound of dripping water first, then the fading echo of heavy footsteps. A lingering coppery taste coated my mouth—blood. Above the wheezing of what had to be my clogged nostrils, the tang of mold and the reek of mildew scented the damp, cold air. Sharp bits of hay jabbed my cheek. My tongue probed the makings of a split lip, and the movement set my face on fire. Wincing, I opened my eyes, but could only manage to widen them a little—swelling. What I beheld through my undoubtedly black eyes didn't do much for my spirits.

I was in a prison cell. My weapons were gone, and my only sources of light were the torches beyond the door. Amarantha had said a cell was to be where I would spend my time, but even as I sat up—my head so dizzy I almost blacked out again—my heartbeat quickened. A dungeon. I examined the slants of light that crept in through the cracks between the door and the wall, then gingerly touched my face.

It ached—ached worse than anything I'd ever endured. I bit down on a cry as my fingers grazed my nose, flakes of blood crumbling from my nostrils. It was broken. Broken. I would have clenched my teeth had my jaw not been a throbbing mess of agony, too.

I couldn't panic. No, I had to keep my tears in check, had to keep my wits together. I had to survey the damage as best I could, then figure out what to do. Maybe my shirt could be used for bandages—maybe they would give me water at some point to wash out the injuries. Taking a breath that was all too shallow, I explored the rest of my face. My jaw wasn't broken, and though my eyes were swollen and my lip was split, the worst damage was to my nose.

I curled my knees to my chest, grasping them tightly as I reined in my breathing. I'd violated one of Alis's rules. I'd had no choice, though. Seeing Tamlin seated beside Amarantha . . .

My jaw protested, but I ground my teeth anyway. The full moon—it had been a half moon when I left my father's home. How long had I been unconscious down here? I wasn't foolish enough to believe that any amount of time would prepare me for Amarantha's first task.

I didn't allow myself to imagine what she had in mind for me. It was enough to know that she expected me to die—that there wouldn't be enough *left of me* for her to torture.

I gripped my legs harder to keep my hands from shaking. Somewhere—not too far off—screaming began. A high-pitched, pleading bleat, accentuated with crescendos of shrieking that made bile sting in my throat. I might sound like that when faced with Amarantha's first task.

A whip cracked, and the screaming built, hardly pausing for a breath. Clare had probably cried similarly. I had as good as tortured her myself. What had she made of all this—all these faeries lusting after her blood and misery? I deserved this—deserved whatever pain and suffering was in store—if only for what she had endured. But . . . but I would make it right. Somehow.

I must have drifted off at some point, because I awoke to the scrape of my cell door against stone. Forgetting the cascading pain in my face, I scrambled to duck into the shadows of the nearest corner. Someone slipped into my cell and swiftly shut the door—leaving it just a bit ajar.

"Feyre?"

I tried to stand, but my legs shook so badly that I couldn't move. "Lucien?" I breathed, and the hay crunched as he dropped to the ground before me.

"By the Cauldron, are you all right?"

"My face—"

A small light flared by his head, and as his eyes swam into view, the metal one narrowed. He hissed. "Have you lost your mind? What are you doing here?"

I fought the tears—they were pointless, anyway. "I went back to the manor . . . Alis told me . . . told me about the curse, and I couldn't let Amarantha—"

"You shouldn't have come, Feyre," he said sharply. "You weren't meant to be here. Don't you understand what he sacrificed in getting you out? How could you be so foolish?"

"Well, I'm here now!" I said, louder than was wise. "I'm here, and there's nothing that can be done about it, so don't bother telling me about my weak human flesh and my stupidity! I know all that, and I . . ." I wanted to cover my face in my hands, but it hurt too much. "I just . . . I had to tell him that I love him. To see if it wasn't too late."

Lucien sat back on his heels. "So you know everything, then." I managed to nod without blacking out from the pain. My agony must have shown, because he winced. "Well, at least we don't have to lie to you anymore. Let's clean you up a bit."

"I think my nose is broken. But nothing else." As I said it, I looked around him for any signs of water or bandages—and found none. It would be magic, then.

Lucien glanced over his shoulder, checking the door. "The guards are drunk, but their replacements will be here soon," he said, and then studied my nose. I braced myself as I allowed him to gently touch it.

Even the graze of his fingertips sent flashes of burning pain through me. "I'm going to have to set it before I can heal it."

I clamped down on my blind panic. "Do it. Right now." Before I could wallow in my cowardice and tell him to forget about it. He hesitated. "*Now*," I panted.

Too swift for me to follow, his fingers latched onto my nose. Pain lanced through me, and a *crack* burst through my ears, my head, before I fainted.

When I came to, I could open both eyes fully, and my nose—my nose was clear, and didn't throb or send agony splintering through my face. Lucien was crouched over me, frowning. "I couldn't heal you completely—they would know someone helped you. The bruises are there, along with a hideous black eye, but . . . all the swelling's gone."

"And my nose?" I said, feeling it before he answered.

"Fixed—as pert and pretty as before." He smirked at me. The familiar gesture made my chest tighten to the point of pain.

"I thought she'd taken most of your power," I managed to say. I'd barely seen him handle magic at all while at the estate.

He nodded to the little light bobbing over his shoulder. "She gave me back a fraction—to entice Tamlin to accept her offer. But he still refuses her." He jerked his chin to my healed face. "I knew some good would come of being down here."

"So you're trapped Under the Mountain, too?"

A grim nod. "She's summoned all the High Lords to her now—and even those who swore obedience are now forbidden to leave until . . . until your trials are over."

Until I was dead was probably what he truly meant. "That ring," I said. "Is it—is it actually Jurian's eye?"

Lucien cringed. "Indeed. So you really know everything, then?"

"Alis didn't say what happened after Jurian and Amarantha faced each other."

"They wrecked an entire battlefield, using their soldiers as shields, until their forces were nearly all dead. Jurian had been gifted some protection against her, but once they entered into single combat . . . It didn't take her long to render him prone. Then she dragged him back to her camp and took weeks—*weeks*—to torture and kill him. She refused orders to march to the King of Hybern's aid—cost him armies and the War; she refused to do anything until she'd finished Jurian's demise. All that she kept was his finger bone and his eye. Clythia promised him that he would never die—and so long as Amarantha keeps that eye of his preserved through her magic, keeps his soul and consciousness bound to it, he'll remain trapped, watching through it. A fitting punishment for what he did, but"—Lucien tapped his own missing eye—"I'm glad she didn't do the same to me. She seems to have an obsession with that sort of thing."

I shuddered. A huntress—she was little more than an immortal, cruel huntress, collecting trophies from her kills and conquests to gloat over through the ages. The rage and despair and horror Jurian must endure every day, for eternity . . . Deserved, perhaps, but worse than anything I could imagine. I shook the thought from me. "Is Tamlin—"

"He's—" But Lucien shot to his feet at a sound my human ears couldn't hear. "The guards are about to change rotations and are headed this way. Try not to die, will you? I already have a long list of faeries to kill—I don't need to add more to it, if only for Tamlin's sake."

Which was no doubt why he'd even come down here.

Lucien vanished—just *vanished* into the dim light. A moment later, a yellowish eye tinged with red appeared at the peephole in the door, glared at me, and continued onward.

✢

I dozed on and off for what could have been hours or days. They gave me three miserable meals of stale bread and water at no regular interval that I could detect. All I knew when the door to my cell swung open was that my relentless hunger no longer mattered, and it would be wise not to struggle when the two squat, red-skinned faeries half dragged me to the throne room. I marked the path, picking out details in the hall—interesting cracks in the walls, features in the tapestries, an odd bend—anything to remind me of the way out of the dungeons.

I observed more of Amarantha's throne room this time, too, noting the exits. No windows, as we were underground. And the mountain I'd seen depicted on that map at the manor was in the heart of the land—far from the Spring Court, even farther from the wall. If I were to escape with Tamlin, my best chance would be to run for that cave in the belly of the mountain.

A crowd of faeries stood along a far wall. Over their heads, I could make out the arch of a doorway. I tried not to look up at Clare's rotting body as we passed, and instead focused on the assembled court. Everyone was clad in rich, colorful clothing—all of them seeming clean and fed. Dispersed among them were faeries with masks. The Spring Court. If I had any chance of finding allies, it would be with them.

I scanned the crowd for Lucien but didn't find him before I was thrown at the foot of the dais. Amarantha wore a gown of rubies, drawing attention to her red-gold hair and to her lips, which spread in a serpentine smile as I looked up at her.

The Faerie Queen clicked her tongue. "You look positively dreadful." She turned to Tamlin, still at her side. His expression remained distant. "Wouldn't you say she's taken a turn for the worse?"

He didn't reply; he didn't even meet my gaze.

"You know," Amarantha mused, leaning against an arm of her throne, "I couldn't sleep last night, and I realized why this morning." She ran an eye over me. "I don't know your name. If you and I are going to be such close friends for the next three months, I should know your name, shouldn't I?"

I prevented myself from nodding. There was something charming and inviting about her—a part of me began to understand why the High Lords had fallen under her thrall, believed in her lies. I hated her for it.

When I didn't reply, Amarantha frowned. "Come, now, pet. You know my name—isn't it fair that I know yours?" There was movement to my right, and I tensed as the Attor appeared through the parted crowd, grinning at me with row after row of teeth. "After all"—Amarantha waved an elegant hand to the space behind me, the crystal casing around Jurian's eye catching the light—"you've already learned the consequences of giving false names." A black cloud wrapped around me as I sensed Clare's nailed form on the wall behind me. Still, I kept my mouth shut.

"Rhysand," Amarantha said—not needing to raise her voice to summon him. My heart became a leaden weight as those casual, strolling steps sounded from behind. They stopped when they were beside me—far too close for my liking.

From the corner of my eye, I studied the High Lord of the Night Court as he bowed at the waist. Night still seemed to ripple off him, like some near-invisible cloak.

Amarantha lifted her brows. "Is this the girl you saw at Tamlin's estate?"

He brushed some invisible fleck of dust off his black tunic before he surveyed me. His violet eyes held boredom—and disdain. "I suppose."

"But did you or did you *not* tell me *that girl*," Amarantha said, her tone sharpening as she pointed to Clare, "was the one you saw?"

He stuffed his hands into his pockets. "Humans all look alike to me."

Amarantha gave him a saccharine smile. "And what about faeries?"

Rhysand bowed again—so smooth it looked like a dance. "Among a sea of mundane faces, yours is a work of art."

Had I not been straddling the line between life and death, I might have snorted.

Humans all look alike . . . I didn't believe him for a second. Rhysand knew exactly how I looked—he'd recognized me that day at the manor.

I willed my features into neutrality as Amarantha's attention again returned to me.

"What's her name?" she demanded of Rhysand.

"How would I know? She lied to me." Either toying with Amarantha was a joke to him—as much of a joke as impaling a head in Tamlin's garden—or . . . it was just more court scheming.

I braced myself for the scrape of those talons against my mind, braced myself for the order I was sure she was to give next.

Still, I kept my lips sealed. I prayed Nesta had hired those scouts and guards—prayed she'd persuaded my father to take the precautions.

"If you're inclined to play games, girl, then I suppose we can do this the fun way," Amarantha said. She snapped her fingers at the Attor, who reached into the crowd and grabbed someone. Red hair glinted, and I jolted a step as the Attor yanked Lucien forward by the collar of his green tunic. No. *No.*

Lucien thrashed against the Attor but could do nothing against those needlelike nails as it forced him to his knees. The Attor smiled, releasing his tunic, but kept close.

Amarantha flicked a finger in Rhysand's direction. The High Lord of the Night Court lifted a groomed brow. "Hold his mind," she commanded.

My heart dropped to the floor. Lucien went utterly still, sweat gleaming on his neck as Rhysand bowed his head to the queen and faced him.

Behind them, pressing to the front of the crowd, came four tall, red-haired High Fae. Toned and muscled, some of them looking like warriors about to set foot on a battlefield, some like pretty courtiers, they all stared at Lucien—and grinned. The four remaining sons of the High Lord of the Autumn Court.

"Her name, Emissary?" Amarantha asked of Lucien. But Lucien only glanced at Tamlin before closing his eyes and squaring his shoulders. Rhysand began smiling faintly, and I shuddered at the memory of what those invisible claws had felt like as they gripped my mind. How easy it would have been for him to crush it.

Lucien's brothers lurked on the edges of the crowd—no remorse, no fear on their handsome faces.

Amarantha sighed. "I thought you would have learned your lesson, Lucien. Though this time your silence will damn you as much as your tongue." Lucien kept his eyes shut. Ready—he was ready for Rhysand to wipe out everything he was, to turn his mind, his self, into dust.

"Her name?" she asked Tamlin, who didn't reply. His eyes were fixed on Lucien's brothers, as if marking who was smiling the broadest.

Amarantha ran a nail down the arm of her throne. "I don't suppose your handsome brothers know, Lucien," she purred.

"If we did, Lady, we would be the first to tell you," said the tallest. He was lean, well dressed, every inch of him a court-trained bastard. Probably the eldest, given the way even the ones who looked like born warriors stared at him with deference and calculation—and fear.

Amarantha gave him a considering smile and lifted her hand. Rhysand cocked his head, his eyes narrowing slightly on Lucien.

Lucien stiffened. A groan slipped out of him, and—

"Feyre!" I shouted. "My name is Feyre."

It was all I could do to keep from sinking to my knees as Amarantha nodded and Rhysand stepped back. He hadn't even removed his hands from his pockets.

She must have allowed him more power than the others, then, if he could still inflict such harm while leashed to her. Or else his power before she'd stolen it had been . . . extraordinary, for *this* to be considered the basest remnants.

Lucien sagged on the ground, trembling. His brothers frowned—the eldest going so far as to bare his teeth at me in a silent snarl. I ignored him.

"Feyre," Amarantha said, testing my name, the taste of the two syllables on her tongue. "An old name—from our earlier dialects. Well, *Feyre*," she said. I could have wept with relief when she didn't ask for my family name. "I promised you a riddle."

Everything became thick and murky. Why did Tamlin do nothing, say nothing? What had Lucien been about to say before he'd fled my cell?

"Solve this, Feyre, and you and your High Lord, and all his court, may immediately leave with my blessing. Let's see if you are indeed clever enough to deserve one of our kind." Her dark eyes shone, and I cleared my mind as best I could as she spoke.

There are those who seek me a lifetime but never we meet,
And those I kiss but who trample me beneath ungrateful feet.

At times I seem to favor the clever and the fair,
But I bless all those who are brave enough to dare.

By large, my ministrations are soft-handed and sweet,
But scorned, I become a difficult beast to defeat.

For though each of my strikes lands a powerful blow,
When I kill, I do it slow . . .

I blinked, and she repeated herself, smiling when she finished, smug as a cat. My mind was void, a blank mass of uselessness. Could it be some sort of disease? My mother had died of typhus, and her cousin had died of malaria after going to Bharat . . . But none of those symptoms seemed to match the riddle. Maybe it was a person?

A ripple of laughter spread across those assembled behind us, the loudest from Lucien's brothers. Rhysand was watching me, wreathed in night and smiling faintly.

The answer was so close—one little answer and we could all be free.

Immediately, she'd said—as opposed to . . . wait, had the conditions of my trials been different from those of the riddle? She'd emphasized *immediately* only when talking about solving the riddle. No, I couldn't think about that right now. I had to solve this riddle. We could all be free. *Free.*

But I couldn't do it—I couldn't even come up with a possibility. I'd be better off slitting my own throat and ending my suffering there, before she could rip me to shreds. I was a fool—a common human idiot. I looked to Tamlin. The gold in his eyes flickered, but his face betrayed nothing.

"Think on it," Amarantha said consolingly, and flicked a grin down at her ring—at the eye swiveling within. "When it comes to you, I'll be waiting."

I gazed at Tamlin even as I was pulled away to the dungeons, my vacant mind reeling.

As they locked me in my cell once more, I knew I was going to lose.

+

I spent two days in that cell, or at least I figured it was two days, based on the meal pattern I'd begun to work out. I ate the decent parts of the half-moldy food, and though I hoped for it, Lucien never came to see me. I knew better than to wish for Tamlin.

I had little to do other than ponder Amarantha's riddle. The more I thought about it, the less sense it made. I dwelled on various kinds of poisons and venomous animals—and that yielded nothing beyond my growing sense of stupidity. Not to mention the nagging feeling that she might have wound up tricking me with this bargain when she'd emphasized *immediately* regarding the riddle. Maybe she meant she would *not* free us immediately after I finished her trials. That she could take however long she wanted. No—no, I was just being paranoid. I was overthinking it. But the riddle could free us all—instantaneously. I had to solve it.

While I'd sworn not to think too long on what tasks awaited me, I didn't doubt Amarantha's imagination, and I often awoke sweating and panting from my restless dreams—dreams in which *I* was trapped within a crystal ring, forever silent and forced to witness their bloodthirsty, cruel world, cleaved from everything I'd ever loved. Amarantha had claimed there wouldn't be enough left of me to play with if I failed a trial—and I prayed that she hadn't lied. Better to be obliterated than to endure Jurian's fate.

Still, fear like nothing I had ever known swallowed me whole when my cell door opened and the red-skinned guards told me that the full moon had arisen.

CHAPTER 36

The sounds of a teeming crowd reverberated against the passageway. My armed escort didn't bother with drawn weapons as they tugged me forward. I wasn't even shackled. Someone or something would catch me before I moved three feet and gut me where I stood.

The cacophony of laughter, shouting, and unearthly howls worsened when the hall opened into what had to be a massive arena. There had been no attempts to decorate the torch-lit cavern—and I couldn't tell if it had been hewn from the rock or if it was formed by nature. The floor was slick and muddy, and I struggled to keep my footing as we walked.

But it was the enormous, riotous crowd that turned my insides cold as they stared at me. I couldn't decipher what they were shouting, but I had a good-enough idea. Their cruel, ethereal faces and wide grins told me everything I needed to know. Not just lesser faeries but High Fae, too, their excitement making their faces almost as feral as their more unearthly brethren.

I was hauled toward a wooden platform erected above the crowd. Atop it sat Amarantha and Tamlin, and before it . . .

I did my best to keep my chin high as I beheld the exposed labyrinth of tunnels and trenches running along the floor. The crowd stood along the banks, blocking my view of what lay within as I was thrown to my knees before Amarantha's platform. The half-frozen mud seeped into my pants.

I rose on trembling legs. Around the platform stood a group of six males, secluded from the main crowd. From their cold, beautiful faces, from that echo of power still about them, I knew they were the other High Lords of Prythian. I ignored Rhysand as soon as I noticed his feline smile, the corona of darkness around him.

Amarantha had only to raise a hand and the roaring crowd silenced.

It became so quiet that I could almost hear my heart beating. "Well, Feyre," the Faerie Queen said. I tried not to look at the hand she rested on Tamlin's knee, that ring as vulgar as the gesture itself. "Your first task is here. Let us see how deep that human affection of yours runs."

I ground my teeth and almost exposed them to her. Tamlin's face remained blank.

"I took the liberty of learning a few things about you," Amarantha drawled. "It was only fair, you know."

Every instinct, every bit of me that was intrinsically human, screamed to run, but I kept my feet planted, locking my knees to avoid them giving out.

"I think you'll like this task," she said. She waved a hand, and the Attor stepped forward to part the crowd, clearing the way to the lip of a trench. "Go ahead. Look."

I obeyed. The trenches, probably twenty feet deep, were slick with mud—in fact, they seemed to have been dug from mud. I fought to keep my footing as I peered in farther. The trenches ran in a maze along the entire floor of the chamber, and their path made little sense. It was full of pits and holes, which undoubtedly led to underground tunnels, and—

Hands slammed into my back, and I cried out as I had the sickening feeling of falling before being suddenly jerked up by a bone-hard grip—up, up into the air. Laughter echoed through the chamber as I dangled from the Attor's claws, its powerful wing-beats booming across the arena. It swooped down into the trench and dropped me on my feet.

Mud squelched, and I swung my arms as I teetered and slipped. More laughter, even as I remained upright.

The mud smelled atrocious, but I swallowed my gag. I turned to find Amarantha's platform now floating to the lip of the trench. She looked down at me, smiling that serpent's grin.

"Rhysand tells me you're a huntress," she said, and my heartbeat faltered.

He must have read my thoughts again, or . . . or maybe he'd found my family, and—

Amarantha flicked her fingers in my direction. "Hunt this."

The faeries cheered, and I saw gold flash between spindly, multi-hued palms. Betting on my life—on how long I would last once this started.

I raised my eyes to Tamlin. His emerald gaze was frozen, and I memorized the lines of his face, the shape of his mask, the shade of his hair, one last time.

"Release it," Amarantha called. I trembled to the marrow of my bones as a grate groaned, and then a slithering, swift-moving noise filled the chamber.

My shoulders rose toward my ears. The crowd quieted to a murmur, silent enough to hear a guttural kind of grumble, so I could feel the vibrations in the ground as whatever it was rushed at me.

Amarantha clicked her tongue, and I whipped my head to her. Her brows rose. "Run," she whispered.

Then it appeared.

I ran.

It was a giant worm, or what might have once been a worm had its front end not become an enormous mouth filled with ring after ring of razor-sharp teeth. It barreled toward me, its pinkish brown body surging and twisting with horrific ease. These trenches were its lair.

And I was dinner.

Sliding and slipping on the reeking mud, I hurtled down the length of the trench, wishing I'd memorized more of the layout in the few moments I'd had, knowing full well that my path could lead to a dead end, where I would surely—

The crowd roared, drowning out the slurping and gnashing noises of the worm, but I didn't dare a glance over my shoulder. The ever-nearing stench of it told me enough about how close it was. I didn't have the breath for a sob of relief as I found a fork in the pathway and veered sharply left.

I had to get as much distance between us as possible; I had to find a spot where I could make a plan, a spot where I could find an advantage.

Another fork—I veered left again. Perhaps if I took as many lefts as I could, I could make a circle, and somehow come up behind the creature, and—

No, that was absurd. I'd have to be thrice as fast as the worm, and right now, I could barely keep ahead of it. I slid into a wall as I made another left and slammed into the slick muck. Cold, reeking, smothering. I wiped it from my eyes to find the leering faces of faeries floating above me, laughing. I ran for my life.

I reached a straight, flat stretch of trench and threw my strength to my legs as I bolted down its course. I finally dared a look over my shoulder, and my fear became wild and thrashing as the worm surged into the path, hot on my trail.

I almost missed a slender opening in the side of the trench thanks to that look, and I gave up valuable steps as I skidded to a halt to squeeze myself through the gap. It was too small for the worm, but the creature could probably shatter through the mud. If not, its teeth could do the trick. But it was worth the risk.

As I made to pull myself through, a force grabbed me back. No—not a force, but the walls. The crack was too small, and I'd so frantically thrown myself through it that I'd become wedged between it. My back to the worm, and too far between the walls to be able to turn, I couldn't see as it approached. The smell, though—the smell was growing worse.

I pushed and pulled, but the mud was too slick, and held fast.

The trenches reverberated with the thunderous movements of the worm. I could almost feel its reeking breath upon my half-exposed body, could hear those teeth slashing through the air, closer and closer. Not like this. It couldn't end like this.

I clawed at the mud, twisting, tearing at anything to pull me through. The worm neared with each of my heartbeats, the smell nearly overpowering my senses.

I ripped away mud, wriggling, kicking, and pushing, sobbing through my gritted teeth. *Not like this.*

The ground shook. A stench wrapped right around me, and hot air slammed into my body. Its teeth clicked together.

Grabbing onto the wall, I pulled and pulled. There was a squelch, and a sudden release of pressure around my middle, and I fell through the crack, sprawling in the mud.

The crowd sighed. I didn't have time for tears of relief as I found myself in another passageway, and I launched farther into the labyrinth. From the continuing quieted roars, I knew the worm had overshot me.

But that made no sense—the passage offered no place to hide. It would have seen me stuck there. Unless it couldn't break through and was now taking some alternate route, and would spring upon me.

I didn't check my speed, though I knew I wasted momentum by smashing into wall after wall as I made each sharp turn. The worm also had to lose its speed making these bends—a creature that big couldn't take the turns without slowing, no matter how dexterous it might be.

I risked a look at the crowd. Their faces were tight with

disappointment, and turned away entirely from me, toward the other end of the chamber. That was where the worm had to be—that was where that passage had ended. It hadn't seen where I went. It hadn't seen me.

It was blind.

I was so surprised that I didn't notice the enormous pit that opened before me, hidden by a slight rise, and it was all I could do to not scream as I tumbled in. Air, empty air, and—

I slammed into ankle-deep mud, and the crowd cried out. The mud softened the landing, but my teeth still sang with the impact. But nothing was broken, nothing hurt.

A few faeries peered in, leering from high above the gaping mouth of the pit. I whirled around, scanning my surroundings, trying to find the fastest way out. The pit itself opened into a small, dark tunnel, but there was no way to climb up—the wall was too steep.

I was trapped. Gasping for breath, I fumbled a few steps into the blackness of the tunnel. I bit down on my shriek as something beneath my foot crunched hard. I staggered back, and my tailbone wailed in pain. I kept scrambling away, but my hand connected with something smooth and hard, and I lifted it to see a gleam of white.

Through my muddy fingers, I knew that texture all too well. Bone.

Twisting onto my hands and knees, I patted the ground, moving farther into the darkness. Bones, bones, bones, of every shape and size, and I swallowed my scream as I realized what this place was. It was only when my hand landed on the smooth dome of a skull that I jumped to my feet.

I had to get out. *Now.*

"Feyre," I heard Amarantha's distant call. "You're ruining everyone's fun!" She said it as if I were a lousy shuttlecock partner. "Come out!"

I certainly would not, but she told me what I needed to know. The worm didn't know where I was; it couldn't smell me. I had precious seconds to get out.

As my sight adjusted to the darkness of the worm's den, mounds and mounds of bones gleamed, piles rolling away into the gloom. The chalkiness of the mud had to be from endless layers of them decomposing. I had to get out *now*, had to find a place to hide that wasn't a death trap. I stumbled out of the den, bones clattering away.

Once more in the open air of the pit, I groped one of its steep walls. Several green-faced faeries barked curses at me, but I ignored them as I tried to scale the wall, made it an inch, and slid to the floor. I couldn't get out without a rope or a ladder, and plunging farther into the worm's lair to see if there was another way out wasn't an option. Of course, there was a back door. Every animal's den had two exits, but I wasn't about to risk the darkness—effectively blinding myself—and completely eliminate my small edge.

I needed a way *up*. I tried scaling the wall again. The faeries were still murmuring their discontent; as long as they remained that way, I was fine. I again latched onto the muddy wall, digging into the pliable dirt. All I got was freezing mud digging beneath my nails as I slid to the ground yet again.

The stench of the place invaded every part of me. I bit down on my nausea as I tried again and again. The faeries were laughing now. "A mouse in a trap," one of them said. "Need a stepping stool?" another crowed.

A stepping stool.

I whirled toward the piles of bones, then pushed my hand hard against the wall. It felt firm. The entire place was made of packed mud, and if this creature was anything like its smaller, harmless brethren, I could assume that the stench—and therefore the mud itself—was the remnant of whatever had passed through its system after it sucked the bones clean.

Disregarding that wretched fact, I seized the spark of hope and grabbed the two biggest, strongest bones I could quickly find. Both were longer than my leg and heavy—so heavy as I jammed them into the wall. I didn't know what the creature usually ate, but it must have been at least cattle-sized.

"What's it doing? What's it planning?" one of the faeries hissed.

I grabbed a third bone and impaled it deep into the wall, as high as I could reach. I grabbed a fourth, slightly smaller bone and set it into my belt, strapping it across my back. Testing the three bones with a few sharp tugs, I sucked in my breath, ignored the twittering faeries, and began climbing my ladder. My stepping stool.

The first bone held firm, and I grunted as I grabbed the second bone-step and pulled myself up. I was putting my foot on the step when another idea flashed, and I paused.

The faeries—not too far off—began to shout again.

But it could work. It could work, if I played it right. It could work, because it *had* to work. I dropped back to the mud, and the faeries watching me murmured their confusion. I drew the bone from my belt, and with a sharp intake of breath, I snapped it across my knee.

My own bones burned with pain, but the shaft broke, leaving me with two sharp-ended spikes. It was going to work.

If Amarantha wanted me to hunt, I would hunt.

I walked to the middle of the pit opening, calculated the distance, and plunged the two bones into the ground. I returned back to the mound of bones and made quick work of whatever I could find that was sturdy and sharp. When my knee became too tender to use as a breaking point, I snapped the bones with my foot. One by one, I stuck them into the muddy floor beneath the pit opening until the whole area, save for one small spot, was filled with white lances.

I didn't double-check my work—it would succeed, or I would wind up among those bones on the floor. Just one chance. That was all I had. Better than no chances at all.

I dashed to my bone ladder and ignored the sting of the splinters in my fingers as I climbed to the third rung, where I balanced before embedding a fourth bone in the wall.

And just like that, I heaved myself out of the pit mouth, and almost wept to be exposed to the open air once more.

I secured the three bones I'd taken in my belt, their weight a comforting presence, and rushed to the nearest wall. I grabbed a fistful of the reeking mud and smeared it across my face. The faeries hissed as I grabbed more, this time coating my hair, then my neck. Already accustomed to the staggering reek, my eyes watered only a little as I made swift work of painting myself. I even paused to roll on the ground. Every inch of me had to be covered. Every damn inch.

If the creature was blind, then it relied on smell—and my smell would be my greatest weakness.

I rubbed mud on me until I was certain I was nothing more than a pair of blue-gray eyes. I doused myself a final time, my hands so slick that I could barely maintain a grasp on one of the sharp-ended bones as I drew it from my belt.

"What's it doing?" the green-faced faerie whined again.

A deep, elegant voice replied this time. "She's building a trap." Rhysand.

"But the Middengard—"

"Relies on its scent to see," Rhysand answered, and I gave a special glower for him as I glanced at the rim of the trench and found him smiling at me. "And Feyre just became invisible."

His violet eyes twinkled. I made an obscene gesture before I broke into a run, heading straight for the worm.

I placed the remaining bones at especially tight corners, knowing well enough that I couldn't turn at the speed I hoped I would be running. It didn't take much to find the worm, as a crowd of faeries had gathered to taunt it, but I had to get to the right spot—I had to pick my battleground.

I slowed to a stalking pace and flattened my back against a wall as I heard the slithering and grunting of the worm. The crunching.

The faeries watching the worm—ten of them, with frosty blue skin and almond-shaped black eyes—giggled. I could only assume they'd grown bored of me and decided to watch something else die.

Which was wonderful, but only if the worm was still hungry—only if it would respond to the lure I offered. The crowd murmured and grumbled.

I eased around a bend, craning my neck. Too covered in its scent to smell me, the worm continued feasting, stretching its bulbous form upward as one of the faeries dangled what looked like a hairy arm. The worm gnashed its teeth, and the blue faeries cackled as they dropped the arm into its waiting mouth.

I recoiled around the bend and raised the bone-sword I'd made. I reminded myself of the path I'd taken, of the turns I'd counted.

Still, my heart lodged in my throat as I drew the jagged edge of the bone across my palm, splitting open my flesh. Blood welled, bright and shining as rubies. I let it build before clenching my hand into a fist. The worm would smell that soon enough.

It was only then that I realized the crowd had gone silent.

Almost dropping the bone, I leaned around the bend again to see the worm.

It was gone.

The blue faeries grinned at me.

Then, shattering the silence like a shooting star, a voice—*Lucien's*—bellowed across the chamber. "*TO YOUR LEFT!*"

I bolted, getting a few feet before the wall behind me exploded, mud spraying as the worm burst through, a mass of shredding teeth just inches away.

I was already running, so fast that the trenches were a blur of reddish brown. I needed a bit of distance or else it'd fall right on top of me.

But I also needed it close, so it couldn't check itself, so it was in a frenzy of hunger.

I took the first sharp turn, and grabbed onto the bone-rail I'd embedded in the corner wall. I used it to swing around, not breaking my speed, propelling me faster, giving me a few more seconds on the worm.

Then a left. My breath was a flame ravaging my throat. The second hairpin turn came upon me, and I again used the bit of bone to hurtle around the bend.

My knees and ankles groaned as I fought to keep from slipping in the mud. Only one more turn, then a straight run . . .

I flipped around the final turn, and the roar of the faeries became different than it had been earlier. The worm was a raging, crashing force behind me, but my steps were steady as I flew down the last passage.

The mouth of the pit loomed, and with a final prayer, I leaped.

There was only open black air, reaching up to swallow me.

I swung my arms as I careened down, aiming for the spot I'd planned. Pain barked through my bones, my head, as I collided with the muddy ground and rolled. I flipped over myself and screamed as something hit my arm, biting through flesh.

But I didn't have time to think, to even look at it, as I scrambled out of the way, as far into the darkness of the worm's den as I could get. I grabbed another bone and whirled when the worm plummeted into the pit.

It hit the earth and lashed its massive body to the side, anticipating the strike to kill me, but a wet, crunching noise filled the air instead.

And the worm didn't move.

I squatted there, gulping down burning air, staring into the abyss of its flesh-shredding mouth, still open wide to devour me. It took me a few heartbeats to realize the worm wasn't going to swallow me whole, and a few more heartbeats to understand that it was truly impaled on the bone spikes. Dead.

I didn't entirely hear the gasps, then the cheering—didn't quite think or feel very much of anything as I edged around the worm and slowly climbed out of the pit, still holding the bone-sword in my hand.

Silently, still beyond words, I stumbled back through the labyrinth, my left arm throbbing, but my body tingled so much I didn't notice.

But the moment I beheld Amarantha on her platform at the edge of the trench, I clenched my free hand. *Prove my love.* Pain shot through my arm, but I embraced it. I had won.

I looked up at her from beneath lowered brows and didn't check myself as I exposed my teeth. Her lips were thin, and she no longer grasped Tamlin's knee.

Tamlin. *My* Tamlin.

I tightened my grip on the long bone in my hand. I was shaking—shaking all over. But not with fear. Oh, no. It wasn't fear at all. I'd proved my love—and then some.

"Well," Amarantha said with a little smirk. "I suppose anyone could have done that."

I took a few running steps and hurled the bone at her with all my remaining strength.

It embedded itself in the mud at her feet, splattering filth onto her white gown, and remained there, quivering.

The faeries gasped again, and Amarantha stared at the wobbling bone before touching the mud on her bodice. She smiled slowly. "Naughty," she tsked.

Had there not been an insurmountable trench between us, I would have ripped her throat out. Someday—if I lived through this—I would skin her alive.

"I suppose you'll be happy to learn most of my court lost a good deal of money tonight," she said, picking up a piece of parchment. I looked at Tamlin as she scanned the paper. His green eyes were bright, and though his face was deathly pale, I could have sworn there was a ghost of triumph on his face. "Let's see," Amarantha went on, reading the paper as she toyed with Jurian's finger bone at the end of her necklace. "Yes, I'd say almost my entire court bet on you dying within the first minute; some said you'd last five, and"—she turned over the paper—"and just one person said you would win."

Insulting, but not surprising. I didn't fight as the Attor hauled me out of the trenches, dumping me at the foot of the platform before flying off. My arm burned at the impact.

Amarantha frowned at her list, and she waved a hand. "Take her away. I tire of her mundane face." She clenched the arms of her throne hard enough that the whites of her knuckles showed. "Rhysand, come here."

I didn't stay long enough to see the High Lord prowl forward. Red hands grabbed me, holding tightly to keep from sliding off. I'd forgotten the mud caked on me like a second skin. As they yanked me away, a shooting pain shot along my arm, and agony blanketed my senses.

I looked at my left forearm then, and my stomach rose at the trickling blood and ripped tendons, at the lips of my skin pulled back to accommodate the shaft of a bone shard protruding clean through it.

I couldn't even glance back at Tamlin, couldn't find Lucien to say thank you before pain consumed me whole, and I could barely manage to walk back to my cell.

CHAPTER 37

No one, not even Lucien, came to fix my arm in the days following my victory. The pain overwhelmed me to the point of screaming whenever I prodded the embedded bit of bone, and I had no other option but to sit there, letting the wound gnaw on my strength, trying my best not to think about the constant throbbing that shot sparks of poisoned lightning through me.

But worse than that was the growing panic—panic that the wound hadn't stopped bleeding. I knew what it meant when blood continued to flow. I kept one eye on the wound, either out of hope that I'd find the blood clotting, or the terror that I'd spy the first signs of infection.

I couldn't eat the rotten food they gave me. The sight of it aroused such nausea that a corner of my cell now reeked of vomit. It didn't help that I was still covered in mud, and the dungeon was perpetually freezing.

I was sitting against the far wall of my cell, savoring the coolness of the stone beneath my back. I'd awoken from a fitful sleep and found myself burning hot. A kind of fire that made everything a bit muddled. My injured arm dangled at my side as I gazed dully at the cell door. It seemed to sway, its lines rippling.

This heat in my face was some kind of small cold—not a fever from infection. I put a hand on my chest, and dried mud crumbled into my lap. Each of my breaths was like swallowing broken glass. Not a fever. Not a fever. Not a fever.

My eyelids were heavy, stinging. I couldn't go to sleep. I had to make sure the wound wasn't infected, I had to . . . to . . .

The door actually did move then—no, not the door, but rather the darkness around it, which seemed to ripple. Real fear coiled in my stomach as a male figure formed out of that darkness, as if he'd slipped in from the cracks between the door and the wall, hardly more than a shadow.

Rhysand was fully corporeal now, and his violet eyes glowed in the dim light. He slowly smiled from where he stood by the door. "What a sorry state for Tamlin's champion."

"Go to Hell," I snapped, but the words were little more than a wheeze. My head was light and heavy all at once. If I tried to stand, I would topple over.

He stalked closer with that feline grace and dropped into an easy crouch before me. He sniffed, grimacing at the corner splattered with my vomit. I tried to bring my feet into a position more inclined for scrambling away or kicking him in the face, but they were full of lead.

Rhysand cocked his head. His pale skin seemed to radiate alabaster light. I blinked away the haze, but couldn't even turn aside my face as his cold fingers grazed my brow. "What would Tamlin say," he murmured, "if he knew his beloved was rotting away down here, burning up with fever? Not that he can even come here, not when his every move is watched."

I kept my arm hidden in the shadows. The last thing I needed them to know was how weak I was. "Get away," I said, and my eyes stung as the words burned my throat. I had difficulty swallowing.

He raised an eyebrow. "I come here to offer you help, and you have the nerve to tell me to leave?"

"Get away," I repeated. My eyes were so sore that it hurt to keep them open.

"You made me a lot of money, you know. I figured I would repay the favor."

I leaned my head against the wall. Everything was spinning—spinning like a top, spinning like . . . I kept my nausea down.

"Let me see your arm," he said too quietly.

I kept my arm in the shadows—if only because it was too heavy to lift.

"Let me see it." A growl rippled from him. Without waiting for my reaction, he grabbed my elbow and forced my arm into the dim light of the cell.

I bit my lip to keep from crying out—bit it hard enough to draw blood as rivers of fire exploded inside me, as my head swam, and all my senses narrowed down to the piece of bone sticking through my arm. They couldn't know—couldn't know how bad it was, because then they would use it against me.

Rhysand examined the wound, a smile appearing on his sensuous lips. "Oh, that's wonderfully gruesome." I swore at him, and he chuckled. "Such words from a lady."

"Get out," I wheezed. My frail voice was as terrifying as the wound.

"Don't you want me to heal your arm?" His fingers tightened around my elbow.

"At what cost?" I shot back, but kept my head against the stone, needing its damp strength.

"Ah, *that*. Living among faeries has taught you some of our ways."

I focused on the feeling of my good hand on my knee—focused on the dry mud beneath my fingernails.

"I'll make a trade with you," he said casually, and gently set my arm down. As it met with the floor, I had to close my eyes to brace against the flow of that poisoned lightning. "I'll heal your arm in exchange for *you*. For two weeks every month, two weeks of my choosing, you'll live with me at the Night Court. Starting after this messy three-trials business."

My eyes flew open. "No." I'd already made one fool's bargain.

"No?" He braced his hands on his knees and leaned closer. "Really?"

Everything was starting to dance. "Get out," I breathed.

"You'd turn down my offer—and for what?" I didn't reply, so he went on. "You must be holding out for one of your friends—for Lucien, correct? After all, he healed you before, didn't he? Oh, don't look so innocent. The Attor and his cronies broke your nose. So unless you have some kind of magic you're not telling us about, I don't think human bones heal that quickly." His eyes sparkled, and he stood, pacing a bit. "The way I see things, Feyre, you have two options. The first, and the smartest, would be to accept my offer."

I spat at his feet, but he kept pacing, only giving me a disapproving look.

"The second option—and the one only a fool would take—would be for you to refuse my offer and place your life, and thus Tamlin's, in the hands of chance."

He stopped pacing and stared hard at me. Though the world spun and danced in my vision, something primal inside me went still and cold beneath that gaze.

"Let's say I walk out of here. Perhaps Lucien will come to your aid within five minutes of my leaving. Perhaps he'll come in five days. Perhaps he won't come at all. Between you and me, he's been keeping a low profile after his rather embarrassing outburst at your trial. Amarantha's not exactly pleased with him. Tamlin even broke his delightful brooding to beg for him to be spared—such a noble warrior, your High Lord. She listened, of course—but only after she made Tamlin bestow Lucien's punishment. Twenty lashes."

I started shaking, sick all over again to think about what it had to have been like for my High Lord to be the one to punish his friend.

Rhysand shrugged, a beautiful, easy gesture. "So, it's really a question of how much you're willing to trust Lucien—and how much you're willing to risk for it. Already you're wondering if that fever of yours is the first sign of infection. Perhaps they're unconnected, perhaps not. Maybe it's fine. Maybe that worm's mud isn't full of festering filth. And maybe Amarantha will send a healer, and by that time, you'll either be dead, or they'll find your arm so infected that you'll be lucky to keep anything above the elbow."

My stomach tightened into a painful ball.

"I don't need to invade your thoughts to know these things. I already know what you've slowly been realizing." He again crouched in front of me. "You're dying."

My eyes stung, and I sucked my lips into my mouth.

"How much are you willing to risk on the hope that another form of help will come?"

I stared at him, sending as much hate as I could into my gaze. He'd been the one who'd caused all this. He'd told Amarantha about Clare; he'd made Tamlin beg.

"Well?"

I bared my teeth. "Go. To. Hell."

Swift as lightning, he lashed out, grabbing the shard of bone in my arm and twisting. A scream shattered out of me, ravaging my aching throat. The world flashed black and white and red. I thrashed and writhed, but he kept his grip, twisting the bone a final time before releasing my arm.

Panting, half sobbing as the pain reverberated through my body, I found him smirking at me again. I spat in his face.

He only laughed as he stood, wiping his cheek with the dark sleeve of his tunic.

"This is the last time I'll extend my assistance," he said, pausing by the cell door. "Once I leave this cell, my offer is dead." I spat again, and he shook his head. "I bet you'll be spitting on Death's face when she comes to claim you, too."

He began to ripple with darkness, his edges blurring into endless night.

He could be bluffing, trying to trick me into accepting his offer. Or he might be right—I might be dying. My life depended on it. *More* than my life depended on my choice. And if Lucien was indeed unable to come . . . or if he came too late . . .

I *was* dying. I'd known it for some time now. And Lucien had underestimated my abilities in the past—had never quite grasped my limitations as a human. He'd sent me to hunt the Suriel with a few knives and a bow. He'd even admitted to hesitating that day, when I had screamed for help. And he might not even know how bad off I was. Might not understand the gravity of an infection like this. He might come a day, an hour, a minute too late.

Rhysand's moon-white skin began to darken into nothing but shadow.

"Wait."

The darkness consuming him paused. For Tamlin . . . for Tamlin, I would sell my soul; I would give up everything I had for him to be free.

"Wait," I repeated.

The darkness vanished, leaving Rhysand in his solid form as he grinned. "Yes?"

I raised my chin as high as I could manage. "Just two weeks?"

"Just two weeks," he purred, and knelt before me. "Two teensy, tiny weeks with me every month is all I ask."

"Why? And what are to . . . to be the terms?" I said, fighting past the dizziness.

"Ah," he said, adjusting the lapel of his obsidian tunic. "If I told you those things, there'd be no fun in it, would there?"

I looked at my ruined arm. Lucien might never come, might decide I wasn't worth risking his life any further, not now that he'd been punished for it. And if Amarantha's healers cut off my arm . . .

Nesta would have done the same for me, for Elain. And Tamlin had done so much for me, for my family; even if he had lied about the Treaty, about sparing me from its terms, he'd still saved my life that day against the naga, and saved it again by sending me away from the manor.

I couldn't think entirely of the enormity of what I was about to give—or else I might refuse again. I met Rhysand's gaze. "Five days."

"You're going to bargain?" Rhysand laughed under his breath. "Ten days."

I held his stare with all my strength. "A week."

Rhysand was silent for a long moment, his eyes traveling across my body and my face before he murmured: "A week it is."

"Then it's a deal," I said. A metallic taste filled my mouth as magic stirred between us.

His smile became a bit wild, and before I could brace myself, he grabbed my arm. There was a blinding, quick pain, and my scream sounded in my ears as bone and flesh were shattered, blood rushed out of me, and then—

Rhysand was still grinning when I opened my eyes. I hadn't any idea how long I'd been unconscious, but my fever was gone, and my head was clear as I sat up. In fact, the mud was gone, too; I felt as if I'd just bathed.

But then I lifted my left arm.

"What have you done to me?"

Rhysand stood, running a hand through his short, dark hair. "It's custom in my court for bargains to be permanently marked upon flesh."

I rubbed my left forearm and hand, the entirety of which was now covered in swirls and whorls of black ink. Even my fingers weren't spared, and a large eye was tattooed in the center of my palm. It was feline, and its slitted pupil stared right back at me.

"Make it go away," I said, and he laughed.

"You humans are truly grateful creatures, aren't you?"

From a distance, the tattoo looked like an elbow-length lace glove, but when I held it close to my face, I could detect the intricate depictions of flowers and curves that flowed throughout to make up a larger pattern. Permanent. Forever.

"You didn't tell me this would happen."

"You didn't ask. So how am I to blame?" He walked to the door but lingered, even as pure night wafted off his shoulders. "Unless this lack of gratitude and appreciation is because you fear a certain High Lord's reaction."

Tamlin. I could already see his face going pale, his lips becoming thin as the claws came out. I could almost hear the growl he'd emit when he asked me what I had been thinking.

"I think I'll wait to tell him until the moment's right, though," Rhysand said. The gleam in his eyes told me enough. Rhysand hadn't done any of this to save me, but rather to hurt Tamlin. And I'd fallen into his trap—fallen into it worse than the worm had fallen into mine.

"Rest up, Feyre," Rhysand said. He turned into nothing more than living shadow and vanished through a crack in the door.

CHAPTER 38

I tried not to look at my left arm as I scrubbed at the floors of the hallway. The ink—which, in the light, was actually a blue so dark it appeared black—was a cloud upon my thoughts, and those were bleak enough even without knowing I'd sold myself to Rhysand. I couldn't look at the eye on my palm. I had an absurd, creeping feeling that it watched me.

I dunked the large brush into the bucket the red-skinned guards had thrown into my arms. I could barely comprehend them through their mouths full of long yellow teeth, but when they gave me the brush and bucket and shoved me into a long hallway of white marble, I understood.

"If it's not washed and shining by supper," one of them had said, its teeth clicking as it grinned, "we're to tie you to the spit and give you a few good turns over the fire."

With that, they left. I had no idea when supper was, and so I frantically began washing. My back already ached like fire, and I hadn't been scrubbing the marble hall for more than thirty minutes. But the water they'd given me was filthy, and the more I scrubbed the floor, the dirtier it became. When I went to the door to ask for a bucket of clean water, I found it locked. There would be no help.

An impossible task—a task to torment me. The spit—perhaps that was the source of the constant screaming in the dungeons. Would a few turns on the spit melt all the flesh from me, or just burn me badly enough to force me into another bargain with Rhysand? I cursed as I scrubbed harder, the coarse bristles of the brush crinkling and whispering against the tiles. A rainbow of brown was left in their wake, and I growled as I dunked the brush again. Filthy water came out with it, dripping all over the floor.

A trail of brown muck grew with each sweep. Breathing quickly, I hurled the brush to the ground and covered my face with my wet hands. I lowered my left hand when I realized the eye was pressed against my cheek.

I gulped down steadying gasps of air. There had to be a rational way to do this; there had to be some old wives' trick. The spit—tied to a spit like a roast pig.

I grabbed the brush from where it had bounced away and scrubbed at the floor until my hands throbbed. It looked like someone had spilled mud all over the place. The dirt was *actually* turning into mud the harder I scrubbed it. I'd probably wail and beg for mercy when they rotated me on that spit. There had been red lines covering Clare's naked body—what instrument of torture had they come from? My hands trembled, and I set down the brush. I could take down a giant worm, but washing a floor—*that* was the impossible task.

A door clicked open somewhere down the hall, and I shot to my feet. An auburn head peered at me. I sagged with relief. Lucien—

Not Lucien. The face that turned toward me was female—and unmasked.

She looked perhaps a bit older than Amarantha, but her porcelain skin was exquisitely colored, graced with the faintest blush of rose along her cheeks. Had the red hair not been indication enough, when her russet eyes met mine, I knew who she was.

I bowed my head to the Lady of the Autumn Court, and she inclined her chin slightly. I supposed that was honor enough. "For giving her your name in place of my son's life," she said, her voice as sweet as sun-warmed apples. She must have been in the crowd that day. She pointed at the bucket with a long, slender hand. "My debt is paid." She disappeared through the door she'd opened, and I could have sworn I smelled roasting chestnuts and crackling fires in her wake.

It was only after the door shut that I realized I should have thanked her, and only after I looked in my bucket that I realized I'd been hiding my left arm behind my back.

I knelt beside the bucket and dipped my fingers into the water. They came out clean.

I shuddered, allowing myself a moment to slump over my knees before I dumped some of the water onto the floor and watched it wash away the muck.

To the chagrin of the guards, I had completed their impossible task. But the next day, they smiled at me as they shoved me into a massive, dark bedroom, lit only by a few candles, and pointed to the looming fireplace. "Servant spilled lentils in the ash," one of the guards grunted, tossing me a wooden bucket. "Clean it up before the occupant returns, or he'll peel off your skin in strips."

A slammed door, the click of a lock, and I was alone.

Sorting lentils from ash and embers—ridiculous, wasteful, and—

I approached the darkened fireplace and cringed.

Impossible.

I cast a glance about the bedroom. No windows, no exits save the one I'd just been chucked through. The bed was enormous and neatly made, its black sheets of—of silk. There was nothing else in the room beyond basic furniture; not even discarded clothes or books or weapons.

As if its occupant never slept here. I knelt before the fireplace and calmed my breathing.

I had keen eyes, I reminded myself. I could spot rabbits hiding in the underbrush and track most things that wanted to remain unseen. Spotting the lentils couldn't be *that* hard. Sighing, I crawled farther into the fireplace and began.

I was wrong.

Two hours later, my eyes were burning and aching, and even though I combed through every inch of that fireplace, there were always more lentils, more and *more* that I'd somehow not spotted. The guards had never said *when* the owner of this room would return, and so every tick of the clock on the mantel became a death knell, every footstep outside the door causing me to reach for the iron poker leaning against the hearth wall. Amarantha had never said anything about not fighting back—never specified that I wasn't allowed to defend myself. At least I'd go down swinging.

I picked through the ashes again and again. My hands were now black and stained, my clothes covered in soot. Surely there couldn't be any more; surely—

The lock clicked, and I lunged for the poker as I shot to my feet, my back to the hearth and the iron rod hidden behind me.

Darkness entered the room, guttering the candles with a snow-kissed breeze. I gripped the poker harder, pressing against the stone of the fireplace, even as that darkness settled on the bed and took a familiar form.

"As wonderful as it is to see you, Feyre, darling," Rhysand said, sprawled on the bed, his head propped up by a hand, "do I want to know why you're digging through my fireplace?"

I bent my knees slightly, preparing to run, to duck, to do anything to get to the door that felt far, far away. "They said I had to clean out lentils from the ashes, or you'd rip off my skin."

"Did they now." A feline smile.

"Do I have you to thank for this idea?" I hissed. He wasn't allowed to kill me, not with my bargain with Amarantha, but . . . there were other ways to hurt me.

"Oh, no," he drawled. "No one's learned of *our* little bargain yet—and you've managed to keep it quiet. Shame riding you a bit hard?"

I clenched my jaw and pointed to the fireplace with one hand, still keeping the poker tucked behind me. "Is this clean enough for you?"

"Why were there lentils in my fireplace to begin with?"

I gave him a flat look. "One of your mistress's *household chores*, I suppose."

"Hm," he said, examining his nails. "Apparently she or her cronies think I'll find some sport with you."

My mouth dried up. "Or it's a test for you," I managed to get out. "You said you bet on me during my first task. She didn't seem pleased about it."

"And what could Amarantha possibly have to test me about?"

I didn't balk from that violet stare. *Amarantha's whore*, Lucien had once called him. "You lied to her. About Clare. You knew very well what I looked like."

Rhysand sat up in a fluid movement and braced his forearms on his thighs. Such grace contained in such a powerful form. *I was slaughtering on the battlefield before you were even born*, he'd once said to Lucien. I didn't doubt it. "Amarantha plays her games," he said simply, "and I play mine. It gets rather boring down here, day after day."

"She let you out for Fire Night. And you somehow got out to put that head in the garden."

"She asked me to put that head in the garden. And as for Fire Night . . ." He looked me up and down. "I had my reasons to be out then. Do not think, Feyre, that it did not cost me." He smiled again, and it didn't meet his eyes. "Are you going to put down that poker, or can I expect you to start swinging soon?"

I swallowed my curse and brought it out—but didn't put it down.

"A valiant effort, but useless," he said. True—so true, when he didn't even need to take his hands out of his pockets to grip Lucien's mind.

"How is it that you have such power still and the others don't? I thought she robbed all of you of your abilities."

He lifted a groomed, dark brow. "Oh, she took my powers. This . . ." A caress of talons against my mind. I jerked back a step, slamming into the fireplace. The pressure on my mind vanished. "This is just the remnant. The scraps I get to play with. Your Tamlin has brute strength and shape-shifting; my arsenal is a far deadlier assortment."

I knew he wasn't bluffing—not when I'd felt those talons in my mind. "So you can't shape-shift? It's not some High Lord specialty?"

"Oh, all the High Lords can. Each of us has a beast roaming beneath our skin, roaring to get out. While your Tamlin prefers fur, I find wings and talons to be more entertaining."

A lick of cold kissed down my spine. "Can you shift now, or did she take that, too?"

"So many questions from a little human."

But the darkness that hovered around him began to writhe and twist and flare as he rose to his feet. I blinked, and it was done.

I lifted the iron poker, just a little bit.

"Not a full shift, you see," Rhysand said, clicking the black razor-sharp talons that had replaced his fingers. Below the knee, darkness stained his skin—but talons also gleamed in lieu of toes. "I don't particularly like yielding wholly to my baser side."

Indeed, it was still Rhysand's face, his powerful male body, but flaring out behind him were massive black membranous wings—like a bat's, like the Attor's. He tucked them in neatly behind him, but the single claw at the apex of each peeked over his broad shoulders. Horrific, stunning—the face of a thousand nightmares and dreams. That again-useless part of me stirred at the sight, the way the candlelight shone through the wings, illuminating the veins, the way it bounced off his talons.

Rhysand rolled his neck, and it all vanished in a flash—the wings, the talons, the feet, leaving only the male behind, well-dressed and unruffled. "No attempts at flattery?"

I had made a very, very big mistake in offering my life to him.

But I said, "You have a high-enough opinion of yourself already. I doubt the flattery of a little human matters much to you."

He let out a low laugh that slid along my bones, warming my blood. "I can't decide whether I should consider you admirable or very stupid for being so bold with a High Lord."

Only around him did I have trouble keeping my mouth shut, it seemed. So I dared to ask, "Do you know the answer to the riddle?"

He crossed his arms. "Cheating, are you?"

"She never said I couldn't ask for help."

"Ah, but after she had you beaten to hell, she ordered us not to help you." I waited. But he shook his head. "Even if I felt like helping you, I couldn't. She gives the order, and we all bow to it." He picked a fleck of dust off his black jacket. "It's a good thing she likes me, isn't it?"

I opened my mouth to press him—to beg him. If it meant instantaneous freedom—

"Don't waste your breath," he said. "I can't tell you—no one here can. If she ordered us all to stop breathing, we would have to obey that, too." He frowned at me and snapped his fingers. The soot, the dirt, the ash vanished off my skin, leaving me as clean as if I'd bathed. "There. A gift—for having the balls to even ask."

I gave him a flat stare, but he motioned to the hearth.

It was spotless—and my bucket was filled with lentils. The door swung open of its own accord, revealing the guards who'd dragged me here.

Rhysand waved a lazy hand at them. "She accomplished her task. Take her back."

They grabbed for me, but he bared his teeth in a smile that was anything but friendly—and they halted. "No more household chores, no more tasks," he said, his voice an erotic caress. Their yellow eyes went glazed and dull, their sharp teeth gleaming as their mouths slackened. "Tell the others, too. Stay out of her cell, and don't touch her. If you do, you're to take your own daggers and gut yourselves. Understood?"

Dazed, numb nods, then they blinked and straightened. I hid my trembling. Glamour, mind control—whatever it was he had done, it worked. They beckoned—but didn't dare touch me.

Rhysand smiled at me. "You're welcome," he purred as I walked out.

CHAPTER 39

From that point on, each morning and evening, a fresh, hot meal appeared in my cell. I gobbled it down but cursed Rhysand's name anyway. Stuck in the cell, I had nothing to do but ponder Amarantha's riddle—usually only to wind up with a pounding headache. I recited it again and again and again, but to no avail.

Days passed, and I didn't see Lucien or Tamlin, and Rhysand never came to taunt me. I was alone—utterly alone, locked in silence—though the screaming in the dungeons still continued day and night. When that screaming became too unbearable and I couldn't shut it out, I would look at the eye tattooed on my palm. I wondered if he'd done it to quietly remind me of Jurian—a cruel, petty slap to the face indicating that perhaps I was well on my way to belonging to him just as the ancient warrior now belonged to Amarantha.

Every once in a while, I'd say a few words to the tattoo—then curse myself for a fool. Or curse Rhysand. But I could have sworn that as I dozed off one night, it blinked.

If I was counting the schedule of my meals correctly, about four days after I'd seen Rhysand in his room, two High Fae females arrived in my cell.

They appeared through the cracks from slivers of darkness, just as Rhysand had. But while he'd solidified into a tangible form, these faeries remained mostly made of shadow, their features barely discernable, save for their loose, flowing cobweb gowns. They remained silent when they reached for me. I didn't fight them—there was nothing to fight them with, and nowhere to run. The hands they clasped around my forearms were cool but solid—as if the shadows were a coating, a second skin.

They had to have been sent by Rhysand—some servants of his from the Night Court. They could have been mutes for all they said to me as they pressed close to my body and we stepped—physically stepped—*through* the closed door, as if it wasn't even there. As if I had become a shadow, too. My knees buckled at the sensation, like spiders crawling down my spine, my arms, as we walked through the dark, shrieking dungeons. None of the guards stopped us—they didn't even look in our direction. We were glamoured, then; no more than flickering darkness to the passing eye.

The faeries brought me up through dusty stairwells and down forgotten halls until we reached a nondescript room where they stripped me naked, bathed me roughly, and then—to my horror—began to paint my body.

Their brushes were unbearably cold and ticklish, and their shadowy grips were firm when I wriggled. Things only worsened when they painted more intimate parts of me, and it was an effort to keep from kicking one of them in the face. They offered no explanation for why—no hint of whether this was another torment sent by Amarantha. Even if I fled, there was nowhere to escape to—not without damning Tamlin further. So I stopped demanding answers, stopped fighting back, and let them finish.

From the neck up, I was regal: my face was adorned with cosmetics—rouge on my lips, a smearing of gold dust on my eyelids, kohl lining my eyes—and my hair was coiled around a small golden diadem imbedded with lapis lazuli. But from the neck down, I was a heathen god's plaything. They had continued the pattern of the tattoo on my arm, and once the blue-black paint had dried, they placed on me a gauzy white dress.

If you could call it a dress. It was little more than two long shafts of gossamer, just wide enough to cover my breasts, pinned at each shoulder with gold brooches. The sections flowed down to a jeweled belt slung low across my hips, where they joined into a single piece of fabric that hung between my legs and to the floor. It barely covered me, and from the cold air on my skin, I knew that most of my backside was left exposed.

The cold breeze caressing my bare skin was enough to kindle my rage. The two High Fae ignored my demands to be clothed in something else, their impossibly shadowed faces veiled from me, but held my arms firm when I tried to rip the shift off.

"I wouldn't do that," a deep, lilting voice said from the doorway. Rhysand was leaning against the wall, his arms crossed over his chest.

I should have known it was his doing, should have known from the matching designs all over my body. "Our bargain hasn't started yet," I snapped. The instincts that had once told me to be quiet around Tam and Lucien utterly failed me when Rhysand was near.

"Ah, but I need an escort for the party." His violet eyes glittered with stars. "And when I thought of you squatting in that cell all night, alone . . ." He waved a hand, and the faerie servants vanished through the door behind him. I flinched as they walked through the wood—no doubt an ability everyone in the Night Court possessed—and Rhysand chuckled. "You look just as I hoped you would."

From the cobwebs of my memory, I recalled similar words Tamlin had once whispered into my ear. "Is this necessary?" I said, gesturing to the paint and clothing.

"Of course," he said coolly. "How else would I know if anyone touches you?"

He approached, and I braced myself as he ran a finger along my shoulder, smearing the paint. As soon as his finger left my skin, the paint fixed itself, returning the design to its original form. "The dress itself won't mar it, and neither will your movements," he said, his face close to mine. His teeth were far too near to my throat. "And I'll remember precisely where *my* hands have been. But if anyone else touches you—let's say a certain High Lord who enjoys springtime—I'll know." He flicked my nose. "And, Feyre," he added, his voice a caressing murmur, "I don't like my belongings tampered with."

Ice wrapped around my stomach. He owned me for a week every month. Apparently, he thought that extended to the rest of my life, too.

"Come," Rhysand said, beckoning with a hand. "We're already late."

We walked through the halls. The sounds of merriment rose ahead of us, and my face burned as I silently bemoaned the too-sheer fabric of my dress. Beneath it, my breasts were visible to everyone, the paint hardly leaving anything to the imagination, and the cold cave air raised goose bumps on my skin. With my legs, sides, and most of my stomach exposed save for the slender shafts of fabric, I had to clench my teeth to keep them from chattering. My bare feet were half-frozen, and I hoped that wherever we were going would have a giant fire.

Queer, off-kilter music brayed through two stone doors that I immediately recognized. The throne room. *No*. No, anyplace but here.

Faeries and High Fae gawked as we passed through the entrance. Some bowed to Rhysand, while others gaped. I spied several of Lucien's older brothers gathered just inside the doors. The smiles they gave me were nothing short of vulpine.

Rhysand didn't touch me, but he walked close enough for it to be obvious that I was with him—that I *belonged* to him. I wouldn't have been surprised if he'd attached a collar and leash around my neck. Maybe he would at some point, now that I was bound to him, the bargain marked on my flesh.

Whispers snaked under the shouts of celebrating, and even the music quieted as the crowd parted and made a path for us to Amarantha's dais. I lifted my chin, the weight of the crown digging into my skull.

I'd beaten her first task. I'd beaten her menial chores. I could keep my head high.

Tamlin was seated beside her on that same throne, in his usual clothing, no weapons sheathed anywhere on him. Rhysand had said that he wanted to tell him at the right moment, that he'd wanted to *hurt* Tamlin by revealing the bargain I'd made. Prick. Scheming, wretched prick.

"Merry Midsummer," Rhysand said, bowing to Amarantha. She wore a rich gown of lavender and orchid-purple—surprisingly modest. I was a savage before her cultivated beauty.

"What have you done with my captive?" she said, but her smile didn't reach her eyes.

Tamlin's face was like stone—like stone, save for the white-knuckled grip on the arms of his throne. No claws. He was able to keep that sign of his temper at bay, at least.

I'd done such a foolish thing in binding myself to Rhysand. Rhysand, with the wings and talons lurking beneath that beautiful, flawless surface; Rhysand, who could shatter minds. *I did it for you*, I wanted to shout.

"We made a bargain," Rhysand said. I flinched as he brushed a stray lock of my hair from my face. He ran his fingers down my cheek—a gentle caress. The throne room was all too quiet as he spoke his next words to Tamlin. "One week with me at the Night Court every month in exchange for my healing services after her first task." He raised my left arm to reveal the tattoo, whose ink didn't shine as much as the paint on my body. "For the rest of her life," he added casually, but his eyes were now upon Amarantha.

The Faerie Queen straightened a little bit—even Jurian's eye seemed fixed on me, on Rhysand. *For the rest of my life*—he said it as if it were going to be a long, long while.

He thought I was going to beat her tasks.

I stared at his profile, at the elegant nose and sensuous lips. Games—Rhysand liked to play games, and it seemed I was now to be a key player in whatever this one was.

"Enjoy my party" was Amarantha's only reply as she toyed with the bone at the end of her necklace. Dismissed, Rhysand put a hand on my back to steer us away, to turn me from Tamlin, who still gripped the throne.

The crowd kept a good distance, and I couldn't acknowledge any of them, out of fear I might have to look at Tamlin again, or might spy Lucien—glimpse the expression on his face when he beheld me.

I kept my chin up. I wouldn't let the others notice that weakness—wouldn't let them know how much it killed me to be so exposed to them, to have Rhysand's symbols painted over nearly every inch of my skin, to have Tamlin see me so debased.

Rhysand stopped before a table laden with exquisite foods. The High Fae around it quickly cleared away. If there were any other members of the Night Court present, they didn't ripple with darkness the way Rhysand and his servants did; didn't dare approach him. The music grew loud enough to suggest there was probably dancing somewhere in the room. "Wine?" he said, offering me a goblet.

Alis's first rule. I shook my head.

He smiled, and extended the goblet again. "Drink. You'll need it."

Drink, my mind echoed, and my fingers stirred, moving toward the goblet. No. No, Alis said not to drink the wine here—wine that was different from that joyous, freeing solstice wine. "No," I said, and some faeries who were watching us from a safe distance chuckled.

"Drink," he said, and my traitorous fingers latched onto the goblet.

✠

I awoke in my cell, still clad in that handkerchief he called a dress. Everything was spinning so badly that I barely made it to the corner before I vomited. Again. And again. When I'd emptied my stomach, I crawled to the opposite corner of the cell and collapsed.

Sleep came fitfully as the world continued to twirl violently around me. I was tied to a spinning wheel, going around and around and around—

Needless to say, I was sick a fair amount that day.

I'd just finished picking at the hot dinner that had appeared moments before when the door creaked and a golden fox-face appeared—along with a narrowed metal eye. "Shit," said Lucien. "It's freezing in here."

It was, but I was too nauseated to notice. Keeping my head up was an effort, let alone keeping the food down. He unclasped his cloak and set it around my shoulders. Its heavy warmth leaked into me. "Look at all this," he said, staring at the paint on me. Thankfully, it was all intact, save for a few places on my waist. "Bastard."

"What happened?" I got out, even though I wasn't sure I truly wanted the answer. My memory was a dark blur of wild music.

Lucien drew back. "I don't think you want to know." I studied the few smudges on my waist, marks that looked like hands had held me.

"Who did that to me?" I asked quietly, my eyes tracing the arc of the spoiled paint.

"Who do you think?"

My heart clenched and I looked at the floor. "Did—did Tamlin see it?"

Lucien nodded. "Rhys was only doing it to get a rise out of him."

"Did it work?" I still couldn't look Lucien in the face. I knew, at least, that I hadn't been violated beyond touching my sides. The paint told me that much.

"No," Lucien said, and I smiled grimly.

"What—what was I doing the whole time?" So much for Alis's warning.

Lucien let out a sharp breath, running a hand through his red hair. "He had you dance for him for most of the night. And when you weren't dancing, you were sitting in his lap."

"What *kind* of dancing?" I pushed.

"Not the kind you were doing with Tamlin on Solstice," Lucien said, and my face heated. From the murkiness of my memories of last night, I recalled the closeness of a certain pair of violet eyes—eyes that sparkled with mischief as they beheld me.

"In front of everyone?"

"Yes," Lucien replied—more gently than I'd heard him speak to me before. I stiffened. I didn't want his pity. He sighed and grabbed my left arm, examining the tattoo. "What were you thinking? Didn't you know I'd come as soon as I could?"

I yanked my arm from him. "I was *dying*! I had a fever—I was barely able to keep conscious! How was I supposed to know you'd come? That you even understood how quickly humans can die of that sort of thing? You told me you *hesitated* that time with the naga."

"I swore an oath to Tamlin—"

"I had no other choice! You think I'm going to trust you after everything you said to me at the manor?"

"I risked my neck for you during your task. Was that not enough?" His metal eye whirred softly. "You offered up your name for me—after all that I said to you, all I did, you still offered up your name. Didn't you realize I would help you after that? Oath or no oath?"

I hadn't realized it would mean anything to him at all. "I had no other choice," I said again, breathing hard.

"Don't you understand what Rhys *is*?"

"I do!" I barked, then sighed. "I do," I repeated, and glared at the eye in my palm. "It's done with. So you needn't hold to whatever oath you swore to Tamlin to protect me—or feel like you owe me anything for saving you from Amarantha. I would have done it just to wipe the smirk off your brothers' faces."

Lucien clicked his tongue, but his remaining russet eye shone. "I'm glad to see you didn't sell your lively human spirit or stubbornness to Rhys."

"Just a week of my life every month."

"Yes, well—we'll see about *that* when the time comes," he growled, that metal eye flicking to the door. He stood. "I should go. The rotation's about to shift."

He made it a step before I said, "I'm sorry—that she still punished you for helping me during my task. I heard—" My throat tightened. "I heard what she made Tamlin do to you." He shrugged, but I added, "Thank you. For helping me, I mean."

He walked to the door, and for the first time I noticed how stiffly he moved. "It's why I couldn't come sooner," he said, his throat bobbing. "She used her—used *our* powers to keep my back from healing. I haven't been able to move until today."

Breathing became a little difficult. "Here," I said, removing his cloak and standing to hand it to him. The sudden cold sent gooseflesh rippling over me.

"Keep it. I swiped it off a dozing guard on my way in here." In the dim light, the embroidered symbol of a sleeping dragon glimmered. Amarantha's coat of arms. I grimaced, but shrugged it on.

"Besides," Lucien added with a smirk, "I've seen enough of you through that gown to last a lifetime." I flushed as he opened the door.

"Wait," I said. "Is—is Tamlin all right? I mean . . . I mean that spell Amarantha has him under to make him so silent . . ."

"There's no spell. Hasn't it occurred to you that Tamlin is keeping quiet to avoid telling Amarantha which form of your torment affects him most?"

No, it hadn't.

"He's playing a dangerous game, though," Lucien said, slipping out the door. "We all are."

✢

The next night, I was again washed, painted, and brought to that miserable throne room. Not a ball this time—just some evening entertainment.

Which, it turned out, was me. After I drank the wine, though, I was mercifully unaware of what was happening.

Night after night, I was dressed in the same way and made to accompany Rhysand to the throne room. Thus I became Rhysand's plaything, the harlot of Amarantha's whore. I woke with vague shards of memories—of dancing between Rhysand's legs as he sat in a chair and laughed; of his hands, stained blue from the places they touched on my waist, my arms, but somehow, never more than that. He had me dance until I was sick, and once I was done retching, told me to begin dancing again.

I awoke ill and exhausted each morning, and though Rhysand's order to the guards had indeed held, the nightly activities left me thoroughly drained. I spent my days sleeping off the faerie wine, dozing to escape the humiliation I endured. When I could, I contemplated Amarantha's riddle, turning over every word—to no avail.

And when I again entered that throne room, I was allowed only a glimpse of Tamlin before the drug of the wine took hold. But every time, every night, just for that one glance, I didn't hide the love and pain that welled in my eyes when they met his.

✢

I had finished being painted and dressed—my gossamer gown a shade of blood orange that night—when Rhysand entered the room. The shadow maids, as usual, walked through the walls and vanished. But rather than beckon me to come with him, Rhysand closed the door.

"Your second trial is tomorrow night," he said neutrally. The gold-and-silver thread in his black tunic shone in the candlelight. He never wore another color.

It was like a stone to the head. I'd lost count of the days. "So?"

"It could be your last," he said, and leaned against the door frame, crossing his arms.

"If you're taunting me into playing another game of yours, you're wasting your breath."

"Aren't you going to beg me to give you a night with your beloved?"

"I'll have that night, and all the ones after, when I beat her final task."

Rhysand shrugged, then flashed a grin as he pushed off the door and stepped toward me. "I wonder if you were this prickly with Tamlin when you were his captive."

"He never treated me like a captive—or a slave."

"No—and how could he? Not with the shame of his father and brothers' brutality always weighing on him, the poor, noble beast. But perhaps if he'd bothered to learn a thing or two about cruelty, about what it means to be a true High Lord, it would have kept the Spring Court from falling."

"Your court fell, too."

Sadness flickered in those violet eyes. I wouldn't have noticed it had I not . . . *felt* it—deep inside me. My gaze drifted to the eye etched in my palm. What manner of tattoo, exactly, had he given me? But instead I asked, "When you were roaming freely on Fire Night—at the Rite—you said it cost you. Were you one of the High Lords that sold allegiance to Amarantha in exchange for not being forced to live down here?"

Whatever sadness had been in his eyes vanished—only cold, glittering calm remained. I could have sworn a shadow of mighty wings stained the wall behind him. "What I do or have done for my Court is none of your concern."

"And what has she been doing for the past forty-nine years? Holding court and torturing everyone as she pleases? To what end?" *Tell me about the threat she poses to the human world*, I wanted to beg—*tell me what all of this means*, why *so many awful things had to happen.*

"The Lady of the Mountain needs no excuses for her actions."

"But—"

"The festivities await." He gestured to the door behind him.

I knew I was on dangerous ground, but I didn't care. "What do you want with me? Beyond taunting Tamlin."

"Taunting him is my greatest pleasure," he said with a mock bow. "And as for your question, why does any male need a reason to enjoy the presence of a female?"

"You saved my life."

"And through *your* life, I saved Tamlin's."

"Why?"

He winked, smoothing his blue-black hair. "That, Feyre, is the real question, isn't it?"

With that, he led me from the room.

We reached the throne room, and I braced myself to be drugged and disgraced again. But it was Rhysand the crowd looked at—Rhysand whom Lucien's brothers monitored. Amarantha's clear voice rang out over the music, summoning him.

He paused, glancing at Lucien's brothers stalking toward us, their attention pinned on me. Eager, hungry—wicked. I opened my mouth, not too proud to ask Rhysand not to leave me alone with them while he dealt with Amarantha, but he put a hand on my back and nudged me along.

"Just stay close, and keep your mouth shut," he murmured in my ear as he led me by the arm. The crowd parted as if we were on fire, revealing all too soon what was before us.

Not us, I amended, but Rhysand.

A brown-skinned High Fae male was sobbing on the floor before the dais. Amarantha was smiling at him like a snake—so intently that she didn't even spare me a glance. Beside her, Tamlin remained utterly impassive. A beast without claws.

Rhysand flicked his eyes to me—a silent command to stay at the edge of the crowd. I obeyed, and when I lifted my attention to Tamlin, waiting for him to look—just *look* at me—he did not, his focus wholly on the queen, on the male before her. Point taken.

Amarantha caressed her ring, watching every movement that Rhysand made as he approached. "The summer lordling," she said of the male cowering at her feet, "tried to escape through the exit to the Spring Court lands. I want to know why."

There was a tall, handsome High Fae male standing at the crowd's edge—his hair near-white, eyes of crushing, crystal blue, his skin of richest mahogany. But his mouth was drawn as his attention darted between Amarantha and Rhysand. I'd seen him before, during that first task—the High Lord of the Summer Court. Before, he'd been shining—almost leaking golden light; now he was muted, drab. As if Amarantha had leeched every last drop of power from him while she interrogated his subject.

Rhysand slid his hands into his pockets and sauntered closer to the male on the ground.

The Summer faerie cringed, his face shining with tears. My own bowels turned watery with fear and shame as he wet himself at the sight of Rhysand. "P-p-please," he gasped out.

The crowd was breathless, too silent.

His back to me, Rhysand's shoulders were loose, not a stitch of clothing out of place. But I knew his talons had latched onto the faerie's mind the moment the male stopped shaking on the ground.

The High Lord of Summer had gone still, too—and it was pain, real pain, and fear that shone in those stunning blue eyes. Summer was one of the courts that had rebelled, I remembered. So this was a new, untested High Lord, who had not yet had to make choices that cost him lives.

After a moment of silence, Rhysand looked at Amarantha. "He wanted to escape. To get to the Spring Court, cross the wall, and flee south into human territory. He had no accomplices, no motive beyond his own pathetic cowardice." He jerked his chin toward the puddle of piss beneath the male. But out of the corner of my eye I saw the Summer High Lord sag a bit—enough to make me wonder . . . wonder what sort of choice Rhys had made in that moment he'd taken to search the male's mind.

But Amarantha rolled her eyes and slouched in her throne. "Shatter him, Rhysand." She flicked a hand at the High Lord of the Summer Court. "You may do what you want with the body afterward."

The High Lord of the Summer Court bowed—as if he'd been given a gift—and looked to his subject, who had gone still and calm on the floor, hugging his knees. The male faerie was ready—relieved.

Rhys slipped a hand out of his pocket, and it dangled at his side. I could have sworn phantom talons flickered there as his fingers curled slightly.

"I'm growing bored, Rhysand," Amarantha said with a sigh, again fiddling with that bone. She hadn't looked at me once, too focused on her current prey.

Rhysand's fingers curled into a fist.

The faerie male's eyes went wide—then glazed as he slumped to the side in the puddle of his own waste. Blood leaked from his nose, from his ears, pooling on the floor.

That fast—that easily, that irrevocably . . . he was dead.

"I said shatter his mind, not his brain," Amarantha snapped.

The crowd murmured around me, stirring. I wanted nothing more than to fade back into it—to crawl back into my cell and burn this from my mind. Tamlin hadn't flinched—not a muscle. What horrors had he witnessed in his long life if this hadn't broken that distant expression, that control?

Rhysand shrugged, his hand sliding back into his pocket. "Apologies, my queen." He turned away without being dismissed, and didn't look at me as he strode for the back of the throne room. I fell into step beside him, reining in my trembling, trying not to think about the body sprawled behind us, or about Clare—still nailed to the wall.

The crowd stayed far, far back as we walked through it. "Whore," some of them softly hissed at him, out of her earshot; "Amarantha's whore." But many offered tentative, appreciative smiles and words—"Good that you killed him; good that you killed the traitor."

Rhysand didn't deign to acknowledge any of them, his shoulders still loose, his footsteps unhurried. I wondered whether anyone but he and the High Lord of the Summer Court knew that the killing had been a mercy. I was willing to bet that there *had* been others involved in that escape plan, perhaps even the High Lord of the Summer Court himself.

But maybe keeping those secrets had only been done in aid of whatever games Rhysand liked to play. Maybe sparing that faerie male by killing him swiftly, rather than shattering his mind and leaving him a drooling husk, had been another calculated move, too.

He didn't pause once on that long trek across the throne room, but when we reached the food and wine at the back of the room, he handed me a goblet and downed one alongside me. He didn't say anything before the wine swept me into oblivion.

CHAPTER 40

My second task arrived.

Its teeth gleaming, the Attor grinned at me as I stood before Amarantha. Another cavern—smaller than the throne room, but large enough to perhaps be some sort of old entertaining space. It had no decorations, save for its gilded walls, and no furniture; the queen herself only sat on a carved wooden chair, Tamlin standing behind her. I didn't gaze too long at the Attor, who lingered on the other side of the queen's chair, its long, slender tail slashing across the floor. It only smiled to unnerve me.

It was working. Not even gazing at Tamlin could calm me. I clenched my hands at my sides as Amarantha smiled.

"Well, Feyre, your second trial has come." She sounded so smug—so certain that my death hovered nearby. I'd been a fool to refuse death in the teeth of the worm. She crossed her arms and propped her chin on a hand. Within the ring, Jurian's eye turned—*turned* to face me, its pupil dilating in the dim light. "Have you solved my riddle yet?"

I didn't deign to make a response.

"Too bad," she said with a moue. "But I'm feeling generous tonight." The Attor chuckled, and several faeries behind me gave hissing laughs that snaked their way up my spine. "How about a little practice?" Amarantha said, and I forced my face into neutrality. If Tamlin was playing indifferent to keep us both safe, so would I.

But I dared a glance at my High Lord, and found his eyes hard upon me. If I could just hold him, feel his skin for just a moment—smell him, hear him say my name . . .

A slight hiss echoed across the room, dragging my gaze away. Amarantha was frowning up at Tamlin from her seat. I hadn't realized we'd been staring at each other, the cavern wholly silent.

"Begin," Amarantha snapped.

Before I could brace myself, the floor shuddered.

My knees wobbled, and I swung my arms to keep upright as the stones beneath me began sinking, lowering me into a large, rectangular pit. Some faeries cackled, but I found Tamlin's stare again and held it until I was lowered so far down that his face disappeared beyond the edge.

I scanned the four walls around me, looking for a door, for any sign of what was to come. Three of the walls were made of a single sheet of smooth, shining stone—too polished and flat to climb. The other wall wasn't a wall at all, but an iron grate splitting the chamber in two, and through it—

My breath caught in my throat. "Lucien."

Lucien lay chained to the center of the floor on the other side of the chamber, his remaining russet eye so wide that it was surrounded with white. The metal one spun as if set wild; his brutal scar was stark against his pale skin. Again he was to be Amarantha's toy to torment.

There were no doors, no way for me to get to his side except to climb over the gate between us. It had such thick, wide holes that I could probably climb it to jump onto his side. I didn't dare.

The faeries began murmuring, and gold clinked. Had Rhysand bet on me again? In the crowd, red hair gleamed—four heads of red hair—and I stiffened my spine. I knew his brothers would be smiling at Lucien's predicament—but where was his mother? His father? Surely the High Lord of the Autumn Court would be present. I scanned the crowd. No sign of them. Only Amarantha, standing with Tamlin at the edge of the pit, peering in. She bowed her head to me and gestured with an elegant hand to the wall beneath her feet.

"Here, Feyre darling, you shall find your task. Simply answer the question by selecting the correct lever, and you'll win. Select the wrong one to your doom. As there are only three options, I think I gave you an unfair advantage." She snapped her fingers, and something metallic groaned. "That is," she added, "if you can solve the puzzle in time."

Not too high above, the two giant, spike-encrusted grates I'd dismissed as chandeliers began lowering, slowly descending toward the chamber—

I whirled to Lucien. That was the reason for the gate cleaving the chamber in two—so I would have to watch as he splattered beneath, just as I myself was squashed. The spikes, which had been supporting candles and torches, glowed red—and even from a distance, I could see the heat rippling off them.

Lucien wrenched at his chains. This would not be a clean death.

And then I turned to the wall that Amarantha had gestured to.

A lengthy inscription was carved into its smooth surface, and beneath it were three stone levers with the numbers *I*, *II*, and *III* engraved above them.

I began to shake. I recognized only basic words—useless ones like *the* and *but* and *went*. Everything else was a blur of letters I didn't know, letters I'd have to slowly sound out or research to understand.

The spiked grate was still descending, now level with Amarantha's head, and would soon shut off any chance I stood of getting out of this pit. The heat from the glowing iron already smothered me, sweat starting to bead at my temples. Who had told her I couldn't read?

"Something wrong?" She raised an eyebrow. I snapped my attention to the inscription, keeping my breathing as steady as I could. She hadn't mentioned reading as an issue—she would have mocked me more if she'd known about my illiteracy. Fate—a cruel, vicious twist of fate.

The chains rattled and strained, and Lucien cursed as he beheld what was before me. I turned to him, but when I saw his face, I knew he was too far to be able to read it aloud to me, even with his enhanced metal eye. If I could hear the question, I might stand a chance at solving it—but riddles weren't my strong point.

I was going to be skewered by burning-hot spikes and then crushed on the ground like a grape.

The grate now passed over the lip of the pit, filling it entirely—no corner was safe. If I didn't answer the question before the grate passed the levers—

My throat closed up, and I read and read and read, but no words came. The air became thick and stank of metal—not magic but burning, unforgiving steel creeping toward me, inch by inch.

"Answer it!" Lucien shouted, his voice hitched. My eyes stung. The world was just a blur of letters, mocking me with their turns and shapes.

The metal groaned as it scraped against the smooth stone of the chamber, and the faeries' whispers grew more frenzied. Through the holes in the grate, I thought I saw Lucien's eldest brother chuckle. Hot—so unbearably hot.

It would hurt—those spikes were large and blunt. It wouldn't be quick. It would take some force to pierce through my body. Sweat slid down my neck, my back as I stared at the letters, at the *I*, *II*, and *III* that had somehow become my lifeline. Two choices would doom me—one choice would stop the grate.

I found numbers in the inscription—it must be a riddle, a logic problem, a maze of words worse than any worm's labyrinth.

"*Feyre!*" Lucien cried, panting as he stared at the ever-lowering spikes. The gleeful faces of the High Fae and lesser faeries sneered at me above the grate.

Three . . . grass . . . grasshope . . . grasshoppers . . .

The gate wouldn't stop, and there wasn't a full body length between my head and the first of those spikes. I could have sworn the heat devoured the air in the pit.

. . . were . . . boo . . . bow . . . boon . . . king . . . sing . . . bouncing . . .

I should say my good-byes to Tamlin. Right now. This was what my life amounted to—these were my last moments, this was it, the final breaths of my body, the last beatings of my heart.

"*Just pick one!*" Lucien shouted, and some of those in the crowd laughed—his brothers no doubt the loudest.

I reached a hand toward the levers and stared at the three numbers beyond my trembling, tattooed fingers.

I, II, III.

They meant nothing to me beyond life and death. Chance might save me, but—

Two. Two was a lucky number, because that was like Tamlin and me—just two people. One had to be bad, because one was like Amarantha, or the Attor—solitary beings. One was a nasty number, and three was too much—it was three sisters crammed into a tiny cottage, hating each other until they choked on it, until it poisoned them.

Two. It was two. I could gladly, willingly, fanatically believe in a Cauldron and Fate if they would take care of me. I believed in two. Two.

I reached for the second lever, but a blinding pain racked my hand before I could touch the stone. I hissed, withdrawing. I opened my palm to reveal the slitted eye tattooed there. It narrowed. I had to be hallucinating.

The grate was about to cover the inscription, barely six feet above my head. I couldn't breathe, couldn't think. The heat was too much, and metal sizzled, so close to my ears.

I again reached for the middle lever, but the pain paralyzed my fingers.

The eye had returned to its usual state. I extended my hand toward the first lever. Again, pain.

I reached for the third lever. No pain. My fingers met with stone, and I looked up to find the grate not four feet from my head. Through it, I found a star-flecked violet gaze.

I reached for the first lever. Pain. But when I reached for the third lever . . .

Rhysand's face remained a mask of boredom. Sweat slipped down my brow, stinging my eyes. I could only trust him; I could only give myself up again, forced to concede by my helplessness.

The spikes were so enormous up close. All I had to do was lift my arm above my head and I'd burn the flesh off my hands.

"*Feyre, please!*" Lucien moaned.

I shook so badly I could scarcely stand. The heat of the spikes bore down on me.

The stone lever was cool in my hand.

I shut my eyes, unable to look at Tamlin, bracing myself for the impact and the agony, and pulled the third lever.

Silence.

The pulsing heat didn't grow closer. Then—a sigh. *Lucien.*

I opened my eyes to find my tattooed fingers white-knuckled beneath the ink as they gripped the lever. The spikes hovered not inches from my head.

Unmoving—stopped.

I had won—I had . . .

The grate groaned as it lifted toward the ceiling, cool air flooding the chamber. I gulped it down in uneven breaths.

Lucien was offering up some kind of prayer, kissing the ground again and again. The floor beneath me rose, and I was forced to release the lever that had saved me as I was brought to the surface again. My knees wobbled.

I couldn't read, and it had almost killed me. I hadn't even won properly. I sank to my knees, letting the platform carry me, and covered my face in my shaking hands.

Tears burned just before pain seared through my left arm. I would never beat the third task. I would never free Tamlin, or his people. The pain shot through my bones again, and through my increasing hysteria, I heard words inside my head that stopped me short.

Don't let her see you cry.

Put your hands at your sides and stand up.

I couldn't. I couldn't move.

Stand. Don't give her the satisfaction of seeing you break.

My knees and spine, not entirely of my own will, forced me upright, and when the ground at last stopped moving, I looked at Amarantha with tearless eyes.

Good, Rhysand told me. *Stare her down. No tears—wait until you're back in your cell.* Amarantha's face was drawn and white, her black eyes like onyx as she beheld me. I had won, but I should be dead. I should be squashed, my blood oozing everywhere.

Count to ten. Don't look at Tamlin. Just stare at her.

I obeyed. It was the only thing that kept me from giving in to the sobs trapped within my chest, thundering to get out.

I willed myself to meet Amarantha's gaze. It was cold and vast and full of ancient malice, but I held it. I counted to ten.

Good girl. Now walk away. Turn on your heel—good. Walk toward the door. Keep your chin high. Let the crowd part. One step after another.

I listened to him, let him keep me tethered to sanity as I was escorted back to my cell by the guards—who still kept their distance. Rhysand's words echoed through my mind, holding me together.

But when my cell door closed, he went silent, and I dropped to the floor and wept.

✢

I wept for hours. For myself, for Tamlin, for the fact that I should be dead and had somehow survived. I cried for everything I'd lost, every injury I'd ever received, every wound—physical or otherwise. I cried for that trivial part of me, once so full of color and light—now hollow and dark and empty.

I couldn't stop. I couldn't breathe. I couldn't beat her. She won today, and she hadn't known it.

She'd won; it was only by cheating that I'd survived. Tamlin would never be free, and I would perish in the most awful of ways. I couldn't read—I was an ignorant, human fool. My shortcomings had caught up with me, and this place would become my tomb. I would never paint again; never see the sun again.

The walls closed in—the ceiling dropped. I wanted to be crushed; I wanted to be snuffed out. Everything converged, squeezing inward, sucking out air. I couldn't keep myself in my body—the walls were forcing me out of it. I was grasping for my body, but it hurt too much each time I tried to maintain the connection. All I had wanted—all I had dared want, was a life that was quiet, easy. Nothing more than that. Nothing extraordinary. But now . . . now . . .

I felt the ripple in the darkness without having to look up, and didn't flinch at the soft footsteps that approached me. I didn't bother hoping that it would be Tamlin. "Still weeping?"

Rhysand.

I didn't lower my hands from my face. The floor rose toward the lowering ceiling—I would soon be flattened. There was no color, no light here.

"You've just beaten her second task. Tears are unnecessary."

I wept harder, and he laughed. The stones reverberated as he knelt before me, and though I tried to fight him, his grip was firm as he grasped my wrists and pried my hands from my face.

The walls weren't moving, and the room was open—gaping. No colors, but shades of darkness, of night. Only those star-flecked violet eyes were bright, full of color and light. He gave me a lazy smile before he leaned forward.

I pulled away, but his hands were like shackles. I could do nothing as his mouth met with my cheek, and he licked away a tear. His tongue was hot against my skin, so startling that I couldn't move as he licked away another path of salt water, and then another. My body went taut and loose all at once and I burned, even as chills shuddered along my limbs. It was only when his tongue danced along the damp edges of my lashes that I jerked back.

He chuckled as I scrambled for the corner of the cell. I wiped my face as I glared at him.

He smirked, sitting down against a wall. "I figured that would get you to stop crying."

"It was disgusting." I wiped my face again.

"Was it?" He quirked an eyebrow and pointed to his palm—to the place where my tattoo would be. "Beneath all your pride and stubbornness, I could have sworn I detected something that felt differently. Interesting."

"Get out."

"As usual, your gratitude is overwhelming."

"Do you want me to kiss your feet for what you did at the trial? Do you want me to offer another week of my life?"

"Not unless you feel compelled to do so," he said, his eyes like stars.

It was bad enough that my life was forfeited to this Fae lord—but to have a bond where he could now freely read my thoughts and feelings and communicate . . .

"Who would have thought that the self-righteous human girl couldn't read?"

"Keep your damned mouth shut about it."

"Me? I wouldn't dream of telling anyone. Why waste that kind of knowledge on petty gossip?"

If I'd had the strength, I would have leaped on him and ripped him apart. "You're a disgusting bastard."

"I'll have to ask Tamlin if this kind of flattery won his heart." He groaned as he stood, a soft, deep-throated noise that traveled along my bones. His eyes met with mine, and he smiled slowly. I exposed my teeth, almost hissing.

"I'll spare you the escort duties tomorrow," he said, shrugging as he walked to the cell door. "But the night after, I expect you to be looking your finest." He gave me a grin that suggested my finest wasn't very much at all. He paused by the door, but didn't dissolve into darkness. "I've been thinking of ways to torment you when you come to my court. I'm wondering: Will assigning you to learn to read be as painful as it looked today?"

He vanished into shadow before I could launch myself at him.

I paced through my cell, scowling at the eye in my hand. I spat every curse I could at it, but there was no response.

It took me a long while to realize that Rhysand, whether he knew it or not, had effectively kept me from shattering completely.

CHAPTER 41

What followed the second trial was a series of days that I don't care to recall. A permanent darkness settled over me, and I began to look forward to the moment when Rhysand gave me that goblet of faerie wine and I could lose myself for a few hours. I stopped contemplating Amarantha's riddle—it was impossible. Especially for an illiterate, ignorant human.

Thinking of Tamlin made everything worse. I'd beaten two of Amarantha's tasks, but I knew—knew it deep in my bones—that the third would be the one to kill me. After what had happened to her sister, what Jurian had done, she would never let me leave here alive. I couldn't entirely blame her; I doubted I would ever forget or forgive something like that being done to Nesta or Elain, no matter how many centuries had passed. But I still wasn't going to leave here alive.

The future I'd dreamed of was just that: a dream. I'd grow old and withered, while he would remain young for centuries, perhaps millennia. At best, I'd have decades with him before I died.

Decades. That was what I was fighting for. A flash in time for them—a drop in the pool of their eons.

So I greedily drank the wine, and I stopped caring about who I was and what had once mattered to me. I stopped thinking about color, about light, about the green of Tamlin's eyes—about all those things I had still wanted to paint and now would never get to.

I wasn't going to leave this mountain alive.

I was walking to the dressing chamber with Rhysand's two shadow-servants, staring at nothing and thinking of even less, when a hissing noise and the flap of wings sounded from around an upcoming corner. The Attor. The faeries beside me tensed, but their chins rose slightly.

I'd never become accustomed to the Attor, but I had come to accept its malignant presence. Seeing my escorts stiffen awakened a dormant dread, and my mouth turned dry as we neared the bend. Even though we were veiled and hidden by shadow, each step brought me closer to that winged demon. My feet turned leaden.

Then a lower, guttural voice grunted in response to the hissing of the Attor. Nails clicked on stone, and my escorts swapped glances before they swung me into an alcove, a tapestry that hadn't been there a moment before falling over us, the shadows deepening, solidifying. I had a feeling that if someone pulled back that tapestry, they would see only darkness and stone.

One of them covered my mouth with a hand, holding me tightly to her, shadows slithering down her arm and onto mine. She smelled of jasmine—I'd never noticed that before. After all these nights, I didn't even know their names.

The Attor and its companion rounded the bend, still talking—their voices low. It was only when I could understand their words that I realized we weren't merely hiding.

"Yes," the Attor was saying, "good. She'll be most pleased to hear that they're ready at last."

"But will the High Lords contribute their forces?" the guttural voice replied. I could have sworn it snorted like a pig.

They came closer and closer, unaware of us. My escorts pressed in tighter to me, so tense that I realized they were holding their breath. Handmaidens—and spies.

"The High Lords will do as she tells them," the Attor gloated, and its tail slithered and slashed across the floor.

"I heard talk from soldiers in Hybern that the High King is not pleased regarding this situation with the girl. Amarantha made a fool's bargain. She cost him the War the last time because of her madness with Jurian; if she turns her back on him again, he will not be so willing to forgive her. Stealing his spells and taking a territory for her own is one thing. Failure to aid in his cause a second time is another."

There was a loud hiss, and I trembled as the Attor snapped its jaws at its companion. "Milady makes no bargains that are not advantageous to her. She lets them claw at hope—but once it is shattered, they are her beautifully broken minions."

They had to be passing right before the tapestry.

"You had better hope so," the guttural voice replied. What manner of creature was this thing to be so unmoved by the Attor? My escort's shadowy hand clamped tighter around my mouth, and the Attor passed on.

Don't trust your senses, Alis's voice echoed through my mind. The Attor had caught me once before when I thought I was safe . . .

"And you had better hold your tongue," the Attor warned. "Or Milady will do so for you—and her pincers are not kind."

The other creature snorted that pig noise. "I am here on a condition of immunity from the king. If your *lady* thinks she's above the king because she rules this wretched land, she'll soon remember who can strip her powers away—without spells and potions."

The Attor didn't reply—and a part of me wished for it to retort, to snap back. But it was silenced, and fear hit my stomach like a stone dropped into a pool.

Whatever plans the King of Hybern had been working on for these long years—his campaign to take back the mortal world—it seemed he was no longer content to wait. Perhaps Amarantha would soon receive what she wanted: destruction of my entire realm.

My blood went cold. Nesta—I trusted Nesta to get my family away, to protect them.

Their voices faded, and it wasn't until a good extra minute had passed that the two females relaxed. The tapestry vanished, and we slipped back into the hall.

"What *was* that?" I said, looking from one to the other as the shadows around us lightened—but not by much. "*Who* was that?" I clarified.

"Trouble," they answered in unison.

"Does Rhysand know?"

"He will soon," one of them said. We resumed our silent walk to the dressing room.

There was nothing I could do about the King of Hybern, anyway—not while trapped Under the Mountain, not when I hadn't even been able to free Tamlin, much less myself. And with Nesta prepared to flee with my family, there was no one else to warn. So day after day passed, bringing my third trial ever closer.

I suppose I sank so far into myself that it took something extraordinary to pull me out again. I was watching the light dance along the damp stones of the ceiling of my cell—like moonlight on water—when a noise traveled to me, down through the stones, rippling across the floor.

I was so used to the strange fiddles and drums of the faeries that when I heard the lilting melody, I thought it was another hallucination. Sometimes, if I stared at the ceiling long enough, it became the vast expanse of the starry night sky, and I became a small, unimportant thing that blew away in the wind.

I looked toward the small vent in the corner of the ceiling through which the music entered my cell. The source must have been far away, for it was just a faint stirring of notes, but when I closed my eyes, I could hear it more clearly. I could . . . see it. As if it were a grand painting, a living mural.

There was beauty in this music—beauty and goodness. The music folded over itself like batter being poured from a bowl, one note atop another, melting together to form a whole, rising, filling me. It wasn't wild music, but there was a violence of passion in it, a swelling kind of joy and sorrow. I pulled my knees to my chest, needing to feel the sturdiness of my skin, even with the slime of the oily paint upon it.

The music built a path, an ascent founded upon archways of color. I followed it, walking out of that cell, through layers of earth, up and up—into fields of cornflowers, past a canopy of trees, and into the open expanse of sky. The pulse of the music was like hands that gently pushed me onward, pulling me higher, guiding me through the clouds. I'd never seen clouds like these—in their puffy sides, I could discern faces fair and sorrowful. They faded before I could view them too clearly, and I looked into the distance to where the music summoned me.

It was either a sunset or sunrise. The sun filled the clouds with magenta and purple, and its orange-gold rays blended with my path to form a band of shimmering metal.

I wanted to fade into it, wanted the light of that sun to burn me away, to fill me with such joy that I would become a ray of sunshine myself. This wasn't music to dance to—it was music to worship, music to fill in the gaps of my soul, to bring me to a place where there was no pain.

I didn't realize I was weeping until the wet warmth of a tear splashed upon my arm. But even then I clung to the music, gripping it like a ledge that kept me from falling. I hadn't realized how badly I didn't want to tumble into that deep dark—how much I wanted to stay here among the clouds and color and light.

I let the sounds ravage me, let them lay me flat and run over my body with their drums. Up and up, building to a palace in the sky, a hall of alabaster and moonstone, where all that was lovely and kind and fantastic dwelled in peace. I wept—wept to be so close to that palace, wept from the need to be there. Everything I wanted was there—the one I loved was there—

The music was Tamlin's fingers strumming my body; it was the gold in his eyes and the twist of his smile. It was that breathy chuckle, and the way he said those three words. It was *this* I was fighting for, *this* I had sworn to save.

The music rose—louder, grander, faster, from wherever it was played—a wave that peaked, shattering the gloom of my cell. A shuddering sob broke from me as the sound faded into silence. I sat there, trembling and weeping, too raw and exposed, left naked by the music and the color in my mind.

When the tears had stopped but the music still echoed in my every breath, I lay on my pallet of hay, listening to my breathing.

The music flittered through my memories, binding them together, making them into a quilt that wrapped around me, that warmed my bones. I looked at the eye in the center of my palm, but it only stared right back at me—unmoving.

Two more days until my final trial. Just two more days, and then I would learn what the Eddies of the Cauldron had planned for me.

CHAPTER 42

It was a party like any other—even if it would likely be my last. Faeries drank and lounged and danced, laughing and singing bawdy and ethereal songs. No glimmer of anticipation for what might occur tomorrow—what I stood to alter for them, for their world. Perhaps they knew I would die, too.

I lurked by a wall, forgotten by the crowd, waiting for Rhysand to beckon me to drink the wine and dance or do whatever it was he wished of me. I was clothed in my typical attire, tattooed from the neck down with that blue-black paint. Tonight my gossamer gown was a shade of sunset pink, the color too bright and feminine against the whorls of paint on my skin. Too cheery for what awaited me tomorrow.

Rhysand was taking longer than usual to summon me—though it was probably because of the supple-bodied faerie perched in his lap, caressing his hair with her long greenish fingers. He'd tire of her soon.

I didn't bother to look at Amarantha. I was better off pretending she wasn't there. Lucien never spoke to me in public, and Tamlin . . . It had become difficult to look at him in recent days.

I just wanted it done. I wanted that wine to carry me through this last night and bring me to my fate. I was so intent on anticipating Rhysand's order to serve him that I didn't notice that someone stood beside me until the heat from his body leaked onto mine.

I went rigid when I smelled that rain and earthen scent, and didn't dare to turn to Tamlin. We stood side by side, staring out at the crowd, as still and unnoticeable as statues.

His fingers brushed mine, and a line of fire went through me, burning me so badly that my eyes pricked with tears. I wished—wished he wasn't touching my marred hand, that his fingers didn't have to caress the contours of that wretched tattoo.

But I lived in that moment—my life became beautiful again for those few seconds when our hands grazed.

I kept my face set in a mask of cold. He dropped his hand, and, as quickly as he had come, he sauntered off, weaving through the crowd. It was only when he glanced over his shoulder and inclined his head ever so slightly that I understood.

My heart beat faster than it ever had during my trials, and I made myself look as bored as possible before I pushed off the wall and casually strolled after him. I took a different route, but headed toward the small door half hidden by a tapestry near which he lingered. I had only moments before Rhysand would begin looking for me, but a moment alone with Tamlin would be enough.

I could scarcely breathe as I moved nearer and nearer to the door, past Amarantha's dais, past a group of giggling faeries . . . Tamlin disappeared through the door as quick as lightning, and I slowed my steps to a meandering pace. These days no one really paid attention to me until I became Rhys's drugged plaything. All too quickly, the door was before me, and it swung open noiselessly to let me in.

Darkness encompassed me. I saw only a flash of green and gold before the warmth of Tamlin's body slammed into me and our lips met.

I couldn't kiss him deeply enough, couldn't hold him tightly enough, couldn't touch enough of him. Words weren't necessary.

I tore at his shirt, needing to feel the skin beneath one last time, and I had to stifle the moan that rose up in me as he grasped my breast. I didn't want him to be gentle—because what I felt for him wasn't at all like that. What I felt was wild and hard and burning, and so he was with me.

He tore his lips from mine and bit my neck—bit it as he had on Fire Night. I had to grind my teeth to keep myself from moaning and giving us away. This might be the last time I touched him, the last time we could be together. I wouldn't waste it.

My fingers grappled with his belt buckle, and his mouth found mine again. Our tongues danced—not a waltz or a minuet, but a war dance, a death dance of bone drums and screaming fiddles.

I wanted him—here.

I hooked a leg around his middle, needing to be closer, and he ground his hips harder against me, crushing me into the icy wall. I pried the belt buckle loose, whipping the leather free, and Tamlin growled his desire in my ear—a low, probing sort of sound that made me see red and white and lightning. We both knew what tomorrow would bring.

I tossed away his belt and started fumbling for his pants. Someone coughed.

"Shameful," Rhysand purred, and we whirled to find him faintly illuminated by the light that broke in through the doorway. But he stood behind us—farther into the passage, rather than toward the door. He hadn't come in through the throne room. With that ability of his, he had probably walked through the walls. "Just shameful." He stalked toward us. Tamlin remained holding me. "Look at what you've done to my pet."

Panting, neither of us said anything. But the air became a cold kiss upon my skin—upon my exposed breasts.

"Amarantha would be greatly aggrieved if she knew her little warrior was dallying with the human help," Rhysand went on, crossing his arms.

"I wonder how she'd punish you. Or perhaps she'd stay true to habit and punish Lucien. He still has one eye to lose, after all. Maybe she'll put it in a ring, too."

Ever so slowly, Tamlin removed my hands from his body and stepped out of my embrace.

"I'm glad to see you're being reasonable," Rhysand said, and Tamlin bristled. "Now, be a clever High Lord and buckle your belt and fix your clothes before you go out there."

Tamlin looked at me, and, to my horror, did as Rhysand instructed. My High Lord never took his eyes off my face as he straightened his tunic and hair, then retrieved and fastened his belt again. The paint on his hands and clothes—paint from *me*—vanished.

"Enjoy the party," Rhysand crooned, pointing to the door.

Tamlin's green eyes flickered as they continued to stare into mine. He softly said, "I love you." Without another glance at Rhysand, he left.

I was temporarily blinded by the brightness that poured in when he opened the door and slipped out. He did not look back at me before the door snicked shut and darkness returned to the dim hall.

Rhysand chuckled. "If you're that desperate for release, you should have asked me."

"Pig," I snapped, covering my breasts with the folds of my gown.

With a few easy steps, he crossed the distance between us and pinned my arms to the wall. My bones groaned. I could have sworn shadow-talons dug into the stones beside my head. "Do you actually intend to put yourself at my mercy, or are you truly that stupid?" His voice was composed of sensuous, bone-breaking ire.

"I'm not your slave."

"You're a fool, Feyre. Do you have any idea what could have happened had Amarantha found you two in here? Tamlin might refuse to be her lover, but she keeps him at her side out of the hope that she'll break him—dominate him, as she loves to do with our kind." I kept silent.

"You're both fools," he murmured, his breathing uneven. "How did you not think that someone would notice you were gone? You should thank the Cauldron Lucien's delightful brothers weren't watching you."

"What do you care?" I barked, and his grip tightened enough on my wrists that I knew my bones would snap with a little more pressure.

"What do I care?" he breathed, wrath twisting his features. Wings—those membranous, glorious wings—flared from his back, crafted from the shadows behind him. "What do *I* care?"

But before he could go on, his head snapped to the door, then back to my face. The wings vanished as quickly as they had appeared, and then his lips were crushing into mine. His tongue pried my mouth open, forcing himself into me, into the space where I could still taste Tamlin. I pushed and thrashed, but he held firm, his tongue sweeping over the roof of my mouth, against my teeth, claiming my mouth, claiming me—

The door was flung wide, and Amarantha's curved figure filled its space. Tamlin—Tamlin was beside her, his eyes slightly wide, shoulders tight as Rhys's lips still crushed mine.

Amarantha laughed, and a mask of stone slammed down on Tamlin's face, void of feeling, void of anything vaguely like the Tamlin I'd been tangled up with moments before.

Rhys casually released me with a flick of his tongue over my bottom lip as a crowd of High Fae appeared behind Amarantha and chimed in with her laughter. Rhysand gave them a lazy, self-indulgent grin and bowed. But something sparked in the queen's eyes as she looked at Rhysand. Amarantha's whore, they'd called him.

"I knew it was a matter of time," she said, putting a hand on Tamlin's arm. The other she lifted—lifted so Jurian's eye might see as she said, "You humans are all the same, aren't you."

I kept my mouth shut, even as I could have died for shame, even as I ached to explain. Tamlin *had* to realize the truth.

But I wasn't given the luxury of learning whether Tamlin understood as Amarantha clicked her tongue and turned away, taking her entourage with her. "Typical human trash with their inconstant, dull hearts," she said to herself—nothing more than a satisfied cat.

Following them, Rhys grabbed my arm to drag me back into the throne room. It was only when the light hit me that I saw the smudges and smears on my paint—smudges along my breasts and stomach, and the paint that had mysteriously appeared on Rhysand's hands.

"I'm tired of you for tonight," Rhys said, giving me a light shove toward the main exit. "Go back to your cell." Behind him, Amarantha and her court smiled with glee, their grins widening when they beheld the marred paint. I looked for Tamlin, but he was stalking for his usual throne on the dais, keeping his back to me. As if he couldn't stand to look.

I don't know what time it was, but hours later, footsteps sounded inside my cell. I jolted into a sitting position, and Rhys stepped out of a shadow.

I could still feel the heat of his lips against mine, the smooth glide of his tongue inside my mouth, even though I'd washed my mouth out three times with the bucket of water in my cell.

His tunic was unbuttoned at the top, and he ran a hand through his blue-black hair before he wordlessly slumped against the wall across from me and slid to the floor.

"What do you want?" I demanded.

"A moment of peace and quiet," he snapped, rubbing his temples.

I paused. "From what?"

He massaged his pale skin, making the corners of his eyes go up and down, out and in. He sighed. "From this mess."

I sat up farther on my pallet of hay. I'd never seen him so candid.

"That damned bitch is running me ragged," he went on, and dropped his hands from his temples to lean his head against the wall. "You hate me. Imagine how you'd feel if I made you serve in my bedroom. I'm High Lord of the Night Court—not her harlot."

So the slurs were true. And I could imagine very easily how much I would hate him—what it would do to me—to be enslaved to someone like that. "Why are you telling me this?"

The swagger and nastiness were gone. "Because I'm tired and lonely, and you're the only person I can talk to without putting myself at risk." He let out a low laugh. "How absurd: a High Lord of Prythian and a—"

"You can leave if you're just going to insult me."

"But I'm so good at it." He flashed one of his grins. I glared at him, but he sighed. "One wrong move tomorrow, Feyre, and we're all doomed."

The thought struck a chord of such horror that I could hardly breathe.

"And if you fail," he went on, more to himself than to me, "then Amarantha will rule forever."

"If she captured Tamlin's power once, who's to say she can't do it again?" It was the question I hadn't yet dared voice.

"He won't be tricked again so easily," he said, staring up at the ceiling. "Her biggest weapon is that she keeps our powers contained. But she can't access them, not wholly—though she can control us through them. It's why I've never been able to shatter her mind—why she's not dead already. The moment you break Amarantha's curse, Tamlin's wrath will be so great that no force in the world will keep him from splattering her on the walls."

A chill went through me.

"Why do you think I'm doing this?" He waved a hand to me.

"Because you're a monster."

He laughed. "True, but I'm also a pragmatist. Working Tamlin into a senseless fury is the best weapon we have against her. Seeing you enter into a fool's bargain with Amarantha was one thing, but when Tamlin saw my tattoo on your arm . . . Oh, you should have been born with my abilities, if only to have felt the rage that seeped from him."

I didn't want to think much about his abilities. "Who's to say he won't splatter you as well?"

"Perhaps he'll try—but I have a feeling he'll kill Amarantha first. That's what it all boils down to, anyway: even your servitude to me can be blamed on her. So he'll kill her tomorrow, and I'll be free before he can start a fight with me that will reduce our once-sacred mountain to rubble." He picked at his nails. "And I have a few other cards to play."

I lifted my brows in silent question.

"Feyre, for Cauldron's sake. I drug you, but you don't wonder why I never touch you beyond your waist or arms?"

Until tonight—until that damned kiss. I gritted my teeth, but even as my anger rose, a picture cleared.

"It's the only claim I have to innocence," he said, "the only thing that will make Tamlin think twice before entering into a battle with me that would cause a catastrophic loss of innocent life. It's the only way I can convince him I was on your side. Believe me, I would have liked nothing more than to enjoy you—but there are bigger things at stake than taking a human woman to my bed."

I knew, but I still asked, "Like what?"

"Like my territory," he said, and his eyes held a far-off look that I hadn't yet seen. "Like my remaining people, enslaved to a tyrant queen who can end their lives with a single word. Surely Tamlin expressed similar sentiments to you." He hadn't—not entirely. He hadn't been able to, thanks to the curse.

"Why did Amarantha target you?" I dared ask. "Why make you her whore?"

"Beyond the obvious?" He gestured to his perfect face. When I didn't smile, he loosed a breath. "My father killed Tamlin's father—and his brothers."

I started. Tamlin had never said—never told me the Night Court was responsible for that.

"It's a long story, and I don't feel like getting into it, but let's just say that when she stole our lands out from under us, Amarantha decided that she especially wanted to punish the son of her friend's murderer—decided that she hated me enough for my father's deeds that I was to suffer."

I might have reached a hand toward him, might have offered my apologies—but every thought had dried up in my head. What Amarantha had done to him . . .

"So," he said wearily, "here we are, with the fate of our immortal world in the hands of an illiterate human." His laugh was unpleasant as he hung his head, cupping his forehead in a hand, and closed his eyes. "What a mess."

Part of me searched for the words to wound him in his vulnerability, but the other half recalled all that he had said, all that he had done, how his head had snapped to the door before he'd kissed me. He'd known Amarantha was coming. Maybe he'd done it to make her jealous, but maybe . . .

If he hadn't been kissing me, if he hadn't shown up and interrupted us, I would have gone out into that throne room covered in smudged paint. And everyone—especially Amarantha—would have known what I'd been up to. It wouldn't have taken much to figure out whom I'd been with, especially not once they saw the paint on Tamlin. I didn't want to consider what the punishment might have been.

Regardless of his motives or his methods, Rhysand was keeping me alive. And had done so even before I set foot Under the Mountain.

"I've told you too much," he said as he got to his feet. "Perhaps I should have drugged you first. If you were clever, you'd find a way to use this against me. And if you had any stomach for cruelty, you'd go to Amarantha and tell her the truth about her whore. Perhaps she'd give you Tamlin for it." He slid his hands into the pockets of his black pants, but even as he faded into shadow, there was something in the curve of his shoulders that made me speak.

"When you healed my arm . . . You didn't need to bargain with me. You could have demanded every single week of the year." My brows knit together as he turned, already half-consumed by the dark. "Every single week, and I would have said yes." It wasn't entirely a question, but I needed the answer.

A half smile appeared on his sensuous lips. "I know," he said, and vanished.

CHAPTER 43

For my final task, I was given my old tunic and pants—stained and torn and reeking—but despite my stench, I kept my chin high as I was escorted to the throne room.

The doors were flung open, and the silence of the room assaulted me. I waited for the jeers and shouts, waited to see gold flash as the onlookers placed their bets, but this time the faeries just stared at me, the masked ones especially intently.

Their world rested on my shoulders, Rhys had said. But I didn't think it was worry alone that was spread across their features. I had to swallow hard as a few of them touched their fingers to their lips, then extended their hands to me—a gesture for the fallen, a farewell to the honored dead. There was nothing malicious about it. Most of these faeries belonged to the courts of the High Lords—had belonged to those courts long before Amarantha seized their lands, their lives. And if Tamlin and Rhysand were playing games to keep us alive . . .

I strode up the path they'd cleared—straight for Amarantha. The queen smiled when I stopped in front of her throne. Tamlin was in his usual place beside her, but I wouldn't look at him—not yet.

"Two trials lie behind you," Amarantha said, picking at a fleck of dust on her blood-red gown. Her hair shone, a gleaming crimson river that threatened to swallow her golden crown. "And only one more awaits. I wonder if it will be worse to fail now—when you are so close." She gave me a pout, and we both awaited the laughter of the faeries.

But only a few laughs hissed from the red-skinned guards. Everyone else remained silent. Even Lucien's miserable brothers. Even Rhysand, wherever he was in the crowd.

I blinked to clear my burning eyes. Perhaps, like Rhysand's, their oaths of allegiance and betting on my life and nastiness had been a show. And perhaps now—now that the end was imminent—they, too, would face my potential death with whatever dignity they had left.

Amarantha glared at them, but when her gaze fell upon me, she smiled broadly, sweetly. "Any words to say before you die?"

I came up with a plethora of curses, but I instead looked at Tamlin. He didn't react—his features were like stone. I wished that I could glimpse his face—if only for a moment. But all I needed to see were those green eyes.

"I love you," I said. "No matter what she says about it, no matter if it's only with my insignificant human heart. Even when they burn my body, I'll love you." My lips trembled, and my vision clouded before several warm tears slipped down my chilled face. I didn't wipe them away.

He didn't react—he didn't even grip the arms of his throne. I supposed that was his way of enduring it, even if it made my chest cave in. Even if his silence killed me.

Amarantha said sweetly, "You'll be lucky, my darling, if we even have enough left of you to burn."

I stared at her long and hard. But her words were not met with jeers or smiles or applause from the crowd. Only silence.

It was a gift that gave me courage, that made me bunch my fists, that made me embrace the tattoo on my arm. I had beaten her until now, fairly or not, and I would not feel alone when I died. I would not die alone. It was all I could ask for.

Amarantha propped her chin on a hand. "You never figured out my riddle, did you?" I didn't respond, and she smiled. "Pity. The answer is so lovely."

"Get it over with," I growled.

Amarantha looked at Tamlin. "No final words to her?" she said, quirking an eyebrow. When he didn't respond, she grinned at me. "Very well, then." She clapped her hands twice.

A door swung open, and three figures—two male and one female—with brown sacks tied over their heads were dragged in by the guards. Their concealed faces turned this way and that as they tried to discern the whispers that rippled across the throne room. My knees bent slightly as they approached.

With sharp jabs and blunt shoves, the red-skinned guards forced the three faeries to their knees at the foot of the dais, but facing me. Their bodies and clothes revealed nothing of who they were.

Amarantha clapped her hands again, and three servants clad in black appeared at the side of each of the kneeling faeries. In their long, pale hands, they each carried a dark velvet pillow. And on each pillow lay a single polished wooden dagger. Not metal for a blade, but ash. Ash, because—

"Your final task, Feyre," Amarantha drawled, gesturing to the kneeling faeries. "Stab each of these unfortunate souls in the heart."

I stared at her, my mouth opening and closing.

"They're innocent—not that it should matter to you," she went on, "since it wasn't a concern the day you killed Tamlin's poor sentinel. And it wasn't a concern for dear Jurian when he butchered my sister. But if it's a problem . . . well, you can always refuse. Of course, I'll take your life in exchange, but a bargain's a bargain, is it not? If you ask me, though, given your history with murdering our kind, I do believe I'm offering you a gift."

Refuse and die. Kill three innocents and live. Three innocents, for my own future. For my own happiness. For Tamlin and his court and the freedom of an entire land.

The wood of the razor-sharp daggers had been polished so expertly that it gleamed beneath the colored glass chandeliers.

"Well?" she asked. She lifted her hand, letting Jurian's eye get a good look at me, at the ash daggers, and purred to it, "I wouldn't want you to miss this, old friend."

I couldn't. I couldn't do it. It wasn't like hunting; it wasn't for survival or defense. It was cold-blooded murder—the murder of them, of my very soul. But for Prythian—for Tamlin, for all of them here, for Alis and her boys . . . I wished I knew the name of one of our forgotten gods so that I might beg them to intercede, wished I knew any prayers at all to plead for guidance, for absolution.

But I did not know those prayers, or the names of our forgotten gods—only the names of those who would remain enslaved if I did not act. I silently recited those names, even as the horror of what knelt before me began to swallow me whole. For Prythian, for Tamlin, for their world and my own . . . These deaths would not be wasted—even if it would damn me forever.

I stepped up to the first kneeling figure—the longest and most brutal step I'd ever taken. Three lives in exchange for Prythian's liberation—three lives that would not be spent in vain. I could do this. I could do this, even with Tamlin watching. I could make this sacrifice—sacrifice them . . . I could do this.

My fingers trembled, but the first dagger wound up in my hand, its hilt cool and smooth, the wood of the blade heavier than I'd expected. There were three daggers, because she wanted me to feel the agony of reaching for that knife again and again. Wanted me to *mean* it.

"Not so fast." Amarantha chuckled, and the guards who held the first kneeling figure snatched the hood off its face.

It was a handsome High Fae youth. I didn't know him, I'd never seen him, but his blue eyes were pleading. "That's better," Amarantha said, waving her hand again. "Proceed, Feyre, dear. Enjoy it."

His eyes were the color of a sky I'd never see again if I refused to kill him, a color I'd never get out of my mind, never forget no matter how many times I painted it. He shook his head, those eyes growing so large that white showed all around. He would never see that sky, either. And neither would these people, if I failed.

"Please," he whispered, his focus darting between the ash dagger and my face. "Please."

The dagger shook between my fingers, and I clenched it tighter. Three faeries—that's all that stood between me and freedom, before Tamlin would be unleashed upon Amarantha. If he could destroy her . . . *Not in vain*, I told myself. *Not in vain.*

"Don't," the faerie youth begged when I lifted the dagger. *"Don't!"*

I took a gasping breath, my lips shaking as I quailed. Saying "I'm sorry" wasn't enough. I'd never been able to say it to Andras—and now . . . now . . .

"*Please!*" he said, and his eyes lined with silver.

Someone in the crowd began weeping. I was taking him away from someone who possibly loved him as much as I loved Tamlin.

I couldn't think about it, couldn't think about who he was, or the color of his eyes, or any of it. Amarantha was grinning with wild, triumphant glee. Kill a faerie, fall in love with a faerie, then be forced to kill a faerie to keep that love. It was brilliant and cruel, and she knew it.

Darkness rippled near the throne, and then Rhysand was there, arms crossed—as if he'd moved to better see. His face was a mask of disinterest, but my hand tingled. *Do it*, the tingling said.

"*Don't*," the young faerie moaned. I began shaking my head. I couldn't listen to him. I had to do it now, before he convinced me otherwise. *"Please!"* His voice rose to a shriek.

The sound jarred me so much that I lunged.

With a ragged sob, I plunged the dagger into his heart.

He screamed, thrashing in the guards' grip as the blade cleaved through flesh and bone, smooth as if it were real metal and not ash, and blood—hot and slick—showered my hand. I wept, yanking out the dagger, the reverberations of his bones against the blade stinging my hand.

His eyes, full of shock and hate, remained on me as he sagged, damning me, and that person in the crowd let out a keening wail.

My bloody dagger clacked on the marble floor as I stumbled back several steps.

"Very good," Amarantha said.

I wanted to get out of my body; I had to escape the stain of what I'd done; I had to get out—I couldn't endure the blood on my hands, the sticky warmth between my fingers.

"Now the next. Oh, don't look so miserable, Feyre. Aren't you having fun?"

I faced the second figure, still hooded. A female this time. The faerie in black extended the pillow with the clean dagger, and the guards holding her tore off her hood.

Her face was simple, and her hair was gold-brown, like mine. Tears were already rolling down her round cheeks, and her bronze eyes tracked my bloody hand as I reached for the second knife. The cleanness of the wooden blade mocked the blood on my fingers.

I wanted to fall to my knees to beg her forgiveness, to tell her that her death wouldn't be for naught. Wanted to, but there was such a rift running through me now that I could hardly feel my hands, my shredded heart. What I'd done—

"Cauldron save me," she began whispering, her voice lovely and even—like music. "Mother hold me," she went on, reciting a prayer similar to one I'd heard once before, when Tamlin eased the passing of that lesser faerie who'd died in the foyer. Another of Amarantha's victims. "Guide me to you." I was unable to raise my dagger, unable to take the step that would close the distance between us. "Let me pass through the gates; let me smell that immortal land of milk and honey."

Silent tears slid down my face and neck, where they dampened the filthy collar of my tunic. As she spoke, I knew I would be forever barred from that immortal land. I knew that whatever Mother she meant would never embrace me. In saving Tamlin, I was to damn myself.

I couldn't do this—couldn't lift that dagger again.

"Let me fear no evil," she breathed, staring at me—into me, into the soul that was cleaving itself apart. "Let me feel no pain."

A sob broke from my lips. "I'm sorry," I moaned.

"Let me enter eternity," she breathed.

I wept as I understood. *Kill me now*, she was saying. *Do it fast. Don't make it hurt. Kill me now.* Her bronze eyes were steady, if not sorrowful. Infinitely, infinitely worse than the pleading of the dead faerie beside her.

I couldn't do it.

But she held my gaze—held my gaze and nodded.

As I lifted the ash dagger, something inside me fractured so completely that there would be no hope of ever repairing it. No matter how many years passed, no matter how many times I might try to paint her face.

More faeries wailed now—her kinsmen and friends. The dagger was a weight in my hand—my hand, shining and coated with the blood of that first faerie.

It would be more honorable to refuse—to die, rather than murder innocents. But . . . but . . .

"Let me enter eternity," she repeated, lifting her chin. "Fear no evil," she whispered—just for me. "Feel no pain."

I gripped her delicate, bony shoulder and drove the dagger into her heart.

She gasped, and blood spilled onto the ground like a splattering of rain. Her eyes were closed when I looked at her face again. She slumped to the floor and didn't move.

I went somewhere far, far away from myself.

The faeries were stirring now—shifting, many whispering and weeping. I dropped the dagger, and the knock of ash on marble roared in my ears. Why was Amarantha still smiling, with only one person left between myself and freedom? I glanced at Rhysand, but his attention was fixed upon Amarantha.

One faerie—and then we were free. Just one more swing of my arm.

And maybe one more after that—maybe one more swing, up and inward and into my own heart.

It would be a relief—a relief to end it by my own hand, a relief to die rather than face this, what I'd done.

The faerie servant offered the last dagger, and I was about to reach for it when the guard removed the hood from the male kneeling before me.

My hands slackened at my sides. Amber-flecked green eyes stared up at me.

Everything came crashing down, layer upon layer, shattering and breaking and crumbling, as I gazed at Tamlin.

I whipped my head to the throne beside Amarantha's, still occupied by my High Lord, and she laughed as she snapped her fingers. The Tamlin beside her transformed into the Attor, smiling wickedly at me.

Tricked—deceived by my own senses again. Slowly, my soul ripping further from me, I turned back to Tamlin. There was only guilt and sorrow in his eyes, and I stumbled away, almost falling as I tripped over my feet.

"Something wrong?" Amarantha asked, cocking her head.

"Not . . . Not fair," I got out.

Rhysand's face had gone pale—so, so pale.

"Fair?" Amarantha mused, playing with Jurian's bone on her necklace. "I wasn't aware you humans knew of the concept. You kill Tamlin, and he's free." Her smile was the most hideous thing I'd ever seen. "And then you can have him all to yourself."

My mouth stopped working.

"Unless," Amarantha went on, "you think it would be more appropriate to forfeit your life. After all: What's the point? To survive only to lose him?" Her words were like poison. "Imagine all those years you were going to spend together . . . suddenly alone. Tragic, really. Though a few months ago, you hated our kind enough to butcher us—surely you'll move on easily enough." She patted her ring. "Jurian's human lover did."

Still on his knees, Tamlin's eyes turned so bright—defiant.

"So," Amarantha said, but I didn't look at her. "What will it be, Feyre?"

Kill him and save his court and my life, or kill myself and let them all live as Amarantha's slaves, let her and the King of Hybern wage their final war against the human realm. There was no bargain to get out of this—no part of me to sell to avoid this choice.

I stared at the ash dagger on that pillow. Alis had been right all those weeks ago: no human who came here ever walked out again. I was no exception. If I were smart, I would indeed stab my own heart before they could grab me. At least then I would die quickly—I wouldn't endure the torture that surely awaited me, possibly a fate like Jurian's. Alis had been right. But—

Alis—Alis had said something . . . something to *help* me. A final part of the curse, a part they couldn't tell me, a part that would aid me . . . And all she'd been able to do was tell me to *listen*. To *listen* to what I'd heard—as if I'd already learned everything I needed.

I slowly faced Tamlin again. Memories flashed, one after another, blurs of color and words. Tamlin was High Lord of the Spring Court—what did that do to help me? The Great Rite was performed—no.

He lied to me about everything—about why I'd been brought to the manor, about what was happening on his lands. The curse—he hadn't been allowed to tell me the truth, but he hadn't exactly pretended that everything was fine. No—he'd lied and explained as best he could and made it painfully obvious to me at every turn that something was very, very wrong.

The Attor in the garden—as hidden from me as I was from it. But Tamlin had hidden me—he'd told me to stay put and then *led* the Attor right toward me, *let* me overhear them.

He'd left the dining room doors open when he'd spoken with Lucien about—about the curse, even if I hadn't realized it at the time. He'd spoken in public places. He'd *wanted* me to eavesdrop.

Because he wanted me to know, to *listen*—because this knowledge . . . I ransacked each conversation, turning over words like stones. A part of the curse I hadn't grasped, that they couldn't explicitly tell me, but Tamlin had needed me to know . . .

Milady makes no bargains that are not advantageous to her.

She would never kill what she desired most—not when she wanted Tamlin as much as I did. But if I killed him . . . she either knew I couldn't do it, or she was playing a very, very dangerous game.

Conversation after conversation echoed in my memory, until I heard Lucien's words, and everything froze. And that was when I knew.

I couldn't breathe, not as I replayed the memory, not as I recalled the conversation I'd overheard one day. Lucien and Tamlin in the dining room, the door wide open for all to hear—for *me* to hear.

"For someone with a heart of stone, yours is certainly soft these days."

I looked at Tamlin, my eyes flicking to his chest as another memory flashed. The Attor in the garden, laughing.

"Though you have a heart of stone, Tamlin," the Attor said, "you certainly keep a host of fear inside it."

Amarantha would never risk me killing him—because she knew I *couldn't* kill him.

Not if his heart couldn't be pierced by a blade. Not if his heart had been turned to stone.

I scanned his face, searching for any glimmer of truth. There was only that bold rebellion within his gaze.

Perhaps I was wrong—perhaps it was just a faerie turn of phrase. But all those times I'd held Tamlin . . . I'd never felt his heartbeat. I'd been blind to everything until it came back to smack me in the face, but not this time.

That was how she controlled him and his magic. How she controlled all the High Lords, dominating and leashing them just as she kept Jurian's soul tethered to that eye and bone.

Trust no one, Alis had told me. But I trusted Tamlin—and more than that, I trusted myself. I trusted that I had heard correctly—I trusted that Tamlin had been smarter than Amarantha, I trusted that all I had sacrificed was not in vain.

The entire room was silent, but my attention was upon only Tamlin. The revelation must have been clear on my face, for his breathing became a bit quicker, and he lifted his chin.

I took a step toward him, then another. I was right. I had to be.

I sucked in a breath as I grabbed the dagger off the outstretched pillow. I could be wrong—I could be painfully, tragically wrong.

But there was a faint smile on Tamlin's lips as I stood over him, ash dagger in hand.

There was such a thing as Fate—because Fate had made sure I was there to eavesdrop when they'd spoken in private, because Fate had whispered to Tamlin that the cold, contrary girl he'd dragged to his home would be the one to break his spell, because Fate had kept me alive just to get to this point, just to see if I had been listening.

And there he was—my High Lord, my beloved, kneeling before me.

"I love you," I said, and stabbed him.

CHAPTER 44

Tamlin cried out as my blade pierced his flesh, breaking bone. For a sickening moment, when his blood rushed onto my hand, I thought the ash dagger would go clean through him.

But then there was a faint thud—and a stinging reverberation in my hand as the dagger struck something hard and unyielding. Tamlin lurched forward, his face going pale, and I yanked the dagger from his chest. As the blood drained away from the polished wood, I lifted the blade.

Its tip had been nicked, turned inward on itself.

Tamlin clutched his chest as he panted, the wound already healing. Rhysand, at the foot of the dais, grinned from ear to ear. Amarantha climbed to her feet.

The faeries murmured to one another. I dropped the blade, sending it clattering across the red marble.

Kill her now, I wanted to bark at Tamlin, but he didn't move as he pushed his hand against his wound, blood dribbling out. Too slowly—he was healing too slowly. The mask didn't fall off. *Kill her now.*

"She won," someone in the crowd said. "Free them," another echoed.

But Amarantha's face blanched, her features contorting until she looked truly serpentine. "I'll free them whenever I see fit. Feyre didn't specify *when* I had to free them—just that I had to. At some point. Perhaps when you're dead," she finished with a hateful smile. "You assumed that when I said instantaneous freedom regarding the riddle, it applied to the trials, too, didn't you? Foolish, stupid human."

I stepped back as she descended the steps of the dais. Her fingers curled into claws—Jurian's eye was going wild within the ring, his pupil dilating and shrinking. "And you," she hissed at me. "*You.*" Her teeth gleamed—turning sharp. "*I'm going to kill you.*"

Someone cried out, but I couldn't move, couldn't even try to get out of the way as something far more violent than lightning struck me, and I crashed to the floor.

"*I'm going to make you pay for your insolence,*" Amarantha snarled, and a scream ravaged my throat as pain like nothing I had known erupted through me.

My very bones were shattering as my body rose and then slammed onto the hard floor, and I was crushed beneath another wave of torturous agony.

"Admit you don't really love him, and I'll spare you," Amarantha breathed, and through my fractured vision, I saw her prowl toward me. "Admit what a cowardly, lying, inconstant bit of human garbage you are."

I wouldn't—I wouldn't say that even if she splattered me across the ground.

But I was being ripped apart from the inside out, and I thrashed, unable to out-scream the pain.

"*Feyre!*" someone roared. No, not someone—Rhysand.

But Amarantha still neared. "You think you're worthy of him? A *High Lord*? You think you deserve anything at all, human?" My back arched, and my ribs cracked, one by one.

Rhysand yelled my name again—yelled it as though he cared. I blacked out, but she brought me back, ensuring that I felt everything, ensuring that I screamed every time a bone broke.

"What are you but mud and bones and worm meat?" Amarantha raged. "What are you, compared to our kind, that you think you're worthy of us?"

Faeries began calling foul play, demanding Tamlin be released from the curse, calling her a cheating liar. Through the haze, I saw Rhysand crouching by Tamlin. Not to help him, but to grab the—

"You are all pigs—all scheming, filthy *pigs*."

I sobbed between screams as her foot connected with my broken ribs. Again. And again. "Your mortal heart is *nothing* to us."

Then Rhysand was on his feet, my bloody knife in his hands. He launched himself at Amarantha, swift as a shadow, the ash dagger aimed at her throat.

She lifted a hand—not even bothering to look—and he was blasted back by a wall of white light.

But the pain paused for a second, long enough for me to see him hit the ground and rise again and lunge for her—with hands that now ended in talons. He slammed into the invisible wall Amarantha had raised around herself, and my pain flickered as she turned to him.

"You traitorous piece of filth," she seethed at Rhysand. "You're just as bad as these human beasts." One by one, as if a hand were shoving them in, his talons pushed back into his skin, leaving blood in their wake. He swore, low and vicious. "You were planning this all along."

Her magic sent him sprawling, and it then hurled into Rhysand again—so hard that his head cracked against the stones and the knife dropped from his splayed fingers. No one made a move to help him, and she struck him once more with her power. The red marble splintered where he hit it, spiderwebbing toward me. With wave after wave she hit him. Rhys groaned.

"Stop," I breathed, blood filling my mouth as I strained a hand to reach her feet. "Please."

Rhys's arms buckled as he fought to rise, and blood dripped from his nose, splattering on the marble. His eyes met mine.

The bond between us went taut. I flashed between my body and his, seeing myself through his eyes, bleeding and broken and sobbing.

I snapped back into my own mind as Amarantha turned to me again. "Stop? *Stop?* Don't pretend you care, human," she crooned, and curled her finger. I arched my back, my spine straining to the point of cracking, and Rhysand bellowed my name as I lost my grip on the room.

Then the memories began—a compilation of the worst moments of my life, a storybook of despair and darkness. The final page came, and I wept, not entirely feeling the agony of my body as I saw that young rabbit, bleeding out in that forest clearing, my knife through her throat. My first kill—the first life I'd taken.

I'd been starving, desperate. Yet afterward, once my family had devoured it, I had crept back into the woods and wept for hours, knowing a line had been crossed, my soul stained.

"*Say that you don't love him!*" Amarantha shrieked, and the blood on my hands became the blood of that rabbit—became the blood of what I had lost.

But I wouldn't say it. Because loving Tamlin was the only thing I had left, the only thing I couldn't sacrifice.

A path cleared through my red-and-black vision. I found Tamlin's eyes—wide as he crawled toward Amarantha, watching me die, and unable to save me while his wound slowly healed, while she still gripped his power.

Amarantha had never intended for me to live, never intended to let him go.

"Amarantha, stop this," Tamlin begged at her feet as he clutched the gaping wound in his chest. "*Stop*. I'm sorry—I'm sorry for what I said about Clythia all those years ago. Please."

Amarantha ignored him, but I couldn't look away. Tamlin's eyes were so green—green like the meadows of his estate. A shade that washed away the memories flooding through me, that pushed aside the evil breaking me apart bone by bone. I screamed again as my kneecaps strained, threatening to crack in two, but I saw that enchanted forest, saw that afternoon we'd lain in the grass, saw that morning we'd watched the sunrise, when for a moment—just one moment—I'd known true happiness.

"*Say that you don't truly love him*," Amarantha spat, and my body twisted, breaking bit by bit. "*Admit to your inconstant heart.*"

"Amarantha, *please*," Tamlin moaned, his blood spilling onto the floor. "I'll do anything."

"I'll deal with you later," she snarled at him, and sent me falling into a fiery pit of pain.

I would never say it—never let her hear that, even if she killed me. And if it was to be my downfall, so be it. If it would be the weakness that would break me, I would embrace it with all my heart. If this was—

For though each of my strikes lands a powerful blow,
When I kill, I do it slow . . .

That's what these three months had been—a slow, horrible death. What I felt for Tamlin was the cause of this. There was no cure—not pain, or absence, or happiness.

But scorned, I become a difficult beast to defeat.

She could torture me all she liked, but it would never destroy what I felt for him. It would never make Tamlin want her—never ease the sting of his rejection.

The world became dark at the borders of my vision, taking the edge off the pain.

But I bless all those who are brave enough to dare.

For so long, I had run from it. But opening myself to him, to my sisters—that had been a test of bravery as harrowing as any of my trials.

"*Say it, you vile beast*," Amarantha hissed. She might have lied her way out of our bargain, but she'd sworn differently with the riddle—instantaneous freedom, regardless of her will.

Blood filled my mouth, warm as it dribbled out between my lips. I gazed at Tamlin's masked face one last time.

"*Love*," I breathed, the world crumbling into a blackness with no end. A pause in Amarantha's magic. "The answer to the riddle . . . ," I got out, choking on my own blood, "is . . . love."

Tamlin's eyes went wide before something forever cracked in my spine.

CHAPTER 45

I was far away but still seeing—seeing through eyes that weren't mine, eyes attached to a person who slowly rose from his position on a cracked, bloodied floor.

Amarantha's face slackened. There my body was, prostrate on the ground, my head snapped to one side at a horribly wrong angle. A flash of red hair in the crowd. Lucien.

Tears shone in Lucien's remaining eye as he raised his hands and removed the fox mask.

The brutally scarred face beneath was still handsome—his features sharp and elegant. But my host was looking at Tamlin now, who slowly faced my dead body.

Tamlin's still-masked face twisted into something truly lupine as he raised his eyes to the queen and snarled. Fangs lengthened.

Amarantha backed away—away from my corpse. She only whispered "Please" before golden light exploded.

The queen was blasted back, thrown against the far wall, and Tamlin let out a roar that shook the mountain as he launched himself at her. He shifted into his beast form faster than I could see—fur and claws and pound upon pound of lethal muscle.

She had no sooner hit the wall than he gripped her by the neck, and the stones cracked as he shoved her against it with a clawed paw.

She thrashed but could do nothing against the brutal onslaught of Tamlin's beast. Blood ran down his furred arm from where she scratched.

The Attor and the guards rushed for the queen, but several faeries and High Fae, their masks clattering to the ground, jumped into their path, tackling them. Amarantha screeched, kicking at Tamlin, lashing at him with her dark magic, but a wall of gold encompassed his fur like a second skin. She couldn't touch him.

"Tam!" Lucien cried over the chaos.

A sword hurtled through the air, a shooting star of steel.

Tamlin caught it in a massive paw. Amarantha's scream was cut short as he drove the sword through her head and into the stone beneath.

And then closed his powerful jaws around her throat—and ripped it out.

Silence fell.

It wasn't until I was again staring down at my own broken body that I realized whose eyes I'd been seeing through. But Rhysand didn't come any closer to my corpse, not as rushing paws—then a flash of light, then footsteps—filled the air. The beast was already gone.

Amarantha's blood had vanished from his face, his tunic, as Tamlin slammed to his knees.

He scooped up my limp, broken body, cradling me to his chest. He hadn't removed his mask, but I saw the tears that fell onto my filthy tunic, and I heard the shuddering sobs that broke from him as he rocked me, stroking my hair.

"No," someone breathed—Lucien, his sword dangling from his hand. Indeed, there were many High Fae and faeries who watched with damp eyes as Tamlin held me.

I wanted to get to Tamlin. I wanted to touch him, to beg for his forgiveness for what I'd done, for the other bodies on the floor, but I was so far away.

Someone appeared beside Lucien—a tall, handsome brown-haired man with a face similar to his own. Lucien didn't look at his father, though he stiffened as the High Lord of the Autumn Court approached Tamlin and extended a clenched hand to him.

Tamlin glanced up only when the High Lord opened his fingers and tipped over his hand. A glittering spark fell upon me. It flared and vanished as it touched my chest.

Two more figures approached—both handsome and young. Through my host's eyes, I knew them instantly. The brown-skinned one on the left wore a tunic of blue and green, and atop his white-blond head was a garland of roses—the High Lord of the Summer Court. His pale-skinned companion, clad in colors of white and gray, possessed a crown of shimmering ice. The High Lord of the Winter Court.

Chins raised, shoulders back, they, too, dropped those glittering kernels upon me, and Tamlin bowed his head in gratitude.

Another High Lord approached, also bestowing upon me a drop of light. He glowed brightest of them all, and from his gold-and-ruby raiment, I knew him to be High Lord of the Dawn Court. Then the High Lord of the Day Court, clad in white and gold, his dark skin gleaming with an inner light, presented his similar gift, and smiled sadly at Tamlin before he walked away.

Rhysand stepped forward, bringing my shred of soul with him, and I found Tamlin staring at me—at us. "For what she gave," Rhysand said, extending a hand, "we'll bestow what our predecessors have granted to few before." He paused. "This makes us even," he added, and I felt the twinkle of his humor as he opened his hand and let the seed of light fall on me.

Tamlin tenderly brushed aside my matted hair. His hand glowed bright as the rising sun, and in the center of his palm, that strange, shining bud formed.

"I love you," he whispered, and kissed me as he laid his hand on my heart.

CHAPTER 46

Everything was black, and warm—and thick. Inky, but bordered with gold. I was swimming, kicking for the surface, where Tamlin was waiting, where *life* was waiting. Up and up, frantic for air. The golden light grew, and the darkness became like sparkling wine, easier to swim through, the bubbles fizzing around me, and—

I gasped, air flooding my throat.

I was lying on the cold floor. No pain—no blood, no broken bones. I blinked. A chandelier dangled above me—I'd never noticed how intricate the crystals were, how the hushed gasp of the crowd echoed off them. A crowd—meaning I was still in that throne room, meaning I . . . I truly wasn't dead. Meaning I had . . . I had killed those . . . I had . . . The room spun.

I groaned as I braced my hands against the floor, readying myself to stand, but—the sight of my skin stopped me cold. It gleamed with a strange light, and my fingers seemed *longer* where I'd laid them flat on the marble. I pushed to my feet. I felt—felt *strong*, and fast and sleek. And—

And I'd become High Fae.

I went rigid as I sensed Tamlin standing behind me, smelled that rain and spring meadow scent of him, richer than I'd ever noticed. I couldn't turn around to look at him—I couldn't . . . couldn't move. A High Fae—immortal. What had they done?

I could hear Tamlin holding his breath—hear as he loosed it. Hear the breathing, the whispering and weeping and quiet celebrating of everyone in that hall, still watching us—watching *me*—some chanting praise for the glorious power of their High Lords.

"It was the only way we could save you," Tamlin said softly. But then I looked to the wall, and my hand rose to my throat. I forgot about the stunned crowd entirely.

There, beneath Clare's decayed body, was Amarantha, her mouth gaping as the sword protruded from her brow. Her throat gone—and blood now soaked the front of her gown.

Amarantha was dead. They were free. I was free. Tamlin was—

Amarantha was dead. And I had killed those two High Fae; I had—

I shook my head slowly. "Are you—" My voice sounded too loud in my ears as I pushed back against that wall of black that threatened to swallow me. Amarantha was dead.

"See for yourself," he said. I kept my eyes on the ground as I turned. There, on the red marble, lay a golden mask, staring at me with its hollow eyeholes.

"Feyre," Tamlin said, and he cupped my chin between his fingers, gently lifting my face. I saw that familiar chin first, then the mouth, and then—

He was exactly how I dreamed he would be.

He smiled at me, his entire face alight with that quiet joy I had come to love so dearly, and he brushed my hair aside. I savored the feel of his fingers on my skin and raised my own to touch his face, to trace the contours of those high cheekbones and that lovely, straight nose—the clear, broad brow, the slightly arching eyebrows that framed his green eyes.

What I had done to get to this moment, to be standing here . . . I shoved against the thought again. In a minute, in an hour, in a day, I would think about that, force myself to face it.

I put a hand on Tamlin's heart, and a steady beat echoed into my bones.

I sat on the edge of a bed, and while I'd thought being an immortal meant a higher pain threshold and faster healing, I winced a good deal as Tamlin inspected my few remaining wounds, then healed them. We'd scarcely had a moment alone together in the hours that followed Amarantha's death—that followed what I had done to those two faeries.

But now, in this quiet room . . . I couldn't look away from the truth that sounded in my head with each breath.

I'd killed them. Slaughtered them. I hadn't even seen their bodies being taken away.

For it had been chaos in the throne room in the moments after I'd awakened. The Attor and the nastier faeries had disappeared instantly, along with Lucien's brothers, which was a clever move, as Lucien wasn't the only faerie with a score to settle. No sign of Rhysand, either. Some faeries had fled, while others had burst into celebration, and others just stood or paced—eyes distant, faces pale. As if they, too, didn't quite feel like this was real.

One by one, crowding him, weeping and laughing with joy, the High Fae and faeries of the Spring Court knelt or embraced or kissed Tamlin, thanking him—thanking *me*. I kept far enough back that I would only nod, because I had no words to offer them in exchange for their gratitude, the gratitude for the faeries I'd butchered to save them.

Then there had been meetings in the frenzied throne room—quick, tense meetings with the High Lords Tamlin was allied with to sort out next steps; then with Lucien and some Spring Court High Fae who introduced themselves as Tamlin's sentries. But every word, every breath was too loud, every smell too strong, the light too bright. Keeping still throughout it all was easier than moving, than adjusting to the strange, strong body that was now mine. I couldn't even touch my hair without the slight difference in my fingers jarring me.

On and on, until every newly heightened sense was chafing and raw, and Tamlin at last noticed my dull eyes, my silence, and took my arm. He escorted me through the labyrinth of tunnels and hallways until we found a quiet bedroom in a distant wing of the court.

"Feyre," Tamlin said now, looking up from inspecting my bare leg. I had been so accustomed to his mask that the handsome face surprised me each time I beheld it.

This—this was what I had murdered those faeries for. Their deaths had not been in vain, and yet . . . The blood on me had been gone when I'd awoken—as if becoming an immortal, as if surviving, somehow earned me the right to wash their blood off me.

"What is it?" I said. My voice was—quiet. Hollow. I should try—try to sound more cheerful, for him, for what had just happened, but . . .

He gave me that half smile. Had he been human, he might have been in his late twenties. But he wasn't human—and neither was I.

I wasn't certain whether that was a happy thought or not.

It was one of my smallest concerns. I should be begging for his forgiveness, begging the families and friends of those faeries for their forgiveness. I should be on my knees, weeping with shame for all that I had done—

"Feyre," he said again, lowering my leg to stand between my knees. He caressed my cheek with a knuckle. "How can I ever repay you for what you did?"

"You don't need to," I said. Let that be that—let that dark, dank cell fade away, and Amarantha's face forever disappear from my memory. Even if those two dead faeries—even if *their* faces would never fade for me. If I could ever bring myself to paint again, I would never be able to stop seeing those faces instead of the colors and light.

Tamlin held my face in his hands, leaning close, but then released me and grasped my left arm—my tattooed arm. His brows narrowed as he studied the markings. "Feyre—"

"I don't want to talk about it," I mumbled. The bargain I had with Rhysand—another small concern compared to the stain on my soul, the pit inside it. But I didn't doubt I'd see Rhys again soon.

Tamlin's fingers traced the marks of my tattoo. "We'll find a way out of this," he murmured, and his hand traveled up my arm to rest on my shoulder. He opened his mouth, and I knew what he would say—the subject he would try to broach.

I couldn't talk about it, about them—not yet. So I breathed "Later" and hooked my feet around his legs, drawing him closer. I placed my hands on his chest, feeling the heart beating beneath. This—I needed *this* right now. It wouldn't wash away what I'd done, but . . . I needed him near, needed to smell and taste him, remind myself that he was real—*this* was real.

"Later," he echoed, and leaned down to kiss me.

It was soft, tentative—nothing like the wild, hard kisses we'd shared in the hall of throne room. He brushed his lips against mine again. I didn't want apologies, didn't want sympathy or coddling. I gripped the front of his tunic, tugging him closer as I opened my mouth to him.

He let out a low growl, and the sound of it sent a wildfire blazing through me, pooling and burning in my core. I let it burn through that hole in my chest, my soul. Let it raze through the wave of black that was starting to press around me, let it consume the phantom blood I could still feel on my hands. I gave myself to that fire, to him, as his hands roved across me, unbuttoning as he went.

I pulled back, breaking the kiss to look into his face. His eyes were bright—hungry—but his hands had stopped their exploring and rested firmly on my hips. With a predator's stillness, he waited and watched as I traced the contours of his face, as I kissed every place I touched.

His ragged breathing was the only sound—and his hands soon began roaming across my back and sides, caressing and teasing and baring me to him. When my traveling fingers reached his mouth, he bit down on one, sucking it into his mouth. It didn't hurt, but the bite was hard enough for me to meet his eyes again. To realize that he was done waiting—and so was I.

He eased me onto the bed, murmuring my name against my neck, the shell of my ear, the tips of my fingers. I urged him—faster, harder. His mouth explored the curve of my breast, the inside of my thigh.

A kiss for each day we'd spent apart, a kiss for every wound and terror, a kiss for the ink etched into my flesh, and for all the days we would be together after this. Days, perhaps, that I no longer deserved. But I gave myself again to that fire, threw myself into it, into him, and let myself burn.

I was pulled from sleep by something tugging at my middle, a thread deep inside.

I left Tamlin sleeping in the bed, his body heavy with exhaustion. In a few hours, we would be leaving Under the Mountain and returning home, and I didn't want to wake him sooner than I had to. I prayed I would ever get to sleep that peacefully again.

I knew who summoned me long before I opened the door to the hall and padded down it, stumbling and teetering every now and then as I adjusted to my new body, its new balance and rhythms. I carefully, slowly took a narrow set of stairs upward, up and up, until, to my shock, a trickle of sunlight poured into the stairwell and I found myself on a small balcony jutting out of the side of the mountain.

I hissed against the brightness, shielding my eyes. I'd thought it was the middle of the night—I'd completely lost all sense of time in the darkness of the mountain.

Rhysand chuckled softly from where I could vaguely make him out standing along the stone rail. "I forgot that it's been a while for you."

My eyes stung from the light, and I remained silent until I could look at the view without a shooting pain going through my head. A land of violet snowcapped mountains greeted me, but the rock of this mountain was brown and bare—not even a blade of grass or a crystal of ice gleamed on it.

I looked at him finally. His membranous wings were out—tucked behind him—but his hands and feet were normal, no talons in sight. "What do you want?" It didn't come out with the snap I'd intended. Not as I remembered how he'd fought, again and again, to attack Amarantha, to save me.

"Just to say good-bye." A warm breeze ruffled his hair, brushing tendrils of darkness off his shoulders. "Before your beloved whisks you away forever."

"Not forever," I said, wiggling my tattooed fingers for him to see. "Don't you get a week every month?" Those words, thankfully, came out frosty.

Rhys smiled slightly, his wings rustling and then settling. "How could I forget?"

I stared at the nose I'd seen bleeding only hours before, the violet eyes that had been so filled with pain. "Why?" I asked.

He knew what I meant, and shrugged. "Because when the legends get written, I didn't want to be remembered for standing on the sidelines. I want my future offspring to know that *I* was there, and that I fought against her at the end, even if I couldn't do anything useful."

I blinked, this time not at the brightness of the sun.

"Because," he went on, his eyes locked with mine, "I didn't want you to fight alone. Or die alone."

And for a moment, I remembered that faerie who had died in our foyer, and how I'd told Tamlin the same thing. "Thank you," I said, my throat tight.

Rhys flashed a grin that didn't quite reach his eyes. "I doubt you'll be saying that when I take you to the Night Court."

I didn't bother to reply as I turned toward the view. The mountains went on and on, gleaming and shadowed and vast under the open, clear sky.

But nothing in me stirred—nothing cataloged the light and colors.

"Are you going to fly home?" I said.

A soft laugh. "Unfortunately, it would take longer than I can afford. Another day, I'll taste the skies again."

I glanced at the wings tucked into his powerful body, and my voice was hoarse as I spoke. "You never told me you loved the wings—or the flying." No, he'd made his shape-shifting seem . . . base, useless, boring.

He shrugged. "Everything I love has always had a tendency to be taken from me. I tell very few about the wings. Or the flying."

Some color had already come into that moon-white face—and I wondered whether he might once have been tan before Amarantha had kept him belowground for so long. A High Lord who loved to fly—trapped under a mountain. Shadows not of his own making still haunted those violet eyes. I wondered if they would ever fade.

"How does it feel to be a High Fae?" he asked—a quiet, curious question.

I looked out toward the mountains again, considering. And maybe it was because there was no one else to hear, maybe it was because the shadows in his eyes would also forever be in mine, but I said, "I'm an immortal—who has been mortal. This body . . ." I looked down at my hand, so clean and shining—a mockery of what I'd done. "This body is different, but this"—I put my hand on my chest, my heart—"this is still human. Maybe it always will be. But it would have been easier to live with it . . ." My throat welled. "Easier to live with what I did if my heart had changed, too. Maybe I wouldn't care so much; maybe I could convince myself their deaths weren't in vain. Maybe immortality will take that away. I can't tell whether I want it to."

Rhysand stared at me for long enough that I faced him. "Be glad of your human heart, Feyre. Pity those who don't feel anything at all."

I couldn't explain about the hole that had already formed in my soul—didn't want to, so I just nodded.

"Well, good-bye for now," he said, rolling his neck as if we hadn't been talking about anything important at all. He bowed at the waist, those wings vanishing entirely, and had begun to fade into the nearest shadow when he went rigid.

His eyes locked on mine, wide and wild, and his nostrils flared. Shock—pure shock flashed across his features at whatever he saw on my face, and he stumbled back a step. Actually *stumbled*.

"What is—" I began.

He disappeared—simply disappeared, not a shadow in sight—into the crisp air.

Tamlin and I left the way I'd come in—through that narrow cave in the belly of the mountain. Before departing, the High Fae of several courts destroyed and then sealed Amarantha's court Under the Mountain. We were the last to leave, and with a wave of Tamlin's arm, the entrance to the court crumbled behind us.

I still didn't have the words to ask what they'd done with those two faeries. Maybe someday, maybe soon, I would ask who they were, what their names had been. Amarantha's body, I'd heard, had been hauled off to be burned—though Jurian's bone and eye were somehow missing. As much as I wanted to hate her, as much as I wished I could have spat on her burning body . . . I understood what had driven her—a very small part of her, but I understood it.

Tamlin gripped my hand as we strode through the darkness. Neither of us said anything when a glimmer of sunlight appeared, staining the damp cave walls with a silvery sheen, but our steps quickened as the sunlight grew brighter and the cave warmer, and then both of us emerged onto the spring-green grass that covered the bumps and hollows of his lands. Our lands.

The breeze, the scent of wildflowers hit me, and despite the hole in my chest, the stain on my soul, I couldn't stop the smile that spread as we mounted a steep hill. My faerie legs were far stronger than my human ones, and when we reached the top of the knoll, I wasn't nearly as winded as I might once have been. But the breath was knocked from my chest when I beheld the rose-covered manor.

Home.

In all my imaginings in Amarantha's dungeons, I'd never allowed myself to think of this moment—never allowed myself to dream that outrageously. But I'd made it—I'd brought us both home.

I squeezed his hand as we gazed down at the manor, with its stables and gardens, two sets of childish laughter—true, free laughter—coming from somewhere inside its grounds. A moment later, two small, shining figures darted into the field beyond the garden, shrieking as they were chased by a taller, chuckling figure—Alis and her boys. Safe and out of hiding at last.

Tamlin slipped an arm around my shoulders, tucking me close to him as he rested his cheek on my head. My lips trembled, and I wrapped my arm around his waist.

We stood atop the hill in silence, until the setting sun gilded the house and the hills and the world and Lucien called us to dinner.

I stepped out of Tamlin's arms and kissed him softly. Tomorrow—there would be tomorrow, and an eternity, to face what I had done, to face what I shredded into pieces inside myself while Under the Mountain. But for now . . . for today . . .

"Let's go home," I said, and took his hand.

ACKNOWLEDGMENTS

To be honest, I'm not quite sure where to begin these acknowledgments, because this book exists thanks to so many people working on it over so many years. My eternal gratitude and love to:

Susan Dennard, my jaeger copilot and Threadsister, the Leonardo to my Raphael, the Gus to my Shawn, the Blake to my Adam, the Scott to my Stiles, the Aragorn to my Legolas, the Iseult to my Safi, the Schmidt to my Jenko, the Senneth to my Kira, the Elsa to my Anna, the Sailor Jupiter (or Luna!) to my Sailor Moon, the Moss to my Roy, the Martin to my Sean, the Alan Grant to my Ian Malcolm, the Brennan to my Dale, and the Esqueleto to my Nacho: I literally don't know what I'd do without you. Or our inside jokes. Our friendship is the definition of Epic—and I'm pretty sure it was written in the stars. (Like a thousand years before the dinosaurs. It's the prophecy.) See also: Imhotep, Tiny Cups For Tiny Hands, *Ohhhh you do??*, Cryssals, Henry Cavill, Sam Heughan, Claaaassic Peg, and everything ever from Nacho Libre. Sarusan Forever.

To Alex Bracken, who was one of the first friends I made in this industry, and remains one of my best friends to this day. There are moments when it still feels like we're fresh out of college with our first book deals, wondering what is next for us—I'm so happy that we've gotten to share this insane journey with each other. Thank you for all the amazing feedback, the multiple reads (on this book and so many others), and always, always, having my back. I can't tell you how much that means to me. Thanks for believing in this story for so many years.

To Biljana Likic, who read this pretty much as I wrote it chapter by chapter, helped me write all those riddles and limericks, and made me believe this story might not actually sit in a drawer for the rest of my life. So proud to now see you kicking ass and taking names, dude.

To my agent, Tamar Rydzinski, who took a chance on an unpublished twenty-two-year-old writer and changed my life forever with one phone call. You are a supreme badass. Thank you for everything.

To Cat Onder—you are such a delight to work with, and I'm honored to call you my editor. To Laura Bernier—thank you so, so much for helping me transform this book into something that I'm truly proud of. I couldn't have done it without your brilliant feedback.

To the entire worldwide team at Bloomsbury: I cannot tell you how thrilled I am that this series found a home with you. You guys are the ultimate best. Thank you for your hard work, your enthusiasm, and making my dreams come true. I can't imagine being in better hands. Thank you, thank you, thank you.

To Dan Krokos, Erin Bowman, Mandy Hubbard, and Jennifer Armentrout—thank you for being there for everything and anything. I don't know what I would do without you.

To Brigid Kemmerer, Andrea Maas, and Kat Zhang, who read various early drafts of this book and provided such crucial feedback and enthusiasm. I owe you one.

To Elena of NovelSounds, Alexa of AlexaLovesBooks, Linnea of Linneart, and all the *Throne of Glass* Ambassadors: Thank you guys so much for your support and dedication. Getting to know you all has been such a highlight and pleasure.

To my parents: it took me a while to realize it, but I'm tremendously blessed to have you as my Number One fans—and to have you as parents. To my family: thank you for the unconditional love and support.

To Annie, the greatest dog in the history of canine companions: I love you forever and ever and ever.

And lastly, to my husband, Josh—this book is for you. It's always been yours, the same way my heart has been yours from the moment I saw you on the first day of freshman orientation at college. Considering the way our lives mysteriously wove together before we ever set eyes on each other, I have a hard time believing it wasn't fate. Thanks for proving to me that true love exists. I'm the luckiest woman in the world to get to spend my life with you.

FEYRE'S STORY REACHES NEW HEIGHTS IN THIS SPELLBINDING SEQUEL

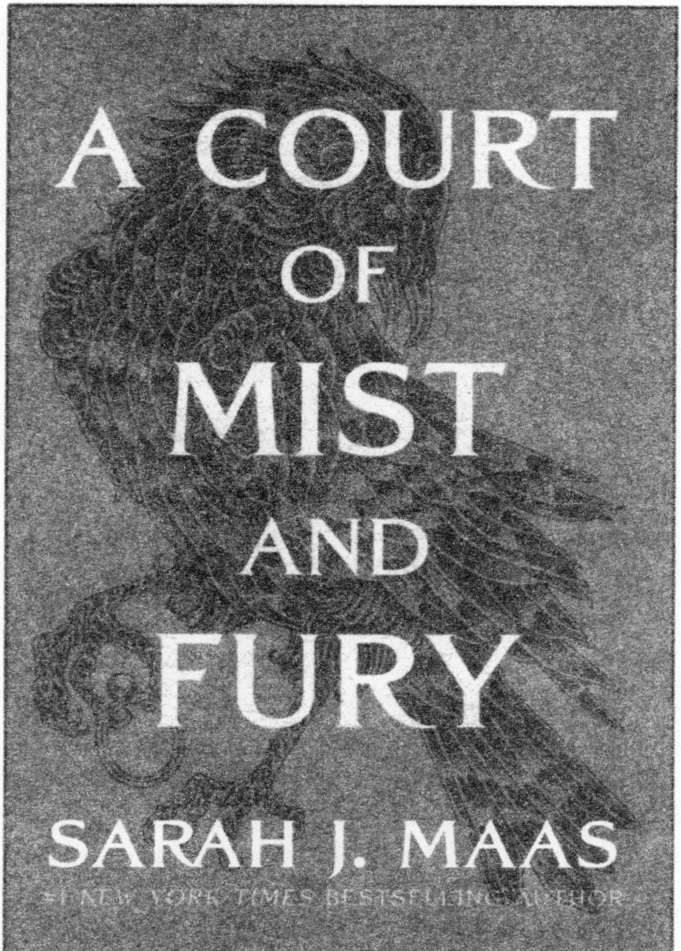

READ ON FOR A SNEAK PEEK AS THE JOURNEY CONTINUES . . .

I agreed to sit at the long, wooden table in a curtained-off alcove only because he had a point. Not being able to read had almost cost me my life Under the Mountain. I'd be damned if I let it become a weakness again, his personal agenda or no. And as for shielding . . . I'd be a damned fool not to take up the offer to learn from him. The thought of anyone, especially Rhys, sifting through the mess in my mind, taking information about the Spring Court, about the people I loved . . . I'd never allow it. Not willingly.

But it didn't make it any easier to endure Rhysand's presence at the wooden table. Or the stack of books piled atop it.

"I know my alphabet," I said sharply as he laid a piece of paper in front of me. "I'm not that stupid." I twisted my fingers in my lap, then pinned my restless hands under my thighs.

"I didn't say you were stupid," he said. "I'm just trying to determine where we should begin." I leaned back in the cushioned seat. "Since you've refused to tell me a thing about how much you know."

My face warmed. "Can't you hire a tutor?"

He lifted a brow. "Is it that hard for you to even try in front of me?"

"You're a High Lord—don't you have better things to do?"

"Of course. But none as enjoyable as seeing you squirm."

"You're a real bastard, you know that?"

Rhys huffed a laugh. "I've been called worse. In fact, I think you've called me worse." He tapped the paper in front of him. "Read that."

A blur of letters. My throat tightened. "I can't."

"Try."

The sentence had been written in elegant, concise print. His writing, no doubt. I tried to open my mouth, but my spine locked up. "What, *exactly*, is your stake in all this? You said you'd tell me if I worked with you."

"I didn't specify *when* I'd tell you." I peeled back from him as my lip curled. He shrugged. "Maybe I resent the idea of you letting those sycophants and war-mongering fools in the Spring Court make you feel inadequate. Maybe I indeed enjoy seeing you squirm. Or maybe—"

"I get it."

Rhys snorted. "Try to read it, Feyre."

Prick. I snatched the paper to me, nearly ripping it in half in the process. I looked at the first word, sounding it out in my head. "Y-you . . . " The next I figured out with a combination of my silent pronunciation and logic. "Look . . . "

"Good," he murmured.

"I didn't ask for your approval."

Rhys chuckled.

"Ab . . . Absolutely." It took me longer than I wanted to admit to figure that out. The next word was even worse. "De . . . Del . . . "

I deigned to glance at him, brows raised.

"Delicious," he purred.

My brows now knotted. I read the next two words, then whipped my face toward him. "*You look absolutely delicious today, Feyre*?! That's what you wrote?"

He leaned back in his seat. As our eyes met, sharp claws caressed my mind and his voice whispered inside my head: *It's true, isn't it?*

I jolted back, my chair groaning. "*Stop that*!"

But those claws now dug in—and my entire body, my heart, my lungs, my *blood* yielded to his grip, utterly at his command as he said, *The fashion of the Night Court suits you.*

I couldn't move in my seat, couldn't even blink.

This is what happens when you leave your mental shields down. Someone with my sort of powers could slip inside, see what they want, and take your mind for themselves. Or they could shatter it. I'm currently standing on the threshold of your mind . . . but if I were to go deeper, all it would take would be half a thought from me and who you are, your very self, would be wiped away.

Distantly, sweat slid down my temple.

You should be afraid. You should be afraid of this, and you should be thanking the gods-damned Cauldron that in the past three months, no one with my sorts of gifts has run into you. Now shove me out.

I couldn't. Those claws were everywhere—digging into every thought, every piece of self. He pushed a little harder.

Shove. Me. Out.

I didn't know where to begin. I blindly pushed and slammed myself into him, into those claws that were everywhere, as if I were a top loosed in a circle of mirrors.

His laughter, low and soft, filled my mind, my ears. *That way, Feyre.*

In answer, a little open path gleamed inside my mind. The road out.

It'd take me forever to unhook each claw and shove the mass of his presence out that narrow opening. If I could wash it away—

A wave. A wave of self, of *me*, to sweep all of him out—

I didn't let him see the plan take form as I rallied myself into a cresting wave and struck.

The claws loosened—reluctantly. As if letting me win this round. He merely said, "Good."

My bones, my breath and blood, they were mine again. I slumped in my seat.

"Not yet," he said. "Shield. Block me out so I can't get back in."

I already wanted to go somewhere quiet and sleep for a while—

Claws at that outer layer of my mind, stroking—

I imagined a wall of adamant snapping down, black as night and a foot thick. The claws retracted a breath before the wall sliced them in two.

Rhys was grinning. "Very nice. Blunt, but nice."

I couldn't help myself. I grabbed the piece of paper and shredded it in two, then four. "You're a pig."

"Oh, most definitely. But look at you—you read that whole sentence, kicked me out of your mind, *and* shielded. Excellent work."

"Don't condescend to me."

"I'm not. You're reading at a level far higher than I anticipated."

That burning returned to my cheeks. "But mostly illiterate."

"At this point, it's about practice, spelling, and more practice. You could be reading novels by Nynsar. And if you keep adding to those shields, you might very well keep me out entirely by then, too."

Nynsar. It'd be the first Tamlin and his court would celebrate in nearly fifty years. Amarantha had banned it on a whim, along with a few other small, but beloved Fae holidays that she had deemed *unnecessary*. But Nynsar was months from now. "Is it even possible—to truly keep you out?"

"Not likely, but who knows how deep that power goes? Keep practicing and we'll see what happens."

"And will I still be bound by this bargain at Nynsar, too?"

Silence.

I pushed, "After—after what happened—" I couldn't mention specifics on what had occurred Under the Mountain, what he'd done for me during that fight with Amarantha, what he'd done after— "I think we can agree that I owe you nothing, and you owe *me* nothing."

His gaze was unflinching.

I blazed on, "Isn't it enough that we're all free?" I splayed my tattooed hand on the table. "By the end, I thought you were different, thought that it was all a mask, but taking me away, *keeping* me here . . . " I shook my head, unable to find the words vicious enough, clever enough to convince him to end this bargain.

His eyes darkened. "I'm not your enemy, Feyre."

"Tamlin says you are." I curled the fingers of my tattooed hand into a fist. "Everyone else says you are."

"And what do *you* think?" He leaned back in his chair again, but his face was grave.

"You're doing a damned good job of making me agree with them."

"Liar," he purred. "Did you even tell your friends about *what I did to you* Under the Mountain?"

So that comment at breakfast *had* gotten under his skin. "I don't want to talk about anything related to that. With you or them."

"No, because it's so much easier to pretend it never happened and let them coddle you."

"I don't *let* them coddle me—"

"They had you wrapped up like a present yesterday. Like you were *his* reward."

"So?"

"So?" A flicker of rage, then it was gone.

"I'm ready to be taken home," I merely said.

"Where you'll be cloistered for the rest of your life, especially once you start punching out heirs. I can't wait to see what Ianthe does when she gets her hands on *them*."

"You don't seem to have a particularly high opinion of her."

Something cold and predatory crept into his eyes. "No, I can't say that I do." He pointed to a blank piece of paper. "Start copying the alphabet. Until your letters are perfect. And every time you get through a round, lower and raise your shield. Until *that* is second nature. I'll be back in an hour."

"What?"

"Copy. The. Alphabet. Until—"

"I heard what you said." Prick. Prick, prick, *prick*.

"Then get to work." Rhys uncoiled to his feet. "And at least have the decency to only call me a prick when your shields are back up."

He vanished into a ripple of darkness before I realized that I'd let the wall of adamant fade again.

✢

By the time Rhys returned, my mind felt like a mud puddle.

I spent the entire hour doing as I'd been ordered, though I'd flinched at every sound from the nearby stairwell: quiet steps of servants, the flapping of sheets being changed, someone humming a beautiful and winding melody. And beyond that, the chatter of birds that dwelled in the unnatural warmth of the mountain or in the many potted citrus trees. No sign of my impending torment. No sentries, even, to monitor me. I might as well have had the entire place to myself.

Which was good, as my attempts to lower and raise that mental shield often resulted in my face being twisted or strained or pinched.

"Not bad," Rhys said, peering over my shoulder.

He'd appeared moments before, a healthy distance away, and if I hadn't known better, I might have thought it was because he didn't want to startle me. As if he'd known about the time Tamlin had crept up behind me, and panic had hit me so hard I'd knocked him on his ass with a punch to his stomach. I'd blocked it out—the shock on Tam's face, how *easy* it had been to take him off his feet, the humiliation of having my stupid terror so out in the open . . .

Rhys scanned the pages I'd scribbled on, sorting through them, tracking my progress.

Then, a scrape of claws inside my mind—that only sliced against black, glittering adamant.

I threw my lingering will into that wall as the claws pushed, testing for weak spots . . .

"Well, well," Rhysand purred, those mental claws withdrawing. "Hopefully I'll be getting a good night's rest at last, if you can manage to keep the wall up while you sleep."

I dropped the shield, sent a word blasting down that mental bridge between us, and hauled the walls back up. Behind it, my mind wobbled like jelly. I needed a nap. Desperately.

"Prick I might be, but look at you. Maybe we'll get to have some fun with our lessons after all."

I was still scowling at Rhys's muscled back as I kept a healthy ten steps behind him while he led me through the halls of the main building, the sweeping mountains and blisteringly blue sky the only witnesses to our silent trek.

I was too drained to demand where we were now going, and he didn't bother explaining as he led me up, up—until we entered a round chamber at the top of a tower.

A circular table of black stone occupied the center, while the largest stretch of uninterrupted gray stone wall was covered in a massive map of our world. It had been marked and flagged and pinned, for whatever reasons I couldn't tell, but my gaze drifted to the windows throughout the room—so many that it felt utterly exposed, breathable. The perfect home, I supposed, for a High Lord blessed with wings.

Rhys stalked to the table, where there was another map spread, figurines dotting its surface. A map of Prythian—and Hybern.

Every court in our land had been marked, along with villages and cities and rivers and mountain passes. Every court . . . but the Night Court.

The vast, northern territory was utterly blank. Not even a mountain range had been etched in. Strange, likely part of some strategy I didn't understand.

I found Rhysand watching me—his raised brows enough to make me shut my mouth against the forming question.

"Nothing to ask?"

"No."

A feline smirk danced on his lips, but Rhys jerked his chin toward the map on the wall. "What do you see?"

"Is this some sort of way of convincing me to embrace my reading lessons?" Indeed, I couldn't decipher any of the writing, only the shapes of things. Like the wall, its massive line bisecting our world.

"Tell me what you see."

"A world divided in two."

"And do you think it should remain that way?"

I whipped my head toward him. "My family—" I halted on the word. I should have known better than to admit to having a family, that I cared for them—

"Your human family," Rhys finished, "would be deeply impacted if the wall came down, wouldn't they? So close to its border . . . If they're lucky, they'll flee across the ocean before it happens."

"*Will* it happen?"

Rhysand didn't break my stare. "Maybe."

"Why?"

"Because war is coming, Feyre."

DON'T MISS
SARAH J. MAAS'S BESTSELLING
COURT OF THORNS AND ROSES SERIES: